T. C. BOYLE
STORIES II

ALSO BY T. CORAGHESSAN BOYLE

NOVELS

San Miguel · When the Killing's Done · The Women
Talk Talk · The Inner Circle · Drop City
A Friend of the Earth · Riven Rock · The Tortilla Curtain
The Road to Wellville · East Is East · World's End
Budding Prospects · Water Music

SHORT STORIES

Wild Child · Tooth and Claw · The Human Fly
After the Plague · T.C. Boyle Stories · Without a Hero
If the River Was Whiskey · Greasy Lake · Descent of Man

T.C. BOYLE
STORIES II

The Collected Stories of
T. Coraghessan Boyle
Volume II

B L O O M S B U R Y
LONDON • NEW DELHI • NEW YORK • SYDNEY

First published in Great Britain 2103

Pages 917–918 constitute an extension of this copyright page

Bloomsbury Publishing plc
50 Bedford Square
London
WC1B 3DP

www.bloomsbury.com

Bloomsbury Publishing, London, New Delhi, New York and Sydney

A CIP catalogue record for this book is available from the British Library

Hardback ISBN 978 1 4088 4456 4
Trade paperback ISBN 978 1 4088 4457 1

10 9 8 7 6 5 4 3 2 1

Set in Arno Pro
Designed by Francesca Belanger
Printed and bound in Great Britain by CPI Group (UK) Ltd, Croydon CR0 4YY

For Spencer, who comes bearing his own stories

I do not know which to prefer,
The beauty of inflections
Or the beauty of innuendoes,
The blackbird whistling
Or just after.

—Wallace Stevens,
"Thirteen Ways of Looking
at a Blackbird"

Contents

Preface

When putting together the first volume of the *Collected Stories* for publication in 1998, I chose a rather whimsical arrangement, in three sections, of the sixty-eight pieces that made the final cut. The sections were titled "Love," "Death," "And Everything in Between," and the stories collected therein represented a period of some twenty-five years' work, from the early 1970s to the mid-1990s. The present volume collects the stories written since then, though some pieces that appeared in the earlier volume—"Mexico," "Juliana Cloth" and "Little Fur People"—should rightly have been included in 2001's *After the Plague* and so in this collection, but were published in the first volume at the suggestion of my editor so as to make *T.C. Boyle Stories* something more than simply a reassemblage. (In keeping with this precedent, Part IV of this book, *A Death in Kitchawank,* presents an entirely new collection of stories written since the publication of *Wild Child* in 2009.)

This time around I've chosen a more straightforward arrangement—that is, roughly chronological—because I suppose I've become ever so slightly less whimsical as I move on down the long dark road that inescapably ends in an even darker place. Still, readers will find here many of the satires, tall tales and excursions into the absurd the first volume provided, though perhaps as a lower percentage of the whole. There are a number of decidedly non-whimsical stories here too, pieces like "When I Woke Up This Morning, Everything I Had Was Gone," "Tooth and Claw," "Rastrow's Island" and "La Conchita," or the odd story drawing on autobiographical elements like "Up Against the Wall" or "Birnam Wood" (as with "If the River Was Whiskey," "The Fog Man" and "Greasy Lake" in the first volume), as well as historical meditations, memory pieces and comedic stories in various valences, from laugh-aloud to the sort of strained laughter that catches in your throat. All well and good. All part of the questing impulse that has pushed me forward into territory I could never have dreamed of when I first set out to write—that is, to understand that there are no limits and everything that exists or existed or might exist in some other time or reality is fair game for exploration.

To me, a story is an exercise of the imagination—or, as Flannery O'Connor has it, an act of discovery. I don't know what a story will be until it begins to unfold, the whole coming to me in the act of composition as a kind of waking dream, and it might begin with the exploration of a subject or a theme or a recollection or something as random as my discovery that the wild creatures in

Tierra del Fuego were going blind as a result of the hole in the ozone layer that opens up there annually ("Blinded by the Light") or that the Shetland Islands are the windiest place on earth ("Swept Away"). The professorial dictum has always been to write what you know, but I say write what you don't know and find something out. And it works. Or can work. After all, a story is a seduction of the reader, and such a seduction can so immerse him or her that everything becomes plausible. And so with "Swept Away." I'd never been to the Shetland Islands, though I'd been near enough—on a fishing boat off Oban, where I nearly froze to death—but the story came to me as if I'd been born and raised there in some other life. After it appeared in *The New Yorker,* I heard from the editors of *The Shetlander,* the magazine of the islands, who wanted to know when and where I'd lived amongst them.

All of the stories collected here were written after my move to Santa Barbara from Los Angeles in 1993, and readers will note that the stories that are not locked into a specific locale—the Fresno of "The Underground Gardens," where Baldasare Forestiere constructed his fantastic maze of subterranean rooms, for instance, or "The Unlucky Mother of Aquiles Maldonado," which takes place in Caracas, or "Dogology" in India—have moved north as well. And west, if you take into account the many stories set in the New York of my younger days, most of which appear in the previous volume. To that degree, I suppose I am writing what I know, at least in terms of exploring the history, ecology, emotional temperature and socioeconomics of whatever environment I find myself in, and this includes the many stories that I've set in the Sequoia National Monument (formerly "Forest"), a place to which I've been escaping since I first moved to the West Coast. "My Pain Is Worse Than Your Pain," for instance, grows directly out of an incident I'd heard rumor of up there in a microcosmic community I like to call "Big Timber" by way of eliding the real and actual. I don't know the people involved in that incident and I don't want to know them. All I want, from that story or any other, is to hear a single resonant bar of truth or mystery or what-if-ness, so I can hum it back and play a riff on it.

Los Angeles, Santa Barbara, the Sierra Nevada, the desert, the chaparral, the sunstruck chop of the Pacific, jagged agaves and wind-ravaged palms—until I was in my twenties I'd never been west of the Hudson, and when I did go west it was first to Iowa City and the Iowa Writers' Workshop and then, finally, to Los Angeles. To say that northern Westchester County, where I was born and raised (in Peekskill, thirty miles up the river from Manhattan) is provincial might seem surprising, but it was when I was a boy, at least in my parents' milieu. I was raised in a working-class household in which we didn't have books or the tradition of them and didn't know much of the outside world, not even the City, with all its cultural glories, which seemed infinitely remote to us. We had TV, and TV dominated our household, the gray screen coming to life when we arrived home from school/work and flicking off when we went to bed. Though the local schools provided a sound egalitarian education, I was pre-literary in those days, a hyperactive kid playing ball and roaming the woods and mainly staying out of trouble. My mother read to me when I was young—it was she who taught me to read, in fact, as I was too impatient and immature to sit still in class—but my earliest memory of the thrill of fiction comes from my eighth-grade English class at Lakeland Junior High, where Mr. (Donald) Grant would read stories aloud to us on Fridays if we were good, and we were very good indeed. Mr. Grant was an amateur actor and he really put the thunder into chestnuts like "To Build a Fire" and "The Most Dangerous Game." We'd leave his class trembling.

Darwin and earth science came tumbling into my consciousness around then, and I told my mother that I could no longer believe in the Roman Catholic doctrine that had propelled us to church on Sundays for as long as I could remember. To her credit, patient woman, she set me free from all that, and I suppose I've been looking for something to replace it ever since. What have I found? Art and nature, the twin deities that sustained Wordsworth and Whitman and all the others whose experience became too complicated for received faith to contain it. At seventeen I found myself at SUNY Potsdam, the New York State university system's music school, where I had gone as an ardent disciple of John Coltrane and lightning-fast technician of saxophone and clarinet. Unfortunately, I had no feel for the sort of music we were expected to play and I flunked my audition. But still, there I was in college, and I fell directly into the cold embrace of the existentialists on the one hand and the redeeming grace of Flannery O'Connor, John Updike, Saul Bellow and the playwrights of the absurd on the other. If I had to choose a defining moment it was when I first read O'Connor's "A Good Man Is Hard to Find" for an English class: here was the sort of story that subverted expectations, that began in one mode—situation comedy, familiar from TV—and ended wickedly and deliciously in another. And I'd thought there were rules.

I lived then in a rooming house on a canopied avenue of trees, enduring Potsdam's arctic temperatures, the gales that battered the storm windows and the rain that froze over everything in a glistening sheet so that the world became crystalline and treacherous. Once the temperature hit twenty below, no car would start, even when plied with ether sprayed generously into the steel maw of the carburetor. It wasn't a problem, or not at first, not until I began to discover romance and the vital significance of the back seat. We lived—variously six, seven or eight of us, males exclusively—in three upstairs rooms of a frame house owned by a widow who had been Potsdam's homecoming queen in 1911 and referred to us as "my boys." The rooms were dense with ancient furniture that gave off an odor of times long gone, but they were adequate to the purpose, and it was here that I began my first rudimentary essays into this form—the form of the short story—that would come to dominate my life. That said, I have to admit that I was not a good student or a dutiful one. Still, I read vastly, read what was current rather than what was prescribed, and came away with a spotty education (a double major in history and English, with a junior-year swoop into Krishna Vaid's creative writing class), but with a real fever for art. What do I remember of that time? A fear of the nausea that Sartre dropped in my lap and a gnawing unformed desire that had me haunting the high steel rafters of the partly constructed library building, alone, in the spectral hours after the bars had closed, trying to taste the future on a sub-zero wind.

I remember Wite-Out, the very acme of technological perfection, made all the more irresistible because of the rumor that Bob Dylan's mother had invented it. I remember Dylan and the instruction rock and roll gave me, years before I coalesced my musical impulses and fronted a band myself, howling out my rage and bewilderment till my body went rigid and my throat clenched. I remember the feel of the Olivetti portable on which I composed everything I'd ever written—stories, essays, letters, notes—until computers made it redundant. And I can still summon up the satisfaction of typing a clean finished copy of something that seemed to have value, great value, value for me and the world too, on fresh crinkled sheets of Corrasable Bond.

Hippie times came along, and that's where memory solidifies. I've always been single-minded (to a fault, many would say), and I do tend to plunge in with everything I've got. I was a hippie's hippie, so blissed-out and outrageously accoutered that people would stop me on the street and ask if I could sell them acid. Which I couldn't. And wouldn't. That would be too . . . grasping. Music pounded in my brain, the music that *was* the culture of the time. I lived in various houses with various people, but I settled into a relationship with a graceful and encouraging woman who had her finger on the pulse of the day, my wife through all these years and moves and books and children, and I read hungrily, madly, looking for something I couldn't define. My fumbling attempts at stories in those times were in the mode then called "experimental," a playful thrust at parrying the traditional narrative and fracturing it into its discrete elements. It was then that I discovered Robert Coover and his clean, lyrical, ultra-smart and wickedly funny stories, and I saw what I had been blindly striving toward made perfection. Next came Barthelme, Borges, Cortázar, Pynchon, Barth, Calvino, García Márquez, writers of a period in which no one ever said never and there was no form that couldn't be squeezed and milked and molded.

I published my first story—in the "experimental" mode—in the *North American Review* in 1972, under the aegis of Robley Wilson Jr., to whom I will forever be grateful. On the strength of that, I applied to Iowa and was accepted and my life as a writer really began to begin. Now I'd been bitten. Now I was an adult. Now I knew what I wanted from my life and I pursued it with devotion and purpose. My professors at the Workshop—Vance Bourjaily, John Irving and John Cheever—gave me exactly what I most needed, a boost of confidence, and my professors in the English Department, where I completed my Ph.D. in nineteenth-century British literature, gave me the foundation I hadn't been able to build during my years as a disaffected undergrad. My rationale? I felt if I wanted to be a writer, it might actually be helpful to know something.

And yes, I was well aware that formal study, at least to writers of the generation before mine, was anathema. Cheever, who was unfailingly kind and generous to me, was positively acidic on the subject of my academic pursuits, which he felt had no real place in an artistic repertoire, but I persisted, because, for better or worse, no one and nothing can turn me once I've got a notion in my head. And so, on graduating, I went to Los Angeles and founded the creative writing program at USC, where I continued to teach until becoming writer in residence in the fall of 2012. The university turned out to be a blessing. It grounded me, got me out of the house and out of myself, and gave me the precious opportunity of assessing, encouraging and discussing the art of fiction on a regular basis with people, mostly young and still in the formative stages, who were as excited about it as I.

It was Cheever too who gently chastised me for using that bludgeoning term "experimental," as did Tom Whittaker, who then edited *The Iowa Review,* where I worked first as assistant fiction editor (to Robert Coover) and then, during my last year, as fiction editor in my own right. Cheever insisted that all good fiction was experimental—and, of course, it is—adducing his own "The Death of Justina" as an example. I took his point. And during the 1980s and into the 1990s I came under the influence of his stories and those of Raymond Carver, who became a friend during the years I was at Iowa. If in the beginning I was more interested in language, design and idea than in character (and this is reflected, I think, in volume one), as I grew as a novelist and came to admire what Carver and Cheever and so many others were accomplishing in a less "experimental" and more traditional vein, I became more at ease with building stories around character as well.

While at Iowa, I kept after the business of sending stories to magazines, big and small, insisting on walking to the post office the very day a story came back to me unloved and unwanted and sending it out to the next prospect on my list, hoping to match story to editor in a way that was by turns futile, masochistic and defiantly optimistic. During the five and a half years I was there, I saw some thirty stories accepted, each acceptance an occasion for the kind of fête that involved a rereading of the story aloud to whomever I could rope into listening and an excursion to some dark watering hole that offered up exotic fare like pizza and beer in exchange for mere money. Exciting times. I became so attuned to the arrival of the mail I could detect the annunciatory squeal of the delivery truck's brakes from two blocks away. There was plenty of rejection, of course—I taped the rejection letters on poster boards and tacked them to the wall of the bedroom that served as my office till all four walls were covered and I resorted to the more practical but less self-righteous system of secreting them in file folders.

I was fortunate to place stories early on in *Esquire, The Paris Review, The Atlantic* and *Harper's*—and later in *The New Yorker* and *Playboy*—and to develop close working relationships with editors like George Plimpton and Lewis Lapham. It meant whole worlds and universes to feel that I wasn't sending things blind, that there were editors out there who actually looked forward to seeing what I might turn out next. George Plimpton took so many of my stories for *The Paris Review* in the seventies and eighties that he once joked he was thinking of renaming the magazine *The Boyle Review,* and his influence and friendship were of incalculable value. He made me feel necessary, not to mention appreciated. On the other hand, the editors of *The New Yorker* gave me a cold shoulder in those days, finally accepting one of my pieces in the early nineties, but once the magazine changed hands and Tina Brown and her fiction editor, Bill Buford, came to the fore—and now their successors, David Remnick and Deborah Treisman—I have seen the bulk of my stories appear in its pages. So yes, I've been very fortunate, but most of all in my editor, Paul Slovak, with whom I've worked on the last fourteen books, and my agent, Georges Borchardt, who took me on while I was a student still and has been my advocate, intercessor and salver of wounds ever since. If it weren't for Georges, I wouldn't be sitting here writing this apologia pro vita sua.

Finally, in reading through the stories collected in this volume, I see that there's a need here to address the question of why, of what it is that impels me and so many of the writers around me to create stories even in the face of the world's general indifference. As students at Iowa we thrilled to the notion that we were part of something important, all-important, and we thrilled too to the readings and public displays of the masters of the form who came through town to entertain us—Borges, Updike, Vonnegut, Barthelme, Leonard Michaels, John Gardner, Grace Paley and many, many others. And yet I remember a student raising his hand after one of Stanley Elkin's astonishing performances (we knew enough not to sit in the first three rows because of the flying spittle as Stanley worked himself up into an actor's rage) and asking this: "Mr. Elkin, you've written a terrific collection of stories—why don't you write more of them?" Stanley's answer: "No money in it. Next question."

Money or no, a writer writes. The making of art—the making of *stories*—is a kind of addiction, as I've pointed out in an earlier essay, "This Monkey, My Back." You begin with nothing, open yourself up, sweat and worry and bleed, and finally you have something. And once you do, you want to have it all over again. And again. And again. There is an elemental power in a good short story, an awakening to something new and unexpected, whether it's encountered on the page or from the lips of an actor in a darkened theater where the words stand naked and take you all the way back to the first voice that ever resonated inside you. In my own way, I've become an actor too, regularly presenting my stories onstage and feeling the pulse of the audience beating steadily there in the darkness before me. In the beginning, I didn't fully trust the relationship and performed only comic pieces, hooked on the easy gratification of the celebratory wash of laughter flowing from the audience. But then I began to read darker things, like "Chicxulub," and felt the command of tragedy, of horror, of putting myself and the audience in a place we never hope to be in the life we lead outside of fiction. I will never forget the woman in Miami who began one night to sob openly a third of the way into the story and whose terrible harrowing grief riveted us all. I wanted to stop and tell her not to worry, that it was just make-believe, a kind of voodoo charm to keep the randomness of the world at bay, but there was no stopping and no consolation: she'd lived the story and I hadn't.

There is a daunting power in that and a daunting responsibility too. We each receive the world according to our lights and what the sparking loop of our senses affords us, and all I can do is hope to capture it in an individual way, to represent the phenomena that crowd in on us through every conscious moment as they appear and vanish again. I want to be playful and serious, investigative and imaginative, curious and more curious still, and I don't want distractions. I don't make music anymore, I don't write articles or film scripts or histories, I don't play sports or do crossword puzzles or tinker with engines—it's all too much. The art—the doing of it—that's what absorbs me to the exclusion of all else. Each day I have the privilege of reviewing the world as it comes to me and transforming it into another form altogether, the very form I would have wrought in the first place if only it were I who'd been the demiurge and the original creator—the one, the being, the force, whether spirit or random principle, that set all this delirious life in motion.

PART I

After the Plague

Termination Dust

There were a hundred and seven of them, of all ages, shapes and sizes, from twenty-five- and thirty-year-olds in dresses that looked like they were made of Saran Wrap to a couple of big-beamed older types in pantsuits who could have been somebody's mother—and I mean somebody grown, with a goatee beard and a job at McDonald's. I was there to meet them when they came off the plane from Los Angeles, I and Peter Merchant, whose travel agency had arranged the whole weekend in partnership with a Beverly Hills concern, and there were a couple other guys there too, eager beavers like J. J. Hotel, and the bad element, by which I mean Bud Withers specifically, who didn't want to cough up the hundred fifty bucks for the buffet, the Malibu Beach party and the auction afterward. They were hoping for maybe a sniff of something gratis, but I was there to act as a sort of buffer and make sure that didn't happen.

Peter was all smiles as we came up to the first of the ladies, Susan Abrams, by her nametag, and started handing out corsages, one to a lady, and chimed out in chorus, "Welcome to Anchorage, Land of the Grizzly and the True-Hearted Man!" Well, it was pretty corny—it was Peter's idea, not mine—and I felt a little foolish with the first few (hard-looking women, divorcées for sure, maybe even legal secretaries or lawyers into the bargain), but when I saw this little one with eyes the color of glacial melt about six deep in the line, I really began to perk up. Her nametag was done in calligraphy, hand-lettered instead of computer-generated like the rest of them, and that really tugged at me, the care that went into it, and I gave her hand a squeeze and said, "Hi, Jordy, welcome to Alaska," when I gave her the corsage.

She seemed a little dazed, and I chalked it up to the flight and the drinks and the general party atmosphere that must certainly have prevailed on that plane, one hundred and seven single women on their way for the Labor Day weekend in a state that boasted two eligible bachelors for every woman, but that wasn't it at all. She'd hardly had a glass of chablis, as it turned out—what I took to be confusion, lethargy, whatever, was just wonderment. As I was later to learn, she'd been drawn to the country all her life, had read and dreamed about it since she was a girl growing up in Altadena, California, within sight of the Rose Bowl. She was bookish—an English teacher, in fact—and she had a new worked-leather high-grade edition of *Wuthering Heights* wedged under the arm that held her suitcase and traveling bag. I guessed her to be maybe late twenties, early thirties.

"Thank you," she said, in this whispery little voice that made me feel about thirteen years old all over again, and then she squinted those snowmelt eyes to take in my face and the spread of me (I should say I'm a big man, one of the biggest in the bush around Boynton, six-five and two-forty-two and not much of that gone yet to fat), and then she read my name off my nametag and added, in a deep-diving puff of a little floating wisp of a voice, "Ned."

Then she was gone, and it was the next woman in line (with a face like a topographic map and the grip of a lumberjack), and then the next, and the next, and all the while I'm wondering how much Jordy's going to go for at the auction, and if a hundred and twenty-five, which is about all I'm prepared to spend, is going to be enough.

The girls—women, ladies, whatever—rested up at their hotel for a while and did their ablutions and ironed their outfits and put on their makeup, while Peter and Susan Abrams fluttered around making sure all the little details of the evening had been worked out. I sat at the bar drinking Mexican beer to get in the mood. I'd barely finished my first when I looked up and who did I see but J.J. and Bud with maybe half a dozen local types in tow, all of them looking as lean and hungry as a winter cat. Bud ignored me and started chatting up the Anchorage boys with his eternal line of bullshit about living off the land in his cabin in the bush outside Boynton—which was absolutely the purest undiluted nonsense, as anybody who'd known him for more than half a minute could testify—but J.J. settled in beside me with a combination yodel and sigh and offered to buy me a drink, which I accepted. "Got one picked out?" he said, and he had this mocking grin on his face, as if the whole business of the Los Angeles contingent was a bad joke, though I knew it was all an act and he was as eager and sweetly optimistic as I was myself.

The image of a hundred and seven women in their underwear suddenly flashed through my mind, and then I pictured Jordy in a black brassiere and matching panties, and I blushed and ducked my head and tried on an awkward little smile. "Yeah," I admitted.

"I'll be damned if Mr. Confidence down there"—a gesture for Bud, who was neck-deep in guano with the weekend outdoorsmen in their L. L. Bean outfits—"doesn't have one too. Says he's got her room number already and told her he'd bid whatever it takes for a date with her, even if he had to dip into the family fortune."

My laugh was a bitter, strangled thing. Bud was just out of jail, where he'd done six months on a criminal mischief charge for shooting out the windows in three cabins and the sunny side of my store on the main street—the only street—in downtown Boynton, population 170. He didn't have a pot to piss in, except what he got from the VA or welfare or whatever it was—it was hard to say, judging from the way he seemed to confuse fact and fiction. That and the rattrap cabin he'd built on federal land along the Yukon River, and that was condemned. I didn't even know what he'd done with his kid after Linda left him, and I didn't want to guess. "How'd he even get here?" I said.

J.J. was a little man with a bald pate and a full snow-white beard, a widower and a musician who cooked as mean a moose tri-tip with garlic and white gravy as any man who'd come into the country in the past ten years. He shrugged, set his beer mug down on the bar. "Same as you and me."

I was incredulous. "You mean he drove? Where'd he get the car?"

"All I know's he told me last week he had this buddy was going to lend him a brand-new Toyota Land Cruiser for the weekend and that furthermore, he was planning on going home to Boynton with the second Mrs. Withers, even if he did have to break down and shell out the one fifty for the party and all. It's an investment, he says, as if any woman'd be crazy enough to go anyplace with him, let alone a cabin out in the hind end of nowhere."

I guess I was probably stultified with amazement at this point, and I couldn't really manage a response. I was just looking over the top of my beer at the back of Bud's head and his elbow resting on the bar and then the necks of his boots as if I could catch a glimpse of the plastic feet he's got stuffed in there. I'd seen them once, those feet, when he first got back from the hospital and he came round the store for a pint of something, already half drunk and wearing a pair of shorts under his coat though it was minus thirty out. "Hey, Ned," he said to me in this really nasty, accusatory voice, "you see what you and the rest of them done to me?," and he flipped open the coat to show his ankles and the straps and the plastic feet that were exactly like the pink molded feet of a mannequin in a department store window.

I was worried. I didn't want to let on to J.J., but I knew Bud, I knew how smooth he was—especially if you weren't forewarned—and I knew women found him attractive. I kept thinking, What if it's Jordy he's after?, but then I told myself the chances were pretty remote, what with a hundred and seven eager women to choose from, and even if it was—even if it *was*—there were still a hundred and six others and one of them had to be for me.

Statistics:

There were thirty-two women out of a population of 170 in Boynton, all of them married and all of them invisible, even when they were sitting around the bar I run in the back room of the store. Average winter temperature was minus twelve, and there was a period of nearly two months when we hardly saw the sun. Add to that the fact that seven out of ten adults in Alaska have a drinking problem, and you can imagine what life was like on the bad days.

I was no exception to the rule. The winter was long, the nights were lonely, and booze was a way to take the edge off the loneliness and the boredom that just slowed you down and slowed you down till you felt like you were barely alive. I was no drunk, don't get me wrong—nothing like Bud Withers, not even close—and I tried to keep a check on myself, going without even so much as a whiff of the stuff every other day at least and trying my best to keep a hopeful outlook. Which is why I left the bar after two beers to go back to Peter's place and douse myself with aftershave, solidify the hair round my bald spot with a blast of hair spray and slip into the sport coat I'd last worn at Chiz Peltz's funeral (he froze to death the same night Bud lost his feet, and I was the one who had to pry him away from the back door of the barroom in the morning; he was like a bronze statue, huddled over the bottle with his parka pulled up over his head, and that was how we had to bury him, bottle and all). Then I made my way back through the roaring streets to the hotel and the ballroom that could have contained all of Boynton and everybody in it, feeling like an overawed freshman pressed up against the wall at the weekly social. But I wasn't a freshman anymore, and this was no social. I was thirty-four years old and I was tired of living like a monk. I needed someone to talk to—a companion, a helpmeet, a wife—and this was my best chance of finding one.

As soon as I saw Jordy standing there by the hors d'oeuvres table, the other hundred and six women vanished from sight, and I knew I'd been fooling myself back there at the bar. She was the one, the only one, and the longing for her was a continuous ache that never let up from that moment on. She was with another woman, and they had their heads together, talking, but I couldn't have honestly told you whether this other woman was tall or short, blond, brunette or redhead: I saw Jordy, and nothing more. "Hi," I said, the sport coat gouging at my underarms and clinging to my back like a living thing, "remember me?"

She sure did. And she reached up to take hold of my hand and peck a little kiss into the outer fringe of my beard. The other woman—the invisible one—faded away into the background before she could be introduced.

I found myself at a loss for what to say next. My hands felt big and cumbersome, as if they'd just been stapled on as I came through the door, and the sport coat flapped its wings and dug its talons into my neck. I wanted a drink. Badly.

"Would you like a drink?" Jordy whispered, fracturing the words into tiny little nuggets of meaning. She was holding a glass of white wine in one hand and she was wearing a pair of big glittery dangling earrings that hung all the way down to the sculpted bones of her bare shoulders.

I let her lead me up to the long folding table with the four bartenders hustling around on one side and all the women pressed up against the other while the rawboned bush crazies did their best to talk them to death, and then I had a double scotch in my hand and felt better. "It's beautiful country," I said, toasting her, it, the ballroom and everything beyond with a clink of our glasses, "especially out my way, in Boynton. Peaceful," I said, "you know?"

"Oh, I know," she said, and for the first time I noticed a hint of something barely contained bubbling just below the surface of that smoky voice, "or at least I can imagine. I mean, from what I've read. That's in the Yukon watershed, isn't it—Boynton?"

This was my cue, and I was grateful for it. I went into a rambling five-minute oration on the geographic and geological high points of the bush around Boynton, with sidelights on the local flora, fauna and human curiosities, tactfully avoiding any reference to the sobering statistics that made me question what I was doing there myself. It was a speech, all right, one that would have done any town booster proud. When I was through with it, I saw that my glass was empty and that Jordy was squirming in her boots to get a word in edgewise. "Sorry," I said, dipping my head in apology, "I didn't mean to talk your ear off. It's just that"—and here I got ahead of myself, my tongue loosened by the seeping burn of the scotch—"we don't get to talk much to anybody new, unless we make the trek into Fairbanks, and that's pretty rare—and especially not to someone as good-looking, I mean, as attractive, as you."

Jordy managed to flush prettily at the compliment, and then she was off on a speech of her own, decrying the lack of the human dimension in city life, the constant fuss and hurry and hassle, the bad air, the polluted beaches, and—this really got my attention—the lack of men with old-fashioned values, backbone and grit. When she delivered this last line—I don't know if that's how she phrased it exactly, but that was the gist of it—she leveled those glaciated eyes on me and I felt like I could walk on water.

We were standing in line at the buffet table when Bud Withers shuffled in. It was surprising how well he managed to do on those plastic feet—if you didn't know what was wrong with him, you'd never guess. You could see something wasn't quite right—every step he took looked like a recovery, as if he'd just been shoved from behind—but as I say, it wasn't all that abnormal. Anyway, I maneuvered myself in between Jordy and his line of sight, hunkering over her like an eagle masking its kill, and went on with our conversation. She was curious about life in Boynton, really obsessing over the smallest details, and I'd been telling her how much freedom you have out in the bush, how you can live your life the way you want, in tune with nature instead of shut up in some stucco box next to a shopping mall. "But what about you?" she said. "Aren't you stuck in your store?"

"I get antsy, I just close the place down for a couple days."

She looked shocked, or maybe skeptical is a better word. "What about your customers?"

I shrugged to show her how casual everything was. "It's not like I run the store for the public welfare," I said, "and they do have The Nougat to drink at, Clarence Ford's place." (Actually, Clarence meant to call it The Nugget, but he's a terrible speller, and I always go out of my way to give it a literal pronunciation just to irritate him.) "So anytime I want, dead of winter, whatever, I'll just hang out the Gone Trappin' sign, dig out my snowshoes, and go off and run my trap-line."

Jordy seemed to consider this, the hair round her temples frizzing up with the steam from the serving trays. "And what are you after—" she said finally, "mink?"

"Marten, lynx, fox, wolf." The food was good (it ought to have been for what we were paying), and I heaped up my plate, but not so much as to make her think I was a hog or anything. There was a silence. I became aware of the music then, a Beach Boys song rendered live by a band from Juneau at the far end of the room. "With a fox," I said, and I didn't know whether she wanted to hear this or not, "you come up on him and he's caught by the foot and maybe he's tried to gnaw that foot off, and he's snarling like a chainsaw . . . well, what you do is you just rap him across the snout with a stick, like this"—gesturing with my free hand—"and it knocks him right out. Like magic. Then you just put a little pressure on his throat till he stops breathing and you get a nice clean fur, you know what I mean?"

I was worried she might be one of those animal liberation nuts that want to protect every last rat, tick and flea, but she didn't look bothered at all. In fact, her eyes seemed to get distant for a minute, then she bent over to dish up a healthy portion of the king crab and straightened up with a smile. "Just like the pioneers," she said.

That was when Bud sniffed us out. He butted right in line, put a hand round Jordy's waist and drew her to him for a kiss, full plate and all, which she had to hold out awkwardly away from her body or there would have been king crab and avocado salad all down the front of that silky black dress she was wearing. "Sorry I'm late, babe," Bud said, and he picked up a plate and began mounding it high with cold cuts and smoked salmon.

Jordy turned to me then, and I couldn't read her face, not at all, but of course I knew in that instant that Bud had got to her and though the chances were a hundred and seven to one against it, she was the one who'd given him her room number. I was dazed by the realization, and after I got over being dazed, I felt the anger coming up in me like the foam in a loose can of beer. "Ned," she murmured, "do you know Bud?"

Bud gave me an ugly look, halfway between a "fuck you" and a leer of triumph. I tried to keep my cool, for Jordy's sake. "Yeah," was all I said.

She led us to a table in back, right near the band—one of those long banquet-type tables—and Bud and I sat down on either side of her, jockeying for position. "Bud," she said, as soon as we were settled, "and Ned"—turning to me and then back to him again—"I'm sure you can both help me with this, and I really want to know the truth of it because it's part and parcel of my whole romance with Alaska and now I've read somewhere that it isn't true." She had to raise her voice to be heard over the strains of "Little Deuce Coupe"—this was the Malibu Beach party, after all, replete with the pile of sand in the corner and a twenty-foot-high poster of Gidget in a bikini—and we both leaned in to hear her better. "What I want to know is, do you really have seventy-two different words for snow—in the Eskimo language, I mean?"

Bud didn't even give me a glance, just started in with his patented line of bullshit, how he'd spent two years with the Inuit up around Point Barrow, chewing walrus hides with the old ladies and dodging polar bears, and how he felt that seventy-two was probably a low estimate. Then he fell into some dialect he must have invented on the spot, all the while giving Jordy this big moony smile that made me want to puke, till I took her elbow and she turned to me and the faux Eskimo caught like a bone in his throat. "We call it termination dust," I said.

She lifted her eyebrows. Bud was on the other side of her, looked bored and greedy, shoveling up his food like a hyperphagic bear. It was the first moment he'd shut his mouth since he'd butted in. "It's because of the road," I explained. "We're at the far end of it, a two-lane gravel road that runs north from the Alaska Highway and dead-ends in Boynton, the last place on the continent you can drive to."

She was still waiting. The band fumbled through the end of the song and the room suddenly came alive with the buzz of a hundred conversations. Bud glanced up from his food to shoot me a look of unadulterated hate. "Go on," she said.

I shrugged, toyed with my fork. "That's it," I said. "The first snow, the first good one, and it's all over till spring, the end, it's all she wrote. If you're in Boynton, you're going to stay there—"

"And if you're not?" she asked, something satirical in her eyes as she tucked away a piece of crab with a tiny two-pronged fork.

Bud answered for me. "You're not going to make it."

The auction was for charity, all proceeds to be divided equally among the Fur Trappers' Retirement Home, the AIDS Hospice and the Greater Anchorage Foodbank. I had no objection to that—I was happy to do my part—but as I said, I was afraid somebody would outbid me for a date with Jordy. Not that the date was anything more than just that—a date—but it was a chance to spend the better part of the next day with the woman of your choice, and when you only had two and a half days, that was a big chunk of it. I'd talked to J.J. and some of the others, and they were all planning to bid on this woman or that and to take them out on a fishing boat or up in a Super Cub to see the glaciers east of town or even out into the bush to look over their cabins and their prospects. Nobody talked about sex—that would demean the spirit of the thing—but it was there, under the surface, like a burning promise.

The first woman went for seventy-five dollars. She was about forty or so, and she looked like a nurse or dental technician, somebody who really knew her way around a bedpan or saliva sucker. The rest of us stood around and watched while three men exercised their index fingers and the auctioneer (who else but Peter?) went back and forth between them with all sorts of comic asides until they'd reached their limit. "Going once, going twice," he chimed, milking the moment for all it was worth, "sold to the man in the red hat." I watched the guy, nobody I knew, an Anchorage type, as he mounted the three steps to the stage they'd set up by the sandpit, and I felt something stir inside me when this dental technician of forty smiled like all the world was melting and gave him a kiss right out of the last scene of a movie and the two of them went off hand in hand. My heart was hammering like a broken piston. I couldn't see Bud in the crowd, but I knew what his intentions were, and as I said, a hundred twenty-five was my limit. There was no way I was going past that, no matter what.

Jordy came up ninth. Two or three of the women that preceded her were really something to look at, secretaries probably or cocktail waitresses, but Jordy easily outclassed them. It wasn't only that she was educated, it was the way she held herself, the way she stepped up to the platform with a private little smile and let those unquenchable eyes roam over the crowd till they settled on me. I stood a head taller than anyone else there, so I guess it wasn't so hard to pick me out. I gave her a little wave, and then immediately regretted it because I'd tipped my hand.

The first bid was a hundred dollars from some clown in a lumberjack shirt who looked as if he'd just been dragged out from under a bush somewhere. I swear there was lint in his hair. Or worse. Peter had said, "Who'll start us off here, do I hear an opening bid?," and this guy stuck up his hand and said, "A hundred," just like that. I was stunned. Bud I was prepared for, but this was something else altogether. What was this guy thinking? A lumberjack shirt and he was bidding on *Jordy?* It was all I could do to keep myself from striding through the crowd and jerking the guy out of his boots like some weed along the roadside, but then another hand popped up just in front of me, and this guy must have been sixty if he was a day, the back of his neck all rutted and seamed and piss-yellow hairs growing out of his ears, and he spoke up just as casually as if he was ordering a drink at the bar: "One twenty." I was in a panic, beset on all sides, and I felt my tongue thickening in my throat as I threw up my arm. "One—" I gasped. "One twenty-five!"

Then it was Bud's turn. I heard him before I saw him slouching there in the second row, right up near the stage. He didn't even bother raising his hand. "One fifty," he said, and right away the old bird in front of me croaked out, "One seventy-five." I was in a sweat, wringing my hands till I thought the left would crush the right and vice versa, the sport coat digging into me like a hair-shirt, like a straitjacket, too small under the arms and across the shoulders. One twenty-five was my limit, absolutely and unconditionally, and even then I'd be straining to pay for the date itself, but I felt my arm jerking up as if it was attached to a wire. "One seventy-six!" I shouted, and everybody in the room turned around to stare at me.

I heard a laugh from the front, a dirty sniggering little stab of a laugh that shot hot lava through my veins, Bud's laugh, Bud's mocking hateful naysaying laugh, and then Bud's voice crashed through the wall of wonder surrounding my bid and pronounced my doom. "Two hundred and fifty dollars," he said, and I stood there stupefied as Peter called out, "Going once, going twice," and slammed down the gavel.

I don't remember what happened next, but I turned away before Bud could shuffle up to the stage and take Jordy in his arms and receive the public kiss that was meant for me, turned away, and staggered toward the bar like a gutshot deer. I try to control my temper, I really do—I know it's a failing of mine—but I guess I must have gotten a little rough with these two L. L. Bean types that were blocking my access to the scotch. Nothing outrageous, nothing more than letting them know in no uncertain terms that they were in my path and that if they liked the way their arms still fit in their sockets, they'd dance on out of there like the sugarplum fairy and her court, but still, I regretted it. Nothing else that night rings too clear, not after Jordy went to Bud for the sake of mere money, but

I kept thinking, over and over, as if a splinter was implanted in my brain, *How in Christ's name did that unemployed son of a bitch come up with two hundred and fifty bucks?*

I rang Jordy's room first thing in the morning (yes, there was that, at least: she'd given me her room number too, but now I wondered if she wasn't just playing mind games). There was no answer, and that told me something I didn't want to know. I inquired at the desk and the clerk said she'd checked out the night before, and I must have had a look on my face because he volunteered that he didn't know where she'd gone. It was then that the invisible woman from the cocktail party materialized out of nowhere, visible suddenly in a puke-green running suit, with greasy hair and a face all pitted and naked without a hint of makeup. "You looking for Jordy?" she said, and maybe she recognized me.

The drumming in my chest suddenly slowed. I felt ashamed of myself. Felt awkward and out of place, my head windy and cavernous from all that sorrowful scotch. "Yes," I admitted.

She took pity on me then and told me the truth. "She went to some little town with that guy from the auction last night. Said she'd be back for the plane Monday."

Ten minutes later I was in my Chevy half-ton, tooling up the highway for Fairbanks and the gravel road to Boynton. I felt an urgency bordering on the manic and my foot was like a cement block on the accelerator, because once Bud got to Boynton I knew what he was going to do. He'd ditch the car, which I wouldn't doubt he'd borrowed without the legitimate owner's consent, whoever that might be, and then he'd load up his canoe with supplies and Jordy and run down the river for his trespasser's cabin. And if that happened, Jordy wouldn't be making any plane. Not on Monday. Maybe not ever.

I tried to think about Jordy and how I was going to rescue her from all that and how grateful she'd be once she realized what kind of person she was dealing with in Bud and what his designs were, but every time I summoned her face, Bud's rose up out of some dark hole in my consciousness to blot it out. I saw him sitting at the bar that night he lost his feet, sitting there drinking steadily though I'd eighty-sixed him three times over the course of the past year and three times relented. He was on a tear, drinking with Chiz Peltz and this Indian I'd never laid eyes on before who claimed to be a full-blooded Flathead from Montana. It was January, a few days after New Year's, and it was maybe two o'clock in the afternoon and dark beyond the windows. I was drinking too—tending bar, but helping myself to the scotch—because it was one of those days when time has no meaning and your life drags like it has brakes on it. There were maybe eight other people in the place: Ronnie Perrault and his wife, Louise, Roy Treadwell, who services snow machines and sells cordwood, Richie Oliver and some others—I don't know where J.J. was that day, playing solitaire in his cabin, I guess, staring at the walls, who knows?

Anyway, Bud was on his tear and he started using language I don't tolerate in the bar, not anytime, and especially not when ladies are present, and I told him to can it and things got nasty. The upshot was that I had to pin the Indian to the back wall by his throat and rip Bud's parka half off him before I convinced the three of them to finish up their drinking over at The Nougat, which is where they went, looking ugly. Clarence Ford put up with them till around seven or so, and then he kicked them out and barred the door and they sat in Chiz Peltz's car with the engine running and the heater on full, passing a bottle back and forth till I don't know what hour. Of course, the car eventually ran out of gas with the three of them passed out like zombies and the overnight temperature went down to something like minus sixty, and as I said, Chiz didn't make it, and how he wound up outside my place I'll never know. We helicoptered Bud to the hospital in Fairbanks, but they couldn't save his feet. The Indian—I've never seen him since—just seemed to shake it off with the aid of a dozen cups of coffee laced with free bourbon at The Nougat.

Bud never forgave me or Clarence or anybody else in town. He was a sorehead and griper of the first degree, the sort of person who blames all his miseries on everybody but himself, and now he had Jordy, this sweet dreamy English teacher who probably thought Alaska was all *Northern Exposure* and charmingly eccentric people saying witty things to each other. I knew Bud. I knew how he would have portrayed that ratty illegal tumbledown cabin to her and how he would have told her it was just a hop, skip and jump down the river and not the twelve miles it actually was—and what was she going to do when she found out? Catch a cab?

These were my thoughts as I passed through Fairbanks, headed southeast on the Alaska Highway, and finally turned north for Boynton. It was late in the afternoon and I still had a hundred and eighty miles of gravel road to traverse before I even hit Boynton, let alone caught up with Bud—I could only hope he'd stopped off at The Nougat for his usual fix of vodka, but the chances of that were slim because he'd want to hustle Jordy down the river before she got a good idea of who he was and what was going on. And that was another thing: I just didn't understand her. Just didn't. He'd put in the highest bid and she was a good sport, okay—but to drive all night with that slime? To put up with his bullshit for all those crippling hours, maybe even fall for it? Poor Jordy. Poor, poor Jordy.

I pulled into Boynton in record time, foot to the floor all the way, and skidded to a halt in the gravel lot out front of my store. There were only three other cars there, each as familiar as my own, and Ronnie Perrault, who I'd asked to help out for the weekend, was presiding over a very quiet bar (half the men in town had gone to Anchorage for the big event, thanks to Peter and his unflagging salesmanship). "Ronnie," I said, coming into the bar to the strains of Lyle Lovett singing "Mack the Knife" like he was half dead, "you seen Bud?"

Ronnie was hunched lovingly over a cigarette and a Meyers and Coke, holding hands with Louise. He was wearing a Seattle Mariners cap backwards on his head, and his eyes were distant, the eyes of a man in rum nirvana. Howard Walpole, seventy years old and with a bad back and runny eyes, was at the far end of the bar, and Roy Treadwell and Richie Oliver were playing cards at the table by the stove. Ronnie was slow, barely flowing, like the grenadine in the back pantry that hardly gets any heat. "I thought," he said, chewing over the words, "I thought you wasn't going to be back till Tuesday?"

"Hey, Neddy," Doug shouted, squeezing out the diminutive until it was like a screech, "how many you bring back?"

"Bud," I repeated, addressing the room at large. "Anybody seen Bud?"

Well, they had to think about that. They were all pretty hazy, while the cat's away the mice will play, but it was Howard who came out of it first. "Sure," he said, "I seen him," and he leaned so far forward over his drink I thought he was going to fall into it, "early this morning, in a brand-new Toyota Land Cruiser, which I don't know where he got, and he had a woman with him." And then, as if remembering some distant bit of trivia: "How was that flesh bazaar anyway? You married yet?"

Louise snickered, Ronnie guffawed, but I was in no mood. "Where'd he go?" I said, hopeful, always hopeful, but I already knew the answer.

Howard did something with his leg, a twitch he'd developed to ease the pain in his back. "I didn't talk to him," he said. "But I think he was going downriver."

The river wasn't too rough this time of year, but it was still moving at a pretty good clip, and I have to admit I'm not exactly an ace with the canoe. I'm too big for anything that small—give me a runabout with an Evinrude engine any day—and I always feel awkward and top-heavy. But there I was, moving along with the current, thinking one thing and one thing only: Jordy. It would be a bitch coming back up, but there'd be two of us paddling, and I kept focusing on how grateful she was going to be for getting her out of there, more grateful than if I'd bid a thousand dollars for her and took her out for steak three nights in a row. But then the strangest thing happened: the sky went gray and it began to snow.

It just doesn't snow that early in the year, not ever, or hardly ever. But there it was. The wind came up the channel of the river and threw these dry little pellets of ice in my face and I realized how stupid I'd been. I was already a couple miles downriver from town, and though I had a light parka and mittens with me, a chunk of cheese, loaf of bread, couple Cokes, that sort of thing, I really hadn't planned on any weather. It was a surprise, a real surprise. Of course, at that point I was sure it was only a squall, something to whiten the ground for a day and then melt off, but I still felt stupid out there on the river without any real protection, and I began to wonder how Jordy would see it, the way she was worried about all the names for snow and how sick at heart she must have been just about then with Bud's shithole of a cabin and no escape and the snow coming down like a life sentence, and I leaned into the paddle.

It was after dark when I came round the bend and saw the lights of the cabin off through the scrim of snow. I was wearing my parka and mittens now, and I must have looked like a snowman propped up in the white envelope of the canoe and I could feel the ice forming in my beard where the breath froze coming out of my nostrils. I smelled woodsmoke and watched the soft tumbling sky. Was I angry? Not really. Not yet. I'd hardly thought about what I was doing up to this point—it all just seemed so obvious. The son of a bitch had gotten her, whether it was under false pretenses or not, and Jordy, sweet Jordy with Emily Brontë tucked under her arm, couldn't have imagined in her wildest dreams what she was getting into. No one would have blamed me. For all intents and purposes, Bud had abducted her. He had.

Still, when I actually got there, when I could smell the smoke and see the lamps burning, I felt shy suddenly. I couldn't just burst in and announce that I'd come to rescue her, could I? And I could hardly pretend I just happened to be in the neighborhood . . . plus, that was Bud in there, and he was as purely nasty as a rattlesnake with a hand clamped round the back of its head. There was no way he was going to like this, no matter how you looked at it.

So what I did was pull the canoe up on the bank about a hundred yards from the cabin, the scrape of the gravel masked by the snow, and creep up on the place, as stealthy as a big man can be—I didn't want to alert Bud's dog and blow the whole thing. But that was just it, I realized, tiptoeing through the snow like an ice statue come to life—what thing would I blow? I didn't have a plan. Not even a clue.

In the end, I did the obvious: snuck up to the window and peered in. I couldn't see much at first, the window all smeared with grime, but I gingerly rubbed the pane with the wet heel of my mitten, and things came into focus. The stove in the corner was going, a mouth of flame with the door flung open wide for the fireplace effect. Next to the stove was a table with a bottle of wine on it and two glasses, one of them half full, and I saw the dog then—a malamute-looking thing—asleep underneath it. There was some homemade furniture—a sort of couch with an old single mattress thrown over it, a couple of crude chairs of bent aspen with the bark still on it. Four or five white plastic buckets of water were lined up against the wall, which was festooned with the usual backcountry junk: snowshoes, traps, hides, the mangy stuffed head of a caribou Bud must have picked up at a fire sale someplace. But I didn't see Bud. Or Jordy. And then I realized they must be in the back room—the bedroom—and that made me feel strange, choked up in the pit of my throat as if somebody was trying to strangle me.

It was snowing pretty steadily, six inches on the ground at least, and it muffled my footsteps as I worked my way around the cabin to the back window. The night was absolute, the sky so close it was breathing for me, in and out, in and out, and the snow held everything in the grip of silence. A candle was burning in the back window—I could tell it was a candle from the way the light wavered even before I got there—and I heard the music then, violins all playing in unison, the sort of thing I wouldn't have expected from a lowlife like Bud, and voices, a low, intimate murmur of voices. That almost stopped me right there, that whispery blur of Jordy's voice and the deeper resonance of Bud's, and for a moment everything hung in the balance. A part of me wanted to back away from that window, creep back to the canoe, and forget all about it. But I didn't. I couldn't. I'd seen her first—I'd squeezed her hand and given her the corsage and admired the hand-lettered nametag—and it wasn't right. The murmur of those voices rose up in my head like a scream, and there was nothing more to think about.

My shoulder hit the back door just above the latch and blew the thing off the hinges like it was a toy, and there I was, breathing hard and white to the eyebrows. I saw them in the bed together and heard this little birdlike cry from Jordy and a curse from Bud, and then the dog came hurtling in from the front room as if he'd been launched from a cannon. (And I should say here that I like dogs and that I've never lifted a finger to hurt any dog I've ever owned, but I had to put this one down. I didn't have any choice.) I caught him as he left the floor and slammed him into the wall behind me till he collapsed in a heap. Jordy was screaming now, actually screaming, and you would have thought that I was the bad guy, but I tried to calm her, her arms bare and the comforter pulled up over her breasts and Bud's plastic feet set there like slippers on the floor, telling her a mile a minute that I'd protect her, it was all right, and I'd see that Bud was prosecuted to the fullest extent, the fullest extent, but then Bud was fumbling under the mattress for something like the snake he was, and I took hold of his puny slip of a wrist with the blue-black snubnose .22 in it and just squeezed till his other hand came up and I caught that one and squeezed it too.

Jordy made a bolt for the other room and I could see she was naked, and I knew right then he must have raped her because there was no way she'd ever consent to anything with a slime like that, not Jordy, not my Jordy, and the thought of what Bud had done to her made me angry. The gun was on the floor now and I kicked it under the bed and let go of Bud's wrists and shut up his stream of curses and vile foul language with a quick stab to the bridge of his nose, and it was almost like a reflex. He went limp under the force of that blow and I was upset, I admit it, I was furious over what he'd done to that girl, and it just seemed like the most natural thing in the world to reach out and put a little pressure on his throat till the raw-looking stumps of his legs lay still on the blanket.

That was when I became aware of the music again, the violins swelling up and out of a black plastic boombox on the shelf till they filled the room and the wind blew through the doorway and the splintered door groaned on its broken latch. Jordy, I was thinking, Jordy needs me, needs me to get her out of this, and I went into the front room to tell her about the snow and how it was coming down out of season and what that meant. She was crouched in the corner across from the stove and her face was wet and she was shivering. Her sweater was clutched up around her neck, and she'd got one leg of her jeans on, but the other leg was bare, sculpted bare and white all the way from her little painted toenails to the curve of her thigh and beyond. It was a hard moment. And I tried to explain to her, I did. "Look outside," I said. "Look out there into the night. You see that?"

She lifted her chin then and looked, out beyond the doorway to the back room, beyond Bud on his bed and the dog on the floor and into the gaping hole where the door had been. And there it was, coming down like the end of everything, snow, and there was only one name for it now. I tried to tell her that. Because we weren't going anywhere.

(1994)

She Wasn't Soft

She wasn't tender, she wasn't soft, she wasn't sweetly yielding or coquettish, and she was nobody's little woman and never would be. That had been her mother's role, and look at the sad sack of neuroses and alcoholic dysfunction she'd become. And her father. He'd been the pasha of the living room, the sultan of the kitchen, and the emperor of the bedroom, and what had it got him? A stab in the chest, a tender liver, and two feet that might as well have been stumps. Paula Turk wasn't born for that sort of life, with its domestic melodrama and greedy sucking babies—no, she was destined for something richer and more complex, something that would define and elevate her, something great. She wanted to compete and she wanted to win—always, shining before her like some numinous icon was the glittering image of triumph. And whenever she flagged, whenever a sniffle or the flu ate at her reserves and she hit the wall in the numbing waters of the Pacific or the devilish winds at the top of San Marcos Pass, she pushed herself through it, drove herself with an internal whip that accepted no excuses and made no allowances for the limitations of the flesh. She was twenty-eight years old, and she was going to conquer the world.

On the other hand, Jason Barre, the thirty-three-year-old surf-and-dive shop proprietor she'd been seeing pretty steadily over the past nine months, didn't really seem to have the fire of competition in him. Both his parents were doctors (and that, as much as anything, had swayed Paula in his favor when they first met), and they'd set him up in his own business, a business that had continuously lost money since its grand opening three years ago. When the waves were breaking, Jason would be at the beach, and when the surf was flat he'd be stationed behind the counter on his tall swivel stool, selling wax remover to bleached-out adolescents who said things like "gnarly" and "killer" in their penetrating adenoidal tones. Jason liked to surf, and he liked to breathe the cigarette haze in sports bars, a permanent sleepy-eyed, widemouthed California grin on his face, flip-flops on his feet, and his waist encircled by a pair of faded baggy shorts barely held in place by the gentle sag of his belly and the twin anchors of his hipbones.

That was all right with Paula. She told him he should quit smoking, cut down on his drinking, but she didn't harp on it. In truth, she really didn't care all that much—one world-beater in a relationship was enough. When she was in training, which was all the time now, she couldn't help feeling a kind of moral superiority to anyone who wasn't—and Jason most emphatically wasn't. He was no threat, and he didn't want to be—his mind just didn't work that way. He was cute, that was all, and just as she got a little frisson of pleasure from the swell of his paunch beneath the oversized T-shirt and his sleepy eyes and his laid-back ways, he admired her for her drive and the lean, hard triumph of her beauty and her strength. She never took drugs or alcohol—or hardly ever—but he persuaded her to try just a puff or two of marijuana before they made love, and it seemed to relax her, open up her pores till she could feel her nerve ends poking through them, and their love-making was like nothing she'd ever experienced, except maybe breaking the tape at the end of the twenty-six-mile marathon.

It was a Friday night in August, half-past seven, the sun hanging in the window like a piñata, and she'd just stepped out of the shower after a two-hour tuneup for Sunday's triathlon, when the phone rang. Jason's voice came over the wire, low and soft. "Hey, babe," he said, breathing into the phone like a sex maniac (he always called her babe, and she loved it, precisely because she wasn't a babe and never would be—it was their little way of mocking the troglodytes molded into the barstools beside him). "Listen, I was just wondering if you might want to join me down at Clubber's for a while. Yeah, I know, you need your sleep and the big day's the day after tomorrow and Zinny Bauer's probably already asleep, but how about it. Come on. It's my birthday."

"Your birthday? I thought your birthday was in December?"

There was the ghost of a pause during which she could detect the usual wash of background noise, drunken voices crying out as if from the netherworld, the competing announcers of the six different games unfolding simultaneously on the twelve big-screen TVs, the insistent pulse of the jukebox thumping faintly beneath it all. "No," he said, "my birthday's today, August twenty-sixth—it is. I don't know where you got the idea it was in December . . . but come on, babe, don't you have to load up on carbohydrates?"

She did. She admitted it. "I was going to make pancakes and penne," she said, "with a little cheese sauce and maybe a loaf of that brown-and-serve bread. . . ."

"I'll take you to the Pasta Bowl, all you can eat—and I swear I'll have you back by eleven." He lowered his voice. "And no sex, I know—I wouldn't want to drain you or anything."

She wasn't soft because she ran forty-five miles a week, biked two hundred and fifty, and slashed through fifteen thousand yards of the crawl in the Baños del Mar pool. She was in the best shape of her life, and Sunday's event was nothing, less than half the total distance of the big one—the Hawaii Ironman—in October.

She wasn't soft because she'd finished second in the women's division last year in Hawaii and forty-fourth over all, beating out one thousand three hundred and fifty other contestants, twelve hundred of whom, give or take a few, were men. Like Jason. Only fitter. A whole lot fitter.

She swung by Clubber's to pick him up—he wasn't driving, not since his last D.U.I. anyway—and though parking was no problem, she had to endure the stench of cigarettes and the faint sour odor of yesterday's vomit while he finished his cocktail and wrapped up his ongoing analysis of the Dodgers' chances with an abstract point about a blister on somebody or other's middle finger. The guy they called Little Drake, white-haired at thirty-six and with a face that reminded her of one of those naked drooping dogs, leaned out of his Hawaiian shirt and into the radius of Jason's gesticulating hands as if he'd never heard such wisdom in his life. And Paula? She stood there at the bar in her shorts and Lycra halter top, sucking an Evian through a straw while the sports fans furtively admired her pecs and lats and the hard hammered musculature of her legs, for all the world a babe. She didn't mind. In fact, it made her feel luminous and alive, not to mention vastly superior to all those pale lumps of flesh sprouting out of the corners like toadstools and the sagging abrasive girlfriends who hung on their arms and tried to feign interest in whatever sport happened to be on the tube.

But somebody was talking to her, Little Drake, it was Little Drake, leaning across Jason and addressing her as if she were one of them. "So Paula," he was saying. "Paula?"

She swiveled her head toward him, hungry now, impatient. She didn't want to hang around the bar and schmooze about Tommy Lasorda and O.J. and Proposition 187 and how Phil Aguirre had broken both legs and his collarbone in the surf at Rincon; she wanted to go to the Pasta Bowl and carbo-load. "Yes?" she said, trying to be civil, for Jason's sake.

"You going to put them to shame on Sunday, or what?"

Jason was snubbing out his cigarette in the ashtray, collecting his money from the bar. They were on their way out the door—in ten minutes she'd be forking up fettucine or angel hair with black olives and sun-dried tomatoes while Jason regaled her with a satiric portrait of his day and all the crazies who'd passed through his shop. The little man with the white hair didn't require a dissertation, and besides, he couldn't begin to appreciate the difference between what she was doing and the ritualistic farce of the tobacco-spitting, crotch-grabbing "athletes" all tricked out in their pretty unblemished uniforms up on the screen over his head, so she just smiled, like a babe, and said, "Yeah."

Truly, the race was nothing, just a warm-up, and it would have been less than nothing but for the puzzling fact that Zinny Bauer was competing. Zinny was a professional, from Hamburg, and she was the one who'd cranked past Paula like some sort of machine in the final stretch of the Ironman last year. What Paula couldn't fathom was why Zinny was bothering with this small-time event when there were so many other plums out there. On the way out of Clubber's, she mentioned it to Jason. "Not that I'm worried," she said, "just mystified."

It was a fine, soft, glowing night, the air rich with the smell of the surf, the sun squeezing the last light out of the sky as it sank toward Hawaii. Jason was wearing his faded-to-pink 49ers jersey and a pair of shorts so big they made his legs look like sticks. He gave her one of his hooded looks, then got distracted and tapped at his watch twice before lifting it to his ear and frowning. "Damn thing stopped," he said. It wasn't until they were sliding into the car that he came back to the subject of Zinny Bauer. "It's simple, babe," he said, shrugging his shoulders and letting his face go slack. "She's here to psych you out."

He liked to watch her eat. She wasn't shy about it—not like the other girls he'd dated, the ones on a perpetual diet who made you feel like a two-headed hog every time you sat down to a meal, whether it was a Big Mac or the Mexican Plate at La Fondita. No "salad with dressing on the side" for Paula, no butterless bread or child's portions. She attacked her food like a lumberjack, and you'd better keep your hands and fingers clear. Tonight she started with potato gnocchi in a white sauce puddled with butter, and she ate half a loaf of crusty Italian bread with it, sopping up the leftover sauce till the plate gleamed. Next it was the fettucine with Alfredo sauce, and on her third trip to the pasta bar she heaped her plate with mostaccioli marinara and chunks of hot sausage—and more bread, always more bread.

He ordered a beer, lit a cigarette without thinking, and shoveled up some spaghetti carbonara, thick on the fork and sloppy with sauce. The next thing he knew, he was staring up into the hot green gaze of the waitperson, a pencil-necked little fag he could have snapped in two like a breadstick if this weren't California and everything so copacetic and laid back. It was times like this when he wished he lived in Cleveland, even though he'd never been there, but he knew what was coming and he figured people in Cleveland wouldn't put up with this sort of crap.

"You'll have to put that out," the little fag said.

"Sure, man," Jason said, gesturing broadly so that the smoke fanned out around him like the remains of a pissed-over fire. "Just as soon as I"—puff, puff—"take another drag and"—puff, puff—"find me an ashtray somewhere . . . you wouldn't happen"—puff, puff—"to have an ashtray, would you?"

Of course the little fag had been holding one out in front of him all along, as if it were a portable potty or something, but the cigarette was just a glowing stub now, the tiny fag end of a cigarette—fag end, how about that?—and Jason reached out, crushed the thing in the ashtray and said, "Hey, thanks, dude—even though it really wasn't a cigarette but just the *fag* end of one."

And then Paula was there, her fourth plate of the evening mounded high with angel hair, three-bean salad, and wedges of fruit in five different colors. "So what was that all about? Your cigarette?"

Jason ignored her, forking up spaghetti. He took a long swig of his beer and shrugged. "Yeah, whatever," he said finally. "One more fascist doing his job."

"Don't be like that," she said, using the heel of her bread to round up stray morsels on her plate.

"Like what?"

"You know what I mean. I don't have to lecture you."

"Yeah?" He let his eyes droop. "So what do you call this then?"

She sighed and looked away, and that sigh really irritated him, rankled him, made him feel like flipping the table over and sailing a few plates through the window. He was drunk. Or three-quarters drunk anyway. Then her lips were moving again. "Everybody in the world doesn't necessarily enjoy breathing through a tube of incinerated tobacco, you know," she said. "People are into health."

"Who? You maybe. But the rest of them just want to be a pain in the ass. They just want to abrogate my rights in a public place"—abrogate, now where did that come from?—"and then rub my nose in it." The thought soured him even more, and when he caught the waitperson pussyfooting by out of the corner of his eye he snapped his fingers with as much pure malice as he could manage. "Hey, dude, another beer here, huh? I mean, when you get a chance."

It was then that Zinny Bauer made her appearance. She stalked through the door like something crossbred in an experimental laboratory, so rangy and hollow-eyed and fleshless she looked as if she'd been pasted onto her bones. There was a guy with her—her trainer or husband or whatever—and he was right out of an X-Men cartoon, all head and shoulders and great big beefy biceps. Jason recognized them from Houston—he'd flown down to watch Paula compete in the Houston Ironman, only to see her hit the wall in the run and finish sixth in the women's while Zinny Bauer, the Amazing Bone Woman, took an easy first. And here they were, Zinny and Klaus—or Olaf or whoever—here in the Pasta Bowl, carbo-loading like anybody else. His beer came, cold and dependable, green in the bottle, pale amber in the glass, and he downed it in two gulps. "Hey, Paula," he said, and he couldn't keep the quick sharp stab of joy out of his voice—he was happy suddenly and he didn't know why. "Hey, Paula, you see who's here?"

The thing that upset her was that he'd lied to her, the way her father used to lie to her mother, the same way—casually, almost as a reflex. It wasn't his birthday at all. He'd just said that to get her out because he was drunk and he didn't care if she had to compete the day after tomorrow and needed her rest and peace and quiet and absolutely no stimulation whatever. He was selfish, that was all, selfish and unthinking. And then there was the business with the cigarette—he knew as well as anybody in the state that there was an ordinance against smoking in public places as of January last, and still he had to push the limits like some cocky immature chip-on-the-shoulder surfer. Which is exactly what he was. But all that was forgivable—it was the Zinny Bauer business she just couldn't understand.

Paula wasn't even supposed to be there. She was supposed to be at home, making up a batch of flapjacks and penne with cheese sauce and lying inert on the couch with the remote control. This was the night before the night before the event, a time to fuel up her tanks and veg out. But because of him, because of her silver-tongued hero in the baggy shorts, she was at the Pasta Bowl, carbo-loading in public. And so was Zinny Bauer, the last person on earth she wanted to see.

That was bad enough, but Jason made it worse, far worse—Jason made it into one of the most excruciating moments of her life. What happened was purely crazy, and if she hadn't known Jason better she would have thought he'd planned it. They were squabbling over his cigarette and how unlaid-back and uptight the whole thing had made him—he was drunk, and she didn't appreciate him when he was drunk, not at all—when his face suddenly took on a conspiratorial look and he said, "Hey, Paula, you see who's here?"

"Who?" she said, and she shot a glance over her shoulder and froze: it was Zinny Bauer and her husband Armin. "Oh, shit," she said, and she lowered her head and focused on her plate as if it were the most fascinating thing she'd ever seen. "She didn't see me, did she? We've got to go. Right now. Right this minute."

Jason was smirking. He looked happy about it, as if he and Zinny Bauer were old friends. "But you've only had four plates, babe," he said. "You sure we got our money's worth? I could go for maybe just a touch more pasta—and I haven't even had any salad yet."

"No joking around, this isn't funny." Her voice withered in her throat. "I don't want to see her. I don't want to talk to her. I just want to get out of here, okay?"

His smile got wider. "Sure, babe, I know how you feel—but you're going to beat her, you are, no sweat. You don't have to let anybody chase you out of your favorite restaurant in your own town—I mean, that's not right, is it? That's not in the spirit of friendly competition."

"Jason," she said, and she reached across the table and took hold of his wrist. "I mean it. Let's get out of here. Now."

Her throat was constricted, as if everything she'd eaten was about to come up. Her legs ached, and her ankle—the one she'd sprained last spring—felt as if someone had driven a nail through it. All she could think of was Zinny Bauer, with her long muscles and the shaved blond stubble of her head and her eyes that never quit. Zinny Bauer was behind her, at her back, right there, and it was too much to bear. "*Jason,*" she hissed.

"Okay, okay," he was saying, and he tipped back the dregs of his beer and reached into his pocket and scattered a couple of rumpled bills across the table by way of a tip. Then he rose from the chair with a slow drunken grandeur and gave her a wink as if to indicate that the coast was clear. She got up, hunching her shoulders as if she could compress herself into invisibility and stared down at her feet as Jason took her arm and led her across the room—if Zinny saw her, Paula wouldn't know about it because she wasn't going to look up, and she wasn't going to make eye contact, she wasn't.

Or so she thought.

She was concentrating on her feet, on the black-and-white checked pattern of the floor tiles and how her running shoes negotiated them as if they were attached to somebody else's legs, when all of a sudden Jason stopped and her eyes flew up and there they were, hovering over Zinny Bauer's table like casual acquaintances, like neighbors on their way to a P.T.A. meeting. "But aren't you Zinny Bauer?" Jason said, his voice gone high and nasal as he shifted into his Valley Girl imitation. "The great triathlete? Oh, God, yes, yes, you are, aren't you? Oh, God, could I have your autograph for my little girl?"

Paula was made of stone. She couldn't move, couldn't speak, couldn't even blink her eyes. And Zinny—she looked as if her plane had just crashed. Jason was playing out the charade, pretending to fumble through his pockets for a pen, when Armin broke the silence. "Why don't you just fock off," he said, and the veins stood out in his neck.

"Oh, she'll be so thrilled," Jason went on, his voice pinched to a squeal. "She's so adorable, only six years old, and, oh, my God, she's not going to believe this—"

Armin rose to his feet. Zinny clutched at the edge of the table with bloodless fingers, her eyes narrow and hard. The waiter—the one Jason had been riding all night—started toward them, crying out, "Is everything all right?" as if the phrase had any meaning.

And then Jason's voice changed, just like that. "Fuck you too, Jack, and your scrawny fucking bald-headed squeeze."

Armin worked out, you could see that, and Paula doubted he'd ever pressed a cigarette to his lips, let alone a joint, but still Jason managed to hold his own—at least until the kitchen staff separated them. There was some breakage, a couple of chairs overturned, a whole lot of noise and cursing and threatening, most of it from Jason. Every face in the restaurant was drained of color by the time the kitchen staff came to the rescue, and somebody went to the phone and called the police, but Jason blustered his way out the door and disappeared before they arrived. And Paula? She just melted away and kept on melting until she found herself behind the wheel of the car, cruising slowly down the darkened streets, looking for Jason.

She never did find him.

When he called the next morning he was all sweetness and apology. He whispered, moaned, sang to her, his voice a continuous soothing current insinuating itself through the line and into her head and right on down through her veins and arteries to the unresisting core of her. "Listen, Paula, I didn't mean for things to get out of hand," he whispered, "you've got to believe me. I just didn't think you had to hide from anybody, that's all."

She listened, her mind gone numb, and let his words saturate her. It was the day before the event, and she wasn't going to let anything distract her. But then, as he went on, pouring himself into the phone with his penitential, self-pitying tones as if he were the one who'd been embarrassed and humiliated, she felt the outrage coming up in her: didn't he understand, didn't he know what it meant to stare into the face of your own defeat? And over a plate of pasta, no less? She cut him off in the middle of a long digression about some surfing legend of the fifties and all the adversity he'd had to face from a host of competitors, a blood-sucking wife and a fearsome backwash off Newport Beach.

"What did you think," she demanded, "that you were protecting me or something? Is that it? Because if that's what you think, let me tell you I don't need you or anybody else to stand up for me—"

"Paula," he said, his voice creeping out at her over the wire, "Paula, I'm on your side, remember? I love what you're doing. I want to help you." He paused. "And yes, I want to protect you too."

"I don't need it."

"Yes, you do. You don't think you do but you do. Don't you see: I was trying to psych her."

"Psych her? At the Pasta Bowl?"

His voice was soft, so soft she could barely hear him: "Yeah." And then, even softer: "I did it for you."

It was Saturday, seventy-eight degrees, sun beaming down unmolested, the tourists out in force. The shop had been buzzing since ten, nothing major—cords, tube socks, T-shirts, a couple of illustrated guides to South Coast hot spots that nobody who knew anything needed a book to find—but Jason had been at the cash register right through lunch and on into the four-thirty breathing spell when the tourist mind tended to fixate on ice-cream cones and those pathetic sidecar bikes they pedaled up and down the street like the true guppies they were. He'd even called Little Drake in to help out for a couple of hours there. Drake didn't mind. He'd grown up rich in Montecito and gone white-haired at twenty-seven, and now he lived with his even whiter-haired old parents and managed their two rental properties downtown—which meant he had nothing much to do except prop up the bar at Clubber's or haunt the shop like the thinnest ghost of a customer. So why not put him to work?

"Nothing to shout about," Jason told him, over the faint hum of the oldies channel. He leaned back against the wall on his high stool and cracked the first beer of the day. "Little stuff, but a lot of it. I almost had that one dude sold on the Al Merrick board—I could taste it—but something scared him off. Maybe mommy took away his Visa card, I don't know."

Drake pulled contemplatively at his beer and looked out the window on the parade of tourists marching up and down State Street. He didn't respond. It was that crucial hour of the day, the hour known as cocktail hour, two for one, the light stuck on the underside of the palms, everything soft and pretty and winding down toward dinner and evening, the whole night held out before them like a promise. "What time's the Dodger game?" Drake said finally.

Jason looked at his watch. It was a reflex. The Dodgers were playing the Mets at five-thirty, Astacio against the Doc, and he knew the time and channel as well as he knew his A.T.M. number. The Angels were on Prime Ticket, seven-thirty, at home against the Orioles. And Paula—Paula was at home too, focusing (do not disturb, thank you very much) for the big one with the Amazing Bone Woman the next morning. "Five-thirty," he said, after a long pause.

Drake said nothing. His beer was gone, and he shuffled behind the counter to the little reefer for another. When he'd cracked it, sipped, belched, scratched himself thoroughly, and commented on the physique of an overweight Mexican chick in a red bikini making her way up from the beach, he ventured an opinion on the topic under consideration: "Time to close up?"

All things being equal, Jason would have stayed open till six, or near six anyway, on a Saturday in August. The summer months accounted for the lion's share of his business—it was like the Christmas season for everybody else—and he tried to maximize it, he really did, but he knew what Drake was saying. Twenty to five now, and they had to count the receipts, lock up, stop by the night deposit at the B. of A., and then settle in at Clubber's for the game. It would be nice to be there, maybe with a tall tequila tonic and the sports section spread out on the bar, before the game got under way. Just to settle in and enjoy the fruits of their labor. He gave a sigh, for form's sake, and said, "Yeah, why not?"

And then there was cocktail hour and he had a couple of tall tequila tonics before switching to beer, and the Dodgers looked good, real good, red hot, and somebody bought him a shot. Drake was carrying on about something—his girlfriend's cat, the calluses on his mother's feet—and Jason tuned him out, ordered two soft chicken tacos, and watched the sun do all sorts of amazing pink and salmon things to the storefronts across the street before the gray finally settled in. He was thinking he should have gone surfing today, thinking he'd maybe go out in the morning, and then he was thinking of Paula. He should wish her luck or something, give her a phone call at least. But the more he thought about it, the more he pictured her alone in her apartment, power-drinking her fluids, sunk into the shell of her focus like some Chinese Zen master, and the more he wanted to see her.

They hadn't had sex in a week. She was always like that when it was coming down to the wire, and he didn't blame her. Or yes, yes, he did blame her. And he resented it too. What was the big deal? It wasn't like she was playing ball or anything that took any skill, and why lock him out for that? She was like his overachieving, straight-arrow parents, Type A personalities, early risers, joggers, let's go out and beat the world. God, that was anal. But she had some body on her, as firm and flawless as the Illustrated Man's—or Woman's, actually. He thought about that and about the way her face softened when they were in bed together, and he stood at the pay phone seeing her in the hazy soft-focus glow of some made-for-TV movie. Maybe he shouldn't call. Maybe he should just . . . surprise her.

She answered the door in an oversized sweatshirt and shorts, barefooted, and with the half-full pitcher from the blender in her hand. She looked surprised, all right, but not pleasantly surprised. In fact, she scowled at him and set the pitcher down on the bookcase before pulling back the door and ushering him in. He didn't even get the chance to tell her he loved her or to wish her luck before she started in on him. "What are you doing here?" she demanded. "You know I can't see you tonight, of all nights. What's with you? Are you drunk? Is that it?"

What could he say? He stared at the brown gloop in the pitcher for half a beat and then gave her his best simmering droopy-eyed smile and a shrug that radiated down from his shoulders to his hips. "I just wanted to see you. To wish you luck, you know?" He stepped forward to kiss her, but she dodged away from him, snatching up the pitcher full of gloop like a shield. "A kiss for luck?" he said.

She hesitated. He could see something go in and out of her eyes, the flicker of a worry, competitive anxiety, butterflies, and then she smiled and pecked him a kiss on the lips that tasted of soy and honey and whatever else was in that concoction she drank. "Luck," she said, "but no excitement."

"And no sex," he said, trying to make a joke of it. "I know."

She laughed then, a high girlish tinkle of a laugh that broke the spell. "No sex," she said. "But I was just going to watch a movie if you want to join me—"

He found one of the beers he'd left in the refrigerator for just such an emergency as this and settled in beside her on the couch to watch the movie—some inspirational crap about a demi-cripple who wins the hurdle event in the Swedish Special Olympics—but he was hot, he couldn't help it, and his fingers kept wandering from her shoulder to her breast, from her waist to her inner thigh. At least she kissed him when she pushed him away. "Tomorrow," she promised, but it was only a promise, and they both knew it. She'd been so devastated after the Houston thing she wouldn't sleep with him for a week and a half, strung tight as a bow every time he touched her. The memory of it chewed at him, and he sipped his beer moodily. "Bullshit," he said.

"Bullshit what?"

"Bullshit you'll sleep with me tomorrow. Remember Houston? Remember Zinny Bauer?"

Her face changed suddenly and she flicked the remote angrily at the screen and the picture went blank. "I think you better go," she said.

But he didn't want to go. She was his girlfriend, wasn't she? And what good did it do him if she kicked him out every time some chickenshit race came up? Didn't he matter to her, didn't he matter at all? "I don't want to go," he said.

She stood, put her hands on her hips, and glared at him. "I have to go to bed now."

He didn't budge. Didn't move a muscle. "That's what I mean," he said, and his face was ugly, he couldn't help it. "I want to go to bed too."

Later, he felt bad about the whole thing. Worse than bad. He didn't know how it happened exactly, but there was some resentment there, he guessed, and it just snuck up on him—plus he was drunk, if that was any excuse. Which it wasn't. Anyway, he hadn't meant to get physical, and by the time she'd stopped fighting him and he got her shorts down he hadn't even really wanted to go through with it. This wasn't making love, this wasn't what he wanted. She just lay there beneath him like she was dead, like some sort of zombie, and it made him sick, so sick he couldn't even begin to apologize or excuse himself. He felt her eyes on him as he was zipping up, hard eyes, accusatory eyes, eyes like claws, and he had to stagger into the bathroom and cover himself with the noise of both taps and the toilet to keep from breaking down. He'd gone too far. He knew it. He was ashamed of himself, deeply ashamed, and there really wasn't anything left to say. He just slumped his shoulders and slouched out the door.

And now here he was, contrite and hungover, mooning around on Ledbetter Beach in the cool hush of 7:00 a.m., waiting with all the rest of the guppies for the race to start. Paula wouldn't even look at him. Her mouth was set, clamped shut, a tiny little line of nothing beneath her nose, and her eyes looked no farther than her equipment—her spidery ultra-lightweight bike with the triathlon bars and her little skullcap of a helmet and water bottles and what-not. She was wearing a two-piece swimsuit, and she'd already had her number—23—painted on her upper arms and the long burnished muscles of her thighs. He shook out a cigarette and stared off past her, wondering what they used for the numbers: Magic Marker? Greasepaint? Something that wouldn't come off in the surf anyway—or with all the sweat. He remembered the way she looked in Houston, pounding through the muggy haze in a sheen of sweat, her face sunk in a mask of suffering, her legs and buttocks taut, her breasts flattened to her chest in the grip of the clinging top. He thought about that, watching her from behind the police line as she bent to fool with her bike, not an ounce of fat on her, nothing, not even a stray hair, and he got hard just looking at her.

But that was short-lived, because he felt bad about last night and knew he'd have to really put himself through the wringer to make it up to her. Plus, just watching the rest of the four hundred and six fleshless masochists parade by with their Gore-Tex T-shirts and Lycra shorts and all the rest of their paraphernalia was enough to make him go cold all over. His stomach felt like a fried egg left out on the counter too long, and his hands shook when he lit the cigarette.

He should be in bed, that's where he should be—enough of this seven o'clock in the morning. They were crazy, these people, purely crazy, getting up at dawn to put themselves through something like this—one mile in the water, thirty-four on the bike, and a ten-mile run to wrap it up, and this was a walk compared to the Ironman. They were all bone and long, lean muscle, like whippet dogs or something, the women indistinguishable from the men, stringy and titless. Except for Paula. She was all right in that department, and that was genetic—she referred to her breasts as her fat reserves. He was wondering if they shrank at all during the race, what with all that stress and water loss, when a woman with big hair and too much makeup asked him for a light.

She was milling around with maybe a couple hundred other spectators—or sadists, he guessed you'd have to call them—waiting to watch the crazies do their thing. "Thanks," she breathed, after he'd leaned in close to touch the tip of his smoke to hers. Her eyes were big wet pools, and she was no freak, no bone woman. Her lips were wet too, or maybe it was his imagination. "So," she said, the voice caught low in her throat, a real smoker's rasp, "here for the big event?"

He just nodded.

There was a pause. They sucked at their cigarettes. A pair of gulls flailed sharply at the air behind them and then settled down to poke through the sand for anything that looked edible. "My name's Sandra," she offered, but he wasn't listening, not really, because it was then that it came to him, his inspiration, his moment of grace and redemption: suddenly he knew how he was going to make it up to Paula. He cut his eyes away from the woman and through the crowd to where Paula bent over her equipment, the take-no-prisoners look ironed into her face. And what does she want more than anything? he asked himself, his excitement so intense he almost spoke the words aloud. What would make her happy, glad to see him, ready to party, celebrate, dance till dawn and let bygones be bygones?

To win. That was all. To beat Zinny Bauer. And in that moment, even as Paula caught his eye and glowered at him, he had a vision of Zinny Bauer, the Amazing Bone Woman, coming into the final stretch with her legs and arms pumping, in command, no problem, and the bright green cup of Gatorade held out for her by the smiling volunteer in the official volunteer's cap and T-shirt—yes—and Zinny Bauer refreshing herself, drinking it down in midstride, running on and on until she hit the wall he was already constructing.

Paula pulled the red bathing cap down over her ears, adjusted her swim goggles and strode across the beach, her heartbeat as slow and steady as a lizard's. She was focused, as clearheaded and certain as she'd ever been in her life. Nothing mattered now except leaving all the hotshots and loudmouths and macho types behind in the dust—and Zinny Bauer too. There were a couple of pros competing in the men's division and she had no illusions about beating them, but she was going to teach the rest of them a hard lesson, a lesson about toughness and endurance and will. If anything, what had happened with Jason last night was something she could use, the kind of thing that made her angry, that made her wonder what she'd seen in him in the first place. He didn't care about her. He didn't care about anybody. That was what she was thinking when the gun went off and she hit the water with the great thundering herd of them, the image of his bleary apologetic face burning into her brain—date rape, that's what they called it—and she came out of the surf just behind Zinny Bauer, Jill Eisen, and Tommy Roe, one of the men's pros.

All right. Okay. She was on her bike now, through the gate in a flash and driving down the flat wide concourse of Cabrillo Boulevard in perfect rhythm, effortless, as if the blood were flowing through her legs and into the bike itself. Before she'd gone half a mile she knew she was going to catch Zinny Bauer and pass her to ride with the men's leaders and get off first on the run. It was preordained, she could feel it, feel it pounding in her temples and in the perfect engine of her heart. The anger had settled in her legs now, a bitter, hot-burning fuel. She fed on the air, tucked herself into the handlebars, and flew. If all this time she'd raced for herself, for something uncontainable inside her, now she was racing for Jason, to show him up, to show him what she was, what she really was. There was no excuse for him. None. And she was going to win this event, she was going to beat Zinny Bauer and all those hundreds of soft, winded, undertrained, crowing, chest-thumping jocks too, and she was going to accept her trophy and stride right by him as if he didn't exist, because she wasn't soft, she wasn't, and he was going to find that out once and for all.

By the time he got back to the beach Jason thought he'd run some sort of race himself. He was breathing hard—got to quit smoking—and his tequila headache was heating up to the point where he was seriously considering ducking into Clubber's and slamming a shot or two, though it was only half past nine and all the tourists would be there buttering their French toast and would you pass the syrup please and thank you very much. He'd had to go all the way out to Drake's place and shake him awake to get the Tuinal—one of Drake's mother's six thousand and one prescriptions to fight off the withering aches of her seventy-odd years. Tuinal, Nembutal, Dalmane, Darvocet: Jason didn't care, just so long as there was enough of it. He didn't do barbiturates anymore—probably hadn't swallowed a Tooey in ten years—but he remembered the sweet numb glow they gave him and the way they made his legs feel like tree trunks planted deep in the ground.

The sun had burned off the fog by now, and the day was clear and glittering on the water. They'd started the race at seven-thirty, so that gave him a while yet—the first men would be crossing the finish line in just under three hours, and the women would be coming in at three-ten, three-twelve, something like that. All he needed to do now was finesse himself into the inner sanctum, pick up a stray T-shirt and cap, find the Gatorade and plant himself about two miles from the finish. Of course there was a chance the Amazing Bone Woman wouldn't take the cup from him, especially if she recognized him from the other night, but he was going to pull his cap down low and hide behind his Ray-Bans and show her a face of devotion. One second, that's all it would take. A hand coming out of the crowd, the cup beaded with moisture and moving right along beside her so she didn't even have to break stride—and what was there to think about? She drinks and hits the wall. And if she didn't go for it the first time, he'd hop in the car and catch her a mile farther on.

He'd been watching one of the security volunteers stationed outside the trailer that served as a command center. A kid of eighteen maybe, greasy hair, an oversized cross dangling from one ear, a scurf of residual acne. He was a carbon copy of the kids he sold wetsuits and Killer Beeswax to—maybe he was even one of them. Jason reminded himself to tread carefully. He was a businessman, after all, one of the pillars of the downtown community, and somebody might recognize him. But then so what if they did? He was volunteering his time, that was all, a committed citizen doing his civic best to promote tourism and everything else that was right in the world. He ducked under the rope. "Hey, bro," he said to the kid, extending his hand for the high five—which the kid gave him. "Sorry I'm late. Jeff around?"

The kid's face opened up in a big beaming half-witted grin. "Yeah, sure—I think he went up the beach a ways with Everardo and Linda and some of the press people, but I could maybe look if you want—"

Jeff. It was a safe bet—no crowd of that size, especially one consisting of whippets, bone people and guppies, would be without a Jeff. Jason gave the kid a shrug. "Nah, that's all right. But hey, where's the T-shirts and caps at?"

Then he was in his car, and forget the D.U.I., the big green waxed cup cold between his legs, breaking Tuinal caps and looking for a parking space along the course. He pulled in under a huge Monterey pine that was like its own little city and finished doctoring the Gatorade, stirring the stuff in with his index finger. What would it take to make her legs go numb and wind up a Did Not Finish without arousing suspicion? Two? Three? He didn't want her to pass out on the spot or take a dive into the bushes or anything, and he didn't want to hurt her either, not really. But four—four was a nice round number, and that ought to do it. He sucked the finger he'd used as a swizzle stick to see if he could detect the taste, but he couldn't. He took a tentative sip. Nothing. Gatorade tasted like such shit anyway, who could tell the difference?

He found a knot of volunteers in their canary-yellow T-shirts and caps and stationed himself a hundred yards up the street from them, the ice rattling as he swirled his little green time bomb around the lip of the cup. The breeze was soft, the sun caught in the crowns of the trees and reaching out to finger the road here and there in long, slim swatches. He'd never tell Paula, of course, no way, but he'd get giddy with her, pop the champagne cork, and let her fill him with all the ecstasy of victory.

A cheer from the crowd brought him out of his reverie. The first of the men was cranking his way round the long bend in the road, a guy with a beard and wraparound sunglasses—the Finn. He was the one favored to win, or was it the Brit? Jason tucked the cup behind his back and faded into the crowd, which was pretty sparse here, and watched the guy propel himself past, his mouth gaping black, the two holes of his nostrils punched deep into his face, his head bobbing on his neck as if it wasn't attached right. Another guy appeared round the corner just as the Finn passed by, and then two others came slogging along behind him. Somebody cheered, but it was a pretty feeble affair.

Jason checked his watch. It would be five minutes or so, and then he could start watching for the Amazing Bone Woman, tireless freak that she was. And did she fuck Klaus, or Olaf, or whoever he was, the night before the big event, or was she like Paula, all focus and negativity and no, no, no? He fingered the cup lightly, reminding himself not to damage or crease it in any way—it had to look pristine, fresh-dipped from the bucket—and he watched the corner at the end of the street till his eyes began to blur from the sheer concentration of it all.

Two more men passed by, and nobody cheered, not a murmur, but then suddenly a couple of middle-aged women across the street set up a howl, and the crowd chimed in: the first woman, a woman of string and bone with a puffing heaving puppetlike frame, was swinging into the street in distant silhouette. Jason moved forward. He tugged reflexively at the bill of his hat, jammed the rims of the shades back into his eyesockets. And he started to grin, all his teeth on fire, his lips spread wide: Here, take me, drink me, have me!

As the woman closed, loping, sweating, elbows flailing and knees pounding, the crowd getting into it now, cheering her, cheering this first of the women in a man's event, the first Iron-woman of the day, he began to realize that this wasn't Zinny Bauer at all. Her hair was too long, and her legs and chest were too full—and then he saw the number clearly, No. 23, and looked into Paula's face. She was fifty yards from him, but he could see the toughness in her eyes and the tight little frozen smile of triumph and superiority. She was winning. She was beating Zinny Bauer and Jill Eisen and all those pathetic jocks laboring up the hills and down the blacktop streets behind her. This was her moment, this was it.

But then, and he didn't stop to think about it, he stepped forward, right out on the street where she could see him, and held out the cup. He heard her feet beating at the pavement with a hard merciless slap, saw the icy twist of a smile and the cold, triumphant eyes. And he felt the briefest fleeting touch of her flesh as the cup left his hand.

(1995)

Killing Babies

When I got out of rehab for the second time, there were some legal complications, and the judge—an old jerk who looked like they'd just kicked him out of the Politburo—decided I needed a sponsor. There was a problem with some checks I'd been writing for a while there when all my resources were going up the glass tube, and since I didn't have a record except for traffic infractions and a juvenile possession when I was fifteen, the court felt inclined to mercy. Was there anybody who could speak up for me, my attorney wondered, anybody financially responsible? Philip, I said, my brother Philip. He's a doctor.

So Philip. He lived in Detroit, a place I'd never been to, a place where it gets cold in winter and the only palm trees are under glass in the botanical gardens. It would be a change, a real change. But a change is what I needed, and the judge liked the idea that he wouldn't have to see me in Pasadena anymore and that I'd have a room in Philip's house with Philip's wife and my nephews, Josh and Jeff, and that I would be gainfully employed doing lab work at Philip's obstetrical clinic for the princely sum of six dollars and twenty-five cents an hour.

So Philip. He met me at the airport, his thirty-eight-year-old face as trenched with anal-retentive misery as our father's was in the year before he died. His hair was going, I saw that right away, and his glasses were too big for his head. And his shoes—he was wearing a pair of brown suede boatlike things that would have had people running for the exits at the Rainbow Club. I hadn't seen him in six years, not since the funeral, that is, and I wouldn't have even recognized him if it wasn't for his eyes—they were just like mine, as blue and icy as a bottle of Aqua Velva. "Little brother," he said, and he tried to gather a smile around the thin flaps of his lips while he stood there gaping at me like somebody who hadn't come to the airport specifically to fetch his down-on-his-luck brother and was bewildered to discover him there.

"Philip," I said, and I set down my two carry-on bags to pull him to me in a full-body, back-thumping, chest-to-chest embrace, as if I was glad to see him. But I wasn't glad to see him. Not particularly. Philip was ten years older than me, and ten years is a lot when you're a kid. By the time I knew his name he was in college, and when I was expressing myself with my father's vintage Mustang, a Ziploc baggie of marijuana, and a can of high-gloss spray paint, he was in medical school. I'd never much liked him, and he felt about the same toward me, and as I embraced him there in the Detroit airport I wondered how that was going to play out over the course of the six months the judge had given me to stay out of trouble and make full restitution or serve the next six in jail.

"Have a good flight?" Philip asked when I was done embracing him.

I stood back from him a moment, the bags at my feet, and couldn't help being honest with him; that's just the way I am. "You look like shit, Philip," I said. "You look like Dad just before he died—or maybe after he died."

A woman with a big shining planetoid of a face stopped to give me a look, then hitched up her skirt and stamped on by in her heels. The carpeting smelled of chemicals. Outside the dirt-splotched windows was snow, a substance I'd had precious little experience of. "Don't start, Rick," Philip said. "I'm in no mood. Believe me."

I shouldered my bags, stooped over a cigarette, and lit it just to irritate him. I was hoping he'd tell me there was a county ordinance against smoking in public places and that smoking was slow suicide, from a physician's point of view, but he didn't rise to the bait. He just stood there, looking harassed. "I'm not starting," I said. "I'm just . . . I don't know. I'm just concerned, that's all. I mean, you look like shit. I'm your brother. Shouldn't I be concerned?"

I thought he was going to start wondering aloud why *I* should be concerned about *him,* since I was the one on the run from an exasperated judicial system and twelve thousand and some-odd dollars in outstanding checks, but he surprised me. He just shrugged and shifted that lipless smile around a bit and said, "Maybe I've been working too hard."

Philip lived on Washtenaw Street, in an upscale housing development called Washtenaw Acres, big houses set back from the street and clustered around a lake glistening with black ice under a weak sky and weaker sun. The trees were stripped and ugly, like dead sticks rammed into the ground, and the snow wasn't what I'd expected. Somehow I'd thought it would be fluffy and soft, movie snow, big pillows of it cushioning the ground while kids whooshed through it on their sleds, but it wasn't like that at all. It lay on the ground like a scab, clots of dirt and yellow weed showing through in mangy patches. Bleak, that's what it was, but I told myself it was better than the Honor Rancho, a whole lot better, and as we pulled into the long sweeping driveway to Philip's house I put everything I had into feeling optimistic.

Denise had put on weight. She was waiting for us inside the door that led from the three-car garage into the kitchen. I didn't know her well enough to embrace her the way I'd embraced Philip, and I have to admit I was taken aback by the change in her—she was fat, there was nothing else to say about it—so I just filtered out the squeals of welcome and shook her hand as if it was something I'd found in the street. Besides which, the smell of dinner hit me square in the face, so overpowering it almost brought me to my knees. I hadn't been in a real kitchen with a real dinner in the oven since I was a kid and my mother was alive, because after she died, and with Philip away, it was just my father and me, and we tended to go out a lot, especially on Sundays.

"You hungry?" Denise asked while we did an awkward little dance around the gleaming island of stainless steel and tile in the middle of the kitchen. "I'll bet you're starved," she said, "after all that bachelor cooking and the airplane food. And look at you—you're shivering. He's shivering, Philip."

I was, and no denying it.

"You can't run around in a T-shirt and leather jacket and expect to survive a Michigan winter—it might be all right for L.A. maybe, but not here." She turned to Philip, who'd been standing there as if someone had crept up on him and nailed his shoes to the floor. "Philip, haven't you got a parka for Rick? How about that blue one with the red lining you never wear anymore? And a pair of gloves, for God's sake. Get him a pair of gloves, will you?" She came back to me then, all smiles: "We can't have our California boy getting frostbite now, can we?"

Philip agreed that we couldn't, and we all stood there smiling at one another till I said, "Isn't anybody going to offer me a drink?"

Then it was my nephews—red-faced howling babies in dirty yellow diapers the last time I'd seen them, at the funeral that had left me an orphan at twenty-three, little fists glomming onto the cold cuts while drool descended toward the dip—but here they were, eight and six, edging up to me in high-tops and oversized sweatshirts while I threw back my brother's scotch. "Hey," I said, grinning till I thought my head would burst, "remember me? I'm your Uncle Rick."

They didn't remember me—how could they?—but they brightened at the sight of the two yellow bags of M&M's peanut candies I'd thought to pick up at the airport newsstand. Josh, the eight-year-old, took the candy gingerly from my hand, while his brother looked on to see if I was going to sprout fangs and start puking up black vomit. We were all sitting around the living room, very clean, very *Home & Garden,* getting acquainted. Philip and Denise held on to their drinks as if they were afraid somebody was going to steal them. We were all grinning. "What's that on your eyebrow?" Josh said.

I reached up and fingered the thin gold loop. "It's a ring," I said. "You know, like an earring, only it's in my eyebrow."

No one said anything for a long moment. Jeff, the younger one, looked as if he was going to start crying. "Why?" Josh said finally, and Philip laughed and I couldn't help myself—I laughed too. It was all right. Everything was all right. Philip was my brother and Denise was my sister-in-law and these kids with their wide-open faces and miniature Guess jeans were my nephews. I shrugged, laughing still. "Because it's cool," I said, and I didn't even mind the look Philip gave me.

Later, after I'd actually crawled into the top bunk and read the kids a Dr. Seuss story that set off all sorts of bells in my head, Philip and Denise and I discussed my future over coffee and homemade cinnamon rolls. My immediate future, that is—as in tomorrow morning, 8 a.m., at the clinic. I was going to be an entry-level drudge despite my three years of college, my musical background and family connections, rinsing out test tubes and sweeping the floors and disposing of whatever was left in the stainless-steel trays when my brother and his colleagues finished with their "procedures."

"All right," I said. "Fine. I've got no problem with that."

Denise had tucked her legs up under her on the couch. She was wearing a striped caftan that could have sheltered armies. "Philip had a black man on full time, just till a week ago, nicest man you'd ever want to meet—and bright too, very bright—but he, uh, didn't feel . . ."

Philip's voice came out of the shadows at the end of the couch, picking up where she'd left off. "He went on to something better," he said, regarding me steadily through the clear walls of his glasses. "I'm afraid the work isn't all that mentally demanding—or stimulating, for that matter—but, you know, little brother, it's a start, and, well—"

"Yeah, I know," I said, "beggars can't be choosers." I wanted to add to that, to maybe soften it a bit—I didn't want him to get the idea I wasn't grateful, because I was—but I never got the opportunity. Just then the phone rang. I looked up at the sound—it wasn't a ring exactly, more like a bleat, *eh-eh-eh-eh-eh*—and saw that my brother and his wife were staring into each other's eyes in shock, as if a bomb had just gone off. Nobody moved. I counted two more rings before Denise said, "I wonder who that could be at this hour?" and Philip, my brother with the receding hairline and the too-big glasses and his own eponymous clinic in suburban Detroit, said, "Forget it, ignore it, it's nobody."

And that was strange, because we sat there in silence and listened to that phone ring over and over—twenty times, twenty times at least—until whoever it was on the other end finally gave up. Another minute ticked by, the silence howling in our ears, and then Philip stood, looked at his watch, and said, "What do you think—time to turn in?"

I wasn't stupid, not particularly—no stupider than anybody else anyway—and I was no criminal either. I'd just drifted into a kind of thick sludge of hopelessness after I dropped out of school for a band I put my whole being into, a band that disintegrated within the year, and one thing led to another. Jobs came and went. I spent a lot of time on the couch, channel-surfing and thumbing through books that used to mean something to me. I found women and lost them. And I learned that a line up your nose is a dilettante's thing, wasteful and extravagant. I started smoking, two or three nights a week, and then it was five or six nights a week, and then it was every day, all day, and why not? That was how I felt. Sure. And now I was in Michigan, starting over.

Anyway, it wouldn't have taken a genius to understand why my brother and his wife had let that phone ring—not after Philip and I swung into the parking lot behind the clinic at seven forty-five the next morning. I wasn't even awake, really—it was four forty-five West Coast time, an hour that gave me a headache even to imagine, much less live through. Beyond the misted-up windows, everything was gloom, a kind of frozen fog hanging in air the color of lemon ice. The trees, I saw, hadn't sprouted leaves overnight. Every curb was a repository of frozen trash.

Philip and I had been making small talk on the way into town, very small talk, out of consideration for the way I was feeling. Denise had given me coffee, which was about all I could take at that hour, but Philip had gobbled a big bowl of bran flakes and sunflower seeds with skim milk, and the boys, shy around me all over again, spooned up Lucky Charms and Frosted Flakes in silence. I came out of my daze the minute the tires hit the concrete apron separating the private property of the lot from the public space of the street: there were people there, a whole shadowy mass of shoulders and hats and steaming faces that converged on us with a shout. At first I didn't know what was going on—I thought I was trapped in a bad movie, *Night of the Living Dead* or *Zombies on Parade.* The faces were barking at us, teeth bared, eyes sunk back in their heads, hot breath boiling from their throats. "Murderers!" they were shouting. "Nazis!" "Baby-killers!"

We inched our way across the sidewalk and into the lot, working through the mass of them as if we were on a narrow lane in a dense forest, and Philip gave me a look that explained it all, from the lines in his face to Denise's fat to the phone that rang in the middle of the night no matter how many times he changed the number. This was war. I climbed out of the car with my heart hammering, and as the cold knife of the air cut into me I looked back to where they stood clustered at the gate, lumpish and solid, people you'd see anywhere. They were singing now. Some hymn, some self-righteous churchy Jesus-thumping hymn that bludgeoned the traffic noise and the deep-frozen air with the force of a weapon. I didn't have time to sort it out, but I could feel the slow burn of anger and humiliation coming up in me. Philip's hand was on my arm. "Come on," he said. "We've got work to do, little brother."

That day, the first day, was a real trial. Yes, I was turning over a new leaf, and yes, I was determined to succeed and thankful to my brother and the judge and the great giving, forgiving society I belonged to, but this was more than I'd bargained for. I had no illusions about the job—I knew it would be dull and diminishing, and I knew life with Philip and Denise would be one long snooze—but I wasn't used to being called a baby-killer. Liar, thief, crackhead—those were names I'd answered to at one time or another. Murderer was something else.

My brother wouldn't talk about it. He was busy. Wired. Hurtling around the clinic like a gymnast on the parallel bars. By nine I'd met his two associates (another doctor and a counsellor, both female, both unattractive); his receptionist; Nurses Tsing and Hempfield; and Fred. Fred was a big rabbity-looking guy in his early thirties with a pale reddish mustache and hair of the same color climbing up out of his head in all directions. He had the official title of "technician," though the most technical things I saw him do were drawing blood and divining urine for signs of pregnancy, clap, or worse. None of them—not my brother, the nurses, the counsellor, or even Fred—wanted to discuss what was going on at the far end of the parking lot and on the sidewalk out front. The zombies with the signs—yes, signs, I could see them out the window, ABORTION KILLS and SAVE THE PREBORNS and I WILL ADOPT YOUR BABY—were of no more concern to them than mosquitoes in June or a sniffle in December. Or at least that was how they acted.

I tried to draw Fred out on the subject as we sat together at lunch in the back room. We were surrounded by shadowy things in jars of formalin, gleaming stainless-steel sinks, racks of test tubes, reference books, cardboard boxes full of drug samples and syringes and gauze pads and all the rest of the clinic's paraphernalia. "So what do you think of all this, Fred?" I said, gesturing toward the window with the ham-and-Swiss on rye Denise had made me in the dark hours of the morning.

Fred was hunched over a newspaper, doing the acrostic puzzle and sucking on his teeth. His lunch consisted of a microwave chili-and-cheese burrito and a quart of root beer. He gave me a quizzical look.

"The protesters, I mean. The Jesus-thumpers out there. Is it like this all the time?" And then I added a little joke, so he wouldn't think I was intimidated: "Or did I just get lucky?"

"Who, them?" Fred did something with his nose and his upper teeth, something rabbity, as if he were tasting the air. "They're nobody. They're nothing."

"Yeah?" I said, hoping for more, hoping for some details, some explanation, something to assuage the creeping sense of guilt and shame that had been building in me all morning. Those people had pigeonholed me before I'd even set foot in the door, and that hurt. They were wrong. I was no baby-killer—I was just the little brother of a big brother, trying to make a new start. And Philip was no baby-killer either—he was a guy doing his job, that was all. Shit, somebody had to do it. Up to this point I guess I'd never really given the issue much thought—my girlfriends, when there were girlfriends, had taken care of the preventative end of things on their own, and we never really discussed it—but my feeling was that there were too many babies in the world already, too many adults, too many suet-faced Jesus-thumping jerks ready to point the finger, and didn't any of these people have better things to do? Like a job, for instance? But Fred wasn't much help. He just sighed, nibbled at the wilted stem of his burrito, and said, "You get used to it."

I wondered about that as the afternoon crept by, and then my mind went numb from jet lag and the general wash of misery and I let my body take over. I scrubbed out empty jars and test tubes with Clorox, labeled and filed the full ones on the racks that lined the walls, stood at Fred's elbow and watched as he squeezed drops of urine onto strips of litmus paper and made notations in a ledger. My white lab coat got progressively dirtier. Every once in a while I'd come to and catch a glimpse of myself in the mirror over the sinks, the mad scientist exposed, the baby-killer, the rinser of test tubes and secreter of urine, and have an ironic little laugh at my own expense. And then it started to get dark, Fred vanished, and I was introduced to mop and squeegee. It was around then, when I just happened to be taking a cigarette break by the only window in the room, that I caught a glimpse of one of our last tardy patients of the day hurrying up the sidewalk elbow to elbow with a grim middle-aged woman whose face screamed *I am her mother!*

The girl was sixteen, seventeen maybe, a pale face, pale as a bulb, and nothing showing on her, at least not with the big white doughboy parka she was wearing. She looked scared, her little mouth clamped tight, her eyes fixed on her feet. She was wearing black leggings that seemed to sprout from the folds of the parka and a pair of furry white ankle boots that were like house slippers. I watched her glide through the dead world on the flowing stalks of her legs, a spoiled pouty chalk-cheeked sweetness to her face, and it moved something in me, something long buried beneath a mountain of grainy little yellow-white rocks. Maybe she was just coming in for an examination, I thought, maybe that was it. Or she'd just become sexually active—or was thinking of it—and her mother was one step ahead of her. Either way, that was what I wanted to believe. With this girl, with her quick fluid step and downcast eyes and all the hope and misery they implied, I didn't want to think of "procedures."

They'd almost reached the building when the zombies began to stir. From where I was standing I couldn't see the front of the building, and the Jesus-thumpers had already begun to fade out of my consciousness, dim as it was. But they came crashing back into the picture now, right there at the corner of the building, shoulders and heads and placards, and one in particular. A shadow that separated itself from the mass and was instantly transformed into a hulking bearded zealot with snapping teeth and eyes like hard-boiled eggs. He came right up to the girl and her mother, rushing at them like a torpedo, and you could see how they shied away from him and how his head raged back on his shoulders, and then they ducked past the corner of the building and out of my line of sight.

I was stunned. This wasn't right, I was thinking, and I didn't want to get angry or depressed or emotional—keep on an even keel, that's what they tell you in rehab—but I couldn't help snuffing the cigarette and stepping quietly out into the hallway that ran the length of the building and gave me an unobstructed view of the front door. I moved forward almost against my will, my feet like toy cars on a track, and I hadn't got halfway down the hall before the door opened on the dwindling day and the dead sticks of the trees, and suddenly there she was, pale in a pale coat and her face two shades paler. We exchanged a look. I don't know what she saw in my eyes—weakness, hunger, fear—but I know what I saw in hers, and it was so poignant and so everlastingly sad I knew I'd never have another moment's rest till I took hold of it.

In the car on the way home Philip was so relaxed I wondered if he wasn't prescribing something for himself. Here was the antithesis of the ice man who'd picked me up at the airport, watched me eat pork chops, read to his children and brush my teeth in the guest bathroom, and then thrown me to the wolves at the clinic. "Sorry about all that commotion this morning," he said, glancing at me in the glowing cubicle of the car. "I would have warned you, but you can never tell when they're going to pull something like that."

"So it gets better, is that what you're saying?"

"Not much," he said. "There's always a couple of them out there, the real hard-core nuts. But the whole crew of the walking dead like you saw today, that's maybe only once a week. Unless they go on one of their campaigns, and I can't figure out what provokes them—the weather, the tides in the lake, the phases of the moon—but then they go all out, theater in the street, schoolchildren, the works. They throw themselves under the wheels, handcuff themselves to the front door—it's a real zoo."

"But what about the cops? Can't you get a restraining order or something?"

He shrugged, fiddled with the tape player—opera, he was listening to opera, a thin screech of it in the night—and turned to me again, his gloved hands rigid on the wheel. "The cops are a bunch of pro-lifers, and they have no objection to those people out there harassing my patients and abridging their civil rights, and even the women just coming in for an exam have to walk the gauntlet. It's hell on business, believe me. And it's dangerous too. They scare me, the real crazies, the ones that shoot people. You've heard of John Britton? David Gunn? George Tiller?"

"I don't know," I said. "Maybe. You've got to realize I've been out of touch for a while."

"Shot down by people like the ones you saw out there today. Two of them died."

I didn't like hearing that. The thought of one of those nutballs attacking my brother, attacking me, was like throwing gasoline on a bed of hot coals. I'd never been one to turn the other cheek, and I didn't feature martyrdom, not at all. I looked out on a blur of brake lights and the crust of ice that seemed to narrow the road into a funnel ahead of us. "Why don't you shoot them first?" I said.

My brother's voice was hard. "Sometimes I wish I could."

We stopped to pick up a few things at the market, and then we were home, dinner stabbing at my salivary glands, the whole house warm and sugary with it, and Philip sat down to watch the news and have a scotch with me. Denise was right there at the door when we came in—and now we embraced, no problem, sister- and brother-in-law, one big happy family. She wanted to know how my day was, and before I could open my mouth, she was answering for me: "Not much of a challenge, huh? Pretty dull, right? Except for the crazies—they never fail to liven things up, do they? What Philip goes through, huh, Philip? Philip?"

I was beat, but the scotch smoked through my veins, the kids came and sat beside me on the couch with their comics and coloring books, and I felt good, felt like part of the family and no complaints. Denise served a beef brisket with oven-roasted potatoes, carrots and onions, a fresh green salad, and coconut creme pie for dessert. I was planning on turning in early, but I drifted into the boys' room and took over the *Winnie-the-Pooh* chores from my brother because it was something I wanted to do. Later, it must have been about ten, I was stretched out on my own bed—and again I had to hand it to Denise, because the room was homey and private, done up with little knickknacks and embroidery work and whatnot—when my brother poked his head in the door. "So," he said, mellow with the scotch and whatever else, "you feeling okay about everything?"

That touched me. It did. Here I'd come into the airport with a chip on my shoulder—I'd always been jealous of Philip, the great shining success my father measured me against—thinking my big brother was going to be an asshole and that assholery would rule the day, but it wasn't like that at all. He was reaching out. He was a doctor. He knew about human foibles and addictions and he knew about his little brother, and he cared, he actually cared. "Yeah," was all I could manage, but I hoped the quality of my voice conveyed a whole lot more than that.

"Good," he said, framed in the light from the hallway, his sunken orbits and rucked face and flat, shining eyes giving him a look of wisdom and calm that reminded me of our father on his good days.

"That girl," I said, inspired by the intimacy of the moment, "the last one that came in today?"

His expression changed. Now it was quizzical, distant, as if he were looking at me through the wrong end of a telescope. "What girl? What are you talking about?"

"The young-looking one in the white parka and furry boots? The last one. The last one in. I was just wondering if, uh, I mean, what her problem was—if she was, you know, coming in for a procedure or whatever. . . ."

"Listen, Rick," he said then, and his voice was back in the deep freeze, "I'm willing to give you a chance here, not only for Dad's sake but for your own sake too. But there's one thing I ask—stay away from the patients. And I'm not really asking."

It was raining the next morning, a cold rain that congealed on the hood of the car and made a cold pudding of the sidewalk out front of the house. I wondered if the weather would discourage the Jesus-thumpers, but they were there, all right, in yellow rain slickers and green gum boots, sunk into their suffering with gratitude. Nobody rushed the car when we turned into the lot. They just stood there, eight of them, five men and three women, and looked hate at us. As we got out of the car, the frozen rain pelting us, I locked eyes across the lot with the bearded jerk who'd gone after the girl in the white parka. I waited till I was good and certain I had his attention, waited till he was about to shout out some hoarse Jesus-thumping accusation, and then I gave him the finger.

We were the first ones at the clinic, what with the icy roads, and as soon as my brother disappeared into the sanctum of his office I went straight to the receptionist's desk and flipped back the page of the appointment book. The last entry, under four-thirty the previous day, was staring me in the face, neat block letters in blue metalpoint: "Sally Strunt," it read, and there was a phone number jotted beneath the name. It took me exactly ten seconds, and then I was in the back room, innocently slipping into my lab coat. Sally Strunt, I whispered to myself, Sally Strunt, over and over. I'd never known anyone named Sally—it was an old-fashioned name, a hokey name, Dick and Jane and Sally, and because it was old-fashioned and because it was hokey it seemed perfect for a teenager in trouble in the grim sleety washed-out navel of the Midwest. This was no downtown Amber, no Crystal or Shanna—this was Detroit Sally, and that really appealed to me. I'd seen the face attached to the name, and the mother of that face. *Sally, Sally, Sally.* Her name sang through my head as I schmoozed with Fred and the nurses and went through the motions of the job that already felt as circumscribed and deadening as a prison sentence.

That night, after dinner, I excused myself and strolled six cold wintry blocks to the convenience store. I bought M&M's for the boys, some white chocolate for Denise, and a liter of Black Cat malt liquor for myself. Then I dialed Sally's number from the phone booth out front of the store.

A man answered, impatient, harassed. "Yeah?"

"Sally there?" I said.

"Who's this?"

I took a stab at it: "Chris Ryan. From school?"

Static. Televised dialogue. The roar of Sally's name and the sound of approaching feet and Sally's approaching voice: "Who is it?" And then, into the receiver: "Hello?"

"Sally?" I said.

"Yes?" There was hope in that voice, eagerness. She wanted to hear from me—or from whoever. This wasn't the voice of a girl concealing things. It was open, frank, friendly. I felt expansive suddenly, connected, felt as if everything was going to be all right, not only for me but for Sally too.

"You don't know me," I said quickly, "but I really admire you. I mean, your courage. I admire what you're doing."

"Who is this?"

"Chris," I said. "Chris Ryan. I saw you yesterday, at the clinic, and I really admire you, but I just wanted to know if, uh, if you need anything."

Her voice narrowed, thin as wire. "What are you talking about?"

"Sally," I said, and I didn't know what I was doing or what I was feeling, but I couldn't help myself, "Sally, can I ask you something? Are you pregnant, or are you—?"

Click. She hung up on me. Just like that.

I was frozen through by the time I got back with the kids' M&M's and Denise's white chocolate, and I'd finished off the beer on the way and flung the empty bottle up under a squat artificial-looking spruce on the neighbor's lawn. I'd tried Sally twice more, after an interval of fifteen or twenty minutes, but her father answered the first time and when I dialed again the phone just rang and kept on ringing.

A week went by. I scrubbed out test tubes and jars that smelled powerfully of the urine of strange women and learned that Fred didn't much care for Afro-Americans, Mexicans, Haitians, Cubans, Poles, or Hmong tribesmen. I tried Sally's number three more times and each time I was rebuffed—threatened, actually—and I began to realize I was maybe just a bit out of line. Sally didn't need me—she had her father and mother and maybe a gangling big-footed slam-dunking brother into the bargain—and every time I glanced through the blinds in the back room I saw another girl just like her. Still, I was feeling itchy and out of sorts despite all Denise and Philip and my nephews were doing for me, and I needed some sort of focus, a plan, something to make me feel good about myself. They'd warned us about this in rehab, and I knew this was the trickiest stage, the time when the backsliders start looking up their old friends and hanging out on the street corner. But I didn't have any old friends, not in Detroit anyway, and the street corner was about as inviting as the polar ice cap. On Saturday night I went out to a bar that looked as if it had been preserved under Plexiglas in a museum somewhere, and I came on to a couple of girls and drank too much and woke up the next morning with a headache.

Then it was Monday and I was sitting at the breakfast table with my brother and my two nephews and it was raining again. Sleeting, actually. I wanted to go back to bed. I toyed with the idea of telling Philip I was sick, but he'd probably insist on inserting the rectal thermometer himself. He sat across from me, expressionless, crunching away at his bran flakes and sunflower seeds, the newspaper spread out before him. Denise bustled around the kitchen, brewing coffee and shoving things into the microwave while the boys and I smeared Eggo waffles with butter and syrup. "So," I said, addressing my nephews over the pitcher of pure Grade A maple syrup, "you know why the California kids have it all over the Midwestern kids when it comes to baseball?"

Josh looked up from his waffles; Jeff was still on dreamtime.

"Because of this," I said, gesturing toward the dark windows and the drooling panes. "In L.A. now it's probably seventy degrees, and when the kids wake up they can go straight out and play ball."

"After school," Josh corrected.

"Yeah," I said. "Whatever. But that's the reason your California and Arizona players dominate the big leagues."

"The Tigers suck," Josh said, and his brother glanced up to add his two cents. "They *really* suck," he said.

It was then that I became aware of the background noise, a thin droning mewl from beyond the windows as if someone were drowning kittens in the street. Philip heard it then too, and the boys and Denise, and in the next moment we were all at the window. "Oh, shit," Philip hissed. "Not again. Not today, of all days."

"What?" I said. "What is it?" And then I saw, while my nephews melted away and Denise gritted her teeth and my brother swore: the zombies were out there at the edge of the lawn, a hundred of them at least. They were singing, locked arm in arm and swaying to the beat, stretched across the mouth of the driveway in a human chain.

Philip's face was drawn tight. He told Denise to call the police, and then he turned to me. "Now you're going to see something, little brother," he said. "Now you're going to see why I keep asking myself if I shouldn't just close down the clinic and let the lunatics take over the asylum."

The kitchen was gray, a weak, played-out light pasted on every surface. Sleet rattled the windows and the conjoined voices mewled away in praise of mercy and forgiveness. I was about to ask him why he didn't do just that—close up and move someplace friendlier, someplace like California, for instance—but I already knew the answer. They could harass all the chalk-faced Sallys and thump all the Bibles they wanted, but my brother wasn't going to bow down to them—and neither was I. I knew whose team I was on, and I knew what I had to do.

It took the police half an hour to show up. There were three squad cars and a bus with wire mesh over the windows, and the cops knew the routine. They'd been here before—how many times you could guess from the deadness in their eyes—and they'd arrested these very people, knew them by name. Philip and I waited in the house, watching the *Today* show at an uncomfortable volume, and the boys stayed in their room, already late for school. Finally, at quarter past eight, Philip and I shuffled out to the garage and climbed into the car. Philip's face was like an old paper sack with eyes poked in it. I watched him hit the remote for the garage door and watched the door lift slowly on the scene.

There they were, right there on the street, the whole bug-eyed crew from the clinic, and ninety more. I saw squat, brooding mothers with babies, kids who should have been in school, old people who should have known better. They jerked their signs up and down and let out with a howl when the door cranked open, and though the cops had cleared them from the mouth of the drive they surged in now to fill the gap, the big Jesus-thumper with the beard right in front. The cops couldn't hold them back, and before we'd got halfway down the drive they were all over us, pounding on the windows and throwing themselves down in the path of the car. My brother, like a jerk, like the holy fool who automatically turns the other cheek, stepped on the brake.

"Run them over," I said, and all my breath was gone. "Run the fuckers over."

Philip just sat there, hanging his head in frustration. The cops peeled them away, one by one, zipped on the plastic cuffs and hauled them off, but for every one they lifted out of the way another dove in to take his place. We couldn't go forward, we couldn't back up. "Your neighbor kills babies!" they were shouting. "Dr. Beaudry is a murderer!" "Kill the butchers, not the babies!" I tried to stay calm, tried to think about rehab and jail and the larger problems of my life, but I couldn't. I couldn't take this. I couldn't.

Before I knew what I was doing I was out of the car. The first face I saw belonged to a kid of eighteen maybe, a tough guy with veins standing out in his neck and his leather jacket open to the sleet to show off a white T-shirt and a gold cross on a gold chain. He was right there, right in my face, shouting, "Jesus! Jesus!" and he looked genuinely surprised when I pitched into him with everything I had and shoved him back into a pair of dumpy women in matching scarves and earmuffs. I went right for the next guy—a little toadstool who looked as if he'd been locked in a closet for the last forty years—and flung him away from the car. I heard shouts, saw the cops wading through the crowd, and then I was staring into the face of the big guy, the king yahoo himself—Mr. Beard—and he was so close I knew what he'd had for breakfast. In all that chaos he just stood there rigid at the bumper of the car, giving me a big rich phony Jesus-loving smile that was as full of hate as anything I'd ever seen, and then he ducked down on one knee and handcuffed himself to the bumper.

That put me over the line. I wanted to make a martyr out of him, wanted to kick him to death right there, right in the driveway and with the whole world looking on, and who knows what would have happened if Philip hadn't grabbed me from behind. "Rick!" he kept shouting. "Rick! Rick!" And then he wrestled me up the walk and into the house, Denise's scared white face in the door, the mob howling for blood and then lurching right into another weepy, churchy song as if they were in a cathedral somewhere.

In the safety of the hallway, the door closed and locked behind us, my brother turned on me. "Are you crazy?" he shouted, and you would have thought *I* was the enemy. "You want to go back to jail? You want lawsuits? What were you thinking anyway—are you stoned on something, is that it?"

I looked away from him, but I wanted to kill him too. It was beating in my veins, along with the Desoxyn I'd stolen from the clinic. I saw my nephews peeking out of their room down the hall. "You can't let these people push you around," I said.

"Look at me, Rick," he said. "Look at me."

I was dodging around on my feet, tight with it, and I lifted my eyes grudgingly. I felt like a kid all over again, Rick the shoplifter, the pothead, the fuckup.

"You're just playing into their hands, don't you see that? They want to provoke you, they want you to go after them. Then they put you back in jail and they get the headlines." His voice broke. Denise tried to say something, but he shut her up with a wave of his hand. "You're back on the drugs, aren't you? What is it—cocaine? Pot? Something you lifted from the clinic?"

Outside I could hear them, "We Shall Overcome," and it was a cruel parody—this wasn't liberation, it was fascism. I said nothing.

"Listen, Rick, you're an ex-con and you've got to remember that, every step you take. I mean, what did you think, you were protecting me out there?"

"Ex-con?" I said, amazed. "Is that what you think of me? I can't believe you. I'm no ex-con. You're thinking of somebody in the movies, some documentary you saw on PBS. I'm a guy who made a mistake, a little mistake, and I never hurt anybody. I'm your brother, remember?"

That was when Denise chimed in. "Philip," she said, "come on, Philip. You're just upset. We're all upset."

"You keep out of this," he said, and he didn't even turn to look at her. He just kept his Aqua Velva eyes on me. "Yeah," he said finally, "you're my brother, but you're going to have to prove it to me."

I can see now the Desoxyn was a mistake. It was exactly the sort of thing they'd warned us about. But it wasn't coke and I just needed a lift, a buzz to work behind, and if he didn't want me to be tempted, then why had he left the key to the drug cabinet right there in the conch-shell ashtray on the corner of his desk? *Ex-con.* I was hurt and I was angry and I stayed in my room till Philip knocked at the door an hour later to tell me the police had cleared the mob away. We drove to work in silence, Philip's opera chewing away at my nerves like a hundred little sets of teeth.

Philip didn't notice it, but there was something different about me when I climbed back into that car, something nobody could notice unless they had X-ray vision. I was armed. Tucked inside the waistband of my gray Levi's, underneath the flap of my shirt where you couldn't see it, was the hard black stump of a gun I'd bought from a girl named Corinne at a time when I was feeling especially paranoiac. I had money lying around the apartment then and people coming and going—nobody desperate, nobody I didn't know or at least know through a friend—but it made me a little crazy. Corinne used to drop by once in a while with my roommate's girlfriend, and she sold me the thing—a .38 Special—for three hundred bucks. She didn't need it anymore, she said, and I didn't want to know what that meant, so I bought it and kept it under my pillow. I'd only fired it once, up a canyon in Tujunga, but it made me feel better just to have it around. I'd forgotten all about it, actually, but when I got my things out of storage and shipped them to Philip's house, there it was, hidden away in a box of CDs like some poisonous thing crouching under a rock.

What I was feeling is hard to explain. It had to do with Philip, sure—ex-con, that really hurt—and with Sally and the clinic and the whole Jesus-thumping circus. I didn't know what I was going to do—nothing, I hoped—but I knew I wasn't going to take any shit from anybody, and I knew Philip didn't have it in him to protect himself, let alone Denise and the kids and all the knocked-up grieving teenage Sallys of the world. That was all. That was it. The extent of my thinking. I walked into the clinic that morning just as I had for the past week and a half, and nobody knew the difference.

I cleaned the toilets, washed the windows, took out the trash. Some blood work came back from an outside lab—we only did urine—and Fred showed me how to read the results. I discussed the baseball strike with Nurse Tsing and the prospects of an early spring with Nurse Hempfield. At noon I went out to a deli and had a meatball wedge, two beers, and a breath mint. I debated dialing Sally just once more—maybe she was home from school, headachy, nauseous, morning sickness, whatever, and I could get past the brick wall she'd put up between us and talk to her, really talk to her for the first time—but when I got inside the phone booth, I just didn't feel like it. As I walked back to the clinic I was wondering if she had a boyfriend or if it was just one of those casual encounters, blind date, back seat of the car—or rape, even. Or incest. Her father's voice could have been the voice of a child abuser, easily—or who even knew if he was her father? Maybe he was the stepfather. Maybe he was a Humbert Humbert type. Maybe anything.

There were no protesters out front when I got back—they were all in jail—and that lightened my mood a bit. I even joked with Fred and caught myself whistling over my work. I forgot the morning, forgot the gun, forgot Pasadena and the life that was. Coffee kept me awake, coffee and Diet Coke, and I stayed away from the other stuff just to prove something to myself—and to Philip too. For a while there I even began to suffer from the delusion that everything was going to work out.

Then it was late, getting dark, and the day was almost done. I pictured the evening ahead—Denise's cooking, *Winnie-the-Pooh,* my brother's scotch, six wind-blown blocks to the store for a liter of Black Cat—and suddenly I felt like pulling out the gun and shooting myself right then and there. Uncle Rick, little brother, ex-con: who was I kidding? I would have been better off in jail.

I needed a cigarette. Badly. The need took me past the waiting room—four scared-looking women, one angry-looking man—through the lab, and into the back corner. The fluorescent lights hissed softly overhead. Fred was already gone. I stood at the window, staring into the nullity of the drawn blinds till the cigarette was a nub. My hands were trembling as I lit another from the butt end of the first, and I didn't think about the raw-looking leftovers in the stainless-steel trays that were like nothing so much as skinned frogs, and I didn't think about Sally or the fat-faced bearded son of a bitch shackling himself to the bumper either. I tried hard to think nothing, to make it all a blank, and I was succeeding, I was, when for some reason—idle curiosity, boredom, fate—I separated two of the slats and peered out into the lot.

And there she was, just like that: Sally.

Sally in her virginal parka and fluffy boots, locked in her mother's grip and fighting her way up the walk against a tide of chanting zombies—and I recognized them too, every one of them, the very ones who'd been dragged away from my brother's door in the dark of the morning. Sally wasn't coming in for an exam—there weren't going to be any more exams. No, Sally meant business. You could see that in the set of her jaw and in the way she lowered her head and jabbed out her eyes like swords, and you could see it in every screaming line of her mother's screaming face.

The light was fading. The sky hung low, like smoke. And then, in that instant, as if some god had snapped his fingers, the streetlights went on, sudden artificial burst of illumination exploding in the sky above them. All at once I felt myself moving, the switch turned on in me too, all the lights flaring in my head, burning bright, and I was out the door, up the corridor, and pushing through the double glass doors at the front entrance.

Something was blocking the doors—bodies, deadweight, the zombies piled up on the steps like corpses—and I had to force my way out. There were bodies everywhere, a minefield of flesh, people stretched out across the steps, obliterating the sidewalk and the curb in front of the clinic, immobilizing the cars in the street. I saw the punk from this morning, the teenage tough guy in his leather jacket, his back right up against the door, and beside him one of the dumpy women I'd flung him into. They didn't learn, these people, they didn't know. It was a game. A big joke. Call people baby-killers, sing about Jesus, pocketful of posies, and then the nice policeman carries you off to jail and Mommy and Daddy bail you out. I tried to kick them aside, lashing out with the steel toes of my boots till my breath was coming in gasps. "Sally!" I cried. "Sally, I'm coming!"

She was stalled at the corner of the building, standing rigid with her mother before the sea of bodies. "Jesus loves you!" somebody cried out and they all took it up till my voice was lost in the clamor, erased in the everlasting hiss of Jesus. "We're going to come looking for you, brother," the tough guy said then, looking up at me out of a pair of seething blue eyes. "You better watch your back."

Sally was there. Jesus was there. Hands grabbed at me, snaked round my legs till I couldn't move, till I was mired in flesh. The big man came out of nowhere, lithe on his feet, vaulting through the inert bodies like the shadow of something moving swiftly overhead, and he didn't so much as graze me as he went by. I was on the third step down, held fast, the voices chanting, the signs waving, and I turned to watch him handcuff himself to the door and flash me a tight little smile of triumph.

"Sally!" I shouted. "Sally!" But she was already turning around, already turning her back to me, already lost in the crowd.

I looked down at my feet. A woman was clutching my right leg to her as if she'd given birth to it, her eyes as loopy as any crackhead's. My left leg was in the grip of a balding guy who might have been a clerk in a hardware store and he was looking up at me like a toad I'd just squashed. "Jesus," they hissed. "Jesus!"

The light was burning in my head, and it was all I needed. I reached into my pants and pulled out the gun. I could have anointed any one of them, but the woman was first. I bent to her where she lay on the unyielding concrete of the steps and touched that snubnose to her ear as tenderly as any man of healing. The noise of it shut down Jesus, shut him down cold. Into the silence, and it was the hardware man next. Then I swung round on Mr. Beard.

It was easy. It was nothing. Just like killing babies.

(1995)

Captured by the Indians

At the lecture that night they learned that human life was expendable. Melanie had sat there in shocked silence—the silence of guilt, mortification and paranoia (what if someone should see her there in the crowd?)—while Dr. Toni Brinsley-Schneider, the Stanford bioethicist, had informed them that humans, like pigs, chickens and guppies, were replaceable. In the doctor's view, the infirm, the mentally impaired, criminals, premature infants and the like were non-persons, whose burden society could no longer be expected to support, especially in light of our breeding success. "We're hardly an endangered species," she said with a grim laugh. "Did you know, all of you good and earnest people sitting here tonight, that we've just reached the population threshold of six billion?" She was cocked back from the lectern in a combative pose, her penurious little silver-rimmed reading glasses flinging fragments of light out into the audience. "Do any of you really want more condominiums, more shantytowns and favelas, more cars on the freeway, more group homes for the physically handicapped right around the corner from you? On your street? Next door?" She leveled her flashing gaze on them. "Well, do you?"

People shifted in their seats, a muted moist surge of sound that was like the timid lapping of waves on a distant shore. No one responded—this was a polite crowd, a liberal crowd dedicated to free expression, a university crowd, and besides, the question had been posed for effect only. They'd have their chance to draw blood during the Q&A.

Sean sat at attention beside Melanie, his face shining and smug. He was midway through the Ph.D. program in literary theory, and the theoreticians had hardened his heart: Dr. Brinsley-Schneider was merely confirming what he already knew. Melanie took his hand, but it wasn't a warm hand, a hand expressive of comfort and love—it was more like something dug frozen from the earth. She hadn't yet told him what she'd learned at two thirty-three that afternoon, special knowledge, a secret as magical and expansive as a loaf of bread rising in a pan. Another sort of doctor had brought her the news, a doctor very different from the pinched and angry-looking middle-aged woman at the podium, a young dark-haired sylph of a woman, almost a girl, with a wide beatific face and congratulatory eyes, dressed all in white like a figure out of a dream.

They walked to the car in silence, the mist off the ocean redrawing the silhouettes of the trees, the streetlights softly glowing. Sean wanted a burger—and maybe a beer—so they stopped off at a local bar and grill the students hadn't discovered yet and she watched him eat and drink while the television over the bar replayed images of atrocities in the Balkans, the routine bombing of Iraq and the itinerary of the railroad killer. In between commercials for trucks that were apparently capable of scaling cliffs and fording rivers, they showed the killer's face, a mug shot of a slightly built Latino with an interrupted mustache and two dead eyes buried like artifacts in his head. "You see that?" Sean said, nodding at the screen, the half-eaten burger clenched in one hand, the beer in the other. "That's what Brinsley-Schneider and these people are talking about. You think this guy worries much about the sanctity of human life?"

Can we afford compassion? Melanie could hear the lecturer's droning thin voice in the back of her head, and she saw the dour pale muffin of a face frozen in the spotlight when somebody in back shouted *Nazi!* "I don't know why we have to go to these lectures anyway," she said. "Last year's series was so much more—do I want to say 'uplifting' here? Remember the woman who'd written that book about beekeeping? And the old professor—what was his name?—who talked about Yeats and Maud Gonne?"

"Stevenson Elliot Turner. He's emeritus in the English Department."

"Yeah," she said, "that's right, and why can't we have more of that sort of thing? Tonight—I don't know, she was so depressing. And so wrong."

"Are you kidding me? Turner's like the mummy's ghost—that talk was stupefying. He was probably giving the same lecture in English 101 thirty years ago. At least Brinsley-Schneider's controversial. At least she keeps you awake."

Melanie wasn't listening, and she didn't want to argue—or debate, or discuss. She wanted to tell Sean—who wasn't her husband, not yet, because they had to wait till he got his degree—that she was pregnant. But she couldn't. She already knew what he would say, and it was right on the same page with Dr. Toni Brinsley-Schneider.

She watched his eyes settle on the screen a moment, then drift down to the burger in his hand. He drew back his lips and took a bite, nostrils open wide, the iron muscles working in his jaw. "We live by the railroad tracks," Melanie said, by way of shifting the subject. "You think we have anything to worry about?"

"What do you mean?"

"The train killer."

Sean gave her a look. He was in his debating mode, his put-down mode, and she could see it in his eyes. "He doesn't kill trains, Mel," he said, "—he kills people. And yes, everybody has something to worry about, everybody on this planet. And if you were listening to half of what Brinsley-Schneider was saying tonight, I wouldn't be surprised if every third person out there on the street was a serial killer. There's too many of us, Mel, let's face it. You think things are going to get better? You think things are better now than when we were kids? When our parents were kids? It's over. Face it."

Something corny and ancient was on the jukebox—Frank Sinatra, Tony Bennett, somebody like that—because the place smacked of the kind of authenticity people were looking for, the kind of authenticity that cried out from the fallen arches, ravaged faces and sclerotic livers of the regulars, to whom she and Sean—at twenty-nine and thirty, respectively—were as inauthentic as newborns.

At home, she changed into a cotton nightgown and got into bed with a book. She wasn't feeling anything, not elation or pain or disappointment, only the symptoms of a headache coming on. The book was something she'd discovered at a yardsale two days earlier—*Captured by the Indians: 15 Firsthand Accounts, 1750–1870*—and the minute she opened it she was swept up into a voyeuristic world of pain and savagery that trumped any horror she could conceive of. It wasn't a good thing to be captured by the Indians, as Sean had snidely observed on seeing her poised behind the cover the night before last, not good at all. There were no notions here of the politically correct, of revisionist history or the ethics of one people forcibly displacing another: no, it was the hot flash of murder and reprisal, the thump of the musket ball hitting home, the operation of knife and tomahawk on unresisting flesh. To die, to be murdered, to be robbed of your life and consciousness and being, that was the stuff of morbid fascination, and she couldn't get enough of it.

Sean was in his underwear, the briefs he preferred over boxers, the sort of thing she'd always associated with boys—little boys, children, that is—and as she watched him pad across the carpet on his way to the bathroom and his nightly ritual of cleansing, clipping, flossing, brushing, tweezering and shaving, it struck her that she'd never in her life been in an intimate situation with a man—or boy—in boxers. "The last they heard," Sean was saying, and he paused now to gaze at her over the mound of the bedspread and her tented knees, "he was in the Midwest someplace—after leaving Texas, I mean. That's a long ways from California, Mel, and besides, his whole thing is so random—"

"He rides freight trains—or hops them, isn't that the terminology?" she said, peering over the cover of the book. "He hops freight trains, Sean, and that means he could be anywhere in twenty-four hours—or forty-eight. How long does it take to drive from Kansas to Isla Vista? Two days? Three?" She wanted to tell him about the doctor, and what the doctor had said, and what it was going to mean for them, but she didn't want to see the look on his face, didn't want to have to fight him, not now, not yet. He'd go pale and tug involuntarily at the grown-over hole in his left earlobe where the big gold hoop used to reside before he got serious about his life, and then he'd tell her she couldn't have her baby for the same reason she couldn't have a dog or even a cat—at least until he'd done his dissertation, at least until then.

"I don't know, Mel," he said, all the tiredness and resignation in the world crept into his voice, as if a simple discussion could martyr him, "what do you want me to say? He's coming through the window tonight? Of the two hundred seventy million potential victims in the country, he's singled us out, zeroed right in on us like a homing pigeon—?"

"Statistics," she said, and she was surprised at her own vehemence. "That's like saying you have about the same chance of getting attacked by a shark as you do of getting hit by lightning, and yeah, sure, but anybody anywhere can get hit by lightning, but how many people live by the ocean, how many actually go in it, and of them, how many are crazy enough—or foolhardy, that's the word I want here—how many are foolhardy enough to go out where the sharks are? Probably a hundred percent of *them* get eaten, and we live right by the tracks, don't we?"

As if in answer, there was the sudden sharp blast of the north-bound's whistle as it neared the intersection two blocks away, and then the building thunder of the train itself, the fierce clatter of the churning wheels and everything in the room trembling with the rush of it. Sean rolled his eyes and disappeared into the bathroom. When the thunder subsided and he could be heard again, he poked his head round the doorframe. "It's the Indians," he said.

"It has nothing to do with the Indians." She wouldn't give him this, though he was right, of course—or partially anyway. "It's Brinsley-Schneider, who you seem to think is so great. Brinsley-Schneider and eugenics and euthanasia and all the rest of the deadly *u*'s."

He was smiling the smile of the literary theorist in a room full of them, the smile that made him look like a toad with an oversized insect clamped in its jaws. "The deadly *u*'s?" he repeated. And then, softening, he said, "All right, if it'll make you feel any better I'll check the doors and windows, okay?"

Her eyes were on the book. Way off in the night she could hear the dying rattle of the last car at the end of the train. Her life was changing, and why couldn't she feel good about it—why shouldn't she?

He was in the doorway still, his face settling into the lines and grooves he'd dug for it over the past two and a half years of high seriousness. He looked exactly like himself. "Okay?" he said.

She didn't have to be in at work till twelve the next day—she was an assistant to the reference librarian at the university library, and her schedule was so flexible it was all but bent over double—and after Sean left for class she sat in front of the TV with the sound off and read the account of Lavina Eastlick, who was twenty-nine and the mother of five when the Sioux went on a rampage near Acton, Minnesota, in the long-forgotten year of 1862. There was a moment's warning, no more than that. A frightened neighbor shouting in the yard, first light, and suddenly Lavina Eastlick—a housewife, a hopeful young woman her own age rudely jolted from sleep—was running barefooted through the wet grass, in her nightgown, herding her children before her. The Indians soon overtook them and cut down her husband, her children, her neighbors and her neighbors' children, taking the women captive. She'd been shot twice and could barely stand, let alone walk. When she stumbled and fell, a Sioux brave beat her about the head and shoulders with the stock of his rifle and left her for dead. Later, when they'd gone, she was able to crawl off and hide herself in the brush through the long afternoon and interminable night that followed. The wounded children—hers and her neighbors'—lay sprawled in the grass behind her, crying out for water, but she couldn't move to help them. On the second afternoon the Indians returned to dig at the children's wounds with sharpened sticks till the terrible gargling cries choked off and the locusts in the trees filled the void with their mindless chant.

And what would Dr. Toni Brinsley-Schneider have thought of that? She'd probably applaud the Indians for eliminating the useless and weak, who would only have grown up crippled around their shattered limbs in any case. That was what Melanie was thinking as she closed the book and glanced up at the casual violence scrolling across the TV screen, but once she was on her feet she realized she was hungry and headed off in the direction of the kitchen, thinking tuna fish on rye with roasted sunflower seeds and red bell pepper. She supposed she'd be putting on weight now, eating for two, and wouldn't that be the way to announce the baby to Sean six months down the road, like the prom mom who hid it till the last fatal minute: *And you thought I was just going to fat, didn't you, honey?*

Outside, beyond the windows, the sun washed over the flowers in the garden, all trace of the night's mist burned off. There were juncos and finches at the feeder she shared with the upstairs neighbor, a dog asleep at the curb across the street, pure white fortresses of cloud building over the mountains. It was still, peaceful, an ordinary day, no Indians in sight, no bioethicists, no railroad killers hopping off freight trains and selecting victims at random, and she chopped onions and diced celery with a steady hand while something inexpressibly sad came over the radio, a cello playing in minor key, all alone, until it was joined by a single violin that sounded as if a dead man were playing it, playing his own dirge—and maybe he was dead, maybe the recording was fifty years old, she was thinking, and she had a sudden image of a man with a long nose and a Gypsy face, serenading the prisoners at Auschwitz.

Stop it, she told herself, *just stop it.* She should be filled with light, shouldn't she? She should be knitting, baking, watching the children at the playground with the greedy intensity of a connoisseur.

The sunflower seeds were in the pan, the one with the loose handle and the black non-stick surface, heat turned up high, when the doorbell rang. The violin died at that moment—literally—and the unctuous, breathless voice of the announcer she hated (the one who always sounded as if he were straining over a bowel movement) filled the apartment as she crossed the front room and stepped into the hall. She was about to pull open the door—it would be the mailman at this hour, offering up a clutch of bills and junk mail and one of Sean's articles on literary theory (or Theory, as he called it, "Just Theory, with a capital *T,* like Philosophy or Physics"), returned from an obscure journal with postage due—but something stopped her. "Who is it?" she called from behind the door, and she could smell the sunflower seeds roasting in the pan.

There was no answer, so she moved to the window beside the door and parted the curtains. A man stood on the concrete doorstep, staring at the flat plane of the door as if he could see through it. He was small and thin, no more than five-five or -six, tanned to the color of the copper teakettle on the stove and dressed in the oily jeans and all-purpose long-sleeved shirt of the bums who lined Cabrillo Boulevard with their Styrofoam cups and pint bottles—or should she call them panhandlers or the homeless or the apartmentally challenged? Sean called them bums, and she guessed she'd fallen into the habit herself. They said crude things to you when you walked down the street, gesturing with fingers that were as black as the stubs of cigars. They were bums, that was all, and who needed them?

But then the man turned to her, saw her there at the window and turned to her, and she had a shock: he was Hispanic, a Latino just like the man on TV, the killer, with the same dead cinders for eyes. He put three fingers together and pushed them at his open mouth, and she saw then that he had no mustache—no, no mustache, but what did that mean? Anybody could shave, even a bum. "What do you want?" she called, feeling trapped in her own apartment, caught behind the wall of glass like a fish in an aquarium.

He looked surprised by the question. What did he want? He wanted food, money, sex, booze, drugs, her car, her baby, her life, her apartment. "Hungry," he said. And then, when she didn't respond: "You got work?"

She just shook her head—No, she didn't have any work—and all the time she had to give this man, this stranger, this bum, had already been used up, because there was smoke in the kitchen and the seeds were burning in the pan.

It was past eight when she drove home from work, feeling exhausted, as if she were in her eighth month instead of the second. The day was softening into night, birds dive-bombing the palms along the boulevard, joggers and in-line skaters reduced to shadows on the periphery of her vision. All through the afternoon the mist had been rolled up like a carpet on the horizon, but it was moving closer now and she could smell it on the air—it was going to be another dense, compacted night. She parked and came up the walk and saw that the upstairs neighbor—Jessica, Jessica-something, who'd been there only a month and was so pathologically shy she cupped both hands to her face when she talked to you as if a real live moving mouth were somehow offensive—had been doing something in the flower garden. The earth was raw in several spots, as if it had been turned over, and there was a spade leaning against the side of the house. Not that it mattered to Melanie—she'd never had a green thumb and plants were just plants to her. If Jessica wanted to plant flowers, that was fine; if she wanted to dig them up, that was fine too.

Sean was in the kitchen, banging things around and singing—bellowing—along with one of Wagner's operas, the only music he ever listened to. And which one was it?—she'd heard them all a thousand times. There it was, yes, Siegfried going down for the count: *Götterdämmerung.* Sean was making his famous shrimp and avocado salad, and he was in the throes of something—Wagner, Theory, some sort of testosterone rush—and he barely glanced up at her as she trudged into the bedroom. Her mistake was in taking off her shoes, the flats she wore for the sake of her feet while propping up an automatic smile behind the reference desk, because once her shoes were off she felt out of balance and had to rest her head on the pillow, just for a minute.

The gods of Valhalla had been laid to rest and the house was silent when she awoke to the soft click of the bedroom door. Sean was standing there framed in the doorway, the tacky yellow globe of the hallway light hanging over his shoulder like a captive moon. It was dark beyond the windows. "What," he said, "are you sick or something?"

Was she? Now was her chance, now was the time to tell him, to share the news, the joyous news, pop the cork on the bottle of champagne and let's go out to a nice place, a really nice place, and save the famous shrimp and avocado salad for tomorrow. "No," she said. "No. Just tired, that's all."

At dinner—Sean and Lacan and a scatter of papers, the shrimp salad, lemonade from the can and an incongruous side dish of Ranch Style barbecue beans, also from the can—she did tell him about the man at the door that morning. "He said he wanted work," she said, waving a forkful of shrimp and beans in an attempt to delineate the scene for the third time, "and I told him I didn't have any work for him. That was it. The whole thing."

Sean had begun to develop a groove just over the bridge of his nose, a V-shaped gouge that might have been a scar or the mark of a hot branding iron. It vanished when he was asleep or sunk into the couch with a beer and the *New York Times*, but it was there now, deeper than ever. "You mean he was Mexican?"

"I don't know," she said, "he was a Latino. I was scared. He really scared me."

There was a long silence, the clock her mother had given her ticking dramatically from atop the brick-and-board bookcase in the hall, someone's sprinklers going on outside, the muted rumble of Jessica-something's TV seeping down through the ceiling—Melanie half-expected to hear the blast of the train's whistle, but it was too early yet. "It could be," Sean said finally, "—I mean, why not? You're right. The guy takes a train, he could be anywhere. And then there's the aleatory factor—"

She just stared at him.

"Chance. Luck. Fate. You can't buck fate." And then a look came over his face: two parts high seriousness, one part vigilante. "But you can be ready for it when it comes—you can be prepared." Suddenly he was on his feet. "You just wait here, just sit tight"—and his voice had an edge to it, as if she'd been arguing with him, as if she had to be restrained from running off into the night like one of the screaming teenagers in a cheap horror film—"I'll be right back."

She wanted a glass of wine, but she knew she couldn't drink anymore, not if she was going to keep the baby, and if she hadn't known, the doctor had taken her down a smiling anfractuous road full of caveats and prohibitions, the sort of thing she—the doctor—must go through ten times a day, albeit tailoring her tone to the educational level of the patient. Outside, the sprinklers switched off with an expiring wheeze. She could hear Sean in the bedroom, rummaging around for something. Tonight, she would tell him tonight.

Because the knowledge was too big for her to contain, and she wanted to call her mother and have a long, confidential chat, and call her sisters too—but before that, before there could be any possibility of that, she had to tell Sean, and

Sean had to say the things she needed to hear. During her five o'clock break, she'd confided in one of the girls she worked with, Gretchen Mohr, but it did nothing to reassure her. Gretchen was only twenty-three, in no way serious about the guy she was dating, and Melanie could tell from the way she squeezed her eyes shut over the news that the idea of a baby was about as welcome to her as paraplegia or epilepsy. Oh, she tried to cover herself with a flurry of congratulations and a nonstop barrage of platitudes and one-liners, but the final thing she said, her last and deepest thought, gave her away. "I don't know," she sighed, staring down into the keyhole of her Diet Coke can as if she were reading tea leaves, "but I just don't think I'd be comfortable bringing a baby into a world like this."

When Melanie looked up, Sean was standing over her. He was wearing a T-shirt with a picture of Freud on it, over a legend that read "Dr. Who?" His hair was slicked down, and the left side of his face, up to and encircling the ear, was inflamed with the skin condition he was forever fighting. But that was ordinary, that was the way he always looked. What was different were his eyes—proud, incandescent, lit up like fireworks—and his hands, or what was in his hands. Swaddled in coarse white cloth that was stained with what might have been olive oil lay an object she recognized from the movies, from TV and pawnshop display cases: a gun.

"What is that?" she said, edging away from him. "What are you showing me?"

"Come on, Mel, give me a break."

"It's a gun, isn't it?"

"We're on the ground floor here, and we're going to lock the windows tonight, even if it's hot, which I doubt because already the fog's coming in, and we're going to keep this by the bed, on the night table, that's all."

She'd drawn up her legs and hugged them to her, as far away from him on the couch as she could manage to be. "I don't *believe* you," she said, and she could hear the thin whine of complaint in her own voice. "You know what my father would say if he saw you now? Where did you get it? Why didn't you tell me?" she demanded, and she couldn't help herself—her voice broke on the final syllable.

He drew the thing back, took it from its cradle and raised it up in one hand till it grazed the ceiling. The muscles of his forearm flexed, the soiled rag dropped to the carpet. "Son of a bitch," he said, "son of a fucking bitch. Tell me this," he said, "would you rather be the killer or the killee?"

She was asleep and dreaming the image of a baby floating in amniotic fluid, the cord attached, eyes shut tight—a big baby, an enormous glowing baby floating free like the interstellar embryo of *2001*—when a sudden sharp explosion of noise jolted her awake. It took her a moment, heart pounding, breath coming quick, to understand what it was—it was a scream, a woman's scream, improvised and fierce. The room was dark. Sean was asleep beside her. The scream—a single rising note tailing off into what might have been a sob or gasp—seemed to have come from above, where Jessica-something lived alone with her potted plants and two bloated pampered push-faced cats that were never allowed out of the apartment for fear of the world and its multiplied dangers. Melanie sat up and caught her breath.

Nothing. The alarm clock on the night table flashed 1:59 and then 2:00.

Earlier, after a dessert of tapioca pudding with mandarin orange slices fresh from the can, she and Sean had watched a costume drama on the public station that gave her a new appreciation for the term *mediocre* (*mediocre,* as she observed to Sean, didn't come easy—you had to work at it), and then she'd slipped into bed with her book while the station went into pledge-break mode and Sean sat there paralyzed on the couch. She hadn't read two paragraphs before he tiptoed into the room, naked and in full amatory display. She left the light on, the better to admire him, but the book dropped to the floor, and then it didn't matter. She felt new, re-created. His body was so familiar, but everything was different now—she'd never been so aroused, rising up again and again to hold him deep inside her in the place where the baby was. Afterward, immediately afterward, almost as if he'd been drugged, he fell asleep with his head on her breast, and it was left to her to reach up awkwardly and kill the lamp. They hadn't discussed a thing.

But now—now there was chaos, and it erupted all at once. There was a thump overhead, the caustic burn of a man's voice, and then another scream, and another, and Melanie was out of bed, the walls pale and vague, the dark shadow that was Sean lurching up mechanically, and "What?" he was saying. "What is it?"

Footsteps on the stairs. More screams. Melanie flicked on the light, and there was Sean, dressed only in his briefs, the long muscles of his legs, all that skin, and the gun in his hand, the pistol, the nasty gleaming black little thing he'd bought at a gun show six months ago and never bothered to tell her about. "Sean," she said, "Sean, don't!" but he was already out the door, racing down the hall in the sick yellow wash of the overhead light, already at the front door, the screams from above rising, rising. She was in her nightgown, barefooted, but she had no thought for anything but to get out that door and put an end to whatever this was.

There was a streetlight out front, but the fog had cupped a hand over it and blotted the light from the windows and the stairway too. Melanie shot a glance up the stairs to where Jessica stood bracing herself against the railing, in nothing but panties and a brassiere torn off one shoulder, and then she saw the glint of Sean's back across the lawn where the cars threw up a bank of shadow against the curb. He was shouting something, ragged, angry syllables that could have made no sense to anyone, even a Theorist, and she saw then that there was somebody else there with him, a dark, shifting figure rallying round a shuffle of feet on the pavement. She was closer now, running, Sean's feet glowing in the night, the long white stalks of his legs and expanse of his back—he seemed to be wrestling with a shadow, but no, it was an animate thing, a man, a dark little man in bum's clothes with a shovel clenched in both hands and Sean fighting him for it. Where was the gun? There was no gun. Both Sean's hands were on the shovel and both the little man's, and now Jessica was screaming again. "The gun," Sean said. "In the grass. Get the gun."

In that moment the little man managed to wrench the shovel free, and in the next—it happened so quickly she wasn't sure she actually saw it—he caught Sean under the chin with the haft, and then the blade, and Sean was on the ground. She never hesitated. Before the man could bring the blade down—and that was what he meant to do, no mistake about it, his arms already raised high for a savage stabbing thrust—she took hold of the haft with all the strength in her and pulled it tight to her chest.

She could smell him. She could feel him. He hung on, the little man, the bum, the one who'd been on the doorstep that afternoon with his reeking breath and greasy clothes, and then he jerked so violently at the shovel she almost pitched headlong into him, into the spill of his flesh and the dankness of the grass. But she didn't. She jerked back, and Jessica screamed, and Sean, reeling like a drunk, began to pick himself up off the lawn, and for the instant before the man let go of the shovel and flung himself into the shadows across the street she was staring him full in the face—yes, but she wasn't seeing the man on the TV or the man on the porch or any one of the army of bums lined up along the street in their all-purpose shirts and sweat-stained caps, she was seeing Dr. Toni Brinsley-Schneider, Dr. Brinsley-Schneider the bioethicist, just her.

There were two policemen. From where she was sitting at the end of the couch, Melanie could see their cruiser reined in at the curb, the interior a black pit, the slowly revolving light on top chopping up the night over and over again. They were built like runners or squash players, both of them—crisp, efficient men in their thirties who looked away from her bare legs and feet and into her eyes. "So you heard screams, and this was about what time?"

They'd already taken Jessica-something's statement—Jessica Fortgang, and she had a name now: *Ms.* Fortgang, as the policemen referred to her—and Sean, hunched in the armchair with an angry red weal under his chin, had given his version of events too. The man in the night, the bum, the one who'd been the cause of all this, had escaped, at least for the time being, and they were denied the satisfaction of seeing him handcuffed in the back of the cruiser, bowed and contrite. Sean had been in a state when the police arrived, clenching his jaws as if he were biting down hard on something, gesturing with a closed fist and wide sweeps of his arm. "The railway killer, it was him, the railway killer," he kept repeating, till the policeman with the mustache, the taller one, told him the railway killer had turned himself in at the Mexican border some fifteen hours earlier. "That was the Texas border," he added, and then his partner, in a flat professional voice, said that they were treating this as an assault in any case, possibly an attempted rape. "Your neighbor, Ms. Fortgang? She apparently hired this individual to do some yard work this afternoon and then invited him in for iced tea and a sandwich when he was done. Then he comes back at night—and this is a cultural thing, you understand, a woman looks at one of these guys twice and he expects a whole lot more. He's a transient, that's all, nobody from around here. But we'll get him."

Melanie answered their questions patiently, though her heart was still jumping in her chest, and she kept glancing at Sean, as if for guidance. But Sean was sullen, distant, withdrawn into some corner of himself—the gun was an embarrassment, the man had knocked him down, he'd been involved in an ordinary altercation with an ordinary bum, and the railway killer had already given himself up. She saw the lines in his face, saw the way his lower lip pushed his chin down into the soft flesh beneath it. Theory couldn't help here. Theory deconstructs, theory has no purpose, no point, no overview or consolation—it was a kind of intellectual masturbation. If she hadn't known it before, she knew it now.

The police thanked them, tried on the briefest of smiles, and then Sean showed them to the door and Melanie got up from the couch with the vague idea of making herself a cup of herbal tea to help her unwind. Just as the door closed, she called Sean's name aloud, and she almost said it, almost said, "Sean, there's something I've been wanting to tell you," but there was no use in that now.

Sean turned away from the door, shoulders slumped, the corners of his mouth drawn down. After the skirmish on the lawn, he'd shrugged into a pair of jeans and the first shirt he could find—a Hawaiian print, festive with palm fronds and miniature pineapples—and she saw that he'd misbuttoned it. He looked hopeless. He looked lost in his own living room.

She held that picture of him, and then she was thinking, unaccountably, of another captive of the Sioux, a young woman taken from her husband to be bride to a chief, the business settled in the smoke and confusion of a desperate fight, her daughter crying out over the cacophony of shouts and curses and the rolling thunder of a hundred rifles firing at once. Months later, fleeing with her captors after a loss in battle, she watched a brave from another party come up to them on his pony, in full regalia, trailing the shawl she'd knitted for her daughter and a tiny shrunken scalp with the hair—the blond shining hair—still attached.

(1999)

Achates McNeil

My father is a writer. A pretty well-known one too. You'd recognize the name if I mentioned it, but I won't mention it, I'm tired of mentioning it—every time I mention it I feel as if I'm suffocating, as if I'm in a burrow deep in the ground and all these fine grains of dirt are raining down on me. We studied him in school, in the tenth grade, a story of his in one of those all-purpose anthologies that dislocate your wrists and throw out your back just to lift them from the table, and then again this year, my freshman year, in college. I got into a Contemporary American Lit class second semester and they were doing two of his novels, along with a three-page list of novels and collections by his contemporaries, and I knew some of them too—or at least I'd seen them at the house. I kept my mouth shut though, especially after the professor, this blond poet in her thirties who once wrote a novel about a nymphomaniac pastry maker, made a joke the first day when she came to my name in the register.

"Achates McNeil," she called out.

"Here," I said, feeling hot and cold all over, as if I'd gone from a sauna into a snowbank and back again. I knew what was coming; I'd been through it before.

She paused, looking up from her list to gaze out the window on the frozen wastes of the campus in the frozen skullcap of New York State, and then came back to me and held my eyes a minute. "You wouldn't happen by any chance to be a relation of anybody on our reading list, would you?"

I sat cramped in the hard wooden seat, thinking about the faceless legions who'd sat there before me, people who'd squirmed over exams and unfeeling professorial remarks and then gone on to become plastic surgeons, gas station attendants, insurance salesmen, bums and corpses. "No," I said. "I don't think so."

She gave me a mysterious little smile. "I was thinking of Teresa Golub or maybe Irving Thalamus?" It was a joke. One or two of the literary cretins in back gave it a nervous snort and chuckle, and I began to wonder, not for the first time, if I was really cut out for academic life. This got me thinking about the various careers available to me as a college dropout—rock and roller, chairman of the board, center for the New York Knicks—and I missed the next couple of names, coming back to the world as the name Victoria Roethke descended on the room and hung in the air like the aftershock of a detonation in the upper atmosphere.

She was sitting two rows up from me, and all I could see was her hair, draped in a Medusan snarl of wild demi-dreadlocks over everything within a three-foot radius. Her hair was red—red as in pink rather than carrot-top—and it tended to be darker on the ends but running to the color of the stuff they line Easter baskets with up close to her scalp. She didn't say here or present or yes or even nod her amazing head. She just cleared her throat and announced, "He was my grandfather."

I stopped her in the hallway after class and saw that she had all the usual equipment as well as a nose ring and two eyes the color of the cardboard stiffeners you get as a consolation prize when you have to buy a new shirt. "Are you really—?" I began, thinking we had a lot in common, thinking we could commiserate, drown our sorrows together, have sex, whatever, but before I could finish the question, she said, "No, not really."

"You mean you—?"

"That's right."

I gave her a look of naked admiration. And she was looking at me, sly and composed, looking right into my eyes. "But aren't you afraid you're going to be on Professor What's-Her-Face's shitlist when she finds out?" I said finally.

Victoria was still looking right into me. She fiddled with her hair, touched her nose ring and gave it a quick squeeze with a nervous flutter of her fingers. Her fingernails, I saw, were painted black. "Who's going to tell her?" she said.

We were complicitous. Instantly. Half a beat later she asked me if I wanted to buy her a cup of ramen noodles in the Student Union, and I said yeah, I did, as if it was something I had any choice about.

We ran through a crust of dead snow in a stiff wind and temperatures that hadn't risen above minus ten in the past two weeks, and there were a lot of people running with us, a whole thundering herd—up here everybody ran everywhere; it was a question of survival.

In the Union she shook out her hair, and five minutes after we'd found a table in the corner and poured the hot water into the Styrofoam containers of dehydrated mystery food I could still smell the cold she'd trapped there. Otherwise I smelled the multi-layered festering odors of the place, generic to college cafeterias worldwide: coffee, twice-worn underwear, cream of tomato soup. If they enclosed the place in plastic and sealed it like a tomb, it'd smell the same two thousand years from now. I'd never been in the kitchen, but I remembered the kitchen from elementary school, with its big aluminum pots and microwave ovens and all the rest, and pictured them back there now, the cafeteria ladies with their dyed hair and their miserable small-town loutish-husband lives, boiling up big cauldrons of cream of tomato soup. Victoria's nose was white from the cold, but right where the nose ring plunged in, over the flange of her left nostril, there was a spot of flesh as pink as the ends of her hair.

"What happens when you get a cold?" I said. "I mean, I've always wondered."

She was blowing into her noodles, and she looked up to shoot me a quick glance out of her cardboard eyes. Her mouth was small, her teeth the size of individual kernels of niblet corn. When she smiled, as she did now, she showed acres of gum. "It's a pain in the ass." Half a beat: that was her method. "I suffer it all for beauty."

And of course this is where I got all gallant and silver-tongued and told her how striking it was, she was, her hair and her eyes and—but she cut me off. "You really are his son, aren't you?" she said.

There was a sudden eruption of jock-like noises from the far end of the room—some athletes with shaved heads making sure everybody knew they were there—and it gave me a minute to compose myself, aside from blowing into my noodles and adjusting my black watchcap with the Yankees logo for the fourteenth time, that is. I shrugged. Looked into her eyes and away again. "I really don't want to talk about it."

But she was on her feet suddenly and people were staring at her and there was a look on her face like she'd just won the lottery or the trip for two to the luxurious Spermata Inn on the beach at Waikiki. "I don't believe it," she said, and her voice was as deep as mine, strange really, but with a just detectable breathiness or hollowness to it that made it recognizably feminine.

I was holding onto my Styrofoam container of hot noodles as if somebody was trying to snatch it away from me. A quick glance from side to side reassured me that the people around us had lost interest, absorbed once again in their plates of reheated stir fry, newspapers and cherry Cokes. I gave her a weak smile.

"You mean, you're like really Tim McNeil's son, no bullshit?"

"Yes," I said, and though I liked the look of her, of her breasts clamped in the neat interwoven grid of a blue thermal undershirt and her little mouth and the menagerie of her hair, and I liked what she'd done in class too, my voice was cold. "And I have a whole other life too."

But she wasn't listening. "Oh, my God!" she squealed, ignoring the sarcasm and all it was meant to imply. She did something with her hands, her face; her hair helicoptered round her head. "I can't believe it. He's my hero, he's my god. I want to have his baby!"

The noodles congealed in my mouth like wet confetti. I didn't have the heart to point out that I *was* his baby, for better or worse.

It wasn't that I hated him exactly—it was far more complicated than that, and I guess it got pretty Freudian too, considering the way he treated my mother and the fact that I was thirteen and having problems of my own when he went out the door like a big cliché and my mother collapsed into herself as if her bones had suddenly melted. I'd seen him maybe three or four times since and always with some woman or other and a fistful of money and a face that looked like he'd just got done licking up a pile of dogshit off the sidewalk. What did he want from me? What did he expect? At least he'd waited till my sister and brother were in college, at least they were out of the house when the cleaver fell, but what about me? I was the one who had to go into that classroom in the tenth grade and read that shitty story and have the teacher look at me like I had something to share, some intimate little anecdote I could relate about what it was like living with a genius—or having lived with a genius. And I was the one who had to see his face all over the newspapers and magazines when he published *Blood Ties,* his post-modernist take on the breakdown of the family, a comedy no less, and then read in the interviews about how his wife and children had held him back and stifled him—as if we were his jailers or something. As if I'd ever bothered him or dared to approach the sanctum of his upstairs office when his genius was percolating or asked him to go to a Little League game and sit in the stands and yabber along with the rest of the parents. Not me. No, I was the dutiful son of the big celebrity, and the funny thing was, I wouldn't have even known he was a celebrity if he hadn't packed up and left.

He was my father. A skinny man in his late forties with kinky hair and a goatee who dressed like he was twenty-five and had a dead black morbid outlook on life and twisted everything into the kind of joke that made you squirm. I was proud of him. I loved him. But then I saw what a monster of ego he was, as if anybody could give two shits for literature anymore, as if he was the center of the universe while the real universe went on in the streets, on the Internet, on TV and in the movie theaters. Who the hell was he to reject me?

So: Victoria Roethke.

I told her I'd never licked anybody's nose ring before and she asked me if I wanted to go over to her apartment and listen to music and have sex, and though I felt like shit, like my father's son, like the negative image of something I didn't want to be, I went. Oh, yes: I went.

She lived in a cramped drafty ancient wreck of a nondescript house from the wood-burning era, about five blocks from campus. We ran all the way, of course—it was either that or freeze to the pavement—and the shared effort, the wheezing lungs and burning nostrils, got us over any awkwardness that might have ensued. We stood a minute in the superheated entryway that featured a row of tarnished brass coathooks, a dim hallway lined with doors coated in drab shiny paint and a smell of cat litter and old clothes. I followed her hair up a narrow stairway and into a one-room apartment not much bigger than a prison cell. It was dominated by a queen-size mattress laid out on the floor and a pair of speakers big enough to double as end tables, which they did. Bricks and boards for the bookcases that lined the walls and pinched them in like one of those shrinking rooms in a sci-fi flick, posters to cover up the faded nineteenth-century wallpaper, a greenish-looking aquarium with one pale bloated fish suspended like a mobile in the middle of it. The solitary window looked out on everything that was dead in the world. Bathroom down the hall.

And what did her room smell like? Like an animal's den, like a burrow or a hive. And female. Intensely female. I glanced at the pile of brassieres, panties, body stockings and sweatsocks in the corner, and she lit a joss stick, pulled the curtains and put on a CD by a band I don't want to name here, but which I like—there was no problem with her taste or anything like that. Or so I thought.

She straightened up from bending over the CD player and turned to me in the half-light of the curtained room and said, "You like this band?"

We were standing there like strangers amidst the intensely personal detritus of her room, awkward and insecure. I didn't know her. I'd never been there before. And I must have seemed like some weird growth sprung up on the unsuspecting flank of her personal space. "Yeah," I said, "they're hot," and I was going to expand on that with some technical praise, just to let her see how hip and knowing I was, when she threw out a sigh and let her arms fall to her sides.

"I don't know," she said, "what I really like is soul and gospel—especially gospel. I put this on for you."

I felt deflated suddenly, unhip and uncool. There she was, joss stick sweetening the air, her hair a world of its own, my father's fan—my absent famous self-absorbed son of a bitch of a father actually pimping for me—and I didn't know what to say. After an awkward pause, the familiar band slamming down their chords and yowling out their shopworn angst, I said, "Let's hear some of your stuff then."

She looked pleased, her too-small mouth pushed up into something resembling a smile, and then she stepped forward and enveloped me in her hair. We kissed. She kissed me, actually, and I responded, and then she bounced the two steps to the CD player and put on Berna Berne and the Angeline Sisters, a slow thump of tinny drums and an organ that sounded like something fresh out of the muffler shop, followed by a high-pitched blur of semihysterical voices. "Like it?" she said.

What could I say? "It's different," I said.

She assured me it would grow on me, like anything else, if I gave it half a chance, ran down the other band for their pedestrian posturing, and invited me to get into her bed. "But don't take off your clothes," she said, "not yet."

I had a three o'clock class in psychology, the first meeting of the semester, and I suspected I was going to miss it. I was right. Victoria made a real ritual of the whole thing, clothes coming off with the masturbatory dalliance of a strip show, the covers rolling back periodically to show this patch of flesh or that, strategically revealed. I discovered her breasts one at a time, admired the tattoo on her ankle (a backward *S* that proved, according to her, that she was a reincarnated Norse skald), and saw that she really was a redhead in the conventional sense. Her lips were dry, her tongue was unstoppable, her hair a primal encounter. When we were done, she sat up and I saw that her breasts pointed in two different directions, and that was human in a way I can't really express, a very personal thing, as if she was letting me in on a secret that was more intimate than the sex itself. I was touched. I admit it. I looked at those mismatched breasts and they meant more to me than her lips and her eyes and the deep thrumming instrument of her voice, if you know what I mean.

"So," she said, sipping from a mug of water she produced from somewhere among a stack of books and papers scattered beside the mattress, "what do I call you? I mean, Achates—right?—that's a real mouthful."

"That's my father," I said. "One of his bullshit affectations—how could the great one have a kid called Joe or Evan or Jim-Bob or Dickie?" My head was on the pillow, my eyes were on the ceiling. "You know what my name means? It means 'faithful companion,' can you believe that?"

She was silent a moment, her gray eyes locked on me over the lip of the cup, her breasts dimpling with the cold. "Yeah," she said, "I can see what you mean," and she pulled the covers up to her throat. "But what do people call you?"

I stared bleakly across the room, fastening on nothing, and when I exhaled I could see my breath. Berna Berne and the Angeline Sisters were still at it, punishing the rhythm section and charging after the vocals till you'd think somebody had set their dresses on fire. "My father calls me Ake," I said finally, "or at least he used to when I used to know him. And in case you're wondering how you spell that, that's Ake with a *k*."

Victoria dropped out of the blond poet-novelist's lit class, but I knew where she lived and you couldn't miss her hair jogging across the tundra. I saw her maybe two or three times a week, especially on weekends. When things began to get to me—life, exams, too many shooters of Jack or tequila, my mother's zombielike voice on the telephone—I sank into the den of Victoria's room with its animal funk and shrinking walls as if I'd never climb back out, and it was nothing like the cold, dry burrow I thought of when I thought of my father. Just the opposite: Victoria's room, with Victoria in it, was positively tropical, whether you could see your breath or not. I even began to develop a tolerance for the Angeline Sisters.

I avoided class the day we dissected the McNeil canon, but I was there for Delmore Schwartz and his amazing re-creation of his parents' courtship unfolding on a movie screen in his head. In dreams begin responsibilities—yes, sure, but whose responsibility was I? And how long would I have to wait before we got to the sequel and *my* dreams? I'd looked through the photo albums, my mother an open-faced hippie in cutoffs and serape with her seamless blond hair and Slavic cheekbones and my father cocky and staring into the lens out of the shining halo of his hair, everything a performance, even a simple photograph, even then. The sperm and the egg, that was a biological concept, that was something I could envision up there on the big screen, the wriggling clot of life, the wet glowing ball of the egg, but picturing them coming together, his coldness, his arrogance, his total absorption in himself, that was beyond me. Chalk it up to reticence. To DNA. To the grandiosity of the patriarchal cock. But then he was me and I was him and how else could you account for it?

It was Victoria who called my attention to the poster. The posters, that is, about six million of them plastered all over every stationary object within a two-mile orbit of the campus as if he was a rock star or something, as if he really counted for anything, as if anybody could even read anymore let alone give half a shit about a balding, leather-jacketed, ex-hippie wordmeister who worried about his image first, his groin second, and nothing else after that. How did I miss it? A nearsighted dwarf couldn't have missed it—in fact, all the nearsighted dwarves on campus had already seen it and were lining up with everybody even vaguely ambulatory for their $2.50 Student Activities Board–sponsored tickets:

TIM McNEIL
READING FROM ELECTRONIC
ORPHANS & BLOOD TIES
FEB. 28, 8:00 P.M.
DUBOFSKY HALL

Victoria was right there with me, out front of the Student Union, the poster with his mugshot of a photo staring out at me from behind the double-insulated glass panel that reflected the whole dead Arctic world and me in the middle of it, and we had to dance on our toes and do aerobics for a full two minutes there to stave off hypothermia while I let the full meaning of it sink in. My first response was outrage, and so was my second. I bundled Victoria through the door and out of the blast of the cold, intimately involved in the revolution of her hair, the smell of her gray bristling fake fur coat that looked like half a dozen opossums dropped on her from high, even the feel of her breasts beneath all that wintry armament, and I howled in protest.

"How in Christ's name could he do this to me?" I shouted across the echoing entranceway, pink-nosed idiots in their hooded parkas coming and going, giving me their eat-shit-and-die looks. I was furious, out of control. Victoria snatched at my arm to calm me, but I tore away from her.

"He planned this, you know. He had to. He couldn't leave well enough alone, couldn't let me get away from him and be just plain nobody up here among the cowflops in this podunk excuse for a university—no, it's not Harvard, it's not Stanford, but at least I didn't take a nickel of his money for it. You think he'd ever even consider reading here even if the Board of Regents got down and licked his armpits and bought him a new Porsche and promised him all the co-eds in Burge to fuck one by one till they dropped dead from the sheer joy of it?"

Victoria just stood there looking at me out of her flat gray eyes, rocking back and forth on the heels of her red leather boots with the cowgirl filigree. We were blocking the doors and people were tramping in and out, passing between us, a trail of yellow slush dribbling behind them in either direction. "I don't know," Victoria said over the heads of two Asian girls wrapped up like corpses, "I think it's kind of cool."

A day later, the letter came. Personalized stationery, California address. I tore it open in the hallway outside the door of my overheated, overlit, third-floor room in the sad-smelling old dorm:

Querido Ake:

I know it's been a while but my crazy life just gets crazier what with the European tour for *Orphans* and Judy and Josh, but I want to make it up to you however I can. I asked Jules to get me the gig at Acadia purposely to give me an excuse to see how you're getting along. Let's do dinner or something afterward—bring one of your girlfriends along. We'll do it up. We will.

Mucho,
Dad

This hit me like a body blow in the late rounds of a prizefight. I was already staggering, bloodied from a hundred hooks and jabs, ten to one against making it to the bell, and now this. Boom. I sat down on my institutional bed and read the thing over twice. Judy was his new wife, and Josh, six months old and still shitting in his pants, was my new brother. Half brother. DNA rules. Shit, it would have been funny if he was dead and I was dead and the whole world a burned-out cinder floating in the dead-black hole of the universe. But I wasn't dead, and didn't want to be, not yet at least. The next best thing was being drunk, and that was easy to accomplish. Three Happy Hours and a good lip-splitting, sideburn-thumping altercation with some mountainous asshole in a pair of Revo shades later, and I was ready for him.

You probably expect me to report that my father, the genius, blew into town and fucked my lit professor, Victoria, the cafeteria ladies and two or three dogs he stumbled across on the way to the reading, but that's not the way it fell out. Not at all. In fact, he was kind of sorry and subdued and old-looking. Real old-looking, though by my count he must have been fifty-three or maybe fifty-four. It was as if his whole head had collapsed like a rotten jack-o'-lantern, his eyes sucked down these volcanoes of wrinkles, his hair standing straight up on his head like a used toilet brush. But I'm getting ahead of myself. According to my roommate, Jeff Heymann, he'd called about a hundred times and finally left a message saying he was coming in early and wanted to have lunch too, if that was okay with me. It wasn't okay. I stayed away from the telephone, and I stayed away from my room. In fact, I didn't even go near the campus for fear of running into him as he long-legged his way across the quad, entourage in tow. I blew off my classes and sank into Victoria's nest as if it was an opium den, sleep and forgetfulness, Berna Berne and the Angeline Sisters keeping me company, along with a bottle of Don Q Victoria's dad had brought back from Puerto Rico for her. What was my plan? To crash and burn. To get so fucked up I'd be in a demi-coma till the lunch was eaten, the reading read and dinner forgotten. I mean, fuck him. Really.

The fatal flaw in my plan was Victoria.

She didn't stay there to comfort me with her hair, her neat little zipper of a mouth and her mismatched breasts. No, she went to class, very big day, exams and papers and quizzes. So she said. But do I have to tell you where she really was? Can't you picture it? The fan, the diehard, somebody who supposedly cared about me, and there she was, camped outside his hotel in the Arctic wind with the snot crusted round her nose ring. They wouldn't tell her what room he was in, and when she took exception to the attitude of the girl behind the desk, they told her she'd have to wait outside—on the public sidewalk. While she was waiting and freezing and I was attempting to drink myself comatose, he was making phone calls. Another hundred to my room and then to the registrar and the dean and anybody else who might have had a glimmer of my whereabouts, and of course they all fell over dead and contacted my professors, the local police—Christ, probably even the FBI, the CIA and TRW.

And then it was lunchtime and all the cheeses and honchos from the English Department wanted to break bread with him, so out the door he went, not with Judy on his arm or some more casual acquaintance who might have been last night's groin massager or the flight attendant who'd served him his breakfast, but his biographer. His biographer. Arm in arm with this bald guy half his height and a face depleted by a pair of glasses the size of the ones Elton John used to wear onstage, trailing dignitaries and toadies, and who does he run into?

Ten minutes later he's coming up the stairs at Victoria's place, and beneath the wailing of the Sisters and the thump of the organ I can hear his footsteps, his and nobody else's, and I know this: after all these years my father has come for me.

Lunch was at the Bistro, one of the few places in town that aspired to anything more than pizza, burgers and burritos. My father sat at the head of the table, of course, and I, three-quarters drunk on white rum, sat at his right hand. Victoria was next to me, her expression rapt, her hair snaking out behind me in the direction of the great man like the tendrils of some unkillable plant, and the biographer, sunk behind his glasses, hunched beside her with a little black notepad. The rest of the table, from my father's side down, was occupied by various members of the English Department I vaguely recognized and older lawyer types who must have been deans or whatever. There was an awkward moment when Dr. Delpino, my American Lit professor, came in, but her eyes, after registering the initial surprise and recalculating our entire relationship from the first day's roll call on, showed nothing but a sort of fawning, shimmering awe. And how did I feel about that? Sick. Just plain sick.

I drank desperate cups of black coffee and tried to detoxify myself with something called Coquilles Saint Jacques, which amounted to an indefinable rubbery substance sealed in an impenetrable layer of baked cheese. My father held forth, witty, charming, as pleased with himself as anybody alive. He said things like "I'm glad you're asking me to speak on the only subject I'm an authority on—me," and with every other breath he dropped the names of the big impressive actors who'd starred in the big impressive movie version of his last book. "Well," he'd say, "as far as that goes, Meryl once told me . . . ," or, "When we were on location in Barbados, Brad and Geena and I used to go snorkeling practically every afternoon, and then it was conch ceviche and this rum drink they call Mata-Mata, after the turtle, and believe me, kill you it does. . . ."

Add to this the fact that he kept throwing his arm round the back of my chair (and so, my shoulders) as if I'd been there with him through every scintillating tête-à-tête and sexual and literary score, and you might begin to appreciate how I felt. But what could I do? He was playing a role that would have put to shame any of the big-gun actors he named, and I was playing my role too, and though I was seething inside, though I felt betrayed by Victoria and him and all the stupid noshing doglike faces fawning round the table, I played the dutiful and proud son to Academy Award proportions. Or maybe I wasn't so great. At least I didn't jump up and flip the table over and call him a fraud, a cheat and a philanderer who had no right to call anybody his son, let alone me. But oh, how those deans and professors sidled up to me afterward to thoroughly kiss my ass while Dr. Delpino glowed over our little secret and tried to shoulder Victoria out of the way. And Victoria. That was another thing. Victoria didn't seem to recall that I was still alive, so enthralled was she by the overblown spectacle of my father the genius.

He took me aside just before we stepped back out into the blast of the wind, confidential and fatherly, the others peeling back momentarily in deference to the ties of the blood, and asked me if I was all right. "Are you all right?" he said.

Everything was in a stir, crescendoing voices, the merry ritual of the zippers, the gloves, the scarves and parkas, a string quartet keening through the speakers in some weird key that made the hair stand up on the back of my neck. "What do you mean?" I said.

I looked into his face then, and the oldness dropped away from him: he was my pal, my dad, the quick-blooded figure I remembered from the kitchen, den and bedroom of my youth. "I don't know," he said, shrugging. "Victoria said—that's her name, right, Victoria?"

I nodded.

"She said you were feeling sick, the flu or something," and he let it trail off. Somebody shouted, "You should have seen it in December!" and the string quartet choked off in an insectlike murmur of busy strings and nervous fingers. "Cute kid, Victoria," he said. "She's something." And then a stab at a joke: "Guess you inherited my taste, huh?"

But the dutiful son didn't smile, let alone laugh. He was feeling less like Achates than Oedipus.

"You need any money?" my father said, and he was reaching into the pocket of his jeans, an automatic gesture, when the rest of the group converged on us and the question fell dead. He threw an arm round me suddenly and managed to snag Victoria and the proud flag of her hair in the other. He gave a two-way squeeze with his skinny arms and said, "See you at the reading tonight, right?"

Everyone was watching, right on down to the busboys, not to mention the biographer, Dr. Delpino and all the by-now stunned, awed and grinning strangers squinting up from their coquilles and fritures. It was a real biographical moment. "Yeah," I said, and I thought for a minute they were going to break into applause, "sure."

The hall was packed, standing room only, hot and stifled with the crush of bodies and the coats and scarves and other paraphernalia that were like a second shadowy crowd gathered at the edges of the living and breathing one, students, faculty and townspeople wedged into every available space. Some of them had come from as far away as Vermont and Montreal, so I heard, and when we came through the big main double doors, scalpers were selling the $2.50 Student Activities Board–sponsored tickets for three and four times face value. I sat in the front row between my father's vacant seat and the biographer (whose name was Mal, as in Malcolm) while my father made the rounds, pumping hands and signing books, napkins, sheets of notebook paper and whatever else the adoring crowd thrust at him. Victoria, the mass of her hair enlarged to even more stupendous proportions thanks to some mysterious chemical treatment she'd undergone in the bathroom down the hall from her room, sat sprouting beside me.

I was trying not to watch my father, plunging in and out of the jungle of Victoria to make small talk, unconcerned, unflappable, no problem at all, when Mal leaned across the vacant seat and poked my arm with the butt of his always handy Scripto pen. I turned to him, Victoria's hand clutched tightly in mine—she hadn't let go, not even to unwrap her scarf, since we'd climbed out of the car—and stared into the reflected blaze of his glasses. They were amazing, those glasses, like picture windows, like a scuba mask grafted to his hairless skull. "Nineteen eighty-nine," he said, "when he wrecked the car? The BMW, I mean?" I sat there frozen, waiting for the rest of it, the man's voice snaking into my consciousness till it felt like the voice of my innermost self. "Do you remember if he was still living at home then? Or was that after he . . . after he, uh, moved out?"

Moved out. Wrecked the car.

"Do you remember what he was like then? Were there any obvious changes? Did he seem depressed?"

He must have seen from my face how I felt about the situation because his glasses suddenly flashed light, he tugged twice at his lower lip, and murmured, "I know this isn't the time or place, I was just curious, that's all. But I wonder, would you mind—maybe we could set up a time to talk?"

What could I say? Victoria clutched my hand like a trophy hunter, my fellow students rumbled and chattered and stretched in their bolted-down seats and my father squatted here, sprang up there, lifted his eyebrows and laid down a layer of witty banter about half a mile thick. I shrugged. Looked away. "Sure," I said.

Then the lights dimmed once, twice, and went all the way down, and the chairman of the English Department took the podium while my father scuttled into the seat beside me and the audience hushed. I won't bother describing the chairman—he was generic, and he talked for a mercifully short five minutes or so about how my father needed no introduction and et cetera, et cetera, before giving the podium over to Mal, as in Malcolm, the official hagiographer. Mal bounced up onto the stage like a trained seal, and if the chairman was selfless and brief, Mal was windy, verbose, a man who really craved an audience. He softened them up with half a dozen anecdotes about the great man's hyperinflated past, with carefully selected references to drug abuse, womanizing, unhinged driving and of course movies and movie stars. By the time he was done he'd made my father sound like a combination of James Dean, Tolstoy and Enzo Ferrari. They were thrilled, every last man, woman and drooling freshman—and me, the only one in the audience who really knew him? I wanted to puke, puke till the auditorium was filled to the balcony, puke till they were swimming in it. But I couldn't. I was trapped, just like in some nightmare. Right there in the middle of the front row.

When Mal finally ducked his denuded head and announced my father, the applause was seismic, as if the whole auditorium had been tipped on end, and the great man, in one of his own tour T-shirts and the omnipresent leather jacket, took the stage and engaged in a little high-fiving with the departing biographer while the thunder gradually subsided and the faces round me went slack with wonder. For the next fifteen minutes he pranced and strutted across the stage, ignoring the podium and delivering a preprogrammed monologue that was the equal of anything you'd see on late-night TV. At least all the morons around me thought so. He charmed them, out-hipped them, and they laughed, snorted, sniggered and howled. Some of them, my fellow freshmen, no doubt, even stamped their feet in thunderous unison as if they were at a pep rally or something. And the jokes—the sort of thing he'd come on with at lunch—were all so self-effacing, at least on the surface, but deep down each phrase and buttressed pause was calculated to remind us we were in the presence of one of the heroes of literature. There was the drinking-with-Bukowski story, which had been reproduced in every interview he'd done in the last twenty years, the traveling-through-Russia-with-nothing-but-a-pair-of-jeans-two-socks-

and-a-leather-jacket-after-his-luggage-was-stolen story, the obligatory movie star story and three or four don't-ask-me-now references to his wild past. I sat there like a condemned man awaiting the lethal injection, a rigid smile frozen to my face. My scalp itched, both nostrils, even the crotch of my underwear. I fought for control.

And then the final blow fell, as swift and sudden as a meteor shrieking down from outer space and against all odds blasting through the roof of the auditorium and drilling right into the back of my reeling head. My father raised a hand to indicate that the jokes were over, and the audience choked off as if he'd tightened a noose around each and every throat. Suddenly he was more professorial than the professors—there wasn't a murmur in the house, not even a cough. He held up a book, produced a pair of wire-rim glasses—a prop if ever I saw one—and glanced down at me. "The piece I want to read tonight, from *Blood Ties,* is something I've wanted to read in public for a long time. It's a deeply personal piece, and painful too, but I read it tonight as an act of contrition. I read it for my son."

He spread open the book with a slow, sad deliberation I'm sure they all found very affecting, but to me he was like a terrorist opening a suitcase full of explosives, and I shrank into my seat, as miserable as I've ever been in my life. He can't be doing this, I thought, he can't. But he was. It was his show, after all.

And then he began to read. At first I didn't hear the words, didn't want to—I was in a daze, mesmerized by the intense weirdness of his voice, which had gone high-pitched and nasal all of a sudden, with a kind of fractured rhythm that made it seem as if he was translating from another language. It took me a moment, and then I understood: this was his reading voice, another affectation. Once I got past that, there were the words themselves, each one a little missile aimed at me, the hapless son, the victim who only wanted to be left lying in the wreckage where he'd fallen. He was reading a passage in which the guilt-racked but lusty father takes the fourteen-year-old son out to the best restaurant in town for a heart-to-heart talk about those lusts, about dreams, responsibilities and the domestic life that was dragging him down. I tried to close myself off, but I couldn't. My eyes were burning. Nobody in the auditorium was watching him anymore—how could they be? No, they were watching me. Watching the back of my head. Watching the fiction come to life.

I did the only thing I could. When he got to the part where the son, tears streaming into his chocolate mousse, asks him why, why, Dad, why, I stood up, right there, right in the middle of the front row, all those eyes drilling into me. I tore my hand away from Victoria's, stared down the biographer and Dr. Delpino and all the rest of them, and stalked straight out the nearest exit even as my father's amplified voice wavered, faltered, and then came back strong again, nothing wrong, nothing the matter, nothing a little literature wouldn't cure.

I don't know what happened between him and Victoria at the muted and minimally celebratory dinner later that night, but I don't suspect it was much, if anything. That wasn't the problem, and both of us—she and I, that is—knew it. I spent the night hiding out in the twenty-four-hour laundromat wedged between Brewskies Pub and Taco Bell, and in the morning I ate breakfast in a greasy spoon only the townies frequented and then caught up on some of Hollywood's distinguished product at the local cineplex for as long as I could stand it. By then, I was sure the great man would have gone on to his many other great appointments, all his public posturing aside. And that was just what happened: he canceled his first flight and hung around till he could hang around no longer, flying out at four-fifteen with his biographer and all the sympathy of the deeply yearning and heartbroken campus. And me? I was nobody again. Or so I thought.

I too dropped out of Dr. Delpino's class—I couldn't stand the thought of that glazed blue look of accusation in her eyes—and though I occasionally spotted Victoria's hair riding the currents around campus, I avoided her. She knew where to find me if she wanted me, but all that was over, I could see that—I wasn't his son after all. A few weeks later I noticed her in the company of this senior who played keyboards in one of the local bands, and I felt something, I don't know what it was, but it wasn't jealousy. And then, at the end of a lonely semester in a lonely town in the lonely hind end of nowhere, the air began to soften and a few blades of yellow grass poked up through the rotting snow and my roommate took me downtown to Brewskies to celebrate.

The girl's name was Marlene, but she didn't pronounce it like the old German actress who was probably dead before she was born, but Mar-*lenna,* the second syllable banged out till it sounded as if she was calling herself Lenny. I liked the way her smile showed off the gold caps on her molars. The band I didn't want to mention earlier was playing through the big speakers over the bar, and there was a whole undercurrent of noise and excitement mixed with the smells of tap beer, Polish sausage and salt-and-vinegar chips. "I know you," she said. "You're, um, Tim McNeil's son, right?"

I never looked away from her, never blinked. All that was old news now, dead and buried, like some battle in the Civil War.

"That's right," I said. "How did you guess?"

(1999)

The Love of My Life

They wore each other like a pair of socks. He was at her house, she was at his. Everywhere they went—to the mall, to the game, to movies and shops and the classes that structured their days like a new kind of chronology—their fingers were entwined, their shoulders touching, their hips joined in the slow triumphant sashay of love. He drove her car, slept on the couch in the family room at her parents' house, played tennis and watched football with her father on the big thirty-six-inch TV in the kitchen. She went shopping with his mother and hers, a triumvirate of tastes, and she would have played tennis with his father, if it came to it, but his father was dead. "I love you," he told her, because he did, because there was no feeling like this, no triumph, no high—it was like being immortal and unconquerable, like floating. And a hundred times a day she said it too: "I love you. I love you."

They were together at his house one night when the rain froze on the streets and sheathed the trees in glass. It was her idea to take a walk and feel it in their hair and on the glistening shoulders of their parkas, an otherworldly drumming of pellets flung down out of the troposphere, alien and familiar at the same time, and they glided the length of the front walk and watched the way the power lines bellied and swayed. He built a fire when they got back, while she toweled her hair and made hot chocolate laced with Jack Daniel's. They'd rented a pair of slasher movies for the ritualized comfort of them—"Teens have sex," he said, "and then they pay for it in body parts"—and the maniac had just climbed out of the heating vent, with a meat hook dangling from the recesses of his empty sleeve, when the phone rang.

It was his mother, calling from the hotel room in Boston where she was curled up—shacked up?—for the weekend with the man she'd been dating. He tried to picture her, but he couldn't. He even closed his eyes a minute, to concentrate, but there was nothing there. Was everything all right? she wanted to know. With the storm and all? No, it hadn't hit Boston yet, but she saw on the Weather Channel that it was on its way. Two seconds after he hung up—before she could even hit the Start button on the VCR—the phone rang again, and this time it was her mother. Her mother had been drinking. She was calling from a restaurant, and China could hear a clamor of voices in the background. "Just stay put," her mother shouted into the phone. "The streets are like a skating rink. Don't you even think of getting in that car."

Well, she wasn't thinking of it. She was thinking of having Jeremy to herself, all night, in the big bed in his mother's room. They'd been having sex ever since they started going together at the end of their junior year, but it was always sex in the car or sex on a blanket or the lawn, hurried sex, nothing like she wanted it to be. She kept thinking of the way it was in the movies, where the stars ambushed each other on beds the size of small planets and then did it again and again until they lay nestled in a heap of pillows and blankets, her head on his chest, his arm flung over her shoulder, the music fading away to individual notes plucked softly on a guitar and everything in the frame glowing as if it had been sprayed with liquid gold. That was how it was supposed to be. That was how it was going to be. At least for tonight.

She'd been wandering around the kitchen as she talked, dancing with the phone in an idle slow saraband, watching the frost sketch a design on the window over the sink, no sound but the soft hiss of the ice pellets on the roof, and now she pulled open the freezer door and extracted a pint box of ice cream. She was in her socks, socks so thick they were like slippers, and a pair of black leggings under an oversized sweater. Beneath her feet, the polished floorboards were as slick as the sidewalk outside, and she liked the feel of that, skating indoors in her big socks. "Uh-huh," she said into the phone. "Uh-huh. Yeah, we're watching a movie." She dug a finger into the ice cream and stuck it in her mouth.

"Come on," Jeremy called from the living room, where the maniac rippled menacingly over the Pause button. "You're going to miss the best part."

"Okay, Mom, okay," she said into the phone, parting words, and then she hung up. "You want ice cream?" she called, licking her finger.

Jeremy's voice came back at her, a voice in the middle range, with a congenital scratch in it, the voice of a nice guy, a very nice guy who could be the star of a TV show about nice guys: "What kind?" He had a pair of shoulders and pumped-up biceps too, a smile that jumped from his lips to his eyes, and close-cropped hair that stood up straight off the crown of his head. And he was always singing—she loved that—his voice so true he could do any song, and there was no lyric he didn't know, even on the oldies station. She scooped ice cream and saw him in a scene from last summer, one hand draped casually over the wheel of his car, the radio throbbing, his voice raised in perfect synch with Billy Corgan's, and the night standing still at the end of a long dark street overhung with maples.

"Chocolate. Swiss chocolate almond."

"Okay," he said, and then he was wondering if there was any whipped cream, or maybe hot fudge—he was sure his mother had a jar stashed away somewhere, *Look behind the mayonnaise on the top row*—and when she turned around he was standing in the doorway.

She kissed him—they kissed whenever they met, no matter where or when, even if one of them had just stepped out of the room, because that was love, that was the way love was—and then they took two bowls of ice cream into the living room and, with a flick of the remote, set the maniac back in motion.

It was an early spring that year, the world gone green overnight, the thermometer twice hitting the low eighties in the first week of March. Teachers were holding sessions outside. The whole school, even the halls and the cafeteria, smelled of fresh-mowed grass and the unfolding blossoms of the fruit trees in the development across the street, and students—especially seniors—were cutting class to go out to the quarry or the reservoir or to just drive the back streets with the sunroof and the windows open wide. But not China. She was hitting the books, studying late, putting everything in its place like pegs in a board, even love, even that. Jeremy didn't get it. "Look, you've already been accepted at your first-choice school, you're going to wind up in the top ten G.P.A.-wise, and you've got four years of tests and term papers ahead of you, and grad school after that. You'll only be a high school senior once in your life. Relax. Enjoy it. Or at least *experience* it."

He'd been accepted at Brown, his father's alma mater, and his own G.P.A. would put him in the top ten percent of their graduating class, and he was content with that, skating through his final semester, no math, no science, taking art and music, the things he'd always wanted to take but never had time for—and Lit., of course, A.P. History, and Spanish 5. "*Tú eres el amor de mi vida,*" he would tell her when they met at her locker or at lunch or when he picked her up for a movie on Saturday nights.

"*Y tú también,*" she would say, "or is it '*yo también?*' "—French was her language. "But I keep telling you it really matters to me, because I know I'll never catch Margery Yu or Christian Davenport, I mean they're a lock for val and salut, but it'll kill me if people like Kerry Sharp or Jalapy Seegrand finish ahead of me—you should know that, you of all people—"

It amazed him that she actually brought her books along when they went backpacking over spring break. They'd planned the trip all winter and through the long wind tunnel that was February, packing away freeze-dried entrées, Power Bars, Gore-Tex windbreakers and matching sweatshirts, weighing each item on a handheld scale with a dangling hook at the bottom of it. They were going up into the Catskills, to a lake he'd found on a map, and they were going to be together, without interruption, without telephones, automobiles, parents, teachers, friends, relatives and pets, for five full days. They were going to cook over an open fire, they were going to read to each other and burrow into the double sleeping bag with the connubial zipper up the seam he'd found in his mother's closet, a relic of her own time in the lap of nature. It smelled of her, of his mother, a vague scent of her perfume that had lingered there dormant all these years, and maybe there was the faintest whiff of his father too, though his father had been gone so long he didn't even remember what he looked like, let alone what he might have smelled like. Five days. And it wasn't going to rain, not a drop. He didn't even bring his fishing rod, and that was love.

When the last bell rang down the curtain on Honors Math, Jeremy was waiting at the curb in his mother's Volvo station wagon, grinning up at China through the windshield while the rest of the school swept past with no thought for anything but release. There were shouts and curses, T-shirts in motion, slashing legs, horns bleating from the seniors' lot, the school buses lined up like armored vehicles awaiting the invasion—chaos, sweet chaos—and she stood there a moment to savor it. "Your mother's car?" she said, slipping in beside him and laying both arms over his shoulders to pull him to her for a kiss. He'd brought her jeans and hiking boots along, and she was going to change as they drove, no need to go home, no more circumvention and delay, a stop at McDonald's, maybe, or Burger King, and then it was the sun and the wind and the moon and the stars. Five days. Five whole days.

"Yeah," he said, in answer to her question, "my mother said she didn't want to have to worry about us breaking down in the middle of nowhere—"

"So she's got your car? She's going to sell real estate in your car?"

He just shrugged and smiled. "Free at last," he said, pitching his voice down low till it was exactly like Martin Luther King's. "Thank God Almighty, we are free at last."

It was dark by the time they got to the trailhead, and they wound up camping just off the road in a rocky tumble of brush, no place on earth less likely or less comfortable, but they were together, and they held each other through the damp whispering hours of the night and hardly slept at all. They made the lake by noon the next day, the trees just coming into leaf, the air sweet with the smell of the sun in the pines. She insisted on setting up the tent, just in case—it could rain, you never knew—but all he wanted to do was stretch out on a gray neoprene pad and feel the sun on his face. Eventually, they both fell asleep in the sun, and when they woke they made love right there, beneath the trees, and with the wide blue expanse of the lake giving back the blue of the sky. For dinner, it was étouffée and rice, out of the foil pouch, washed down with hot chocolate and a few squirts of red wine from Jeremy's bota bag.

The next day, the whole day through, they didn't bother with clothes at all. They couldn't swim, of course—the lake was too cold for that—but they could bask and explore and feel the breeze out of the south on their bare legs and the places where no breeze had touched before. She would remember that always, the feel of that, the intensity of her emotions, the simple unrefined pleasure of living in the moment. Woodsmoke. Duelling flashlights in the night. The look on Jeremy's face when he presented her with the bag of finger-sized crayfish he'd spent all morning collecting.

What else? The rain, of course. It came midway through the third day, clouds the color of iron filings, the lake hammered to iron too, and the storm that crashed through the trees and beat at their tent with a thousand angry fists. They huddled in the sleeping bag, sharing the wine and a bag of trail mix, reading to each other from a book of Donne's love poems (she was writing a paper for Mrs. Masterson called "Ocular Imagery in the Poetry of John Donne") and the last third of a vampire novel that weighed eighteen-point-one ounces.

And the sex. They were careful, always careful—*I will never, never be like those breeders that bring their puffed-up squalling little red-faced babies to class,* she told him, and he agreed, got adamant about it, even, until it became a running theme in their relationship, the breeders overpopulating an overpopulated world and ruining their own lives in the process—but she had forgotten to pack her pills and he had only two condoms with him, and it wasn't as if there was a drugstore around the corner.

In the fall—or the end of August, actually—they packed their cars separately and left for college, he to Providence and she to Binghamton. They were separated by three hundred miles, but there was the telephone, there was e-mail, and for the first month or so there were Saturday nights in a motel in Danbury, but that was a haul, it really was, and they both agreed that they should focus on their course work and cut back to every second or maybe third week. On the day they'd left—and no, she didn't want her parents driving her up there, she was an adult and she could take care of herself—Jeremy followed her as far as the Bear Mountain Bridge and they pulled off the road and held each other till the sun fell down into the trees. She had a poem for him, a Donne poem, the saddest thing he'd ever heard. It was something about the moon. *More than moon,* that was it, lovers parting and their tears swelling like an ocean till the girl—the woman, the female—had more power to raise the tides than the moon itself, or some such. More than moon. That's what he called her after that, because she was white and round and getting rounder, and it was no joke, and it was no term of endearment.

She was pregnant. Pregnant, they figured, since the camping trip, and it was their secret, a new constant in their lives, a fact, an inescapable fact that never varied no matter how many home pregnancy kits they went through. Baggy clothes, that was the key, all in black, cargo pants, flowing dresses, a jacket even in summer. They went to a store in the city where nobody knew them and she got a girdle, and then she went away to school in Binghamton and he went to Providence. "You've got to get rid of it," he told her in the motel room that had become a prison. "Go to a clinic," he told her for the hundredth time, and outside it was raining—or, no, it was clear and cold that night, a foretaste of winter. "I'll find the money—you know I will."

She wouldn't respond. Wouldn't even look at him. One of the *Star Wars* movies was on TV, great flat thundering planes of metal roaring across the screen, and she was just sitting there on the edge of the bed, her shoulders hunched and hair hanging limp. Someone slammed a car door—two doors in rapid succession—and a child's voice shouted, "Me! Me first!"

"China," he said. "Are you listening to me?"

"I can't," she murmured, and she was talking to her lap, to the bed, to the floor. "I'm scared. I'm so scared." There were footsteps in the room next door, ponderous and heavy, then the quick tattoo of the child's feet and a sudden thump against the wall. "I don't want anyone to know," she said.

He could have held her, could have squeezed in beside her and wrapped her in his arms, but something flared in him. He couldn't understand it. He just couldn't. "What are you thinking? Nobody'll know. He's a doctor, for Christ's sake, sworn to secrecy, the doctor-patient compact and all that. What are you going to do, keep it? Huh? Just show up for English 101 with a baby on your lap and say, 'Hi, I'm the Virgin Mary'?"

She was crying. He could see it in the way her shoulders suddenly crumpled and now he could hear it too, a soft nasal complaint that went right through him. She lifted her face to him and held out her arms and he was there beside her, rocking her back and forth in his arms. He could feel the heat of her face against the hard fiber of his chest, a wetness there, fluids, her fluids. "I don't want a doctor," she said.

And that colored everything, that simple negative: life in the dorms, roommates, bars, bullshit sessions, the smell of burning leaves and the way the light fell across campus in great wide smoking bands just before dinner, the unofficial skateboard club, films, lectures, pep rallies, football—none of it mattered. He couldn't have a life. Couldn't be a freshman. Couldn't wake up in the morning and tumble into the slow steady current of the world. All he could think of was her. Or not simply her—her and him, and what had come between them. Because they argued now, they wrangled and fought and debated, and it was no pleasure to see her in that motel room with the queen-size bed and the big color TV and the soaps and shampoos they made off with as if they were treasure. She was pigheaded, stubborn, irrational. She was spoiled, he could see that now, spoiled by her parents and their standard of living and the socioeconomic expectations of her class—of his class—and the promise of life as you like it, an unscrolling vista of pleasure and acquisition. He loved her. He didn't want to turn his back on her. He would be there for her no matter what, but why did she have to be so *stupid?*

Big sweats, huge sweats, sweats that drowned and engulfed her, that was her campus life, sweats and the dining hall. Her dormmates didn't know her, and so what if she was putting on weight? Everybody did. How could you shovel down all those carbohydrates, all that sugar and grease and the puddings and nachos and all the rest, without putting on ten or fifteen pounds the first semester alone? Half the girls in the dorm were waddling around like the Doughboy, their faces bloated and blotched with acne, with crusting pimples and whiteheads fed on fat. So she was putting on weight. Big deal. "There's more of me to love," she told her roommate, "and Jeremy likes it that way. And, really, he's the only one that matters." She was careful to shower alone, in the early morning, long before the light had begun to bump up against the windows.

On the night her water broke—it was mid-December, almost nine months, as best as she could figure—it was raining. Raining hard. All week she'd been having tense rasping sotto voce debates with Jeremy on the phone—arguments, fights—and she told him that she would die, creep out into the woods like some animal and bleed to death, before she'd go to a hospital. "And what am I supposed to do?" he demanded in a high childish whine, as if he were the one who'd been knocked up, and she didn't want to hear it, she didn't.

"Do you love me?" she whispered. There was a long hesitation, a pause you could have poured all the affirmation of the world into.

"Yes," he said finally, his voice so soft and reluctant it was like the last gasp of a dying old man.

"Then you're going to have to rent the motel."

"And then what?"

"Then—I don't know." The door was open, her roommate framed there in the hall, a burst of rock and roll coming at her like an assault. "I guess you'll have to get a book or something."

By eight, the rain had turned to ice and every branch of every tree was coated with it, the highway littered with glistening black sticks, no moon, no stars, the tires sliding out from under her, and she felt heavy, big as a sumo wrestler, heavy and loose at the same time. She'd taken a towel from the dorm and put it under her, on the seat, but it was a mess, everything was a mess. She was cramping. Fidgeting with her hair. She tried the radio, but it was no help, nothing but songs she hated, singers that were worse. Twenty-two miles to Danbury, and the first of the contractions came like a seizure, like a knife blade thrust into her spine. Her world narrowed to what the headlights would show her.

Jeremy was waiting for her at the door to the room, the light behind him a pale rinse of nothing, no smile on his face, no human expression at all. They didn't kiss—they didn't even touch—and then she was on the bed, on her back, her face clenched like a fist. She heard the rattle of the sleet at the window, the murmur of the TV: *I can't let you go like this,* a man protested, and she could picture him, angular and tall, a man in a hat and overcoat in a black-and-white world that might have been another planet, *I just can't.* "Are you—?" Jeremy's voice drifted into the mix, and then stalled. "Are you ready? I mean, is it time? Is it coming now?"

She said one thing then, one thing only, her voice as pinched and hollow as the sound of the wind in the gutters: "Get it out of me."

It took a moment, and then she could feel his hands fumbling with her sweats.

Later, hours later, when nothing had happened but pain, a parade of pain with drum majors and brass bands and penitents crawling on their hands and knees till the streets were stained with their blood, she cried out and cried out again. "It's like *Alien,*" she gasped, "like that thing in *Alien* when it, it—"

"It's okay," he kept telling her, "it's okay," but his face betrayed him. He looked scared, looked as if he'd been drained of blood in some evil experiment in yet another movie, and a part of her wanted to be sorry for him, but another part, the part that was so commanding and fierce it overrode everything else, couldn't begin to be.

He was useless, and he knew it. He'd never been so purely sick at heart and terrified in all his life, but he tried to be there for her, tried to do his best, and when the baby came out, the baby girl all slick with blood and mucus and the lumped white stuff that was like something spilled at the bottom of a garbage can, he was thinking of the ninth grade and how close he'd come to fainting while the teacher went around the room to prick their fingers one by one so they each could smear a drop of blood across a slide. He didn't faint now. But he was close to it, so close he could feel the room dodging away under his feet. And then her voice, the first intelligible thing she'd said in an hour: "Get rid of it. Just get rid of it."

Of the drive back to Binghamton he remembered nothing. Or practically nothing. They took towels from the motel and spread them across the seat of her car, he could remember that much . . . and the blood, how could he forget the blood? It soaked through her sweats and the towels and even the thick cotton bathmat and into the worn fabric of the seat itself. And it all came from inside her, all of it, tissue and mucus and the shining bright fluid, no end to it, as if she'd been turned inside out. He wanted to ask her about that, if that was normal, but she was asleep the minute she slid out from under his arm and dropped into the seat. If he focused, if he really concentrated, he could remember the way her head lolled against the doorframe while the engine whined and the car rocked and the slush threw a dark blanket over the windshield every time a truck shot past in the opposite direction. That and the exhaustion. He'd never been so tired, his head on a string, shoulders slumped, his arms like two pillars of concrete. And what if he'd nodded off? What if he'd gone into a skid and hurtled over an embankment into the filthy gray accumulation of the worst day of his life? What then?

She made it into the dorm under her own power, nobody even looked at her, and no, she didn't need his help. "Call me," she whispered, and they kissed, her lips so cold it was like kissing a steak through the plastic wrapper, and then he parked her car in the student lot and walked to the bus station. He made Danbury late that night, caught a ride out to the motel, and walked right through the Do Not Disturb sign on the door. Fifteen minutes. That was all it took. He bundled up everything, every trace, left the key in the box at the desk, and stood scraping the ice off the windshield of his car while the night opened up above him to a black glitter of sky. He never gave a thought to what lay discarded in the Dumpster out back, itself wrapped in plastic, so much meat, so much cold meat.

He was at the very pinnacle of his dream, the river dressed in its currents, the deep hole under the cutbank, and the fish like silver bullets swarming to his bait, when they woke him—when Rob woke him, Rob Greiner, his roommate, Rob with a face of crumbling stone and two policemen there at the door behind him and the roar of the dorm falling away to a whisper. And that was strange, policemen, a real anomaly in that setting, and at first—for the first thirty seconds, at least—he had no idea what they were doing there. Parking tickets? Could that be it? But then they asked him his name, just to confirm it, joined his hands together behind his back, and fitted two loops of naked metal over his wrists, and he began to understand. He saw McCaffrey and Tuttle from across the hall staring at him as if he were Jeffrey Dahmer or something, and the rest of them, all the rest, every head poking out of every door up and down the corridor, as the police led him away.

"What's this all about?" he kept saying, the cruiser nosing through the dark streets to the station house, the man at the wheel and the man beside him as incapable of speech as the seats or the wire mesh or the gleaming black dashboard that dragged them forward into the night. And then it was up the steps and into an explosion of light, more men in uniform, stand here, give me your hand, now the other one, and then the cage and the questions. Only then did he think of that thing in the garbage sack and the sound it had made—its body had made—when he flung it into the Dumpster like a sack of flour and the lid slammed down on it. He stared at the walls, and this was a movie too. He'd never been in trouble before, never been inside a police station, but he knew his role well enough, because he'd seen it played out a thousand times on the tube: deny everything. Even as the two detectives settled in across from him at the bare wooden table in the little box of the overlit room he was telling himself just that: *Deny it, deny it all.*

The first detective leaned forward and set his hands on the table as if he'd come for a manicure. He was in his thirties, or maybe his forties, a tired-looking man with the scars of the turmoil he'd witnessed gouged into the flesh under his eyes. He didn't offer a cigarette ("I don't smoke," Jeremy was prepared to say, giving them that much at least), and he didn't smile or soften his eyes. And when he spoke his voice carried no freight at all, not outrage or threat or cajolery—it was just a voice, flat and tired. "Do you know a China Berkowitz?" he said.

And she. She was in the community hospital, where the ambulance had deposited her after her roommate had called 911 in a voice that was like a bone stuck in the back of her throat, and it was raining again. Her parents were there, her mother red-eyed and sniffling, her father looking like an actor who's forgotten his lines, and there was another woman there too, a policewoman. The policewoman sat in an orange plastic chair in the corner, dipping her head to the knitting in her lap. At first, China's mother had tried to be pleasant to the woman, but pleasant wasn't what the circumstances called for, and now she ignored her, because the very unpleasant fact was that China was being taken into custody as soon as she was released from the hospital.

For a long while no one said anything—everything had already been said, over and over, one long flood of hurt and recrimination—and the antiseptic silence of the hospital held them in its grip while the rain beat at the windows and the machines at the foot of the bed counted off numbers. From down the hall came a snatch of TV dialogue, and for a minute China opened her eyes and thought she was back in the dorm. "Honey," her mother said, raising a purgatorial face to her, "are you all right? Can I get you anything?"

"I need to—I think I need to pee."

"Why?" her father demanded, and it was the perfect non sequitur. He was up out of the chair, standing over her, his eyes like cracked porcelain. "Why didn't you tell us, or at least tell your mother—or Dr. Fredman? Dr. Fredman, at least. He's been—he's like a family member, you know that, and he could have, or he would have . . . What were you *thinking,* for Christ's sake?"

Thinking? She wasn't thinking anything, not then and not now. All she wanted—and she didn't care what they did to her, beat her, torture her, drag her weeping through the streets in a dirty white dress with "Baby Killer" stitched over her breast in scarlet letters—was to see Jeremy. Just that. Because what really mattered was what he was thinking.

The food at the Sarah Barnes Cooper Women's Correctional Institute was exactly what they served at the dining hall in college, heavy on the sugars, starches, and bad cholesterol, and that would have struck her as ironic if she'd been there under other circumstances—doing community outreach, say, or researching a paper for her sociology class. But given the fact that she'd been locked up for more than a month now, the object of the other girls' threats, scorn, and just plain *nastiness,* given the fact that her life was ruined beyond any hope of redemption, and every newspaper in the country had her shrunken white face plastered across its front page under a headline that screamed MOTEL MOM, she didn't have much use for irony. She was scared twenty-four hours a day. Scared of the present, scared of the future, scared of the reporters waiting for the judge to set bail so that they could swarm all over her the minute she stepped out the door. She couldn't concentrate on the books and magazines her mother brought her or even on the TV in the rec room. She sat in her room—it was a room, just like a dorm room, except that they locked you in at night—and stared at the walls, eating peanuts, M&M's, sunflower seeds by the handful, chewing for the pure animal gratification of it. She was putting on more weight, and what did it matter?

Jeremy was different. He'd lost everything—his walk, his smile, the muscles of his upper arms and shoulders. Even his hair lay flat now, as if he couldn't bother with a tube of gel and a comb. When she saw him at the arraignment, saw him for the first time since she'd climbed out of the car and limped into the dorm with the blood wet on her legs, he looked like a refugee, like a ghost. The room they were in—the courtroom—seemed to have grown up around them, walls, windows, benches, lights and radiators already in place, along with the judge, the American flag and the ready-made spectators. It was hot. People coughed into their fists and shuffled their feet, every sound magnified. The judge presided, his arms like bones twirled in a bag, his eyes searching and opaque as he peered over the top of his reading glasses.

China's lawyer didn't like Jeremy's lawyer, that much was evident, and the state prosecutor didn't like anybody. She watched him—Jeremy, only him—as the reporters held their collective breath and the judge read off the charges and her mother bowed her head and sobbed into the bucket of her hands. And Jeremy was watching her too, his eyes locked on hers as if he defied them all, as if nothing mattered in the world but her, and when the judge said "First-degree murder" and "Murder by abuse or neglect," he never flinched.

She sent him a note that day—"I love you, will always love you no matter what, More than Moon"—and in the hallway, afterward, while their lawyers fended off the reporters and the bailiffs tugged impatiently at them, they had a minute, just a minute, to themselves. "What did you tell them?" he whispered. His voice was a rasp, almost a growl; she looked at him, inches away, and hardly recognized him.

"I told them it was dead."

"My lawyer—Mrs. Teagues?—she says they're saying it was alive when we, when we put it in the bag." His face was composed, but his eyes were darting like insects trapped inside his head.

"It was dead."

"It looked dead," he said, and already he was pulling away from her and some callous shit with a camera kept annihilating them with flash after flash of light, "and we certainly didn't—I mean, we didn't slap it or anything to get it breathing. . . ."

And then the last thing he said to her, just as they were pulled apart, and it was nothing she wanted to hear, nothing that had any love in it, or even the hint of love: "You told me to get rid of it."

There was no elaborate name for the place where they were keeping him. It was known as Drum Hill Prison, period. No reform-minded notions here, no verbal gestures toward rehabilitation or behavior modification, no benefactors, mayors or role models to lend the place their family names, but then who in his right mind would want a prison named after him anyway? At least they kept him separated from the other prisoners, the gangbangers and dope dealers and sexual predators and the like. He was no longer a freshman at Brown, not officially, but he had his books and his course notes, and he tried to keep up as best he could. Still, when the screams echoed through the cellblock at night and the walls dripped with the accumulated breath of eight and a half thousand terminally angry sociopaths, he had to admit it wasn't the sort of college experience he'd bargained for.

And what had he done to deserve it? He still couldn't understand. That thing in the Dumpster—and he refused to call it human, let alone a baby—was nobody's business but his and China's. That's what he'd told his attorney, Mrs. Teagues, and his mother and her boyfriend, Howard, and he'd told them over and over again: *"I didn't do anything wrong."* Even if it was alive, and it was, he knew in his heart that it was, even before the state prosecutor presented evidence of blunt-force trauma and death by asphyxiation and exposure, it didn't matter, or shouldn't have mattered. There was no baby. There was nothing but a mistake, a mistake clothed in blood and mucus. When he really thought about it, thought it through on its merits and dissected all his mother's pathetic arguments about where he'd be today if she'd felt as he did when she was pregnant herself, he hardened like a rock, like sand turning to stone under all the pressure the planet can bring to bear. Another unwanted child in an overpopulated world? They should have given him a medal.

It was the end of January before bail was set—three hundred and fifty thousand dollars his mother didn't have—and he was released to house arrest. He wore a plastic anklet that set off an alarm if he went out the door, and so did she, so did China, imprisoned like some fairy-tale princess at her parents' house. At first, she called him every day, but mostly what she did was cry—"I want to see it," she sobbed. "I want to see our daughter's *grave.*" That froze him inside. He tried to picture her—her now, China, the love of his life—and he couldn't. What did she look like? What was her face like, her nose, her hair, her eyes and breasts and the slit between her legs? He drew a blank. There was no way to summon her the way she used to be or even the way she was in court, because all he could remember was the thing that had come out of her, four limbs and the equipment of a female, shoulders rigid and eyes shut tight, as if she were a mummy in a tomb . . . and the breath, the shuddering long gasping rattle of a breath he could feel ringing inside her even as the black plastic bag closed over her face and the lid of the Dumpster opened like a mouth.

He was in the den, watching basketball, a drink in his hand (7Up mixed with Jack Daniel's in a ceramic mug, so no one would know he was getting shit-faced at two o'clock on a Sunday afternoon), when the phone rang. It was Sarah Teagues. "Listen, Jeremy," she said in her crisp, equitable tones, "I thought you ought to know—the Berkowitzes are filing a motion to have the case against China dropped."

His mother's voice on the portable, too loud, a blast of amplified breath and static: "On what grounds?"

"She never saw the baby, that's what they're saying. She thought she had a miscarriage."

"Yeah, right," his mother said.

Sarah Teagues was right there, her voice as clear and present as his mother's. "Jeremy's the one that threw it in the Dumpster, and they're saying he acted alone. She took a polygraph test day before yesterday."

He could feel his heart pounding the way it used to when he plodded up that last agonizing ridge behind the school with the cross-country team, his legs sapped, no more breath left in his body. He didn't say a word. Didn't even breathe.

"She's going to testify against him."

Outside was the world, puddles of ice clinging to the lawn under a weak afternoon sun, all the trees stripped bare, the grass dead, the azalea under the window reduced to an armload of dead brown twigs. She wouldn't have wanted to go out today anyway. This was the time of year she hated most, the long interval between the holidays and spring break, when nothing grew and nothing changed—it didn't even seem to snow much anymore. What was out there for her anyway? They wouldn't let her see Jeremy, wouldn't even let her talk to him on the phone or write him anymore, and she wouldn't be able to show her face at the mall or even the movie theater without somebody shouting out her name as if she was a freak, as if she was another Monica Lewinsky or Heidi Fleiss. She wasn't China Berkowitz, honor student, not anymore—she was the punchline to a joke, a footnote to history.

She wouldn't mind going for a drive, though—that was something she missed, just following the curves out to the reservoir to watch the way the ice cupped the shore, or up to the turnout on Route 9 to look out over the river where it oozed through the mountains in a shimmering coil of light. Or to take a walk in the woods, just that. She was in her room, on her bed, posters of bands she'd outgrown staring down from the walls, her high school books on two shelves in the corner, the closet door flung open on all the clothes she'd once wanted so desperately she could have died for each individual pair of boots or the cashmere sweaters that felt so good against her skin. At the bottom of her left leg, down there at the foot of the bed, was the anklet she wore now, the plastic anklet with the transmitter inside, no different, she supposed, than the collars they put on wolves to track them across all those miles of barren tundra or the bears sleeping in their dens. Except that hers had an alarm on it.

For a long while she just lay there gazing out the window, watching the rinsed-out sun slip down into the sky that had no more color in it than a TV tuned to an unsubscribed channel, and then she found herself picturing things the way they were an eon ago, when everything was green. She saw the azalea bush in bloom, the leaves knifing out of the trees, butterflies—or were they cabbage moths?—hovering over the flowers. Deep green. That was the color of the world. And she was remembering a night, summer before last, just after she and Jeremy started going together, the crickets thrumming, the air thick with humidity, and him singing along with the car radio, his voice so sweet and pure it was as if he'd written the song himself, just for her. And when they got to where they were going, at the end of that dark lane overhung with trees, to a place where it was private and hushed and the night fell in on itself as if it couldn't support the weight of the stars, he was as nervous as she was. She moved into his arms, and they kissed, his lips groping for hers in the dark, his fingers trembling over the thin yielding silk of her blouse. He was Jeremy. He was the love of her life. And she closed her eyes and clung to him as if that were all that mattered.

(1999)

Rust

That was the sky up above, hot, with a fried egg of a sun stuck in the middle of it, and this was the ground down here, hard, with a layer of parched grass and a smell of dirt and leaf mold, and no matter how much he shouted there didn't seem to be much else in between. What he could use was a glass of water. He'd been here, what—an hour, maybe?—and the sun hadn't moved. Or not that he could see, anyway. His lips were dry, and he could feel all that ultraviolet radiation cooking the skin off his face, a piece of meat on the grill, turkey skin, crisp and oozing, peeling away in strips. But he wasn't hungry—he was never hungry anymore. It was just an image, that was all. He could use a chair, though, and somebody to help him up and put him in it. And some shade. Some iced tea, maybe, beads of moisture sliding down the outside of the glass.

"Eunice!" he called out in a voice that withered in his throat. "Eunice, goddamnit, Eunice!" And then, because he was old and he was angry and he didn't give a damn anymore, he cried out for help. "Help!" he croaked. "Help!"

But nobody was listening. The sky hung there like a tattered curtain, shreds of cloud draped over the high green crown of the pepper tree he'd planted forty years ago, the day his son was born, and he could hear the superamplified rumble of the TV from behind the shut and locked windows and the roar of the air conditioner, and where was the damn dog anyway? That was it. He remembered now. The dog. He'd come out to look for the dog—she'd been gone too long, too long about her business, and Eunice had turned her parched old lampshade of a head away from the TV screen and said, "Where's the dog?" He didn't know where the dog was, though he knew where his first bourbon and water of the day was—right there on the TV tray in front of him—and it was 11:00 a.m. and plenty late enough for it. "How the hell would I know," he'd said, "you were the one let her out," and she'd come right back at him with something smart, like "Well you'd better just get yourself out there in the yard and see, hadn't you?"

He hadn't actually been out in the yard in a long while—years, it seemed—and when he went out the back door and down the steps he found himself gaping at the bushes all in flower, the trumpet vine smothering the back of the house, and he remembered a time when he cared about all that, about nature and flowers, steer manure and potting soil. Now the yard was as alien to him as the Gobi Desert. He didn't give a damn for flowers or trees or the stucco peeling off the side of the house and all the trim destroyed with the blast of the sun or anything else. "Booters!" he'd called, angry suddenly, angry at he didn't know what. "Booters! Here, girl!"

And that was when he fell.

Maybe the lawn dipped out from under him, maybe he stepped in a gopher hole or tripped over a sprinkler head—that must have been it—but the long and short of it was that he was here, on the grass, stretched out like a corpse under the pepper tree, and he couldn't for the life of him seem to get up.

I've never wanted anybody more in my life, from the minute I came home from Rutgers and laid eyes on you, and I don't care if you are my father's wife, I don't care about anything anymore. . . . Eunice sipped at her drink—vodka and soda, bland as all get-out, but juice gave her the runs—and nodded in complete surrender as the former underwear model-turned-actress fell into the arms of the clip-jawed actor with the ridge of glistening hair that stood up from his crown like a meat loaf just turned out of the pan. The screen faded for the briefest nanosecond before opening on a cheery ad for rectal suppositories, and she found herself drifting into a reverie about the first time Walt had ever taken her in his arms.

They were young then. Or younger. A whole lot younger. She was forty-three and childless, working the checkout desk at the library while her husband ran a slowly failing quick-printing business, and Walt, five years her junior and with the puffed-up chest and inflated arms of the inveterate body builder, taught phys ed at the local high school. She liked to stop in at the Miramar Hotel after work, just to see who was there and unwind a bit after a day of typing out three-by-fives for the card catalogue and collecting fifteen- and twenty-cent fines from born-nasty rich men's wives with beauty parlor hair and too much time on their hands. One day she came in out of the flaming nimbus of the fog and there was Walt, sitting at the bar like some monument to manhood, his tie askew and the sleeves of his white dress shirt rolled up to reveal the squared-off blocks of his forearms. She sat at one of the tables, ordered a drink—it was vodka and grapefruit in those days, tall—and lit a cigarette. When she looked up, he was standing over her. "Don't you know smoking's bad for your health?"

She took her time, crossed her legs under the table and squirmed her bottom around till she was comfortable. She'd seen Ava Gardner in the movies. And Lauren Bacall too. "Tell me that," she said, slow and languid, drawing it out with the smoke, "when I'm an old lady."

Well, he laughed and sat down and they got to talking and before long he was meeting her there every afternoon at five while her husband moaned and fretted over last-minute rush jobs and his wife drank herself into oblivion in her own kitchen. And when that moment came—their first embrace—she reached out for his arms as if she were drowning.

But now the screen flickered and *The Furious Hours* gave way to *Riddle Street* and she eased back in her chair, the vodka and soda at her lips like recirculated blood flowing back into her, and watched as the heroine—one of the towering sluts of daytime television—carved up another man.

The funny thing was that nothing hurt, or not particularly or any more than usual, what with the arthritis in both knees and the unreconstructed hernia that felt as if some animal was living under his skin and clawing to get out—no, he hadn't broken anything, he was pretty sure of that. But there was something wrong with him. Desperately wrong. Or why else would he be lying here on his back listening to the grass grow while the clouds became ghosts in winding sheets and fled away to nothing and the sun burned the skin right off his face?

Maybe he was dying, maybe that was it. The thought didn't alarm him, not especially, not yet, but it was there, a hard little bolus of possibility lodged in his brain. He moved the fingers of his right hand, one by one, just to see if the signals still carried that far, and then he tried the other side, the left, and realized after a long moment that there was nothing there, nothing he could feel anyway. Something whispered in his ear—a single word, *stroke*—and that was when he began to be afraid. He heard a car go by on the street out front of the house, the soughing of the tires, the clank of the undercarriage, the smooth fuel-injected suck of the engine. "Help!" he cried. "Somebody help!"

And then he was looking up into the lace of the pepper tree and remembering a moment on a bus forty-five years ago, some anonymous stop in Kansas or Nebraska, and he on his way to California for the first time and every good thing awaiting him. An old man got on, dazed and scrawny and with a long whittled pole of a neck and a tattered straw hat set way back on his head, and he just stood there in the middle of the aisle as if he didn't know where he was. Walt was twenty-nine, he'd been in the service and college too, and he wasn't acquainted with any old people or any dead people either—not since the war anyway. He lifted weights two hours every morning, rain or shine, hot or cold, sick or well, and the iron suffused him with its power like some magic potion.

He looked up at the old man and the old man looked right through him. That was when the driver, oblivious, put the bus in gear and the old man collapsed in his shiny worn suit like a puppet with the strings cut. No one seemed to know what to do, the mother with her mewling baby, the teenager with the oversized shoes, the two doughy old hens with the rolled-in-butter smiles fixed on their faces, but Walt came up out of his seat automatically and pulled the old man to his feet, and it was as if the old guy wasn't even there, nothing more than a suit stuffed with wadding—he could have propped up ten old men, a hundred, because he was a product of iron and the iron flowed through his veins and swelled his muscles till there was nothing he couldn't do.

Eunice refreshed her drink twice during *Riddle Street,* and then she sat through the next program with her eyes closed, not asleep—she couldn't sleep anymore, sleep was a dream, a fantasy, the dimmest recollection out of an untroubled past—but in a state suspended somewhere between consciousness and its opposite. The sound of a voice, a strange voice, speaking right to her, brought her out of it—*It was amazing, just as if she knew me and my whole life and she told me I was going to come into some money soon, and I did, and the very next day I met the man of my dreams*—and the first thing she focused on was her husband's empty chair. Now where had he got himself off to? Maybe he'd gone to lie down, maybe that was it. Or maybe he was in the kitchen, his big arms that always seemed to be bleeding pinioning the wings of the newspaper, a pencil in his big blunt fingers, his drink like liquid gold in the light through the window and the crossword all scratched over with his black, glistening scrawl. Those were skin cancers on his arms, she knew that, tiny dots of fresh wet blood stippling the places where his muscles used to be, but he wouldn't do anything about it. He didn't care. It was like his hernia. "I'm going to be dead soon anyway," he said, and that got her down, it did, that he should talk like that. "How can you talk like that?" she'd say, and he'd throw it right back at her. "Why not? What have I got to live for?" And she'd blink at him, trying desperately to focus, because if she couldn't focus she couldn't give him a look, all pouty and frowning, like Marlene Dietrich in *Destry Rides Again.* "For me, baby," she'd say. "For me."

The idea of the kitchen sent her there, a little shaky on her feet after sitting so long, and her ankles weren't helping, not at all—it felt as if somebody'd snuck in and wrapped truck tires around them while she sat watching her programs. The kitchen was glowing, the back windows glazed with sun, and all the clutter of their last few half-eaten meals invested with a purity and beauty that took her breath away and made her feel like crying, the caramel of the maple syrup bottle and the blue of the Windex and red of the ketchup as vibrant and natural there as flowers in a field. It was a pretty kitchen, the prettiest kitchen in the world. Or it had been once. They'd remodeled in '66—or was it '69? Double aluminum sink, self-cleaning oven, cabinets in solid oak and no cheap lamination, thank you very much. She'd loved that kitchen. It was a kitchen that made her feel loved in return, a place she could retreat to after all the personal nastiness and gossip at the library and wait for her man to come home from coaching football or basketball or whatever it was, depending on the season.

The thought came to her then—or not a thought, actually, but a feeling because feelings were what moved her now, not thoughts—that she ought to maybe fix a can of tomato soup for lunch, and wouldn't it be nice, for a change, to fix some for Walt too? Though she knew what his reaction would be. "I can't eat that," he'd say, "not with my stomach. What do you think, I'm still thirty-eight?"

Well, yes, she did, as a matter of fact. And when he was thirty-eight and he took her away from Stan Sadowsky and blackened both of his eyes for him when he tried to get rough about it, he'd eat anything she put down on the table in front of him, shrimp cocktail in horseradish sauce right out of the jar, pickled cherry peppers, her special Tex-Mex tamales with melted cheese and Tabasco. He loved her then too. Loved her like she'd never been loved before. His fingers—his fingers were magic, the fingers of a masseur, a man who knew what a deep rub was, who knew muscle and ligament and the finer points of erectile tissue and who could manipulate her till she was limp as a rag doll and tingling all over.

Sure, sure he could. But where in Lord's name was he?

The sun had moved. No doubt about it. He'd been asleep, unconscious, delirious, dehydrated, sun-poisoned—pick an adjective—and now he was awake again and staring up at that yellow blot in the sky that went to deep blue and then black if you stared at it too long. He needed water. He needed bourbon. Aspirin. Ibuprofen. Two of those little white codeine tablets the doctor gave him for the pain in his knees. More than anything, though, he needed to get up off this damn lawn before the grass grew through the back of his head. Furious suddenly, raging, he gave it everything he had and managed to lift his right shoulder and the dead weight of his head from the ground—and hold it there, hold it there for a full five seconds, as if he were bench-pressing his own body—before he sank back down again. It wasn't going to work, he could see that now, nothing was going to work, ever again, and he felt himself filling up with despair, a slow dark trickle of it leaking into the black pool that was already inside him.

With the despair came Jimmy. That was the way it always was. When he felt blue, when he felt that life was a disease and not worth the effort of drawing the next contaminated breath, Jimmy was there. Seven years, six months, and fourteen days old, sticks for legs, his head too big for his body and his hair like something you'd scour pans with. Jimmy. His son. The boy who grew up teething on a catcher's mitt and was already the fastest kid in the second grade. Walt had been at school the day he was killed, spotting for the gymnastics club as they went through their paces on the parallel bars. Somebody said there was smoke up the street—the paint store was on fire, the whole block going up, maybe even the bank—and the vaulted cathedral of the gym went silent. Then they smelled the smoke, musty and sharp at the same time, and then they heard the sirens. By the time Walt got out to the street, his gymnasts leading the way in a blur of flying heels, the fire engine was skewed across the sidewalk in the oddest way, three blocks at least from the fire, and he remembered thinking they must have been drunk or blind, one or the other. When he got there, to where the fire company was, smoke crowding the sky in the distance and the taste of it, acid and bitter, on his tongue, he asked the first person he saw—Ed Bakey, the assistant principal—what was the matter. "One of the kids," Ed said, and he was shaking so badly he could hardly get the words out, "one of the kids got hit by the truck."

He drifted off again, mercifully, and when he came to this time the sun was playing peekaboo with the crown of the pepper tree, and the field of shade, healing redemptive shade, spread almost to his feet. What time was it anyway? Three, at least. Maybe four. And where the hell was Eunice? Inside, that's where she was, where time was meaningless, a series of half-hour slices carved out of the program guide, day melding into night, breakfast into dinner, the bright electrons dancing eternally across the screen. He dug his elbows into the lawn then, both of them, and yes, he could feel his left side all of a sudden and that was something, and he flexed every muscle in his body, pecs, delts, biceps, the long striated cords of his back and the lump of nothing that was his left leg, but he couldn't sit up, couldn't so much as put an inch between him and the flattened grass. That frustrated him. Made him angry. And he cried out again, the driest, faintest bleat of rage and bewilderment from the desert throat of a man who'd never asked anybody for anything.

She called him for lunch, went to the foot of the stairs and called out his name twice, but it was next to impossible to wake him once he went off, soundest sleeper in the world—you'd need a marching band just to get him to blink his eyes—so she heated the tomato soup, cleared a place at the table, and ate by herself. The soup was good, really hit the spot, but they put too much salt in it, they all did, didn't matter which brand you bought. It made her thirsty, all that salt, and she got up to make herself a fresh vodka and soda—there was no sense in traipsing round the house looking for the other glass, which, as she knew from experience, could be anywhere. She couldn't count the hours she'd spent shuffling through the bathroom, kitchen and living room on her feet that felt as if they'd been crimped in a vise, looking for one melted-down watery drink or another. So she took a fresh glass, and she poured, and she drank. Walt was up in the bedroom, that's where he was, napping, and no other possibility crossed her mind, because there was none.

There was the usual ebb and flow of afternoon programming, the stupid fat people lined up on a stage bickering about their stupid fat lives and too stupid to know the whole country was laughing at them, the game shows and teenage dance shows and the Mexican shows stocked with people as fat and stupid as the Americans, only bickering in Spanish instead of English. Then it was evening. Then it was dusk. She was watching a Mickey Rooney/Judy Garland picture on the classic movie channel when a dog began barking on the screen, and she was fooled, just for a second, into thinking it was Booters. That was when she noticed that Booters was gone. And Walt: whatever could he be doing all this time?

She went up the stairs, though each step seemed to rise up insidiously to snatch at her just as she lifted her foot, and saw that the bedroom was empty and that neither dog nor man was in the upstairs bathroom enjoying the monotonous drip-drip-drip of the faucet that never seemed to want to shut itself off. Twice more she went round the house, utterly bewildered, and she even looked in the pantry and the broom closet and the cabinet under the sink. It was nearly dark, the ice cubes of her latest vodka and soda tinkling like chimes in her hand, when she thought to look out back.

"Walt?" she called, thrusting her head out the door. "Booters?"

The frail bleating echo of her own voice came back to her, and then, slipping in underneath it, the faintest whisper of a sound, no louder than the hum of a mosquito's wings or the muffled cry of a bird strangled in the dark. "Help!" she heard, or thought she heard, a sound so weak and constrained it barely registered.

"Walt?" she tried again.

And then: "Eunice, goddamnit, over here!"

She was so startled she dropped her drink, the glass exploding on the flagstones at her feet and anointing her ankles with vodka. The light was fading, and she didn't see very well anymore, not without her glasses anyway, and she was puzzled, truly puzzled, to hear her husband's voice coming out of nowhere. "Walt?" she murmured, moving across the darkened lawn as through a minefield, and when she tripped, and fell, it wasn't over a sprinkler head or gopher's mound or a sudden rise in the lawn, it was over the long, attenuated shadow of her husband's still and recumbent form.

Eunice cried out when she went down, a sharp rising exhalation of surprise, followed by an aquiescent grunt and the almost inevitable elision of some essential bone or joint giving way. He'd heard that sound before, too many times to count, on the football field, the baseball diamond, the basketball court, and he knew right away it was trouble. Or more trouble, if that was possible. "Eunice," he croaked, and his face was cooked right down to the bone, "are you hurt?"

She was right there, right there beside him, one of her legs thrust awkwardly over his, her face all but planted in the turf. She was trying to move, to turn over, to right herself—all that he could feel, though he couldn't for the life of him swivel his head to see—but she wasn't having much success. When finally, after a protracted effort, she managed to drag her living leg across his dead one, she took what seemed like an hour to gulp at the air before her lips, tongue and mouth could form a response. "Walt," she gasped, or moaned actually, that's what it was, moaning, "my . . . I think . . . oh, oh, it hurts . . ."

He heard a car race up the street, the swift progress of life, places to go, people to meet. Somewhere a voice called out and a door slammed.

"My hip, I think it's my hip—"

It was all he could do to keep from cursing, but he didn't have the strength to curse, and there was no use in it, not now. He gritted his teeth. "Listen, I can't move," he said. "And I've been laying here all day waiting for somebody to notice, but do you think anybody'd even poke their damn head out the door to see if their husband was dead yet and fried up in the sun like a damn pork rind?"

She didn't answer. The shadows thickened round them. The lawn went from gray to black, the color drained out of the treetops and the sky grew bigger by the minute, as if invisible forces were inflating it with the stuff of the universe. He was looking up at the emerging stars—he had no choice, short of closing his eyes. It had been a long time since he'd looked at the stars, indifferent to any space that didn't have a roof over it, and he was strangely moved to see that they were all still there. Or most of them anyway, but who was counting? He could hear Eunice sobbing in the dark just to the left of him, and for a long while she didn't say anything, just sniffed and snuffled, gagging on every third or fourth breath. Finally her voice came at him out of the void: "You always blame me for everything."

Well, there was truth in that, he supposed, but no sense in getting into it now. "I don't know what's wrong with me, Eunice," he said, trying to keep his voice level, though his heart was hammering and he foresaw every disaster. "I can't get up. I can't even move. Do you understand what I'm saying?"

There was no response. A mosquito lighted on his lower eyelid, soft as a snowflake, and he didn't have the power to brush it away. "Listen," he said, speaking to the sky and all the spilled paint of the stars, "how bad are you? Can you—do you think you can crawl?"

"It hurts," she gasped, "Walt, it hurts," and then she was sobbing again, a broken dry nagging rasp that cut into him like the teeth of a saw.

He softened his voice. "It's okay, Eunice. Everything's going to be okay, you'll see."

It was then, just as the words passed his lips, that the familiar music of Booters' jingling tags rang out ecstatically from the far corner of the yard, followed by a joyful woof and the delirious patter of approaching paws. "Booters!" they cried out simultaneously. "Good girl, Booters. Come here, come here, girl!"

Eunice was expecting a miracle, nothing less—she was an optimist, always was, always would be—and the minute she heard the dog she thought of all the times Lassie had come to the rescue, Rin Tin Tin, Old Yeller, Buck, Toto and she didn't know who else. She was lying face-down on the lawn, and her cheek had begun to itch where it was pressed into the grass and the grass made its snaking intaglio in the flesh, but she didn't dare move because of the pain in her hip and lower back that made her feel as if she were being torn in two. She was scared, of course she was, for herself and for Walt, but when Booters stood over her and began to lick the side of her face, she felt a surge of hope. "That's a girl," she said. "Now speak, Booters, speak!"

Booters didn't speak. She settled her too-big paws down in the grass beside Eunice's head and whined in a soft, puppyish way. She wasn't much more than a puppy, after all, a big lumpish stupid dog of indeterminate breed that couldn't seem to resist soiling the carpet in the hallway no matter how many times she was punished for it. The last dog they'd had, Booters the First, the original Booters, now that was a dog. She was a border collie, her eyes bright with alertness and suspicion, and so smart you could have taught her the multiplication tables if you had a mind to. It was a sad day when they had to have her put down, fifteen years old and so stiff it was like she was walking on stilts, and Walt felt it as much as she did herself, but all he said was "You measure your life in dogs, and if you're lucky you'll get five or six of them," and then he threw the dirt in the hole.

For the next hour, while the mosquitoes had a field day with her face and the back of her neck and her unprotected legs, Eunice kept trying. "Speak, girl!" she said. "Go get help. Get help! Speak!" At first, Walt did his part too, growling out one command after another, but all Booters did was whine through her slushy jowls and shift position to be near whichever one of them was exhorting her the most passionately. And when the automatic sprinklers came on with a hiss of air and the first sputtering release of subterranean pressure, the dog sprang up and trotted over to the porch, smart enough at least to come in out of the rain.

He was dozing when the sprinklers came on. He'd long since given up on the dog—what did Eunice expect her to do, flag down an ambulance?—and he was dreaming about nothing more complicated than his bed, his bed and a glass of water, half a glass, anything to soothe his throat, when the deluge began. It was a mixed blessing. He'd never been so thirsty in his life, baked and bleached under the sun till he felt mummified, and he opened his mouth reflexively. Unfortunately, none of the sprinklers had been adjusted to pinpoint the gaping maw of a supine old man stretched out in the middle of the lawn, and while the odd drop did manage to strike his lips and even his tongue, it did nothing to relieve his thirst, and he was soon soaked through to the skin and shivering. And yet still the water kept coming like some sort of Oriental water torture until finally the pipes heaved a sigh and the flow cut off as abruptly as it had begun.

He felt bad for Eunice, felt powerless and weak, felt dead, but he fought down the despair and tried to sit up again. Or his brain tried. The rest of him, aside from the sting of his sun-scorched face and the persistent ache of his knees and the shivers that shook him like a rag, seemed to belong to somebody else, some stranger he couldn't communicate with. After a while, he gave it up and called out softly to his wife. There was no response. Then he was asleep, and the night came down to lie on him with all its crushing weight.

Toward morning he woke and saw that Eunice had managed to crawl a few feet away; if he rolled his eyes all the way to the left, he could just make her out, a huddled lump in the shining grass. He held his breath, fearing the worst, but then he heard her breathing—or snoring, actually—a soft glottal insuck of air followed by an even softer puff of exhalation. The birds started in then, recommencing their daily argument, and he saw that the sky had begun to grow light, a phenomenon he hadn't witnessed in ages, not since he was in college and stayed up through the night bullshitting about women and metaphysics and gulping beer from the can.

He could shake it off then. Push himself up out of the damp grass, plow through ten flapjacks and half a dozen sausage links, and then go straight to class and after that to the gym to work out. He built himself up then, every day, with every repetition and every set, and there was the proof of it staring back at him in the weight-room mirror. But there was no building now, no collecting jazz albums and European novels, no worrying about brushing between meals or compound interest or life insurance or anything else. Now there was only this, the waiting, and whether you waited out here on the lawn like breakfast for the crows or in there in the recliner, it was all the same. Nothing mattered anymore but this. This was what it all came down to: the grass, the sky, the trumpet vine and the pepper tree, the wife with her bones shot full of air and her hip out of joint, the dog on the porch, the sun, the stars.

Stan Sadowsky had tried to block the door on him the day he came to take Eunice away, but he held his ground because he'd made up his mind and when he made up his mind he was immovable. "She doesn't want to be with you anymore, Stan," he said. "She's not going to be with you."

"Yeah?" Stan's neck was corded with rage and his eyes leapt right out of his head. Walt didn't hate him. He didn't feel anything for him, one way or the other. But there behind him, in the soft light of the hall, was Eunice, her eyes scared and her jaw set, wearing a print dress that showed off everything she had. "Yeah?" Stan repeated, barking it like a dog. "And what the fuck do you know about it?"

"I know this," Walt said, and he hit him so hard he went right through the screen door and sprawled out flat on his back in the hallway. And when he got up, Walt hit him again.

But now, now there was the sun to contend with, already burning through the trees. He smelled the rich wet chlorophyll of the grass and the morning air off the sea, immemorial smells, ancient as his life, and when he heard the soft matitudinal thump of the paper in the front drive, he called out suddenly, but his voice was so weak he could scarcely hear it himself. Eunice was silent. Still and silent. And that worried him, because he couldn't hear her snoring anymore, and when he found his voice again, he whispered, "Eunice, honey, give me your hand. Can you give me your hand?"

He could have sworn he saw her lift her shoulder and swivel toward him, her face alive and glowing with the early light, but he must have been fooling himself. Because when he summoned everything he had left in him and somehow managed to reach out his hand, there was nothing there.

(1997)

Peep Hall

I like my privacy. My phone is unlisted, my mailbox locks with a key, and the gate across the driveway automatically shuts behind me when I pull in. I've got my own little half-acre plot in the heart of this sunny little university town, and it's fenced all the way round. The house is a Craftsman-era bungalow, built in 1910, and the yard is lush with mature foliage, including the two grand old oaks that screen me from the street out front, a tsunami of Bougainvillea that long ago swallowed up the chainlink on both sides of the place, half a dozen tree ferns in the fifteen-foot range, and a whole damp, sweet-earth-smelling forest of pittosporum, acacia, and blue gum eucalyptus crowding out what's left of the lawn.

When I sit on the porch in the afternoon, all I see is twenty shades of green, and when someone bicycles by or the couple across the way get into one of their biweekly wrangles, I'm completely invisible, though I'm sitting right here with my feet propped up, taking it all in. I haven't been to a concert or a sporting event for as long as I can remember, or even a play or the movies, because crowds irritate me, all that jostling and hooting, the bad breath, the evil looks, not to mention the microbes hanging over all those massed heads like bad money on a bad bet. And no, I'm not a crank. I'm not crazy. And I'm not old, or not particularly (I'll be forty-one in November). But I do like my privacy, and I don't think there's any crime in that, especially when you work as hard as I do. Once I pull my car into the driveway, I just want to be left alone.

Six nights a week, and two afternoons, I stir *mojitos* and shake martinis at the El Encanto Hotel, where I wear a bowtie and a frozen smile. I don't have any pets, I don't like walking, my parents are dead, and my wife—my *ex*-wife—may as well be. When I'm not at the El Encanto, I read, garden, burn things in a pan, clean spasmodically, and listen to whatever the local arts station is playing on the radio. When I feel up to it, I work on my novel (working title, *Grandma Rivers*)—either that or my master's thesis, "Claustrophobia in Franz Kafka's Fictive Universe," now eleven years behind schedule.

I was sitting on the porch late one afternoon—a Monday, my day off, the sun suspended just above the trees, birds slicing the air, every bud and flower entertaining its individual bee—when I heard a woman's voice raised in exasperation from the porch next door. She was trying to reel herself in, fighting to keep her voice from getting away from her, but I couldn't quite make out what she was saying. The woman's voice rose and fell, and then I recognized the voice of my next-door neighbor saying something in reply, something curt and dismissive, punctuated by the end stop of the front door slamming shut.

Next it was the sharp hammer-and-anvil ring of spike heels on pavement—*toing, toing, toing*—as they retreated down the Schusters' macadam driveway, turned left on the sidewalk, and halted at my gate, which was, of course, locked. I was alert now in every fiber. I slipped a finger between the pages of the novel I'd been reading and held my breath. I heard the gate rattle, my eyes straining to see through the dense leathery mass of the oaks, and then the voice called, "Hello, hello, *hello!*" It was a young voice, female, a take-charge and brook-no-nonsense sort of voice, a very attractive voice, actually, but for some reason I didn't reply. Habit, I suppose. I was on my own porch in my own yard, minding my own business, and I resented the intrusion, no matter what it turned out to be, and I had no illusions on that score either. She was selling something, circulating a petition, organizing a Neighborhood Watch group, looking for a lost cat; she was out of gas, out of money, out of luck. I experienced a brief but vivid recollection of the time the gardener had left the gate ajar and a dark little woman in a sari came rushing up the walk holding a balsawood replica of the *Stars & Stripes* out in front of her as if it were made of sugar-frosted air, looked me in the eye, and said, "P'raps maybe you buy for a hunnert dollah good coin monee?"

"I'm your neighbor," the voice called, and the gate rattled again. "Come on," she said, "I can see you, you know—I can see your feet—and I know you're there. I just want to take a minute of your time, that's all, just a minute—"

She could see me? Self-consciously I lifted my feet from the floorboards and propped them up on the rail. "I can't," I said, and my voice sounded weak and watered down, "I'm busy right now."

The fraction of a moment passed, all the sounds of the neighborhood butting up against one another—crows cursing in the trees, a jet revealing itself overhead with the faintest distant whine of its engines, a leaf blower starting up somewhere—and then she sang out, "I like your shoes. Where'd you get them? Not in this town, right?"

I said nothing, but I was listening.

"Come on, just a minute, that's all I ask."

I may live alone, by preference, but don't get me wrong, I'm no eunuch. I have the same needs and urges as other men, which I've been able to satisfy sporadically with Stefania Porovka, the assistant pastry chef at the hotel. Stefania is thirty-two, with a smoky deep Russian voice that falls somewhere in the range between magnetic and aphrodisiacal and two children in elementary school.

The children are all right, as children go, aside from a little caterwauling when they don't get their way (which seems to be about a hundred percent of the time), but I can't manage to picture them in my house, and by the same token, I can't picture myself in Stefania's psychotically disordered two-bedroom walk-up. So what I'm saying is that I got up from the porch and ambled down the walk to the gate and the girl of twenty or so standing there in blue jeans, heels and a V-neck top.

She was leaning over the gate, her arms crossed at the wrists, rings glinting from her fingers. Her eyes and hair were the exact same shade of brown, as if the colors had been mixed in the same vat, which in a sense I guess they were, and she had unusually thick and expressive eyebrows of the same color. From where I was standing, five feet back from the locked gate, I could see down the front of her blouse. She wasn't wearing a brassiere. "Hello," I said, regaling her with a cautious nod and the same approximation of a smile I put on for my customers at the bar.

"Oh, *hi*," she returned, giving it the sort of emphasis that said she was surprised and impressed and very, very friendly. "I'm Samantha. I live up at the end of the block—the big white house with the red trim?"

I nodded. At this point I was noncommittal. She was attractive—pretty and beyond, actually—but too young for me to be interested in anything more than a neighborly way, and as I say, I wasn't especially neighborly to begin with.

"And you are—?"

"Hart," I said, "Hart Simpson," and I put my hands on my hips, wondering if she could translate body language.

She never moved, but for a slight readjustment of her hands that set her bracelets ajingle. She was smiling now, her eyebrows arching up and away from the sudden display of her teeth. "Hart," she repeated, as if my name were a curious stone she'd found in the street and was busy polishing on the sleeve of her blouse. And then: "Hart, are we bothering you? I mean, are we really bothering you all that much?"

I have to admit the question took me by surprise. Bothering me? I never even knew she existed until thirty seconds ago—and who was this *we* she was referring to? "*We?*" I said.

The smile faded, and she gave me a long, slow look. "So you're not the one who complained—or one of the ones?"

"You must have me confused with somebody else. I don't have the faintest idea what you're talking about."

"Peep Hall—" she said, "you know, like *peephall.com?*"

It was warm, midsummer, the air charged with the scent of rosemary and lavender and the desiccated menthol of the eucalyptus trees. I felt the sun on my face. I slowly shook my head.

She rubbed the palms of her hands together as if she were washing with soap and water, shifted her eyes away, and then came back to me again. "It's nothing dirty," she said. "It's not like it's some sleazoid club with a bunch of Taiwanese businessmen shoving dollar bills up our crotches or we're lap-dancing or anything like that—we don't even take our clothes off that much, because that totally gets old—"

I still had no idea what she was talking about, but I was beginning to warm to the general drift of it. "Listen," I said, trying to unhinge my smile a bit, "do you want to come in for a beer or maybe a glass of wine or something?"

My house—not the one I grew up in, but this one, the one I inherited from my grandmother—is a shrine to her conventional, turn-of-the-last-century taste, as well as a kind of museum of what my parents left behind when they died. There isn't too much of me in it, but I'm not one for radical change, and the Stickley furniture, the mica lamps, and even the ashtrays and bric-a-brac are wearing well, as eternal as the king's ankus or the treasure buried with Tutankhamen. I keep the place neat—my parents' books commingled with my own on the built-in bookshelves, rugs squared off against the couches and chairs, cups and dishes neatly aligned in the glass-front cabinets—but it's not particularly clean, I'm afraid. I'm not much for dusting. Or vacuuming. The toilets could use a little more attention. And the walls on either side of the fireplace feature long, striated, urine-colored stains where the water got in around the chimney flashing last winter.

"Nice place," Samantha breathed as I handed her a beer and led her into the living room, the house as dark and cool as a wine cellar though it must have been ninety out there in the sun. She settled into the big oak chair by the window, kicked off her heels and took first one foot, then the other, into her hands and slowly rubbed it. "I hate heels," she said, "especially these. But that's what they want us to wear."

I was having a beer too, and I cradled it in my lap and watched her.

"No running shoes—they hate running shoes—and no sweats. It's in our contract." She laughed. "But you don't know what I'm talking about, do you?"

I was thinking about Stefania and how long it had been since I'd had her over, how long it had been since she'd sat in that chair and done something as unselfconscious as rubbing her bare white feet and laughing over a beer. "Tell me," I said.

It was a long story, involving so many digressions that the digressions became stories in themselves, but finally I began to gather that the big white house on the corner, where she lived with six other girls, was meant to represent a college dorm—that's where the "Peep Hall" designation came in—and that the business of the place was to sell subscriptions on the Internet to overlathered voyeurs who could click on any time of day or night to watch the girls going about their business in living color. "So you've got all these video cameras around," I said, trying to picture it. "Like at the bank or the 7-Eleven—that sort of thing?"

"Yeah, but much better quality, and instead of just like two of them or whatever, you've got cameras all over the place."

"Even in the bathroom?"

Another laugh. "*Especially* the bathroom, what do you think?"

I didn't have anything to say to that. I guess I was shocked. I *was* shocked. I definitely was. But why not admit it? I was titillated too. Women in the shower, I was thinking, women in the tub. I drained my beer, held the bottle up to the light, and asked her if she'd like another one.

She was already slipping her feet back into the shoes. "No, no thanks—I've got to go," she said, rising to her feet. "But thanks for the beer and all—and if they do come around with a petition, you tell them we're not doing anything wrong, okay?" She was smiling, swaying slightly over her heels. "And I don't know if you're into it—you're online, right?—but you should check us out, see for yourself."

We were at the door. She handed me the empty beer bottle, still warm from the embrace of her hand. "You really should," she said.

After she left, I opened another beer and wandered through the downstairs rooms, picking up magazines and tossing them back down again, opening and shutting doors for no good reason, until I found myself in the kitchen. There were dishes in the sink, pans encrusted with one thing or another on the stove. The drainboard looked like an artifact, the one incomprehensible object left behind by a vanished civilization, and was it merely decorative or was it meant for some utilitarian purpose? The windows were a smudge of light. The plants needed water. I'd been planning to make myself an omelet and then go up to the university for the Monday Night Film Society's showing of *The Seventh Seal,* a film so bleak it always brought tears of hysterical laughter to my eyes, but instead, on an impulse, I dialed Stefania's number. When she answered, there was an edge to her voice, all the Russian smoke blown right out of it by the winds of complexity and turmoil, and in the background I could hear the children shrieking as if the skin were being peeled from their bodies in long, tapering strips.

"Hello?" Stefania demanded. "Who is it? Is anybody there? Hello?" Very carefully, though my hand was trembling, I replaced the receiver in its cradle.

And this was strange: it was my day off, the only day of the week when I could really relax, and yet I was all worked up, as if I'd had one too many cups of coffee. I found myself drifting through the house again, thoughtfully pulling at my beer, studying a lamp or a painting or an old family photo as if I'd never seen it before, all the while making a wide circuit around the little room off the front hall where the computer sat on my desk like a graven idol. I resisted it for half an hour or more, until I realized I was resisting it, and then I sat down, booted it up and clicked on *www.peephall.com.*

A Web page gradually took shape on the screen. I saw the house on the corner, a big shapeless stucco box against a neutral background, and in front of it, as the image filled in from top to bottom, the girls began to materialize. There were seven of them, squeezed shoulder-to-shoulder to fit in the frame, and they were dressed in low-cut tops and smiling as if they were selling lip gloss or plaque remover. Samantha was second from the left, staring right at me. "*Twenty-four hours a day!*" screamed the teaser. "*Watch our young sexy College Girls take bubble baths, throw sexy Lingerie parties and sunbathe Nude poolside! You'll never miss an Intimate Moment!*" To the left, in a neat pulsating sidebar, were come-ons for related sites, like *See Me Pee* and *Hot Sexy Teen Vixens.* The subscription fee was $36 a month. I never hesitated.

Once I was in, I was presented with an array of choices. There were forty cameras in all, and I could choose among the two bathrooms, three bedrooms, the pool, kitchen, living room and deck. I was working on my third beer—on an empty stomach, no less—and I wasn't really thinking, just moving instinctively toward something I couldn't have defined. My pulse was racing. I felt guilty, paranoiac, consumed with sadness and lust. The phrase *dirty old man* shot through my head, and I clicked on "The Kitchen" because I couldn't go to "Upstairs Bath," not yet anyway.

The room that came into view was neat, preternaturally neat, like the set for a cooking show, saucepans suspended from hooks, ceramic containers of flour, sugar, tea and coffee lined up along a tile counter, matching dishtowels hanging from two silver loops affixed to the cabinet beneath the sink. But of course it *was* a set, the whole house was a set, because that was what this was all about: seeing through walls like Superman, like God. I clicked on Camera 2, and suddenly a pair of shoulders appeared on the screen, female shoulders, clad in gray and with a blond ponytail centered in the frame. The shoulders ducked out of view, came back again, working vigorously, furiously, over something, and now the back of a blond head was visible, a young face in profile, and I experienced my first little *frisson* of discovery: she was beating eggs in a bowl. The sexy young teen college vixens were having omelets for dinner, just like me . . . but no, another girl was there now, short hair, almost boyish, definitely not Samantha, and she had a cardboard box in her hand, and they were—what were they doing?—they were making brownies. *Brownies.* I could have cried for the simple sweet irreducible beauty of it.

That night—and it was a long night, a night that stretched on past the declining hours and into the building ones—I never got out of the kitchen. Samantha appeared at twenty past six, just as the blonde (Traci) pulled the brownies from the oven, and in the next five minutes the entire cast appeared, fourteen hands hovering over the hot pan, fingers to mouths, fat dark crumbs on their lips, on the front of their T-shirts and clingy tops, on the unblemished tiles of the counter and floor. They poured milk, juice, iced tea, Coke, and they flowed in and out of chairs, propped themselves up against the counter, the refrigerator, the dishwasher, every movement and gesture a revelation. And more: they chattered, giggled, made speeches, talked right through one another, their faces animated with the power and fluency of their silent words. What were they saying? What were they thinking? Already I was spinning off the dialogue ("Come on, don't be such a pig, leave some for somebody else!"; "Yeah, and who you think went and dragged her ass down to the store to pick up the mix in the first place?"), and it was like no novel, no film, no experience I'd ever had. Understand me: I'd seen girls together before, seen them talk, overheard them, and men and women and children too, but this was different. This was for me. My private performance. And Samantha, the girl who'd come up my walk in a pair of too-tight heels, was the star of it.

The next morning I was up at first light, and I went straight to the computer. I needed to shave, comb my hair, dress, eat, micturate; I needed to work on my novel, jog up and down the steps at the university stadium, pay bills, read the paper, take the car in for an oil change. The globe was spinning. People were up, alert, ready for the day. But I was sitting in a cold dark house, wrapped in a blanket, checking in on Peep Hall.

Nobody was stirring. I'd watched Samantha and the short-haired girl (Gina) clean up the kitchen the night before, sweeping up the crumbs, stacking plates and glasses in the dishwasher, setting the brownie pan out on the counter to soak, and then I'd watched the two of them sit at the kitchen table with their books and a boombox, turning pages, taking notes, rocking to the beat of the unheard music. Now I saw the pan sitting on the counter, a peach-colored band of sunlight on the wall behind it, plates stacked in the drainboard, the silver gleam of the microwave—and the colors weren't really true, I was thinking, not true at all. I studied the empty kitchen in a kind of trance, and then, without ceremony, I clicked on "Upstairs Bath." There were two cameras, a shower cam and a toilet cam, and both gazed bleakly out on nothing. I went to "Downstairs Bath" then, and was rewarded by a blur of motion as the stone-faced figure of one of the girls—it was Cyndi, or no, Candi—slouched into the room in a flannel nightdress, hiked it up in back, and sat heavily on the toilet. Her eyes were closed—she was still dreaming. There was the sleepy slow operation with the toilet paper, a perfunctory rinsing of the fingertips, and then she was gone. I clicked on the bedrooms then, all three of them in succession, until I found Samantha, a gently respiring presence beneath a quilt in a single bed against the far wall. She was curled away from me, her hair spilled out over the pillow. I don't know what I was feeling as I watched her there, asleep and oblivious, every creep, sadist, pervert and masturbator with thirty-six dollars in his pocket leering at her, but it wasn't even remotely sexual. It went far beyond that, far beyond. I just watched her, like some sort of tutelary spirit, watched her till she turned over and I could see the dreams invade her eyelids.

I was late for work that day—I work lunch on Tuesdays and Thursdays, then come back in at five for my regular shift—but it was slow and nobody seemed to notice. A word on the hotel: it's a pretty little place on the European model, perched at the top of the tallest hill around, and it has small but elegant rooms, and a cultivated—or at least educated—staff. It features a restaurant with pretensions to three-star status, a cozy bar and a patio with a ten-million-dollar view of the city and the harbor spread out beneath it. The real drinkers—university wives, rich widows, department heads entertaining visiting lecturers—don't come in for lunch till one o'clock or later, so in my absence the cocktail waitress was able to cover for me, pouring two glasses of sauvignon blanc and uncapping a bottle of non-alcoholic beer all on her own. Not that I didn't apologize profusely—I might have been eleven years late with my thesis, but work I took seriously.

It was a typical day on the South Coast, seventy-two at the beach, eighty or so on the restaurant patio, and we did get busy for a while there. I found myself shaking martinis and Manhattans, uncorking bottles of merlot and viognier, cutting up whole baskets of fruit for the sweet rum drinks that seemed to be in vogue again. It was work—simple, repetitive, nonintellectual—and I lost myself in it. When I looked up again, it was ten of three and the lunch crowd was dispersing. Suddenly I felt exhausted, as if I'd been out on some careening debauch the night before instead of sitting in front of my computer till my eyes began to sag. I punched out, drove home and fell into bed as if I'd been hit in the back of the head with a board.

I'd set the alarm for four-thirty, to give myself time to run the electric razor over my face, change my shirt and get back to work, and that would have been fine, but for the computer. I checked the walnut clock on the mantel as I was knotting my tie—I had ten minutes to spare—and sat down at my desk to have a quick look at Peep Hall. For some reason—variety's sake, I guess—I clicked on "Living Room Cam I," and saw that two of the girls, Mandy and Traci, were exercising to a program on TV. In the nude. They were doing jumping jacks when the image first appeared on the screen, hands clapping over their heads, breasts flouncing, and then they switched, in perfect unison, to squat thrusts, their faces staring into the camera, their arms flexed, legs kicking out behind. It was a riveting performance. I watched, in awe, as they went on to aerobics, some light lifting with three-pound dumbbells and what looked to be a lead-weighted cane, and finally concluded by toweling each other off. I was twenty minutes late for work.

This time it wasn't all right. Jason, the manager, was behind the bar when I came in, and the look on his face told me he wasn't especially thrilled at having this unlooked-for opportunity to dole out cocktail onions and bar mix to a roomful of sunburned hotel guests, enchanted tourists and golfers warming up for dinner. He didn't say a word. Just dropped what he was doing (frothing a mango margarita in the blender), brushed past me and hurried down the corridor to his office as if the work of the world awaited him there. He was six years younger than I, he had a Ph.D. in history from a university far more prestigious than the one that ruled our little burg, and he wielded a first-rate vocabulary. I could have lived without him. At any rate, I went around to each customer with a smile on my face—even the lunatic in tam-o'-shanter and plus fours drinking rum and Red Bull at the far end of the bar—and refreshed drinks, bar napkins and the bowls of pretzels and bar mix. I poured with a heavy hand.

Around seven, the dining room began to fill up. This was my favorite hour of the day, the air fragrant and still, the sun picking out individual palms and banks of flowers to illuminate as it sank into the ocean, people bending to their hors d'oeuvres with a kind of quiet reverence, as if for once they really were thankful for the bounty spread out before them. Muted snatches of conversation drifted in from the patio. Canned piano music—something very familiar—seeped out of the speakers. All was well, and I poured myself a little Irish whiskey to take some of the tightness out of my neck and shoulders.

That was when Samantha walked in.

She was with two other girls—Gina, I recognized; the other one, tall, athletic, with a nervous, rapid-blinking gaze that seemed to reduce the whole place and everything in it to a series of snapshots, was unfamiliar. All three were wearing sleek ankle-length dresses that left their shoulders bare, and as they leaned into the hostess' stand there was the glint of jewelry at their ears and throats. My mouth went dry. I felt as if I'd been caught out at something desperate, something furtive and humiliating, though they were all the way across the room and Samantha hadn't even so much as glanced in my direction. I fidgeted with the wine key and tried not to stare, and then Frankie, the hostess, was leading them to a table out on the patio.

I realized I was breathing hard, and my pulse must have shot up like a rocket, and for what? She probably wouldn't even recognize me. We'd shared a beer for twenty minutes. I was old enough to be her—her what? Her uncle. I needed to get a grip. She wasn't the one watching *me* through a hidden lens. "Hart? Hart, are you there?" a voice was saying, and I looked up to see Megan, the cocktail waitress, hovering over her station with a drink order on her lips.

"Yeah, sure," I said, and I took the order and started in on the drinks. "By the way," I said as casually as I could, "you know that table of three—the girls who just came in? Tell me when you take their order, okay? Their drinks are on me."

As it turned out, they weren't having any of the sweet rum drinks garnished with fruit and a single orange nasturtium flower or one of our half dozen margaritas or even the house chardonnay by the glass. "I carded them," Megan said, "and they're all legal, but what they want is three sloe gin fizzes. Do we even have sloe gin?"

In the eight years I'd been at the El Encanto, I doubt if I'd mixed more than three or four sloe gin fizzes, and those were for people whose recollections of the Eisenhower administration were still vivid. But we did have a vestigial bottle of sloe gin in the back room, wedged between the peppermint schnapps and the Benedictine, and I made them their drinks. Frankie had seated them around the corner on the patio, so I couldn't see how the fizzes went over, and then a series of orders came leapfrogging in, and I started pouring and mixing and forgot all about it. The next time I looked up, Samantha was coming across the room to me, her eyebrows dancing over an incipient smile. I could see she was having trouble with her heels and the constriction of the dress—or gown, I suppose you'd call it—and I couldn't help thinking how young she looked, almost like a little girl playing dress-up. "Hart," she said, resting her hands on the bar so that I could admire her sculpted fingers and her collection of rings—rings even on her thumbs—"I didn't know you worked here. This place is really nice."

"Yeah," I said, grinning back at her while holding the picture of her in my head, asleep, with her hair splayed out over the pillow. "It's first-rate. Top-notch. Really fantastic. It's a great place to work."

"You know, that was really sweet of you," she said.

I wanted to say something like "Aw, shucks" or "No problem," but instead I heard myself say, "The gesture or the drink?"

She looked at me quizzically a moment, and then let out a single soft flutter of a laugh. "Oh, you mean the gin fizzes?" And she laughed again—or giggled, actually. "I'm legal today, did you know that? And my gramma made me promise to have a sloe gin fizz so she could be here tonight in spirit—she passed last winter?—but I think we're having like a bottle of white wine or something with dinner. That's my sister I'm with—she's taking me out for my birthday, along with Gina—she's one of my roommates? But you probably already know that, right?"

I shot my eyes left, then right, up and down the bar. All the drinks were fresh, and no one was paying us the least attention. "What do you mean?"

Her eyebrows lifted, the silky thick eyebrows that were like two strips of mink pasted to her forehead, and her hair was like some exotic fur too, rich and shining and dark. "You didn't check out the Web site?"

"No," I lied.

"Well, you ought to," she said. The air was a stew of smells—a couple at the end of the bar were sharing the warm spinach and scallop salad, there was the sweet burned odor of the Irish whiskey I was sipping from a mug, Samantha's perfume (or was it Megan's?) and a medley of mesquite-grilled chops and braised fish and Peter Oxendine's famous sauces wafting in from the kitchen. "Okay," she said, shaking out her hair with a flick of her head and running a quick look around the place before bringing her eyes back to me. "Okay, well—I just wanted to say thanks." She shrugged. "I guess I better be getting back to the girls."

"Yeah," I said. "Nice seeing you again. And hey, happy birthday."

She'd already turned away from the bar, earrings swaying, face composed, but she stopped to give me a smile over her shoulder, and then she made her way across the room and out onto the darkened patio.

And that would have been it, at least until I could get home and watch her shimmy out of that gown and paint her toenails or gorge on cake or whatever it was she was going to do in the semi-privacy of her own room, but I couldn't let it go and I sent over dessert too, a truly superior raspberry-kiwi tart Stefania had whipped up that afternoon. That really put them in my debt, and after dessert the three of them came to the bar to beam at me and settle in for coffee and an after-dinner drink. "You're really just twenty-one today?" I said, grinning at

Samantha till the roots of my teeth must have showed. "You're sure I don't have to card you, now, right?"

I watched the hair swirl round her shoulders as she braced herself against the bar and reached down to ease off her heels, and then she was fishing through her purse till she came up with her driver's license and laid it out proudly on the bar. I picked it up and held it to the light—there she was, grinning wide out of the bottom right-hand corner, date of birth clearly delineated, and her name, Jennifer B. Knickish, spelled out in bold block letters. "Jennifer?" I said.

She took the card back with a frown, her eyebrows closing ranks. "Everybody calls me Samantha," she said. "Really." And to her companions: "Right, guys?" I watched them nod their glossy heads. The older one, the sister, giggled. "And besides, I don't want any of the creeps to know my real name—even my first name—you know what I mean?"

Oh, yes, yes I did. And I smiled and bantered and called up reserves of charm I hadn't used in years, and the drinks were on me all night long. It was Samantha's birthday, wasn't it? And her twenty-first, no less—a rite of passage if ever there was one. I poured Grand Marnier and Rémy till the customers disappeared and the waiters and busboys slipped out the back and the lights drew down to nothing.

I woke with a headache. I'd matched them, round for round, and, as I say, I'd started in on the Irish whiskey earlier in the night—and yes, I'm all too well aware that the concrete liver and stumbling tongue are hazards of the profession, but I'm pretty good at keeping all that in check. I do get bored, though, and wind up overdoing it from time to time, especially when the novel isn't going well, and it hadn't been going well in a long while. The problem was, I couldn't get past the initial idea—the setup—which was a story I'd come across in the newspaper two or three years ago. It had to do with an old woman's encounter with the mysterious forces of nature (I don't recall her real name, not that it would matter, but I called her Grandma Rivers, to underscore the irony that here was a woman with eight children, thirty-two grandchildren and six great-grandchildren and she was living alone in a trailer park in a part of the country so bleak no one who wasn't condemned to it would ever even deign to glance down on it from the silvered window of a jetliner at thirty-five thousand feet). One night, when the wind was sweeping up out of the south with the smell of paradise on it and all her neighbors were mewed up in their aluminum boxes lulled by booze, prescription drugs and the somnolent drone of the tube, she stepped outside to take in the scent of the night and indulge in a cigarette (she always smoked outside so as not to pollute the interior of her own little aluminum box set there on the edge of the scoured prairie). No sooner had she lit up than a fox—a red fox, *Vulpes fulva*—shot out of the shadows and latched onto her ankle. In the shock and confusion of that moment, she lurched back, lost her balance and fell heavily on her right side, dislocating her hip. But the fox, which later proved to be rabid, came right back at her, at her face this time, and the only thing she could think to do in her panic was to seize hold of it with her trembling old arms and pin it beneath her to keep the snapping jaws away from her.

Twelve hours. That's how long she lay there, unable to move, the fox snarling and writhing beneath her, its heartbeat joined to hers, its breathing, the eloquent movement of its fluids and juices and the workings of its demented little vulpine brain, until somebody—a neighbor—happened to glance beyond the hedge and the hump of the blistered old Jeep Wagoneer her late husband had left behind to see her there, stretched out in the gravel drive like a strip of discarded carpet. Yes. But what then? That was what had me stumped. I thought of going back and tracing her life up to that point, her girlhood in the Depression, her husband's overseas adventures in the war, the son killed in Vietnam . . . or maybe just to let her sink into the background while I focused on the story of the community, the benighted neighbors and their rat-faced children, so that the trailer park itself became a character. . . .

But, as I say, I woke with a headache, and when I did sit down at the computer, it wasn't to call up Grandma Rivers and the imperfect dream of her life, but to click onto *peephall.com* and watch another sort of novel unfold before my eyes, one in which the plot was out of control and the details were selected and shaped only by the anonymous subscriber with his anonymous mouse. I went straight to Samantha's bedroom, but her bed was empty save for the jumbled topography of pillows and bedclothes, and I stared numbly at the shadows thickening round the walls, at the limp form of the gown tossed over a chair, and checked my watch. It was ten-thirty. *Breakfast,* I thought. I clicked on "Kitchen," but that wasn't her staring into the newspaper with a cup of coffee clenched in one hand and a Power Bar in the other, nor was that her bent at the waist and peering into the refrigerator as if for enlightenment. I went to the living room, but it was empty, a dully flickering static space caught in the baleful gaze of my screen. Had she gone out already? To an early class maybe?

But then I remembered she was taking only one class—"Intermediate Sketching," paid for by the Web site operators, who were encouraging the Sexy Teen College Coeds actually to enroll so that all the voyeurs out there could live the fantasy of seeing them hitting the books in their thong bikinis and lacy push-up bras—and that the class met in the afternoon. She was getting paid too, incidentally—five hundred dollars a month, plus the rent-free accommodations at Peep Hall and a food allowance—and all for allowing the world to watch her live hot sexy young life through each scintillating minute of the over-inflated day, the orotund month and the full, round year. I thought of the girls who posed naked for the art classes back when I was an undergraduate (specifically, I thought of Nancy Beckers, short, black hair, balls of muscle in her calves and upper arms and a look in her eyes that made me want to strip to my socks and join her on the dais), and then I clicked on "Downstairs Bath," and there she was.

This wasn't a hot sexy moment. Anything but. Samantha—my Samantha—was crouched over the toilet on her knees, the soles of her feet like single quotes around the swell of her buttocks, her hair spilling over the bright rim of the porcelain bowl. I couldn't see her face, but I watched the back of her head jerk forward as each spasm racked her, and I couldn't help playing the sound track in my mind, feeling sorrowful and guilty at the same time. Her feet—I felt sorry for her feet—and the long sudden shiver of her spine and even the dangling wet ends of her hair. I couldn't watch this. I couldn't. My finger was on the mouse—I took one more look, watched one last shudder ascend her spine and fan out across her shoulder blades, watched her head snap forward and her hair slide loose, and then I clicked off and left her to suffer in private.

A week rolled by, and I hardly noticed. I wasn't sleeping well, wasn't exercising, wasn't sitting on the porch with a book in my hand and the world opening up around me like a bigger book. I was living the life of the screen, my bones gone hollow, my brain dead. I ate at my desk, microwave pizza and chili-cheese burritos, nachos, whiskey in a glass like a slow, sweet promise that was never fulfilled. My scalp itched. My eyes ached. But I don't think I spent a waking moment outside work when I wasn't stalking the rooms of Peep Hall, clicking from camera to camera in search of a new angle, a better one, the view that would reveal all. I watched Gina floss her teeth and Candi pluck fine translucent hairs from the mole at the corner of her mouth, sat there in the upstairs bath with Traci as she bleached her roots and shaved her legs, hung electrified over the deck as Cyndi perched naked on the railing with a bottle of vodka and a cigarette lighter, breathing fire into the gloom of the gathering night. Mainly, though, I watched Samantha. When she was home, I followed her from room to room, and when she picked up her purse and went out the door, I felt as if Peep Hall had lost its focus. It hurt me, and it was almost like a physical hurt, as if I'd been dealt an invisible blow.

I was pulling into the drive one afternoon—it must have been a Monday or Wednesday, because I'd just worked lunch—when a rangy, tall woman in a pair of wraparound sunglasses came out of nowhere to block my way. She was wearing running shorts and a T-shirt that advertised some fund-raising event at the local elementary school, and she seemed to be out of breath or out of patience, as if she'd been chasing after me for miles. I was trying to place her as the gate slowly cranked open on its long balky chain to reveal the green depths of the yard beyond—she was someone I knew, or was expected to know. But before I could resolve the issue, she'd looped around the hood of the car and thrust her face in the open window, so close to me now I could see the fine hairs catching the light along the parabola of her jawbone and her shadowy eyes leaping at the lenses of her sunglasses. "I need you to sign this," she said, shoving a clipboard at me.

The gate hit the end of the chain with a clank that made the posts shudder. I just stared at her. "It's me," she said, removing the sunglasses to reveal two angry red welts on the bridge of her nose and a pair of impatient eyes, "Sarah. Sarah Schuster—your next-door neighbor?"

I could smell the fumes of the car as it rumbled beneath me, quietly misfiring. "Oh, yeah," I said, "sure," and I attempted a smile.

"You need to sign this," she repeated.

"What is it?"

"A petition. To get rid of them. Because this is a residential neighborhood—this is a *family* neighborhood—and frankly Steve and I are outraged, just outraged, I mean, as if there isn't enough of this sort of thing going on in town already—"

"Get rid of who?" I said, but I already knew.

I watched her face as she filled me in, the rolling eyes, the clamp and release of the long mortal jaws, moral outrage underscored by a heavy dose of irony, because she was an educated woman, after all, a liberal and a Democrat, but this was just—well, it was just too much.

I didn't need this. I didn't want it. I wanted to be in my own house minding my own business. "All right, yeah," I said, pushing the clipboard back at her, "but I'm real busy right now—can you come back later?"

And then I was rolling up the driveway, the gate already rumbling shut behind me. I was agitated and annoyed—*Sarah Schuster,* who did she think she was?—and the first thing I did when I got in the house was pull the shades and turn on the computer. I checked Peep Hall to be sure Samantha was there—and she was, sunk into the couch in T-shirt and jeans, watching TV with Gina—and then I smoothed back my hair in the mirror and went out the front door. I looked both ways before swinging open the gate, wary of Sarah Schuster and her ilk, but aside from two kids on bikes at the far end of the block, the street was deserted.

Still, I started off in the opposite direction from the big white house on the corner, then crossed the street and kept going—all the way up the next block over—so as to avoid any prying eyes. The sun was warm on my face, my arms were swinging, my feet knew just what to do—I was walking, actually walking through the neighborhood, and it felt good. I noticed things the view from the car window wouldn't have revealed, little details, a tree in fruit here, a new flowerbed there, begonias blooming at the base of three pale silvery eucalypti at the side of a neighbor's house, and all that would have been fine but for the fact that my heart seemed to be exploding in my chest. I saw myself ringing the doorbell, mounting the steps of the big white house and ringing the bell, but beyond that I couldn't quite picture the scene. Would Samantha—or Traci or Candi or whoever—see me as just another one of the creeps she had to chat with online for two hours each week as part of her job description? Would she shut the door in my face? Invite me in for a beer?

As it turned out, Cyndi answered the door. She was shorter than I'd imagined, and she was dressed in a red halter top and matching shorts, her feet bare and toenails painted blue—or aquamarine, I suppose you'd call it. I couldn't help thinking of the way she looked without her clothes on, throwing back her head and spewing flames from her lips. "Hi," I said, "I was looking for Samantha? You know, *Jennifer,*" I added, by way of assuring her I was on intimate terms here and not just some psychotic who'd managed to track them all down.

She didn't smile. Just gave me a look devoid of anything—love, hate, fear, interest, or even civility—turned her head away and shouted, "Sam! Sammy! It's for you!"

"Tell her it's Hart," I said, "she'll know who—" but I broke off because I was talking to myself: the doorway was empty. I could hear the jabber and squawk of the TV and the thump of bass-heavy music from one of the upstairs bedrooms, then a whisper of voices in the hall.

In the next moment a shadow fell across the plane of the open door, and Samantha slid into view, her face pale and tentative. "Oh," she said, and I could hear the relief in her voice. "Oh, hi."

"I've got something to tell you," I said, coming right out with it, "—bad news, I think. This woman just stopped me when I was pulling into the driveway—my next-door neighbor—and they're circulating a petition." I watched her eyebrows, her eyes, saw the glint of the rings on her right hand as she swept it through her hair. "But I didn't sign. I blew her off."

She looked distracted, staring out over my shoulder as if she hadn't heard me. "Louis warned us there might be trouble," she said finally, "but it really isn't fair. I mean, do I look like some kind of slut to you? Do I?"

I wanted to make a speech, or at least a confession, and now was the time for it, now, but the best I could do was shake my head slowly and emphatically. *Louis?* Who was Louis?

Her eyes were burning. I heard a blast of gunfire from the TV, and then the volume went dead. "I'm sorry, Hart," Samantha said, lifting one bare foot from the floor to scratch the other with a long casual stroke of her instep, "but do you want to come in? You want a beer?"

And then I was in, following the sweep of Samantha's shoulders and hair and the sweet balsam scent of her into the living room I knew so well—and that was strange, surpassing strange, to know a place in its every apparent detail and yet never to have been there in the flesh. It was like a dream made concrete, a vision come to life. I felt like a character in a play, walking onto the set for the first time—and I was, I *was.* Don't look at the camera, isn't that what they tell you on TV? I glanced up, and there it was, staring me in the face. Gina stuck her head through the swinging door to the kitchen. "Hi," she said, for form's sake, and then she disappeared—out onto the deck, I supposed, to tan her hot sexy young limbs. I sat in the chair facing the dead TV screen and Samantha went out of the frame and into the kitchen for the beer, and I couldn't help wondering how many hundreds of perverts went with her.

She came back with two beers and sat opposite me, in the armchair facing "Living Room Cam 2," and gave me a smile as she settled into the chair.

I took a sip of beer, smiled back, and said, "Who's Louis?"

Samantha was sitting with one leg tucked under her, her back arched, the beer pinioned between her legs. "He's one of the operators—of the site? He's got something like thirty of them around the country, and he's like—"

"A cyber-pimp?" It was out before I could think.

She frowned and looked down into the neck of the bottle a minute, then brought her head back up and flicked the hair out of her face. "I was going to say he's like used to this sort of thing, people hassling him over zoning laws and sex-oriented businesses and all that, but really, I mean, what's the big deal?"

"I watch," I said suddenly, looking directly into her eyes. "I watch you."

Her smile blossomed into a grin. "You do?"

I held her eyes. I nodded.

"Really? Well, that's—that's great. But you've never seen me do anything dirty, have you? Some of the girls get off on it, but I figure I'm just going to live, you know, and get my end out of it—it's a good deal. I need the money. I *like* the money. And if I'm nude in the shower or when I'm changing clothes and all these guys are jerking off or whatever, I don't care, that's life, you know what I mean?"

"You know when I like to watch you best? When you're asleep. You look so—I don't want to say angelic, but that's part of it—you just look so peaceful, I guess, and I feel like I'm right there with you, watching over you."

She got up from the chair then and crossed the room to me. "That's a sweet thing to say," she said, and she set her beer down on the coffee table and settled into the couch beside me. "Really sweet," she murmured, slipping an arm round my neck and bringing her face in for a close-up. Everything seemed transformed in that moment, every object in the room coming into sudden focus, and I saw her with a deep and revelatory clarity. I kissed her. Felt the soft flutter of her lips and tongue against mine and forgot all about Stefania, my ex-wife, Sarah Schuster and Grandma Rivers. I broke away and then kissed her again, and it was a long, slow, sweet, lingering kiss and she was rubbing my back and I had my hands on her hips, just dreaming and dreaming. "Do you want to—?" I breathed. "Can you—?"

"Not here," she said, and she looked right into the camera. "They don't like it. They don't even like this."

"All right," I said, "all right," and I looked up too, right into the glassy eye of Camera 1. "What do we do now?"

"I don't know," she said. "Just hold me."

(1999)

Going Down

He started the book at two-fifteen on a Saturday afternoon in early December. There were other things he'd rather be doing—watching the Notre Dame game, for instance, or even listening to it on the radio—but that was freezing rain slashing down outside the window, predicted to turn to snow by nightfall, and the power had been out for over an hour. Barb was at the mall, indulging her shopping disorder, Buck was away at college in Plattsburgh, and the dog lay in an arthritic bundle on the carpet in the hall. He'd built a fire, checked the hurricane lamps for fuel and distributed them round the house, washed up the breakfast dishes by hand (the dishwasher was just an artifact now, like the refrigerator and the furnace), and then he'd gone into Buck's room in search of reading material.

His son's room was another universe, an alien space contained within the walls of the larger, more familiar arena of the house he knew in all its smallest details, from the corroding faucet in the downstairs bathroom to the termite-riddled front porch and the balky light switch in the guest bedroom. Nobody had been in here since September, and the place smelled powerfully of mold—refrigerated mold. It was as cold as a meat locker, and why not? Why heat an unoccupied room? John felt for the light switch and actually flicked it twice, dumbfounded, before he realized it wasn't working for the same reason the dishwasher wasn't working. That was what he was doing in here in the first place, getting a book to read, because without power there was no TV, and without TV, there was no Notre Dame.

He crossed the faintly glutinous carpet and cranked open the blinds; a bleak pale rinsed-out light seeped into the room. When he turned back round he was greeted by the nakedly ambitious faces of rap and rock stars leering from the walls and the collages of animals, cars and various body parts with which Buck had decorated the ceiling. One panel, just to the left of the now-useless overhead light, showed nothing but feet and toes (male, female, androgyne), and another, the paws of assorted familiar and exotic animals, including what seemed to be the hooked forefeet of a tree sloth. Buck's absence was readily apparent—the heaps of soiled clothes were gone, presumably soiled now in Plattsburgh. In fact, the sole sartorial reminder of his son was a pair of mud-encrusted hiking boots set against the wall in the corner. Opposite them, in the far corner, a broken fly rod stood propped against the bed above a scattering of yellowed newspapers and the forlorn-looking cage where a hamster had lived out its days. The bed itself was like a slab in the morgue. And that was it: Buck was gone now, grown and gone, and it was a fact he'd just have to get used to.

For a long moment John stood there at the window, taking it all in, and then he shivered, thinking of the fire in the living room, the inoperative furnace and the storm. And then, almost as an afterthought, he bent to the brick-and-board bookcase that climbed shakily up the near wall.

Poking through his son's leftover books took him a while, longer than he would have thought possible, and it gave him time to reflect on his own adolescent tastes in literature, which ran basically in a direct line from Heinlein to Vonnegut and detoured from there into the European exotica, like *I Jan Cremer* and *Death on the Installment Plan,* which he'd never finished. But books were a big factor in his life then, the latest news, as vital to day-to-day existence as records and movies. He never listened to music anymore, though—it seemed he'd heard it all before, each band a regurgitation of the last, and he and Barb rarely had the time or energy to venture out to the wasteland of the cineplex. And books—well, he wasn't much of a reader anymore, and he'd be the first to admit it. Oh, he'd find himself stuck in an airport someplace, and like anybody else he'd duck apologetically into the bookshop for something fat and insipid to kill the stupefying hours on the ground and in the air, but whatever he seemed to choose, no matter how inviting the description on the cover, it was invariably too fat and too insipid to hold his attention. Even when he was strapped in with two hundred strangers in a howling steel envelope thirty-five thousand feet above the ground and there was no space to move or think or even shift his weight from one buttock to the other.

Finally, after he'd considered and rejected half a dozen titles, a uniform set of metallic spines caught his eye—gold, silver, bronze, a smooth gleaming polished chromium—and he slid a shining paperback from the shelf. The title, emblazoned in a hemoglobic shade of red that dripped off the jacket as if gravity were still at work on it, was *The Ravishers of Pentagord.* He'd never heard of the author, a man by the name of Filéncio Salmón, described on the inside flap as "The preeminent Puerto Rican practitioner of speculative fiction," which, as even John knew, was the preferred term for what he and his dormmates used to call sci-fi. He looked over each of the glittering metallic books that constituted the Salmón oeuvre and settled finally on one called *Fifty Going Down (Cincuenta y retrocetiendo).* And why that one? Well, because he'd just turned fifty himself, an age fraught with anxiety and premonitory stirrings, and the number in the title spoke to him. He'd always been attracted to titles that featured numbers—*One Hundred Years of Solitude; Two Years Before the Mast; 2001: A Space Odyssey*—and maybe that was because of his math background. Sure it was. He felt safe with numbers, with the order they represented in a disordered world—that was all.

When he reemerged from the narcotic gloom of Buck's sanctuary, he had the book clutched in his hand, and there was a nostalgic feel to it—to the book and the whole business of it, opening the cover and seeing the title there in bold black letters, and the epigraph ("Death is something I only want to do once"—Oliver Niles)—and he opened a can of chicken corn chowder, thought briefly of heating it in the fireplace, then dismissed the idea and settled into the couch to spoon it up cold and attack the book. It was quiet, preternaturally quiet, no hum of the household machinery or drone of the TV to distract him, and he began, as if it were the most natural thing in the world, to read.

My mother was my child. I mean this in no metaphoric sense, but literally, because my universe is not strictly like yours, the universe of decay and decrepitude, in which one sinks each day closer and closer to the yawning mouth of the grave. I loved my mother—she raised me and then I raised her—and my memories of her are inextricably bound up with the cradle, the nursery, toys and playthings and the high ecstatic thrill of juvenile laughter. And sadness. Infinite sadness. But it is not my mother I wish to tell you about, but my wife and lover, Sonia, the mature woman of fifty with the voice of smoke and the eyes of experience, the silky girl of twenty who would bound ahead of me along the banks of the Río Luminoso as if she had been granted a second childhood. Which she had.

Let me explain. You see, in our scheme of things the Creator has been much more generous than in yours. In His wisdom, He has chosen the age of fifty as the apex of existence, and not a debilitated and toothless ninety or an even more humbling ninety-five or a hundred. (And what is more obscene than the wasted old man with his mouth full of mush and crumbs on his lapels, or the gaping hag staring round her in the street as if she's misplaced some vital part of herself?) We do not progress inexorably in age as you do, but when we reach the magical plateau, that golden age of fifty, we begin, as we say, to go down. That is, one is forty-nine the year before one turns fifty, and one is forty-nine the year after.

When Sonia was forty-nine for the second time, I was thirty-one for the first. She had been a dancer, a model, a photographer and a sculptress, and she was looking forward to going down, and, as I presumed, doing it all over again. She'd known some of the great younging minds of her day—they were history now, all of them—and I admired her for that and for her accomplishments too, but I wanted a wife who would stand by me, fix me paella and roast veal in the languorous evenings and hand me a crisply ironed shirt each morning. I broached the subject one afternoon just after our engagement. We were sitting at an outdoor café, sipping aperitifs and nibbling at a plate of fried squid. "Sonia," I murmured, reaching across the table to entwine my fingers in hers, "I want a wife, not a career woman. Can you be that for me?"

Her eyes seemed to grow until they ate up her face. Her cheekbones were monuments, her lips like two sweet desert fruits. "Oh, Faustito," she murmured, "poor little boy. Of course I'll be a wife to you. I have no interest in society anymore, really I don't—I'm retired from all that now." She sighed. Patted her lips with a snowy napkin and leaned forward to kiss me. "I just want to be young again, that's all—young and carefree."

The room had grown cold and the darkness was coming down when John next looked up. It was the darkness, more than anything, that did it: he couldn't see to read. He woke as if from a dream and saw that the windows had gone pale with the storm—it was snow now, and no doubt about it. The can of soup, the spoon still transfixed in a bit of congealed goop at the bottom, stood frigidly on the end table beside him. When he let out a breath, he could see it condense in a cloud at the tip of his nose. Stirring himself—this was a crisis, the pipes would freeze, and just look at that fire, nothing but embers and ash—he stoked the fire impatiently, laid on an armful of kindling and two massive slabs of split oak. It was four forty-five, he was a hundred pages into the book and the snow was raging down over the slick heart of the ice that lay beneath it. And where was Barb? Stuck in a drift somewhere? Abandoned in a darkened mall? Dead? Mutilated? Laid out on a slab at the county hospital?

The anxiety came up in him like a sort of fuel, pure-burning and high of octane, and he'd actually lifted the phone to his ear before he realized it was dead. There was no dial tone, no sound of any kind, just the utter nullity of the void. He went to the window again. The sky was dark now, moiling with the flecks and bits of itself it was shedding over the earth. He could barely see to the end of the drive, and the lightless houses across the street were invisible. He thought of the car then—his car, the compulsively restored MGA roadster with the fifteen-hundred-dollar paint job in British racing green—but he couldn't risk that on streets as slick as these were bound to be. He hardly drove it in winter at all—just enough to keep it in trim—and it certainly wouldn't get him far on a night like this, even in an emergency. And he couldn't call Barb's absence an emergency, not yet. They were having a storm. The lines were down. There was no way she could get to him or he to her. He couldn't call the police, couldn't call her sister or that restaurant in the mall or that store, Things & Oddments, that featured so prominently in his monthly credit card bill. He was powerless. And like the pioneers before him, he would just have to batten down the hatches—the doors and windows, that is—and wait out the storm.

And where better to do it than stretched out on the sofa in front of the fireplace, with a hurricane lamp and a book? He gave the fire a poke, spread a comforter over his legs, and settled back to read.

"Sonia," I cried, exasperated, "you're behaving like a child!"

She was dancing through the town square, riding high up off the lithe and juvenile stems of her legs, laughing in the astonished faces of the shopkeepers and making rude flatulent noises with her tongue and her pouting underlip. Even Don Pedro C———, the younging commandant of our fair city, who was in that moment taking the air with his aging bride of twenty, had to witness this little scene. "I am *a child!" Sonia shrieked, tailing the phrase with a cracked and willful schoolgirl's laugh that mounted the walls to tremble in every fishbowl and flowerpot on the square. "And you're an old tightwad!" And then she was off again, singing it through the side streets and right on up to the house where my mother had been twice an infant: "Don Fausto's a tightwad, Don Fausto's a tightwad!"*

It was my fault, actually—at least partly—because I'd denied her a bauble at the jewelry merchant's, but still, you can imagine my consternation, not to mention my embarrassment. I bit my lip and cursed myself. I should have known better, marrying a woman going down when I was going up. But I'd always been attracted to maturity, and when I was a young, aging man of thirty, I found her fifty-year-old's wrinkles and folds as attractive as her supple wit and her voice of authority and experience. Then she was forty-five and I was thirty-five and we were closer than ever, till we celebrated our fortieth birthdays together and I thought I had found heaven, truly and veritably.

But now, now she's running through the streets like a little wanton, fifteen years old and you'd think she'd never been fifteen before, her slip showing, her feet a mad dancing blur and something in her hair—chocolate, the chocolate she ate day and night and never mind the pimples sprouting in angry red constellations all over her face and pretty little chin. And there she is, just ahead of me, running her hands through all the bowls of fighting fish poor Leandro Mopa has put out on display—and worse, upsetting Benedicta Moreno's perfectly proportioned pyramid of mangoes.

And what am I thinking, all out of breath and my lungs heaving like things made of leather? When we get home—this is what I am thinking—when we get home, I will spank her.

There was a sudden thump on the front porch, an ominous thump, ponderous and reverberative, and it resounded through the empty house like the clap of doom. John sat up, startled. It sounded as if someone had dropped down dead on the planks—or been murdered. But there it was again, not just a single thump now but a whole series of them, as if the local high school were staging a sack race on his front porch. He glanced at the clock on the mantel—eight-forty already, and where had the time gone?—then set the book down and rose from the couch to investigate.

As he approached the front door, the thumping became louder and more insistent, as if someone were kicking snow from their boots—that was it, yes, of course. It was Barb, the car was stuck in a drift someplace and she'd walked the whole way, he could see it already, and she'd be annoyed, of course she would, but not too annoyed, because of the magic and romance of the storm, and she'd warm herself by the fire, share a brandy with him and something they could heat over the open flames—hot dogs, whatever—and then, then he could go back to his book. But all that, the elaborate vision called up by the sound of thumping feet, the comfort and rationalization of it, went for nothing. Because at that moment, just as he reached his hand out for the doorknob, he heard the murmur of a man's voice and the high assaultive giggle of a female, definitely not Barb.

And then the door stood open, the keen knife of the air, the immemorial smell of the snow and the whole world transformed and transforming still, and there was Buck, home from college in a snow-shrouded ski jacket and a girl with him, a girl with fractured blue eyes and a knit cap pulled down to her eyebrows. "Hey, Dad," Buck breathed in passing, and then he and the vigorously stomping girl were in the hall and the old dog was wagging her tail and attempting a puppyish yip of greeting.

"Jesus"—and Buck was shouting suddenly, his voice gone high with enthusiasm—"you ever see anything like this? Must've taken us twelve hours from Plattsburgh and the only thing moving on the Northway was the bus. Good old Greyhound, huh?"

John wasn't thinking clearly. He was still in the book, or part of him was. "You didn't flunk out, did you?" he said, throwing his hands out, as if for balance.

Buck gave him a look, the narrow eyes he'd inherited from his mother, the beak of the nose and the cheeks flushed with the cold—or drink, hard liquor, and that was all they did up in Plattsburgh, as far as John had heard anyway. "No," Buck said finally, a hurt and sorrowful expression clouding his features, "I just thought I'd come home for the weekend, you know, see how everybody was . . . oh, this is Bern." He indicated the girl, who reached up to tear off the knit cap and shake out a blazing head of white-blond hair.

John was impressed. He snatched a quick look at her breasts and her slim legs rising out of a pair of slick red boots. This was the sort of girl he'd wanted in college, lusted after, howled to the moon over, but to no avail. He'd been a nerd, a math nerd, the kind of guy who got excited over cryptography and differential equations, and he'd wound up with Barb. Thankfully. And he wasn't complaining. But his son, look at his son: Buck was no nerd, no sir, not with a girl like—"What was your name?" he heard himself asking.

A final shake of the hair, a soft cooed greeting for the reeking old dog. "Bern," she said evenly, and she had a smile for him, wonderful teeth, staggering lips, pink and youthful gums.

The door was shut now. The hallway was cold. And dark. He was smiling till his own teeth must have glowed in the dim glancing light of the fire in the other room. "Short for Bernadette?" he ventured.

They were moving instinctively, as a group, toward the fire—even the dog. "Nope," she said. "Just Bern."

Well, fine. And would she like a drink? Suddenly, for some reason, it was vitally important to John that she have a drink, crucial even. No, she said, looking to Buck, no, she didn't drink. There was a silence. "And how's school?" he asked finally, just to say something.

Neither of them rushed to answer. Buck, alternately warming his hands over the fire and stroking the old dog, just shrugged, and the girl, Bern, turned to John and said, "Frankly, it sucks."

"That's why we're here," Buck murmured.

John was puzzled. "You mean—?"

"Aw, shit." Buck spoke with real vehemence, but softly, almost under his breath, and he rose tumultuously from his place by the fire. "We're going to hang in my room for a while, okay, Dad?" His arm found Bern's shoulder and they were gone, or almost, two shadows touching and melding and then slowly receding down the dark hall. But then Buck hung back a moment, the shadows separating, and his face was floating there in the unsteady light of the hurricane lamp. "Where's Mom?" he asked.

When she was twelve, she began to lose her breasts. I would put my arm round her in a restaurant and feel like a child molester, and when we went to bed together I had to keep reminding myself that she was a younging *twelve, which actually gave her some eighty-eight years of worldly wiles and experience, at least seventy-five of them enlivened by venereal pleasures. (I never fooled myself into thinking I was the only one, though I wanted to be. She'd been married and separated before I met her, and when she was young the first time, there had been a succession of lovers, a whole mighty tide of them.) She'd begun taking a rag doll to bed—and crunching hard candy between her dwindling molars or snapping gum in my face whenever I began to feel amorous—and this just intensified my feelings of jealousy and resentment.*

"Tell me about your first," I would demand. "What was his name, Eduardo, wasn't it?"

"Don't!" She would giggle, because I was stroking the soft white doeskin of her belly or the silk of her upper arm, and then, blowing a pink bubble with her gum, she would correct me. "It wasn't Eduardo, silly, it was Armando. I told you. Silly." And it would become a chant—"Silly, silly, silly!"—till I sprang up off the bed and chased her round the room, through the apartments and past the maid's quarters, and only then, when I was out of breath and half spent, would she give me my pleasure.

And then came the day, the inevitable day, when she was no longer a woman. Her breasts had disappeared entirely, not even the tiniest bud left, and between her legs she was as bald as an apple. Of course, I'd known all along the day was coming, and I'd tried to prepare myself as so many before me had done, watching soap operas and reading the great tragedies, but the pain and disillusionment were more than I could bear—yes, disillusionment. Here was the woman I loved, the woman who could talk all day of the books of Mangual and Garci-Crespo, make love all night to the sensual drone of Rodriguez's Second Cello Concerto and cry out in joy at the dawn as if she'd created it herself. And now, now she sat Indian style in the middle of the bed and called out for me in a piping little singsong voice that made my blood boil. And what did she call me? Fausto, or even Faustito? No, she called me Daddy. "Daddy, Daddy," *she called,* "read me a story."

Buck's question was a good one: where *was* Barb? Though Buck hardly seemed concerned—irritated was more like it, as if he'd expected his mother to spring out of the woodwork and wash his socks or whip him up a lemon meringue pie from scratch. John had already sunk back into the couch, the book clutched like a living thing in his hand, and he just stared up at the glowing ball of his son's face. "I don't know," he said, drawing up his lip and shrugging a little more elaborately than was necessary, "—she went shopping."

Buck's face just hung there at the mouth of the dark hallway as if it had been sliced from his shoulders. "Shopping?" he repeated, knitting his brows and working a querulous edge into his voice. "When? When did she leave?"

John felt guilty now—he was the accused, the accused on the witness stand and the district attorney hammering away at him—and he felt afraid suddenly too, afraid for his wife and his son and the whole withering masquerade of his second-rate engineer's life, numbers turned vile and accusatory, job shopping, one deadening plant after another. "I don't know," he said. "Sometime this afternoon—or this morning, I mean. Late this morning."

"This morning? Jesus, Dad, are you losing your mind? That's a blizzard out there—she could be dead for all we know."

And now he was standing, his son's face shining fiercely with the reds and ambers of combustion, and he was ordering his apologies and excuses, ever rational, ever precise, till he realized that Buck was no longer there—he'd receded down the hallway to the refrigerated room, where even now the door slammed behind him in finality. That was when John struggled with himself, when it all came to the surface—his fears, his needs, his love for Barb, or respect for her, or whatever you wanted to call it—and he actually threw on his coat, muffler and hat and went to the little jade box on the mantel for the keys to the MG, before he caught himself. It was a fool's errand. A recipe for disaster. How could he go out in this—there must have been two and a half feet of snow out there, and it was drifting—and in a car made for summer roads, no less? It was crazy. Irresponsible. And she could be anywhere—what was he supposed to do, go house to house and shop to shop?

Finally, and it was past nine now, he convinced himself that the only rational thing was to wait out the storm. He'd been through blizzards before—he was fifty years old, after all—and they'd always come out right, aside from maybe a fender bender here or there, or a minor case of back strain from leaning into the snow shovel, running out of bread and milk and the like. But the storms always blew themselves out and the sun came back and the snow receded from the roads. No, he'd been right all along—there was nothing to do but wait, to curl up with a good book, and just, well, see what developed, and he'd shrugged off his coat, found his place on the couch and taken up the book again, when he heard the creak of the floorboards in the hall and glanced up.

Bern was standing there, hands at her sides. The primitive light attacked her hair, hair so white it reminded him of death, and she showed him her palms in a humble gesture of submission, amicability, engagement. "Buck's asleep," she said.

"Already?" The book was in his lap, his left index finger marking the place. "That was fast."

"It was a long trip."

"Yes," he said, and he didn't know why he was saying it, "yes." The wind came up suddenly and twisted round the corner of the house, spraying the windowpanes with compact pellets of snow.

She was in the room now, hovering over the couch. "I was just—I mean, I'm not sleepy at all, and I thought it would be nice, you know, just to sit by the fire . . . for a while, I mean."

"Sure," he said, and she squatted by the fire and threw her head back to curb her hair, and a long moment went by—five minutes, ten, he couldn't tell—before she spoke again. He'd just folded back the page of the book when she turned round and said, in a low murmur, "Buck's been very depressed. I mean, like clinically."

Her face was broad and beautiful, with a high forehead and the nose of a legislator or poet. That face stunned him, so beautiful and new and floating there like an apparition in his living room, and he couldn't think of how to respond. The snow ticked at the windows. The old dog let out an audible fart. "He can't—" John began, and then he faltered. "What do you mean, depressed? How? Why?"

She'd been watching him, focusing a clear, steady gaze on him that seemed to say all sorts of things—erotic things, crazy things—but now she dropped her eyes. "He thinks he's going to die."

Something clutched suddenly at him, something deep, but he ignored it. He was going to say, "Don't be ridiculous," but aimed for something lighter instead. "Well, he is," he said. "I mean, it's a rational fear. We're all going to die." He stared into her eyes, a pillar of strength and wisdom. "Eventually," he added, and tried for a smile. "Look at me—I'm fifty already. But Buck—you kids, the two of you—what have you got to worry about? It's a long way off. Forget about it, enjoy yourselves, dance to the music of life." *Dance to the music of life?* The phrase had just jumped into his head, and now he felt a little silly, a little quaint, but seductive too and wise and so full of, of love and maybe fear that he was ready to get up from the couch and embrace her.

The only problem was, she was no longer there. She'd heard something—and he'd heard it too, Buck calling out, the wind dragging its nails across the windowpane—and had risen like a ghost and silently vanished into the black hole of the hallway. John looked round him a moment, listening for the smallest sounds. The snow ticked away at the roof, the gutters, the window frame. The dog groaned in her sleep. He glanced down absently and saw the book there in his lap, turned back the page with a single autonomous sweep of his hand, and began, again, to read.

I'd never wanted to be a father—it was enough to have been father to my own diminishing parents, and I vowed I would never repeat the experience. Sonia felt as I did, and we took precautions to avoid any chance of conception, especially as she began younging and found herself menstruating again. I'd seen my own beloved mother dwindle to the size of a doll, a glove, an acorn, to nothing recognizable except to a scientist with a high-powered microscope, and the idea of it—of parenthood, little people, babies—terrified me.

But what could I do? I loved Sonia with all my being and I'd sworn before the Creator and Father Benitez to minister to her in sickness and health, if not in age and youth. It was my duty and my obligation to care for her when she could no longer care for herself—some would say it was my privilege, and perhaps it was, but it made me no less miserable for all that. For, you see, the inevitable had come to pass and she was an infant now, my Sonia, a baby, a squally, colicky, wide-eyed, little niñita *sucking greedily on a bottle of formula and howling through the sleepless nights with miniature tears of rage and impotence rolling down her ugly red cheeks.*

"Sonia!" I would cry. "Sonia, snap out of it! I know you're in there, I know you understand me—now just stop that bawling, stop it right now!"

But, of course, she didn't. How could she? She was only a baby, eight months old, six months, two. I held her in my arms, my lover, my Sonia, and watched her shrink away from me day by day. I picked her up by her naked ankles as if she were nothing more than a skinned rabbit ready for the pan, and I laid her out on a clean diaper after swabbing her privates and the little cleft that had once been my joy and my life.

Don't think I didn't resent it. Oh, I knew the rules, we all did, but this was cruel, too cruel, and I wept to see her reduced to this sucking, grasping, greedy little thing. "Sonia!" I cried. "Oh, Sonia!" And for all that she just stared at me out of her eyes the color of hazelnuts, eyes as brimming and lucid as her adult eyes, eyes that must have seen and known and felt. I lost weight. I couldn't sleep. My boss at the Banco Nacional, an eminently reasonable man, took me aside and informed me in so many words that I was in danger of losing the position I'd held for nearly sixty years.

Then one evening, after Sonia had soiled herself so thoroughly and repulsively I had no choice but to draw her a bath, there came a knock at the door. I had her in my arms, Sonia, my Sonia, the water in the tub as mild as a breeze and only two inches deep, but rising, rising, and she gave me a look that ate right through to my soul. It was a plea, a very particular and infinitely sad request that sprang like fire from the depths of her wide and prescient hazelnut eyes. . . .

The knock came again, louder and more insistent now, and I set her down on her back in the slowly accumulating water, all the while watching her eyes as her spastic little legs kicked out and her fists clenched. Then I rose—just for a second, only a second—wiped my hands on my pants, and called, "I'm coming, I'm . . . coming!"

The knock at the door roused John momentarily—Good God, it was past one in the morning, the fire was dead, and Barb, where was Barb?—but he was caught up in something here, and he tried to fight down his anxiety, compartmentalize it, tuck it away in a corner of his brain for future reference. When the knock came again, he didn't hear it, or not consciously, and *Sonia,* he was thinking, *what's going to become of Sonia?* till Buck was there and the door stood open like the mouth of a cave, freezing, absolutely freezing, and a figure loomed in the doorway in a great wide-brimmed felt hat above a gaunt and harried face.

"Dad," Buck was saying, "Dad, there's been an accident—"

John barely heard him. He held the book to his face like a screen, and over the tumult and the confusion and the sudden slashing movement that swept up the room in a hurricane of shouts and moans and the frantic sobbing bark of the old dog, he finally found his voice. "Fifteen pages," he said, waving a frantic hand to fend them off, all of them, even the dog. "I've just got fifteen pages to go."

(1997)

Friendly Skies

When the engine under the right wing began to unravel a thin skein of greasy, dark smoke, Ellen peered out the abraded Plexiglas window and saw the tufted clouds rising up and away from her and knew she was going to die. There was a thump from somewhere in the depths of the fuselage, the plane lurched like a balsawood toy struck by a rock, and the man in the seat in front of her lifted his head from the tray table and cried, "Mama!" in a thin, disconsolate wail. On went the "Fasten Seat Belts" sign. The murmur of the cabin became a roar. Every muscle in her body seized.

She thought distractedly of cradling her head—isn't that what you were supposed to do, cradle your head?—and then there was a burst of static, and the captain's voice was chewing calmly through the loudspeakers: "A little glitch there with engine number three, I'm afraid, folks. Nothing to worry about." The plane was obliterating the clouds with a supersonic howl, and every inanimate fold of metal and crease of plastic had come angrily to life, sloughed shoes, pieces of fruit, pretzels, paperback books and handbags skittering by underfoot. Ellen stole a glance out the window: the smoke was dense now, as black and rich as the roiling billows rising from a ship torpedoed at sea, and stiff raking fingers of yellow flame had begun to strangle the massive cylinder of the engine. The man in the seat next to hers—late twenties, with a brass stud centered half an inch beneath his lower lip, and hair the exact color and texture of meringue—turned a slack face to her. "What is that? Smoke?"

She was so frightened that she could only nod, her head filled with the sucking dull hiss of the air jets and the static of the speakers. The man leaned across her and squinted through the gray aperture of the window to the wing beyond. "Fuck, that's all we need. There's no way I'm going to make my connection now."

She didn't understand. Connection? Didn't he realize they were all going to die?

She braced herself and murmured a prayer. Voices rose in alarm. Her eyes felt as if they were going to implode in their sockets. But then the flames flickered and dimmed, and she felt the plane lifted up as if in the palm of some celestial hand, and for all the panic, the dimly remembered prayers, the cries and shouts, and the sudden, potent reek of urine, the crisis was over almost as soon as it had begun. "I hate to do this to you, folks," the captain drawled, "but it looks like we're going to have to turn around and take her back into LAX."

And now there was a collective groan. The man with the meringue hair let out a sharp, stinging curse and slammed the back of the seat in front of him with his fist. Not LAX. Not that. They'd already been delayed on the ground for two and a half hours because of mechanical problems, and then they'd sat on the runway for another forty minutes because they'd lost their slot for takeoff—or at least that's what the pilot had claimed. Everyone had got free drinks and peanuts, but nobody wanted peanuts, and the drinks tasted like nothing, like kerosene. Ellen had asked for a scotch-and-soda—she was trying to pace herself, after sitting interminably at the airport bar nursing a beer that had gone stale and warm—but the man beside her and the woman in the aisle seat had both ordered doubles and flung them down wordlessly. "Shit!" the man cursed now, and slammed his fist into the seat again, pounding it as if it were a punching bag, until the man in front of him lifted a great, swollen dirigible of a head over the seat back and growled, "Give it a rest, asshole. Can't you see we got an emergency here?"

For a moment, she thought the man beside her was going to get up out of his seat and start something—he was certainly drunk enough—but mercifully the confrontation ended there. The plane rocked with the weight of the landing gear dropping into place, the big-headed man swiveled around and settled massively in his seat, and beyond the windows Los Angeles began to scroll back into view, a dull brown grid sunk at the bottom of a muddy sea of air. "Did you hear that?" the man beside Ellen demanded of her. "Did you hear what he called me?"

Ellen sat gazing straight ahead, rigid as a catatonic. She could feel him staring at the side of her face. She could smell him. And everyone else too. She narrowed her shoulders and emptied her lungs of air, as if she could collapse into herself, dwindle down to nothing, and disappear.

The man shifted heavily in his seat, muttering to himself now. "Courtesy," he spat, "common courtesy," over and over, as if it were the only phrase he knew. Ellen leaned her head back and shut her eyes.

There was the usual wait on the ground, the endless taxiing, the crush of the carry-on luggage, and the densely packed, boviform line creeping up the aisles and into the steel tube that fed the passenger terminal. Ellen inched along, her head down, shoulders slumped, her over-the-shoulder bag like a cannonball in a sling, and followed the crowd out into the seething arena of the terminal. She'd been up since five, climbing aboard the airport bus in the dark and sitting stiffly through the lurching hour-and-a-half trip in bumper-to-bumper traffic; she'd choked down a dry six-dollar bagel and three-fifty cup of espresso at one of the airport kiosks, and then there was the long wait for the delayed flight, the pawed-over newspapers, the mobbed restroom, and the stale beer. Now she was back where she'd started, and a flight agent was rewriting her ticket and shoving her in the direction of a distant gate, where she would hook up with the next flight out to Kennedy, where her mother would be waiting for her. Was it a direct flight? No, the agent was afraid not. She'd have a two-hour layover in Chicago, and she'd have to switch planes. On top of that, there was weather, a fierce winter storm raking the Midwest and creeping toward New York at a slow, sure pace that was almost certain to coincide with her arrival.

She moved through the corridors like an automaton, counting off the gates as she passed them. The terminal was undergoing renovation—perpetually, it seemed—and up ahead plywood walls narrowed the corridors to cattle chutes. There was raw concrete underfoot here, and everything had a film of dust on it. She looked anxiously to the bottleneck ahead—she had only ten minutes to make the flight—and she was just shifting the bag from her left shoulder to her right when she was jostled from behind. Or not simply jostled—if it hadn't been for the woman in front of her, she would have lost her footing on the uneven surface and gone down in a heap. She glanced up to see the man who'd been sitting beside her on the aborted flight hurrying past—what should she call him? Stud Lip? Meringue Head?—even as she braced herself against the woman and murmured, "Excuse me, I'm so sorry." The man never gave her so much as a glance, let alone a word of apology. On he went, a pair of shoulders in some sort of athletic jacket, the bulb of his head in the grip of his hair, a bag too big for the overhead compartment swinging like a weapon at his side.

She saw him again at the gate—at the front of the line, a head taller than anyone else—and what was he doing? There were at least twenty people ahead of her, and the flight was scheduled to depart in three minutes. He was just standing there, immovable, waving his ticket in the attendant's face and gesticulating angrily at his bag. Ellen wasn't a violent person—she was thirty-two years old, immured in the oubliette of a perpetual diet, with limp blond hair, a plain face, and two milky blue eyes that oozed sympathy and regret—but if she could have thrown a switch that would put an instant, sizzling end to Meringue Head's existence, she wouldn't have hesitated. "What do you mean, I have to check it?" he demanded, in a voice that was like the thumping of a mallet.

"I'm sorry, Mr. Lercher," the man behind the desk was saying, "but federal regulations require—"

"Ler*share,* you idiot, Ler*share*—didn't you ever take French? And fuck the regulations. I've already been held up for two and a half hours and damn near killed when the goddamn engine caught fire, and you're trying to tell me I can't take my bag on the airplane, for Christ's sake?"

The other passengers hung their heads, consulted their watches, worked their jaws frantically over thin bands of flavorless gum, the people-movers moved people, the loudspeakers crackled, and the same inane voices repeated endlessly the same inane announcements in English and in Spanish. Ellen felt faint. Or no, she felt nauseated. It was as if there were something crawling up her throat and trying to get out, and all she could think of was the tarantula creeping through the clear plastic tubes of the terrarium in the classroom she'd left behind for good.

Waldo, the kids had called it, after the *Where's Waldo?* puzzles that had swept the fifth graders into a kind of frenzy for a month or two until something else—some computer game she couldn't remember the name of—had superseded them. She'd never liked the big, lazy spider, the slow, stalwart creep of its legs and abdomen as it patrolled its realm, seeking out the crickets it fed on, the alien look of it, like a severed hand moving all on its own. It's harmless, the assistant principal had assured her, but when Tommy Ayala sneaked a big dun trap-door spider into school and dropped it into the terrarium, Waldo had reacted with a swift and deadly ferocity. A lesson had come of that—about animal behavior and territoriality, and nearly every child had a story of cannibalistic guppies or killer hamsters to share—but it wasn't a happy lesson. Lucy Fadel brought up road rage, and Jasmyn Dickers knew a teenager who was stabbed in the neck because he had to live in a converted garage with twelve other people, and somebody else had been bitten by a pit bull, and on and on and on. Fifth graders. Ten years of fifth graders.

"Chicago passengers only," a flight attendant was saying, and the line melted away as Ellen found herself in yet another steel tube, her heart racing still over the image of that flaming engine and the fatal certainty that had gripped her like the death of everything. Was it an omen? Was she crazy to get on this flight? And what of the prayer she'd murmured—where had that come from? *Hail, Mary, full of grace, the Lord is with thee.* Prayers were for children, and for the old and hopeless, and she'd grown up to discover that they were addressed not to some wise and recumbent God on high but to the cold gaps between the stars. *Pray for us, now and at the hour of our—*

Up ahead, she saw the open door of the plane, rivets, the thin steel sheet of its skin, flight attendants in their blue uniforms and arrested smiles, and then she was shuffling down the awkward aisle like a mismatched bride—"The overhead bins are for secondary storage only. . . . A very full flight . . . Your cooperation, please"—and she was murmuring another sort of prayer now, a more common and profane one: *Christ, don't let me sit next to that idiot again.*

She glanced down at her boarding pass—18B—and counted off the rows, so tired, suddenly, that she felt as if she had been drained of blood. ("Anemic," the doctor had said, clucking her tongue, that was the problem, that and depression.) The line had come to a halt, Ellen's fellow passengers slumped under the weight of their bags like penitents, and all she could see down the length of the aisle was their shoulders, their collars and the hair that sprouted from their heads in all its multi-ethnic variety. The lucky ones—the ones already settled in their seats—gazed up at her with irritation, as if she were responsible for the delays, as if she had personally spun out the weather system over the Midwest, put the lies in the pilots' mouths, and flouted the regulations for carry-ons. "All right, all right, give me a minute, will you?" a voice raged out, and through a gap in the line she saw him, six or seven rows down, blocking the aisle as he fought to stuff his bag into the overhead compartment. Force, that was all he could think to use, because he was spoiled, bullying, petulant, like an overgrown fifth grader. She hated him. Everyone on the plane hated him.

And then the flight attendant was there, assuring him that she would find a place for his bag up front, even as an amplified voice hectored them to take their seats and the engines rumbled to life. Ellen caught a glimpse of his face, blunt and oblivious, as he swung ponderously into his seat, and then the line shuffled forward and she saw that her prayer had been answered—she was three rows ahead of him. She'd been assigned a middle seat, of course, as had most of the passengers bumped from the previous flight, but at least it wasn't a middle seat beside him. She waited as the woman in the aisle seat (mid-fifties, with a saddlebag face and a processed pouf of copper hair) unfastened her seat belt and laboriously rose to make way for her. There was no one in the window seat—not yet, at least—and even as she settled in, elbow to elbow with the saddlebag woman, Ellen was already coveting it.

Could she be so lucky? No, no, she couldn't, and here was another layer of superstition rising up out of the murk of her subconscious, as if luck had anything to do with her or what she'd been through already today or in the past week or month or year—or, for that matter, through the whole course of her vacant and constricted life. A name came to her lips then, a name she'd been trying, with the help of the prescription the doctor had given her, to suppress. She held it there for a moment, enlarged by her grief until she felt like the heroine of some weepy movie, a raped nun, an airman's widow, sloe-eyed and wilting under the steady gaze of the camera. She shouldn't have had the beer, she told herself. Or the scotch either. Not with the pills.

The plane quieted. The aisles cleared. She fought down her exhaustion and kept her eyes fixed on the far end of the aisle, where the last passenger—a boy in a reversed baseball cap—was fumbling into his seat. Surreptitiously, with her feet only, she shifted her bag from the space under her seat to the space beneath the window seat, and then, after a moment, she unfastened her seat belt and slipped into the unoccupied seat. She stretched her legs, adjusted her pillow and blanket, watched the flight attendants work their way up the aisle, easing shut the overhead bins. She was thinking that she should have called her mother with the new flight information—she'd call her from Chicago, that's what she'd do—when there was movement at the front of the plane and one final passenger came through the door, even as the attendants stood by to screw it shut. Stooping to avoid the TV monitors, he came slowly down the aisle, sweeping his eyes right and left to check the row numbers, an overcoat over one arm, a soft computer bag slung over the opposite shoulder. He was dressed in a sport coat and a T-shirt, his hair cut close, after the fashion of the day, and his face seemed composed despite what must have been a mad dash through the airport. But what mattered most about him was that he seemed to be coming straight to her, to 18A, the seat she'd appropriated. And what went through her mind? A curse, that was all. Just a curse.

Sure enough, he paused at Row 18, glanced at the saddlebag woman, and then at Ellen, and said, "Excuse me, I believe I'm in here?"

Ellen reddened. "I thought . . ."

"No, no," he said, holding Ellen's eyes even as the saddlebag woman rolled up and out of her seat like a rock dislodged from a crevice, "stay there. It's okay. Really."

The pilot said something then, a garble of the usual words, the fuselage shuddered, and the plane backed away from the gate with a sudden jolt. Ellen put her head back and closed her eyes.

She woke when the drinks cart came around. There was a sour taste in her mouth, her head was throbbing, and the armrest gouged at her ribs as if it had come alive. She'd been dreaming about Roy, the man who had dismembered her life like a boy pulling the legs off an insect, Roy and that elaborate, humiliating scene in the teachers' lounge, her mother there somehow to witness it, and then she and Roy were in bed, the stiff insistence of his erection (which turned out to be the armrest), and his hand creeping across her ribcage until it was Waldo, Waldo the tarantula, closing in on her breast. "Something to drink?" the broad-faced flight attendant was asking, and both Ellen's seatmates seemed to be hanging on her answer. "Scotch-and-soda," she said, without giving it a second thought.

The man beside her, the new man, the one who had offered up his seat to her, was working on his laptop, the gentle blue glow of the screen softly illuminating his lips and eyes. He looked up at the flight attendant, his fingers still poised over the keys, and murmured, "May I have a chardonnay, please?" Then it was the saddlebag woman's turn. "Sprite," she said, the dull thump of her voice swallowed up in the drone of the engines.

The man flattened himself against the seat back as the flight attendant leaned in to pass Ellen her drink, then he typed something hurriedly, shut down the computer, and slipped it into his lap, beneath the tray table. He took the truncated bottle, the glass, napkin and peanuts from the attendant, arranged them neatly before him, and turned to Ellen with a smile. "I never know where to put my elbows on these things," he said, shrinking away from the armrest they shared. "It's kind of like being in a coffin—or one of those medieval torture devices, you know what I mean?"

Ellen took a sip of her drink and felt the hot smoke of the liquor in the back of her throat. He was good-looking, handsome—more than handsome. At that moment, the engines thrumming, the flat, dull earth fanning out beneath the plane, he was shining and beautiful, as radiant as an archangel come flapping through the window to roost beside her. Not that it would matter to her. Roy was handsome too, but she was done with handsome, done with fifth graders, done with the whole failed experiment of living on her own in the big, smoggy, palm-shrouded city. Turn the page, new chapter. "Or maybe a barrel," she heard herself say, "going over Niagara Falls."

"Yeah," he said, laughing through his nose. "Only in the barrel you don't get your own personal flotation device."

Ellen didn't know what to say to that. She took another pull at her drink for lack of anything better to do. She was feeling it, no doubt about it, but what difference would it make if she was drunk or sober as she wandered the labyrinthine corridors of O'Hare, endlessly delayed by snow, mechanical failure, the hordes of everybody going everywhere? Three sheets to the wind, right—isn't that what they said? And what, exactly, did that mean? Some old sailing expression, she supposed, something from the days of the clipper ships, when you vomited yourself from one place to another.

Their meals had come. The broad-faced flight attendant was again leaning in confidentially, this time with the eternal question—"Chicken or pasta?"—on her lips. Ellen wasn't hungry—food was the last thing she wanted—but on an impulse she turned to her neighbor. "I'm not really very hungry," she said, her face too close to his, their elbows touching, his left knee rising up out of the floor like a stanchion, "but if I get a meal, would you want it—or some of it? As an extra, I mean?"

He gave her a curious look, then said, "Sure, why not?" The flight attendant was waiting, the sealed-in smile beginning to crack at the corners with the first fidgeting of impatience. "Chicken for me," the man said, "and pasta for the lady." And then, to Ellen, as he shifted the tray from one hand to the other: "You sure, now? I know it's not exactly three-star cuisine, but you've got to eat, and the whole reason they feed you is to make the time pass so you don't realize how cramped and miserable you are."

The smell of the food—salt, sugar and animal fat made palpable—rose to her nostrils, and she felt nauseated again. Was it the pills? The alcohol? Or was it Roy—Roy, and life itself? She thought about that, and the instant she did, there he was—Roy—clawing his way back into her mind. She could see him now, his shoulders squared in his black polyester suit with the little red flecks in it—the suit she'd helped him pick out, as if he had any taste or style he could call his own—his eyes swollen out of their sockets, his lips reduced to two thin, ungenerous flaps of skin grafted to his mouth. *Shit-for-brains.* That's what he'd called her, right there in the teachers' lounge with everybody watching—Lynn Bendall and Lauren McGimpsey and that little teacher's aide, what was her name? He was shouting, and she was shouting back, no holds barred, not anymore. *So what if I am sleeping with her? What's it to you? You think you own me? Do you? Huh, shit-for-brains? Huh?* Lauren's face was dead, but Ellen saw Lynn exchange a smirk with the little teacher's aide, and that smirk said it all, because Lynn, it seemed, knew more about who he was sleeping with than Ellen did herself.

The man beside her—her neighbor—was eating now. He was hungry, and that was good. She felt saintly, watching him eat and listening to him chatter on about his work—he was some sort of writer or journalist, on his way to Philadelphia for the holidays. She'd renounced the pasta and given it to him, and he was grateful—he hadn't eaten all day, and he was a growing boy, he said, with a smile, though he must have been in his early thirties. And unmarried, judging from his naked fingers. When the drinks cart came by, Ellen ordered another scotch.

They were talking about movies, maybe the only subject people had in common these days, when Ellen glanced up to see Lercher, his face twisted in a drunken scowl, looming over them as he made his unsteady way to the forward lavatories. She and her companion—his name was Michael, just Michael, that was all he offered—had struck a real chord when it came to the current cinema (no movies with explosions, no alien life-forms, no geriatric lovers, no sappy kids), and she'd begun to feel something working inside her. She was interested, genuinely interested in something, for maybe the first time in months. Michael. She held the name on her tongue like the thinnest wafer, repeating it silently, over and over. And then it came to her: he was the anti-Roy, that's who he was, so polite and unassuming, a soul mate, somebody who could care, really care—she was sure of it.

"You see that man?" she asked, lowering her voice. "The one with the hair? He was sitting right next to me on the last flight, the one where, well, I was telling you, I was looking out the window and the engine caught fire? And I've never been so scared in my life."

The wind shrieked along the length of the fuselage, the lights dimmed and went up again, Michael poured himself a second glass of wine and made sympathetic noises. "You actually saw this? Flames? Or was it like sparks or something?"

She went cold with the memory of it. "Flames," she said, pursing her lips and nodding her head. "I was so scared I started praying." She glanced out the window, as if to reassure herself. "You're not religious, are you?" she said, turning back to him.

"No," he said, and he raised his hand to cut the throat of the subject before it could take hold of him. "I'm an atheist. I mean, we had no set religion in our house, that's just the way my parents were."

"Me too," she said, remembering religious instruction, the icy dip of the holy water, her mother in a black veil, and the priest intoning the sleepy immemorial phrases of her girlhood, "but we went to church when I was little."

He didn't ask what church, and a silence fell between them as the plane rocked gently and the big man oscillated back from the lavatory. Ellen closed her eyes again, for just a moment, the swaying of the cabin and the pills and the scotch pulling her down toward some inky dark place that was like the mouth of an abandoned well, like a cave deep in the earth. . . .

She was startled awake by a sudden explosion of voices behind her. "The fuck I will!" snarled a man's voice, and even through the fog of her waking she recognized it.

"But, sir, I've already told you, the plane is full. You can see for yourself."

"Then put me up front—and don't try to tell me that's full, because I was up there to use the restroom, and there's all sorts of space up there. This is bullshit. I'm not going to sit here squeezed in like a rat. I paid full fare, and I'm not going to take this shit anymore, you hear me?"

Heads had begun to turn. Ellen glanced at Michael, but he was absorbed with his computer, some message she couldn't read, some language she didn't know; for a moment she stared at the ranks of dark symbols floating across the dull firmament of the screen, then she craned her neck to see over the seat back. Lercher was standing in the aisle, his shoulders hunched, his head cocked forward against the low ceiling. Two flight attendants, the broad-faced woman and another, slighter woman with her hair in a neat French braid, stood facing him.

"There's nothing we can do, sir," the slight woman said, an edge of hostility in her voice. "I've already told you, you don't qualify for an upgrade. Now, I'm going to have to ask you to take your seat."

"This is bullshit," he reiterated. "Two and a half fucking hours on the ground, and then we get sent back to LAX, and now I'm stuck in this cattle car, and you won't even serve me a fucking drink? Huh? What do you call this?" He flailed his arms, appealing to the people seated around him; to a one, they looked away. "Well, I call it bullshit!" he roared.

The women held their ground. "Sit down, sir. Now. Or we'll have to call the captain."

The big man's face changed. The crease between his eyes deepened; his lips drew back as if he were about to spit down the front of the first woman's crisp blue jacket. "All right," he said ominously, "if that's how you want to play it," and he was already swinging around and staggering toward the rear of the plane, the flight attendants trailing along helplessly in his wake. Ellen shifted in her seat so she could follow their progress, her hips straining against the seat belt, her right hand inadvertently braced against Michael's forearm. "Oh, I'm sorry," she murmured, even as Lercher disappeared into the galley at the rear and she turned her face to Michael's. He looked startled, his eyes so blue and electric they reminded her of the fish in the classroom aquarium—the neon tetras, with their bright lateral stripes. "Did you see that? I mean, did you hear him—the man, the one I was telling you about?"

He hesitated a moment, just staring into her eyes. "No," he said finally, "I didn't notice. I was—I guess I was so absorbed in my work I didn't know where I was."

Ellen's face darkened. "He's the worst kind of trash," she said. "Just mean, that's all, like the bullies on the playground."

And now there was the sound of a commotion from the rear of the plane, and Ellen turned to see Lercher emerge from the galley on the far side of the plane, the flight attendants cowering behind him. In each hand he wielded a gleaming stainless-steel coffeepot, and he was moving rapidly up the aisle, his eyes gone hard with hate. "Out of my way!" he screamed, elbowing a tottering old lady aside. "Anybody fucks with me gets scalded, you hear me?"

People awoke with a snort. A hundred heads ducked down protectively, and on every face was an expression that said *not now, not here, not me.* No one said a word. And then, suddenly, a male flight attendant came hurtling down the aisle from the first-class section and attempted to tackle the big man, gripping him around the waist, and Ellen heard a woman cry out as hot coffee streamed down the front of her blouse. Lercher held his ground, bludgeoning the flight attendant to the floor with the butt of the wildly splashing pot he clutched in his right fist, and then the two female attendants were on him, tearing at his arms, and a male passenger, heavyset and balding, sprang savagely up out of his seat to enter the fray.

For a moment, they achieved a sort of equilibrium, surging forward and falling back again, but Lercher was too much for them. He stunned the heavyset man with a furious, slashing blow, then flung off the flight attendants as if they were nothing. The scalded woman screamed again, and Ellen felt as if a knife were twisting inside her. She couldn't breathe. Her arms went limp. Lercher was dancing in the aisle, shouting obscenities, moving backward now, toward the galley, and God only knew what other weapons he might find back there.

Where was the captain? Where were the people in charge? The cabin was in an uproar, babies screaming, voices crying out, movement everywhere—and Lercher was in the galley, dismantling the plane, and no one could do anything about it. There was the crash of a cart being overturned, a volley of shouts, and suddenly he appeared at the far end of Ellen's aisle, his face contorted until it was no human face at all. "Die!" he screamed. "Die, you motherfuckers!" The rear exit door was just opposite him, and he paused in his fury to kick at it with a big booted foot, and then he was hammering at the Plexiglas window with one of the coffeepots as if he could burst through it and sail on out into the troposphere like some sort of human missile.

"You're all going to die!" he screamed, pounding, pounding. "You'll be sucked out into space, all of you!" Ellen thought she could hear the window cracking—wasn't anybody going to do anything?—and then he dropped both coffeepots and made a rush up the aisle for the first-class section.

Before she could react, Michael rose in a half-crouch, swung his laptop out across the saddlebag lady's tray table, and caught Lercher in the crotch with the sharp, flying corner of it. She saw his face then, Lercher's, twisted and swollen like a sore, and it came right at Michael, who could barely maneuver in his eighteen inches of allotted space. In a single motion, the big man snatched the laptop from Michael's hand and brought it whistling down across his skull, and Ellen felt him go limp beside her. At that point, she didn't know what she was doing. All she knew was that she'd had enough, enough of Roy and this big, drunken, testosterone-addled bully and the miserable, crimped life that awaited her at her mother's, and she came up out of her seat as if she'd been launched—and in her hand, clamped there like a flaming sword, was a thin steel fork that she must have plucked from the cluttered dinner tray. She went for his face, for his head, his throat, enveloping him with her body, the drug singing in her heart and the scotch flowing like ichor in her veins.

They made an emergency stop in Denver, and they sat on the ground in a swirling light snow as the authorities boarded the plane to take charge of Lercher. He'd been overpowered finally and bound to his seat with cloth napkins from the first-class dining service, a last napkin crammed into his mouth as a gag. The captain had come on the loudspeaker with a mouthful of apologies, and then, to a feeble cheer from the cabin, pledged free headphones and drinks on the house for the rest of the flight. Ellen sat, dazed, over yet another scotch, the seat beside her vacant. Even before the men in uniforms boarded the plane to handcuff and shackle Lercher, the paramedics had rushed down the aisle to evacuate poor Michael to the nearest hospital, and she would never forget the way his eyes had rolled back in his head as they laid him out on the stretcher. And Lercher, big and bruised, his head drunkenly bowed and the dried blood painted across his cheek where the fork had gone in and gone in again, as if she'd been carving a roast with a dull knife, Lercher led away like Billy Tindall or Lucas Lopez in the grip of the principal on a bad day at La Cumbre Elementary.

She sipped her drink, her face gone numb, eyes focused on nothing, as the whole plane murmured in awe. People stole glances at her, the saddlebag woman offered up her personal copy of the January *Cosmopolitan,* the captain himself came back to pay homage. And the flight attendants—they were so relieved they were practically genuflecting to her. It didn't matter. Nothing mattered. There would be forms to fill out, a delay in Chicago, an uneventful flight into New York, eight hours behind schedule. Her mother would be there, with a face full of pity and resignation, and she'd be too delicate to mention Roy, or teaching, or any of the bleak details of the move itself, the waste of a new microwave, and all that furniture tossed in a Dumpster. She would smile, and Ellen would try to smile back. "Is that it?" her mother would say, eyeing the bag slung over her shoulder. "You must have some baggage?" And then, as they were heading down the carpeted corridor, two women caught in the crush of humanity, with the snow spitting outside and the holidays coming on, her mother would take her by the arm, smile up at her, and just to say something, anything, would ask, "Did you have a nice flight?"

(1999)

The Black and White Sisters

I used to cut their lawn for them, before they paved it over, that is. It was the older one, Moira, the one with the white hair and vanilla skirt, who gave me the bad news. "Vincent," she said, "Caitlin and I have decided to do without the lawn—and the shrubs and flowers too." (We were in her kitchen at the time, a place from which every hint of color had been erased, Caitlin was hovering in the doorway with her vulcanized hair and cream-pie face, and my name is Larry, not Vincent—just to give you some perspective.)

I shuffled my feet and ducked my head. "So you won't be needing a gardener anymore then?"

Moira exchanged a look with her sister, who was my age exactly: forty-two. I know, because we were in school together, all three of us, from elementary through junior high, when their parents took them to live in New York. Not long after that the parents died and left them a truckload of money, and eventually they made their way back to California to take up residence in the family manse, which has something like twenty rooms and two full acres of lawns and flower-beds, which I knew intimately. Moira wasn't much to look at anymore—too pinned-back and severe—but Caitlin, if you caught her in the right light, could be very appealing. She had a sort of retro-ghoulish style about her, with her dead black clinging dress and Kabuki skin and all the rest of it. Black fingernails, of course. And toenails. I could just see the glossy even row of them peeping out from beneath the hem of her dress.

"Well," Moira demurred, coming back to me in her brisk grandmotherly way, though she wasn't a grandmother, never even married, and couldn't have been more than forty-four or -five, "I wouldn't be too hasty. We're going to want all the shrubs and trees removed—anything that shows inside the fence, that is."

I'd been around in my time (in and out of college, stint in the merchant marine, twice married and twice divorced, and I'd lived in Poughkeepsie, Atlanta, Juneau, Cleveland and Mazatlán before I came home to California and my mother), and nothing surprised me. Or not particularly. I studied Moira's face, digging the toe of my workboot into the square of linoleum in front of me. "I don't know," I said finally, "it's going to be a big job—the trees anyway. I can handle the shrubs and flowers myself, but the treework's going to have to go to a professional. I can make some calls, if you want."

Moira came right back at me, needling and sharp. "You know the rule: black jeans, white T-shirt, black caps. No exceptions."

I was wearing black jeans myself—and a white T-shirt and black cap, from which I'd removed the silver Raiders logo at her request. I was clear on the parameters here. But the money was good, very good, and I was used to dealing with the eccentric rich—that was pretty much all we had in this self-consciously quaint little town by the sea. And eccentric, as we all know, is just a code word for pure cold-water crazy. "Sure," I said. "No problem."

"You'll bill us?" Moira asked, smoothing down her skirt and crossing the room in a nervous flutter to pull open the refrigerator and peer inside.

Ten percent, I could see it already—and the treework would be eleven or twelve thousand, easy, maybe more. It wasn't gouging, not really, just my commission for catering to their whims—or needs. Black jeans and white T-shirts. Sure. I just nodded.

"And no Mexicans. I know there's practically nothing but on any work crew these days, and I have nothing against them, nothing at all, but you know how I feel, Vincent, I think. Don't you?" She removed a clear glass pitcher of milk from the refrigerator and took a glass from the cupboard. "A black crew I'd have no objection to—or a white one either. But it's got to be one or the other, no mixing, and you know"—she paused, the glass in one hand, the pitcher in the other—"if it's a black crew, I think I'd like to see them in *white* jeans and *black* T-shirts. Would there be a problem with that, if the question should arise?"

"No," I said, slowly shaking my head, as if I could barely sustain the weight of it, "no problem at all."

"Good," she said, pouring out a clean white glass of milk and setting it down on the counter beside the pitcher as if she were arranging a still life. She clasped her hands over her breast, flashed a look at her sister, and then smiled as if I'd just carved up the world like a melon and handed it to her, piece by dripping piece. "We'll begin A.S.A.P. then, hmm? The sooner the better?"

"Sure," I said.

"All right, then. Do you have anything to add, Caitlin?"

Caitlin's voice, soft as the beat of a cabbage moth's wing: "No, nothing."

I started digging out the bushes myself—fuchsia, oleander, mock orange—but I had to go pretty far afield for the tree crew. There were three grand old oaks in the front yard, a mature Australian tea tree on the east side of the house, and half a dozen citrus trees in the back. It would take a crew of ten at least, with climbers, a cherry picker, shredder and cleanup, and as I say, it was going to be expensive. And wasteful. A real shame, really, to strip and pave a yard like that, but if that was what they wanted, I was in no position to argue. I stood to make eleven hundred or so on the trees and another five digging out the shrubs and tilling up the lawn.

The problem, though, as Moira had foreseen, was in finding a non-Mexican crew in San Roque. It just didn't exist. Nor were there many white guys on the dirty end of the tree business—they basically just bid the jobs and sent you the bill—and there were no blacks in town at all. Finally, I drove down to Los Angeles and talked to Walt Tremaine, of Walt's Stump & Tree, and he agreed to come up and bid the job, writing in three hundred extra for the aesthetic considerations—i.e., the white jeans and black T-shirts.

Walt Tremaine was a man of medium size with a firm paunch and a glistening bald sweat-speckled crown. He looked to be in his fifties, and he was wearing a pair of cutoff blue jeans and one of those tight-fitting shirts with the little alligator logo over the left nipple. The alligator was green, and the shirt was the color of a crookneck squash—a bright, glowing, almost aniline yellow. We were both contemplating the problem of the tea tree, a massive snaking thing that ran its arms out into a tangle of neglected Victorian Box, when the two women appeared round the corner of the house. Moira was in white—high-heeled boots, ankle-length dress and sweater, though it was a golden temperate day, like most days here—and Caitlin was in her customary black. Both of them had parasols, but Caitlin had taken the white one and Moira the black for some reason—maybe they were trying to impress Walt Tremaine with their improvisatory daring.

I introduced them, and Moira, beaming, took Walt Tremaine's hand and said, "So, you're a black man."

He just stared at the picture of her white-gloved hand in the shadow of his for a minute and then corrected her. "African American."

"Yes," Moira said, still beaming, "exactly. And I very much like the color of your shirt, but you do understand I hope that it's much too much of an excitation and will simply have to go. Yes?" And then she turned to me. "Vincent, have you explained to this gentleman what we require?"

Walt Tremaine gave me a look. It was a look complicated by the fact that I'd introduced myself as Larry when he climbed out of his pickup truck, not to mention Moira's comment about his shirt and the dead white of Moira's dress and the nullifying black of her sister's lipstick, but it went further than that too—it was the way Moira was talking, taking elaborate care with each syllable, as if she were an English governess with a board strapped to her back. He operated out of Van Nuys, and I figured he didn't run across many women like Moira in an average day. But he was equal to the challenge, no problem there.

"Sure," he said, pressing a little smile onto his lips. "Your man here—whatever his name is—outlined the whole thing for me. I can do the job for you, but I have to say I'm an equal-opportunity employer, and I have eight Mexicans, two Guatemalans, a Serb and a Fiji Islander working for me, as well as my African Americans. And I don't particularly like it, but I can split off one crew of black men and bring them up here, if that's what you want." He paused. Toed the grass a minute, touched a finger to his lips. When he spoke, it was with a rising inflection, and his eyes rolled up like loose windowshades and then came back down again: "White jeans?"

Caitlin gave a little laugh and gazed out across the lawn. Her sister shot her a fierce look and then clamped the grandmotherly smile back on her face. "Indulge us," she said. "We're just trying to—well, let's say we're trying to simplify our environment."

Later that afternoon, sweating buckets, I stopped to strip off my soaked-through T-shirt and hose some of the grit off me. I stood there a moment, my mind blank, the scent of everything that lives and grows rising to my nostrils, the steady stream of the hose now dribbling from my fingertips, now distending my cheeks, when the front gate cranked open and Caitlin's black Mercedes rolled up the drive and came to a silent, German-engineered halt beside me. I'd been hacking away at an ancient plumbago bush for the past half hour, and I wasn't happy. It seemed wrong to destroy all this living beauty, deeply wrong, a desecration of the yard and the neighborhood and a violation of the principles I try to live by—I hadn't started up a gardening business to maim and uproot things, after all. I wanted to nurture new growth. I wanted healing. Rebirth. All of that. Because I'd seen some bad times, especially with my second wife, and all I can say is thank God we didn't have any children.

Anyway, there I was and there she was, Caitlin, stepping out of the car with a panting dog at her heels (no, it wasn't a Scottie or a black Lab, but a Hungarian puli that was so unrelievedly black it cut a moving hole out of the scenery). She lifted two bulging plastic sacks from the seat beside her—groceries—and I remember wondering if the chromatic obsession extended to foods too. There would be eggplant in one of those bags, I was thinking, vanilla ice cream in another, devil's food cake, Béchamel, week-old bananas, coffee, Crisco . . . but inspiration began to fail me when I realized she was standing two feet from me, watching the water roll off my shoulders and find its snaking way down my chest and into the waist of my regulation black jeans.

"Hi, Larry," she murmured, smiling at me with as sweet an expression as you could expect from a woman with black-rimmed eyes and lips the color of a dead streetwalker's. "How's it going?"

I tried to wipe every trace of irritation from my face—as I say, I wasn't too pleased with what she and her sister were doing here, but I tried to put things in perspective. I'd had crazier clients by a long shot. There was Mrs. Boutilier du Plessy, for one, who had me dig a pond twenty feet across for a single goldfish she'd been handed by a stranger at the mall, and Frank and Alma Fortressi, who paid me to line the floor of their master bedroom with Visqueen and then dump thirty bags of planting mix on top of it so I could plant peonies right at the foot of the bed. I smiled back at Caitlin. "All right, I guess."

She shaded her eyes from the sun and squinted at me. "Is that sweat? All over you, I mean?"

"It was," I said, holding her eyes. I was remembering her as a child, black hair in braids, like Pocahontas, dimpled knees, the plain constricting chute of a little girl's dress, but a dress that was pink or moss-green or Lake Tahoe blue. "I just hosed off."

"Hard work, huh?" she said, looking off over my shoulder as if she were addressing someone behind me. And then: "Can I get you something to drink?"

"It wouldn't be milk, would it?" I said, and she laughed.

"No, no milk, I promise. I can give you juice, soda, beer—would you like a beer?"

The dog sniffed at my leg—or at least I hope he was sniffing, since he was so black and matted you couldn't tell which end of him was which. "A beer sounds real nice," I said, "but I don't know how you and your sister are supposed to feel about it—I mean, beer's not white." I let it go a beat. "Or black."

She held her smile, not fazed in the least. "For one thing," she said, "Moira always takes a nap after lunch, so she won't be involved. And for another"—she was looking right into my eyes now, the smile turned up a notch—"we only serve Guinness in this house."

We sat in the kitchen—black-and-white tile, white cabinets, black appliances—and had three bottles each while the sun slid across the windowpanes and the plumbago withered over its hacked and naked roots. I don't know what it was—the beer, the time of day, the fact that she was there and listening—but I really opened up to her. I told her about Janine, my second wife, and how she picked at me all the time—I was never good enough for her, no matter what I did—and I got off on a tangent about a transformative experience I'd had in Hawaii, when I first realized I wanted to work with the earth, with the whole redemptive process of digging and planting, laying out flowerbeds, running drip lines, setting trees in the ground. (I was on top of Haleakala Crater, in the garden paradise of the world, and there was nothing but volcanic debris all around me, a whole sour landscape of petrified symbols. It was dawn and I hadn't slept and Janine and I stood there in the wind, bleary tourists gazing out on all that nullity, and suddenly I understood what I wanted in life. I wanted things to be green, that was all. It was as simple as that.)

Caitlin was a good listener, and I liked the way she tipped the glass back in delicate increments as she drank, her eyes shining and her free hand spread flat on the tabletop, as if we were at sea and she needed to steady herself. She kept pushing the hair away from her face and then leaning forward to let it dangle loose again, and whenever I touched on anything painful or sensitive (and practically everything about Janine fell into that category), a sympathetic little crease appeared between her eyebrows and she clucked her tongue as if there were something stuck to the roof of her mouth. After the second beer, we turned to less personal topics: the weather, gardening, people we knew in common. When we cracked the third, we began reminiscing about the lame, halt and oddball teachers we'd had in junior high and some of the more memorable disasters from those days, like the time it rained day and night for the better part of a week and boulders the size of Volkswagens rolled up out of the streambeds and into the passing lane of the freeway.

I was having a good time, and good times had been in precious short supply since my divorce. I felt luxurious and calm. The shrubs, I figured, could wait until tomorrow—and the trees and the grass and the sky too. It was nice, for a change, to let the afternoon stretch itself over the window like a thin skin and not have to worry about a thing. I was drunk. Drunk at three in the afternoon, and I didn't care. We'd just shared a laugh over Mr. Clemens, the English teacher who wore the same suit and tie every day for two years and pronounced *poem* as "poim," when I set my glass down and asked Caitlin what I'd been wanting to ask since I first left my card in her mailbox six months back. "Listen, Caitlin," I said, riding the exhilaration of that last echoing laugh, "I hope you won't take this the wrong way, but what is it with the black-and-white business—I mean, is it some sort of political statement? A style? A religious thing?"

She leaned back in her chair and made an effort to hold on to her smile. The dog lay asleep in the corner, as shabby and formless as an old alpaca coat slipped from a hanger. He let out a long, heaving sigh, lifted his head briefly, and then dropped it again. "Oh, I don't know," she said, "it's a long story—"

That was when Moira appeared, right on cue. She was wearing a gauzy white pantsuit she might have picked up at a beekeepers' convention, and she hesitated at the kitchen door when she saw me sitting there with her sister and a thick black beer, but only for an instant. "Why, Vincent," she said, more the governess than ever, "what a nice surprise."

The next morning, at eight, Walt Tremaine showed up with seven black men in white jeans, black T-shirts and white caps and enough heavy machinery to take down every tree within half a mile before lunch. "And how are you this fine morning, Mr. Vincent Larry," he said, "—or is it Larry Vincent?"

I blew the steam off a cup of McDonald's coffee and worked my tongue round the remnants of an Egg McMuffin. "Just call me Larry," I said. "It's her," I added, by way of explanation. "Moira, the older one. I mean, she's . . . well, I don't have to tell you—I'm sure you can draw your own conclusions."

Walt Tremaine planted his feet and wrapped his arms round his chest. "Oh, I don't know," he said, waxing philosophical as his crew scuttled past us with ropes, chainsaws, blowers and trimmers. "Sometimes I wish I could get a little simplicity in *my* life, if you know what I mean. Up in a tree half the day, sawdust in my hair, and when I come home to my wife she expects me to mow the lawn and break out the hedge clippers." He looked down at his feet and then out across the lawn. "Hell, I'd like to pave my yard over too."

I was going to say *I know what you mean,* because that's the sort of thing you say in a situation like that, but that would have implied agreement, and I didn't agree, not at all. So I just shrugged noncommittally and watched Walt Tremaine's eyes follow his climbers up the biggest, oldest and most venerable oak in the yard.

Later, when the tree was in pieces and the guy I'd hired for the day and I had rototilled the lawn and raked the dying fragments into three top-heavy piles the size of haystacks, Moira, in her beekeeper's regalia, appeared with a pitcher of milk and a tray of Oreo cookies. It was four in the afternoon, the yard was raw with dirt, and the air shrieked with the noise of Walt Tremaine's shredder as his men fed it the remains of the oak's crown. The other two oaks, smaller but no less grand, had been decapitated preparatory to taking them down, and the tea tree had been relieved of its limbs. All in all, it looked as if a bomb had hit the yard while miraculously sparing the house (white, of course, with whiter trim and a dead black roof). I watched Moira circulate among the bewildered sweating men of Walt Tremaine's crew, pouring out milk, offering cookies.

When she got around to me and Greg (black jeans, white T-shirt, black cap, white skin), she let her smile waver and flutter twice across her lips before settling in. We were taking a hard-earned break, stretched out in comfort on the last besieged patch of grass and trying to muster the energy to haul all that yellowing turf out to my pickup. We'd really humped it all afternoon, so caught up in the rhythm of destruction we never even stopped for a drink from the hose, but we couldn't help but look guilty now—you always do when the client catches you on your rear end. I introduced her to Greg, who didn't bother to get up.

"I'm very pleased to meet you," she said, and Greg just grunted in return, already tucking a cookie inside his cheek. I passed on the cookies myself, and the milk too—I was beginning to resent being reduced to a figure in some crazy composition. She smiled at me, though, a full-on interplanetary dreamer's smile that really made me wonder if there was anyone home, at least for that instant, and then she turned back to Greg. "You're, uh, how can I put this?" she murmured, studying his deeply tanned face and arms. "You're not Mexican, by any chance, are you?"

Greg looked surprised and maybe a bit shocked too—she might as well have asked him if he was a Zulu. He gave me a quick glance, then shifted his gaze to Moira. "My last name's Sorenson," he said, struggling to keep his voice under control, and he took off his cap to show her the blond highlights in his hair. He replaced the cap indignantly and held out his arms. "I'm a surfer," he said, "every chance I get. This is what's known as a *tan*."

I watched the sun touch her hair as she straightened up with the tray and struggled with her smile. She must bleach her hair, I was thinking, because nobody under seventy has hair that white—and it was amazing hair, white right on through to the scalp, sheep-white, bone-white, paper-white—when she squared her shoulders and looked down at Greg as if he were some panting animal she'd discovered in a cage at the zoo. "Well, that's nice," she said finally. "Very nice. It's a nice sport. Will you be working here long? For us, I mean?"

"We'll be done this time tomorrow, Moira," I said, cutting in before Greg could say something I might wind up regretting. "We've just got to rake out the lawn—the dirt, that is—for the blacktop guy, and take out the rest of the pittosporum under the tea tree. Walt Tremaine and his people are going to need two more days."

Moira wavered on the cusp of this news, the gauzy beekeeper's outfit inflating with a sudden breath of wind. She held the tray of milk and cookies rigidly before her, and I noticed her hands for the first time, a young woman's hands, sleek and unlined, the fingernails heavily enameled in cake-frosting white. "Vincent," she said after a moment, raising her voice to be heard over the dopplering whine of the shredder out on the street, "could I have a word with you in private?" She moved off then without waiting for an answer, and I was left to push myself up and tag after her, like the hired help I was.

We'd marched forty feet across the ravaged yard before she turned to me. "This Sorenson," she said. "Your associate?"

"Yeah?"

"I presume he's just casual labor?"

I nodded.

She glanced up toward the house and I followed her line of sight to one of the second-story windows. Caitlin was there, in her funereal black, looking down on the wreckage of the yard with a fixed stare. "I don't want to put you out, Vincent," Moira was saying, and she was still staring up at the image of her sister, "but couldn't you find someone a little less *sallow* for tomorrow?"

There wouldn't be any gardening going on around here for some time to come, and I didn't really have to kowtow to this woman anymore—or humor her either—but I went along with her just the same. Call it a reflex. "Sure," I said, and I had to keep myself from tipping my hat. "No problem."

A week later the yard was an empty parking lot surrounded by a ten-foot-high clapboard fence (whitewashed, of course). From inside you couldn't see a trace of green anywhere—or yellow, red, pink or tangerine, for that matter. I wondered how they felt, Moira and her sweet sad sister, when they stepped outside on their perfectly contoured blacktop plateau and looked up into the airy blue reaches of the sky with that persistent golden sun hanging in the middle of it. Disappointed? Frustrated? Sorry God hadn't made us all as color-blind as dogs? Maybe they ought to just go ahead and dome the place—sure, just like a baseball stadium, and they could paint the underside of the thing Arctic white. Or avoid daylight altogether. A good starlit night wouldn't interfere with the scheme at all.

Do I sound bitter? I was bitter—and disgusted with myself for being party to the whole fiasco. It was so negative, so final, so life-quenching and drab. Moira was sick, and her heart and mind must have been as black as her sister's dresses, but Caitlin—I couldn't believe she was that far gone. Not after the day we'd spent drinking beer and reminiscing or the way she smiled at me and spoke my name, my real name, and not some bughouse invention (and who *was* Vincent, I'd like to know?). No, there was feeling there, I was sure of it, and sensitivity and sweetness too. And need. A whole lot of need. That was why I found myself slowing outside their fence as I came and went from one job or another, hoping to catch a glimpse of Caitlin backing her Mercedes out into the street or collecting the mail, but all I ever saw was the blank white field of the fence.

Then, early one evening as I lay soaking in the tub, trying to scrub the deep verdigris stains of Miracle-Gro off my hands and forearms, the phone rang. I got to it, dripping, on the fifth ring. Caitlin was on the other end. "Larry," she said, "hi. Listen," she said, her voice soft and breathy, "I kind of miss you, I mean, not seeing you around. I'd like to offer you a beer sometime—"

"Be right over," I said.

It was high summer and still light out when I got there, the streets bathed in a soft, milky luminescence, swallowtails leaping in the air, bougainvillea, hibiscus, Euryops and oleander blazing against the fall of night. I'd automatically thrown on a pair of black jeans and an unadorned white T-shirt, but as I was going out the door I reached in the coat closet and pulled out a kelly-green sport coat I'd bought for St. Patrick's Day one year, the sort of thing you regret having spent good money on the minute the last beer is drained and the fiddler stops fiddling. But by my lights, what Caitlin needed was a little color in her life, and I was the man to give it to her. I stopped by the florist's on my way and got her a dozen long-stemmed roses, and I didn't look twice at the white ones. No, the roses I picked were as deep and true as everything worth living for, red roses, bright red roses, roses that flowed up out of their verdant stems like blood from an open artery.

I punched in the code at the gate and wheeled my pickup into the vast parking lot that was their yard and parked beside the front steps (the color of my truck, incidentally, is white, albeit a beat-up, battered and very dirty shade of it). Anyway, I climbed out of my white truck in my black jeans, white shirt and kelly-green jacket and moved across the blacktop and up the white steps with the blood-red roses clutched under one arm.

Caitlin answered the door. "Larry," she murmured, letting her eyes stray from my face to the jacket and back again, "I'm glad you could come. Did you eat yet?"

I had. A slime burger, death fries and a side dish of fermented slaw at the local greasy spoon. I could have lied, trying to hold the picture of her whipping up a mud pie or blackened sole with mashed potatoes or black beans, but food wasn't what I'd come for. "Yeah," I said, "on my way home from work. Why? You want to go out?"

We were in the front hall now, in a black-and-white world, no shade of gray even, the checkered tiles gleaming, ebony chairs, a lacquered Japanese cabinet. She gave me her black-lipped smile. "Me?" she said. "Uh-uh. No. I don't want to go out." A pause. "I want to go to bed."

In bed, after I discovered she was black and white without her clothes on too, we sipped stout and porter and contemplated the scintillating roses, set in a white vase against a white wall like a trompe l'oeil. And we talked. Talked about love and need and loss, talked about the world and its tastes and colors, and talked round and round the one subject that stood between us. We'd become very close for the second time and were lying in each other's arms, all the black lipstick kissed off her, when I came back to the question I'd posed in the kitchen the last time we'd talked. "So," I said. "Okay. It's a long story, but the night's long too, and I tell you, I don't feel the least bit sleepy. Come on, the black and white. Tell me."

It would make a better story if there was some sort of "Rose for Emily" thing going on, if Moira had been left at the altar in her white satin and veil or seduced and abandoned by some neon hippie in an iridescent pink shirt and tie-dyed jacket, but that wasn't it at all. She was just depressed. Afraid of the world. In need of control. "But what about you?" I said, searching Caitlin's eyes. "You feel that way too?"

We were naked, in each other's arms, stretched the length of the bed. She shrugged. "Sort of," she said. "When we were girls, before we moved to New York, Moira and I used to watch TV, everything in black and white, Fred MacMurray, Donna Reed, *Father Knows Best,* and we had a game, a competition really, to see who could make her room like that, like the world of those shows, where everything turned out right in the end. I wanted white, but Moira was older, so I got black."

There was more, but the next line—"Our parents didn't like it, of course"—didn't come from Caitlin, but her sister. Maybe I'd closed my eyes a minute, I don't know, but suddenly there she was, all in white and perched at the end of the bed. Her mouth was drawn up in a little bow, as if the whole scene was distasteful to her, but she looked at me without blinking. "In New York, everything was pink, chiffon and lace, peach, champagne, the pink of little girls and blushing maidens. That was what Daddy wanted—and his wife too. Little girls. Normal, sweet, curtsying and respectfully whispering little girls who'd climb up into his lap for a bedtime story. I was sixteen at the time, Vincent; Caitlin was fourteen. Can you see? Can you?"

I pulled the black sheets up to my hips, trying to calm the pounding in my chest. This was an unusual situation, to say the least—as I say, I'd been around, but this was out of my league altogether. I wanted to say something, but I couldn't for the life of me guess what that might be. My right arm lay under the luxurious weight of Caitlin's shoulders; I gave them a squeeze to reassure myself.

"Oh, it's nothing like that, Larry," Caitlin said, anticipating me. "Nothing dirty. But Daddy wanted an end to black and white, and we—we didn't. Did we, Moira?"

Moira was staring off across the room to where the night hung in the windows, absolute and unadulterated. "No, Caitly, we didn't. And we showed them, didn't we?"

I felt Caitlin tense beside me. I wanted nothing in that moment but to leap up out of the bed, pull the ridiculous green jacket over my head and sprint for my truck. But instead I heard myself asking, "How?"

Both sisters laughed then, a low rasping laugh caught deep in their throats, and there wasn't a whole lot of hilarity in it. "Oh, I don't know, Vincent," Moira said, throwing her head back to laugh again, and then coming back to me with a hand pattering at her breast. "Let's just say that colors can get out of hand sometimes, if you know what I mean."

"Fire is our friend," Caitlin said, leaving a little hiatus after the final syllable.

"If you *respect* it," Moira chimed in, and they both laughed again. I pulled the sheet up a little farther. Caitlin had lit a pair of tapering black candles when the sky had gone dark, and I stared into the unsteady flame of them now, watching the yellow ribbons of light die back and re-create themselves over and over. There wasn't a sound in the world.

"And Vincent," Moira said, turning back to me, "if you're going to be seeing my sister on any sort of regular basis, I have to tell you you're simply not white enough. There'll be no more outdoor work, that's out of the question." She let out another laugh, but this one at least had a little life in it. "You wouldn't want to end up looking like your surfer friend, would you?"

The silence held. I could hear the two sisters breathing gently, almost in unison, and it was as if they were breathing for me, and I'd never felt so tranquil and volitionless in my life. Whiteness loomed, the pale ethereality of nothingness, and blackness too, the black of a dreamless sleep. I closed my eyes. I could feel my head sinking into the pillow as if into the ancient mud of an untracked forest.

"Oh, and Vincent, one more thing," Moria said, and I opened my eyes long enough to see her cross the room and dump the roses in the wastebasket. "Dye your hair, will you?"

(1997)

Death of the Cool

First there were the kids on the beach. What were they, fifteen, sixteen? Big ugly kids in big shorts with haircuts right out of a 1963 yearbook, all thatch and no shag, but what did they know about 1963? They were drunk, one-thirty in the afternoon, and they'd lifted a pint of tequila and a forty-ouncer from the convenience store or raided somebody's mother's liquor cabinet, and so what if he'd done the same sort of thing himself when he was their age, so *what?*—that was then and this was now. Drunk, and they had a dog with them, a retriever that had something else in it around the ears and snout and in the frantic splay of the rear legs. They were throwing a stick—an old scrap of flotsam spotted with tar and barnacles—and the dog was bringing it back to them. Every time the exchange was made and the stick went hurtling back into the ribbon of the surf, they collapsed with the hilarity of it, pounded each other's freshly tattooed shoulders and melted right into the sand, because there was nothing under the sun funnier than this. Come to think of it, they were probably stoned too.

"You want to buy a dog?" they were shouting at everybody who came up the beach. "Cheap. He's real cheap."

They asked him—they asked Edison, Edison Banks—as he kicked through the sand to lay out his towel in the place tucked into the rocks where he'd been coming every afternoon for a week now to stretch out and ease the ache in his knee. He'd just had arthroscopic surgery on the right knee and it was weak and the Tylenol-codeine tabs they'd given him were barely scratching the surface of the pain. But walking in the sand was a good thing—it strengthened the muscles, or so the surgeon told him. "Hey, man," the ugliest of the three kids had shouted, "you want to buy a dog?"

Edison was wearing a pair of shorts nearly as big as the stiffened shrouds they'd somehow managed to prop up on their nonexistent hips, and he had his Lakers cap on backwards and an oversized T-shirt and beads, the beads he'd been wearing since beads were invented back in 1969. "No, thanks," he said, a little ruffled, a little pissed off at the world in general and these three kids in particular, "—I had one for breakfast."

That was the end of the exchange, and on a better day, that would have been the end of the encounter and let's turn the page and get on with it. Edison wanted to lie in the sun, shuffle through the deep sand above tideline for maybe a hundred yards in each direction, thrash his arms in the surf a bit and let the codeine work on the pain till cocktail hour, and that was it, that was the day he was envisioning, with dinner out and maybe a movie after that. But the kids wouldn't let it rest. They didn't recognize Edison as one of their own, didn't appreciate his wit, his graying soul beard and the silver stud in his left ear. They saw him as a gimpy, pinch-faced old relic, in the same camp as their facially rejuvenated mothers, vanished fathers, and the various teachers, principals, deputy sheriffs and dance club bouncers who washed through their lives each day like some stinking red tide. They gave him a cold sneer and went back to the dog.

And *that* would have been it, but no sooner had Edison stretched out on his towel and dug out the sunblock and his book than the stick came rocketing his way. And after the stick, half a beat later, came the dog, the wet dog, the heaving, whimpering, sand-spewing whipcrack of a wet dog with a wet smell all its own. The stick vanished, only to come thumping back at him, this time landing no more than two feet away, so that the sand kicked up in his face. Were they trying to provoke him, was that it? Or were they just drunk and oblivious? Not that it mattered. Because if that stick came his way one more time, he was going to go ballistic.

He tried to focus on the page, his eyes stinging with sweat, the smell of the sunblock bringing him back to the beaches of the past, the sun like a firm hot hand pressing down on his shoulders and the heavy knots of his calves. The book wasn't much—some tripe about a one-armed lady detective solving crimes in a beach town full of rich people very much like the one he was living in—but it had been there on the hall table when he was limping out the door, a relic of Kim. Kim had been gone three weeks now, vanished along with the Z3 he'd bought her, an armload of jewelry and a healthy selection of off-the-shoulder dresses and open-toed shoes. He expected to hear from her lawyer any day now. And the credit card company. Them too, of course.

When it came this time, the final time, the stick was so close it whirred in his ears like a boomerang, and before he could react—or even duck—it was there, right at his elbow, and the black panting form of the dog was already hurtling over him in an explosion of sand and saliva. He dropped the book and shoved himself up out of the sand, the tide pulling back all along the beach with a long, slow sigh, gulls crying out, children shrieking in the surf. They were smirking, the three of them, laughing at him, though now that he was on his feet, now that he was advancing on them, the line of his mouth drawn tight and the veins pounding in his neck, the smirks died on their faces. "Hey, Jack," he snarled in his nastiest New York-transplanted-to-California voice, "would you mind throwing that fucking stick someplace else? Or do I have to shove it up your ass?"

They were kids, lean and loose, flat stomachs, the beginner's muscles starting to show in their upper arms and shoulders like a long-delayed promise, just kids, and he was a man—and a man in pretty good shape too, aside from the knee. He had the authority here. This was his beach—or the community's, and he was a member of the community, paying enough in taxes each year to repave all the roads personally and buy the entire police force new uniforms and gold-capped nightsticks to boot. There were no dogs allowed on this beach, unless they were leashed (*Dogs Required on Leash,* the sign said, and he would joke to Kim that they had to get a dog and leash him or they were out of compliance with the law), and there was no drinking here either, especially underage drinking.

One of the kids, the one with the black crewcut and dodgy eyes, murmured an apology—"We didn't realize," or something to that effect—but the big one, the ugly one, the one who'd started all this in the first place by giving him that wiseass crap about did he want to buy a dog, just stood his ground and said, "My name isn't Jack."

Nobody moved. Edison swayed over the prop of his good leg, the right knee still red and swollen, and the two blond kids—they were brothers, he saw that in a flash, something in the pinched mouths and the eyes that were squeezed too close together, as if there weren't enough room on the canvas—crossed their arms over their tanned chests and gave him a look of contempt.

"All right," he said, "fine. Maybe you want to tell me what your name is then, huh?"

Up on the street, on the ridge behind the beach, a woman in an aquamarine Porsche Boxster swung into the last open spot in a long line of parked cars, pausing to let a trio of cyclists glide silently past. The palms rose rigid above her. There was no breath of wind. "I don't have to tell you nothing," the kid said, and his hands were shaking as he drew the stub of a joint out of one of the pouches in his shorts and put a match to it. "You know what I say? I say fuck you, Mister."

And here was the dog, trembling all over, a flowing rill of muscle, dropping the stick at the kid's feet, and "No," Edison said, his voice like an explosion in his own ears, "no, fuck *you!*"

He was ten feet from them, fifteen maybe, so imprisoned in the moment he couldn't see the futility of it, standing there on the public beach trading curses with a bunch of drunk and terminally disaffected kids, kids a third his age, mere kids. What was it? What did they see in him? And why him? Why him and not one of the real geeks and geezers strung out up and down the beach with their potbellies and skinny pale legs and the Speedos that clung to their cracks like geriatric diapers?

That was when the tall kid snatched the stick out of the dog's mouth and flung it directly at Edison with everything he had, a savage downward chop of the arm that slammed the thing into his chest with so much force he found himself sprawling backwards in the sand even as the kids took to their feet and the harsh, high laughter rang in his ears.

Then it was the bar, the scene at the bar at four o'clock in the afternoon, when the sun was still high and nobody was there. Edison didn't even bother to go home and change. He hadn't gone near the water—he was too furious, too pissed off, burned up, rubbed raw—and aside from a confectioner's sprinkle of dry sand on his ankle and the dark stain in the center of his T-shirt, no one would have guessed he'd been to the beach, and what if they did? This was California, beach city, where the guy sitting next to you in the bleached-out shirt and dollar-twenty-nine Kmart flip-flops was probably worth more than the GNP of half a dozen third world countries. But there was nobody sitting next to him today—the place was deserted. There was only the bartender, the shrine to booze behind him, and a tall slim cocktail waitress with blue eyes, dimples and hair that glistened like the black specks of tar on the beach.

He ordered a top-shelf margarita on the rocks, no salt, and morosely chewed a handful of bar mix that looked and tasted like individual bits of laminated sawdust, his dark blood-flecked eyes sweeping the room, from TV to waitress to the mirror behind the bar and back again. His heart was still pounding, though he'd left the beach half an hour ago, humiliated, decrepit, feeling like the thousand-year-old man as he gathered up his things and limped up the steps to his car. It was irrational, he knew it, a no-win situation, but all he could think about was revenge—Revenge? Murder was more like it—and he methodically combed the street along the beach, up one narrow lane and down another, looking for any sign of his three antagonists. Every time he came round a bend and saw movement up ahead, he was sure it would be them, drunk and stoned and with their guard down, whacking one another with rolled-up towels, shoving and jostling, crowing at the world. He'd take them by surprise, jerk the wheel, and slice in at the curb to cut them off, and then he'd be on them, slamming the tall kid's face, over and over, till there was no more smirk left in him. . . .

"You want another one?" the bartender was asking. Edison had seen him before—he was the day man and Edison didn't know his name and he didn't know Edison's—and he had no opinion about him one way or the other. He was young, twenty-eight, thirty maybe, with a deep tan and the same basic haircut as the kids on the beach, though it wasn't cut so close to the scalp. Edison decided he liked him, liked the look of him, with his surfer's build and the streaks of gold in his hair and the smile that said he was just enjoying the hell out of every goddamned minute of life on this earth.

"Yeah, sure," Edison said, and he found that the first drink, in combination with the codeine, had made his words run down like an unoiled machine, all the parts gummed up and locked in place, "and let me maybe see the bar menu. You got a bar menu?"

The cocktail waitress—she was stunning, she really was, a tall girl, taller than the bartender, with nice legs and outstanding feet perched up high on a pair of black clogs—flashed her dimpled smile when Edison cocked his head to include her in the field of conversation.

Sure they had a bar menu, sure, but they really wouldn't have anything more than crudités or a salad till the kitchen opened up for dinner at six—was that all right, or would he rather wait? Edison caught sight of himself in the mirror in back of the bar then, and it shook him. At first he didn't even recognize himself, sure that some pathetic older guy had slipped onto the stool beside him while he was distracted by the waitress, but no, there was the backwards Lakers cap and the shades and the drawn-down sinkhole of his mouth over the soul beard and the chin that wasn't nearly as firm as it should have been. And his skin—how had his skin got so yellow? Was it hepatitis? Was he drinking too much?

The bartender moved off down the bar to rub at an imaginary speck on the mahogany surface and convert half a dozen limes into neat wedges, and the cocktail waitress was suddenly busy with the cash register. On the TV, just above the threshold of sound, somebody was whispering about the mechanics of golf while the camera flowed over an expanse of emerald fairways and a tiny white ball rose up into the sky in a distant looping trajectory. A long moment hung suspended, along with the ball, and Edison was trying not to think about what had happened on the beach, but there it was, nagging at him like grief, and then the bartender was standing in front of him again. "You decide yet?"

"I think I'll," Edison began, and at that moment the door swung open and a woman with a wild shag of bleached hair slipped in and took a seat three stools down, "I'll . . . I don't know, I think I'll wait."

Who was she? He'd seen her around town, he was sure of it.

"Hi, Carlton," she said, waving two fingers at the bartender while simultaneously swinging round to chirp "Hi, Elise" at the waitress. And then, shifting back into position on the stool, she gave Edison a long cool look of appraisal and said hi to him too. "Martini," she instructed the bartender, "three olives, up. And give me a water back. I'm dying."

She was a big girl, big in the way of the jeans model who'd married that old tottering cadaver of a millionaire a few years back and then disappeared from the face of the earth, big but sexy, very sexy, showing off what she had in a tight black top—and how long had it been since Kim had left? Edison, the T-shirt still damp over his breastbone, smiled back.

He initiated the conversation. He'd seen her around, hadn't he? Yes, she had a condo just down the street. Did she come in here often? A shrug. The roots of her hair were black, and she dug her fingers deep into them, massaging as she talked. "Couple times a week maybe."

"I'm Edison," he said, smiling like he meant it, and he did. "And you're—?"

"I'm Sukie."

"Cool," Edison said, in his element now, smiling, smiling. "I've never known anybody named Sukie. Is that your real name?"

She dug her fingers into her scalp, gave her head a snap so that the whole towering shako of her hair came to life. "No," she said.

"It's a nickname?"

"No."

"You don't want to tell me your real name? Is that it?"

She shrugged, an elegant big-shouldered gesture that rippled all the way down her body and settled in one gently rocking ankle. She was wearing a long blue print skirt and sandals. Earrings. Makeup. And how old was she? Thirty-five, he figured. Thirty-five and divorced. "What about you?" she said. "What kind of name is Edison?"

Now it was his turn. He lifted both hands and flashed open the palms. "My father thought I was going to be an inventor. But maybe you've heard of me, my band, I mean—I had an eponymous rock band a few years back."

She just blinked.

"*Edison Banks.* You ever hear of them—of us, I mean? Early eighties? Warner Brothers? The *Downtown* LP?"

No, she hadn't heard of anything.

All right. He knew how to play this, though he was out of practice. Back off—"We weren't all that big, really, I don't know"—and then a casual mention of the real firepower he could bring to the table. "That was before I got into TV."

And now the scene shifted yet again, because before she could compress her lips in a little moue and coo "Tee-vee?" the door swung open, loudly, and brought in the sun and the street and three guys in suits, all of them young, with haircuts that chased them around the ears and teeth that should have been captured on billboards for the dental hygienists' national convention. One of them, as it turned out, would turn out to be Lyle, and when she saw him come through the door, Sukie froze just for the briefest slice of an instant, but Edison saw it, and registered it, and filed it away.

The roar went down the other end of the bar, and Edison asked her if she'd like another drink. "No," she said, "I don't think so. But it's been nice talking to you," and already she was shifting away from the stool to reach for her purse.

"How about a phone number?" he said. "We could do dinner or something—sometime, I mean."

She was on her feet now, looking down at him, the purse clutched in her hand. "No," she said, and she shook her head till her hair snatched up all the light in the room, "no, I don't think so."

Edison had another drink. The sun slid down the sky to where it should have been all along. He gazed out idly across the street and admired the way the sunlight sat in the crowns of the palms and sank into the grip of the mountains beyond. Cars drifted lazily by. He watched a couple turn the corner and seat themselves under a green umbrella on the patio of the restaurant across the way. For the briefest moment the face of his humiliation rose up in his mind—the kid's face, the poised stick—but he fought it down and thumbed through a copy of the village paper, just to have something to do while he sucked at his sweet-sour drink and chewed his way through another dish of sawdust pellets.

He read of somebody's elaborate wedding ("fifteen thousand dollars on sushi alone"), the booming real estate market, and the latest movie star to buy up one of the estates in the hills, browsed the wine column ("a dramatic nose of dried cherries and smoked meat with a nicely defined mineral finish"), then settled on an item about a discerning burglar who operated by daylight, entering area homes through unlocked doors and ground-floor windows to make off with all the jewelry he could carry—as long as it was of the very highest quality, that is. Paste didn't interest him, nor apparently did carpets, electronics, vases or artwork. Edison mulled that over: a burglar, a discerning burglar. The brazenness it must take—just strolling up the walk and knocking on the front door, hello, is anybody home? And if they were, he was selling magazine subscriptions or looking for a lost cat. What a way to make a living. Something for those little shits on the beach to aspire to.

By the time he looked up to order his fourth drink, the place had begun to fill up. The cocktail waitress—Elise, he had to remember her name, and the bartender's too, but what was it?—was striding back and forth on her long legs, a tray of drinks held high above the jostling crowd. Up on the TV in the corner the scene had shifted from golf to baseball, fairways and greens giving way to the long, dense grass of the outfield—or was it artificial turf, a big foam mat with Easter basket fluff laid over it? He was thinking he should just eat and get it over with, ask what's his name for the menu and order something right at the bar and then hang out for a while and see what developed. Home was too depressing. All that was waiting for him at home was the channel changer and a thirty-two-ounce packet of frozen peas to wrap around his bad knee. And that killed him: where was Kim when he needed her, when he was in pain and could barely get around? What did she care? She had her car and her credit cards and probably by now some new sucker to take to the dance—

"Excuse me," somebody was saying at his elbow, and he looked up into the face of one of the men who'd come in earlier, the one the big blonde had reacted to. "I don't mean to bother you, but aren't you Edison Banks?"

The codeine was sludge in his veins, and his knee—he'd forgotten he had a knee—but he peeled off his sunglasses and gave the man a smile. "That's right," he said, and he would never admit to himself that he was pleased, but he was. He'd lived here three years now, and nobody knew who he was, not even the mailman or the girl who counted out his money at the bank.

"I'm Lyle," the man was saying, and then they were locked palm to palm in a rollicking soul shake, "Lyle Hansen, and I can't tell you how cool this is. I mean, I'm a big fan. *Savage Street* was the coolest thing in the history of TV, and I mean that—it got me through high school, and that was a bad time for me, real adolescent hell, with like all the rules and the regimentation and my parents coming down on me for every little minor thing—shit, *Savage Street* was my *life*."

Edison took hold of his drink, the comforting feel of the glass in his hand, the faces at the bar, dark blue shadows leaning into the building across the street. There was a trip-hop tune playing on the jukebox, a languid slow female vocal over an industrial storm of guitars and percussion that managed to be poignant and ominous at the same time, and it felt right. Just right.

"Listen, I didn't mean to intrude or anything—"

Edison waved a hand. "No problem, man, it's cool, it's all right."

Lyle looked to be about the same age as the bartender, which meant he would have been out of high school for ten or twelve years. He wore his hair longer than the bartender's, combed back up off his forehead with enough mousse to sustain it and the odd strand dangling loose in front. He kept shifting from foot to foot, rattling the keys in his pocket, tugging at his tie, and his smile flashed and flashed again. "Hey, Carlton," he spoke into the din, "give me another one, will you—and one for Mr. Banks here too. On me."

"No, no," Edison protested, "you don't have to do that," but the money was on the bar, and the drink appeared in a fresh glass.

"So you wrote *and* produced that show, right?"

"Shit, I *created* it. You know, when you see the titles and it says 'Created By'? I wrote the first two seasons, then left it to them. Why work when you can play, right?"

Lyle was drinking shooters of Herradura out of a slim tube of a glass. He threw back the current one, then slapped his forehead as if he'd been stung. "I can't believe it. Here I am talking to Edison Banks. You know, when you moved into town, like what was it, three, four years ago?"

"Three."

"Yeah, I read that article in the paper about you and I thought wow—you were the guitarist for Edison Banks too, right? I had both their albums, New Wave, right? But what I really dig is jazz. Miles Davis. Monk. That era stuff."

Edison felt a weight lift off him. "I've been a jazz fan all my life," he said, the alcohol flaring up in him till the whole place was on fire with it, mystical fire, burning out of the bottles and the light fixtures and the golden shining faces lined up at the bar. "Since I was a kid of fifteen anyway, hopping the subway up to Harlem and bullshitting my way into the clubs. I've got everything—*Birth of the Cool, Sketches,* all the Coltrane stuff, Sonny Rollins, Charles Lloyd, Ornette, Mulligan—and all of it on the original LPs too."

Lyle set both hands down on the bar, as if to brace himself. He was wearing a pinkie ring that featured a silver skull, and the rough edge of a tattoo showed at the base of his left wrist where the cuff climbed up his arm. "You might think I'm just some suit or something," he said, "but that's not me at all." He plucked at his lapels. "See this? This is my first day on the job. Real estate. That's where the money is. But I tell you, I'd love to hear some of that shit with you—I mean, *Miles*. Wow. And I know what you're saying—CDs just don't cut it like vinyl."

And Edison, in the shank of a bad evening that had begun to turn clement after all, turned to him and said, "I'm up at the corner of Dolores and San Ignacio—big Spanish place with the tile roof? Come by anytime, man—anytime, no problem." And then he looked up to see the waitress—Elise—glide by like a ballerina, that's what she was like, a ballerina, with her bare arms held high and the tray levitating above her head. He had to get home. Had to eat. Feed the cat. Collapse in front of the tube. "Just don't come between maybe one and four—that's when I'm down at the beach."

In the morning, the dryness in the back of his throat told him he'd drunk too much the night before—that and a fuzziness between his ears, as if his head were a radio caught between stations—and he took two of the Tylenol-codeine tabs to ease his transition into the day. Theoretically, he was working on a screenplay about the adventures of a rock band on the road as seen through the eyes of the drummer's dog, but the work had stalled even before Kim walked out, and now there was nothing there on the screen but words. He took the newspaper and a glass of orange juice out on the patio, and then he swam a couple of laps and began to feel better. The maid came at eleven and fixed him a plate of eggs and chorizo before settling into her routine with the bucket, the mop and the vacuum cleaner. Two hours later, as he sat frozen at his desk, playing his eighteenth game of computer solitaire, there was a tap at the door.

It was Orbalina, the maid. "Mr. Banks," she said, poking her head into the room, "I don't want to bother you, but I can't, I can't—" He saw that she was crying, her face creased with the geography of her grief, tears wetting her cheeks. This was nothing new—she was always sobbing over one thing or another, the tragedies that constantly befell her extended family, the way a man on TV had looked right at her as if he'd come alive right there in her own living room, the hollowness of the sky over the graveyard in Culiacán where her mother lay buried under a wooden cross. Kim used to handle her moods with a mixture of compassion and firmness that bordered on savagery; now it was up to him. "What is it?" he said. "What's the matter?"

She was in the room now, a whittled-down woman in her thirties whose weight had migrated to her haunches. "The elephants," she sobbed.

"Elephants? What elephants?"

"You know what they do to them, to the elephants?" She buried her face in her hands, then looked up at him out of eyes that were like two pools of blood. "Do you?" she demanded, her frame shaken with the winds of an unceasing emotional storm.

He didn't. His knee hurt. He had a headache. And his screenplay was shit.

"They beat them. With big, with big *sticks!*" Her hands flailed at the air. "Like this! And this! And when they get too old to work, when they fall down in the jungle with their big trees in their noses, you know what they do then? They beat them more! They do! They do! And I know what I'm saying because I saw it on the, on the"—and here her voice failed her, till her final words were so soft and muted they might have been a prayer—"on the TV."

He was on his feet now, the screen behind him displaying seven neat rows of electronic cards, a subtle crepitating pain invading his knee, as if a rodent were trapped beneath the patella and gnawing to get out. "Listen," he said, "it's okay, don't worry about it." He wanted to take her in his arms and press her to him, but he couldn't do that because she was the maid and he the employer, so he limped past her to the door and said, "Look, I'm going to the beach, okay? You finish up here and take the rest of the day off—and tomorrow, tomorrow too."

The morning haze had burned off by the time he stepped out into the drive. The sky was a clear, depthless blue, the blue of childhood adventures, picnics, outings to Bear Mountain and the Island, the blue of good times, and he was thinking of his first wife, Sarah, thinking of Cap d'Antibes, Isla Mujeres, Molokai. They traveled in those days, on the beaten path and off it. There was no end to what he wanted to see: the Taj Mahal, the snow monkeys of Hokkaido, prayer wheels spinning idly on the naked slopes above Lhasa. They went everywhere. Saw it all. But that turned sour too, like everything else. He took a minute to duck behind a bank of Bougainvillea and empty his bladder—there was no place to pee on the beach, unless you did it surreptitiously in the flat water beyond the breakers, and since he'd hit forty he couldn't seem to go more than an hour at a time without feeling that nagging pressure in his lower abdomen. And was that cool? No, no part of it was even remotely cool—it was called getting old.

There was a discolored place on the floor of the garage where Kim's car had been, a kind of permanent shadow, but he didn't dwell on it. He decided to take the sports car—a mint Austin-Healey 3000 he'd bought from a guy in the movie business with a garage full of them—because it made him feel good, and feeling good had been in short supply lately. The top was down, so he took a moment to rub a palmful of sunblock into the soft flesh under his eyes—no reason to wind up looking like one of the unwrapped mummies nodding over their white wine and appetizers in every café and trattoria in town. Then he adjusted his sunglasses, turned his cap backwards, and shot down the street with a modulated roar.

He'd nearly got to the beach—had actually turned into the broad, palm-lined boulevard that fronted it—before he remembered the three kids from yesterday. What if they showed up again? What if they were already there? The thought made him brake inappropriately, and the next thing he knew some jerk in a four-by-four with the frame jacked up eight feet off the ground was giving him the horn—and the finger. Normally, he would have had a fit—it was a New York thing, turf wars, attitude—but he was so put out he just pulled over meekly and let the jerk go by.

But then he told himself he wasn't about to be chased off his own beach by anybody, especially not some punk-ass kids who wouldn't know one end of hip from the other. He found a spot to park right across from the steps down to the beach and pulled his things out of the trunk with a quick angry jerk of his arm—if he could run, if he could only run, he'd chase them down till their stinking weed-choked little punk lungs gave out, even if it took miles. The shits. The little shits. He was breathing hard, sweating under the band of the cap.

Then he was on the concrete steps, the Pacific opening up before him in an endless array of waves, that cool, fathomless smell on the air, the white crescent of the beach, blankets and umbrellas spread out across the sand as far as he could see in either direction. There was something about the scene that always lightened his mood, no matter how sorry for himself he was feeling. That was one thing he could never understand about Kim. Kim didn't like the beach. Too much sun. Bad for the skin. And the sand—the sand was just another kind of grit, and she always bitched when she found a white spill of it on the carpet in the hall. But she liked it when he came home to her all aflame because he'd just watched a hundred women strip down to the essentials and rub themselves all over with the sweetest unguents and emollients an eight-ounce tube could hold. She liked that, all right.

He was halfway down the steps, studying a pair of girls descending ahead of him, when he heard the high, frenzied barking of the dog. There they were, the three of them, in their boxcar shorts and thatch haircuts, laughing and jiving, throwing the stick as if nothing had happened. And nothing had, not to them anyway. Edison froze, right there, six steps down. It was as if he were paralyzed, as if he'd suffered a stroke as he reached for the iron rail and set one gimpy leg down in front of the other. An older couple, trainwrecks of the flesh, brushed past him, then a young mother trailing kids and plastic buckets. He could not move. The dog barked. There was a shout from down the beach. The stick flew.

And then, patting down his pockets as if he'd forgotten something, he swung slowly round and limped up the steps. For a long moment he sat in the car, fiddling with the tuner until he found a rap station, and he cranked it as loud as it would go, though he hated the music, hated it. Finally he slammed the car in gear and took off with a lurch, the thunderous bass and hammering lyrics thrusting a dagger into the corpse of the afternoon, over and over, all the way down the street.

He thought of the bar—of lunch at the bar and a cocktail to pull the codeine up out of whatever hole it was hiding in—but he didn't have the heart for it. He was Edison Banks. He'd had his own band. He'd created *Savage Street.* He didn't eat lunch at one-thirty in the afternoon, and he didn't eat lunch alone either—or drink anything, even wine, before five o'clock. That was what the rest of them did, all his hopeless washed-out diamond-encrusted neighbors: they ate lunch. And then they had a couple of cocktails and bought flowers from the flower girl in the short skirt before picking up their prescriptions at the drugstore, and by then it was cocktail hour and they drank cocktails and ate dinner. Or ordered it anyway.

He burned up the tires for the next half hour, taking the turns like a suicide—or a teenager, a thatch-headed, flat-stomached, stick-throwing teenager—and then the engine started to overheat and he switched off the radio and crawled back home like one of the living dead in their ancient Jags and Benzes. A nap, that was what he was thinking, elevate the knee, wrap the frozen peas round it, and doze over a book by the pool—where at least it was private. He winced when he climbed out of the car and put some weight on his right leg, but the peas and another codeine tab would take care of that, and he came up the back walk feeling nothing. He was digging for his keys, the sun pushing down like a weight on his shoulders while a pair of hummingbirds stitched the air with iridescent feints and dodges and the palms along the walk nodded in the faintest stirrings of a breeze, when he saw that the back door was open.

And that was odd, because he was sure he'd shut and locked it when he left. Kim might have been clueless about security, leaving her handbag on the front seat of the car where anybody could see it, running out of the house with her makeup half on and never thinking twice about the door gaping behind her, but he was a rock. He never forgot anything, even when his brain was fuzzed with the little white pills the doctor kept feeding him. He wouldn't have left the door open. He couldn't have. His next thought was for the maid—she must not have left yet. But then he glanced over his shoulder, down the slope and past the fence to the spot out on the public road where she always parked her dirt-brown Corolla. It wasn't there.

He shut the door behind him, thinking he'd have to talk to her about that, about walking off and leaving the place wide open—there was no excuse for it, even if she was distraught about the fate of the elephants or her sister's latest lumpectomy. In the kitchen, he fought the childproof cap of the prescription bottle and chased down a pill with a glass of cranberry juice. He'd just pulled open the freezer to reach for the peas when a sound from above made him catch his breath. It was a furtive sound, the soft friction of wood on wood—as of a dresser drawer, antique oak, slightly balky, sliding open. He didn't breathe again until he heard the faint squeal of the drawer going back in, and the answering echo of the next one falling open.

Edison kept three guns in the house, identical Smith & Wesson 9mm stainless steel pistols, two of which had never been fired, and he went now for the one he kept in a cubicle in the pantry, behind the old telephone books. He held it in his hand a long while, listening, then made sure it was loaded, flicked off the safety, and started up the stairs. It was very quiet. Shadows collided on the walls above him, and the air was thick with motes of dust and the lazy circling attentions of the flies at the upstairs window. He was in his own house, among familiar things, but everything seemed distorted and unfamiliar, because he'd never before gone up these stairs with a gun in his hand—and yet he didn't feel nervous or tense, or not particularly. He felt like a hunter in an air-conditioned forest.

When he crept into the bedroom—the master bedroom, the place where he'd slept alone in the big antique bed for the past three weeks—there was a man there, his back to the door, his arms and shoulders busy with the work at hand. A phrase came into Edison's head: *rifling the drawers.* And then another one, one he'd heard on TV a thousand times—used himself in too many episodes of *Savage Street* to count: *Freeze.* And that's what he said now, in a kind of bark, and he couldn't help appending an epithet to it, for maximum effect. "Freeze, motherfucker," that's what he said. "Freeze, motherfucker!"

That was when Lyle, dressed in the same pale European-cut suit he'd been wearing the night before, turned around, his hands at his sides. "Hey, man," he said, all the sunshine in the world distilled in his voice, no worries, no problems, and how do you spell California? "I just stopped by to see you, take you up on your invitation, you know? Cool house. I really dig your antiques—you the collector, or is it your wife?"

Edison had a gun in his hand. A gun he'd fired just once, at the indoor firing range, twelve bucks an hour, no target big enough for him to nail—or maybe it wasn't this gun at all. Maybe it was the one under the sink in the master bath or the one behind the drapes in the front hall. The gun was cold. It was heavy. He didn't know what to do with it now that he was holding it there in his hand like some party favor.

"Hey, come on, man, put that thing away, all right? You're scaring me." Lyle was wearing two-tone shoes and a hand-painted tie, very cool. He swept the hair back from his brow with a hand that betrayed him—a hand that was shaking. "I mean I knocked and all, but nobody answered, right? So I came in to wait for you, so we could maybe spin some sides—isn't that what you say, 'spin some sides'?"

It came to him then that Lyle was exactly like the kid on the beach, the kid grown up, all mockery and hate, all attitude. "You're the guy," Edison said. "You're the guy, aren't you?"

And there it was, the curled lip, the dead blue vacancy of the eyes. "What guy? I don't know what you're talking about, man—I mean, I come over, at *your* invitation, to, to—"

"The jewelry thief. 'The discerning burglar.' You're him, aren't you?" The knowledge went right through him, hot knowledge, knowledge like the burning needle his mother would use to probe his flesh when he came in screaming with a splinter embedded in his finger. "Let me see your pockets. Pull out your pockets."

"Spin some sides," Lyle said, but the phrase was bitter now, nasal and venomous. "Isn't that what you hepcats say, you hipsters and thin white dukes? Too cool, right?" And he pulled a necklace out of his pocket, one of the things Kim, in her haste, had left behind. He held it out for a moment, a gentle silken dangle of thin hammered gold with a cluster of jewels, and let it drop to the carpet. "Let me tell you something, *Edison*—your show sucked. Even back then it was a joke—me and my buds'd get stoned and laugh at it, you know that? And your band—your pathetic band—was even worse."

Outside, beyond Lyle, beyond the blinds and the curtains, the sun was spread over everything like the richest cream, and the window that framed it all was like nothing so much as an outsized TV screen. Edison felt something in him die, droop down and die like some wilted plant, and he wondered if it was the codeine or what it was. It came almost as a surprise to him to glance down and see that he was still holding on to the gun.

Lyle leaned back against the dresser and fumbled in his pocket for a cigarette, stuck it between his lips, and lit it with a quick flick of his lighter. "So what are you going to do, shoot me?" he said. "Because it's my word against yours. I mean, where's your witness? Where's the stolen property? You invited me over, right? 'Anytime, man,' isn't that what you said? And here I am, an honored guest, and maybe we had an argument and you got a little crazy—old guys are like that, aren't they? Don't they go a little crazy every once in a while?" He exhaled a blue veil of smoke. "Or shit, I mean I was just up here checking out my listings, I thought this was going to be an open house, and I wander in, innocent, totally innocent, and suddenly there's this guy with a gun . . . and who is it? It's you."

"That's right," Edison said, "it's me. Edison Banks. And who the fuck are you? What did you ever write? How many albums did you record? Huh?"

Lyle put the cigarette to his lips, and Edison watched the coal go red with the rush of oxygen. He had nothing to say, but his look—it was the look of the kid on the beach all over again. Exactly. Exactly that. But this time there would be no footrace, because Edison had already caught up.

(1999)

My Widow

Cat Person

My widow likes cats. No one knows exactly how many cats inhabit the big solid old redwood house I left her, but after several generations of inbreeding and depositing fecal matter in select corners and in an ever-growing mound on the mantelpiece, their numbers must reach into the thirties, perhaps even the forties. There are cats draped like bunting over every horizontal surface in the house, and when they mew in concert for their cat chow and their tins of mashed fish heads, the noise is enough to wake the dead, if you'll pardon the expression. She sleeps with these cats, my widow does, or at least as many of them as the antique bed, with its questionable sheets and cat-greased quilt, can accommodate, and all night and into the burgeoning sun-dappled hours of the early morning, there is a ceaseless movement of limb and tongue and the lazy twitching of feline tails. In addition to the cats, my widow once had a pair of vocal and energetic little dogs, of a breed whose name I could never remember, but both have long since run off or been crushed to marrow out on the busy street that winds up from the village and past the rear gate of the house. She had a ferret too, for a while, though ferrets are illegal in the state of California. It didn't last long. After throttling and partially dismembering a litter of week-old kittens, the animal secreted itself in the crawl space under the house, where it took sick and died. Even now, its mummified corpse subsides gradually into the immemorial dust beneath the floorboards of the kitchen, just under the place where the refrigerator rests, going quietly about its work.

One afternoon, a day or two after the first rain of the winter has converted the dry creek bed out back into a sluice of braided, sepia-colored ripples and long, trailing ropes of eucalyptus bark, my window is startled by a persistent thumping from the far end of the house. She is, as always, in the kitchen, peering into a steaming pot of chicken-vegetable soup, the only thing she ingests these days, aside from the odd slab of indifferently grilled flank steak and coffee so acidic it's taken the glaze off the ceramic cup our son made her when he was in the sixth grade. The doorbell, which in my day chimed a carillon from Beethoven's "Ode to Joy," is long since defunct, and so my widow takes a while to register the notion that someone is knocking at the front door. The front door, is, after all, a good sixty paces from the kitchen, out the kitchen door and down the long L-shaped hall that leads to the entryway and the grand room beyond it, now a refuge for cats. Still, that is unmistakably the sound of knocking, and you can see the alertness come into her eyes—it could be the postman, she's thinking, who just the other day (or was it the other week?) brought her a letter from our son, who lives and works in Calcutta, dispensing cornmeal mush and clean bandages to the mendicants there. "I'm coming!" my widow calls in her creaking, octave-challenged voice, and she sets down the stirring spoon amidst the debris of what once was the kitchen counter, wipes her hands on her flannel nightgown, and moves slowly but resolutely down the hall to answer the door.

Standing on the brick doorstep, plainly visible through the ancient flowing glass of the front door, is a young woman in shorts, leggings and some sort of athletic jersey, with stringy black hair, terrible posture, and what appears to be a fur muff tucked under one arm. As my widow gets closer and the indefinite becomes concrete, she sees that the young woman's eyes are heavily made up, and that the muff has become a kitten of indeterminate breed—black, with a white chest and two white socks. Curious, and pursing her lips in the way she used to when she was a young woman herself, my widow swings open the door and stands there blinking and mute, awaiting an explanation.

"Oh, hi," the young woman says, squeezing the words through an automatic smile, "sorry to disturb you, but I was wondering . . ." Unaccountably, the young woman trails off, and my widow, whose hearing was compromised by the Velvet Underground and Nico during a period of exuberance in the last century, watches her lips for movement. The young woman studies my widow's face a moment, then decides to change tack. "I'm your neighbor, Megan Capaldi?" she says finally. "Remember me? From the school-lunch drive last year?"

My widow, dressed in an old flannel shirt over the faded and faintly greasy flannel nightgown, does not, in fact, remember her. She remains noncommittal. Behind her, from the depths of the house, a faint mewling arises.

"I heard that you were a real cat person, and I just thought—well, my daughter April's cat had kittens, and we're looking for good homes for them, with people who really care, and this one—we call her Sniggers—is the last one left."

My widow is smiling, her face transformed into a girl's, the striations over her lip pulling back to reveal a shining and perfect set of old lady's teeth—the originals, beautifully preserved. "Yes," she says, "yes," before the question has been asked, already reaching out for the kitten with her regal old hands. She holds it to her a moment, then looks up myopically into the young woman's face. "Thanks for thinking of me," she says.

The Roof

The roof, made of a composite material guaranteed for life, leaks. My widow is in the bedroom, in bed, crocheting neat four-inch granny squares against some larger need while listening to the murmur of the TV across the room and the crashing impact of yet another storm above her, when the dripping begins. The cats are the first to notice it. One of them, a huge, bloated, square-headed tom with fur like roadkill, shifts position to avoid the cold stinging drops, inadvertently knocking two lesser cats off the west slope of the bed. A jockeying for space ensues, the cats crowding my widow's crocheting wrists and elbows and leaving a vacant spot at the foot of the bed. Even then, she thinks nothing of it. A voice emanating from the TV cries out, *They're coming—they're coming through the walls!,* followed by the usual cacophony of screams, disjointed music and masticatory sounds. The rain beats at the windows.

A long slow hour hisses by. Her feet are cold. When she rubs them together, she discovers that they are also wet. Her first thought is for the cats—have they been up to their tricks again? But no, there is a distinct patter now, as of water falling from a height, and she reaches out her hand to confront the mystery. There follows a determined shuffle through the darkened arena of the house, the close but random inspection of the ceilings with a flashlight (which itself takes half an hour to find), and then the all-night vigil over the stewpot gradually filling itself at the foot of the bed. For a while, she resumes her crocheting, but the steady mesmeric drip of the intruding rain idles her fingers and sweeps her off into a reverie of the past. She's revisiting other roofs—the attic nook of her girlhood room, the splootching nightmare of her student apartment with the dirty sit-water drooling down the wall into the pan as she heated brown rice and vegetables over the stove, the collapse of the ceiling in our first house after a pipe burst when we were away in Europe—and then she's in Europe herself, in the rain on the Grand Canal, with me, her first and most significant husband, and before long the stewpot is overflowing and she's so far away she might as well exist in another dimension.

The roofer, whose name emerged from the morass of the Yellow Pages, arrives some days later during a period of tumultuous weather and stands banging on the front door while rain drools from the corroded copper gutters (which, incidentally, are also guaranteed for life). My widow is ready for him. She's been up early each day for the past week, exchanging her flannel nightgown for a pair of jeans and a print blouse, over which she wears an old black cardigan decorated with prancing blue reindeer she once gave me for Christmas. She's combed out her hair and put on a dab of lipstick. Like Megan Capaldi before him, the roofer pounds at the redwood frame of the front door until my widow appears in the vestibule. She fumbles a moment with the glasses that hang from a cord around her neck, and then her face assumes a look of bewilderment: *Who is this infant banging at the door?*

"Hello!" calls the roofer, rattling the doorknob impatiently as my widow stands there before him on the inside of the glass panel, looking confused. "It's me—the roofer?" He's shouting now: "You said you had a leak?"

The roofer's name is Vargas D'Onofrio, and the minute he pronounces it, it's already slipped her mind. He has quick, nervous eyes, and his face is sunk into a full beard of tightly wound black hairs threaded with gray. He's in his early forties, actually, but anyone under seventy looks like a newborn to my widow, and understandably so.

"You're all wet," she observes, leading him into the house and up the slow heaving stairs to reveal the location of the leak. She wonders if she should offer to bake him cookies and maybe fix a pouch of that hot chocolate that only needs microwaved water to complete it, and she sees the two of them sitting down at the kitchen table for a nice chat after he's fixed the roof—but does she have any hot chocolate? Or nuts, shortening, brown sugar? How long has it been since she remembered to buy flour, even? She had a five-pound sack of it in the pantry—she distinctly remembers that—but then wasn't that the flour the weevils got into? She's seeing little black bugs, barely the size of three grains of pepper cobbled together, and then she understands that she doesn't want to chat with this man—or with anybody else, for that matter. She just wants the roof repaired so she can go back to the quiet seep of her old lady's life.

"Rotten weather," the roofer breathes, thumping up the stairs in his work boots and trundling on down the upper hallway to the master bedroom, scattering cats as he goes.

My widow has given up on the stewpot and has been sleeping downstairs, in what was once our son's room. As a result, the antique bed is now soaked through to the springs and oozing water the color of tobacco juice.

"I can patch it," the roofer says, after stepping out onto the sleeping porch and assaying the roof from the outside, "but you really should have the whole thing replaced once summer comes—and I can do that for you too, and give you a good price. Best price in town, in fact." The roofer produces a wide bearded closer's grin that is utterly lost on my widow.

"But that roof," she says, "was guaranteed for life."

The roofer just shrugs. "Aren't they all?" he sighs, and disappears through the door to the sleeping porch. As she pulls the door shut, my widow can smell the keen working scent of the rain loosening the earth around the overgrown flowerbeds and the vaguely fishy odor of wet pavement. The air is alive. She can see her breath in it. She watches the roofer's legs ride up past the window as he hoists himself up the ladder and into the pall of the rain. And then, as she settles into the armchair in the bedroom, she hears him up there, aloft, his heavy tread, the pounding of nails, and through it all a smell of hot burning tar.

Shopping

In her day my widow was a champion shopper. She'd been a student of anthropology in her undergraduate years, and she always maintained that a woman's job—her need, calling and compulsion—was to accumulate things against the hard times to come. Never mind that we didn't experience any hard times—aside from maybe having to pinch a bit in grad school or maxing out our credit cards when we were traveling in Japan back in the eighties—my widow was ready for anything. She shopped with a passion matched by few women of her generation. Her collections of antique jewelry, glassware, china figurines and the like would, I think, be truly valuable if she could ever find them in the cluttered caverns and dark byways of the house and basement, and the fine old Craftsman-era couches and chairs strewn through the main rooms are museum pieces, or would be, if the cats hadn't gotten to them. Even now, despite the fact that she's become increasingly withdrawn and more than a bit impatient with the fuss and hurry of the world, my widow can still get out and shop with the best of them.

On a day freshened by a hard cold breeze off the ocean, she awakens in my son's narrow bed to a welter of cats and a firm sense of purpose. Her sister, Inge, ten years her junior and unmarried, is driving up from Ventura to take her shopping at the mall for the pre-Christmas sales, and she is galvanized into action. Up and out of bed at first light, cats mewling at her feet, the crusted pot set atop the crusted burner, coffee brewing, and she slips into a nice skirt and blouse (after a prolonged search through the closet in the master bedroom, where the mattress, unfortunately, continues to ooze a brownish fluid), pulls her hair back in a bun and sits down to a breakfast of defrosted wheat bread, rancid cream cheese and jam so old it's become a culture medium. In my time, there were two newspapers to chew through and the morning news on the radio, but my widow never bothered herself much with the mechanism of receiving and paying bills (the envelope, the check, the stamp), and the newspapers have been discontinued. As for the radio, my widow prefers silence. She is thinking nothing, staring into space and slowly rotating the coffee cup in her hands, when there is a sharp rap at the kitchen door and Inge's face appears framed there in the glass panel.

Later, hours later, after lunch at the Thai Palace, after Pic 'n Save, Costco, Ruby's Thrift Shoppe and the Bargain Basement, my widow finds herself in the midst of a crush of shoppers at Macy's. She doesn't like department stores, never has—no bargains to be had, or not usually—but her sister was looking at some tableware for one of their grandnieces, and she finds herself, unaccountably, in the linen department, surrounded by women poking through sheets and pillowcases and little things for the bathroom. There will be a white sale in January, she knows that as well as she knows there will be valentines for Valentine's Day and lilies for Easter, and since the maid died ten years back she really hasn't had much need of linens—nobody to change the beds, really—but she can't help herself. The patterns are so unique, the fabric so fresh and appealing in its neat plastic packaging. Voices leap out around her. Christmas music settles on the air. My widow looks round for a salesperson.

Second Husband

His name is—*was*—Roland Secourt. He was one of those types who never really strain themselves with such trivialities as earning a living during their younger years, and he wound up being a pretty impressive old man, replete with teeth, hair and the ability to walk unaided from the car to the house. I remember him only slightly—he used to give piano lessons to our son a thousand years ago, and I think he managed a parking lot or something like that. At any rate, five years after I bowed out, he began showing up at the front door with one excuse or another—he was driving past and saw the gate was open; he'd picked up six cases of cranberry juice at a sale and didn't know what to do with it all; he was just wondering if my widow might want to go down to the village for maybe a cocktail and dinner—and before long, my widow, who'd succumbed to the emptiness that afflicts us all, took him in.

She never loved him, though. He was a man, a presence in a deteriorating house full of cats, my shadowy simulacrum. What did he bring with him? Three cardboard boxes full of out-of-date shoes, belt buckles, underwear, a trophy he'd once won in a piano competition. Nine months into the marriage he sucked up his afflatus to crack the holy living hell out of a golf ball on the fourth tee at La Cumbre Country Club (he was golf-fixated, another strike against him), felt a stab under his arm as if someone had inserted one of those gleaming biopsy needles between his ribs, and fell face forward into the turf, dead, without displacing the ball from the tee.

That was a long time ago. My widow didn't have him around long enough to really get used to him in the way she was used to the walls and the furniture and the cats, so his death, though a painful reminder of what awaits us all, wasn't the major sort of dislocation it might have been. He was there, and then he was gone. I have no problem with that.

Her Purse

Her purse was always a bone of contention between us—or her *purses,* actually. She seemed to have a limitless number of them, one at least for every imaginable occasion, from dining at the White House to hunting boar in Kentucky, and all of them stuffed full of ticket stubs, charge card receipts, wadded-up tissues, cat collars, gum wrappers, glasses with broken frames, makeup in various states of desiccation, crushed fortune cookies, fragments of our son's elementary school report cards, dice, baby teeth, empty Tic Tac cases, keychains, cans of Mace and a fine detritus of crumbs, dandruff, sloughed skin and chipped nail polish. Only one of these, however, contained her checkbook and wallet. That was the magical one, the essential one, the one she spent a minimum of half an hour looking for every time we left the house, especially when we were on our way to the airport or the theater or a dinner date with A-type personalities like myself who'd specified *eight p.m., sharp.*

Not that I'm complaining. My widow lived a placid, unhurried existence, no slave to mere schedules, as so many of us were. She radiated calm in a crisis. When things went especially bad—during the '05 earthquake, for instance—she would fix herself a nice meal, some stir-fry or chicken-vegetable soup, and take a nap in order to put things in their proper perspective. And so what if the movie started at 7:45 and we arrived at 8:30? It was all the more interesting for having to piece together what must have transpired with this particular set of characters while we were looking for purses, parking the car and sprinting hand in hand down the crowded street. The world could wait. What was the hurry?

At any rate, it is that very same totemic purse that turns up missing after her shopping trip. She and her sister arrive at home in a blizzard of packages, and after sorting them out in the driveway and making three trips from car to house, they part just as dusk is pushing the birds into the trees and thickening the shadows in the fronds of the tree ferns I planted thirty years ago. Inge won't be staying for dinner, nor will she be spending the night. She is eager to get home to her own house, where a pot of chicken-vegetable soup and her own contingent of cats await her. "Well," she says, casting a quick eye over the welter of packages on the table, "I'm off," and the door closes on silence.

Days pass. My widow goes through her daily routine without a thought to her purse, until, with the cat food running low, she prepares for a trip to the market in the ancient, battered, *hennarot* BMW M3 that used to be my pride and joy, and discovers that none of the purses she is able to locate contains her wallet, her keys, her glasses (without which she can't even see the car, let alone drive it). While the cats gather round her, voicing their complaint, she attempts to retrace her steps of the past few days and concludes finally that she must have left the purse in her sister's car. Certainly, that's where it is. Of course it is. Unless she left it on the counter at Ruby's or the Bargain Basement or even Macy's. But if she had, they would have called, wouldn't they?

She tries her sister, but Inge isn't much for answering the phone these days, a quirk of her advancing years. Why bother?, that's what she thinks. Who is there she wants to hear from? At her age, is there any news that can't wait? Any news that could even vaguely be construed as good? My widow is nothing if not persistent, however, and on the twelfth ring Inge picks up the phone. "Hello?" she rasps in a voice that was never especially melodious but is now just a deflated ruin. My widow informs her of the problem, accepts a scolding that goes on for at least five minutes and incorporates a dozen ancient grievances, and then she waits on the line for another fifteen minutes while Inge hobbles out to the garage to check the car. *Click, click,* she's back on the line and she has bad news for my widow: the purse is not there. Is she sure? Yes, yes, she's sure. She's no idiot. She still has two eyes in her head, doesn't she?

For the next two hours my widow searches for the phone book. Her intention is to look up the phone number of the stores they'd visited, and the Thai Palace too—she's concerned, and the cats are hungry. But the phone book is elusive. After evicting a dozen cats from the furniture in the main room, digging through the pantry and the closet and discovering any number of things she'd misplaced years ago, she loses track of what she's looking for, lost in a reverie over an old photo album that turns up in the cabinet under the stove, amidst the pots and pans. She sits at the table, a crescent of yellow lamplight illuminating her features, and studies the hard evidence of the way things were. There are pictures of the two of us, smiling into the camera against various exotic backdrops, against Christmas trees and birthday cakes, minarets and mountains, a succession of years flipping by, our son, his dog, the first cat. Her heart—my widow's heart—is bursting. It's gone, everything is gone, and what's the sense of living, what's it all about? The girlhood in Buffalo, the college years, romance and love and hope and the prospect of the future—what was the sense in it, where had it gone? The pictures cry out to her. They scream from the page. They poke her and prod her till she's got no breath left in her body. And just then, when the whole world seems to be closing down, the phone rings.

Bob Smith, A. K. A. Smythe Roberts, Robert P. Smithee, Claudio Noriega and Jack Frounce

"Hello?" my widow answers, her voice like the clicking of the tumblers in an old lock.

"Mrs. B.?" a man's voice inquires.

My widow is cautious but polite, a woman who has given out her trust, time and again, and been rewarded, for the most part, with kindness and generosity in return. But she hates telephone solicitors, especially those boiler-room types that prey on the elderly—the TV news has been full of that sort of thing lately, and the A.A.R.P. newsletter too. She hesitates a moment, and then, in a barely audible voice, whispers, "Yes?"

"My name is Bob Smith," the caller returns, "and I've found your purse. Somebody apparently dumped it in a trash bin outside of Macy's—no cash left, of course, but your credit cards are intact, and your license and whatnot. Listen, I was wondering if I might bring it to you—I mean, I could mail it, but who can trust the mail these days, right?"

My widow makes a noise of assent. She doesn't trust the mail either. Or, actually, she's never really thought about it one way or another. She shuts her eyes and sees the mailman in his gray-blue shorts with the black stripe up the side, his neatly parted hair cut in the old-fashioned way, his smile, and the way his eyes seem to register everything about everybody on his route as if he took it personally, as if he were policing the streets out front and back of her house and stuffing mailboxes at the same time. Maybe she does trust the mail. Maybe she does.

Bob Smith says, "The mail'd take three days, and I'd have to find a box for the thing—"

My widow says what Bob Smith has been hoping she'll say: "Oh, you don't have to go to all that bother. Honestly, I'd come to you, but without my driving glasses—they're in the purse, you see, and I do have another pair, several pairs, but I can't seem to, I can't—"

"That's all right," he croons, his voice flowing like sugar water into a child's cup, "I'm just glad to help out. Now, is this address on your driver's license still current?"

My widow is waiting at the door for him when he steps through the front gate, a pair of legs like chopsticks in motion, his hair a dyed fluff of nothing combed straight up on his head as if he were one of those long-pants comedians of her father's era, a face gouged with wrinkles and a smile that makes his eyes all but disappear into two sinkholes of flesh. He wouldn't have got any farther than the gate if I was around, and I don't care how old I might have been, or how frail—this man is trouble, and my widow doesn't know it. Look out, honey, I want to say. Watch out for this one.

But she's smiling her beautiful smile, the smile that even after all these years has the two puckered dimples in it, her face shining and serene, and "Hello, hello, Mr. Smith," she's saying, "won't you come in?"

He will. He ducks reflexively on stepping through the door, as if his head would crack the doorframe, a tall man with dangling hands, a grubby white shirt and a tie that looks as if it'd been used to swab out the deep fryer at McDonald's. In his left hand, a plain brown shopping bag, and as she shuts the door behind him and six or seven cats glance up suspiciously from their perch on the mantel, he holds it out to her. "Here it is," he says, and sure enough, her purse is inside, soft black leather with a silver clasp and the ponzu sauce stain etched into the right panel like an abstract design. She fumbles through the purse for her wallet, thinking to offer him a reward, but then she remembers that there's no money in it—hadn't he said on the phone that the money was gone? "I wanted to—" she begins, "I mean, you've been so nice, and I—"

Bob Smith is not listening. He's wandered out into the arena of the grand room, hands clasped behind his back, dodging mounds of discarded magazines, balled-up skeins of yarn, toppled lamps and a cat-gutted ottoman. He has the look of a prospective buyer, interested, but not yet committed. "Pretty old place," he says, taking his time.

My widow, plumped with gratitude, is eager to accommodate him. "Nineteen-oh-nine," she says, working the purse between her hands. "It's the only Prairie style—"

"The rugs and all," he says, "they must be worth something. And all this pottery and brass stuff—you must have jewelry too."

"Oh, yes," my widow says, "I've been collecting antique jewelry for, well, since before I was an antique myself," and she appends a little laugh. What a nice man, she's thinking, and how many out there today would return a lady's purse? Or anything, for that matter? They'd stolen the lawnmower right out of the garage, stripped the tires off the car that time she'd broken down in Oxnard. She's feeling giddy, ready to dial Inge the minute he leaves and crow about the purse that's come back to her as if it had wings.

"Your husband here?" Bob Smith asks, picking his way back to her like a man on the pitching deck of a ship. There seems to be something stuck to the bottom of his left shoe.

"My husband?" Another laugh, muted, caught deep in her throat. "He's been gone twenty years now. Twenty-one. Or no, twenty-two."

"Kids?"

"Our son, Philip, lives in Calcutta, India. He's a doctor."

"So there's nobody here but you," Bob Smith says, and that's when my widow feels the first faint stirring of alarm. A cat rises slowly on the periphery of her vision, stretching itself. The sun slants through the windows, irradiating the skeleton of the dead palm in the big pot in the corner. Everything is still. She just nods her head in response to the question and clutches the purse to her, thinking, It's all right, just show him to the door now, and thank him, tell him the reward's coming, in the mail, just leave an address . . .

But Bob Smith isn't ready to leave. In fact, he's hovering over her now, his face as rucked and seamed as an old mailbag, his eyes glittering like something that's been crushed in the street. "So where's the jewelry then?" he says, and there's nothing of the good Samaritan left in his voice now, no bonhomie, no fellow feeling or even civility. "Can you even find it in this shithole? Huh?"

My widow doesn't say a word.

He has a hand on her wrist suddenly, clamped there like a manacle, and he's tugging at her, shouting in her face. "You stupid old bitch! You're going to pay—shit, yes, you're going to pay. Any cash? Huh? Cash? You know what that is?" And then, before she has time to answer, he snakes out his other hand, the right one, and slaps her till she jerks back from the grip of him like an animal caught in the jaws of a trap.

My widow hasn't been slapped in seventy-odd years, not since she got into a fight with her sister over a pan of brownies when their mother stepped out of the kitchen to answer the phone. She's in shock, of course—everything's happened so fast—but she's tough, my widow, as tough in the core of her as anybody on earth. Nobody slaps her. Nobody comes into her house on false pretenses and—well, you get the picture. And in the next instant her free hand comes up out of the purse with an ancient can of Mace clutched in it, and because this is a good and fitting universe I'm constructing here, the aerosol spray still works despite an expiration date ten years past, and before she can think, Bob Smith is writhing on the floor in a riot of cat feces, dust balls and lint, cursing and rubbing at his eyes. And more: when my widow turns for the door, ready to scurry out onto that brick porch and scream till her dried-up old lungs give out, who should be standing there at the door but Megan Capaldi, screaming herself.

In Her Own Words

As I say, my widow doesn't get the newspaper, not anymore. But Megan Capaldi brings her two copies the next day, because her picture is on the front page under the caption, "FEISTY OCTOGENARIAN THWARTS BURGLARY." There she is, hunched and squinting into the camera, arm in arm with Megan Capaldi, who dialed 911 on her cell phone and escorted my widow to safety while the San Roque Municipal Police handcuffed Bob Smith and secured him in the back of their cruiser. In the photograph, which shows off the front of the house to real advantage, I think, the windows especially, with their intricate design and the wooden frames I scraped, sanded and painted at least three times in the course of my tenure here, my widow is smiling. So too is Megan Capaldi, who wouldn't be bad-looking at all if only she'd stand up straight. Posed there, with the house mushrooming over them in grainy black and white, you can hardly tell them apart.

On page 2, at the end of the article, my widow is given an opportunity to reflect on her ordeal. "It's a shame, is what it is," she is quoted as saying, "the way people like this prey on the elderly—and don't forget the telemarketers, they're just as bad. It didn't used to be this way, before everybody got so suspicious of everybody else, and you didn't have to triple-lock your doors at night either."

There was more, much more, because the young woman reporter they sent out to the house had been so sympathetic—a cat person herself—but there were space limitations, and the story, while novel, didn't have the sort of grit and horror the paper's readers had come to expect. Any number of times during the interview, for instance, my widow had begun with the phrase "When my husband was alive," but none of that made the cut.

Night

It is Christmas, a clear cold night, the sky above the house staggering under the weight of the stars. My widow doesn't know about the stars—or if she does, it's only theoretically. She doesn't leave the house much, except for shopping, of course, and shopping is almost exclusively a daytime activity. At the moment, she is sitting in the grand room, on the cherrywood couch in front of the fireplace, where the ashes lie heaped, twenty-two years cold. She has been knitting, and the electric blue needles and balls of yarn lie in her lap, along with three or four cats. Her head is thrown back, resting on the broad wooden plane of the couch, and she is staring up at the high sloping ceiling above her, oblivious to the sky beyond and the cold pinpoints of light crowding the plane of the ecliptic. She's not thinking about the roof, or the roofer, or rain. She's not thinking about anything.

There is little evidence of the holidays here—a few Christmas cards scattered across the end table, a wreath of artificial pine she draped over one of the light sconces six years ago. She doesn't bother anymore with the handcrafted elves and angels from Gstaad, the crèche made of mopane wood, or even the colored lights and bangles. All that was peerless in its time, the magic of the season, our son coming down the stairs in his pajamas, year after year, growing taller and warier, the angels tarnished, the pile of gift-wrapped presents growing in proportion, but that time is past. She and Inge had planned to get together and exchange gifts in the afternoon, but neither of them had felt much enthusiasm for it, and besides, Inge's car wouldn't start. What I'd wanted here was for our son to pull up front in a cab, having flown in all the way from the subcontinent to be with his mother for Christmas—and he'd been planning on it too, planning to surprise her, but a new and cruelly virulent strain of cholera swept through the refugee camps, and he couldn't get away.

So she sits there by the ashes of the cold fire, listening to the furtive groans and thumps of the old house. The night deepens, the stars draw back, higher and higher, arching into the backbone of the sky. She is waiting for something she can't name, a beautiful old lady clothed in cats, my widow, just waiting. It is very still.

(2000)

The Underground Gardens

But you do not know me if you think I am afraid. . . .

—Franz Kafka, "The Burrow"

All he knew, really, was digging. He dug to eat, to breathe, to live and sleep. He dug because the earth was there beneath his feet, and men paid him to move it. He dug because it was a sacrament, because it was honorable and holy. As a boy in Sicily he stood beside his brothers under the sun that was like a hammer and day after day stabbed his shovel into the skin of the ancient venerable earth of their father's orchards. As a young man in Boston and New York he burrowed like a rodent beneath streets and rivers, scouring the walls of subway tubes and aqueducts, dropping his pick, lifting his shovel, mining dirt. And now, thirty-two years old and with the deed to seventy bleak and hard-baked acres in his back pocket, he was in California. Digging.

> FRIENDS! COME TO THE LAND OF FERTILITY WHERE THE SUN SHINES THE YEAR ROUND AND THE EARTH NEVER SUBMITS TO FROST! COME TO THE LAND THE ANGELS BLESSED! COME TO CALIFORNIA! WRITE NOW, C/O EUPHRATES MEAD, Box 9, Fresno, California.

Yes, the land never froze, that was true and incontrovertible. But the sun scorched it till it was like stone, till it was as hard and impenetrable as the adobe brick the Indians and Mexicans piled up to make their shabby, dusty houses. This much Baldasare discovered in the torporific summer of 1905, within days of disembarking from the train with his pick and shovel, his cardboard suitcase, and his meager supply of dried pasta, flour and beans. He'd come all the way across the country to redeem the land that would bloom with the serrate leaves and sweetly curling tendrils of his own grapes, the grapes of the Baldasare Forestiere Vineyards.

When he got down off the train, the air hot and sweet with the scent of things growing and multiplying, he was so filled with hope it was a kind of ecstasy. There were olive trees in California, orange and lemon and lime, spreading palms, fields of grapes and cotton that had filled the rushing windows of the train with every kind of promise. No more sleet and snow for him, no more wet feet and overshoes or the grippe that took all the muscle out of your back and arms, but heat, good Sicilian heat, heat that baked you right down to the grateful marrow of your happy Sicilian bones.

The first thing he did was ask directions at the station, his English a labyrinth of looming verbs and truncated squawks that sounded strange in his ears, but was serviceable for all that, and he soon found himself walking back in the direction he'd come, following the crucified grid of the tracks. Three miles south, then up a dry wash where two fire-scarred oaks came together like a pair of clasped arms, he couldn't miss it. At least that was what the man on the platform had told him. He was a farmer, this man, unmistakably a farmer, in faded coveralls and a straw hat, long of nose and with two blue flecks for eyes in a blasted face. "That's where all the Guineas are," he said, "that's where Mead sold 'em. Seventy acres, isn't it? That's what I figured. Same as the rest."

When he got there and set his cardboard suitcase in the dust, he couldn't help but pace off the whole seventy acres with the surveyor's map Euphrates Mead had sent in the mail held out before him like a dowsing stick. The land was pale in a hundred shades of brown and a sere gray-green, and there was Russian thistle everywhere, the decayed thorny bones of it already crushed to chaff in his tracks. It crept down the open neck of his shirt and into his socks and shoes and the waist of his trousers, an itch of the land, abrasive and unforgiving. Overhead, vultures rose on the air currents like bits of winged ash. Lizards scuttered underfoot.

That night he ate sardines from a tin, licking the oil from his fingers and dipping soda crackers in the residue that collected in the corners, and then he spread a blanket under one of his new oak trees and slept as if he'd been knocked unconscious. In the morning he walked into town and bought a wheelbarrow. He filled the wheelbarrow with provisions and two five-gallon cans that had once held olive oil and now contained water—albeit an oleaginous and tinny-tasting variant of what he knew water to be. Then he hefted the twin handles of the new wheelbarrow till he felt the familiar flex of the muscles of his lower back, and he guided it all the long way back out to the future site of the Baldasare Forestiere Vineyards.

He'd always thought big, even when he was a boy wandering his father's orchards, the orchards that would never be his because of a simple confluence of biology and fate—his brothers had been born before him. If, God forbid, either Pietro or Domenico should die or emigrate to Argentina or Australia, there was always the other one to stand in his way. But Baldasare wasn't discouraged—he knew he was destined for greatness. Unlike his brothers, he had the gift of seeing things as they would one day be, of seeing himself in America, right here in Fresno, his seventy acres buried in grapes, the huge oak fermenting barrels rising above the cool cellar floors, his house of four rooms and a porch set on a hill and his wife on the porch, his four sons and three daughters sprinting like colts across the yard.

He didn't even stop to eat, that first day. Sweating till his eyes burned with the sting of salt, his hands molded to the shape of the wheelbarrow's polished handles, he made three more trips into town and back—twelve miles in all, and half of them pushing the overladen wheelbarrow. People saw him there as they went about their business in carriages and farm wagons, a sun-seared little man in slept-in clothes following the tread of a single sagging tire along the shoulder of the broad dirt road. Even if he'd looked up, they probably wouldn't have nodded a greeting, but he never took his eyes off the unwavering line the tire cut in the dirt.

By the end of the week a one-room shanty stood beneath the oak, a place not much bigger than the bed he constructed of planks. It was a shelter, that was all, a space that separated him from the animals, that reminded him he was a man and not a beast. *Men are upright,* his father had told him when he was a boy, *and they have dominion over the beasts. Men live in houses, don't they? And where do the beasts live,* mio figlio? *In the ground, no? In a hole.*

It was some day of the following week when Baldasare began digging (he didn't have a calender and he didn't know Sunday from Monday, and even if he did, where was the church and the priest to guide him?). He wanted the well to be right in front of the shack beneath the tree where his house would one day stand, but he knew enough about water to know that it wouldn't be as easy as that. He spent a whole morning searching the immediate area, tracing dry watercourses, observing the way the hill of his shack and the one beside it abutted each other like the buttocks of a robust and fecund woman, until finally, right there, right in the cleft of the fundament, he pitched his shovel into the soil.

Two feet down he hit the hardpan. It didn't disconcert him, not at all—he never dreamed it would extend over all of the seventy acres—and he attacked the rocky substrate with his pick until he was through it. As he dug deeper, he squared up the sides of his excavation with mortared rock and devised a pulley system to haul the buckets of superfluous earth clear of the hole. By the close of the second day, he needed a ladder. A week later, at thirty-two feet, he hit water, a pure sweet seep of it that got his shoes wet and climbed up the bottom rungs of his homemade ladder to a depth of four feet. And even as he set up the hand pump and exulted over the flow of shimmering sun-struck water, he was contriving his irrigation system, his pipes, conduits and channels, a water tank, a reservoir. Yes. And then, with trembling hands, he dug into the earth in the place where the first long row of canes would take root, and his new life, his life of disillusionment, began.

Three months later, when his savings began to dwindle down to nothing, Baldasare became a laboring man all over again. He plowed another man's fields, planted another man's trees, dug irrigation channels and set grape canes for one stranger after another. And on his own property, after those first few weeks of feverish activity, all he'd managed, after working the soil continuously and amending it with every scrap of leaf-mold and bolus of chicken manure he could scrounge, was a vegetable garden so puny and circumscribed a housewife would have been ashamed of it. He'd dreamed of independence—from his father and brothers, from the hard-nosed Yankee construction bosses of Boston and Manhattan Island—and what had he gotten but wage slavery all over again?

He was depressed. Gloomy. Brooding and morose. It wasn't so much Mr. Euphrates Mead who'd betrayed him, but the earth, the earth itself. Plying his shovel, sweating in a long row of sweating men, he thought of suicide in all its gaudy and elaborate guises, his eyes closed forever on his worthless land and his worthless life. And then one rainy afternoon, sitting at the counter in Siagris' Drugstore with a cup of coffee and a hamburger sandwich, he had a vision that changed all that. The vision was concrete, as palpable as flesh, and it moved with the grace and fluidity of a living woman, a woman he could almost reach out and . . . "Can I get you anything else?" she asked.

He was so surprised he answered her in Italian. Olive eyes, hair piled up on her head like a confection, skin you could eat with a spoon—and hadn't it been old Siagris, the hairy Greek, who'd fried his hamburger and set it down on the counter before him? Or was he dreaming?

She was giving him a look, a crease between her eyebrows, hands on hips. "What did you say?"

"I mean"—fumbling after his English—"no, no, thank you . . . but who, I mean . . . ?"

She was serene—a very model of serenity—though the other customers, men in suits, two boys and their mother lingering over their ice cream, were all watching her and quietly listening for her answer. "I'm Ariadne," she said. "Ariadne Siagris." She looked over her shoulder to the black-eyed man standing at the grill. "That's my uncle."

Baldasare was charmed—and a bit dazed too. She was beautiful—or at least to his starved eyes she was—and he wanted to say something witty to her, something flirtatious, something that would let her know that he wasn't just another sorrowful Italian laborer with no more means or expectations than the price of the next hamburger sandwich, but a man of substance, a landowner, future proprietor of the Baldasare Forestiere Vineyards. But he couldn't think of anything, his mind impacted, his tongue gone dead in the sleeve of his mouth. Then he felt his jaws opening of their own accord and heard himself saying, "Baldasare Forestiere, at your service."

He would always remember that moment, through all the digging and lifting and wheelbarrowing to come, because she looked hard at him, as if she could see right through to his bones, and then she turned up the corners of her mouth, pressed two fingers to her lips, and giggled.

That night, as he lay in his miserable bed in his miserable shack that was little more than a glorified chicken coop, he could think of nothing but her. Ariadne Siagris. She was the one. She was what he'd come to America for, and he spoke her name aloud as the rain beat at his crude roof and insinuated itself through a hundred slivers and cracks to drizzle down onto his already damp blankets, spoke her name aloud and made the solemnest pledge that she would one day be his bride. But it was cold and the night beyond the walls was limitless and black and his teeth were chattering so forcefully he could barely get the words out. He was mad, of course, and he knew it. How could he think to have a chance with her? What could he offer her, a girl like that who'd come all the way from Chicago, Illinois, to live with her uncle, the prosperous Greek—a school-educated girl used to fine things and books? Yes, he'd made inquiries—he'd done nothing but inquire since he'd left the drugstore that afternoon. Her parents were dead, killed at a railway crossing, and she was nineteen years old, with two younger sisters and three brothers, all of them farmed out to relatives. Ariadne. Ariadne Siagris.

The rain was relentless. It spoke and sighed and roared. He was wearing every stitch of clothing he possessed, wrapped in his blankets and huddled over the coal-oil lamp, and still he froze, even here in California. It was an endless night, an insufferable night, but a night in which his mind was set free to roam the universe of his life, one thought piled atop another like bricks in a wall, until at some point, unaccountably, he was thinking of the grand tunnels he'd excavated in New York and Boston, how clean they were, how warm in winter and cool in summer, how they smelled, always, of the richness of the earth. Snow could be falling on the streets above, the gutters frozen, wind cutting into people's eyes, but below ground there was no weather, none at all. He thought about that, pictured it—the great arching tubes carved out of the earth and the locomotive with a train of cars standing there beneath the ground and all the passengers staring placidly out the windows—and then he was asleep.

The next morning, he began to dig again. The rain had gone and the sun glistened like spilled oil over his seventy acres of mire and hardpan. He told himself he was digging a cellar—a proper cellar for the house he would one day build, because he hadn't given up, not yet, not Baldasare Forestiere—but even then, even as he spat on his hands and raised the pick above his head, he knew there was more to it than that. The pick rose and fell, the shovel licked at the earth with all the probing intimacy of a tongue, and the wheelbarrow groaned under one load after another. Baldasare was digging. And he was happy, happier than he'd been since the day he stepped down from the train, because he was digging for her, for Ariadne, and because digging was what he'd been born to do.

But then the cellar was finished—a fine deep vaulted space in which he could not only stand erect—at his full height of five feet and four inches—but thrust his right arm straight up over his head and still only just manage to touch the ceiling—and he found himself at a loss for what to do next. He could have squared up the corners and planed the walls with his spade till all the lines were rectilinear, but he didn't want that. That was the fashion of all the rooms he'd ever lived in, and as he scraped and smoothed and tamped, he realized it didn't suit him. No, his cellar was dome-shaped, like the apse of the cathedral in which he'd worshipped as a boy, and its entrance was protected from the elements by a long broad ramp replete with gutters that drained into a small reflecting pool just outside the wooden door. And its roof, of course, was of hardpan, impervious to the rain and sun, and more durable than any shingle or tile.

He spent two days smoothing out the slope of the walls and tidying and leveling the floor, working by the light of a coal-oil lantern while in the realm above the sky threw up a tatter of cloud and burned with a sun in the center of it till the next storm rolled in to snuff it out like a candle. When the rain came, it seemed like the most natural thing in the world to move his clothes and his bed and his homemade furniture down into the new cellar, which was snug and watertight. Besides, he reasoned, even as he fashioned himself a set of shelves and broke through the hardpan to run a stovepipe out into the circumambient air, what did he need a cellar for—a strict cellar, that is—if he couldn't grow the onions, apples, potatoes and carrots to store in it?

Once the stove was installed and had baked all the moisture out of the place, he lay on the hard planks of his bed through a long rainy afternoon, smoking one cigarette after another and thinking about what his father had said—about the animals and how they lived in the ground, in holes. His father was a wise man. A man of character and substance. But he wasn't in California and he wasn't in love with Ariadne Siagris and he didn't have to live in a shack the pigeons would have rejected. It took him a while, but the conclusion Baldasare finally reached was that he was no animal—he was just practical, that was all—and he barely surprised himself when he got up from the bed, fetched his shovel and began to chip away at the east wall of his cellar. He could already see a hallway there, a broad grand hallway, straight as a plumb line and as graceful and sensible as the arches the Romans of antiquity put to such good use in their time. And beyond that, as the dirt began to fall and the wheelbarrow shuddered to receive it, he saw a kitchen and bedroom opening onto an atrium, he saw grape and wisteria vines snaking toward the light, camellias, ferns and impatiens overflowing clay pots and baskets—and set firmly in the soil, twenty feet below the surface, an avocado tree, as heavy with fruit as any peddler's cart.

The winter wore on. There wasn't much hired work this time of year—the grapes had been picked and pressed, the vines cut back, the fig trees pruned, and the winter crops were in the ground. Baldasare had plenty of time on his hands. He wasn't idle—he just kept right on digging—nor was he destitute. Modest in his needs and frugal by habit, he'd saved practically everything he'd earned through the summer and fall, repairing his own clothes, eating little more than boiled eggs and pasta, using his seventy acres as a place to trap rabbits and songbirds and to gather wood for his stove. His one indulgence was tobacco—that, and a weekly hamburger sandwich at Siagris' Drugstore.

Chewing, sipping coffee, smoking, he studied his future bride there, as keen as any scholar intent on his one true subject. He made little speeches to her in his head, casual remarks he practiced over and over till he got them right—or thought he did anyway. Lingering over his coffee after cleaning the plate of crumbs with a dampened forefinger, he would wait till she came near with a glass or washcloth in hand, and he would blurt: "One thinks the weather will change, is that not true?" Or: "This is the most best sandwich of hamburger my mouth will ever receive." And she? She would show her teeth in a little equine smile, or she would giggle, then sometimes sneeze, covering her nose and mouth with one hand as her late mother had no doubt taught her to do. All the while, Baldasare feasted on the sight of her. Sometimes he would sit there at the counter for two or three hours till Siagris the Greek would make some impatient remark and he would rise in confusion, his face suffused with blood, bowing and apologizing till he managed to find his way to the door.

It was during this time of close scrutiny that he began to detect certain small imperfections in his bride-to-be. Despite her education, for instance, she seemed to have inordinate difficulty in making change or reading off the menu from the chalkboard on the wall behind her. She'd begun to put on weight too, picking at bits of doughnut or fried potatoes the customers left on their plates. If she'd been substantial when Baldasare first laid eyes on her, she was much more than that now—stout, actually. As stout as Signora Cardino back home in Messina, who was said to drink olive oil instead of wine and breakfast on sugared cream and cake. And then there were her eyes—or rather, her right eye. It had a cast in it, and how he'd missed that on the day he was first smitten, he couldn't say. But he had to look twice to notice the hairs on her chin—as stiff as a cat's whiskers and just as translucent—and as far as he was concerned, the red blotches that had begun to appear on the perfect skin of her hands and throat might have been nothing more than odd splashes of marinara sauce, as if she'd gotten too close to the pot.

Another lover, less blinded by the light of certitude than Baldasare, might have found these blemishes a liability, but Baldasare treasured them. They were part of her, part of that quiddity that made her unique among women. He watched with satisfaction as her hips and buttocks swelled so that even at nineteen she had to walk with a waddle, looked on with a soaring heart as the blotches spread from her throat to her cheeks and brow and her right eye stared out of her head, across the room and out the window, surer each day that she was his. After all, who else would see in her what he saw? Who else could love her the way he did? Who but Baldasare Forestiere would come forward to declare himself? And he would declare himself soon—as soon as he finished digging.

Two years passed. He worked for other men and saved every cent of his wages, worse than any miser, and in his free time, he dug. When he completed a passage or a room or carved his way to the sky for light, he could already see the next passage and the next room beyond that. He had a vision, yes, and he had Ariadne to think of, but even so, he wasn't the sort to sit around idle. He didn't have the gift of letters, he didn't play violin or mouth organ, and he rarely visited among his neighbors. The vaudeville theater was a long way off, too far to walk, and he went there only once, with Lucca Albanese, a vineyard worker with whom he'd struck up a friendship. There were comedians and jugglers and pretty women all dancing like birds in flight, but all the while he was regretting the two cents the streetcar had cost him and the fifteen-cent admission, and he never went back. No, he stayed home with his shovel and his vision, and many days he didn't know morning from night.

Saturdays, though, he kept sacred. Saturday was the day he walked the three and a half miles to Siagris' Drugstore, through winter rains and summer heat that reached a hundred and sixteen degrees Fahrenheit. He prided himself on his constancy, and he was pleased to think that Ariadne looked forward to his weekly visits as much as he did. His place at the end of the counter was always vacant, as if reserved for him, and he relished the little smiles with which she greeted him and the sweet flow of familiar phrases that dropped so easily from her supple American lips: "So how've you been?" "Nice day." "Think it's coming on to rain?"

As time went on, they became increasingly intimate. She told him of her uncle's back pain, the illness of her cat, the ascension of her oldest brother to assistant floor supervisor at the Chicago Iron Works, and he told her of his ranch and of the elegance and spaciousness of his living quarters. "Twelve room," he said. "Twelve room, and all to myself." And then came the day when he asked her, in his runaway English, if she would come with him to the ranch for a picnic. "But not just the picnic," he said, "but also the scene, how do you say, the scene of the place, and my, my house, because I want—I need—you see, I . . ."

She was leaning over the counter, splotchy and huge. Her weight had stabilized in the past year—she'd reached her full growth, finally, at the age of twenty-one—and she floated above her feet like one of the airships the Germans so prized. "Yes," she said, and she giggled and sneezed, a big mottled hand pressed to her mouth, "I'd love to."

The following Sunday he came for her, lightly ascending the sun-bleached steps to the walkup above the drugstore where she lived with uncle and aunt and their five children. It was a hot September morning, all of Fresno and the broad dusty valley beyond held in the grip of something stupendous, a blast of air so sere and scorching you would have thought the whole world was a pizza oven with the door open wide. Siagris the Greek answered his knock. He was in his shirtsleeves and the sweat had made a washcloth of his garments, the white field of his shirt stuck like a postage stamp to the bulge of his belly. He didn't smile but he didn't look displeased either, and Baldasare understood the look: Siagris didn't like him, not one bit, and in other circumstances might have gone out of his way to squash him like a bug, but then he had a niece who took up space and ate like six nieces, and Baldasare could just maybe deliver him from that. "Come in," he said, and there was Baldasare, the cave-dweller, in a room in a house two stories above the ground.

Up here, inside, it was even hotter. The Siagris children lay about like swatted flies, and Mrs. Siagris, her hair like some wild beast clawing at her scalp, poked her head around the corner from the kitchen. It was too hot to smile, so she grimaced instead and pulled her head back out of sight. And then, in the midst of this suffocating scene, the voice of a ventriloquist cried out, "He's here," and Ariadne appeared in the hallway.

She was all in white, with a hat the size of a tabletop perched atop the mighty pile of her hair. He was melting already, from the heat, but when she focused her wild eye on him and turned up her lips in the shyest of smiles, he melted a little more.

Outside, in the street, she gave him her arm, which was something of a problem because she was so much taller than he was, and he had to reach up awkwardly to take it. He was wearing his best suit of clothes, washed just the evening before, and the unfamiliar jacket clung to him like dead skin while the new celluloid collar gouged at his neck and the tie threatened to throttle him. They managed to walk the better part of a block before she put her feet together and came to a halt. "Where's your carriage?" she asked.

Carriage? Baldasare was puzzled. He didn't have any carriage—he didn't even have a horse. "I no got," he said, and he strained to give her his best smile. "We walk."

"Walk?" she echoed. "In this heat? You must be crazy."

"No," he said, "we walk," and he leaned forward and exerted the most delicate but insistent pressure on the monument of her arrested arm.

Her cheeks were splotched under the crisp arc of shadow the hat brim threw over her face and her olive eyes seemed to snatch at his. "You mean," and her voice was scolding and intemperate, "you ain't even got a wagon? You, with your big house you're always telling me about?"

The following Sunday, though it wounded him to throw his money away like some Park Avenue millionaire, he pulled up to Siagris' Drugstore in a hired cabriolet. It was a clear day, the sun high and merciless, and the same scenario played itself out in the walkup at the top of the stairs, except that this time Baldasare seemed to have things in hand. He was as short with Siagris as Siagris was with him, he made a witticism regarding the heat for the benefit of the children, and he led Ariadne (who had refused the previous week to go farther than a bench in the park at the end of the street) out the door, down the steps, and into the carriage like a *cavaliere* of old.

Baldasare didn't like horses. They were big and crude and expensive and they always seemed to need grooming, shoeing, doctoring, and oats—and the horse attached to the cabriolet was no exception. It was a stupid, flatulent, broad-flanked, mouse-colored thing, and it did its utmost to resist every touch of the reins and thwart every desire of the man wielding them. Baldasare was in a sweat by the time they reached his property, every square inch of his clothing soaked through like a blotter, and his nerves were frayed raw. Nor had he made any attempt at conversation during the drive, so riveted was he on the task at hand, and when they finally pulled up in the shade of his favorite oak, he turned to Ariadne and saw that she hadn't exactly enjoyed the ride either.

Her hat was askew, her mouth set in a thin unyielding line. She was glistening with sweat, her hands like doughballs fried in lard, and a thin integument of moistened dust clung to her features. She gave him a concentrated frown. "Well, where is it?" she demanded. "Why are we stopping here?"

His tongue ran ahead of him, even as he sprang down from the carriage and scurried to her side to assist her in alighting. "This is what I have want for to show you, and so long, because—well, because I am making it for you."

He studied the expression of her face as she looked from the disreputable shack to the hummock of the well and out over the heat-blasted scrub to where the crown of his avocado tree rose out of the ground like an illusion. And then she saw the ramp leading down to the cellar. She was stunned, he could see it in her face and there was no denying it, but he watched her struggle to try on a smile and focus her eyes on his. "This is a prank, ain't it? You're just fooling with me and your house is really over there behind that hill"—pointing now from her perch atop the carriage—"ain't it?"

"No, no," he said, "no. It's this, you see?" And he indicated the ramp, the crown of the avocado, the bump where the inverted cone of a new atrium broke the surface. "Twelve room, I tell you, twelve room." He'd become insistent, and he had his hand on her arm, trying to lead her down from the carriage—if only she would come, if only she would see—and he wanted to tell her how cool and fresh-smelling it was down there beneath the earth, and how cheap it was to build and expand, to construct a nursery, a sewing room, anything she wanted. All it took was a strong back and a shovel, and not one cent wasted on nails and lumber and shingles that fell apart after five years in the sun. He wanted to tell her, but the words wouldn't come, and he tried to articulate it all through the pressure of his hand on her arm, tugging, as if the whole world depended on her getting down from that carriage—and it did, it did!

"Let go!" she cried, snatching her arm away, and then she was sobbing, gasping for breath as if the superheated air were some other medium altogether and she was choking on it. "You said . . . you said . . . *twelve rooms!*"

He tried to reach for her again—"Please," he begged, "please"—but she jerked back from him so violently the carriage nearly buckled on its springs. Her face was furious, streaked with tears and dirt. "You bully!" she cried. "You Guinea, Dago, Wop! You, you're no better than a murderer!"

Three days later, in a single paragraph set off by a black border, the local paper announced her engagement to Hiram Broadbent, of Broadbent's Poultry & Eggs.

An engagement wasn't a marriage, that's what Baldasare was thinking when Lucca Albanese gave him the news. An engagement could be broken, like a promise or a declaration or even a contract. There was hope yet, there had to be. "Who is this Hiram Broadbent?" he demanded. "Do you know him?"

They were sharing a meal of beans and vermicelli in Baldasare's subterranean kitchen, speaking in a low tragic Italian. Lucca had just read the announcement to him, the sharp-edged English words shearing at him like scissors, and the pasta had turned to cotton wadding in his throat. He was going to choke. He was going to vomit.

"Yeah, sure," Lucca said. "I know him. Big, fat man. Wears a straw hat winter and summer. He's a drunk, mean as the devil, but his father owns a chicken farm that supplies all the eggs for the local markets in Fresno, so he's always got money in his pocket. Hell, if you ever came out of your hole, you'd know who I'm talking about."

"You don't think—I mean, Ariadne wouldn't really . . . would she?"

Lucca ducked his head and worked his spoon in the plate. "You know what my father used to say? When I was a boy in Catania?"

"No, what?"

"There's plenty of fish in the sea."

But that didn't matter to Baldasare—he wanted only one fish. Ariadne. Why else had he been digging, if not for her? He'd created an underground palace, with the smoothest of corners and the most elegant turnings and capacious courtyards, just to give her space, to give her all the room she could want after having to live at her uncle's mercy in that cramped walkup over the drugstore. Didn't she complain about it all the time? If only she knew, if only she'd give him a chance and descend just once into the cool of the earth, he was sure she'd change her mind, she had to.

There was a problem, though. An insurmountable problem. She wouldn't see him. He came into the drugstore, hoping to make it all up to her, to convince her that he was the one, the only one, and she backed away from the counter, exchanged a word with her uncle, and melted away through the sun-struck mouth of the back door. Siagris whirled round like some animal startled in a cave, his shoulders hunched and his head held low. "We don't want you in here anymore, understand?" he said. There was the sizzle of frying, the smell of onions, tuna fish, a row of startled white faces staring up from pie and coffee. Siagris leaned into the counter and made his face as ugly as he could. "*Capiche?*"

Baldasare Forestiere was not a man to be easily discouraged. He thought of sending her a letter, but he'd never learned to write, and the idea of having someone write it for him filled him with shame. For the next few days he brooded over the problem, working all the while as a hired laborer, shoveling, lifting, pulling, bending, and as his body went through the familiar motions his mind was set free to achieve a sweated lucidity. By the end of the third day, he'd decided what he had to do.

That night, under cover of darkness, he pushed his wheelbarrow into town along the highway and found his way to the vacant lot behind the drugstore. Then he started digging. All night, as the constellations drifted in the immensity overhead until one by one they fled the sky, Baldasare plied his shovel, his pick, and his rake. By morning, at first light, the outline of his message was clearly visible from the second-story window of the walkup above the store. It was a heart, a valentine, a perfectly proportioned symbol of his love dug three feet deep in the ground and curving gracefully over the full area of what must have been a quarter-acre lot.

When the outline was finished, Baldasare started on the interior. In his mind's eye, he saw a heart-shaped crater there in the lot, six feet deep at least, with walls as smooth as cement, a hole that would show Ariadne the depth of the vacancy she'd left in him. He was coming up the ramp he'd shaped of earth with a full wheelbarrow to spread over the corners of the lot, when he glanced up to see Siagris and two of his children standing there peering down at him. Siagris' hands were on his hips. He looked more incredulous than anything else. "What in Christ's name do you think you're doing?" he sputtered.

Baldasare, swinging wide with his load of dirt so that Siagris and the children had to take a quick step back, never even hesitated. He just kept going to a point in the upper corner of the frame where he was dumping and raking out the dirt. "Digging," he said over his shoulder.

"But you can't. This is private property. You can't just dig up people's yards, don't you know that? Eh? Don't you know anything?"

Baldasare didn't want a confrontation. He was a decent man, mild and pacifistic, but he was determined too. As he came by again with the empty wheelbarrow and eased it down the ramp, he said, "Tell her to look. She is the one. For her, I do this."

After that, he was deaf to all pleas, threats, and remonstrations, patiently digging, shoring up his walls, spreading his dirt. The sun climbed in the sky. He stopped only to take an occasional drink from a jug of water or to sit on his overturned wheelbarrow and silently eat a sandwich from a store of them wrapped in butcher's paper. He worked through the day, tireless, and though the sheriff came and threatened him, even the sheriff couldn't say with any certainty who owned the lot Baldasare was defacing—couldn't say, that is, without checking the records down at the courthouse, which he was going to do first thing in the morning, Baldasare could be sure of that. Baldasare didn't respond. He just kept digging.

It began to get dark. Baldasare had cleared the entire cutout of his heart to a depth of three feet, and he wasn't even close to quitting. Six feet, he was thinking, that's what it would take, and who could blame him if he kept glancing up at the unrevealing window of the apartment atop the drugstore in the hope of catching a glimpse of his inamorata there? If she was watching, if she knew what he was doing for love of her, if she saw the lean muscles of his arms strain and his back flex, she gave no sign of it. Undeterred, Baldasare dug on.

And then there came a moment, and it must have been past twelve at night, the neighborhood as silent as the grave and Baldasare working by the light of a waxing moon, when two men appeared at the northern edge of the excavation, right where the lobes of the heart came together in a graceful loop. "Hey, Wop," one of them yelled down to where Baldasare stood with his shovel, "I don't know who you think you are, but you're embarrassing my fiancée, and I mean to put an end to it."

The man's shadow under that cold moon was immense—it could have been the shadow of a bear or buffalo. The other shadow was thinner, but broad across the shoulders, where it counted, and it danced on shadowy feet. There was no sound but for the slice of Baldasare's shovel and the slap of the dirt as it dropped into the wheelbarrow.

He was a small man, Baldasare, but the hundreds of tons of dirt he'd moved in his lifetime had made iron of his limbs, and when they fell on him he fought like a man twice his size. Still, the odds were against him, and Hiram Broadbent, fueled by good Kentucky bourbon and with the timely assistance of Calvin Tompkins, a farrier and amateur boxer, was able to beat him to the ground. And once he was down, Broadbent and Tompkins kicked him with their heavy boots till he stirred no more.

When Baldasare was released from the hospital, he was a changed man—or at least to the degree that the image of Ariadne Siagris no longer infested his brain. He went back home and sat in a bentwood rocker and stared at the sculpted dirt walls of the kitchen that gave onto the atrium and the striated trunk of its lone avocado tree. His right arm was in a sling, with a cast on it from the elbow down, and he was bound up beneath his shirt like an Egyptian mummy with all the tape it took to keep his cracked ribs in place. After a week or so—his mourning period, as he later referred to it—he found himself one evening in the last and deepest of his rooms, the one at the end of the passage that led to the new atrium where he was thinking of planting a lemon tree or maybe a quince. It was preternaturally quiet. The earth seemed to breathe with and for him.

And then suddenly he began to see things, all sorts of things, a rush of raw design and finished image that flickered across the wall before him like one of Edison's moving pictures. What he saw was a seventy-acre underground warren that beckoned him on, a maze like no other, with fishponds and gardens open to the sky above, and more, much more—a gift shop and an Italian restaurant with views of subterranean grottoes and a lot for parking the carriages and automobiles of the patrons who would flock there to see what he'd accomplished in his time on earth. It was a complete vision, more eloquent than any set of blueprints or elevations, and it staggered him. He was a young man still, healing by the day, and while he had a long way to go, at least now he knew where he was going. *Baldasare Forestiere's Underground Gardens,* he said to himself, trying out the name, and then he said it aloud: "Baldasare Forestiere's Underground Gardens."

Standing there in the everlasting silence beneath the earth, he reached out a hand to the wall in front of him, his left hand, pronating the palm as if to bless some holy place. And then, awkwardly at first, but with increasing grace and agility, he began to dig.

(1997)

After the Plague

After the plague—it was some sort of Ebola mutation passed from hand to hand and nose to nose like the common cold—life was different. More relaxed and expansive, more natural. The rat race was over, the freeways were clear all the way to Sacramento, and the poor dwindling ravaged planet was suddenly big and mysterious again. It was a kind of miracle really, what the environmentalists had been hoping for all along, though of course even the most strident of them wouldn't have wished for his own personal extinction, but there it was. I don't mean to sound callous—my parents are long dead and I'm unmarried and siblingless, but I lost friends, colleagues and neighbors, the same as any other survivor. What few of us there are, that is. We're guessing it's maybe one in ten thousand, here in the States anyway. I'm sure there are whole tribes that escaped it somewhere in the Amazon or the interior valleys of Indonesia, meteorologists in isolated weather stations, fire lookouts, goatherds and the like. But the president's gone, the vice president, the cabinet, Congress, the joint chiefs of staff, the chairmen of the boards and CEOs of the Fortune 500 companies, along with all their stockholders, employees and retainers. There's no TV. No electricity or running water. And there won't be any dining out anytime soon.

Actually, I'm lucky to be here to tell you about it—it was sheer serendipity, really. You see, I wasn't among my fellow human beings when it hit—no festering airline cabins or snaking supermarket lines for me, no concerts, sporting events or crowded restaurants—and the closest I came to intimate contact was a telephone call to my on-and-off girlfriend, Danielle, from a gas station in the Sierra foothills. I think I may have made a kissing noise over the wire, my lips very possibly coming into contact with the molded plastic mouthpiece into which hordes of strangers had breathed before me, but this was a good two weeks before the first victim carried the great dripping bag of infection that was himself back from a camcorder safari to the Ngorongoro Crater or a conference on economic development in Malawi. Danielle, whose voice was a drug I was trying to kick, at least temporarily, promised to come join me for a weekend in the cabin after my six weeks of self-imposed isolation were over, but sadly, she never made it. Neither did anyone else.

I *was* isolated up there in the mountains—that was the whole point—and the first I heard of anything amiss was over the radio. It was a warm, full-bodied day in early fall, the sun caught like a child's ball in the crown of the Jeffrey pine outside the window, and I was washing up after lunch when a smooth melodious voice interrupted *Afternoon Classics* to say that people were bleeding from the eyeballs and vomiting up bile in the New York subways and collapsing en masse in the streets of the capital. The authorities were fully prepared to deal with what they were calling a minor outbreak of swine flu, the voice said, and people were cautioned not to panic, but all at once the announcer seemed to chuckle deep in his throat, and then, right in the middle of the next phrase, he sneezed—a controlled explosion hurtling out over the airwaves to detonate ominously in ten million trembling speakers—and the radio fell silent. Somebody put on a CD of Richard Strauss' *Death and Transfiguration,* and it played over and over through the rest of the afternoon.

I didn't have access to a telephone—not unless I hiked two and a half miles out to the road where I'd parked my car and then drove another six to Fish Fry Flats, pop. 28, and used the public phone at the bar/restaurant/gift shop/one-stop grocery/gas station there—so I ran the dial up and down the radio to see if I could get some news. Reception is pretty spotty up in the mountains—you never knew whether you'd get Bakersfield, Fresno, San Luis Obispo or even Tijuana—and I couldn't pull in anything but white noise on that particular afternoon, except for the aforementioned tone poem, that is. I was powerless. What would happen would happen, and I'd find out all the sordid details a week later, just as I found out about all the other crises, scandals, scoops, coups, typhoons, wars and cease-fires that held the world spellbound while I communed with the ground squirrels and woodpeckers. It was funny. The big events didn't seem to mean much up here in the mountains, where life was so much more elemental and immediate and the telling concerns of the day revolved around priming the water pump and lighting the balky old gas stove without blowing the place up. I picked up a worn copy of John Cheever's stories somebody had left in the cabin during one of its previous incarnations and forgot all about the news out of New York and Washington.

Later, when it finally came to me that I couldn't live through another measure of Strauss without risk of permanent impairment, I flicked off the radio, put on a light jacket and went out to glory in the way the season had touched the aspens along the path out to the road. The sun was leaning way over to the west now, the shrubs and ground litter gathering up the night, the tall trees trailing deep blue shadows. There was the faintest breath of a chill in the air, a premonition of winter, and I thought of the simple pleasures of building a fire, preparing a homely meal and sitting through the evening with a book in one hand and a scotch and Drambuie in the other. It wasn't until nine or ten at night that I remembered the bleeding eyeballs and the fateful sneeze, and though I was half-convinced it was a hoax or maybe one of those fugitive terrorist attacks with a colorless, odorless gas—sarin or the like—I turned on the radio, eager for news.

There was nothing, no Strauss, no crisp and efficient NPR correspondent delivering news of riots in Cincinnati and the imminent collapse of the infrastructure, no right-wing talk, no hip-hop, no jazz, no rock. I switched to AM, and after a painstaking search I hit on a weak signal that sounded as if it were coming from the bottom of Santa Monica Bay. *This is only a test,* a mechanical voice pronounced in what was now just the faintest whispering squeak, *in the event of an actual emergency please stay tuned to . . .* and then it faded out. While I was fumbling to bring it back in, I happened upon a voice shouting something in Spanish. It was just a single voice, very agitated, rolling on tirelessly, and I listened in wonder and dread until the signal went dead just after midnight.

I didn't sleep that night. I'd begun to divine the magnitude of what was going on in the world below me—this was no hoax, no casual atrocity or ordinary attrition; this was the beginning of the end, the Apocalypse, the utter failure and ultimate demise of all things human. I felt sick at heart. Lying there in the fastness of the cabin in the absolute and abiding dark of the wilderness, I was consumed with fear. I lay on my stomach and listened to the steady thunder of my heart pounding through the mattress, attuned to the slightest variation, waiting like a condemned man for the first harrowing sneeze.

Over the course of the next several days, the radio would sporadically come to life (I left it switched on at all times, day and night, as if I were going down in a sinking ship and could shout "Mayday!" into the receiver at the first stirring of a human voice). I'd be pacing the floor or spooning sugar into my tea or staring at a freshly inserted and eternally blank page in my ancient manual typewriter when the static would momentarily clear and a harried newscaster spoke out of the void to provide me with the odd and horrific detail: an oceanliner had run aground off Cape Hatteras and nothing left aboard except three sleek and frisky cats and various puddles of flesh swathed in plaid shorts, polo shirts and sunglasses; no sound or signal had come out of South Florida in over thirty-six hours; a group of survivalists had seized Bill Gates' private jet in an attempt to escape to Antarctica, where it was thought the infection hadn't yet reached, but everyone aboard vomited black bile and died before the plane could leave the ground. Another announcer broke down in the middle of an unconfirmed report that every man, woman and child in Minneapolis was dead, and yet another came over the air early one morning shouting, "It kills! It kills! It kills in three days!" At that point, I jerked the plug out of the wall.

My first impulse, of course, was to help. To save Danielle, the frail and the weak, the young and the old, the chairman of the social studies department at the school where I teach (or taught), a student teacher with cropped red hair about whom I'd had several minutely detailed sexual fantasies. I even went so far as to hike out to the road and take the car into Fish Fry Flats, but the bar/restaurant/gift shop/one-stop grocery/gas station was closed and locked and the parking lot deserted. I drove round the lot three times, debating whether I should continue on down the road or not, but then a lean furtive figure darted out of a shed at the corner of the lot and threw itself—himself—into the shadows beneath the deck of the main building. I recognized the figure immediately as the splay-footed and pony-tailed proprietor of the place, a man who would pump your gas with an inviting smile and then lure you into the gift shop to pay in the hope that the hand-carved Tule Indian figurines and penlight batteries would prove irresistible. I saw his feet protruding from beneath the deck, and they seemed to be jittering or trembling as if he were doing some sort of energetic new contra-dance that began in the prone position. For a long moment I sat there and watched those dancing feet, then I hit the lock button, rolled up the windows and drove back to the cabin.

What did I do? Ultimately? Nothing. Call it enlightened self-interest. Call it solipsism, self-preservation, cowardice, I don't care. I was terrified—who wouldn't be?—and I decided to stay put. I had plenty of food and firewood, fuel for the generator and propane for the stove, three reams of twenty-five percent cotton fiber bond, correction fluid, books, board games—Parcheesi and Monopoly—and a complete set of *National Geographic,* 1947–1962. (By way of explanation, I should mention that I am—or was—a social studies teacher at the Montecito School, a preparatory academy in a pricey suburb of Santa Barbara, and that the serendipity that spared me the fate of nearly all my fellow men and women was as simple and fortuitous a thing as a sabbatical leave. After fourteen years of unstinting service, I applied for and was granted a one-semester leave at half-salary for the purpose of writing a memoir of my deprived and miserable Irish-Catholic upbringing. The previous year a high school teacher from New York—the name escapes me now—had enjoyed a spectacular *succès d'estime,* not to mention *d'argent,* with a memoir about his own miserable and deprived Irish-Catholic boyhood, and I felt I could profitably mine the same territory. And I got a good start on it too, until the plague hit. Now I ask myself what's the use—the publishers are all dead. Ditto the editors, agents, reviewers, booksellers and the great congenial book-buying public itself. What's the sense of writing? What's the sense of anything?)

At any rate, I stuck close to the cabin, writing at the kitchen table through the mornings, staring out the window into the ankles of the pines and redwoods as I summoned degrading memories of my alcoholic mother, father, aunts, uncles, cousins and grandparents, and in the afternoons I hiked up to the highest peak and looked down on the deceptive tranquillity of the San Joaquin Valley spread out like a continent below me. There were no planes in the sky overhead, no sign of traffic or movement anywhere, no sounds but the calling of the birds and the soughing of the trees as the breeze sifted through them. I stayed up there past dark one night and felt as serene and terrible as a god when I looked down at the velvet expanse of the world and saw no ray or glimmer of light. I plugged the radio back in that night, just to hear the fading comfort of man-made noise, of the static that emanates from nowhere and nothing. Because there was nothing out there, not anymore.

It was four weeks later—just about the time I was to have ended my hermitage and enjoyed the promised visit from Danielle—that I had my first human contact of the new age. I was at the kitchen window, beating powdered eggs into a froth for dinner, one ear half-attuned to the perfect and unbroken static hum of the radio, when there was a heavy thump on the deteriorating planks of the front deck. My first thought was that a branch had dropped out of the Jeffrey pine—or worse, that a bear had got wind of the corned beef hash I'd opened to complement the powdered eggs—but I was mistaken on both counts. The thump was still reverberating through the floorboards when I was surprised to hear a moan and then a curse—a distinctly human curse. "Oh, shit-fuck!" a woman's voice cried. "Open the goddamned door! Help, for shit's sake, help!"

I've always been a cautious animal. This may be one of my great failings, as my mother and later my fraternity brothers were always quick to point out, but on the other hand, it may be my greatest virtue. It's kept me alive when the rest of humanity has gone on to a quick and brutal extinction, and it didn't fail me in that moment. The door was locked. Once I'd got wind of what was going on in the world, though I was devastated and the thought of the radical transformation of everything I'd ever known gnawed at me day and night, I took to locking it against just such an eventuality as this. "Shit!" the voice raged. "I can hear you in there, you son of a bitch—I can *smell* you!"

I stood perfectly still and held my breath. The static breathed dismally through the speakers and I wished I'd had the sense to disconnect the radio long ago. I stared down at the half-beaten eggs.

"I'm dying out here!" the voice cried. "I'm starving to death—hey, are you deaf in there or what? I said, I'm *starving!*"

And now of course I was faced with a moral dilemma. Here was a fellow human being in need of help, a member of a species whose value had just vaulted into the rarefied atmosphere occupied by the gnatcatcher, the condor and the beluga whale by virtue of its rarity. Help her? Of course I would help her. But at the same time, I knew if I opened that door I would invite the pestilence in and that three days hence both she and I would be reduced to our mortal remains.

"Open up!" she demanded, and the tattoo of her fists was the thunder of doom on the thin planks of the door.

It occurred to me suddenly that she couldn't be infected—she'd have been dead and wasted by now if she were. Maybe she was like me, maybe she'd been out brooding in her own cabin or hiking the mountain trails, utterly oblivious and immune to the general calamity. Maybe she was beautiful, nubile, a new Eve for a new age, maybe she would fill my nights with passion and my days with joy. As if in a trance, I crossed the room and stood at the door, my fingers on the long brass stem of the bolt. "Are you alone?" I said, and the rasp of my own voice, so long in disuse, sounded strange in my ears.

I heard her draw in a breath of astonishment and outrage from the far side of the thin panel that separated us. "What the hell do you think, you son of a bitch? I've been lost out here in these stinking woods for I don't know how long and I haven't had a scrap for days, not a goddamn scrap, not even bark or grass or a handful of soggy trail mix. *Now will you fucking open this door?!*"

Still, I hesitated.

A rending sound came to me then, a sound that tore me open as surely as a surgical knife, from my groin to my throat: she was sobbing. Gagging for breath, and sobbing. "A frog," she sobbed, "I ate a goddamn slimy little putrid *frog!*"

God help me. God save and preserve me. I opened the door.

Sarai was thirty-eight years old—that is, three years older than I—and she was no beauty. Not on the surface anyway. Even if you discounted the twenty-odd pounds she'd lost and her hair that was like some crushed rodent's pelt and the cuts and bites and suppurating sores that made her skin look like a leper's, and tried, by a powerful leap of the imagination, to see her as she once might have been, safely ensconced in her condo in Tarzana and surrounded by all the accoutrements of feminine hygiene and beauty, she still wasn't much.

This was her story: she and her live-in boyfriend, Howard, were nature enthusiasts—at least Howard was anyway—and just before the plague hit they'd set out to hike an interlocking series of trails in the Golden Trout Wilderness. They were well provisioned, with the best of everything—Howard managed a sporting goods store—and for the first three weeks everything went according to plan. They ate delicious freeze-dried fettuccine Alfredo and shrimp couscous, drank cognac from a bota bag and made love wrapped in propylene, Gore-Tex and nylon. Mosquitoes and horseflies sampled her legs, but she felt good, born again, liberated from the traffic and the smog and her miserable desk in a miserable corner of the electronics company her father had founded. Then one morning, when they were camped by a stream, Howard went off with his day pack and a fly rod and never came back. She waited. She searched. She screamed herself hoarse. A week went by. Every day she searched in a new direction, following the stream both ways and combing every tiny rill and tributary, until finally she got herself lost. All streams were one stream, all hills and ridges alike. She had three Kudos bars with her and a six-ounce bag of peanuts, but no shelter and no freeze-dried entrées—all that was back at the camp she and Howard had made in happier times. A cold rain fell. There were no stars that night, and when something moved in the brush beside her she panicked and ran blindly through the dark, hammering her shins and destroying her face, her hair and her clothes. She'd been wandering ever since.

I made her a package of Top Ramen, gave her a towel and a bar of soap and showed her the primitive shower I'd rigged up above the ancient slab of the tub. I was afraid to touch her or even come too close to her. Sure I was skittish. Who wouldn't be when ninety-nine percent of the human race had just died off on the tailwind of a simple sneeze? Besides, I'd begun to adopt all the habits of the hermit—talking to myself, performing elaborate rituals over my felicitous stock of foodstuffs, dredging bursts of elementary school songs and beer jingles out of the depths of my impacted brain—and I resented having my space invaded. *Still.* Still, though, I felt that Sarai had been delivered to me by some higher power and that she'd been blessed in the way that I was—we'd escaped the infection. We'd survived. And we weren't just errant members of a selfish, suspicious and fragmented society, but the very foundation of a new one. She was a woman. I was a man.

At first, she wouldn't believe me when I waved a dismissive hand at the ridge behind the cabin and all that lay beyond it and informed her that the world was depeopled, that the Apocalypse had come and that she and I were among the solitary survivors—and who could blame her? As she sipped my soup and ate my flapjacks and treated her cuts and abrasions with my Neosporin and her hair with my shampoo, she must have thought she'd found a lunatic as her savior. "If you don't believe me," I said, and I was gloating, I was, sick as it may seem, "try the radio."

She looked up at me out of the leery brooding eyes of the one sane woman in a madhouse of impostors, plugged the cord in the socket and calibrated the dial as meticulously as a safecracker. She was rewarded by static—no dynamics even, just a single dull continuum—but she glared up at me as if I'd rigged the thing to disappoint her. "*So,*" she spat, skinny as a refugee, her hair kinked and puffed up with my shampoo till it devoured her parsimonious and disbelieving little sliver of a face, "that doesn't prove a thing. It's broken, that's all."

When she got her strength back, we hiked out to the car and drove into Fish Fry Flats so she could see for herself. I was half crazy with the terrible weight of the knowledge I'd been forced to hold inside me, and I can't describe the irritation I felt at her utter lack of interest—she treated me like a street gibberer, a psychotic, Cassandra in long pants. She condescended to me. She was *humoring* me, for God's sake, and the whole world lay in ruins around us. But she would have a rude awakening, she would, and the thought of it was what kept me from saying something I'd regret—I didn't want to lose my temper and scare her off, but I hate stupidity and willfulness. It's the one thing I won't tolerate in my students. Or wouldn't. Or didn't.

Fish Fry Flats, which in the best of times could hardly be mistaken for a metropolis, looked now as if it had been deserted for a decade. Weeds had begun to sprout up through invisible cracks in the pavement, dust had settled over the idle gas pumps and the windows of the main building were etched with grime. And the animals—the animals were everywhere, marmots waddling across the lot as if they owned it, a pair of coyotes asleep in the shade of an abandoned pickup, ravens cawing and squirrels chittering. I cut the engine just as a bear the color of cinnamon toast tumbled stupendously through an already shattered window and lay on his back, waving his bloodied paws in the air as if he were drunk, which he was. As we discovered a few minutes later—once he'd lurched to his feet and staggered off into the bushes—a whole host of creatures had raided the grocery, stripping the candy display right down to the twisted wire rack, scattering Triscuits and Doritos, shattering jars of jam and jugs of port wine and grinding the hand-carved Tule Indian figurines underfoot. There was no sign of the formerly sunny proprietor or of his dancing feet—I could only imagine that the ravens, coyotes and ants had done their work.

But Sarai—she was still an unbeliever, even after she dropped a quarter into the public telephone and put the dead black plastic receiver to her ear. For all the good it did her, she might as well have tried coaxing a dial tone out of a stone or a block of wood, and I told her so. She gave me a sour look, the sticks of her bones briefly animated beneath a sweater and jacket I'd loaned her—it was the end of October and getting cold at seventy-two hundred feet—and then she tried another quarter, and then another, before she slammed the receiver down in a rage and turned her seething face on me. "The lines are down, that's all," she sneered. And then her mantra: "It doesn't prove a thing."

While she'd been frustrating herself, I'd been loading the car with canned goods, after entering the main building through the broken window and unlatching the door from the inside. "And what about all this?" I said, irritated, hot with it, sick to death of her and her thick-headedness. I gestured at the bloated and lazy coyotes, the hump in the bushes that was the drunken bear, the waddling marmots and the proprietary ravens.

"I don't know," she said, clenching her jaws. "And I don't care." Her eyes had a dull sheen to them. They were insipid and bovine, exactly the color of the dirt at her feet. And her lips—thin and stingy, collapsed in a riot of vertical lines like a dried-up mud puddle. I hated her in that moment, godsend or no. Oh, how I hated her.

"What are you *doing?*" she demanded as I loaded the last of the groceries into the car, settled into the driver's seat and turned the engine over. She was ten feet from me, caught midway between the moribund phone booth and the living car. One of the coyotes lifted its head at the vehemence of her tone and gave her a sleepy, yellow-eyed look.

"Going back to the cabin," I said.

"You're *what?*" Her face was pained. She'd been through agonies. I was a devil and a madman.

"Listen, Sarai, it's all over. I've told you time and again. You don't have a job anymore. You don't have to pay rent, utility bills, don't have to make car payments or remember your mother's birthday. It's over. Don't you get it?"

"You're insane! You're a shithead! I hate you!"

The engine was purring beneath my feet, fuel awasting, but there was infinite fuel now, and though I realized the gas pumps would no longer work, there were millions upon millions of cars and trucks out there in the world with full tanks to siphon, and no one around to protest. I could drive a Ferrari if I wanted, a Rolls, a Jag, anything. I could sleep on a bed of jewels, stuff the mattress with hundred-dollar bills, prance through the streets in a new pair of Italian loafers and throw them into the gutter each night and get a new pair in the morning. But I was afraid. Afraid of the infection, the silence, the bones rattling in the wind. "I know it," I said. "I'm insane. I'm a shithead. I admit it. But I'm going back to the cabin and you can do anything you want—it's a free country. Or at least it used to be."

I wanted to add that it was a free world now, a free universe, and that God was in the details, the biblical God, the God of famine, flood and pestilence, but I never got the chance. Before I could open my mouth she bent for a stone and heaved it into the windshield, splintering me with flecks and shards of safety glass. "Die!" she shrieked. "*You* die, you shit!"

That night we slept together for the first time. In the morning, we packed up a few things and drove down the snaking mountain road to the charnel house of the world.

I have to confess that I've never been much of a fan of the apocalyptic potboiler, the doomsday film shot through with special effects and asinine dialogue or the cyberpunk version of a grim and relentless future. What these entertainments had led us to expect—the roving gangs, the inhumanity, the ascendancy of machines and the redoubled pollution and ravaging of the earth—wasn't at all what it was like. There were no roving gangs—they were all dead, to a man, woman and tattooed punk—and the only machines still functioning were the automobiles and weed whippers and such that we the survivors chose to put into prosaic action. And a further irony was that the survivors were the least likely and least qualified to organize anything, either for better or worse. We were the fugitive, the misfit, the recluse, and we were so widely scattered we'd never come into contact with one another anyway—and that was just the way we liked it. There wasn't even any looting of the supermarkets—there was no need. There was more than enough for everybody who ever was or would be.

Sarai and I drove down the mountain road, through the deserted small town of Springville and the deserted larger town of Porterville, and then we turned south for Bakersfield, the Grapevine and Southern California. She wanted to go back to her apartment, to Los Angeles, and see if her parents and her sisters were alive still—she became increasingly vociferous on that score as the reality of what had happened began to seep through to her—but I was driving and I wanted to avoid Los Angeles at all costs. To my mind, the place had been a pit before the scourge hit, and now it was a pit heaped with seven million moldering corpses. She carped and moaned and whined and threatened, but she was in shock too and couldn't quite work herself up to her usual pitch, and so we turned west and north on Route 126 and headed toward Montecito, where for the past ten years I'd lived in a cottage on one of the big estates there—the DuPompier place, *Mírame.*

By the way, when I mentioned earlier that the freeways were clear, I was speaking metaphorically—they were free of traffic, but cluttered with abandoned vehicles of all sorts, take your pick, from gleaming choppers with thousand-dollar gold-fleck paint jobs to sensible family cars, Corvettes, Winnebagos, eighteen-wheelers and even fire engines and police cruisers. Twice, when Sarai became especially insistent, I pulled alongside one or another of these abandoned cars, swung open her door and said, "Go ahead. Take this Cadillac"—or BMW or whatever—"and drive yourself any damn place you please. Go on.

What are you waiting for?" But her face shrank till it was as small as a doll's and her eyes went stony with fear: those cars were catacombs, each and every one of them, and the horror of that was more than anybody could bear.

So we drove on, through a preternatural silence and a world that already seemed primeval, up the Coast Highway and along the frothing bright boatless sea and into Montecito. It was evening when we arrived, and there wasn't a soul in sight. If it weren't for that—and a certain creeping untended look to the lawns, shrubs and trees—you wouldn't have noticed anything out of the ordinary. My cottage, built in the twenties of local sandstone and draped in wisteria till it was all but invisible, was exactly as I'd left it. We pulled into the silent drive with the great house looming in the near distance, a field of dark reflective glass that held the blood of the declining sun in it, and Sarai barely glanced up. Her thin shoulders were hunched and she was staring at a worn place on the mat between her feet.

"We're here," I announced, and I got out of the car.

She turned her eyes to me, stricken, suffering, a waif. "Where?"

"Home."

It took her a moment, but when she responded she spoke slowly and carefully, as if she were just learning the language. "I have no home," she said. "Not anymore."

So. What to tell you? We didn't last long, Sarai and I, though we were pioneers, though we were the last hope of the race, drawn together by the tenacious glue of fear and loneliness. I knew there wouldn't be much opportunity for dating in the near future, but we just weren't suited to each other. In fact, we were as unsuited as any two people could ever be, and our sex was tedious and obligatory, a ballet of mutual need and loathing, but to my mind at least, there was a bright side—here was the chance to go forth and be fruitful and do what we could to repopulate the vast and aching sphere of the planet. Within the month, however, Sarai had disabused me of that notion.

It was a silky, fog-hung morning, the day deepening around us, and we'd just gone through the mechanics of sex and were lying exhausted and unsatisfied in the rumple of my gritty sheets (water was a problem and we did what laundry we could with what we were able to haul down from the estate's swimming pool). Sarai was breathing through her mouth, an irritating snort and burble that got on my nerves, but before I could say anything, she spoke in a hard shriveled little nugget of a voice. "You're no Howard," she said.

"Howard's dead," I said. "He deserted you."

She was staring at the ceiling. "Howard was gold," she mused in a languid, reflective voice, "and you're shit."

It was childish, I know, but the dig at my sexual performance really stung—not to mention the ingratitude of the woman—and I came back at her. "You came to me," I said. "I didn't ask for it—I was doing fine out there on the mountain without you. And where do you think you'd be now if it wasn't for me? Huh?"

She didn't answer right away, but I could feel her consolidating in the bed beside me, magma becoming rock. "I'm not going to have sex with you again," she said, and still she was staring at the ceiling. "Ever. I'd rather use my finger."

"You're no Danielle," I said.

She sat up then, furious, all her ribs showing and her shrunken breasts clinging to the remains of them like an afterthought. "Fuck Danielle," she spat. "And fuck you."

I watched her dress in silence, but as she was lacing up her hiking boots I couldn't resist saying, "It's no joy for me either, Sarai, but there's a higher principle involved here than our likes and dislikes or any kind of animal gratification, and I think you know what I'm talking about—"

She was perched on the edge of a leather armchair I'd picked up at a yard sale years ago, when money and things had their own reality. She'd laced up the right boot and was working on the left, laces the color of rust, blunt white fingers with the nails bitten to the quick. Her mouth hung open slightly and I could see the pink tip of her tongue caught between her teeth as she worked mindlessly at her task, reverting like a child to her earliest training and her earliest habits. She gave me a blank look.

"Procreation, I mean. If you look at it in a certain way, it's—well, it's our duty."

Her laugh stung me. It was sharp and quick, like the thrust of a knife. "You idiot," she said, and she laughed again, showing the gold in her back teeth. "I hate children, always have—they're little monsters that grow up to be uptight fussy pricks like you." She paused, smiled, and released an audible breath. "I had my tubes tied fifteen years ago."

That night she moved into the big house, a replica of a Moorish castle in Seville, replete with turrets and battlements. The paintings and furnishings were exquisite, and there were some twelve thousand square feet of living space, graced with carved wooden ceilings, colored tiles, rectangular arches, a loggia and formal gardens. Nor had the DuPompiers spoiled the place by being so thoughtless as to succumb inside—they'd died, Julius, Eleanor and their daughter, Kelly, under the arbor in back, the white bones of their hands eternally clasped. I wished Sarai good use of the place. I did. Because by that point I didn't care if she moved into the White House, so long as I didn't have to deal with her anymore.

Weeks slipped by. Months. Occasionally I would see the light of Sarai's Coleman lantern lingering in one of the high windows of *Mírame* as night fell over the coast, but essentially I was as solitary—and as lonely—as I'd been in the cabin in the mountains. The rains came and went. It was spring. Everywhere the untended gardens ran wild, the lawns became fields, the orchards forests, and I took to walking round the neighborhood with a baseball bat to ward off the packs of feral dogs for which Alpo would never again materialize in a neat bowl in the corner of a dry and warm kitchen. And then one afternoon, while I was at Von's, browsing the aisles for pasta, bottled marinara and Green Giant asparagus spears amidst a scattering of rats and the lingering stench of the perished perishables, I detected movement at the far end of the next aisle over. My first thought was that it must be a dog or a coyote that had somehow managed to get in to feed on the rats or the big twenty-five-pound bags of Purina Dog Chow, but then, with a shock, I realized I wasn't alone in the store.

In all the time I'd been coming here for groceries, I'd never seen a soul, not even Sarai or one of the six or seven other survivors who were out there occupying the mansions in the hills. Every once in a while I'd see lights shining in the wall of the night—someone had even managed to fire up a generator at Las Tejas, a big Italianate villa half a mile away—and every so often a car would go helling up the distant freeway, but basically we survivors were shy of one another and kept to ourselves. It was fear, of course, the little spark of panic that told you the contagion was abroad again and that the best way to avoid it was to avoid all human contact. So we did. Strenuously.

But I couldn't ignore the squeak and rattle of a shopping cart wheeling up the bottled water aisle, and when I turned the corner, there she was, Felicia, with her flowing hair and her scared and sorry eyes. I didn't know her name then, not at first, but I recognized her—she was one of the tellers at the Bank of America branch where I cashed my checks. Formerly cashed them, that is. My first impulse was to back wordlessly away, but I mastered it—how could I be afraid of what was human, so palpably human, and appealing? "Hello," I said, to break the tension, and then I was going to say something stupid like "I see you made it too" or "Tough times, huh?" but instead I settled for "Remember me?"

She looked stricken. Looked as if she were about to bolt—or die on the spot. But her lips were brave and they came together and uttered my name. "Mr. Halloran?" she said, and it was so ordinary, so plebeian, so real.

I smiled and nodded. My name is—was—Francis Xavier Halloran III, a name I've hated since Tyrone Johnson (now presumably dead) tormented me with it in kindergarten, chanting "Francis, Francis, Francis" till I wanted to sink through the floor. But it was a new world now, a world burgeoning and bursting at the seams to discover the lineaments of its new forms and rituals. "Call me Jed," I said.

Nothing happens overnight, especially not in plague times. We were wary of each other, and every banal phrase and stultifying cliché of the small talk we made as I helped her load her groceries into the back of her Range Rover reverberated hugely with the absence of all the multitudes who'd used those phrases before us. Still, I got her address that afternoon—she'd moved into Villa Ruscello, a mammoth place set against the mountains, with a creek, pond and Jacuzzi for fresh water—and I picked her up two nights later in a Rolls Silver Cloud and took her to my favorite French restaurant. The place was untouched and pristine, with a sweeping view of the sea, and I lit some candles and poured us each a glass of twenty-year-old Bordeaux, after which we feasted on canned crab, truffles, cashews and marinated artichoke hearts.

I'd like to tell you that she was beautiful, because that's the way it should be, the way of the fable and the fairy tale, but she wasn't—or not conventionally anyway. She was a little heavier than she might have been ideally, but that was a relief after stringy Sarai, and her eyes were ever so slightly crossed. Yet she was decent and kind, sweet even, and more important, she was available.

We took walks together, raided overgrown gardens for lettuce, tomatoes and zucchini, planted strawberries and snow peas in the middle of the waist-high lawn at Villa Ruscello. One day we drove to the mountains and brought back the generator so we could have lights and refrigeration in the cottage—ice cubes, now there was a luxury—and begin to work our way through the eight thousand titles at the local video store. It was nearly a month before anything happened between us—anything sexual, that is. And when it did, she first felt obligated, out of a sense of survivor's guilt, I suppose, to explain to me how she came to be alive and breathing still when everyone she'd ever known had vanished off the face of the earth. We were in the beamed living room of my cottage, sharing a bottle of Dom Pérignon 1970, with the three-hundred-ten-dollar price tag still on it, and I'd started a fire against the gathering night and the wet raw smell of rain on the air. "You're going to think I'm an idiot," she said.

I made a noise of demurral and put my arm round her.

"Did you ever hear of a sensory deprivation tank?" She was peering up at me through the scrim of her hair, gold and red highlights, health in a bottle.

"Yeah, sure," I said. "But you don't mean—?"

"It was an older one, a model that's not on the market anymore—one of the originals. My roommate's sister—Julie Angier?—she had it out in her garage on Padaro, and she was really into it. You could get in touch with your inner self, relax, maybe even have an out-of-body experience, that's what she said, and I figured why not?" She gave me a look, shy and passionate at once, to let me know that she was the kind of girl who took experience seriously. "They put salt water in it, three hundred gallons, heated to your body temperature, and then they shut the lid on you and there's nothing, absolutely nothing there—it's like going to outer space. Or inner space. Inside yourself."

"And you were in there when—?"

She nodded. There was something in her eyes I couldn't read—pride, triumph, embarrassment, a spark of sheer lunacy. I gave her an encouraging smile.

"For days, I guess," she said. "I just sort of lost track of everything, who I was, where I was—you know? And I didn't wake up till the water started getting cold"—she looked at her feet—"which I guess is when the electricity went out because there was nobody left to run the power plants. And then I pushed open the lid and the sunlight through the window was like an atom bomb, and then, then I called out Julie's name, and she . . . well, she never answered."

Her voice died in her throat and she turned those sorrowful eyes on me. I put my other arm around her and held her. "Hush," I whispered, "it's all right now, everything's all right." It was a conventional thing to say, and it was a lie, but I said it, and I held her and felt her relax in my arms.

It was then, almost to the precise moment, that Sarai's naked sliver of a face appeared at the window, framed by her two uplifted hands and a rock the size of my Webster's unabridged. "What about *me,* you son of a bitch!" she shouted, and there it was again, everlasting stone and frangible glass, and not a glazier left alive on the planet.

I wanted to kill her. It was amazing—three people I knew of had survived the end of everything, and it was one too many. I felt vengeful. Biblical. I felt like storming Sarai's ostentatious castle and wringing her chicken neck for her, and I think I might have if it weren't for Felicia. "Don't let her spoil it for us," she murmured, the gentle pressure of her fingers on the back of my neck suddenly holding my full attention, and we went into the bedroom and closed the door on all that mess of emotion and glass.

In the morning, I stepped into the living room and was outraged all over again. I cursed and stomped and made a fool of myself over heaving the rock back through the window and attacking the shattered glass as if it were alive—I admit I was upset out of all proportion to the crime. This was a new world, a new beginning, and Sarai's nastiness and negativity had no place in it. Christ, there were only three of us—couldn't we get along?

Felicia had repaired dozens of windows in her time. Her little brothers (dead now) and her fiancé (dead too) were forever throwing balls around the house, and she assured me that a shattered window was nothing to get upset over (though she bit her lip and let her eyes fill at the mention of her fiancé, and who could blame her?). So we consulted the Yellow Pages, drove to the nearest window glass shop and broke in as gently as possible. Within the hour, the new pane had been installed and the putty was drying in the sun, and watching Felicia at work had so elevated my spirits I suggested a little shopping spree to celebrate.

"Celebrate what?" She was wearing a No Fear T-shirt and an Anaheim Angels cap and there was a smudge of off-white putty on her chin.

"You," I said. "The simple miracle of you."

And that was fine. We parked on the deserted streets of downtown Santa Barbara and had the stores to ourselves—clothes, the latest (and last) bestsellers, CDs, a new disc player to go with our newly electrified house. Others had visited some of the stores before us, of course, but they'd been polite and neat about it, almost as if they were afraid to betray their presence, and they always closed the door behind them. We saw deer feeding in the courtyards and one magnificent tawny mountain lion stalking the wrong way up a one-way street. By the time we got home, I was elated. Everything was going to work out, I was sure of it.

The mood didn't last long. As I swung into the drive, the first thing I saw was the yawning gap where the new window had been, and beyond it, the undifferentiated heap of rubble that used to be my living room. Sarai had been back. And this time she'd done a thorough job, smashing lamps and pottery, poking holes in our cans of beef stew and chili con carne, scattering coffee, flour and sugar all over everything and dumping sand in the generator's fuel tank. Worst of all, she'd taken half a dozen pairs of Felicia's panties and nailed them to the living room wall, a crude *X* slashed across the crotch of each pair. It was hateful and savage—human, that's what it was, human—and it killed all the joy we'd taken in the afternoon and the animals and the infinite and various riches of the mall. Sarai had turned it all to shit.

"We'll move to my place," Felicia said. "Or any place you want. How about an oceanfront house—didn't you say you'd always wanted to live right on the ocean?"

I had. But I didn't want to admit it. I stood in the middle of the desecrated kitchen and clenched my fists. "I don't want any other place. This is my home. I've lived here for ten years and I'll be damned if I'm going to let *her* drive me out."

It was an irrational attitude—again, childish—and Felicia persuaded me to pack up a few personal items (my high school yearbook, my reggae albums, a signed first edition of *For Whom the Bell Tolls,* a pair of deer antlers I'd found in the woods when I was eight) and move into a place on the ocean for a few days. We drove along the coast road at a slow, stately pace, looking over this house or that, until we finally settled on a grand modern place that was all angles and glass and broad sprawling decks. I got lucky and caught a few perch in the surf, and we barbecued them on the beach and watched the sun sink into the western bluffs.

The next few days were idyllic, and we thought about little beyond love and food and the way the water felt on our skin at one hour of the day or another, but still, the question of Sarai nagged at me. I was reminded of her every time I wanted a cold drink, for instance, or when the sun set and we had to make do with candles and kerosene lanterns—we'd have to go out and dig up another generator, we knew that, but they weren't exactly in demand in a place like Santa Barbara (in the old days, that is) and we didn't know where to look. And so yes, I couldn't shake the image of Sarai and the look on her face and the things she'd said and done. And I missed my house, because I'm a creature of habit, like anybody else. Or more so. Definitely more so.

Anyway, the solution came to us a week later, and it came in human form—at least it appeared in human form, but it was a miracle and no doubt about it. Felicia and I were both on the beach—naked, of course, as naked and without shame or knowledge of it as Eve and Adam—when we saw a figure marching resolutely up the long curving finger of sand that stretched away into the haze of infinity. As the figure drew closer, we saw that it was a man, a man with a scraggly salt-and-pepper beard and hair the same color trailing away from a bald spot worn into his crown. He was dressed in hiking clothes, big-grid boots, a bright blue pack riding his back like a second set of shoulders. We stood there, naked, and greeted him.

"Hello," he said, stopping a few feet from us and staring first at my face, then at Felicia's breasts, and finally, with an effort, bending to check the laces of his boots. "Glad to see you two made it," he said, speaking to the sand.

"Likewise," I returned.

Over lunch on the deck—shrimp salad sandwiches on Felicia-baked bread—we traded stories. It seems he was hiking in the mountains when the pestilence descended—"The mountains?" I interrupted. "Whereabouts?"

"Oh," he said, waving a dismissive hand, "up in the Sierras, just above this little town—you've probably never heard of it—Fish Fry Flats?"

I let him go on awhile, explaining how he'd lost his girlfriend and wandered for days before he finally came out on a mountain road and appropriated a car to go on down to Los Angeles—"One big cemetery"—and how he'd come up the coast and had been wandering ever since. I don't think I've ever felt such exhilaration, such a rush of excitement, such perfect and inimitable a sense of closure.

I couldn't keep from interrupting him again. "I'm clairvoyant," I said, raising my glass to the man sitting opposite me, to Felicia and her breasts, to the happy fishes in the teeming seas and the birds flocking without number in the unencumbered skies. "Your name's Howard, right?"

Howard was stunned. He set down his sandwich and wiped a fleck of mayonnaise from his lips. "How did you guess?" he said, gaping up at me out of eyes that were innocent and pure, the newest eyes in the world.

I just smiled and shrugged, as if it were my secret. "After lunch," I said, "I've got somebody I want you to meet."

(1997)

PART II

Tooth and Claw

When I Woke Up This Morning, Everything I Had Was Gone

The man I want to tell you about, the one I met at the bar at Jimmy's Steak House, was on a tear. Hardly surprising, since this was a bar, after all, and what do people do at bars except drink, and one drink leads to another—and if you're in a certain frame of mind, I suppose, you don't stop for a day or two or maybe more. But this man—he was in his forties, tall, no fat on him, dressed in a pair of stained Dockers and a navy blue sweatshirt cut off raggedly at the elbows—seemed to have been going at it steadily for weeks, months even.

It was a Saturday night, rain sizzling in the streets and steaming the windows, the dinner crowd beginning to rouse themselves over decaf, cheesecake and V.S.O.P. and the regulars drifting in to look the women over and wait for the band to set up in the corner. I was new in town. I had no date, no wife, no friends. I was on something of a tear myself—a mini-tear, I guess you'd call it. The night before I'd gone out with one of my co-workers from the office, who, like me, was recently divorced, and we had dinner, went to a couple places afterward. But nothing came of it—she didn't like me, and I could see that before we were halfway through dinner. I wasn't her type, whatever that might have been—and I started feeling sorry for myself, I guess, and drank too much. When I got up in the morning, I made myself a Bloody Mary with a can of Snap-E-Tom, a teaspoon of horseradish and two jiggers of vodka, just to clear my head, then went out to breakfast at a place by the water and drank a glass or two of chardonnay with my frittata and homemade duck sausage with fennel, and then I wandered over to a sports bar and then another place after that, and I never got any of the errands done I'd been putting off all week—and I didn't have any lunch either. Or dinner. And so I drifted into Jimmy's and there he was, the man in the sweatshirt, on his tear.

There was a space around him at the bar. He was standing there, the stool shoved back and away from him as if he had no use for comfort, and his lips were moving, though nobody I could see was talking to him. A flashlight, a notebook and a cigarette lighter were laid out in front of him on the mahogany bar, and though Jimmy's specialized in margaritas—there were eighteen different types of margaritas offered on the drinks menu—this man was apparently going the direct route. Half a glass of beer sat on the counter just south of the flashlight and he was guarding three empty shot glasses as if he was afraid someone was going to run off with them. The bar was filling up. There were only two seats available in the place, one on either side of him. I was feeling a little washed out, my legs gone heavy on me all of a sudden, and I was thinking I might get a burger or a steak and fries at the bar. I studied him a moment, considered, then took the seat to his right and ordered a drink.

Our first communication came half a second later. He tapped my arm, gave me a long, tunneled look, and made the universal two-fingered gesture for a smoke. Normally this would have irritated me—the law says you can no longer smoke in a public place in this state, and in any case I don't smoke and never have—but I was on a tear myself, I guess, and just gave him a smile and shrugged my shoulders. He turned away from me then to flag down the bartender and order another shot—he was drinking Herradura Gold—and a beer chaser. There was a ritualistic moment during which he took a bite from the wedge of lime the bartender provided, sprinkled salt onto the webbing between the thumb and index finger of his left hand, licked it off and threw back the shot, after which the beer came into play. He exhaled deeply, and then his eyes migrated back to me. "Nice to see you," he said, as if we'd known each other for years.

I said it was nice to see him too. The gabble of voices around us seemed to go up a notch. A woman at the end of the bar began to laugh with a thick, dredging sound, as if she were bringing something up with great reluctance.

He leaned in confidentially. "You know," he said, "people drink for a lot of reasons. You know why I drink? Because I like the taste of it. Sweet and simple. I like the taste."

I told him I liked the taste of it too, and then he made a fist and cuffed me lightly on the meat of the arm. "You're all right, you know that?" He held out his hand as if we'd just closed a deal, and I took it. I've been in business for years—for all but one of the years since I left college—and it was just a reflex to give him my name. He didn't say anything in response, just stared into my eyes, grinning, until I said, "And what do I call you?"

The man looked past me, his eyes groping toward the red and green neon sign with its neatly bunched neon palm trees that glowed behind the bar and apprised everybody of the name of the establishment. It took him a minute, but then he dropped my hand and said, "Just call me Jimmy."

After a couple of drinks at a bar, after the subjects of sports, movies and TV have been exhausted, people tend to talk about liquor, about the people they know who drink too much, fly off the handle, wind up wrecking their lives and the lives of everyone around them, and then they tend to get specific. This man—Jimmy—was no different. Alcoholism ran in his family, he told me. His father had died in the streets when he was younger than Jimmy was now, a transient, a bum, useless to the world and, more emphatically, to his wife and children. And Jimmy himself had a problem. He admitted as much.

A year before, he'd been living on the East Coast, in a town up the Hudson River, just outside of New York. He taught history at the local high school, and he'd come to it late, after working a high-stress job in Manhattan and commuting for years. History was his passion, and he hadn't had time to stagnate in the job like so many of his fellow teachers who went through the motions as if they were the walking dead. He loved sports too. He was a jogger, a tennis player, a mountain-biker, and he coached lacrosse after school. He was married to a girl he'd met in his senior year at the state university at Albany. They had a son—"Call him 'Chris,'" he said, looking to the neon sign again—and he'd coached Chris in high school and watched him go on to college himself as a newly minted freshman at an Ivy League school.

That was all right. Everything was all right. The school year began and he dug out his notes, Xeroxed study guides, looked up and down the class register and saw who he could trust and who he'd have to watch. In the mornings, before it was light, he ate breakfast alone in the kitchen, listening to the soft hum of the classic rock channel, the hits that took him back, hits he hadn't heard in years because Chris always had the radio tuned to hip-hop or the alternative station. Above him, in the master bedroom, Caroline was enjoying the luxury of sleeping late after thirteen years of scrambling eggs and buttering toast and seeing her son off to school. It was still dark when he climbed into his car, and most mornings he was the first one in the building, striding down the wide polished halls in a silence that could have choked on itself.

Fall settled in early that year, a succession of damp glistening days that took the leaves off the trees and fed on the breath of the wind. It seemed to do nothing but rain, day after day. The sky never swelled to flex its glory; the sun never shone. He saw a photo in the paper of a barechested jogger on the beach in Key Biscayne and felt reality slipping away from him. One afternoon he was out on the field in back of the school—the lacrosse team was scrimmaging with a bigger, more talented squad from a prep school upstate—and he couldn't seem to focus on the game. The assistant coach, no more than three or four years out of school himself, stepped up and took over the hectoring and the shoulder patting, managed the stream of substitutions and curbed the erupting tempers—discipline, that's what Jimmy taught above all else, because in a contact sport the team that controls its emotions will win out every time—while the clock ticked off the minutes to the half and the sky drew into itself and the rain whitened to sleet.

The sticks flashed, the players hurtled past him, grunting and cursing. He stood there in the weather, a physical presence, chilled, his hair wet, yet he wasn't there at all. He was reliving an episode from the previous year when his son had been the star player on the team, a moment like this one, the field slick, the players' legs a patchwork of mud, stippled flesh and dark blooming contusions. Chris had the ball. Two defenders converged on him, and Jimmy—the coach, the father—could see it all coming, the collision that would break open the day, bone to bone, the concussion, the shattered femur, injury to the spinal cord, to the brain. The sound of it—the sick wet explosion—froze him so that he couldn't even go to his son, couldn't move. But then, a miracle, Chris pushed himself up from the icy turf, stiff as a rake, and began to walk it off.

Jimmy awoke to the fact that someone was tugging at his arm. "Coach," somebody was saying, Mary-Louise, the principal's secretary, and what was she doing out here in this weather, the sleet caught like dander in the drift of her hairdo that must have cost sixty-five dollars to streak and color and set? "Jimmy," she said. "You need to call your wife." Her face fell, the white pellets pounded her hair. "It's an emergency."

He used the phone in the history chair's office, more weary than anything else. Since Chris had left home, everything seemed to set off alarm bells in Caroline's head—she thought she heard a sound in the front end of the car, the telephone had rung three times in succession but nobody was there, the cat was refusing to eat and she was sure it was feline leukemia because she'd just read an article about it in the local paper. And what was it this time—a furtive scratching in the attic? Mold eating at the caulking around the tub? He thought nothing. Stared at the crescent of white beach on the marked-up calendar tacked to the wall behind Jerry Mortensen's desk as he dialed, and wished he could feel some sun on his face for a change. Florida. Maybe they'd go to Florida for the holidays, if Chris was up for it.

Caroline picked up on the second ring and her words burned a hole right through him. "It's Chris," she said. "He's in the hospital." There was no quaver, no emotion, no cracking around the edges of what she was trying to convey, and it scared him. "He's in the hospital," she repeated.

"The hospital?"

"Jimmy," she said, and her voice cracked now, snapped like a compound fracture. "Jimmy. He's dying."

Dying? An eighteen-year-old athlete with a charmer's smile and no bad habits, heart like a clock, limbs of hammered wire, studious, dutiful, not a wild bone in his body? "What was it," I said, sounding tinny in my own ears, because his pain wasn't mine and there was no confusing the two. "Car crash?"

There had been a fraternity party the night before. The streets were slick, power lines were down, rain turned to ice, ice to snow. Chris was one of twelve pledges at Delta Upsilon, a party-hearty fraternity that offered instant access to the social scene, and it was the pledges' responsibility to pick up the party supplies—beer, vodka, cranberry juice, chips and salsa, and bunting to drape over the doorways of the big white ocean liner of a house, which had belonged to a shipping magnate at the turn of the last century. None of them had a car, so they had to walk into town and back, three trips in all, over sidewalks that were like bobsled runs, the snow so thick it was coming down in clumps, and somebody—it was Sonny Hammerschmitt, twenty-three years old and fresh from four years in the Navy and the only one of them who didn't need fake I.D.—suggested they ought to stop in at the Owl's Eye Tavern and sneak a quick beer to get in the party mood. Chris tried to talk them out of it. "Are you kidding?" he said, a cardboard box bristling with the amber necks of tequila bottles perched up on one shoulder while cars shushed by on the street and the intermediate distance blurred to white. "Dagan'll kill us if he finds out."

"Fuck Dagan. What's he going to do, blackball us? All of us?"

A snowball careened off the box and Chris almost lost his grip on it. Everybody was laughing, breath streaming, faces red with novelty, with hilarity and release. He set down the box and pelted his pledgemates with snowballs, each in his turn. Directly across the street was the tavern, a nondescript shingled building with a steep-pitched roof that might have been there when the Pilgrims came over—ancient, indelible, rooted like the trees. It was getting dark. Snow frosted the roof; the windows were pools of gold. A car crept up the street, chains jingling on the rear tires. Chris threw back his head and closed his eyes a moment, the snow accumulating like a cold compress on his eyelids. "Sure," he said, "okay. Why not? But just one, and then we'd better—" but he never finished the thought.

Inside, it was like another world, like a history lesson, with jars of pickled eggs and Polish sausage lined up behind the bar, a display of campaign buttons from the forties and fifties—*I Like Ike*—and a fireplace, a real fireplace, split oak sending up fantails of sparks against a backdrop of blackened brick. The air smelled sweet—it wasn't a confectionary sweetness or the false scent of air freshener either, but the smell of wood and wood smoke, pipe tobacco, booze. Sonny got them two pitchers of beer and shots of peppermint schnapps all around. They were there no more than half an hour—Dagan Drava, their pledgemaster, would really have their hides if he ever found out—and they drank quickly, greedily, drank as if they were getting away with something. Which they were. The snow mounted on the ledge outside the window. They had two more shots each and refilled the pitchers at least once, or maybe it was twice. Chris couldn't be sure.

Then it was the party, a blur of grinning, lurching faces, the music like a second pulse, the laughter of the girls, the brothers treating the pledges almost like human beings and everything made special by the snow that was still coming down, coming harder, coming like the end of the world. Every time the front door opened, the smell of it took hold of you as if you'd been plunged in a cold stream on the hottest day in August, and there would be two girls, two more girls, in knit hats pulled down to the eyebrows and scarves flung over their shoulders, stamping the snow from their boots and shouting, "A beer! A beer! My kingdom for a beer!"

Time contracted. One minute Chris and his pledgemates were scrambling to replenish the drinks and snacks on the big table in the dining room, everything reeking of spilled beer and tequila, as if a sea of it had washed through the house, from the attic on down to the basement, and the next minute the girls were gone, the night was settling in and Dagan was there, cracking the whip. "All right, you dogs, I want this place clean—spotless, you understand me? You've got ten minutes, ten minutes and all the trash is out of here and every scrap of this shit off the floor." The rest of the brothers were standing around now, post-party, working on the keg—the ones who weren't off getting laid, that is—and they added jeers and head slaps, barking out random orders and making the pledges drop for twenty at the slightest provocation (and being alive, breathing and present seemed provocation enough).

Like any other healthy eighteen-year-old, Chris drank, and he'd tried just about everything at least once. He was no angel on a pedestal, Jimmy knew that, and drinking—the taste for it—ran in his blood, sure it did, but in high school it was beer only and never to excess. Chris was afraid of what alcohol would do to him, to his performance on the field, to his grades, and more often than not he was the one who wound up driving everybody home after the post-game parties. But here he was, dense with it, his head stuffed full of cellulose, a screen pulled down over his eyes. He moved slowly and deliberately, lurching behind a black plastic bag full of wet trash, fumbling with the broom, the dustpan, listening for Dagan's voice in the mélange of shouts and curses and too-loud dance music as if it were the one thing he could cling to, the one thing that would get him through this and into the shelter of his bed in the windowless room behind the stairway on the second floor.

"Wait a minute, what's this? Hey, Dagan. *Dagan.* You see this?" It was the guy they called Pillar, a senior who wore a perpetual look of disappointment on his face and was said to have once won the drinking contest at Harry's Bar in

Key West by outlasting a three-hundred-pound Samoan through sixteen rounds of mojitos. He was holding up two still-sealed bottles of Don José tequila.

Dagan's face floated into the picture. "I see what you mean, bro—the place just isn't clean, is it? I mean, would you want to operate under these conditions?"

"Uh-uh, no way," Pillar said. "Not while these motherfucking bottles are sitting here. I'm offended. I really am. How about you, Dagan? Aren't you offended?"

Dude. That was what they called the drinking game, though Chris had never heard of it before and would never hear of it again. Dude, that was all, and the whole house was chanting it now, "Dude! Dude! Dude!" Dagan marched the pledges down to the game room in the basement, made them line up against the back wall and handed each of them a shot glass. This was where the big-screen TV was, where the whole house gathered to watch the Pats and the Celtics and the porn videos that made your blood surge till you thought it was going to keep on going right out the top of your head.

It was 2:00 a.m. Chris couldn't feel his legs. Everything seemed funny suddenly, and he was laughing so hard he thought he was going to bring it all up, the beer, the schnapps, the pepperoni pizza and the chips and salsa and Cheez Doodles, and his pledgemates were laughing too, Dude, the funniest thing in the world. Then Dagan slipped the video into the VCR—*Bill & Ted's Excellent Adventure*—and gave them their instructions, serious business now, a ritual, and no fooling around ("I'm serious, people, and wipe the smirks off your faces—you are in deep shit now"). Music, a flash of color, and there was Keanu Reeves, with his slice of an Asiatic face and disappearing eyes, playing the fool, or maybe playing to type, and every time he uttered the monosyllabic tag that gave the game its name, the pledge class had to lift the glasses to their lips and down a shot—"Hey, dude; 'S up, dude"—till both bottles were drained.

Benny Chung was the first one to break. He was seventeen, a Merit Scholarship finalist, with narrow shoulders, wrists you could loop two fingers around and a head that seemed to float up like a balloon from the tether of his neck. His shoulders dipped forward as if he were trying to duck under a low-hanging limb, then his lips pulled back and he spewed all over the floor and his pant legs and his black high-top Converse sneakers. It was a heroic effort, so much of that umber chowder coming out of so frail a vessel, and Benny had to go down on one knee to get it all out. Nobody said anything, and nobody was laughing now. Up on the screen, Keanu Reeves said the magic word, and all the pledges, including Benny, hammered another shot. Benny couldn't hold it, though, and neither could Chris. Chris saw the look on Benny's face—the outrage of an entire organism and all its constituent cells—and he remembered his own legs buckling and the release the first wave of nausea gave him, and then he felt nothing more.

All the Delts were swarming the room now, expostulating over this disgusting display, this pathetic showing on the part of a pledge class that wasn't worthy of the name, and hands took hold of Benny and Chris, people shouting and jostling, the whinny of laughter, cries of "Gross!" and "Don't get any of that shit on me, man," the hands finding purchase at armpit and knee. They laid Benny and Chris side by side on Chris' bed, then thundered back down the three flights of stairs to the game room. Half an hour went by and both bottles of Don José were drained by the time anyone thought to look in on them, and another ten minutes elapsed before Dagan Drava, a premed student, realized that Chris wasn't breathing.

"So he was drunk," Jimmy told me, the band into their opening number now—blues, they were doing a blues tune that seemed vaguely familiar—"and who hasn't been drunk? I've been drunk a thousand times in my life, you know what I mean? So I figure, all the way up there with Caroline hyperventilating and what-if-ing and driving me half crazy, that we're going to walk into the hospital and he'll be sitting up in bed with a sheepish grin on his face, one hell of a headache, maybe, and a lesson learned, but no harm done."

Jimmy was wrong. His son had choked on his own vomit, inhaled it, compromising his lungs. No one knew how long he'd been lying there in the bed next to Benny Chung without drawing a breath before the E.R. team restarted his heart, and no one was sure of how much damage had been done to his brain functions. A CT scan showed edema of the brain tissue. He was in a coma. A machine was breathing for him. Caroline went after the doctors like an inquisitor, relentless, terrifying in her grief. She stalked the halls, chased them to their cars, harangued them on the phone, demanded—and got—the top neurologist in New England. Chris' eyes never opened. Beneath the lids, like a dirty secret, his pupils dilated to full and fixed there, focused on nothing. Two days later he was dead.

I bought Jimmy a drink, watched myself in the mirror behind the bar. I didn't look like anybody I knew, but there I was, slouched over my elbows and a fresh drink, taking in air and letting it seep back out again. The woman with the deep-dredged laugh was gone. A couple in their twenties had settled into the vacant spot on the other side of Jimmy, oblivious to the drama that had just played out here, the woman perched on the barstool while the man stood in place, rocking in her arms to the beat of the music. The band featured a harp player, and he moved round the confines of the stage like a caged animal, riffling the notes till he went all the way from despair to disbelief and back again, the bass player leaning in as if to brace himself, the guitar rising up slow and mournful out of the stew of the backbeat.

"Hey, don't feel sorry for me," Jimmy said. "I'm out here in California having the time of my life." He pointed a finger at the rain-streaked window. "All this sun really cheers me up."

I don't know why I asked—I was drunk, I guess, feeling maudlin, who knows?—but I said, "You got a place to stay tonight?"

He looked into the shot glass as if he might discover a motel key at the bottom of it. "I'm on sabbatical," he said. "Or on leave, actually. I was staying with my brother—up on Olive Mill?—but he got to be a pain in the ass. Caroline couldn't take it. She's back in New York. At least, I think she is."

"Hard luck," I said, just to say something.

"Oh, yeah," he said, "sure, and that's the long and the short of it. But I tell you, I clean up real nice, and what I plan to do is pick up one of these spare women here, like that one over there—the dye job looks like she just crawled out of a coffin? She'll take me home with her, what you want to bet? And what you want to bet she's got a shower, maybe even a Jacuzzi?"

I didn't want to bet anything. I wanted another drink, that was all. And after that, I wanted to have maybe one more, at this place up the street I'd been to a couple of times, just to see what was happening, because it was Saturday night and you never knew.

A week later—it was the next Friday, actually—I went into a place down at the marina for cocktails with a woman I'd almost picked up after I left Jimmy at the steakhouse the previous Saturday. Her name was Steena, she was five-ten, blond, and just getting over a major breakup with a guy named Steve whose name dropped from her lips with the frequency of a speech impediment. She'd agreed to "have a drink" with me, and though I'd hoped for more, I had to assume, after we'd had two glasses each of Piper-Heidsieck at twelve and a half dollars per and a plate of oysters, that I wasn't *her* type either. The whole time she kept glancing at her watch, and finally her cell phone rang and she got up from the table and went out into the anteroom to take the call. It was Steve. She was sorry, but he wanted to meet her later, for dinner, and he sounded so sad and heartbroken and shot through with misery and contrition she couldn't refuse. I had nothing to say. I just stared at her, the plate of desecrated oysters between us. "So," she said, hovering over the table as if she were afraid to sit back down, "I guess I'm going to have to say goodbye. It's been nice, though. Really."

I paid the waitress and moved up to the bar, idly watching the Lakers go through their paces with the sound muted and gazing out the window on the pale bleached forest of the ships' masts gathered there against the night. I was drinking brandy and water, picking through a bowl of artificial snack food and waiting for something to happen, when I ran into the other man I wanted to tell you about. Shaq's monumental head loomed up on the screen and then faded away again, and I turned around and there he was, just settling into the seat beside me. For a minute I thought he was Jimmy—he had the same hangdog look, the rangy height, the air of an athlete gone to seed—and it gave me a start, because the last thing I needed the way I was feeling was another bout of one-way commiseration. He nodded a greeting, then looked up at the screen. "What's the score?"

"The Lakers are killing them," I said. "I think. I'm pretty sure anyway." But this *was* Jimmy, had to be, Jimmy all dressed up and with his hair combed and looking satisfied with himself. It was then that I remembered the brother. "You wouldn't be Jimmy's brother, would you?" I said. "By any chance?"

"*Whose* brother?"

I felt foolish then. Obviously Jimmy hadn't given me his real name, and why would he? The alcohol bloomed in my brain, petals unfolding like a rosebud in time-lapse photography. "It's nothing," I said, "I just thought . . ." and let it die. I went back to watching the game. Helped myself to the artificial snacks. Had another brandy and water. After a while the man beside me ordered dinner at the bar, and I got into a conversation about recycling and the crime of waste with a startled-looking woman and her martini-fueled husband. Gradually, the bar filled up. The startled-looking woman and her husband went in to dinner and somebody else took their place. Nothing was happening. Absolutely nothing. I was thinking I should move on, pick up a pizza, some takeout, make it an early night, and I could envision myself standing at the supercharged counter of Paniagua's Pizza Palace, where you could get two slices with chorizo and jalapeños for three dollars and fifty cents, but instead I found myself turning to the man on my left. "You do have a brother, though, right?" I said.

He gave me a long, slow, deliberate look, then shrugged. "What, does he owe you money?"

So we talked about Jimmy, Jimmy's tragedy, Jimmy's refusal to accept facts and the way Jimmy was running hard up against the sharp edges of the world and was sure to wind up in a coffin just like his father before him and his son too if he didn't get himself into rehab as his number one priority. Then we talked about me, but I didn't reveal much, and then it was general subjects, the look of the people on TV as opposed to the look of the flesh-and-blood people sitting at the tables at our feet like an undiscovered tribe, and then, inevitably, we came back to alcohol. I told him of some of my escapades, he told me of his. I was probably on my sixth or seventh brandy and water when we got back as far as our mutual childhoods lived mutually under the shadow of booze, though on opposite coasts. The brother was in an expansive mood, his wife and six-year-old daughter gone for the weekend to a Little Miss pageant in Sacramento, and the four walls of his house—or eight or sixteen or however many there were—inadequate to contain him. I took a sip of my drink and let him fly.

He was three years older than Jimmy, and they had two other brothers and a sister, all younger. They moved around a lot as kids, but one winter they were living out in the country in Dutchess County, at the junction of two blacktop roads where there were a handful of summer cabins that had been converted to cheap year-round housing, a two-pump gas station where you could get milk, bread and Coke in the eight-ounce bottle, and a five-stool roadhouse with a jukebox and a griddle called the Pine Top Tavern. The weather turned nasty, their father was out of work and about a month from bailing out for good, and neither of their parents left the tavern for more than a shower or a shave or to put a couple cans of chicken broth in a saucepan and dump a handful of rice and sliced wieners in on top of it so the kids would have something to eat. Jimmy's brother had a cough that wouldn't go away. Their little sister had burned her arm on the stove trying to make herself a can of tomato soup and the brother had to change her bandage twice a day and rub ointment into the exfoliated skin. Jimmy spent his time out in the weed-blistered lot behind the house, kicking a football as close to vertical as he could, over and over again, then slanting off to retrieve it before it could hit the ground. Their dog—Gomer, named after the TV character—had been killed crossing the road on Christmas Eve, and their father blamed one of the drunks leaving the tavern, but nobody did anything about it.

It was just after Christmas—or maybe after New Year's, because school had started up again—when a cold front came down out of Hudson Bay and froze everything so thoroughly nobody could stand to be out of doors more than five minutes at a time. The birds huddled under the eaves of the tavern, looking distressed; the squirrels hung like ornaments in the stripped trees. Everybody in the family drank hot tea thick with honey and the oily residue of the bitter lemon juice that came out of the plastic squeeze bottle, and that was the only time their hands seemed to warm up. When they went outside, the bare ground crackled underfoot as if it were crusted with snow, and for a few days there none of the converted cabins had water because the lines from the well had frozen underground. Jimmy's brother, though he had a cough that wouldn't go away, had to take a pail across the road to the pond and break the ice to get water for the stove.

He remembered his father, wizened forearms propped up on the bar in a stained khaki parka he'd worn in Korea, a sheaf of hair canted the wrong way because it hadn't seen a comb in days, the smoke of his cigarette fuming in the dark forge of the bar. And his mother, happiest woman in the world, laughing at anything, laughing till all the glasses were drained and the lights went out and the big-bellied bartender with the caved-in face shooed them out the door and locked the place up for the night. It was cold. The space heater did nothing, less than nothing, and Jimmy's brother could have earned his merit badge as a fire-starter that winter because all he did was comb the skeletal forest for fallen branches, rotten stumps and fence posts, anything that would burn, managing to keep at least a continuous smolder going day and night. And then he got up for school one morning and there was an old woman—or a woman his mother's age anyway—laid out snoring on the couch in front of the fireplace where the dog used to sleep. He went into his parents' room and shook his mother awake. "There's somebody sleeping out there on the couch," he told her, and watched her gather her features together and assess the day. He had to repeat himself twice, the smell of her, of her warmth and the warmth of his father beside her, rising up to him with a sweet-sick odor of sex and infirmity, and then she murmured through her cracked lips, "Oh, that's only Grace. You know Grace—from the tavern? Her car won't start, that's all. Be a good boy, huh, and don't wake her?"

He didn't wake her. He got his brothers and sister out of bed, then huddled with them at the bus stop in the dark, jumping from foot to foot to keep warm and imagining himself on a polar expedition with Amundsen, sled dogs howling at the stars and the ice plates shifting like dominoes beneath their worn and bleeding paws. There was a pot on the stove when he got home from school, some sort of incarnadine stew with a smell of the exotic spices his mother never used—mace, cloves, fennel—and he thought of Grace, with her scraggle of gray-black hair and her face that was like a dried-up field plowed in both directions. He tasted it—they all sampled it, just to see if it was going to be worth eating—and somehow it even managed to taste of Grace, though how could anybody know what Grace tasted like unless they were a cannibal?

His parents weren't at home. They were three hundred feet away, in the tavern, with Grace and the rest of their good-time buddies. A few dispirited snowflakes sifted down out of the sky. He made himself a sandwich of peanut butter and sliced banana, then went into the tavern to see if his parents or anybody else there was in that phase of rhapsodic drunkenness where they gave up their loose change as if they were philanthropists rolling down Park Avenue in an open Rolls-Royce. One guy, hearty, younger than the rest, in a pair of galoshes with the buckles torn off, gave him a fifty-cent piece, and then his father told him to get the hell out of the bar and stay out till he was of legal age or he'd kick his ass for him but good.

The next morning was even colder, and Jimmy's brother was up early, shivering despite the rancid warmth generated by his three brothers and the cheap sleeping bag advertised for comfort even at five below zero, which might as well have been made of shredded newspaper for all the good it did. He put the kettle on to boil so they could have hot tea and instant oatmeal to fortify them out there in the wind while they were waiting for the school bus to come shunting down the hill with its headlights reduced to vestigial eyes and the driver propped up behind the black windshield like a blind cavefish given human form. The house was dark but for the overhead light in the kitchen. There was no sound anywhere, nothing from his parents or his brothers and sister, everybody locked in a sleep that was like a spell in a fairy tale, and he missed the dog then, if only to see it stretch and yawn and nose around in its dish. The kettle came to a boil and he'd actually put three tea bags in the pot and begun pouring the water before he realized that something was wrong. What was it? He strained his ears but there was nothing to hear. Not even the tick of the stove or the creak and whine of the house settling into the cold, no sound of stirring birds or tires revolving on the blacktop road. It was then that he thought to check the time.

There was a clock built into the stove, foreshortened hands painted gold behind a greased-over plastic lens. It read 3:35 a.m. Jimmy's brother could have kicked himself. He sat in the kitchen, shivering, and had a cup of tea, wishing it would snow so they'd call off school and he could sleep all day. After a while he decided to build up the fire in the living room and sit there on the couch and terrify himself with *Dracula*—he was halfway through, though he'd started it at Halloween—and then maybe he'd drift off for a while till it was time to get up. He shrugged into his coat and went to the kitchen door, thinking of the punky wood he and Jimmy had stacked in the shed over the weekend.

But then—and I was ahead of him here, because you'd have to be as blind as a cavefish yourself not to see where this was going—the storm door wouldn't give. There was something there, an immovable shadow stretched long and dark across the doorstep, and it took everything the brother had to wedge the door open enough to squeeze out into the night. And when he did pull himself out into the cold, and the killing, antipathetic breath of it hit him full in the face, he willed the shadow at his feet to take shape until he could distinguish the human form there, with her dried-out skin and fixed eyes and the dirty scraggle of gray-black hair.

"Grace?" I said.

Jimmy's brother nodded.

"Jesus," I said. "And your brother—did he see her there?"

He shrugged. "I don't know. I don't remember. She was a drunk, that was all, just another drunk."

We sat for a moment, looking past our drinks to the marina and the black unbroken plane of the sea beyond it. I had an impulse to open up to him, to tell him my story, or one of my stories, as if we were clasping hands at an AA meeting, but I didn't. I made a clucking sound, meant to signify sympathy and understanding, threw some money on the bar and went out the door, feeling for my keys. What I didn't tell him, though he might have known it himself, was that Jimmy had put his son in a crematory box at the hospital and he put the box in the back of his Suburban and drove it home and into the garage, and all night, while his wife lay stiff and sedated in the big queen-sized bed upstairs, Jimmy hugged the coffin to him. I didn't tell him that life is a struggle against weakness, fought not in the brain or in the will but in the cells, in the enzymes, in the key the DNA inserts into the tumbler of our personalities. And I didn't tell him that I had a son myself, just like Jimmy, though I didn't see him as much as I would have wanted to, not anymore.

The fact was that I hadn't wanted a son, hadn't planned on it or asked or prayed or hoped for or even imagined it. I was twenty-four. My wife was pregnant and I raged at her, *Get rid of it, you're ruining my life, we can't afford it, you're crazy, get rid of it, get rid of it.* She was complete in herself, sweet-faced and hard-willed, and mine was a voice she couldn't hear. She went to Lamaze classes, quit drinking, quit smoking, did her exercises, read all the books. My son was born in the Kaiser hospital in Panorama City, eight pounds, six ounces, as healthy as a rat and beautiful in his own way, and I was his father, though I wasn't ready to be. He was nine months old when one of my drinking buddies—call him Chris, why not?—came for the weekend and we went on a tear. My wife put up with it, even joined in a bit, and on Monday morning, when she had to go in early to work, Chris and I took her out for breakfast.

The day beat down like a hammer and everything in the visible world shone as if it had been lit from within. We'd been up till four, and now it was seven, and while we were waiting for a table Chris and I ducked into the men's room and alternated hits from a pint of Smirnoff we were planning to doctor our fresh-squeezed orange juice with. So we were feeling fine as we chased the waffles around our plates and my wife smiled and joked and the baby unfurled his arms and grabbed at things in high baby spirits. Then my wife touched up her makeup and left, and right away the mood changed—here was this baby, my son, with his multiplicity of needs, his diapers and his stroller and all the rest of it, and I was in charge.

We finally hit upon the plan of taking him to the beach, to get a little sun, throw a Frisbee, let the sand mold itself to us through the long, slow-simmering morning and into the afternoon and the barbecue I was planning for Chris' send-off. The beach was deserted, a board-stretched canvas for gulls and pelicans and snapping blue waves, and as soon as we stepped out of the car I felt everything was all right again. My son was wearing nothing but his diaper, and Chris and I were laughing over something, and I tossed my son up in the air, a game we played, and he loved it, squealing and crying out in baby ecstasy. I tossed him again, and then I tossed him to Chris and Chris tossed him back, and that was when I lost my balance and the black sea-honed beak of a half-buried rock loomed up on me and I saw my future in that instant: I was going to drop my son, let him slip through my fingers in a moment of aberration, and he was going to be damaged in a way that nobody could repair.

It didn't happen. I caught him, and held on, and I never let go.

(2002)

Swept Away

People can talk, they can gossip and cavil and run down this one or the other, and certainly we have our faults, our black funks and suicides and crofters' wives running off with the first man who'll have them and a winter's night that stretches on through the days and weeks like a foretaste of the grave, but in the end the only real story here is the wind. The puff and blow of it. The ceaselessness. The squelched keening of air in movement, running with its currents like a new sea clamped atop the old, winnowing, harrowing, pinching everything down to nothing. It rakes the islands day and night, without respect to season, though if you polled the denizens of Yell, Funzie and Papa Stour, to a man, woman, lamb and pony they would account winter the worst for the bite of it and the sheer frenzy of its coming. One January within living memory the wind blew at gale force for twenty-nine days without remit, and on New Year's Eve back in '92 the gusts were estimated at 201 mph at the Muckle Flugga lighthouse here on the northernmost tip of the Isle of Unst. But that was only an estimate: the weather service's wind gauge was torn from its moorings and launched into eternity that day, along with a host of other things, stony and animate alike.

Junie Ooley should have known better. She was an American woman—*the American ornithological woman* is the way people around town came to refer to her, or sometimes just *the bird woman*—and she hadn't just barely alighted from the ferry when she was blindsided by Robbie Baikie's old one-eyed tom, which had been trying to inveigle itself across the roof tiles of the kirk after an imaginary pigeon. Or perhaps the pigeon wasn't imaginary, but by the time the cat blinked his eyes whatever he had seen was gone with the wind. At any rate, Junie Ooley, who was at this juncture a stranger to us all, came banking up the high street in a store-bought tartan skirt and a pair of black tights climbing her queenly legs, a rucksack flailing at the small of her back and both hands clamped firmly to her knit hat, and she never saw the cat coming, for all her visual acuity and the fine-ground photographic lenses she trucked with her everywhere. The cat—his name was Tiger and he must have carried a good ten or twelve pounds of pigeon-fed flesh on his bones—caught a gust and flew off the kirk tiles like a heat-seeking missile locked in on Junie Ooley's hunched and flapping form.

The impact was dramatic, as you would have had reason to testify had you been meditating over a pint of bitter at the rattling window of Magnuson's Pub that day, and the bird woman, before she'd had a chance even to discover the whereabouts of her lodgings or offer up a "good day" or "how do you do?" to a single soul, was laid out flat on the flagstones, her lips quivering unconsciously over the lyrics to a tune by the Artist Formerly Known as Prince. At least that was what Robbie claimed afterward, and he's always been dead keen on the Artist, ever since he came by the CD of *Purple Rain* in the used-disc bin of a record shop in Aberdeen and got it for less than half of what it would have cost new. We had to take his word for it. He was the first one out the door and come to her aid.

There she was, flung down on the stones like a wilted flower amidst the crumpled stalks of her limbs, the rucksack stuffed full of spare black tights and her bird-watching paraphernalia, her kit and dental floss and all the rest, and Tiger just pulling himself up into a ball to blink his eyes and lick at his spanned paws in a distracted way, when Duncan Stout, ninety-two years on this planet and in possession of the first Morris automobile ever manufactured, came down the street in that very vehicle at twice his normal speed of five and a half miles per hour, and if he discerned Junie Ooley lying there it was anybody's guess. Robbie Baikie flailed his arms to head off Duncan's car, but Duncan was the last man in these islands to be expecting anything unexpected out there in the middle of the high street designed and reserved exclusively for the traffic of automobiles and lorries and the occasional dithering bicycle. He kept coming. His jaw was set, the cap pulled down to the orbits of his milk-white eyes. Robbie Baikie was not known for thinking on his feet—like many of us, he was a deliberative type—and by the time he thought to scoop Junie Ooley up in his arms the car was on them. Or just about.

People were shouting from the open door of the pub. Magnus Magnuson himself was in the street now, windmilling his arms and flinging out his feet in alarm, the bar rag still clutched in one hand like a flag of surrender. The car came on. Robbie stood there. Hopeless was the way it looked. But then we hadn't taken the wind into account, and how could any of us have forgotten its caprices, even for a minute? At that crucial instant, a gust came up the canyon of the high street and bowled Robbie Baikie over atop the bird woman even as it lifted the front end of Duncan's car and flung it into the near streetlamp, which never yielded.

The wind skreeled off down the street, carrying bits of paper, cans, bottles, old bones and rags and other refuse along with it. The bird woman's eyes blinked open. Robbie Baikie, all fifteen stone of him, lay pressed atop her in a defensive posture, anticipating the impact of the car, and he hadn't even thought to prop himself on his elbows to take some of the crush off her. Junie Ooley smelled the beer on him and the dulcet smoke of his pipe tobacco and the sweetness of the peat fire at Magnuson's and maybe even something of the sheep he kept, and she couldn't begin to imagine who this man was or what he was doing on top of her in the middle of the public street. "Get off me," she said in a voice so flat and calm Robbie wasn't sure he'd heard it at all, and because she was an American woman and didn't commonly make use of the term "clod," she added, "you big doof."

Robbie was shy with women—we all were, except for the women themselves, and they were shy with the men, at least for the first five years after the wedding—and he was still fumbling with the notion of what had happened to him and to her and to Duncan Stout's automobile and couldn't have said one word even if he'd wanted to.

"Get off," she repeated, and she'd begun to add physical emphasis to the imperative, writhing beneath him and bracing her upturned palms against the great unmoving slabs of his shoulders.

Robbie went to one knee, then pushed himself up even as the bird woman rolled out from under him. In the next moment she was on her feet, angrily shifting the straps of her rucksack where they bit into the flesh, cursing him softly but emphatically and with a kind of fluid improvisatory genius that made his face light up in wonder. Twenty paces away, Duncan was trying to extricate himself from his car, but the wind wouldn't let him. Howith Clarke, the greengrocer, was out in the street now, surveying the damage with a sour face, and Magnus was right there in the middle of things, his voice gone hoarse with excitement. He was inquiring after Junie Ooley's condition—"Are you all right, lass?"—when a gust lifted all four of them off their feet and sent them tumbling like ninepins. That was enough for Robbie. He picked himself up, took hold of the bird woman's arm and frog-marched her into the pub.

In they came, and the wind with them, packets of crisps and beer coasters sailing across the polished surface of the bar, and all of us instinctively grabbing for our hats. Robbie's head was bowed and his hair blown straight up off his crown as if it had been done up in a perm by some mad cosmetologist, and Junie Ooley heaving and thrashing against him till he released her to spin away from him and down the length of the bar. No one could see how pretty she was at first, her face all deformed with surprise and rage and the petulant crease stamped between her eyes. She didn't even so much as look in our direction, but just threw herself back at Robbie and gave him a shove as if they were children at war on the playground.

"What the hell do you think you're doing?" she demanded, her voice piping high with her agitation. And then, glancing round at the rest of us: "Did you see what this big *idiot* did to me out there?"

No one said a word. The smoke of the peat fire hung round us like a thin curtain. Tim Maconochie's Airedale lifted his head from the floor and laid it back down again.

The bird woman clenched her teeth, set her shoulders. "Well, isn't anybody going to do anything?"

Magnus was the one to break the silence. He'd slipped back in behind the bar, unmindful of the chaff and bits of this and that that the wind had deposited in his hair. "The man saved your life, that's about all."

Robbie ducked his head out of modesty. His ears went crimson.

"Saved—?" A species of comprehension settled into her eyes. "I was . . . something hit me, something the wind blew . . ."

Tim Maconochie, though he wasn't any less tightfisted than the rest of us, cleared his throat and offered to buy the girl a drop of whisky to clear her head, and her face opened up then like the sun coming through the clouds so that we all had a good look at the beauty of her, and it was a beauty that made us glad to be alive in that moment to witness it. Whiskies went round. A blast of wind rattled the panes till we thought they would burst. Someone led Duncan in and sat him down in the corner with his pipe and a pint of ale. And then there was another round, and another, and all the while Junie Ooley was perched on a stool at the bar talking Robbie Baikie's big glowing ears right off him.

That was the beginning of a romance that stood the whole island on its head. Nobody had seen anything like it, at least since the two maundering teens from Cullivoe had drowned themselves in a suicide pact in the Ness of Houlland, and it was the more surprising because no one had ever suspected such depths of passion in a poor slug like Robbie Baikie. Robbie wasn't past thirty, but it was lassitude and the brick wall of introspection that made him sit at the bar till he carried the weight of a man twice his age, and none of us could remember him in the company of a woman, not since his mother died anyway. He was the sort to let his sheep feed on the blighted tops of the heather and the wrack that blew up out of the sea and he kept his heart closed up like a lockbox. And now, all of a sudden, right before our eyes, he was a man transformed. That first night he led Junie Ooley up the street to her lodgings like a gallant out of the picture films, the two of them holding hands and leaning into the wind while cats and flowerpots and small children flew past them, and it seemed he was never away from her for five minutes consecutive after that.

He drove her all the wind-blasted way out to the bird sanctuary at Herma Ness and helped her set up her equipment in an abandoned crofter's cottage of such ancient provenance that not even Duncan Stout could say who the landlord might once have been. The cottage had a thatched roof, and though it was rotted through in half a dozen places and perfervid with the little lives of crawling things and rodents, she didn't seem particular. It was in the right place, on a broad barren moor that fell off into the sea among the cliffs where the birds made their nests, and that was all that mattered.

There was no fuss about Junie Ooley. She was her own woman, and no doubt about it. She'd come to see and study the flocks that gathered there in the spring—the kittiwakes, the puffins, terns and northern fulmars nesting the high ledges and spreading wide their wings to cruise out over the sea—and she had her array of cameras and telephoto lenses with her to take her photographs for the pricey high-grade magazines. If she had to rough it, she was prepared. There were the cynical among us who thought she was just making use of Robbie Baikie for the convenience of his Toyota minivan and the all-purpose, wraparound warmth of him, and there was no end to the gossip of the biddies and the potboilers and the kind who wouldn't know a good thing if it fell down out of Heaven and conked them on the head, but there were those who saw it for what it was: love, pure and simple.

If Robbie never much bothered about the Moorits and Cheviots his poor dead and buried father had bred up over the years, now he positively neglected them. If he lost six Blackface ewes stranded by the tide or a Leicester tup caught on a bit of wire in his own yard, he never knew it. He was too busy elsewhere. The two of them—he and the bird woman—would be gone for a week at a time, scrabbling over the rock faces that dropped down to the sea, she with her cameras, he with the rucksack and lenses and the black bottles of stout and smoked-tongue sandwiches, and when we did see them in town they were either taking tea at the hotel or holding hands in the back nook of the pub. They scandalized Mrs. Dunwoodie, who let her rooms over the butcher's shop to Junie Ooley on a monthly basis, because she'd seen Robbie coming down the stairs with the girl on more than one occasion and once in the night heard what could only have been the chirps and muffled cries of coital transport drifting down from above. And a Haroldswick man—we won't name him here, for decency's sake—even claims that he saw the two of them cavorting in the altogether outside the stone cottage at Herma Ness.

One night when the wind was up they lingered in Magnuson's past the dinner hour, murmuring to each other in a soft indistinguishable fusion of voices, and Robbie drinking steadily, pints and whiskies both. We watched him rise for another round, then weave his way back to the table where she awaited him, a pint clutched in each of his big red hands. "You know what we say this time of year when the kittiwakes first return to us?" he asked her, his voice booming out suddenly and his face aflame with the drink and the very joy of her presence.

Conversations died. People looked up. He handed her the beer and she gave him a sweet inquisitive smile and we all wished the smile was for us and maybe we begrudged him it just the smallest bit. He spread his arms and recited a little poem for her, a poem we all knew as well as we knew our own names, the heart stirrings of an anonymous bird lover lost now to the architecture of time:

> Peerie mootie! Peerie mootie!
> O, du love, du joy, du Beauty!
> Whaar is du came frae? Whaar is du been?
> Wi di swittlin feet and di glitterin een?

It was startling to hear these sentiments from Robbie Baikie, a man's man who was hard even where he was soft, a man not given to maundering, and we all knew then just how far overboard he'd gone. Love was one thing—a rose blooming atop a prickly stem risen up out of the poor soil of these windswept islands, and it was a necessary thing, to be nourished, surely—but this was something else altogether. This was a kind of fealty, a slavery, a doom—he'd given her *our* poem, and in public no less—and we all shuddered to look on it.

"Robbie," Magnus cried out in a desperation that spoke for us all, "Robbie, let me stand you a drop of whisky, lad," but if Robbie heard him, he gave no sign of it. He took the bird woman's hand, a little bunch of chapped and wind-blistered knuckles, and brought it to his lips. "That's the way I feel about you," he said, and we all heard it.

It would be useless to deny that we were all just waiting for the other shoe to drop. There was something inhuman in a passion so intense as that—it was a rabbity love, a tup's love, and it was bound to come crashing down to earth, just as the Artist lamented so memorably in "When Doves Cry." There were some of us who wondered if Robbie even listened to his own CDs anymore. Or heeded them.

And then, on a gloomy gray dour day with the wind sitting in the north and the temperatures threatening to take us all the way back to the doorstep of winter again, Robbie came thundering through the front door of the pub in a hurricane of flailing leaves, thistles, matchbooks and fish-and-chips papers and went straight to the bar for a double whisky. It was the first time since the ornithological woman had appeared among us that anyone had seen him alone, and if that wasn't sign enough, there were those who could divine by the way he held himself and the particular roseate hue of his ears that the end had come. He drank steadily for an hour or two, deflecting any and all comments—even the most innocuous observations about the weather—with a grunt or even a snarl. We gave him his space and sat at the window to watch the world tumble by.

Late in the day, the light of the westering sun slanted through the glass, picking out the shadow of the mullions, and for a moment it laid the glowing cross of our Saviour in the precise spot where Robbie's shoulder blades conjoined. He heaved a sigh then—a roaring, single-malt, tobacco-inflected groan it was, actually—and finally those massive shoulders began to quake and heave. The barmaid (Rose Ellen MacGooch, Donal MacGooch's youngest) laid a hand on his forearm and asked him what the matter was, though we all knew. People made their voices heard so he wouldn't think we were holding our breath; Magnus made a show of lighting his pipe at the far end of the bar; Tim Maconochie's dog let out an audible fart. A calm settled over the pub, and Robbie Baikie exhaled and delivered up the news in a voice that was like a scouring pad.

He'd asked her to marry him. Up there, in the crofter's hut, the wind keening and the kittiwakes sailing through the air like great overblown flakes of snow. They'd been out all morning, scaling the cliffs with numb hands, fighting the wind, and now they were sharing a sandwich and the stout over a turf fire. Robbie had kissed her, a long, lingering lover's kiss, and then, overcome by the emotion of the moment, he'd popped the question. Junie Ooley had drawn herself up, the eyes shining in her heaven-sent face, and told him she was flattered by the proposal, flattered and moved, deeply moved, but that she just wasn't ready to commit to something like that, like marriage, that is, what with him being a Shetland sheepman and she an American woman with a college degree and a rover at that. Would he come with her to Patagonia to photograph the *chimango* and the *ñandú*? Or to the Okefenokee Swamp in search of the elusive ivory bill? To Singapore? São Paolo? Even Edinburgh? He said he would. She called him a liar. And then they were shouting and she was out in the wind, her knit cap torn from her head in a blink and her hair beating mad at her green eyes, and he tried to pull her to him, to snatch her arm and hold her, but she was already at the brink of the cliff, already edging her way down amidst the fecal reek and the raucous avian cries. "Junie!" he shouted. "Junie, take my hand, you'll lose your balance in this wind, you know you will! Take my hand!"

And what did she say then? "I don't need any man to cling to." That was it. All she said and all she wrote. And he stood in the blast, watching her work her way from one handhold to another out over the yawning sea as the birds careened round her and her hair strangled her face, and then he strode back to the minivan, fired up the engine, and drove back into town.

That night the wind soughed and keened and rattled like a set of pipes through the canyon of the high street on till midnight or so, and then it came at us with a new sound, a sound people hadn't heard in these parts since '92. It was blowing a gale. Shingles fled before the gusts, shrubs gave up their grip on the earth, the sheep in the fields were snatched up and flung across the countryside like so many puffs of lint. Garages collapsed, bicycles raced down the street with no more than a ghost at the pedals. Robbie was unconscious in the sitting room of his cottage at the time, sad victim of drink and sorrow. He'd come home from the pub before the wind rose up in its fury, boiled himself a plate of liver muggies, then conked out in front of the telly before he could so much as lift a fork to them.

It was something striking the side of the house that brought him to his senses. He woke to darkness, the electric gone with the first furious gusts, and at first he didn't know where he was. Then the house shuddered again and the startled bellow of the Ayrshire cow he kept for her milk and butter roused him up out of the easy chair and he went to the door and stuck his head out into that wild night. Immediately the door was torn from his grasp, straining back on its hinges with a shriek even as the pale form of the cow shot past and rose up to tear away like a cloud over the shingles of the roof. He had one thought then, and one thought only: *Junie. Junie needs me.*

It was his luck that he carried five hundred pounds of coal in the back of his minivan as ballast, as so many of us do, because without it he'd never have kept the thing to the road. As it was, he had to dodge the hurtling sheep, rabbits that flew out of the shadows like nightjars, posts torn from their moorings, the odd roof or wall, even a boat or two lashed up out of the heaving seas. He could barely see the road for the blowing trash, the wind slammed at him like a fist and he had to fight the wheel to keep the car from flipping end over end. If he was half-looped still when he climbed into the car, now he was as sober as a foude, all the alcohol burned away in his veins with the terrible anxiety that drove him. He put his foot to the floor. He could only pray that he wouldn't be too late.

Then he was there, fighting his way out of the car, and he had to hold to the door to keep from being blown away himself. The moor was as black as the hide of an Angus bull. The wind shrieked in every passage, scouring the heather till it lay flat and cried out its agony. He could hear the sea battering the cliffs below. It was then that the door of the minivan gave way and in the next instant he was coasting out over the scrub like a tobogganer hurtling down Burrafirth Hill, and there'll be men to tell you it was a tree saved him from going over, but what tree could grow on an island as stingy as this? It was a thornbush is what it was, a toughened black unforgiving snarl of woody pith combed down to the ground with fifty years of buffeting, but it was enough. The shining white door of the minivan ran out to sea as if it would run forever, an awkward big plate of steel that might as well have been a Frisbee sailing out over the waves, but Robbie Baikie was saved, though the thorns dug into his hands and the wind took the hair off his head and flailed the beard from his cheeks. He squinted against it, against the airborne dirt and the darkness, and there it was, two hundred yards away and off behind him to the left: the crofter's cottage, and with her in it. "Junie!" he cried, but the wind beat at the sound of his voice and carried it away till it was no voice at all. "Junie!"

As for her, the bird woman, the American girl with the legs that took the breath out of you and the face and figure that were as near perfection as any man here had ever dreamed of on the best night of his life, she never knew Robbie had come for her. What she did know was that the wind was bad. Very bad. She must have struggled against it and realized how futile it was to do anything more than to succumb to it, to huddle and cling and wait it out. Where were the birds? she wondered. How would they weather this—on their wings? Out at sea? She was cold, shivering, the fire long since consumed by the gusts that tore at the chimney. And then the chimney went, with a sound of claws raking at a windowpane. There was a crack, and the roof beams gave way, and then it was the night staring down at her from above. She clung to the andirons, but the andirons blew away, and then she clung to the stones of the hearth but the stones were swept away as if they were nothing more than motes of dust, and what was she supposed to cling to then?

We never found her. Nobody did. There are some who'll say she was swept all the way to the coast of Norway and came ashore speaking Norse like a native or that a ship's captain, battened down in a storm-sea, found her curled round the pocked safety glass of the bridge like a living figurehead, but no one really believes it. Robbie Baikie survived the night and he survived the mourning of her too. He sits even now over his pint and his drop of whisky in the back nook at Magnuson's, and if anybody should ask him about the only love of his life, the bird woman from America, he'll tell you he's heard her voice in the cries of the kittiwakes that swarm the skies in spring, and seen her face there too, hanging over the black crashing sea on the stiff white wings of a bird. Poor Robbie.

(2001)

Dogology

Rumors

It was the season of mud, drainpipes drooling, the gutters clogged with debris, a battered and penitential robin fixed like a statue on every lawn. Julian was up early, a Saturday morning, beating eggs with a whisk and gazing idly out the kitchen window and into the colorless hide of the day, expecting nothing, when all at once the scrim of rain parted to reveal a dark, crouching presence in the far corner of the yard. At first glance, he took it to be a dog—a town ordinance he particularly detested disallowed fences higher than three feet, and so the contiguous lawns and flowerbeds of the neighborhood had become a sort of open savanna for roaming packs of dogs—but before the wind shifted and the needling rain closed in again, he saw that he was wrong. This figure, partially obscured by the resurgent forsythia bush, seemed out of proportion, all limbs, as if a dog had been mated with a monkey. And what was it, then? Raccoons had been at the trash lately, and he'd seen a opossum wavering down the street like a pale ghost one late night after a dreary overwrought movie Cara had insisted upon, but this was no opossum. Or raccoon either. It was dark in color, whatever it was—a bear, maybe, a yearling strayed down from the high ridges along the river, and hadn't Ben Ober told him somebody on F Street had found a bear in their swimming pool? He put down the whisk and went to fetch his glasses.

A sudden eruption of thunder set the dishes rattling on the drainboard, followed by an uncertain flicker of light that illuminated the dark room as if the bulb in the overhead fixture had gone loose in the socket. He wondered how Cara could sleep through all this, but the wonder was short-lived, because he really didn't give a damn one way or the other if she slept all day, all night, all week. Better she should sleep and give him some peace. He was in the living room now, the gloom ladled over everything, shadows leeching into black holes behind the leather couch and matching armchairs, the rubber plant a dark ladder in the corner and the shadowy fingers of the potted palms reaching out for nothing. The thunder rolled again, the lightning flashed. His glasses were atop the TV, where he'd left them the night before while watching a sorry documentary about the children purportedly raised by wolves in India back in the nineteen twenties, two stringy girls in sepia photographs that revealed little and could have been faked in any case. He put his glasses on and padded back into the kitchen in his stocking feet, already having forgotten why he'd gone to get them in the first place. Then he saw the whisk in a puddle of beaten egg on the counter, remembered, and peered out the window again.

The sight of the three dogs there—a pair of clownish chows and what looked to be a shepherd mix—did nothing but irritate him. He recognized this trio—they were the advance guard of the dog army that dropped their excrement all over the lawn, dug up his flowerbeds, and, when he tried to shoo them, looked right through him as if he didn't exist. It wasn't that he had anything against dogs per se—it was their destructiveness he objected to, their arrogance, as if they owned the whole world and it was their privilege to do as they liked with it. He was about to step to the back door and chase them off, when the figure he'd first seen—the shadow beneath the forsythia bush—suddenly emerged. It was no animal, he realized with a shock, but a woman, a young woman dressed all in black, with her black hair hanging wet in her face and the clothes stuck to her like a second skin, down on all fours like a dog herself, sniffing. He was dumbfounded. As stunned and amazed as if someone had just stepped into the kitchen and slapped him till his head rolled back on his shoulders.

He'd been aware of the rumors—there was a new couple in the neighborhood, over on F Street, and the woman was a little strange, dashing through people's yards at any hour of the day or night, baying at the moon and showing her teeth to anyone who got in her way—but he'd dismissed them as some sort of suburban legend. Yet here she was, in his yard, violating his privacy, in the company of a pack of dogs he'd like to see shot—and their owners too. He didn't know what to do. He was frozen there in his own kitchen, shadows undermining the flicker of the fluorescent tubes he'd installed over the counters, the omelet pan sending up a metallic stink of incineration. And then the three dogs lifted their heads as if they'd heard something in the distance, the thunder boomed overhead, and suddenly they leapt the fence in tandem and were gone. The woman rose up out of the mud at this point—she was wearing a sodden turtleneck, jeans, a watch cap—locked eyes with him across the expanse of the rain-screened yard for just an instant, or maybe he was imagining this part of it, and then she turned and took the fence in a single bound, vanishing into the rain.

Cynomorph

Whatever it was they'd heard, it wasn't available to her, though she'd been trying to train her hearing away from the ceaseless clatter of the mechanical and tune it to the finer things, the wind stirring in the grass, the alarm call of a fallen nestling, the faintest sliver of a whimper from the dog three houses over, begging to be let out. And her nose. She'd made a point of sticking it in anything the dogs did, breathing deep of it, rebooting the olfactory receptors of a brain that had been deadened by perfume and underarm deodorant and all the other stifling odors of civilization. Every smell was a discovery, and every dog discovered more of the world in ten minutes running loose than a human being would discover in ten years of sitting behind the wheel of a car or standing at the lunch counter in a deli or even hiking the Alps. What she was doing, or attempting to do, was nothing short of reordering her senses so that she could think like a dog and interpret the whole world—not just the human world—as dogs did.

Why? Because no one had ever done it before. Whole hordes wanted to be primatologists or climb into speedboats and study whales and dolphins or cruise the veldt in a Land Rover to watch the lions suckle their young beneath the baobabs, but none of them gave a second thought to dogs. Dogs were beneath them. Dogs were common, pedestrian, no more exotic than the housefly or the Norway rat. Well, she was going to change all that. Or at least that was what she'd told herself after the graduate committee rejected her thesis, but that was a long time ago now—two years and more—and the door was rapidly closing on it.

But here she was moving again, and movement was good, it was her essence: up over the fence and into the next yard, dodging a clothesline, a cooking grill, a plastic trike, a sandbox, reminding herself always to keep her head down and go quadrupedal whenever possible, because how else was she going to hear, smell and see as the dogs did? Another fence, and there, at the far end of the yard, a shed, and the dense rust-colored tails of the chows wagging. The rain spat in her face, relentless. It had been coming down steadily most of the night, and now it seemed even heavier, as if it meant to drive her back indoors where she belonged. Lightning forked overhead. There was a rumble of thunder. She was shivering—had been shivering for the past hour, shivering so hard she thought her teeth were coming loose—and as she ran, doubled over in a crouch, she pumped her knees and flapped her arms in an attempt to generate some heat.

And what were the dogs onto now? She saw the one she called Barely disappear behind the shed and snake back out again, her tail rigid, sniffing now, barking, and suddenly they were all barking—the two chows and the semi-shepherd she'd named Factitious because he was such a sham, pretending he was a rover when he never strayed more than five blocks from his house on E Street. There was a smell of freshly turned earth, of compost and wood ash, of the half-drowned worms Snout the Afghan loved to gobble up off the pavement. She glanced toward the locked gray vault of the house, concerned that the noise would alert whoever lived here, but it was early yet, no lights on, no sign of activity. The dogs' bodies moiled. The barking went up a notch. She ran, hunched at the waist, hurrying.

And then, out of the corner of her eye, she caught a glimpse of A.1., the big-shouldered husky who'd earned his name by consuming half a bottle of steak sauce beside an overturned trash can one bright January morning. He was running—but where had he come from? She hadn't seen him all night and assumed he'd been wandering out at the limits of his range, over in Bethel or Georgetown. She watched him streak across the yard, ears pinned back, head low, her path converging on his until he disappeared behind the shed. Angling round the back of the thing—it was aluminum, one of those prefab articles they sell in the big warehouse stores—she found the compost pile her nose had alerted her to (good, good: she was improving) and a tower of old wicker chairs stacked up six feet high. A.1. never hesitated. He surged in at the base of the tower, his jaws snapping, and the second chow, the one she called Decidedly, was right behind him—and then she saw: there was something under there, a face with incendiary eyes, and it was growling for its life in a thin continuous whine that might have been the drone of a model airplane buzzing overhead.

What was it? She crouched low, came in close. A straggler appeared suddenly, a fluid sifting from the blind side of the back fence to the yard—it was Snout, gangly, goofy, the fastest dog in the neighborhood and the widest ranger, A.1.'s wife and the mother of his dispersed pups. And then all five of the dogs went in for the kill.

The thunder rolled again, concentrating the moment, and she got her first clear look: cream-colored fur, naked pink toes, a flash of teeth and burdened gums. It was a opossum, unlucky, doomed, caught out while creeping back to its nest on soft marsupial feet after a night of foraging among the trash cans. There was a roil of dogs, no barking now, just the persistent unraveling growls that were like curses, and the first splintering crunch of bone. The tower of wicker came down with a clatter, chairs upended and scattered, and the dogs hardly noticed. She glanced around her in alarm, but there was nobody to be seen, nothing moving but the million silver drill bits of the rain boring into the ground. Just as the next flash of lightning lit the sky, A.1. backed out from under the tumble of chairs with the carcass clenched in his jaws, furiously shaking it to snap a neck that was already two or three times broken, and she was startled to see how big the thing was—twenty pounds of meat, gristle, bone and hair, twenty pounds at least. He shook it again, then dropped it at his wife's feet as an offering. It lay still, the other dogs extending their snouts to sniff at it dispassionately, and they were scientists themselves, studying and measuring, remembering. And when the hairless pink young emerged from the pouch, she tried not to feel anything as the dogs snapped them up one by one.

Cara

"You mean you didn't confront her?"

Cara was in her royal purple robe—her "wrapper," as she insisted on calling it, as if they were at a country manor in the Cotswolds entertaining Lord and Lady Muckbright instead of in a tract house in suburban Connecticut—and she'd paused with a forkful of mushroom omelet halfway to her mouth. She was on her third cup of coffee and wearing her combative look.

"Confront her? I barely had time to recognize she was human." He was at the sink, scrubbing the omelet pan, and he paused to look bitterly out into the gray vacancy of the yard. "What did you expect me to do, chase her down? Make a citizen's arrest? What?"

The sound of Cara buttering her toast—she might have been flaying the flesh from a bone—set his teeth on edge. "I don't know," she said, "but we can't just have strangers lurking around anytime they feel like it, can we? I mean, there are *laws*—"

"The way you talk you'd think I invited her. You think I like mental cases peeping in the window so I can't even have a moment's peace in my own house? On a Saturday morning, no less?"

"So do something."

"What? You tell me."

"Call the police, why don't you? That should be obvious, shouldn't it? And that's another thing—"

"I thought she was a bear."

"A bear? What, are you out of your mind? Are you drunk or something? A bear? I've never heard anything so asinine."

That was when the telephone rang. It was Ben Ober, his voice scraping through the wires like a set of hard chitinous claws scrabbling against the side of the house. "Julian?" he shouted. "Julian?"

Julian reassured him. "Yeah," he said, "it's me. I'm here."

"Can you hear me?"

"I can hear you."

"Listen, she's out in my yard right now, out behind the shed with a, I don't know, some kind of wolf it looks like, and that Afghan nobody seems to know who's the owner of—"

"Who?" he said, but even as he said it he knew. "Who're you talking about?"

"The dog woman." There was a pause, and Julian could hear him breathing into the mouthpiece as if he were deep underwater. "She seems to be—I think she's killing something out there."

The Wolf Children of Mayurbhanj

It was high summer, just before the rains set in, and the bush had shriveled back under the sun till you could see up the skirts of the sal trees, and all that had been hidden was revealed. People began to talk of a disturbing presence in the jungle outside of the tiny village of Godamuri in Mayurbhanj district, of a *bhut,* or spirit, sent to punish them for their refusal to honor the authority of the maharaja. This thing had been twice seen in the company of a wolf, a vague pale slash of movement in the incrassating twilight, and it was no wolf itself, of that the eyewitnesses were certain. Then came the rumor that there were two of them, quick, nasty, bloodless things of the night, and that their eyes flamed with an infernal heat that incinerated anyone who looked into them, and panic gripped the countryside. Mothers kept their children close, fires burned in the night. Then, finally, came the news that these things were concrete and actual and no mere figments of the imagination: their den—the demons' den itself—had been found in an abandoned termitarium in the dense jungle seven miles south of the village.

The rumors reached the Reverend J. A. L. Singh, of the Anglican mission and orphanage at Midnapore, and in September, after the monsoon clouds had peeled back from the skies and the rivers had receded, he made the long journey to Godamuri by bullock cart. One of his converts, a Kora tribesman by the name of Chunarem, who was prominent in the area, led him to the site. There, the Reverend, an astute and observant man and an amateur hunter acquainted with the habits of beasts, saw evidence of canine occupation of the termite mound—droppings, bones, tunnels of ingress and egress—and instructed that a *machan* be built in an overspreading tree nearby. Armed with his dependable twenty-bore Westley Richards rifle, the Reverend sat breathlessly in the *machan* and concentrated his field glasses on the main entrance to the den. The Reverend Singh was not one to believe in ghosts, other than the Holy Spirit, perhaps, and he expected nothing more remarkable than an albino wolf or perhaps a sloth bear gone white with age or dietary deficiency.

Dusk filtered up from the forest floor. Shadows pooled in the undergrowth, and then an early moon rose up pregnant from the horizon to soften them. Langurs whooped in the near distance, cicadas buzzed, a hundred species of beetles, moths and biting insects flapped round the Reverend's ears, but he held rigid and silent, his binoculars fixed on the entrance to the mound. And then suddenly a shape emerged, the triangular head of a wolf, followed by a smaller canine head and then something else altogether, with a neatly rounded cranium and foreshortened face. The wolf—the dam—stretched herself and slunk off into the undergrowth, followed by a pair of wolf cubs and the two other creatures, which were too long-legged and rangy to be canids; that was clear at a glance. Monkeys, the Reverend thought at first, or apes of some sort. But then, even though they were moving swiftly on all fours, the Reverend could see, to his amazement, that these weren't monkeys at all, or wolves or ghosts either.

Denning

She no longer bothered with a notepad or the pocket tape recorder she'd once used to document the telling yip or strident howl. These were the accoutrements of civilization, and civilization got in the way of the kind of freedom she required if she was ever going to break loose of the constraints that had shackled field biologists from the beginning. Even her clothes seemed to get in the way, but she was sensible enough of the laws of the community to understand that they were necessary, at least for now. Still, she made a point of wearing the same things continuously for weeks on end—sans underwear or socks—in the expectation that her scent would invest them, and the scent of the pack too. How could she hope to gain their confidence if she smelled like the prize inside a box of detergent?

One afternoon toward the end of March, as she lay stretched out beneath a weak pale disc of a sun, trying to ignore the cold breeze and concentrate on the doings of the pack—they were excavating a den in the vacant quadrangle of former dairy pasture that was soon to become the J and K blocks of the ever-expanding development—she heard a car slow on the street a hundred yards distant and lifted her head lazily, as the dogs did, to investigate. It had been a quiet morning and a quieter afternoon, A.1. and Snout, as the alpha couple, looking on placidly as Decidedly, Barely and Factitious alternated the digging and a bulldog from B Street she hadn't yet named lay drooling in the dark wet earth that flew from the lip of the burrow. Snout had been chasing cars off and on all morning—to the dogs, automobiles were animate and ungovernable, big unruly ungulates that needed to be curtailed—and she guessed that the fortyish man climbing out of the sedan and working his tentative way across the lot had come to complain, because that was all her neighbors ever did: complain.

And that was a shame. She really didn't feel like getting into all that right now—explaining herself, defending the dogs, justifying, forever justifying—because for once she'd gotten into the rhythm of dogdom, found her way to the sacred place where to lie flat in the sun and breathe in the scents of fresh earth, dung, sprouting grass, was enough of an accomplishment for an entire day. Children were in school, adults at work. Peace reigned over the neighborhood. For the dogs—and for her too—this was bliss. Hominids had to keep busy, make a buck, put two sticks together, order and structure and *complain,* but canids could know contentment—and so could she if she could only penetrate deep enough.

Two shoes had arrived now. Loafers, buffed to brilliance and decorated with matching tassels of stripped hide. They'd come to rest on a trampled mound of fresh earth no more than twenty-four inches from her nose. She tried to ignore them, but there was a bright smear of mud or excrement gleaming on the toe of the left one; it *was* excrement, dog—the merest sniff told her that—and she was intrigued despite herself, though she refused to lift her eyes. And then a man's voice was speaking from somewhere high above the shoes, so high up and resonant with authority it might have been the voice of the alpha dog of all alpha dogs—God Himself.

The tone of the voice, but not the sense of it, appealed to the dogs, and the bulldog, who was present and accounted for because Snout was in heat, hence the den, ambled over to gaze up at the trousered legs in lovesick awe. "You know," the voice was saying, "you've really got the neighborhood in an uproar, and I'm sure you have your reasons, and I know these dogs aren't yours—" The voice faltered. "But Ben Ober—you know Ben Ober? Over on C Street?—well, he's claiming you're killing rabbits or something. Or you were. Last Saturday. Out on his lawn?" Another pause. "Remember, it was raining?"

A month back—two weeks ago, even—she would have felt obligated to explain herself, would have soothed and mollified and dredged up a battery of behavioral terms—proximate causation, copulation solicitation, naturalistic fallacy—to cow him, but today, under the pale sun, in the company of the pack, she just couldn't seem to muster the energy. She might have grunted—or maybe that was only the sound of her stomach rumbling. She couldn't remember when she'd eaten last.

The cuffs of the man's trousers were stiffly pressed into jutting cotton prows, perfectly aligned. The bulldog began to lick at first one, then the other. There was the faintest creak of tendon and patella, and two knees presented themselves, and then a fist, pressed to the earth for balance. She saw a crisp white strip of shirt cuff, the gold flash of watch and wedding band.

"Listen," he said, "I don't mean to stick my nose in where it's not wanted, and I'm sure you have your reasons for, for"—the knuckles retrenched to balance the movement of his upper body, a swing of the arm perhaps, or a jerk of the head—"all this. I'd just say live and let live, but I can't. And you know why not?"

She didn't answer, though she was on the verge—there was something about his voice that was magnetic, as if it could adhere to her and pull her to her feet again—but the bulldog distracted her. He'd gone up on his hind legs with a look of unfocused joy and begun humping the near leg of the man who belonged to the loafers, and her flash of epiphany deafened her to what he was saying. The bulldog had revealed his name to her: from now on she would know him as Humper.

"Because you upset my wife. You were out in our yard and I, she—Oh, Christ," he said, "I'm going about this all wrong. Look, let me introduce myself—I'm Julian Fox. We live on B Street, 2236? We never got to meet your husband and you when you moved in, I mean, the development's got so big—and impersonal, I guess—we never got the chance. But if you ever want to stop by, maybe for tea, a drink—the two of you, I mean—that would be, well, that would be great."

A Drink on B Street

She was upright and smiling, though her posture was terrible and she carried her own smell with her into the sterile sanctum of the house. He caught it immediately, unmistakably, and so did Cara, judging from the look on her face as she took the girl's hand. It was as if a breeze had wafted up from the bog they were draining over on G Street to make way for the tennis courts; the door stood open, and here was a raw infusion of the wild. Or the kennel. That was Cara's take on it, delivered in a stage whisper on the far side of the swinging doors to the kitchen as she fussed with the hors d'oeuvres and he poured vodka for the husband and tap water for the girl: *She smells like she's been sleeping in a kennel.* When he handed her the glass, he saw that there was dirt under her nails. Her hair shone with grease and there were bits of fluff or lint or something flecking the coils of it where it lay massed on her shoulders. Cara tried to draw her into small talk, but she wouldn't draw—she just kept nodding and smiling till the smile had nothing of greeting or joy left in it.

Cara had got their number from Bea Chiavone, who knew more about the business of her neighbors than a confessor, and one night last week she'd got through to the husband, who said his wife was out—which came as no surprise—but Cara had kept him on the line for a good ten minutes, digging for all she was worth, until he finally accepted the invitation to their "little cocktail party." Julian was doubtful, but before he'd had a chance to comb his hair or get his jacket on, the bell was ringing and there they were, the two of them, arm in arm on the doormat, half an hour early.

The husband, Don, was acceptable enough. Early thirties, bit of a paunch, his hair gone in a tonsure. He was a computer engineer. Worked for IBM. "Really?" Julian said. "Well, you must know Charlie Hsiu, then—he's at the Yorktown office?"

Don gave him a blank look.

"He lives just up the street. I mean, I could give him a call, if, if—" He never finished the thought. Cara had gone to the door to greet Ben and Julie Ober, and the girl, left alone, had migrated to the corner by the rubber plant, where she seemed to be bent over now, sniffing at the potting soil. He tried not to stare—tried to hold the husband's eye and absorb what the husband was saying about interoffice politics and his own role on the research end of things ("I guess I'm what you'd call the ultimate computer geek, never really get away from the monitor long enough to put a name to a face")—but he couldn't help stealing a glance under cover of the Obers' entrance. Ben was glad-handing, his voice booming, Cara was cooing something to Julie, and the girl (the husband had introduced her as Cynthia, but she'd murmured, "Call me C.f., capital C, lowercase f") had gone down on her knees beside the plant. He saw her wet a finger, dip it into the soil and bring it to her mouth.

While the La Portes—Cara's friends, dull as woodchips—came smirking through the door, expecting a freak show, Julian tipped back his glass and crossed the room to the girl. She was intent on the plant, rotating the terra-cotta pot to examine the saucer beneath it, on all fours now, her face close to the carpet. He cleared his throat, but she didn't respond. He watched the back of her head a moment, struck by the way her hair curtained her face and spilled down the rigid struts of her arms. She was dressed all in black, in a ribbed turtleneck, grass-stained jeans and a pair of canvas sneakers that were worn through at the heels. She wasn't wearing socks, or, as far as he could see, a brassiere either. But she'd clean up nicely, that was what he was thinking—she had a shape to her, anybody could see that, and eyes that could burn holes right through you. "So," he heard himself say, even as Ben's voice rose to a crescendo at the other end of the room, "you, uh, like houseplants?"

She made no effort to hide what she was doing, whatever it may have been—studying the weave of the carpet, looking to the alignment of the baseboard, inspecting for termites, who could say?—but instead turned to gaze up at him for the first time. "I hope you don't mind my asking," she said in her hush of a voice, "but did you ever have a dog here?"

He stood looking down at her, gripping his drink, feeling awkward and foolish in his own house. He was thinking of Seymour (or "See More," because as a pup he was always running off after things in the distance), picturing him now for the first time in how many years? Something passed through him then, a pang of regret carried in his blood, in his neurons: Seymour. He'd almost succeeded in forgetting him. "Yes," he said. "How did you know?"

She smiled. She was leaning back against the wall now, cradling her knees in the net of her interwoven fingers. "I've been training myself. My senses, I mean." She paused, still smiling up at him. "Did you know that when the Ninemile wolves came down into Montana from Alberta they were following scent trails laid down years before? Think about it. All that weather, the seasons, trees falling and decaying. Can you imagine that?"

"Cara's allergic," he said. "I mean, that's why we had to get rid of him. Seymour. His name was Seymour."

There was a long braying burst of laughter from Ben Ober, who had an arm round the husband's shoulder and was painting something in the air with a stiffened forefinger. Cara stood just beyond him, with the La Portes, her face glowing as if it had been basted. Celia La Porte looked from him to the girl and back again, then arched her eyebrows wittily and raised her long-stemmed glass of viognier, as if toasting him. All three of them burst into laughter. Julian turned his back.

"You didn't take him to the pound—did you?" The girl's eyes went flat. "Because that's a death sentence, I hope you realize that."

"Cara found a home for him."

They both looked to Cara then, her shining face, her anchorwoman's hair. "I'm sure," the girl said.

"No, really. She did."

The girl shrugged, looked away from him. "It doesn't matter," she said with a flare of anger, "dogs are just slaves anyway."

Kamala and Amala

The Reverend Singh had wanted to return to the site the following afternoon and excavate the den, convinced that these furtive night creatures were in fact human children, children abducted from their cradles and living under the dominion of beasts—unbaptized and unsaved, their eternal souls at risk—but urgent business called him away to the south. When he returned, late in the evening, ten days later, he sat over a dinner of cooked vegetables, rice and *dal,* and listened as Chunarem told him of the wolf bitch that had haunted the village two years back after her pups had been removed from a den in the forest and sold for a few *annas* apiece at the Khuar market. She could be seen as dusk fell, her dugs swollen and glistening with extruded milk, her eyes shining with an unearthly blue light against the backdrop of the forest. People threw stones, but she never flinched. Everywhere she left diggings in the earth for farmers to step into on their way out to the fields, attempting, some said, to memorialize that den that had been robbed—or to avenge it. And she howled all night from the fringes of the village, howled so that it seemed she was inside the walls of every hut simultaneously, crooning her sorrow into the ears of each sleeping villager. The village dogs kept hard by, and those that didn't were found in the morning, their throats torn out. "It was she," the Reverend exclaimed, setting down his plate as the candles guttered and moths beat at the netting. "She was the abductress—it's as plain as morning."

A few days later he got up a party that included several railway men and returned to the termite mound, bent on rescue. In place of the rifle he carried a stout cudgel cut from a *mahua* branch, and he'd thought to bring a weighted net along as well. The sun hung overhead. All was still. And then the hired beaters started in, the noise of them racketing through the trees, coming closer and closer until they converged on the site, driving hares and bandicoots and the occasional gaur before them. The railway men tensed in the *machan,* their rifles trained on the entrance to the burrow, while Reverend Singh stood by with a party of diggers to effect the rescue when the time came. It was unlikely that the wolves would have been abroad in daylight, and so it was no surprise to the Reverend that no large animal was seen to run before the beaters and seek the shelter of the den. "Very well," he said, giving the signal. "I am satisfied. Commence the digging."

As soon as the blades of the first shovels struck the mound, a protracted snarling could be heard emanating from the depths of the burrow. After a few minutes of the tribesmen's digging, the she-wolf sprang out at them, ears flattened to her head, teeth flashing. One of the diggers went for her with his spear just as the railway men opened fire from the *machan* and turned her, snapping, on her own wounds; a moment later she lay stretched out dead in the dust of the laterite clay. In a trice the burrow was uncovered, and there they were, the spirits made flesh, huddled in a defensive posture with the two wolf cubs, snarling and panicked, scrabbling at the clay with their broken nails to dig themselves deeper. The tribesmen dropped their shovels and ran, panicked themselves, even as the Reverend Singh eased himself down into the hole and tried to separate child from wolf.

The larger of the wolf children, her hair a feral cap that masked her features, came at him biting and scratching, and finally he had no recourse but to throw the net over the pullulating bodies and restrain each of the creatures separately in one of the long, winding *gelaps* the local tribesmen use for winter wear. On inspection it was determined that the children were females, aged approximately three and six, of native stock, and apparently, judging from the dissimilarity of their features, unrelated. And this puzzled the Reverend, so far as he was concerned with the she-wolf's motives and behavior—she'd abducted the children on separate occasions, perhaps even from separate locales, and over the course of some time. Was this the bereaved bitch Chunarem had reported? Was she acting out of revenge? Or merely trying, in her own unknowable way, to replace what had been taken from her and ease the burden of her heart?

In any case, he had the children confined to a pen so that he could observe them, before caging them in the back of the bullock cart for the trip to Midnapore and the orphanage, where he planned to baptize and civilize them. He spent three full days studying them and taking notes in a leatherbound book he kept always at his side. He saw that they persisted in going on all fours, as if they didn't know any other way, and fled from the sunlight as if it were an instrument of torture. They thrust forward to lap water like the beasts of the forest and took nothing in their mouths but bits of twig and stone. At night they came to life and stalked the enclosure with shining eyes like the *bhuts* half the villagers still believed them to be. They did not know any of the languages of the human species, but communicated with each other—and with their sibling wolves—with a series of grunts, snarls and whimpers. When the moon rose, they sat on their haunches and howled.

It was Mrs. Singh who named them, some weeks later. They were pitiful, filthy, soiled with their own urine and excrement, undernourished and undersized. They had to be caged to keep them from harming the other children, and Mrs. Singh, though it broke her heart to do it, ordered them put in restraints so that the filth and the animal smell could be washed from them, even as their heads were shaved to defeat the ticks and fleas they'd inherited from the only mother they'd ever known. "They need delicate names," Mrs. Singh told her husband, "names to reflect the beauty and propriety they will grow into." She named the younger sister Amala, after a bright yellow flower native to Bengal, and she named the elder Kamala, after the lotus that blossoms deep in the jungle pools.

Running with the Pack

The sun stroked her like a hand, penetrated and massaged the dark yellowing contusion that had sprouted on the left side of her ribcage. Her bones felt as if they were about to crack open and deliver their marrow and her heart was still pounding, but she was here, among the dogs, at rest, and all that was winding down now. It was June, the season of pollen, the air supercharged with the scents of flowering, seeding, fruiting, and there were rabbits and squirrels everywhere. She lay prone at the lip of the den and watched the pups—long-muzzled like their mother and brindled Afghan peach and husky silver—as they worried a flap of skin and fur that Snout had peeled off the hot black glistening surface of the road and dropped at their feet. She was trying to focus on the dogs—on A.1., curled up nose to tail in the trampled weeds after regurgitating a mash of kibble for the pups, on Decidedly, his eyes half-closed as currents of air brought him messages from afar, on Humper and Factitious—but she couldn't let go of the pain in her ribs and what that pain foreshadowed from the human side of things.

Don had kicked her. Don had climbed out of the car, crossed the field and stood over her in his suede computer-engineer's ankle boots with the waffle bottoms and reinforced toes and lectured her while the dogs slunk low and rumbled deep in their throats. And, as his voice had grown louder, so too had the dogs' voices, till they were a chorus commenting on the ebb and flow of the action. When was she going to get her ass up out of the dirt and act like a normal human being? That was what he wanted to know. When was she going to cook a meal, run the vacuum, do the wash—his underwear, for Christ's sake? He was wearing dirty underwear, did she know that?

She had been lying stretched out flat on the mound, just as she was now. She glanced up at him as the dogs did, taking in a piece of him at a time, no direct stares, no challenges. She was in no mood. "All I want," she said, over the chorus of growls and low, warning barks, "is to be left alone."

"Left alone?" His voice tightened in a little yelp. "Left alone? You need help, that's what you need. You need a shrink, you know that?"

She didn't reply. She let the pack speak for her. The rumble of their response, the flattened ears and stiffened tails, the sharp, savage gleam of their eyes should have been enough, but Don wasn't attuned. The sun seeped into her. A grasshopper she'd been idly watching as it bent a dandelion under its weight suddenly took flight, right past her face, and it seemed the most natural thing in the world to snap at it and break it between her teeth.

Don let out some sort of exclamation—"My God, what are you doing? Get up out of that, get up out of that now!"—and it didn't help matters. The dogs closed in. They were fierce now, barking in savage recusancy, their emotions twisted in a single cord. But this was Don, she kept telling herself, Don from grad school, bright and buoyant Don, her mate, her husband, and what harm was there in that? He wanted her back home, back in the den, and that was his right. The only thing was, she wasn't going.

"This isn't research. This is bullshit. Look at you!"

"No," she said, giving him a lazy, sidelong look, though her heart was racing, "it's dog shit. It's on your shoes, Don. It's in your face. In your precious computer—"

That was when he'd kicked her. Twice, three times maybe. Kicked her in the ribs as if he were driving a ball over an imaginary set of uprights in the distance, kicked and kicked again—before the dogs went for him. A.1. came in first, tearing at a spot just above his right knee, and then Humper, the bulldog who belonged to the feathery old lady up the block, got hold of his pantleg while Barely went for the crotch. Don screamed and thrashed all right—he was a big animal, two hundred and ten pounds, heavier by far than any of the dogs—and he threatened in his big-animal voice and fought back with all the violence of his big-animal limbs, but he backed off quickly enough, threatening still, as he made his way across the field and into the car. She heard the door slam, heard the motor scream, and then there was the last thing she heard: Snout barking at the wheels as the wheels revolved and took Don down the street and out of her life.

Survival of the Fittest

"You know he's locked her out, don't you?"

"Who?" Though he knew perfectly well.

"Don. I'm talking about Don and the dog lady?"

There was the table, made of walnut varnished a century before, the crystal vase full of flowers, the speckless china, the meat, the vegetables, the pasta. Softly, so softly he could barely hear it, there was Bach too, piano pieces—partitas—and the smell of the fresh-cut flowers.

"Nobody knows where she's staying, unless it's out in the trash or the weeds or wherever. She's like a bag lady or something. And what she's eating. Bea said Jerrilyn Hunter said she saw her going through the trash at dawn one morning. Do you hear me? Are you even listening?"

"I don't know. Yeah. Yeah, I am." He'd been reading lately. About dogs. Half a shelf of books from the library in their plastic covers—behavior, breeds, courting, mating, whelping. He excised a piece of steak and lifted it to his lips. "Did you hear the Leibowitzes' Afghan had puppies?"

"*Puppies?* What in God's name are you talking about?" Her face was like a burr under the waistband, an irritant, something that needed to be removed and crushed.

"Only the alpha couple gets to breed, you know that, right? And so that would be the husky and the Leibowitzes' Afghan, and I don't know who the husky belongs to—but they're cute, real cute."

"You haven't been—? Don't tell me. Julian, use your sense: she's out of her mind. You want to know what else Bea said?"

"The alpha bitch," he said, and he didn't know why he was telling her this, "she'll actually hunt down and kill the pups of any other female in the pack who might have got pregnant, a survival of the fittest kind of thing—"

"She's crazy, bonkers, out of her *fucking* mind, Julian. They're going to have her committed, you know that? If this keeps up. And it will keep up, won't it, Julian? Won't it?"

The Common Room at Midnapore

At first they would take nothing but water. The wolf pups, from which they'd been separated for reasons both of sanitation and acculturation, eagerly fed on milk-and-rice pap in their kennel in one of the outbuildings, but neither of the girls would touch the pan-warmed milk or rice or the stewed vegetables Mrs. Singh provided for them—even at night, when they were most active and their eyes spoke a language of desire all their own. Each morning and each evening before retiring, she would place a bowl on the floor in front of them, trying to tempt them with biscuits, confections, even a bit of boiled meat, though the Singhs were vegetarians themselves and repudiated the slaughter of animals for any purpose. The girls drew back into the recesses of the pen the Reverend had constructed in the orphanage's common room, showing their teeth. Days passed. They grew weaker. He tried to force-feed them balls of rice, but they scratched and tore at him with their nails and their teeth, setting up such a furious caterwauling of hisses, barks and snarls as to give rise to rumors among the servants that he was torturing them—or trying to exorcise the forest demons that inhabited them, as if he, an educated man, had given in to the superstitions of the tribesmen. Finally, in resignation, and though it was a risk to the security of the entire orphanage, he left the door to the pen standing open in the hope that the girls, on seeing the other small children at play and at dinner, would soften.

In the meanwhile, though the girls grew increasingly lethargic—or perhaps because of it—the Reverend was able to make a close and telling examination of their physiology and habits. Their means of locomotion had transformed their bodies in a peculiar way. For one thing, they had developed thick pads of callus at their elbows and knees, and toes that were of abnormal strength and inflexibility—indeed, when their feet were placed flat on the ground, all five toes stood up at a sharp angle. Their waists were narrow and extraordinarily supple, like a dog's, and their necks dense with the muscle that had accrued there as a result of leading with their heads. And they were fast, preternaturally fast, and stronger by far than any other child of their respective ages the Reverend and his wife had ever seen. In his diary, for the sake of posterity, the Reverend noted it all down.

Still, all the notes in the world wouldn't matter a whit if the wolf children didn't end their hunger strike, if that was what this was, and the Reverend and his wife had begun to lose hope for them, when the larger one—the one who would become known as Kamala—finally asserted herself. It was early in the evening, the day after the Reverend had ordered the door to the pen left open, and the children were eating their evening meal while Mrs. Singh and one of the servants looked on and the Reverend settled in with his pipe on the veranda. The weather was typical for Bengal in that season, the evening heavy and close, every living thing locked in the grip of the heat, nothing moving, not even the birds, and all the mission's doors and windows stood open to receive even the faintest breath of a breeze. Suddenly, without warning, Kamala bolted out of the pen, through the door and across the courtyard to where the orphanage dogs were being fed scraps of uncooked meat, gristle and bone left over from the preparation of the servants' meal, and before anyone could stop her she was down among them, slashing with her teeth, fighting off even the biggest and most aggressive of them until she'd bolted the red meat and carried off the long, hoofed shinbone of a gaur to gnaw in the farthest corner of her pen.

And so the Singhs, though it revolted them, fed the girls on raw meat until the crisis had passed, and then they gave them broth, which the girls lapped from their bowls, and finally meat that had been at least partially cooked. As for clothing—clothing for decency's sake—the girls rejected it as unnatural and confining, tearing any garment from their backs and limbs with their teeth, until Mrs. Singh hit on the idea of fashioning each of them a single tight-fitting strip of cloth they wore knotted round the waist and drawn up over their privates, a kind of diaper or loincloth they were forever soiling with their waste. It wasn't an ideal solution, but the Singhs were patient—the girls had suffered a kind of deprivation no other humans had ever suffered—and they understood that the ascent to civilization and light would be steep and long.

When Amala died, shortly after the wolf pups succumbed to what the Reverend presumed was distemper communicated through the orphanage dogs, her sister wouldn't let anyone approach the body. Looking back on it, the Reverend would see this as Kamala's most human moment—she was grieving, grieving because she had a soul, because she'd been baptized before the Lord and was no wolfling or jungle *bhut* but a human child after all, and here was the proof of it. But poor Amala. Her, they hadn't been able to save. Both girls had been dosed with sulfur powder, which caused them to expel a knot of roundworms up to six inches in length and as thick as the Reverend's little finger, but the treatment was perhaps too harsh for the three-year-old, who was suffering from fever and dysentery at the same time. She'd seemed all right, feverish but calm, and Mrs. Singh had tended her through the afternoon and evening. But when the Reverend's wife came into the pen in the morning, Kamala flew at her, raking her arms and legs and driving her back from the straw in which the cold body of her sister lay stretched out like a figure carved of wood. They restrained the girl and removed the corpse while Mrs. Singh retired to bandage her wounds and the Reverend locked the door of the pen to prevent any further violence. All that day Kamala lay immobile in the shadows at the back of the pen, wrapped in her own limbs. And then night fell, and she sat back on her haunches behind the rigid geometry of the bars and began to howl, softly at first, and then with increasing force and plangency until it was the very sound of desolation itself, rising up out of the compound to chase through the streets of the village and into the jungle beyond.

Going to the Dogs

The sky was clear all the way to the top of everything, the sun so thick in the trees he thought it would catch there and congeal among the motionless leaves. He didn't know what prompted him to do it exactly, but as he came across the field he balanced first on one leg, and then the other, to remove his shoes and socks. The grass—the weeds, wildflowers, puffs of mushroom, clover, swaths of moss—felt clean and cool against the lazy progress of his bare feet. Butterflies shifted and flapped, grasshoppers shone gold, the false bees hung suspended from invisible wires. Things rose up to greet him, things and smells he'd forgotten all about, and he took his time among them, moving forward only to be distracted again and again. He found her finally in the tall nodding weeds that concealed the entrance of the den, playing with the puppies. He didn't say hello, didn't say anything—just settled in on the mound beside her and let the pups surge into his arms. The pack barely raised its collective head.

Her eyes came to him and went away again. She was smiling, a loose, private smile that curled the corners of her mouth and lifted up into the smooth soft terrain of the silken skin under her eyes. Her clothes barely covered her anymore, the turtleneck torn at the throat and sagging across one clavicle, the black jeans hacked off crudely—or maybe chewed off—at the peaks of her thighs. The sneakers were gone altogether, and he saw that the pale yellow soles of her feet were hard with callus, and her hair—her hair was struck with sun and shining with the natural oil of her scalp.

He'd come with the vague idea—or no, the very specific idea—of asking her for one of the pups, but now he didn't know if that would do exactly. She would tell him that the pups weren't hers to give, that they belonged to the pack, and though each of the pack's members had a bed and a bowl of kibble awaiting it in one of the equitable houses of the alphabetical grid of the development springing up around them, they were free here, and the pups, at least, were slaves to no one. He felt the thrusting wet snouts of the creatures in his lap, the surge of their animacy, the softness of the stroked ears and the prick of the milk teeth, and he smelled them too, an authentic smell compounded of dirt, urine, saliva and something else also: the unalloyed sweetness of life. After a while, he removed his shirt, and so what if the pups carried it off like a prize? The sun blessed him. He loosened his belt, gave himself some breathing room. He looked at her, stretched out beside him, at the lean, tanned, running length of her, and he heard himself say, finally, "Nice day, isn't it?"

"Don't talk," she said. "You'll spoil it."

"Right," he said. "Right. You're right."

And then she rolled over, bare flesh from the worried waistband of her cutoffs to the dimple of her breastbone and her breasts caught somewhere in between, under the yielding fabric. She was warm, warm as a fresh-drawn bath, the touch of her communicating everything to him, and the smell of her too—he let his hand go up under the flap of material and roam over her breasts, and then he bent closer, sniffing.

Her eyes were fixed on his. She didn't say anything, but a low throaty rumble escaped her throat.

Waiting for the Rains

The Reverend Singh sat there on the veranda, waiting for the rains. He'd set his notebook aside, and now he leaned back in the wicker chair and pulled meditatively at his pipe. The children were at play in the courtyard, an array of flashing limbs and animated faces attended by their high, bright catcalls and shouts. The heat had loosened its grip ever so perceptibly, and they were all of them better for it. Except Kamala. She was indifferent. The chill of winter, the damp of the rains, the full merciless sway of the sun—it was all the same to her. His eyes came to rest on her where she lay across the courtyard in a stripe of sunlight, curled in the dirt with her knees drawn up beneath her and her chin resting atop the cradle of her crossed wrists. He watched her for a long while as she lay motionless there, no more aware of what she was than a dog or an ass, and he felt defeated, defeated and depressed. But then one of the children called out in a voice fluid with joy, a moment of triumph in a game among them, and the Reverend couldn't help but shift his eyes and look.

(2002)

The Kind Assassin

What you hope for
Is that at some point of the pointless journey . . .
The kind assassin Sleep will draw a bead
And blow your brains out.

—Richard Wilbur

I was having trouble getting to sleep. Nothing serious, just the usual tossing and turning, the pillow converted to stone, every whisper of the night amplified to a shriek. I heard the refrigerator click on in the kitchen, the soft respiration of the dust-clogged motor that kept half a six-pack, last week's takeout Chinese and the crusted jar of capers at a safe and comfortable temperature, and then I heard it click off. Every seven and a half minutes—I timed it by the glowing green face of the deep-sea diver's watch my ex-wife gave me for Christmas last year—the neighbors' dog let out a single startled yelp, and twenty seconds later I heard the car of some drunk or shift worker laboring up the hill with an intermittent wheeze and blast of exhaust (and couldn't *anybody* in this neighborhood afford a new car—or at least a trip to the muffler shop?). It was three o'clock in the morning. Then it was four. I tried juggling invisible balls, repeating the names of my elementary school teachers, Mrs. Gold, Mrs. Cochrane, Miss Mandia, Miss Slivovitz, summoned their faces, the faces of as many of my classmates as I could remember, the faces of everybody in the neighborhood where I grew up, of everybody in New York, California, China, but it didn't do any good. I fell asleep ten minutes before the alarm hammered me back to consciousness.

By the time I got both legs into a pair of jeans and both arms through the armholes of my favorite Hawaiian shirt, I was running late for work. I didn't bother with gelling my hair or even looking at it, just grabbed a stocking cap and pulled it down to my eyebrows. Some sort of integument seemed to have been interposed between me and the outside world, some thick dullish skin that made every movement an ordeal, as if I were swimming in a medium ten times denser than water—and how the scalding twelve-ounce container of Starbuck's triple latte wound up clenched between my legs as I gripped the steering wheel of the car that didn't even feel like my own car—that felt borrowed or stolen—I'll never know.

All this by way of saying I was late getting to the studio. Fifteen minutes late, to be exact. The first face I saw, right there, stationed at the battered back door with the call letters KFUN pasted at eye level in strips of peeling black electrical tape, seemed to belong to Cuttler Ames, the program director. Seemed to, that is, because the studio was filled to the ceiling with this new element I had to fight my way through, at least until the caffeine began to take hold and the integument fell away like so much sloughed skin. Cuttler made his lemon-sucking face. "Don't tell me you overslept," he said. "Not today of all days. Tell me I'm wrong. Tell me your car threw a rod, tell me you got a speeding ticket, tell me your house burned down."

Cuttler was a Brit. He wore his hair long and his face baggy. His voice was like Karo syrup poured through an echo box. He'd limped through the noon-hour "Blast from the Past" show for six months before he was elevated to program director over the backs of a whole troop of more deserving men (and women). I didn't like him. Nobody liked him. "My house burned down," I said.

"Why don't you pull your head up out of your ass, will you? For once? Would that be too much to ask?" He turned to wheel away, resplendent in his black leather bell bottoms with the silver medallions sewed into the seams, then stopped to add, "Anthony's already in there, going it alone, which makes me wonder what we're paying *you* for, but let's not develop a sense of urgency here or anything—let's just linger in the corridor and make small talk, shall we?" A pause. The man was in a time warp. The leather pants, the wide-collared shirt, the pointy-toed boots: it was 1978 and Pink Floyd was ascendant. His eyes flamed briefly. "How did you sleep?"

Anthony was Tony, my morning-show partner. Sometimes, depending on his mood, Cuttler called him "Tony" like everybody else, except that he pronounced it "Tunny." The question of how I'd slept was of vital import on this particular morning, because I'd been in training for the past week under the direction of Dr. Laurie Pepper of the Sleep Institute, who was getting some high-profile publicity for her efforts, not to mention a reduced rate on her thirty-second spots. "You need to build up your sleep account," she told me, perched on the edge of the couch in my living room, and she prescribed long hot baths and sipping tepid milk before bed. "White noise helps," she said. "One of my clients, a guitarist in an A-list band whose name I can't reveal because of confidentiality issues, and I hope you'll understand, used to make a tape loop of the toilet flushing and play it back all night." She was in her mid-thirties and she had a pair of dramatic legs she showed off beneath short skirts and Morning Mist stockings, and in case anybody failed to take note she wore a gold anklet that spelled out *Somnus* in linked letters. "Roman god of sleep," she said when she saw where my eyes had wandered. She had a notepad in her lap. She consulted it and uncrossed her legs. "Sex helps," she said, coming back to the point she was pursuing. I told her I wasn't seeing anybody just then. She shrugged, an elegant little shift of the shoulders. "Masturbation, then."

There was a coffeepot and a tray of two-days'-stale doughnuts set up on a table against the wall just behind Cuttler, the remnants of a promotion for the local Krazy Kreme franchise. I went for them like a zombie, pausing only to reference his question. "Like shit," I said.

"Oh, smashing. Super. Our champion, our hero. I suppose you'll be drooling on the table ten minutes into the marathon."

I wanted a cigarette, though it was an urge I had to fight. Since Cuttler's accession we'd become a strictly tobacco-free workplace and I had to hide my Larks out of sight and blow smoke into a screw-top bottle when Tony and I were on the air. I could feel the caffeine working its way up the steep grades and inclines of my circulatory system like a train of linked locomotives, chugging away. In a burst of exhilaration I actually drew the pack from my pocket and shook out a cigarette, just to watch Cuttler's face go into isolation. I made as if to stick the cigarette between my lips, but then thought better of it and tucked it behind my ear. "No way," I said. "You want me to go twelve days, I'll go twelve days. Fourteen, fifteen, whatever you want. Jesus, I don't sleep anyway." And then I was in the booth with Tony, ad-libbing, doing routines, cueing up records and going to commercials I'd heard so many times I could have reprised them in my sleep—if I ever slept, that is.

In the mid-sixties, Dr. Allan Rechtschaffen of the University of Chicago devised an experiment in sleep deprivation, using rats as his subject animals. He wired their rodent brains to an EEG machine and every time their brain waves showed them drifting off he ducked them in cold water. The rats didn't like this. They were in a lab, with plenty to eat and drink, a nice equitable temperature, no predators, no danger, nothing amiss but for the small inconvenience of the wires glued to the patches shaved into their skulls, but whenever they started dreaming they got wet. Normally, a rat will sleep thirteen hours a day on average, midway on the mammalian scale between the dolphin (at seven) and the bat (at twenty). These rats didn't sleep at all. A week went by. Though they ate twice as much as normal, they began to lose weight. Their fur thinned, their energy diminished. The first died after thirteen days. Within three weeks all of them were gone.

I mention it here because I want to emphasize that I went into all this with my eyes wide open. I was informed. I knew that the Chinese Communists had used sleep deprivation as a torture device and that the physiological and psychological effects of continual wakefulness can be debilitating, if not fatal. Like the rats, sleep-deprived people tend to eat more, and like the rats, to lose weight nonetheless. Their immune systems become compromised. Body temperatures drop. Disorientation occurs. Hallucinations are common. Beyond that, it was anybody's guess what would happen, though the fate of the rats was a pretty fair indication as far as I was concerned. And yet still, when Cuttler and Nguyen Tranh, the station's owner and manager, came up with the idea of a marathon—a "Wake-A-Thon," Tony was calling it—to boost ratings and coincidentally raise money for the National Narcolepsy Association, I was the first to volunteer. Why not?, was what I was thinking. At least it would be something different.

Thus, Dr. Laurie. If I was going to challenge the world record for continuous hours without sleep, I would need to be coached and monitored, and before I stepped into that glass booth at the intersection of Chapala and Oak in downtown San Roque at the conclusion of today's edition of "The Gooner & Boomer Morning-Drive Show" I would have built up my sleep account, replete with overdraft protection, to ease me on my way. Call it nerves, butterflies, anticipatory anxiety—whatever it was, I'd never slept worse in my life than during the past week, and my sleep account was bankrupt. Even before the last puerile sexual-innuendo-laden half-witted joke of the show was out of my mouth, I could picture myself out cold in the glass booth five minutes into the marathon, derisive faces pressed up against the transparent walls, all the bright liquid hopes and aspirations of what was once a career unstoppered and leaching off into the pipes. I cued up the new Weezer single and backed out of the booth.

There was a photographer from the local paper leaning up against the shoulder-greased wall in the corridor, the telltale traces of doughnut confection caught in the corners of his mouth. He glanced up at me with dead eyes, tugged at the camera strap as if it had grown into his flesh. "You ready for this, man?" Tony crowed, slipping out of the booth like a knife pulled from a corpse, and he threw an arm round my shoulder, grinning for the photographer. Tony's job was to represent the control group. Every morning, after our show, which we'd be broadcasting live from the glassed-in booth, he would go home to bed, then pop in at odd hours to sign autographs, hand out swag and keep me going with ever newer jokes and routines, which we would then work into the next morning's show. He'd spent the past week trying to twist Polish jokes to fit the insomnia envelope, as in how many insomniacs does it take to screw in a lightbulb and what did the insomniac say to the bartender? Tony squeezed my shoulder. "How you feeling?"

I just nodded in response. I felt all right, actually. Not rested, not calm, not confident, but all right. The sun slanted in through one of the grimy skylights and hit me in the face and it was like throwing cold water on a drunk. Plus I'd had two more cups of coffee and a Diet Coke while we were on the air, and the assault of the caffeine made me feel almost human. When Dr. Laurie, Nguyen and Cuttler stepped out of the shadows and locked arms with me and Tony to pose for the photographer, I braved the flash and showed every tooth I had.

The first masochist to subject himself to sleep withdrawal for the sake of ratings was a DJ named Peter Tripp, who had a daily show on WMGM in New York back in 1959. His glassed-in booth was in Times Square, and he made it through the two hundred hours of sleeplessness his program director had projected for him, though not without experiencing his share of delusions and waking nightmares. Toward the end of his trial, he somehow mistook the physician monitoring him for an undertaker come to pump him full of formaldehyde and they had to read him the riot act to get him back into the glass booth and finish out his sentence. Two hundred hours is just over eight days, but what Cuttler was shooting for here was twelve days, two hundred eighty-eight hours—a full twenty-four hours longer than the mark set by the *Guinness Book of World Records* champ, a high school senior from San Diego named Randy Gardner who'd employed himself as the test subject in a science project to monitor the effects of sleep deprivation. He was seventeen at the time, gifted with all the recuperative powers of the young, and he came out of it without any lasting adverse effects.

As I stood in the back hallway at KFUN, simulating insouciance for the photographer, I was thirty-three years old, sapped of enthusiasm after twelve years on the air, sleep-deprived and vulnerable, with the recuperative powers of a corpse. I was loveless, broke, bored to the point of rage, so fed up with KFUN, microphones, recording engineers and my drive-time partner I sometimes thought I'd choke him to death on the air the next time he opened his asinine mouth to spout one more asinine crack, to which I, an ass myself, would be obligated to respond. My career was a joke. The downmarket slide had begun. I didn't have a chance.

Outside, in the parking lot, there was a random aggregation of sixth-grade girls in KFUN T-shirts, flanked by their slack-jawed, work-worn mothers. When Tony, Dr. Laurie and I stepped out the door and made for the classic KFUN-yellow Eldorado convertible that would take us downtown to the glass booth, they let out a series of halfhearted shrieks and waved their complimentary KFUN bumper stickers like confetti. I slipped into the embrace of my wraparound shades and treated them to a grand wave in return, and then we were out in traffic, and people who may or may not have been KFUN listeners looked at us as if we were prisoners on the way to the gallows.

It was early yet, just before nine, but there were four or five bums already camped against the walls of the glass cubicle—it was Plexiglas, actually—and a pair of retirees in golf hats gaping at the thing as if it had been manufactured by aliens. The sun, softened by a trace of lingering fog, made a featherbed of the sidewalk, the parked cars shone dully and the palms stood watch in silhouette up and down both sides of the street. The photographer got a shot of me in conference with the more emaciated of the retirees, who informed me that he'd once stayed up forty-six hours straight, hunting Japs on Iwo Jima, then Dr. Laurie, whose function had now abruptly switched from sleep induction to prevention, led me into the booth where Tony had already stowed my satchel stuffed with clean underwear, shaving kit, two fresh shirts, a burlap bag of gravel (to sit on when I felt drowsy: Cuttler's idea) and eighteen thrillers plucked at random from the shelves of Walmart. The format was simple: every fifteen minutes I would go live to the studio and update the time and remind everybody out there in KFUN land just how many consecutive waking hours I'd racked up. Every other hour I was allowed a five-minute break to visit the toilet facilities across the street at the Soul Shack Dance Club, which was co-sponsoring the event, but aside from that I was to remain on full public display, upright and attentive, and no matter what happened, my eyelids were never to close, even for an instant.

It may seem hard to believe—especially now, looking at it in retrospect—but those first few hours were the worst. Once the excitement of setting up in the booth (and cutting into Armageddon Annie's mid-morning show for a sixty-second exchange of canned jocularities—"How're you hanging, Boomer? Still awake after fifteen minutes?"), the effect of the last few sleepless nights hit me like an avalanche. I was sitting there at the console they'd set up for me, staring off down the avenue and thinking of Dr. Laurie's legs and what she could do for me in a strictly therapeutic way when all this was over and I really did have to get back to sleep, and I think I may have drifted for a minute. I wasn't asleep. I know that. But it was close, my eyelids listing, the image of Dr. Laurie slipping off her undies replaced by a cold sweeping wall of gray as if someone had suddenly flipped channels on me, and then I was no longer staring down the avenue but into the eyes, the deep sea–green startled eyes, of a girl of twenty or so in what looked to be a homemade knit cap with long trailing ear flaps. At first I thought I'd gone over the edge, already dreaming and not thirty minutes into the deal, because why would anyone be wearing a knit cap with earflaps in downtown San Roque where the sun was shining and the temperature stuck at seventy-two, day and night, as if there were a thermostat in the sky? But then she waved, touched two fingers to her lips and pressed them to the glass, and I knew I was awake.

I gave her my best radio-personality smile, ran a hand through my hair (now combed and gelled, just as my cheeks were smooth-shaven and my Hawaiian shirt wrinkle-free, because this was a performance above all else and I was representing KFUN to the public here, as Cuttler had reminded me sixteen times already that morning, lest I forget). She smiled back, and I noticed then that a crowd had begun to gather, maybe twenty people or so—shoppers, delivery truck drivers, mothers and babes, granddads, slope-shouldered truants from San Roque High, and even a solitary cop perched over his motionless bicycle—all drawn to the image of this woman pressed against the glass in a place on the sidewalk where no glass had been just a day ago. They saw her there, people who might have just strolled on obliviously by, and then they saw me, in my glass cage. I watched their faces, the private looks of absorption metamorphosing to surprise and then amusement, and something else too—recognition, and maybe even admiration. *Oh, yeah, they were thinking, I heard about this—that's Boomer in there, from KFUN, and he's setting the world record for staying awake. It's been almost an hour now. Cool.*

At least that's what I imagined, and I wasn't delusional yet, not by a long shot. That girl standing there had turned things around for me, and for the first time I felt a surge of pride, a sense of accomplishment and worth—enthusiasm, real enthusiasm—but of course, I was tired to the marrow already and experiencing a kind of hypnotic giddiness that could have been the precursor to any level of mental instability. In my exuberance I waved to the assembled crowd, mothers, bums and truants alike, and that seemed to break the spell—their eyes shifted away from me, they began to move off, and the new people who might have been their reinforcements just kept on walking past the glass booth as if it didn't exist. The girl tore a sheet from a loose-leaf notebook then and bent over it in concentration. I watched her write out a message in block letters as the pigeons dodged and ducked round her feet and the seagulls cut white flaps out of the sky overhead, and then she looked up, held my eyes, and pressed the paper to the glass. The message was simple, terse, to the point: YOU ARE MY GOD.

I fought sleep through the morning and into the early afternoon, so wired on caffeine my knees were sore from knocking together under the table. There are two low points in our circadian cycle, one to four in the morning, which seems self-evident, and, more surprisingly, the same hours in the afternoon. Or maybe it's not so surprising when you take into account the number of cultures that indulge the post-prandial nap or afternoon siesta. At any rate, on a normal day at this hour I'd be doing voice-overs on ads or dozing off in one of the endless meetings Cuttler and Nguyen seemed to call every other day to remind us of the cost of postage, long-distance phone calls and the paper towels in the restroom. The afternoon lull hit me. My head lolled on my shoulders like a bowling ball. I thought if I ate something it would help, so when Tony stopped in to glad-hand the bums and the half-dozen lingerers and gawkers gathered round the booth, I asked him to get me some Chinese takeout. I did the one forty-five spot ("Hey, out there in KFUN land, this is the Boomer, and yes, I'm still awake after three hours and forty-five minutes, and when you hear the tone it will be exactly—"), then bent to the still-warm cartons of kung pao chicken, scallops in black bean sauce and mu shu pork.

I couldn't eat. I lifted the first dripping forkful to my mouth and a dozen pairs of eyes locked on mine. The bums had been stretched out in comfort all morning, passing a short dog of Gallo white port, cadging change and hawking gobs of mucus onto the pavement, making merry at my expense, and now they just turned their heads to stare as if they somehow expected me to provide for them too. A trio of middle-aged women with Macy's bags looped over their wrists took one look at me and pulled up short as if they'd forgotten something (lunch, most likely). And one of the old men from the morning reappeared suddenly, licking his lips. I tried to smile and chew at the same time, but it wasn't working. I toyed with the food awhile, even picked up one of the thrillers and tried to block them out, but finally I set down the fork and pushed the cartons away. That was when the girl in the earflaps popped up out of nowhere—she must have been lurking in the bushes along the median or watching from the window of the Soul Shack—to painstakingly indite a second message. She pressed it to the glass. EAT, it read, YOU'RE GOING TO NEED YOUR STRENGTH.

The girl's name was Hezza Moore. She was of medium height, medium weight, medium coloring and medium attractiveness. We met formally just after the sun went down the evening of that first day. I'd got my second wind around seven or so (the second period of alertness in our circadian cycle, by the way, corresponding to the one we experience in the morning), and by the time the sun went down I felt as energized as Nosferatu climbing out of his coffin. I paced round the glass box, spanked off my quarter-hour spots with the rumbling monitory gusto that had won me my on-air moniker ten years back when I was an apprentice jock at KSOT in San Luis Obispo, did a few sets of jumping jacks, flossed my teeth and unlatched the glass door at the rear of the booth to embrace the night air.

I was thinking this is a lark, this is nothing, thinking I could go a month, a year, and who needed sleep anyway, when she materialized at the open door. She was still in the knit cap, but she seemed to be wearing mittens now too, and an old Salvation Army overcoat that dropped to the toes of her Doc Martens. "Hey," she said.

"Hey."

"You remember that Dishwalla promo you guys did six years ago?"

I gave her a blank look. The temperature reading on the display over the Bank of America down the street was 71°.

She'd edged partway into the booth, one foot on the plywood floor, her shoulders bridging the Plexiglas doorframe. "You know, the new CD and dinner for two at the Star of India? I was the fourteenth caller."

"Really?"

She beamed at me now, two dimples sucked down into her smile. The knit hat cut a slash just above her eyes, and her eyes jumped and settled, then jumped again. "Yeah," she went on, "but I was only fifteen and I didn't have anybody to go with. I wound up going with my mom, and that was a drag. You should have been the prize, though. I mean, it was you telling us all that the fourteenth caller would win the free chapatis and the lime pickle and all the rest of it, and if it'd been you going to dinner with the fourteenth caller I would've died. Really, I would have. You know, I've never missed your show, not even once, ever since you went on the air? I even used to listen in school, in homeroom and first period, with headphones."

I held out my hand. "It's a real pleasure," I said, just to say it, and that was when she gave me her name. "You want an autograph? Or some of this swag?" I gestured to the heap of KFUN T-shirts, beanies, CDs and concert tickets we were giving away as part of the Wake-A-Thon, teen treasure mounded in the corner of the glass booth just above the spot on the pavement outside where one of the bums—the one with the empty pantleg where his left foot should have been—was stretched out in bum nirvana, snoring lustily.

Her eyes changed. She looked down and then away. "Oh, no," she breathed finally. "No, I didn't come for any of that. Don't you realize what I'm saying?"

I didn't. A wave of exhaustion crashed inside of me and pulled back from the naked shingle with a long slow suck and moan.

"I came for you. I'm here for you. For as long as it takes." She lifted her eyes and gave me a searching look. "I'm your *angel,*" she said, and then she backed away and vanished into the night.

I made it through the first week without closing my eyes once, not even in the privacy of the Soul Shack's unisex restroom, resorting to the Freon horn and the safety pin whenever I felt myself giving way. My body temperature dropped to 94.2 degrees at one point, but Dr. Laurie wrapped me in one of those thermal survival blankets and brought it back up to normal. Like the rats, I ate. Over-ate, actually, and by the second day I couldn't have cared if Mother Teresa and all the starving bald-headed waifs of Calcutta were camped outside the glass cube, I was eating and there were no two ways about it. Whereas before I'd made do like any other bachelor fending for himself, skipping breakfast most days and going to the deli for a meatball wedge in the afternoon and one fast-food venue or another in the evening, now I found myself gorging almost constantly. Tony and Dr. Laurie were bringing me pizza, sushi, tandoori chicken and supersizer burritos around the clock. I was thirsty too. Couldn't get enough of the power drinks, of Red Bull, Jolt and Starbucks. The caffeine made me sizzle and it hollowed out its own place in the lining of my stomach, a low gastrointestinal burning that made me know I was alive. For the first few nights I felt a bit shaky during the down hours, from one to maybe five or so, but I never faltered, and there was always somebody there to monitor me, whether it was Dr. Laurie or one of our interns at the station. As the hours fell away, I felt stronger, more alive and awake, though the integument was back, draped over the world like a transparent screen, and everything—the way Hezza's mouth moved when she spoke, Tony's animated thrusts and jabs as he sat emoting beside me from six to nine each morning, even the way people and cars moved along the street—seemed to be happening at the bottom of the sea.

Cuttler made himself scarce the first week, chary of associating himself with failure, I suppose, but on the eighth day, when I was a mere seventy-three hours from the record, he showed up just after Tony and I had signed off and the blitzkrieg of ads leading into Annie's slot had begun cannonading over the airwaves. I was experiencing a little difficulty in recognizing people at this juncture—my eyes couldn't seem to focus and the pages of the thrillers were just an indecipherable blur—and I guess I didn't place him at first. He was standing there at the open door of the booth, a vaguely familiar figure in a canary-yellow long-sleeved shirt and trailing cerulean scarf, threads of graying blond hair hanging in his eyes—his small, piglike eyes—and two mugs of piping hot coffee in his hands. Or maybe he was wearing a pullover that day, done up in psychedelic blots of color, or nothing at all. Maybe he was standing there naked, pale as a dead fish, loose and puffy and without definition beyond the compact swell of his gut and the shriveled little British package of his male equipment. Who was I to say? I was hallucinating at this point, experiencing as reality what Dr. Laurie called "hypnogogic reveries," the sort of images you summon up just before nodding off to Dreamland.

"Boomer, you astonish me, you really do," Cuttler might have said, and I think, in reconstructing events, he did. His figure loomed there in the doorway, the two coffee mugs emblazoned with the KFUN logo outstretched to Tony and me. "We all took bets, and I tell you, really, I've been on the losing end all week. Not that I didn't have faith, but knowing you, knowing your performance, that is, and the level of your attachment to, uh, *procedure* down at KFUN, I just didn't think—well, as I say, you do astonish me. Bravo. And keep it up, old chip."

My focus was wavering. I couldn't really feel the cup in my hands, couldn't tell if it was cold or hot, ceramic or Styrofoam (I was suffering from astereognosis, the inability to identify objects through the sense of touch, the very same condition that had afflicted Randy Gardner from the second day on). I felt irritated suddenly. Hot. Outraged. The feeling came up in me like a brush fire, and I couldn't have put the two proper nouns "Cuttler" and "Ames" together if they were the key to taking home the million-dollar prize on a quiz show. "Who the fuck are *you*?" I snarled, and the coffee seemed to snake out of the cup of its own accord.

Cuttler's canary-yellow shirt was canary no longer, if, in fact, that was what he was wearing that day. He snarled something back at me, something offensive and threatening, something about my status at the station, but then Tony, glad-faced, big-headed, cliché-spouting moron that he was, stepped in on my side. "Lay off him, Cutt," he might have said. "Can't you see the strain he's under here? Give us a break, will you?"

And now I felt warm to the bottom of my heart. Tony, good old reliable witty Tony, my partner and my fortress, was coming to my aid. "Tony," I said. "Tony." And left it at that.

Then somehow it was night and my mood shifted to the valedictory because I knew I was going to die just like the rats. My quarter-hour spots lacked vitality, or that was my sense of them ("Helloooo, you ladies and baboons out there in K-whatever land, do you know what the time is? Do you care? Because the Boomer doesn't"). The street outside the booth wasn't a street anymore but a portal to the underworld and the bums weren't bums either, but dark agents of death and decay. I saw my wife and her second husband rise up out of the fog, sprout fangs and wings and flap off into the night. My dead mother appeared briefly, rattling the ice cubes in her cocktail glass till the sound exploded around me like a train derailment. I shoved a gyro into my face, fascinated by the pooling orange grease on the console that seemed to have risen up out of the floor beneath me just to receive it. When Dr. Laurie, who might have been dressed that night like a streetwalker or maybe a nun, came in to monitor me, I may have grabbed for her breasts and hung on like a pair of human calipers until she slapped me back to my senses. And Hezza. My angel in earflaps. Hezza was there, always there, as sleepless as I, sometimes crouched in the bushes, sometimes manifesting herself in the booth with me, rubbing my shoulders and the small of my back with her medium-sized mittened hands and talking nonstop of bands, swag and the undying glamour of FM radio. Christ was in the desert. I was in the booth. My fingers couldn't feel and my eyes couldn't see.

On the tenth day, I achieved clarity. Suddenly the ever-thickening skin of irreality was gone. I saw the street transformed, the fog dissipating that seemed to have been there all week pushing up against the glass walls like the halitosis of defeat, each wisp and tendril burnished by the sun till it glowed. I went live to the studio for my quarter-hour update and let my voice ooze out over the airwaves with such plasticity and oleaginous joy you would have thought I was applying for the job. When I got up to visit the facilities at the Soul Shack, a whole crowd of starry-eyed fans thumped and patted me and held out their hands in supplication even as the chant *Boomer, Boomer, Boomer* rose up like a careening wave to engulf us all in triumph and ecstasy. One more day to set the record, and then we'd see about the day beyond that—the twelfth day, the magic one, the day no other DJ or high school science nerd or speed freak would ever see or match, not as long as the Guinness Brewing Company kept its records into the burgeoning and glorious future.

I was running both taps, trying to make out the graffiti over the toilet and staring into my cratered eyes as if I might tumble into them and never emerge again, when there came a soft insistent rapping at the door. Clear-headed though I was, I felt a surge of irritation. Who in hell could this be? Didn't everybody in town, from the people in their aluminum rockers at the nursing home to the Soul Shack's ham-fisted bouncers, know that I had to have my five minutes of privacy here? Five minutes. Was that too much to ask? Sixty stinking minutes a day? Did they have to see me squatting over the toilet? Unzipping my fly? What did they want, blood? "Who is it?" I boomed.

The smallest voice: "It's me, Hezza."

I opened the door. Hezza's face was drawn and white, pale as a gutter leaf bleached by the winter rains. Beyond her I could see Rudy, our prissiest intern, studying the stopwatch that kept me strictly to my five minutes and not a second more. "Nazi!" I shouted at him, then pulled Hezza into the bathroom with me and shut the door.

She was shivering. Her eyes were red-rimmed, the irises faded till you couldn't tell what color they were anymore. She'd been keeping vigil. She was as tranced as I was. "Take your clothes off," I told her.

How much hesitation was there—half a second?

"Hurry!" I barked.

She was wearing blue jeans, a blouse under the long coat, nothing under that. The coat fell to the floor, the blouse parted, the jeans grabbed at her thighs, and her panties—yellow and gold butterflies and hovering bees, the panties of a child—slid to her knees. Hypnogogic reverie indeed. I tore the buttons off my third-favorite Hawaiian shirt, yanked at my belt, but it was too late, too far gone and lost, because Rudy was pounding on the door like the Gestapo with instructions from Cuttler to knock it off its hinges and snap an amyl nitrite cap under my nostrils if I lingered even a heartbeat too long.

I don't know. I can't remember. But I don't think I even touched her.

Day eleven was a circus. A zoo. I was in the cage, hallucinating, suffering from dissociated thinking, ataxia, blurred vision and homicidal rage, and the KFUN fans—a hundred of them at least, maybe two hundred—blocked the street, pressed up against the glass walls, gyrated and danced and shouted. Tony was with me full-time now, counting down to the moment of Randy Gardner's annihilation, the KFUN sound truck blasting up-to-the-minute KFUN hits to the masses, the police, the city council and the mayor getting in on the act—taking credit, even, though at a safe distance. The stores up and down the block were doing a brisk business in everything from T-shirts to birdcages to engagement rings, and the fast-food outlets were putting on extra shifts.

Hezza was in the booth with us, the booth that had grown crowded now because Dr. Laurie and Nguyen were hovering over the console like groupies, milking every moment for all it was worth, and nobody wanted Hezza there but me. I insisted. Got angry. Maybe even violent. So, though Cuttler and Rudy the intern bit their lips and looked as sour as spoiled milk, Hezza was right there in a plastic chair between me and Tony, her medium-sized mittened hand clutched in my own. And why not? I was the star here, I was the anchorite, I was the one nailed to the cross and hung out to dry for the public's amusement and edification and maybe even redemption. I was feeling grandiose. Above everybody and everything. Transcendent, I guess you'd call it. I wanted Hezza in the booth. Hezza was in the booth.

Tony and I stumbled our way through the show, the Boomer anything but, my wit dried up, my voice a freeze-dried rasp, a whisper. We played more music than usual, cueing up one insomnia tune after another, the Talking Heads' "Stay Up Late," the Beastie Boys' "No Sleep Till Brooklyn," a Cuttler Ames' blast from the past "Wake Me, Shake Me." The ads came fast and furious. Tony counted down the minutes in a voice that got increasingly hysterical. The record was in sight. I was going to make it—and what's more I was ready to shoot for the whole banana, the twelfth day, the immortal day, and I'd already told Cuttler as much. "It's in the bag," I told him, waving my arms over my head like an exercise guru. "No fears."

And then the final countdown, live on the air, 5–4–3–2–1, and a shout went up from the crowd, all those delirious bobbing heads, Hezza grinning up at me out of her parchment face and squeezing my hand as if she were milking it, Dr. Laurie beaming, Cuttler, Tony and the mayor jostling for position with Nick Nixon from the local TV station and a smattering of crews from as far away as Fresno and Bakersfield. "Speech!" somebody shouted, and they all took it up: "Speech, speech, speech!"

I rose from the chair, bits of pea stone gravel stuck to the backside of my sweaty trousers, Hezza rising with me. Tony was chanting along with the crowd now—or no, he was leading the chant, his voice booming out through the big speakers of the sound truck. It was my moment of glory. My first in a whole long dry spell that stretched all the way back to high school and a lead role in the Thespian Club's production of *The Music Man*. I lifted the mike to my lips, took a deep breath. "I just want to say"—my voice was thunderous, godlike—"I just want to say, Goodbye, Randy Gardner, R.I.P.!"

Then I was alone again and it was dark. The morning had bled into afternoon and afternoon into evening, the world battened on the fading light, and with every sleepless minute a new record was being forged. Dr. Laurie begged me to quit at noon, three hours into the new record (actually six, if you consider that I'd been awake and alive for the show that first day before sequestering myself in the glass box). She reminded me of the rats—"They had hemorrhages in their brain tissue, Boomer; enough is enough"—but I ignored her. Cuttler wanted me to go twelve full days, and though I knew on some level he didn't care if I lived or died, I had to show him—show everybody—what I was made of. It was only sleep. I could sleep for a week when I was done. A month. But to stay awake just one more minute was to make history, and the next minute would make history all over again, and the next after that.

Hezza had melted away with the crowd. Dr. Laurie had gone home to sleep. Tony had a date. Cuttler was cuddled up at home with his snaggle-toothed British wife, listening to Deep Purple or some such crap. Even the bums had deserted me, taking their moveable feast down the avenue to a less strenuous venue. The funny thing was, I felt fine. I didn't think sleep, not for a minute. What I saw and what I thought I saw were one and the same and I no longer cared to differentiate. I was living inside a dream and the dream was real life, and what was wrong with that?

I watched the KFUN fans line up outside the Soul Shack, watched the line swell and shrink, and fixated on the taillights of the cars moving silently down the boulevard. I couldn't read, couldn't watch the portable TV Tony had set up for me, couldn't even listen to the chatter of it. Everything seemed so inconsequential. I would say that my mind wandered, but the phrase doesn't begin to do justice to the state I was in—I no longer inhabited my body, no longer had a mind or a being. I felt a great peace descend on me, and I just sat there in silence, studying the red LED display on the console as it chopped and diced the hours, moving only to lift a listless hand to acknowledge the thumbs-up from one or another of the baggy-pantsed teens drifting by on the sidewalk. The club emptied, the streets went silent. I didn't even bother to take my restroom breaks.

In the morning, the light climbed down from the tops of the buildings, a light full of pigeons and hope, and Tony appeared, as usual, at quarter of six, with two cups of coffee. There was something wrong with him, I could see that right away. His face lacked dimension. It wasn't a face at all, but a flat screen painted with Tony-features. He looked worried. "Listen, Boom," he said, "you've got to give this up. No offense, but it's like having a dead man here doing the show with me. You know what you said yesterday, on the air, when I asked you how it felt to set the record? You remember that?"

I didn't. I gave him a numb look.

"You said, 'Fuck you, Dog Face.'"

"I said 'fuck'? On the air?"

Tony didn't respond. He handed me a coffee, sat down and put his headphones on. A moment fluttered by. I couldn't feel the paper cup in my hand. I studied Tony in profile, hoping to see how he was Tony, *if* he was Tony. "Just keep out of my way today, will you?" he said, turning on me abruptly. "And when the show's over, when you've got your twelve days in, you go home to bed. You hear me? Rudy's going to take over for you the next two days, so you get a little vacation here to get your head straight." And then, as if he felt he'd been too harsh, he put a hand on my shoulder and leaned in to me. "You deserve it, man."

I don't remember anything of the show that day, except that Tony—Gooner, as the KFUN audience knew him—kept ringing down the curtain on my record, reminding everybody in KFUN land that the Boomer would be going on home to bed at the conclusion of the show, and what would the Boomer like? A foot massage? A naked blonde? A teddy bear? Couple of brewskies? Ha-ha, ha-ha. One more day, one more show, one more routine. But what Tony didn't know, or Cuttler Ames or Dr. Laurie either, was that I had no intention of giving up the microphone: I was shooting for thirteen days now, and after that it would be fourteen, maybe fifteen. Who could say?

A handful of people were milling around outside the glass booth as we closed out the show, but there was none of the ceremony of the preceding day. The record had been broken, the ratings boosted, and the stunt was over as far as anybody was concerned. The mayor certainly didn't show. Nor did Dr. Laurie. Tony let out a long trailing sigh after we signed off ("This is the Gooner—and the Boomer—saying *adiós, amigos,* and keep the faith, baby—at least till tomorrow morning, same time, same place") and made as if to help me out of the chair, but I shoved him away. He was standing, I was sitting. I was trembling all over, trembling as if I'd just been hosed down on an ice floe in the middle of the Arctic Ocean. *Don't touch me,* I muttered to myself. *Don't even think about it.* He dropped his face to mine, his big bloated moronic moon face that I wanted to smash till it shattered. "Come on, man," he said, "it's over. Beddy-bye. Time to crash."

I didn't move. Wouldn't look at him.

"Don't get psychotic on me now," he said, and he took hold of my left arm, but I shrugged him off. The people on the street stopped what they were doing. Heads turned, eyes zeroed in. He gave them a lame smile, as if it was all part of the act. "You're tired," he said, "that's all," but there was no conviction in his voice. "Boomer?" he said, as if I were floating away from him. "Boomer?" A minute later I heard the glass door at the back of the booth swing open and then shut.

At quarter past nine I went to do my update, but the mike was dead: they'd cut the power on me. I flicked the on/off button a couple of times, then shifted in my seat to glare at the engineer in the sound truck, but the engineer wasn't there—nobody was. So that was it. They were going to isolate me, the sons of bitches. Cut me off. Use me and discard me. I got up from my seat, and who was watching? Nobody. Or no, there was a six-year-old kid standing there gawking at me while his mother jawed with some other mother in front of the Burger

King outlet across the street, and I locked eyes with him for an instant before I jerked the mike out of the socket. What came next I don't remember too clearly, or maybe I've repressed it, but it seems I began to pound the mike against the Plexiglas walls, whipping it like a lariat, and when that was in fragments, I went for the console.

When they finally got me out of there, I'm told, it was past noon and I was well into my thirteenth day—a record that has yet to be surpassed, incidentally, though I'm told there's a fakir in India who claims he hasn't slept in three months, but of course that's unofficial. Not to mention impossible. At any rate, Dr. Laurie had to come down and reason with me in a rigorous way, a squad car began circling the block, and Cuttler ordered Rudy and the sound engineer to cover up the glass walls with black plastic sheeting from the Home Depot up the street. We were getting publicity now, all right, but it wasn't exactly the touchy-feely sort of publicity our august program director had in mind. I'd latched the door from the inside and forced the remains of the console up against it as a makeshift barricade. Rudy was on the roof of the glass cage, unscrolling sheets of black plastic as if it were bunting. I watched Dr. Laurie's face on the other side of the transparent door, watched her mouth work professionally, noted and discarded each of her patent phrases, her false pleas and admonitions. Anything could have happened, because I wasn't going anywhere. And if it wasn't for Hezza I might still be in that glass box—or in the Violent Ward down at the County Hospital. It was that close.

I wasn't aware of how or when it occurred, but at some point I realized that Hezza's face had been transposed over Dr. Laurie's, and that Hezza was smiling at me out of the screwholes of her dimples. I don't know what it was—psychosis, terminal exhaustion or the simple joy of being alive—but I'd never seen anything more beautiful than the earflaps of her knit hat and the way they tucked into her cheeks and made her face into the face of a cut-out doll in a children's book. I smiled back. Then she bent her head, scribbled a moment, and pressed a sheet of paper to the glass. I LOVE YOU, it read.

Of course, this is the sort of resolution we all hope for, even the sleep-deprived, but it wasn't as easy as all that. When we got to my place, when we got to the bed I hadn't seen in thirteen days, the skin of irreality was so thick I couldn't be sure who it was at my side—Hezza, Dr. Laurie, my ex-wife, one of the lean shopping machines I'd watched striding down the avenue from the confines of my glass cage. There was a stripe of sun on the carpet. I pulled the curtains. It vanished. "Who are you?" I said, though the earflaps were a dead giveaway. Something began buzzing from the depths of the house. Outside in the alley the neighbor's dog barked sharply, once, twice, three times. She looked puzzled, looked hurt. "Hezza," she said. "I'm Hezza, don't you remember?"

This time I didn't have to shout, didn't have to do anything really except fall into her where she lay naked on the bed, the blissful bed, the place of sex and sleep. I made love to her through the sheath of exhaustion and afterward watched her eyes slip toward closure and listened to her breathing deepen into sleep. I was tired. Had never been so tired in my life. No one on this earth—no one, ever, not even Randy Gardner—had been so tired. I closed my eyes. Nothing happened. My eyes blinked open as if they'd been trip-wired. For a moment I lay there staring at the ceiling, then I closed them again and by force of will kept them closed. Still nothing. Hezza stirred in her sleep, kicked out at an imaginary something. And then a figure stepped out of the mist and I didn't see him. He had a gun, and I didn't see that either. Swiftly, a shadow moving over open ground, he came up behind me and fired, hitting the gap between the parietal plates.

Boom: I was gone.

(2002)

The Swift Passage of the Animals

She was trying to tell him something about eels, how it had rained eels one night on a town in South America—in Colombia, she thought it was—but he was only half-listening. He was willing himself to focus on the road, the weather getting worse by the minute, and he had to keep one hand on the tuner because the radio was fading in and out as they looped higher into the mountains. "It was a water spout," she said, her face a soft pale shell floating on the undersea glow of the dash lights, "or that's what they think anyway. I mean, that's the rational explanation—the eels congregating to feed or mate and then this eruption that flings them into the air. But imagine the people. Imagine them."

He could feel the rear wheels slipping away from him each time he steered into a curve, and there was nothing but curves, one switchback after another all the way up the flank of the mountain. The night was absolute, no lights, no habitation, nothing—they'd passed the last ranch house ten miles back and were deep into the national forest now, at fifty-five hundred feet and making for the Big Timber Lodge at seventy-two. There was a winter storm watch out for the Southern Sierras, he knew that, and he knew that the back road would be closed as soon as the first snow hit, but the alternative route—up the front of the mountain—was even more serpentine than this one, and a good half hour longer too. His feeling was that they'd make it before the rain turned to snow—or before anything accumulated anyway. Was he a risk taker? Sure he was. And he was always in a hurry. Especially tonight. Especially with her.

"Zach—you listening to me?"

The radio caught a surging throb of chords and a wicked guitar lead burning over the top of them as if the guitarist's fingers had suddenly burst into flame, but before he could enjoy it or even recognize the tune, a wall of static shut it out and was suddenly replaced by a snatch of mariachi and a superslick DJ booming something in Spanish—used cars probably, judging from the tone of it. Or Viagra. *Estimados Señores! Tienen Vds. problemas con su vigor?* His fingers tweaked the dial as delicately as a recording engineer's. But the static came back and persisted. "Shit," he muttered, and punched the thing off.

Now there was nothing but the wet slash of the wheels and the rise and fall of the engine—gun it here, lay off there, gun it, lay off—and the mnemonic echo of the question he'd yet to answer: *You listening to me?* "Yeah," he said, reaching for his buoyant tone—he *was* listening and there was nothing or no one he'd rather listen to because he was in love and the way she bit off her words, the dynamics of her voice, the whisper, the intonation, the soft sexy scratch of it shot from his eardrums right to his crotch, but this was sleet they were looking at now and the road was dark and he was pressing to get there. "The eels. And the people. They must've been surprised, huh?"

She feasted on that a moment and he snatched a glimpse at her, the slow satisfied smile floating on her uplifted face, and the wheels grabbed and slipped and grabbed again. "That's the thing," she said, her voice rich with the telling, "that's the whole point, to imagine that. They're in their huts, frame houses, whatever—tin roofs, maybe just thatch. But the tin roofs are cooler. Way cooler. Think of the tin roofs. It's like, 'Daddy! Mommy!' the kids call out, 'it's *really* raining!'"

This was hilarious—the picture of it, the way she framed it for him, carrying it into falsetto for the kids' voices—and they both broke up, laughing like kids themselves, kids set free in the back of the bus on a school trip. But then there was the road and a black tree-thick turn he nearly didn't make and the last spasm of laughter died in his throat.

A minute fled by, the wipers beating, sleet trapped in the headlights. She readjusted herself in the seat and he saw her hand—a white furtive ghost in the dark of the cab—reach down to check the seatbelt. "The tires are okay, aren't they?" she asked, trying—and failing—to keep the concern out of her voice.

"Oh, yeah," he said, "yeah, plenty of tread," though he'd begun to think he should have sprung for chains. The last sign he'd seen, way back, had said *Cars Required With Chains,* and that stabbed him with the first prick of worry, but chains were something like seventy-five bucks a set and you didn't need chains to get to work in Santa Monica. It seemed excessive to him. If he could have *rented* them, maybe—

And there went the back wheels again, fishtailing this time, a broad staggered Z inscribing itself across both sides of the road and thank God there was nobody else out here tonight, no chance of running into a vehicle coming down the opposite way, not with a winter storm watch and a road closure that was all but certain to go into effect at some point in the night . . .

"You're really skidding," she observed. He glanced at her a moment—sweet and compact in her black leggings and the sweater with the two reindeer prancing across her breasts—and then his eyes shot back to the road. Which was whitening before them, as if some cosmic hand had swept on ahead with a two-lane paintbrush.

"You know my theory?" he said, accelerating out of a turn and leaning into the pitch of the road—up and up, always up.

"No, what?"

"If you go fast enough"—he gave her a quick glance, straight-faced—"I mean really fast . . ."

"Yeah, uh-huh?"

"Well, it's obvious, isn't it? You won't have time to skid."

There was the briefest hesitation—one beat, and he loved that about her, that moment of process—and then they were laughing again, laughing so hard he thought he'd have to pull over to keep from collapsing.

He'd met her three weeks ago, just before Thanksgiving, at a party in Silver Lake. Friends of friends. A Craftsman house, restored down to the last lick of varnish, good wines, hors d'oeuvres from the caterer, a roomful of studiously hip people who if they weren't rockers or filmmakers or poets had to be training to swim the Java Strait or climb solo up the South Col of Mount Diablo. He figured he'd tank up on the hors d'oeuvres, get smashed on somebody else's thirty-two-dollars-a-bottle cabernet, then duck home and watch a movie on DVD, because he wasn't really interested in much more than that. Not yet. He'd been with Christine for two and a half years and then she met somebody at work, and that had shaved him right on down to the root.

Ontario was standing by the fire with his best friend Jared's sister, Mindy, and when he came to think of it later, he saw that there might have been more than a little matchmaking going on here from Mindy's perspective—she knew Ontario from her book club, and she knew that Ontario, sweet and shy and reposing on a raft of arcane information about meteorological events and the swift passage of the various animal species from this sore and wounded planet, was six months divorced and in need of diversion. As he was himself, at least in Mindy's eyes. The wine sang in his veins. He made his way over to the fire.

"So I suppose you must hear this all the time," he said, trying to be clever, trying to impress her after Mindy had embraced him and made the introductions, "but are your parents Canadian?"

"You guessed it."

"So your brother must be Saskatchewan, right? Or B.C., how about B.C.?"

Her hair shone. She was dressed all in black. Her eyes assessed him a moment—from behind the narrow plastic-frame glasses that were like a provocation, as if at any moment she would throw them off and dazzle the room with her unfettered beauty—and she very deliberately shifted the wineglass from one hand to the other. "Unfortunately, I don't have a brother," she said. "Or a sister either." Then she smiled, fully radiant. "If I did, though, I'd think my parents would have gone for Alberta if it was a girl—"

"And what, let me guess—*Newfoundland* if it was a boy."

She looked pleased. Her lips parted and she bit the tip of her tongue in anticipation of the punchline. "Right," she said, "and we'd call him Newf for short."

He'd phoned her the next night and taken her to dinner, and then to a concert two nights later, all the correspondences in alignment. She had a three-year-old daughter. Her ex paid alimony. She worked part-time as a receptionist and was taking courses at UCLA toward an advanced degree in environmental studies. One entire wall in her apartment, floor to ceiling, was dedicated to nature books, from Thoreau to Leopold to Wilson, Garrett, Quammen and Gould.

He fell. And fell hard.

Each turn was a duplicate of the one he'd just negotiated, hairpin to the right, hairpin to the left, more trees, more snow, more distance. The road was gone now altogether, replaced by a broad white featureless plain without discernible limits. He used the trunks of the trees as guideposts, trying to keep the car equidistant from those on the left and the ones that clipped by on the right like so many slats in a fence. It really wouldn't do to skid into any of these trees—they were yellow pines, sugar pines, Jeffreys and ponderosas, as wide around as the pillars of the Lincoln Memorial—but the gaps between them were what caught his attention. Go off the road there and no one could say how far you would drop. Guardrails? Not out here.

They were silent a moment, so he took up the eels again—just to hear his own voice by way of distraction. "So I suppose there's an upside—the villagers must have enjoyed a little fried eel and plantains. Or maybe they smoked them."

"You'd get awfully sick of eel after a couple days, don't you think?" She wasn't staring out the windshield into the white fury of the headlights, but watching him as if they were cruising down the Coast Highway under a ripe and delicate sun. "No, I think they went ahead and buried them—the ones that were too injured to crawl off."

"The stink, huh?"

"Or slither off. Did you know that eels—the American eel, which is what these were—can crawl overland? Like a snake?"

He squinted into the sleet, reached out to flick the radio back on, but thought better of it. "No, I don't think so. Or maybe. Maybe I did. I remember they used to be in every creek when I was a kid—you'd fish for trout and catch this big slick whipping thing that always seemed to swallow the hook and then you couldn't do anything but cut it loose. Because of the slime factor."

"They're all born in the Sargasso Sea, you know that, right? And that it's the females that migrate inland?"

He did. Because he was something of a nature buff himself, hiking up the canyons on weekends, poking under rocks and in the willows along the streambeds, trying to learn the lore, and his own bookshelves featured many of the same titles he'd found on hers. Which was one of the reasons they were going to Big Timber for the weekend—so he could show her the trails he'd discovered the past summer, take her on the Trail of a Hundred Giants and then down the Freeman Creek Trail to the Freeman Grove. She was from Boston and she'd never seen the redwoods and sequoias except in photographs. When she'd told him that, over a plate of mussels marinara at a semi-hip, overpriced place on Wilshire with red banquette seats and votive candles on the tables, he began to rhapsodize Big Timber till he'd made it out to be the earthly paradise itself. Which it was, for all he knew. He'd only been there twice, both times with Jared, on their mountain bikes, but it was as wild and beautiful as it must have been in Muir's time—sure it was—and he'd persuaded her to have her girlfriend babysit for the weekend so they could hike the trails and cross-country ski if there was enough snow, and then sit at the bar at the lodge till it was time to go to bed.

And that was the other reason for the trip, the unspoken promise percolating beneath the simple monosyllable of her assent—going to bed. On their first date she'd told him she was feeling fragile still—her word, not his—and wanted to take things slowly. All right. He respected that. But three weeks had gone by and when she'd agreed to come with him—for two days and two nights—he felt something pull loose inside of him.

"Right," he said, "and then they all return to the Sargasso Sea to mate."

"Amazing, isn't it?"

"All those eels," he said. "Eels from Ohio, Pennsylvania, Texas"—he gave her a look—"Ontario even."

That was when the wheels got away from him and the car spun across the road to glance off a white-capped boulder and into a glistening white ditch that undulated gracefully away from the hidden surface of the road, which was where he really and truly wanted to be.

That they were stuck was a given. The passenger's side wheels were in the ditch, canting the car at an unfortunate angle, and beneath the furiously accumulating snow there was a glaze of ice that gave no purchase. He cursed under his breath—"Shit, shit, shit"—and slammed the wheel with his fist, and she said, "Are we stuck?" For a long moment he didn't respond, the wipers stupidly beating, the snow glossy in the headlights and driving down like a hard white rain.

"Are you all right?" he said finally. "Because I—I mean, it just got away from me there. The road—it's like a skating rink or something." Her face was ghost-lit. He couldn't see her eyes. "Yeah," she said softly, "I'm fine."

When he cracked the door to get out and have a look, the snow stung his eyes and drove the breath from his lips. He caught a quick glimpse of her, huddled there in the passenger's seat—and there was the smell of her perfume too, of the heat of her body and the sleepy warmth of the car's interior—and then he slammed the door and walked round the car to assess the damage. The front fender on the passenger's side had been staved in where it had hit the boulder, but it didn't seem to be interfering with the wheel at all—and that was the good news. For the rest of it, the rear tires had dug themselves a pair of craters in the ice beneath the snow and the axle was resting on a scraped-bald patch of dirt just beneath the tailpipe. And the snow. The snow was coming down and the road was certain to be closed—till spring maybe—and he wasn't sure how many miles yet it was to the lodge. Five? Ten? Twenty? He couldn't begin to guess, and as he looked up into the thin streaming avenue of illumination the car's headlights afforded him, he realized he didn't recognize a thing. There were just trees. Trees and more trees.

Then the car door slammed and she was standing there beside him, the hood of her parka drawn tight over the oval of her face. "You know, I grew up in snow, so this is nothing to me." She was grinning, actually grinning, the glow of the taillights giving her features a weird pinkish cast. "I'll tell you what we have to do, we have to jack up this back wheel here and put something under it."

"Like what?" The engine coughed softly, twice, three times, and then settled into its own rhythm. There was the smell of the exhaust and the sound of the miniature ice pellets in all their trillion permutations hissing off the hood of his jacket, off the trunk of the car, off her hood and the boughs of the trees. He looked round him bleakly—there was nothing, absolutely nothing, to see but for the hummocks of the snow, white fading to gray and then to a drifting pale nullity beyond the range of the headlights.

"I don't know," she said, "a log or something. You have a shovel in the trunk?"

He didn't have a shovel in the trunk—no shovel and no chains. He began to feel less a risk taker and more a fool, callow, rash, without foresight or calculation, the sort of blighted individual whose genetic infirmities get swallowed up in the food chain before he can reproduce and pass them on to vitiate the species. That was the way an evolutionist would see it—that was the way *she* would see it. "No, uh-uh, no shovel," he breathed, and then he was slogging round the car to reach in the driver's door, cut the engine and retrieve the keys—the jack was in the trunk anyway. Or at least it had been, the last time he'd looked, but who obsessed over the contents of the trunk of their car? It was a place to put groceries, luggage, the big purchase at the mall.

Without the rumble of the engine, the night seemed to close in, the ceaseless hiss of the snow the only sound in the universe. He left the lights on, though the buzzer warned him against it, and then he was back with her, flinging open the trunk of the car, the interior of which immediately began to whiten with the descending snow. There were their bags—his black, hers pink—and there was the jack laid in against the inner panel where he'd flung it after changing a flat last summer. Or was it summer before last?

"Okay, great," she said, the pale puff of her breath clinging at her lips, "why don't you jack it up and I'll look for something to—pine boughs, we could use pine boughs. Do you have a knife with you? A hatchet? Anything to cut with?"

He was standing there, two feet from her, staring into the whitening trunk. There were two plastic quarts of motor oil in the back, a grease-stained T-shirt, half a dozen CDs he was afraid the valet at the Italian restaurant might have wanted to appropriate for himself, but no knives, no tools of any kind, other than the jack handle. "No, I don't think so."

She gave him a look then—the dark slits of her glasses, the pursed lips—but all she said was, "We could use the carpet. I mean, look"—and she was reaching in, experimentally lifting the fitted square of it from the mottled steel beneath.

The car was two years old and he was making monthly payments on it. It was the first car he'd ever bought new in his life and he'd picked it out over Christine's objections. He liked the sportiness of it, the power—he could blow by most cars on the freeway without really pushing it—and the color, a magnetic red that stood out a hundred yards away. He didn't want to tear out the carpeting—that was not an option, because they'd get out of this and laugh about it over drinks at the lodge, and there was no sense in getting panicky, no sense in destroying things unnecessarily—but she already had hold of it with one hand and was shoving the bags back away from it with the other, and he had no choice but to pitch in and help.

Inside the car with the engine running, he was in a dream, a trance, as if he'd plunged to the bottom of the sea with Cousteau in his bathyscaphe and all the world had been reduced to this dim cab with the faint green glow of the dash lights and the hum of the heater. Ontario was there beside him, a dark presence in the passenger's seat, her head nestled in the crook of his arm. They'd agreed to run the car every fifteen minutes or so—and then only briefly—in order to conserve gas and still keep the engine warm enough to deliver up heat. And that was all right, though he kept waking from his dream to a kind of frantic beating in his chest because they were in trouble here, deep trouble, he knew that no matter how much he told himself the storm would tail off and they could wade through the snow to the lodge. And what of the car? With this heavy a snowfall the road would be closed till spring and the car would be abandoned until the snow melted away and revealed it there at the side of the road, in the ditch, and he'd have to beg a ride to work or squeeze onto one of those noxious buses with all the dregs of humanity. Still, it could be worse—at least he'd filled the gas tank before they'd started up the hill.

"Zach?" Her voice was murmurous with sleep.

"Yeah?"

"There's nothing to worry about, you know. I've got two strong legs. We can walk out in the morning and get somebody to help—snowmobilers. There's sure to be snowmobilers out—"

"Yeah," he said, "yeah, I'm sure," and he wanted to add, gloomily, that this wasn't suburban Massachusetts, that this was the wild, or at least as wild as it got in Southern California. There were mountain lions here, bears, pine martens, the ring-tailed cat. Last summer, with Jared, he'd seen a bear cub—a yearling, he guessed, a pretty substantial animal—out on the highway, this very highway, scraping the carcass of a crushed squirrel off the pavement with its teeth. They averaged twenty-plus feet of snow per season at this altitude and as much as forty during an El Niño year, and with his luck this would turn out to be an El Niño, no doubt about it, because it was coming down as if it wasn't going to stop till May. *Snowmobilers.* Fat chance. Still, there was the lodge, and if they could get there—when they got there—they'd be all right. And the car would keep—he felt sick about it and he'd need a new battery maybe, but that was something he could live with. The cold he didn't think about. Or the killing effort of slogging through knee-deep snow. That was for tomorrow. That was for daylight.

They'd spent a good hour or more trying to get the car out, the carpets expendable, his Thomas Guide, even his spare jacket and two back issues of *Nature* she'd brought along to pore over by the fire, but the best they'd been able to do was give the rear wheels a moment's purchase in order to shove the front end in deeper. By the time they gave up, he'd lost all sensation in his toes and fingertips, and that was when she thought of her cell phone—and he let her take it out and dial 911 because he didn't have the heart to tell her that cell phones were useless up here, out of range, just like the radio.

"Tell me a story," she said now. "Talk to me."

He cut the engine. The snow had long since turned to powder and it fell silently, the only sound the creak and groan of the automobile shutting down. The dark was all-embracing and the humps of the gathering snow clung to it. "I don't know," he said. "I don't know any stories."

"Tell me about the animals. Tell me about the bears."

He shrugged in the darkness, drew her to him. "They're all asleep now. But last summer—at the lodge?—there was one out back, a big cinnamon sow they said that must have weighed three hundred pounds or more. Jared and I were playing eight ball—there's a nice table there, by the way, and I'm challenging you to the world championship tomorrow afternoon, so you better limber up your fingers—and somebody said, *The bear's out there again,* and we must have watched the thing for half an hour before it lumbered off, and lumber it did. I mean, now I can understand the meaning of that word in a whole new way."

She was silent a moment, then she said, "The California grizzly's extinct, but you knew that, right?"

"Oh, yeah, yeah, I meant this was a black bear."

"They shot the last grizzly in Fresno, probably sniffing around somebody's sheep ranch, in 1922. Boom. And it was gone forever." There was a hitch in her voice, a sort of downbeat, as she settled into the arena of certainty, of what is and what was. The snow sifted down around them, a white sea in fragments—the dandruff of God, as his father used to call it when they went skiing at Mammoth over Christmas break each year. She paused a beat, then her voice came to him, soft as a prayer. "Did I ever tell you about the Carolina parakeet?"

It was still snowing at first light and the wind had come up in the night and sculpted a drift that rose as high as the driver's side window, though he didn't know that yet. He woke from a dream that dissolved as soon as he opened his eyes, replaced by a sudden sharp apprehension of loss: his car to be abandoned, the indeterminate walk ahead of them, the promise of the weekend crushed like a bag full of nothing. All because he was an idiot. Because he'd taken a chance and the chance had failed him. He thought back to yesterday afternoon, the unalloyed pleasure in her face as she tucked her bag into the trunk and settled in beside him, the palms nodding in a breeze off the ocean, the traffic light—lighter than he'd ever seen it—one great tune after another on the radio, all beat and attitude, his fingertips drumming on the steering wheel and how was work and did the boss say anything about ducking out early? He wished he could go back there, back to that moment when she slid in beside him and the precipitation hadn't started in yet and he could have chosen the main road, the one he knew would get them there, snow or no snow. He wished he'd sprung for chains too. He wished a lot of things. Wished he was at the lodge, waking up beside her in bed. Or lingering over breakfast by the fire, big white oval plates of eggs and ham and home fries, mimosas, Bloody Marys, the snow hanging in the windows like a wraparound mural . . .

The car was cold—he could see the breath trailing from his lips—and the windshield was opaque with the accumulation of snow and the intricate frozen swirls of condensation that clung to the inner surface of the glass. Ontario was asleep, the hood framing her face, her lips parted to expose the neat arc of her upper teeth, and for a long moment he just stared at her, afraid to wake her, afraid to start whatever was to come. What had she told him the night before? That the wild was shrinking away and the major species of the earth were headed for oblivion and there was nothing anyone could do about it. He tried to dissuade her, pointing to the reintroduction of the wolf in Yellowstone, the resilience of the puma and black bear populations in these woods, the urban invasion of deer, opossums and raccoons, but she wouldn't listen. This was her obsession, everything dead or dying, the oceans depleted, the skies bereft, the plains and the forests gone preternaturally silent, and she fell asleep in his arms reciting the names of the creatures gone down as if she were saying her prayers.

He listened to her breathing, the soft rattle of the air circulating through her nostrils and lifting and deflating her chest in a slow regular rhythm, and he watched her face, composed around dreams of the animals deserting their niches one by one. He didn't want to wake her. But he was cold and he had to relieve himself and then formulate some sort of plan or at least figure out where they were and how far they were going to have to walk, and so he turned over the engine to get some heat and cracked his door to discover the drift and the chill blue light trapped within it.

She sat up with a start, even as he put his shoulder to the door and the breath of the storm rode in on a cold whip of wind-flung snow. "Where are we?" she murmured, as if they could have been anyplace else, and then, vaguely pushing at the hood of her parka as if to run her fingers through her hair, "Is it still snowing?"

They relieved themselves privately, he on his side of the car—after planing off the drift with the dull knife-edge of the door—and she on hers. He stood there, the snow in his face, whiteness unrelieved, and drilled a steaming cavity into the drift while she squatted out of sight and the road revealed itself as a featureless river flowing away between the cleft banks of the trees. It took them a while to divide up their things—anything left behind, extra clothes, toiletry articles, makeup, jewelry, would go into the trunk, where they'd recover it next spring as if they were digging up a time capsule—and they shared one of the two power bars she'd brought along in her purse and a stick each of the beef jerky he found in his backpack. They ate in the car, talking softly, warming their fingers in the blast of the heater, the gas gauge run nearly all the way down now, but he'd worry about that later. Much later. He brooded as he worked his jaws over a plug of dried meat, kicking himself all over again, but she was unfazed. In fact, given the circumstances, given how miserable he was, she seemed inordinately cheerful, as if this was a big adventure—but then it wasn't her car, was it?

"Oh, come on, Zach," she said, her eyes startled and wide behind the constricting lenses, a faint trace of chocolate defining her upper lip, "we'll make the most of it. We were going to hike anyway, weren't we? And when we get to the lodge we'll see if maybe somebody can tow the car out—all right? And then we can play that game of pool you promised me."

His voice dropped to a croak. He was feeling sorry for himself and the more upbeat she was the more sorry he felt. "They can't," he said. "It's miles from the lodge and they don't plow here, there's no point in it. I mean, how would they get a tow truck in?"

The smile still clung to her lips, a patient smile, serene, beautiful. "Maybe you can get them to just plow one lane or something—or somebody with a snowplow on his pickup, something like that."

He turned his head, stared at the frosted-over side window. "Forget it," he said. "The car's here till May. Unless the yahoos come out and strip it."

"All right, then. Have it your way. But we'd better get walking or we'll be here till May ourselves, right?"

He didn't answer.

"It's that way, I assume," she said, pointing a gloved finger at the windshield.

He just looked at her, then shoved open the door and stepped out into the snow.

He was twenty-eight years old, in reasonably good shape—he worked out once or twice a week at the gym, made a point of walking the eight blocks to the grocery store every other day and went mountain biking in season—but the major part of his waking life was spent motionless in front of the computer screen, and that was what afflicted him now. The snow was thigh-deep, the air thin, and they hadn't gone half a mile before his clothes were damp with sweat and his legs felt like dead things grafted on at the hip. She followed three steps behind in the narrow gauge of the trail he broke for her, her eyes sharp and attuned, the pink bag thrown over one shoulder, thrusting out her arms for balance every so often as if she were walking a tightrope. Nothing moved ahead of them, not a bird or squirrel even. The silence pinned them in, as if they were in an infinite bed under a blanket as big as the sky.

"You look like a snowman," she said. "A walking snowman."

He took this as a signal to stop, and he planted his feet and rotated to face her. She seemed reduced somehow, as small as a child sent out to play with her sled on a day when the superintendent had closed down the schools, and he wanted to hug her to him protectively, wanted to make amends for his mood and the mess he'd gotten them into, but he didn't. The snow drove down, burying everything. There was a crown of it atop her hood, individual flakes caught like drift in her eyelashes and softening the frames of her glasses. "You too," he said, pulling for air as if he were drowning. "Both of us," he gasped. "Snowmen. Or snow man and snow woman."

Later on—and maybe they'd gone another mile—he made a discovery that caused his heart to leap up and then almost simultaneously closed it down again. They'd come to a place he recognized even through the blowing snow and the shifting, subversive contours of the landscape—an intersection, with a half-buried stop sign. Straight ahead the road pushed deeper into the wilderness; to the left, it led to the Big Timber Lodge, and at least he knew where they were now, even if it wasn't nearly as close as he'd imagined. He'd been fooling himself, he knew that, but all along he'd been hoping they'd passed here in the disorientation of the night. "I know this place," he said. "The lodge is this way."

She was panting now too, though not ten minutes ago she'd been telling him how she never missed a day on the Stairmaster—or almost never. "Fantastic," she said. "See, it wasn't so bad." She stamped in place, shook the snow from her shoulders. "How far from here?"

His voice sank. "Pretty far," he said.

"How far?"

He shrugged. Looked away from her even as a gust flung a fist of snow in his face. "Thirteen miles."

There came a point—it might have been half an hour later, forty-five minutes, he couldn't say—when he gave in and let her break trail ahead of him. He was wiped. He could barely lift his legs. And when he wasn't moving—if he paused even for a minute to catch his breath—the wind dug into him and he felt the sweat go cold under his arms and across his back. He couldn't believe how fast the snow was accumulating—it was up to his crotch now and even deeper in the drifts, the wind raking the trees till the needles whipped and sang, the temperature falling as if it were night already, though it was just past one. He watched her move ahead of him, head bobbing, arms churning, six steps and then a recuperative pause, her lower body sheared off at the waist as if she were wading across a river. She'd slipped a pair of jeans on over her leggings in the fastness of the car but she must have been cold, whether she'd grown up in the snow or not. He was thinking he'd have to catch her by the arm and reverse positions with her—he was the one who'd gotten her into this and he was going to lead her out of it—when suddenly she stopped and swung round on him, heaving for breath.

"Wow," she said, "this is something, huh?" Her face was chapped, blazing, the cord of the hood gone hard with a knot of ice; her nose was running and her mouth was set.

"Let me," he said, "it's my turn."

Her eyes gave him permission. Slowly, with the wind in his face and his feet shuffling like a drunk's, he waded on ahead of her.

"I wish we had snowshoes," she said at his back.

"Yeah, me too."

"Or skis."

"How about a snowmobile? Wouldn't that be nice?"

"Hot coffee," she said. "I'd settle for that."

"With a shot of brandy—or Kahlúa. How does Kahlúa sound?"

The wind came up. She didn't answer. After a while she asked him if he thought it was much farther and he halted and swung round on her. His fingers throbbed, his feet were dead. "I don't know—it can't be that much farther."

"How far do you think we've come? I mean, from where the road forked?"

He shrugged. "A couple miles, I guess, right?"

Her eyes narrowed against the wind. She ran a mittened hand under her nose. "You know what killed off the glyptodont?"

He hugged his arms to his chest and watched her, the wind-blown snow riding up his legs.

"Stupidity," she said, and then they moved on.

Near the end, when the sky shaded perceptibly toward night and the ravens began to call from their hidden perches, she complained of numbness in her fingers and toes. Neither of them had spoken for a long while—speech was superfluous, a waste of energy in the face of what was turning out to be more of a trial than either of them could have imagined—and all he could say was that he was sorry for getting her into this and reassure her that they'd be there soon. The snow hadn't slackened all day—if anything, perversely, it seemed to be coming down even harder now—and the going was ever slower as the drifts mounted ahead of them. Earlier, they'd stopped to share the remaining power bar and she'd been sufficiently energetic still to regale him with stories of the last passenger pigeon dying on its perch in the Cincinnati Zoo and the last wolf shot in these mountains, of the aurochs and the giant sloth and half a dozen other poor doomed creatures winging by on their way to extinction even as he silently calculated their own chances. People froze to death out here, that much he knew. Hikers forever lost in the echoing canyons, snowmobilers awaiting rescue by their disabled machines, the unlucky and unprepared. But they weren't lost, he kept telling himself—they were on the road and it was just a matter of time and effort before they got to the lodge. Nothing to worry about. Nothing at all.

She was ahead of him, breaking trail, the snow up to her waist. "It's not just numb," she said, her breath trailing behind her. "It stings. It stings so bad."

The gloom deepened. He went on another five steps and pulled up short. "Maybe we should stop," he said, breathing so hard he felt as if his lungs had been turned inside out. "Just for a couple minutes. I have a tarp in my pack and we could make a little shelter. If we get out of the wind we can—"

"What?" she swung round on him, her face savage. "We can what—freeze to death? Is that what you want, huh?"

The snow absorbed them. Everything, even the trunks of the trees, faded to colorlessness. He didn't know what to do. He was the one at fault here and there was no way to make that right, but still, couldn't she see he was doing his best?

"No," he said, "that's not what I mean. I mean we could recoup our energy—it can't be much farther—and I could warm your feet. I mean, on my chest, under my parka—isn't that what you're supposed to do? Flesh to flesh?"

She snatched off her glasses and all her beauty flashed out, but it was a disengaged beauty, a bedraggled and fractious beauty. Her lips clenched, her eyes penetrated him. "Are you crazy? I'm going to take off my boots in this? Are you out of your mind?"

"Ontario," he whispered, "listen, come on, please," and he was shuffling forward to take her in his arms and press her to him, to have that at least, human warmth and comfort and all the trailing sorrowful release that comes with it, when the air suddenly bloomed with sound and they both turned to see the single Cyclopean eye of a snowmobile bounding toward them through the drifts.

A moment, and it was over. The engine screamed and then the driver saw them and let off on the throttle, the machine skidding to a halt just in front of them. The driver peeled back his goggles. There was a rime of ice in his beard. The exhaust took hold of the air and paralyzed it. "Jesus," he said, his eyes shying away from them, "I damn near run you down. You people lost or what?"

He could have stayed where he was, could have waited while the man in the goggles sped Ontario back to the lodge and then returned for him, but he trudged on anyway, a matter of pride now, the man's incredulous laugh still echoing in his ears. *You mean you come up the back road? In this? Oh, man, you are really in the shits.* He was less than a mile from the lodge when the noise of the machine tore open the night and the headlight pinned him where he was. Then it was the wind and the exhaust and the bright running flash of the meaningless snow.

She was propped up by the fire with her boots off and a mug of coffee wrapped in her hands when he dragged himself in the door, shivering violently from that last wind-whipped run through the drifts. Her wet parka was flung over the chair beside her and one of her mittens lay curled on the floor beneath the chair. A group of men in plaid shirts and down vests were gathered at the bar, roaring over the weather and their tall drinks, and a subsidiary group hovered around Ontario, plying her with their insights as to the advisability of bringing a vehicle up the back road in winter and allowing as how you should never go anywhere this time of year without snowshoes, a GPS beacon and the means of setting up a shelter and building yourself a fire in the event you had to hole up. She was lucky, they were telling her, not to mention crazy. In fact, this was the craziest thing any of them had ever heard of. And they all—every man in the place—turned their heads to give him a look as he clumped toward the fire.

Someone shoved a hot drink in his hands and he tried to be a sport about it, tried to be grateful and humble as they crowded around him and offered up their mocking congratulations on his having made it—"You're a snow marathoner, isn't that a fact?" one of them shouted in his face—but humility had never been his strong suit and the longer it went on the angrier he felt. And it did go on, he and Ontario the entertainment for the night, the drinks circulating and the fire snapping, a woman at the bar now, heavyset and hearty and louder than any of the men, until finally the owner of the place came in the door, snow to his eyes, to get a look at this marvel. He was a big man, bearded like the rest of them, his face lit with amusement, proprietor of the Big Timber Lodge and king of all he surveyed. "Hello and welcome," he called in a hoarse, too-loud voice, gliding across the room to the fireplace, where Zach sat slumped and shivering beside Ontario. He took a minute, bending forward to poke solicitously at the coals. "So I hear you two took a little hike out there today."

Zach reddened. The laughter rose and ebbed. Ontario sat hunched over her coffee as the fire stirred and settled. Beyond the windows it was dark now, the snow reduced to a collision of particles beating across the cone of light cast by a single lamp nailed to the trunk of one of the massive trees that presided over the parking lot. "Yeah," Zach said, looking up into the man's face and allowing him half a smile, "a little stroll."

"But you're okay, right—both of you? You need anything—dinner? We can make you dinner, full menu tonight."

For the first time, Ontario spoke up. "Dinner would be nice," she murmured. Her hair was tangled and wet, her face bleached of color. "We haven't really eaten since lunch yesterday, I guess."

"Except for some beef jerky," Zach put in, just for the record. "And two power bars."

The big man straightened up. He was beaming at them, his eyes jumping from Zach to Ontario and back again. "Good," he said, rubbing his hands as if he'd just stepped away from the grill, as if the steaks had already been flipped and the potatoes were browning in the pan, "fine. Well, listen, you make yourselves comfortable, and if there's anything else, you just holler." He paused. "By the way," he added, leaning in to brace himself on the back of the chair, "you have a place to stay for the night?"

The fire snapped and spat. It was all winding down now. Zach put the mug to his lips and felt the hot jolt of the coffee like a bullet in the back of his throat. He didn't look at Ontario, didn't pat her hand or slip an arm round her shoulders. "We're going to need a room," he said, gazing up at the man, and in the space of that instant he could hear the faint hum of the wings and the beat of the paws and the long doomed drumming of the hooves before Ontario corrected him.

"No," she said. "Two rooms."

(2004)

Jubilation

I've been living in Jubilation for almost two years now. There's been a lot of change in that time, both for the better and the worse, as you might expect in any real and authentic town composed of real and authentic people with their iron-clad personalities and various personal agendas, but overall I'd say I'm happy I chose the Contash Corp's vision of community living. I've got friends here, neighbors, people who care about me the way I care about them. We've had our crises, no question about it—Mother Nature has been pretty erratic these past two years—and there isn't a man, woman or child in Jubilation who isn't worried about maintaining property values in the face of all the naysaying and criticism that's come our way. Still, it's the *people* this whole thing is about, and the people I know are as determined and forward-looking a bunch as any you'd ever hope to find. We've built something here, something I think we can all be proud of.

It wasn't easy. From the beginning, everybody laughed behind my back. Everybody said, "Oh, sure, Jackson, you get divorced and the first thing you do is fly down to Florida and live in some theme park with Gulpy Gator and whoever—Chowchy the Lizard, right?—and you defend it with some tripe about community and the New Urbanists and we're supposed to say you're behaving rationally?" My ex-wife was the worst. Lauren. She made it sound as if I was personally going to drive the Sky Lift or slip into a Gulpy suit and greet people at the gates of Contash World, but the truth is I was a pioneer, I had a chance to get into something on the ground floor and make it work—*sacrifice* to make it work—and all the cynics I used to call friends just snickered in their apple martinis as if my post-divorce life was some opera bouffe staged for their amusement.

Take the lottery. They all thought I was crazy, but I booked my ticket, flew down to Orlando and took my place in line with six thousand strangers while the sun peeled the skin off the tip of my nose and baked through the soles of my shoes. There was sleet on the runway at LaGuardia when the plane took off, a foot and a half of snow expected in the suburbs, and it meant nothing to me, not anymore. The palms were nodding in a languid tropical breeze, the chiggers, no-see-ums and mosquitoes were all on vacation somewhere, children scampered across the emerald grass and vigorous little birds darted in and out of the jasmine and hibiscus. It was early yet, not quite eight. People shuffled their feet, tapped their watches, gazed hopefully off into the distance while a hundred Contash greeters moved up and down the line with crullers and Styrofoam cups of coffee.

The excitement was contagious, and yet it was inseparable from a certain element of competitive anxiety—this was a random drawing, after all, and there would necessarily have to be winners and losers. Still, people were outgoing and friendly, chatting among themselves as if they'd known one another all their lives, sharing around cold cuts and homemade potato salad, swapping stories. Everybody knew the rules—there was no favoritism here. Charles Contash was founding a town, a prêt-à-porter community set down in the middle of the vacation wonderland itself, with Contash World on one side and Game Park U.S.A. on the other, and if you wanted in—no matter who you were or who you knew—you had to stand in line like anybody else.

Directly in front of me was a single mother in a powder-blue halter top designed to show off her assets, which were considerable, and in front of her were two men holding hands; immediately behind me, silently masticating crullers, was a family of four, mom, pop, sis and junior, their faces haggard and interchangeable, and behind them, a black couple burying their heads in a glossy brochure. The single mother—she'd identified herself only as Vicki—had one fat ripe creampuff of a baby slung over her left shoulder, where it (he? she?) was playing with the thin band of her spaghetti strap, while the other child, a boy of three or so decked out in a striped polo shirt and a pair of shorts he could grow into, clung to her knee as if he'd been fastened there with a strip of Velcro. "So what did you say your name was?" she asked, swinging round on me for what must have been the hundredth time in the past hour. The baby, in this view, was a pair of blinding white diapers and two swollen, rooting legs.

I told her my name was Jackson, and that I was pleased to meet her, and before she could say *Is that your first name or last?* I clarified the issue for her: "Jackson Peters Reilly. That's my mother's maiden name. Jackson. And her mother's maiden name was Peters."

She seemed to consider this a moment, her eyes drifting in and out of focus. She patted the baby's bottom for no good reason. "Wish I'd thought of that," she said. "This one's Ashley, and my son's Ethan—Say hello, Ethan. Ethan?" And then she laughed, a hearty, hopeful laugh that had nothing to do with rejection, abandonment or a night spent on the pavement with two exhausted children while holding a place something like four hundred deep in the lottery line. "Of course, my maiden name's Silinski, so it wouldn't exactly sound too feminine for little baby Ashley, now would it?"

She was flirting with me, and that was okay, that was fine, because wasn't that what I'd come down here for in the first place—to upgrade my social life? I was tired of New York. Tired of L.A. Tired of the anonymity, the hassle, the grab and squeeze and the hostility snarling just beneath the surface of every transaction, no matter how small or insignificant. "I don't know," I said, "sounds kind of chic to me. The doorbell rings and there's all these neighborhood kids chanting, 'Can Silinski come out to play?' Or the modeling agency calls. 'So what about Silinski,' they say, 'is she available?' "

I was doing fine, grinning and smooth-talking and sailing right along, though my back felt misaligned and my right hip throbbed where the pavement had bitten into it during a mostly sleepless night under the amber glow of the newly installed Contash streetlamps. I took a swig from my Evian bottle, tugged the plastic brim of my visor down to keep the sun from irradiating the creases at the corners of my eyes. There was one more Silinski trope on my tongue, the one that would bring her to her knees in adoration of my wit and charm, but I never got to utter it because at that moment the rolling blast of a Civil War cannon announced the official opening of the lottery, and everybody in line crowded closer as ten thousand balloons, in the powder-blue and sun-kissed orange of the Contash Corp, rose up like a mad flock into the sky.

"Welcome, all you friends and neighbors," boomed an amplified voice, and all eyes went to the head of the line. There, atop the four-story tower of the sales preview center, a tiny figure in the Contash colors held out his arms in benediction. "And all you little ones too—and remember, Gulpy Gator and Chowchy love you one and all, and so does our founder, Charles Contash, whose vision of community, of health and vigor and good schools and good neighbors, has never shone more brightly than it does today in Jubilation! No need to crowd, no need to fret. We've got two thousand Village Homes, Cottage Homes, Little Adobes and Mercado Street mini–luxury apartments available today, and three thousand more to come. So welcome, folks, and just step up and draw your lucky number from the hopper."

The press moved forward in all its human inevitability, and I had to brace myself to avoid trampling the young woman in front of me. As it was, the family of four gouged their angles into my flesh and I found myself making a nest of my arms for her, for Vicki, who in turn was shoved up against the hand-holding men in front of her. I could smell her, her breath sweet with the mints she'd been sucking all morning and the odor of her sweat and perfume rising up out of the confinement of her halter top. "Oh, God," she whispered, "God, I just pray—"

Her hair was in my mouth, caught in the bristles of my mustache. It was as if we were dancing, doing the Macarena or forming up a conga line, back to front. "Pray what?"

Her breath caught and then released in a respiratory tumult that was almost a sob: "That there's just one Mercado Street mini–luxury apartment left, just one, that's all I ask." And then she paused, the shining new moon of her face rising over her shoulder to gaze up into mine. "And you," she breathed, "I pray you get what you want too."

What I wanted was a detached home in the North Village section of town, on the near side of the artificial lake, a cool four hundred fifty thousand dollars for a ninety-by-thirty-foot lot and a wraparound porch that leered promiscuously at the wraparound porches of my neighbors, ten feet away on either side—one of the Casual Contempos or even one of the Little Adobes—and I wanted it so badly I would have taken Charles Contash himself hostage to get it. "A Casual Contempo," I said, and the family of four strained against me.

She was fighting for position. The child underfoot clung like a remora to the long tapered muscle of her leg. The baby began to fuss. She was put out, overwrought, not at all at her best, I could see that, but still her eyebrows lifted and she let out a low whistle. "Wow," she said, "you must be rich."

I wasn't rich, not by the standards I'd set for myself, but I'd sold my company to a bigger company and bought off my ex-wife, and what was left was more than adequate to set me up in a new life in a new house—and no, I wasn't retiring to Florida to play golf till I dropped dead of boredom, but just looking for what was missing in my life, for the values I'd grown up with in the suburbs, where there were no fences, no walls, no gated communities and private security guards, where everybody knew everybody else and democracy wasn't just a tattered banner the politicians unfurled for their convenience every four years. That was what the Jubilation Company promised. That and a rock-solid property valuation, propped up by Charles Contash and all the fiscal might of his entertainment and merchandising empire. The only catch was that you had to occupy your property a minimum of nine months out of the year and nobody could sell within two years of purchase, so as to discourage speculators, but to my way of thinking that wasn't a catch at all, if you were committed. And if you weren't, you had no business taking up space in line to begin with. "Not really," I said, enjoying the look on her face, the unconscious widening of her eyes, the way her lips parted in expectation. "Comfortable, I guess you'd say."

Then the line jerked again and we all revised our footing. "Mercado Street!" somebody shouted. "Penny Lane!" countered another, and there was a flicker of nervous laughter.

From where I was standing, I could barely see over the crush. A girl in a short blue skirt and orange heels stood on a platform at the head of the line, churning a gleaming stainless-steel hopper emblazoned with the Contash logo, and an LED display stood ready to flash the numbers as people extracted the little digitized cards from the depths of it. There was a ripple of excitement as the first man in line, a phys ed teacher from Las Vegas, New Mexico, climbed the steps of the platform. Rumor had it he'd been camped on the unforgiving concrete for over a month, eating his meals out of a microwave and doing calisthenics to keep in shape. I saw a running suit (blue with orange piping, what else?) surmounted by yard-wide shoulders and a head like a wrecking ball. The man bent to the hopper, straightened up again and handed a white plastic card to the girl, who in turn ran it under a scanner. The display flickered, and then flashed the number: 3,347. "Oh, God," Vicki muttered under her breath. My pulse was racing. I couldn't seem to swallow. The sun hung overhead like an over-ripe orange on a limb just out of reach as the crowd released a long slow withering exhalation. So what if the phys ed teacher had camped out for a month? He was a loser, and he was going to have to wait for Phase II construction to begin before he could even hope to become part of this.

None of the next five people managed to draw under 1,000, but at least they were in, at least there was that. "They look like they want houses, don't they?" Vicki said, a flutter of nerves undermining her voice. "I don't mean Casual Contempos," she said, "I wouldn't want to jinx that for you, but maybe the Little Adobes or the Courteous Coastals. But not apartments. No way."

Then a couple who looked as if they belonged on one of the Contash Corp's billboards drew number 5 and the crowd let out a collective groan before people recovered themselves and a spatter of applause went up. I shut my eyes. I hadn't eaten since the previous afternoon on the plane and I felt dizzy suddenly. *Get lucky,* I told myself. *Just get lucky, that's all.*

A breeze came up. The line moved forward step by step, slab by slab. As each number was displayed, a thrill ran through the crowd, and they were all neighbors, or potential neighbors, but that didn't mean they weren't betting against you. It took nearly an hour before the men in front of Vicki—Mark and his partner, Leonard, nicest guys in the world—mounted the steps to the platform and drew number 222. I watched in silence as they fell into each other's arms and improvised a little four-legged jig around the stage, and then Vicki was up there with the sun bringing out the highlights in her hair and drawing the color from her eyes as if they'd been inked in. The boy fidgeted. The baby squalled. She bent forward to draw her number, and when the display flashed 17 she flew down the steps and collapsed for sheer joy in the arms of the only man she knew in that whole astonished crowd—me—and everybody must have assumed I was the father of those creamy pale children until I climbed the steps myself and thrust my own arm into the hopper.

The stage seemed to go quiet suddenly, all that tumult of voices reduced to a whisper, tongues arrested, lips frozen in mid-sentence. I was going to get what I wanted. I was sure of it. My fingers closed on a card, one of thousands, and I fished it out and handed it to the girl; an instant later the number flashed on the board—4,971—and Vicki, poised at the foot of the steps with a glazed smile, looked right through me.

There are people in this world who are content with the lot they're given, content to bow their heads and accept what comes, to wait, sacrifice and look to the future. I'm not one of them. Within an hour of the drawing, I'd traded number 4,971 and $10,000 cash for Mark and Leonard's number 222, and within a month of that I was reclining in a new white wicker chaise longue on the wraparound porch of my Casual Contempo discussing interior decoration with a very determined—and attractive—young woman from Coastal Design. The young woman's name was Felicia, and she wore her hair in a French braid that exposed the long cool nape of her neck. She was looking into my eyes and telling me in her soft breathy reconstructed tones what I needed vis-à-vis the eclectic neo-traditional aesthetic of the Jubilation Community—"Really, Mr. Reilly, you can mix and match to your heart's content, a Stickley sofa to go with your Craftsman windows set right next to a Chinese end table of lacquered rosewood with an ormolu inlay"—when I interrupted her. I listened to the ice cubes clink in my glass a moment, then asked her if she wouldn't prefer discussing my needs over a nice étoufée on the deck of the Cajun Kitchen overlooking lovely Lake Allagash. "Oh, I would love that, Mr. Reilly," she said, "more than practically anything I can think of, but Jeffrey—my sweet little husband of six months?—might just voice an objection." She crossed her legs, let one heel dangle strategically. "No, I think we'd better confine ourselves to the business at hand, don't you?"

I wrote her a check, and within forty-eight hours I was inhabiting a color plate torn out of one of the Jubilation brochures, replete with throw rugs, armoires, sideboards, a set of kitchen chairs designed by a Swedish sadist and a pair of antique brass water pitchers—or were they spittoons?—stuffed with the Concours d'Elegance mix of dried coastal wildflowers. It hadn't come cheap, but I wasn't complaining. This was what I'd wanted since the breath had gone out of my marriage and I'd begun living the nomadic life of the motor court, the high-rise hotel and the inn round the corner. I was home. For the first time in as long as I could remember, I felt oriented and secure.

I laid in provisions, rode my Exercycle, got into a couple of books I'd always meant to read (*Crime and Punishment*, *Judgment at Nuremberg*, *The Naked and the Dead*), took a divorcée named Cecily to the Chowchy Grill for dinner and afterward to a movie at the art deco palace designed by Cesar Pelli as the centerpiece of the Mercado Street pedestrian mall, and enjoyed the relatively bugless spring weather in a rented kayak out on Lake Allagash. By the end of the second month I'd lost eight pounds, my arms felt firmer and my face was as tan as a tennis pro's. I wished my wife could see me now, but even as I wished it, the image of her—the heavy, pouting lips and irascible lines etched into the corners of her mouth, the flaring eyes and belligerent stab of her chin—rose up to engulf me in sorrow. Raymond, that was the name of the man she was dating—Raymond, who owned his own restaurant and had a boat out on Long Island Sound.

At any rate, I was standing over the vegetable display at the Jubilation Market one afternoon watching my ex-wife's face superimpose itself on the gleaming epidermis of an oversized zucchini, when a familiar voice called out my name. It was Vicki. She was wearing a transparent blouse over a bikini top and she'd had her hair done up in a spill of tinted ringlets. A plastic shopping basket dangled from one hand. There were no children in sight. "I heard you got your Casual Contempo," she said. "How're you liking it?"

"A dream come true. And you?"

Her smile widened. "I got a job. At the company office? I'm assistant facilitator for tour groups."

"Tour groups? You mean here? Or over at Contash World?"

"You haven't noticed all the people in the streets?" she asked, holding her smile. "The ones with the cameras and the straw hats coming down to check us out and see what a model city looks like, works like? Look right there, right out the window there on the sidewalk in front of the Chowchy Grill. See that flock of Hawaiian shirts? And those women with the legs that look like they've just been pulled out of the deep freeze?"

I followed her gaze and there they were, tourists, milling around as if on a stage set. How had I failed to notice them? Even now one of them was backing away from the front of the grocery with a movie camera. "Tourists?" I murmured.

She nodded.

Maybe I was a little sour that morning, maybe I needed love and affection, not to mention sex, and maybe I was lonely and frustrated and beginning to feel the first stab of disappointment with my new life, but before I could think, I said, "They're worse than the ants. Do you have ants, by the way—in your apartment, I mean? The little minuscule ones that make ant freeways all over the floor, the kitchen counter, the walls?"

Her face fell, but then the smile came back, because she was determined to be chirpy and positive. "I wouldn't say they were worse than the ants—at least the ants clean up after themselves."

"And cockroaches. Or palmetto bugs—isn't that what we call them down here? I saw one the size of a frog the other day, right out on Penny Lane."

She had nothing to say to this, so I changed the subject and asked how her kids were doing.

"Oh, fine. Terrific. They're thriving." A pause. "My mother's down from Philadelphia—she's babysitting for me until I can find somebody permanent. While I'm at work, that is."

"Really," I said, reaching down to shift the offending zucchini to the bottom of the bin. "So are you free right now? For maybe a drink? Unless you have to rush home and cook or something."

She looked doubtful.

"What I mean is, don't you want to see what a neo-retro Casual Contempo looks like when it's fully furnished?"

The first real bump in the road came a week or two later. I'd been called away to consult with the transition team at my former company, and when I got back I found a notice in the mailbox from the Contash Corp's subsidiary, the Jubilation Company, or as we all knew it in short—and somewhat redundantly—the TJC. It seemed they were advising against our spending too much time on our wraparound porches, especially at sunrise and sunset, and to take all precautions while using the jogging trail round Lake Allagash or even window-shopping on Mercado Street. The problem was mosquitoes. Big, outsized Central Floridian mosquitoes that were found to be carrying encephalitis and dengue fever. The TJC was doing all it could vis-à-vis vector control, and they were contractually absolved from any responsibility—just read your Declaration of Covenants, Deeds and Restrictions—but in the interest of public safety they were advising everyone to stay indoors. Despite the heat. And the fact that staying in defeated the whole idea of the Casual Contempo, the wraparound porch and the free interplay between neighbors that lies at the core of what makes a real and actual town click.

I was brooding in the kitchen, idly scratching at the constellation of angry red welts on my right wrist and waiting for the meninges to start swelling in my brainpan, when a movement on the porch caught my eye. Two cloaked figures there, one large, one small, and a cloaked baby carriage. For a moment I didn't know what to make of it all, but the baby carriage was a dead giveaway: it was Vicki, dressed like a beekeeper, with little Ethan in his own miniature beekeeper's outfit beside her and baby Ashley imprisoned behind a wall of gauze in the depths of the carriage. “Christ,” I said, ushering them in, “is this what we’re going to have to start wearing now?”

She pulled back the veil to reveal that hopeful smile and the small shining miracle of her hair. “No, I don’t think so,” she said, bending to remove her son’s impedimenta (“I don’t want,” he kept saying, “I don’t want”). “There,” she said, addressing the pale dwindling oval of his face, “there, it’s all right now. And you can have a soda, if Jackson still has any left in the refrigerator—”

“Oh, yeah, sure,” I said, and I was bending too. “Root beer? Or Seven-Up?”

We wound up sitting in the kitchen, drinking white wine and sharing a box of stale Triscuits while the baby slept and Ethan sucked at a can of Hires in front of the tube in the living room. Out back was the low fence that gave onto the nature preserve, with its bird-friendly marsh that also coincidentally happened to serve as a maternity ward for the mosquitoes, and beyond that was Lake Allagash. “At the office they’re saying the mosquitoes are just seasonal,” Vicki said, working a hand up under the tinted ringlets and giving them a shake, “and besides, they’re pretty much spraying around the clock now, so I would think—well, I mean, they’ve had to close down some of the outdoor rides over at Contash World, and that means money lost, big money.”

I wasn’t a cynic, or I tried not to be, because a pioneer can’t afford cynicism. Look on the bright side, that was what I maintained—there was no alternative. “Okay, fine, but have you seen my wrist? I mean, should I be concerned? Should I go to the doctor, do you think?”

She took my wrist in her cool grip, traced the bumps there with her index finger. She gave a little laugh. “Chigger bites, that’s all. Nothing to worry about. And the mosquitoes’ll just be a bad memory in a week or two, I guarantee it.”

There was a moment of silence, during which we both gazed out the window on the marsh—or swamp, as I’d mistakenly called it before Vicki corrected me. We watched an egret rise up out of nowhere and sail off into the trees. Clouds massed on the horizon in a swell of pure, unadulterated white; the palmettos gathered and released the faintest trace of a breeze. Next door, the wraparound porch of my neighbors—the black couple, Sam and Ernesta Fills—was deserted. Ditto the porch of the house on the other side, into which Mark and Leonard, having traded $2,500 of the cash I’d given them for number 632 and a prime chance at a Casual Contempo, had recently moved. “No,” she said finally, draining her wine glass and holding it out in one delicate hand so that I could refill it for her, “what I’d be concerned about if I was you is your neighbors across the street—the Weekses?”

I gave her a dumb stare.

“You know them—July and Fili Weeks and their three sons?”

"Yeah," I said, "sure." Everybody knew everybody else here. It was a rule.

From the TV in the other room came the sound of canned laughter, followed by Ethan's stuttering high whinny of an underdeveloped laugh. "What about the red curtains?" she said. "And that car? That whatever it is, that race car painted in the three ugliest shades of magenta they keep parked out there on the street where the whole world can see it? They're in violation of the code on something like eight counts already and they haven't been here a month yet."

I felt a prickle of alarm. We were all in this together, and if everybody didn't pitch in—if everybody didn't subscribe to the letter as far as the Covenants and Restrictions were concerned—what was going to happen to our property values? "Red curtains?" I said.

Her eyes were steely. "Just like in a whorehouse. And you know the rules—white, off-white, beige and taupe only."

"Has anybody talked to them? Can't anybody do anything?"

She set the glass down, drew her gaze away from the window and looked into my eyes. "You mean the Citizens' Committee?"

I shrugged. "Yeah. Sure. I guess."

She leaned in close. I could smell the rinse she used in her hair, and it was faintly intoxicating. I loved her eyes, loved the shape of her, loved the way she aspirated her *h*'s like an elocution teacher. "Don't you worry," she whispered. "We're already on it."

Once Vicki had mentioned the Weekses and the way they were flouting the code, I couldn't get them out of my head. July Weeks was a salesman of some sort, aviation parts, I think it was—he worked for Cessna—and he seemed to spend most of his time, despite the mosquito scare, buried deep in his own white wicker chaise longue out on the wraparound porch of his Courteous Coastal directly across the street from me. He was a Southerner, and that was all right because this *was* the South, after all, but he had one of those accents that just went on clanging and jarring till you could barely understand a word he was saying. Not that I harbor any prejudices—he was my neighbor, and if he wanted to sound like an extra from *Deliverance,* that was his privilege. But I looked out the front window and saw that race car—*No excessive or unsightly vehicles, including campers, RVs, moving vans or trailers, shall be parked on the public streets for a period exceeding forty-eight continuous hours,* Section III, Article 12, Declaration of Covenants, Deeds and Restrictions—and the sight of it became an active irritation. Which was compounded by the fact that the eldest son, August, pulled up one afternoon in a pickup truck that sat about six feet up off its Bayou Crawler tires and deposited a boat trailer at the curb. The boat was painted puce with lime-green trim and it had a staved-in hull. Plus, there were those curtains.

A week went by. Two weeks. I got updates from Vicki—we were seeing each other just about every day now—and of course the Citizens' Committee, as an arm of the TJC, was threatening the Weekses with a lawsuit and the Weekses had hired an attorney and were threatening back, but nothing happened. I couldn't enjoy my wraparound porch or the view out my mullioned Craftsman windows. Every time I looked up, there was the boat, there was the car, and beyond them, the curtains. The situation began to weigh on me, so one night after dinner I strolled down the three broad inviting steps of my wraparound porch, waved a greeting to the Fills on my right and Mark and Leonard on my left, and crossed the street to mount the equally inviting steps of the Weekses' wraparound porch with the intention of setting Mr. Weeks straight on a few things. Or no, that sounds too harsh. I wanted to block out a couple issues with him and see if we couldn't resolve things amicably for all concerned.

He was sitting in the chaise longue, his wife in the wicker armchair beside him. An Atlanta Braves cap that looked as if it had just come off the shelf at Gulpy's Sports Emporium hid his brow and the crown of his head and he was wearing a pair of those squared-off black sunglasses for people with cataracts, and that reduced the sum of his expression to the sharp beak of his nose and an immobile mouth. The wife was a squat Korean woman whose name I could never remember. She was peeling the husk off of a dark pungent pod or tuber. It was a homey scene, and the moment couldn't have been more neighborly.

"Hi," I said (or maybe, prompted by the ambience, I might even have managed a "Howdy").

Neither of them said a word.

"Listen," I began, after standing there for an awkward moment (and what had I been expecting—mint juleps?). "Listen, about the curtains and the car and all that—the boat—I just wanted to say, well, I mean, it might seem like a small thing, it's ridiculous, really, but—"

He cut me off then. I don't know what he said, but it sounded something like "Rabid rabid gurtz."

The wife—her name came to me suddenly: Fili—translated. She carefully set aside the root or pod or whatever it was and gave me a flowering smile that revealed a set of the whitest and evenest teeth I'd ever seen. "He say you can blow it out you ass."

"No, no," I said, brushing right by it, "you misunderstand me. I'm not here to complain, or even to convince you of anything. It's just that, well, I'm your neighbor, and I thought if we—"

Here he spoke again, a low rumble of concatenated sounds that might have been expressive of digestive trouble, but the wife—Fili—seeing my blank expression, dutifully translated: "He say his gun—you know gun?—he say he keep gun loaded."

Things are not perfect. I never claimed they were. And if you're going to have a free and open town and not one of these gated neo-racist enclaves, you've got to be willing to accept that. The TJC sued the Weekses and the Weekses sued them back, and still the curtains flamed behind the windows and the garish race car and the unseaworthy boat sat at the curb across the street. So what I did to make myself feel better, was buy a dog. A Scottie. Lauren would never let me have a dog—she claimed to be allergic, but in fact she was pathologically averse to any intrusion on the rigid order she maintained around the house—and we never had any children either, which didn't affect me one way or the other, though I should say I was one of the few single men in Jubilation who didn't view Vicki's kids as a liability. I grew to like them, in fact—or Ethan anyway; the baby was just a baby, practically inert if it wasn't shrieking as if it had just had the skin stripped from its limbs. But Ethan was something else. I liked the feel of his tiny bunched little sweating hand in mine as we strolled down to the Benny Tarpon Old Tyme Ice Cream Parlor in the evening or took a turn round Lake Allagash. He was always tugging me one way or the other, chattering, pointing like a tour director: "Look," he would say. "Look!"

I named the dog Bruce, after my grandfather on my mother's side. He was a year old and housetrained, and I loved the way the fur hid his paws so that he seemed to glide over the grass of the village green as if he had no means of locomotion beyond willpower and magic.

That was around the time we began to feel the effects of the three-year drought that none of the TJC salespeople had bothered to mention in their all-day seminars and living-color brochures. The wind came up out of the south carrying a freight of smoke (apparently the Everglades were on fire) and a fine brown dust that obliterated our lawns and flowerbeds and made a desert of the village green. The heat seemed to increase too, as if the fires had somehow turned up the thermostat, but the worst of it was the smell. Everywhere you went, whether you were standing on line at the bank, sunk into one of the magic-fingers lounge chairs at the movie theater or pulling your head up off the pillow in the morning, the stale smell of old smoke assaulted your nostrils.

I was walking Bruce up on Golfpark Drive one afternoon, where our select million-dollar-plus homes back up onto the golf course—and you have to realize that this is part of the Contash vision too, millionaires living cheek by jowl with single mothers like Vicki and all the others struggling to pay mortgages that were thirty-five percent higher than those in the surrounding area, not to mention special assessments and maintenance fees—when a man with a camera slung round his neck stopped me and asked if he could take my picture. The sky was marbled with smoke. Dust fled across the pavement. The birds were actually shrieking in the trees. "Me?" I said. "Why me?"

"I don't know," he said, snapping the picture. "I like your dog."

"You do?" I was flattered, I admit it, but I was on my guard too. Journalists from all over the world had descended on the town en masse, mainly to cook up dismissive articles about a legion of Stepford wives and robotic husbands living on a Contash movie set and doing daily obeisance to Gulpy Gator. None of them ever bothered to mention our equanimity, our openness and shared ideals. Why would they? Hard work and sacrifice never have made for good copy.

"Yeah, sure," he said, "and would you mind posing over there, by the gate to that gingerbread mansion? That's good. Nice." He took a series of shots, the camera whirring through its motions. He wore a buzz cut, a two-day growth of nearly translucent beard and a pair of tri-colored Nikes. "You do live here, don't you?" he asked finally. "I mean, you're an actual resident, right, and not a tourist?"

I felt a surge of pride. "That's right," I said. "I'm one of the originals."

He gave me an odd look, as if he were trying to sniff out an impostor. "Do they really pay you to walk the dog around the village green six times a day?"

"*Pay* me? Who?"

"You know, the town, the company. You can't have a town without people in it, right?" He looked down at Bruce, who was sniffing attentively at a dust-coated leaf. "Or dogs?" The camera clicked again, several times in succession. "I hear they pay that old lady on the moped too—and the guy that sets up his easel in front of the Gulpy monument every morning."

"Don't be ridiculous. You're out of your mind."

"And I'll tell you another thing—don't think just because you bought into the Contash lifestyle you're immune from all the shit that comes down in the real world, because you're not. In fact, I'd watch that dog if I were you—"

Somewhere the fires were burning. A rag of smoke flapped at my face and I began to cough. "You're one of those media types, aren't you?" I said, pounding at my breastbone. "You people disgust me. You don't even make a pretense of unbiased reporting—you just want to ridicule us and tear us down, isn't that right?" My dander was up. Who were these people to come in here and try to undermine everything we'd been working for? I shot him a look of impatience. "It wouldn't be jealousy, would it? By any chance?"

He shrugged, shifted the camera to one side and dug a cigarette out of his breast pocket. I watched him cup his hands against the breeze and light it. He flung the match in the bushes, a symbolic act, surely. "We used to have a Scottie when I was a kid," he said, exhaling. "So I'm just telling you—you'd be surprised what I know about this town, what goes on behind closed doors, the double-dealing, the payoffs, the flouting of the environmental regs, all the dirt the TJC and Charles Contash don't want you to know about. View me as a resource, your diligent representative of the fourth estate. Keep the dog away from the lake, that's all."

I was stubborn. I wasn't listening. "He can swim."

The man let out a short, unpleasant laugh. "I'm talking about alligators, my friend, and not the cuddly little cartoon kind. You might or might not know it because I'm sure it's not advertised in any of the TJC brochures, but when they built Contash World back in the sixties they evicted all the alligators, not to mention the coral snakes and cane rattlers and snapping turtles—and where do you think they put them?"

All right. I was forewarned. And what happened should never have happened, I know that, but there are hazards in any community, whether it be South Central L.A. or Scarsdale or Kuala Lumpur. I took Bruce around Lake Allagash—twice—and then went home and barbecued a platter of wings and ribs for Vicki and the kids and I thought no more about it. Alligators. They were there, sure they were, but so were the mosquitoes and the poison toads that looked like deflated kick balls and chased the dogs off their kibble. This was Florida. It was muggy. It was hot. We had our share of sand fleas and whatnot. But at least we didn't have to worry about bronchial pneumonia or snow tires.

The rains came in mid-September, a series of thunderstorms that rolled in off the Gulf and put out the fires. We had problems with snails and slugs for a while there, armadillos crawling up half-drowned on the lawn, snakes in the garage, walking catfish, that sort of thing—I even found a opossum curled up in the dryer one morning amidst my socks and boxer shorts. But the Citizens' Committee was active in picking up strays, nursing them back to health and restoring them to the ecosystem, so it wasn't as bad as you'd think. And after that, the sun came out and the earth just seemed to steam till every trace of mold and mud was erased and the flowers went mad with the glory of it. The smoke was gone, the snails had crawled back into their holes or dens or wherever they lived when they weren't smearing the windows with slime, and the air was scented so sweetly it was as if the Contash Corp had hired a fleet of crop dusters to spray air freshener over the town. Even the thermometer cooperated, the temperature holding at a nice equitable seventy-eight degrees for three days running. Tear the page out of the brochure: this was what we'd all come for.

I was sitting out on my wraparound porch, trying to ignore the decrepit boat and magenta car across the street, *Crime and Punishment* spread open in my lap (Raskolnikov was just climbing the steps to the old lady's place and I was waiting for the axe to fall), when Vicki called and proposed a picnic. She'd made up some sandwiches on the brown nut bread I like, Asiago cheese, sweet onion and roasted red pepper, and she'd picked up a nice bottle of Chilean white at the Contash Liquor Mart. Was I ready for some sun? And maybe a little backrub afterward at her place?

Ethan wanted to go out on the water, but when we got to the Jubilation dock the sound of the ratcheting motors scared him, so we settled on an aluminum rowboat, and that was better—or would have been better—because we could hear ourselves think and didn't have to worry about all that spew of fumes, and that was a real concern for Vicki. We might have been raised in houses where our parents smoked two packs a day and sprayed Raid on the kitchen counter every time an ant or roach showed its face—or head or feelers or whatever—but there was no way any toxins were entering her children's systems, not if she could help it. So I rented the rowboat. "No problem," I told Vicki, who was looking terrific in a sunbonnet, her bikini top and a pair of skimpy shorts that showed off her smooth solid legs and the Gulpy tattoo on her ankle. The fact was I hadn't been kayaking since the rains started and the exercise was something I was looking forward to.

It took me a few strokes to reacquaint myself with the apparatus of oars and oarlocks, and we lurched away from the dock as if we'd been torpedoed, but I got into the rhythm of it soon enough and we glided cleanly out across the mirrored surface of the lake. Vicki didn't want me to go more than twenty or thirty feet from shore, and that was all right too, except that I found myself dredging up noxious-smelling clumps of pondweed that seemed to cast a powerful olfactory spell over Bruce. He kept snapping at the weed as I lifted first one oar and then the other to try to shake it off, and once or twice I had to drop the oars and discipline him because he was leaning so far out over the bow I thought we were going to lose him. Still, we saw birdlife everywhere we looked, herons, egrets, cormorants and anhingas, and Ethan got a real kick out of a clutch of painted turtles stacked up like dinner plates on a half-submerged log.

We'd gone half a mile or so, I guess, to the far side of the lake where the wake of the motorboats wouldn't interfere overmuch with the mustarding of the sandwiches and the delicate operation of pouring the wine into long-stemmed crystal glasses. The baby, wrapped up like a sausage in her life jacket—or life-cradle, might be more accurate—was asleep, a blissful baby smile painted on her lips. Bruce curled up at my feet in the brown swill at the bottom of the boat and Vicki sipped wine and gave me a look of contentment so deep and pure I was beginning to think I wouldn't mind seeing it across the breakfast table for the rest of my life. It was tranquil. Dragonflies hovering, fish rising, not a mosquito in sight. Even little Ethan, normally such a clingy kid, seemed to be enjoying himself tracing the pattern of his finger in the water as the boat rocked and drifted in a gentle airy dance.

About that water. The TJC assured us it was unpolluted by human waste and uncontaminated by farm runoff, and that its rusty color—it was nearly opaque and perpetually blooming with the microscopic creatures that comprise the bottom of the food chain in a healthy and thriving aquatic ecosystem—was perfectly natural. Though the lake had been dredged out of the swampland some forty years earlier, this was the way its waters had always looked, and the creatures that lived and throve here were grateful for it—like all of us in Jubilation, they had Charles Contash to thank for that too.

Well. We drifted, the dog and the baby snoozed, Vicki kept up a happy chatter on any number of topics, all of which seemed to have a subtext of sexual innuendo, and I just wasn't prepared for what came next, and I blame myself, I do. Maybe it was the wine or the influence of the sun and the faint sweet cleansing breeze, but I wasn't alert to the dangers inherent in the situation—I was an American, raised in a time of prosperity and peace, and I'd been spared the tumult and horror visited on so many of the less fortunate in this world. New York and L.A. might have been nasty places, and Lauren was certainly a plague in her own right, but nobody had ever bombed my village or shot down my family in the street, and when my parents died they died quietly, in their own beds.

I was in the act of extracting the wine bottle from its cradle of ice in the cooler when the boat gave a sudden lurch and I glanced up just in time to see the broad flat grinning reptilian head emerge from the water, pluck Ethan off the gunwale and vanish in the murk. It was like an illusion in a magic show, now he's here, now he isn't, and I wasn't able to respond until my brain replayed the scene and I felt the sudden horror knife at my heart. "Did you—?" I began, but Vicki was already screaming.

The sequence of events becomes a little confused for me at this juncture, but looking back on it, I'm fairly certain the funeral service preceded the thrashing we took from Hurricane Albert—I distinctly remember the volunteerism the community showed in dredging the lake, which would have been impossible after the hurricane hit. Sadly, no trace of little Ethan was ever found. No need to tell you how devastated I was—I was as hurt and wrung out as I've ever been in my life, and I'll never give up second-guessing myself—but even more, I was angry. Angry over the Contash Corp's failure to disclose the hazards lurking around us and furious over the way the press jumped on the story, as if the life of a child was worth no more than a crude joke or a wedge to drive between the citizens of the community and the rest of the so-called civilized world. *Alligator Mom.* That was what they called Vicki in headlines three inches high, and could anyone blame her for packing up and going back to her mother in Philadelphia? I took her place on the Citizens' Committee, though I'd never been involved in community affairs in my life to this point, and I was the one who pushed through the initiative to remove *all* the dangerous animals from the lake, no matter what their size or species (and that was a struggle too, the environmentalists crying foul in all their puritanical fervor, and one man—I won't name him here—even pushing to have the alligators' teeth capped as a compromise solution).

It wasn't all bad, though. The service at the Jubilation Non-Denominational Chapel, for all its solemnity, was a real inspiration to us all, a public demonstration of our solidarity and determination. Charles Contash himself flew in from a meeting with the Russian premier to give the eulogy, every man, woman and child in town turned out to pay their respects, and the cards and flowers poured in from all over the country. Even July Weeks turned up, despite his friction with the TJC, and we found common ground in our contempt for the reporters massed on the steps out front of the chapel. He stood tall that day, barring the door to anyone whose face he didn't recognize, and I forgave him his curtains, for the afternoon at least.

If anything, the hurricane brought us together even more than little Ethan's tragedy. I remember the sky taking on the deep purple-black hue of a bruise and the vanguard of the rain that lashed down in a fusillade of wind-whipped pellets and the winds that sucked the breath right out of your body. Sam and Ernesta Fills helped me board up the windows of my Casual Contempo, and together we helped Mark and Leonard and the Weekses with their places and then went looking to lend a hand wherever we could. And when the storm hit in all its intensity, just about everybody in town was bundled up safe and sound in the bastion of the movie palace, where the emergency generator allowed the TJC to lift the burden from our minds with a marathon showing of the Contash Corp's most-beloved family films. Of course, we emerged to the devastation of what the National Weather Service was calling the single most destructive storm of the past century, and a good proportion of Jubilation had been reduced to rubble or swept away altogether. I was luckier than most. I lost the back wall that gives onto the kitchen, which in turn was knee-deep in roiling brown water and packed to the ceiling with wind-blown debris, and my wraparound porch was wrapped around the Weekses' house, but on the plus side the offending race car and the boat were lifted right up into the sky and for all we know dropped somewhere over the Atlantic, and the Weekses' curtains aren't really an issue anymore.

As for myself, I've been rebuilding with the help of a low-interest loan secured through the Contash Corp, and I've begun, in a tentative way, to date Felicia, whose husband was one of the six fatalities we recorded once the storm had moved on. Beyond that, my committee work keeps me pretty busy, I've been keeping in touch with Vicki both by phone and e-mail, and every time I see Bruce chase a palmetto bug up the side of the new retaining wall, I just want to smile. And I do. I do smile. Sure, things could be better, but they could be worse too. I live in Jubilation. How bad can it be?

(2002)

Rastrow's Island

A car radio bleats,
"Love, O careless Love. . . ."

—Robert Lowell,
"Skunk Hour"

She called and he was ready if not eager to sell, because he'd had certain reverses, the market gone sour, Ruth in bed with something nobody was prepared to call cancer, and his daughter, Charlene, waiting for his check in her dorm room with her unpacked trunk full of last year's clothes and the grubby texts with the yellow scars of the USED stickers seared into their spines. "That's right," she said, her old lady's voice like the creak of oarlocks out on the bay in the first breath of dawn, "Mrs. Rastrow, Alice Rastrow, and I used to know your mother when she was alive." There was a sharp crackling jolt of static, as if an electrical storm were raging inside the wires, then her voice came back at him: "I never have put much confidence in realtors. Do you want to talk or not?"

"So go," Ruth said. Her face had taken on the shine and color of the elephant-ear fungus that grew out of the sodden logs in the ravine at the foot of the park. "Don't worry about me. Just go."

"You know what she's doing, don't you?"

"I know what she's doing."

"I never wanted to sell the place. I wanted it for Charlene, for Charlene's kids. To experience it the way I did, to have that, at least—" He saw the house then, a proud two-story assertion of will from the last century, four rooms down, four rooms up, the wood paintless now and worn to a weathered silver, the barn subsiding into its angles in a bed of lichen-smeared rock, the hedges gone to straw in the absence of human agency. And when was the last time—? Two summers ago? Three?

"It's just a summer house." She reached out a hand you could see right through and lifted the rimed water glass from the night table. He watched the hand tremble, fumble for the pills, and he looked away, out the window and down the row of townhouses and the slouching, copper-flagged maples. "Isn't that the first thing to go when you—?"

"Yeah," he said. "Yeah, I guess it is."

"I mean," and she paused to draw the water down, gulp the pills, "it's not as if we really need the place or anything."

The water was choppy, the wind cold, and he sat in his car with the engine running and the heater on full as the ferry slammed at the seething white roil of the waves and the island separated itself from the far shore and began to fan out across the horizon. When the rain came up, first as a spatter that might have been nothing more than the spray thrown up by the bow and then as a moving scrim that isolated him behind the wheel, he thought of switching on the windshield wipers, but he didn't. There was something about the opaque windows and the pitch of the deck tugging at the corners of the light that relaxed him—he could have been underwater, in a submarine, working his way along the bottom of the bay through the looming tangle of spars and timbers of the ships gone to wrack a hundred years ago. He laid his hand idly on the briefcase beside him. Inside were all the relevant papers he could think of: the deed, signed in his father's ecstatic rolling hand, termite, electrical, water rights. But what did she care about termites, about water or dry rot?—she wasn't going to live there. She wasn't going to live anywhere but the white-washed stone cottage she was entombed in now, the one she'd been born in, and after that she had her place reserved in the cemetery beside her husband and two drowned children. She must have been eighty, he figured. Eighty, or close to it.

Ronald Rastrow—he was a violinist, or no, a violist—and his sister, Elyse. At night, in summer, above the thrum of the insects and the listless roll of the surf, you could hear his instrument tuned to some ancient sorrow and floating out across the water. He was twenty-two or -three, a student at Juilliard, and his sister must have been twenty or so. They went sailing under a full moon, rumors of a party onshore and Canadian whiskey and marijuana, the sea taut as a bedspread, a gentle breeze out of the east, and they never came back. He was twelve the summer it happened, and he used to thrill himself leaning out over the stern of the dinghy till the shadow of his head and shoulders made the sea transparent and the dense architecture of the bottom rushed up at him in a revulsion of disordered secrets. He remembered the police divers gathered in a dark clump at the end of the pier. Volunteers. Adults, kids in sailboats, Curtis Mayhew's father in his fishing boat fitted out with a dragline, working up and down the bay as if he were plowing it for seed. It was a lobsterman who found them, both of them, tangled in his lines at the end of a long cold week that was like December in July.

He drove along the shore, past the saltbox cottages with their weathered shingles and the odd frame house that had acquired a new coat of paint, the trees stripped by the wind, nothing in the fields but pale dead stalks and the refulgent slabs of granite that bloomed in all seasons. There were a few new houses clustered around the village, leggy things, architecturally wise, but the gas station hadn't changed or the post office/general store or Dorcas' House of Clams (*Closed for the Season*). The woman behind the desk at The Seaside Rest (*Sep Units Avail by Day or Week*) took his money and handed him the key to the last cottage in a snaking string of them, though none of the intervening cottages seemed to be occupied. That struck him as a bit odd—she must have marked him down for a drug fiend or a prospective suicide—but it didn't bother him, not really. She didn't recognize him and he didn't recognize her, because people change and places change and what once was will never be again. He entered the cottage like an acolyte taking possession of his cell, a cold little box of a room with a bed, night table and chair, no TV. He spent half an hour down on his knees worshipping the AC/heater unit, but could raise no more than the faintest stale exhalation out of it. At quarter of one he got back in the car and drove out to Mrs. Rastrow's place.

There was a gate to be negotiated where the blacktop gave way to the dirt drive, and then there was the drive itself, unchanged in two hundred years, a pair of beaten parallel tracks with a yellow scruff of dead vegetation painted down the center of it. He parked beneath a denuded oak, went up the three stone steps and rang the bell. Standing there on the doorstep, the laden breeze in his face and the bay spread out before him in a graceful arc to Colson's Head, where the summer house stood amidst the fortress of trees like a chromatic miscalculation on a larger canvas, he felt the anxiety let go of him, eased by the simple step-by-step progress of his day, the business at hand, the feel of the island beneath his feet. She hadn't mentioned a price. But he had a figure in mind, a figure that would at least stanch his wounds, if not stop the bleeding altogether, and she had the kind of capital to take everything down to the essentials, everybody knew that—Mrs. Rastrow, Alice Rastrow, widow of Julius, the lumber baron. He'd prepared his opening words, and his smile, cool and at ease, because he wasn't going to be intimidated by her or let her see his need, and he listened to the bell ring through the house that was no mansion, no showplace, no testament to riches and self-aggrandizement but just what it was, and he pictured her moving through the dimness on her old lady's limbs like a deep-sea diver in his heavy, confining suit. A moment passed. Then another. He debated, then rang again.

His first surprise—the first in what would prove to be an unraveling skein of them—was the face at the door. The big pitted brown slab of oak pulled back and Mrs. Rastrow, ancient, crabbed, the whites of her eyes gone to yellow and her hair flown away in the white wisps of his recollection, was nowhere to be seen. A young Asian woman was standing there at the door, her eyes questioning, brow wrinkled, teeth bundled beneath the neat bow of her lips. Her hair shone as if it had been painted on. "I came to see Mrs. Rastrow," he said. "About the house?"

The woman—she looked to be in her late twenties, her body squeezed into one of those luminous silk dresses the hostess in a Chinese restaurant might wear—showed no sign of recognition.

He gave her his name. "We had an appointment today," he said, "—for one?" Still nothing. He wondered if she spoke English. "I mean, me and Mrs. Rastrow? You know Mrs. Rastrow? Do you work for her?"

She pressed a hand to her lips in a flurry of painted nails and giggled through her fingers, and the curtain dropped. She was just a girl, pretty, casual, and she might have been standing in the middle of her own dorm room, sharing a joke with her friends. "It's just—you look like a potato peeler salesman or something standing there like that." Her smile opened up around even, white teeth. "I'm Rose," she said, and held out her hand.

There was a mudroom, flagstone underfoot, firewood stacked up like breastworks on both sides, and then the main room with its bare oak floors and plaster walls. A few museum pieces, braided rug, a plush sofa with an orange cat curled up in the middle of it. Two lamps, their shades as thin as skin, glowed against the gray of the windows. Rose bent to the stove in the corner, opened the grate and laid two lengths of wood on the coals, and he stood there in the middle of the room watching the swell of her figure in the tight wrap of her dress and the silken flex and release of the muscles in her shoulders. The room was cold as a meat locker.

He was watching Rose, transfixed by the incongruity of her bent over the black stove in her golden Chinese restaurant dress that clung to her backside as if it had been sewn over her skin, and the old lady's voice startled him, for all the pep talk he'd given himself. "You came," she said, and there she was in the doorway, looking no different from the picture he'd held of her.

She waited for him to say something in response, and he complied, murmuring "Yes, sure, it's my pleasure," and then she was standing beside him and studying him out of her yellowed eyes. "Did you bring the papers?" she said.

He patted the briefcase. They were both standing, as if they'd just run into each other in a train station or the foyer at the theater, and Rose was standing too, awaiting the moment of release. "Rose," she said then, her eyes snapping sharply to her, "fetch my reading glasses, will you?"

The car had developed a cough on the drive up from Boston, a consumptive wheeze that rattled the floorboards when he depressed the accelerator, and now, with the influence of the sea, it had gotten worse. He turned the key in the ignition and listened to the slow seep of strangulation, then put the car in gear, backed out from beneath the oak and made his hesitant way down the drive, wondering how much they were going to take him for this time when he brought it into the shop—if he made it to the shop, that is. There was no reward in any of this—he'd tried to keep the shock and disappointment from rising to his face when the old lady named her price—but at least, for now, there was the afternoon ahead and the rudimentary animal satisfaction of lunch, food to push into his maw and distract him, and he took the blacktop road back into the village and found a seat at the counter in the diner.

There were three other customers. The light through the windows was like concrete, like shale, the whole place hardened into its sediments. He didn't recognize anyone, and he ate his grilled cheese on white with his head down, gathering from the local newspaper that the creatures had deserted the sea en masse and left the lobstermen scrambling for government handouts and the cod fleet stranded at anchor. He'd countered the old lady's offer, but she'd held firm. At first he thought she hadn't even heard him. They'd moved to the sofa and she was looking through the papers, nodding her head like a battered old sea turtle fighting the pull of gravity, but she turned to him at last and said, "My offer is final. You might have known that." He fought himself, tried to get hold of his voice. He told her he'd think about it—sleep on it, he'd sleep on it—and have an answer for her in the morning.

It was raining again, a pulsing hard-driven rain that sheathed the car and ran slick over the pavement till the parking lot gleamed like the sea beyond it. He didn't want to go back to the cottage in the motor court, not yet anyway—the thought of it entered his mind like a closed box floating in the void, and he had to squeeze his eyes shut to make it disappear—and he wasn't much of a drinker, so there wasn't any solace in the lights of the bar across the street. Finally, he decided to do what he'd known he was going to do all along: drive out to the house and have a last look at it. Things would have to be sold, he told himself, things stored, winnowed, tossed into the trash.

As soon as he pulled into the dirt drive that dropped off the road and into the trees, he could see he'd been fooling himself. The place was an eyesore, vandalized and vandalized again, the paint gone, windows shattered, the porch skewed away from the foundation as if it had been shoved by the hand of a giant. He switched off the ignition and stepped out into the rain. Inside, there was nothing of value: graffiti on the walls, a stained mattress in the center of the living room, every stick of furniture broken down and fed to the fire, the toilet bowl smashed and something dead in the pit of it, rodent or bird, it didn't matter. He wandered through the rooms, stooping to pick things up and then drop them again. For a long while he stood at the kitchen sink, staring out into the rain.

The summer the Rastrows drowned, he'd lived primitive, out on the water all day every day, swimming, fishing, crabbing, racing from island to shore and back again under the belly of his sail. That was the year his parents had their friends from the city out to stay, the Morses—Mr. Morse, ventricose and roaring, with his head set tenuously atop the shaft of his neck, as if they'd given him the wrong size at birth, and Mrs. Morse, her face drawn to a point beneath the bleached bird fluff of her hair—and a woman who worked with his mother as a secretary, a divorcée with two shy pretty daughters his own age. And what was the woman's name? Jean. And the daughters? He could no longer remember, but they wore sunsuits that left their legs and midriffs bare, the field of their taut browned flesh a thrill and revelation to him. He couldn't look them in the face, couldn't even pretend. But they went off after a week to be with their father, and the Morses—and Jean—stayed on with his parents, sunning outside in the vinyl lawn chairs, drinking and playing cards so late in the night that their voices—murmurous, shrill suddenly, murmurous again—were like the disquisitions of the birds that wakened him at dawn to go down to the shore and the boat and the sun that burned the chill off the water.

There was something tumultuous going on among them—all five of them—but he didn't understand what it was till he looked back on it years later. It was something sexual, that much he knew, something forbidden and shameful and emotionally wrought. He lay in his bed upstairs, twelve years old and discovering his own body, and they shouted recriminations at each other a floor down. Mr. Morse took him and Jean out fishing for pollack one afternoon, the big man shirtless and rowing, Jean in the bow, an ice bucket sprouting a bristle of green-necked bottles between them. He fished. Baited his hook with squid and dropped the weighted line into the shifting gray deep. Behind him, Mr. Morse slipped his hand up under Jean's blouse and they kissed and wriggled against each other until they couldn't seem to catch their breath, even as he peered down into the water and pretended he didn't notice. He remembered a single voice raised in agony that night, a voice caught between a sob and a shriek, and in the morning Mrs. Morse was gone. A few days later, her husband got behind the wheel of Jean's car and the two of them pulled out of the drive. Nobody said a word. He sat with his parents at dinner—coleslaw, corn on the cob, hamburgers his father seared on the grill—and nobody said a word.

He was back at the motor court by five and he called Ruth just to hear the sound of her voice and to lie to her about the old lady's offer. Yes, he told her, yes, it was just what he'd expected and he'd close the deal tomorrow, no problem.

Yes, he loved her. Yes, good night. Then, though he wasn't a drinker, he walked into the village and sat at the bar while the Celtics went through the motions up on the television screen and the six or seven patrons gathered there either cheered or groaned as the occasion demanded. He let two beers grow warm by the time he got to the bottom of them and he had a handful of saltines to steady his stomach. He was hoping someone would mention Mrs. Rastrow, offer up some information about her, some gossip about what she was doing to the island, about Rose, but nobody spoke to him, nobody even looked at him. By seven-thirty he was back in the cottage paging through half a dozen back issues of a news magazine the woman at the desk had given him with an apologetic thrust of her hand, and she was sorry they didn't have any TV for him to watch but maybe he'd be interested in these magazines?

He was reading of things that had happened five years ago—big stories, crises, and he couldn't for the life of him remember how any of them had turned out—when there was a knock at the door. It was Rose, dressed in a bulky sweater and blue jeans. The black patent-leather pumps she'd been wearing earlier had been replaced by tennis shoes. Her ankles were bare. "Hi," she said. "I thought I'd drop by to see how you were doing."

Everything in him seemed to seize up. How he was doing? He was doing poorly, feeling trapped and bereft, pressed for money, for luck, for hope, so worried about Ruth and her doctors and the tests and prescriptions and bills he didn't know how he was going to survive the night ahead, let alone the rest of the winter and the long unspooling year to come. Mrs. Rastrow—her employer, her *ally*—had cut the heart out of him. So how was he doing? He couldn't even open his mouth to tell her.

They were both standing at the open door. The night smelled like an old dishrag that had been frozen and defrosted again. "Because I felt bad this afternoon," she said, "I mean, not even offering you something to drink or a sandwich. Alice can be pretty abrupt, and I wanted to apologize."

"Okay," he said, "sure, I appreciate that." He was in his stocking feet, his shirt open at the collar to reveal the T-shirt beneath, and was it clean? His hair. Had he combed his hair? "Okay," he said again, not knowing what else to do.

"Do you have a minute?" She peered into the room as if it might conceal something she needed to be wary of. Her shoulders were bunched, her eyes gone wide. The night air leaked in around her, carrying a sour lingering odor now of panic and attrition—a skunk, somebody had surprised a skunk somewhere out on the road. Suddenly she was smiling. "I guess I'm the potato peeler salesman now, huh?"

"No," he said, "no," too forcefully, and he didn't know what he was up to—what *she* was up to, a young woman who lived with an old woman and wore tight silk Chinese dresses on an island that had no Chinese restaurants and no need of them—and then he was pulling the door back and inviting her in, their bodies pressed close in passing, and the door shutting behind them.

She took the chair, he the bed. "I'd offer you something," he said, "but—" and he threw up his hands and they both laughed. Was he drunk—two beers on an empty stomach? Was that it?

"I brought you something," she said, snapping open her purse to remove a brown paper bag and set it on the night table. There were oil stains on the bag, translucent continents, headlands, isthmuses painted across the surface in a random geography. "Tuna," she said. "Tuna on rye. I made them myself. And these"—lifting the sandwiches in their opaque paper from the bag and holding two cans of beer aloft. "I thought you'd be hungry. With the diner closing early, I mean." She pushed a beer across the table and handed him a sandwich. "I didn't know if you'd know that—that they close early this time of year?"

He told her he hadn't known, or he'd forgotten—or hadn't even thought of it, really—and he thanked her for thinking of him. They sipped their beers in silence a moment, the light on the night table the only illumination in the room, and then he said, "You know, that house belonged to my father. That's his signature on the deed. We spent summers here when I was a kid, best summers of my life. I was here when Mrs. Rastrow's—when Ronald and Elyse drowned. I was maybe twelve at the time, and I didn't really—I didn't understand you *could* die. Not if you were young. Up till that point it was old people who'd died, the lady next door—Mrs. Jennings—my grandmother, a great-aunt."

She just nodded, but he could see she was right there with him, the brightness in her eyes, the way she chewed, sipped. He felt the beer go to his head. He wanted to ask about her, how she'd come to the island—was it an ad in the paper, lumber heiress in need of a companion to wear silk Chinese dresses in a remote cottage, room and board and stipend and all the time in the world to paint, write, dream?—but he didn't want to be obvious. She was exotic. Chinese. The only Chinese person on the island, and it would be rude, maybe even faintly racist, to ask.

He watched her tuck the last corner of the sandwich in her mouth and tilt back the can to drain it. She wiped her lips with a paper napkin, then settled her hands over her knees and said, "You know, it's no use. She's never going to go any higher."

He was embarrassed suddenly—to bring all that into this?—and he just shrugged. It was a fait accompli. He was defeated and he knew it.

"She knows about your wife. And you know she could pay a fair price, even though the place is run-down, because it's not the money—she has all the money anybody could want—but she won't. I know her. She won't budge." She lifted her face so that the light cut it in two, the ridge of her nose and one eye shining, the rest in shadow. "She's just going to let it rot anyway. That's what she's doing with all of them."

"Spoils her view?"

She smiled. "Something like that."

Then the question he'd been swallowing since she'd appeared at the door, finally pried up off his tongue by the beer: "This isn't some kind of negotiation, is it? I mean, she didn't send you, did she?"

The question left a space for all the little sounds of the night to creep in: the cry of a shorebird, the wind scouring the beach, something ticking in the depths of the heater. She dropped her eyes. "No, that's not it at all," she murmured.

Well, what is it then? he wanted to say—almost said—but he felt a tightening across the surface of him, his flesh prickling and contracting as if all his defenses were going down at once, and the answer came to him. She was here for him, for a quick fix for loneliness and despair, here to listen to a voice besides Mrs. Rastrow's, to sleep in another bed, any bed, make contact where before there had been none. He got up from the bed, moved awkwardly toward her, and she got up too. They were as close as they'd been at the door. He could smell her, a sweet heat rising from the folds of the sweater, caught in the coils of her hair. "Did you want to maybe go over to the tavern?" she said. "For another beer, I mean? I only brought the two."

He didn't want another beer, hadn't wanted the first one. "No," he said in a whisper, and then he was holding her, pulling her to him as if she had no bones in her body, everything new and soft and started from scratch. Her cheek was pressed to his, scintillating, electric, *her cheek,* and she let him kiss her and her bones were gone and she was melting down away from the chair and into the bed. She didn't taste like Ruth. Didn't feel like her. Didn't conform to him the way Ruth had through all those years when she was well and alive and lit up like a meteor, and he had to say something, he didn't have any choice. "I don't think so," he said. "I'm sorry. I really don't."

She was beneath him on the bed, her hair in a sprawl. He pulled away from her—pushed himself up as if he were doing some sort of exercise, calisthenics of the will, the heaviest of heavy lifting—and before he knew what he was doing he was out the door and into the night. He thought he heard her call out his name, but the surf took it away. He was furious, raging, pounding his way down the dark strand as if every step was a murder—*That dried-up old bitch, and who does she think she is anyway?*

A sudden wind came up off the shore to rake the trees, the branches rattling like claws, and the smell assaulted him again, the smell of rottenness and corruption, of animals and their glands. He kept walking, the wind in his face. Head down, shoulders pumping, he followed his legs till he got beyond the lights of the farthest house and the sky closed down and melded with the shore. There was something there ahead on the beach, a shape spawned from the shadows, and it took him a moment to see what it was: a trash can, let's all pitch in and keep the island clean, turned on its side in a spill of litter. And inside the can, the animal itself, coiled round the wedge of its head and the twin lights of its eyes. "Get out of that!" he shouted, looking for something to throw. "Get out!"

In the morning he made his way back up the long dirt drive and signed away the property. By noon, he was gone.

(2002)

Chicxulub

My daughter is walking along the roadside late at night—too late, really, for a seventeen-year-old to be out alone even in a town as safe as this—and it is raining, the first rain of the season, the streets slick with a fine immiscible glaze of water and petrochemicals so that even a driver in full possession of her faculties, a driver who hasn't consumed two apple martinis and three glasses of Hitching Post pinot noir before she gets behind the wheel of the car, will have trouble keeping the thing off the sidewalk and out of the gutters, the shrubbery, *the highway median,* for Christ's sake. . . . But that's not really what I want to talk about, or not yet anyway.

Have you heard of Tunguska? In Russia?

This was the site of the last-known large-body impact on the earth's surface, nearly a hundred years ago. Or that's not strictly accurate—the meteor, an estimated sixty yards across, never actually touched down. The force of its entry—the compression and superheating of the air beneath it—caused it to explode some twenty-five thousand feet above the ground, but then the term "explode" hardly does justice to the event. There was a detonation—a flash, a thunderclap—equal to the explosive power of eight hundred Hiroshima bombs. Thirty miles away, reindeer in their loping herds were struck dead by the blast wave, and the clothes of a hunter another thirty miles beyond that burst into flame even as he was poleaxed to the ground. Seven hundred square miles of Siberian forest were leveled in an instant. If the meteor had hit only four hours later it would have exploded over St. Petersburg and annihilated every living thing in that glorious and baroque city. And this was only a rock. And it was only sixty yards across.

My point? You'd better get down on your knees and pray to your gods, because each year this big spinning globe we ride intersects the orbits of some twenty million asteroids, at least a thousand of which are bigger than a mile in diameter.

But my daughter. She's out there in the dark and the rain, walking home. Maureen and I bought her a car, a Honda Civic, the safest thing on four wheels, but the car was used—pre-owned, in dealer-speak—and as it happens it's in the shop with transmission problems and, because she just had to see her friends and gossip and giggle and balance slick multicolored clumps of raw fish and pickled ginger on conjoined chopsticks at the mall, Kimberly picked her up and Kimberly will bring her home. Maddy has a cell phone and theoretically she could have called us, but she didn't—or that's how it appears. And so she's walking. In the rain. And Alice K. Petermann of 16 Briar Lane, white, divorced, a realtor with Hyperion who has picked at a salad and left her glasses on the bar, loses control of her car.

It is just past midnight. I am in bed with a book, naked, and hardly able to focus on the clustered words and rigid descending paragraphs, because Maureen is in the bathroom slipping into the sheer black negligee I bought her at Victoria's Secret for her birthday, and her every sound—the creak of the medicine cabinet on its hinges, the susurrus of the brush at her teeth, the tap running—electrifies me. I've lit a candle and am waiting for Maureen to step into the room so I can flick off the light. We had cocktails earlier, a bottle of wine with dinner, and we sat close on the couch and shared a joint in front of the fire because our daughter was out and we could do that and no one the wiser. I listen to the little sounds from the bathroom, seductive sounds, maddening. I am ready. More than ready. "Hey," I call, pitching my voice low, "are you coming or not? You don't expect me to wait all night, do you?"

Her face appears in the doorway, the pale lobes of her breasts and the dark nipples visible through the clinging black silk. "Oh, are you waiting for me?" she says, making a game of it. She hovers at the door, and I can see the smile creep across her lips, the pleasure of the moment, drawing it out. "Because I thought I might go down and work in the garden for a while—it won't take long, couple hours, maybe. You know, spread a little manure, bank up some of the mulch on the roses. You'll wait for me, won't you?"

Then the phone rings.

We stare blankly at each other through the first two rings and then Maureen says, "I better get it," and I say, "No, no, forget it—it's nothing. It's nobody."

But she's already moving.

"Forget it!" I shout, and her voice drifts back to me—"What if it's Maddy?"—and then I watch her put her lips to the receiver and whisper, "Hello?"

The night of the Tunguska explosion the skies were unnaturally bright across Europe—as far away as London people strolled in the parks past midnight and read novels out of doors while the sheep kept right on grazing and the birds stirred uneasily in the trees. There were no stars visible, no moon—just a pale, quivering light, as if all the color had been bleached out of the sky. But of course that midnight glow and the fate of those unhappy Siberian reindeer were nothing at all compared to what would have happened if a larger object had invaded the earth's atmosphere. On average, objects greater than a hundred yards in diameter strike the planet once every five thousand years and asteroids half a mile across thunder down at intervals of three hundred thousand years. Three hundred thousand years is a long time in anybody's book. But if—when—such a collision occurs, the explosion will be in the million megaton range and will cloak the atmosphere in dust, thrusting the entire planet into a deep freeze and effectively stifling all plant growth for a period of a year or more. There will be no crops. No forage. No sun.

There has been an accident, that is what the voice on the other end of the line is telling my wife, and the victim is Madeline Biehn, of 1337 Laurel Drive, according to the I.D. the paramedics found in her purse. (The purse, with the silver clasp that has been driven half an inch into the flesh under her arm from the force of the impact, is a little thing, no bigger than a hardcover book, with a ribbon-thin strap, the same purse all the girls carry, as if it's part of a uniform.) Is this her parent or guardian speaking?

I hear my wife say, "This is her mother." And then, the bottom dropping out of her voice, "Is she—?"

Is she? They don't answer such questions, don't volunteer information, not over the phone. The next ten seconds are thunderous, cataclysmic, my wife standing there numbly with the phone in her hand as if it's some unidentifiable object she's found in the street while I fumble out of bed to snatch for my pants—and my shoes, where are my shoes? The car keys? My wallet? This is the true panic, the loss of faith and control, the nameless named, the punch in the heart and the struggle for breath. I say the only thing I can think to say, just to hear my own voice, just to get things straight, "She was in an accident. Is that what they said?"

"She was hit by a car. She's—they don't know. In surgery."

"What hospital? Did they say what hospital?"

My wife is in motion now too, the negligee ridiculous, unequal to the task, and she jerks it over her head and flings it to the floor even as she snatches up a blouse, shorts, flip-flops—anything, anything to cover her nakedness and get her out the door. The dog is whining in the kitchen. There is the sound of the rain on the roof, intensifying, hammering at the gutters. I don't bother with shoes—there are no shoes, shoes do not exist—and my shirt hangs limply from my shoulders, misbuttoned, sagging, tails hanging loose, and we're in the car now and the driver's side wiper is beating out of sync and the night closing on us like a fist.

And then there's Chicxulub. Sixty-five million years ago, an asteroid (or perhaps a comet—no one is quite certain) collided with the earth on what is now the

Yucatán Peninsula. Judging from the impact crater, which is one hundred and twenty miles wide, the object—this big flaming ball—was some six miles across. When it came down, day became night and that night extended so far into the future that at least seventy-five percent of all known species were extinguished, including the dinosaurs in nearly all their forms and array and some ninety percent of the oceans' plankton, which in turn devastated the pelagic food chain. How fast was it traveling? The nearest estimates put it at 54,000 miles an hour, more than sixty times the speed of a bullet. Astrophysicists call such objects "civilization enders," and calculate the chances that a disaster of this magnitude will occur during any individual's lifetime at roughly one in ten thousand, the same odds as dying in an auto accident in the next ten months—or, more tellingly, living to be a hundred in the company of your spouse.

All I see is windows, an endless grid of lit windows climbing one atop the other into the night, as the car shoots through the *Emergency Vehicles Only* lane and slides in hard against the curb. Both doors fling open simultaneously. Maureen is already out on the sidewalk, already slamming the door behind her and breaking into a trot, and I'm right on her heels, the keys still in the ignition and the lights stabbing at the pale underbelly of a diagonally parked ambulance—and they can have the car, anybody can have it and keep it forever, if they'll just tell me my daughter is all right. *Just tell me,* I mutter, hurrying, out of breath, soaked through to the skin, *just tell me and it's yours,* and this is a prayer, the first of them in a long discontinuous string, addressed to whomever or whatever may be listening. Overhead, the sky is having a seizure, black above, quicksilver below, the rain coming down in wind-blown arcs, and I wouldn't even notice but for the fact that we are suddenly—instantly—wet, our hair knotted and clinging and our clothes stuck like flypaper to the slick tegument of our skin.

In we come, side by side, through the doors that jolt back from us in alarm, and all I can think is that the hospital is a death factory and that we have come to it like the walking dead, haggard, sallow, shoeless. "My daughter," I say to the nurse at the admittance desk, "she's—they called. You called. She's been in an accident."

Maureen is at my side, tugging at the fingers of one hand as if she's trying to remove an invisible glove, her shoulders slumped, mouth set, the wet blouse shrink-wrapping her. "A car. A car accident."

"Name?" the nurse asks. (About this nurse: she's young, Filipina, with opaque eyes and the bone structure of a cadaver; every day she sees death and it blinds her. She doesn't see us. She sees a computer screen, she sees the TV monitor mounted in the corner and the shadows that pass there, she sees the walls, the floor, the naked light of the fluorescent tube. But not us. Not us.)

For one resounding moment that thumps in my ears and then thumps again, I can't remember my daughter's name—I can picture her leaning into the mound of textbooks spread out on the dining room table, the glow of the overhead light making a nimbus of her hair as she glances up at me with a glum look and half a rueful smile, as if to say, *It's all in a day's work for a teenager, Dad, and you're lucky you're not in high school anymore,* but her name is gone.

"Maddy," my wife says. "Madeline Biehn."

I watch, mesmerized, as the nurse's fleshless fingers maneuver the mouse, her eyes fixed on the screen before her. A click. Another click. The eyes lift to take us in, even as they dodge away again. "She's still in surgery," she says.

"Where is it?" I demand. "What room? Where do we go?"

Maureen's voice cuts in then, elemental, chilling, and it's not a question she's posing, not a statement or demand, but a plea: "What's wrong with her?"

Another click, but this one is just for show, and the eyes never move from the screen. "There was an accident," the nurse says. "She was brought in by the paramedics. That's all I can tell you."

It is then that I become aware that we are not alone, that there are others milling around the room—other zombies like us, hurriedly dressed and streaming water till the beige carpet is black with it, shuffling, moaning, clutching at one another with eyes gone null and void—and why, I wonder, do I despise this nurse more than any human being I've ever encountered, this young woman not much older than my daughter, with her hair pulled back in a bun and the white cap like a party favor perched atop it, *who is just doing her job?* Why do I want to reach across the counter that separates us and awaken her to a swift sure knowledge of hate and fear and pain? Why?

"Ted," Maureen says, and I feel her grip at my elbow, and then we're moving again—hurrying, sweeping, practically running—out of this place, down a corridor under the glare of the lights that are a kind of death in themselves, and into a worse place, a far worse place.

The thing that disturbs me about Chicxulub, aside from the fact that it erased the dinosaurs and wrought catastrophic and irreversible change, is the deeper implication that we, and all our works and worries and attachments, are so utterly inconsequential. Death cancels our individuality, we know that, yes, but ontogeny recapitulates phylogeny and the kind goes on, human life and culture succeed us—that, in the absence of God, is what allows us to accept the death of the individual. But when you throw Chicxulub into the mix—or the next Chicxulub, the Chicxulub that could come howling down to obliterate all and everything even as your eyes skim the lines of this page—where does that leave us?

"You're the parents?"

We are in another room, gone deeper now, the walls closing in, the loudspeakers murmuring their eternal incantations, *Dr. Chandrasoma to Emergency, Dr. Bell, paging Dr. Bell,* and here is another nurse, grimmer, older, with deader eyes and lines like the strings of a tobacco pouch pulled tight round her lips. She's addressing us, me and my wife, but I have nothing to say, either in denial or affirmation. I'm paralyzed, struck dumb. If I claim Maddy as my own—and I'm making deals again—then I'm sure to jinx her, because those powers that might or might not be, those gods of the infinite and the minute, will see how desperately I love her and they'll take her away just to spite me for refusing to believe in them. *Voodoo, Hoodoo, Santeria, Bless me, Father, for I have sinned.* I hear Maureen's voice, emerging from a locked vault, the single whispered monosyllable, and then: "Is she going to be all right?"

"I don't have that information," the nurse says, and her voice is neutral, robotic even. This is not her daughter. Her daughter's at home, asleep in a pile of teddy bears, pink sheets, fluffy pillows, the night light glowing like the all-seeing eye of a sentinel.

I can't help myself. It's that neutrality, that maddening clinical neutrality, and can't anybody take any responsibility for anything? "What information *do* you have?" I say, and maybe I'm too loud, maybe I am. "Isn't that your job, for Christ's sake, to know what's going on here? You call us up in the middle of the night—our daughter's hurt, she's been in an accident, and you tell me you don't have *any fucking information*?"

People turn their heads, eyes burn into us. They're slouched in orange plastic chairs, stretched out on the floor, praying, pacing, their lips moving in silence. They want information too. We all want information. We want news, good news: it was all a mistake, minor cuts and bruises—contusions, that's the word—and your daughter, son, husband, grandmother, first cousin twice removed will be walking through that door over there any minute . . .

The nurse drills me with a look, and then she's coming out from behind the desk, a short woman, dumpy—almost a dwarf—and striding briskly to the door, which swings open on another room, deeper yet. "If you'll just follow me, please," she says.

Sheepish suddenly, I duck my head and comply, two steps behind Maureen.

This room is smaller, an examining room, with a set of scales and charts on the walls and its slab of a table covered with a sheet of antiseptic paper. "Wait here," the nurse tells us, already shifting her weight to make her escape. "The doctor'll be in in a minute."

"What doctor?" I want to know. "What for? What does he want?"

But the door is already closed.

I turn to Maureen. She's standing there in the middle of the room, afraid to touch anything or to sit down or even move for fear of breaking the spell. She's listening for footsteps, her eyes fixed on the other door, the one at the rear of the room. I hear myself murmur her name, and then she's in my arms, sobbing, and I know I should hold her, know that we both need it, the human contact, the love and support, but all I feel is the burden of her—there is nothing or no one that can make this better, can't she see that? I don't want to console or be consoled. I don't want to be touched. I just want my daughter back, that's all, nothing else.

Maureen's voice comes from so deep in her throat I can barely make out what she's saying. It takes a second to register, even as she pulls away from me, her face crumpled and red, and this is her prayer, whispered aloud: "She's going to be all right, isn't she?"

"Sure," I say, "sure she is. She'll be fine. She'll have some bruises, that's for sure, maybe a couple broken bones even . . ." and I trail off, trying to picture it, the crutches, the cast, Band-Aids, gauze: our daughter returned to us in a halo of shimmering light.

"It was a car," she says. "A car, Ted. A car hit her."

The room seems to tick and buzz with the fading energy of the larger edifice, and I can't help thinking of the congeries of wires strung inside the walls, the cables bringing power to the X-ray lab, the EKG and EEG machines, the life-support systems, and of the myriad pipes and the fluids they drain. A car. Three thousand pounds of steel, chrome, glass, iron.

"What was she even doing walking like that? She knows better than that."

My wife nods, the wet ropes of her hair beating at her shoulders like the flails of the penitents. "She probably had a fight with Kimberly, I'll bet that's it. I'll bet anything."

"Where is the son of a bitch?" I snarl. "This doctor—where is he?"

We are in that room, in that purgatory of a room, for a good hour or more. Twice I thrust my head out the door to give the nurse an annihilating look, but there is no news, no doctor, no nothing. And then, at quarter past two, the inner door swings open, and there he is, a man too young to be a doctor, an infant with a smooth bland face and hair that rides a wave up off his brow, and he doesn't have to say a thing, not a word, because I can see what he's bringing us and my heart seizes with the shock of it. He looks to Maureen, looks to me, then drops his eyes. "I'm sorry," he says.

When it comes, the meteor will punch through the atmosphere and strike the earth in the space of a single second, vaporizing on impact and creating a fireball several miles wide that will in that moment achieve temperatures of 60,000 degrees Kelvin, or ten times the surface reading of the sun. If it is Chicxulub-sized and it hits one of our landmasses, some two hundred thousand cubic kilometers of the earth's surface will be thrust up into the atmosphere, even as the thermal radiation of the blast sets fire to the planet's cities and forests. This will be succeeded by seismic and volcanic activity on a scale unknown in human history, and then the dark night of cosmic winter. If it should land in the sea, as the Chicxulub meteor did, it would spew superheated water into the atmosphere instead, extinguishing the light of the sun and triggering the same scenario of seismic catastrophe and eternal winter, while simultaneously sending out a rippling ring of water three miles high to rock the continents as if they were saucers in a dishpan.

So what does it matter? What does anything matter? We are powerless. We are bereft. And the gods—all the gods of all the ages combined—are nothing but a rumor.

The gurney is the focal point in a room of gurneys, people laid out as if there's been a war, the beaked noses of the victims poking up out of the maze of sheets like a series of topographic blips on a glaciated plane. These people are alive still, fluids dripping into their veins, machines monitoring their vital signs, nurses hovering over them like ghouls, but they'll be dead soon, all of them. That much is clear. But *the* gurney, the one against the back wall with the sheet pulled up over the impossibly small and reduced form, this is all that matters. The doctor leads us across the room, talking in a low voice of internal injuries, a ruptured spleen, trauma to the brain stem, and I can barely control my feet. Maureen clings to me. The lights dim.

Can I tell you how hard it is to lift this sheet? Thin percale, and it might as well be made of lead, iron, iridium, might as well be the repository of all the dark matter in the universe. The doctor steps back, hands folded before him. The entire room or triage ward or whatever it is holds its breath. Maureen moves in beside me till our shoulders are touching, till I can feel the flesh and the heat of her pressing into me, and I think of this child we've made together, this thing under the sheet, and the hand clenches at the end of my arm, the fingers there, prehensile, taking hold. The sheet draws back millimeter by millimeter, the slow striptease of death—and I can't do this, I can't—until Maureen lunges forward and jerks the thing off in a single violent motion.

It takes us a moment—the shock of the bloated and discolored flesh, the crusted mat of blood at the temple and the rag of the hair, this obscene violation of everything we know and expect and love—before the surge of joy hits us. Maddy is a redhead, like her mother, and though she's seventeen, she's as rangy and thin as a child, with oversized hands and feet, and she never did pierce that smooth sweet run of flesh beneath her lower lip. I can't speak. I'm rushing still with the euphoria of this new mainline drug I've discovered, soaring over the room, the hospital, the whole planet. Maureen says it for me: "This is not our daughter."

Our daughter is not in the hospital. Our daughter is asleep in her room beneath the benevolent gaze of the posters on the wall, Britney and Brad and Justin, her things scattered around her as if laid out for a rummage sale. Our daughter has in fact gone to Hana Sushi at the mall, as planned, and Kimberly has driven her home. Our daughter has, unbeknownst to us or anyone else, fudged the rules a bit, the smallest thing in the world, nothing really, the sort of thing every teenager does without thinking twice, loaning her I.D. to her second-best friend, Kristi Cherwin, because Kristi is sixteen and Kristi wants to see—is dying to see—the movie at the Cineplex with Brad Pitt in it, the one rated NC17. Our daughter doesn't know that we've been to the hospital, doesn't know about Alice K. Petermann and the pinot noir and the glasses left on the bar, doesn't know that even now the phone is ringing at the Cherwins'.

I am sitting on the couch with a drink, staring into the ashes of the fire. Maureen is in the kitchen with a mug of Ovaltine, gazing vacantly out the window where the first streaks of light have begun to limn the trunks of the trees. I try to picture the Cherwins—they've been to the house a few times, Ed and Lucinda—and I draw a blank until a backlit scene from the past presents itself, a cookout at their place, the adults gathered around the grill with gin and tonics, the radio playing some forgotten song, the children—our daughters—riding their bikes up and down the cobbled drive, making a game of it, spinning, dodging, lifting the front wheels from the ground even as their hair fans out behind them and the sun crashes through the trees. Flip a coin ten times and it could turn up heads ten times in a row—or not once. The rock is coming, the new Chicxulub, hurtling through the dark and the cold to remake our fate. But not tonight. Not for me.

For the Cherwins, it's already here.

(2003)

Here Comes

He didn't know how it happened, exactly—lack of foresight on his part, lack of caring, planning, holding something back for a rainy day—but in rapid succession he lost his job, his girlfriend and the roof over his head, waking up one morning to find himself sprawled out on the sidewalk in front of the post office. The sun drilled him where he lay. Both knees were torn out of his jeans and the right sleeve of his jacket was gone altogether. People were skirting him, clopping by like a whole herd of self-righteous Republicans, though they were mostly Latino—and mostly illegal—in this part of town. He sat up, feeling around for his hat, which he seemed to be sitting on. The pavement glistened minutely.

What was motivating him at the moment was thirst, the kind of thirst that made him suspect everything and everybody, because somebody had to have done this to him, deprived him of fluids, dredged his throat with a swab, left him here stranded like a nomad in the desert. Just beyond his reach, and he noticed this in the way of a detective meditating on a crime scene, was a brown paper bag with the green neck of a Mogen David 20/20 bottle peeping out of it. The bag had been crushed, and the bottle with it; ants had gathered for the feast. In real time, the time dictated by the sun in the sky and the progressive seep of movement all around him, a woman who must have had three hundred pounds packed like mocha fudge into the sausage skin of her monumental blue-and-white-flecked top and matching toreador pants stepped daintily over the splayed impediment of his legs and shot him a look of disgust. Cars pulled up, engines ticking, then rattled away. Exhaust hovered in a poisonous cloud. Two gulls, perched atop the convenient drive-up mail depository, watched him out of their assayers' eyes, big birds, vagrant and opportunistic, half again as tall as the boombox he'd left behind at Dana's when she drilled him out the door.

It wasn't an alcoholic beverage he wanted, though he wouldn't turn down a beer, but water, just that, something to wet his mouth and dribble down his throat. He made a failed effort to rise, and then somehow his feet found their place beneath him and he shoved himself up and snatched his cap off the pavement in a single graceless lurch. He let the blood pound in his ears a minute, then scanned the street for a source of H_2O.

To be homeless, in July, in a tourist-infested city on the coast of Southern California, wasn't as bad maybe as being homeless in Cleveland or Bogotá, but it wasn't what he was used to. Even at his worst, even when he got going on the bottle and couldn't stop, he was used to four walls and a bed, and if not a kitchen, at least a hot-plate. A chair. A table. A place to put his things, wash up, have a smoke and listen to music while dreaming over a paperback mystery—he loved mysteries and police procedurals, and horror, nothing better than horror when you're wrapped up in bed and the fog transfigures the streets and alleyways outside till anything could be lurking there. Except you. Because you're in bed, in your room, with the door shut and locked and the blankets pulled up to your chin, reading. And smoking. But Dana's face was like a cleaver, sharp and shining and merciless, and it cleaved and chopped till he had no choice but to get out the door or leave his limbs and digits behind. So now he was on the street, and everything he did, every last twitch and snort and furtive palpation of his scrotum, was a public performance, open to interpretation and subject to the judgment of strangers. Idiotic strangers. Strangers who were no better than him or anybody else, but who made way for him in a parting wave as if he was going to stick to the bottom of their shoes.

Across the street, kitty-corner to where he found himself at the moment, was a gas station—it floated there like a mirage, rippling gently in the convection waves rising up off the blacktop—and a gas station was a place where all sorts of fluids were dispensed, including water. Or so he reasoned. All right, then. He began to move, one scuffing sneaker following the other.

He was running the hose over the back of his head when he became aware that someone was addressing him. He didn't look up right away—he knew what was coming—but he made sure to twist off the spigot without hesitation. Then he ran his fingers through his hair, because if there was one thing that made him feel the strain of his circumstances it was unwashed hair, knocked the hat twice on his thigh and clapped it on his head like a helmet. He wasn't presentable, he knew that. He looked like a bum—for all intents and purposes he *was* a bum, or at least making a pretty fair run at becoming one—and it just didn't pay to make eye contact. Raymond rose slowly to his feet.

A man was standing there in the alley amidst the debris of torn-up boxes and discarded oil cans, the sun cutting into his eyes. Five minutes from picking himself up off the burning sidewalk, Raymond was in no condition to make fine distinctions, but he could see that whatever he was the man was no outraged service station attendant or hostile mechanic, no cop or security guard. He had a dog with him, for one thing, a little buff and yellow mutt that seemed to be composed entirely of hacked-off whiskers, and for another, he was dressed all in blue jeans, including two blue-jean jackets but no shirt, and none of the ensemble looked as if it had been washed and tumble-dried in recent memory. Raymond relaxed. He was in the presence of a fellow loser.

"Nice hat," the man said. He looked to be in his thirties, long hair slicked back close to his scalp and tucked behind his ears, the beard neatly clipped, big hands dangling from his doubled-up sleeves. He was grinning. At least there was that.

"Oh, this?" Raymond's hand went reflexively to his head. "It's just . . . it's nothing. It used to belong to my girlfriend."

"Yeah, I guess so, because why would a guy wear a hat like that, right?"

The hat—it was a cheap baseball cap made of plastic mesh—featured a black badge on the crown, and a legend, in a tiny, looping, gold script, that read: *You Can Pet My Cat, But Don't Touch My Pussy.* To Dana's mind, this was the height of subversive humor and she insisted on wearing the thing whenever they went out barhopping, which was every night except when they gave up all pretense and got a bottle at Von's and drank at home in front of the TV. He'd snatched it off her head the night she shoved him out the door with nothing but the clothes on his back, and it served her right, because she had his boombox and his other pair of shoes and his books and bedroll and shaving kit, and by the next afternoon the locks had been changed and every time he went over to demand his things back she just sat there in the window with her knife blade of a face and waited for one of the neighbors to call the cops.

Raymond was new to all this. He was shy, lonely, angry. It had been something like five or six days now, and during that time he'd kept away from the street people, bedding down wherever he could (but not on the sidewalk, that was crazy, and he still didn't know how that happened), eating when he felt like it and steadily drinking up what was left of his last and final paycheck. He ducked his head. "Right," he murmured.

The man introduced himself through his shining wet-toothed grin, because he was just there to get a little drink of fresh H_2O himself, and then he was thinking about maybe going into the convenience store on the corner and picking up a nice twelve-pack of Keystone and maybe sitting down by the beach and watching the A-types jog by with their dogs and their two-hundred-dollar running shoes. His name was Schuyler, Rudolph Schuyler, though everybody called him Sky for short, and his dog was Pal.

The light was like a scimitar, cutting the alley in two. Raymond didn't think he'd ever seen a line so sharp, a shadow so deep, and that was a kind of revelation, a paean to what man had built—a rectilinear gas station and a neatly proportionate fence topped with a spray of pink-tinged trumpet flowers—and how

God had come to light it like a photographer setting up the trickiest shot of his life. And there was a shot just as tricky played out over and over throughout the city, the country, the world even. He patted down his pockets, felt something there still, a few bucks anyway. When he looked up at Sky, when he finally looked him in the eye, he heard his own voice crawling out of his throat as if there were somebody else in there speaking for him. "Am I hearing you right, or is that an invitation?"

After the first twelve-pack, there was another—Raymond's treat—because the great and wise and all-knowing people who brewed the beer in their big vats and sealed it in the shining aluminum cans that were like little pills, little individual doses delivered up in the convenient twelve-ounce format, had foreseen the need and stocked the shelves to overflowing. "You know," Raymond said, easing back the flip-top on a fresh can, "I read in the paper a couple years ago about that time the mudslides put Big Sur out of business, I mean going both ways on Highway 1—did you hear about that? They had no beer, I mean—they ran out. You remember that?"

Sky was leaning back against one of the polished boulders the city had dumped along the beach as a seawall, both jackets spread out beneath him, his bare chest and arms exposed to the sun. He was tanned right down to the roots of his hair, tanned like a tennis pro or maybe a diving instructor, somebody vigorous and clean making a clean living under the sun. Out here, on the beach, he didn't look like a bum—or at least not one of the mental cases you saw on the streets, immured in the walking dungeon of their own stink. "Yeah," he said. "Maybe. I mean, I don't know—no beer?" He laughed. "How'd they survive?"

Raymond shrugged. He was looking out to sea, out to where the shimmer of the waves met the horizon in an explosion of light as if diamonds were being ground up in a thin band that stretched laterally as far as you could see. "They're all rich people up there. I guess they just dug the single-malt scotch and green Chartreuse out of their liquor cabinets and forgot about it. Or their wine cellars, or whatever. But the trucks couldn't get through, so there was no beer, no potato chips, no Slim Jims."

"What, no Pampers and underarm deodorant? What's a young mother to do?"

"No Kotex," Raymond said, tipping back his beer and reaching for another one. The cans were getting warm, though he'd stowed them in the shade, in a crevice between two boulders the size of Volkswagens, but he didn't mind: warm was better than nothing. He was enjoying himself. "No condoms. No Preparation-H."

"Yeah," Sky said, "but let me tell you, those people suck up there. Big-time. And I know from experience, because if you haven't got a motel key on you to show the cops—right there, show me a motel key, motherfucker—they put you in the car and drive you out to the city limits, period, no arguments. As if this wasn't America or something."

Raymond had nothing to say to that. He understood where the city fathers were coming from: who wanted an army of bums camped out on the streets? It turned off the tourists, and the tourists were what made a place like Big Sur click in the first place. Or this town. This town right here.

"So how long?" Sky asked, turning to him with eyes drawn down to slits against the sun.

Raymond took a pull at the fresh beer in his hands and felt warm all over, felt good, felt superior. "I don't know, a couple days. A week maybe. I had a place but my girlfriend—she's a bitch, a real queen bitch—kicked me out."

A rope of muscle flashed across Sky's shoulders as he reached for another beer and felt for the pop-top. "No," he said, "I mean how long were the roads closed down, like a week, two weeks, what?"

"Months. Months at least."

"Wow. Picture that. But if you had beer and jug wine—and maybe a little stash of canned food, Dinty Moore and the like, it must have been like paradise, if not for the cops, I mean. But even the cops. What are they going to do, kick you out of a place that's already closed off? Kick you out of nowhere? Like, I'm sorry, officer, I'd really like to accommodate you here, but where the fuck you expect me to go, huh, motherfucker? Like, suck on this."

Raymond took a moment to think about that, about the kind of paradise that must have been, or might have been—or could have been under the right conditions—and then, unaccountably, he found himself staring into the glazed brown eyes of a German shepherd with a foam-flecked muzzle and a red bandanna looped round its neck. One minute there'd been nothing there but the open vista of the sea, and now here was this big panting animal crowding his frame of reference and looking at him as if it expected him to get down on all fours and chase it round the beach. "Nice dog," Raymond said, giving the broad triangular head a pat. The dog panted, stray grains of sand glistening along the black seam of its lips. Pal, curled up at Sky's feet, never even so much as twitched a muscle. In the next moment two girls in tube tops and shorts jogged by on the compacted sand at the foot of the waves, beautiful girls with their hair and everything else bouncing in the shattered light, and they shouted for the dog and Raymond eased back and popped another beer, wondering why anybody would want to go to work nine-to-five and live in an apartment you had to kill yourself just to make the rent on when you could just kick back, like this, and let the dogs and the women present themselves to you as if you were a potentate on his throne.

The next thing he knew, the sun was going down. It balanced there on the flat cobalt palm of the ocean, trembling like the flame of a gas stove, till the water took hold of it and spread it across the surface in even, rippling strokes. The palms turned pink overhead. Birds—or were they bats?—hurled themselves from one shadow to another. Raymond was drunk, deeply, blissfully drunk, the original pair of twelve-packs transubstantiated into short-necked pints of wine, then into liters of Black Cat and finally wine again, out of the gallon jug. Somewhere along the line there had been food—Stagg chili, cold, straight from the can—and there was an interlude during which he sat by the fountain at the foot of the pier while Pal, tricked out in a little blue crepe doll's dress Sky had dug out of the bottom of a Dumpster, danced and did backflips for the tourists. Now there was the beach, the deep-anchored palm against which he was resting his complicit spine, and the sun drowning itself in color.

The jug came to him, fat and heavy as a bowling ball, and he lifted it to his lips and drank, then passed it on to Sky, who lingered over it before passing it to a tall, mad-haired, slit-eyed guy named Dougie—or was it Droogie? Droogie, yeah. That was it. Like in that old movie, the Kubrick one, and why couldn't he remember the name of it? Not that it mattered. Not really. Not anymore. All that—movies, books, the knowledge you could wield like a hammer—belonged to another world. Things were more immediate here, more elemental, like where you were going to relieve yourself without getting busted and where the next bottle was coming from.

During the afternoon, he'd spent a fruitful hour removing the left sleeve of his jacket, to give the thing proportion—to make it look as if it were a fashion statement instead of a disaster—but now, as the sun faded, he began to feel a chill at his back and wished he'd left it alone. There was still the problem of where he was going to sleep. It was one thing to sit around and pass a bottle in a circle of like-minded souls, the sun on your face and the sea breeze ruffling the hair at the back of your neck, and another thing altogether to wake up on the sidewalk like some terminal-stage loser with Swiss cheese for a brain.

Droogie—or maybe it *was* Dougie after all—was going on about the Chumash Casino, how he'd hit a thousand-dollar payoff on a slot machine there one night and booked himself into the bridal suite with a lady and a case of champagne and couldn't find so much as a nickel in his pocket come morning. Another guy—beard, tattoos, one lens gone from his glasses so it looked as if his eye had been staved in—said that was nothing, he'd scored five g's at Vegas one time, and then Sky cut in with a question for the group, which had grown to six now, including a woman about thirty who kept picking at the dirty yellow dress she wore over her jeans as if she were trying to break it down into its constituent fibers. Sky wanted to know if anybody felt like a nice pepperoni pizza—or maybe one of those thick-crust Hawaiian jobs, with the pineapple and ham?

Nobody said anything. The jug went round. Finally, from the echoing depths of his inner self, Raymond heard a voice saying, "Yeah, sure. I could go for it."

"All right, my man," Sky said, rising up from the cradle of his tree, "you are elected."

It was all coming from very far off. Raymond didn't know what was required, didn't have a clue.

"Come on, man, let's hump it. I said pizza. Didn't you hear me? Pizza!"

Then they were making their way through the deep sand above tide line and into the parking lot with its shrouded cars and drifting trash, Pal clicking along behind them. The last pay phone in the world stood at the far end of the lot. Sky dropped two coins into it and gave him his instructions: "Be forceful, be a man who knows what he wants, with his feet up on the padded stool in his condo—and don't slur. They'll want a call-back number, but they never call back. Make one up. Or your girlfriend. Use your girlfriend's number."

Later, much later, when the fog had settled in like an amphibious skin stretched over everything and the driftwood fire had burned down to coals, Sky pushed himself up from the sand and stretched his arms out in front of him. "Well," he said, "how about that pizza?" Raymond blinked up at him. The others had wandered off separately, ghosts dissolving in the mist, all except for the woman. At one point, Dougie had bent over her and tugged at her arm as if he were trying to tear a fistful of weeds up out of the ground, but she wasn't giving an inch and they'd hissed at each other for what seemed like a week before Sky said, "Why don't you just give it up already," and Dougie stalked off into the mist. She was sitting beside Raymond now, her lips wet on the neck of the bottle, nothing but dregs and saliva left at this point. "I don't know if I could eat," she said.

"Everybody's got to eat, right, Ray? Am I right?"

Raymond didn't have an opinion. He wanted to go get another bottle before the stores closed, but his money was gone.

"I don't know," the woman said doubtfully.

But Sky roused them, and a moment later they were all three stumbling through the sand to the sidewalk and along the sidewalk to the boulevard, Pal leading the way with his tail thrust up like a banner. It was unnaturally quiet, everything held fast in the grip of the fog. Cars drifted silently by as if towed on a wire, one pulled along after the other, their headlights barely visible. There was a faint music playing somewhere, saxophone and drums, and it came to them in snatches as they walked in the deep shadow of a bank of condos thrown up for the convenience of the tourists. Raymond didn't know what he was doing or where he was going, and he didn't care, because Sky was there and Sky was in command. His feet hit the pavement and he tried to keep from lurching into the shrubs that bristled along the high stucco walls of the condos. At one point the woman bumped up against him and he put his arm out to steady her, and in that moment of casual intimacy, he mumbled something along the lines of "You know, I don't even know what to call you."

"Her name's Knitsy," Sky said over his shoulder. "Because her fingers are always knitting in the air—isn't that right, Knitsy? I mean, knitting nothing, right?"

Her voice was breathy and shallow, with a sharp rural twang to it. "Sure," she said, "that's right."

"And what's that rhyme with—ditzy, right?"

"Sure, whatever."

Raymond wanted to ask her about that, make a joke, but it would have been a cruel joke, and so he kept it to himself. *Knitsy.* Let her knit, and let the guy with the broken glasses stare out at the world like an ambassador with a pince-nez and let Sky lord it over everybody. What difference did it make? The world was nothing but cruelty and stupidity anyway. And he himself? He was drunk, very drunk. Too drunk to keep walking and too drunk to lie down.

They were away from the beach now, trailing down the alley behind Giulio's Pizza Kitchen and the One-Stop Travel Shop. Sky motioned for silence, and they hung back in the shadows, whispering—hide-and-seek, that's what it was, hide-and-seek—while Pal trotted across the pavement to reconnoiter the Dumpster. Reeling, watching the spots swell and explode before his eyes, Raymond felt Knitsy's cold rough hand snake out and take hold of his own. His heart was thrumming. The fog sifted through the alley, etherized and unreal. Lit by the dull yellow glow of the streetlight on the corner, the dog might have been onstage somewhere, on TV, in a video, going through the repertoire of his tricks, and they watched as he sniffed and squirmed, prancing back and forth, till he finally went up on his hind legs and began to paw at the belly of the Dumpster. And then Sky was there, lifting the metal lid and retrieving the two large pies, still snug in their boxes, one decorated with pepperoni, the other with pineapple and ham.

In the morning—the morning, that was the hurtful time—Raymond woke to a shifting light, the peeling tan upthrust trunks of a grove of eucalyptus, and the sky revealed in a frame of leaves. He was on his back, something underneath him—a plastic tarp—and a blanket, heavy with dew, thrown over the cage of his chest. Beside him, snoring lightly and twitching in her sleep, was a woman with dirty fanned-out blondish hair and the deep indigo tattoo of a scorpion crawling up her neck. But that was no surprise—nothing was a surprise, unless it was the sidewalk, and this wasn't the sidewalk. This was—he lifted his head to take in the half-collapsed teepee fashioned of blue tarps backed up against a chain-link fence, the scrub at his feet, the trash scattered over the leaf litter and the pregnant rise of the mound giving onto the railroad tracks—this was the woods. He saw Pal then, Pal poking his whiskered head out of the teepee to give him an unfathomable look, and beyond Pal, Sky's red Mongoose mountain bike, for which—and it was all coming back to him now—Sky had paid nearly a third of his monthly SSI disability check. So this was Knitsy, then, and that was Sky inside the collapsing teepee. Or wigwam. Call it a wigwam. Better sound to it.

His head slipped back to the tarp. He tried to close his eyes, to fight down the stirring in his lower abdomen that was like the first stab of stomach distress—what his mother used to call the runs—but the thirst wouldn't let him. It was there again, powerful, imperious, parching him all the way from his throat up into the recesses of his skull. *I've got to get out of here,* he was thinking, *got to get up and out of here, find money, find work, a toilet, a tap, four walls to hide myself in.* But he couldn't move. Not yet.

That first night, the night she locked the door on him, they'd been drinking bourbon with beer chasers, and all his muscles were sapped—or his bones, his bones seemed to have melted away so that all he wanted to do was seek the lowest point, like water—and the best he could do was hammer on the door and shout the sort of incoherent things you shout at times like that until the police came and she told them she paid the rent around here and she didn't know him anymore and didn't want to. He wound up sleeping in the back of the building, under the oleanders against the fence, which made his face and hands break out in shining welts that were like fresh burns. He was planning on using his key after she left for work, but she didn't leave for work, just sat there in the window drinking bourbon and waiting for the locksmith. That night he pounded on the door again, but he melted away when he saw the police cruiser coming up the street, and after that, he gave it up. First month, last month, security: where was he going to get that? He tried calling his brother collect in Tampa but his brother wouldn't take the call. The bars were open though, and the corner stores with the Coors signs flashing in the windows. He got loaded, got hammered, wound up on the sidewalk. Now he was here.

He dozed. Came to. Dozed. And then, out of some beaten fog of a dream, he heard footsteps crunching gravel, a yip from Pal, and a voice—Sky's voice—raised in song: "Here comes Santa Claus, here comes Santa Claus, right down Santa Claus Lane."

Knitsy stirred, and they both came up simultaneously into the bewilderment of the day. Her hair was bunched on one side, her dress torn at the collar to reveal a stained thermal T-shirt beneath it. A warm, brewing odor rose from her. She looked at Raymond and her eyes retreated into her head.

Sky was standing over them now, a silver twelve-pack of beer in each hand. "Hey, you two lovebirds, Christmas came early this year," he said, handing a can first to Raymond, then Knitsy. The can was cold; the top peeled back with a hiss. Raymond didn't want a beer—he wanted to clean up his act, go back to Dana and beg her to let him in, if only for a shower and a shave and a change of clothes so he could go back to his boss—his ex-boss, the smug, fat, self-satisfied son of a bitch who'd canned him because he had a couple of drinks and came back late from lunch once or twice—and grovel at his feet, at anybody's feet, because he was out of money and out of luck and this was no way to live. But he took that beer and he thanked Sky for it, and for the next one after that, and before long the sun got caught in the trees and every single thing, every little detail, seemed just as fine as fine could be.

When the beer was gone and he could taste nothing in his throat but the rinsed-out metallic sourness of it, he pushed himself up and stood unsteadily in the high weeds. Judging from the sun, it must have been past noon, not that it mattered, because Dana didn't get home from work till five and if he went over there and tried the door or the windows or even sat out back in the lawn chair, the old lady next door would have the cops on him in a heartbeat. She was his enemy, in collusion with Dana, and the two of them were out to destroy him, he saw that much now. And what had he done to deserve it? He'd got drunk a couple times, that was all, and when Dana came needling at him, he'd defended himself—with his hands, not his fists, his hands—and she'd gone running next door to Mrs. Ruiz and Mrs. Ruiz had called the cops for her. So he couldn't go there, not till Dana came home, and even then it was a stretch to think she'd open the door to him, but what choice did he have?

There was a smell of menthol on the air, and he couldn't place it at first, until he looked down and saw the litter of eucalyptus buds scattered underfoot, every one a perfectly formed little nugget awaiting a layer of dirt and a little rain. They were beautiful in their way, all these silver nuggets spread out before him like spare change, and he fumbled open his fly and gave them a little dose of salts and urea to help them along, a real altruist, a nature boy all the way. Was he laughing? Yes, sure he was, and why not? Nature boy. "There was a boy, a very strange and *something* boy," he sang, and then he was singing "Here Comes Santa Claus," because Sky had put it in his head and he couldn't get it out.

Beyond the railroad tracks was the freeway, and he could hear the continuous rush of tires like white noise in the background of the film that was his life, a confused film begun somewhere in the middle with a close-up of his dangling empty hands and pulling back for a shot of Knitsy passed out on the tarp, her head thrown back and her mouth hanging open so you could see that at least at some point in her life she'd been to the dentist. Pal wasn't in the frame. Or Sky either. Half an hour ago he'd slipped a couple of beers in his pockets, whistled for the dog, and headed up the tracks in the direction of the pier. Raymond looked off down the tracks a long moment, looked to Knitsy, sprawled there in the weeds as if she'd been flung off the back of the train as it roared by—*Lovebirds? What in Christ's name had Sky meant by that?*—then started up the slope to where the rails burned in the light.

He wasn't a bum and he wasn't a drunk, not the way these others were, and he kept telling himself that as he made his way along the tracks, lit up on Sky's beer under the noonday sun that was peeling the skin off the tip of his nose. He'd always had a place to stay, always fended for himself, and that was the way it was going to be this time too. All it was was a binge, and the binge was over—it was over now—even if he didn't want it to be. He was out of money, and that was that. He was going to walk into town, find the unemployment office, and put in an application, and then he was going to see if he could patch things up with Dana, at least until he could collect his first check and find himself a room someplace—and no sense kidding himself, Dana was nothing but a pain in the ass, dragging him down with her bourbon, bourbon, bourbon, and he was through with her. Finally and absolutely. He didn't even like bourbon. Please. Give him vodka any day.

The tracks swept around a bend ahead and followed a trestle over the boulevard that ran along the beach, and he was thinking he didn't want to risk the trestle—you were always reading about somebody getting hit by a train out here, the last time a deaf-mute who couldn't hear the whistle, and that was pathetic—when he saw a figure approaching him in the distance. It was Dougie—or Droogie—and he had something in his hand, a pole or a stick, that caught the sun in a metallic shimmer. When he got closer, Raymond saw that it was a length of pipe ripped out of one of the public restrooms in the park or lifted from a construction site, and Dougie kept swinging it out away from his body and clapping it back in again as if he were trying to tenderize the flesh of his leg. He stopped ten feet from Raymond, and Raymond stopped too. "You seen Knitsy? Because I'm going to kill the bitch."

Raymond didn't answer. The beer had made him slow.

"What are you, deaf, motherfucker? I said, you seen Knitsy?"

It took him a minute, staring into the slits of the man's eyes as if he could find the answer there. He was conflicted. He was. But the pipe focused his attention. "I don't know, I think she's"—he gestured with a jerk of his head—"back there, you know, in the trees back there."

The man took a step closer and swiped at the near rail with the pipe till it clanged and clanged again. "Son of a bitch. It's Sky, then, right? She's with Sky? Because I'm going to kill his ass too."

Raymond didn't have anything to say to this. He just shrugged and moved on, even as Dougie cursed at his back. "I won't forget you either, you sorry son of a bitch. Payback time, I'm telling you, *payback,*" but Raymond just kept going, all the way down the tracks and across the trestle and into town. It was nothing to him. He was out of this. He was gone. Let them work it out among themselves, that's what he figured.

He waited till six, when he was sure she'd be there, and walked up the familiar street with its kids and dogs and beat-up cars and the men home from work and sitting out on the porch with a beer to take in the lingering sun, another day down, a job well done and a beer well deserved. Nobody waved to him, nobody said a word or even looked at him twice, and you would have thought he'd never lived here, never paid rent or electric bills or brought back a distillery's worth of bourbon in the plastic two-liter jug, night after night for a year and more. All right. Well, fuck them. He didn't need them or anybody else, except maybe Dana and a little sympathy. A shower, a shave, a couple of bucks to get him back on his feet again, that was all, because he'd had enough of sleeping in the bushes like some vagrant.

The only problem was, Dana wasn't home. He didn't hear the buzz of the TV she switched on the minute she came in the door and kept going till she passed out in front of it at midnight, or the canned diarrhea of the easy-listening crap she played on the radio in the kitchen all the time. He knocked. Rang the buzzer. Leaned out away from the porch to cup his hands over the shifting mirror of the front window and peer inside. But by this time Mrs. Ruiz was out on her own porch, twenty feet away, giving him an uncompromising look out of her flat black old-lady's eyes.

He thought of the Wildcat then—that's where she'd be, sitting at the bar with one of her hopeless, titanic, frizzy-haired friends from work with their dried-blood fingernails and greasy lipstick, knocking back bourbon and water as if they were afraid Prohibition was going to start up again at the stroke of the hour. It would be a walk—two miles, at least, but he was used to walking since his last DUI, and he had nothing better to do. The afternoon had been an exercise in futility, because by the time he got to the head of the line at the unemployment office he realized he was wearing the pussy hat (no choice, what with the state of his hair) and that they'd probably laugh him out of the place, so he just turned around and walked out the door. He was hungry—he hadn't put anything on his stomach since the pizza the night before—but he wouldn't go to the soup kitchen or the mission or whatever it was. That was where the bums went, and he was no bum, not yet anyway. Once the effects of the beer wore off, he wanted a drink, but without money or an ATM card or a bank account to go with it, he just couldn't see how he was going to get one. For a while there he'd lingered in the back of the liquor department at the grocery store, thinking to liberate something from the cooler, but they had television monitors mounted on the walls and a vigilant little smooth-skinned guy with a mustache and a tie who kept asking if he could help him find anything, and that was probably the low point of his day. Till now. Because now he just backed down off the porch, shot Mrs. Ruiz a look of burning hate, and started walking.

There was some coming and going at the Wildcat, people milling around the door in schools like fish, like barracuda—or no, like guppies, bloated and shining with all their trumped-up colors—but he peered in the window and didn't see Dana there at the bar. In the off chance she was in the ladies' or in the back room, he went in to have a look for himself. She wasn't there. It was crowded, though, the speakers were putting out music and there was a pervasive rising odor of rum and sour mix that brought him back to happier times, like the week before last. He took the opportunity to duck into the men's and wash some of the grit off his face and hands and smooth back the gray-flecked scrub of a beard that made him look about sixty years old, though he was only thirty-two—or no, thirty-three. Thirty-three, last birthday. He thought to reverse the hat, too, just for the sake of respectability, and then he stood at the bar awhile, hoping somebody would turn up and stand him a couple of drinks. Nobody did. Steve, the bartender, asked him if he wanted anything, and he asked Steve if he'd seen Dana. Yeah, she'd been in earlier. Did he want anything?

"Double vodka on the rocks."

"You going to pay for it this time?"

"When did I never pay?"

There was a song on he hated. Somebody jostled him, gave him a look. Steve didn't answer.

"Can I put it on Dana's tab?"

"Dana doesn't have a tab. It's cash only, my friend."

He got loud then, because he wanted that drink, and they knew him, didn't they? What did they think he was, some kind of deadbeat or something? But when Steve came out from behind the bar he felt it all go out of him in a long hissing rush of air. "All right," he said. "Okay, I hear you," and then he was back out on the street.

His feet hurt. He was at the tail end of a week-long drunk and he felt sick and debilitated, his stomach clenched around a hard little ball of nothing, his head full of beating wings, the rasp of feathers, a hiss that was no sound at all. Dana was out there somewhere—it wasn't that big a town, a grid of palmy streets configured around the tourist haven of the main drag, and a bar and T-shirt shop on every corner—and if he could only find her, go down on his knees to her, abase himself, beg and whine and lie and wheedle, she would relent, he knew she would. He was heading back up the street with the appealing idea of forcing a back window at the house, climbing in, making a sandwich and washing it down with bourbon and just crawling into bed and let come what will, when he spotted Dana's car in the lot behind the movie theater.

That was her car, no doubt about it, a ravaged brown Corolla with a rearranged front bumper and the dark slit at the top of the passenger's side window where it wouldn't roll up all the way. He crossed the street, sidled through the lot like any other carefree moviegoer and casually worked his arm through the crack of the window till he caught the handle and popped open the door. There was change in the glove compartment, maybe twelve or thirteen dollars' worth of quarters, dimes and nickels—and one Sacajawea dollar—she kept there against emergencies, and it took him no more than thirty seconds to scoop it up and weigh down his pockets. Then he relocked the door, eased it shut and headed back down the block, looking for the nearest liquor store.

It was getting dark when he made his way down to the beach, hoping to find Sky there, singing one of his Christmas songs, singing "Rudolph the Red-Nosed Reindeer" or "I Saw Mommy Kissing Santa Claus," singing just for the sheer joy of it, because every day was Christmas when you had your SSI check in your pocket and an ever-changing cast of lubricated tourists to provide you with doggie bags of veal piccata and a fistful of change. He had a pint of Popov in one hand and a Big Mac in the other, and he was alternately taking a swig from the bottle and a bite of the sandwich, feeling good all over again. A police cruiser came down the street as he was crossing at the light, but the bottle was clothed in its brown paper bag and the eyes of the men behind the windshield passed over him as if he didn't exist.

The cool breath of a breeze rode up off the water. He could hear the waves lifting and falling against the plane of the beach with a low reverberant boom, could feel the concussion radiating through the worn-out soles of his sneakers and up into his feet and ankles like a new kind of friction. The parking lot was deserted, five cars exactly, and the gulls had taken over as if he'd walked into that other movie, the Hitchcock one, what was it called? With Tippi Hedren? They were grouped at the edge of the pavement, a hundred of them or more, pale and motionless as statues. "Tippi, Tippi, Tippi," he said aloud. "The Tipster." There was a smell of iodine and whatever the tide had brought in.

He went from fire to fire on the beach, shared a swig of vodka in exchange for whatever the huddled groups were drinking, saw the guy with the broken glasses—Herbert, his name was Herbert—and a few other faces he vaguely recognized, but no Sky and no Pal. The night was clear, the stars alive and spread over the deepening sky all the way out to the Channel Islands and down as far as Rincón to the east. He shuffled through the still-warm sand in a kind of bliss, the second pint of vodka pressed to his lips, all the rough edges of things worn smooth, all his problems reduced to zero. He was going to find Sky, Sky his benefactor, the songbird, and see if he wanted a hit or two of vodka, and maybe they could sit around the fire and sing, order up another pizza, lie there and stare up at the stars as if they owned them all. It was early yet. The night was young.

The train gave him his first scare. He'd just come across the trestle and stepped to one side, careful of his footing in the loose stone, when the whistle sounded behind him. He was drunk and slow to react, sure, but it just about scared him out of his skin nonetheless. There was a rush of air and then the train—it was a freight, a thousand dark, clanking cars—went by like thunder, like war. He twisted his right ankle trying to lurch out of the way and went down hard in the bushes, but he held on to the bottle, that was the important thing, because the bottle—and most of it was left—was an offering for Sky, and maybe Knitsy too, if she was there. For a long while, as the sound of the train faded in the distance, he sat there in the dark, rubbing his ankle and laughing softly to himself—he could have been like the deaf-mute, somebody Dana would read about in the morning paper. *Raymond Leitner, cut down by the southbound. After a week-long illness. Currently—make that permanently—unemployed. Survived by his loving mother. Wherever she might be.*

When he got close enough to the camp to see the glow of candlelight suffusing the walls of the wigwam, he was startled by a sudden harsh shout and then Pal started barking, and there was movement there, framed against the drizzle of the light. "I said you ever touch her I'm going to kill your ass, because she's my soul mate, you motherfucker, my *soul mate,* and you know it!"

Sky's voice sang out, harsh and ragged, "Get off of me, get out of here, go on, get out!" And the barking. The barking rose to a frenzy, high-pitched, breathless, and then suddenly there was the dull wet thump of a blow, and the barking ceased, even as the movement shook the floating walls and the light snuffed out. "Here comes, you son of a bitch," Dougie's voice shouted out, "I'll give you here comes," and there was that wet sound again, the percussion of unyielding metal and yielding flesh, and again, and again.

Raymond froze. He took a step back in the dark, collided with something that shouldn't have been there, a solid immovable shape stretched out across the flat of the ground—and the tarp, the tarp he'd slept on—and the ankle gave way. He went down again, and the bottle with him, the sudden explosion of its shattering like gunfire in the night. His blood raced. He felt around him for a branch, a rock, anything, and that was when his hands told him what it was he'd tripped over. Her hair was the first thing, then the slick cotton of the dress, and everything wet and cold.

The night went silent. He couldn't see, all the shadings of uncommitted dark swelling and shrinking around him. A shadow rose up then out of the black pool of the ground no more than twenty feet away, rose to full height, and began to slash at the darkness where the wigwam would have been, and Dougie was cursing, raging, beating at everything in the night till the galvanized post rang out against the stones. Raymond was no longer drunk. He didn't move, didn't breathe. The post rose and fell till the shadows changed shape and the curses subsided into sobs and choked, half-formed phrases, to barks and whispers, and then there was another sound, the clangor of the post flung away against the stones of the railway bed and a new metallic sound, the whirring of gears, and suddenly the shadow was moving off down the deserted tracks on the dark skeleton of a mountain bike.

It took him nearly an hour, hobbled by the ankle that felt as if it had been snapped off the bone, sharpened to a point and jammed back in again, an hour treading along the railway ties, through the sand, up the sidewalks still full of safe, oblivious people passing from one appointment to another. He just kept walking, rotating up off the bad ankle, and they saw his face and stood aside for him. Dogs barked. Cars shot past. There were shouts and voices in the night. He had never been down there by the railroad tracks, never been to any bum's encampment, never passed a bottle with a bunch of derelicts, and there'd never been any question in his mind about going to Sky's aid or calling the police or anything else. He was just walking, that was all, walking home. And when he got there, when he saw Dana just getting out of her car, her face softened with drink and her hair newly cut, cut short as an acolyte's, he got down on his knees and crawled to her.

(2002)

All the Wrecks I've Crawled Out Of

All I wanted, really, was to attain mythic status. Along the lines, say, of James Dean, Brom Bones, Paul Bunyan, my father. My father was a giant among men, with good-sized trees for arms and fists like buckets of nails, and I was not a giant among men. I wasn't even a man, though I began to look like one as I grew into my shoulders and eventually found something to shave off my cheeks after a close and patient scrutiny, and I manfully flunked out of three colleges and worked at digging graves at the Beth-El cemetery and shoveling chicken shit at the Shepherd Hill Egg Farm till I got smart and started bartending. That was a kind of wreckage, I suppose—flunking out—but there was much more to come, wrecks both literal and figurative, replete with flames, blood, crushed metal and broken hearts, a whole swath of destruction and self-immolation, my own personal skid marks etched into the road of my life and maybe yours too.

So. Where to start? With Helen, I suppose, Helen Kreisler. She was a cocktail waitress at the restaurant where I was mixing drinks six and a half days a week, four years older than I when I met her—that is, twenty-seven—and with a face that wasn't exactly pretty in any conventional sense, but more a field for the play of psychodrama, martyrdom and high-level neurosis. It was an old face, much older than her cheerleader's body and her still relatively tender years, a face full of worry, with lines scored around her eyes and dug deep into the corners of her mouth. She wore her hair long and parted in the middle, after the fashion of the day, and her eyes—the exact color of aluminum foil—jumped out of her tanned face from a hundred feet away. They were alien eyes, that's what I called them. And her too. *Alien,* that was my pet name for her, and I used it to urge her on when she was on top of me and my hands were on her breasts and her mouth had gone slack with the feeling of what I was doing to her.

It was about a month after I started working at Brennan's Steakhouse that we decided to move in together. We found a two-bedroom house dropped down in a blizzard of trees by the side of a frozen lake. This was in suburban New York, by the way, in the farthest, darkest reaches of northern Westchester, where the nights were black-dark and close. The house was cheap, so far as rent was concerned, because it was a summer house, minimally insulated, but as we were soon to discover, two hundred dollars a month would go up the chimney or stovepipe or whatever it was that was connected to the fuel-evaporating furnace in the basement. Helen was charmed despite the water-stained exterior walls and the stink of frozen mouseshit and ancient congealed grease that hit you in the face like a two-by-four the minute you stepped in the door, and we lied to the landlady (a mustachioed widow with breasts the size of New Jersey and Connecticut respectively) about our marital status, got out our wallets and put down our first and last months' rent. It was a move up for me at any rate, because to this point I'd been living in a basement apartment at my parents' house, sleeping late as bartenders will do, and listening to the heavy stolid tread of my father's footsteps above me as he maneuvered around his coffee cup in the morning before leaving for work.

Helen fixed the place up with some cheap rugs and prints and a truckload of bric-a-brac from the local head shop—candles, incense burners, ceramic bongs, that sort of thing. We never cooked. We were very drunk and very stoned. Meals, in which we weren't especially interested, came to us out of a saucepan at the restaurant—except for breakfast, a fuzzy, woozy meal heavy on the sugars and starches and consumed languidly at the diner. Our sex was youthful, fueled by hormonal rushes, pot and amyl nitrite, and I was feeling pretty good about things—about myself, I mean—for the first time in my life.

But before I get into all that, I ought to tell you about the first of the wrecks, the one from which all the others seemed to spool out like fishing line that's been on the shelf too long. It was my first night at work, at Brennan's, that is. I'd done a little bartending weekends in college, but it was strictly beer, 7&7, rum and Coke, that sort of thing, and I was a little tentative about Brennan's, a big softly lit place that managed to be intimate and frenziedly public at the same time, and Ski Sikorski, the other bartender, gave me two shots of 151 and a Tuinol to calm me before the crush started. Well, the crush started, and I was still about as hyper as you can get without strictly requiring a straitjacket, but way up on the high end of that barely controlled hysteria there was a calm plateau of rum, Tuinol and the beer I sipped steadily all night long—and this was a place I aspired to reach eventually, once the restaurant closed down and I could haul myself up there and fade into a warm, post-conscious glow. We did something like a hundred and ten dinners that night, I met and flirted with Helen and three other cocktail waitresses and half a dozen partially lit female customers, and, all things considered, acquitted myself well. Ski and I had the door locked, the glasses washed and tomorrow's fruit cut and stowed when Jimmy Brennan walked in.

Helen and one of the other waitresses—Adele-something—were sitting at the bar, the stereo was cranked and we were having a celebratory nightcap at the time. It didn't faze Jimmy. He was the owner, only thirty-two years old, and he'd really stepped in it with this place, the first West Coast–style steak-and-salad-bar restaurant in the area. He drove a new Triumph, British racing green, and he drank martinis, straight up with a twist. "How'd it go tonight, Lester?" he asked, settling his lean frame on a barstool even as Ski set a martini, new-born and gleaming with condensation, before him.

I gave the waitresses a look. They were in their skimpy waitress outfits, long bare perfect legs crossed at the knee, cigarettes propped between the elegantly bunched knuckles that in turn propped up their weary silken heads. I was a man among men—and women—and I feared no evil and felt no pain. "Fine," I said, but I was already amending what seemed a much-too-modest assessment. "No, better than fine: great. Stupendous. Magnificent."

Jimmy Brennan wore glasses, the thin silver-framed discs made popular two years earlier by John Lennon. His eyes were bright behind them and I attributed that brightness to the keenness of mind and Darwinian fortitude that had made him rich at thirty-two, but I was wrong. That gleam was the gleam of alcohol, nothing more. Jimmy Brennan was, as I would discover, an alcoholic, though at the time that seemed just fine to me—anything that altered your consciousness and heightened your perceptions was cool in the extreme, as far as I was concerned.

Jimmy Brennan bought us a round, and then another. Helen gave me a look out of her silver-foil eyes—a look of lust, complicity, warning?—picked up her bag and left with Adele. It was three-thirty in the morning. Ski, who at twenty-seven was married and a father, pleaded his wife. The door closed behind him and I remember vividly the sound of the latch clicking into place as he turned his key from the outside. "Well," Jimmy said, slapping my back, "I guess it's just us, huh?"

I don't remember much of the rest of it, except this: I was in my car when I woke up, there was a weak pale sun draped over everything like a crust of vomit, and it was very, very hot. And more: there was a stranger in a yellow slicker beating out the glass of the driver's side window and I was trying to fight him off till the flames licking away at my calves began to make their point more emphatically than he could ever have. As I later reconstructed it, or as it was reconstructed for me, I'd apparently left the bar in the cold glow of dawn, fired up the engine of my car and then passed out with my foot to the floor. But as Jimmy said when he saw me behind the bar the next night, "It could have been worse—think what would've happened if the thing had been in gear."

My father seemed to think the whole affair was pretty idiotic, but he didn't deliver any lectures. It was idiotic, but by some convoluted way of thinking, it was manly too. And funny. Deeply, richly, skin-of-the-teeth and laughing-in-the-face-of-Mr.-D. funny. He rubbed his balding head with his nail-bucket hands and said he guessed I could take my mother's car to work until I could find myself another heap of bolts, but he hoped I'd show a little more restraint and maybe pour a drop or two of coffee into my brandy before trying to make it home on all that glare ice.

Helen—the new and exciting Helen with the silver-foil eyes—didn't seem particularly impressed with my first-night exploits, which had already entered the realm of legend by the time I got to work at four the following afternoon, but she didn't seem offended or put off in any way either. We worked together through the cocktail-hour rush and into the depths of a very busy evening, exchanging the thousand small quips and intimacies that pass between bartender and cocktail waitress in the course of an eight-hour shift, and then it was closing time and there was Jimmy Brennan, at the very hub of the same unfolding scenario that had played itself out so disastrously the night before. Had I learned my lesson? Had the two-paragraph story in the local paper crediting Fireman Samuel L. Calabrese with saving my sorry life had any effect? Or the loss of my car and the humiliation of having to drive my mother's? Not a whit. Jimmy Brennan bought and I poured, and he went off on a long soliloquy about beef suppliers and how they weren't competent to do a thing about the quality of the frozen lobster tails for Surf 'n' Turf, and I probably would have gone out and wrecked my mother's car if it wasn't for Helen.

She was sitting down at the end of the bar with Adele, Ski, another cocktail waitress and two waiters who'd stayed on to drink deep after we shut down the kitchen. What she was doing was smoking a cigarette and drinking a Black Russian and watching me out of those freakish eyes as if I were some kind of wonder of nature. I liked that look. I liked it a lot. And when she got up to whisper something in my ear, hot breath and expressive lips and an invitation that electrified me from my scalp to my groin, I cut Jimmy Brennan off in the middle of an aside about what he was paying per case for well-vodka and said, "Sorry, gotta go. Helen's having car trouble and she needs a ride, isn't that right, Helen?"

She already had her coat on, a complicated thing full of pleats and buckles that drove right down to the toes of her boots, and she shook out her hair with a sideways flip of her head before clapping a knit hat over it. "Yeah," she said. "That's right."

There were no wrecks that night. We left my mother's car in the lot out front of Brennan's and Helen drove me to the apartment she and Adele shared on the second floor of an old frame house in Yorktown. It was dark—intensely, preternaturally dark (or maybe it was just the crust of salt, sand and frozen slush on the windshield that made it seem that way)—and when we swung into a narrow drive hemmed in by long-legged pines, the house suddenly loomed up out of nowhere like the prow of a boat anchored in the night. "This is it?" I said, just to hear the sound of my own voice, and she said something like "Home sweet home" as she cut the engine and the lights died.

The next thing I knew we were on the porch, bathed in the dull yellow glow of a superfluous bug light, locked out and freezing; she gave me a ghostly smile, dug through her purse, dropped her keys twice, then her gloves and compact, and finally announced that the house key was missing. In response, I drew her to me and kissed her, my mind skewed by vodka and the joint we'd shared in the car, our breath steaming, heavy winter coats keeping our bodies apart—and then, with a growing sense of urgency, I tried the door. It was locked, all right. But I was feeling heroic and reckless, and I put my shoulder to it—just once, but with real feeling—and the bolt gave and we were in.

Upstairs, at the end of the hallway, was Helen's superheated lair, a place that looked pretty much the way our mutual place would look, but which was a revelation to me at the time. There was order here, femininity, floors that gave back the light, books and records arranged alphabetically on brick-and-board shelves, prints on the walls, a clean sink and a clean toilet. And there was a smell connected to and interwoven with it all, sweet and astringent at the same time. It might have been patchouli, but I didn't know what patchouli was or how it was supposed to smell, just that it was exotic, and that was enough for me. There were cats—two of them, Siamese or some close approximation—but you can't have everything. I was hooked. "Nice place," I said, working at the buttons of my coat while the cats yowled for food or attention or both, and Helen fluttered around the living room, lighting candles and slipping a record on the stereo.

I didn't know what to do with myself, so I eased my haunches down on the floor in a pile of pillows—there was no furniture in the usual sense—and shrugged out of my coat. It was hot as a steambath, Helen had left the room through a set of bead curtains that were still clacking, and a beer had magically appeared in my hand. I tried to relax, but the image of what was to come and what was expected of me and how exactly to go about it without ruining everything weighed on me so heavily even the chugging of the beer had no effect. Then Helen returned in a white terrycloth robe, her hair freshly brushed and shining. "So," she said, settling into the pillows beside me and looking suddenly as vulnerable and uncertain as I, "you want to get high?"

We smoked hash. We listened to music, very loud music—Buffalo Springfield; Blood, Sweat and Tears; the Moody Blues—and that provided an excuse for not saying much of anything beyond the occasional murmur as the pipe was passed or the lighter sprang to life. The touch of her hand as we shared the pipe set me on fire though and the music invested me with every nuance and I thought for a while I was floating about three feet above the floor. I was thinking sex, she was thinking sex, but neither of us made a move.

And then, somehow, Adele was there, compact, full-breasted Adele, with her sheenless eyes and the dark slash of her bangs obliterating her eyebrows. She was wearing a pair of black pantyhose and nothing else, and she settled into the pillows on my left, languidly reaching for the pipe. She didn't say anything for a long while—none of us did—and I don't know what she was thinking, so natural and naked and warm, but I was suffering from sensory overload. Two women, I was thinking, and the image of my father and my sad dumpy mother floated up in my brain just as one of the cats climbed into Adele's lap and settled itself between her breasts.

That was when I felt Helen's hand take hold of mine. She was standing, and she pulled me to my feet with surprising force, and then she led me through the bead curtains and down a hall and into her bedroom. And the first thing she did, before I could take hold of her and let all the rest unfold, was shut the door—and lock it.

And so we moved in together, in the house that started off smelling of freeze-dried mouseshit and wound up taking on the scent of patchouli. I was content. For the first time I was off on my own, independent, an adult, a man. I had a woman. I had a house. Two cats. Heating bills. And I came home to all that pretty religiously for the first month or two, but then, on the nights when I was working and Helen wasn't, I started staying after closing with Jimmy Brennan and a few of the other employees. The term Quaalude speaks to me now when I think back on it, that very specific term that calls up the image of a little white pill that kicked your legs out from under you and made your voice run down like a wind-up motor in need of rewinding. Especially when you judiciously built your high around it with a selection of high-octane drinks, pot, hash, and anything else you could get your hands on.

There we were, sitting at the bar, the music on full, the lights down low, talking into the night, bullshitting, getting stoned and progressively more stoned, and Helen waiting for me in our little house at the end of the road by the frozen lake. That was the setting for the second wreck—or it wasn't a wreck in the fundamental, literal sense of the word, because Helen's VW bus was barely damaged, aside from some unexpected wear and tear on the left front fender and a barely noticeable little twist to the front bumper. It was four or five in the morning, the sky a big black puddle of nothing, three feet of dogshit-strewn snow piled up on either side of the road till it looked like a long snaking bobsled run.

The bus fired up with a tinny rattle and I took off, but I was in a state of advanced confusion, I guess, and I went right by the turnoff for our road, the one that led to the little house by the frozen lake, and instead found myself out on the main highway, bouncing back and forth between the snow berms like a poolball that can't decide on a pocket.

There was something in the urgency of the lights flashing behind me that got me to pull over, and then there was a cop standing there in his jackboots and wide-brimmed hat, shining a flashlight in my face. "Out of the car," he said, and I complied, or tried to, but I missed my footing and pitched face-forward into the snow. And when I awoke this time, there were no firemen present and no flames, just an ugly pale-gray concrete-block room with graffiti scrawled over it and three or four hopeless-looking jerks sitting around on the floor. I got shakily to my feet, glanced around me and went instinctively to the door, a heavy sliding affair with a little barred window set in the center of it at eye level. My hands took hold of the handle and I gave the door a tug. Nothing. I tried again. Same lack of result. And then I turned round on my companions, these pathetic strangers with death masks for faces and seriously disarranged hair, and said, as if I was in a dream, "Hey, it's locked."

That was when one of the men on the floor stirred himself long enough to glance up at me out of blood-flecked eyes and a face that was exactly like a bucket of pus. "What the fuck you think, mother fucker," he said. "Your ass is in jail."

Then it was spring and the ice receded from the shore of the lake to reveal a black band of dead water, the driveway turned to mud and the ditches along the blacktop road began to ululate with the orgasmic cries of the nondescript little toads known as spring peepers. The heating bill began to recede too, and to celebrate that minor miracle and the rebirth of all things green and good, I took my Alien—Helen, that is—out for dinner at Capelli's, where all the waiters faked an Italian accent, whether they were Puerto Ricans or Swedes, and you couldn't pick up a cigarette without one of them rushing over to light it for you. It was dark. It smelled good. Somebody's grandmother was out in the kitchen, cooking, and we ate the usual things—cannelloni, baked ziti, pasta primavera—and paid about twice what we would have paid in the usual places. I was beginning to know a little about wine, so I ordered a bottle of the second-highest-priced red on the menu, and when we finished that, I ordered another. For dessert, my balled fist presented Helen with two little white Rorer Quaaludes.

She was looking good, silver-eyed and tanned from an early-spring ski trip to Vermont with Adele and one of the other waitresses. I watched the rings glitter on her fingers as she lifted her glass to wash down the pills, and then she set the glass down and eased back into her chair under the weight of all that food and wine. "I finally met Kurt," she said.

I was having a scotch and Drambuie as an after-dinner drink, no dessert thanks, and enjoying the scene, which was very formal and adult, old guys in suits slurping up linguine, busty wives with poodle hair and furs, people of forty and maybe beyond out here in the hinterlands living the good life. "Kurt who?" I said.

"Kurt Ramos? Adele's ex?" She leaned forward, her elbows splayed on the tabletop. "He was bartending at this place in Stowe—he's a Sagittarius, very creative. Funny too. He paints and writes poetry and had one of his poems almost published in the *Hudson Review,* and of course, Adele knew he was going to be there, I mean that was the whole point. He's thirty-four, I think. Or thirty-five. You think that's too much? Age-wise, I mean? Adele's only twenty-four."

"*Almost* published?" I said.

Helen shrugged. "I don't know the details. The editor wrote him a long letter or something."

"He is pretty old. But then so are you, and you don't mind having a baby like me around, do you?"

"Four years, kiddo," she said. "Three years and nine months, actually. I'm not an old lady yet. But what do you think—is he too old for her?"

I didn't think anything. Helen was always giving these speeches about so-and-so and their sex life, who was cheating on who, the I Ching, reincarnation, cat-breeding, UFOs and the way people's characters could be read like brownie recipes according to their astrological charts. I gave her a sly smile and put my hand on her leg. "Age is relative," I said. "Isn't it?"

And then the strangest thing happened, by way of coincidence, that is—there was a flurry of activity in the foyer, the bowing and scraping of waiters, the little tap dance of leather soles as coats were removed, and suddenly the maître d' was leading Adele and the very same Kurt Ramos past our table.

Helen saw them first. "Adele!" she chirped, already rising up out of the chair with a big stoned grin on her face, and then I glanced up and saw Adele there in a sweater so tight she must have been born in it (but no, no, I had vivid proof to the contrary). Beside her, loping along with an athletic stride, was Kurt Ramos, half-German, half–Puerto Rican, with crazily staring eyes and slick black hair that hung to his shoulders. He was wearing a tan trenchcoat, bell-bottoms and a pair of red bowling shoes he'd borrowed from a bowling alley one night. There were exclamations of surprise all around, the girls embraced as if they hadn't seen each other in twelve years and I found myself wrapping my hand round

Kurt Ramos' in a complicated soul shake. "Good to meet you, man," I said in my best imitation of a very hip adult, but he just stared right through me.

In May, Ski Sikorski quit to move up to Maine and live among goats and liberated women on a commune, leaving his wife and kid behind, and I found myself elevated to head bartender at the ripe age of twenty-three. I was making good money, getting at least a modicum of exercise rowing Helen around the defrosted lake every afternoon, and aside from the minorest of scrapes, I hadn't really wrecked anything or anybody in a whole long string of weeks. Plus, I was ascending to the legendary status I'd sought all along, stoked by the Fireman Calabrese incident and the high drama of my unconscious dive into the hands of the state police. I'd begun dealing Quaaludes in a quiet way, I tripped and had revelatory visions and went to concerts with Helen, Adele and Kurt, and I pretty generally felt on top of things. The prevailing ethos was simple in those days—the more drugs you ingested, the hipper you were, and the hipper you were, the more people sought you out for praise, drugs and admiration. I even got to the point where I could match Jimmy Brennan drink for drink and still make it home alive—or at least partially so.

Anyway, Ski quit and on my recommendation we hired Kurt Ramos as second bartender, and the two of us made quite a pair behind the bar, he with his shower-curtain hair and staring eyes and me with my fixed grin that was impervious to anything life or the pharmaceutical industry could throw at it. We washed glasses, cut fruit, mixed drinks, talked about everything and nothing. He told me about Hawaii and Amsterdam, drugs, women he'd known, and he showed me his poetry, which seemed pretty banal to me, but who was I to judge? When work was over, he and Adele would come over to our place for long stoned discussions and gleeful drug abuse, or we'd go to a late movie or another bar. I liked him. He had heart and style and he never tried to pull rank on me by virtue of his greater age and wisdom, as Jimmy Brennan and his drinking cronies never failed to do.

It was a month or so after Kurt started working behind the bar that my parents came in for the first time. They'd been threatening to make an appearance ever since I'd got the job—my mother wanted to check the place out because she'd heard so much about it, everybody had, and my father seemed amused by the idea of his son officially making him a drink and pushing it across the bar to him on a little napkin. "You'd have to give me a discount," he kept saying. "Wouldn't you?" And then he'd laugh his high husky laugh till the laugh became a smoker's cough and he'd cross the kitchen to the sink and drop a ball of sputum in the drain.

I was shaking a martini for a middle-aged guy at the end of the bar when I glanced up and saw my father looming there in the doorway. The sun was setting, a fat red disc on the horizon, and my father extinguished it with the spread of his shoulders as he maneuvered my mother through the door. The hostess—a terminally pretty girl by the name of Jane Nardone—went up to him with a dripping smile and asked if he'd like a table for two. "Yeah, sure," I heard him say in his rasping voice, "but only after my son makes me a vodka gimlet—or maybe two." He put his hands on his hips and looked down at the little painted doll that was Jane Nardone. "That okay with you?" Then he made his way across the room to where I stood behind the bar in white shirt and tie.

"Nice place," he grunted, helping my mother up onto a barstool and settling in beside her. My mother was heavily made-up and liquid-eyed, which meant she'd already had a couple of drinks, and she was clutching a black patent-leather purse the size of a refrigerator. "Hi, honey," she said, "working hard?"

For a minute I was frozen there at the bar, one hand on the shaker, the other on the glass. There went my cool, the legend dissolved, Lester the ultra-wild one nothing more than a boy-faced boy—and with parents, no less. It was Kurt who saved the day. He was thirty-five years old after all, with hollow cheeks and the faintest weave of gray in his mustache, and he had nothing to prove. He was cool, genuinely cool, and I was an idiot. "Mr. Rifkin," he said, "Mrs. Rifkin. Lester's told me a lot about you"—a glowing, beautiful, scintillating lie. "What can I get you?"

"Yeah," I said, adjusting the edges of my fixed smile just a degree, "what'll it be?"

And that was fine. My father had three drinks at the bar and got very convivial with Kurt, and my mother, perched on the edge of the stool and drinking Manhattans, corralled anybody she could—Jane, Adele, Helen, random customers, even one of the busboys—and told them all about my potty training, my elementary school triumphs and the .417 batting average I carried one year in Little League. Jimmy Brennan came in and bought everybody a round. We were very busy. I was glowing. My father was glowing. Jane showed him and my mother to the best table in the house and they kept Helen and two waiters schmoozing over a long, lingering, three-course dinner with dessert, after-dinner drinks and coffee. Which I paid for. Happily.

The summer that year was typical—heat, mosquitoes, fat green flies droning aimlessly round the kitchen, the air so dense with moisture even the frogs were sweating. Helen and I put off going to bed later and later each night, hoping it would cool off so we could actually sleep instead of sweating reservoirs on each other, and we saw dawn more times than I'd like to remember. Half the time I wound up passed out on the couch, and I would wake at one or two in the afternoon in a state of advanced dehydration. Iced coffee would help, especially with a shot or two of Kahlúa in it, and maybe a Seconal to kill some of the pain of the previous night's afflictions, but by the time we got around to the deli for a sandwich to go, it was four and we were on our way to work. That became a real grind, especially when I only got Monday nights off. But then, right in the middle of a heat wave, Jimmy Brennan's mother died and the restaurant closed down for three days. It was a tragedy for Jimmy, and worse for his mother, but for us—Helen, Kurt, Adele and me—it was like Christmas in July. Three whole days off. I couldn't believe it.

Jimmy flew back to California, somebody pinned a notice to the front door of the restaurant, and we took advantage of the fact that Kurt had recently come into twenty hits of blotter acid to plan a day around some pastoral activities. We filled a cooler with sangria and sandwiches and hiked into the back end of Wiccopee Reservoir, deep in Fahnestock Park, a place where swimming was prohibited and trespassing forbidden. Our purpose? To swim. And trespass. We could have spent the day on our own muddy little lake, but there were houses, cabins, people, cars, boats and dogs everywhere, and we wanted privacy, not to mention adventure. What we wanted, specifically, was to be nude, because we were very hip and the puritanical mores of the false and decrepit society our parents had so totteringly constructed didn't apply to us.

We parked off the Taconic Parkway—far off, behind a thick screen of trees where the police wouldn't discover the car and become overly curious as to the whereabouts of its former occupants—shouldered our day packs, hefted the cooler, and started off through the woods. As soon as we were out of sight of the road, Kurt paused to strip off his T-shirt and shorts, and it was immediately evident that he'd done this before—and often—because he had no tan line whatever. Adele was next. She threw down her pack, dropped her shorts, and in a slow tease unbuttoned her shirt, watching me all the time. The woods were streaked with sun, deerflies nagged at us, I was sweating. I set down the cooler, and though I'd begun to put on weight and was feeling self-conscious about it, I tried to be casual as I rolled the sweaty T-shirt up over my gut and chest and then kicked free of my shorts. Helen was watching me too, and Kurt—all three of them were—and I clapped on my sunglasses to mask my eyes. Then it was Helen's turn. She gave me a look out of her silver-foil eyes, then laughed—a long musical girlish laugh—before pulling the shirt over her head and dropping her shorts and panties in a single motion. *"Voilà!"* she said, and laughed again.

And what was I thinking? "How about a hit of that acid, Kurt?" I said, locked away behind my shades.

He looked dubious. Lean, naked and suntanned and caught between two impulses. "Sure," he said, shrugging, the green mottled arena of the untrodden woods opening up around him, "why not? But the lake's maybe a mile off and I can still hear the parkway, for Christ's sake, but yeah, sure, it's going to take a while to kick in anyway."

It was a sacramental moment. We lined up naked under the trees and Kurt tore off a hit for each of us and laid it on our tongues, and then we hoisted our packs, I picked up the cooler, and we started off down the path. Kurt, who'd been here before, was in front, leading the way; the two girls were next, Adele and then Helen; and I brought up the rear, seeing nothing of the sky, the trees, the ferns or the myriad wonders of nature. No, I saw only the naked buttocks of the naked women as they eased themselves down the path or climbed over a downed tree or a spike of granite, and it was all I could do to keep cool in a vigilantly hip and matter-of-fact way, and fight down an erection.

After a while, the lake began to peek through the trees, a silver sheen cut up in segments, now shining in a gap over here, now over there. We came down to it like pilgrims, the acid already starting to kick in and alter the colors and texture ever so subtly, and the first thing we did was drop our packs and the cooler and cannonade into the water in an explosion of hoots and shouts that echoed out over the lake like rolling thunder. There was splashing and frolicking and plenty of incidental and not-so-incidental contact. We bobbed like seals. The sun hung fat in the sky. There was no finer moment. And then, at some point, we found ourselves sitting cross-legged on a blanket and passing round the bota bag of sangria and a joint, before falling to the sandwiches. After that, we lay back and stared up into the shifting shapes of the trees, letting the natural world sink slowly in.

I don't remember exactly what happened next—maybe I was seeing things, maybe I was dozing—but when I came back to the world, what I saw was no hallucination. Kurt was having sex with Helen, my Helen, my Alien, and Adele was deeply involved too, very busy with her hands and tongue. I was thoroughly stoned—tripping, and so were they—but I wasn't shocked or surprised or jealous, or not that I would admit to myself. I was hip. I was a man. And if Kurt could fuck Helen, then I could fuck Adele. A quid pro quo, right? That was only fair.

Helen was making certain small noises, whispery rasping intimate noises that I knew better than anyone in the world, and those noises provoked me to get up off the blanket and move over to where Adele was lying at the periphery of all that passionate action as if she were somehow controlling it. I put one hand on her shoulder and the other between her legs, and she turned to me with her black eyes and the black slash of her bangs caught in the depths of them, and she smiled and pulled me down.

What happened next, of course, is just another kind of wreckage. It wasn't as immediate maybe as turning over a car or driving it into the trees, but it cut just as wide a swath and it hurt, ultimately, beyond the capacity of any wound that can be closed with stitches. Bang up your head, it's no problem—you're a man, you'll grow another one. Broken leg, crushed ribs—you're impervious. But if there's one thing I've learned, it's that the emotional wrecks are the worst. You can't see the scars, but they're there, and they're a long time healing.

Anyway, later that day, sunburned and sated, we all came back to our house at the end of the lane on the muddy lake, showered—individually—and ordered up takeout Chinese, which we washed down with frozen margaritas while huddling on the floor and watching a truly hilarious old black-and-white horror film on the tube. Then there came a moment when we all looked at one another—consenting adults, armored in hip—and before we knew it we were reprising the afternoon's scenario. Finally, very late, I found my way to bed, and it was Adele, not Helen, who joined me there. To sleep.

I was stupid. I was inadequate. I was a boy playing at being a man. But the whole thing thrilled me—two women, two women at my disposal—and I never even heard Helen when she told me she wanted to break it off. "I don't trust myself," she said. "I don't love him, I love you. You're my man. This is our house." The aluminum eyes fell away into her head and she looked older than ever, older than the mummy's ghost, older than my mother. We were in the kitchen, staring into cups of coffee. It was a week after the restaurant had opened up again, four in the morning, impossibly hot, the night alive with the shriek of every disturbed and horny insect, and we'd just got done entertaining Kurt and Adele in the way that had become usual and I didn't want to hear her, not a word.

"Listen," I said, half-stoned and rubbed raw between the legs, "listen, Alien, it's okay, there's nothing wrong with it—you don't want to get yourself buried in all that bourgeois shit. I mean, that's what started the War. That's what our parents are like. We're above that. We are."

The house was still. Her voice was very quiet. "No," she said, shaking her head slowly and definitively, "no we're not."

A month went by, and nothing changed. Then another. The days began to grow shorter, the nights took on a chill and the monster in the basement clanked and rumbled into action, devouring fuel oil once again. I was tending bar one night at the end of September, maybe twenty customers sitting there staring at me,

Jimmy Brennan and a few of his buddies at the end of the bar, couples lingering over the tables, when the phone rang. It had been a slow night—we'd only done maybe fifty dinners—but the bar had filled up after we shut the kitchen down, and everybody seemed unnaturally thirsty. Helen had gone home early, as had Adele and Kurt, and I was getting drinks at the bar and taking orders at the tables too. I picked the phone up on the second ring. "Brennan's," I said, "how can I help you?"

It was Helen. Her voice was thick, gritty, full of something I hadn't heard in it before. "That you, Les?" she said.

"Yeah, what's up?" I pinned the phone to one shoulder with my chin to keep my hands free, and began dipping glasses in the rinse water and stacking them to dry. I kept my eyes on the customers.

"I just wanted to tell you I'm moving out."

I watched Jimmy Brennan light a cigarette and lean out over the bar to fetch himself an ashtray. I caught his eye and signaled "just a minute," then turned my back to the bar. "What do you mean?" I said, and I had to whisper. "What are you saying?"

"What am I saying? You want to know what I'm saying, Les—do you really?" There it was, the grit in her voice, and more than that—anger, hostility. "What I'm saying is I'm moving in with Kurt and Adele because I'm in love with Kurt. You understand that? You understand what I'm saying? It's over. Totally. Adioski."

"Sure," I whispered, and I was numb, no more capable of thought or feeling than the empty beer mug I was turning over in my hands, "—if that's what you want. But when, I mean, when are you—?"

There was a pause, and I thought I heard her catch her breath, as if she were fighting back the kind of emotion I couldn't begin to express. "I won't be there when you get home," she said.

Somebody was calling me—"Hey, bartender!"—and I swung round on a big stupid-looking guy with a Fu Manchu mustache who came in every night for two or three drinks and never left more than a quarter tip. "Another round here, huh?"

"And, Les," she was saying through that cold aperture molded to my ear like a compress, "the rent's only paid through the thirtieth, so I don't know what you're going to do—"

"Hey, bartender!"

"—and you know what, Les? I don't care. I really don't."

I stayed late that night. The bar was alive, roaring, seething with camaraderie, chaos, every kind of possibility. My friends were there, my employer, customers I saw every night and wanted to embrace. I drank everything that came my way. I went out to the kitchen and smoked a joint with the busboys. Muddy Waters thumped through the speakers with his mojo workin' ("All you womens, stand in line, / I'll make love to you, babe, / In five minutes' time, / Ain't that a man?"). I talked a couple of people comatose, smoked a whole pack of cigarettes. Then came the moment I'd been dreading since I'd hung up the phone—Jimmy Brennan got up off his barstool and shut down the lights and it was time to go home.

Outside, the sky seemed to rise up out of itself and pull the stars taut like separate strands of hair till everything blurred and there was no more fire, just ice. It was cold. My breath steamed in the sick yellow glow of the streetlights. I must have stood in the empty parking lot for a full five minutes before I realized Helen had the van—her van—and I had no way to get home and nobody to call. But then I heard a noise behind me, the rattle of keys, a slurred curse, and there was Jimmy Brennan, locking up, and I shouted, "Jimmy, hey, Jimmy, how about a ride?" He looked puzzled, as if the pavement had begun to speak, but the light caught the discs of his glasses and something like recognition slowly transformed his face. "Sure," he said, unsteady on his feet, "sure, no problem."

He drove like a zombie, staring straight ahead, the radio tuned so low all I could hear was the dull muted snarl of the bass. We didn't say much, maybe nothing at all. He had his problems, and I had mine. He let me off at the end of the dark lane and I fumbled my way into the dark house and fled away to unconsciousness before I could think to turn the lights on.

Two days later I put down five hundred dollars on a used Dodge the color of dried blood and moved in with Phil Cherniske, one of the waiters at Brennan's, who by a cruel stroke of fate happened to live on the next street over from the one I'd just vacated, right on the shore of the same muddy lake. Phil's place stank of mouseshit too, and of course it lacked the feminine touches I'd grown accustomed to and cleanliness wasn't all that high on the list of priorities, but who was I to complain? It was a place in which to breathe, sleep, shit, brood and get stoned.

In the meanwhile, I tried to get hold of Helen. She'd quit Brennan's the day after our phone conversation, and when I called Kurt and Adele's, she refused to talk to me. Adele wouldn't say a word the next day at work and it was awkward in the extreme going through an eight-hour shift behind the bar with Kurt, no matter how hip and impervious I tried to be. We dodged round each other a hundred times, made the smallest of small talk, gave elaborate consideration to customers at the far end of the bar. I wanted to kill him, that's what I wanted to do, and I probably would have too, except that violence was so unhip and immature. Helen's name never passed my lips. I froze Kurt out. And Adele too. And to everybody else I was a combination of Mahatma Gandhi and Santa Claus, my frozen smile opening up into a big slobbering insincere grin. "Hey, man," I said to the cheapazoid with the mustache, "how you doin'?"

On my break and after work, I called Kurt and Adele's number over and over, but Helen wasn't answering. Twice I drove my Dodge down the street past their house, but nobody was home the first time and then all three of them were there the next, and I couldn't face going up those steps. For a while I entertained a fantasy of butting down the door, kicking Kurt in the crotch and dragging Helen out to the car by her hair, but it faded away in a pharmaceutical haze. I didn't run through a checklist of emotions, like one of those phony Ph.D.s in the women's magazines Helen stacked up on the coffee table like miniature Bibles and Korans—that wasn't my way at all. I didn't even tell my parents we weren't together anymore. I just got high. And higher.

That was what brought about the culminating wreck—of that series anyway. I was feeling bad one day, bad in every sense of the word, and since it was my day off, I spent the afternoon chasing down drugs in every house and apartment I could think of in Westchester and Putnam Counties, hitting up friends, acquaintances and acquaintances of acquaintances. Phil Cherniske was with me for part of the time, but then he had to go to work, and I found myself driving around the back roads, stoned on a whole smorgasbord of things, a bottle of vodka propped between my legs. I was looking at leaves, flaming leaves, and I was holding a conversation with myself and letting the car take me wherever it wanted. I think I must have pulled over and nodded out for a while, because all of a sudden (I'd say "magically," but this was more like treachery) the leaves were gone and it was dark. There was nothing to do but head for the restaurant.

I came through the door in an envelope of refrigerated air and the place opened up to me, warm and frank and smelling of cigarettes, steak on the grill, fresh-cut lime. I wasn't hungry myself, not even close to it, so I settled in at the bar and watched people eat dinner. Kurt was bartending, and at first he tried to be chummy and unctuous, as if nothing had happened, but the look on my face drove him to the far end of the bar, where he tried to keep himself urgently occupied. It was good sitting there with a cigarette and a pocketful of pills, lifting a finger to summon him when my drink needed refreshing—once I even made him light my cigarette, and all the while I stared hate into his eyes. Adele was waitressing, along with Jane Nardone, recently elevated from hostess. I never even looked at Adele, but at some point it seemed I tried to get overly friendly with Jane in the corner and Phil had to come out of the kitchen and put a hand on my arm. "Brennan'll be in soon, you know," Phil said, his hand like a clamp on the meat of my arm. "They'll eighty-six you. They will."

I gave him a leer and shook him off. "Hey, barkeep," I shouted so that the whole place heard me, all the Surf 'n' Turf gnashers and their dates and the idiots lined up at the bar, "give me another cocktail down here, will you? What, do you want me to die of thirst?"

Dinner was over and the kitchen closed by the time things got ugly. I was out of line and I knew it, and I deserved what was coming to me—that's not to say it didn't hurt, though, getting tossed out of my own restaurant, my sanctuary, my place of employ, recreation and release, the place where the flame was kept and the legend accruing. But tossed I was, cut off, eighty-sixed, banned. I don't know what precipitated it exactly, something with Kurt, something I said that he didn't like after a whole long night of things he didn't like, and it got physical. Next thing I knew, Phil, Kurt, Jimmy Brennan and two of the busboys had ten arms around me and we were all heaving and banging into the walls until the door flew open and I was out on the pavement where some bleached-out overweight woman and her two kids stepped over me as if I were a leper. I tried to get back in—uncool, unhip, raging with every kind of resentment and hurt—but they'd locked the door against me, and the last thing I remember seeing was Kurt Ramos' puffed-up face peering out at me through the little window in the door.

I climbed into my car and fired it up with a roar that gave testimony to a seriously compromised exhaust system. When the smoke cleared—and I hoped they were all watching—I hit the gas, jammed the lever into gear and shot out onto the highway on screaming tires. Where was I headed? I didn't know. Home, I guessed. There was no place else to go.

Now, to set this up properly, I should tell you that there was one wicked turn on the long dark blacktop road that led to that dark lane on the muddy lake, a ninety-degree hairpin turn the Alien had christened "Lester's Corner" because of the inevitability of the forces gathered there, and that was part of the legend too. I knew that corner was there, I was supremely conscious of it, and though I can't say I always coasted smoothly through it without some last-minute wheel-jerking and tire-squealing, it hadn't really been a problem. Up to this point.

At any rate, I wasn't really paying attention that night and my reaction time must have been somewhere in the range of the Alzheimer's patient on medication—in fact, for those few seconds I *was* an Alzheimer's patient on medication—and I didn't even know where I was until I felt the car slip out from under me. Or no, that isn't right. It was the road—the road slipped out from under me, and it felt just as if I were on a roller coaster, released from the pull of gravity. The car ricocheted off a tree that would have swatted me down like a fly if I'd hit it head-on, blasted down an embankment and wound up on its roof in a stew of skunk cabbage and muck. I wasn't wearing a seatbelt, of course—I don't even know if they'd been invented yet, and if they had, there wouldn't have been one in that car—and I found myself puddled up in the well of the roof like an egg inside a crushed shell.

There was no sense in staying there, underneath two tons of crumpled and drooling machinery—that wasn't the way things were supposed to be, even I could see that—so I poked my hands through the gap where the driver's side window had formerly been and felt them sink into the cold ooze. There was a smell of gasoline, but it was overpowered by the reek of deconstructed skunk cabbage, and I didn't give the situation any more thought or calculation than a groundhog does when he pulls himself out of his burrow, and the next thing I knew I was standing up to my ankles in cold muck, looking up in the direction of the road. There were lights there, and a shadowy figure in a long winter coat. "You all right?" a voice called down to me.

"Yeah, sure," I said, "no problem," and then I was lurching up the embankment on splayed feet, oozing muck. When I got to the top, a guy my age was standing there. He looked a little bit like Kurt—same hair, same slope to the shoulders—but he wasn't Kurt, and that was a good thing. "What happened?" he said. "You lose control?"

It was a ridiculous question, but I answered it. "Something like that," I said, my voice thick with alcohol and methaqualone.

"Sure you're not hurt? You want to go to the hospital or anything?"

I took a minute to pat myself down, the night air like the breath of some expiring beast. "No," I said, slowly shaking my head in the glare of the headlights, "I'm not hurt. Not that I know of anyway."

We stood there in silence a moment, contemplating the overturned hulk of the car. One wheel, persistent to the point of absurdity, kept spinning at the center of a gulf of shadow. "Listen," I said finally, "can you give me a lift?"

"A lift? But what about—?"

"Tomorrow," I said, and I let one hand rise and then drop.

There was another silence, and he was thinking it over, I could see that. From his point of view, this was no happy occasion. I wasn't bleeding, but I stank like a corpse and I was leaving the scene of an accident and he was a witness and all the rest of it. But he was a good man, and he surprised me. "Yeah, sure," he said, after a minute. "Climb in."

That was when things got very strange. Because as I directed him to my house at the end of the lane by the side of the soon-to-be-refrozen lake, a curtain fell over my mind. It was a dense curtain, weighted at the ends, and it admitted no glimmer of light. "Here," I said, "stop here," and the curtain fell over that part of my life that played itself out at Phil Cherniske's house.

A moment later, I found myself alone in the night, the taillights of the good samaritan's car winking once at the corner and then vanishing. I walked down the dark lane thinking of Helen, Helen with her silver-foil eyes and smooth sweet smile, and I mounted the steps and turned the handle of the door thinking of her, but it wouldn't turn, because it was locked. I knocked then, knocked at my own door, knocked until my knuckles bled, but there was no one home.

(1998)

Blinded by the Light

So the sky is falling. Or, to be more precise, the sky is emitting poisonous rays, rays that have sprinkled the stigmata of skin cancer across both of Manuel Banquedano's cheeks and the tip of his nose and sprouted the cataracts in Slobodan Abarca's rheumy old eyes. That is what the tireless Mr. John Longworth, of Long Beach, California, U.S.A., would have us believe. I have been to Long Beach, California, on two occasions, and I give no credence whatever to a man who would consciously assent to live in a place like that. He is, in fact, just what my neighbors say he is—an alarmist, like the chicken in the children's tale who thinks the sky is falling just because something hit him on the head. On *his* head. On his individual and prejudicial head. And so the barnyard goes into a panic—and to what end? Nothing. A big fat zero.

But let me tell you about him, about Mr. John Longworth, Ph.D., and how he came to us with his theories, and you can judge for yourself. First, though, introductions are in order. I am Bob Fernando Castillo and I own an *estancia* of 50,000 acres to the south of Punta Arenas, on which I graze some 9,000 sheep, for wool and mutton both. My father, God rest his soul, owned Estancia Castillo before me and his father before him, all the way back to the time Punta Arenas was a penal colony and then one of the great trading towns of the world—that is, until the Americans of the North broke through the Isthmus of Panama and the ships stopped rounding Cape Horn. In any case, that is a long and venerable ownership in anybody's book. I am fifty-three years old and in good health and vigor and I am married to the former Isabela Mackenzie, who has given me seven fine children, the eldest of whom, Bob Fernando Jr., is now twenty-two years old.

It was September last, when Don Pablo Antofagasta gave his annual three-day *fiesta primavera* to welcome in the spring, that Mr. John Longworth first appeared among us. We don't have much society out here, unless we take the long and killing drive into Punta Arenas, a city of 110,000 souls, and we look forward with keen anticipation to such entertainments—and not only the adults, but the children too. The landowners from several of the *estancias,* even the most far-flung, gather annually for Don Pablo's extravaganza and they bring their children and some of the house servants as well (and even, as in the case of Don Benedicto Braun, their dogs and horses). None of this presents a problem for Don Pablo, one of the wealthiest and most generous among us. As we say, the size of his purse is exceeded only by the size of his heart.

I arrived on the Thursday preceding the big weekend, flying over the *pampas* in the Piper Super Cub with my daughter, Paloma, to get a jump on the others and have a quiet night sitting by the fire with Don Pablo and his eighty-year-old Iberian *jerez*. Isabela, Bob Fernando Jr. and the rest of the family would be making the twelve-hour drive over washboard roads and tortured gullies the following morning, and frankly, my kidneys can no longer stand that sort of pounding. I still ride—horseback, that is—but I leave the Suburban and the Range Rover to Isabela and to Bob Fernando Jr. At any rate, the flight was a joy, soaring on the back of the implacable wind that rakes our country day and night, and I taxied right up to the big house on the airstrip Don Pablo scrupulously maintains.

Don Pablo emerged from the house to greet us even before the prop had stopped spinning, as eager for our company as we were for his. (Paloma has always been his favorite, and she's grown into a tall, straight-backed girl of eighteen with intelligent eyes and a mane of hair so thick and luxuriant it almost seems unnatural, and I don't mind saying how proud I am of her.) My old friend strode across the struggling lawn in boots and puttees and one of those plaid flannel shirts he mail-orders from Boston, Teresa and two of the children in tow. It took me half a moment to shut down the engine and stow away my aeronautical sunglasses for the return flight, and when I looked up again, a fourth figure had appeared at Don Pablo's side, matching him stride for stride.

"Cómo estás, mi amigo estimado?" Don Pablo cried, taking my hand and embracing me, and then he turned to Paloma to kiss her cheek and exclaim on her beauty and how she'd grown. Then it was my turn to embrace Teresa and the children and press some sweets into the little ones' hands. Finally, I looked up into an untethered North American face, red hair and a red mustache and six feet six inches of raw bone and sinew ending in a little bony afterthought of a head no bigger than a tropical coconut and weighted down by a nose to end all noses. This nose was an affliction and nothing less, a tool for probing and rooting, and I instinctively looked away from it as I took the man's knotty gangling hand in my own and heard Don Pablo pronounce, "Mr. John Longworth, a scientist from North America who has come to us to study our exemplary skies."

"Mucho gusto en conocerle," he said, and his Spanish was very good indeed, but for the North American twang and his maddening tendency to over-pronounce the consonants till you felt as if he were battering both sides of your head with a wet root. He was dressed in a fashion I can only call bizarre, all cultural differences aside, his hands gloved, his frame draped in an ankle-length London Fog trenchcoat and his disproportionately small head dwarfed by a pair of wraparound sunglasses and a deerstalker cap. His nose, cheeks and hard horny chin were nearly fluorescent with what I later learned was sunblock, applied in layers.

"A pleasure," I assured him, stretching the truth for the sake of politesse, after which he made his introductions to my daughter with a sort of slobbering formality, and we all went in to dinner.

There was, as I soon discovered, to be one topic of conversation and one topic only throughout the meal—indeed, throughout the entire three days of the *fiesta,* whenever and wherever Mr. John Longworth was able to insinuate himself, and he seemed to have an almost supernatural ability to appear everywhere at once, as ubiquitous as a cockroach. And what was this penetrating and all-devouring topic? The sky. Or rather the hole he perceived in the sky over Magallanes, Tierra del Fuego and the Antarctic, a hole that would admit all the poisons of the universe and ultimately lead to the destruction of man and nature. He talked of algae and krill, of acid rain and carbon dioxide and storms that would sweep the earth with a fury unknown since creation. I took him for an enthusiast at best, but deep down I wondered what asylum he'd escaped from and when they'd be coming to reclaim him.

He began over the soup course, addressing the table at large as if he were standing at a podium and interrupting Don Pablo and me in a reminiscence of a salmon-fishing excursion to the Penitente River undertaken in our youth. "None of you," he said, battering us with those consonants, "especially someone with such fair skin as Paloma here or Señora Antofagasta, should leave the house this time of year without the maximum of protection. We're talking ultraviolet-B, radiation that increases by as much as one thousand percent over Punta Arenas in the spring because of the hole in the ozone layer."

Paloma, a perspicacious girl educated by the nuns in Santiago and on her way to the university in the fall, gave him a deadpan look. "But, Mr. Longworth," she said, her voice as clear as a bell and without a trace of intimidation or awe, "if what you say is true, we'll have to give up our string bikinis."

I couldn't help myself—I laughed aloud and Don Pablo joined me. Tierra del Fuego is hardly the place for sunbathers—or bikinis either. But John Longworth didn't seem to appreciate my daughter's satiric intent, nor was he to be deterred. "If you were to go out there now, right outside this window, for one hour unprotected under the sun, that is, without clothing—or, er, in a bikini, I mean—I can guarantee you that your skin would blister and that those blisters could and would constitute the incipient stages of melanoma, not to mention the damage to your eyes and immune system."

"Such beautiful eyes," Don Pablo observed with his customary gallantry. "And is Paloma to incarcerate them behind dark glasses, and my wife too?"

"If you don't want to see them go blind," he retorted without pausing to draw breath.

The thought, as we say, brought my kettle to a boil: who was this insufferable person with his stabbing nose and deformed head to lecture us? And on what authority? "I'm sorry, señor," I said, "but I've heard some far-fetched pronouncements of doom in my time, and this one takes the cake. Millenarian hysteria is what I say it is. Proof, sir. What proof do you offer?"

I realized immediately that I'd made a serious miscalculation. I could see it in the man's pale leaping eyes, in the way his brow contracted and that ponderous instrument of his nose began to sniff at the air as if he were a bloodhound off after a scent. For the next hour and a half, or until I retreated to my room, begging indigestion, I was carpet-bombed with statistics, chemical analyses, papers, studies, obscure terms and obscurer texts, until all I could think was that the end of the planet would be a relief if only because it would put an end to the incessant, nagging, pontificating, consonant-battering voice of the first-class bore across the table from me.

At the time, I couldn't foresee what was coming, though if I'd had my wits about me it would have been a different story. Then I could have made plans, could have arranged to be in Paris, Rio or Long Beach, could have been in the hospital, for that matter, having my trick knee repaired after all these years. Anything, even dental work, would have been preferable to what fell out. But before I go any further I should tell you that there are no hotels in the Magallanes region, once you leave the city, and that we have consequently developed among us a strong and enduring tradition of hospitality—no stranger, no matter how personally obnoxious or undeserving, is turned away from the door. This is open range, overflown by caracara and condor and haunted by *ñandú,* guanaco and puma, a waste of dwarf trees and merciless winds where the unfamiliar and the unfortunate collide in the face of the wanderer. This is to say that three weeks to the day from the conclusion of Don Pablo's *fiesta,* Mr. John Longworth arrived at the Estancia Castillo in all his long-nosed splendor, and he arrived to stay.

We were all just sitting down to a supper of lamb chops and new potatoes with a relish of chiles and onions in a white sauce I myself had instructed the cook to prepare, when Slobodan Abarca, my foreman and one of the most respected *huasos* in the province, came to the door with the news that he'd heard a plane approaching from the east and that it sounded like Don Pablo's Cessna. We hurried outside, all of us, even the servants, and scanned the iron slab of the sky. Don Pablo's plane appeared as a speck on the horizon, and I was astonished at the acuity of Slobodan Abarca's hearing, a sense he's developed since his eyes began to go bad on him, and before we knew it the plane was passing over the house and banking for the runway. We watched the little craft fight the winds that threatened to flip it over on its back at every maneuver, and suddenly it was on the ground, leaping and ratcheting over the greening turf. Don Pablo emerged from the cockpit, the lank raw form of John Longworth uncoiling itself behind him.

I was stunned. So stunned I was barely able to croak out a greeting as the wind beat the hair about my ears and the food went cold on the table, but Bob Fernando Jr., who'd apparently struck up a friendship with the North American during the *fiesta,* rushed to welcome him. I embraced Don Pablo and numbly took John Longworth's hand in my own as Isabela looked on with a serene smile and Paloma gave our guest a look that would have frozen my blood had I only suspected its meaning. "Welcome," I said, the words rattling in my throat.

Don Pablo, my old friend, wasn't himself, I could see that at a glance. He had the shamed and defeated look of Señora Whiskers, our black Labrador, when she does her business in the corner behind the stove instead of outside in the infinite grass. I asked him what was wrong, but he didn't answer—or perhaps he didn't hear, what with the wind. A few of the men helped unload Mr. John Longworth's baggage, which was wound so tightly inside the aircraft I was amazed it had been able to get off the ground, and I took Don Pablo by the arm to escort him into the house, but he shook me off. "I can't stay," he said, staring at his shoes.

"Can't stay?"

"Don Bob," he said, and still he wouldn't look me in the eye, "I hate to do this to you, but Teresa's expecting me and I can't—" He glanced up then at John Longworth, towering and skeletal in his huge flapping trenchcoat, and he repeated "I can't" once more, and turned his back on me.

Half an hour later I sat glumly at the head of the table, the departing whine of Don Pablo's engine humming in my ears, the desiccated remains of my reheated chops and reconstituted white sauce laid out like burnt offerings on my plate, while John Longworth addressed himself to the meal before him as if he'd spent the past three weeks lashed to a pole on the *pampas.* He had, I noticed, the rare ability to eat and talk at the same time, as if he were a ventriloquist, and with every bite of lamb and potatoes he tied off the strings of one breathless sentence and unleashed the next. The children were all ears as he and Bob Fernando Jr. spoke mysteriously of the sport of basketball, which my son had come to appreciate during his junior year abroad at the University of Akron, in Ohio, and even Isabela and Paloma leaned imperceptibly toward him as if to catch every precious twist and turn of his speech. This depressed me, not that I felt left out or that I wasn't pleased on their account to have the rare guest among us as a sort of linguistic treat, but I knew that it was only a matter of time before he switched from the esoterica of an obscure and I'm sure tedious game to his one and true subject—after all, what sense was there in discussing a mere sport when the sky itself was corrupted?

I didn't have long to wait. There was a pause just after my son had expressed his exact agreement with something John Longworth had said regarding the "three-point shot," whatever that might be, and John Longworth took advantage of the caesura to abruptly change the subject. "I found an entire population of blind rabbits on Don Pablo's ranch," he said, apropos of nothing and without visibly pausing to chew or swallow.

I shifted uneasily in my chair. Serafina crept noiselessly into the room to clear away the plates and serve dessert, port wine and brandy. I could hear the wind at the panes. Paloma was the first to respond, and at the time I thought she was goading him on, but as I was to discover it was another thing altogether. "Inheritance?" she asked. "Or mutation?"

That was all the encouragement he needed, this windbag, this doomsayer, this howling bore with the pointed nose and coconut head, and the lecture it precipitated was to last through dessert, cocoa and *maté* in front of the fire and the first, second and third strokes of the *niñitos*' bedtime. "Neither," he said, "though if they were to survive blind through countless generations—not very likely, I'm afraid—they might well develop a genetic protection of some sort, just as the sub-Saharan Africans developed an increase of melanin in their skin to combat the sun. But, of course, we've so radically altered these creatures' environment that it's too late for that." He paused over an enormous forkful of cheesecake. "Don Bob," he said, looking me squarely in the eye over the clutter of the table and the dimpled faces of my little ones, "those rabbits were blinded by the sun's radiation, though you refuse to see it, and I could just stroll up to them and pluck them up by the ears, as many as you could count in a day, and they had no more defense than a stone."

The challenge was mine to accept, and though I'd heard rumors of blind salmon in the upper reaches of the rivers and birds blinded and game too, I wasn't about to let him have his way at my own table in my own house. "Yes," I observed drily, "and I suppose you'll be prescribing smoked lenses for all the creatures of the *pampas* now, am I right?"

He made no answer, which surprised me. Had he finally been stumped, bested, caught in his web of intrigue and hyperbole? But no: I'd been too sanguine. Calamities never end—they just go on spinning out disaster from their own imperturbable centers. "Maybe not for the rabbits," he said finally, "but certainly this creature here could do with a pair . . ."

I leaned out from my chair and looked down the length of the table to where Señora Whiskers, that apostate, sat with her head in the madman's lap. "What do you mean?" I demanded.

Paloma was watching, Isabela too; Bob Fernando Jr. and the little ones sat rigid in their chairs. "Call her to you," he said.

I called. And the dog, reluctant at first, came down the length of the table to her master. "Yes?" I said.

"Do you see the way she walks, head down, sniffing her way? Haven't you noticed her butting into the furniture, scraping the doorframes? Look into her eyes, Don Bob: she's going blind."

The next morning I awoke to a sound I'd never before heard, a ceaseless rapid thumping, as of a huge penitential heart caught up in the rhythm of its sorrows. Isabela awoke beside me and I peered through the blinds into the courtyard that was still heavy with shadow under a rare crystalline sky. Figures moved there in the courtyard as if in a dream—my children, all of them, even Paloma—and they fought over the swollen globe of a thumping orange ball and flung it high against an orange hoop shrouded in mesh. They were shouting, crying out in a kind of naked joy that approached the ecstatic, and the trenchcoat and the nose and the shrunken bulb of the bobbing head presided over all: *basketball.*

Was I disturbed? Yes. Happy for them, happy for their fluid grace and their joy, but struck deep in my bowels with the insidiousness of it: first basketball and then the scripture of doom. Indeed, they were already dressed like the man's disciples, in hats with earmuffs and the swirling greatcoats we'd long since put away for winter, and the exposed flesh of their hands and faces glistened with his sunblock. Worse: their eyes were visored behind pairs of identical black sunglasses, Mr. John Longworth's gift to them, along with the gift of hopelessness and terror. The sky was falling, and now they knew it too.

I stood there dumbfounded at the window. I didn't have the heart to break up their game or to forbid the practice of it—that would have played into his hands, that would have made me the voice of sanity and restraint (and clearly, with this basketball, sanity and restraint were about as welcome as an explosion at *siesta* time). Nor could I, as *dueño* of one of the most venerable *estancias* in the country, attempt to interdict my guest from speaking of certain worrisome and fantastical subjects, no matter how distasteful I found them personally. But what could I do? He was clearly deluded, if not downright dangerous, but he had the ready weight of his texts and studies to counterbalance any arguments I might make.

The dog wasn't blind, any fool could see that. Perhaps her eyes were a bit cloudy, but that was to be expected in a dog of her age, and what if she was losing her sight, what did that prove? I'd had any number of dogs go blind, deaf, lame and senile over the years. That was the way of dogs, and of men too. It was sad, it was regrettable, but it was part of the grand design and there was no sense in running round the barnyard crowing your head off about it. I decided in that moment to go away for a few days, to let the basketball and the novelty of Mr. John Longworth dissipate like the atmospheric gases of which he spoke so endlessly.

"Isabela," I said, still standing at the window, still recoiling from that subversive thump, thump, thump, "I'm thinking of going out to the upper range for a few days to look into the health of Manuel Banquedano's flock—pack up my things for me, will you?"

This was lambing season, and most of the *huasos* were in the fields with the flocks to discourage eagle and puma alike. It is a time that never fails to move me, to strengthen my ties to the earth and its rejuvenant cycles, as it must have strengthened those ties for my father and his father before him. There were the lambs, appeared from nowhere on tottering legs, suckling and frolicking in the waste, and they were money in my pocket and the pockets of my children, they were provender and clothing, riches on the hoof. I camped with the men, roasted a haunch of lamb over the open fire, passed a bottle of *aguardiente.* But this time was different, this time I found myself studying the pattern of moles, pimples, warts and freckles spread across Manuel Banquedano's face and thinking the worst, this time I gazed out over the craggy *cerros* and open plains and saw the gaunt flapping figure of Mr. John Longworth like some apparition out of Apocalypse. I lasted four days only, and then, like Christ trudging up the hill to the place of skulls, I came back home to my fate.

Our guest had been busy in my absence. I'd asked Slobodan Abarca to keep an eye on him, and the first thing I did after greeting Isabela and the children was to amble out to the bunkhouse and have a private conference with the old *huaso.* The day was gloomy and cold, the wind in an uproar over something. I stepped in the door of the long low-frame building, the very floorboards of which gave off a complicated essence of tobacco, sweat and boot leather, and found it deserted but for the figure of Slobodan Abarca, bent over a chessboard by the window in the rear. I recognized the familiar sun-bleached *poncho* and *manta,* the spade-like wedge of the back of his head with its patches of parti-colored hair and oversized ears, and then he turned to me and I saw with a shock that he was wearing dark glasses. Inside. Over a chessboard. I was speechless.

"Don Bob," Slobodan Abarca said then in his creaking, unoiled tones, "I want to go back out on the range with the others and I don't care how old and feeble you think I am, anything is better than this. One more day with that devil from hell and I swear I slit my throat."

It seemed that when John Longworth wasn't out "taking measurements" or inspecting the teeth, eyes, pelt and tongue of every creature he could trap, coerce or pin down, he was lecturing the ranch hands, the smith and the household help on the grisly fate that awaited them. They were doomed, he told them—all of mankind was doomed and the drop of that doom was imminent—and if they valued the little time left to them they would pack up and move north, north to Puerto Montt or Concepción, anywhere away from the poisonous hole in the sky. And those spots on their hands, their throats, between their shoulderblades and caught fast in the cleavage of their breasts, those spots were cancerous or at the very least pre-cancerous. They needed a doctor, a dermatologist, an oncologist. They needed to stay out of the sun. They needed laser surgery. Sunblock. Dark glasses. (The latter he provided, out of a seemingly endless supply, and the credulous fools, believers in the voodoo of science, dutifully clamped them to their faces.) The kitchen staff was threatening a strike and Crispín Mansilla, who looks after the automobiles, had been so terrified of an open sore on his nose that he'd taken his bicycle and set out on the road for Punta Arenas two days previous and no one had heard from him since.

But worse, far worse. Slobodan Abarca confided something to me that made the blood boil in my veins, made me think of the braided bullhide whip hanging over the fireplace and the pearl-handled dueling pistols my grandfather had once used to settle a dispute over waterfowl rights on the south shore of Lake Castillo: Mr. John Longworth had been paying his special attentions to my daughter. Whisperings were overheard, tête-à-têtes observed, banter and tomfoolery taken note of. They were discovered walking along the lakeshore with their shoulders touching and perhaps even their hands intertwined (Slobodan Abarca couldn't be sure, what with his failing eyes), they sought each other out at meals, solemnly bounced the basketball in the courtyard and then passed it between them as if it were some rare prize. He was thirty if he was a day, this usurper, this snout, this Mr. John Longworth, and my Paloma was just out of the care of the nuns, an infant still and with her whole life ahead of her. I was incensed. Killing off the natural world was one thing, terrifying honest people, gibbering like a lunatic day and night till the whole *estancia* was in revolt, but insinuating himself in my daughter's affections—well, this was, quite simply, the end.

I stalked up the hill and across the yard, blind to everything, such a storm raging inside me I thought I would explode. The wind howled. It shrieked blood and vengeance and flung black grains of dirt in my face, grains of the unforgiving *pampas* on which I was nurtured and hardened, and I ground them between my teeth. I raged through the house and the servants quailed and the children cried, but Mr. John Longworth was nowhere to be found. Pausing only to snatch up one of my grandfather's pistols from its velvet cradle in the great hall, I flung myself out the back door and searched the stables, the smokehouse, the generator room. And then, rounding the corner by the hogpen, I detected a movement out of the corner of my eye, and there he was.

Ungainly as a carrion bird, the coat ends tenting round him in the wind, he was bent over one of the hogs, peering into the cramped universe of its malicious little eyes as if he could see all the evil of the world at work there. I confronted him with a shout and he looked up from beneath the brim of his hat and the fastness of his wraparound glasses, but he didn't flinch, even as I closed the ground between us with the pistol held out before me like a homing device. "I hate to be the bringer of bad news all the time," he called out, already lecturing as I approached, "but this pig is in need of veterinary care. It's not just the eyes, I'm afraid, but the skin too—you see here?"

I'd stopped ten paces from him, the pistol trained on the nugget of his head. The pig looked up at me hopefully. Its companions grunted, rolled in the dust, united their backsides against the wind.

"Melanoma," he said sadly, shaking his visored head. "Most of the others have got it too."

"We're going for a ride," I said.

His jaw dropped beneath the screen of the glasses and I could see the intricate work of his front teeth. He tried for a smile. "A ride?"

"Your time is up here, *señor,*" I said, and the wind peeled back the sleeve of my jacket against the naked thrust of the gun. "I'm delivering you to Estancia Braun. Now. Without your things, without even so much as a bag, and without any goodbyes either. You'll have to live without your basketball hoop and sunblock for a few days, I'm afraid—at least until I have your baggage delivered. Now get to your feet—the plane is fueled and ready."

He gathered himself up then and rose from the ground, the wind beating at his garments and lifting the hair round his glistening ears. "It'll do no good to deny it, Don Bob," he said, talking over his shoulder as he moved off toward the shed where the Super Cub stood out of the wind. "It's criminal to keep animals out in the open in conditions like these, it's irresponsible, mad—think of your children, your wife. The land is no good anymore—it's dead, or it will be. And it's we who've killed it, the so-called civilized nations, with our air conditioners and underarm deodorant. It'll be decades before the CFCs are eliminated from the atmosphere, if ever, and by then there will be nothing left here but blind rabbits and birds that fly into the sides of rotting buildings. It's over, Don Bob—your life here is finished."

I didn't believe a word of it—naysaying and bitterness, that's all it was. I wanted to shoot him right then and there, on the spot, and have done with it—how could I in good conscience deliver him to Don Benedicto Braun, or to anyone, for that matter? He was the poison, he was the plague, he was the ecological disaster. We walked grimly into the wind and he never stopped talking. Snatches of the litany came back to me—ultraviolet, ozone, a hole in the sky bigger than the United States—but I only snarled out directions in reply: "To the left, over there, take hold of the doors and push them inward."

In the end, he didn't fight me. He folded up his limbs and squeezed into the passenger seat and I set aside the pistol and started up the engine. The familiar throb and roar calmed me somewhat, and it had the added virtue of rendering Mr. John Longworth's jeremiad inaudible. The wind assailed us as we taxied out to the grassy runway—I shouldn't have been flying that afternoon at all, but as you can no doubt appreciate, I was a desperate man. After a rocky takeoff we climbed into a sky that opened above us in all its infinite glory but which must have seemed woefully sad and depleted to my passenger's degraded eyes. We coasted high over the wind-whipped trees, the naked rock, the flocks whitening the pastures like distant snow, and he never shut up, not for a second. I tuned him out, let my mind go blank, and watched the horizon for the first weathered outbuildings of Estancia Braun.

They say that courtesy is merely the veneer of civilization, the first thing sacrificed in a crisis, and I don't doubt the truth of it. I wonder what became of my manners on that punishing wind-torn afternoon—you would have thought I'd been raised among the Indians, so eager was I to dump my unholy cargo and flee. Like Don Pablo, I didn't linger, and I could read the surprise and disappointment and perhaps even hurt in Don Benedicto's face when I pressed his hand and climbed back into the plane. "Weather!" I shouted, and pointed to the sky, where a wall of cloud was already sealing us in. I looked back as he receded on the ground beneath me, the inhuman form of Mr. John Longworth at his side, long arms gesticulating, the lecture already begun. It wasn't until I reached the verges of my own property, Estancia Castillo stretched out beneath me like a worn carpet and the dead black clouds moving in to strangle the sky, that I had my moment of doubt. What if he was right? I thought. What if Manuel Banquedano truly was riddled with cancer, what if the dog had been blinded by the light, what if my children were at risk? What then?

The limitless turf unraveled beneath me and I reached up a hand to rub at my eyes, weary suddenly, a man wearing the crown of defeat. A hellish vision came to me then, a vision of 9,000 sheep bleating on the range, their fleece stained and blackened, and every one of them, every one of those inestimable and beloved animals, my inheritance, my life, imprisoned behind a glistening new pair of wraparound sunglasses. So powerful was the vision I could almost hear them baa-ing out their distress. My heart seized. Tears started up in my eyes. Why go on? I was thinking. What hope is there?

But then the sun broke through the gloom in two pillars of fire, the visible world come to life with a suddenness that took away my breath, color bursting out everywhere, the range green all the way to the horizon, trees nodding in the wind, the very rock faces of the *cerros* set aflame, and the vision was gone. I listened to the drone of the engine, tipped the wings toward home, and never gave it another thought.

(1994)

Tooth and Claw

The weather had absolutely nothing to do with it—though the rain had been falling off and on throughout the day and the way the gutters were dripping made me feel as if despair was the mildest term in the dictionary—because I would have gone down to Daggett's that afternoon even if the sun was shining and all the fronds of the palm trees were gilded with light. The problem was work. Or, more specifically, the lack of it. The boss had called at six-thirty a.m. to tell me not to come in, because the guy I'd been replacing had recovered sufficiently from his wrenched back to feel up to working, and no, he wasn't firing me, because they'd be onto a new job next week and he could use all the hands he could get. "So take a couple days off and enjoy yourself," he'd rumbled into the phone in his low hoarse uneven voice that always seemed on the verge of morphing into something else altogether—squawks and bleats or maybe just static. "You're young, right? Go out and get yourself some tail. Get drunk. Go to the library. Help old ladies across the street. You know what I mean?"

It had been a long day: breakfast out of a cardboard box while cartoon images flickered and faded and reconstituted themselves on the TV screen, and then some desultory reading, starting with the newspaper and a couple of *National Geographics* I'd picked up at a yard sale, lunch at the deli where I had ham and cheese in a tortilla wrap and exchanged exactly eleven words with the girl behind the counter (*Number 7, please, no mayo; Have a nice day; You too*), and a walk to the beach that left my sneakers sodden. And after all that it was only three o'clock in the afternoon and I had to force myself to stay away from the bar till five, five at least.

I wasn't stupid. And I had no intention of becoming a drunk like all the hard-assed old men in the shopping mall–blighted town I grew up in, silent men with hate in their eyes and complaint eating away at their insides—like my own dead father, for that matter—but I was new here, or relatively new (nine weeks now and counting) and Daggett's was the only place where I felt comfortable. And why? Precisely because it was filled with old men drinking themselves into oblivion. It made me think of home. Or feel at home anyway.

The irony wasn't lost on me. The whole reason I'd moved out to the Coast to live, first with my Aunt Kim and her husband, Waverley, and then in my own one-bedroom apartment with kitchenette and a three-by-six-foot balcony with a partially obscured view of the Pacific, half a mile off, was so that I could inject a little excitement into my life and mingle with all the college students in the bars that lined State Street cheek to jowl, but here I was hanging out in an old man's bar that smelled of death and vomit and felt as closed-in as a submarine, when just outside the door were all the exotic sun-struck glories of California. Where it never rained. Except in winter. And it was winter now.

I nodded self-consciously at the six or seven regulars lined up at the bar, then ordered a Jack-and-Coke, the only drink besides beer I liked the taste of, and I didn't really like the taste of beer. There were sports on the three TVs hanging from the ceiling—this was a sports bar—but the volume was down and the speakers were blaring the same tired hits of the sixties I could have heard back home. Ad nauseam. When the bartender—*he* was young at least, as were the waitresses, thankfully—set down my drink, I made a comment about the weather, "Nice day for sunbathing, isn't it?" and the two regulars nearest me glanced up with something like interest in their eyes. "Or maybe bird-watching," I added, feeling encouraged, and they swung their heads back to the familiar triangulation of their splayed elbows and cocktail glasses and that was the end of that.

It must have been seven or so, the rain still coming down and people briefly enlivened by the novelty of it as they came and went in spasms of umbrella furling and unfurling, when a guy about my own age—or no, he must have been thirty, or close to it—came in and took the seat beside me. He was wearing a baseball cap, a jeans jacket and a T-shirt that said *Obligatory Death,* which I took to be the name of a band, though I'd never heard of them. His hair was blond, cut short around the ears, and he wore a soul beard that was like a pale stripe painted under his lip by a very unsteady hand. We exchanged the standard greeting—*What's up?*—and then he flagged down the bartender and ordered a draft beer, a shot of tomato juice and two raw eggs.

"Raw eggs?" the bartender echoed, as if he hadn't heard him right.

"Yeah. Two raw eggs, in the shell."

The bartender—his name was Chris, or maybe it was Matt—gave a smile and scratched the back of his head. "We can do them over-easy or sunny-side up or poached even, but *raw,* I don't know. I mean, nobody's ever requested raw before—"

"Ask the chef, why don't you?"

The bartender shrugged. "Sure," he said, "no problem." He started off in the direction of the kitchen, then pulled up short. "You want toast with that, home fries, or what?"

"Just the eggs."

Everybody was watching now, any little drama worth the price of admission, especially on a night like this, but the bartender—Chris, his name was definitely

Chris—just went down to the other end of the bar and communicated the order to the waitress, who made a notation in her pad and disappeared into the kitchen. A moment went by, and then the man turned to me and said in a voice loud enough for everybody to hear, "Jesus, this music sucks. Are we caught in a time warp here, or what?"

The old men—the regulars—glanced up from their drinks and gave him a look, but they were gray-haired and slack in the belly and they knew their limits. One of them said something about the game on the TV and one of the others chimed in and the conversation started back up in an exclusionary way.

"Yeah," I heard myself say, "it really sucks," and before I knew it I was talking passionately about the bands that meant the most to me even as the new guy poured tomato juice in his beer and sipped the foam off the top, while the music rumbled defiantly on and people came in the door with wet shoes and dripping umbrellas to crowd in behind us. The eggs, brown-shelled and naked in the middle of a standard dinner plate, were delivered by Daria, a waitress I'd had my eye on, though I hadn't yet worked up the nerve to say more than hello and goodbye to her. "Your order, sir," she said, easing the plate down on the bar. "You need anything with that? Ketchup? Tabasco?"

"No," he said, "no, that's fine," and everyone was waiting for him to crack the eggs over his beer, but he didn't even look at them. He was looking at Daria, holding her with his eyes. "So what's your name?" he asked, grinning.

She told him, and she was grinning too.

"Nice to meet you," he said, taking her hand. "I'm Ludwig."

"Ludwig," she repeated, pronouncing it with a hard *v*, as he had, though as far as I could tell—from his clothes and accent, which was pure Southern California—he wasn't German. Or if he was, he sure had his English down.

"Are you German?" Daria was flirting with him, and the realization of it began to harden me against him in the most rudimentary way.

"No," he said, "I'm from Hermosa Beach, born and raised. It's the name, right?"

"I had this German teacher last year? His name was Ludwig, that's all."

"You're in college?"

She told him she was, which was news to me. Working her way through. Majoring in business. She wanted to own her own restaurant someday.

"It was my mother's idea," he said, as if he'd been mulling it over. "She was listening to the 'Eroica' Symphony the night I was born." He shrugged. "It's been my curse ever since."

"I don't know," she said, "I think it's kind of cute. You don't get many Ludwigs, you know?"

"Yeah, tell me about it," he said, sipping at his beer.

She lingered, though there were other things she could have been doing. The sound of the rain intensified so that for a moment it overcame the drone of the speakers. "So what about the eggs," she said, "you going to need utensils, or—"

"Or what? Am I going to suck them out of the shell?"

"Yeah," she said, "something like that."

He reached out a hand cluttered with silver to embrace the eggs and gently roll them back and forth across the gleaming expanse of the plate. "No, I'm just going to fondle them," he said, and he got the expected response: she laughed. "But does anybody still play dice around here?" he called down the bar as the eyes of the regulars slid in our direction and then away again.

In those days—and this was ten years ago or more—the game of Horse was popular in certain California bars, as were smoking, unprotected sex and various other adult pleasures that may or may not have been hazardous to your health. There were five dice, shaken in a cup, and you slammed that cup down on the bar, trying for the highest cumulative score, which was thirty. Anything could be bet on, from the next round of drinks to ponying up for the jukebox.

The rain hissed at the door and it opened briefly to admit a stamping, umbrella-less couple. Ludwig's question hung unanswered on the air. "No? How about you, Daria?"

"I'm working, actually."

He turned to me. I had no work in the morning or the next morning either—maybe no work at all. My apartment wasn't what I'd thought it would be, not without anybody to share it with, and I'd already vowed to myself that I'd rather sleep on the streets than go back to my aunt's because going back there would represent the worst kind of defeat. *Take good care of my baby, Kim,* my mother had said when she'd dropped me off. *He's the only one I've got.*

"Sure," I said, "I guess. What're we playing for—for drinks, right?" I began fumbling in my pockets, awkward, shoulders dipping—I was drunk, I could feel it. "Because I don't have, well, maybe ten bucks—"

"No," he said, "no," already rising from his seat, "you just wait here, just one minute, you'll see," and then he was out the door and into the grip of the rain.

Daria hadn't moved. She was dressed in the standard outfit for Daggett's employees, shorts, white ankle socks and a T-shirt with the name of the establishment blazoned across the chest, her legs pale and silken in the flickering light of the fake fireplace in the corner. She gave me a sympathetic look and I shrugged to show her I was ready for anything, a real man of the world.

There was a noise at the door—a scraping and shifting—and we all looked up to see Ludwig struggling with something against the backdrop of the rain.

His hat had been knocked askew and water dripped from his nose and chin. It took a moment, one shoulder pinning the door open, and then he lifted a cage—a substantial cage, two and a half feet high and maybe four long—through the doorway and set it down against the wall. No one moved. No one said a word. There was something in the cage, the apprehension of it as sharp and sudden as the smell it brought with it, something wild and alien and very definitely out of the ordinary on what to this point had been a painfully ordinary night.

Ludwig wiped the moisture from his face with a swipe of his sleeve, straightened out his hat and came back to the bar, looking jaunty and refreshed. "All right," he said, "don't be shy—go have a look. It won't bite. Or it will, it definitely will, but just don't get your fingers near it, that's all—"

I saw coiled limbs, claws, yellow eyes. Whatever it was, the thing hadn't moved, not even to blink. I was going to ask what it was, when Daria, still at my side, said, "It's a cat, some kind of wild cat. Right? A what—a lynx or something?"

"You can't have that thing in here," one of the regulars said, but already he was getting up out of his seat to have a look at it—everyone was getting up now, shoving back chairs and rising from the tables, crowding around.

"It's a serval," Ludwig was saying. "From Africa. Thirty-five pounds of muscle and quicker than a snake."

And where had he gotten it? He'd won it, in a bar in Arizona, on a roll of the dice.

How long had he had it? Two years.

What was its name? Cat. Just Cat. And yes, it was a male, and no, he didn't want to get rid of it but he was moving overseas on a new job and there was just no way he could take it with him, so he felt it was apropos—that was the word he used, *apropos*—to give it up in the way he'd gotten it.

He turned to me. "What was your name again?"

"Junior," I said. "James Jr. Turner, I mean. James Turner Jr. But everybody calls me Junior." I wanted to add, "Because of my father, so people wouldn't confuse us," but I left it at that, because it got even more complicated considering that my father was six months dead and I could be anybody I wanted.

"Okay, Junior, here's the deal," Ludwig said. "Your ten bucks against the cat, one roll, what do you say?"

I wanted to say that I had no place for the thing, that I didn't want a cat of any kind or even a guinea pig or a fish in a bowl and that the ten dollars was meaningless, but everyone was watching me and I couldn't back out without feeling the shame rise to my face—and there was Daria to consider, because she was watching me too. "Yeah," I said. "Yeah, okay, sure."

Sixty seconds later I was still solvent and richer by one cat and one cage. I'd gotten lucky—or unlucky, depending on how you want to look at it—and rolled three fives and two fours; Ludwig rolled a combined eleven. He finished his beer in a gulp, took my hand to seal the deal and offer his congratulations, and then started toward the door. "But what do I feed it?" I called. "I mean, what does it eat?"

"Eggs," he said, "it loves eggs. And meat. Raw. No kibble, forget kibble. This is the real deal, this animal, and you need to treat it right." He was at the door, looking down at the thing with what might have been wistfulness or satisfaction, I couldn't tell which, then he reached down behind the cage to unfasten something there—a gleam of black leather—and toss it to me: it was a glove, or a gauntlet actually, as long as my arm. "You'll want to wear this when you feed him," he said, and then he was gone.

For a long moment I stared at the door, trying to work out what had happened, and then I looked at the regulars—the expressions on their faces—and at the other customers, locals or maybe even tourists who'd come in for a beer or burger or the catch of the day and had all this strangeness thrust on them, and finally at the cage. Daria was bent beside it, cooing to the animal inside, Ludwig's eggs cradled in one hand. She was short and compact, conventionally pretty, with the round eyes and symmetrical features of an anime heroine, her running shoes no bigger than a child's, her blond hair pulled back in a ponytail, and I'd noticed all that before, over the course of weeks of study, but now it came back to me with the force of revelation. She was beautiful, a beautiful girl propped on one knee while her shorts rode up in back and the T-shirt bunched beneath her breasts, offering this cat—my cat—the smallest comfort, as if it were a kitten she'd found abandoned on the street.

"Jesus, what are you going to do with the thing?" Chris had come out from behind the bar and he was standing beside me now, looking awed.

I told him I didn't know. That I hadn't planned on owning a wild cat, hadn't even known they existed—servals, that is—until five minutes ago.

"You live around here?"

"Bayview Apartments."

"They accept pets?"

I'd never really given it much thought, but they did, they must have—the guy next door to me had a pair of yapping little dogs with bows in their hair and the woman down the hall had a Doberman that was forever scrabbling its nails on the linoleum when she came in and out with it, which she seemed to do about a hundred times a day. But this was something different. This was something that might push at the parameters of the standard lease. "Yeah," I said, "I think so."

There was a single slot where the door of the cage fastened that was big enough to receive an egg without crushing its shell, and Daria, still cooing, rolled first one egg, then the other, through the aperture. For a moment, nothing happened. Then the cat, hunched against the mesh, shifted position ever so slightly and took the first egg in its mouth—two teeth like hypodermics, a crunch, and then the soft frictive scrape of its tongue.

Daria rose and came to me with a look of wonder. "Don't do a thing till I get off, okay?" she said, and in her fervor she took hold of my arm. "I get off at nine, so you wait, okay?"

"Yeah," I said. "Sure."

"We can put him in the back of the storage room for now, and then, well, I guess we can use my pickup—"

I didn't have the leisure to reflect on how complex things had become all of a sudden, and even if I had I don't think I would have behaved any differently. I just nodded at her, stared into her plenary eyes and nodded.

"He's going to be all right," she said, and added, "He will," as if I'd been disagreeing with her. "I've got to get back to work, but you wait, okay? You wait right here." Chris was watching. The manager was watching. The regulars had all craned their necks and half the dinner customers too. Daria patted down her apron, smoothed back her hair. "What did you say your name was again?"

So I had a cat. And a girl. We put the thing in the back of her red Toyota pickup, threw a tarp over it to keep the rain off, and drove to Von's, where I watched Daria march up and down the aisles seeking out kitty litter and the biggest cat pan they had (we settled for a dishpan, hard blue plastic that looked all but indestructible), and then it was on to the meat counter. "I've only got ten bucks," I said.

She gave me a withering look. "This animal's got to eat," she informed me, and she reached back to slip the band from her ponytail so that her hair fell glistening across her shoulders, a storm of hair, fluid and loose, the ends trailing down her back like liquid in motion. She tossed her head impatiently. "You do have a credit card, don't you?"

Ten minutes later I was directing her back to my building, where I had her park next to the Mustang I'd inherited when my father died, and then we went up the outside stairs and along the walkway to my apartment on the second floor. "I'm sorry," I said, swinging open the door and hitting the light switch, "but I'm afraid I'm not much of a housekeeper." I was going to add that I hadn't expected company either, or I would have straightened up, but Daria just strode right in, cleared a spot on the counter and set down the groceries. I watched her shoulders as she reached into the depths of one bag after another and extracted the forty-odd dollars' worth of chicken parts and ribeye steak (marked down for quick sale) we'd selected in the meat department.

"Okay," she said, turning to me as soon as she'd made space in the refrigerator for it all, "now where are we going to put the cat, because I don't think we should leave it out there in the truck any longer than we have to, do you? Cats don't like the rain, I know that—I have two of them. Or one's a kitten really." She was on the other side of the kitchen counter, a clutter of crusted dishes and glasses sprouting various colonies of mold separating us. "You have a bedroom, right?"

I did. But if I was embarrassed by the state of the kitchen and living room—this was my first venture at living alone, and the need for order hadn't really seemed paramount to me—then the thought of the bedroom, with its funk of dirty clothes and unwashed sheets, the reeking workboots and the duffel bag out of which I'd been living, gave me pause. Here was this beautiful apparition in my kitchen, the only person besides my aunt who'd ever stepped through the door of my apartment, and now she was about to discover the sad lonely disorder at the heart of my life. "Yeah," I said, "that door there, to the left of the bathroom," but she was already in the room, pushing things aside, a frown of concentration pressed between her eyes.

"You're going to have to clear this out," she said. "The bed, everything. All your clothes."

I was standing in the doorway, watching her. "What do you mean 'clear it out'?"

She lifted her face. "You don't think that animal can stay caged up like that, do you? There's hardly room for it to turn around. And that's just cruel." She drilled me with that look again, then put her hands on her hips. "I'll help you," she said. "It shouldn't take ten minutes—"

Then it was up the stairs with the cat, the two of us fighting the awkwardness of the cage. We kept the tarp knotted tightly in place, both to keep the rain off the cat and disguise it from any of my neighbors who might happen by, and though we shifted the angle of the thing coming up the stairs, the animal didn't make a sound. We had a little trouble getting the cage through the doorway—the cat seemed to concentrate its weight as if in silent protest—but we managed, and then we maneuvered it into the bedroom and set it down in the middle of the rug. Daria had already arranged the litter box in the corner, atop several sheets of newspaper, and she'd taken my biggest stewpot, filled it with water and placed it just inside the door, where I could get to it easily. "Okay," she said, glancing up at me with a satisfied look, "it's time for the unveiling," and she bent to unfasten the tarp.

The overhead light glared, the tarp slid from the cage and puddled on the floor, and there was the cat, pressed to the mesh in a compression of limbs, the yellow eyes seizing on us. "Nice kitty," Daria cooed. "Does he want out of that awful cage? Hmm? Does he? And meat—does he want meat?"

So far, I'd gone along with everything in a kind of daze, but this was problematic. Who knew what the thing would do, what its habits were, its needs? "How are we going to—?" I began, and left the rest unspoken. The overhead light glared down on me and the alcohol whispered in my blood. "You remember what that guy said about feeding him, right?" In the back of my head, there was the smallest glimmer of a further complication: once he was out of the cage, how would we—how would I—ever get him back into it?

For the first time, Daria looked doubtful. "We'll have to be quick," she said.

And so we were. Daria stood at the bedroom door, ready to slam it shut, while I leaned forward, my heart pounding, and slipped the release bolt on the cage. I was nimble in those days—twenty-three years old and with excellent reflexes despite the four or five Jack-and-Cokes I'd downed through the course of the evening—and I sprang for the door the instant the bolt was released. Exhilaration burned in me. And it burned in the cat too, because at the first click of the bolt it came to life as if it had been hot-wired. A screech tore through the room, the cage flew open and the thing was an airborne blur slamming against the cheap plywood panel of the bedroom door, even as Daria and I fought to force it shut.

In the morning (she'd slept on the couch, curled up in the fetal position, faintly snoring; I was stretched out on the mattress we'd removed from the bedroom and tucked against the wall under the TV) I was faced with a number of problems. I'd awakened before her, jolted out of a dreamless sleep by a flash of awareness, and for a long while I just lay there watching her. I could have gone on watching her all morning, thrilled by her presence, her hair, the repose of her face, if it weren't for the cat. It hadn't made a sound, and it didn't stink, not yet, but its existence was communicated to me nonetheless—it was there, and I could feel it. I would have to feed it, and after the previous night's episode, that was going to require some thought and preparation, and I would have to offer Daria something too, if only to hold her here a little longer. Eggs, I could scramble some eggs, but there was no bread for toast, no milk, no sugar for the coffee. And she would want to freshen up in the bathroom—women always freshened up in the morning, I was pretty sure of that. I thought of the neatly folded little matching towels in the guest bathroom at my aunt's and contrasted that image with the corrugated rag wadded up on the floor somewhere in my own bathroom. Maybe I should go out for muffins or bagels or something, I thought—and a new towel. But did they sell towels at the 7-Eleven? I didn't have a clue.

We'd stayed up late, sharing the last of the hot cocoa out of the foil packet and talking in a specific way about the cat that had brought us to that moment on my greasy couch in my semi-darkened living room and then more generally about our own lives and thoughts and hopes and ambitions. I'd heard about her mother, her two sisters, the courses she was taking at the university. Heard about Daggett's, the regulars, the tips—or lack of them. And her restaurant fantasy. It was amazingly detailed, right down to the number of tables she was planning on, the dinnerware, the cutlery and the paintings on the walls, as well as the decor and the clientele—"Late twenties, early thirties, career people, no kids"—and a dozen or more of the dishes she would specialize in. My ambitions were more modest. I told her how I'd finished community college without any particular aim or interest, and how I was working setting tile for a friend of my aunt and uncle's; beyond that, I was hoping to maybe travel up the coast and see Oregon. I'd heard a lot about Oregon, I told her. Very clean. Very natural up there. Had she ever been to Oregon? No, but she'd like to go. I remembered telling her that she ought to open her restaurant up there, someplace by the water, where people could look out and take in the view. "Yeah," she said, "yeah, that would be cool," and then she'd yawned and dropped her head to the pillow.

I was just getting up to go to the bathroom and to see what I could do about the towel in there, thinking vaguely of splashing some aftershave on it to fight down any offensive odors it might have picked up, when her eyes flashed open. She didn't say my name or wonder where she was or ask for breakfast or where the bathroom was. She just said, "We have to feed that cat."

"Don't you want coffee or anything—breakfast? I can make breakfast."

She threw back the blanket and I saw that her legs were bare—she was wearing the Daggett's T-shirt over a pair of shiny black panties; her running shoes, socks and shorts were balled up on the rug beneath her. "Sure," she said, "coffee sounds nice," and she pushed her fingers through her hair on both sides of her head and then let it all fall forward to obscure her face. She sat there a moment before leaning forward to dig a hair clip out of her purse, arch her back and pull the hair tight in a ponytail. "But I am worried about the cat, in new surroundings and all. The poor thing—we should have fed him last night."

Perhaps so. And certainly I didn't want to contradict her—I wanted to be amicable and charming, wanted to ingratiate myself in any way I could—but we'd both been so terrified of the animal's power in that moment when we'd released it from the cage that neither of us had felt up to the challenge of attempting to feed it. Attempting to feed it would mean opening that door again and that was going to take some thought and commitment. "Yeah," I said. "We should have. And we will, we will, but coffee, coffee first—you want a cup? I can make you a cup?"

So we drank coffee and ate the strawberry Pop-Tarts I found in the cupboard above the sink and made small talk as if we'd awakened together a hundred mornings running and it was so tranquil and so domestic and so right I never wanted it to end. We were talking about work and about what time she had to be in that afternoon, when her brow furrowed and her eyes sharpened and she said, "I wish I could see it. When we feed it, I mean. Couldn't you like cut a peephole in the door or something?"

I was glad for the distraction, damage deposit notwithstanding. And the idea appealed to me: now we could see what the thing—my pet—was up to, and if we could see it, then it wouldn't seem so unapproachable and mysterious. I'd have to get to know it eventually, have to name it and tame it, maybe even walk it on a leash. I had a brief vision of myself sauntering down the sidewalk, this id with claws at my side, turning heads and cowing the weight lifters with their Dobermans and Rottweilers, and then I fished my power drill out from under the sink and cut a neat hole, half an inch in diameter, in the bedroom door. As soon as it was finished, Daria put her eye to it.

"Well?"

"The poor thing. He's pacing back and forth like an animal in a zoo."

She moved to the side and took my arm as I pressed my eye to the hole. The cat flowed like molten ore from one corner of the room to the other, its yellow eyes fixed on the door, the dun, faintly spotted skin stretched like spandex over its seething muscles. I saw that the kitty litter had been upended and the hard blue plastic pan reduced to chewed-over pellets, and wondered about that, about where the thing would do its business if not in the pan. "It turned over the kitty pan," I said.

She was still holding to my arm. "I know."

"It chewed it to shreds."

"Metal. We'll have to get a metal one, like a trough or something."

I took my eye from the peephole and turned to her. "But how am I going to change it—don't you have to change it?"

Her eyes were shining. "Oh, it'll settle down. It's just a big kitty, that's all"—and then for the cat, in a syrupy coo—"Isn't that right, kittums?" Next, she went to the refrigerator and extracted one of the steaks, a good pound and a half of meat. "Put on the glove," she said, "and I'll hold on to the doorknob while you feed him."

"What about the blood—won't the blood get on the carpet?" The gauntlet smelled of saddle soap and it was gouged and pitted down the length of it; it fit me as if it had been custom-made.

"I'll press the blood out with a paper towel—here, look," she said, dabbing at the meat in the bottom of the sink and then lifting it on the end of a fork. I took the fork from her and together we went to the bedroom door.

I don't know if the cat scented the blood or whether it heard us at the door, but the instant I turned the knob it was there. I counted three, then jerked the door back just enough to get my arm and the dangle of meat into the room even as the cat exploded against the doorframe and the meat vanished. We pulled the door to—Daria's face was flushed and she seemed to be giggling or gasping for air—and then we took turns watching the thing drag the steak back and forth across the rug as if it still needed killing. By the time it was done, there was blood everywhere, even on the ceiling.

After Daria left for work I didn't know what to do with myself. The cat was ominously silent and when I pressed my eye to the peephole I saw that it had dragged its cage into the far corner and was slumped behind it, apparently asleep. I flicked on the TV and sat through the usual idiocy, which was briefly enlivened by a nature show on the Serengeti that gave a cursory glimpse of a cat like mine—*The serval lives in rocky kopjes where it keeps a wary eye on its enemies, the lion and hyena, feeding principally on small prey, rabbits, birds, even snakes and lizards,* the narrator informed me in a hushed voice—and then I went to the sandwich shop and ordered the Number 7 special, no mayo, and took it down to the beach. It was a clear day, all the haze and particulate matter washed clean of the air by the previous day's deluge, and I sat there with the sun on my face and watched the waves ride in on top of one another while I ate and considered the altered condition of my life. Daria's face had gotten serious as she stood at the door, her T-shirt rumpled, her hair pulled back so tightly from her scalp I could make out each individual strand. "Take care of our cat now, okay?" she said. "I'll be back as soon as I get off." I shrugged in a helpless, submissive way, the pain of her leaving as acute as anything I'd ever felt. "Sure," I said, and then she reached for my shoulders and pulled me to her for a kiss—on the lips. "You're sweet," she said.

So I was sweet. No one had ever called me sweet before, not since childhood anyway, and I have to admit the designation thrilled me, bloomed inside me like the promise of things to come. I began to see her as a prime mover in my life, her naked legs stretched out on the couch, the hair falling across her shoulders at the kitchen table, her lips locked on mine. But as I sat there eating my ham-and-cheese wrap, a conflicting thought came to me: there had to be someone in her life already, a girl that beautiful, working in a bar, and I was deluding myself to think I had a chance with her. She had to have a boyfriend—she could even be engaged, for all I knew. I tried to focus on the previous night, on her hands and fingers—had she been wearing a ring? And if she had, then where was the fiancé, the boyfriend, whoever he was? I hated him already, and I didn't know if he even existed.

The upshot of all this was that I found myself in the cool subterranean glow of Daggett's at three-thirty in the afternoon, nursing a Jack-and-Coke like one of the regulars while Daria, the ring finger of her left hand as unencumbered as mine, went round clearing up after the lunch crowd and setting the tables for the dinner rush. Chris came on at five, and he called me by my name and refreshed my drink before he even glanced at the regulars, and for the next hour or so, during the lulls, we conversed about any number of things, beginning with the most obvious—the cat—but veering into sports, music, books and films, and I found myself expanding into a new place altogether. At one point, Daria stopped by to ask if the cat was settling in—Was he still pacing around neurotically or what?—and I could tell her with some assurance that he was asleep. "He's probably nocturnal," I said, "or something like that." And then, with Chris looking on, I couldn't help adding, "You're still coming over, right? After work? To help me feed him, I mean."

She looked to Chris, then let her gaze wander out over the room. "Oh, yeah," she said, "yeah," and there was a catch of hesitation in her voice, "I'll be there."

I let that hang a moment, but I was insecure and the alcohol was having its effect and I couldn't leave it alone. "We can drive over together," I said, "because I didn't bring my car."

She was looking tired by the end of her shift, the bounce gone out of her step, her hair a shade duller under the drab lights, and even as I switched to coffee I noticed Chris slipping her a shot of something down at the end of the bar. I'd had a sandwich around six, and then, so as not to seem overanxious, I'd taken a walk, which brought me into another bar down the street, where I had a Jack-and-Coke and didn't say a word to anyone, and then I'd returned at eight to drink coffee and watch her and hold her to her promise.

We didn't say much on the way over to my place. It was only a five-minute drive, and there was a song on we both liked. Plus, it seemed to me that when you were comfortable with someone you could respect the silences. I'd gone to the cash machine earlier and in a hopeful mood stocked up on breakfast things—eggs, English muffins, a quart each of no-fat and two-percent milk, an expensive Chinese tea that came in individual foil packets—and I'd picked up two bottles of a local chardonnay that was supposed to be really superior, or at least that was what the guy in the liquor department had told me, as well as a bag of corn chips and a jar of salsa. There were two new bathroom towels hanging on the rack beside the medicine cabinet and I'd given the whole place a good vacuuming and left the dishes to soak in a sink of scalding water and the last few molecules of dish soap left in the plastic container I'd brought with me from my aunt's. The final touch was a pair of clean sheets and a light blanket folded suggestively over the arm of the couch.

Daria didn't seem to notice—she went straight to the bedroom door and affixed her eye to the peephole. "I can't see anything," she said, leaning into the door in her shorts, the muscles of her calves flexing as she went up on her toes. "It's too bad we didn't think of a night light or something—"

I was watching her out of the corner of my eye—admiring her, amazed all over again at her presence—while working the corkscrew in the bottle. I asked her if she'd like a glass of wine. "Chardonnay," I said. "It's a local one, really superior."

"I'd love a glass," she said, turning away from the door and crossing the room to me. I didn't have wine glasses, so we made do with the milky-looking water glasses my aunt had dug out of a box in her basement. "But I wonder if you could maybe slip your arm in the door and turn on the light in there," she said. "I'm worried about him. And plus, we've got to feed him again, right?"

"Sure," I said, "yeah, no problem," but I was in no hurry. I refilled our glasses and broke out the corn chips and salsa, which she seemed happy enough to see. For a long while we stood at the kitchen counter, dipping chips and savoring the wine, and then she went to the refrigerator, extracted a slab of meat, and began patting it down with paper towels. I took her cue, donned the gauntlet, braced myself and jerked the bedroom door open just enough to get my hand in and flick on the light. The cat, which of course had sterling night vision, nearly tore the glove from my arm, and yet the suddenness of the light seemed to confuse it just long enough for me to salvage the situation. The door slammed on a puzzled yowl.

Daria immediately put her eye to the peephole. "Oh my God," she murmured.

"What's he doing?"

"Pacing. But here, you have a look."

The carpeting—every last strip of it—had been torn out of the floor, leaving an expanse of dirty plywood studded with nails, and there seemed to be a hole in the plasterboard just to the left of the window. A substantial hole. Even through the closed door I could smell the reek of cat piss or spray or whatever it was. "There goes my deposit," I said.

She was right there beside me, her hand on my shoulder. "He'll settle down," she assured me, "once he gets used to the place. All cats are like that—they have to establish their territory, is all."

"You don't think he can get inside the walls, do you?"

"No," she said, "no way, he's too big—"

The only thing I could think to do, especially after an entire day of drinking, was to pour more wine, which I did. Then we repeated the ritual of the morning's feeding—the steak on the fork, the blur of the cat, the savage thump at the door—and took turns watching it eat. After a while, bored with the spectacle—or "sated," maybe that's a better word—we found ourselves on the couch and there was a movie on TV and we finished the wine and the chips and we never stopped talking, a comment on this movie leading to a discussion of movies in general, a reflection on the wine dredging up our mutual experiences of wine tastings and the horrors of Cribari red and Boone's Farm and all the rest. It was midnight before we knew it and she was yawning and stretching.

"I've really got to get home," she said, but she didn't move. "I'm wiped. Just wiped."

"You're welcome to stay over," I said, "I mean, if you don't want to drive, after all the wine and all—"

A moment drifted by, neither of us speaking, and then she made a sort of humming noise—"Mmmm"—and held out her arms to me even as she sank down into the couch.

I was up before her in the morning, careful not to wake her as I eased myself from the mattress where we'd wound up sleeping because the couch was too narrow for the two of us. My head ached—I wasn't used to so much alcohol—and the effigy of the cat lurked somewhere behind that ache, but I felt buoyant and optimistic. Daria was asleep on the mattress, the cat was hunkered down in his room, and all was right with the world. I brewed coffee, toasted muffins and fried eggs, and when she woke I was there to feed her. "What do you say to breakfast in bed?" I murmured, easing down beside her with a plate of eggs over-easy and a mug of coffee.

I was so intent on watching her eat I barely touched my own food. After a while, I got up and turned on the radio and there was that song again, the one we'd heard coming home the night before, and we both listened to it all the way through without saying a word. When the disc jockey came on with his gasping juvenile voice and lame jokes, she got up and went to the bathroom, passing right by the bedroom door without a thought for the cat. She was in the bathroom a long while, running water, flushing, showering, and I felt lost without her. I wanted to tell her I loved her, wanted to extend a whole list of invitations to her: she could move in with me, stay here indefinitely, bring her cats with her, no problem, and we could both look after the big cat together, see to its needs, tame it and make it happy in its new home—no more cages, and meat, plenty of meat. I was scrubbing the frying pan when she emerged, her hair wrapped in one of the new towels. She was wearing her makeup and she was dressed in her Daggett's outfit. "Hey," I said.

She didn't answer. She was bent over the couch now, stuffing things into her purse.

"You look terrific," I said.

There was a sound from the bedroom then, a low moan that might have been the expiring gasp of the cat's prey and I wondered if it had found something in there, a rat, a stray bird attracted to the window, an escaped hamster or lizard. "Listen, Junior," she said, ignoring the moaning, which grew higher and more attenuated now, "you're a nice guy, you really are."

I was behind the Formica counter. My hands were in the dishwater. Something pounded in my head and I knew what was coming, heard it in her voice, saw it in the way she ducked her head and averted her eyes.

"I can't—I have to tell you something, okay? Because you're sweet, you are, and I want to be honest with you."

She raised her face to me all of a sudden, let her eyes stab at mine and then dodge away again. "I have a boyfriend. He's away at school. And I don't know why . . . I mean, I just don't want to give you the wrong impression. It was nice. It was."

The moaning cut off abruptly on a rising note. I didn't know what to say—I was new at this, new and useless. Suddenly I was desperate, looking for anything, any stratagem, the magic words that would make it all right again. "The cat," I said. "What about the cat?"

Her voice was soft. "He'll be all right. Just feed him. Be nice to him." She was at the door, the purse slung over one shoulder. "Patience," she said, "that's all it takes. A little patience."

"Wait," I said. "Wait."

"I've got to go."

"Will I see you later?"

"No," she said. "No, I don't think so."

As soon as her pickup pulled out of the lot, I called my boss. He answered on the first ring, raising his voice to be heard over the ambient noise. I could hear the tile saw going in the background, the irregular banging of a hammer, the radio tuned to some jittery rightwing propagandist. "I want to come in," I said.

"Who is this?"

"Junior."

"Monday, Monday at the earliest."

I told him I was going crazy cooped up in my apartment, but he didn't seem to hear me. "What is it?" he said. "Money? Because I'll advance you on next week if you really need it, though it'll mean a trip to the bank I wasn't planning on. Which is a pain in the ass. But I'll do it. Just say the word."

"No, it's not the money, it's just—"

He cut me off. "Don't you ever listen to anything I say? Didn't I tell you to go out and get yourself laid? That's what you're supposed to be doing at your age. It's what I'd be doing."

"Can't I just, I don't know, help out?"

"Monday," he said.

I was angry suddenly and I slammed the phone down. My eyes went to the hole cut in the bedroom door and then to the breakfast plates, egg yolk congealing there in bright yellow stripes, the muffin, Daria's muffin, untouched but for a single neat bite cut out of the round. It was Friday. I hated my life. How could I have been so stupid?

There was no sound from the bedroom, and as I laced my sneakers I fought down the urge to go to the peephole and see what the cat had accomplished in the night—I just didn't want to think about it. Whether it had vanished like the bad odor of a bad dream or chewed through the wall and devoured the neighbor's yapping little dogs or broken loose and smuggled itself onto a boat back to Africa, it was all the same to me. The only thing I did know was that there was no way I was going to attempt to feed that thing on my own, not without Daria there. It could starve for all I cared, starve and rot.

Eventually, I fished a jean jacket out of a pile of clothes on the floor and went down to the beach. The day was overcast and a cold wind out of the east scoured the sand. I must have walked for hours and then, for lack of anything better to do, I went to a movie, after which I had a sandwich at a new place downtown where the college students were rumored to hang out. There were no students there as far as I could see, just old men who looked exactly like the regulars at Daggett's, and they had their square-shouldered old wives with them and their squalling unhappy children. By four I hit my first bar, and by six I was drunk.

I tried to stay away from Daggett's—*Give her a day or two,* I told myself, *don't nag, don't be a burden*—but at quarter of nine I found myself at the bar, ordering a Jack-and-Coke from Chris. Chris gave me a look, and everything had changed since yesterday. "You sure?" he said.

I asked him what he meant.

"You look like you've had enough, buddy."

I craned my neck to look for Daria, but all I saw were the regulars, hunched over their drinks. "Just pour," I said.

The music was there like a persistent annoyance, dead music, ancient, appreciated by no one, not even the regulars. It droned on. Chris set down my drink and I lifted it to my lips. "Where's Daria?" I asked.

"She got off early. Said she was tired. Slow night, you know?"

I felt a stab of disappointment, jealousy, hate. "You have a number for her?"

Chris gave me a wary look, because he knew something I didn't. "You mean she didn't give you her number?"

"No," I said, "we never—well, she was *at* my house . . ."

"We can't give out personal information."

"To me? I said she was at my house. Last night. I need to talk to her, and it's urgent—about the cat. She's really into the cat, you know?"

"Sorry."

I threw it back at him. "You're sorry? Well, fuck you—I'm sorry too."

"You know what, buddy—"

"Junior, the name's Junior."

He leaned into the bar, both arms propped before him, and in a very soft voice he said, "I think you better leave now."

It had begun to rain, a soft patter in the leaves that grew steadier and harder as I walked home. Cars went by on the boulevard with the sound of paper tearing, and they dragged whole worlds behind them. The streetlights were dim. There was nobody out. When I came up the hill to my apartment I saw the Mustang standing there under the carport, and though I'd always been averse to drinking and driving—a lesson I'd learned from my father's hapless example—I got behind the wheel and drove up to the jobsite with a crystalline clarity that would have scared me in any other state of mind. There was an aluminum ladder there, and I focused on that—the picture of it lying against the building—till I arrived and hauled it out of the mud and tied it to the roof of the car without a thought for the paint job or anything else.

When I got back, I fumbled in the rain with the overzealous knots I'd tied until I got the ladder free and then I hauled it around the back of the apartment.

I was drunk, yes, but cautious too—if anyone had seen me, in the dark, propping a ladder against the wall of an apartment building, even my own apartment building, things could have gotten difficult in a hurry. I couldn't very well claim to be painting, could I? Not at night. Not in the rain. Luckily, though, no one was around. I made my way up the ladder, and when I got to the level of the bedroom the odor hit me, a rank fecal wind sifting out of the dark slit of the window. The cat. The cat was in there, watching me. I was sure of it. I must have waited there in the rain for fifteen minutes or more before I got up the nerve to fling the window open, and then I ducked my head and crouched reflexively against the wall. Nothing happened. After a moment, I made my way down the ladder.

I didn't want to go in the apartment, didn't want to think about it, didn't know if a cat of that size could climb down the rungs of a ladder or leap twenty feet into the air or unfurl its hidden wings and fly. I stood and watched the dense black hole of the window for a long while and then I went back to the car and sat listening to the radio in the dark till I fell asleep.

In the morning—there were no heraldic rays of sunshine, nothing like that, just more rain—I let myself into the apartment and crept across the room as stealthily as if I'd come to burgle it. When I reached the bedroom door, I put my eye to the peephole and saw a mound of carpet propped up against an empty cage—a den, a makeshift den—and only then did I begin to feel something for the cat, for its bewilderment, its fear and distrust of an alien environment: this was no rocky kopje, this was my bedroom on the second floor of a run-down apartment building in a seaside town a whole continent and a fathomless ocean away from its home. Nothing moved inside. Surely it must be gone, one great leap and then the bounding limbs, grass beneath its feet, solid earth. It was gone. Sure it was. I steeled myself, pulled open the door and slipped inside. And then—and I don't know why—I pulled the door shut behind me.

(2003)

Almost Shooting an Elephant

So we went in there with Meghalaya Cable, a subsidiary of Verizon (don't ask, because I couldn't begin to tell you: just think multinational, that's all), and put in the grid so these people could have color TV and DSL hookups in their huts, and I brought a couple rifles with me. I like to hunt, all right? So crucify me. I grew up in Iowa, in Ottumwa, and it was a rare day when I didn't bring something home for my mother, whether it was ringneck or rabbit or even a gopher or muskrat, which are not bad eating if you stew them up with tomatoes and onions, and plus you get your fur. I had to pay an excess baggage charge, which the company declined to pick up, but there was no way I was going to India without my guns. Especially since this leg of the project was in the West Garo Hills, where they still have the kind of jungle they had in Kipling's day. Or at least remnants of it.

Anyway, it was my day off and I was lying up in my tent, slapping mosquitoes and leafing through a back issue of *Guns & Ammo,* the birds screeching in the trees, the heat delivering one knockout punch after another till I could barely hold my head up. I wouldn't say I was bored—I was putting in a six-day workweek stringing wire to one ramshackle village after another, and just to lie there and feel the cot give under my bones was a luxury. Still, it felt as if the hands of my watch hadn't moved in the last hour and as I drifted in and out of sleep the birds always seemed to be hitting the same note. I tried to relax, enjoy the moment and the magazine, but I was only waiting for the heat to let up so I could take my .22 and a jar of the local rice beer down the hill to the swamp and see what was stirring in the bushes.

I was studying the ads in the back of the magazine—a party in Wishbone, Montana, was offering a classic Mannlicher-Schoenauer carbine with a Monte Carlo stock for sale or trade, a weapon I would have killed for—when I heard the sound of footsteps approaching on the path up from the village. Flip-flops. You could hear them a mile away, a slap, a shuffle, another slap, and then a quick burst: *slap, slap, slap.* There was a pause and I felt the bamboo platform rock ever so slightly.

The birds stopped screeching, all at once, as if the point of contention, whatever it was, had slipped their bird brains. A smell of meat roasting over the open fire came wafting up the hill on the first hint of an evening breeze. In the sudden hush I heard the frogs belching in the ditch behind me and the faintest thumping strains of Lynyrd Skynyrd's "Free Bird" from a radio in one of the other tents. "Randall? You in there?" came a voice just outside the front flap.

This was a female voice, and my hope (notwithstanding the fact that I was, and am, totally attached to Jenny, who I'm saving to buy a condo with in Des Moines) was that it was Poonam. Poonam was from Bombay, she wore tight jeans and little knit blouses that left her midriff bare, and she was doing her Ph.D. thesis on the Garos and their religious beliefs. She'd been waiting for me with a bottle of gin and a plate of curry when I got off work two days earlier, and I have to admit that the sound of her voice—she spoke very softly, so you had to strain to hear—put me in a sort of trance that wouldn't seem to let up, and I'd begun to entertain thoughts about what she might look like without the jeans and blouse. All she could talk about was her research, of course, and that was fine by me, because with the gin and the curry and the sweet, soft music of her voice she could have been lecturing on the Bombay sewer system and I would have been rooted to the spot. (And what *did* the Garos believe in? Well, they called themselves Christians—they'd been converted under the British Raj—but in actuality they were animists, absolutely dead certain that spirits inhabited the trees, the earth, the creatures of the forest, and that those spirits were just about universally evil. That is, life was shit—rats in the granaries, elephants obliterating the fields, kraits and cobras killing the children the leopards hadn't made off with, floods and droughts and diseases that didn't even have names—and whoever was responsible for it had to be as malicious as a whole squad of devils.)

So I said, "Yeah, I'm here," expecting Poonam, expecting gin, religion, and a sweet little roll of belly flesh I could almost taste with the tip of a stiff tongue going south, and who should part the flaps but Candi Berkee, my co-worker from New Jersey whose presence there, in my tent in the West Garo Hills, was a real testimony to Verizon's commitment to equal-opportunity employment.

"Hi," she said.

"'S up?" I said.

She gave a sort of full-body shrug, her lips crushed together under the weight of her nose and the *Matrix*-style shades that never left her face, then ducked through the flaps and flopped down in my camp chair. Which was piled high with six or seven sedimentary layers of used socks, underwear, and T-shirts I refrained from tossing on the floor for fear of what might end up living inside them. "I don't know," she said, dropping her face as if she were emptying a pan of dishwater, "I'm just bored. This is a boring place. The most boring place in the world. Number one. Know what I mean?"

It wasn't that she was unattractive—bodywise, she was off the charts—but there was something about her that irritated me, and it went beyond her unrelenting whining about the heat, the mosquitoes, the food, the tedium, and anything else she could think of. For one thing, she was a militant vegetarian who regarded anyone who even thought of hunting as the lowest of the low, a step below the average Al Qaeda terrorist ("At least they *believe* in something"). For another, her taste in music—Britney, Whitney, and Mariah—was as pathetic as you could get. The fact that she was in my tent was a strong indicator that everybody else must have gone into Tura, the nearest excuse for a city. Either that or committed suicide.

I didn't respond. The cot cupped my bones. She was wearing shorts and a bikini top, and there was a bright sheen of sweat on her exposed flesh that made her look as if she'd been greased for the flagpole event at the county fair. The birds started in again: *screech, screech, screech.*

"You want to smoke out?"

She knew I had pot. I knew she had pot. Everybody had pot. The whole country was made out of it. I was about to beg off on the grounds that I had to keep my senses sharp for putting bullets into whatever might be creeping down to the river to sneak a drink, be it muntjac or macaque, but thought better of it—I was in no mood for a lecture. "Nah," I said finally, sucking all the enthusiasm out of my voice. "I don't think so. Not today."

"Why not?" She shoved her sweat-limp hair out of her eyes and gave me an accusatory look. "Come on, don't be a pussy. Help me out here. I'm bored. Did I tell you that? Bored with a capital *B*."

I don't know whether the birds cut off before or after the sound of a second pair of flip-flops came to me, but there it was—the slap, the shuffle, and then the give of the bamboo floor. "Hello?" Poonam's voice. "Hello, Randall?"

Poonam wasn't exactly overjoyed to see Candi there, and for her part, Candi wasn't too thrilled either. I'd been up front with both of them about Jenny, but when you're away from home and affection long enough, strange things begin to happen, and I suppose hunting can only take you so far. As a distraction, that is.

"Oh . . . hi," Poonam murmured, shifting her eyes from me to Candi and back again. "I was just—" She looked down at the floor. "I was just coming for Randall, because the Wangala celebration is about to begin, or the drumming anyway—we won't see the dancing till tomorrow, officially—and I wondered if, well" (up came the eyes, full and bright, like high beams on a dark country road), "if you wanted to come with me to the village and see what they're doing—the ritual, I mean. Because it's, well, I find it stimulating. And I think you would too, Randall." She turned to Candi then, because Poonam was graceful and pretty and she had manners to spare. "And you too, Candi. You're welcome too."

I'm no expert, but from what Poonam told me, the Garos have a number of celebrations during the year, no different from the puffed-up Christians of Ottumwa and environs, and this one—Wangala—was a harvest festival. Think Thanksgiving, but a whole lot more primitive. Or maybe "rootsier" is a better word. Who are *we* thanking? God, supposedly, but in Ottumwa, it's more like Walmart or Hy-Vee. The Garos, on the other hand, are doing obeisance to Saljong, god of fertility, who provides nature's bounty in the forms of crops and fish and game. Of course, Poonam never did tell me what they expected to happen if they didn't give their abundant thanks to this particular god, but I could guess.

Anyway, the three of us went down the hill to the village amidst the bird-screech and the smell of dung and cook-fires, and Candi fired up a bowl and passed it round and Poonam and I took our turns, because I figured, why not? The muntjacs could wait till tomorrow, and this, whatever it might turn out to be, was something different at least, not to mention the fact that Poonam was there at my side with her slim, smooth limbs and the revelation of flesh that defined her hipbones and navel. "Do you feel anything?" Candi kept saying. "You want to do another hit? Randall? Poonam?" Half a dozen chickens fanned out across the path and vanished in the undergrowth. The sun inflamed the trees.

In the village itself—foot-tamped dirt, cane and thatch huts on raised platforms of bamboo, lurking rack-ribbed dogs, more bird-screech—people were preparing the evening meal in their courtyards. The smoke was fragrant with curry and vindaloo, triggering my salivary glands to clench and clench again. A pig gave us a malicious look from beneath one of the huts and I couldn't help laughing—the thing wouldn't have even come up to the hocks of one of our Iowa hogs. "What are you talking, *drums*?" Candi said. "I don't hear any drums."

Overhead, the high-voltage wires bellied between the electric poles, at least half of which we'd had to replace with the new high-resin-compound model that resists rot and termite damage, and you wouldn't believe what the climate here can do to a piece of creosote-soaked wood stuck in the ground—but don't get me started. Just looking at the things made my back ache. Poonam was about to say something in response, something cutting or at least impatient—I could tell from the way she bit her underlip—when all at once the drums started up from the rear of the village, where the bachelors had their quarters. There was a hollow booming and then a deeper thump that seemed to ignite a furious, palm-driven rhythm pulsing beneath it. Children began to sprint past us.

Instantly I was caught up in the excitement. I felt like a kid at the start of the Memorial Day parade, with the high school band warming up the snare drums, the horses beating at the pavement in impatience, and the mayor goosing his white Cadillac convertible with the beauty queen arrayed in back. I'd heard some of the local music before—my best bud in the village, Dakgipa, played a thing like an oversized recorder, and he could really do on it too, knocking out the melodies to "Smells Like Teen Spirit" and "Paranoid Android" as if he'd written them himself—but it was nothing like the ferment of those drums. I glanced at Poonam and she gave me a smile so muscular it showed all her bright, perfect teeth and lifted her right nostril so that her nose ring caught the light and winked at me. "All right," I said. "Party time!"

And that was how it went. Everybody knew us—the Garos are not in the least bit standoffish or uptight or whatever you want to call it—and before long we were sitting cross-legged in the courtyard with plates of food in our laps and jars of rice beer in hand while the bachelors went at it on every sort of drum imaginable—the *Ambengdama,* the *Chisakdama, Atong dama, Ruga* and *Chibok dama,* the *Nagra* and *Kram.* And gongs. They were big on gongs too. Candi wouldn't touch the food—she'd been down with one stomach ailment after another, right from orientation on—but she drained that beer as if she were at a kegger on Long Beach Island, while Poonam sat beside me on a clump of grass with her flawless posture and sweet, compressed smile.

At one point—my recollection isn't too clear here, I'm afraid, after the weed and the beer, not to mention the flamingest curry I've ever yet to this day run across—Dakgipa came and sat with us and we made a date to go hunting the following day after work. Dakgipa spent all his free time out in the bush, snaring squirrels, bandicoots, and the black-napped hare and the like, potting green pigeons in the trees and crow pheasants out in the fields, and he'd acted as a sort of guide for me, teaching me the habits of the local game and helping me tan the hides to ship back home so Jenny and I could stretch them decoratively over the walls of our condo-to-be. There was a quid pro quo, of course—Dak was a Counter-Strike addict and all he could talk about was the DSL capability he fervently hoped we were bringing him and the 10Base-T Ethernet network interface cards he expected we'd hand out to go with the new modems we were seeding the village with. But that was okay. That was cool. He gave me the binturong and the masked palm civet and I gave him the promise of high-speed Internet.

It grew dark. The mosquitoes settled in for their own feast, and even as the screeching day birds flew off to their roosts the night creatures took up the complaint, which sizzled through the quieter moments of the drummers' repertoire like some sort of weird natural distortion, as if the gods of the jungle had their amps cranked too high. I was aware of Poonam beside me, Dak was sounding out Candi on the perennial question of Mac versus PC, and the drums had sunk down to the hypnotic pulse of water flowing in its eternal cycle—everything gone calm and mellow. After a long silence, Poonam turned to me. "Did you know the auntie of my host family was carried off by a *bhut* the other night?"

I didn't know. Hadn't heard. Poonam's skin glowed in the light of the bonfire somebody had lit while I was dreaming the same dream as the drummers, and her eyes opened up to me so that I wanted to crawl inside them and forever forget Jenny and Des Moines and the Appleseed Condo Corp. Inc. "What's a *bhut*?" I asked.

"A forest spirit."

"A what? Don't tell me you actually—?" I caught myself and never finished the thought. I didn't want to sound too harsh because we were just starting to have a real meeting of the minds and a meeting of the minds is—or can be, or ought to be—a prelude to a meeting of the flesh.

Her smile was softer, more serene than ever. "It was in the form of a leopard," she said. "*Bhuts* often take on the shape of that sneaking thief of the night. They come for adulterers, Randall, false-promisers, moneylenders, for the loose and easy. Some nights, they just take what they can get."

I stared off into the fire, at the shapes that shifted there like souls come to life. "And the auntie—what did she do?"

Poonam gave an elaborate shrug. "They say she ate the flesh of the forest creatures without making sacrifice. But you'd have to believe, wouldn't you, to put any credence in a primitive speculation like that?" The drums flowed, things crept unseen through the high grass. "Just think of it, Randall," she said, rotating her hips so that she was facing me square on, "all these people through all these eons and when they go out to make water at night they might never come back, grandmother vanished on her way to the well, your childhood dog disappeared like smoke, your own children carried off. And you ask me if I *believe*?"

Maybe it was the pot, maybe that was it, but suddenly I felt uneasy, as if the whole world were holding its breath and watching me and me alone. "But you said it yourself—it's only a leopard."

"Only?"

I didn't know what to say to this. The fact was I'd never shot anything larger than a six-point buck on the edge of a soybean field; the biggest predators we had in Iowa were fox, bobcat, and coyote, nothing that could creep up on you without a sound and crush your skull in its jaws while simultaneously raking out your intestines with swift, knifing thrusts of its hind claws. That was a big "only."

"Would you hunt such a thing, Randall? In the night? Would you?"

Candi was deep in conversation with Dak when Poonam and I excused ourselves to stroll back up the hill to my tent ("Yes," Dak was saying, "but what sort of throughput speed can you offer?"). I'd felt so mellow and so—detached, I'd guess you'd call it, from Jenny that I found myself leaning into Poonam and putting my lips to her ear just as the drummers leapfrogged up the scale of intensity and the ground and the thatch and even the leaves of the bushes began to vibrate. It was hot. I was sweating from every pore. There was nothing in the world but drums. Drums were my essence, drums were the rain and the sunshine after a storm, they were the beginning and the end, the stars, the deeps—but I don't want to get too carried away here. You get the idea: my lips, Poonam's ear. "Would you—" I began, and I had to shout to hear myself, "I mean, would you want to come back to the tent for a nightcap maybe? With me?"

She smelled of palm oil—or maybe it was Nivea. She was shy, and so was I. "Yes," she whispered, the sound all but lost in the tumult around us. But then she shrugged for emphasis and added, "Sure, why not?"

The night sustained us, the hill melted away. Her hand found mine in the dark. For a long while we sat side by side on my cot, mixing fresh-squeezed lime juice, confectioners' sugar, and Tanqueray in my only glass and taking turns watching each other drink from it, and then she subsided against me, against my chest and the circulatory organ that was pounding away there—my heart, that is—and eventually I got to see what she looked like without the little knit blouse and the tight jeans and I fell away to the pulse of the drums and the image of a swift, spotted *bhut* stalking the night.

I woke with a jolt. It was dark still, the drums silent, the birds and monkeys nodding on their hidden perches, the chirring of the insects fading into the background like white noise. Somewhere, deep in my dream, someone had been screaming—and this was no ordinary scream, no mere wringing out of fear or excitement, but something darker, deeper, more hurtful and wicked—and now, awake, I heard it again. Poonam sat up beside me. "Jesus," I said. "What was that?"

She didn't say I told you so, didn't say it was a leopard or a *bhut* or the creeping manifestation of the Christian Devil himself, because there was no time for that or anything else: the platform swayed under the weight of an animate being and I never thought to reach for my rifle or even my boxers. For an interminable time I sat there rigid in the dark, Poonam's nails digging into my shoulder, neither of us breathing—*Jenny,* I was thinking, *Jenny*—until the flaps parted on the gray seep of dawn and Dak thrust his agitated face into the tent. "Randall," he barked. "Randall—oh, shit! Shit! Have you got your gun, your rifle? Get your rifle. Bring it! Quick!" I could hear the birds now—first one started in and then they were all instantaneously competing to screech it down—and Poonam loosened her grip on my arm.

"What is it? What's the problem?" I couldn't really hear myself, but I have no doubt my voice was unsteady, because on some level—scratch that: on every level—I didn't want to know and certainly didn't want to have to go off into the bush after whatever it was that had made that unholy rupture in the fabric of the night.

Dak's face just hung there, astonished, a caricature of impatience and exasperation, though I couldn't see his eyes (for some reason—and this struck me as maybe the oddest thing about the whole situation—he was wearing Candi's *Matrix* shades). "The big one," he said. "The biggest bore you have."

"For what? Why? What's the deal?" Though our entire exchange could have been compacted into the space of maybe ten seconds, I was stalling, no doubt about it.

His response, delivered through clenched teeth, completely threw me. I don't know what I'd expected—demons, man-eaters, Bangladeshi terrorists—but probably the last thing was elephants. "Elephants?" I repeated stupidly. To tell you the truth, I'd pretty much forgotten they even had elephants out there in the bush—sure, people still used them to haul things, like telephone poles, for instance, but those elephants were as tame as lapdogs and no more noticeable or threatening than a big gray stucco wall.

I still hadn't moved. Poonam shielded herself from Dak—as if, in this moment of fomenting crisis, he would have been interested in the shape of her breasts—and before I'd even reached for my shorts she had the knit blouse over her head and was smoothing it down under her ribcage.

What had happened, apparently, was that the wild elephants had come thundering out of the jungle at first light to ravage the village and raid the crops. All I could think of were those old Tarzan movies—I mean, really: *elephants*? "You're joking, right, Dak?" I said, reaching for my clothes. "It's like April Fool's, right—part of the whole Wangala thing? Tell me you're joking."

I'd never heard Dak raise his voice before—he was so together, so calm and focused, he was almost holy—but he raised it now. "Will you fucking wake up to what I'm telling you, Randall—they're wrecking the place, going for the granary, trampling the fields. Worse—they're drunk!"

"Drunk?"

His face collapsed, his shoulders sank. "They got the rice beer. All of it."

And so, that was how I found myself stalking the streets of the village ten minutes later, the very sweaty stock of a very inadequate rifle in my hand. The place was unrecognizable. Trees had been uprooted, the huts crushed, the carcasses of pigs, chickens, and goats scattered like trash. Smoke rose from the ruins where early-morning cook-fires had gone out of control and begun to swallow up the splinters of the huts, even as people ran around frantically with leaking buckets of water. There was one man dead in the street and I'd never seen a dead human being before, both sets of my grandparents having opted for cremation to spare us the mortuary and the open casket and the waxen effigies propped within. He was lying on his face in the dirt, the skin stripped from his back like the husk of a banana, his head radically compressed. I couldn't be sure, but I thought I recognized him as one of the drummers from the previous night. I felt something rise in my throat, a lump of it burning there.

That was when the villagers caught sight of me, caught sight of the rifle. Within minutes I'd attracted a vengeful, hysterical crowd, everybody jabbering and gesticulating and singing their own little song of woe, and me at the head of the mob, utterly clueless. The rifle in my hands—a 7mm Remington—was no elephant gun. Far from it. It packed some stopping power, sure, and I'd brought it along in the unlikely event I could get a shot at something big, a gaur or maybe even a leopard or (crucify me) a tiger. Back in Ottumwa I suppose I'd entertained a fantasy about coming down some sun-spangled path and seeing a big flat-headed Bengal tiger making off with somebody's dog and dropping him with a single, perfect heart shot and then paying a bunch of worshipful coolies or natives or whoever they might be to skin it out so Jenny and I could hang it on the wall and I could have a story to tell over the course of the next thousand backyard barbecues. But that was the fantasy and this was the reality. To stop an elephant—even to put a scare into one—you needed a lot more firepower than I had. And experience—experience wouldn't hurt either.

The noise level—people squabbling and shouting, the eternal birds, dogs howling—was getting to me. How could anybody expect me to stalk an animal with this circus at my back? I looked around for Dak, hoping he could do something to distract the mob so that I could have some peace to prop myself up and stop the heaviness in my legs from climbing up over my belt and paralyzing me. I'd never been more afraid in my life, and I didn't know what was worse—having to shoot something the size of a house without getting trampled or looking like a fool, coward and wimp in the face of all these people. Like it or not, I was the one with the gun, the white man, the pukka sahib; I was the torchbearer of Western superiority, the one with everything to prove and everything to lose.

How had I gotten myself into this? Just because I liked to hunt? Because I'd potted a bandicoot or two and the entire village knew it? And this wasn't just one elephant, which would have been bad enough, but a whole herd—and they were drunk, and who knew what that would do to their judgment?

The crowd pushed me forward like the surge of the tide and I looked in vain for Dak—for a friendly face, for anybody—until finally I spotted him at the rear of the press, with Candi and Poonam at his side, all three of them looking as if they'd just vomited up breakfast. I gave them a sick wave—there was nothing else I could do—and came round a corner to see two other corpses laid out in the street as if they were sleeping on very thin mattresses. And then, suddenly, the crowd fell silent.

There before me was an elephant. Or the truck-high back end of one. It was standing in the shell of a hut, its head bent forward as it sucked rice beer up its trunk from an open cask that somehow, crazily, had remained upright through all the preceding chaos. I remember thinking what an amazing animal this was—a kind of animate bulldozer, and it lived right out there in the jungle, invisible to everybody but the birds, as stealthy as a rat—and wondered what we'd do if we had things like this back home, ready to burst out of the river bottom and lay waste to the cornfields on their way to Kenny's Bar and Grill to tap half a dozen kegs at a time. The thought was short-lived. Because the thing had lifted its head and craned its neck—if it even had a neck—to look back over its shoulder and fan its ears, which were like big tattered flags of flesh. Reflexively I looked over my shoulder and discovered that I was alone—the villagers had cleared off to a distance of five hundred feet, as if the tide had suddenly receded. How did I feel about that? For one thing, it made my legs go even heavier—they were pillars, they were made of concrete, marble, lead, and I couldn't have run if I'd wanted to. For another, I began a grisly calculation—as long as the crowd had been with me, the elephant would have had a degree of choice as to just who it wanted to obliterate. Now that choice had been drastically reduced.

Very slowly—infinitely slowly, millimeter by millimeter—I began to move to my right, the rifle at my shoulder, the cartridge in the chamber, my finger frozen at the trigger. I needed to get broadside of the thing, which had gone back to drinking beer now, pausing to snort or to tear up a patch of long grass and beat it against its knees in a nice calm undrunken grandmotherly kind of way that lulled me for an instant. But really, I didn't have a clue. I remembered the Orwell essay, which *Guns & Ammo* reprinted every couple of years by way of thrilling the reading public with the fantasy of bringing down the ultimate trophy animal, and how Orwell said he'd thought the thing's brain was just back of the eyes. My right arm felt as if it was in a cast. My trigger finger swelled up to the size of a baseball bat. I couldn't seem to breathe.

That was when the elephant gave a sudden lurch and swung around amidst the shattered bamboo and the tatters of thatch to face me head-on. Boom: it happened in an instant. There the thing was, fifty feet away—four quick elephantine strides—stinking and titanic, staggering from one foot to the other like one of the street people you see on the sidewalks of San Francisco or New York. It seemed perplexed, as if it couldn't remember what it was doing there with all that wreckage scattered around it—and I had to credit the beer for that. Those fermenting tubs hold something like fifty gallons each, and that's a lot of beer by anybody's standards, even an elephant's. The smallest ray of hope stirred in me—maybe, if I just stood rock still, the thing wouldn't see me. Or couldn't. Maybe it would just stagger into the jungle to sleep it off and I could save face by blowing a couple shots over its retreating butt.

But that wasn't what happened.

The unreadable red-rimmed eyes seemed to seize on me and the thing threw back its head with one of those maniacal trumpeting blasts we all recognize, anybody who's got a TV anyway, and then, quite plainly berserk, it came for me. I'd like to say I stood my ground, calmly pumping off round after round until the thing dropped massively at my feet, but that didn't happen either. All at once my legs felt light again, as if they weren't legs at all but things shaped out of air, and I dropped the gun and ran like I'd never run before in my life. And the crowd—all those irate Garo tribesmen, Dak and Candi and Poonam and whoever else was crazy enough to be out there watching this little slice of drama—they turned and ran too, but of course they had a good head start on me, and even if I'd just come off a first-place finish in the hundred meters at the Olympics, the elephant would have caught up to me in a heartbeat and transformed me into a section of roadway and all the money my parents had laid out on orthodontics and tuition and just plain food would have been for naught. I hadn't gone ten paces before an errant fragment of thatch roof caught hold of my foot and down I went, expecting imminent transformation (or pancakeization, as Poonam later phrased it, and I didn't think it was that funny, believe me).

The elephant had been trumpeting madly but suddenly the high notes shot right off the scale and I lifted my fragile head to see what I at first thought was some sort of giant black snake cavorting with the thing. I'll tell you, the elephant was lively now, dancing right up off its toes as if it wanted to fly away. It took a moment to come together for me: that was no snake—that was the high-voltage cable and that thing at the other end of it was the snapped-off, bobbing remnant of a high-resin-compound utility pole. The dance was energetic, almost high-spirited, but it was over in an instant, and when the thing came down—the elephant, big as an eighteen-wheeler—the ground shook as if a whole city had collapsed.

There was dust everywhere. The cable whipped and sparked. I heard the crowd roar and reverse itself, a hundred feet pounding at the dirt, and then, in the midst of it all, there was that scream again, the one I'd heard in the night; it was like someone slipping a knife up under my ribcage and twisting it. My gaze leapt past the hulk of the elephant, past the ruin of the village and the pall of smoke, to the shadowy architecture of the jungle. And there it was, the spotted thing, crouching on all fours with its eyes fastened on me, raging yellow, raging, until it rose on two legs and vanished.

(2004)

The Doubtfulness of Water: Madam Knight's Journey to New York, 1702

Boston to Dedham

The road was dark, even at six in the evening, and if it held any wonders aside from the odd snug house or the stubble field, she couldn't have said because all that was visible was the white stripe of heaven overhead. Her horse was no more than a sound and a presence now, the heat of its internal engine rising round her in a miasma of sweat dried and reconstituted a hundred times over, even as she began to feel the repetition of its gait in the deep recesses of her seat and that appendage at the base of the spine her mother used to call the tailbone. Cousin Robert was some indeterminate distance ahead of her, the slow crepitating slap of his mount's hooves creating a new kind of silence that fed off the only sound in the world and then swallowed it up in a tower of vegetation as dense and continuous as the waves of the sea. Though it was only the second of October, there had been frost, and that was a small comfort in all of this hurt and upset, because it drew down the insects that a month earlier would have eaten her alive. The horse swayed, the stars staggered and flashed. She wanted to call out to Robert to ask if it was much farther yet, but she restrained herself. She'd talked till her throat went dry as they'd left town in the declining sun and he'd done his best to keep up though he wasn't naturally a talker, and eventually, as the shadows came down and the rhythmic movement of the animals dulled their senses, they'd fallen silent. She resigned herself. Rode on. And just as she'd given up hope, a light appeared ahead.

At Dedham

Robert her cousin leaving her to await the Post at the cottage of the Reverend and Madam Belcher before turning round for Boston with a dozen admonitions on his lips—She should have gone by sea as there was no telling what surprises lay ahead on the road in that savage country and she was to travel solely with trusted companions and the Post, et cetera—she settled in by the fire with a cup of tea and explained her business to Madam Belcher in her cap and the Reverend with his pipe. Yes, she felt responsible. And yes, it was she who'd introduced her boarder, a young widow, to her kinsman, Caleb Trowbridge, only to have him die four months after the wedding and leave the poor woman twice widowed. There were matters of the estate to be settled in both New Haven and New York, and it was her intention to act in the widow's behalf, being a widow herself and knowing how cruel such divisions of property can be.

An old dog lay on the rug. A tallow candle held a braided flame above it. There was a single ornament on the wall, a saying out of the Bible in needlepoint: *He shall come down like rain upon the mown grass: as showers that water the earth.* After a pause, the Reverend's wife asked if she would like another cup.

Sarah's eyes rose from the fire to the black square of the window. "You're very kind," she said, "but no thank you." She was concerned about the Post. Shouldn't he have been here by now? Had she somehow managed to miss him? Because if she had, there was no sense in going on—she might just as well admit defeat and find a guide back to Boston in the morning. "But where can the Post be?" she asked, turning to the Reverend.

The Reverend was a big block of a man with a nose to support the weight of his fine-ground spectacles. He cleared his throat. "Might be he's gone on to the Billingses, where he's used to lodge."

She listened to the hiss of the water trapped in a birch stick on the fire. Her whole body ached with the soreness of the saddle. "And how far would that be?"

"Twelve mile on."

At Dedham Tavern

She sat in a corner in her riding clothes while the Reverend brought the hostess to her, the boards of the floor unswept, tobacco dragons putting their claws into the air and every man with a black cud of chew in his mouth. The woman came to her with her hair in a snarl and her hands patting at her hips, open-faced and wondering. The Reverend stood beside her with his nose and his spectacles, the crown of his hat poking into the timbers overhead. Could she be of assistance?

"Yes, I'd like some refreshment, if you please. And I'll need a guide to take me as far as the Billingses' to meet up with the Post."

"The Billingses? At this hour of night?"

The hostess had raised her voice so that every soul in the place could appreciate the clear and irrefragable reason of what she was saying, and she went on to point out that it was twelve miles in the dark and that there would be none there to take her, but that her son John, if the payment was requisite to his risking life and limb, might be induced to go. Even at this unholy hour.

And where was John?

"You never mind. Just state your price."

Madam Knight sat as still as if she were in her own parlor with her mother and daughter and Mrs. Trowbridge and her two boarders gathered round her. She was thirty-eight years old, with a face that had once been pretty, and though she was plump and her hands were soft, she was used to work and to hard-dealing and she was no barmaid in a country tavern. She gazed calmly on the hostess and said nothing.

"Two pieces of eight," the woman said. "And a dram."

A moment passed, every ear in the place attuned to the sequel. "I will not be accessory to such extortion," Sarah pronounced in an even voice, "not if I have to find my own way, alone and defenseless in the dark."

The hostess went on like a singing Quaker, mounting excuse atop argument, and the men stopped chewing and held the pewter mugs arrested in their hands, until finally an old long-nosed cadaver who looked to be twice the hostess's age rose up from the near table and asked how much she *would* pay him to show her the way.

Sarah was nonplussed. "Who are you?"

"John," he said, and jerked a finger toward the hostess. "'Er son."

Dedham to the Billingses'

If the road had been dark before, now it was as if she were blind and afflicted and the horse blind too. Clouds had rolled in to pull a shade over the stars and planets while she'd sat listening to the hostess at the tavern, and if it weren't for the sense of hearing and the feel of a damp breeze on her face, she might as well have been locked in a closet somewhere. John was just there ahead of her, as Cousin Robert had been earlier, but John was a talker and the strings of his sentences pulled her forward like a spare set of reins. Like his mother, he was a monologuist. His subject was himself and the myriad dangers of the road—savage Indians, catamounts, bears, wolves and common thieves—he'd managed to overthrow by his own cunning and heroism in the weeks and months just recently passed. "There was a man 'ere, on this very spot, murdered and drawn into four pieces by a Pequot with two brass rings in 'is ears," he told her. "Rum was the cause of it. If I'd passed by an hour before it would have been me." And: "The catamount's a wicked thing. Gets a horse by the nostrils and then rakes out the innards with 'is hinder claws. I've seen it myself." And again: "Then you've got your shades of the murdered. When the wind is down you hear them hollowin' at every crossroads."

She wasn't impressed. They'd hanged women for witches in her time, and every corner, even in town, seemed to be the haunt of one goblin or another. Stories and wives' tales, legends to titillate the children before bed. There were real dangers in the world, dangers here in the dark, but they were overhead and underfoot, the nagging branch and open gully, the horse misstepping and coming down hard on her, the invisible limb to brain her as she levitated by, but she tried not to think of them, tried to trust in her guide—John the living cadaver—and the horse beneath her. She gripped the saddle and tried to ease the ache in her seat, which had radiated out to her limbs now and her backbone, even her neck, and she let her mind go numb with the night and the sweet released odors of the leaves they crushed underfoot.

At the Billingses'

She would never have known the house was there but for the sudden scent of wood smoke and the narrowest ribbon of light that hung in the void like the spare edge of something grander. "If you'll just alight, then, Missus," John was saying, and she could feel his hand at her elbow to help her down, "and take yourself right on through that door there."

"What door?"

"There. Right before your face."

He led her forward even as the horses stamped in their impatience to be rid of the saddle. She felt stone beneath her feet and focused on the ribbon of light till the door fell inward and she was in the room itself, low beams, plank floor, a single lantern and the fire dead in the hearth. In the next instant a young woman of fifteen or so rose up out of the inglenook with a contorted face and demanded to know who she was and what she was doing in her house at such an hour. The girl stood with her legs apart, as if ready to defend herself. Her voice was strained. "I never seen a woman on the road so dreadful late. Who are you? Where are you going? You scared me out of my wits."

"This *is* a lodging house, or am I mistaken?" Sarah drew herself up, sorer than she'd ever been in her life, the back of a horse—any horse—like the Devil's own rack, and all she wanted was a bed, not provender, not company, not even civility—just that: a bed.

"My ma's asleep," the girl said, standing her ground. "So's my pa. And William too."

"It's William I've come about. He's the Post, isn't he?"

"I suspect."

"Well, I'll be traveling west with him in the morning and I'll need a bed for the night. You *do* have a bed?" Even as she said it she entertained a vision of sleeping rough, stretched out on the cold ground amidst the dried-out husks of the fallen leaves, prey to anything that stalked or crept, and she felt all the strength go out of her. She never pleaded. It wasn't in her nature. But she was slipping fast when the door suddenly opened behind her and John stepped into the room.

The girl's eyes ran to him. "Lawful heart, John, is it you?" she cried, and then it was all right, and she offered a chair and a biscuit and darted away upstairs only to appear a moment later with three rings on her fingers and her hair brushed back from her brow. And then the chattering began, one topic flung down as quickly as the next was taken up, and all Sarah wanted was that bed, which finally she found in a little back lean-to that wasn't much bigger than the bedstead itself. As for comfort, the bed was like a mound of bricks, the shuck mattress even worse. No matter. Exhaustion overcame her. She undressed and slid in under the counterpane even as the bed lice stole out for the feast.

The Billingses' to Foxvale

She arose stiff in the morning, feeling as if she'd been pounded head to toe with the flat head of a mallet, and the girl was nowhere to be seen. But William was there, scooping porridge out of a bowl by the fire, and the mistress of the house. Sarah made her own introductions, paid for her bed, a mug of coffee that scalded her palate, and her own wooden bowl of porridge, and then she climbed back into the rack of the saddle and they were gone by eight in the morning.

The country they passed through rolled one way and the other, liberally partitioned by streams, creeks, freshets and swamps, the hooves of the horses eternally flinging up ovals of black muck that smelled of things dead and buried. There were birds in the trees still, though the summer flocks were gone, and every branch seemed to hold a squirrel or chipmunk. The leaves were in color, the dragonflies glazed and hovering over the shadows in the road ahead, and in the clearings goldenrod nodding bright on a thousand stalks. For the first time she found herself relaxing, settling into the slow-haunching rhythm of the horse as she followed the Post's back and the swishing tail of his mount through one glade after another. There were no houses, no people. She heard a gabbling in the forest and saw the dark-clothed shapes there—turkeys, in all their powers and dominions, turkeys enough to feed all of Boston—and she couldn't help thinking of the basted bird in a pan over the fire.

At first she'd tried to make conversation with William (a man in his twenties, kempt, lean as a pole, taciturn) just to be civil, but talk seemed superfluous out here in the wild and she let her thoughts wander as if she were at prayer or drifting through the mutating moments before sleep comes. *You should have gone by sea,* Cousin Robert had said, and he was right of course, except that the rollicking of the waters devastated her—she'd been once with her father in a dinghy to Nantucket when she was a girl, and once was enough. She could still remember the way her stomach heaved and the fear she'd felt of the implacable depths where unseen things—leviathan, the shark, the crab and suckerfish—rolled in darkness. She'd never learned to swim. Why would she, living in town, and when even the water of the lakes and the river was like the breath of mid-winter, and the sea worse, far worse, with men falling overboard from the fishing boats and drowning from the shock of it? No, she would keep the solid earth under her feet. Or her horse's feet, at any rate.

Sure progress, the crown of the day: there was the sun, the solemn drapery of the forest, birdsong. She was lulled, half asleep, expecting nothing but more of the same, when suddenly a small thicket of trees detached itself from the wood and ambled out into the road so that her mount pulled up and flung its near eye back at her. It took two catapulting moments for the image to jell, and then she let out a scream that was the only human sound for twenty miles around.

The thing—the walking forest—was bearded and antlered and had eyes that shone like the Indian money they made of shells. It produced a sound of its own—a blunt bewildered bleat of alarm—and then it was gone and William, taciturn William, was there at her side. "It's nothing to worry yourself over," he said, and she saw that he was grinning as if he'd just heard a joke—or formulated one. He had a story to tell at the tavern that night, that's what it was, and she was the brunt of it, the widow from Boston who wouldn't recognize a—what was it, a moose?—if it came right up and grazed out of her hand.

At Foxvale

The board was primitive, to say the least, Sarah sitting at table with William while William discharged his letters to Nathan, the western Post, and the hostess bringing in a cheese that was like no cheese she'd ever seen. Eating was one of her small pleasures, and at home she always took care with the menu, serving up fish or viands in a savory sauce or peas boiled with a bit of salt meat, fresh roasted venison, Indian corn and squashes and pies—her speciality—made from the ripe fruit of the season, blueberry, raspberry, pumpkin, apple. But here the woods gathered close so that it was like night in the middle of a towering bright day, and there were none of the niceties of civilization, either in the serving or the quality. The cheese—harder than the bed she'd slept in the night before—barely took to the knife, and then it was a dish of pork and cabbage, which looked to be the remains of dinner. She found that she was hungry despite herself—ravenous, actually, with the exercise and air—and she took a larger portion than she would have liked.

"Tucking in there, Missus, eh?" William observed, giving her that same grin even as he nudged Nathan, and here was another story.

"We've been on the road since eight in the morning," she said, wondering for the life of her what was so amusing about sheltering in a hovel in the woods fit only for a band of naked savages, "and it's now past two in the afternoon. A woman has got to eat, if only to keep up her strength." She was throwing it back at them, and why not—that was how she felt. And she *was* hungry, nothing to be ashamed of there. But the sauce was the strangest color—a purple so deep it was nearly black—and the thought came to her that the hostess had stewed the meal in her dye kettle.

William was watching her. As was Nathan. The hostess had vanished in the back room and the sound of the fowl scratching in the dirt of the yard came to her as if she were standing there among them. Very slowly a branch outside the sole window dipped in the breeze and parted the dense shadow on the wall. She hesitated, the spoon hovering over the dish—they were both of them grinning like fools—and then she plunged in.

Foxvale to Providence

This was the leg of the journey that wore on her most. The new man—Nathan—rode hard and she had to struggle to keep up with him, or at least keep him in sight. Though he'd seen her discharge William handsomely enough and pay for his refreshment too, he didn't seem in the least solicitous. He was a hat and pair of shoulders and a back, receding, always receding. Her mount wasn't much taller than a pony and tended to lag no matter how much encouragement she gave him, running to his own head and not a pace faster. The clouds closed in. A light rain began to awaken the dust. Nathan was gone.

She'd never been out alone in the wilderness in her life. When she was younger she'd gone berrying on the outskirts of town or spent a warm afternoon sitting by a cool brook, but the wild was nothing she wanted or recognized. It was a waste, all of it, and the sooner it was civilized and cultivated, the sooner people could live as they did in England, with security and dignity—and cleanliness—the better. To her mind, aside from the dangers that seemed to multiply with every step they took—a moose, indeed—it was the dirt that damned the wild more than anything. She hadn't felt even remotely clean since she'd left town, though she'd done her best to beat the soil from her skirts, brush her shoes of mud and see to the demands of her hair. And now she was wet and the horse was wet and her baggage and the road before her, and every leaf on every tree shone and dripped.

She tried to concentrate her thoughts on easeful things, the tea set in her parlor and her daughter and Mrs. Trowbridge pouring out the tea and artfully arranging the pastries on the platter, because it was teatime now, and if it was raining there they'd have built up the fire to take the damp out of the air—but she couldn't hold the picture long. Her thoughts kept coming back to the present and the dangers of the road. Every stump seen at a distance seemed to transform itself into a bear or wolf, every copse was the haunt of Indians mad with rum and lust, the birds fallen silent now and the rain awakening the mosquitoes that dove at her hands and face where they'd coarsened in the sun. She'd thought she was going on an adventure, a respite from town and gossip and all the constraints of widowhood, something she could look back on and tell over and over again to her daughter and the grandchildren she saw as clearly as if they'd already come into existence—but she wasn't foolish, and she wasn't blindered. She'd expected a degree of hardship, an untenanted road, insects and the like, wild animals, and yet in her mind the road always ran between inns with reasonable beds and service and a rough but hardy and well-tendered fare. But this was impossible. This rain, these bugs, this throbbing ache in her seat that was like a hot poker applied to her backside by one of Satan's own fiends. She hated this. Hated it.

At Providence Ferry

It got worse.

Nathan's silhouette presented itself to her at the top of a rise, unkempt now and dripping. Slowly, with the testudineous progress of something you might crush underfoot, she made her way up the hill to him, and when she got there he pointed down at the lashing dun waves of the Seekonk River and the distant figure of the ferryman. She didn't say a word, but when they got there, when the water was beating to and fro and the ferryman accepting her coin, she held back. "The water looks doubtful," she said, trying to keep her voice from deserting her.

"This?" Nathan looked puzzled. "I'd call this calm, Missus," he said. "And the quicker we're over it, the better, because there's worse to come."

She closed her eyes fast, drew in a single breath and held it till they were across and she knew she was alive still and climbing back into the saddle even as the rain quickened its pace and the road ahead turned to sludge.

Providence Ferry to the Havenses'

They hadn't gone on a quarter of an hour when they came to a second river, the name of which she never did learn. It was dark as a brew with the runoff of the rain and ran in sheets over the submerged rocks and boiled up again round the visible ones. She felt herself seize at the sight of it, though Nathan assured her it wasn't what it seemed—"No depth to it at all and we're used to ride across it even at spring thaw"—and when they were there at the crossing and Nathan's mount already hock-deep in the surge, she just couldn't go on. He remonstrated with her—they were late on the road already, dusk was falling, there was another crossing after this one and fourteen miles more to the next stage—but she was adamant. There was no inducement in the world that would make her risk that torrent.

The rain had begun to let up now and a few late faltering streaks of sun shone through the clouds across the river. But wasn't that a house there on the far shore? A cabin, crudely made of logs with the bark peeled back and smoke rising palely from the stacked stone of the chimney? The current sang. Nathan swung his horse round on the shingle and gave her a look of hatred. "Does someone live there?" she asked. "In that cabin there?"

He didn't answer. Just thrust his horse into the current and floundered through it with a crashing like cymbals and she was so furious she would have shot him right through his pinched shoulder blades if only she'd had the means. He was deserting her. Leaving her to the wolves, the murderers and the haunts. "You come back here!" she shouted, but there were only his shoulders, receding.

That was her low point. She tried, at first, to screw up her courage and follow him—it wasn't so deep, after all, she could see that—but the way the water seemed to speak and hiss and mock her was enough to warn her off. She dismounted. There was a chill in the air, her clothes wet still, the night descending. She should have stayed home. Should have listened to Robert and her daughter and everyone else she talked to—women simply did not travel the Post Road, not without their husbands or brothers or kinsmen there to guide and protect them, and even then, it was a risk. Something settled in the back of her throat, a hard bolus of self-pity and despair. She couldn't swallow. One more minute of this, one more minute of this water and these trees, these endless trees, and she was going to break down and sob like a child. But then, out there on the naked back of the water, she saw the envelope of the birchbark canoe coming toward her and a boy in it and Nathan beckoning to her from the far shore.

What to say? That the crossing—eyes tight shut and her grip on the papery gunwales like the grip of death—was the single worst moment of her life, at least until the next crossing, through which they plunged in a pit of darkness so universal that it was only the tug of the reins, the murmur of the current and the sudden icy stab of the water at her calves to let her know she was in it and through it? Or that the fourteen miles remaining were so tedious she could scarcely stay awake and upright in the saddle despite the horripilating shivers that tossed her from one side to the other like a ball in a child's game? Say it. And say that she thought she was dreaming when the Post sounded his horn and the snug, well-lit house of the Havenses materialized out of the night.

At the Havenses'

As weary as she was, as worn and dispirited, she couldn't help feeling her soul rise up and shout when she stepped through the door. There was Mr. Havens, solicitous and stout, and Mrs. Havens beside him with a welcoming smile, the fire going hard in the hearth and a smell of beef broth to perfume the air. She saw immediately that these were people civil and clean, with a well-ordered house and every sign of a demanding mistress, a picture on one wall of the sitting room and a glass vase of dried flowers set atop an oiled sideboard on the other. Chairs were drawn up to the fire and a number of people cozily ensconced there with their mugs and pipes and they all had a greeting on their lips. Mrs. Havens helped her off with her riding clothes and hung them up to dry and then asked if she could get her anything by way of refreshment, Sarah answering that she had a portion of chocolate with her and wondered if she might have some milk heated in a pan. And then she was shown to her room—small but sufficient and tidy—and the door was shut and she felt as if she'd come through a storm and shipwreck and washed up safe.

She must have dozed, because she came back with a start when Mrs. Havens rapped at the door. "Yes?" Sarah called, and for a moment she didn't know where she was.

A murmur from the other side of the door: "Your chocolate, Missus."

The milk had been boiled with the chocolate in a clean brass kettle, and there was enough of it to give her three cups full. And there were corn cakes, still warm from the griddle. This was heaven, she was thinking, very heaven, dipping the cakes into the chocolate and warming her hands at the cup, but then the voices began to intrude. It seemed that her apartment, separated from the kitchen by a board partition, wasn't quite as private as she'd supposed. Next door to her—just beyond that thin rumor of a wall—were three, or was it four, of the town's topers, and all of them arguing a single point at once.

She listened, frozen on the starched white field of the bed, and she might as well have been right out there among them.

"No," a voice declared, "that's not it at all. Narragansett means 'briar' in the Indian language, and the patch of it was right out there on Peter Parker's place, twenty feet high and more—"

"I beg to differ, but it was a spring here—and that's where the country gets its name. Waters of a healing property, I'm told."

"Yes? And where is it, then? Why aren't you drinking the waters now—why aren't we all?"

A scuffle of mugs, the scrape of chair legs. "But we are—only it's been distilled out of cane." Laughter rang out, there was a dull booming as fists pounded the tabletop, and then someone followed it up with a foul remark, in foul language.

And so it went, for what seemed like hours. Exhausted as she was, there was no hope of sleep as long as the rum held out, and she began to pray the keg would run dry, though she was a practical soul who'd never had the calling and she never expected her prayers to be answered since there were so many worthier than she calling on the same power at the same moment. But the voices next door grew thicker, as if they'd started chewing maple sap boiled to gum, and the argument settled into a faintly disputatious murmur and then finally a pure drugged intake and outlay of breath that formed the respiratory foundation of her dreams.

The Havenses' to the Paukataug

The next knock came at four in the morning, black as pitch and no breakfast but what was portable, and here they were, back out on the road in the dark and cold, deep in the Narragansett country now, which to Sarah's mind was just more of the same: the hard road, the shadowy trees and the reptatory murmur of the waters that were all running underfoot to gather in some terrible place ahead. "Narragansett," she whispered to herself, as if it were an incantation, but she had to be forgiven if she couldn't seem to muster much enthusiasm for the origins of the name.

They'd been joined at the Havenses' by a French doctor, a slight man with a limp and a disproportionate nose, whose name she couldn't pronounce and whose accent made him difficult to understand, so that they were a party of three now for this leg of the journey. Not that it made a particle of difference, except that Nathan and the doctor rode on at such a furious pace as to leave her a mile and more behind, alone with her thoughts and whatever frights the unbroken wood might harbor. From time to time she'd spy them on a hill up ahead of her, waiting to see that she was still on the road and not lying murdered in a ditch, and then they'd tug at the reins again and vanish over the rise.

The Post had warned her that there was no accommodation or refreshment on this stretch of the road—no human habitation at all—for a full twenty-two miles, but as the morning wore on it seemed as if they'd gone a hundred miles before she saw the two figures poised on a ridge up ahead, looking back at her and pointing to a tight tourniquet of smoke in the distance. She'd been down on foot and leading her mount at that point, just to ease the soreness of her seat and thighs, but now she remounted with some effort and found her way to the source of the smoke: an ordinary set down beside a brook in a clearing of the trees.

Painfully she dismounted and painfully accepted the refreshment the landlady had to offer—stewed meat and Indian bread, unleavened—and then sat over the journal she'd determined to keep while the landlady went on to the doctor about her physical complaints in a voice loud enough to be heard all the way to Kingston town and back. The woman spoke of her privates as if they were public, and perhaps they were, but just hearing it was enough to turn Sarah's stomach and she had to take her book and sit out in the courtyard among the flies, which were especially thick here, as if they'd gathered for some sort of convention. She sat on a stump and swatted and shooed and blotted her precious paper with the effort until the Frenchman and the Post, still chewing a cud of stewed meat, saddled up and moved on down the road, and she had no choice but to rouse herself and follow on in their wake.

The country was unremarkable, the road boggy, the sun an affliction. Her hands and face were burned where they were exposed and the pain of it was like being freshly slapped every ten seconds. She saw a pair of foxes and what might have been a wolf, loping and rangy, with something dangling from its jaws. The sight of it gave her a start, but the thing ignored her and went about its business, which was slipping into a ravine with its prey in order to feed in some dark den, and then she almost wished it would emerge round the next bend to attack her, if only to put an end to the ceaseless swaying and battering of the horse beneath her. Nothing of the sort happened, however, and at around one in the afternoon she found the Post and doctor waiting for her on the shores of a broad tidal river she knew she would never get across, not in this lifetime.

At the Paukataug

"Well, the road ends here, then, Missus, because the doctor has his business in Kingston town and I've got the letters to deliver." The Post was leaning across his saddle, giving her a look of indifference. He was going to desert her and it didn't bother him a whit.

The doctor said something then about the ebbing tide, but she couldn't quite fathom what he was getting at until Nathan translated: "He says it's easier crossing at low tide—"

"Well, when is that, pray?"

"Three hour. Maybe more."

"And you won't wait?"

Neither man spoke. They were both of them like the boys she used to teach at school, caught out at something—doing wrong and knowing it—but unequal to admitting it. She felt her jaws clench. "You'd desert me, then?"

It took a moment, and then Nathan pointed an insolent finger at what at first she'd taken to be a heap of flood-run brush, but which she now saw was some sort of habitation. "Old Man Cotter lives there," he said, and at the sound of his voice a great gray-winged bird rose out of the shallows at river's edge and ascended like a kite on the currents of the air. "He'll take you in."

Stunned, she just sat there astride her horse and watched the Post and doctor slash into the current until the water was at their waists and all that was visible of their mounts were their heads and a flat sheen of pounding rump, and then she made her way to the ramshackle collection of weathered boards and knocked at the door. The old man who answered gave her a startled look, as if he'd never seen a woman before, or a lady at any rate, but she steeled herself, and trusting in human kindness, offered him a coin and asked if she might shelter with him until the tide drew off. Very slowly, as if it were coming from a long way off, the old man discovered a smile and then stood back and held the door open for her. She hesitated—the floor was bare earth and there were animal skins on the wall, the place as dank and cold as a cellar. She turned to look back at the river, but the Post and his companion were already gone and the day was blowing away to the east in a tatter of cloud. She stepped inside.

The Paukataug to Stoningtown

There was a wife inside that hut and two children, both girls and ill-favored, and the whole miserable family dressed in rags and deerskin, and no furniture but for the rounds of logs cut for stools, a bed with a glass bottle hanging at the head of it for what purpose she could only imagine (decoration?), an earthen cup, a pewter basin and a board supported on rough-cut props to serve as a table. The hearth was a crude array of blackened stone, and as Sarah stepped through the door the wife was just setting a few knots of wood to the flame. "I don't mean to intrude," she said, all the family's starved blue eyes on her, "but I've been deserted here at the river and I don't know what else to do—"

The wife looked down at her feet and murmured that she was welcome and could make herself at home and that they were very honored to have her. "Here," she said, "you just sit here," and she indicated the bed. After that, no one said a word, the girls slipping out the door as soon as they could and the old man responding to Sarah's questions and observations ("It must be solitary out here" and "Do you get into Stoningtown much?") with a short sharp grunt of denial or affirmation. The dirt of the floor was pounded hard. The fire was meager. A draft flowed continuously through the gaps in the river-run boards that made the walls of the place. She was cold, hungry, tired, uncomfortable. She closed her eyes and endured.

When she opened them, there was a new person in the room. At first she took him to be a wild Indian because there was no stitch of civilized clothing about him, from his moccasins to his buckskin shirt and crude hat tanned with the fur of some creature still on it, but she gathered from the conversation—what little of it there was—that he was the son-in-law of the old man and woman and living off in the deeper wild in a hovel of his own with their daughter, also named Sarah. No introductions were made, and the man all but ignored her, till finally Mr. Cotter rose to his feet and said, "Well, the river'll be down now and I expect it's time you wanted to go, Missus."

Sarah began to gather herself up, thanking them for their hospitality, such as it was, but then wondered aloud who was to escort her across the river? And beyond, on the road to Stoningtown?

The old man gestured toward his son-in-law, who looked up at her now from out of the depths of his own cold blue eyes. "If you'd give him something, Missus, I'm sure George here could be persuaded."

Stoningtown to New London Ferry

It was past dark when they limped into Stoningtown and her guide (no, he hadn't murdered her along the road or robbed her or even offered up an uncivil remark, and she reminded herself the whole way not to judge people by their appearances, though she could hardly help herself) showed her to the Saxtons', where she was to spend the night in the cleanest and most orderly house she'd yet seen since leaving Boston. Will Saxton was a kinsman on her mother's side and he and his wife had been expecting her, and they sat her before the fire and fed her till she could eat no more. Oysters, that was what she was to remember of Stoningtown, dripping from the sea and roasted over the coals till the shells popped open, and a lobster fish as long as her arm. And a featherbed she could sink into as if it were a snowdrift, if only the snow were a warm and comforting thing and not the particles of ice flung down out of the sky by a wrathful God.

She left at three the following afternoon—Thursday, her fourth day on the road—in the company of the Saxtons' neighbor, Mr. Polly, and his daughter, Jemima, who looked to be fourteen or so. The road here was clear and dry but for the dull brown puddles that spotted the surface like a geographical pox, but they were easy enough to avoid and the weather was cool and fair with scarcely the breath of a breeze. They looked out to the sea and moved along at a reasonable rate—Mr. Polly, a man her own age and cultivated, a farmer and schoolmaster, setting a pace to accommodate his daughter. All went well for the first hour or so, and then the daughter—Jemima—began to complain.

The saddle was too hard for her. The horse was lame and couldn't keep to a regular gait. She was bored. The countryside was ill-favored—or no, it wasn't just ill-favored but what you'd expect to see on the outskirts of hell. Could she get down and walk now? For just a hundred yards? Her backside was broken. Couldn't they stop? Couldn't they buy that man's farm over there and live in it for the rest of their lives?

Finally—and this when they were in sight of New London and the ferry itself—she got down from the horse in the middle of the road and refused to go a step farther.

Sarah was herself in a savage mood, wishing for the hundredth time that she'd stayed home in her parlor and let Mrs. Trowbridge worry over her own affairs, and each second she had to sit on that horse without moving forward was a goad to her temper. Mr. Polly gave her a look as if to say *What am I to do?* and before she could think she said that if it was her daughter she'd give her a whipping she'd never forget.

Jemima, big in the shoulder, with a broad red face beneath her bonnet, informed her that she wasn't her daughter and glad of it too. "You're an old hag from hell," she spat, her face twisted in a knot, "and I wouldn't live with you—or listen to you either—if I was an orphan and starving."

The trees stood still. In the near distance there was a farm and a pen and a smell of cattle. Then the father dismounted, took the daughter by the arm and marched into a thicket of the woods, where both their voices were raised in anger until the first blow descended. And then there were screams, raw, outraged, crescendoing, until you would have thought the savages had got hold of her to strip the skin from her limbs with their bloody knives. The blows stopped. Silence reigned. And Jemima, looking sullen and even redder in the face and probably elsewhere too, followed her father out of the thicket and climbed wearily back into the saddle. She didn't speak another word till they arrived at the ferry.

At New London

She would just as soon forget about that careening ride over the Thames on the ferry, with the wind coming up sudden and hard and the horses jerking one way and the other and Jemima screaming like a mud hen and roaring out at her father to save her because she was afraid of going overboard and Sarah's own stomach coming up on her till there was nothing left in it and the certainty that she would die stuck there in her throat like a criminal's dagger, because here she was handsomely lodged at the house of the Reverend Gordon Saltonstall, minister of the town, and he and the Reverend Mrs. Saltonstall entertained her with their high-minded conversation and a board fit for royalty. Her bed was hard, the room Spartan. But she was among civilized people now, in a real and actual town, and she slept as if she were stretched out in her own bed at home.

New London to Saybrook and on to Killingworth

For all that, she awoke early and anxious. She felt a lightness in her head, which was the surest sign she was catching cold, and she thought of those long hours in the rain on the road to the Havenses' and the unwholesome night airs she'd been compelled to breathe through the traverse of a hundred bogs and low places along the road, and all at once she saw herself dying there in the Reverend's bed and buried in his churchyard so many hard miles from home. She pictured her daughter then, pale, sickly, always her mother's child and afraid of her own shadow, having to make this grueling journey just to stand over her mother's grave in an alien place, and she got up out of the bed choking back a sob. Her nose dripped. Her limbs ached. She was a widow alone in the world and in a strange place and she'd never felt so sorry for herself in her life. Still, she managed to pull on her clothes and boots and find her way to the kitchen where the servant had got the fire going and she warmed herself and had a cup of the Reverend's Jamaica coffee and felt perceptibly better. As soon as the Reverend appeared, she begged him to find her a guide to New Haven, where she could go to her kinsmen and feel safe from all illness and accident.

The Reverend said he knew just the man and went out to fetch him, and by eight o'clock in the morning she was back in the saddle and enjoying the company of Mr. Joshua Wheeler, a young gentleman of the town who had business in New Haven. He was educated and had a fresh look about him, but was crippled in the right arm as the result of a riding accident when he was a boy. He talked of *The Pilgrim's Progress, Paradise Lost* and *The Holy Bible* as if he'd written them himself, and though her acquaintance with all three was not what it was once or should have been, she was able to quote him three lines of Milton—"And fast by, hanging in a golden chain, / This pendent world, in bigness as a star / Of smallest magnitude close by the moon"—and he rewarded her with a smile that made the wilderness melt away to nothing. He was like her own husband, the late, lamented Mr. Knight, when he was twenty and two, that was what she was thinking, and her nose stopped dripping and the miles fell away behind them without effort or pain.

Until they came to the bridge near Lyme. It was a doubtful affair at best, rickety and swaybacked, and it took everything she had in her to urge her mount out onto it. The horse stepped forward awkwardly, the bridge dipped, the river ran slick and hard beneath it. Her heart was in her mouth. "Get on," she told the horse, but she kept her voice low for fear of startling him, and the animal moved forward another five paces and froze there as if he'd been turned to stone. From the far side, where the trees framed him on his mount and the sun shone sick and pale off the naked rock, Mr. Wheeler called out encouragement. "Come ahead, Sarah," he urged. "It's as safe as anything." If she hadn't been so scared, suspended there over the river and at the mercy of a dumb beast that could decide to stagger sideways as easily as go forward, she might have reflected on how easy it was for him to say since he was already over on solid ground and didn't have her fear of water. Or bridges. She gave him a worried glance and saw from the look on his face that he could have dashed across the bridge time and again without a thought and that he knew how to swim like a champion and trusted his horse and was too young yet to know how the hurts of the world accumulate. A long moment passed. She leaned close to the horse's ear and made a clicking noise. Nothing happened. Finally, in exasperation, she resorted to the whip—just the merest flicker of it across the animal's hindquarters—and the horse bucked and the world spun as if it were indeed hanging from a pendant and she knew she was dead. Somehow, though, she'd got to the other side, and somehow she managed to fight down her nerves and forge on, even to Saybrook Ferry and beyond.

She must not have said two words to Mr. Wheeler the rest of the way, but when they disembarked from the ferry he suggested they stop at the ordinary there to bait the horses and take this opportunity of refreshment. It was two in the afternoon. Sarah had had nothing since breakfast, and that she couldn't keep down for worry over falling sick on the road, and so she agreed and they found themselves at a table with one respectable diner and three or four local idlers. The landlady—in a dirty apron, hair hanging loose and scratching at her scalp with both hands as if to dislodge some foreign thing clinging there—told them she'd broil some mutton if they'd like, but as good as that sounded, Sarah couldn't muster much enthusiasm. She kept thinking of the landlady's hands in her hair, and when the dish did come—the mutton pickled, with cabbage and a bit of turnip in a sauce that was so ancient it might have been scraped together from the moss grown on the skulls of the Christian martyrs—she found she had no appetite. Nor did Mr. Wheeler, who tried gamely to lift the spoon a second time to his lips, but wound up pushing the dish to the corner of the table while Sarah paid sixpence apiece for their dinners, or rather the smell of dinner.

They pressed on after that for Killingworth and arrived by seven at night. It was Friday now, the end of her fifth day on the road. She didn't care about the bed or the food—though the former was soft and the latter savory, roasted venison, in fact—but only the road ahead and the sanctuary of Thomas Trowbridge's house in New Haven. If she could have flown, if she could have mounted on the back of some great eagle or griffin, she would have done it without a second thought. *New Haven,* she told herself as she drifted off to sleep despite the noise and furor of the inn and the topers who seemed to have followed her all the way from Dedham Tavern, *New Haven tomorrow.*

Killingworth to New Haven

They set out early after a satisfactory breakfast, and though there were the Hammonasett, the East and West Rivers to cross and a dozen lesser waters, the fords were shallow and she barely hesitated. It was overcast and cool, the breeze running in off the sea to loosen her hair and beat it about her bonnet, Mr. Wheeler giving her a second day's course in literature, the way relatively easy. And what did she see in that country on the far side of the Connecticut River? Habitations few and far between, a clutch of small boats at sea, two Indians walking along the roadway in their tatters with scallop shells stuck in their ears and dragging the carcass of some dead half-skinned animal in the dirt behind them. She saw shorebirds, a spouting whale out to sea, a saltwater farm on a promontory swallowed up in mist, and, as they got closer to their destination, boys and dogs and rude houses and yards chopped out of the surrounding forest, stubble fields and pumpkins still fat on the vine and scattered like big glowing cannonballs across the landscape. And then they were arrived and she was so relieved to see her cousin Thomas Trowbridge standing there outside his considerable stone house with his wife, Hannah, and a sleek black dog that she nearly forgot to introduce Mr. Wheeler properly, but they were all in the parlor by then and tea was brewing and something in the pot so ambrosial she could have fainted for the very richness of the smell.

At New Haven

She stayed two months, or one day short of it, having arrived on Saturday, the seventh of October, and leaving for New York on the sixth of December in the company of Mr. Trowbridge. In the interim, she vanquished her cold, wrote in her journal and prosecuted her business, at the same time taking advantage of this period of quiet to learn something of the people and customs of the Connecticut Colony, which to her mind at least, seemed inferior in most respects to the Massachusetts. The leaves brightened and fell, the weather grew bitter. She spun wool. Sat by the fire and chatted with Mrs. Trowbridge while the servants made a show of being busy and the slaves skulked in the kitchen to escape the cold of the fields. There were savages here aplenty, more even than at home, and they were a particularly poor and poorly attired lot, living on their own lands but suffering from a lack of Christian charity on the part of the citizenry. And the people themselves could have benefited from even the most rudimentary education—there wasn't a man or woman walking the streets who was capable of engaging in a conversation that stretched beyond the limits of a sow's indigestion or the salting of pilchards for the barrel.

One afternoon she happened to be at a merchant's house, looking to acquire a few articles to give the Trowbridges in thanks for their hospitality, when in walked a rangy tall bumpkin dressed in skins and Indian shoes and with his cheeks distended by a black plug of tobacco. He stood in the middle of the room, barely glancing at the articles on display, spitting continually into the dirt of the floor and then covering it over again with the sole of his shoe till he'd made his own personal wallow. The merchant looked inquiringly at him, but he wasn't able to raise his eyes from the floor. Finally, after what must have been five full minutes of silence, he blurted out, "Have you any ribbands and hatbands to sell, I pray?" The merchant avowed he did and then the bumpkin wanted to know the price and the ribbons were produced; at that very instant, in came his inamorata, dropping curtsies and telling him how pretty the ribbon was and what a gentleman he was to buy it for her and did they have any hood silk and thread silk to sew it with? Well, the merchant did, and they bartered over that for half the hour, the bumpkin all the while spitting and spitting again and his wife—if she was his wife—simpering at his arm.

That night, at supper, she remarked to Mrs. Trowbridge that some of her neighbors seemed to lack breeding and Mrs. Trowbridge threw her eyes to the ceiling and said she didn't have to tell *her.*

New Haven to Fairfield

The saddle again. If she'd begun to harden herself to it on the long road from Boston to New Haven, now her layover with the Trowbridges had softened her and the pains that had lain dormant these two months began to reassert themselves. And it was bitter out of doors, a taut curtain of iron-gray cloud pinning them to the earth even as the wind stabbed at her bones and jerked loose every bit of chaff and ordure in the road and flung it in her face. The breath of the horse was palpable. Her fingers and toes lost all feeling and never regained them, not for two days running.

There was a brief contretemps at the Stratford Ferry—water, more water—and she froze upright with fear and at first wouldn't budge from the horse, Thomas Trowbridge's wide lunar face floating somewhere beneath her as he pleaded and reasoned and tried repeatedly to take hold of her hand, but in the end she mastered herself and the expedition went forward. The water beat at the flat bottom of the boat and she buried her face in her hands to keep herself from screaming, and then she thought she was screaming but it was only the gulls, white ghosts crying in the gloom. After that, she was only too glad to dismount at the ordinary two miles up the road and sit by the fire while the horses were baited and the hostess served up a hot punch and a pumpkin/Indian bread that proved, unfortunately, to be inedible.

By seven at night they came to Fairfield, and lodged there.

Fairfield to Rye

They set out early, arriving just after noon at Norowalk, where the food, for once, was presentable and fresh, though the fried venison the landlady served up could have used more pepper in the seasoning and the tea was as weak as dishwater. The road from there to Rye was eight hours and more, a light snow swirling round them and the last four hours of the journey prosecuted in utter darkness, with only the faint tracks of a previous traveler to show them the way through the pale gauze of the night. And here she had a new sensation—her feet ached, aside from having gone numb with the cold, that is. For there was a prodigious high hill along the road, a mile or more in length, and they had to go afoot here, leading their horses behind them. Her legs took on all of her weight. They sank beneath her. She couldn't lift them. Couldn't breathe. And there was Thomas Trowbridge plodding ahead of her like a spirit risen in his winding sheet and his horse white too and the snow still falling as if it had been coming down since the beginning of creation and everything else—the sun, the fields, high summer and green crops—had been an illusion. "Is it much farther yet?" she asked, gasping for breath, and she must have asked a thousand times. "Na much," came the reply, blown back in the wind.

A French family kept the ordinary at Rye, and this was a novelty to her. She sat by the fire, shivering till she thought she would split in two, and then, so famished from the ordeal of the road and the cold and the weather she could have eaten up every last scrap of food in the county, she asked for a fricassee, which the Frenchman claimed as his speciality. "Oh, Madame," he told her, all the while drawing at his pewter cup, "I can prepare a fricassee to fit a king, your king or mine." But when it came it was like no fricassee she'd ever seen or tasted, its sauce like gluten and spiced so even a starving dog would have spat it out. She was outraged and she told him so, even as Thomas Trowbridge shoveled a simple dinner of salt pork and fried eggs into his groaning maw and pronounced it as good as he'd ever tasted. "I won't eat this," Sarah said, piercing the Frenchman with a look. "You'll cook me eggs."

"I will cook you nothing," the Frenchman said. "I go to bed now. And so do you."

Rye to Spuyten Duyvil

The night was sleepless and miserable, the bed an instrument of torture, Thomas Trowbridge and another gentleman making their beds in the same room and keeping her awake and furious with their blowing and snorting till she thought she'd have to get up and stuff rags down their throats, and they were away at first light, without breakfast. The previous day's snow had accumulated only to three or four inches but it had frozen hard during the night so that each step of her horse groaned and crackled underfoot. To say that she ached would be an understatement, and there was the cold—bitterer even than yesterday—and the scare her horse gave her every two minutes when its feet skewed away and it made a slow, heaving recovery that at any moment could have been its last. Did she picture herself down beneath the beast with her leg fractured so that the bone protruded and the unblemished snow ran red with her blood? She did. Repeatedly.

By seven in the morning they reached the French town of New Rochelle, and her previous experience of Frenchmen notwithstanding, had an excellent breakfast at an ordinary there. She was so frozen she could scarcely lift the fork to her mouth and found she had no desire to leave the fireside ever again, no matter that her family would never more lay eyes on her and the widowed Mrs. Trowbridge would die in penury and the life of Boston—and its gossip—would go on without Sarah Kemble Knight ever seeing or knowing of it. But within an hour of their alighting, they were back on the road even as she cursed Thomas Trowbridge under her breath and her horse stumbled and slid and made risk of her life and limb with every clumsy faltering step.

They rode all day, through an increasingly civilized country, from time to time meeting other people on the road, people on foot, on horseback, in wagons. Cold, sore and miserable as she was, she nonetheless couldn't help feeling her spirits lighten as they came closer to their destination—here was real progress, in a peopled country, the wilderness falling away to the axe on both sides of the road. She took it all in and thought to memorialize it in her journal when they were arrived at New York late that night. All well and good. But then came the final crisis, the one that nearly prevented her from laying eyes on that so nearly foreign city with its Dutchmen pulling at their clay pipes and playing at draughts in stifling taverns, the women in their peculiar dress and jeweled earrings—even the dogs that looked to be from another world—and the amenable society of the Governor Lord Cornbury from the Jerseys and the solid brick buildings built cheek to jowl all through the lower town and a hundred other things. The sleighing parties. The shops. The houses of entertainment in a place called the Bowery and the good drink—choice beer, metheglin and cider—and a standard board that consisted of five and six dishes served hot and steaming from the fire. All this. All this and more.

But when they came to Spuyten Duyvil, the Spitting Devil, at the crossing to the north end of Manhattoes Island, with the night coming down and the wind blowing a gale and the waters surging as if it were the Great Flood all over again, she couldn't go on. There was a bridge here, narrow and unreliable, perched high up out over the waters, and it was slick with a coating of ice that lay black and glistening in the fading light. She got down to lead her horse, because if she led him she'd be lower to the ground—or the planking—and wouldn't be at the mercy of his uncertain footing. Thomas Trowbridge, hulking in his coats, paid the gatekeeper the sixpence for the two of them, and started across, mounted and oblivious; Sarah held back.

He was halfway across to the far shore, nearly invisible to her in the accumulating dark and the hard white pellets of ice that seemed to have come up with the wind, and the gatekeeper was huddled back in his hut giving her an odd look. All she could hear was the thunder of the roiling water where the river hit the surge of the tide even as the skin of it, black and unforgiving, stretched taut beneath her and exploded again. She was going to die. She was certain of it. She'd come all this way only to have the horse panic and trample her or bump her over the rail and into the spume or the bridge collapse beneath her. Thomas Trowbridge was gone now, enfolded in the mist, and he hadn't even so much as glanced back. The city was on the far shore, somewhere to the south of the island, and it was what she'd come for. There was lodging there. Fire. Food. Die or not, she stepped out onto the bridge.

It quaked and quailed. The wind thrashed. The horse jerked at her arm like a dead weight come to life. But she steeled herself and put one foot in front of the other and never looked down, a whole eternity passing till she was halfway across and then another eternity till she made the far side in a hard pale swirl of spray thrown up off the rocks and frozen in mid-air. For a long while she just stood there looking back the way she'd come, the bridge fading away into the blow till it might not have been there at all. But it was there, because this was no child's tale struck with magic, and she knew, even as she turned her mount and swung out onto the road, that she would have to cross it again.

(2003)

Up Against the Wall

My childhood wasn't exactly ideal, and I mention it here not as an excuse, but a point of reference. For the record, both my parents drank heavily, and in the early days, before my father gave up and withered away somewhere deep in the upright shell of himself, there was shouting, there were accusations, tears, violence. And smoke. The house was a factory of smoke, his two packs of Camels a day challenging the output of her two packs of Marlboros. I spent a lot of time outside. I ran with the kids in the neighborhood, the athletic ones when I was younger, the sly and disaffected as I came into my teens, and after an indifferent career at an indifferent college, I came back home to live rent-free in my childhood room in the attic as the rancor simmered below me and the smoke rose up through the floorboards and seeped in around the doorframe.

After a fierce and protracted struggle, I landed a job teaching eighth-grade English in a ghetto school, though I hadn't taken any of the required courses and had no intention of doing so. That job saved my life. Literally. Teaching, especially in a school as desperate as this, was considered vital to the national security and it got me a deferment two weeks short of the date I was to report for induction into the U.S. Army, with Vietnam vivid on the horizon. All well and fine. I had a job. And a routine. I got up early each morning, though it was a strain, showered, put on a tie and introspectively chewed Sugar Pops in the car on the way to work. I ate lunch out of a brown paper bag. Nights, I went straight to my room to play records and hammer away at my saxophone and vocals.

Then a day came—drizzling, cold, the wet skin of dead leaves on the pavement and nothing happening anywhere in the world, absolutely nothing—when I was in the local record store turning over albums to study the bright glare of the product and skim the liner notes, killing time till the movie started in the mall. Something with a monumental bass line was playing over the speakers, something slow, delicious, full of hooks and grooves and that steamroller bass, and when I looked up vacantly to appreciate it, I found I was looking into the face of a guy I recalled vaguely from high school.

I saw in a glance he'd adopted the same look I had—the greasy suede jacket, bell-bottoms and Dingo boots, his hair gone long over the collar in back, the shadowy beginnings of a mustache—and that was all it took. "Aren't you—Cole?" I said. "Cole, right?" And there he was, wrapping my hand in a cryptic soul shake, pronouncing my name without hesitation. We stood there catching up while people drifted by us and the bass pounded through the speakers. Where had he been? Korea, in the Army. Living with his own little mama-san, smoking opium every night till he couldn't feel the floor under his futon. And I was a teacher now, huh? What a gas. And should he start calling me professor or what?

We must have talked for half an hour or so, the conversation ranging from people we knew in common to bands, drugs and girls we'd hungered for in school, until he said, "So what you doing tonight? Later, I mean?"

I was ashamed to tell him I was planning on taking in a movie alone, so I just shrugged. "I don't know. Go home, I guess, and listen to records."

"Where you living?"

Another shrug, as if to show it was nothing, a temporary arrangement till I could get on my feet, find my own place and begin my real life, the one I'd been apprenticing for all these years: "My parents'."

Cole said nothing. Just gave me a numb look. "Yeah," he said, after a moment, "I hear you. But listen, you want to go out, drive around, smoke a number? You smoke, right?"

I did. Or I had. But I had no connection, no stash of my own, no privacy. "Yeah," I said. "Sounds good."

"I might know where there's a party," he said, letting his cold blue eyes sweep the store as if the party might materialize in the far corner. "Or a bar," he said, coming back to me, "I know this bar—"

I was late for homeroom in the morning. It mattered in some obscure way, in the long run, that is, because funding was linked to attendance and there had to be somebody there to check off the names each morning, but the school was in such an advanced state of chaos I don't know if anyone even noticed. Not the first time anyway. But homeroom was the least of my worries—it was mercifully brief and no one was expected to do anything other than merely exist for the space of ten minutes. It was the rest of the slate that was the trial, one swollen class after another shuffling into the room, hating school, hating culture, hating me, and I hated them in turn because they were brainless and uniform and they didn't understand me at all. I was just like them, couldn't they see that? I was no oppressor, no tool of the ruling class, but an authentic rebel, twenty-one years old and struggling mightily to grow a mustache because Ringo Starr had one and George Harrison and Eric Clapton and just about anybody else staring out at you from the front cover of a record album. But none of that mattered. I was the teacher, they were the students. Those were our roles, and they were as fixed and mutually exclusive as they'd been in my day, in my parents' day, in George Washington's day for all I knew.

From the minute the bell rang the rebellion began to simmer. Two or three times a period it would break out in riot and I would find myself confronting some wired rangy semi-lunatic who'd been left back twice and at sixteen already had his own mustache grown in as thick as fur, and there went the boundaries in a hard wash of threat and violence. Usually I'd manage to get the offender out in the hall, away from the eyes of the mob, and if the occasion called for it I would throw him against the wall, tear his shirt and use the precise language of the streets to let him know in excruciating detail just who was the one with the most at stake here. A minute later we'd return to the room, the victor and the vanquished, and the rest of them would feel something akin to awe for about ten minutes, and then it would all unwind again.

Stress. That's what I'm talking about. One of the other new teachers—he looked to be thirty or so, without taste or style, a drudge who'd been through half a dozen schools already—used to get so worked up he'd have to dash into the lavatory and vomit between classes, and there was no conquering that smell, not even with a fistful of breath mints. The students knew it, and they came at him like hyenas piling on a kill. He lasted a month, maybe less. This wasn't pedagogy—it was survival. Still, everybody got paid and they were free to go home when the bell rang at the end of the day, and some of them—some of us—even got to avoid the real combat zone, the one they showed in living color each night on the evening news.

When I got home that afternoon, Cole was waiting for me. He was parked out front of my house in his mother's VW Bug, a cigarette clamped between his teeth as he beat at the dashboard with a pair of drumsticks, the radio cranked up high. I could make out the seething churn of his shoulders and the rhythmic bob of his head through the oval window set in the back of the Bug, the sticks flashing white, the car rocking on its springs, and when I killed the engine of my own car—a 1955 Pontiac that had once been blue, but was piebald now with whitish patches of blistered paint—I could hear the music even through the safety glass of the rolled-up window. "Magic Carpet Ride," that was the song, with its insistent bass and nagging vocal, a tune you couldn't escape on AM radio, and there were worse, plenty worse.

My first impulse was to get out of the car and slide in beside him—here was adventure, liberation, a second consecutive night on the town—but then I thought better of it. I was dressed in my school clothes—dress pants I wouldn't wish on a corpse, button-down shirt and tie, a brown corduroy sport coat—and my hair was slicked down so tightly to my scalp it looked as if it had been painted on, a style I'd adopted to disguise the length and shagginess of it toward the end of appeasing the purse-mouthed principal and preserving my job. And life. But I couldn't let Cole see me like this—what would he think? I studied the back of the Bug a moment, waiting for his eyes to leap to the rearview mirror, but he was absorbed, oblivious, stoned no doubt—and I wanted to be stoned too, share the sacrament, shake it out—but not like this, not in these clothes. What I finally did was ease out of the car, slip down the block and cut through the neighbor's to our backyard, where the bulk of the house screened me from view.

I came up the cellar stairs from the garage, my father sunk into the recliner in the living room with the TV going—the news grim and grimmer—and my mother rattling things around in the kitchen. "You going to eat tonight?" she asked, just to say something. I ate every night—I couldn't afford not to. She had a cigarette at her lips, a drink in her hand—scotch and water. There were dishes set out on the table, a pot of something going on the stove. "I'm making chili con carne."

I had a minute, just a minute, no more, because I was afraid Cole would wake up to the fact that he was waiting for nothing and then it would be the room upstairs, the hypnosis of the records, the four walls and the sloping ceiling and a gulf of boredom so deep you could have sailed a fleet into it. "No," I said, "I think I might go out."

She stirred the pot, went to set the cigarette in the ashtray on the stove and saw that there was another there, already burning and rimmed red with lipstick. "Without dinner?" (I have to give her her due here—she loved me, her only son, and my father must have loved me too, in his own way, but I didn't know that then, or didn't care, and it's too late now to do anything about it.)

"Yeah, I might eat out, I guess. With Cole."

"Who?"

"Cole Harman. He was in high school with me?"

She just shrugged. My father said nothing, not hello or goodbye or you look half-starved already and you tell me you're going to miss dinner? The TV emitted the steady whipcrack of small-arms fire, and then the correspondent came on with the day's body count. Four minutes later—the bells, the boots, a wide-collared shirt imprinted with two flaming outsized eyeballs under the greasy jacket and my hair kinked up like Hendrix's—and I was out the door.

"Hey," I said, rapping at the window of the Bug. "Hey, it's me."

Cole looked up as if he'd been asleep, as if he'd been absorbed in some other reality altogether, one that didn't seem to admit or even recognize me. It took him a moment, and then he leaned across the passenger's seat and flipped the lock, and I went round the car and slid in beside him. I said something like,

"Good to see you, man," and reached out for the soul shake, which he returned, and then I said, "So, what's up? You want to go to Chase's, or what?"

He didn't reply. Just handed me the tight white tube of a joint, put the car in gear and hit the accelerator with the sound of a hundred eggbeaters all rattling at once. I looked back to see my house receding at the end of the block and felt as if I'd been rescued. I put the lighter to the joint.

The night before we'd gone to Chase's, a bar in town I'd never been to before, an ancient place with a pressed-tin ceiling and paneled booths gone the color of beef jerky with the smoke of a hundred thousand cigarettes. The music was of the moment, though, and the clientele mostly young—women were there, in their low-slung jeans and gauzy tops, and it was good to see them, exciting in the way of an afterthought that suddenly blooms into prominence (I'd left a girlfriend behind at college, promising to call, visit, write, but long distance was expensive, she was five hundred miles away and I wasn't much of a writer). My assumption—my hope—was that we'd go back there tonight.

But we didn't. Cole just drove aimlessly past bleached-out lawns and squat houses, down the naked tunnels of trees and into the country, where the odd field—crippled cornstalks, rotting pumpkins—was squeezed in among the housing developments and the creep of shopping malls. We smoked the joint down to the nub, employed a roach clip and alternated hits till it was nothing but air. An hour stole by. The same hits thumped through the radio, the same commercials. It was getting dark.

After a while we pulled up at a deserted spot along a blacktop road not two miles from my house. I knew the place from when I was a kid, riding my bike out to the reservoir to fish and throw rocks and fool around. There was a waist-high wall of blackened stone running the length of a long two blocks, and behind that a glimpse of a cluster of stone cottages through the dark veins of the trees. We'd been talking about something comforting—a band or a guitar player—and I'd been drifting, wheeling round and round the moment, secure, calm, and now suddenly we were stopped out on the road in the middle of nowhere. "So, what's the deal?" I said.

A car came up the street in the opposite direction and the lights caught Cole's face. He squinted, put a hand up to shield his eyes till the car had passed, and he craned his neck to make sure it was still moving, watching for the flash of brake lights as it rounded the curve at the corner behind us and vanished into the night. "Nothing," he said, a spark of animation igniting his voice as if it were a joke—the car, the night, the joint—"I just wanted you to meet some people, that's all."

"What people? Out here?" I gave it a beat. "You don't mean the little people, do you? The elves? Where are they—crouching behind the wall there? Or in their burrows, is that where they are—asleep in their burrows?"

We both had a laugh, one of those protracted, breast-pounding jags of hilarity that remind you just how much you've smoked and how potent it was. "No," he said, still wheezing, "no. Big people. Real people, just like you and me." He pointed to the faintest glow of light from the near cottage. "In there."

I was confused. The entrance to the place—the driveway, which squeezed under a stone arch somebody had erected there at some distant point in our perfervid history—was up on the cross street at the end of the block, where the car had just turned. "So why don't we just go in the driveway?" I wanted to know.

Cole took a moment to light a cigarette, then he cracked the door and the dark pure refrigerated smell of the night hit me. "Not cool," he said. "Not cool at all."

I made a real effort the next day, and though I had less than three hours' sleep, I made homeroom with maybe six seconds to spare. The kids—the students, my charges—must have scented the debauch on me, the drift away from the straight and narrow they demanded as part of the social contract, because they were more restive than usual, more boisterous and slippery, as if the seats couldn't contain them. There was one—there's always one, memorable not for excellence or scholarship but for weakness, only that—and he spoke up now. Robert, his name was, Robert Rowe. He was fifteen, left back once, and he was no genius but he had more of a spark in him than the others could ever hope for, and that made him stand out—it gave him power, but he didn't know what to do with it. "Hey, Mr. Caddis," he called from the back of the room where he was slumped into one of the undersized desks we'd inherited from another era when the average student was shorter, slimmer, more attentive and eager. "You look like shit, you know that?"

The rest of them—this was only homeroom, where, as I've indicated, nothing was expected—froze for a moment. The interaction was delicious for them, I'm sure—they were scientists dissecting the minutest gradations of human behavior: would I explode? Overheat and run for the lavatory like Mr. James, the puker? Ignore the comment? Pretend I hadn't heard?

I was beat, truly. Two nights running with less than three hours' sleep. But I was energized too because something new was happening to me, something that shone over the bleakness of this job, this place, my parents' damaged lives, as if I'd suddenly discovered the high beams along a dark stretch of highway. "Yeah, Robert," I said, holding him with my eyes, though he tried to duck away, "thanks for the compliment." A tutorial pause, flatly instructive. "You look like shit too."

The cottage, the stone cottage on the far side of the stone wall in the featureless mask of the night that had given way to this moment of this morning, was a place I felt I'd come home to after a long absence. I'd been to war, hadn't I? Now I was home. How else to describe it, what that place meant to me from the minute the door swung back and I stepped inside?

I hadn't known what to expect. We vaulted the stone wall and picked our way through a dark tangle of leafless sumac and stickers that raked at our boots and the oversized flaps of our pants, and then there was another, lower wall, and we were in the yard. Out front was a dirt bike with its back wheel missing, skeletal under the porch light, and there were glittering fragments of other things there too, machines in various states of disassembly—a chain saw minus the chain, an engine block decorated with lit candles that flickered like votives in the dark cups of the cylinders, a gutted amplifier. And there was music. Loud now, loud enough to rattle the glass in the windowpanes. Somebody inside was playing along with the bass line of "Ob-La-Di, Ob-La-Da."

Cole went in without knocking, and I followed. Through a hallway and into the kitchen, *obladi oblada life goes on bra!* There were two women there—girls—rising up from the table in the kitchen with loopy grins to wrap their arms around Cole, and then, after the briefest of introductions—"This is my friend, John, he's a *professor*"—to embrace me too. They were sisters, both tall, with the requisite hair parted in the middle and trailing down their shoulders. Suzie, the younger, darker and prettier one, and JoJo, two years older, with hair the color of rust before it flakes. There was a Baggie of pot on the table, a pipe and what looked to be half a bar of halvah candy but wasn't candy at all. Joss sticks burned among the candles that lit the room. A cat looked up sleepily from a pile of newspaper in the corner. "You want to get high?" JoJo asked, and I was charmed instantly—here she was, the consummate hostess—and a portion of my uncertainty and awkwardness went into retreat.

I looked to Cole, and we both laughed, and this was a laugh of the same quality and flavor as the one we'd shared in the car.

"What?" Suzie said, leaning back against the stove now, grinning wide. "Oh, I get it—you're already stoned, both of you, right? High as kites, right?"

From the living room—the door was closed and I had to presume it was the living room—there was the sudden screech of the needle lifting off the record, then the superamplified rasp of its dropping down again, and "Ob-La-Di, Ob-La-Da" came at us once more. JoJo saw my quizzical look and paused in putting the match to the pipe. "Oh, that's Mike—my boyfriend? He's like obsessed with that song."

I don't know how much time slid by before the door swung open—we were just sitting there at the table, enveloped in the shroud of our own consciousness, the cat receding into the corner that now seemed half a mile away, candles flickering and sending insubstantial shadows up the walls. I turned round to see Mike standing in the doorframe, wearing the strap of his bass like a bandolier over a shirtless chest. He was big, six feet and something, two hundred pounds, and he was built, pectorals and biceps sharply defined, a stripe of hard blue vein running up each arm, but he didn't do calisthenics or lift weights or anything like that—it was just the program of his genes. His hair was long, longer than either of the women's. He wore a Fu Manchu mustache. He was sweating. "That was hot," he said, "that was really hot."

JoJo looked up vacantly. "What," she said, "you want me to turn down the heat?"

He gave a laugh and leaned into the table to pluck a handful of popcorn out of a bowl that had somehow materialized there. "No, I mean the—Didn't you hear me? That last time? That was hot, that's what I'm saying."

It was only then that we got around to introductions, he and Cole swapping handclasps, and then Cole cocking a finger at me. "He's a professor," he said.

Mike took my hand—the soul shake, a pat on the shoulder—and stood there looking bemused. "A professor?" he said. "No shit?"

I was too stoned to parse all the nuances of the question, but still the blood must have risen to my face. "A teacher," I corrected. "You know, just to beat the draft? Like because if you—" and I went off on some disconnected monologue, talking because I was nervous, because I wanted to fit in, and I suppose I would have kept on talking till the sun came up but for the fact that everyone else had gone silent and the realization of it suddenly hit me.

"No shit?" Mike repeated, grinning in a dangerous way. He was swaying over the table, alternately feeding popcorn into the slot of his mouth and giving me a hooded look. "So how old are you—what, nineteen, twenty?"

"Twenty-one. I'll be twenty-two in December."

There was more. It wasn't an inquisition exactly—Cole at one point spoke up for me and said, "He's cool"—but a kind of scientific examination of this rare bird that had mysteriously turned up at the kitchen table. What did I think? I thought Cole should ease up on the professor business—as I got to know him I realized he was inflating me in order to inflate himself—and that we should all smoke some of the hash, though I wasn't the host here and hadn't brought anything to the party.

Eventually, we did smoke—that was what this was all about, community, the community of mind and spirit and style—and we moved into the living room where the big speakers were to listen to the heartbeat of the music and feel the world settle in around us. There were pillows scattered across the floor, more cats, more incense, ShopRite cola and peppermint tea in heavy homemade mugs and a slow sweet seep of peace. I propped my head against a pillow, stretched my feet out before me. The music was a dream, and I closed my eyes and entered it.

A week or two later my mother asked me to meet her after work at a bar /restaurant called the Hollander. This was a place with pretensions to grander things, where older people—people my mother's age—came to drink Manhattans and smoke cigarettes and feel elevated over the crowd that frequented taverns with sawdust on the floors, the sort of places my father favored. Teachers came to the Hollander, lawyers, people who owned car dealerships and dress shops. My mother was a secretary, my father a bus driver. And the Hollander was an ersatz place, with pompous waiters and a fake windmill out front.

She was at the bar, smoking, sitting with a skinny white-haired guy I didn't recognize, and as I came up to them I realized he could have been my father's double, could have been my father, but he wasn't. There were introductions—his name was Jerry Reilly and he was a teacher just like me—and a free beer appeared at my elbow, but I couldn't really fathom what was going on here or why my mother would want me to join her in a place like this. I played it cool, ducked my head and answered Jerry Reilly's interminable questions about school as best I could—*Yeah, sure, I guess I liked it; it was better than being executed in Vietnam, wasn't it?*—without irritating him to the point at which I would miss out on a free dinner, but all I wanted to do was get out of there and meet Cole at the cottage in the woods. As expeditiously as possible. Dinner down, goodbyes and thankyous on file, and out the door and into the car.

That wasn't how it worked out. Something was in the air and I couldn't fathom what it was. I kept looking at Jerry Reilly, with his cufflinks and snowy collar and whipcord tie and thinking, *No, no way—my mother wouldn't cheat on my father, not with this guy.* But her life and what she did with it was a work in progress, as unfathomable to me as my own life must have been to my students—and tonight's agenda was something else altogether, something that came in the form of a very special warning, specially delivered. We were on our third drink, seated in the dining room now, eating steak all around, though my mother barely touched hers and Jerry Reilly just pushed his around the plate every time I lifted my eyes to look at him. "Listen, John," my mother said finally, "I just wanted to say something to you. About Cole."

All the alarm bells went off simultaneously in my head. "Cole?" I echoed.

She gave me a look I'd known all my life, the one reserved for missteps and misdeeds. "He has a record."

So that was it. "What's it to you?"

My mother just shrugged. "I just thought you ought to know, that's all."

"I know. Of course I know. And it's nothing, believe me—a case of mistaken identity. They got the wrong guy is all." The fact was that Cole had been busted for selling marijuana to an undercover agent and they were trying to make a felony out of it even as his mother leaned on a retired judge she knew to step in and quash it. I put on a look of offended innocence. "So what'd you do, hire a detective?"

A thin smile. "I'm just worried about you, that's all."

How I bristled at this. I wasn't a child—I could take care of myself. How many times had her soft dejected voice come at me out of the shadows of the living room at three and four in the morning, where she sat smoking in the dark while I roamed the streets with my friends? *Where had I been?* she always wanted to know. *Nowhere,* I told her. There was the dark, the smell of her cigarette, and then, even softer: *I was worried.* And what did I do now? I worked my face and gave her a disgusted look to show her how far above all this I was.

She looked to Jerry Reilly, then back to me. I became aware of the sound of traffic out on the road. It was dark beyond the windows. "You're not using drugs," she asked, drawing at her cigarette, so that the interrogative lift came in a fume of smoke, "are you?"

The first time I ever saw anyone inject heroin was in the bathroom of that stone cottage in the woods. It was probably the third or fourth night I'd gone there with Cole to hang out, listen to music and be convivial on our own terms (he was living at his parents' house too, and there was no percentage in that). Mike greeted us at the door—he'd put a leather jacket on over a T-shirt and he was all business, heading out to the road to meet a guy named Nicky and they were going on into town to score and we should just hang tight because they'd be right back and did we happen to have any cash on us?—and then we went in and sat with the girls and smoked and didn't think about much of anything until the front door jerked back on its hinges half an hour later and Mike and Nicky came storming into the room as if their jackets had been set afire.

Then it was into the bathroom, Mike first, the door open to the rest of us lined up behind him, Nicky (short, with a full beard that did nothing to flesh out a face that had been reduced to the sharp lineaments of bone and cartilage) and the two sisters, Cole and me. I'd contributed five dollars to the enterprise, though I had my doubts. I'd never done anything like this and I was scared of the consequences, the droning narration of the anti-drug films from high school riding up out of some backwater of my mind to assert itself, to take over, become shrill even. Mike threw off his jacket, tore open two glassine packets with his teeth and carefully—meticulously—shook out the contents into a tablespoon. It was a white powder, and it could have been anything, baking soda, confectioners' sugar, Polident, but it wasn't, and I remember thinking how innocuous it looked, how anonymous. In the next moment, Mike sat heavily on the toilet, drew some water up into the syringe I'd seen lying there on a shelf in the medicine cabinet last time I'd used the facilities, squeezed a few drops into the powder, mixed it around and then held a lighter beneath the spoon. Then he tied himself off at the biceps with a bit of rubber tubing, drew the mixture from the spoon through a ball of cotton and hit a vein. I watched his eyes. Watched the rush take him, and then the nod. Nicky was next, then Suzie, then JoJo, and finally Cole. Mike hit them, one at a time, like a doctor. I watched each of them rush and go limp, my heart hammering at my ribcage, the record in the living room repeating over and over because nobody had bothered to put the changer down, and then it was my turn. Mike held up the glassine packet. "It's just a taste," he said. "Three-dollar bag. You on for it?"

"No," I said, "I mean, I don't think I—"

He studied me a moment, then tossed me the bag. "It's a waste," he said, "a real waste, man." His voice was slow, the voice of a record played at the wrong speed. He shook his head with infinite calm, moving it carefully from side to side as if it weighed more than the cottage itself. "But hey, we'll snort it this time. You'll see what you're missing, right?"

I saw. Within the week I was getting off too, and it was my secret—my initiation into a whole new life—and the tracks, the bite marks of the needle that crawled first up one arm and then the other, were my testament.

It was my job to do lunch duty one week a month, and lunch duty consisted of keeping the student body out of the building for forty-five minutes while they presumably went home, downtown or over to the high school and consumed whatever nourishment was available to them. It was necessary to keep them out of the junior high building for the simple reason that they would destroy it through an abundance of natural high spirits and brainless joviality. I stood in the dim hallway, positioned centrally between the three doors that opened from the southern, eastern and western sides of the building, and made my best effort at chasing them down when they burst in howling against the frigid collapse of the noon hour. On the second day of my third tour of duty, Robert Rowe sauntered in through the front doors and I put down my sandwich—the one my mother had made me in the hour of the wolf before going off to work herself—and reminded him of the rules.

He opened his face till it bloomed like a flower and held out his palms. He was wearing a T-shirt and a sleeveless parka. I saw that he'd begun to let his hair go long. "I just wanted to ask you a question is all."

I was chewing tunafish on rye, standing there in the middle of all that emptiness in my ridiculous pants and rumpled jacket. The building, like most institutions of higher and lower learning, was overheated, and in chasing half a dozen of my charges out the door I'd built up a sweat that threatened to break my hair loose of its mold. Without thinking, I slipped off the jacket and let it dangle from one hand; without thinking, I'd pulled a short-sleeved button-down shirt out of my closet that morning because all the others were dirty. That was the scene. That was the setup. "Sure," I said. "Go ahead."

"I was just wondering—you ever read this book, *The Man with the Golden Arm*?"

"Nelson Algren?"

He nodded.

"No," I said. "I've heard of it, though."

He took a moment with this, then cocked his head back till it rolled on his shoulders and gave me a dead-on look. "He shoots up."

"Who?"

"The guy in the book. All the time." He was studying me, gauging how far he could go. "You know what that's like?"

I played dumb.

"You don't? You really don't?"

I shrugged. Dodged his eyes.

There was a banging at the door behind us, hilarious faces there, then the beat of retreating footsteps. Robert moved back a pace, but he held me with his gaze. "Then what's with the spots on your arms?"

I looked down at my arms as if I'd never seen them before, as if I'd been born without them and they'd been grafted on while I was napping. "Mosquito bites," I said.

"In November? They must be some tough-ass mosquitoes."

"Yeah," I said, shifting the half-eaten sandwich from one hand to the other so I could cover up with the jacket, "yeah, they are."

Mike liked the country. He'd grown up in the projects on the Lower East Side, always pressed in by concrete and blacktop, and now that he was in the wilds of northern Westchester he began to keep animals. There were two chickens in a rudely constructed pen and a white duck he'd hatched from the egg, all of which met their fate one bitter night when a fox—or more likely, a dog—sniffed them out. He had a goat too, chained to a tree from which it had stripped the bark to a height of six feet or more, its head against the palm of your hand exactly like a rock with hair on it, and when he thought about it he'd toss it half a bale of hay or a loaf of stale bread or even the cardboard containers the beer came in. Inside, he had a fifty-gallon aquarium with a pair of foot-long alligators huddled inside it under a heat lamp, and these he fed hamburger in the form of raw meatballs he'd work between his palms. Every once in a while someone would get stoned and expel a lungful of smoke into the aquarium to see what effect it would have on a pair of reptiles and the things would scrabble around against the glass enclosure, hissing.

I was there one night without Cole—he was meeting with his lawyer, I think; I remember he'd shaved his mustache and trimmed his hair about that time—and I parked out on the street so as to avoid suspicion and made my way over the stone wall and through the darkened woods to the indistinct rumble of live music, the pulse of Mike's bass buoyed by the chink-chink of a high hat, an organ fill and cloudy vocals. My breath steamed around me. A sickle moon hung over the roof of the cottage and one of the cats shot along the base of the outer wall as I pushed through the door.

Everyone was gathered in the living room, JoJo and Suzie stretched out on the floor, Mike and his band, his new band, manning the instruments. I stood in the doorway a moment, feeling awkward. Nicky was on keyboards and a guy I'd met a few times—Skip—was doing the drumming. But there was a stranger, older, in his late twenties, with an out-of-date haircut and the flaccid beginnings of jowls, up at the mike singing lead and playing guitar. I leaned against the doorframe and listened, nodding my head to the beat, as they went through a version of "Rock and Roll Woman," Mike stepping up to the microphone to blend his voice effortlessly with the new guy's on the complex harmonies, and it wasn't as if they were rehearsing at all. They could have been onstage playing the tune for the hundredth time. When the song finished, I ducked into the room, nodding to Mike and saying something inane like, "Sounding good, man."

As it turned out, the new guy—his name was either Haze or Hayes, I never did get that straight—had played with Mike in a cover band the year before and then vanished from sight. Now he was back and they were rehearsing for a series of gigs at a club out on Route 202, where eventually they'd become the house band. I sat there on the floor with the girls and listened and felt transported—I wanted to get up and sing myself, ask them if they couldn't use a saxophone to cut away from the guitar leads, but I couldn't work up the nerve. Afterward, in the kitchen, when we were all stoned and riding high on the communion of the music, Haze launched into "Sunshine of My Love" on his acoustic guitar and I lost my inhibitions enough to try to blend my voice with his, with mixed results. But he kept on playing, and I kept on singing, till Mike went out to the living room and came back with the two alligators, one clutched in each hand, and began banging them together like tambourines, their legs scrambling at the air and tails flailing, the white miniature teeth fighting for purchase.

Then there was parent/teacher night. I got home from work and went straight to bed, and then, cruelly, had to get back up, put the tie on all over again and drive to school right in the middle of cocktail hour, or at the tail end of it anyway. I make a joke of it now, but I was tentative about the whole thing, afraid of the parents' scrutiny, afraid I'd be exposed for the impostor I was. I pictured them grilling me about the rules of grammar or Shakespeare's plays—the ones I hadn't read—but the parents were as hopeless as their offspring. Precious few of them turned up, and those who did looked so intimidated by their surroundings I had the feeling they would have taken my word for practically anything. In one class—my fifth period—a single parent turned up. His son—an overweight, well-meaning kid mercilessly ragged by his classmates—was one of the few in the class who weren't behavioral problems, but the father kept insisting that his son was a real hell-raiser, "just like his old man." He sat patiently, work-hardened hands folded on the miniature desk, through my fumbling explanation of what I was trying to accomplish with this particular class and the lofty goals to which each and every student aspired and more drivel of a similar nature, before interrupting me to say, "He gives you a problem, you got my permission to just whack him one. All right? You get me?"

I was stuffing papers into my briefcase just after the final bell rang at 8:15, thinking to meet Cole at Chase's as soon as I could change out of my prison clothes, when a woman in her thirties—a mother—appeared in the doorway. She looked as if she'd been drained of blood, parchment skin and a high sculpted bluff of bleached-blond hair gone dead under the dehumanizing wash of the overhead lights. "Mr. Caddis?" she said in a smoker's rasp. "You got a minute?"

A minute? I didn't have thirty seconds. I wanted nothing but to get out of there and get loose before I fell into my bed for a few hours of inadequate dreamless sleep and then found myself right here all over again. "I'm in a hurry," I told her. "I have—well, an appointment."

"I only want a minute." There was something about her that looked vaguely familiar, something about the staring cola-colored eyes and the way her upper teeth pushed at her lip, that reminded me of somebody, somewhere—and then it came to me: Robert Rowe. "I'm Robert's mother," she said.

I didn't say anything, just parked my right buttock on the nearest desk and waited for her to go on. Robert wasn't in any of my classes, just homeroom. I wasn't his teacher. He wasn't my responsibility. The fat kid, yes. The black kid who flew around the room on the wings beating inside his brain chanting *He's white, he's right* for hours at a time, the six months' pregnant girl whose head would have fallen off if she stopped chewing gum for thirty seconds, yes and yes. But not Robert. Not Robert Rowe.

She was wearing a dirty white sweater, misbuttoned. A plaid skirt. Loafers. If I had been older, more attuned, more sympathetic, I would have seen that she was pretty, pretty still, and that she was desperately trying to communicate something to me, some nascent hope grown up out of the detritus of welfare checks and abandonment. "He looks up to you," she said, her voice choked, as if suddenly she couldn't breathe.

This took me by surprise. I didn't know how to respond, so I threw it back at her, stalling a moment to assimilate what she was saying. "Me?" I said. "He looks up to *me*?"

Her eyes were pooling. She nodded.

"But why me? I'm not even his teacher."

"Ever since his father left," she began, but let that thought trail off as she struggled to summon a new one, the thought—the phrase—that would bring me around, that would touch me in the way she wanted to. "He talks about you all the time. He thinks you're cool. That's what he say, 'Mr. Caddis is cool.' "

Robert Rowe's face rose up to hover before me in the seat of my unconscious, a compressed little nugget of a face, with the extruded teeth and Coca-Cola eyes of this woman, his mother, Mrs. Rowe. That was who she was, Mrs. Rowe, I reminded myself, and I seized on the proper form of address in that moment: "Mrs. Rowe, look, he's a great kid, but I'm not, I mean—well, I'm not his *teacher,* you know that—"

The room smelled of adolescent fevers and anxieties, of socks worn too long, unwashed hair, jackets that had never seen the inside of a dry cleaner's. There was a fading map of the United States on the back wall, chalkboards so old they'd faded to gray. The linoleum was cracked and peeled. The desks were a joke. Her voice was so soft I could barely hear her over the buzz of the fluorescent lights. "I know," she said. "But he's not . . . he's getting F's—D's and F's. I don't know what to do with him. He won't listen to me—he hasn't listened to me in years."

"Yeah," I said, just to say something. He looked up to me, sure, but I had a date to meet Cole at Chase's.

"Would you just, I don't know, look out for him? Would you? That's all I ask."

I suppose there are several layers of irony here, not the least of which is that I wasn't capable of looking out for myself, but I buried all that at the bar and when I saw Robert Rowe in homeroom the next morning, I felt nothing more than a vague irritation. He was wearing a tie-dyed shirt—starbursts of pink and yellow—under the parka and he'd begun to kink his hair out in the way I wore mine at night, but that had to be a coincidence, because to my knowledge he'd never seen me outside of school. It was possible, of course. Anything was possible. He could have seen me coming out of Chase's or stopped in my car along South Street with Mike or Cole, looking to score. I kept my head down, working at my papers—the endless, hopeless, scrawled-over tests and assignments—but I felt his eyes on me the whole time. Then the bell rang and he was gone with the rest of them.

I was home early that evening, looking for sustenance—hoping to find my mother in the kitchen stirring something in a pot—because I was out of money till payday and Cole was lying low because his mother had found a bag of pot in his underwear drawer and I felt like taking a break from the cottage and music and dope. Just for the night. I figured I'd stay in, read a bit, get to bed early. My mother wasn't there, though. She had a meeting. At school. One of the endless meetings she had to sit through, taking minutes in shorthand, while the school board debated yet another bond issue. I wondered about that and wondered about Jerry Reilly too.

My father was home. There was no other place he was likely to be—he'd given up going to the tavern or the diner or anyplace else. TV was his narcotic. And there he was, settled into his chair with a cocktail, watching *Victory at Sea* (his single favorite program, as if he couldn't get enough of the war that had robbed him of his youth and personality), the dog, which had been young when I was in junior high myself, curled up stinking at his feet. We exchanged a few words—*Where's Mom? At a meeting. You going to eat? No. A sandwich? I'll make you a sandwich? I said no.*—and then I heated a can of soup and went upstairs with it. For a long while I lay on the floor with my head sandwiched between the speakers, playing records over and over, and then I drifted off.

It was late when I woke—past one—and when I went downstairs to use the toilet, my mother was just coming in the door. The old dog began slapping his tail on the carpet, too arthritic to get up; the lamp on the end table flicked on, dragging shadows out of the corners. "You just getting in?" I said.

"Yes," she said, her voice hushed. She was in her work clothes: flocked dress, stockings and heels, a cloth coat, no gloves, though the weather had turned raw.

I stood there a moment, listening to the thwack of the dog's tail, half-asleep, summoning the beat of an internal rhythm. I should have mounted the stairs, should have gone back to bed; instead, I said, "Late meeting?"

My mother had set her purse down on the little table inside the door reserved for the telephone. She was slipping out of her coat. "We went out for drinks afterward," she said. "Some of us—me and Ruth, Larry Abrams, Ted Penny."

"And Jerry? What about him—was he there?"

It took a moment, the coat flung over the banister, the dog settled back in his coil, the clank of the heat coming on noisy out of all proportion, and then she turned to me, hands on her hips, and said, "Yes, Jerry was there. And you know what—I'm glad he was." A beat. She swayed slightly, or maybe that was my imagination. "You want to know why?"

There was something in her voice that should have warned me off, but I was awake now, and instead of going back upstairs to bed I just stood there in the dim arc of light the lamp cast on the floor and shrugged my shoulders. She lifted her purse from the telephone stand and I saw that there was something else there, a metal case the size of the two-tiered deluxe box of candy I gave her for Christmas each year. It was a tape recorder, and she bent a moment to fit the plug in the socket next to the phone outlet. Then she straightened up and gave me that look again—the admonitory look, searing and sharp. "I want you to listen to something," she said. "Something a friend of Jerry's—he works for the Peterskill police department, he's a detective—thought you ought to hear."

I froze. There was no time to think, no time to fabricate a story, no time to wriggle or plead, because my own voice was coming at me out of the miniature speaker. *Hey,* I was saying, *you coming over or what? It's like past nine already and everybody's waiting—*

There was music in the background, cranked loud—"Spinning Wheel," the tune of that fall, and we were all intoxicated by David Clayton Thomas and the incisiveness of those punched-up horns—and my mind ran through the calendar of the past week, Friday or Saturday at the cottage in the woods, Cole running late, the usual party in progress . . .

Yeah, sure, I heard Cole respond. He was at his mother's—it was his mother's birthday. *Just as soon as I can get out of here.*

Okay, man, I said. *Catch you later, right?*

That was it. Nothing incriminating, but incrimination wasn't the point of the exercise. It took me a moment, and then I thought of Haze, his sudden appearance in our midst, the glad-handing and the parceling out of the cool, and then I understood why he'd come to us—the term "infiltrated" soared up out of nowhere—and just who had put him up to it. I couldn't think of what to say.

My mother could, though. She clicked off the tape with a punch of her index finger. "My friend said if you knew what was good for you, you'd stay clear of that place for a while. For good." We stood five feet apart. There was no embrace—we weren't an embracing family—no pat on the back, no gesture of any kind. Just the two of us standing there in the half-dark. When she spoke finally her voice was muted. "Do you understand what I'm telling you?"

As soon as I got out of work the next day I changed my clothes and went straight to the cottage. It was raining steadily, a cold gray rain that drooled from the branches of the trees and braided in the gutters. Cole's Bug was parked on the street as I drove up, but I didn't park beside him—I drove another half mile on and parked on a side street, a cul-de-sac where nobody would see the car. Then I put my head down and walked up the road in the rain, veering off into the woods the minute I saw a car turn into the street. I remember how bleak everything looked, the summer's trash revealed at the feet of the denuded trees, the weeds bowed and frost-burned, leaves clinging to my boots as if the ground were made of paste. My heart was pounding. It was a condition we called paranoia when we were smoking, the unreasoning feeling that something or somebody is about to pounce, that the world has become intractably dangerous and your own vulnerability has been flagged. But no, this wasn't paranoia: the threat was real.

The hair was wet to my scalp and my jacket all but ruined by the time I pushed through the front door. The house was quiet, no music bleeding through the speakers, no murmur of voices or tread of footsteps. There was the soft fading scratch of one of the cats in the litter pan in the kitchen, and that was it, nothing, silence absolute. I stood in the entryway a moment, trying to scrape the mud and leaves from my boots, but it was hopeless, so finally I just stepped out of them in my stocking feet and left them there at the door. I suppose that was why Suzie and Cole didn't hear me coming—I hadn't meant to creep up on them, hadn't meant anything except to somehow come round to tell them what I knew, what I'd learned, warning them, sparing them, and as I say my heart was going and I was risking everything myself just to be there, just to be present—and when I stepped into the living room they gave me a shock. They were naked, their clothes flung down beside them, rolling on a blanket in sexual play—or the prelude to it. I suppose it doesn't really matter at this juncture to say that I'd found her attractive—she was the pretty one, always that—or that I felt all along that she'd favored me over Cole or Nicky or any of the others? That didn't matter. That had nothing to do with it. I'd come with a warning, and I had to deliver it.

"Who's that?" Suzie's voice rose up out of the stillness. Cole was atop her and she had to lift her head to fix her eyes on me. "John? Is that you?"

Cole rolled off her and flipped a fold of the blanket over her. "Jesus," he said, "you picked a great moment." His eyes burned, though I could see he was trying to be cool, trying to minimize it, no big thing.

"Jesus," Suzie said, "you scared me. Do you always creep around like that?"

"My boots," I said. "They just—or actually, I just came by to tell you something, that's all—I can't stay . . ."

The rain was like two cupped palms holding the place in its grip. The gutters rattled. Pinpricks needled the roof. "Shit," Cole said, and Suzie reached out to gather up her clothes, shielding her breasts in the crook of one arm, "I mean, shit, John. Couldn't you wait in the kitchen, I mean, for like ten fucking minutes? Huh? Couldn't you?"

I swung round without a word and padded out to the kitchen even as the living room door thundered shut at my back. For a long while I sat at the familiar table with its detritus of burned joss sticks, immolated candles, beer bottles, mugs, food wrappers and the like, thinking I could just write them a note—that would do it—or maybe I'd call Cole later, from home, when he got home, that was, at his mother's. But I couldn't find a pencil—nobody took notes here, that was for sure—and finally I just pushed myself up, tiptoed to the door and fell back into my boots and the sodden jacket.

It was just getting dark when I pulled up in front of the house. My father's car was parked there at the curb, but my mother's wasn't and it wasn't in the driveway either. The rain kept coming down—the streets were flooding, broad sheets of water fanning away from the tires and the main road clogged with slow-moving cars and their tired headlights and frantically beating wipers. I ran for the house, kicked off my boots on the doorstep and flung myself inside as if I'd been away for years. My jacket streamed and I hurried across the carpet to the accompaniment of the dog's thwacking tail and hung it from the shower head in the bathroom. Then I went to the kitchen to look in the refrigerator, feeling desolate and cheated. I didn't have a habit despite the stigmata of my arms—I was a neophyte still, a twice- or three-times-a-week user—but I had a need, and that need yawned before me, opening up and opening up again, as I leaned over the sink. The cottage was over. Cole was over. Life, as I'd come to know it, was finished.

It was then that I noticed the figure of my father moving through the gloom of the backyard. He had on a pair of galoshes I'd worn as a kid, the kind with the metal fasteners, and he was wearing a yellow rain slicker and one of those winter hats with the fold-down earmuffs. I couldn't quite tell what he was doing out there, raking dirt or leaves, something to do with the rain, I guessed—the driveway was eroding, maybe that was it. It never crossed my mind that he might need help. And Robert Rowe never crossed my mind either, nor the fact that his speech had been garbled and slow at the noon hour and his eyes drifting toward a point no one in this world could see but him.

No. I was hungry for something, I didn't know what. It wasn't food, because I mechanically chewed a handful of saltines over the sink and washed them down with half a glass of milk that tasted like chalk. I paced round the living room, snuck a drink out of my mother's bottle—Dewar's, that was what she drank; my father stuck with vodka, the cheaper the better, and I'd never acquired a taste for it. I had another drink, and then another. After a while I eased myself down in my father's chair and gazed around the room where I'd spent the better part of my life, the secondhand furniture, the forest-green wallpaper gone pale around the windowframes, the peeling sheet-metal planter I'd made for my mother in shop class, the plants within it long since expired, just curls of dead things now. Finally I got up and turned on the TV, then settled back in my father's chair as the jets came in low and the village went up in flames.

(2003)

PART III

Wild Child

Balto

There were two kinds of truths, good truths and hurtful ones. That was what her father's attorney was telling her, and she was listening, doing her best, her face a small glazed crescent of light where the sun glanced off the yellow kitchen wall to illuminate her, but it was hard. Hard because it was a weekday, after school, and this was her free time, her chance to breeze into the 7-Eleven or Instant Message her friends before dinner and homework closed the day down. Hard too because her father was there, sitting on a stool at the kitchen counter, sipping something out of a mug, not coffee, definitely not coffee. His face was soft, the lines at the corners of his eyes nearly erased in the gentle spill of light—his *crow's-feet,* and how she loved that word, as if the bird's scaly claws had taken hold there like something out of a horror story, Edgar Allan Poe, the Raven, Nevermore, but wasn't a raven different from a crow and why not call them raven's-feet? Or hawk's-feet? People could have a hawk's nose—they always did in stories—but they had crow's-feet, and that didn't make any sense at all.

"Angelle," the attorney said—*Mr. Apodaca*—and the sound of her own name startled her, "are you listening to me?"

She nodded her head. And because that didn't seem enough, she spoke up too. "Yes," she said, but her voice sounded strange in her ears, as if somebody else were speaking for her.

"Good," he said, "good," leaning into the table so that his big moist dog's eyes settled on her with a baleful look. "Because this is very important, I don't have to stress that—"

He waited for her to nod again before going on.

"There are two kinds of truths," he repeated, "just like lies. There are bad lies, we all know that, lies meant to cheat and deceive, and then there are white lies, little fibs that don't really hurt anybody"—he blew out a soft puff of air, as if he were just stepping into a hot tub—"and might actually do good. Do you understand what I'm saying?"

She held herself perfectly still. Of course she understood—he was treating her like a nine-year-old, like her sister, and she was twelve, almost thirteen, and this was an act of rebellion, to hold herself there, not answering, not nodding, not even blinking her eyes.

"Like in this case," he went on, "your father's case, I mean. You've seen TV, the movies. The judge asks you for the truth, the whole truth and nothing but the truth, and you'll swear to it, everybody does—your father, me, anybody before the court." He had a mug too, one she recognized from her mother's college days—B.U., it said in thick red letters, *Boston University*—but there was coffee in his, or there had been. Now he just pushed it around the table as if it were a chess piece and he couldn't decide where to play it. "All I want you to remember—and your father wants this too, or no, he needs it, needs you to pay attention—is that there are good truths and bad truths, that's all. And your memory only serves to a point; I mean, who's to say what really happened, because everybody has their own version, that woman jogger, the boy on the bike—and the D.A., the district attorney, he's the one who might ask you what happened that day, just him and me, that's all. Don't you worry about anything."

But she was worried, because Mr. Apodaca was there in the first place, with his perfect suit and perfect tie and his doggy eyes, and because her father had been handcuffed along the side of the road and taken to jail and the car had been impounded, which meant nobody could use it, not her father or her mother when she came back from France or Dolores the maid or Allie the au pair. There was all that, but there was something else too, something in her father's look and the attorney's sugary tones that hardened her: they were talking down to her. Talking down to her as if she had no more sense than her little sister. And she did. She did.

That day, the day of the incident—or accident, he'd have to call it an accident now—he'd met Marcy for lunch at a restaurant down by the marina where you could sit outside and watch the way the sun struck the masts of the ships as they rocked on the tide and the light shattered and regrouped and shattered again. It was one of his favorite spots in town—one of his favorite spots, period. No matter how overburdened he felt, no matter how life beat him down and every task and deadline seemed to swell up out of all proportion so that twenty people couldn't have dealt with it all—a team, an army—this place, this table in the far corner of the deck overlooking the jungle of masts, the bleached wooden catwalks, the glowing arc of the harbor and the mountains that framed it, always had a calming effect on him. That and the just-this-side-of-too-cold local chardonnay they served by the glass. He was working on his second when Marcy came up the stairs, swaying over her heels like a model on the runway, and glided down the length of the deck to join him. She gave him an uncomplicated smile, a smile that lit her eyes and acknowledged everything—the day, the locale, the sun and the breeze and the clean pounded smell of the ocean and him perched there in the middle of it all—and bent to kiss him before easing herself into the chair beside him. "That looks nice," she said, referring to the wine dense as struck gold in the glass before him, and held up a finger for the waiter.

And what did they talk about? Little things. Her work, the pair of shoes she'd bought and returned and then bought all over again, the movie they'd seen two nights ago—the last time they'd been together—and how she still couldn't believe he liked that ending. "It's not that it was cheesy," she said, and here was her wine and should they get a bottle, yeah, sure, a bottle, why not? "and it was, but just that I didn't believe it."

"Didn't believe what—that the husband would take her back?"

"No," she said. "Or yes. It's idiotic. But what do you expect from a French movie? They always have these slinky-looking heroines in their thirties—"

"Or forties."

"—with great legs and mascara out of, I don't know, a KISS revival, and then even though they're married to the greatest guy in the world they feel unfulfilled and they go out and fuck the whole village, starting with the butcher."

"Juliette Binoche," he said. He was feeling the wine. Feeling good.

"Yeah, right. Even though it wasn't her, it could have been. Should have been. Has been in every French movie but this one for the past what, twenty years?" She put down her glass and let out a short two-note laugh that was like birdsong, a laugh that entranced him, and he wasn't worried about work now, not work or anything else, and here was the bottle in the bucket, the wine cold as the cellar it came from. "And then the whole village comes out and applauds her at the end for staying true to her romantic ideals—and the *husband,* Jesus."

Nothing could irritate him. Nothing could touch him. He was in love, the pelicans were gliding over the belly of the bay and her eyes were lewd and beautiful and pleased with themselves, but he had to pull the stopper here for just a minute. "Martine's not like that," he said. "I'm not like that."

She looked over her shoulder before digging out a cigarette—this was California, after all—and when she bent to light it her hair fell across her face. She came up smiling, the smoke snatched away from her lips and neutralized on the breeze the moment she exhaled. Discussion over.

Marcy was twenty-eight, educated at Berkeley, and she and her sister had opened an artists' supply shop on a side street downtown. She'd been a double major in art and film. She rode a bike to work. She was Asian. Or Chinese, she corrected him. Of Chinese descent anyway. Her family, as she'd informed him on the first date with enough irony in her voice to foreground and bury the topic at the same time, went back four generations to the honorable great-grandfather who'd smuggled himself across the Pacific inside a clichéd flour barrel hidden in the clichéd hold of a clichéd merchant ship. She'd grown up in Syracuse, in a suburban development, and her accent—the *a*'s flattened so that his name came out *Eelan* rather than Alan—just killed him, so incongruous coming from someone, as, well—the words out of his mouth before he knew what he was saying—as *exotic*-looking as her. And then, because he couldn't read her expression—had he gone too far?—he told her he was impressed because he only went back three generations, his grandfather having come over from Cork, but if it was in a barrel it would have been full of whiskey. "And Martine's from Paris," he'd added. "But you knew that already, didn't you?"

The bottle was half-gone by the time they ordered—and there was no hurry, no hurry at all, because they were both taking the afternoon off, and no argument—and when the food came they looked at each other for just the briefest fleeting particle of a moment before he ordered a second bottle. And then they were eating and everything slowed down until all of creation seemed to come into focus in a new way. He sipped the wine, chewed, looked into her unparalleled eyes and felt the sun lay a hand across his shoulders, and in a sudden blaze of apprehension he glanced up at the gull that appeared on the railing behind her and saw the way the breeze touched its feathers and the sun whitened its breast till there was nothing brighter and more perfect in the world—this creature, his fellow creature, and he was here to see it. He wanted to tell Marcy about it, about the miracle of the moment, the layers peeled back, revelatory, joyous, but instead he reached over to top off her glass and said, "So tell me about the shoes."

Later, after Mr. Apodaca had backed out of the driveway in his little white convertible with the Mercedes sign emblazoned on the front of it and the afternoon melted away in a slurry of phone calls and messages—*OMG! Chilty likes Alex Turtieff, can you believe it?*—Dolores made them *chiles rellenos* with carrot and jícama sticks and ice cream for dessert. Then Allie quizzed her and Lisette over their homework until the house fell quiet and all she could hear was the faint pulse of her father's music from the family room. She'd done her math and was working on a report about Aaron Burr for her history teacher, Mr. Compson, when she got up and went to the kitchen for a glass of juice or maybe hot chocolate in the microwave—and she wouldn't know which till she was standing there in the kitchen with the recessed lights glowing over the stone countertops and the refrigerator door open wide. She wasn't thinking about anything in particular—Aaron Burr was behind her now, upstairs, on her desk—and when she passed the archway to the family room the flash of the TV screen caught her eye and she paused a moment. Her father was there still, stretched out on the couch with a book, the TV muted and some game on, football, baseball, and the low snarl of his music in the background. His face had that blank absorbed look he got while reading and sometimes when he was just sitting there staring across the room or out the window at nothing, and he had the mug cradled in one hand, balanced on his chest beside the book.

He'd sat with them over dinner, but he hadn't eaten—he was going out later, he told her. For dinner. A late dinner. He didn't say who with, but she knew it was the Asian woman. Marcy. She'd seen her exactly twice, behind the window of her car, and Marcy had waved at her both times, a little curl of the fingers and a flash of the palm. There was an Asian girl in her class—she was Chinese—and her name was Xuan. That seemed right for an Asian girl, Xuan. Different. A name that said who she was and where she was from, far away, a whole ocean away. But Marcy? She didn't think so.

"Hey," her father said, lifting his head to peer over the butt of the couch, and she realized she'd been standing there watching him, "what's up? Homework done? Need any help? How about that essay—want me to proof that essay for you? What's it on, Madison? Or Burr. Burr, right?"

"That's okay."

"You sure?" His voice was slow and compacted, as if it wasn't composed of vibrations of the vocal cords, the air passing through the larynx like in her science book, but made of something heavier, denser. He would be taking a taxi tonight, she could see that, and then maybe she—*Marcy*—would drive him back home. "Because I could do it, no problem. I've got"—and she watched him lift his watch to his face and rotate his wrist—"half an hour or so, forty-five minutes."

"That's okay," she said.

She was sipping her hot chocolate and reading a story for English by William Faulkner, the author's picture in her textbook a freeze-frame of furious eyes and conquered hair, when she heard her father's voice riding a current down the hall, now murmurous, now pinched and electric, then dense and sluggish all over again. It took her a minute: he was reading Lisette her bedtime story. The house was utterly still and she held her breath, listening, till all of a sudden she could make out the words. He was reading *Balto,* a story she'd loved when she was little, when she was Lisette's age, and as his voice came to her down the hall she could picture the illustrations: Balto, the lead dog of the sled team, radiating light from a sunburst on his chest and the snowstorm like a monstrous hand closing over him, the team fighting through the Alaskan wind and ice and temperatures of forty below zero to deliver serum to the sick children in Nome—and those children would die if Balto didn't get through. Diphtheria. It was a diphtheria epidemic and the only plane available was broken down—or no, it had been dismantled for the winter. *What's diphtheria?* she'd asked her father, and he'd gone to the shelf and pulled down the encyclopedia to give her the answer, and that was heroic in itself, because as he settled back onto her bed, Lisette snuggled up beside her and rain at the windows and the bedside lamp the only thing between them and darkness absolute, he'd said, *You see, there's everything in books, everything you could ever want.*

Balto's paws were bleeding. The ice froze between his toes. The other dogs kept holding back, but he was the lead dog and he turned on them and snarled, fought them just to keep them in their traces, to keep them going. *Balto.* With his harnessed shoulders and shaggy head and the furious unconquerable will that drove him all through that day and into the night that was so black there was no way of telling if they were on the trail or not.

Now, as she sat poised at the edge of her bed, listening to Lisette's silence and her father's limping voice, she waited for her sister to pipe up in her breathy little baby squeak and frame the inevitable questions: *Dad, Dad, how cold is forty below?* And: *Dad, what's diphtheria?*

The sun had crept imperceptibly across the deck, fingering the cracks in the varnished floorboards and easing up the low brass rail Marcy was using as a backrest. She was leaning into it, the rail, her chair tipped back, her elbows splayed behind her and her legs stretched out to catch the sun, shapely legs, stunning legs, legs long and burnished and firm, legs that made him think of the rest of her and the way she was in bed. There was a scar just under the swell of her left kneecap, the flesh annealed in an irregular oval as if it had been burned or scarified, and he'd never noticed that before. Well, he was in a new place, half a glass each left of the second bottle and the world sprung to life in the fullness of its detail, everything sharpened, in focus, as if he'd needed glasses all these years and just clapped them on. The gull was gone but it had been special, a very special gull, and there were sparrows now, or wrens, hopping along the floor in little streaks of color, snatching up a crumb of this or that and then hurtling away over the rail as if they'd been launched. He was thinking he didn't want any more wine—two bottles was plenty—but maybe something to cap off the afternoon, a cognac maybe, just one.

She'd been talking about one of the girls who worked for her, a girl he'd seen a couple of times, nineteen, soft-faced and pretty, and how she—her name was Bettina—was living the party life, every night at the clubs, and how thin she was.

"Cocaine?" he wondered, and she shrugged. "Has it affected her work?"

"No," she said, "not yet anyway." And then she went on to qualify that with a litany of lateness in the morning, hyper behavior after lunch and doctor's appointments, too many doctor's appointments. He waited a moment, watching her mouth and tongue, the beautiful unspooling way the words dropped from her lips, before he reached down and ran a finger over the blemish below her kneecap. "You have a scar," he said.

She looked at her knee as if she wasn't aware it was attached to her, then withdrew her leg momentarily to scrutinize it before giving it back to the sun and the deck and the waiting touch of his hand. "Oh, that?" she said. "That's from when I was a kid."

"A burn or what?"

"Bicycle." She teased the syllables out, slow and sure.

His hand was on her knee, the warmth of the contact, and he rubbed the spot a moment before straightening up in the chair and draining his glass. "Looks like a burn," he said.

"Nope. Just fell in the street." She let out that laugh again and he drank it in. "You should've seen my training wheels—or the one of them. It was as flat"—*flaat*—"as if a truck had run me over."

Her eyes flickered with the lingering seep of the memory and they both took a moment to picture it, the little girl with the wheel collapsed under her and the scraped knee—or it had to have been worse than that, punctured, shredded—and he didn't think of Lisette or Angelle, not yet, because he was deep into the drift of the day, so deep there was nothing else but this deck and this slow sweet sun and the gull that was gone now. "You want something else?" he heard himself say. "Maybe a Rémy, just to cap it off? I mean, I'm wined out, but just, I don't know, a taste of cognac?"

"Sure," she said, "why not?" and she didn't look at her watch and he didn't look at his either.

And then the waiter was there with two snifters and a little square of dark chocolate for each of them, compliments of the house. *Snifter,* he was thinking as he revolved the glass in his hand, what a perfect designation for the thing, a name that spoke to function, and he said it aloud, "Isn't it great that they have things like snifters, so you can stick your nose in it and sniff? And plus, it's named for what it is, unlike, say, a napkin or a fork. You don't nap napkins or fork forks, right?"

"Yeah," she said, and the sun had leveled on her hair now, picking out the highlights and illuminating the lobe of one ear, "I guess. But I was telling you about Bettina? Did you know that guy she picked up I told you about—not the boyfriend, but the one-night stand? He got her pregnant."

The waiter drifted by then, college kid, hair in his eyes, and asked if there'd be anything else. It was then that he thought to check his watch and the first little pulse of alarm began to make itself felt somewhere deep in the quiet lagoon of his brain: *Angelle,* the alarm said. *Lisette.* They had to be picked up at school after soccer practice every Wednesday because Wednesday was Allie's day off and Martine wasn't there to do it. Martine was in Paris, doing whatever she pleased. That much was clear. And today—today was Wednesday.

Angelle remembered waiting for him longer than usual that day. He'd been late before—he was almost always late, because of work, because he had such a hectic schedule—but this time she'd already got through half her homework, the blue backpack canted away from her and her notebook spread open across her knees as she sat at the curb, and still he wasn't there. The sun had sunk into the trees across the street and she felt a chill where she'd sweated through her shorts and T-shirt at soccer. Lisette's team had finished before hers and for a while her sister had sat beside her, drawing big *x*'s and *o*'s in two different colors on a sheet of loose-leaf paper, but she'd got bored and run off to play on the swings with two other kids whose parents were late.

Every few minutes a car would round the turn at the top of the street, and her eyes would jump to it, but it wasn't theirs. She watched a black SUV pull up in front of the school and saw Dani Mead and Sarah Schuster burst through the doors, laughing, their backpacks riding up off their shoulders and their hair swaying back and forth as they slid into the cavernous back seat and the door slammed shut. The car's brake lights flashed and then it rolled slowly out of the parking lot and into the street, and she watched it till it disappeared round the corner. He was always working, she knew that, trying to dig himself out from under all the work he had piled up—that was his phrase, *dig himself out,* and she pictured him in his office surrounded by towering stacks of papers, papers like the Leaning Tower of Pisa, and a shovel in his hands as if he were one of those men in the orange jackets bent over a hole in the road—but still, she felt impatient. Felt cold. Hungry. And where was he?

Finally, after the last two kids had been picked up by their mothers and the sun reduced to a streak that ran across the tile roof of the school and up into the crowns of the palms behind it, after Lisette had come back to sit on the curb and whine and pout and complain like the baby she was (*He's just drunk, I bet that's it, just drunk like Mom said*) and she had to tell her she didn't know what she was talking about, there he was. Lisette saw the car first. It appeared at the top of the street like a mirage, coming so slowly round the turn it might have been rolling under its own power, with nobody in it, and Angelle remembered what her father had told her about always setting the handbrake, always, no matter what. She hadn't really wanted a lesson—she'd have to be sixteen for that—but they were up in the mountains, at the summer cabin, just after her mother had left for France, and there was nobody around. "You're a big girl," he'd told her, and she was, tall for her age—people always mistook her for an eighth grader or even a freshman. "Go ahead, it's easy," he told her. "Like bumper cars. Only you don't bump anything." And she'd laughed and he laughed and she got behind the wheel with him guiding her and her heart was pounding till she thought she was going to lift right out of the seat. Everything looked different through the windshield, yellow spots and dirt, the world wrapped in a bubble. The sun was in her eyes. The road was a black river, oozing through the dried-out weeds, the trees looming and receding as if a wave had passed through them. And the car crept down the road the way it was creeping now. Too slow. Much too slow.

When her father pulled up to the curb, she saw right away that something was wrong. He was smiling at them, or trying to smile, but his face was too heavy, his face weighed a thousand tons, carved of rock like the faces of the presidents on Mount Rushmore, and it distorted the smile till it was more like a grimace. A flare of anger rose in her—Lisette was right—and then it died away and she was scared. Just scared.

"Sorry," he murmured, "sorry I'm late, I—" and he didn't finish the thought or excuse or whatever it was because he was pushing open the door now, the driver's door, and pulling himself out onto the pavement. He took a minute to remove his sunglasses and polish them on the tail of his shirt before leaning heavily against the side of the car. He gave her a weak smile—half a smile, not even half—and carefully fitted them back over his ears, though it was too dark for sunglasses, anybody could see that. Plus, these were his old sunglasses—two shining blue disks in wire frames that made his eyes disappear—which meant that he must have lost his good ones, the ones that had cost him two hundred and fifty dollars on sale at the Sunglass Hut. "Listen," he said, as Lisette pulled open the rear door and flung her backpack across the seat, "I just—I forgot the time, is all. I'm sorry. I am. I really am."

She gave him a look that was meant to burn into him, to make him feel what she was feeling, but she couldn't tell if he was looking at her or not. "We've been sitting here since four," she said, and she heard the hurt and accusation in her own voice. She pulled open the other door, the one right beside him, because she was going to sit in back as a demonstration of her disapproval—they'd both sit in back, she and Lisette, and nobody up front—when he stopped her with a gesture, reaching out suddenly to brush the hair away from her face.

"You've got to help me out here," he said, and a pleading tone had come into his voice. "Because"—the words were stalling, congealing, sticking in his throat—"because, hey, why lie, huh? I wouldn't lie to you."

The sun faded. A car went up the street. There was a boy on a bicycle, a boy she knew, and he gave her a look as he cruised past, the wheels a blur.

"I was, I had lunch with Marcy, because, well, you know how hard I've been—and I just needed to kick back, you know? Everybody does. It's no sin." A pause, his hand going to his pocket and then back to her hair again. "And we had some wine. Some wine with lunch." He gazed off down the street then, as if he were looking for the tapering long-necked green bottles the wine had come in, as if he were going to produce them for evidence.

She just stood there staring at him, her jaw set, but she let his hand fall to her shoulder and give her a squeeze, the sort of squeeze he gave her when he was proud of her, when she got an A on a test or cleaned up the dishes all by herself without anybody asking.

"I know this is terrible," he was saying, "I mean I hate to do this, I hate to . . . but Angelle, I'm asking you just this once, because the thing is?"—and here he tugged down the little blue discs so that she could see the dull sheen of his eyes focused on her—"I don't think I can drive."

When the valet brought the car round, the strangest thing happened, a little lapse, and it was because he wasn't paying attention. He was distracted by Marcy in her low-slung Miata with the top down, the redness of it, a sleek thing, pin your ears back and fly, Marcy wheeling out of the lot with a wave and two fingers kissed to her lips, her hair lifting on the breeze. And there was the attendant, another college kid, shorter and darker than the one upstairs frowning over the tip but with the same haircut, as if they'd both been to the same barber or stylist or whatever, and the attendant had said something to him—*Your car, sir; here's your car, sir*—and the strange thing was that for a second there he didn't recognize it. Thought the kid was trying to put something over on him. Was this his car? Was this the sort of thing he'd own? This mud-splattered charcoal-gray SUV with the seriously depleted tires? And that dent in the front fender, the knee-high scrape that ran the length of the body as if some metallic claw had caught hold of it? Was this some kind of trick?

"Sir?"

"Yeah," he'd said, staring up into the sky now, and where were his shades? "Yeah, what? What do you want?"

The smallest beat. "Your car. Sir."

And then it all came clear to him the way these things do, and he flipped open his wallet to extract two singles—finger-softened money, money as soft and pliable as felt—and the valet accepted them and he was in the car, looking to connect the male end of the seatbelt to the female, and where was the damned thing? There was still a sliver of sun cutting in low over the ocean and he dug into the glove compartment for his old sunglasses, the emergency pair, because the new ones were someplace else altogether, apparently, and not in his pocket and not on the cord round his neck, and then he had them fitted over his ears and the radio was playing something with some real thump to it and he was rolling on out of the lot, looking to merge with the traffic on the boulevard.

That was when everything turned hard-edged and he knew he was drunk. He waited too long to merge—too cautious, too tentative—and the driver behind him laid on the horn and he had no choice but to give him the finger and he might have leaned his head out the window and barked something too, but the car came to life beneath him and somebody swerved wide and he was out in traffic. If he was thinking anything at all it probably had to do with his last DUI, which had come out of nowhere when he wasn't even that drunk, or maybe not drunk at all. He'd been coming back from Johnny's Rib Shack after working late, gnawing at a rib, a beer open between his legs, and he came down the slope beneath the underpass where you make a left to turn onto the freeway ramp and he was watching the light and didn't see the mustard-colored Volvo stopped there in front of him until it was too late. And he was so upset with himself—and not just himself, but the world at large and the way it presented these problems to him, these impediments, the unforeseen and the unexpected just laid out there in front of him as if it were some kind of conspiracy—that he got out of the car, the radiator crushed and hissing and beer pissed all over his lap, and shouted, "All right, so sue me!" at the dazed woman behind the wheel of the other car. But that wasn't going to happen now. Nothing was going to happen now.

The trees rolled by, people crossed at the crosswalk, lights turned yellow and then red and then green, and he was doing fine, just sailing, thinking he'd take the girls out for burritos or In-N-Out burgers on the way home, when a cop passed him going in the other direction and his heart froze like a block of ice and then thawed instantaneously, hammering so hard he thought it would punch right through his chest. *Signal, signal,* he told himself, keeping his eyes on the rearview, and he did, he signaled and made the first turn, a road he'd never been on before, and then he made the next turn after that, and the next, and when he looked up again he had no idea where he was.

Which was another reason why he was late, and there was Angelle giving him that hard cold judgmental look—her mother's look exactly—because she was perfect, she was dutiful and put-upon and the single best kid in the world, in the history of the world, and he was a fuckup, pure and simple. It was wrong, what he asked her to do, but it happened nonetheless, and he guided her through each step, a straight shot on the way home, two and a half miles, that was all, and forget stopping at In-N-Out, they'd just go home and have a pizza delivered. He remembered going on in that vein, "Don't you girls want pizza tonight? Huh, Lisette? Peppers and onions? And those little roasted artichokes? Or maybe you'd prefer wormheads, mashed wormheads?"—leaning over the seat to cajole her, make it all right and take the tightness out of her face, and he didn't see the boy on the bicycle, didn't know anything about him until Angelle let out a choked little cry and there was the heart-stopping thump of something glancing off the fender.

The courtroom smelled of wax, the same kind of wax they used on the floors at school, sweet and acrid at the same time, a smell that was almost comforting in its familiarity. But she wasn't at school—she'd been excused for the morning—and she wasn't here to be comforted or to feel comfortable either. She was here to listen to Mr. Apodaca and the judge and the D.A. and the members of the jury decide her father's case and to testify in his behalf, tell what she knew, tell a kind of truth that wasn't maybe whole and pure but necessary, a necessary truth. That was what Mr. Apodaca was calling it now, *necessary,* and she'd sat with him and her father in one of the unused rooms off the main corridor—another courtroom—while he went over the whole business one more time for her, just to be sure she understood.

Her father had held her hand on the way in and he sat beside her on one of the wooden benches as his attorney went over the details of that day after school, because he wanted to make sure they were all on the same page. Those were his words exactly—"I want to make sure we're all on the same page on this"—as he loomed over her and her father, bracing himself on the gleaming wooden rail, his shoes competing with the floor for the brilliance of their shine, and she couldn't help picturing some Mexican boy, some dropout from the high school, laboring over those shoes while Mr. Apodaca sat high in a leatherbacked chair, his feet in the stainless steel stirrups. She pictured him behind his newspaper, looking stern, or going over his brief, the details, *these* details. When he was through, when he'd gone through everything, minute by minute, gesture by gesture, coaching her, quizzing her—"And what did he say? What did you say?"—he asked her father if he could have a minute alone with her.

That was when her father gave her hand a final squeeze and then dropped it and got up from the bench. He was wearing a new suit, a navy so dark and severe it made his skin look like raw dough, and he'd had his hair cut so tight round the ears it was as if a machine had been at work there, an edger or a riding mower like the one they used on the soccer field at school, only in miniature, and for an instant she imagined it, tiny people like in *Gulliver's Travels,* buzzing round her father's ears with their mowers and clippers and edgers. The tie he was wearing was the most boring one he owned, a blue fading to black, with no design, not even a stripe. His face was heavy, his crow's-feet right there for all the world to see—gouges, tears, slits, a butcher's shop of carved and abused skin—and for the first time she noticed the small gray dollop of loose flesh under his chin. It made him look old, worn-out, past his prime, as if he weren't the hero anymore but playing the hero's best friend, the one who never gets the girl and never gets the job. And what role was she playing? The star. She was the star here, and the more the attorney talked on and the heavier her father's face got, the more it came home to her.

Mr. Apodaca said nothing, just let the silence hang in the room till the memory of her father's footsteps had faded. Then he leaned over the back of the bench directly in front of her, the great seal of the state of California framed over the dais behind him, and he squeezed his eyes shut a moment so that when he opened them and fixed her with his gaze, there were tears there. Or the appearance of tears. His eyelashes were moist and the moistness picked each of them out individually until all she could think of was the stalks of cane against the fence in the back corner of the yard. "I want you to listen very carefully to what I'm about to say, Angelle," he breathed, his voice so soft and constricted it was like the sound of the air being let out of a tire. "Because this concerns you and your sister. It could affect your whole life."

Another pause. Her stomach was crawling. She didn't want to say anything but he held the pause so long she had to bow her head and say, "Yeah. Yeah, I know."

And then suddenly, without warning, his voice was lashing out at her: "But you don't know it. Do you know what's at stake here? Do you really?"

"No," she said, and it was a whisper.

"Your father is going to plead no contest to the charge of driving under the influence. He was wrong, he admits it. And they'll take away his driving privileges and he'll have to go to counseling and find someone to drive you and your sister to school, and I don't mean to minimize that, that's very serious, but here's the thing you may not know." He held her eyes, though she wanted to look away. "The second charge is child endangerment, not for the boy on the bike, who barely even scraped a knee, luckily, luckily, and whose parents have already agreed to a settlement, but for you, for allowing you to do what you did. And do you know what will happen if the jury finds him guilty on that charge?"

She didn't know what was coming, not exactly, but the tone of what he was conveying—dark, ominous, fulminating with anger and the threat about to be revealed in the very next breath—made her feel small. And scared. Definitely scared. She shook her head.

"They'll take you and Lisette away from him." He clenched both hands, pushed himself up from the rail and turned as if to pace off down the aisle in front of her, as if he was disgusted with the whole thing and had no more to say. But then, suddenly, he swung round on her with a furious twist of his shoulders and a hard accusatory stab of his balled-up right hand and a single rigid forefinger. "And no," he said, barely contained, barely able to keep his voice level, "in answer to your unasked question or objection or whatever you want to call it, your mother's not coming back for you, not now, maybe not ever."

Was he ashamed? Was he humiliated? Did he have to stop drinking and get his life in order? Yes, yes and yes. But as he sat there in the courtroom beside Jerry Apodaca at eleven-thirty in the morning, the high arched windows pregnant with light and his daughter, Marcy, Dolores and the solemn-faced au pair sitting shoulder-to-shoulder on the gleaming wooden bench behind him, there was a flask in his inside pocket and the faint burning pulse of single-malt scotch rode his veins. He'd taken a pull from it in the men's room not ten minutes ago, just to steady himself, and then he'd rinsed out his mouth and ground half a dozen Tic Tacs between his teeth to knock down any trace of alcohol on his breath. Jerry would have been furious with him if he so much as suspected . . . and it was a weak and cowardly thing to do, no excuse, no excuse at all, but he felt adrift, felt scared, and he needed an anchor to hold on to. Just for now. Just for today. And then he'd throw the thing away, because what was a flask for anyway except to provide a twenty-four-hour teat for the kind of drunk who wore a suit and brushed his teeth.

He began to jiggle one foot and tap his knees together beneath the table, a nervous twitch no amount of scotch would cure. The judge was taking his time, the assistant D.A. smirking over a sheaf of papers at her own table off to the right. She wore a permanent self-congratulatory look, this woman, as if she were queen of the court and the county too, and she'd really laid into him before the recess, and that was nasty, purely nasty. She was the prosecution's attack dog, that was what Jerry called her, her voice tuned to a perpetual note of sarcasm, disbelief and petulance, but he held to his story and never wavered. He was just glad Angelle hadn't had to see it.

She was here now, though, sitting right behind him, missing school—missing school because of him. And that was one more strike against him, he supposed, *because what kind of father would . . . ?*—but the thought was too depressing and he let it die. He resisted the urge to turn round and give her a look, a smile, a wink, the least gesture, anything. It was too painful to see her there, under constraint, his daughter dragged out of school for this, and then he didn't want anybody to think he was coaching her or coercing her in any way. Jerry had no such scruples, though. He'd drilled her over and over and he'd even gone to the extreme of asking her—or no, *instructing* her—to wear something that might conform to the court's idea of what a good, honest, straightforward child was like, something that would make her look younger than she was, too young to bend the truth and far too young even to think about getting behind the wheel of a car.

Three times Jerry had sent her back to change outfits until finally, with a little persuasion from the au pair (*Allie,* and he'd have to remember to slip her a twenty, a twenty at least, because she was gold, pure gold), she put on a lacy white high-collared dress she'd worn for some kind of pageant at school, with matching white tights and patent-leather shoes. There was something wrong there in the living room, he could see that, something in the way she held her shoulders and stamped up the stairs to her room, her face clenched and her eyes burning into him, and he should have recognized it, should have given her just a hair more of his attention, but Marcy was there and she had her opinion and Jerry was being an autocrat and he himself had his hands full—he couldn't eat or think or do anything other than maybe slip into the pantry and tip the bottle of Macallan over the flask. By the time he thought of it, they were in the car, and he tried, he did, leaning across the seat to ply her with little jokes about getting a free day off and what her teachers were going to think and what Aaron Burr might have done—he would've just shot somebody, right?—but Jerry was drilling her one last time and she was sunk into the seat beside Marcy, already clamped up.

The courtroom, this courtroom, the one she was in now, was a duplicate of the one in which her father's attorney had quizzed her an hour and a half ago, except that it was filled with people. They were all old, or older anyway, except for one woman in a formfitting plaid jacket Angelle had seen in the window at Nordstrom who must have been in her twenties. She was in the jury box, looking bored. The other jurors were mostly men, businessmen, she supposed, with balding heads and recessed eyes and big meaty hands clasped in their laps or grasping the rail in front of them. One of them looked like the principal of her school, Dr. Damon, but he wasn't.

The judge sat up at his desk in the front of the room, which they called a bench but wasn't a bench at all, the flag of the state of California on one side of him and the American flag on the other. She was seated in the front row, between Dolores and Allie, and her father and Mr. Apodaca sat at a desk in front of her, the shoulders of their suits puffed up as if they were wearing football pads. Her father's suit was so dark she could see the dandruff there, a little spray of it like dust on the collar of his jacket, and she felt embarrassed for him. And sorry for him, sorry for him too—and for herself. And Lisette. She looked up at the judge and then the district attorney with his grim gray tight-shaven face and the scowling woman beside him, and couldn't help thinking about what Mr. Apodaca had told her, and it made her shrink into herself when Mr. Apodaca called her name and the judge, reading the look on her face, tried to give her a smile of encouragement.

She wasn't aware of walking across the floor or of the hush that fell over the courtroom or even the bailiff who asked her to hold up her right hand and swear to tell the truth—all this, as if she were recalling a fragmented dream, would come to her later. But then she was seated in the witness chair and everything was bright and loud suddenly, as if she'd just switched channels on the TV. Mr. Apodaca was right there before her, his voice rising sweetly, almost as if he were singing, and he was leading her through the questions they'd rehearsed over and over again. Yes, she told him, her father was late, and yes, it was getting dark, and no, she didn't notice anything strange about him. He was her father and he always picked her sister and her up on Wednesdays, she volunteered, because Wednesdays were when Allie and Dolores both had their day off and there was no one else to do it because her mother was in France.

They were all watching her now, the court gone absolutely silent, so silent you would have thought everyone had tiptoed out the door, but there they all were, hanging on her every word. She wanted to say more about her mother, about how her mother was coming home soon—had promised as much the last time she'd called long distance from her apartment in Saint-Germain-des-Prés—but Mr. Apodaca wouldn't let her. He kept leading her along, using his sugary voice now, talking down to her, and she wanted to speak up and tell him he didn't have to treat her like that, tell him about her mother, Lisette, the school and the lawn and the trees and the way the interior of the car smelled and the heat of the liquor on her father's breath—anything that would forestall the inevitable, the question that was tucked in just behind this last one, the question on the point of which everything turned, because now she heard it, murmurous and soft and sweet on her father's attorney's lips: "Who was driving?"

"I just wanted to say one thing," she said, lifting her eyes now to look at Mr. Apodaca and only Mr. Apodaca, his dog's eyes, his pleading soft baby-talking face, "just because, well, I wanted to say you're wrong about my mother, because she *is* coming home—she told me so herself, on, on the phone—" She couldn't help herself. Her voice was cracking.

"Yes," he said too quickly, a hiss of breath, "yes, I understand that, Angelle, but we need to establish . . . you need to answer the question."

Oh, and now the silence went even deeper, the silence of the deep sea, of outer space, of the arctic night when you couldn't hear the runners of the sled or the feet of the dogs bleeding into the snow, and her eyes jumped to her father's then, the look on his face of hopefulness and fear and confusion, and she loved him in that moment more than she ever had.

"Angelle," Mr. Apodaca was saying, murmuring. "Angelle?"

She turned her face back to him, blotting out the judge, the D.A., the woman in the plaid jacket who was probably a college student, probably cool, and waited for the question to drop.

"Who," Mr. Apodaca repeated, slowing it down now, "was"—slower, slower still—"driving?"

She lifted her chin then to look at the judge and heard the words coming out of her mouth as if they'd been planted there, telling the truth, the hurtful truth, the truth no one would have guessed because she was almost thirteen now, almost a teenager, and she let them know it. "*I* was," she said, and the courtroom roared to life with so many people buzzing at once she thought at first they hadn't heard her. So she said it again, said it louder, much louder, so loud she might have been shouting it to the man with the camera at the back of the long churchy room with its sweat-burnished pews and the flags and emblems and all the rest. And then she looked away from the judge, away from the spectators and the man with the camera and the court recorder and the bank of windows so brilliant with light you would have thought a bomb had gone off there, and looked directly at her father.

(2005)

La Conchita

In my business, where you put something like forty to forty-five thousand miles a year on your vehicle and the sweet suck of the engine at 3,500 rpm is like another kind of breathing, you can't afford distractions. Can't afford to get tired or lazy or lift your eyes from the road to appreciate the way the fog reshapes the palms on Ocean Avenue or the light slips down the flanks of the mountains on that mind-blowing stretch of Highway 1 between Malibu and Oxnard. Get distracted and you could wind up meat. I know that. The truckers know that. But just about everybody else—Honda drivers, especially, and I'm sorry—don't even know they're behind the wheel and conscious half the time. I've tried to analyze it, I have. They want value, the Honda drivers, value and reliability, but they don't want to pay for the real deal—German engineering is what I'm talking about here—and yet they still seem to think they're part of some secret society that allows them to cut people off at will, to take advantage because they're so in the know. So hip. So Honda. And yes, I carry a gun, a Glock 9 I keep in a special compartment I had built into the leather panel of the driver's side door, but that doesn't mean I want to use it. Or would use it again. Except in extremis.

The only time I did fire it, in fact, was during that rash of freeway shootings a few months back—a statistical bubble, the police called it—when people were getting popped at the rate of two a week in the greater L.A. area. I could never figure it, really. You see some jerk swerving in and out of traffic, tailgating, and maybe you give him the finger and maybe he comes up on you, but you're awake, aren't you? You've got an accelerator and a brake pedal, right? But most people, I guess, don't even know they're alive in the world or that they've just made the driver charging up alongside them homicidal or that their engine is on fire or the road is dropping off into a crater the size of the Sea of Tranquility because they've got the cell clamped to the side of their head and they're doing their nails or reading the paper. Don't laugh. I've seen them watching TV, gobbling kung pao out of the carton, doing crossword puzzles and talking on two cells at once—and all at eighty miles an hour. Anyway, I just fired two slugs—*blip blip.* Didn't even know my finger was on the trigger. Plus, of course, I was aiming low—just trying to perforate his rocker panels or the idiotic big-dick off-road Super Avenger tires that had him sitting about twelve feet up off the ground. I'm not proud of it. And I probably shouldn't have gone that far. But he cut me off—twice—and if he'd given me the finger it would have been one thing, but he didn't even know it, didn't even know he'd nearly run me into the median two times in the space of a minute.

On this particular day, though, everybody seemed to keep their distance. It was just past noon and raining, the ocean stretching out on my left like a big seething cauldron, the surface of the roadway slick beneath the wheels—so slick and soft and ill-defined I had to slow to seventy in places to keep from hydroplaning. But this wasn't just rain. This was one cell in a string of storms that had stalled over the coast for the past week, sucking load after load of moisture up out of the sea and dropping it on the hills that had burned clear of vegetation the winter before. I was already running late because of a slide at Topanga Canyon, boulders the size of SUVs in the middle of the road, cops in slickers waving their flashlights, down to two lanes, then one, and finally—I heard this on the radio after I got through, feeling stressed for time, but lucky I guess—down to none. Road closed. All she wrote.

I didn't like driving in the rain—it was just asking for disaster. My fellow drivers, riding their brakes and clinging to the wheel as if it were some kind of voodoo fetish that would protect them against drunks, curves, potholes, errant coyotes and sheet metal carved into knives, went to pieces the minute the first drop hit the windshield. As you might expect, the accident rate shot up something like three hundred percent every time it rained, and as I say, this wasn't just rain in the ordinary sense. But I had a delivery to make in Santa Barbara, an urgent delivery, and if I couldn't guarantee door-to-door faster than FedEx or Freddie Altamirano (my major competitor, who rode a ProStreet FXR and moved like a spirit raptured to heaven), then I was out of business. Plus, this wasn't just the usual packet of bonds or stock certificates or the blockbuster screenplay passing from writer to director and back again, this was the kind of thing I handled maybe two or three times a month at most—and it never failed to give me a thrill. In the trunk, anchored firmly between two big blocks of Styrofoam, was a human liver packed in a bag of ice slurry inside a Bud Light Fun-in-the-Sun cooler, and if that sounds ridiculous, I'm sorry. That's how it's done. Simple fact. Ninety minutes earlier I'd picked it up at LAX because the S.B. airport was closed due to flooding, and if you want a definition of time sensitive, this was it. The recipient, a twenty-seven-year-old mother of three, was on life support at University Hospital, and I was running late and there wasn't much I could do about it.

At any rate, I was coming up on La Conchita, a little town no bigger than a trailer court carved out of the hill where the freeway dips down to the ocean, rounding the big curve at Mussel Shoals and dropping down to fourth to blow past a U-Haul truck (the worst, the very worst, but that's another story), when the hillside gave way. There was a series of sharp cracks I at first took to be lightning hitting the hill, and then a deep reverberant concussion, as if all the air had been knocked out of the day. By this point I was shifting down, hyper-aware of the chain of brake lights flung up across the road in front of me and the U-Haul, piloted by a zombie on his way to Goleta or Lompoc with his zombie girlfriend at his side and their little white dog in her lap, bearing down on me from behind. I was able to stop. They weren't. They barely had time to flash their brake lights before skidding past me and hammering the back end of a Mercedes with its panic lights on, lifting the whole shimmering orange-and-white truck up on two wheels before it crashed down on its side.

I'll say right up front I've never been much in an emergency—and when you're behind the wheel as often as I am, you see plenty of emergencies, believe me. I don't know CPR, don't know how to stay calm or counsel anybody else to stay calm either and I've been lucky because it's never been me wrapped around the telephone pole or nodding over the windshield and nobody I know has ever choked at the dinner table or clutched their heart or started hemorrhaging from the mouth and ears. I saw the dog lying there in the road like a heap of rags, saw the driver of the moving truck haul himself up out of the driver's side window like a pearl diver coming up for air, saw the rain eclipse him. And the first thing I did—for my own sake and for the sake of whoever else might be tooling up behind me—was pull the car off the road, as far up on the shoulder as I could take it without fear of getting stuck. I was just reaching for my cell to dial 911, the road blocked, the day shot, my mind churning and the donor organ sitting there undelivered and unincorporated and getting staler by the minute, when things got worse, a whole lot worse.

I don't know if the average person really has much of an idea of what a mudslide involves. I certainly didn't—not before I started driving for a living anyway. You'd see footage on the six o'clock news, telephone poles down, trees knocked askew, a car or two flattened and a garage staved in, but it didn't seem like much. It wasn't hot lava, wasn't an earthquake or one of the firestorms that burned through this or that subdivision and incinerated a couple hundred homes every fall. Maybe it was the fault of the term itself—*mudslide.* It sounded innocuous, almost cozy, as if it might be one of the new attractions at Magic Mountain, or vaguely sexy, like the mud-wrestling that was all the rage when I was in high school and too young to get in the door. But that was the thinking of a limited imagination. A mudslide, as I now know, is nothing short of an avalanche, but instead of snow you've got 400,000 tons of liquefied dirt bristling with rock and tree trunks coming at you with the force of a tsunami. And it moves fast, faster than you would think.

The sound I'd heard, even through the rolled-up windows and the ready voice of the narrator of the book-on-tape I'd checked out of the library because I never go anywhere without a good story to take my mind off the raging idiots all around me, was the sudden angry shriek of the bulkhead in back of La Conchita giving way. Steel beams snapped like chicken bones, railroad ties went airborne. Up ahead of me, beyond the overturned U-Haul, a few of the cars had got through, but now a vanguard of boulders came sluicing across the freeway, followed by a soupy river of mud. A rock the size of a cannonball thumped into the underside of the U-Haul truck and a fistful of pellets—gravel, I guess—sprayed the side of my car, and that was going to mean a new paint job, I knew it, maybe even bodywork. The rain quickened. The mud spread out across the pavement, seething round the tires and underneath the car and beyond, and soon dark tongues of it had pushed across the southbound lanes too.

What did I do? I got out of the car, the normal reaction, and immediately my shoes filled with sludge. The mud was no more than a foot or so deep, and here, at the far verge of the slide, it was the consistency of pancake batter. But darker. And it smelled of something long buried and dug up again, damp and raw as an open grave, and for a moment there I flashed on my father's funeral, the squared-off edges of the hole with its fringe of roots, my mother trying to be stoic and my uncle putting an arm round my shoulders as if that could help. Let me say it wasn't a pleasant smell and leave it at that.

Doors slammed. Somebody was shouting. I turned my head to look up the road and there was the driver of the U-Haul, pulling his wife or girlfriend or whoever she was up out of the cab even as she reacted to the sight of the dog lying there on a clean stretch of pavement, and the mud, working to its own logic, flowed around it. Behind me were at least a hundred cars, bottled up and idling, their lights dully illuminating the scene, windshield wipers clapping in the way of a very tired audience. People were running up the street. A pickup just north of the overturned U-Haul began to float off, sustained on a wave of mud as if it were a dinghy drifting away on the tide. My jacket was soaked through, the hair hanging in my face. The liver wasn't getting any fresher.

Suddenly, unaccountably, I found myself at the trunk of the car. I inserted the key and flipped it open, and I don't really know why—just to reassure myself, I guess. The lid of the cooler eased back and there it was, the liver, smooth and burnished, more pink than red—and it wasn't like meat, not at all, more like something sculpted out of very soft stone. But it was okay, it was fine, I told myself, and I should just stay calm. I figured we had an hour, more or less, before things began to get critical. It was then that the woman with the dog—she was bent over it in the rain, wailing, and the water dripping from the end of her nose was pink with the blood leaching out of her scalp—looked up and shouted something to me. She might have been asking if I knew anything about dogs. Or if she could use my cell to call the vet. Or if I had a knife, an oxygen mask, a GPS locator, a blanket. I don't know what she said, actually. She wanted something, but I couldn't hear her over the rattle of all those idling engines, the hiss of the rain, the shouts and curses, and in the next moment somebody else was there, some stranger, and he was taking care of it. I ducked back into the car, just to get out of the rain—mud everywhere, mud on the carpets, the doorframe, the console—and punched in the cell number of the assisting physician at the hospital.

"There's a problem," I said.

His voice came back at me in a thinly amplified yelp. "What do you mean? Where are you?"

"I'm maybe fifteen miles south, at La Conchita, that's what I mean, but I can't get through because there's some kind of slide—it just happened—and it's blocking the road. Totally." For the first time I looked up at the mountain outside the window and saw the scar there and the trail of displaced earth and the crushed houses. Everything was gray with the rain.

"How long before they clear it?"

"Actually? Could be a while."

He was silent and I tried to picture him, nobody I knew, an intern maybe, glasses, short hair because it was easier to maintain when your life wasn't your own, biting his lip and staring out the window into the pall of rain. "Is there any way I can get to *you*? I mean, if I jump in the car and—"

"Maybe," I said, and I wanted this to work in the worst way because my reputation was on the line here and that woman needed her liver she'd been waiting for for Christ knew how long, somebody freshly dead in Phoenix and this was the best match and I'd walk it there if I could, no doubt about it, walk till my feet turned to stumps, but I had to be honest with him. "You got to realize the traffic's already backed up in both directions," I said, and I wasn't calm, wasn't calm at all. "I mean nothing's going through, there's an accident just in front of me and there's mud and rocks all over the road. In both directions. Even if you leave now you're not going to be able to get within five miles of here, so you tell me. Tell me what you want me to do. Tell me."

Another silence. "All right," he said finally. His voice was pinched. "You know how urgent this is. How crucial. We'll get this done. We will. Just keep your cell on, all right? And don't do anything till I get back to you."

I must have sat there for five minutes at least, just staring out into the rain, the cell clutched in my hand. I was wet through and I'd begun to shiver, so I turned the engine over and got the heater going. The mud was still flowing, I could see that much, and the white dog had disappeared, along with the couple from the U-Haul. Apparently they'd found shelter somewhere, in the little gas station–cum–grocery that was La Conchita's sole commercial establishment, or maybe in one of the cars stalled behind me. There were people out on the pavement, hunched-over forms wading through the mud and shouting at one another, and I thought I heard the distant keening of a siren—police, fire, ambulance—and wondered how they expected to get through. You might find it hard to believe, but I really didn't think much about the danger, though if another section of the hillside were to let go we'd all be buried, no doubt about that—no, I was more concerned with the package in the trunk. Why hadn't they called me back? What were they waiting for? I could have been slogging down the road already, the cooler propped up on one shoulder, and somebody—I thought of an ambulance from the hospital—could have met me a couple miles up the freeway. But no, the ambulances would all be busy with the wreckage in front of me, with people trapped in their cars, bleeding from head wounds, their own organs ruptured, bones broken. Or in those houses. I turned my head to look out the passenger's side window at the ghost of La Conchita, a rectangular grid of split-level homes and trailers bereft of electricity and burdened by rain, and the ones up against the hillside, the ones that had been there ten minutes ago and were gone now. Just then, just as I turned, a streaming dark figure surged up against the car and a woman's face appeared at the window. "Open up!" she demanded. "Open up!"

I was caught off-guard—startled, actually, the way she came up on me. It took a minute to react, but she didn't have a minute, because she was pounding at the window now, frantic, both hands in motion, her eyes cutting into me through the smeared-over glass. I hit the button for the window and that smell came at me, that graveyard stink, and there she was, a woman in her twenties with smudged makeup, mud in her hair and her hair wet and hanging loose like the frayed ends of a rope. Before the window was all the way down she thrust her head in and reached across the seat to grab hold of my wrist as if to tug me out of the car, going on about her husband, her husband and her little girl, her baby, her little girl, her little girl, her voice so strained and constricted I could barely make out what she was saying. "You've got to help," she said, jerking at my arm. "Help me. *Please.*"

And then, before I knew what I was doing, I was out the driver's side door and into the mud again and I never even thought to crank the window back up, her urgency gone through me like an electric jolt, and why I thought to take the gun, to tuck it into my waistband, I'll never know. Maybe because panic is infectious and violence the only thing to soothe it. I don't know. Maybe I was thinking of looters—or of myself, of insulating myself from whatever was out there, good, bad or indifferent. I came round the front of the car, the mud to my knees, and without a word she grabbed hold of my hand and started pulling me forward. "Where're we going?" I shouted into the rain, but she just tugged at me and slashed through the debris until we were across the inundated railroad tracks—running now, both of us—and into La Conchita, where the mud flowed and the houses lay buried.

Though I must have passed by the place a hundred times, doing eighty, eighty-five, with one eye out for the CHP and the other for the inevitable moron blocking the fast lane, I don't think I'd actually stopped there more than once or twice—and then only to get gas and only in an emergency situation when I'd been so intent on a delivery I'd forgotten to check the fuel gauge. What I knew of La Conchita was limited to what I'd heard—that it was cheap, or relatively cheap, because the hillside had given way in '95, obliterating a few houses and scaring off buyers and realtors alike, and that people kept coming back to it because they had short memories and the little community there, a hundred fifty houses or so and the store I mentioned, exerted a real pull on the imagination. This was the last of the Southern California beach towns anybody could afford, a throwback to earlier, happier times before the freeways came and the megalopolis ate everything up. I'd always meant to stop and look around and yet never seemed to find the time—the whole place couldn't have been more than a quarter mile from one end to the other, and that goes by in a heartbeat at eighty-five.

But I was here now, right in the thick of it, skirting the tentacles of mud and hurrying past houses that just sat there dark and untouched, fumbling on up the street to where the slide had broken through, and this woman, her bare legs mud-streaked and her shoulders pinched with urgency, never let go of my wrist. And that was strange, a strange feeling, as if I were back in elementary school and bound to one of the other kids in some weird variant of the three-legged race. Except that this woman was a total stranger and this was no game. I moved without thinking, without question, my legs heavy with the mud. By the time we reached the top of the street, a long block and a half in, all of it uphill, I was out of breath—heaving, actually—but whether my lungs burned or my shoes were ruined beyond salvage or repair or the finish on the car was damaged to the tune of five hundred bucks or more didn't matter, because the whole thing suddenly came clear to me. This was the real deal. This was affliction and loss, horror unfolding, the houses crushed like eggshells, cars swallowed up, sections of roof flung out across the street and nothing visible beneath but tons of wet mud and a scatter of splintered beams. I was staggered. I was in awe. I became aware of a dog barking somewhere, a muffled sound, as if it were barking through a gag. "Help," the woman repeated, choking on her own voice, "goddamnit, do something, *dig*," and only then did she let go of my wrist. She gave me one frantic look and threw herself down in the muck, flailing at the earth with her bare hands.

Again, as I said, I'm no hero—I'm barely capable of taking care of myself, if you want to know the truth—but I fell in beside her without a word. She was sobbing now, her face slack with shock and the futility of it all—we needed a shovel, a pick, a backhoe for Christ's sake—but the tools were buried, everything was buried. "I was at the store," she kept saying, chanting it as her fingers raked and bled and her nails tore and the blouse clung wet to the hard frenetic muscles of her digging, "at the store, at the store," and my mind flew right out of my body. I snatched up a length of two-by-four and began to tear at the earth as if I'd been born to it. The dirt flew. I knew nothing. I was in a trench up to my knees, up to my waist, the mud sliding back in almost as fast as I could fling it out, and she was right there beside me with her martyred hands, looking like Alice, like my Alice when I first met her with her snaking hair and the smile that pulled you across the room, Alice before things went bad. And I wondered: Would Alice dig me out? Would she even care?

Back, shoulders, bending, flinging, gouging at the face of the earth: will it sound ridiculous if I say that in that hard labor, that digging, that sweat and panic and the headlong burning rush of adrenaline, I found my wife again? And that I saw something there, something in the fierceness of her need and the taint of her smeared limbs I found incredibly sexy? I didn't know the husband. I didn't know the little girl. I was digging, yes—in my place, the average person would have done the same—but I was no hero. I wasn't digging to save anybody. I was digging for her. And there came a point, ten, fifteen minutes into it, when I saw what was going to happen as clearly as if I could predict the future. Those people were dead down there, long dead, choked and asphyxiated, and she was going to grieve, this hot young woman, this girl in the muddy shorts and soaked-through top whose name I didn't even know, who kept saying over and over that she'd gone to the store for a can of tomato paste to add to the sauce, the sauce simmering on the stove while her husband set the table and the little girl bent over her coloring book. I saw that. The grief. The grief was only to be expected. And I saw that in time—six months, a year maybe—she was going to get over it, very gradually, in a tender and fragile way, and then I would be there for her, right there at her side, and she could cleave to me the way Alice couldn't and wouldn't. It was biblical, is what it was. And I was a seer—a fortune teller—for fifteen hard minutes. But let me tell you, digging for somebody's life is a desperate business, and you don't know your thoughts, you just don't.

At some point a neighbor appeared with a shovel, and I couldn't tell you whether this guy was thirty or eighty, ten feet tall or a hunchbacked dwarf, because in one unbroken motion I flung down the two-by-four, snatched the shovel from him, and started stabbing at the earth all on my own, feeling the kind of ecstasy only the saints must know. I was shoulder-deep, slamming at something—a window frame, shattered mullions and teeth of glass—when the cell in my right front pocket began to ring. It rang on and on, five times, six times, and I couldn't stop myself, the motion of pitching forward and heaving back all I knew, the dirt looser now, fragments of shingle appearing at the bottom of the hole like treasure. The ringing stopped. Shingle gave way to splintered wood, chicken wire and fragments of stucco, an interior wall—was that an interior wall? And then the cell began to ring again and I dropped the shovel, just for an instant, to pull the thing out of my pocket and shout into the receiver. "Yeah?" my voice boomed out, and all the while I was looking to the woman, to her hopeless eyes and bloodied hands, and there was the hillside poised above us like the face of death.

"It's Joe Liebowitz. Where are you?"

"Who?"

"Dr. Liebowitz. At the hospital."

It took a moment, shifting gears. "Yeah," I said. "I'm here."

"Good. All right. Now, listen: we found somebody and he's on his way to you, on a motorcycle, so we think—he thinks—he can get through, and all you have to do is hand the package over to him. Are you all right? You think you can do that?"

Yes, I was going to say, *of course I can do that,* but I didn't have the chance. Because at that moment, somebody—some guy in a blue windbreaker and a Dodgers cap gone black with the rain—made a grab for the shovel, and they're saying I brandished the gun, but I don't know, I truthfully don't. What I do know is that I dropped the cell and wrestled the shovel away from him and began to dig with everything I had, and I could have been made of steel and rivets, a digging machine, a robot, all sensation fled out of my limbs and hands and back. I dug. And the woman—the wife, the young mother—collapsed in the mud, giving up her grief in a chain of long shuddering sobs that fed me like an intravenous drip and people were gathering now to comfort her and some guy with a pick starting in beside me. The cell rang again. It was right there, at my feet, and I paused only to snatch it up and jam it down the front of my pants, mud and all.

I don't know how long it was after that—five minutes maybe, no more—until I broke through. I was stabbing at the bottom of the hole like a fencer parrying with an invisible opponent, thrusting away, when all at once the shovel plunged in all the way to my fist and everything went still. This was the miracle: he was in there, the husband, and the little girl with him, preserved in a pocket where the refrigerator and stove had gone down under a section of the wall and held it in place. As soon as I jerked the blade of the shovel back his arm came thrusting out of the hole, and it was a shock to see this grasping hand and the arm so small and white and unexpected in that sea of mud. I could hear him now—he was shouting his wife's name, *Julie! Julie!*—and the arm vanished to show a sliver of his face, one eye so intensely green it was as if all the vegetation of the hillside had been distilled and concentrated there underground, and then his hand thrust out again and she was there, the wife, clinging to it.

I stood back then and let the guy with the pick work at the hole, the rain settling into a thin drizzle and a long funnel of cloud clinging to the raw earth above us as if the mountain had begun to breathe. People were crowding around all of a sudden, and there must have been a dozen or more, wet as rats, looking shell-shocked, the hair glued to their heads. Their voices ran away like kites blown on the wind. Somebody had a movie camera. And my cell was ringing, had been ringing for I don't know how long. It took me a minute to wipe the scrim of mud from the face of it, then I pressed the talk button and held it to my ear.

"Gordon? Is this Gordon I'm talking to?"

"I'm here," I said.

"Where? Where are you, that's what I want to know. Because the man we got has been there for ten minutes now, looking for you. Don't you realize what's going on here? There's a woman's life at stake—"

"Yeah," I said, and I was already starting down the hill, my car up to the frame in mud and debris, the police there, lights revolving, somebody with a plow on the front of his pickup trying to make the smallest dent in the mudflow that stretched on as far as I could see, "yeah, I'm on it."

The doctor's voice ran at me, hard as a knife. "You know that, don't you? You know how much longer that organ's got? Till it's not viable? You know what that means?"

He didn't want an answer. He was venting, that was all, hyped-up on caffeine and frustrated and looking for somebody to take it out on. I said, "Yeah," very softly, more as an interjection than anything else, and then asked him who I was supposed to hand the package off to.

I could hear him breathing into the phone, ready to go off on another rant, but he managed to control himself long enough to say: "Altamirano. Freddie Altamirano. He's on a motorcycle and he says he's wearing a silver helmet."

Even before I could answer I saw Freddie, legging his way through the mud, the Harley looking more like a dirt bike in the motocross than a street machine.

He gave me a thumbs-up sign and gestured to the trunk of my car, even as I waded through the muck and dug in my pocket for the keys. I was soaked through to the skin. My back began to signal its displeasure and my arms felt as if all the bone and sinew had been cored out of them. Did I mention that I don't have much respect for Freddie Altamirano? That I don't like him? That he lives to steal my clients?

"Hey, brother," he said, treating me to a big wet phony grin, "where you been keeping? I been here like fifteen minutes and they are *pissed* up there at the hospital. Come on, come on," he urged as I worked through the muddy keys, and the grin was gone now.

It took maybe three minutes, no more, before Freddie had the cooler secured—minutes that were ticking down till the donor organ was just a piece of meat you could have laid out on the stainless steel counter at the market—and then he was off, kicking up mud, the blast of his exhaust like the first salvo in a war of attrition. But I didn't care about any of that. I cared about the liver and where it was going. I cared about the woman who'd taken hold of my wrist and her husband and the little girl I never did get to lay eyes on. And though I was wet through and shivering and my car was stuck and my shoes ruined and my hands so blistered I couldn't make a fist with either one, I started back up the hill—and not, as you might think, to watch the lucky man emerge from the hole in the ground or to take a bow or anything like that, but just to see if anybody else needed digging out.

(2005)

Question 62

She was out in the flowerbed, crushing snails—and more on them later—when she happened to glance up into the burning eyes of an optical illusion. Without her glasses and given the looming obstruction of the brim of her straw gardener's hat, which kept slipping down the crest of her brow every time she bent forward, she couldn't be sure what she was seeing at first. She was wearing the hat even though it was overcast because the doctor had removed a basal cell carcinoma from the lobe of her left ear six months ago and she wasn't taking any chances, not with the hole in the ozone layer and the thinning—or was it thickening?—of the atmosphere. She was wearing sunblock too, though it had been raw and gray all week, grayer than she would have imagined last winter when she was living in Waunakee, Wisconsin, with her sister Anita and thinking of palm trees and a fat glowing postcard sun that melted everything away in its wake. It never rained in Southern California, except that it had been raining all week, all month, and the snails, sliding along on their freeways of slime, loved it. They were everywhere, chewing holes in her nasturtiums, yellowing the tips of her Kaffir lilies and sucking at the bright orange flowers till the delicate petals turned brown and dropped off.

Which was why she was out here this morning, early, before Doug was awake, while the mist clung like gauze to the ground and the *L.A. Times* landed with a resounding thump in the driveway, down on her hands and knees crushing snails with the garden trowel. She was a vegetarian, like her sister—they'd made a vow when they were in junior high—and she didn't like to kill anything, not even the flies that gathered in fumbling flotillas on the windowsill, but this was different, this was a kind of war. The snails were an invasive species, the very same escargot people paid fifteen dollars a plate for in the restaurant, brought here at the turn of the last century by a French chef who was a little lax in keeping them in their pens or cages or wherever. They were destroying her plants, so she was destroying them. The tip of the trowel closed over the whorl of the shell and then she pressed down and was rewarded by an audible pop as the shell gave way. She didn't want to look, didn't want to see the naked dollop of meat trying to follow its probing antennae out of the ruin of its shell, and so she pressed down again until the thing was buried, each snail following the next to its grave.

And then she looked up. And what she saw didn't compute, not at first. Right there, right behind the wrought-iron fence Doug had put up to keep the deer out of her garden, there seemed to be a big cat watching her, a big striped cat the size of a pony—a tiger, that was what it was, a tiger from India with a head as wide across as the pewter platter she trucked out each Thanksgiving for the veggie cornucopia. She was startled—who wouldn't be? She'd seen tigers at the zoo, on the Nature Channel, in cages at the circus, but not in her own backyard in Moorpark, California—might as well expect a polar bear in the Bahamas or a warthog at the Dorothy Chandler Pavilion. It took her a minute, staring into the yellow eyes and the blistered snout from thirty feet away, her vision blurred, the hat slipping down over her eyebrows, before she thought to be afraid. "Doug," she called in a low voice, as if he could hear her across the yard and through the pink stucco wall of the house, "Doug, Doug." She wondered if she should move, come out of her crouch and wave her arms and shout—wasn't that what you were supposed to do, wave your arms and shout? But the tiger, improbable as it was, didn't lift its lip in a snarl or leap over the fence or drift away into a corner of her imagination. No, it only twitched its tail and lifted its ears at the sound of her voice.

Two thousand miles away, under a sky of hammered granite, Anita Nordgarden was kicking across the frozen expanse of the drive, two bags of groceries clutched in her arms. She was on the midnight shift at the Page Center for Elder Care, midnight to eight a.m., and she'd had a few drinks after work with some of the other nurses, then sifted through the aisles at the supermarket for the things she'd forgotten she needed. Now, the wind in her face, her fingertips stinging with the cold, she wasn't thinking very clearly, but if she was thinking anything, it was the fish, Lean Cuisine, pop it in the microwave, wash it down with two glasses of chardonnay and then read till she fell away into the deeps of her mid-day sleep that was all but indistinguishable from a coma. Or maybe she'd watch a movie, because she was exhausted and a movie required less effort than a book, though she'd seen each of the twenty-three cassettes on the shelf over the TV so many times she could have stopped her ears and cinched a blindfold over her eyes and watched them all the same.

She was just mounting the steps to her trailer when a shadow detached itself from the gloom beneath the doorstep and presented a recognizable face to her. This was One-Eye, the feral tom that lived with his various paramours in the secret fastness beneath the trailer, an animal she neither encouraged nor discouraged. She'd never had a cat. Never especially liked them. And Robert, when he was alive, wouldn't have an animal in the house. Every once in a while, she'd toss a handful of kibble out in the yard, feeling charitable, but the cat was a bird killer—more than once she'd come home to find feathers scattered round the steps—and she probably would have got rid of it if it weren't for the mice. Since he'd moved in beneath the trailer she'd stopped finding the slick black mouse pellets in the cupboards and scattered across the kitchen counter and she didn't like to think of the disease they carried. At any rate, there he was, One-Eye, just staring at her as if she'd somehow intruded on him, and she was about to say something, to raise her voice in a soft, silly half-lubricated falsetto and murmur *Kitty, kitty,* when the cat suddenly darted back under the steps and she looked up to see a man coming round the corner of the trailer opposite hers.

He walked in a jaunty, almost demented way, closing quickly on her with a big artificial grin on his face—he was selling something, that was it—and before she could get her key in the door he was right there. "Good morning," he boomed, "lovely morning, huh? Don't you love the cold?" He was tall, she saw, nearly as tall as she was perched atop the third step, and he was wearing some sort of animal-skin hat with the ragged frizz of a tail dangling in back—coonskin, she wanted to call it, only she saw right away that this wasn't raccoon but something else. "Need a hand?"

"No," she said, and she would have closed out the scene right there, but for the look in his eyes: he wanted something, but he didn't want it desperately and he wasn't selling anything, she could see that now. There was a mystery here, and at this hour of the morning, with two Dewar's and sodas in her and nothing to look forward to but the fish and the chardonnay and the sleep of the dead, she felt the prick of it. "No, thanks," she added, "I can manage," and she was pushing open the door when he made his pitch.

"I was just wondering if you might have a minute to spare—? To talk. Just a minute, that's all?"

A Jesus freak, she was thinking. All I need. She was halfway through the door, looking back at him, down at him, but he must have been six-five, six-six, and his fixed blue eyes were nearly on a level with hers. "No," she said, "I don't think so. I work nights and—"

He lifted his eyebrows and the corners of his mouth went up a notch. "Oh, no, no, no," he said, "I'm not a Bible-thumper or anything like that. I'm not selling anything, nothing at all. I'm your neighbor, is all? Todd Gray? From over on Betts Street?"

The wind was at war with the heater and the soft warm slightly rancid smell of home that emanated from the pillows of the built-in couch and the cheap floorboards and the kitchen counter and the molded plastic strips of the ceiling. She was half-in and half-out and he was standing there on the frozen ground.

"No," he said, "no," as if she were protesting, "I just wanted to talk to you about Question 62, that's all. And I won't take a minute of your time."

She was down on her hands and knees for so long her back began to ache—her lower back, right at the base of the spine, where gravity tugged at the bunched muscles there and her stomach sagged beneath them—and she could feel the burden of her torso in her shoulders and wrists. She was there so long the mist began to lift and an oblivious snail slid out from the furls of one of the plants and etched a trail across the knuckles of her right hand. But she didn't want to move. She couldn't move. She was beyond fear now and deep into the realm of fascination, of magic and wonder and the compelling strangeness of the moment. A tiger. A tiger in her garden. No one would believe it. No one, not Doug snoring in the bedroom or Anita locked away in her trailer with its frozen skirt of snow and the wind sitting in the north.

The tiger hadn't moved. It sat there on its haunches like a dog anticipating a treat, braced on its big buff paws, ears erect, tail twitching, watching her. She'd been talking to it in a low voice for some time now, offering up blandishments against the dwindling nugget of her fear, saying, *Good boy, good cat, that's right, yes*—and here her voice contracted to a syrupy chirp—*he just wants a little love, doesn't he? A little love, yeah?*

The animal made no sign it understood, but it stayed there, pressed to the fence, apparently as fascinated as she, and as the mist clotted round the smooth lanceolate leaves of the oleanders and steamed from the wet shingles of the Hortons' across the way, she understood that this was somebody's pet, the ward of some menagerie owner or private collector like that man in the Bronx or Brooklyn or wherever it was with the full-grown tiger in his apartment and the six-foot alligator in the bathtub. Of course it was. This wasn't Sumatra or the Sunderbans—aliens hadn't swooped down overnight in one of their radiant ships and set loose a plague of tigers across the land. The animal was a pet. And it had got loose. It was probably hungry. Bewildered. Tired. It was probably as surprised to see her in her straw hat and faded green overalls as she was to see it—or him. It was definitely a him—she could see the crease where his equipment lay against his groin and the twin bulbs of his testicles.

But she couldn't crouch like this forever—her back was killing her. And her wrists. Her wrists had gone numb. Very slowly, as if she were doing yoga to a tape running at half-speed, she lowered her bottom down in the damp soil and felt the pressure ease in her arms, and that was all right, except that her new posture seemed to confound the cat—or excite him. He moved up off his haunches and slid silkily down the length of the iron fence, then swung round and came back again, the muscles tensed in his shoulders as he rubbed against the bars, and she was sure that he'd been in a cage, that he wanted a cage now—the security of it, the familiarity, probably the only environment he'd ever known—and all she could think of was how to get him in here, inside the fence and maybe into the garage, where she could lock the door and hide him away.

Since Robert died—was killed, that is—she hadn't had many visitors. There was Tricia, who lived with her boyfriend three trailers down—she sometimes came in for a cup of tea in the evening when Anita was just waking up and trying to consolidate her physical resources for the shift ahead, but her schedule kept her pretty much to herself. She was only thirty-five, widowed less than a year, the blood still ran in her veins and she liked a good time as much as anybody else. Still, it was hard to find people who wanted to make the rounds of the bars at eight a.m., other than congenital losers and pinch-faced retirees hunched over a double vodka as if it was going to give them back the key to their personalities, and the times she'd tried to go out at night on her days off she'd found herself drifting over her first beer while everybody else got up and danced. And so she invited him in, this man, Todd, and here he was sprawled on the couch in his faded cowboy boots with his legs that ran on forever, and she was offering him some stale Triscuits and a bright orange block of cheddar she'd surreptitiously shaved the mold off of and she was just wondering if he might like a glass of chardonnay.

He'd let his grin flag, but it came back now, a boy's grin, the grin that had no doubt got him whatever he wanted wherever he went. He pushed the hat back till the roots of his hair showed in front, squared his shoulders and gathered in his legs. She saw that he was her age, or close enough, and she saw too that he wasn't wearing a wedding ring. "A little early for me," he said, and his laugh was genuine. "But if you're going to have one—"

She was already pouring. "I told you," she said, "I work nights."

The wine was one of her few indulgences—it was from a little California vineyard in the Santa Ynez Valley. She and her sister Mae had gone wine-tasting when she was visiting over Christmas and she liked the faint dry echo of the chardonnay so much she had two cases shipped back to Wisconsin. Her impulse was to hoard it, but she was feeling generous this morning, expansive in a way that had nothing to do with the two scotches or the way the trailer ticked and hummed over its heating element and a feeble cone of rinsed-out sunshine poked through the blinds. "This is cocktail hour for me," she said, handing him the glass, "my chance to kick back before dinner."

"Right," he said, "just about the time everybody else is getting to work with crumbs in their lap and a cardboard cup of lukewarm coffee. I used to work nights," he said. "At a truck stop. I know how it is."

She'd eased into the chair opposite him, his legs snaking out again as if he couldn't contain them, boots crossed at the ankles, then uncrossed and crossed again. "So what do you do now?" she asked, wishing she'd had a chance to put on some lipstick, brush her hair. In time, though. In time she would. Especially if he stayed for a second glass.

His eyes, which had never strayed from hers since he hunched through the door, slipped away and then came back again. He shrugged. "This and that."

She had nothing to say to this and they were silent a moment as they sipped their wine and listened to the wind run at the trailer. "You like it?" she said finally.

"Hm?"

"The wine."

"Oh, sure, yeah. I'm not much of a connoisseur, I'd say . . . but yeah, definitely."

"It's a California wine. My sister lives out there. Got it right from the winery itself."

"Nice," he said, and she could see he was just being polite. Probably the next thing he would say was that he was more of a beer man himself.

She wanted to say more, wanted to tell him about the vineyard, the neat braided rows of grapevines curling round the hills and arcing down into the little valleys like the whorls of a shell, about the tasting room and the feel of the sun on her face as she and Mae sat outside at a redwood table and toasted each other and the power of healing and the beginning of a new life for them both, but she sensed he wouldn't be interested. So she leaned in then, elbows propped on the knees of the pale blue cotton scrubs she wore to work every night, his legs splayed out in front of her as if he'd been reclining there all his life, and said, "So what is this question you wanted to ask me about anyway?"

The more she talked, the more the tiger seemed to settle down. Before long it stopped pacing, leaned into the rails of the fence and let its body melt away till it was lying there in the dirt and devil grass as if it had somehow found the one place in the world that suited it best. There was the sound of the birds—a jay calling harshly from the next yard over, a songbird swapping improvisations with its mate—and the soughing rumble of a car going up the street behind the house, and then she could hear the tiger's breathing as clearly as if she were sitting in the living room listening to it come through Doug's stereo speakers. It wasn't purring, not exactly, but there was a glottal sound there, deep and throaty, and after a moment she realized the animal was asleep and that what she was hearing was a kind of snore, a sucking wheeze, in and out, in and out. She was amazed. Struck dumb. How many people had heard a tiger snore? How many people in the world, in the history of the world, let alone Moorpark? What she felt then was grace, a grace that descended on her from the gray roof of the morning, a sense of privilege and intimacy no one on earth was feeling. This animal didn't belong to her, she knew that—it had an owner somewhere and he would be out looking for it, the police would be here soon, dogs, trackers, guns—but the moment did.

"Well, let me put it this way," he was saying, "I see you got some ferals living under your trailer . . ."

"Ferals?" At first she thought he'd meant ferrets and she gave his hat a closer scrutiny. Was that what that was, ferret fur?

"Cats. Stray cats."

He was studying her intently, challenging her with his eyes. She shrugged. "Three or four of them. They come and go."

"You're not feeding them, are you?"

"Not really."

"Good," he said, and then repeated himself with a kind of religious fervor, his voice echoing off the molded plastic of the ceiling. She saw that his glass was empty, clutched in one oversized hand and balanced delicately over the crotch of his jeans. "Because they're bird killers, you know. Big time. You ever notice feathers scattered around?"

"Not really." This was the moment to look at her own empty glass and hold it up to the light. "But hey, I'm going to have another—help me sleep. How about you?"

He waved his hand in a vague way, which she took to mean yes, and she lifted the bottle from the coffee table and held it aloft a moment so that the pale light through the window caught the label, then leaned forward, way out over the gulf of his parted thighs, to pour for him. He didn't thank her. Didn't even seem to notice. "I like birds," he said. "I love birds. I've been a member of the Audubon Society since I was in sixth grade, did you know that?"

She didn't know that, how could she?—she'd just met him ten minutes ago. But she'd always liked tall men and she liked the way he'd settled in, liked the way things were going. His brow furrowed, his eyes leapt out at her: he *was* a preacher, after all. So what did she do? She poured herself a glass of wine and shrugged again. *Let him talk.*

"Anyway," he said, and he drank off half the glass in a gulp, "anyway—this *is* good stuff, I see what you mean. But the cats. Did you know there are something like two million stray cats in this state alone and that they're responsible for killing between forty-seven million to a hundred and thirty-nine million native songbirds a year, depending on the estimate? A hundred and thirty-nine million." He drew up his legs, the boots sliding away from her and clapping lightly together as he sat up erect in the chair. "Now that's outrageous, don't you think?"

"Yeah," she said, sipping California, tasting the sun on her tongue, the earth, the trees, the vines that wove the hills into a big green fruit-hung tapestry. Robert had been five-eleven, an inch taller than she, and that was fine, that was all right, because she'd had her fill of blind dates and friends of friends who came up to her clavicle, but she'd always wondered what it would be like to date a man who made her feel short. And vulnerable. Somebody who could pull her head to his chest and just squeeze till she felt the weight go out of her legs.

"So that's why I'm here," he said, studying the pale gold of the wine in the clear crystal of the glass, before tilting his head to throw back what remained. "That's why I'm going house to house to drum up support for Question 62—for the birds. To save the birds."

She felt as if she were drifting, uncontained, floating right up and out through the ceiling of the trailer to blow off on the wind as if she were a bird herself—two scotches and two glasses of wine on a mostly empty stomach, the Lean Cuisine Salmon Gratin with Lemon & Dill sitting frozen on the counter. Still, she had the presence of mind to lean back in the chair, let out a deep breath and focus a smile on him. "All right," she said, "you got me—what's Question 62?"

The answer consumed the next ten minutes, during which she put on her listening expression and poured them each another half glass of wine and the presence of the sun grew firmer as it sliced the blinds into plainly delineated stripes that began ever so slowly to creep across the carpet. Question 62, he told her, was coming up for a vote in seventy-two counties on the twelfth of April and it was as simple as this: should cats be listed as an unprotected species like skunks and gophers and other nuisance animals? They were coldly efficient predators and they were interfering with the ecosystem. They were killing off birds and outcompeting native animals like hawks, owls and foxes for prey, and the long and short of it was that any cat found roaming without a collar could be hunted without a license or season or bag limit.

"Hunted?" she said. "You mean, with a gun? Like deer or something?"

"Like gophers," he said. "Like rats." His eyes were fierce and he leaned over his empty glass as if he were about to snatch it up and grind it between his teeth. He was sweating, a translucent runnel of fluid leaching out of his hairline and into the baffle of his right eyebrow; in a single motion he shrugged out of his parka and pulled off the hat to reveal a full head of russet hair streaked blond at the tips. He was staring right into her.

"I don't like guns," she said.

"Guns're a fact of life."

"My husband was killed by a gun." As she said it, a flat statement of fact, she saw Robert lying in the dirt not fifty feet from where they were sitting now and she heard the sirens and the gunshots, and the face of Tim Palko from the trailer across the way came back to her, Tim Palko, drunk for a week after he lost his job and gone crazy with his deer rifle till the SWAT team closed in and he put the barrel of it in his own mouth and jerked the trigger one last time. But she'd seen death—she saw it every week at the Page Center—and when she looked out the window of the trailer after the first shot thumped through the afternoon like the beat of a bass drum that never reverberated, she could see from the way Robert was lying there that it had come for him and come instantly. Mae had said, *How could you be sure?*, but she had two eyes and she knew absolutely and incontrovertibly, and that knowledge, cold as it was, grim as it was, saved her. *If I'd run out there, Mae,* she told her, *we wouldn't be sitting here now.*

The man—Todd—dropped his eyes, made a noise in the back of his throat. They were silent a moment, just listening to the wind, and then the clouds closed in and the sun failed and the room grew a shade darker, two shades, and she reached for the pull on the lamp. "I'm sorry," he said. "It must be hard."

She didn't answer. She studied his face, his hands, the nervous bounce of his right heel. "What I was thinking," she said finally, "is maybe opening another bottle. Just one more glass. What do you say?"

He looked up at her with that grin, the grin resurrected in the space of a heartbeat to make everything all right again. "I don't know," he sighed, and he was watching her now, watching her as intently as he'd been a moment ago when he was delivering his speech, "but if I have another glass I'm going to want to lay down. How about you? You feel like laying down?"

For a long while Mae crouched there in the wet earth, toying with the idea of backing noiselessly across the lawn so she could slip next door to the Kaprielians' and see if she could maybe borrow or purchase some meat—steak, rump roast, whatever they had—and she'd pay them later because this was an emergency and she couldn't talk about it now. Meat, that was what she needed. Any kind of meat. She had a fantasy of dropping wet slabs of it across the lawn in a discontinuous path that snaked up the gravel walk and through the open door of the garage, the big cat lured inside where it would settle down to sleep over a full belly between the dryer and the Toyota. But no. She hardly knew the Kaprielians. And what she did know of them she didn't like, the husband a big-bellied inimical presence bent perpetually over the hood of his hot rod or whatever it was and the wife dressed like some sort of hooker even in the morning when she went out to the driveway to retrieve the newspaper. . . .

She didn't believe in meat and neither did Doug. That was one of the things that had attracted her to him, one of the things they had in common, though there were other things—mountains of them, replete with ridges and declensions and towering heights—in which they were polar opposites. But Doug had worked two summers in a chicken plant in Tennessee, snatching the chickens up out of their cages to suspend them on a cable by their clamped feet so they could proceed to the pluckers and gutters, and he'd vowed never again to touch a piece of meat as long as he lived. He'd strung up tens of thousands of bewildered birds, their wings flapping in confusion amidst the chicken screech and the chicken stink, one after another heading down the line to have their heads removed and their innards ripped out. What did they ever do to us, he said, his face twisted with the memory of it, to deserve that?

She was still down on her knees, her eyes fixed on the swell of the tiger's ribs as they rose and fell in the decelerating rhythm of sleep, thinking maybe she could give it eggs, a stainless steel pan with raw egg and then a line of individual eggs just tapped enough to show the yolk, when the back door of the neighbors' house jerked open with a pneumatic wheeze and there was the Kaprielian woman, in her bathrobe and heels no less, letting the two yapping Pomeranians out into the yard. That was all it took to break the spell. The door wheezed shut, the dogs blew across the grass like down in a stiff wind, and the tiger was gone.

Later, after the dogs had got through sniffing and yapping and the neighborhood woke to the building clangor of a Saturday morning in March—doors slamming, voices rising and falling and engines of every conceivable bore and displacement screaming to life—she sat with Doug at the kitchen table and stared out into the gray vacancy of the backyard, where it had begun to rain. Doug was giving the paper his long squint. He'd lit a cigarette and he alternated puffs with delicate abbreviated sips of his second cup of overheated coffee. He was wearing his pajama bottoms and a sweatshirt stained with the redwood paint he'd used on the picnic table. At first he hadn't believed her. "What," he'd said, "it's not April Fools', not yet." But then, there it was in the paper—a picture of a leathery white-haired man, a tracker, bent over a pugmark in the mud near a dude ranch in Simi Valley, and then they turned on the TV and the reporter was standing there in the backwash of the helicopter's blades, warning people to stay inside and keep their pets with them because some sort of exotic cat had apparently got loose and could be a potential danger—and they'd both gone out back and studied the ground along the fence in silence.

There was nothing there, no sign, nothing. Just dirt. The first few spatters of rain feathered the brim of her hat, struck at her shoulders. For a moment she thought she could smell it, the odor released in a sprinkle of rain, the smell of litter, fur, the wild, but then she couldn't be sure.

Doug was staring at her, his eyes pale and wondering. "You really saw it?" he said. "Really? You're not shitting me, right?" In the next moment he went down on his heels and thrust his hand through the slats of the fence to pat the ground as if it were the striped hide of the animal itself.

She looked down at the top of his head, the hair matted and poorly cut, his bald spot spinning in a whorl of its own, galactic, a whole cosmos there. She didn't bother to answer.

Todd barely fit the bed, which occupied its own snug little cubbyhole off the wall of the master bedroom, and twice, in his passion, he sat up abruptly and cracked his head on the low-slung ceiling, and she had to laugh, lying there naked beneath him, because he was so earnest, so eager in his application. But he was tender too, and patient with her—it had been a long time, too long, and she'd almost forgotten what a man could make her feel like, a man other than Robert, a stranger with a new body, new hands and tongue and groin. New rhythm. New smell. Robert had smelled of his mother, of the sad damp house he'd grown up in, carpet slippers and menthol, the old dog and the mold under the kitchen sink and the saccharine spice of the aftershave he tried to cover it all up with. Todd's smell was different, fresher somehow, as if he'd just come back from a roll in the snow, but there was something else too, something darker and denser, and she held him a long while, her face pressed to the back of his head, before she understood what it was: the lingering scent of the fur hat that was lying now on the couch in the other room. She thought of that and then she was gone, deep in her coma, the whole world closing down on her cubbyhole in the wall.

He left her a note on the kitchen table. She saw it there when she got up for work, the windows dark and the heater ticking away like a Geiger counter. His hand was free-flowing, shapely, and that pleased her, the care that went into it, what it said about him as an individual. The words were pretty special too. He said that she was the most beautiful woman he'd ever met in his life and that he was going to take her out to breakfast in the morning, make it a date, if that was all right with her, and he signed his full name, Todd Jefferson Gray, and wrote out his address and phone number beneath it.

Next morning, when her shift was over, she walked across the snow-scabbed lot to her car, her spirits rising with every step. She never doubted he'd be there, not for a minute, but she couldn't help craning her neck to sweep the lot, expecting him to emerge from one car or another, tall and quick-striding, his smile widening. As it was, she didn't notice him until she was nearly on him—he wasn't in a car; he didn't have a car. He was standing just beyond the front bumper of her Saturn with a solemn look on his face, rooted to the ground like one of the trees that rose up behind him in a black tangle. When she was right there, right at the door of the car with the keys in her hand and he still hadn't moved, she felt confused. "Todd?" she heard herself say. "Is everything all right?"

He smiled then and swept the fur hat from his head with a mock bow. "I believe we have a date, don't we?" he said, and without waiting for an answer he moved forward to hold the door for her before sliding into the passenger's seat.

At the diner—already busy with the Sunday-morning church crowd—they ordered two large orange juices, which Todd discreetly reinforced with vodka from the bottle he produced from the inside pocket of his parka. She drained the first one all the way to the bottom before she lit her first cigarette of the day and ordered another. Only then did she look at the menu.

"Go on," Todd told her, "it's on me. Order anything you want. Have a steak, anything. Steak and eggs—"

She was feeling the vodka, the way it seemed to contract her insides and take the lingering chill out of her fingers and toes. She took another sip of her screwdriver, threw back her head to shake out her hair. "I'm a vegetarian," she said.

It took him a minute. She watched his eyes narrow, as if he were trying for a better perspective. The waitress stalked by, decaf in one hand, regular in the other, giving them a look. "So what does that mean?"

"It means I don't eat any meat."

"Dairy?"

She shrugged. "Not much. I take a calcium supplement."

A change seemed to come over him. Where a moment ago he'd been loose and supple, sunk into the cushion of the fake-leather banquette as if his spine had gone to sleep, now suddenly he went rigid. "What," he said, his voice saturated with irony, "you feel sorry for the cows, is that it? Because they have to have their poor little teats pulled? Well, I'll tell you, I was raised on a dairy farm and if you didn't milk those cows every morning they'd explode—and that's cruelty, if you want to know."

She didn't say anything, didn't really want to get into it. Whether she drank milk or ate sloppy joes and pig's feet was nobody's business but hers and it was a decision she'd made so long ago it was just part of her now, like the shape of her eyes and her hair color. She picked up the menu, just to do something.

"So what," he said. "I'm just wasting my time here, is that it? You're one of these save the animals people? You hate hunting, isn't that right?" He drew in a breath. "And hunters."

"I don't know," she said, and she felt a spark of irritation rising in her, "what difference does it make?"

She saw him clench his fist, and he almost brought it down on the table before he caught himself. He was struggling to control his voice: "What *difference* does it make? Have you been listening to me? I've had *death* threats over Question 62—from your cat lovers, the pacifists themselves."

"Right," she said. "Like the cats under my trailer are some big threat, aren't they? Invasive species, right? Well, we're an invasive species. Mrs. Merker I was telling you about, the one that gets up twenty times a night to find the bathroom and twenty times a night asks me who I am and what I think I'm doing in her house? She's part of the problem, isn't she? Why not hunt old ladies too?"

His eyes jumped round the room before they came back to her, exasperated eyes, irritated, angry. "I don't know. I'm not into that. I mean, that's people."

She told herself to shut it down, to pick up the menu and order something innocuous—waffles, with fake maple syrup that spared even the maple trees—but she couldn't. Maybe it was the drinks, maybe that was it. "But don't people kill birds? Habitat destruction and whatever, mini-malls, diesel engines and what, plastics. Plastics kill birds, don't they?"

"Don't get crazy on me. Because that's nuts. Just nuts."

"Just asking."

"Just *asking*?" Now the fist did come down on the table, a single propulsive thump that set the silverware rattling and heads turning. "We're talking death threats and you think this is some kind of game?" He was on his feet suddenly, the tallest man in the world, the jacket riding up over his belt, his face soaring, all that displacement of air and light. He bent for his hat, then straightened up again, his face contorted. "Some date," he said, and then he was gone.

The night of the tiger, a night that collapsed across the hills like a wet sack under the weight of yet another storm, Mae kept the television on late, hoping for news. Earlier, she and Doug had thought of going out to dinner and then maybe a movie, but with the rain showing no sign of letting up Doug didn't think he wanted to risk it and so she'd got creative with some leftover marinara sauce, zucchini and rice and they'd wound up watching an old pastel movie on the classic channel. The movie—they missed the first ten minutes and she never did catch the title—featured Gene Kelly in a sailor suit. Doug, who was working on the last beer of his six-pack, said it should have been *Singin' in the Rain.*

That was funny, and though she was distracted—had been distracted all day—she laughed. There was a silence then and they both listened to the rain hammering at the roof—it was so loud, so persistent, that for a moment it drowned out the dialogue on the TV.

"I guess this is it," Doug said, leaning back in his recliner with a sigh, "—the monsoon. The real deal, huh?" He gestured to the ceiling with the can of beer.

"Yeah," she said, watching the bright figures glide across the screen, "but I just hope it doesn't float us away. You think the car's going to be all right in the driveway?"

He gave her a look of irritation. "It's only rain."

"It seems so strange, though, because there's no thunder, no lightning. It just keeps coming as if somebody'd turned on a big spigot in the sky." She made a face. "I don't know. I don't like it. I don't think I'll ever get used to it—even the word, *monsoon*. It's so bizarre, like something out of some jungle someplace."

He just shrugged. They'd looked to his career and chosen California—Moorpark—over Atlanta, because, and they were both in absolute agreement here, they didn't want to live in the South. And while she loved the idea of year-round gardening—flowers in February and trees that never lost their leaves—she was still feeling her way around the way the seasons seemed to stall and the earth hardened to clay under the unblinking summer sun till it was like brick and nothing would grow along the fence but devil grass and tumbleweeds. *Tumbleweeds.* She might as well have been in the Wild West.

She'd had two beers herself and her attention was drifting—she couldn't really focus on the movie, all that movement, singing, dancing, the earnest plot, as if any of this meant anything—and when Doug got up without a word and steadied himself against the arm of the chair before moving off toward the bedroom, she picked up the remote and began flicking through the channels. She was looking for something, anything that might bring her back to what she'd felt that morning, on her knees in the garden with the mist rising round her. The tiger was out there, in the black of the night, the rain steaming round it. That was a thing she could hold on to, an image that grew inside her like something that had been planted there. And they wouldn't be able to track it, she realized, not now, not in this. After a while she muted the sound and just sat there listening to the rain, hoping it would never stop.

A week went by. The temperature took a nosedive and then it began to snow, off and on, until Saturday, when Anita came out of work to the smell of diesel and the flashing lights of the snowplow and had to struggle through a foot of fresh snow to her car. Her mood was desolate. Mrs. Merker had torn off her Depends and squatted to pee right in front of the nurses' station and Mr. Pohnert ("Call me Alvin") kept pressing his buzzer every five minutes to complain that his feet were cold despite the fact that both his legs had been removed five years ago due to complications from diabetes. And there were the usual aggravations, the moans and whimpers and the gagging and retching and people crying out in the dark—the strangeness of the place, insulated and overheated, with its ticking machines and dying bodies and her at the center of it. And now this. The sky was dark and roiled, the snow flung on the wind in sharp stinging pellets. It took her fifteen minutes to get her car out. And she drove home like a zombie, both hands clenching the wheel even as the tires floated and shimmied over the patches of ice.

There were tracks punched in the snow around her doorstep, cat tracks, amidst a scattering of blue feathers tipped with black. And a flyer, creased down the middle and shoved into the crack of the door. NO ON 62, it said, SAVE OUR PETS. She didn't have the heart to open a bottle of chardonnay—that she would save for brighter times—but she did make herself a cup of tea and spike it with a shot of Dewar's while she thought about what she wanted to eat, soup maybe, just a can of Chunky Vegetable and some wheat toast to dip in it. She had the TV on and her feet up before she noticed the blinking light on her message machine. There were two messages. The first was from Mae—"Call me," delivered in a tragic voice—and the second, the one she'd been waiting all week for, was from Todd. He was sorry about the blowup, but he'd been under a lot of pressure lately and he hoped they could get together again—soon, real soon—despite their differences, because they really did have a lot in common and she was the most beautiful woman he'd ever met and he'd really like to make it up to her. If she would let him. *Please.*

She was wondering about that—what exactly they had in common aside from two semi-drunken go-arounds on her bed and the fact that they were both tall and both lived in Waunakee—when the phone rang. She picked it up on the first ring, thinking it was him. "Hello?" she whispered.

"Anita?" It was Mae. Her voice was cored out and empty, beyond tragic, beyond tears. "Oh, Anita, Anita." She broke off, gathered herself. "They shot the tiger."

"Who? What tiger?"

"It didn't even have claws. This beautiful animal, somebody's pet, and it couldn't have—"

"Couldn't have what? What tiger? What are you talking about?"

But the conversation ended there. The connection was broken, either on Mae's end or hers—she couldn't be sure until she tried to dial her sister and the phone gave back nothing but static. Somebody had skidded into a telephone pole, that was it, and she wondered how much longer the lights would be on—that would be next, no power—and she got up out of the chair to pull open the tab on the top of the soup can, disgorge the contents into a ceramic bowl and hit the microwave while she could. She punched in the three digits and was rewarded by the mechanical roar of the thing starting up, the bowl rotating inside and the visual display of the numbers counting down, 3:30, 3:29, 3:28, until suddenly, in the space of the next second, the microwave choked off and the TV died and the fluorescent strip under the cabinet flickered once and buried its light in a dark tube.

For a long while she sat there in the shadows, sipping her tea, which had already crossed the threshold from hot to lukewarm, and then she got up and dumped a handful of ice in it and filled it to the rim with Dewar's. She was sipping her drink and thinking vaguely about food, a sandwich, she'd make a sandwich when she felt like it, cheese, lettuce, wheat bread—that she could do with or without power—when a sound from beneath the trailer brought her back, a scrabbling there, as of an animal, on its four paws, making a quiet meal.

She'd have to sacrifice the cats, she could see that now, because as soon as they hooked the phones back up she was going to call Todd. She wished he were here now, wished they were in bed together, under the quilt, drinking chardonnay and listening to the snow sift down on the aluminum roof of the trailer. She didn't care about the cats. They were nothing to her. And she wanted to please him, she did, but she couldn't help wondering—and she'd ask him too, she'd put it to him—What had Question 61 been, or Question 50, Question 29? Pave over the land? Pollute the streams? Kill the buffalo? Or what about Question 1, for that matter. Question 1—and she pictured it now, written on a slate in chalk and carried from village to village in a time of want and weather just like this, the snow coming down and people peering out from behind heavy wooden doors with a look of suspicion and irritation—Question 1 must have been something really momentous, the kick start of the whole program of the Department of Natural Resources. And what could it have been? Cut down the trees, flay the hides, pull the fish from the rivers? Or no, she thought, tipping back the mug, it would have been even more basic than that: Kill off the Indians. Yeah. Sure. That must have been it: Kill off the Indians.

She got up then and made herself a sandwich, then poured herself another little drop of scotch and took the plate and the mug with her to the cubbyhole of her bed, where she sat cross-legged against the pillow that still smelled of him and chewed and drank and listened to the cold message of the snow.

(2005)

Sin Dolor

He came into the world like all the rest of them—like us, that is—brown as an iguana and flecked with the detritus of afterbirth, no more remarkable than the date stamped on the morning's newspaper, but when I cleared his throat and slapped his infant buttocks, he didn't make a sound. Quite the contrary. His eyes snapped open with that searching myopia of the newborn and he began to breathe, calmly and quietly, with none of the squalling or fuss of the others. My nurse, Elvira Fuentes, who had spent fifteen years working on the cancer ward at the hospital in Guadalajara before coming home to devote herself to me, both as lover and helpmeet, frowned as I handed the infant to his mother. She was thinking exactly the same thing I was: there must have been some constriction or deformation of the child's vocal apparatus. Or perhaps he'd been born without it. We've seen stranger things, all manner of defects and mutations, especially among the offspring of the migrant workers, what with the devil's brew of herbicides, pesticides and genetically engineered foodstuffs to which they've been routinely exposed. There was one man I won't name here who came back from the cotton fields of Arizona looking like one of Elvira's oncological ghosts, and whose wife gave birth nine months later to a monster without a face—no eyes, ears, mouth or nose, just a web of translucent skin stretched tight over a head the size of an avocado. Officially, we labeled it a stillbirth. The corpse—if you could call it that—was disposed of with the rest of the medical waste.

But that's neither here nor there. What I mean to say is that we were wrong. Happily, at least as it appeared. The child—he was born to Francisco and Mercedes Funes, street vendors whose *tacos de chivo* are absolutely poisonous to the digestive tract, and I advise all who read this to avoid their stall at the corner of Independencia and Constitución if you value your equilibrium—was soon groping at his mother's breast and making the usual gurgling and sucking noises. Mercedes Funes, twenty-seven years old at the time, with six children already to her credit, a pair of bow legs, the shoulders of a fullback and one continuous eyebrow that made you think of Frida Kahlo (stripped of artistry and elegance, that is), was back at her stall that evening, searing goat over a charcoal grill for the entertainment of the unwary, and, as far as Elvira and I were concerned, that was that. One more soul had entered the world. I don't remember what we did that night, but I suppose it was nothing special. Usually, after we closed the clinic, we would sit in the courtyard, exhausted, and watch the doves settle on the wires while the serving girl put together a green salad and a *caldereta de verduras* or a platter of fried artichoke hearts, Elvira's favorite.

Four years slipped by before I next saw the child or gave more than a glancing thought to the Funes clan except when I was treating cases of vomiting and diarrhea, and as a matter of course questioning my patients as to what and where they'd eaten. "It was the oysters, Doctor," they'd tell me, looking penitent. "Onions, definitely the onions—they've never agreed with me." "Mayonnaise, I'll never eat mayonnaise again." And, my favorite: "The meat hardly smelled at all." They'd blame the Chinese restaurant, the Mennonites and their dairy, their own wives and uncles and dogs, but more often than not I was able to trace the source of the problem to the Funes stall. My patients would look at me with astonishment. "But that can't be, Doctor—the Funes make the best tacos in town."

At any rate, Mercedes Funes appeared at the clinic one sun-racked morning with her son in tow. She came through the door tugging him awkwardly by the wrist (they'd named the boy Dámaso, after her husband's twin brother, who sent small packets of chocolate and the occasional twenty-dollar bill from Los Angeles when the mood took him), and settled into a chair in the waiting room while Elvira's parrot gnawed at the wicker bars of its cage and the little air conditioner I keep in the front window churned out its hyperborean drafts. I was feeling especially good that morning, at the top of my game, certain real estate investments having turned out rather well for me, and Elvira keeping her eye on a modest little cottage at the seashore, which we hoped to purchase as a getaway and perhaps, in the future, as a place of retirement. After all, I was no longer as young as I once was and the Hippocratic *frisson* of healing the lame and curing the incurable had been replaced by a sort of repetitious drudgery, nothing a surprise anymore and every patient who walked through the door diagnosed before they even pulled up a chair. I'd seen it all. I was bored. Impatient. Fed up. But, as I say, on this particular day, my mood was buoyant, my whole being filled with an inchoate joy over the prospect of that little frame cottage at the seashore. I believe I may even have been whistling as I entered the examining room.

"And what seems to be the problem?" I asked.

Mercedes Funes was wrapped in a shawl despite the heat. She'd done up her hair and was wearing the shoes she reserved for mass on Sundays. In her lap was the child, gazing up at me out of his father's eyes, eyes that were perfectly round, as if they'd been created on an assembly line, and which never seemed to blink. "It's his hands, Doctor," Mercedes said in a whisper. "He's burned them."

Before I could say "Let's have a look" in my paternal and reassuring tones, the boy held out his hands, palms up, and I saw the wounds there. The burns were third degree, right in the center of each palm, and involved several fingers as well. Leathery scabs—eschars—had replaced the destroyed tissue and were seeping a deep wine-colored fluid around the margins. I'd seen such burns before, of course, on innumerable occasions, the result of a house fire, smoking in bed, a child blundering against a stove, but these seemed odd, as if they'd been deliberately inflicted. I glanced up sharply at the mother and asked what had happened.

"I was busy with a customer," she said, dropping her eyes as if to summon the image, "a big order, a family of seven, and I wasn't watching him—and Francisco wasn't there; he's out selling bicycle tires now, you know, just so we can make ends meet. Dámaso must have reached into the brazier when my back was turned. He took out two hot coals, Doctor, one in each hand. I only discovered what he'd done when I smelled the flesh burning." She gave me a glance from beneath the continuous eyebrow that made her look as if she were perpetually scowling. "It smelled just like goat. Only different."

"But how—?" I exclaimed, unable to finish the question. I didn't credit her for a minute. No one, not even the fakirs of India (and they are fakers), could hold on to a burning coal long enough to suffer third-degree burns.

"He's not normal, Doctor. He doesn't feel pain the way others do. Look here"—and she lifted the child's right leg as if it weren't even attached to him, rolling up his miniature trousers to show me a dark raised scar the size of an adult's spread hand—"do you see this? This is where that filthy pit bull Isabel Briceño keeps came through the fence and bit him, and we've gone to the lawyer over it too, believe me, but he never cried out or said a word. The dog had him down in the dirt, chewing on him like he was a bone, and if my husband hadn't gone out into the yard to throw his shaving water on the rosebushes I think he would have been torn to pieces."

She looked out the window a moment, as if to collect herself. The boy stared at me out of his unblinking eyes. Very slowly, as if he were in some perverse way proud of what had befallen him or of how stoically he'd endured, he began to smile, and I couldn't help thinking he'd make a first-rate soldier in whatever war we were prosecuting when he grew up.

"And do you see this?" she went on, tracing her index finger over the boy's lips. "These scars here?" I saw a tracery of pale jagged lines radiating out from his mouth. "This is where he's bitten himself—bitten himself without knowing it."

"Señora Funes," I said in my most caustic tone, the tone I reserve for inebriates with swollen livers and smokers who cough up blood while lighting yet another cigarette, and right there in my office, no less, "I don't think you're telling me the whole truth here. This boy has been abused. I've never seen a more egregious case. You should be ashamed of yourself. Worse: you should be reported to the authorities."

She rolled her eyes. The boy sat like a mannequin in her lap, as if he were made of wood. "You don't understand: he doesn't feel pain. Nothing. Go ahead. Prick him with your needle—you can push it right through his arm and he wouldn't know the difference."

Angry now—what sort of dupe did she take me for?—I went straight to the cabinet, removed a disposable syringe, prepared an injection (a half-dose of the B_{12} I keep on hand for the elderly and anemic) and dabbed a spot on his stick of an arm with alcohol. They both watched indifferently as the needle slid in. The boy never flinched. Never gave any indication that anything was happening at all. But that proved nothing. One child out of a hundred would steel himself when I presented the needle (though the other ninety-nine would shriek as if their fingernails were being pulled out, one by one).

"Do you see?" she said.

"I see nothing," I replied. "He didn't flinch, that's all. Many children—some anyway—are real little soldiers about their injections." I hovered over him, looking into his face. "You're a real little solider, aren't you, Dámaso?" I said.

From the mother, in a weary voice: "We call him Sin Dolor, Doctor. That's his nickname. That's what his father calls him when he misbehaves, because no amount of spanking or pinching or twisting his arm will even begin to touch him. Sin Dolor, Doctor. The Painless One."

The next time I saw him he must have been seven or eight, I don't really recall exactly, but he'd grown into a reedy, solemn boy with great, devouring eyes and his father's Indian hair, still as thin as a puppet and still looking anemic. This time the father brought him in, carrying the boy in his arms. My first thought was worms, and I made a mental note to dose him before he left, but then it occurred to me that it must only have been his mother's cooking and I dismissed the idea. A stool sample would do. But of course we'd need to draw blood to assess hemoglobin levels—if the parents were willing, that is. Both of them were notoriously tightfisted and I rarely saw any of the Funes clan in my offices unless something were seriously amiss.

"What seems to be the problem?" I asked, rising to take Francisco Funes' hand in my own.

With a grunt, he bent down to set the boy on his feet. "Go ahead, Dámaso," he said, "walk for the doctor."

I noticed that the boy stood unevenly, favoring his right leg. He glanced first at his father, then at me, dipped his shoulder in resignation and walked to the door and back, limping as if he'd dislocated his knee. He looked up with a smile. "I think something's wrong with my leg," he said in a voice as reduced and apologetic as a confessor's.

I cupped him beneath his arms and swung him up onto the examining table, giving the father a look—if this wasn't child abuse, then what was?—and asked, "Did you have an accident?"

His father answered for him. "He's broken his leg, can't you see that? Jumping from the roof of the shed when he should know better—" Francisco Funes was a big man, powerfully built, with a low but penetrating voice, and he leveled a look of wrath on his son, as if to say that the truth of the matter was evident and the boy would have a whipping when he got home, broken leg or no.

I ignored him. "Can you stretch out here for me on your back?" I said to the boy, patting the examining table. The boy complied, lifting both his legs to the table without apparent effort, and the first thing I noticed were the scars there, a constellation of burns and slashes uncountable running from his ankles to his thighs, and I felt the outrage come up in me all over again. Abuse! The indictment flared in my head. I was about to call for Elvira to come in and evict the father from my offices so that I could treat the son—and quiz him too—when I ran my hand over the boy's left shin and discovered the swelling there. He did indeed have a broken leg—a fractured tibia, from the feel of it. "Does this hurt?" I asked, putting pressure on the spot.

The boy shook his head.

"Nothing hurts him," the father put in. He was hovering over me, looking impatient, expecting to be cheated and wanting only to extract the pesos from his wallet as if his son's injury were a sort of tax and then get on with the rest of his life.

"We'll need X-rays," I said.

"No X-rays," he growled. "I knew I should have taken him to the *curandero,* I knew it. Just set the damn bone and get it over with."

I felt the boy's gaze on me. He was absolutely calm, his eyes like the motionless pools of the rill that brought the water down out of the mountains and into the cistern behind our new cottage at the seashore. For the first time it occurred to me that something extraordinary was going on here, a kind of medical miracle: the boy had fractured his tibia and should have been writhing on the table and crying out with the pain of it, but he looked as if there were nothing at all the matter, as if he'd come into the friendly avuncular doctor's office just to have a look around at the skeleton on its stand and the framed diplomas on the whitewashed walls and to bask in the metallic glow of the equipment Elvira polished every morning before the patients started lining up outside the door.

It hit me like a thunderclap: he'd walked on a broken leg. Walked on it and didn't know the difference but for the fact that he was somehow mysteriously limping. I couldn't help myself. I gripped his leg to feel the alignment of the bone at the site of the fracture. "Does this hurt?" I asked. I felt the bone slip into place. The light outside the window faded and then came up again as an unseen cloud passed overhead. "This?" I asked. "This?"

After that day, after I'd set and splinted the bone, put the boy in a cast and lent him a couple of old mismatched crutches before going out to the anteroom and telling Francisco Funes to forget the bill—"Free of charge," I said—I felt my life expand. I realized that I was staring a miracle in the face, and who could blame me for wanting to change the course of my life, to make my mark as one of the giants of the profession to be studied and revered down through the ages instead of fading away into the terminal ennui of a small-town practice, of the doves on the wire, the *caldereta* in the pot and the cottage at the seaside? The fact was that Dámaso Funes must have harbored a mutation in his genes, a positive mutation, superior, progressive, nothing at all like the ones that had given us the faceless infant and all the other horrors that paraded through the door of the clinic day in and day out. If that mutation could be isolated—if the genetic sequence could be discovered—then the boon for our poor suffering species would be immeasurable. Imagine a pain-free old age. Painless childbirth, surgery, dentistry. Imagine Elvira's patients in the oncology ward, racing round in their wheelchairs, grinning and joking to the last. What freedom! What joy! What an insuperable coup over the afflictions that twist and maim us and haunt us to the grave!

I began to frequent the Funes stall in the hour before siesta, hoping to catch a glimpse of the boy, to befriend him, take him into my confidence, perhaps even have him move into the house and take the place of the child Elvira and I had never had because of the grinding sadness of the world. I tried to be casual. *"Buenas tardes,"* I would say in my heartiest voice as Mercedes Funes raised her careworn face from the grill. "How are you? And how are those mouthwatering tacos? Yes, yes, I'll take two. Make it three." I even counterfeited eating them, though it was only a nibble and only of the tortilla itself, while whole legions of my patients past and present lined up for their foil-wrapped offerings. Two months must have gone by in this way before I caught sight of Dámaso. I ordered, stepped aside, and there he was, standing isolated behind the grill, even as his younger siblings—there were three new additions to the clan—scrabbled over their toys in the dirt.

His eyes brightened when he saw me and I suppose I said something obvious like "I see that leg has healed up well. Still no pain, eh?"

He was polite, well-bred. He came out from behind the stall and took my hand in a formal way. "I'm fine," he said, and paused. "But for this." He lifted his dirty T-shirt (imprinted with the logo of some North American pop band, three sneering faces and a corona of ragged hair) and showed me an open wound the size of a fried egg. Another burn.

"Ooh," I exclaimed, wincing. "Would you like to come back to the office and I'll treat that for you?" He just looked at me. The moment hovered. The smoke rose from the grill. "Gratis?"

He shrugged. It didn't matter to him one way or the other—he must have felt himself immortal, as all children do until they become sufficiently acquainted with death and all the miseries that precede and attend it, but of course he was subject to infection, loss of digits, limbs, the sloughing of the flesh and corruption of the internal organs, just like anyone else. Though he couldn't feel any of it. Mercifully. He shrugged again. Looked to his mother, who was shifting chunks of goat around the cheap screen over the brazier as the customers called out their orders. "I need to help my mother," he said. I was losing him.

It was then that I hit on a stratagem, the sort of thing that comes on a synaptical flutter like the beating of internal wings: "Do you want to see my scorpions?"

I watched his face change, the image of a foreshortened arachnid with its claws and pendent stinger rising miasmic before him. He gave a quick glance to where his mother was making change for Señora Padilla, an enormous woman of well over three hundred pounds whom I've treated for hypertension, adult-onset diabetes and a virulent genital rash no standard medication seemed able to eradicate, and then he ducked behind the brazier, only to emerge a moment later just up the street from where I was standing. He signaled impatiently with his right hand and I gave up the ruse of lunching on his mother's wares, turned my back on the stall and fell into step with him.

"I keep one in a jar," he said, and it took me a moment to realize he was talking of scorpions. "A brown one."

"Probably *Vaejovis spinigeris,* very common in these parts. Does it show dark stripes on its tail?"

He nodded in a vague way, which led me to believe he hadn't looked all that closely. It was a scorpion—that was enough for him. "How many do you have?" he asked, striding along without the slightest suggestion of a limp.

I should say, incidentally, that I'm an amateur entomologist—or, more specifically, arachnologist—and that scorpions are my specialty. I collect them in the way a lepidopterist collects butterflies, though my specimens are very much alive. In those days, I kept them in terraria in the back room of the clinic, where they clung contentedly to the undersides of the rocks and pottery shards I'd arranged there for their benefit.

"Oh, I don't know," I said. We were just then passing a group of urchins goggling at us from an alleyway, and they all, as one, called out his name—and not in mockery or play, but reverentially, in homage. He was, I was soon to discover, a kind of hero among them.

"Ten?" he guessed. He was wearing sandals. His feet shone in the glare of the sunlight, kicking out ahead of him on the paving stones. It was very hot.

"Oh, a hundred or more, I'd say. Of some twenty-six species." And then, slyly: "If you have the time, I'll show you them all."

Of course, I insisted on first treating the burn as a kind of quid pro quo. It wouldn't do to have him dying of a bacterial infection, or of anything else for that matter—for humanitarian reasons certainly, but also with respect to the treasure he was carrying for all of mankind. His excitement was palpable as I led him into the moist, dim back room, with its concrete floor and its smell of turned earth and vinegar. The first specimen I showed him—*Hadrurus arizonensis pallidus,* the giant desert scorpion, some five inches long and nearly indistinguishable in color from the sand it rested on—was clutching a cricket in its pedipalps as I lifted the screen at the top of the terrarium. "This is the largest scorpion in North America," I told him, "though its venom is rather weak compared to what *Centruroides exilicauda* delivers. The bark scorpion, that is. They live around here too and they can be very dangerous."

All he said was, "I want to see the poison one."

I had several specimens in a terrarium set against the back wall and I shut down the lights, pulled the shades and used a black light to show him how they glowed with their own natural phosphorescence. As soon as I flicked on the black light and he'd had a moment to distinguish the creatures' forms as they crawled round their home, he let out a whoop of delight and insisted on shining it in each of the terraria in succession until he finally led me back to *Centruroides.* "Would they sting me?" he asked. "If I reached in, I mean?"

I shrugged. "They might. But they're shy creatures and like most animals want to avoid any sort of confrontation—and they don't want to waste their venom. You know, it takes a great deal of caloric resources to make the toxin—they need it for their prey. So they can eat."

He turned his face to me in the dark, the glow of the black light erasing his features and lending a strange blue cast to his eyes. "Would I die?" he asked.

I didn't like where this was leading—and I'm sure you've already guessed what was to come, the boy who feels no pain and the creatures who come so well equipped to inflict it—and so I played up the danger. "If one were to sting you, you might become ill, might vomit, might even froth at the mouth. You know what that is, frothing?"

He shook his head.

"Well, no matter. The fact is, a sting of this species might kill someone very susceptible, an infant maybe, a very old person, but probably not a boy of your age, though it would make you very, very sick—"

"Would it kill my grandfather?"

I pictured the grandfather. I'd seen him dozing behind the stall on occasion, an aggregation of bones and skin lesions who must have been in his nineties. "Yes," I said, "it's possible—if he was unlucky enough to step on one on his way to the bathroom one night . . ."

It was then that the bell sounded in the clinic, though we were closed, except for emergencies, during the afternoon. I called for Elvira, but she must have been taking her lunch in the garden or dozing in the apartment upstairs. "Come with me," I said to the boy and I led him out of the back room, through the examining room and into the office, where I found one of the men of the neighborhood, Dagoberto Domínguez, standing at the counter, his left hand wrapped in a bloody rag and a small slick gobbet of meat, which proved to be the tip of his left index finger, clutched in the other. I forgot all about Dámaso.

When I'd finished bandaging Señor Domínguez's wound and sent him off in a taxi to the hospital with the tip of his finger packed in ice, I noticed that the door to the back room stood open. There, in the dark, with the black light glowing in its lunar way, stood little Dámaso, his shirt fluorescing with the forms of my scorpions—half a dozen at least—as they climbed across his back and up and down the avenues of his arms. I didn't say a word. Didn't move. Just watched as he casually raised a hand to his neck where my *Hadrurus*—the giant—had just emerged from the collar of his shirt, and I watched as it stung him, repeatedly, while he held it between two fingers and then tenderly eased it back into its cage.

Was I irresponsible? Had I somehow, in the back of my mind, hoped for just such an outcome—as a kind of perverse experiment? Perhaps so. Perhaps there was that part of me that couldn't help collapsing the boundary between detachment and sadism, but then did the term even apply? How could one be sadistic if the victim felt nothing? At any rate, from that day on, even as I wrote up my observations and sent them off to Boise State University, where Jerry Lemongello, one of the world's premier geneticists and an old friend from my days at medical school in Guadalajara, had his state-of-the-art research lab, Dámaso became my constant companion. He seemed to revel in the attention Elvira and I gave him, coming as he did from a large and poor family, and over the course of time he began to dine with us frequently, and even, on occasion, to spend the night on a cot in the guest bedroom. I taught him everything I knew about scorpions and their tarantula cousins too and began to instruct him in the natural sciences in general and medicine in particular, a subject for which he seemed to have a special affinity. In return he did odd jobs about the place, sweeping and mopping the floors of the clinic, seeing that the scorpions had sufficient crickets to dine on and the parrot its seed and water and bits of fruit.

In the meantime, Jerry Lemongello pressed for a DNA sample and I took some scrapings from inside the boy's mouth (which had been burned many times over—while he could distinguish hot and cold, he had no way of registering what was *too* hot or *too* cold) and continued my own dilatory experiments, simple things like reflex tests, pinpricks to various parts of the anatomy, even tickling (to which he proved susceptible). One afternoon—and I regret this still—I casually remarked to him that the paper wasps that had chosen to build a massive nest just under the eaves of the clinic had become a real nuisance. They were strafing my patients as they ducked through the screen door and had twice stung poor Señora Padilla in a very tender spot when she came in for her medication. I sighed and wished aloud that someone would do something about it.

When I glanced out the window fifteen minutes later, there he was, perched on a ladder and shredding the nest with his bare hands while the wasps swarmed him in a roiling black cloud. I should have interfered. Should have stopped him. But I didn't. I simply watched as he methodically crushed the combs full of pupae underfoot and slapped the adults dead as they futilely stung him. I treated the stings, of course—each of them an angry swollen red welt—and cautioned him against ever doing anything so foolish again, lecturing him on the nervous system and the efficacy of pain as a warning signal that something is amiss in the body. I told him of the lepers whose fingers and toes abrade away to nothing because of the loss of feeling in the extremities, but he didn't seem to understand what I was driving at. "You mean pain is good?" he asked.

"Well, no," I said. "Pain is bad, of course, and what we do in my profession is try to combat it so people can go on with their lives and be productive and so on. . . ."

"My mother has pain," he said, running a finger over the bumps on his forearm as if they were nothing more than a novelty. "In her back. From bending over the grill all day, she says."

"Yes," I said—she suffered from a herniated disk—"I know."

He was quiet a moment. "Will she die?"

I told him that everyone would die. But not today and not from back pain.

A slow smile bloomed on his lips. "Then may I stay for dinner?"

It was shortly after this that the father came in again and this time he came alone, and whether his visit had anything to do with the wasp adventure or not, I can't say. But he was adamant in his demands, almost rude. "I don't know what you're doing with my boy—or what you think you're doing—but I want him back."

I was sitting at my desk. It was eleven in the morning and beyond the window the hummingbirds were suspended over the roseate flowers of the trumpet vine as if sculpted out of air. Clouds bunched on the horizon. The sun was like butter. Elvira was across the room, at her own desk, typing into the new computer while the radio played so softly I could distinguish it only as a current in the background. The man refused to take a seat.

"Your son has a great gift," I said after a moment. And though I'm an agnostic with regard to the question of God and a supernatural Jesus, I employed a religious image to reinforce the statement, thinking it might move a man like Francisco Funes, imbued as he was with the impoverished piety of his class: "He can redeem mankind—redeem us from all the pain of the ages. I only want to help."

"Bullshit," he snarled, and Elvira looked up from her typing, dipping her head to see over her glasses, which slipped down the incline of her nose.

"It's the truth," I said.

"Bullshit," he repeated, and I reflected on how unoriginal he was, how limited and ignorant and borne down under the weight of the superstition and greed that afflicts all the suffering hordes like him. "He's *my* son," he said, his voice touching bottom, "not yours. And if I ever catch him here again, I'll give him such a whipping—" He caught himself even as I flashed my bitterest smile. "You don't know, but I have my ways. And if I can't beat him, I can beat you, Doctor, with all respect. And you'll feel it like any other man."

"Are you threatening me? Elvira"—I turned to her—"take note."

"You bet your ass I am," he said.

And then, quite simply, the boy disappeared. He didn't come into the clinic the following morning or the morning after that. I asked Elvira about it and she shrugged as if to say, "It's just as well." But it wasn't. I found that I missed having him around, and not simply for selfish reasons (Jerry Lemongello had written to say that the DNA sample was unusable and to implore me to take another), but because I'd developed a genuine affection for him. I enjoyed explaining things to him, lifting him up out of the stew of misinformation and illiteracy into which he'd been born, and if I saw him as following in my footsteps as a naturalist or even a physician, I really didn't think I was deluding myself. He was bright, quick-witted, with a ready apprehension of the things around him and an ability to observe closely, so that, for instance, when I placed a crab, a scorpion and a spider on a tray before him he was able instantly to discern the relationship between them and apply the correct family, genus and species names I'd taught him. And all this at nine years of age.

On the third morning, when there was still no sign of him, I went to the Funes stall in the marketplace, hoping to find him there. It was early yet and Mercedes Funes was just laying the kindling on the brazier while half a dozen slabs of freshly (or at least recently) slaughtered goat hung from a rack behind her (coated, I might add, in flies). I called out a greeting and began, in a circuitous way, to ask about her health, the weather and the quality of her goat, when at some point she winced with pain and put her hand to her back, slowly straightening up to shoot me what I can only call a hostile look. "He's gone off to live with his grandmother," she said. "In Guadalajara."

And that was that. No matter how hard I pressed, Mercedes Funes would say no more, nor would her donkey of a husband, and when they had the odd medical emergency they went all the way to the other side of the village to the clinic of my rival, Dr. Octavio Díaz, whom I detest heartily, though that's another story. Suffice to say that some years went by before I saw Dámaso again, though I heard the rumors—we all did—that his father was forcing him to travel from town to town like a freak in a sideshow, shamelessly exploiting his gift for the benefit of every gaping rube with a few pesos in his pocket. It was a pity. It was criminal. But there was nothing that I or Jerry Lemongello or all the regents of Boise State University could do about it. He was gone and we remained.

Another generation of doves came to sit on the wires, Elvira put on weight around the middle and in the hollow beneath her chin, and as I shaved each morning I watched the inevitable progress of the white hairs as they crept up along the slope of my jowls and into my sideburns and finally colonized the crown of my head. I got up from bed, ran the water in the sink and saw a stranger staring back at me in the mirror, an old man with a blunted look in his reconstituted eyes. I diagnosed measles and mumps and gonorrhea, kneaded the flesh of the infirm, plied otoscope, syringe and tongue depressor as if the whole business were some rarefied form of punishment in a Sophoclean drama. And then one afternoon, coming back from the pet shop with a plastic sack of crickets for my brood, I turned a corner and there he was.

A crowd of perhaps forty or fifty people had gathered on the sidewalk outside the Gómez bakery, shifting from foot to foot in the aspiring heat. They seemed entranced—none of them so much as glanced at me as I worked my way to the front, wondering what it was all about. When I spotted Francisco Funes, the blood rushed to my face. He was standing to one side of a makeshift stage—half a dozen stacked wooden pallets—gazing out on the crowd with a calculating look, as if he were already counting up his gains, and on the stage itself, Dámaso, shirtless, shoeless, dressed only in a pair of clinging shorts that did little to hide any part of his anatomy, was heating the blade of a pearl-handled knife over a charcoal brazier till it glowed red. He was stuck all over like a kind of hedgehog with perhaps twenty of those stainless steel skewers people use for making shish kebab, including one that projected through both his cheeks, and I watched in morbid fascination as he lifted the knife from the brazier and laid the blade flat against the back of his hand so that you could hear the sizzling of the flesh. A gasp went up from the crowd. A woman beside me fainted into the arms of her husband. I did nothing. I only watched as Dámaso, his body a patchwork of scars, found a pinch of skin over his breastbone and thrust the knife through it.

I wanted to cry out the shame of it, but I held myself in check. At the climactic moment I turned and faded away into the crowd, waiting my chance. The boy—he was an adolescent now, thirteen or fourteen, I calculated—performed other feats of senseless torture I won't name here, and then the hat went round, the pesos were collected, and father and son headed off in the direction of their house. I followed at a discreet distance, the crickets rasping against the sides of the bag. I watched the father enter the house—it was grander now, with several new rooms already framed and awaiting the roofer's tar paper and tiles—as the boy went to a yellow plastic cooler propped up against the front steps, extracted a bottle of Coca-Cola and lowered himself into the battered armchair on the porch as if he were a hundred and fifty years old.

I waited a moment, till he'd finished his poor reward and set the bottle down between his feet, and then I strolled casually past the house as if I just happened to be in the neighborhood. When I drew even with him—when I was sure he'd seen me—I stopped in my tracks and gave him an elaborate look of surprise, a double take, as it were. "Dámaso?" I exclaimed. "Can it really be you?"

I saw something light up in his eyes, but only the eyes—he seemed incapable of forming a smile with his lips. In the next moment he was out of the chair and striding across the yard to me, holding out his hand in greeting. "Doctor," he said, and I saw the discoloration of the lips, the twin pinpoints of dried blood on either cheek amidst a battlefield of annealed scars, and I couldn't have felt more shock and pity if he were indeed my own son.

"It's been a long time," I said.

"Yes," he agreed.

My mind was racing. All I could think of was how to get him out of there before Francisco Funes stepped through the door. "Would you like to come over to the clinic with me—for dinner? For old times' sake? Elvira's making an eggplant lasagna tonight, with a nice crisp salad and fried artichokes, and look"—I held up the bag of crickets and gave it a shake—"we can feed the scorpions. Did you know that I've got one nearly twice as big as *Hadrurus*—an African variety? Oh, it's a beauty, a real beauty—"

And there it was, the glance over the shoulder, the very same gesture he'd produced that day at the stall when he was just a child, and in the next moment we were off, side by side, and the house was behind us. He seemed to walk more deliberately than he had in the past, as if the years had weighed on him in some unfathomable way (or fathomable, absolutely fathomable, right down to the corrosive depths of his father's heart), and I slowed my pace to accommodate him, worrying over the thought that he'd done some irreparable damage to muscle, ligament, cartilage, even to the nervous system itself. We passed the slaughterhouse where his mother's first cousin, Refugio, sacrificed goats for the good of the family business, continued through the desiccated, lizard-haunted remains of what the city fathers had once intended as a park, and on up the long sloping hill that separates our village by class, income and, not least, education.

The holy aroma of Elvira's lasagna bathed the entire block as we turned the corner to the clinic. We'd been talking of inconsequential things, my practice, the parrot—yes, she was well, thank you—the gossip of the village, the weather, but nothing of his life, his travels, his feelings. It wasn't till I'd got him in the back room under the black light, with a glass of iced and sweetened tea in his hand and a plate of *dulces* in his lap, that he began to open up to me. "Dámaso," I said at one point, the scorpions glowing like apparitions in the vestibules of their cages, "you don't seem to be in very high spirits—tell me, what's the matter? Is it—your travels?"

In the dark, with the vinegary odor of the arachnids in our nostrils and the promise of Elvira's cuisine wafting in the wings, he carefully set down his glass and brushed the crumbs from his lap before looking up at me. "Yes," he said softly. And then with more emphasis, *"Yes."*

I was silent a moment. Out of the corner of my eye I saw my *Hadrurus* probing the boundaries of its cage. I waited for him to go on.

"I have no friends, Doctor, not a single one. Even my brothers and sisters look at me like I'm a stranger. And the boys all over the district, in the smallest towns, they try to imitate me." His voice was strained, the tones of the adult, of his father, at war with the cracked breathy piping of a child. "They do what I do. And it hurts them."

"You don't have to do this anymore, Dámaso." I felt the heat of my own emotions. "It's wrong, deeply wrong, can't you see that?"

He shrugged. "I have no choice. I owe it to my family. To my mother."

"No," I said, "you owe them nothing. Or not that. Not your own self, your own body, your heart—"

"She brought me into the world."

Absurdly, I said, "So did I."

There was a silence. After a moment, I went on, "You've been given a great gift, Dámaso, and I can help you with it—you can live here, with us, with Elvira and me, and never have to go out on the street and, and *damage* yourself again, because what your father is doing is evil, Dámaso, *evil,* and there's no other word for it."

He raised a wounded hand and let it fall again. "My family comes first," he said. "They'll always come first. I know my duty. But what they'll never understand, what you don't understand, is that I do hurt, I do feel it, I *do.*" And he lifted that same hand and tapped his breastbone, right over the place where his heart constricted and dilated and shot the blood through his veins. "Here," he said. "Here's where I hurt."

He was dead a week later.

I didn't even hear of it till he was already in the ground and Jerry Lemongello buckled in for the long flight down from Boise with the hope of collecting the DNA sample himself, too late now, Mercedes Funes inhaling smoke and tears and pinning one hopeless hand to her lower back as she bent over the grill while her husband wandered the streets in a dirty *guayabera,* as drunk as any derelict. They say the boy was showing off for the urchins who followed him around as if he were some sort of divinity, the kind of boys who thrive on pain, who live to inflict and extract it as if it could be measured and held, as if it were precious, the kind of boys who carve hieroglyphs into their skin with razor blades and call it fashion. It was a three-story building. "Jump!" they shouted. "Sin Dolor! Sin Dolor!" He jumped, and he never felt a thing.

But what I wonder—and God, if He exists, have mercy on Francisco Funes and the mother too—is if he really knew what he was doing, if it was a matter not so much of bravado but of grief. We will never know. And we will never see another like him, though Jerry Lemongello tells me he's heard of a boy in Pakistan with the same mutation, another boy who stands in the town square and mutilates himself to hear the gasps and the applause and gather up the money at his feet.

Within a year, Dámaso was forgotten. His family's house had burned to ashes around the remains of a kerosene heater, the goats died and the brazier flared without him, and I closed up the clinic and moved permanently, with Elvira and her parrot, to our cottage by the sea. I pass my days now in the sunshine, tending our modest garden, walking the sugar-white beach to see what the tide has brought in. I no longer practice medicine, but of course I'm known here as *El Estimado Doctor,* and on occasion, in an emergency, a patient will show up on my doorstep. Just the other day a little girl of three or four came in, swaddled in her mother's arms. She'd been playing in the tide pools down by the lava cliffs that rise up out of the sand like dense distant loaves and had stepped on a sea urchin. One of the long black spikes the animal uses for defense had broken off under the child's weight and embedded itself in the sole of her foot.

I soothed her as best I could, speaking softly to distract her, speaking nonsense really—all that matters in such circumstances is the intonation. I murmured. The sea murmured along the shore. As delicately as I could, I held her miniature heel in my hand, took hold of the slick black fragment with the grip of my forceps and pulled it cleanly from the flesh, and I have to tell you, that little girl shrieked till the very glass in the windows rattled, shrieked as if there were no other pain in the world.

(2007)

Bulletproof

The Sticker

I don't have any children—I'm not even married, not anymore—but last month, though I was fried from my commute and looking forward to nothing more complicated than the bar, the TV and the microwave dinner, in that order, I made a point of attending the Thursday-evening meeting of the Smithstown School Board. On an empty stomach. Sans alcohol. Why? Because of Melanie Albert's ninth-grade biology textbook—or, actually, the sticker affixed to the cover of it. This is the book with the close-up of the swallowtail butterfly against a field of pure environmental green, standard issue, used in ten thousand schools across the land, and it came to my attention when her father, Dave, and I were unwinding after work at the Granite Grill a week earlier.

The Granite is our local watering hole, and it doesn't have much to recommend it, beyond the fact that it's there. Its virtues reside mainly in what it doesn't offer, I suppose—no waiters wrestling with their consciences, no chef striving to demonstrate his ability to fuse the Ethiopian and Korean culinary traditions, no music other than the hits of the eighties, piped in through a service that plumbs the deep cuts so that you get to hear The Clash doing "Wrong 'Em Boyo" and David Byrne's "Swamp," from his days with Talking Heads, instead of the same unvarying eternal crap you get on the radio. And it's dimly lighted. Very dimly lighted. All you see, really, beyond the shifting colors of the TV, is the soft backlit glow of the bottles on display behind the bar dissolving into a hundred soothing glints of gold and copper. It's relaxing—so relaxing I've found myself drifting off to dreamland right there in the grip of my barstool, one hand clenched round the stem of the glass, the other bracing up a chin as heavy as all the slag heaps of the earth combined. You could say it's my second home. Or maybe my first.

We'd just settled onto our stools, my right hand going instinctively to the bowl of artificial bar snacks while the Mets careened round the bases on the wide-screen TV and Rick, the bartender, stirred and strained my first Sidecar of the evening, when I became aware of Dave, off to my left, digging something out of his briefcase. There was a thump beside me and I turned my head. "What's that?" I said. The title, in fluorescent orange, leapt out at me: *An Introduction to Biology.* "A little light reading?"

Dave—he was my age, forty-three, and he didn't bother to dye his hair or counteract the wrinkles eroding his forehead and chewing away at the corners of his eyes because he accepted who he was and he had no qualms about letting the world in on it—just stared at me. He'd given up tennis. Given up poker. And when I called him on a Saturday morning to go out for a hike or a spin up the river in my speedboat with the twin Merc 575s that'll shear the hair right off your head, he was always busy.

"What?" I said.

He tapped the cover of the book. "Don't you notice anything?"

My drink had come, iced, sugared, as necessary as oxygen. The Mets scored again. I took a sip.

"The sticker," he said. "Don't you see the sticker?"

Prodded, I took notice of it, a lemon-yellow circle the size of a silver dollar, inside of which was a disclaimer printed in sober black letters. *The theory of evolution as put forth in this text,* it read, *is just that, a theory, and should not be confused with fact.* "Yeah," I said. "So?"

He clenched his jaw. Gave me a long hard look. "Don't you know what this means?"

I thought about that a moment, turning the book over in one hand before setting it back down on the bar. I worked at the sticker with my thumbnail. It was immovable, as if it had been fused to the cover using a revolutionary new process. "Sucker's really on there," I said. I gave him a grin. "You wouldn't happen to have any sandpaper on you, would you?"

"It's not fucking funny, Cal. You can laugh—you haven't got a kid in school. But if you believe in anything, if you believe in what's happening to this country, what's happening right here in our own community—" He broke off, so wrought up he couldn't go on. His face was flushed. He picked up his beer and set it down again.

"You're talking about the fact that we're living in a theocracy now, right? A theocracy at war with another theocracy?"

"Why do you always have to make a joke out of everything?"

"Bible-thumpers," I said, but without conviction. I was in a bar. It had been a long day. I wanted to talk about nothing, sports, women, the subtle manipulations of the commercials for beer, cars, Palm Pilots. I didn't want to delve beneath the surface. It was too cold down there, too dark and claustrophobic. "You can't be serious," I said finally, giving ground. "Here? Thirty-five miles up the river from Manhattan?"

He was nodding, his eyes fixed on mine. "I don't pay that much attention, I guess," he said finally. "Or Katie either. I don't even think we voted in the last school board election. . . . I mean, it's our own fault. It was just a slate of names, you know. Like the judges. Does anybody ever know the slightest thing about any of the judges on the ballot that comes round every November? Or the town supervisors? Shit. You'd have to devote your life to it, know what I'm saying?"

Feelings were stirring in me—anger, resentment, helplessness. My drink had gone warm. I said the only thing I could think to say: "So what are you going to do?"

Jesus, and Where He Resides

It was raining that Thursday night, though the air was warm still, a last breath of summer before September gave way to October and the days began to wind down till the leaves littered the streets and the boat would have to come out of the water. I had a little trouble finding the place where they were holding the meeting—they've built a whole city's worth of new buildings since I went to school, the population ratcheting up relentlessly even around here where there are zero jobs to be had and all everybody talks about is preserving the semi-rural feel, as if we were all dipping our own candles and greasing the wheels of our buggies. Which is another reason why I couldn't find the place. It's dark. The streetlights give out within a block of the junction of the state road and Main Street, and the big old black-barked oaks and elms everybody seems to love soak up the light till the roads might as well be tunnels in a coal mine. And I admit it: my eyes aren't what they used to be. I've put off getting glasses because of the kind of statement they make—weakness, that is—and I've heard that once you begin to rely on them you can never go back to the naked eye, that's it, and here's your crutch forever. The next thing is reading glasses, and then you're pottering around with those pathetic lanyards looped round your neck, murmuring, *Has anybody seen my glasses?*

Anyway, it was the cars that clued me. There must have been a hundred or more of them jamming every space in the parking lot behind the new elementary school, with the overflow parked on a lawn that was just a wet black void sucked out of the shadows. I pulled up within inches of the last car squeezed in on the grass—a cobalt-blue Suburban, humped and mountainous—and felt the wheels give ever so slightly before I shut down the ignition, figuring I'd worry about it later. I pulled up the collar of my coat and hurried along the walk toward the lights glowing in the distance.

The auditorium was packed, standing room only, and everybody looked angry—from the six school board members seated behind a collapsible table up onstage to the reporter from the local paper and the concerned parents and students warming the chairs and lining the walls like extras on a movie set. I caught a nostalgic whiff of floor wax, finger paint and formaldehyde, but it was short-lived, overwhelmed by the working odor of all that crush of humanity. The fact that everybody was wet to one degree or another didn't help matters, the women's hair hanging limp, the men's jackets clinging at the shoulders and under the arms, umbrellas drooling, smears of wet black mud striping the linoleum underfoot. I could smell myself—what I was adding to the mix—in the bad cheese of my underarms and the sweet reek of mango-pineapple rising from the dissolved gel in my hair. It was very hot.

The door closed softly behind me and I found myself squeezed in between a gaunt leathery woman with a starburst of shellacked hair and a pock-faced man who looked as if he'd had a very bad day made worse by the dawning awareness that he was going to have to stand here amidst all these people, in this stink and this heat, till the last word was spoken and the doors opened to deliver him back out into the rain. I hunched my shoulders to make room and let my eyes roam over the crowd in the hope of spotting Dave and his wife. Not that it would matter—even if they'd saved a seat for me I couldn't have got to them. But still, it gave me the smallest uptick of satisfaction to see them sitting there in the third row left, Katie's head shrouded in a black scarf, as if she were attending a funeral, and Dave's bald spot glowing like a poached egg in the graying nest of his hair.

What can I say? This was the most normal scene in the world, a scene replicated through the generations and across the continent, the flag drooping to one side of the podium, red velvet curtains disclosing the stage beyond, student art buckling away from the freshly painted walls while parents, teachers and students gathered in a civic forum to weigh all the pedagogical nuances of the curriculum. Standing there, the fluorescent lights glaring in my eyes and the steam of my fellow humans rising round me, I was plunged into a deep pool of nostalgia, thinking of my own parents, now dead, my own teachers, mostly dead, and myself, very much alive and well though in need of a drink. On some level it was strangely moving. I shifted my feet. Looked to the tiles of the ceiling as a way of neutering my emotions. It was then that I felt the door open behind me—a cold draft, the sizzle of rain—as a newcomer even tardier than I slipped in to join the gathering. A female. Young, pretty, with an overload of perfume. I gave her a glance as she edged in beside me. "Sorry," she whispered. "No problem," I said under my breath, and because I felt awkward and didn't want to stare, I turned my attention back to the stage.

There was a general coughing and rustling, and then one of the school board members—a sour-looking woman with reading glasses dangling from her throat—leaned forward and reached for the microphone perched at the edge of the table. There was a thump followed by the hiss of static as she wrestled the thing away from its stand, and then her amplified voice came at us as if it had been there all along, just under the surface: "And since that concludes the formal business for the evening, we're prepared to take your questions and comments at this point. One person at a time, please, and please come to the center aisle and use the microphone there so everybody can hear."

The first speaker—a man in his thirties, narrow eyes, narrow shoulders, a cheap sport coat and a turquoise bola tie he must have worn in the hope somebody would think him hip—rose to a spatter of applause and a cascade of hoots from the students against the wall. "Ba-oom!" they chanted. "Ba-oom!" In an instant the mood had been transformed from nervous anticipation to a kind of ecstasy. "Ba-oom!"

He took hold of the microphone, glanced over his shoulder at the students behind him and snapped, "That'll be enough now, and I *mean* it," until the chant died away. Then he half-turned to the audience—and this was awkward because he was addressing the board up onstage as well—and began by introducing himself. "My name is Robert Tannenbaum"—a burst of *Ba-oom, Ba-oom!*—"and as many of you know, I teach ninth-grade biology at Smithstown High. And I have a statement here, signed not only by the entire science department—with one notable exception—but the majority of the rest of the faculty as well."

It was just a paragraph or so—he knew to keep it short—and as he read I couldn't help watching the faces of the board members. They were four men and two women, with the usual hairstyles and appurtenances, dressed in shades of brown and gray. They held themselves so stiffly their bones might have been fused, and they gazed out over the crowd while the teacher read his statement, their eyes barely registering him. The statement said simply that the faculty rejected the warning label the board had imposed on *An Introduction to Biology* as a violation of the Constitution's separation of church and state. "No reputable scientist anywhere in the world," the teacher went on, lifting his head to stare directly at the woman with the microphone, "subscribes to the notion of Intelligent Design—or let's call it by its real name, *Creationism*—as a viable scientific theory." And now he swung round on the crowd and spread his arms wide: "Get real, people. There's no debate here—just science and anti-science."

A few members of the audience began stamping their feet. The man beside me pulled his lips back and hissed.

"And that's the key phrase here, *scientific* theory—that is, testable, subject to peer review—and not a theological one, because that's exactly what this is, trying to force religion into the classroom—"

"Atheist!" a woman cried out, but the teacher waved her off. "No theory is bulletproof," he said, raising his voice now, "and we in the scientific community welcome debate—legitimate, scientific debate—and certainly theories mutate and evolve just like life on this planet, but—"

"Ba-oom, Ba-oom!"

There was a building ferment, a muted undercurrent of dissent and anger, the students chanting, people shouting out, until the sour-looking woman—the chairwoman, or was she the superintendent?—slammed the flat of her hand down on the table. "You'll all get your chance," she said, pinching her voice so that it shot splinters of steel through the microphone and out into the audience on a blast of feedback, "because everybody's got the right to an opinion." She glared down at the teacher, then lifted the reading glasses to the bridge of her nose and squinted at a sheet of paper she held up before her in an attempt to catch the light. "Thank you, Mr. Tannenbaum," she said. "We'll hear now from the Reverend Doctor Micah Stiller, of the First Baptist Church. Reverend Stiller?"

I was transfixed. I'd had no idea. Here I'd taken the train into the city every day and slogged on back every night, lingered at the Granite, hiked the trails and rocketed my way up the river to feel the wind in my face and impress whatever woman I'd managed to cajole along with me, and all the while this Manichean struggle had been going on right up the street. The reverend (beard, off-the-rack suit, big black shoes the size of andirons) invoked God, Jesus and the Bible as the ultimate authorities on matters of creation, and then a whole snaking line of people trooped up to the microphone one after another to voice their opinions on everything from the Great Flood to the age of the earth (*Ten thousand years! Are you out of your mind?* the biology teacher shouted as he slammed out the side exit to a contrapuntal chorus of cheers and jeers), to recent advancements in space travel and the unraveling of the human genome and how close it was to the chimpanzee's. And the garden slug's.

At one point, Dave even got into the act. He stood abruptly, his face frozen in outrage, stalked up to the microphone and blurted, "If there's no evolution, how come we all have to get a new flu shot each year?" Before anyone could answer him he was back in his seat and the chairwoman was clapping her hands for order. How much time had gone by I couldn't say—an hour, an hour at least. My left leg seemed to have gone dead at the hip. I breathed perfume. Stole a look at the woman beside me and saw that she had beautiful hands and feet and a smile that sought out my own. She was thirty-five or so, blond, no hat, no coat, in a blue flocked dress cut just above her knees, and we were complicit. Or so I thought.

Finally, when things seemed to be winding down, a girl dressed in a white sweater and plaid skirt, with her hair cut close and her arms folded palm to elbow, came down the aisle as if she were walking a bed of hot coals and took hold of the microphone. Her hands trembled as she tried to adjust it to her height, but she couldn't seem to loosen the catch. She stood there a moment, working at it, and when she saw that no one was going to help her, she went up on her tiptoes. "I just wanted to say," she breathed, clutching the mike as if it were a wall she was trying to climb, "that my name is Mary-Louise Mohler and I'm a freshman at Smithstown High—"

Hoots, catcalls, two raw-faced kids in baseball hats leering from the far side of the auditorium, adult faces swiveling angrily, the clatter of the rain beyond the windows.

She stood there patiently till the noise died down and the sour-faced woman, attempting a smile, gestured for her to go ahead. "I want everyone to know that the theory of evolution is only a theory, just like the sticker says—"

"What about Intelligent Design?" someone called out, and I was startled to see that it was Dave, half-risen from his seat. "I suppose that's fact?" I couldn't help laughing, but softly, softly, and turned to the woman beside me—the blonde. "To all the Jesus freaks, maybe," I whispered, and gave her an unequivocal grin. Which she ignored. Her gaze was fixed on the girl. The auditorium had grown quiet. I raised my hand to my mouth to suppress an imaginary cough, shifted my weight and looked back down the aisle.

"It is," the girl said quietly, dropping her eyes so she wouldn't have to look Dave in the face. "It *is* fact and I'm the one to know it." She clenched her hands in front of her, rocked back on her heels and then rose up once more on point to let her soft feathery voice inhabit the microphone: "I know it because Jesus lives in my heart."

The Weak

I was the first one out the door. The rain had let up, nothing more than a persistent drizzle now, the shrubs along the walk black with moisture and the air dense with the smell of it—the smell of nature, that is, wet, fungal, chaotic. And sweet. Infinitely sweet after the reek of that auditorium. I hurried down the walk and across the lot, thinking to get out ahead of the traffic. I was meeting Dave and Katie at the Granite for burgers and a drink or two and I could hardly wait for the postmortem, because I'd wanted to flag my hand and put a question to the girl in the plaid skirt, wanted to ask her just how provable her contention was. Could we thread one of those surgical mini-cameras up through the vein in her thigh and into her left ventricle just to see if we could find the Redeemer there? And what would He be doing? Sitting down to dinner? Frying up fish in a pan? At least Jonah had some elbow room. But then I guessed Jesus was capable of making himself very, very small—sub-microscopic even.

High comedy—Dave and I would have a real laugh over this one. My feet sailed on down the walk, across the lot and through the drizzle of the world, and I was thinking cold beer, medium-rare burger with extra cheese and two slices of Bermuda onion, until I reached my car and saw that I wasn't going anywhere. The rear tires had sunk maybe half an inch into the grass-turned-to-mud, but that wasn't the problem, or not the immediate problem. The immediate problem was the Mini Cooper (two-tone, red and black) backed up against my bumper and blocking me as effectively as if a wall had been erected round my car while the meeting was going down.

I was wearing a tan leather three-quarter-length overcoat that had caught my eye in the window of a shop on Fifth Avenue a month back and for which I'd paid too much, and it was on its way to being ruined. I didn't have an umbrella. And I'd ignored the salesgirl, who'd given me a four-ounce plastic bottle of some waterproofing agent and made me swear to spray the coat with it the minute I got home. I could feel the coat drinking up the wet. A thin trickle, smelling of mango-pineapple, began to drip from the tip of my nose. I looked round me, thinking of the blond woman—this was her car, I was sure of it, and where in hell was she and how could she just block me in like that?—and then I opened the door of my car and slid in to wait.

Twenty of the longest minutes of my life crumbled round me as I sat there in the dark, smoking one of the cigarettes I'd promised myself to give up while the radio whispered and the windshield fogged over. Headlights illuminated me as one car after another backed out, swung round and rolled on out of the lot to freedom. I reminded myself, not for the first time, that patience, far from being a virtue, was just weakness in disguise. A mosquito beat itself up out of nowhere to settle on the back of my neck so I could put an end to its existence before it had its opportunity to produce more mosquitoes to send out into a world of exposed necks, arms and midriffs. Midriffs. I began to think about midriffs and then the blond woman and what hers might look like if she were wearing something less formal than a flocked blue dress that buttoned all the way up to the collar and I pulled on my cigarette and drummed my fingers on the dash and felt my lids grow heavy.

Finally—and it was my bad luck that the last two cars left in the whole place were the ones blocking me in—I heard voices and glanced in the rearview mirror to see three figures emerging from the gloom. Women. "All right, then," one of them called out, and here she was—the chairwoman, her big white block of a face looming up on the passenger side of my car like a calving glacier as the Suburban flashed its lights and gurgled in appreciation of her—"you have a good night. And feel good. You did real well tonight, honey."

The door slammed. The Suburban roared. Red brake lights, a great powerful churning of tires and the song of the steering mechanism, and then she was gone. I shifted my eyes to the other side, and there she was, the blonde, framed in the driver's side mirror. Right next to her daughter, in the plaid skirt and damp white sweater.

I froze. Absolutely. I was motionless. I didn't draw breath. The girl and her mother climbed into the Mini Cooper and I wanted to shrink down in my seat, crawl into the well under the steering wheel, vanish altogether, but I couldn't do a thing. I heard the engine start up—they were on their way; in a second they'd be gone—and for all I'd been through, for all the rumbling of my stomach and the craving for alcohol that was almost like a need and the strangeness of that overstuffed auditorium and the testimony I'd witnessed, I felt a yearning so powerful it took me out of myself till I didn't know where I was. And then I heard the harsh message of the wheels slipping and then an accelerating whine as they fought for purchase in the mud. She had no idea, this woman—not the faintest notion—of how to rock a car out of a hole in a yielding surface. She accelerated. The wheels spun. Then she did it again. And again.

I watched the door swing open, watched her legs emerge from the car as she reached down to remove her shoes and step out onto the grass to assess the situation while her daughter's torso faded in soft focus behind the fogged-over windshield. And because I was weak, because I hadn't dated anybody in a month and more and couldn't stand to see those shining bare legs and glistening feet stained with mud and didn't care whether Jesus and all the saints in heaven were involved in the equation or not, I got out of my car, looked her full in the face over the glare of the headlights and said, "Can I help?"

The Fit

I never did get to the Granite that night. I called Dave on my cell and he sounded annoyed—wound up from the meeting and eager to take it out on somebody—but the Mini Cooper was in deeper than it looked and by the time we were able to free it I was in no shape for anything but bed. My coat was ruined. Ditto my shoes. Both pantlegs were greased with mud, my hands dense with it, my fingernails blackened. I should have given up, the term *lost cause* hammered like a spike into the back of my brain, but I was feeling demonstrative—and maybe just a little bit ashamed of myself over the Jesus freak comment. We were ten minutes into it, the drizzle thickening to rain, the miniature wheels digging deeper and the daughter and I straining against the rear bumper, when the woman behind the wheel—the blonde, the mother—stuck her head out the window and gave me my out. "You know," she called over the ticking of the engine and the soft beat of the rain, "maybe I should just call Triple A?"

I came up alongside the car so I could see the pale node of her face wrapped in her shining hair and her eyes like liquid fire. The interior of the car sank away into the shadows beyond her. I couldn't see her shoulders or her torso or her legs. Just her face, like a picture in a frame. "No," I said, "no need. We can get it out."

The daughter chimed in then—Mary-Louise. She was standing on the far side of the car, hands on hips. There was a spatter of mud on her sweater. "Come on, Mom," she said with an edge of exasperation. "Try it again." She looked to me, then bent to brace herself against the bumper. "Come on," she said, "one more time."

I watched the mother's face. She squeezed her eyes shut a moment so that a little hieroglyph of flesh appeared over the bridge of her nose, then she gave me the full benefit of her gaze and it came to me that she hadn't heard what I'd said back in the auditorium, that there was no animosity, none at all. I wasn't on trial. I was just a helpful stranger, the Good Samaritan himself. "I'm Lynnese Mohler," she said, and here was her hand, the nails done in a metallic shade of blue or lavender, slipping free of the darkness to take hold of my own. "And this is my daughter, Mary-Louise."

"Calvin Jessup." I leaned toward her, toward the smell of her, her perfume and what lay beneath it. "But people call me Cal. My friends anyway." I was smiling. Broadly. Stupidly. The rain quickened.

"Come on, Mom."

"I want to thank you for your help—you're really sweet. I mean it. But are you sure I shouldn't call Triple A? It's nothing. I mean, they don't even charge—"

I straightened up and gave her an elaborate shrug, feeling the accumulated weight of every cell and fiber of my one hundred and eighty-seven pounds. I didn't need alcohol. Didn't need a burger. All I needed was to push this car out of the ditch. "If you want to wait here in the dark," I said. "But I really think we can get you out if you just—"

"You have to rock the car, Mom." The girl—what was she, fourteen, fifteen? Was that ninth grade? I couldn't remember—slapped the side of the car with her open palm. "We almost had it there that last time, so just, come on, start it up and then you go back and forth—you know, the way Dad showed us."

Lynnese glanced up at me, then ducked her head and shook it side to side so that her hair, dense with moisture, fell loose to screen her face. "I'm divorced," she said.

Behind us, across the lot, the lights of the auditorium faded briefly and then blinked out. "Yeah," I said. "So am I."

The Fittest

A week later I was sitting with Dave at the Granite, enjoying my second Sidecar of the evening and watching the first round of the playoffs that wouldn't feature the Mets (this year anyway), thinking about Lynnese while Dave went on about the lawsuit he and twelve of the other parents were filing against the school district. I liked Dave. He was one of my oldest friends. And I agreed with him both in principle and fact, but when he got on his high horse, when he got *Serious* with a capital *S*, he tended to repeat himself to the point of stupefaction. I was listening to him, feeding him the appropriate responses ("Uh-huh, uh-huh—really?") at the appropriate junctures, yet I was tuning him out too.

I wanted to talk about Lynnese and what had happened between us in the past week, but I couldn't. I'd never been comfortable exposing my feelings, which was why people like Dave accused me of making a joke of everything, and I couldn't even mention her—not to Dave—without feeling like a traitor to the cause. "I'm a Christian," she told me on the occasion of our first date, before I'd even had a chance to ice the beer or rev up the engines or ask her if she'd like to release the stern line and help cast us off (which was a simple way to involve anybody in the process of what we were about to do, because there's no pretense in boating and the thrill of being out on the water takes you right back to your childhood, automatically—boom—just like that). The sun was high, Indian summer, a Saturday delivered from the heavens, and I was planning to take her up the river to a floating restaurant-cum-club where we could have cocktails on the deck, listen to reggae (and dance, maybe dance, if she was up for it) and get dinner too. She was wearing shorts. Her hair was its own kind of rapture. "Hi," I said. "Hi," she said back. "Where's Mary-Louise?" I asked, secretly thrilled that she'd come alone and all the while dreading the intrusion of that child with Jesus in her heart, half-expecting her to pop up out of the back seat of the Mini Cooper or come strolling out of the bushes, and she told me that Mary-Louise was out in the woods hiking—"Up Breakneck Ridge? Where that trail loops behind the mountain to where those lakes are? She loves nature," she said. "Every least thing, the way she focuses on it—it's just a shame they won't let her alone in school, in biology. She could be a scientist, a doctor, anything." I didn't have much to say to that. I held out a hand to help her into the boat. She anchored her legs, the hull rocking beneath us, and leveled her eyes on me. "I'm a Christian," she said.

Well, all right. I'd seen her twice since, and she was as lively, smart and well-informed as anybody I knew—and if I'd expected some sort of sackcloth-and-ashes approach to the intimate moments of an exploratory relationship, well, there went another prejudice. She was hot. And I was intrigued. Really intrigued. (Though I wouldn't want to call it love or infatuation or anything more specific than that after what I'd gone through with my ex-wife and the three or four women who came after her.)

"We're going to break them," Dave was saying. "I swear to you. There was that case in Pennsylvania and before that in Kansas, but these people just don't learn. And they've got bucks behind them. Big bucks."

"You want to call them fanatics," was what I said.

"That's right," he said. "They're fanatics."

The Petitions

Before the trial, there were the petitions. Trials require a whole lot of steam, time to maneuver for position, war chests, thrusts and counterthrusts, but petitions require nothing more than footwork and a filing fee. Within a week of the meeting, petitioners were everywhere. You couldn't go into the grocery, the post office or the library without sidestepping a fold-up table with two or three clench-jawed women sitting behind it in a welter of pens, Styrofoam cups, ledgers and homemade signs. And men, men too. Men like Dave, and on the other side of the issue, men like the reverend and the pockmarked man who'd stood beside me in the auditorium distending his lips and puffing up his cheeks to express his opinion of the proceedings. I'd taken a lot of things for granted. Some of us might have lived at the end of long driveways and maybe we didn't get involved in community issues because that sort of rah-rah business didn't mesh with our personalities, but as far as I knew we'd always been a community in agreement—save the trees, confine the tourists, preserve the old houses on Main Street, clean up the river and educate the kids to keep them from becoming a drag on society. Now I saw how wrong I was.

Of course, Dave came into the Granite and laid his petition right out on the bar and I was one of the first to sign it—and not just out of social pressure, Rick and half a dozen of the regulars looking over my shoulder while Elvis Costello sang "My Aim Is True" and my burger sizzled on the grill and the late sun melted across the wall, but because it was the right thing to do. "People can believe what they want," Dave said, giving a little speech for the bar, "but that doesn't make it the truth. And it sure as shit doesn't make it science." I signed. Sure, I signed. He would have killed me if I didn't.

And then I was coming up the hill from the station, the trees fired with the season and dusk coming down over the river behind me, everything so changeless and pure it was as if I'd stepped back in time, when I remembered I needed to pick up a few things at the deli. I didn't cook much—I let Tom Scoville, the chef at the Granite, take care of that—but I ate cereal for breakfast, slipped the odd frozen dinner into the microwave or went through the elaborate ritual of slicing Swiss and folding it between two slices of rye. I was out of milk, butter, bread. And as I'd walked down the hill to the train that morning I'd reminded myself to remind myself when I came back up.

I was deep in my post-work oblivion, thinking nothing, and the pockmarked man took me by surprise. Suddenly he was standing there, right in front of the door of Gravenites' Deli, not exactly blocking my access, but taking up space in a way I didn't like. Up close, I saw that the pockmarks were a remnant of an epidermal war he was fighting not only on his face but his scalp and throat as well. He smelled like roast beef. "Hello, brother," he said, thrusting a clipboard at me.

I was in no mood. "I'm an only child," I said.

Unfazed—I don't even think he heard me—he just kept talking, "There's a battle going on here for the souls of our children. And we all have to get involved."

"Not me," I said, trying to maneuver past him. "What I have to get is a quart of milk."

"I saw you at the meeting," he said, and now he was blocking my way. "You know damn well what this is all about." Behind him, in the depths of the store, I could see people lined up waiting for cold cuts, sandwiches, a slice of pizza. Thirty seconds had gone by, thirty seconds out of my life. I moved for the door and the clipboard flew up like a bird. "What side you on?" he said. "Because there's only one side to this—God's side."

"Get the fuck out of my way."

His eyes jumped and steadied and something hard settled into his face. "Don't use that language with me."

The whole world dissolved in that instant, as if the movie had slipped off the reel, and a long sorrow opened up inside me. What was going on here had nothing to do with Dave or school boards or Lynnese or her daughter either—it was just some stranger getting in my face, and nobody gets in my face. Some redneck. Some yahoo with a complexion like a cheese grater and bad breath on top of it. So I shoved him and he lurched back against the window and everybody in Gravenites' Deli looked up at the concussion as the plate glass contracted and snapped back again. He came at me before I could get a second shove in, his hands at the collar of my shirt, bunching the material there, and he was the one cursing now, "Jesus, Jesus, Jesus!"

It was over in a minute, the way most fights are. I grabbed both his hands and flung them away from me even as my shirt—green Tencel, in a banana-leaf pattern, eighty-seven bucks on sale—ripped down the front and I gave him a parting shove that sent him into the empty steel framework of the bicycle rack, where his legs got tangled up and he went down hard on the sidewalk. Then I was stalking up the street, the blood screaming in my ears and everything so distorted I thought I was losing my sight.

I felt contaminated. Angry with myself but more angry with him and everybody like him, the narrow, the bigoted, the *fanatics,* because that was what they were, their hope masquerading as certainty, desperation plucking at your sleeve, plucking, always plucking and pushing. In college—I think it was my sophomore year—I took a course called "Philosophy of Religion" by way of fulfilling an elective requirement, but also because I wanted ammunition against my Catholic mother and the fraud the priests and rabbis and mullahs were perpetrating on people too ignorant and scared to know better. Throughout my childhood I'd been the victim of a scam, of the panoply of God and His angels, of goodness everlasting and the answer to the mystery Mary-Louise carried in her heart and laid out for all to see, and I wanted this certified college course and this middle-aged professor with a pouf of discolored hair and a birthmark in the shape of Lake Erie on his forehead to confirm it. I knew Paley's argument from design, knew about the watch and the watchmaker, and I knew now that these people—these Jesus freaks—were trundling out the same old argument dressed in new clothes. Intricacy requires design, that was what they said. And design requires a designer. That was as far as they could see, that was it, case closed: God exists. And the earth is ten thousand years old, just like the Bible says.

I went up the sidewalk, my legs churning against the grade with the fierce regularity of my rage, my quadriceps muscles flexing and releasing, the anterior cruciate ligaments aligning and realigning themselves in my knees, the chambers of my Jesus-less heart pumping like the slick-working intricate parts of the intricate machine they were, and the whole debate reduced to a naked clipboard and a torn shirt. I was two blocks from the Granite. I couldn't see. I couldn't think. I crossed one street, then the next, and the hill sank ahead of me until the familiar yellow awning of the bar came into view, cars parked out front, lights glowing against the twilight and all the trees down the block masked in shadow.

That was when my vision suddenly came clear and I spotted Lynnese. She was sitting behind a card table in front of the bookstore, Mary-Louise perched on a folding chair beside her with her back arched so perfectly she might have been auditioning for junior cotillion. They were fifty feet from me. I saw a mug imprinted with the hopeful yellow slash of a smiley face, front and center, right in the middle of the table, saw Mary-Louise's pink backpack at her feet and the sprawl of her books and homework. And I saw the clipboard. Cheap dun plastic, the shining metallic clip. Saw it all at the very moment Lynnese lifted her eyes and flashed me a smile with wings on it.

My reaction? Truthfully? I made as if I didn't see her. Suddenly I had to cross the street—this was very compelling, an absolute necessity, because even though crossing the street would take me away from the Granite and I'd have to walk a block in the opposite direction and then double back, I had an urgent errand over there on the other side of the street, in that antique shop I'd passed a hundred times and never yet set foot in.

Mutation, and How It Operates in Nature

And then it was a Sunday toward the end of the month, warmer than it should have been at this time of year, and I was out in the woods on the trail behind Breakneck Ridge, enjoying the weight of my daypack and the way the trees caught the wind and shook out their colors. I had two hot dog buns with me, two all-beef wieners, yellow mustard in a disposable packet and a bottle of red wine I'd decanted into my bota bag, and I was planning on a good six- or seven-mile loop and lunch beside a creek I liked to visit, especially in the fall when the bugs were down. The World Series was on, but it featured two teams that didn't excite me all that much and I figured the Granite could do without me, at least for the afternoon—I'd been in and out all week anyway, mostly when Dave wasn't there. Nothing against Dave—I just needed a little time to myself. Nights were getting cold. The season was almost gone.

I felt the climb as a burn in my lungs and I realized I wasn't in the kind of shape I should have been—the walk up from the train was one thing, but the ridge was another thing altogether. I was thinking about the philosophy of religion professor and a trick he'd played on the class one Friday afternoon when all we wanted, collectively, was to get out the door and head downtown for beer, loud music and whatever association we could make with the opposite sex. He put a drawing up on the blackboard, nothing very elaborate, just lines and shadings, that appeared to be a scene out of nature, a crag, a pine tree, a scattering of boulders. He didn't identify it as a trompe l'oeil, but that was what it was, a trick of the eye, a deception, sweet and simple. *There's a hidden figure here,* he told us, *and when you see it—and please don't reveal it to anyone else—you're welcome to leave. Just concentrate. That's all it takes.* One by one, my classmates gave out with expressions of surprise, wondered a moment over the subtlety of the lesson, packed up their books and left. I was the last one. I stared at that crag, that pine tree, till they were imprinted on my brain, increasingly frustrated—there was nothing there, I was sure of it, and the others were faking it in order to curry favor and not least to get out of the classroom and into the sunlit arena of that Friday afternoon. When finally I did see it—a representation of Jesus leaping clear of the background, his halo a pine bough, a boulder for his cheek—all I felt was disappointment. It was a cheap trick, that was all. What did it prove? That anybody can be fooled? That we can't trust the evidence of our five senses when five senses are all we've got?

It had rained the night before and the path was slick beneath my feet. I came within an ace of losing my balance on a switchback with a considerable drop to it and that drove the professor and his drawing right out of my head. There was the sound of running water everywhere, a thousand little streams sprung up overnight to churn away at the side of the mountain, and the wind picked up so that the branches of the trees rattled overhead and the leaves came down like confetti. I was almost to the creek where I was planning to gather up some damp twigs and get a fire going so I could roast my wieners and take in the glory of the day from a new perspective, when I came around a bend in the trail and saw a figure up ahead. A girl. Dressed in khaki shorts and a denim jacket. Her back was to me and she was bent at the waist in a patch of sun just off the trail, as if she were looking for something.

I stopped where I was. It was always awkward meeting people on the trail—they'd come for solitude and so had I, and a woman alone would always view a man with suspicion, and rightfully so. There'd been attacks, even out here. It took me a moment, poised there with my feet still in their tracks, before I recognized her, Mary-Louise, bent over in a column of sunlight with her blond hair clipped short and the back of her neck so white it was like an ache. For a moment, I didn't know what to do—I was about to turn away and tiptoe back down the trail, but she turned her face to me as if she'd known all along that I was there and I scuffed my hiking boots on the dirt just to make some noise, and said, "Hi. Hi, Mary-Louise." And then a joke, lame, admittedly, but the best I could manage under the circumstances: "I see you've stepped up in the world."

She'd turned back to whatever it was that had caught her attention and when she looked at me again she put a single finger to her lips and then gestured for me to come closer. I moved up the path as stealthily as I could, one slow step at a time. When I reached her, when I was standing over her and seeing what she was seeing—a snake, a blacksnake stretched out across a fallen log in the full glare of the sun, its scales trapping the light like a fresh coat of paint—she gave me such a look of pride you'd think she'd created it herself. "It's a blacksnake," I said. "A big one too. They can get to be ten feet long, you know."

"Eight feet," she said. "Maximum. The record's a hundred and one inches."

"And you didn't have to shush me—I mean, it's not as if they can hear."

"They feel the vibrations. And they can see."

We both looked down at it. Its eyes were open, its tongue flicking. There was no hurry in it because the sun was a thing it needed and the season was going fast and soon it would be underground. Or dead. "You know," I said, "it's really a black racer—"

"Coluber constrictor," she said without turning her head. "That's the scientific name."

The wind beat at the trees and a shadow chased violently across the ground, but the snake never moved. "Yeah," I said, out of my league now. "It's amazing how fast they can move if they want to. I saw one once, when I was a kid, and it was in this swamp. A couple of inches of water anyway, and it went after a frog like you couldn't believe."

"They move by contracting the muscles of their ribs. All snakes have at least a hundred vertebrae and some as many as four hundred, did you know that?"

"But no legs. Their lizard cousins have legs, though, and how do you think they got them? And out west—I saw one once in the Sierras—they have a legless lizard, just like a snake, but it's not." I should have left it, but I couldn't. "Why do you suppose that is? I think—no, I know—it's because of evolution, and that legless lizard is a link between the snakes, who don't need legs to crawl into tight spaces, and the lizards that can get up and run. Like us." She didn't say anything. The trees dipped and rose again. The snake lay still.

"Once," she said, turning all the way round to stare at me as if I were the wonder of nature and the snake no more than incidental, "in the spring? I was with my mother and we were standing outside my friend Sarah's house, a farmhouse, but it's not a farm really, just an old stone place with a barn. Right there, while we were saying goodbye and getting ready to walk to our car, these snakes began to come out of a hole in the ground right where we were standing. Garter snakes."

I wanted to tell her that they balled up like a skein of yarn to survive the winter, hundreds of them sometimes, that they gave birth to live young and that the babies were on their own after that, but I didn't. "Red and yellow stripes," I said. "And black."

She nodded. Her eyes went distant at the memory. "They were like ribbons," she said. "Ribbons of God."

(2007)

Hands On

She liked his hands. His eyes. The way he looked at her as if he could see beneath the skin, as if he were modeling her from clay, his fingers there at her jawline, at the orbits of her eyes, feeling their way across her brow. She'd stepped in out of the hard clean light of early summer, announced herself to the receptionist and barely had time to leaf through one of the magazines on the end table before she'd been ushered into this room, with its quiet shadows and the big black-leather reclining chair in the middle of the floor—it was like a dentist's chair, that was her impression, only without all the rest of the paraphernalia. And that was good, because she hated the dentist, but then who didn't? Pain, necessary pain, pain in the service of improvement and health, that was what the dentist gave you, and she wondered about this—what would this give her? The recliner said nothing to her, but it intimidated her all the same, and so she'd taken a seat in a straight-backed chair just under the single shaded window. And then he was there, soft-voiced and smiling, and he pulled up a second chair and sat close, studying her face.

"It was the Botox I was interested in," she heard herself say, the walls soaking up her words as if she were in a confessional. "These frown marks, right here?"—she lifted a hand to run two fingers along the rift between her eyes—"and maybe my eyes too, underneath them? I thought—well, looking in the mirror I thought they looked a little tired or saggy or something. Right here? Right along here? And maybe you could—if there's some procedure, nothing radical, just some smoothing out there? Is that possible?" She couldn't help herself: she laughed then, a laugh of nerves, yes, because all this was strange to her and he hadn't said a word beyond that first soft hello, just fixed those eyes of his on the lines of her face and hadn't let go even to blink. "I guess it's because I'm coming up on my birthday—next week, I mean. I'll be thirty-five, if you can believe it, so I just—"

"Yes," he said, rising, "why don't you have a seat here"—indicating the leather recliner—"and we'll have a look?"

On the way out, she stopped at the desk to make an appointment for the Botox treatment. Both secretaries—or no, one was a nurse flipping through files in the far corner—had flawless faces, not a line or wrinkle visible, and she wondered about that. Did they get a discount? Was that one of the perks of the job? There was a color brochure to take home and study, forms to sign. The Botox was nothing, he'd assured her—simplest thing in the world, and it wouldn't take more than fifteen minutes—and the procedure on her eyes was very routine too, a snip of the excess skin and removal of the fat pads, the whole thing done in-office, though she'd be under sedation. It would take a month to heal, two to three months till it was perfect. He had run his fingers under her chin, stroked the flesh below her ears and pressed his thumbs into the hollows there. "You've got beautiful skin," he said. "Stay out of the sun and you won't need anything major for fifteen, twenty years."

"I was just wondering," she said to the secretary, feeling bright now, hopeful, "Dr. Mellors' wife—did he work on her? I mean, the kind of procedure we're talking about for me?" She pushed her credit card across the counter. "It's no big deal, I was just wondering if he would, you know, on his own wife . . . ?"

The secretary—*Maggie,* her nametag read—was in her thirties, or maybe forties, it was hard to say. She'd put her hair up in a bun and she wore a low-cut blouse over a pair of suspiciously full breasts, but then she was an advertisement, wasn't she? Her smile—the complicitous sunny smile that had beamed out continuously to this point—faded suddenly. The eyes—too round, too tight at the corners—dodged away. "I wouldn't know," she said. "He got a divorce five years ago and I've only been here three. But I don't see why not."

The procedure—the injection of the botulin toxin under the skin between her eyes and then creeping on up to her hairline, one needle prick after another—hurt more than she thought it would. He numbed the area first with a packet of ice, but the ice gave her an instant headache and still she felt the sting of the needle. On the second or third prick she must have flinched. "Are you comfortable?" he asked, inches from her, his pale gray eyes probing hers, and she said, "Yes," and tried to nod, but that only made it worse. "I guess I don't handle pain well." She tried to compose herself, tried to keep it light, because she wasn't a whiner—that wasn't her image of herself. Not at all. "Too sensitive, I guess," she said, and she meant it as a joke.

The purpose of the toxin, as he'd explained to her in his sacerdotal tones, was to paralyze the muscles between her eyes and the ones that lifted her brow too, so that when she squinted in the bright sun or frowned over her checkbook, the skin wouldn't crease—it wouldn't move at all. She could be angry, raging, as furious as she'd ever been in her life, and certainly her body language would show that—her mouth, her eyes—but her brow would remain as smooth and untroubled as if she were asleep and dreaming of a boat drifting across a placid lake. Of course, the effect would last an average of three months or so and then she'd have to undergo the procedure all over again. And he had to warn her that a small percentage of patients reported side effects—headaches, nausea, that sort of thing. A very small percentage, negligible really. This was the safest thing in the world—in the right hands, that is. These Botox parties she'd read about? Not a good idea.

Now he took her hand to lift it to her forehead and the patch of gauze she was to hold there, just till the pinpricks closed up. "There," he was saying, "that wasn't so bad, was it?"

Lying back in the chair, staring into his eyes, she felt something give way inside her, the thin tissue of susceptibility, of surrender: she was in his hands now. This was his domain, this darkened room with its examining chair, the framed degrees on the wall, the glint of polished metal. How old was he? she wondered. She couldn't say, and she realized with a jolt that he wore the same expression as the nurse and the secretary, that his brow was immobile and his eyes rounded as if they'd been shaped out of dough. Forty, she guessed. Forty-five, maybe. But he had a spread to his shoulders—and those hands. His hands were like electric blankets on a cold night in a cabin deep in the woods. "No," she lied. "No, not bad at all."

"All right, good," he said, rising from the chair though he hadn't shifted his gaze from her. "Any problems, you call me right away, day or night, okay?" He drifted to the table in the corner and came back with a card imprinted with his name, the number of the office and an after-hours number. "And let's get a date set up for that blepharoplasty—we'll plan it around your schedule."

She was about to get up too, but before she could move he reached forward to take the pad of gauze from her and she saw that it was flecked with minuscule spots of blood. "Here," he said, handing her a mirror. "You see, there's nothing there—if you want, you can cover up with a dab of makeup. And you should expect results within a day or two."

"Wonderful," she said, giving him a smile. In the background—and she'd been faintly aware of it all along, even through her minor assault of nerves—a familiar piano piece was sifting through speakers hidden somewhere in the walls, as orderly and precise as the beating of a young heart. Bach. The partitas for keyboard, and she could hear the pianist—what was his name?—humming over them. She rose and stood there a moment in the still, shadowy room with the bright light focused on the chair in the middle of the floor, absorbing the music as if she'd just awakened to it. "Do you like classical music?" she murmured.

He gave her a smile. "Yes, sure."

"Bach?"

"Is that what this is? I never know—it's the music service. But they're good and I think it helps the patients relax—soothing, you know? Hey, better than heavy metal, right?"

She made a leap here, and everything to come was the result of it, as inevitable and indisputable as if she'd planned it all out beforehand: "The reason I ask is because I have two tickets for Saturday night—at the Music Academy? It's an all-Bach program, and"—she lifted her eyebrows, she could still do that—"my girlfriend just told me this morning she can't make it. She was—she had to go out of town unexpectedly—and I was wondering: would you like to go?"

After the concert—he'd begged off, said he'd love to go but had to check with Maggie, the secretary, to see if he was free, and then he wasn't—she went into Andalusia, a restaurant she liked because it had a good feel and a long bar where people gathered to have tapas and drinks while a guitarist worked his way through the flamenco catalogue in a nook by the fireplace. She knew people here—the bartender, Enrique, especially—and she didn't feel out of place coming in alone. Or she did, but not to the extent she felt elsewhere. Enrique took care of her, made sure nobody crowded her. He was protective, maybe a little obsessive even, and if he had a thing for her, well, she could use that to her advantage. A little mutual flirtation, that was all, but she wasn't seriously looking—or she hadn't been, not since she'd got her divorce. She had a house, money in the bank, the freedom to eat when and where she liked, to travel, make her own schedule, and she was enjoying it, that was what she kept telling herself.

She was having ceviche and a salad, sipping a glass of Chilean red and looking through the local newspaper—she couldn't resist the Personals: they were so tacky, so dishonest and nakedly self-serving, and how pathetic could people be?—when she felt a tap at her shoulder and there he was, Dr. Mellors, in a pale gold sport coat and a black silk shirt open at the collar. "Hello," he said, "or should I say *buenas noches,*" and there was nothing even faintly medicinal in his tone.

"Oh, hi," she said, taken by surprise. Here he was, looming over her again, and though she'd been thinking of him all through the concert, trying to fit him into the empty seat beside her, for one flustered second she couldn't summon his name. "How are you?"

He just smiled in answer. A beat went by, Enrique giving her a sidelong glance from the near end of the bar. "You look terrific," he said finally. "All dressed up, huh?"

"The concert," she said.

"Oh, right, yeah—how was that?"

"All right, I guess." It had served its purpose, giving her an excuse to put on some makeup and leave the house, to do something, anything. "A little dreary, actually. Organ music." She let her smile bloom. "I left at the intermission."

His smile opened up now too. "So what do I say—I'm glad I couldn't make it? But you look great, you do. No complications, right? The headache's gone away? No visual problems?"

"No," she said, "no, I'm fine," and then she saw Maggie, with her hair down and a pair of silver chandelier earrings dangling above her bare shoulders, watching them from a table in the dining room.

"Good," he said, "good. Well, listen, nice to see you—and I guess we'll be seeing you next week, then?"

The first thing she did when she got home was put on some music, because she couldn't stand the silence of an empty house, and it wasn't Bach, anything but Bach, her hand going to the first disc on the shelf, which turned out to be a reggae compilation her husband had left behind. She poured herself a glass of wine as the chords fell like debris into the steadily receding sea of the bass line, a menace there, menace in the vocals and the unshakable rhetoric of the dispossessed. Reggae. She'd never much liked it, but here it was, background music to her own awakening drama of confusion and disappointment. And anger, anger too. He'd blown her off. Dr. Mellors. Said he was busy, too busy to sit beside her in a dim auditorium and listen to a professor from the local college sweat over the keyboard, but not in the least embarrassed to be caught out in a lie. Or even contrite. He'd tried to make a joke of it, as if she were nobody, as if her invitation counted for nothing—and for what? So he could fuck his secretary?

The windows were black with the accumulation of the night and she went around pulling the shades, too many shades, too many windows. The house—it was what she'd wanted, or thought she wanted, new construction, walk-in closets, three-car garage and six thousand square feet of views opening out to the hills and the ocean beyond—was too big for her. Way too big. Even when Rick was around, when she was wound up twenty-four/seven with selecting carpets and furniture and poring over catalogues and landscaping books, the place had seemed desolate. There were no nooks—it was nookless, a nookless house that might as well have been a barn in Nebraska—no intimate corners, no place where she could feel safe and enclosed. She went through the dining room to the kitchen and then back round again to what the architect called "the grand room," turning on all the lights, then she poured herself another glass of wine, went into the bathroom and closed and locked the door.

For a long while she stared at herself in the mirror. The lines—the two vertical furrows between her eyes—didn't seem appreciably different, but maybe they were shallower, maybe that was it. She put a finger there, ran it over the skin. Then she smiled, seductively at first—"Hello, Dr. Mellors," she said to her reflection, "and what do I call you, Ed? Eddie? Ted?"—and then goofily, making faces at herself the way she used to when she was growing up with her three sisters and they'd pull at their lips and nostrils and ears, giggling and screeching till their mother had to come in and scoot them out of the bathroom. It didn't do any good. She snatched the glass up off the marble countertop, drained it and looked at herself the way she really was, a not-so-young woman wearing a permanent scowl, her nose too big, her chin too narrow, her eyes crystallizing in wariness and suspicion. But she was interesting. She was. Interesting and pretty too, in her own way. Prettier than the secretary or the nurse or half the other women in town. At least she looked real.

Or did she? And what was real worth anyway?

She shrugged out of her clothes then and for a long while studied herself in the full-length mirror on the door. In profile her stomach swelled out and away from her hips, a hard little ball of fat—but she'd just eaten, that was it—and her buttocks seemed to be sagging, from this angle anyway. Her breasts—they weren't like the breasts of the women in the porn videos her ex-husband seemed so turned on by—and she wondered about that, about the procedure there, about liposuction, a tummy tuck, maybe even a nose job. She didn't want to look like the secretary, like Maggie, because she didn't care about Maggie, Maggie was beneath her, Maggie wasn't even pretty, but the more she looked in the mirror the less she liked what she was seeing.

On Tuesday, the day of her pre-op appointment, she woke early and for a long while lay in bed watching the sun search out the leaves of the flowering plum beyond the window. She made herself two cups of coffee but no eggs or toast or anything else because she'd resolved to eat less and she didn't even lighten the coffee with a splash of non-fat milk. She took her time dressing. The night before she'd laid out a beige pantsuit she thought he might like, but when she saw it there folded over the chair like a vacated skin, she knew it wasn't right. After trying on half the things in the closet she decided finally on a black skirt, a cobalt-blue blouse that buttoned up the back and a pair of matching heels. She looked fine, she really did. But she spent so much time on her makeup she had to speed down the narrow twisting roads to the town spread out below and she ran a couple of lights on the yellow and still she was ten minutes late for her appointment.

Maggie greeted her with a plastic smile. She was wearing another revealing top—borderline tacky for business dress—and she seemed to have lightened her hair, or no, she'd streaked it, that was it. "If you'll just follow me," she chirped, and came out from behind the counter to lead her down the hallway in a slow hip-grinding sashay and then she was in the examining room again, and the door closed softly behind her. *Awaiting an audience,* she thought, and this was part of the mystique doctors cultivated, wasn't it, and why couldn't they just be there in the flesh instead of lurking somewhere down the corridor in another hushed room identical to this one? She set her purse down on the chair in the corner and settled herself into the recliner. She resisted the impulse to lift the hand mirror from the table and touch up her eyes.

"So," he was saying, gliding through the doorway on noiseless feet, "how are we today?"

"Okay, I guess."

"Okay? Just okay?"

"Listen," she said, ignoring the question, "before we go any further I just wanted to ask you something—"

"Sure," he said, and he pulled up a stool on wheels, the sort of thing dentists use, so he could sit beside her, "anything you want. Any concerns you have, that's what I'm here for."

"I just wanted to ask you, do you think I'm pretty?"

The question seemed to confound him and it took him a moment to recover himself. "Of course," he said. "Very pretty."

She said nothing and he moved into her then, his hands on her face, under her eyes, probing along the occipital bone, kneading, weighing the flesh while she blinked into his unwavering gaze. "Which is not to say that we can't improve on it," he said, "because it was your perception, and I agree with you, that right here"—his fingers tightened—"there's maybe just a few millimeters of excess skin. And—"

"I don't care about my eyes," she said abruptly, cutting him off. "I want you to look at my breasts. And my hips, and, and"—the formal term ran in and out of her head—"my tummy. It's fat. I'm fat."

She watched his eyes drop away. "I don't, uh," he began, fumbling now for the right words. "You appear to be fine, maybe a pound or two—but if you're interested, of course, we can consult on that too, and I've got brochures—"

"I don't want brochures," she said, and she began to unbutton her blouse. "I want you to tell me, right here, right now, face to face, because I don't believe you. You say I'm pretty but when I asked you to—to what, accompany me to hear Bach of all people?—you said you were busy, too busy, and then I see you out on the town. How am I supposed to feel?"

"Whoa," he said, "let's just back up a minute—and don't do anything, don't unbutton your . . . because I have to ask Maggie into the room. For legal reasons." He was at the door suddenly, the door swinging open, and he was calling down the hall for his secretary.

"I don't want Maggie," she said, and she had her brassiere off now and was working at the hook of her skirt. "I want to look real, not like some mannequin, not like her. Leave her out of this."

She was looking over her shoulder at him as he stood at the door, the skirt easing down her thighs, and she hadn't worn any stockings because they were just an encumbrance and she was here to be examined, to feel his hands on her, to set the conditions and know what it would take to improve. That was what this was all about, wasn't it? Improvement?

(2005)

The Lie

I'd used up all my sick days and the two personal days they allowed us, but when the alarm went off and the baby started squalling and my wife threw back the covers to totter off to the bathroom in a hobbled two-legged trot, I knew I wasn't going in to work. It was as if a black shroud had been pulled over my face: my eyes were open but I couldn't see. Or no, I could see—the pulsing LED display on the clock radio, the mounds of laundry and discarded clothes humped round the room like the tumuli of the dead, a hard-driving rain drooling down the dark vacancy of the window—but everything seemed to have a film over it, a world coated in Vaseline. The baby let out a series of scaled-back cries. The toilet flushed. The overhead light flicked on.

Clover was back in the room, the baby flung over one shoulder. She was wearing an old Cramps T-shirt she liked to sleep in and nothing else. I might have found this sexy to one degree or another but for the fact that I wasn't at my best in the morning and I'd seen her naked save for one rock-and-roll memento T-shirt for something like a thousand consecutive mornings now. "It's six-fifteen," she said. I said nothing. My eyes eased shut. I heard her at the closet, and in the dream that crashed down on me in that instant she metamorphosed from a rippling human female with a baby slung over one shoulder to a great shining bird springing from the brink of a precipice and sailing on great shining wings into the void. I woke to the baby. On the bed. Beside me. "You change her," my wife said. "You feed her. I'm late as it is."

We'd had some people over the night before, friends from the pre-baby days, and we'd made margaritas in the blender, watched a movie and stayed up late talking about nothing and everything. Clover had shown off the baby—Xana, we'd named her Xana, after a character in one of the movies I'd edited, or actually, logged—and I'd felt a rush of pride. Here was this baby, perfect in every way, beautiful because her parents were beautiful, and that was all right. Tank—he'd been in my band, co-leader, co-founder, and we'd written songs together till that went sour—said she was fat enough to eat and I'd said, "Yeah, just let me fire up the barbie," and Clover had given me her little drawn-down pout of disgust because I was being juvenile. We stayed up till the rain started. I poured one more round of margaritas and then Tank's girlfriend opened her maw in a yawn that could have sucked in the whole condo and the street out front too and the party broke up. Now I was in bed and the baby was crawling up my right leg, giving off a powerful reek of shit.

The clock inched forward. Clover got dressed, put on her makeup and took her coffee mug out to the car and was gone. There was nothing heroic in what I did next, dealing with the baby and my own car and the stalled nose-to-tail traffic that made the three miles to the babysitter's seem like a trek across the wastelands of the earth—it was just life, that was all. But as soon as I handed Xana over to Violeta at the door of her apartment that threw up a wall of cooking smells, tearful Telemundo dialogue and the diachronic yapping of her four Chihuahuas, I slammed myself into the car and called in sick. Or no: not sick. My sick days were gone, I reminded myself. And my personal days too. My boss picked up the phone. "Iron House Productions," he said, his voice digging out from under the *r*'s. He had trouble with *r*'s. He had trouble with English, for that matter.

"Hello, Radko?"

"Yes, it is he—who is it now?"

"It's me, Lonnie."

"Let me guess—you are sick."

Radko was one of that select group of hard chargers in the production business who kept morning hours, and that was good for me because with Clover working days and going to law school at night—and the baby, the baby, of course—my own availability was restricted to the daylight hours when Violeta's own children were at school and her husband at work operating one of the cranes that lifted the beams to build the city out till there was nothing green left for fifty miles around. But Radko had promised me career advancement, moving up from logging footage to actual editing, and that hadn't happened. On this particular morning, as on too many mornings in the past, I felt I just couldn't face the editing bay, the computer screen, the eternal idiocy of the dialogue repeated over and over through take after take, frame after frame, "No, Jim, stop/No—Jim, stop!/No! Jim, Jim: *stop!!*" I used to be in a band. I had a college degree. I was no drudge. Before I could think, it was out: "It's the baby," I said.

There was a silence I might have read too much into. Then Radko, dicing the interrogative, said, "What baby?"

"Mine. My baby. Remember the pictures Clover e-mailed everybody?" My brain was doing cartwheels. "Nine months ago? When she was born?"

Another long pause. Finally, he said, "Yes?"

"She's sick. Very sick. With a fever and all that. We don't know what's wrong with her." The wheel of internal calculus spun one more time and I made another leap, the one that would prove to be fatal: "I'm at the hospital now."

As soon as I hung up I felt as if I'd been pumped full of helium, giddy with it, rising right out of my seat, but then the slow seepage of guilt, dread and fear started in, drip by drip, like bile drained out of a liver gone bad. A delivery truck pulled up next to me. Rain beat at the windshield. Two cholos rolled out of the apartment next to Violeta's, the green block tattoos they wore like collars glistening in the light trapped beneath the clouds. I had the whole day in front of me. I could do anything. Go anywhere. An hour ago it was sleep I wanted. Now it was something else. A pulse of excitement, the promise of illicit thrills, started up in my stomach.

I drove down Ventura Boulevard in the opposite direction from the bulk of the commuters. They were stalled at the lights, a single driver in every car, the cars themselves like steel shells they'd extruded to contain their resentments. They were going to work. I wasn't. After a mile or so I came to a diner where I sometimes took Clover for breakfast on Sundays, especially if we'd been out the night before, and on an impulse, I pulled into the lot. I bought a newspaper from the machine out front and then I took a copy of the free paper too and went on in and settled into a seat by the window. The smell of fresh coffee and home fries made me realize how hungry I was and I ordered the kind of breakfast I used to have in college after a night of excess—salt, sugar and grease, in quantity—just to open my pores. While I ate, I made my way through both newspapers, item by item, because this was luxurious, kingly, the tables clean, the place brightly lit and warm to the point of steaming with the bustle of the waitresses and the rain at the windows like a plague. Nobody said a word to me. Nobody even looked at me, but for my waitress. She was middle-aged, wedded to her uniform, her hair dyed shoe-polish black. "More coffee?" she asked for the third or fourth time, no hurry, no rush, just an invitation. I glanced at my watch and couldn't believe it was only nine-thirty.

That was the thing about taking a day off, the way the time reconfigured itself and how you couldn't help comparing any given moment with what you'd be doing at work. At work, I wouldn't have eaten yet, wouldn't even have reached the coffee break—*Jim, stop! No, no!*—and my eyelids would have weighed a hundred tons each. I thought about driving down to the ocean to see what the surf looked like under the pressure of the storm—not that I was thinking about surfing; I hadn't been surfing more than a handful of times since the baby was born. It was just that the day was mine and I wanted to fill it. I made my way down through Topanga Canyon, the commuter traffic dissipated by now, and I saw how the creek was tearing at the banks and there were two or three places where there was water on the road and the soft red dough of the mud was like something that had come out of a mold. There was nobody on the beach but me. I walked along the shore till the brim of my baseball cap was sodden and the legs of my jeans as heavy as if they'd just come out of the washing machine.

I drove back up the canyon, the rain a little worse, the flooding more obvious and intense, but it wasn't anything really, not like when the road washes out and you could be driving one minute and the next flailing for your life in a chute full of piss-yellow water. There was a movie at two I was interested in, but since it was only just past twelve and I couldn't even think about lunch after the Lumberjack's Special I'd had for breakfast, I went back to the condo, parked the car and walked down the street, getting wetter and wetter and enjoying every minute of it, to a bar I knew. The door swung in on a denseness of purpose, eight or nine losers lined up on their barstools, the smell of cut lime and the sunshine of the rum, a straight shot of Lysol from the toilet in back. It was warm. Dark. A college basketball game hovered on the screen over the cash register. "A beer," I said, and then clarified by specifying the brand.

I didn't get drunk. That would have been usual, and I didn't want to be usual. But I did have three beers before I went to the movie and after the movie I felt a vacancy in my lower reaches where lunch should have been and so I stopped at a fast-food place on my way to pick up the baby. They got my order wrong. The employees were glassy-eyed. The manager was nowhere to be seen. And I was thirty-five minutes late for the baby. Still, I'd had my day, and when I got home I fed the baby her Cream of Wheat, opened a beer, put on some music and began chopping garlic and dicing onions with the notion of concocting a marinara sauce for my wife when she got home. Thoughts of the following morning, of Radko and what he might think or expect, never entered my mind. Not yet.

All was well, the baby in her crib batting at the little figurines in the mobile over her head (the figurines personally welded to the wires by Clover's hippie mother so that there wasn't even the faintest possibility the baby could get them lodged in her throat), the sauce bubbling on the stove, the rain tapping at the windows. I heard Clover's key in the door. And then she was there with her hair kinked from the rain and smelling like everything I'd ever wanted and she was asking me how my day had gone and I said, "Fine, just fine."

Then it was morning again and the same scene played itself out—Clover stutter-stepping to the bathroom, the baby mewling, rain whispering under the soundtrack—and I began to calculate all over again. It was Thursday. Two more days to the weekend. If I could make it to the weekend, I was sure that by Monday, Monday at the latest, whatever was wrong with me, this feeling of anger, hopelessness, turmoil, whatever it was, would be gone. Just a break. I just needed a break, that was all. And Radko. The thought of facing him, of the way he would mold the drooping dog-like folds of his Slavic flesh around the suspicion in his eyes while he told me he was docking me a day's pay and expected me to work overtime to make up for yesterday, was too much to hold on to. Not in bed. Not now. But then the toilet flushed, the baby squalled and the overhead light went on. "It's six-fifteen," my wife informed me.

The evening before, after we'd dined on my marinara sauce with porcini mushrooms and Italian-style turkey sausage over penne pasta, in the interval before she put the baby down for the night, while the dishwasher murmured from the kitchen and we lingered over a second glass of Chianti, she told me she was thinking of changing her name. "What do you mean?" I was more surprised than angry, but I felt the anger come up in me all the same. "My name's not good enough for you? Like it was my idea to get married in the first place?"

She had the baby in her lap. The baby was in high spirits, grinning her toothless baby grin and snatching for the wine glass my wife held just out of reach. "You don't have to get nasty about it. It's not your name that's the problem—it's mine. My first name."

"What's wrong with Clover?" I said, and even as I said it, I knew how stupid I sounded. She was Clover. I could close my eyes and she was Clover, go to Africa and bury myself in mud and she'd still be Clover. Fine. But the name was a hippie affectation of her hippie parents—they were glassblowers, with their own gallery—and it was insipid, I knew that, down deep. They might as well have named her Dandelion or Fescue.

"I was thinking of changing it to Cloris." She was watching me, her eyes defiant and insecure at the same time. "Legally."

I saw her point—she was a legal secretary, studying to be a lawyer, and Clover just wouldn't fly on a masthead—but I hated the name, hated the idea. "Sounds like something you clean the toilet with," I said.

She shot me a look of hate.

"With bleach in it," I said. "With real scrubbing power."

But now, though I felt as if I'd been crucified and wanted only to sleep for a week, or till Monday, just till Monday, I sat up before she could lift the baby from the crib and drop her on the bed, and in the next moment I was in the bathroom myself, staring into the mirror. As soon as she left I was going to call Radko. I would tell him the baby was worse, that we'd been in the hospital all night. And if he asked what was wrong with her I wasn't going to equivocate because equivocation—any kind of uncertainty, a tremor in the voice, a tonal shift, playacting—is the surest lie detector. Leukemia, that was what I was going to tell him. "The baby has leukemia."

This time I waited till I was settled into the booth at the diner and the waitress with the shoe-polish hair had got done fussing over me, the light of recognition in her eyes and a maternal smile creasing her lips—I was a regular, two days in a row—before I called in. And when Radko answered, the deepest consonant-battering pall of suspicion lodged somewhere between his glottis and adenoids, I couldn't help myself. "The baby," I said, holding it a beat, "the baby . . . passed." Another beat. The waitress poured. Radko breathed fumes through the receiver. "Last night. At—at four a.m. There was nothing they could do."

"Past?" his voice came back at me. "What is this *past*?"

"The baby's dead," I said. "She died." And then, in my grief, I broke the connection.

I spent the entire day at the movies. The first show was at eleven and I killed time pacing round the parking lot at the mall till they opened the doors, and then I was inside, in the anonymous dark. Images flashed by on the screen. The sound was amplified to a killing roar. The smell of melted butter hung over everything. When the lights came up I ducked into the men's room and then slipped into the next theater and the next one after that. I emerged at quarter of four, feeling shaky.

I told myself I was hungry, that was all, but when I wandered into the food court and saw what they had arrayed there, from chapattis to corn dogs to twice-cooked machaca, pretzels and Szechuan eggplant in a sauce of liquid fire, I pushed through the door of a bar instead. It was one of those oversanitized, too-bright, echoing spaces the mall designers, in their wisdom, stuck in the back of their plastic restaurants so that the average moron, accompanying his wife on a shopping expedition, wouldn't have to kill himself. There was a basketball game on the three TVs encircling the bar. The waitresses were teenagers, the bartender had acne. I was the only customer and I knew I had to pick up the baby, that was a given, that was a fact of life, but I ordered a Captain and Coke, just for the smell of it.

I was on my second, or maybe my third, when the place began to fill up and I realized, with a stab of happiness, that this must have been an after-work hangout, with a prescribed happy hour and some sort of comestibles served up gratis on a heated tray. I'd been wrapped up in my grief, a grief that was all for myself, for the fact that I was twenty-six years old and going nowhere, with a baby to take care of and a wife in the process of flogging a law degree and changing her name because she wasn't who she used to be, and now suddenly I'd come awake. There were women everywhere, women my age and older, leaning into the bar with their earrings swaying, lined up at the door, sitting at tables, legs crossed, feet tapping rhythmically to the canned music. Me? I had to pick up the baby. I checked my watch and saw that I was already late, late for the second day running, but I was hungry all of a sudden and I thought I'd just maybe have a couple of the taquitos everybody else was shoving into their mouths while I finished my drink, and then I'd get in the car, take the back streets to Violeta's and be home just before my wife and see if we could get another meal out of the marinara sauce. With porcini mushrooms. And turkey sausage.

That was when I felt a pressure on my arm, my left arm, and I lifted my chin to glance over my shoulder into the face of Joel Chinowski, who occupied the bay next to mine at Iron House Productions. At first, I didn't recognize him—one of those tricks of the mind, the inebriated mind, especially, in which you can't place people out of context, though you know them absolutely. "Joel," I said.

He was shaking his head, very slowly, as if he were tolling a bell, as if his eyes were the clappers and his skull the ringing shell of it. He had a big head, huge—he was big all around, one of those people who aren't obese, or not exactly, but just overgrown to the extent that his clothes seemed inflated, his pants, his jacket, even his socks. He was wearing a tie—the only one of the seventy-six employees at Iron House to dress in shirt and tie—and it looked like a toy trailing away from his supersized collar. "Shit, man," he said, squeezing tighter. "Shit."

"Yeah," I said, and my head was tolling too. I felt caught out. Felt like the very essence he was naming—like shit, that is.

"We all heard," he said. He removed his hand from my arm, peered into his palm as if trying to divine what to say next. "It sucks," he said. "It really sucks."

"Yeah," I said.

And then, though his face never changed expression, he seemed to brighten around the eyes for just an instant. "Hey," he said, "can I buy you a drink? I mean, to drown the sorrow—I mean, that's what you're doing, right? And I don't blame you. Not at all. If it was me . . ." He let the thought trail off. There was a girl two stools down from me, her hair pulled up in a long trailing ponytail, and she was wearing a knit jumper over a little black skirt and red leggings. She glanced up at me, two green swimming eyes above a pair of lips pursed at the straw of her drink. "Or maybe," Joel said, "you'd rather be alone?"

I dragged my eyes away from the girl. "The truth is," I said, "I mean, I really appreciate it, but like I'm meeting Clover at the—well, the funeral parlor. You know, to make the arrangements? And it's—I just stopped in for a drink, that's all."

"Oh, man"—Joel was practically erupting from his shoes, his face drawn down like a curtain and every blood vessel in his eyes gone to waste—"I understand. I understand completely."

On the way out the door I flipped open my cell and dialed Violeta to tell her my wife would be picking up the baby tonight because I was working late, and then I left a message to the same effect at my wife's law office. Then I went looking for a bar where I could find something to eat and maybe one last drink before I went home to lie some more.

The next day—Friday—I didn't even bother to call in, but I was feeling marginally better. I had a mild hangover, my head still clanging dully and my stomach shriveled up around a little nugget of nothing so that after I dropped the baby off I wasn't able to take anything more than dry toast and black coffee at the diner that was fast becoming my second home, and yet the force of the lie, the enormity of it, was behind me, and here, outside the windows, the sun was shining for the first time in days. I'd been listening to the surf report in the car on the way over—we were getting six-foot swells as a result of the storm—and after breakfast I dug out my wetsuit and my board and let the Pacific roll on under me until I forgot everything in the world but the taste of salt and the smell of the breeze and the weird, strangled cries of the gulls. I was home by three and I vacuumed, washed the dishes, scrubbed the counters. I was twenty minutes early to pick up Xana and while dinner was cooking—meat loaf with boiled potatoes in their skins and asparagus vinaigrette—I took her to the park and listened to her screech with baby joy as I held her in my lap and rocked higher and higher on the swings.

When Clover came home she was too tired to fight and she accepted the meat loaf and the wine I'd picked out as the peace offerings they were and after the baby was asleep we listened to music, smoked a joint and made love in a slow deep plunge that was like paddling out on a wave of flesh for what seemed like hours. We took a drive up the coast on Saturday and on Sunday afternoon we went over to Tank's for lunch and saw how sad his apartment was with its brick-and-board bookcases, the faded band posters curling away from the walls and the deep-pile rug that was once off-white and was now just plain dirty. In the car on the way home, Clover said she never could understand people who treated their dog as if they'd given birth to it and I shook my head—tolling it, but easily now, thankfully—and said I couldn't agree more.

I woke on Monday before the alarm went off and I was showered and shaved and in the car before my wife left for work, and when I pulled up in front of the long windowless gray stucco edifice that housed Iron House Productions, I was so early Radko himself hadn't showed up yet. I took off my watch and stuffed it deep in my pocket, letting the monotony of work drag me down till I was conscious of nothing, not my fingers at the keyboard or the image on the screen or the dialogue I was capturing frame by frozen frame. Log and capture, that was what I was doing, hour, minute, second, frame, transcribing everything that had been shot so the film's editor could locate what he wanted without going through the soul-crushing drudgery of transcribing it himself.

At some point—it might have been an hour in, two hours, I don't know—I became aware of the intense gland-clenching aroma of vanilla chai, hot, spiced, blended, the very thing I wanted, caffeine to drive a stake into the boredom. Vanilla chai, available at the coffeehouse down the street, but a real indulgence because of the cost—usually I made do with the acidic black coffee and artificial creamer Radko provided on a stained cart set up against the back wall. I lifted my head to search out the aroma and there was Jeannie, the secretary from the front office, holding a paperboard Venti in one hand and a platter of what turned out to be homemade cannoli in the other. "What?" I said, thinking Radko had sent her to tell me he wanted to see me in his office. But she didn't say anything for a long excruciating moment, her eyes full, her face white as a mask, and then she shoved the chai into my hand and set the tray down on the desk beside me. "I'm so sorry for your loss," she said, and then I felt her hand on my shoulder and she was dipping forward in a typhoon of perfume to plant a lugubrious kiss just beneath my left ear.

What can I say? I felt bad about the whole business, felt low and despicable, but I cracked the plastic lid and sipped the chai, and as if I weren't even conscious of what my fingers were doing, I started in on the cannoli, one by one, till the platter was bare. I was just sucking the last of the sugar from my fingertips when Steve Bartholomew, a guy of thirty or so who worked in special effects, a guy I barely knew, came up to me and without a word pressed a tin of butter cookies into my hand. "Hey," I said, addressing his retreating shoulders, "thanks, man, thanks. It means a lot." By noon my desk was piled high with foodstuffs—sandwiches, sweets, a dry salami as long as my forearm—and at least a dozen gray-jacketed sympathy cards inscribed by one co-worker or another. I wanted to hide. Wanted to quit. Wanted to go home, tear the phone out of the wall, get into bed and never leave. But I didn't. I just sat there, trying to work, giving one person after another a zombie smile and my best impression of the thousand-yard stare.

Just before quitting time, Radko appeared, his face like an old paper bag left out in the rain. He was flanked by Joel Chinowski. I glanced up at them out of wary eyes and in a flash of intuition I realized how much I hated them both, how much I wanted only to jump to my feet like a cornered animal and punch them out, both of them. Radko said nothing. He just stood there gazing down at me and then, after a moment, he pressed one hand to my shoulder in Slavic commiseration, turned and walked away. "Listen, man," Joel said, shifting his eyes away from mine, "we all wanted to . . . Well, we got together, me and some of the others, and I know it isn't much, but—"

I saw now that he was holding a plastic grocery sack in one hand. I knew what was in the sack. I tried to wave it away, but he thrust it at me and I had no choice but to take it. Later, when I got home and the baby was in her high chair smearing her face with Cream of Wheat and I'd slipped the microwave pizza out of its box, I sat down and emptied the contents of the bag on the kitchen table. It was mainly cash, but there were maybe half a dozen checks too. I saw one for twenty-five dollars, another for fifty. The baby made one of those expressions of baby joy, sharp and sudden, as if the impulse had seized her before she could process it. It was five-thirty and the sinking sun was pasted over the windows. I sifted the bills through my hands, tens and twenties, fives—a lot of fives—and surprisingly few singles, thinking how generous my co-workers were, how good and real and giving, but I was grieving all the same, grieving beyond any measure I could ever have imagined or contained. I was in the process of counting the money, thinking I'd give it back—or donate it to some charity—when I heard Clover's key in the lock and I swept it all back into the bag and tucked that bag in the deep recess under the sink where the water persistently dripped from the crusted-over pipe and the old sponge there smelled of mold.

The minute my wife left the next morning I called Radko and told him I wasn't coming in. He didn't ask for an excuse, but I gave him one anyway. "The funeral," I said. "It's at eleven a.m., just family, very private. My wife's taking it hard." He made some sort of noise on the other end of the line—a sigh, a belch, the faintest cracking of his knuckles. "Tomorrow," I said. "I'll be in tomorrow without fail."

And then the day began, but it wasn't like that first day, not at all. I didn't feel giddy, didn't feel liberated or even relieved—all I felt was regret and the cold drop of doom. I deposited the baby at Violeta's and went straight home to bed, wanting only to clear some space for myself and think things out. There was no way I could return the money—I wasn't that good an actor—and I couldn't spend it either, even to make up for the loss of pay. That would have been low, lower than anything I'd ever done in my life. I thought of Clover then, how furious she'd be when she found out my pay had been docked. If it had been docked. There was still a chance Radko would let it slide, given the magnitude of my tragedy, a chance that he was human after all. A good chance.

No, the only thing to do was bury the money someplace. I'd burn the checks first—I couldn't run the risk of anybody uncovering them; that would really be a disaster, magnitude 10. Nobody could explain that, though various scenarios were already suggesting themselves—a thief had stolen the bag from the glove box of my car; it had blown out the window on the freeway while I was on my way to the mortuary; the neighbor's pet macaque had come in through the open bathroom window and made off with it, wadding the checks and chewing up the money till it was just monkey feces now. *Monkey feces.* I found myself repeating the phrase, over and over, as if it were a prayer. It was a little past nine when I had my first beer. And for the rest of the day, till I had to pick up the baby, I never moved from the couch.

I tried to gauge Clover's mood when she came in the door, dressed like a lawyer in her gray herringbone jacket and matching skirt, her hair pinned up and her eyes in traffic mode. The place was a mess. I hadn't picked up. Hadn't put on anything for dinner. The baby, asleep in her molded plastic carrier, gave off a stink you could smell all the way across the room. I looked up from my beer. "I thought we'd go out tonight," I told her. "My treat." And then, because I couldn't help myself, I added: "I'm just trashed from work."

She wasn't happy about it, I could see that, lawyerly calculations transfiguring her face as she weighed the hassle of running up the boulevard with her husband and baby in tow before leaving for her eight o'clock class. I watched her reach back to remove the clip from her hair and shake it loose. "I guess," she said. "But no Italian." She'd set down her briefcase in the entry hall, where the phone was, and she put a thumb in her mouth a moment—a habit of hers; she was a fingernail chewer—before she said, "What about Chinese?" She shrugged before I could. "As long as it's quick, I don't really care."

I was about to agree with her, about to rise up out of the grip of the couch and do my best to minister to the baby and get us out the door, en famille, when the phone rang. Clover answered. "Hello? Uh-huh, this is she."

My right knee cracked as I stood, a reminder of the torn ACL I'd suffered in high school when I'd made the slightest miscalculation regarding the drop off the backside of a boulder while snowboarding at Mammoth.

"Jeannie?" my wife said, her eyebrows lifting in two perfect arches. "Yes," she said. "Yes, *Jeannie*—how are you?"

There was a long pause as Jeannie said what she was going to say and then my wife said, "Oh, no, there must be some mistake. The baby's fine. She's right here in her carrier, fast asleep." And her voice grew heartier, surprise and confusion riding the cusp of the joke, "She could use a fresh diaper, judging from the smell of her, but that's her daddy's job, or it's going to be if we ever expect to—"

And then there was another pause, longer this time, and I watched my wife's gaze shift from the form of the sleeping baby in her terry-cloth jumpsuit to where I was standing beside the couch. Her eyes, in soft focus for the baby, hardened as they climbed from my shoetops to my face, where they rested like two balls of granite.

Anybody would have melted under that kind of scrutiny. My wife, the lawyer. It would be a long night, I could see that. There would be no Chinese, no food of any kind. I found myself denying everything, telling her how scattered Jeannie was and how she must have mixed us up with the Lovetts—she remembered Tony Lovett, worked in sfx? Yeah, they'd just lost their baby, a little girl, yeah. No, it was awful. I told her we'd all chipped in—"Me too, I put in a fifty, and that was excessive, I know it, but I felt I had to, you know? Because of the baby. Because what if it happened to us?" I went on in that vein till I ran out of breath and when I tried to be nonchalant about it and go to the refrigerator for another beer, she blocked my way. "Where's the money?" she said.

We were two feet apart. I didn't like the look she was giving me because it spared nothing. I could have kept it up, could have said, "What money?" injecting all the trampled innocence I could summon into my voice, but I didn't. I merely bent to the cabinet under the sink, extracted the white plastic bag and handed it to her. She took it as if it were the bleeding corpse of our daughter—or no, of our relationship that went back three years to the time when I was up onstage, gilded in light, my message elided under the hammer of the guitar and the thump of the bass. She didn't look inside. She just held my eyes. "You know this is fraud, don't you?" she said. "A felony offense. They can lock you up for this. You know that."

She wasn't asking a question, she was making a demand. And I wasn't about to answer her because the baby *was* dead and she was dead too. Radko was dead, Jeannie the secretary whose last name I didn't even know and Joel Chinowski and all the rest of them. Very slowly, button by button, I did up my shirt. Then I set my empty beer bottle down on the counter as carefully as if it were full to the lip and went on out the door and into the night, looking for somebody I could tell all about it.

(2007)

The Unlucky Mother of Aquiles Maldonado

When they took Aquiles Maldonado's mother, on a morning so hot it all but seared the hide off the hundred and twenty thousand stray dogs in Caracas, give or take a few, no one would have guessed they would keep her as long as they did. Her husband was dead, murdered in a robbery attempt six years earlier, and he would remain unconcerned and uncommunicative. But there were the household servants and the employees of the machine shop ready to run through the compound beating their breasts, and while her own mother was as feeble as a dandelion gone to seed, she was supremely capable of worry. As were Marita's four grown sons and Aquiles' six children by five different *aficionadas,* whom she looked after, fed, scolded and sent off to school each morning. There was concern, plenty of concern, and it rose up and raced through the community the minute the news hit the streets. "They took Marita Villalba," people shouted from window to window while others shouted back, "Who?"

"Who?" voices cried out in outrage and astonishment. "Who? Aquiles Maldonado's mother, that's who!"

At that time, Aquiles was playing for Baltimore, in the American League, away from home from the start of spring training in late February to the conclusion of the regular season in the first week of October. He was thirty years old and had worked his way through four teams with a fierce determination to reach the zenith of his profession—he was now the Birds' closer, pitching with grit and fluidity at the end of the first year of his two-year, eleven-point-five-million-dollar contract, despite the sharp burn he felt up under the rotator cuff of his pitching arm every time he changed his release point, about which he had told no one. There were three weeks left in the season, and the team, which had already been eliminated from playoff contention by the aggressive play of the Red Sox and Yankees, was just going through the motions. But not Aquiles. Every time he was handed the ball with a lead to protect, however infrequently, he bore down with a fury so uncompromising you would have thought every cent of his eleven-point-five-million U.S. guaranteed dollars rode on each and every pitch.

He was doing his pre-game stretching and joking with the team's other Venezuelan player, Chucho Rangel, about the two tattooed *güeras* they'd taken back to the hotel the night before, when the call came through. It was from his brother Néstor, and the moment he heard his brother's voice, he knew the news was bad.

"They got Mamí," Néstor sobbed into the receiver.

"Who did?"

There was a pause, as if his brother were calling from beneath the sea and needed to surface to catch his breath. "I don't know," he said, "the gangsters, the FARC, whoever."

The field was the green of dreams, the stands spotted with fans come early for batting practice and autographs. He turned away from Chucho and the rest of them, hunched over his cell. "For what?" And then, because the word slipped into his mouth: "For ransom?"

Another pause, and when his brother came back to him his voice was as pinched and hollow as if he were talking through his snorkel: "What do you think, *pendejo*?"

"It just shouldn't be so hot this time of year," she'd been saying to Rómulo Cordero, foreman of the machine shop her son had bought her when he signed his first big league contract. "I've never seen it like this—have you? Maybe in my mother's time . . ."

The children were at school, under supervision of the nuns and the watchful eye of Christ in heaven, the lathes were turning with their insectoid drone and she was in the back office, both fans going full speed and directed at her face and the three buttons of cleavage she allowed herself on the hottest days. Marita Villalba was forty-seven years old, thirty pounds heavier than she'd like to be, but pretty still and so full of life (and, let's face it, money and respectability) that half the bachelors of the neighborhood—and all the widowers—were mad for the sight of her. Rómulo Cordero, a married man and father of nine, wasn't immune to her charms, but he was an employee first and never allowed himself to forget it. "In the nineteen sixties, when I was a boy," he said, pausing to sweeten his voice, "—but you would have been too young to remember—it was a hundred nineteen degrees by eleven in the morning every day for a week and people were placing bets on when it would break a hundred and twenty—"

He never got to finish the story. At that moment, four men in the uniform of the federal police strode sweating into the office to crowd the little dirt-floored room with its walls of unpainted plywood and the rusting filing cabinets and the oversized Steelcase desk on which Marita Villalba did her accounts. "I've already paid," she said, barely glancing up at them.

Their leader, a tall stoop-shouldered man with a congenitally deformed eye and a reek of the barrio who didn't look anything like a policeman, casually unholstered his gun. "We don't know anything about that. My instructions are to bring you to the station for questioning."

And so it began.

When they got outside, to the courtyard, where the shop stood adjacent to the two-story frame house with its hardwood floors and tile roof, the tall one, who was referred to variously as "Capitán" and "El Ojo" by the others, held open the door of a blistered pale purple Honda with yellow racing stripes that was like no police vehicle Marita Villalba or Rómulo Cordero had ever seen. Marita balked. "Are you sure we have to go through with this?" she said, gesturing to the dusty back seat of the car, to the open gate of the compound and the city festering beyond it. "Can't we settle this right here?" She was digging in her purse for her checkbook, when the tall one said abruptly, "I'll call headquarters." Then he turned to Rómulo Cordero. "Hand me your cell phone."

Alarm signals began to go off in Marita Villalba's head. She sized up the three other men—boys, they were boys, street urchins dressed up in stolen uniforms with automatic pistols worth more than their own lives and the lives of all their ancestors combined clutched in nervous hands—even as Rómulo Cordero unhooked the cell phone from his belt and handed it to the tall man with the drooping eye.

"Hello?" the man said into the phone. "District headquarters? Yes, this is"—and he gave a name he invented out of the scorched air of the swollen morning—"and we have the Villalba woman." He paused. "Yes," he said, "yes, I see: she must come in in person."

Marita glanced at her foreman and they shared a look: the phone was dead, had been dead for two weeks and more, the batteries corroded in the shell of the housing and new ones on order, endlessly on order, and they both broke for the open door of the shop at the same instant. It was hopeless. The weapons spoke their rapid language, dust clawed at her face and Rómulo Cordero went down with two red flowers blooming against the scuffed leather of the tooled boot on his right foot, and the teenagers—the boys who should have been in school, should have been working at some honest trade under an honest master—seized Aquiles Maldonado's mother by the loose flesh of her upper arms, about which she was very sensitive, and forced her into the car. It took a minute, no more. And then they were gone.

Accompanied by a bodyguard and his brother Néstor, Aquiles mounted the five flights of listing stairs at the Central Police Headquarters and found his way, by trial and error, through a dim dripping congeries of hallways to the offices of the Anti-Extortion and Kidnap Division. The door was open. Commissioner Diosado Salas, Chief of the Division, was sitting behind his desk. "It's an honor," he said, rising to greet them and waving a hand to indicate the two chairs set before the desk. "Please, please," he said, and Aquiles and Néstor, with a glance for the bodyguard, who positioned himself just outside the door, eased tentatively into the chairs.

The office looked like any other, bookshelves collapsing under the weight of papers curling at the edges, sagging venetian blinds, a poor pale yellowish light descending from the fixtures in the ceiling, but the desk, nearly as massive as the one Aquiles' mother kept in her office at the machine shop, had been purged of the usual accoutrements—there were no papers, no files, no staplers or pens, not even a telephone or computer. Instead, a white cloth had been spread neatly over the surface, and aside from the two pale blue cuffs of the Chief's shirt-sleeves and the *pelota* of his clenched brown hands, there were but four objects on the table: three newspaper clippings and a single sheet of white paper with something inscribed across it in what looked to be twenty-point type.

All the way up the stairs, his brother and the bodyguard wheezing behind him, Aquiles had been preparing a speech—"I'll pay anything, do anything they say, just so long as they release her unharmed and as soon as possible, or expeditiously, I mean expeditiously, isn't that the legal term?"—but now, before he could open his mouth, the Chief leaned back in the chair and snapped his fingers in the direction of the door at the rear of the room. Instantly, the door flew open and a waiter from the Fundador Café whirled across the floor with his tray held high, bowing briefly to each of them before setting down three white ceramic plates and three Coca-Colas in their sculpted greenish bottles designed to fit the hand like the waist of a woman. In the center of each plate was a steaming *reina pepeada*—a maize cake stuffed with avocado, chicken, potatoes, carrots and mayonnaise, Aquiles' favorite, the very thing he hungered for during all those months of exile in the north. "Please, please," the Chief said. "We eat. Then we talk."

Aquiles was fresh off the plane. There was no question of finishing the season, of worrying about bills, paychecks, the bachelor apartment he shared with Chucho Rangel in a high-rise within sight of Camden Yards or the milk-white Porsche in the parking garage beneath it, and the Orioles' manager, Frank Bowden, had given him his consent immediately. Not that it was anything more than a formality. Aquiles would have been on the next plane no matter what anyone said, even if they were in the playoffs, even the World Series. His mother was in danger. And he had come to save her. But he hadn't eaten since breakfast the previous day, and before he knew what he was doing, the sandwich was gone.

The room became very quiet. There was no sound but for the whirring of the fans and the faint mastication of the Chief, a small-boned man with an overlarge head and a crown of dark snaking hair that pulled away from his scalp as if an invisible hand were eternally tugging at it. Into the silence came the first reminder of the gravity of the situation: Néstor, his face clasped in both hands, had begun to sob in a quiet soughing way. "Our mother," he choked, "she used to cook *reinas* for us, all her life she used to cook. And now, now—"

"Hush," the Chief said, his voice soft and expressive. "We'll get her back, don't you worry." And then, to Aquiles, in a different voice altogether, an official voice, hard with overuse, he said: "So you've heard from them."

"Yes. A man called my cell—and I don't know how he got the number—"

The Chief gave him a bitter smile, as if to say *Don't be naïve.*

Aquiles flushed. "He didn't say hello or anything, just 'We have the package,' that was all, and then he hung up."

Néstor lifted his head. They both looked to the Chief.

"Typical," he said. "You won't hear from them for another week, maybe two. Maybe more."

Aquiles was stunned. "A week? But don't they want the money?"

The Chief leaned into the desk, the black pits of his eyes locked on Aquiles. "What money? Did anybody say anything about money?"

"No, but that's what this is all about, isn't it? They wouldn't"—and here an inadmissible thought invaded his head—"they're not sadists, are they? They're not . . . ," but he couldn't go on. Finally, gathering himself, he said, "They don't kidnap mothers just for the amusement of it, do they?"

Smiling his bitter smile, the Chief boxed the slip of white paper so that it was facing Aquiles and pushed it across the table with the tips of two fingers. On it, in those outsized letters, was written a single figure: ELEVEN-POINT-FIVE MILLION DOLLARS. In the next moment he was brandishing the newspaper clippings, shaking them so that the paper crackled with the violence of it, and Aquiles could see what they were: articles in the local press proclaiming the *beisbol* star Aquiles Maldonado a national hero second only to Simón Bolívar and Hugo Chávez. In each of them, the figure of eleven-point-five million dollars had been underlined in red ink. "This is what they want," the Chief said finally, "money, yes. And now that they have your attention they will come back to you with a figure, maybe five million or so—they'd demand it all and more, except that they know you will not pay them a cent, not now or ever."

"What do you mean?'

"I mean we do not negotiate with criminals."

"But what about my mother?"

He sighed. "We will get her back, don't you worry. It may take time and perhaps even a certain degree of pain"—here he reached down beneath the desk and with some effort set a two-quart pickle jar on the table before him—"but have no fear."

Aquiles stole a look at his brother. Néstor had jammed his forefinger into his mouth and was biting down as if to snap it in two, a habit he'd developed in childhood and had been unable to break. These were not pickles floating in the clear astringent liquid.

"Yes," the Chief said, "this is the next step. It is called proof of life."

It took a moment for the horror to settle in.

"But these fingers—there are four of them here, plus two small toes, one great toe and a left ear—represent cases we have resolved. Happily resolved. What I'm telling you is be prepared. First you will receive the proof of life, then the demand for money." He paused. And then his fist came down, hard, on the desktop. "But you will not pay them, no matter what."

"I will," Aquiles insisted. "I'll pay them anything."

"You won't. You can't. Because if you do, then every ballplayer's family will be at risk, don't you understand that? And, I hate to say this, but you've brought it on yourself. I mean, please—driving a vermilion Hummer through the streets of this town? Parading around with your gold necklaces and these disgraceful women, these *putas* with their great inflated tits and swollen behinds? Did you really have to go and paint your compound the color of a ripe tangerine?"

Aquiles felt the anger coming up in him, but as soon as he detected it, it was gone: the man was right. He should have left his mother where she was, left her to the respectability of poverty, should have changed his name and come home in rags wearing a beard and a false nose. He should never in his life have picked up a baseball.

"All right," the Chief was saying, and he stood to conclude the meeting. "They call you, you call me."

Both brothers rose awkwardly, the empty plate staring up at Aquiles like the blanched unblinking eye of accusation, the jar of horrors grinning beside it. The bodyguard poked his head in the door.

"Oh, but wait, wait, I almost forgot." The Chief snapped his fingers once again and an assistant strode through the rear door with a cellophane package of crisp white baseballs in one hand and a Magic Marker in the other. "If you wouldn't mind," the Chief said. "For my son, Aldo, with Best Wishes."

She was wedged between two of the boys in the cramped back seat of the car, the heat oppressive, the stink of confinement unbearable. El Ojo sat up front beside the other boy, who drove with an utter disregard for life. At first she tried to shout out the window at pedestrians, shrieking till she thought the glass of the windshield would shatter, but the boy to her right—pinch-faced, with two rotted teeth like fangs and a pair of lifeless black eyes—slapped her and she slapped him right back, the guttersnipe, the little hoodlum, and who did he think he was? How dare he? Beyond that she remembered nothing, because the boy punched her then, punched her with all the coiled fury of his pipestem arm and balled fist and the car jolted on its springs and the tires screamed and she passed into unconsciousness.

When she came back to the world she was in a skiff on a river she'd never seen before, its waters thick as paste, all the birds and insects in the universe screaming in unison. Her wrists had been tied behind her and her ankles bound with a loop of frayed plastic cord. The ache in her jaw stole up on her, her tongue probing the teeth there and tasting her own blood, and that made her angry, furious, and she focused all her rage on the boy who'd hit her—there he was, sitting athwart the seat in the bow, crushed beneath the weight of his sloped shoulders and the insolent wedge of the back of his head. She wanted to cry out and accuse him, but she caught herself, because what if the boat tipped, what then? She was helpless. No one, not even the Olympic butterfly champion, could swim with all four limbs bound. So she lay there on the rocking floor of the boat, soaked through with the bilge, the sun lashing her as she breathed the fumes of the engine and stared up into a seared fragment of the sky, waiting her chance.

Finally, and it seemed as if they'd been on that river for days, though that was an impossibility, the engine choked on its own fumes and they cut across the current to the far bank. El Ojo—she saw now that he had been the one at the tiller—sprang out and seized a rope trailing from the branch of a jutting tree, and then the boy, the one who'd assaulted her, reached back to cut the cord at her ankles with a flick of his knife and he too was in the murky water, hauling the skiff ashore. She endured the thumps and bumps and the helpless feeling they gave her and then, when he thrust a hand under her arm to lead her up onto the bank, the best she could do was mutter, "You stink. All of you. Don't you have any pride? Can't you even wash yourselves? Do you wear your clothes till they rot, is that it?" And then, when that got no response: "What about your mothers—what would they think?"

They were on the bank now, El Ojo and the others taking pains to secrete the boat in the undergrowth, where they piled sticks and river-run debris atop it.

The boy who had hold of her just gave her his cold vampire's smile, the two stubs of his teeth stabbing at his lower lip. "We don't got no mothers," he said softly. "We're guerrillas."

"Hoodlums, you mean," she snapped back at him. "Criminals, *narcotraficantes,* kidnappers, cowards."

It came so quickly she had no time to react, the arm snaking out, the wrist uncoiling to bring the flat of his hand across her face, right where it had begun to bruise. And then, for good measure, he slapped her again.

"Hey, Eduardo, shithead," El Ojo rasped, "get your ass over here and give us a hand. What do you think this is, a nightclub?"

The others laughed. Her face stung and already the flies and mosquitoes were probing at the place where it had swelled along the line of her jaw. She dropped her chin to her shoulder for protection, but she didn't say anything. To this point she'd been too indignant to be scared, but now, with the light fading into the trees and the mud sucking at her shoes and the ugly nameless things of the jungle creeping from their holes and dens to lay siege to the night, she began to feel the dread spread its wings inside her. This was about Aquiles. About her son, the major leaguer, the pride of her life. They wanted him, wanted his money he'd worked so hard to acquire since he was a barefoot boy molding a glove out of old milk cartons and firing rocks at a target nailed to a tree, the money he'd earned by his sweat and talent—and the fame, the glory, the pride that came with it. They had no pride themselves, no human decency, but they would do anything to corrupt it—she'd heard the stories of the abductions, the mutilations, the families who'd paid ransom for their daughters, sons, parents, grandparents, even the family dog, only to pay again and again until hope gave way to despair.

But then, even as they took hold of her and began to march her through the jungle, she saw her son's face rise before her, his portrait just as it appeared on his Topps card, one leg lifted in the windup and that little half-smile he gave when he was embarrassed because the photographer was there and the photographer had posed him. *He'll come for me,* she said to herself. *I know he will.*

For Aquiles, the next three weeks were purgatorial. Each day he awoke sweating in the silence of dawn and performed his stretching exercises on the Turkish carpet until the maid brought him his orange juice and the protein drink into which he mixed the contents of three raw eggs, two ounces of wheatgrass and a tablespoon of brewer's yeast. Then he sat dazed in front of the high-definition plasma TV he'd bought his mother for her forty-fifth birthday, surrounded by his children (withdrawn from school for their own protection), and the unforgivably homely but capable girl from the provinces, Suspira Salvatoros, who'd been brought in to see after their welfare in the absence of his mother. In the corner, muttering darkly, sat his *abuela,* the electric ghost of his mother's features flitting across her face as she rattled her rosary and picked at the wart under her right eye till a thin line of serum ran down her cheek. The TV gave him nothing, not joy or even release, each show more stupefyingly banal than the last—how could people go about the business of winning prizes, putting on costumes and spouting dialogue, singing, dancing, stirring soft-shell crabs and cilantro in a fry pan for Christ's sake, when his mother, Marita Villalba, was in the hands of criminals who refused even to communicate let alone negotiate? Even baseball, even the playoffs, came to mean nothing to him.

And then, one bleak changeless morning, the sun like a firebrick tossed in the window and all Caracas up in arms over the abduction—*Free Marita* was scrawled in white soap on the windows of half the cars in town—he was cracking the eggs over his protein drink when Suspira Salvatoros knocked at the door. "Don Aquiles," she murmured, sidling into the room in her shy fumbling way, her eyes downcast, "something has come for you. A missive." In her hand—bitten fingernails, a swell of fat—there was a single dirty white envelope, too thick for a letter and stained with a smear of something he couldn't name. He felt as if his chest had been torn open, as if his still-beating heart had been snatched out of him and flung down on the carpet with the letter that dropped from his ineffectual fingers. Suspira Salvatoros began to cry. And gradually, painfully, as if he were bending for the rosin bag in a nightmare defeat in which he could get no one out and the fans were jeering and the manager frozen in the dugout, he bent for the envelope and clutched it to him, hating the feel of it, the weight of it, the guilt and horror and accusation it carried.

Inside was a human finger, the little finger of the left hand, two inches of bone, cartilage and flesh gone the color of old meat, and at the tip of it, a manicured nail, painted red. For a long while he stood there, weak-kneed, the finger cold in the palm of his hand, and then he reverently folded it back into the envelope, secreted it in the inside pocket of his shirt, closest to his heart, and flung himself out the door. In the next moment he sprang into the car—the Hummer, and so what if it was the color of poppies and arterial blood, so much the worse for them, the desecrators, the criminals, the punks, and he was going to track them down if it was the last thing he did. Within minutes he'd reached the police headquarters and pounded up the five flights of stairs, the ashen-faced bodyguard plodding along behind him. Without a word for anyone he burst into the Chief's office and laid the envelope on the desk before him.

The Chief had been arrested in the act of biting into a sweet cake while simultaneously blowing the steam off a cup of coffee, the morning newspaper propped up in front of him. He gave Aquiles a knowing look, set down the cake and extracted the finger from the envelope.

"I'll pay," Aquiles said. "Just let me pay. Please, God. She's all I care about."

The Chief held the finger out before him, studying it as if it were the most pedestrian thing in the world, a new sort of pen he'd been presented by the Boys' Auxiliary, a stick of that dried-out bread the Italians serve with their antipasto. "You will not pay them," he said without glancing up.

"I will." Aquiles couldn't help raising his voice. "The minute they call, I swear I'll give them anything, I don't care—"

Now the Chief raised his eyes. "Your presumption is that this is your mother's finger?"

Aquiles just stared at him.

"She uses this shade of nail polish?"

"Yes, I—I assume . . ."

"Amateurs," the Chief spat. "We're onto them. We'll have them, believe me. And you—*assume* nothing."

The office seemed to quaver then, as if the walls were closing in. Aquiles had begun to take deep breaths as he did on the mound when the situation was perilous, runner on first, no outs, a one-run ballgame. "My mother's in pain," he said.

"Your mother is not in pain. Not physical pain, at any rate." The Chief had set the severed finger down on the napkin that cradled the sweet bun and brought the mug to his lips. He took a sip of the coffee and then set the mug down too. "This is not your mother's finger," he said finally. "This is not, in fact, even the finger of a female. Look at it. Look closely. This," he pronounced, again lifting the mug to his lips, "is the finger of a man, a young man, maybe even a boy playing revolutionary. They like that, the boys. Dressing up, hiding out in the jungle. Calling themselves"—and here he let out his bitter laugh—"guerrillas."

She was a week in the jungle, huddled over a filthy stewpot thick with chunks of *carpincho,* some with the hide still on it, her digestion in turmoil, the insects burrowing into her, her dress—the shift she'd been wearing when they came for her—so foul it was like a layer of grease applied to her body. Then they took her farther into the jungle, to a crude airstrip—the kind the *narcotraficantes* employ in their evil trade—and she was forced into a Cessna airplane with El Ojo, the boy with the pitiless eyes and an older man, the pilot, and they sailed high over the broken spine of the countryside and up into the mountains. At first she was afraid they were taking her across the border to Colombia to trade her to the FARC rebels there, but she could see by the sun that they were heading southeast, and that was small comfort because every minute they were in the air she was that many more miles from her home and rescue. Their destination—it appeared as a cluster of frame cottages with thatched roofs and the splotched yawning mouth of a dried-up swimming pool—gave up nothing, not a road or even a path, to connect it with the outside world.

The landing was rough, very rough, the little plane lurching and pitching like one of those infernal rides at the fair, and when she climbed down out of the cockpit she had to bend at the waist and release the contents of her stomach in the grass no one had thought to cut. The boy, her tormentor, the one they called Eduardo, gave her a shove from behind so that she fell to her knees in her own mess, so hurt and confused and angry she had to fight to keep from crying in front of him. And then there were other boys there, a host of them, teenagers in dirty camouflage fatigues with the machine rifles slung over their shoulders, their faces blooming as they greeted Eduardo and El Ojo and then narrowing in suspicion as they regarded her. No one said a word to her. They unloaded the plane—beer, rum, cigarettes, pornographic magazines, sacks of rice and three cartons of noodles in a cup—and then ambled over to a crude table set up in the shade of the trees at the edge of the clearing, talking and joking all the while. She heard the hiss of the first beer and then a chorus of hisses as one after another they popped the aluminum tabs and pressed the cans to their lips, and she stood and gazed up at the barren sky and then let her eyes drop to the palisade of the jungle that went on unbroken as far as she could see.

Within a week, they'd accepted her. There was always one assigned to guard her, though for the life of her she couldn't imagine why—unless she could sprout wings like a *turpial* and soar out over the trees she was a prisoner here just as surely as if she'd been locked away in a cell—but aside from that, they gave her free rein. Once she'd recovered from the shock of that inhuman flight, she began to poke through the dilapidated buildings, just to do something, just to keep occupied, and the first thing she found was a tin washtub. It was nothing to collect fragments of wood at the edge of the clearing and to build a fire-ring of loose stone. She heated water in the tub, shaved a bar of soap she found in the latrine, wrapped herself in the blanket they gave her and washed first her hair, then her dress. The boys were drunk on the yeasty warm beer, sporadically shooting at something in the woods until El Ojo rose in a rage from his nap and cursed them, but soon they gathered round and solemnly stripped down to their underwear and handed her their filth-stiffened garments, murmuring,

"Please, *señora*" and "Would you mind?" and "Me too, me too." All except Eduardo, that is. He just sneered and lived in his dirt.

Ultimately, she knew these boys better than they knew themselves, boys playing soldier in the mornings, *beisbol* and *fútbol* in the afternoons, gathering to drink and boast and lie as the sun fell into the trees. They were the spawn of prostitutes and addicts, uneducated, unwanted, unloved, raised by grandmothers, raised by no one. They knew nothing but cruelty. Their teeth were bad. They'd be dead by thirty. As the days accumulated she began to gather herbs at the edge of the jungle and sort through the store of cans and rice and dried meat and beans, sweetening the clearing on the hilltop with the ambrosial smell of her cooking. She found a garden hose and ran it from the creek that gave them their water to the lip of the empty swimming pool and soon the boys were cannon-balling into the water, their shrieks of joy echoing through the trees even as the cool clear water cleansed and firmed their flesh and took the rankness out of their hair. Even El Ojo began to come round to hold out his tin plate or have his shirt washed and before long he took to sitting in the shade beside her just to pass the time of day. "These kids," he would say, and shake his head in a slow portentous way, and she could only cluck her tongue in agreement. "You're a good mother," he told her one night in his cat's tongue of a voice, "and I'm sorry we had to take you." He paused to lick the ends of the cigarette he'd rolled and then he passed it to her. "But this is life."

And then one morning as she was pressing out the corn cakes to bake on a tin sheet over the fire for the *arepas* she planned to serve for breakfast and dinner too, there was a stir among the boys—a knot of them gathered round the table and El Ojo there, brandishing a pair of metal shears. "You," he was saying, pointing the shears at Eduardo, "you're the tough guy. Make the sacrifice."

She was thirty feet from them, crouched over a stump, both hands thick with corn meal. Eduardo fastened his eyes on her. "She's the hostage," he spat. "Not me."

"She's a good person," El Ojo said, "a saint, better than you'll ever be. I won't touch her—no one will. Now hold out your hand."

The boy never flinched. Even when the shears bit, even when metal contacted metal and the blood drained from his face. And all the while he never took his eyes from her.

By the time the call came, the one Aquiles had been awaiting breathlessly through five and a half months of sleepless nights and paralyzed days, spring training was well under way. Twice the kidnappers had called to name their price—the first time it was five million, just as the Chief had predicted, and the next, inexplicably, it had dropped to two—but the voice on the other end of the phone, as hoarse and buzzing as the rattle of an inflamed serpent, never gave directions as to where to deliver it. Aquiles fell into despair, his children turned on one another like demons so that their disputations rang through the courtyard in a continual clangor, his *abuela*'s face was an open sore and Suspira Salvatoros cleaned and cooked with a vengeance even as she waded in among the children like the referee of an eternal wrestling match. And then the call came. From the Chief. Aquiles pressed the cell to his ear and murmured, *"Bueno?"* and the Chief's voice roared back at him: "We've found her!"

"Where?"

"My informants tell me they have her at an abandoned tourist camp in Estado Bolívar."

"But that's hundreds of miles from here."

"Yes," the Chief said. "The amateurs."

"I'm coming with you," Aquiles said.

"No. Absolutely no. Too dangerous. You'll just be in the way."

"I'm coming."

"No," the Chief said.

"I give you my solemn pledge that I will sign one truckload of baseballs for the sons and daughters of every man in the federal police district of Caracas and I will give to your son, Aldo, my complete 2003, 2004 and 2005 sets of Topps baseball cards direct from the U.S.A."

There was a pause, then the Chief's voice came back at him: "We leave in one hour. Bring a pair of boots."

They flew south in a commercial airliner, the Chief and ten of his men in camouflage fatigues with the patch of the Federal Police on the right shoulder and Aquiles in gum boots, blue jeans and an old baseball jersey from his days with the Caracas Lions, and then they took a commandeered produce truck to the end of the last stretch of the last road on the map and got down to hike through the jungle. The terrain was difficult. Insects thickened the air. No sooner did they cross one foaming yellow cataract than they had to cross another, the ground underfoot as slippery as if it had been oiled, the trees alive with the continuous screech of birds and monkeys. And they were going uphill, always uphill, gaining altitude with each uncertain step.

Though the Chief had insisted that Aquiles stay to the rear—"That's all we need," he said, "you getting shot, and I can see the headlines already: 'Venezuelan Baseball Star Killed in Attempt to Save His Sainted Mother' "—Aquiles' training regimen had made him a man of iron and time and again he found himself well out in front of the squad. Repeatedly the Chief had to call him back in a terse whisper and he slowed to let the others catch up. It was vital that they stay together, the Chief maintained, because there were no trails here and they didn't know what they were looking for except that it was up ahead somewhere, high up through the mass of vegetation that barely gave up the light, and that it would reveal itself when they came close enough.

Then, some four hours later, when the men had gone gray in the face and they were all of them as soaked through as if they'd been standing fully clothed under the barracks shower, the strangest thing happened. The Chief had called a halt to check his compass reading and allow the men to collapse in the vegetation and squeeze the blood, pus and excess water from their boots, and Aquiles, though he could barely brook the delay, paused to slap mosquitoes on the back of his neck and raise the canteen of Gatorade to his mouth. That was when the scent came to him, a faint odor of cooking that insinuated itself along the narrow olfactory avenue between the reeking perfume of jungle blooms and the fecal stench of the mud. But this was no ordinary smell, no generic scent you might encounter in the alley out back of a restaurant or drifting from a barrio window—this was his mother's cooking! His mother's! He could even name the dish: tripe stew! *"Jefe,"* he said, taking hold of the Chief's arm and pulling him to his feet, "do you smell that?"

They approached the camp warily, the Chief's men fanning out with their weapons held rigidly before them. Surprise was of the essence, the Chief had insisted, adding, chillingly, that the guerrillas were known to slit the throats of their captives rather than give them up, and so they must be eliminated before they knew what hit them. Aquiles felt the moment acutely. He'd never been so tense, so unnerved, in all his life. But he was a closer and a closer lived on the naked edge of catastrophe every time he touched the ball, and as he moved forward with the rest of them, he felt the strength infuse him and knew he would be ready when the moment came.

There were sounds now—shouts and curses and cries of rapture amidst a great splash and heave of water in motion—and then Aquiles parted the fronds of a palm and the whole scene was made visible. He saw rough huts under a diamond sky, a swimming pool exploding with slashing limbs and ecstatic faces, and there, not thirty feet away, the cookfire and the stooping form of a woman, white-haired, thin as bone. It took him a moment to understand that this was his mother, work-hardened and deprived of her makeup and the Clairol Nice 'n Easy he sent her by the cardboard case from the north. His first emotion, and he hated himself for it, was shame, shame for her and for himself too. And then, as the voices caromed round the pool—*Oaf! Fool! Get off me, Humberto, you ass!*—he felt nothing but anger.

He would never know who started the shooting, whether it was one of the guerrillas or the Chief and his men, but the noise of it, the lethal stutter that saw the naked figures jolted out of the pool and the water bloom with color, started him forward. He stepped from the bushes, oblivious to danger, stopping only to snatch a rock from the ground and mold it to his hand in the way he'd done ten thousand times when he was a boy. That was when the skinny kid with the dead eyes sprang up out of nowhere to put a knife to his mother's throat, and what was the point of that? Aquiles couldn't understand. One night there was victory, another night defeat. But you played the game just the same—you didn't blow up the ballpark or shoot the opposing batter. You didn't extort money from the people who'd earned it through God-given talent and hard work. You didn't threaten mothers. That wasn't right. That was impermissible. And so he cocked his arm and let fly with his fastball that had been clocked at ninety-eight miles an hour on the radar gun at Camden Yards while forty-five thousand people stamped and shouted and chanted his name—*High and inside,* he was thinking, *high and inside*—and, without complicating matters, let's just say that his aim was true.

Unfortunately, Marita Villalba never fully recovered from her ordeal. She would awaken in the night, smelling game roasting over a campfire—smelling *carpincho* with its rodent's hide intact—and she seemed lost in her own kitchen. She gave up dyeing her hair, rarely wore makeup or jewelry. The machine shop was nothing to her and when Rómulo Cordero, hobbled by his wounds, had to step down, she didn't even come downstairs to attend his retirement party, though the smell of the *arepas, empanadas* and *chivo en coco* radiated through the windows and up out of the yard and into the streets for blocks around. More and more she was content to let Suspira Salvatoros look after the kitchen and the children while she sat in the sun with her own mother, their collective fingers, all twenty of them, busy with the intricate needlepoint designs for which they became modestly famous in the immediate neighborhood.

Aquiles went back to the major leagues midway through the season, but after that moment of truth on the hilltop in the jungle of Estado Bolívar, he just couldn't summon the fire anymore. That, combined with the injury to his rotator cuff, spelled disaster. He was shelled each time he went to the mound, the boos rising in chorus till the manager took the ball from him for the last time and he cleared waivers and came home to stay, his glory gone but the contract guaranteed. The first thing he did was take Suspira Salvatoros to the altar, defeating the ambitions of any number of young and not-so-young women whose curses and lamentations could be heard echoing through the streets for weeks to come. Then he hired a team of painters to whitewash every corner of the compound, even to the tiles of the roof. And finally—and this was perhaps the hardest thing of all—he sold the vermilion Hummer to a TV actor known for his sensitive eyes and hyperactive jaw, replacing it with a used van of uncertain provenance and a color indistinguishable from the dirt of the streets.

(2005)

Admiral

She knew in her heart it was a mistake, but she'd been laid off and needed the cash and her memories of the Strikers were mostly on the favorable side, so when Mrs. Striker called—*Gretchen, this is Gretchen? Mrs. Striker?*—she'd said yes, she'd love to come over and hear what they had to say. First, though, she had to listen to her car cough as she drove across town (fuel pump, that was her father's opinion, offered in a flat voice that said it was none of his problem, not anymore, not now that she was grown and living back at home after a failed attempt at life), and she nearly stalled the thing turning into the Strikers' block. And then did stall it as she tried, against any reasonable expectation of success, to parallel park in front of their great rearing fortress of a house. It felt strange punching in the code at the gate and seeing how things were different and the same, how the trees had grown while the flowerbeds remained in a state of suspended animation, everything in perpetual bloom and clipped to within a millimeter of perfection. The gardeners saw to that. A whole battalion of them that swarmed over the place twice a week with their blowers and edgers and trimmers, at war with the weeds, the insects, the gophers and ground squirrels and the very tendency of the display plants to want to grow outside the box. At least that was how she remembered it. The gardeners. And how Admiral would rage at the windows, showing his teeth and scrabbling with his claws—and if he could have chewed through glass he would have done it. "That's right, boy," she'd say, "that's right—don't let those bad men steal all your dead leaves and dirt. You go, boy. You go. That's right."

She rang the bell at the front door and it wasn't Mrs. Striker who answered it but another version of herself in a white maid's apron and a little white maid's cap perched atop her head, and she was so surprised she had to double-clutch to keep from dropping her purse. *A woman of color does not clean house,* that was what her mother always told her, and it had become a kind of mantra when she was growing up, a way of reinforcing core values, of promoting education and the life of the mind, but she couldn't help wondering how much higher a dogsitter was on the socioeconomic scale than a maid. Or a sous-chef, waitress, aerobics instructor, ticket puncher and tortilla maker, all of which she'd been at one time or another. About the only thing she hadn't tried was leech gathering. There was a poem on the subject in her college text by William Wordsworth, the poet of daffodils and leeches, and she could summon it up whenever she needed a good laugh. She developed a quick picture of an old long-nosed white man rolling up his pantlegs and wading into the murk, then squeezed out a miniature smile and said, "Hi, I'm Nisha? I came to see Mrs. Striker? And Mr. Striker?"

The maid—she wasn't much older than Nisha herself, with a placid expression that might have been described as self-satisfied or just plain vacant—held open the door. "I'll tell them you're here," she said.

Nisha murmured a thank-you and stepped into the tiled foyer, thinking of the snake brain and the olfactory memories that lay coiled there. She smelled dog—smelled Admiral—with an overlay of old sock and furniture polish. The great room rose up before her like something transposed from a cathedral. It was a cold room, echoing and hollow, and she'd never liked it. "You mind if I wait in the family room?" she asked.

The maid—or rather the girl, the young woman, the young woman in the demeaning and stereotypical maid's costume—had already started off in the direction of the kitchen, but she swung round now to give her a look of surprise and irritation. For a moment it seemed as if she might snap at her, but then, finally, she just shrugged and said, "Whatever."

Nothing had changed in the paneled room that gave onto the garden, not as far as Nisha could see. There were the immense old high-backed leather armchairs and the antique Stickley sofa rescued from the law offices of Striker and Striker, the mahogany bar with the wine rack and the backlit shrine Mr. Striker had created in homage to the spirits of single-malt scotch whisky, and overseeing it all, the oil portrait of Admiral with its dark heroic hues and golden patina of varnish. She remembered the day the painter had come to the house and posed the dog for the preliminary snapshots, Admiral uncooperative, Mrs. Striker strung tight as a wire and the inevitable squirrel bounding across the lawn at the crucial moment. The painter had labored mightily in his studio to make his subject look noble, snout elevated, eyes fixed on some distant, presumably worthy, object, but to Nisha's mind an Afghan—any Afghan—looked inherently ridiculous, like some escapee from *Sesame Street,* and Admiral seemed a kind of concentrate of the absurd. He looked goofy, just that.

When she turned round, both the Strikers were there, as if they'd floated in out of the ether. As far as she could see, they hadn't aged at all. Their skin was flawless, they held themselves as stiff and erect as the Ituri carvings they'd picked up on their trip to Africa and they tried hard to make small talk and avoid any appearance of briskness. In Mrs. Striker's arms—*Call me Gretchen, please*—was an Afghan pup, and after the initial exchange of pleasantries, Nisha, her hand extended to rub the silk of the ears and feel the wet probe of the tiny snout on her wrist, began to get the idea. She restrained herself from asking after Admiral. "Is this his pup?" she asked instead. "Is this little Admiral?"

The Strikers exchanged a glance. The husband hadn't said, *Call me Cliff,* hadn't said much of anything, but now his lips compressed. "Didn't you read about it in the papers?"

There was an awkward pause. The pup began to squirm. "Admiral passed," Gretchen breathed. "It was an accident. We had him—well, we were in the park, the dog park . . . you know, the one where the dogs run free? You used to take him there, you remember, up off Sycamore? Well, you know how exuberant he was . . ."

"You really didn't read about it?" There was incredulity in the husband's voice.

"Well, I—I was away at college and then I took the first job I could find. Back here, I mean. Because of my mother. She's been sick."

Neither of them commented on this, not even to be polite.

"It was all over the press," the husband said, and he sounded offended now. He adjusted his oversized glasses and cocked his head to look down at her in a way that brought the past rushing back. "*Newsweek* did a story, *USA Today*—we were on *Good Morning America,* both of us."

She was at a loss, the three of them standing there, the dog taking its spiked dentition to the underside of her wrist now, just the way Admiral used to when he was a pup. "For what?" she was about to say, when Gretchen came to the rescue.

"This *is* little Admiral. Admiral II, actually," she said, ruffling the blond shag over the pup's eyes.

The husband looked past her, out the window and into the yard, an ironic grin pressed to his lips. "Two hundred and fifty thousand dollars," he said, "and it's too bad he wasn't a cat."

Gretchen gave him a sharp look. "You make a joke of it," she said, her eyes suddenly filling, "but it was worth every penny and you know it." She mustered a long-suffering smile for Nisha. "Cats are simpler—their eggs are more mature at ovulation than dogs' are."

"I can get you a cat for thirty-two thou."

"Oh, Cliff, stop. Stop it."

He moved to his wife and put an arm round her shoulders. "But we didn't want to clone a cat, did we, honey?" He bent his face to the dog's, touched noses with him and let his voice rise to a falsetto, "Did we now, Admiral? Did we?"

At seven-thirty the next morning, Nisha pulled up in front of the Strikers' house and let her car wheeze and shudder a moment before killing the engine. She flicked the radio back on to catch the last fading chorus of a tune she liked, singing along with the sexy low rasp of the lead vocalist, feeling good about things—or better anyway. The Strikers were giving her twenty-five dollars an hour, plus the same dental and health care package they offered the staff at their law firm, which was a whole solid towering brick wall of improvement over what she'd been making as a waitress at Johnny's Rib Shack, sans health care, sans dental and sans any tip she could remember above ten percent over the pre-tax total because the people who came out to gnaw ribs were just plain cheap and no two ways about it. When she stepped out of the car, there was Gretchen coming down the front steps of the house with the pup in her arms, just as she had nine years ago when Nisha was a high school freshman taking on what she assumed was going to be a breeze of a summer job.

Nisha took the initiative of punching in the code herself and slipping through the gate to hustle up the walk and save Gretchen the trouble, because Gretchen was in a hurry, always in a hurry. She was dressed in a navy-blue suit with a double string of pearls and an antique silver pin in the shape of a bounding borzoi that seemed eerily familiar—it might have been the exact ensemble she'd been wearing when Nisha had told her she'd be quitting to go off to college. *I'm sorry, Mrs. Striker, and I've really enjoyed the opportunity to work for you and Mr. Striker,* she'd said, hardly able to contain the swell of her heart, *but I'm going to college. On a scholarship.* She'd had the acceptance letter in her hand to show her, thinking how proud of her Mrs. Striker would be, how she'd take her in her arms for a hug and congratulate her, but the first thing she'd said was, *What about Admiral?*

As Gretchen closed on her now, the pup wriggling in her arms, Nisha could see her smile flutter and die. No doubt she was already envisioning the cream-leather interior of her BMW (a 750i in Don't-Even-Think-About-It Black) and the commute to the office and whatever was going down there, court sessions, the piles of documents, contention at every turn. Mr. Striker—Nisha would never be able to call him Cliff, even if she lived to be eighty, but then he'd have to be a hundred and ten and probably wouldn't hear her anyway—was already gone, in his matching Beemer, his and hers. Gretchen didn't say *good morning* or *hi* or *how are you?* or *thanks for coming,* but just enfolded her in the umbrella of her perfume and handed her the dog. Which went immediately heavy in Nisha's arms, fighting for the ground with four flailing paws and the little white ghoul's teeth that fastened on the top button of her jacket. Nisha held on. Gave Gretchen a big grateful-for-the-job-and-the-health-care smile, no worries, no worries at all.

"Those jeans," Gretchen said, narrowing her eyes. "Are they new?"

The dog squirming, squirming. "I, well—I'm going to set him down a minute, okay?"

"Of course, of course. Do what you do, what you normally do." An impatient wave. "Or what you used to do, I mean."

They both watched as the pup fell back on its haunches, rolled briefly in the grass and sprang up to clutch Nisha's right leg in a clumsy embrace. "I just couldn't find any of my old jeans—my mother probably threw them all out long ago. Plus"—a laugh—"I don't think I could fit into them anymore." She gave Gretchen a moment to ruminate on the deeper implications here—time passing, adolescents grown into womanhood, flesh expanding, that sort of thing—then gently pushed the dog down and murmured, "But I *am* wearing—right here, under the jacket?—this T-shirt I know I used to wear back then."

Nothing. Gretchen just stood there, looking distracted.

"It's been washed, of course, and sitting in the back of the top drawer of my dresser where my mother left it, so I don't know if there'll be any scent or anything, but I'm sure I used to wear it because Tupac really used to drive my engine back then, if you know what I mean." She gave it a beat. "But hey, we were all fourteen once, huh?"

Gretchen made no sign that she'd heard her—either that or she denied the proposition outright. "You're going to be all right with this, aren't you?" she said, looking her in the eye. "Is there anything we didn't cover?"

The afternoon before, during her interview—but it wasn't really an interview because the Strikers had already made up their minds and if she'd refused them they would have kept raising the hourly till she capitulated—the two of them, Gretchen and Cliff, had positioned themselves on either side of her and leaned into the bar over caramel-colored scotches and a platter of ebi and maguro sushi to explain the situation. Just so that she was clear on it. "You know what cloning is, right?" Gretchen said. "Or what it involves? You remember Dolly?"

Nisha was holding fast to her drink, her left elbow pressed to the brass rail of the bar in the family room. She'd just reached out her twinned chopsticks for a second piece of the shrimp, but withdrew her hand. "You mean the country singer?"

"The sheep," the husband said.

"The first cloned mammal," Gretchen put in. "Or larger mammal."

"Yeah," she said, nodding. "Sure. I guess."

What followed was a short course in genetics and the method of somatic cell nuclear transplant that had given the world Dolly, various replicated cattle, pigs and hamsters, and now Admiral II, the first cloned dog made available commercially through SalvaPet, Inc., the genetic engineering firm with offices in Seoul, San Juan and Cleveland. Gretchen's voice constricted as she described how they'd taken a cell from the lining of Admiral's ear just after the accident and inserted it into a donor egg, which had had its nucleus removed, stimulated the cell to divide through the application of an electric current, and then inserted the developing embryo into the uterus of a host mother—"The sweetest golden retriever you ever saw. What was her name, Cliff? Some flower, wasn't it?"

"Peony."

"Peony? Are you sure?"

"Of course I'm sure."

"I thought it was—oh, I don't know. You sure it wasn't Iris?"

"The point is," he said, setting his glass down and leveling his gaze on Nisha, "you can get a genetic copy of the animal, a kind of three-dimensional Xerox, but that doesn't guarantee it'll be like the one you, well, the one you lost."

"It was so sad," Gretchen said.

"It's nurture that counts. You've got to reproduce the animal's experiences, as nearly as possible." He gave a shrug, reached for the bottle. "You want another?" he asked, and she held out her glass. "Of course we're both older now—and so are you, we realize that—but we want to come as close as possible to replicating the exact conditions that made Admiral what he was, right down to the toys we gave him, the food, the schedule of walks and play and all the rest. Which is where you come in—"

"We need a commitment here, Nisha," Gretchen breathed, leaning in so close Nisha could smell the scotch coming back at her. "Four years. That's how long you were with him last time. Or with Admiral, I mean. The original Admiral."

The focus of all this deliberation had fallen asleep in Gretchen's lap. A single probing finger of sunlight stabbed through the window to illuminate the pale fluff over the dog's eyes. At that moment, in that light, little Admiral looked like some strange conjunction of ostrich and ape. Nisha couldn't help thinking of *The Island of Dr. Moreau,* the cheesy version with Marlon Brando looking as if he'd been genetically manipulated himself, and she would have grinned a private grin, fueled by the scotch and the thundering absurdity of the moment, but she had to hide everything she thought or felt behind a mask of impassivity. She wasn't committing to anything for four years—four years? If she was still living here in this craphole of a town four years from now she promised herself she'd go out and buy a gun and eliminate all her problems with a single, very personal squeeze of the trigger.

That was what she was thinking when Gretchen said, "We'll pay you twenty dollars an hour," and the husband said, "With health care—and dental," and they both stared at her so fiercely she had to look down into her glass before she found her voice. "Twenty-five," she said.

And oh, how they loved that dog, because they never hesitated. "Twenty-five it is," the husband said, and Gretchen, a closer's smile blooming on her face, produced a contract from the folder at her elbow. "Just sign here," she said.

After Gretchen had climbed into her car and the car had slid through the gate and vanished down the street, Nisha sprawled out on the grass and lifted her face to the sun. She was feeling the bliss of déjà vu—or no, not déjà vu, but a virtual return to the past, when life was just a construct and there was nothing she couldn't have done or been and nothing beyond the thought of clothes and boys and the occasional term paper to hamper her. Here she was, gone back in time, lying on the grass at quarter of eight in the morning on a sunstruck June day, playing with a puppy while everybody else was going to work—it was hilarious, that's what it was. Like something you'd read about in the paper—a behest from some crazed millionaire. Or in this case, two crazed millionaires. She felt so good she let out a laugh, even as the pup came charging across the lawn to slam headfirst into her, all feet and pink panting tongue, and he was Admiral all right, Admiral in the flesh, born and made and resurrected for the mere little pittance of a quarter million dollars.

For a long while she wrestled with him, flipping him over on his back each time he charged, scratching his belly and baby-talking him, enjoying the novelty of it, but by quarter past eight she was bored and she pushed herself up to go on into the house and find something to eat. *Do what you used to do,* Gretchen had told her, but what she used to do, summers especially, was nap and read and watch TV and sneak her friends in to tip a bottle of the husband's forty-year-old scotch to their adolescent lips and make faces at one another before descending into giggles. Twice a day she'd take the dog to the doggie park and watch him squat and crap and run wild with the other mutts till his muzzle was streaked with drool and he dodged at her feet to snatch up mouthfuls of the Evian the Strikers insisted he drink. Now, though, she just wanted to feel the weight of the past a bit, and she went in the back door, the dog at her heels, thinking to make herself a sandwich—the Strikers always had cold cuts in the fridge, mounds of pastrami, capicolla, smoked turkey and Swiss, individual slices of which went to

Admiral each time he did his business outside where he was supposed to or barked in the right cadence or just stuck his goofy head in the door. She could already see the sandwich she was going to make—a whole deli's worth of meat and cheese piled up on Jewish rye; they always had Jewish rye—and she was halfway to the refrigerator before she remembered the maid.

There she was, in her maid's outfit, sitting at the kitchen table with her feet up and the newspaper spread out before her, spooning something out of a cup. "Don't you bring that filthy animal in here," she said, glancing up sharply.

Nisha was startled. There didn't used to be a maid. There was no one in the house, in fact, till Mrs. Yamashita, the cook, came in around four, and that was part of the beauty of it. "Oh, hi," she said, "hi, I didn't know you were going to be—I just . . . I was going to make a sandwich, I guess." There was a silence. The dog slunk around the kitchen, looking wary. "What was your name again?"

"Frankie," the maid said, swallowing the syllables as if she weren't ready to give them up, "and I'm the one has to clean up all these paw marks off the floor—and did you see what he did to that throw pillow in the guest room?"

"No," Nisha said, "I didn't," and she was at the refrigerator now, sliding back the tray of the meat compartment. This would go easier if they were friends, no doubt about it, and she was willing, more than willing. "You want anything?" she said. "A sandwich—or, or something?"

Frankie just stared at her. "I don't know what they're paying you," she said, "but to me? This is the craziest shit I ever heard of in my life. You think I couldn't let the dog out the door a couple times a day? Or what, take him to the park—that's what you do, right, take him to the doggie park over on Sycamore?"

The refrigerator door swung shut, the little light blinking out, the heft of the meat satisfying in her hand. "It's insane, I admit it—hey, I'm with you. You think I wanted to grow up to be a dogsitter?"

"I don't know. I don't know anything about you. Except you got your degree—you need a degree for that, dogsitting, I mean?" She hadn't moved, not a muscle, her feet propped up, the cup in one hand, spoon in the other.

"No," Nisha said, feeling the blood rise to her face, "no, you don't. But what about you—you need a degree to be a maid?"

That hit home. For a moment, Frankie said nothing, just looked from her to the dog—which was begging now, clawing at Nisha's leg with his forepaws—and back again. "This is just temporary," she said finally.

"Yeah, me too." Nisha gave her a smile, no harm done, just establishing a little turf, that was all. "Totally."

For the first time, Frankie's expression changed: she almost looked as if she were going to laugh. "Yeah, that's right," she said, "temporary help, that's all we are. We're the temps. And Mr. and Mrs. Striker—dog crazy, plain crazy, two-hundred-and-fifty-thousand-dollar crazy—they're permanent."

And now Nisha laughed, and so did Frankie—a low rumble of amusement that made the dog turn its head. The meat was on the counter now, the cellophane wrapper pulled back. Nisha selected a slice of Black Forest ham and held it out to him. "Sit!" she said. "Go ahead, sit!" And the dog, just like his father or progenitor or donor or whatever he was, looked at her stupidly till she dropped the meat on the tile and the wet plop of its arrival made him understand that here was something to eat.

"You're going to spoil that dog," Frankie said.

Nisha went unerringly to the cabinet where the bread was kept, and there it was, Jewish rye, a fresh loaf, springy to the touch. She gave Frankie a glance over her shoulder. "Yeah," she said. "I think that's the idea."

A month drifted by, as serene a month as Nisha could remember. She was making good money, putting in ten-hour days during the week and half days on the weekends, reading through all the books she hadn't had time for in college, exhausting the Strikers' DVD collection and opening her own account at the local video store, walking, lazing, napping the time away. She gained five pounds and vowed to start swimming regularly in the Strikers' pool, but hadn't got round to it yet. Some days she'd help Frankie with the cleaning and the laundry so the two of them could sit out on the back deck with their feet up, sharing a bottle of sweet wine or a joint. As for the dog, she tried to be conscientious about the whole business of imprinting it with the past—or *a* past—though she felt ridiculous. Four years of college for this? Wars were being fought, people were starving, there were diseases to conquer, children to educate, good to do in the world, and here she was reliving her adolescence in the company of an inbred semi-retarded clown of a cloned Afghan hound because two childless rich people decreed it should be so. All right. She knew she'd have to move on. Knew it was temporary. Swore that she'd work up a new résumé and start sending it out—but then the face of her mother, sick from vomiting and with her scalp as smooth and slick as an eggplant, would rise up to shame her. She threw the ball to the dog. Took him to the park. Let the days fall round her like leaves from a dying tree.

And then one afternoon, on the way back from the dog park, Admiral jerking at the leash beside her and the sky opening up to a dazzle of sun and pure white tufts of cloud that made her feel as if she were floating untethered through the universe along with them, she noticed a figure stationed outside the gate of the Strikers' house. As she got closer, she saw that it was a young man dressed in baggy jeans and a T-shirt, his hair fanning out in rusty blond dreads and a goatee of the same color clinging to his chin. He was peering over the fence. Her first thought was that he'd come to rob the place, but she dismissed it—he was harmless; you could see that a hundred yards off. Then she saw the paint smears on his jeans and wondered if he was a painting contractor come to put in a bid on the house, but that wasn't it either. He looked more like an amateur artist—and here she had to laugh to herself—the kind who specializes in dog portraits. But she was nearly on him now, thinking to brush by him and slip through the gate before he could accost her, whatever he wanted, when he turned suddenly and his face caught fire. "Wow!" he said. "Wow, I can't believe it! You're her, aren't you, the famous dogsitter? And this"—he went down on one knee and made a chirping sound deep in his throat—"this is Admiral. Right? Am I right?"

Admiral went straight to him, lurching against the leash, and in the next instant he was flopping himself down on the hot pavement, submitting to the man's caresses. The rope of a tail whapped and thrashed, the paws gyrated, the puppy teeth came into play. "Good boy," the man crooned, his dreads riding a wave across his brow. "He likes that, doesn't he? Doesn't he, boy?"

Nisha didn't say anything. She just watched, the smallest hole dug out of the canyon of her boredom, till the man rose to his feet and held out his hand even as Admiral sprang up to hump his leg with fresh enthusiasm. "I'm Erhard," he said, grinning wide. "And you're Nisha, right?"

"Yes," she said, taking his hand despite herself. She was on the verge of asking how he knew her name, but there was no point: she already understood. He was from the press. In the past month there must have been a dozen reporters on the property, the Strikers stroking their vanity and posing for pictures and answering the same idiotic questions over and over—*A quarter million dollars: that's a lot for a dog, isn't it?*—and she herself had been interviewed twice already. Her mother had even found a fuzzy color photo of her and Admiral (couchant, lap) on the Web under the semi-hilarious rubric CLONE-SITTER. So this guy was a reporter—a foreign reporter, judging from the faint trace of an accent and the blue-eyed rearing height of him, German, she supposed. Or Austrian. And he wanted some of her time.

"Yes," he said, as if reading her thoughts. "I am from *Die Weltwoche,* and I wanted to ask of you—prevail upon you, beg you—for a few moments? Is that possible? For me? Just now?"

She gave him a long slow appraisal, flirting with him, yes, definitely flirting.

"I've got nothing but time," she said. And then, watching his grin widen: "You want a sandwich?"

They ate on the patio overlooking the pool. She was dressed casually in shorts and flip-flops and her old Tupac tee, and that wasn't necessarily a bad thing because the shirt—too small by half—lifted away from her hips when she leaned back in the chair, showing off her navel and the onyx ring she wore there. He was watching her, chattering on about the dog, lifting the sandwich to his lips and putting it down again, fooling with the lens on the battered old Hasselblad he extracted from the backpack at his feet. The sun made sequins on the surface of the pool. Admiral lounged beneath the table, worrying a rawhide bone. She was feeling good, better than good, sipping a beer and watching him back.

They had a little conversation about the beer. "Sorry to offer you Miller, but that's all we have—or the Strikers have, I mean."

"Miller High Life," he said, lifting the bottle to his mouth. "Great name. What person would not want to live the high life? Even a dog. Even Admiral. He lives the high life, no?"

"I thought you'd want a German beer, something like Beck's or something."

He set down the bottle, picked up the camera and let the lens wander down the length of her legs. "I'm Swiss, actually," he said. "But I live here now. And I like American beer. I like everything American."

There was no mistaking the implication and she wanted to return the sentiment, but she didn't know the first thing about Switzerland, so she just smiled and tipped her beer to him.

"So," he said, cradling the camera in his lap and referring to the notepad he'd laid on the table when she'd served him the sandwich, "this is the most interesting for me, this idea that Mr. and Mrs. Striker would hire you for the dog? This is very strange, no?"

She agreed that it was.

He gave her a smile she could have fallen into. "Do you mind if I should ask what are they paying you?"

"Yes," she said. "I do."

Another smile. "But it is good—worth your while, as they say?"

"I thought this was about Admiral," she said, and then, because she wanted to try it out on her tongue, she added, "Erhard."

"Oh, it is, it is—but I find you interesting too. More interesting, really, than the dog." As if on cue, Admiral backed out from under the table and squatted on the concrete to deposit a glistening yellow turd, which he examined briefly and then promptly ate.

"Bad dog," she said reflexively.

Erhard studied the dog a moment, then shifted his eyes back to her. "But how do you feel about the situation, this concept of cloning a pet? Do you know anything about this process, the cruelty involved?"

"You know, frankly, Erhard, I haven't thought much about it. I don't know really what it involves. I don't really care. The Strikers love their dog, that's all, and if they want to, I don't know, bring him back—"

"Cheat death, you mean."

She shrugged. "It's their money."

He leaned across the table now, his eyes locked on hers. "Yes, but they must artificially stimulate so many bitches to come into heat and then they must take the eggs from the tubes of these bitches, what they call 'surgically harvesting,' if you can make a guess as to what that implies for the poor animals"—she began to object but he held up a peremptory finger—"and that is nothing when you think of the numbers involved. Do you know about Snuppy?"

She thought she hadn't heard him right. "Snuppy? What's that?"

"The dog, the first one ever cloned—it was two years ago, in Korea? Well, this dog, this one dog—an Afghan like your dog here—was the result of over a thousand embryos created in the laboratory from donor skin cells. And they put these embryos into one hundred and twenty-three bitches and only three clones resulted—and two died. So: all that torture of the animals, all that money—and for what?" He glanced down at Admiral, the flowing fur, the blunted eyes. "For this?"

A sudden thought came to her: "You're not really a journalist, are you?"

He slowly shook his head, as if he couldn't bear the weight of it.

"You're what—one of these animal people, these animal liberators or whatever they are. Isn't that right? Isn't that what you are?" She felt frightened suddenly, for herself, for Admiral, for the Strikers and Frankie and the whole carefully constructed edifice of getting and wanting, of supply and demand and all that it implied.

"And do you know why they clone the Afghan hound," he went on, ignoring her, "—the very stupidest of all the dogs on this earth? You don't? Breeding, that is why. This is what they call an uncomplicated genetic line, a pure line all the way back to the wolf ancestor. Breeding," he said, and he'd raised his voice so that Admiral looked up at the vehemence of it, "so that we can have this purity, this stupid hound, this *replica* of nature."

Nisha tugged down her T-shirt, drew up her legs. The sun glared up off the water so that she had to squint to see him. "You haven't answered my question," she said, "Erhard. If that's even your name."

Again, the slow rolling of the head on his shoulders, back and forth in rhythmic contrition. "Yes," he said finally, drawing in a breath, "I am one of 'these animal people.'" His eyes went distant a moment and then came back to her. "But I am also a journalist, a journalist first. And I want you to help me."

That night, when the Strikers came home—in convoy, her car following his through the gate, Admiral lurching across the lawn to bark furiously at the shimmering irresistible disks of the wheels of first one car, then the other—Nisha was feeling conflicted. Her loyalties were with the Strikers, of course. And with Admiral too, because no matter how brainless and ungainly the dog was, no matter how many times he wet the rug or ravaged the flowerbed or scrambled up onto the kitchen table to choke down anything anyone had been foolish enough to leave untended even for thirty seconds, she'd bonded with him—she would have been pretty cold if she hadn't. And she wasn't cold. She was as susceptible as anyone else. She loved animals, loved dogs, loved the way Admiral sprang to life when he saw her walk through the door, loved the dance of his fur, his joyous full-throated bark, the feel of his wet whiskered snout in the cupped palm of her hand. But Erhard had made her feel something else altogether.

What was it? A sexual stirring, yes, absolutely—after the third beer, she'd found herself leaning into him for the first of a series of deep, languid, adhesive kisses—but it was more than that. There was something transgressive in what he wanted her to do, something that appealed to her sense of rebellion, of anarchy, of applying the pin to the swollen balloon . . . but here were the Strikers, emerging separately from their cars as Admiral bounced between them, yapping out his ecstasy. And now Gretchen was addressing her, trying to shout over the dog's sharp vocalizations, but without success. In the next moment, she was coming across the lawn, her face set.

"Don't let him chase the car like that," she called, even as Admiral tore round her like a dust devil, nipping at her ankles and dodging away again. "It's a bad habit."

"But Admiral—I mean, the first Admiral—used to chase cars all the time, remember?"

Gretchen had pinned her hair up so that all the contours of her face stood out in sharp relief. There were lines everywhere suddenly, creases and gouges, frown marks, little embellishments round her eyes, and how could Nisha have missed them? Gretchen was old—fifty, at least—and the realization came home to Nisha now, under the harsh sun, with the taste of the beer and of Erhard still tingling on her lips. "I don't care," Gretchen was saying, and she was standing beside Nisha now, like a figurine the gardeners had set down amidst that perfect landscape.

"But I thought we were going to go for everything, the complete behavior, good or bad, right? Because otherwise—"

"That was how the accident happened. At the dog park. He got through the gate before Cliff or I could stop him and just ran out into the street after some idiot on a motorcycle. . . ." She looked past Nisha a moment, to where Admiral was bent over the pool, slurping up water as if his pinched triangular head worked on a piston. "So no," she said, "no, we're going to have to modify some behavior. I don't want him drinking that pool water, for one thing. Too many chemicals."

"Okay, sure," Nisha said, shrugging. "I'll try." She raised her voice and sang out "Bad dog, bad dog," but it was halfhearted and Admiral ignored her.

The cool green eyes shifted to meet hers again. "And I don't want him eating his own"—she paused to search for the proper word for the context, running through various euphemisms before giving it up—"shit."

Another shrug.

"I'm serious on this. Are you with me?"

Nisha couldn't help herself, and so what if she was pushing it? So what? "Admiral did," she said. "Maybe you didn't know that."

Gretchen just waved her hand in dismissal. "But *this* Admiral," she said. "He's not going to do it. Is he?"

Over the course of the next two weeks, as summer settled in with a succession of cloudless, high-arching days and Admiral steadily grew into the promise of his limbs, Erhard became a fixture at the house. Every morning, when Nisha came through the gate with the dog on his leash, he was there waiting for her, shining and tall and beautiful, with a joke on his lips and always some little treat for Admiral secreted in one pocket or another. The dog worshipped him. Went crazy for him. Pranced on the leash, spun in circles, nosed at his sleeves and pockets till he got his treat, then rolled over on his back in blissful submission. And then it was the dog park, and instead of sitting there wrapped up in the cocoon of herself, she had Erhard to sustain her, to lean into her so that she could feel the heat of him through the thin cotton of his shirt, to kiss her, and later, after lunch and the rising tide of the beer, to make love to her on the divan in the cool shadows of the pool house. They swam in the afternoons—he didn't mind the five pounds she'd put on; he praised her for them—and sometimes Frankie would join them, shedding the maid's habit for a white two-piece and careering through a slashing backstroke with a bottle of beer her reward, because she was part of the family too, Mama and Papa and Aunt Frankie, all there to nurture little Admiral under the beneficent gaze of the sun.

Of course, Nisha was no fool. She knew there was a quid pro quo involved here, knew that Erhard had his agenda, but she was in no hurry, she'd committed to nothing, and as she lay there on the divan smoothing her hands over his back, tasting him, enjoying him, taking him inside her, she felt hope, real hope, for the first time since she'd come back home. It got so that she looked forward to each day, even the mornings that had been so hard on her, having to take a tray up to the ghost of her mother while her father trudged off to work, the whole house like a turned grave, because now she had Admiral, now she had Erhard, and she could shrug off anything. Yes. Sure. That was the way it was. Until the day he called her on it.

Cloudless sky, steady sun, every flower at its peak. She came down the walk with Admiral on his leash at the appointed hour, pulled back the gate, and there he was—but this time he wasn't alone. Beside him, already straining at the leash, was a gangling overgrown Afghan pup that could have been the twin of Admiral, and though she'd known it was coming, known the plan since the very first day, she was awestruck. "Jesus," she said, even as Admiral jerked her forward and the two dogs began to romp round her legs in a tangle of limbs and leashes, "how did you—? I mean, he's the exact, he's totally—"

"That's the idea, isn't it?"

"But where did you find him?"

Erhard gave her a look of appraisal, then his eyes jumped past her to sweep the street. "Let's go inside, no? I don't want that they should see us here, anyone—not right in the front of the house."

He hadn't talked her into it, not yet, not exactly, but now that the moment had come she numbly punched in the code and held the gate open for him. What he wanted to do, what he was in the process of doing with her unspoken complicity, was to switch the dogs—just for a day, two at the most—by way of experiment. His contention was that the Strikers would never know the difference, that they were arrogant exemplars of bourgeois excess, even to the point of violating the laws of nature—and God, God too—simply to satisfy their own solipsistic desires. Admiral wouldn't be harmed—he'd enjoy himself, the change of scenery, all that. And certainly she knew how much the dog had come to mean to him. "But these people will not recognize their own animal," he'd insisted, his voice gone hard with conviction, "and so I will have my story and the world will know it."

Once inside the gate, they let the dogs off their leashes and went round back of the house where they'd be out of sight. They walked hand in hand, his fingers entwined with hers, and for a long while, as the sun rode high overhead and a breeze slipped in off the ocean to stir the trees, they watched as the two dogs streaked back and forth, leaping and nipping and tumbling in doggy rhapsody. Admiral's great combed-out spill of fur whipped round him in a frenzy of motion, and the new dog, Erhard's dog—the impostor—matched him step for step, hair for glorious hair. "You took him to the groomer, didn't you?" she said.

Erhard gave a stiff nod. "Yes, sure: what do you think? He must be exact."

She watched, bemused, for another minute, her misgivings buried deep under the pressure of his fingers, bone, sinew, the wedded flesh, and why shouldn't she go along with him? What was the harm? His article, or exposé or whatever it was, would appear in Switzerland, in German, and the Strikers would never know the difference. Or even if they did, even if it was translated into English and grabbed headlines all over the country, they had it coming to them. Erhard was right. She knew it. She'd known it all along. "So what's his name?" she asked, the dogs shooting past her in a moil of fur and flashing feet. "Does he have a name?"

"Fred."

"Fred? What kind of name is that for a pedigree dog?"

"What kind of name is Admiral?"

She was about to tell him the story of the original Admiral, how he'd earned his sobriquet because of his enthusiasm for the Strikers' yacht and how they were planning on taking Admiral II out on the water as soon as they could, when the familiar rumble of the driveway gate drawing back on its runners startled her. In the next moment, she was in motion, making for the near corner of the house where she could see down the long macadam strip of the drive. Her heart skipped a beat: it was Gretchen. Gretchen home early, some crisis compelling her, mislaid papers, her blouse stained, the flu, Gretchen in her black Beemer, waiting for the gate to slide back so she could roll up the drive and exert dominion over her house and property, her piss-stained carpets and her insuperable dog. "Quick!" Nisha shouted, whirling round, "grab them. Grab the dogs!"

She saw Erhard plunge forward and snatch at them, the grass rising up to meet him and both dogs tearing free. "Admiral!" he called, scrambling to his knees. "Here, boy. Come!" The moment thundered in her ears. The dogs hesitated, the ridiculous sea of fur smoothing and settling momentarily, and then one of them—it was Admiral, it had to be—came to him and he got hold of it even as the other pricked up its ears at the sound of the car and bolted round the corner of the house.

"I'll stall her," she called.

Erhard, all six feet and five inches of him, was already humping across the grass in the direction of the pool house, the dog writhing in his arms.

But the other dog—it was Fred, it had to be—was chasing the car up the drive now, nipping at the wheels, and as Nisha came round the corner she could read the look on her employer's face. A moment and she was there, grabbing for the dog as the car rolled to a stop and the engine died. Gretchen stepped out of the car, heels coming down squarely on the pavement, her shoulders thrust back tightly against the grip of her jacket. "I thought I told you . . . ," she began, her voice high and querulous, but then she faltered and her expression changed. "But where's Admiral?" she said. "And whose dog is *that*?"

In the course of her life, short though it had been, she'd known her share of embittered people—her father, for one; her mother, for another—and she'd promised herself she'd never go there, never descend to that hopeless state of despair and regret that ground you down till you were nothing but raw animus, but increasingly now everything she thought or felt or tasted was bitter to the root. Erhard was gone. The Strikers were inflexible. Her mother lingered. Admiral reigned supreme. When the car had come up the drive and Gretchen had stood there confronting her, she'd never felt lower in her life. Until Admiral began howling in the distance and then broke free of Erhard to come careening round the corner of the house and launch himself in one wholly coordinated and mighty leap right into the arms of his protector. And then Erhard appeared, head bowed and shoulders slumped, looking abashed.

"I don't think I've had the pleasure," Gretchen said, setting down the dog (which sprang right up again, this time at Erhard) and at the same time shooting Nisha a look before stepping forward and extending her hand.

"Oh, this is, uh, Erhard," she heard herself say. "He's from Switzerland, and I, well, I just met him in the dog park and since he had an Afghan too—"

Erhard was miserable, as miserable as she'd ever seen him, but he mustered a counterfeit of his smile and said, "Nice to meet you," even as Gretchen dropped his hand and turned to Nisha.

"Well, it's a nice idea," she said, looking down at the dogs, comparing them, "—good for you for taking the initiative, Nisha . . . but really, you have to know that Admiral didn't have any—*playmates*—here on the property, Afghans or no, and I'm sure he wasn't exposed to anybody from *Switzerland,* if you catch my drift?"

There was nothing Nisha could do but nod her acquiescence.

"So," Gretchen said, squaring her shoulders and turning back to Erhard.

"Nice to meet you," she said, "but I'm going to have to ask that you take your dog—what's his name?"

Erhard ducked his head. "Fred."

"Fred? What an odd name. For a dog, I mean. His does have papers, doesn't he?"

"Oh, yes, he's of the highest order, very well-bred."

Gretchen glanced dubiously down at the dog, then back at Erhard. "Yes, well, he looks it," she said, "and they do make great dogs, Afghans—we ought to know. I don't know if Nisha told you, but Admiral is very special, very, very special, and we can't have any other dogs on the property. And I don't mean to be abrupt"—a sharp look for Nisha—"but strangers of any sort, or species, just cannot be part of this, this . . ." she trailed off, fighting, at the end, to recover the cold impress of her smile. "Nice meeting you," she repeated, and there was nowhere to go from there.

It had taken Nisha a while to put it all behind her. She kept thinking Erhard was lying low, that he'd be back, that there had been something between them after all, but by the end of the second week she no longer looked for him at the gate or at the dog park or anywhere else. And very slowly, as the days beat on, she began to understand what her role was, her true role. Admiral chased his tail and she encouraged him. When he did his business along the street, she nudged the hard little bolus with the tip of her shoe till he stooped to take it up in his mouth. Yes, she was living in the past and her mother was dying and she'd gone to college for nothing, but she was determined to create a new future—for herself and Admiral—and when she took him to the dog park she lingered outside the gate, to let him run free where he really wanted to be, out there on the street where the cars shunted by and the wheels spun and stalled and caught the light till there was nothing else in the world. "Good boy," she'd say. "Good boy."

(2005)

Ash Monday

He'd always loved the smell of gasoline. It reminded him of when he was little, when he was seven or eight and Grady came to live with them. When Grady moved in he'd brought his yellow Chevy Super Sport with him, backing it into the weeds by the side of the garage on a sleek black trailer he must have rented for the day because it was gone in the morning. That first night had fallen over Dill like an absence, like all the nights then and most of the days too, a whole tumble of nothing that sparked with a particle of memory here and there. But he remembered the trailer, and Grady—of course he remembered Grady because Grady was here in this house till he was eleven years old—and he remembered seeing the car mounted on cement blocks the next morning as if it had gone through a wall at a hundred miles an hour and got hung up on the rubble. And he remembered the smell of gasoline. Grady wore it like perfume.

Now Dill was thirteen, with a car of his own, or at least the one he'd have when he was old enough to get his learner's permit, and when he tried to picture Grady, what Grady looked like, he could see Grady's hat, the grease-feathered baseball cap that had a #4 and a star sign on it in a little silver box in front, and he could see Grady's silver shades beneath the bill of that cap, and below that there must have been a nose and a mouth but all he could remember was the mustache that hooked down over the corners of Grady's lips, making him look like the sad face Billy Bottoms used to draw on every available surface when they were in fifth grade.

At the moment, he was in the yard, smelling gasoline, thinking of Grady, looking at his own piece-of-shit car parked there by the garage where the Super Sport had sunk into its cement blocks till his mother had it towed away to the junkyard. He felt the weight of the gas can in his hand, lifted his face to the sun and the hot breath sifting through the canyon, but for just a fraction of a second he forgot what he was doing there, as if he'd gone outside of himself. This was a thing that happened to him, that had always happened to him, another kind of absence that was so usual he hardly noticed it. It irritated his mother. Baffled his teachers. He wished it wouldn't happen or happen so often, but there it was. He was a dreamer, he guessed. That was what his mother called him. A dreamer.

And here came her voice through the kitchen window, her caught-high-in-the-throat voice that snapped like the braided tail of a whip: "Dill, what are you doing standing there? The potatoes are almost done. I need you to light the fire and put up the meat *right this minute*!"

His mother was a teacher. His father didn't exist. His grandmother was dead. And this house, high in the canyon with bleached boulders all around it like the big toes of a hundred buried giants, was his grandmother's house. And his piece-of-shit '97 Toyota Camry with no front bumper, two seriously rearranged fenders and the sun-blistered paint that used to be metallic gold but had turned the color of a fresh dog turd, was his grandmother's car. But then she didn't need a car, not where she was now. And where was that? he'd asked his mother in the hush of the back room at the funeral parlor where they'd burned up his grandmother and made her fit into a squared-off cardboard box. "You know," his mother said. "You know where she is." And he'd said, "Yeah, I know where she is—in that box right there."

So he felt a little thrill. He had a can of gasoline in his hand. He was the man of the house—"You're my man now," his mother had told him when he was eleven years old and Grady's face swelled up like a soccer ball from all the screaming and fuck-you's and fuck-you-too's before he slammed out the door and disappeared for good—and it was his job to light the fire and grill the meat. Every night. Even in winter when the rains came and it was cold and he had to wear his hoodie and watch the flames from under the overhang on the garage. That was all right. He had nothing better to do. And he liked the way the charcoal went up in a flash that sucked the life out of the air after he'd soaked it with gasoline, a thing his mother had expressly forbidden him to do (*It could explode, you know that, don't you?*), but they were out of charcoal lighter and the store was way down the snaking road at the bottom of the canyon and for the past week this was the way he'd done it.

The grill was an old iron gas thing shaped like a question mark with the dot cut off the bottom. The tank was still attached, but it had been empty for years and they just dumped briquettes in on top of the chunks of ancient pumice that were like little burned-up asteroids sent down from space and went ahead and cooked that way. He set down the can, patted the front pocket of his jeans to feel the matches there. Then he lifted the iron lid and let it rest back on its hinges, and he was just bending to the bag of charcoal when he saw something move beneath the slats of the grill. He was startled, his first thought for the snakes coming down out of the chaparral because of the drought, but this was no snake—it was a rat. A stupid dun-colored little thing with a wet black eye and cat's whiskers peering up at him from the gap between two slats, and what was it thinking? That it would be safe in a cooking grill? That it could build a nest in there? He slammed the lid down hard and heard the thing scrambling around in the ashes.

He could feel a quick pulse of excitement coming up in him. He glanced over his shoulder to make sure his mother wasn't watching through the screen door, and he snatched one quick look at the blank stucco wall and sun-glazed windows of the house next door—Itchy-goro's house, Itchy-goro, with his gook face and gook eyes and his big liar's mouth—and then he cracked the lid of the grill just enough to slosh some gasoline inside before slamming it shut. He started counting off the seconds, *one-a-thousand, two-a-thousand,* and there was no sound now, nothing but silence. And when he struck the match and flung it in he felt the way he did when he was alone in his room watching the videos he hid from his mother, making himself hard and then soft and then hard again.

Sanjuro Ichiguro was standing at the picture window, admiring the way the light sifted through the pale yellow-green leaves of the bamboo he'd planted along the pathway to the front door and down the slope to the neighbors' yard. This was a variety of bamboo called Buddha's Belly, for the plump swellings between its joints, perfect for poor soils and dry climates, and he fed and watered it sparingly, so as to produce the maximal swelling. He'd planted other varieties too—the yellow groove, the marbled, the golden—but Buddha's Belly was his favorite because his father had prized it and it reminded him of home. He didn't care so much about the cherry trees on the east side of the house—they were almost a cliché—but Setsuko had insisted on them. If they were going to have to live so far away from home—*Six thousand miles!* she'd kept repeating, riding a tide of woe as they packed and shipped their things and said goodbye to their families in Okutama nearly a decade ago—then she wanted at least to make this house and this sun-blasted yard into something beautiful, something *Japanese* set down amidst the scrub oak and manzanita. He'd hired a carpenter to erect the *torii* to frame her view of the cherry trees and a pair of Mexican laborers to dig a little jigsaw pond out front so she could rest there in the late afternoon and watch the koi break the surface while the lily pads revealed their flowers and the dragonflies hovered and he sat entombed in the steel box of the car, stuck in traffic.

From the kitchen came the smell of dinner—garlic, green onions, sesame oil. His commute from Pasadena had been murder, nearly two hours when it should have been half of that, but some idiot had plowed into the back end of another idiot and then a whole line of cars joined in the fun and the freeway was down to one lane by the time he got there. But he was home now and the light was exquisite, the air was rich with whatever it was Setsuko was preparing and in his hand he held a glass of Onikoroshi, chilled to perfection. He was remembering the pond, the old one, the one he'd made too shallow so that the raccoons had wallowed in it at night and made sashimi of the koi that had cost him a small fortune because he wanted to establish a breeding stock and his salary at JPL allowed him the freedom to purchase the very best of everything.

The raccoons. They were a hazard of living up here, he supposed. Like the coyotes that had made off with Setsuko's cat while she was standing right in front of the house, not ten feet away, watering the begonias. And that bird. A great long-legged thing that might have been a stork but for the pewter glaze of its feathers. He'd come out one morning at dawn to get a head start on the traffic, his car keys dangling from one hand, his lucky ceramic mug and a thermos of green tea in the other, only to see it there up to its knees in the pond, his marble-white *purachina ogon* clasped between the twin levers of its bill as neatly as if the bird were an animated pair of chopsticks, *hashi* with legs and wings. That was his metaphor. His joke. And he used it on his colleagues at work, the whole story, from the snatching of the fish to his outraged shout to the bird's startled flapping as it wrote its way across the sky, refining it in the telling till the fact that the fish had cost him sixteen hundred dollars only underscored the hilarity—he even called Setsuko from his cell on the way home and told her too: *Hashi with wings.*

Suddenly his eyes were drawn to the neighboring yard, to a drift of movement there, and he felt the smallest tick of irritation. It was that kid, that boy, the one who'd insulted him to his face. And what was he up to now? The grill, the nightly ritual with the grill, and why couldn't the mother cook in the oven like anyone else? These weren't feudal times. They weren't cavemen, were they? He raised the glass to his nose to feel the cold rim of it there and inhale the scent of his sake. He took a sip, then another long sniff, and it calmed him. This was the scent of pleasure, of unwinding after work, of civility, the scent of a country where people would never dream of calling their next-door neighbor a gook motherfucker or anything else for that matter. And while he understood perfectly well the term motherfucker, its significance escaped him, unless it had to do with incest or some infantile fixation with marital sex, in which case the preponderance of men were indeed motherfuckers. But it was the gook part of the equation that truly mystified him. Colin Andrews, at work, had flinched when Sanjuro had asked him its meaning, but then put on the bland frozen-eyed look Americans assumed when confronting racial issues and explained that it was a derogatory term for the Vietnamese deriving from the war there in the sixties, but that had only further confused him. How could this boy, even if he was mentally deficient—and he was, he was sure of it—ever confuse him, a Japanese, with one of those spindly little underfed peasants from Vietnam?

Angry now, angry all at once, he called over his shoulder to Setsuko. "He's at it again."

Her face appeared in the kitchen doorway, round as the moon. He saw that she'd had her hair done, two waves cresting on either side of her brow and an elevated dome built up on top of it. She looked almost like an American, like a *gaijin*, and he didn't know whether he liked that or not. "Who?" she asked in Japanese—they always spoke Japanese at home.

"The kid next door. The delinquent. The little shit. Now he's using gasoline to cook his hot dogs or hamburgers or whatever it is, can you imagine?"

She glanced at the window, but from where she was standing the angle was wrong so that she must have seen only the sky and the tips of the bamboo waving in the breeze. If she'd taken five steps forward, she could have seen what he was talking about, the kid dancing round the rusted grill with the red-and-yellow gas can and his box of kitchen matches, but she didn't. "Do you like my hair?" she said. "I went to Mrs. Yamamura at the beauty parlor today and she thought we would try something different. Just for a change. Do you like it?"

"Maybe I should donate a box of lighter fluid—just leave it on the front porch. Because if he keeps this up he's going to burn the whole canyon down, I tell you that."

"It's nothing. Don't let it worry you."

"Nothing? You call this nothing? Wait till your cherry trees go up in smoke, the house, the cars, wait till the fish boil in the pond like it's a pot on the stove, then tell me it's nothing."

The kid struck the match, pulled back the lid and flung it in. There was the muffled concussion of the gasoline going up, flames leaping high off the grill in a jagged corona before sucking themselves back in, and something else, something shooting out like the tail of a rocket and jerking across the ground in a skirt of fire.

It was the coolest thing he'd ever seen. The rat came flying out of there squealing like the brakes on the Camry and before he had a chance to react it was rolling in the dirt, and then, still aflame, trying to bury itself in the high weeds in back of the garage. And then the weeds caught fire. Which was intense. And he was running after the thing with the vague intent of crushing its skull under the heel of his shoe or maybe watching to see how long it would take before it died on its own, when here came Itchy-goro flying down the hill like he was on drugs, screaming, "You crazy? You crazy outta your mind?"

The weeds hissed and popped, burrs and stickers mainly, a few tumbleweeds that were all air, the fire already burning itself out because there was nothing to feed it but dirt and gravel. And the rat was just lying there now, blackened and steaming like a marshmallow that's fallen off the stick and into the coals. But Itchy-goro—he was in his bathrobe and slippers and he had a rake in his hand—jumped over the fence and started beating at the weeds as if he were trying to kill a whole field full of rattlesnakes. Dill just stood there while Itchy-goro cursed in his own language and snatched up the hose that was lying by the side of the garage and sprayed water all over everything like it was some big deal. Then he heard the door slam behind him and he looked over his shoulder to see his mother running toward them in her bare feet and he had a fleeting image of the harsh deep lines that dug in around her toes that were swollen and red from where her shoes pinched her because she was on her feet all day long. "Can't you get up and get the milk?" she'd say. Or "I'm too exhausted to set the table, can't you do it?" And then the kicker: "I've been on my feet all day long."

Itchy-goro's face was twisted out of shape. He looked like one of the dupes in a ninja movie, one of the ten thousand anonymous grimacing fools who rush Jet Li with a two-by-four or tire iron only to be whacked in the throat or the knee and laid out on the ground. "You see?" he was shouting. "You see what he does? Your boy?" Itchy-goro's hands were trembling. He couldn't seem to get the hose right, the water arcing up to spatter the wall of the garage, then drooling down to puddle in the dust. The air stank of incinerated weed.

Before his mother could put on her own version of Itchy-goro's face and say "What on earth are you doing now?" Dill kicked at a stone in the dirt, put his hands on his hips and said, "How was I supposed to know a rat was in there? A rat, Mom. A rat in our cooking grill."

But she took Itchy-goro's side, the two of them yelling back and forth—"Dry tinder!" Itchy-goro kept saying—and pretty soon they were both yelling at him. So he gave his mother a look that could peel hide and stalked off around the corner of the garage and didn't even bother to answer when she called his name out in her shrillest voice three times in a row.

He kept going till he came to the shed where Grady used to keep the chinchillas, and then he went round that too and pushed his way through the door that was hanging by one hinge and into the superheated shadows within. She could cook her own pork chops, that was what he was thinking. Let her give them to Itchy-goro. She always took his side anyway. Why didn't she just go ahead and marry him? That's what he'd say to her later when he was good and ready to come in and eat something and listen to her rag on him about his homework: "Marry Itchy-goro if you love him so much."

It took him a moment, standing slumped in the half-light and breathing in the shit smell of the chinchillas that would probably linger there forever like the smell of the bandages they wrapped the mummies in, before he felt his heartbeat begin to slow. He was sweating. It must have been twenty degrees hotter in there than outside, but he didn't care. This was where he came when he was upset or when he wanted to think or remember what it had been like when Grady was raising the chinchillas and they'd had to work side by side to keep the cages clean and make sure there was enough food and water for each and every one of them. You needed between eighty and a hundred pelts to make one coat, so Grady would always go on about how they had to keep breeding them to get more and more or they'd never turn a profit. That was his phrase, turn a profit. And Dill remembered how his mother would throw it back at him because he wasn't turning a profit and never would, the cost of feed and the animals themselves a constant drain—and that was her phrase—but nothing compared to what they were spending on air-conditioning.

"They've got to be kept cool," Grady insisted.

"What about us?" his mother would say. "We can't afford to run the air-conditioning in the house—you jump down my throat every time I switch it on as if it was some kind of crime—but god forbid your precious rodents should do without it."

"You've got to have patience, Gloria. Any business—"

"Business? You call sitting around in an air-conditioned shed all day a business? How many coats have you made, tell me that? How many pelts have you sold? How many have you even harvested? Tell me that."

Dill was on Grady's side and he never even thought twice about it. His mother didn't know anything. Chinchillas were from South America, high in the Andes Mountains where the temperature was in the cool range and never went over eighty degrees, not even on the hottest day in history. At eighty degrees they'd die of heatstroke. She didn't know that. Or she didn't care. But Dill knew it. And he knew how to feed them their chinchilla pellets and the little cubes of hay, but no cabbage or corn or lettuce because it would give them gas and they would bloat up and die. He knew how to kill them too. Grady showed him. What you did was pull the chinchilla out of its cage by the tail and then take hold of its head in one hand and give the back legs a jerk to break the neck. Then it twitched for a while. Then you skinned it out. Grady didn't like to kill them—they were cute, they were harmless, he didn't like to kill anything—but it was a business and you had to keep sight of that.

That fall, the Santa Ana winds had begun to blow. Dill's science teacher, Mr. Shields, had explained it to them—how, when a high-pressure system built up inland and low pressure settled in over the ocean, all the air got sucked down from the deserts and squeezed through the canyons in gusts of wind that were clocked at as much as a hundred miles an hour, drying everything to the bone—but Dill knew the wind as something more immediate. He felt it in the grit between his teeth, the ring of dirt in his nostrils in the morning. And he could taste it when he was out in the backyard, the whole world baking like the pizza ovens at Giovanni's, only instead of pizza it was sage they were baking, it was the leaves from the sycamore trees along the dried-up streambed and the oil of the poison oak that was everywhere. He came home from school one afternoon and the wind was so strong it shook the bus when he stepped off it. Immediately a fistful of sand raked his face just as if it had been blasted out of a shotgun, and somebody—Billy Bottoms, most likely—shouted "Sucker!" as the doors wheezed shut.

He turned his head to keep the dirt out of his eyes. Tumbleweeds catapulted across the yard. Scraps of paper and plastic bottles spewed from the trash can in a discontinuous stream, like water blown out of a sprinkler, and he could already hear his mother going on about how somebody had been too lazy and too careless to take one extra second to fasten the raccoon clamps on the lid. He pulled down the brim of his cap, the one Grady had given him, with the silver-and-black F-14 Tomcat on the crown, hiked up his backpack to get the weight off his spine, and went on up the walk and into the house.

In the kitchen, he poured himself a tall glass of root beer and drank it down in a gulp, never so thirsty in his life, then poured another one and took his time with it while his Hot Pocket sizzled in the microwave. He was planning on going out to the shed to see what Grady was doing, but first he flicked on the TV in the kitchen just to have something to do while he was eating, and there was nothing but news on. The news was on because everything was burning everywhere, from Malibu through the San Fernando Valley and into L.A. and Orange County too. On every channel there was a woman with a microphone and some seriously blowing hair standing in front of a burning house and trees gone up like candles—change the channel and all you did was change the color of the woman, blond, black, Mexican, Chinese. Mr. Shields had told them a wildfire could come at you faster than you could run and that was why firemen sometimes burned to death and homeowners too—which was why you had to evacuate when the police came round and told you to. But nobody believed him. How could fire go faster than somebody running all out? He thought of Daylon James, the fastest kid in the school—how nobody could even touch him in flag football, let alone swipe the flag—and the idea seemed preposterous. But there were helicopters on the screen now, the camera jumping from one angle to another, and then just the flames, sheets of them rippling from red to orange to yellow and back, and the black crown of the smoke.

He was picturing himself running as hard as he could through a field of burning bushes and trees as a whole mountain of fire came down on him, and he must have zoned out a minute because when he looked up the TV screen was blank and the LED display on the microwave had switched off. That was when Grady burst through the back door. "Quick," he said, and he was panting as if he couldn't catch his breath and his face wasn't Grady's face but the face of some crazy person in a horror flick in the instant before the monster catches up to him. "Grab all the ice you can. Quick! Quick!"

They ran out the back door with every scrap of ice from the ice maker in two black plastic bags and the bags rippled and sang with the wind and the dirt blew in their eyes and the door to the shed didn't want to open and when it did it tore back and slammed against the bleached-out boards like a giant fist. The shed was still cool inside, but the air-conditioning was down—the power was out, through the whole canyon—and already the chinchillas were looking stressed. He and Grady went down all four rows of cages, cages stacked three high with newspapers spread out on top of each row to catch the turds from the cages above, tossing ice cubes inside. Half an hour later, it was up to seventy-eight in the shed and Grady, his eyes jumping in his face like two yellow jackets on a piece of meat, said, "I'm going to make a run down the canyon for ice. You stay here and, I don't know, take off your shirt and fan them, anything to work up some breeze, and maybe run the hose over the roof and the walls, you know? Just to cool it a little. All we need is a little till the sun goes down and we'll be all right."

But they weren't all right. Even though Grady came back with the trunk of the Camry packed full of ice, thirty bags or more, and they filled the cages with the little blue-white machine-made cubes and draped wet sheets over everything, the heat kept rising. Till it was too hot. Till the chinchillas got heatstroke, one after another. First the standard grays started to die, then the mosaics and the black velvets that were worth twice as much. Grady kept reviving them with ice packs he squeezed around their heads till they came to and wobbled across their cages, but the electricity didn't come back on and the ice melted and the sun didn't seem to want to go down that day because it was a sci-fi sun, big and fat and red, and it wanted only to dry out everything in creation. By the time Dill's mother got back from school—"Sorry I'm late; the meeting just dragged on and on"—the chinchillas were dead, all dead, two hundred and seventeen of them. And the shed smelled the way it still smelled now. Like piss. And shit. And death.

It was a thing they did on Fridays, after work, he and some of his colleagues who tracked CloudSat, the satellite that collected data on global cloud formations for the benefit of meteorologists worldwide, not to mention the local weatherman. They met at a sushi bar in Pasadena, one of those novelty places for *gaijin* featuring a long oval bar with the chefs in the middle and a flotilla of little wooden boats circling around in a canal of fresh-flowing water from which you plucked one plate or another from the passing boats till the saucers mounted up and the Filipino busboy slid them into his wet plastic tub. It wasn't authentic. And it wasn't good, or not particularly. But you could special-order if you liked (which he always did, depending on what the head chef told him was best that day), and, of course, the beer and sake never stopped coming. Sanjuro had already put away two sakes and he was thinking about ordering a beer—or splitting one with Colin, because he was going to have to switch to tea eventually, to straighten himself out for the drive home. He gazed absently down the bar, past his co-workers and the mob of other people crowding in to ply their chopsticks and drip cheap sake into their little ceramic cups as if it were some exotic rite, and saw how the sun took the color out of everything beyond the windows. The cars were white with it, the trees black. What was he doing here?

Colin turned to him then and said, "Isn't that right, Sange?"

They'd been discussing sports, the usual topic, before they moved on to women, and, inevitably, work. Sanjuro hated sports. And he hated to be called Sange. But he liked Colin and Dick Wurzengreist and Bill Chen, good fellows all, and he liked being here with them, even if he was feeling the effects of the sake on a mostly empty stomach—or maybe because he was. "What?" he heard himself say. "Isn't what right?"

Colin's face hung there above half a dozen saucers smeared with soya and a bottle of Asahi with a quarter inch of beer left in it. He was grinning. His eyes looked blunted. "SC," he said. "They're thirty-five-point favorites over Stanford, can you believe it? I mean, how clueless do you have to be not to bet against the spread—am I right?"

There was something like merriment in the drawn-down slits of Dick Wurzengreist's eyes—Dick was drunk—but Bill Chen was involved in a conversation about alternate-side-of-the-street parking with the woman seated beside him and everyone knew the question was for show only, part of a long-standing joke at Sanjuro's expense. They were all what the average person would call nerds, but it seemed that Sanjuro was the prince of the nerds simply because he didn't care two pennies for sports. "Yes," he said, and he wanted to flash a smile but couldn't seem to summon the energy, "you're absolutely right."

Everyone had a laugh over that, and he didn't mind—it was part of the routine—and then the beer came and things quieted down and Colin began to talk about work. Or not work, so much as gossip revolving around work, how so-and-so kept a bottle in his desk and how another had tested positive for marijuana and then slammed into a deer right out front of the gate, that sort of thing. Sanjuro listened in silence. He was a good listener. But he was bored with gossip and shoptalk too, and when Colin paused to top off both their glasses, he said, "You know that kid I was telling you about? The one that called me a gook?"

"A gook motherfucker," Colin corrected.

"Well, you know how the wind's been blowing, especially in the canyon—and I told you how the mother sends the kid out there every night to start up the grill?"

Colin nodded. His eyes were like the lenses of a camera, the pupils narrowing and then dilating: click. He was drunk. He'd have to call his wife to drive him home again, Sanjuro could see that. And he himself would soon have to push the beer aside and gear himself up for the freeway.

"You know it's been gasoline all week, as if they couldn't afford charcoal lighter, and I tell you last night he nearly blew the thing up."

Colin let out a short bark of a laugh before he seemed to realize that it wasn't funny, that Sanjuro hadn't meant to be funny, not at all—that he was worried, deeply concerned, nearly hysterical over it and right on the verge of calling the police. Or the fire department, Sanjuro was thinking. The fire marshal. Wasn't there a fire marshal?

"And there was a rat in it, in the grill, and he set the rat on fire."

"A rat? You're joking, right?"

"No joke. The rat was like this flaming ball shooting across the driveway and right on into the weeds behind the garage."

"No," Colin said, because that was the required response. And then he grinned: "Let me guess," he said. "Then the weeds caught fire."

Sanjuro felt weary suddenly, as if an invisible force, cupped to fit round his back and his shoulders and arms like a custom-made suit, were pressing down on him with a weight he couldn't sustain. He was living at the top of a canyon, far from the city, in a high-risk area, because of Setsuko, because Setsuko was afraid of Americans, black Americans, Mexicans, whites too—all the people crowding the streets of Pasadena and Altadena and everyplace else. She watched the TV news, trying to learn the language, and it made her crazy. "I won't live in an apartment," she'd insisted. "I won't live with that kind of people. I want nature. I want to live where it's safe." She'd sacrificed for him in coming here, to this country, for his career, and so he'd sacrificed for her and they bought the house at the end of the road at the very top of a wild canyon and tried to make it just like a house in Mitaka or Okutama.

He paused to give Colin a long look, staring into the weed-green shutters of his eyes—Colin, his friend, his amigo, the man who understood him best of anyone on the team—and he let out a sigh that was deeper and moister and more self-pitying than he'd intended, because he never showed emotion, or never meant to. That wasn't the Japanese way. He looked down. Made his face conform. "Yeah," he said. "That's just what happened."

So tonight it was chicken—and three of those hot Italian sausages he liked, and a piece of fish, salmon with the skin still on it his mother had paid twelve dollars for because they were having a guest for dinner. One of the teachers who worked with her at the elementary school. "His name's Scott," she said. "He's a vegetarian."

It took him a moment to register the information: guest for dinner, teacher, vegetarian. "So what does he eat—spinach? Brussels sprouts? Bean burritos?"

She was busy at the stove. Her wine glass stood half-full on the baked enamel surface between the snow peas sautéing in the pan and the pot where she was boiling potatoes for her homemade potato salad. He could see the smudge of her lipstick on the near side of the glass and he could see through it to the broken clock set in its display above the burners and the shining chrome-framed window on the door of the oven that didn't work anymore because the handle had broken off and there was no way to turn it on, even with a pair of pliers. "Fish," she said, swiveling to give him a look over her shoulder, "he eats fish."

She'd come straight home from school that afternoon, showered, changed her clothes and run the vacuum over the rug in the living room. Then she'd set the table and stuck an empty vase in the middle of it—"He'll bring flowers, you wait and see: that's the kind of person he is, very thoughtful"—and then she'd started chopping things up for a green salad and rinsing the potatoes. Dill was afraid she was going to add, "You're really going to like him," but she didn't and so he didn't say anything either, though after the fish comment he'd thought about pitching his voice into the range of sarcasm and asking, "So is this a date?"

Her last words to him as he slammed out the door with the platter of meat, the matches and the plastic squeeze bottle of lighter fluid that had appeared magically on the doorstep that morning, were, "Don't burn the fish. And don't overcook it either."

He was in the yard. The wind had died, but now it came up again, rattling things, chasing leaves across the driveway and up against the piece-of-shit Toyota, where they gathered with yesterday's leaves and the leaves from last week and the week before that. For a long moment he just stood there, halfway to the grill, feeling the wind, smelling it, watching the way the sun pushed through the air one layer after another and the big bald rock at the top of the canyon seemed to ripple and come clear again. Then he went to the grill, set down the platter of chicken and sausage and the fat red oblong slab of fish, and lifted the heavy iron lid, half-hoping there'd be another rat in there—or a snake, a snake would be even better. But of course there was nothing inside. It was just a grill, not a rat condo. Ash, that was all that was there, just ash.

The wind jumped over the garage then and the ash came to life, sifting out like the sand in *The Mummy Returns,* and that was cool and he let it happen because here was the grill, cleaning itself. And while that was happening and the meat sat there on its platter and the plastic container squeezed in and out like a cold nipple in his hand, he was back in school, last spring, and Billy Bottoms, who wasn't scared of anybody or ever showed any weakness or even a flaw—not a single zit, nothing—had a black thumbprint right in the middle of his forehead. It was an amazing thing, as if Billy had turned Hindu overnight, and Dill couldn't resist calling him out on it. Or no, he didn't call him out on it. He came up behind him and wrestled one arm around his neck, and before Billy knew what was happening Dill had touched his own thumb to the mark there and his thumb came away black. Billy punched him in the side of the head and he punched back and they both got sent to the office and his mother had to come pick him up after detention because there was no late bus and it was your hard luck—part of your punishment—to have to have your mother come for you. Or your father.

Her face was set. She didn't ask, not right away. She was trying to be understanding, trying to make small talk so as not to start in on him before they could both have a minute to calm themselves, so he just came out and said, "He had this spot of ash on his forehead. Like a Hindu, like in *Indiana Jones and the Temple of Doom.* I wanted to see what it was, that was all."

"So? A lot of kids in my class had it too. It's Ash Wednesday." She gave him a glance over the steering wheel. "They're Catholic. It's a Catholic thing."

"But we're not Catholic," he said. There were only seven cars left in the parking lot. He counted them.

"No," she said, shaking her head but keeping her face locked up all the same.

"We're not anything, are we?"

She was busy with the steering wheel, maneuvering her own car, her Nissan Sentra that was only slightly better than the piece-of-shit Toyota, around the elevated islands that divided the parking lot. The radio gave up a soft hum and a weak voice bleated out one of the easy-listening songs she was always playing. She shook her head again. Let out an audible breath. Shrugged her shoulders. "I don't know. I believe in God, if that's what you're asking." He said nothing. "Your grandparents, my parents, I mean, were Presbyterian, but we didn't go to church much. Christmas, Easter. In name only, I guess."

"So what does that make me?"

Another shrug. "You can be anything you want. Why? Are you interested in religion?"

"I don't know."

"Well, you're a Protestant, then. That's all. Just a Protestant."

He was dumping more briquettes into the grill now, the wind teasing the black powder that wasn't ash off the hard-baked stony little things that weren't really charcoal at all. Then he was squirting them with the clear dry-smelling fluid that was nothing like gasoline with its heavy rich petroleum sweetness, soaking them down, thinking every day was made out of ash, Ash Monday, Ash Tuesday, Ash Saturday and Sunday too. He glanced up to see a car pulling into the driveway at the front of the house. The car door slammed, and a man his mother's age stepped out into the wind with an armload of flowers and a bottle that was probably wine or maybe whiskey. Dill looked to Itchy-goro's house, the windows painted over with sun so that he couldn't see whether Itchy-goro was watching or not, and then he lit the match.

It was a Monday and she hated Mondays most of all because on Mondays Sanjuro always went to work early to set an example for the others, stealing out of the house while it was dark yet and the little thieves of the night, the raccoons, coyotes and rats, were just crawling back into their holes. She'd awaken with the first colorless stirrings of light and lie there in the still room, thinking of her parents and the house she'd grown up in, and feel as if the ground had gone out from under her. This morning was no different. She woke to grayness and for a long while stared up at the ceiling as the color crept back into things, and then she pushed herself up and went down the hallway to the kitchen and lit the stove under the kettle. It wasn't till she was blowing softly into her second cup of tea and gazing out the window into the crowded green struts of the bamboo that she remembered that today was different, today was special: *Shūbun-no-hi,* the autumnal equinox, a holiday in Japan even if it passed unnoticed here.

Her spirits lifted. She would make *ohagi,* the rice balls coated in bean paste people left at the graves of their ancestors to honor the spirits of the dead, and she'd put on one of her best kimono and burn incense too, and when Sanjuro came home they'd have a quiet celebration and neither of them would mention the fact that the graves of their ancestors were six thousand miles away. She thought about that while she was in the shower—about that distance and how long a broom she'd have to find to sweep those graves clean—then she put on the rice and went outside to the garden. If she were in Japan she would have arranged flowers on her parents' graves—red flowers, the *Higanbana* of tradition—but here the closest thing she could find was the bougainvillea that grew along the fence.

The wind rattled the bamboo as she went down the slope with her clippers and the cedar-shake roof of the house below rose to greet her. This was the boy's house, and as she bent to cut the brilliant red plumes of the flowers and lay them over one arm, she saw the cooking grill there in the yard and thought back to two nights ago, or was it three? Sanjuro had been beside himself. He'd gone out of his way to buy a plastic squeeze bottle of starter fluid for these people, the boy and his mother, thinking to help them, and then the boy had stood out there in full view, looking up at the windows and smirking as he fed the fire with long iridescent strings of fuel till the strings were fire themselves. He wasn't thankful. He wasn't respectful. He was a bad boy, a delinquent, just as Sanjuro had said all along, and the mother was worse—and a teacher, no less. They were bad people, that was all, no different from the criminals on the news every night, stabbing each other, screaming, their faces opening up in one great maw of despair.

Setsuko felt the weight of the sun. A gust flailed the bamboo and flung grit at her face. She made her way back up the hill, the wind whipping her kimono and sawing at the canes till they were like swords clashing together, and there was wind drift all over the surface of the pond and the koi moiling beneath it like pulsing flames. The mouth of the brass urn took the flowers, a spray of them, and she went down on her knees to get the arrangement just right. But then the wind shifted them and shifted them again, the papery petals flapping against the bamboo that framed the pond, and after a while she gave it up, figuring she'd rearrange them when Sanjuro came home. She was thinking of her mother when she set the incense cone in the burner and put a match to it, the face of the ceramic Buddha glowing through its eye holes as if it were alive.

But the wind, the wind. She got up and was halfway to the house when she heard the first premonitory crackle in the leaves gathered like a skirt at the ankles of the bamboo. She jerked round so violently that her kimono twisted under one foot and she very nearly tripped herself. And she might have caught the fire then, might have dug a frantic scoop of water out of the pond and flung it into the bamboo, might have dashed into the house and dialed 911, but she didn't. She just stood there motionless as the wind took the flames out of the bamboo and into the yard, rolling on across the hill away from her house and her garden and her tea things and the memory of her mother to set them down in a brilliant sparking burst that was exactly like a fireworks display, cleansing and pure and joyful, on the roof of the house below.

(2007)

Thirteen Hundred Rats

There was a man in our village who never in his life had a pet of any kind until his wife died. By my calculation, Gerard Loomis was in his mid-fifties when Marietta was taken from him, but at the ceremony in the chapel he looked so scorched and stricken people mistook him for a man ten or twenty years older. He sat collapsed in the front pew, his clothes mismatched and his limbs splayed in the extremity of his grief, looking as if he'd been dropped there from a great height, like a bird stripped of its feathers in some aerial catastrophe. Once the funeral was over and we'd all offered up our condolences and gone back to our respective homes, rumors began to circulate. Gerard wasn't eating. He wouldn't leave the house or change his clothes. He'd been seen bent over a trash barrel in the front yard, burning patent leather pumps, brassieres, skirts, wigs, even the mink stole with its head and feet still attached that his late wife had worn with pride on Christmas, Easter and Columbus Day.

People began to worry about him, and understandably so. Ours is a fairly close-knit community of a hundred and twenty souls, give or take a few, distributed among some fifty-two stone-and-timber houses erected nearly a century ago in what the industrialist B.P. Newhouse hoped would be a model of Utopian living. We are not Utopians, at least not in this generation, but our village, set as it is in the midst of six hundred acres of dense forest at the end of a consummately discreet road some forty miles from the city, has fostered, we like to think, a closeness and uniformity of outlook you wouldn't find in some of the newer developments built right up to the edges of the malls, gallerias and factory outlets that surround them.

He should have a dog, people said. That sounded perfectly reasonable to me. My wife and I have a pair of shelties (as well as two lorikeets, whose chatter provides a tranquil backdrop to our evenings by the fireplace, and one very fat angelfish in a tank all his own on a stand in my study). One evening, at dinner, my wife glanced at me over her reading glasses and said, "Do you know that according to this article in the paper, ninety-three percent of pet owners say their pets make them smile at least once a day?" The shelties—Tim and Tim II—gazed up from beneath the table with wondering eyes as I fed scraps of meat into their mobile and receptive mouths.

"You think I ought to speak with him?" I said. "Gerard, I mean?"

"It couldn't hurt," my wife said. And then, the corners of her mouth sinking toward her chin, she added, "The poor man."

I went to visit him the next day—a Saturday, as it happened. The dogs needed walking, so I took them both with me, by way of example, I suppose, and because when I'm home—and not away on the business that takes me all over the world, sometimes for weeks or even months at a time—I like to give them as much attention as I can. Gerard's cottage was half a mile or so from our house, and I enjoyed the briskness of the season—it was early December, the holidays coming on, a fresh breeze spanking my cheeks. I let the dogs run free ahead of me and admired the way the pine forest B.P. Newhouse had planted all those years ago framed and sculpted the sky. The first thing I noticed on coming up the walk was that Gerard hadn't bothered to rake the leaves from his lawn or cover any of his shrubs against the frost. There were other signs of neglect: the storm windows weren't up yet, garbage overspilled the two cans in the driveway, and a pine bough, casualty of the last storm, lay across the roof of the house like the severed hand of a giant. I rang the bell.

Gerard was a long time answering. When finally he did come to the door, he held it open just a crack and gazed out at me as if I were a stranger. (And I was nothing of the sort—our parents had known each other, we'd played couples bridge for years and had once taken a road trip to Hyannis Port together, not to mention the fact that we saw each other at the lake nearly every day in the summer, shared cocktails at the clubhouse and basked in an air of mutual congratulation over our separate decisions not to complicate our lives with the burden of children.) "Gerard," I said. "Hello. How are you feeling?"

He said nothing. He looked thinner than usual, haggard. I wondered if the rumors were true—that he wasn't eating, wasn't taking care of himself, that he'd given way to despair.

"I was just passing by and thought I'd stop in," I said, working up a grin though I didn't feel much in the mood for levity and had begun to wish I'd stayed home and let my neighbor suffer in peace. "And look," I said, "I've brought Tim and Tim II with me." The dogs, hearing their names, drew themselves up out of the frost-blighted bushes and pranced across the doormat, inserting the long damp tubes of their snouts in the crack of the door.

Gerard's voice was hoarse. "I'm allergic to dogs," he said.

Ten minutes later, after we'd gone through the preliminaries and I was seated on the cluttered couch in front of the dead fireplace while Tim and Tim II whined from the front porch, I said, "Well, what about a cat?" And then, because I was mortified at the state to which he'd sunk—his clothes were grubby, he smelled, the house was like the lounge in a transient hotel—I found myself quoting my wife's statistic about smiling pet owners.

"I'm allergic to cats too," he said. He was perched uncomfortably on the canted edge of a rocker and his eyes couldn't seem to find my face. "But I understand your concern, and I appreciate it. And you're not the first—half a dozen people have been by, pushing one thing or another on me: pasta salad, a baked ham, profiteroles, and pets too. Siamese fighting fish, hamsters, kittens. Mary Martinson caught me at the post office the other day, took hold of my arm and lectured me for fifteen minutes on the virtues of emus. Can you believe it?"

"I feel foolish," I said.

"No, don't. You're right, all of you—I need to snap out of it. And you're right about a pet too." He rose from the chair, which rocked crazily behind him. He was wearing a stained pair of white corduroy shorts and a sweatshirt that made him look as gaunt as the Masai my wife and I had photographed on our safari to Kenya the previous spring. "Let me show you," he said, and he wound his way through the tumbling stacks of magazines and newspapers scattered round the room and disappeared into the back hall. I sat there, feeling awkward—was this what it would be like if my wife should die before me?—but curious too. And, in a strange way, validated. Gerard Loomis had a pet to keep him company: mission accomplished.

When he came back into the room, I thought at first he'd slipped into some sort of garish jacket or cardigan, but then I saw, with a little jolt of surprise, that he was wearing a snake. Or, that is, a snake was draped over his shoulders, its extremities dangling beyond the length of his arms. "It's a python," he said. "Burmese. They get to be twenty-five feet long, though this one's just a baby."

I must have said something, but I can't really recall now what it was. I wasn't a herpetophobe or anything like that. It was just that a snake wasn't what we'd had in mind. Snakes didn't fetch, didn't bound into the car panting their joy, didn't speak when you held a rawhide bone just above shoulder level and twitched it invitingly. As far as I knew, they didn't do much of anything except exist. And bite.

"So what do you think?" he said. His voice lacked enthusiasm, as if he were trying to convince himself.

"Nice," I said.

I don't know why I'm telling this story—perhaps because what happened to Gerard could happen to any of us, I suppose, especially as we age and our spouses age and we're increasingly set adrift. But the thing is, the next part of what I'm going to relate here is a kind of fiction, really, or a fictive reconstruction of actual events, because two days after I was introduced to Gerard's python—he was thinking then of naming it either Robbie or Siddhartha—my wife and I went off to Switzerland for an account I was overseeing there and didn't return for four months. In the interval, here's what happened.

There was a heavy snowfall the week before Christmas that year and for the space of nearly two days the power lines were down. Gerard woke the first morning to a preternaturally cold house and his first thought was for the snake. The man in the pet shop at the mall had given him a long lecture before he bought the animal. "They make great pets," he'd said. "You can let them roam the house if you want and they'll find the places where they're comfortable. And the nice thing is they'll come to you and curl up on the couch or wherever, because of your body heat, you understand." The man—he wore a nametag that read Bozeman and he looked to be in his forties, with a gray-flecked goatee and his hair drawn back in a patchily dyed ponytail—clearly enjoyed dispensing advice. As well he should, seeing that he was charging some four hundred dollars for a single reptile that must have been as common as a garden worm in its own country. "But most of all, though, especially in this weather, you've got to keep him warm. This is a tropical animal we're talking about here, you understand? Never—and I mean never—let the temperature fall below eighty."

Gerard tried the light on the nightstand, but it was out. Ditto the light in the hall. Outside, the snow fell in clumps, as if it had been preformed into snowballs somewhere high in the troposphere. In the living room, the thermostat read sixty-three degrees, and when he tried to click the heat on, nothing happened. The next thing he knew he was crumpling newspaper and stacking kindling in the fireplace, and where were the matches? A quick search round the house, everything a mess (and here the absence of Marietta bit into him, down deep, like a parasitical set of teeth), the drawers stuffed with refuse, dishes piled high, nothing where it was supposed to be. Finally he retrieved an old lighter from a pair of paint-stained jeans on the floor in the back of the closet and he had the fire going. Then he went looking for Siddhartha. He found the snake curled up under the kitchen sink where the hot water pipe fed into the faucet and dishwasher, but it was all but inanimate, as cold and slick as a garden hose left out in the frost.

It was also surprisingly heavy, especially for an animal that hadn't eaten in the two weeks it had been in the house, but he dragged it, stiff and frigid, from its cachette, and laid it before the fireplace. While he was making coffee in the kitchen, he gazed out the window on the tumble of the day, and thought of all those years he'd gone in to work in weather like this, in all weathers actually, and felt a stab of nostalgia. Maybe he should go back to work—if not in his old capacity, from which he was gratefully retired, then on a part-time basis, just to keep his hand in, just to get out of the house and do something useful. On an impulse he picked up the phone, thinking to call Alex, his old boss, and sound him out, but the phone line was down too.

Back in the living room, he sank into the couch with his coffee and watched the snake as it came slowly back to itself, its muscles shivering in slow waves from head to tail like a soft breeze trailing over a still body of water. By the time he'd had a second cup of coffee and fixed himself an egg on the gas range, the crisis—if that was what it was—had passed. Siddhartha seemed fine. He never moved much even in the best of times, with the heat on high and the electric blanket Gerard had bought for him draped across the big Plexiglas terrarium he liked to curl up in, and so it was difficult to say. Gerard sat there a long while, stoking the fire, watching the snake unfurl its muscles and flick the dark fork of its tongue, until a thought came to him: maybe Siddhartha was hungry. When Gerard had asked the pet shop proprietor what to feed him, Bozeman had answered, "Rats." Gerard must have looked dubious, because the man had added, "Oh, I mean you can give him rabbits when he gets bigger, and that's a savings really, in time and energy, because you won't have to feed him as often, but you'd be surprised—snakes, reptiles in general, are a lot more efficient than we are. They don't have to feed the internal furnace all the time with filet mignon and hot fudge sundaes, and they don't need clothes or fur coats either." He paused to gaze down at the snake where it lay in its terrarium, basking under a heat lamp. "I just fed this guy his rat yesterday. You shouldn't have to give him anything for a week or two anyway. He'll let you know."

"How?" Gerard had asked.

A shrug. "Could be a color thing, where you notice his pattern isn't as bright maybe. Or he's just, I don't know, what you'd call lethargic."

They'd both looked down at the snake then, its eyes like two pebbles, its body all but indistinguishable from the length of rough wood it was stretched out on. It was no more animate than the glass walls of the terrarium and Gerard wondered how anyone, even an expert, could tell if the thing was alive or dead. Then he wrote the check.

But now he found himself chafing at the cusp of an idea: the snake needed to be fed. Of course it did. It had been two weeks—why hadn't he thought of it before? He was neglecting the animal and that wasn't right. He got up from the couch to close off the room and build up the fire, then went out to shovel the driveway and take the car down the long winding community road to the highway and on into Newhouse and the mall. It was a harrowing journey. Trucks threw blankets of slush over the windshield and the beating of the wipers made him dizzy. When he arrived, he was relieved to see that the mall had electricity, the whole place lit up like a Las Vegas parade for the marketing and selling of all things Christmas, and with a little deft maneuvering he was able to wedge his car between a plowed drift and the handicapped space in front of the pet store.

Inside, Pets & Company smelled of nature in the raw, every creature in every cage and glassed-in compartment having defecated simultaneously, just to greet him, or so he imagined. The place was superheated. He was the only customer. Bozeman was up on a footstool, cleaning one of the aquariums with a vacuum tube. "Hey, man," he said, his voice a high singsong, "Gerard, right? Don't tell me." He reached back in a practiced gesture to smooth down his ponytail as if he were petting a cat or a ferret. "You need a rat. Am I right?"

Gerard found himself fumbling round the answer, perhaps because the question had been put so bluntly—or was it that Bozeman had become clairvoyant in the instant? "Well," he heard himself say, and he might have made a joke, might have found something amusing or at least odd in the transaction, but he didn't because Marietta was dead and he was depressed, or so he reminded himself, "I guess so."

The rat—he didn't see it; Bozeman had gone into the back room to fetch it—came in a cardboard container with a molded carrying handle on top, the sort of thing you got if you asked for a doggie bag at a restaurant. The animal was heavier than he'd expected, shifting its weight mysteriously from one corner of the box to another as he carried it out into the snow and set the box on the seat beside him. He turned on the fan after he'd started up the engine, to give it some heat—but then it was a mammal, he figured, with fur, and it didn't have as much of a need because it could warm itself. And in any case it was dinner, or soon to be. The roads were slick. Visibility was practically zero. He crawled behind the snowplow all the way back to Newhouse Gardens and when he came in the door he was pleased to see that the fire was still going strong.

All right. He set down the box and then dragged the python's terrarium across the floor from the bedroom to the living room and set it to one side of the fireplace. Then he lifted the snake—it was noticeably warm to the touch on the side that had been closest to the fire—and laid it gently in the terrarium. For a moment it came to life, the long run of muscles tensing, the great flat slab of the head gearing round to regard him out of its stony eyes, and then it was inert again, dead weight against the Plexiglas floor. Gerard bent cautiously to the rat's box—would it spring out, bite him, scrabble away across the floor to live behind the baseboard forever as in some cartoon incarnation?—and, with his heart pounding, lowered the box into the terrarium and opened the lid.

The rat—it was white, with pink eyes, like the lab rats he'd seen arrayed in their cages in the biology building when he was a student—slid from the box like a lump of gristle, then sat up on its haunches and began cleaning itself as if it were the most natural thing in the world to be transported in a doggie bag and dumped into a glass-walled cavern in the presence of a tongue-flicking reptile. Which might or might not be hungry.

For a long while, nothing happened. Snow ticked at the windows, the fire sparked and settled. And then the snake moved ever so slightly, the faintest shifting of the bright tube of its scales, energy percolating from the deepest core of its musculature, and suddenly the rat stiffened. All at once it was aware of the danger it was in. It seemed to shrink into itself, as if by doing so it could somehow become invisible. Gerard watched, fascinated, wondering how the rat—reared in some drowsy pet warehouse, slick and pink and suckling at its mother's teats in a warm gregarious pack of its pink siblings, generations removed from the wild and any knowledge of a thing like this snake and its shining elongate bulk—could recognize the threat. Very slowly, by almost imperceptible degrees, the snake lifted its head from the Plexiglas floor, leveling on the rat like a sculpture come to life. Then it struck, so quickly Gerard nearly missed it, but the rat, as if it had trained all its life for just this moment, was equal to it. It sprang over the snake's head in a single frantic leap and shot to the farthest corner of the terrarium, where it began to emit a series of bird-like cries, all the while fastening its inflamed eyes on the white hovering face of Gerard. And what did he feel? He felt like a god, like a Roman emperor with the power of fatality in his thumb. The rat scrabbled at the Plexiglas. The snake shifted to close in on it.

And then, because he was a god, Gerard reached into the terrarium and lifted the rat up out of the reach of his python. He was surprised by how warm the animal was and how quickly it accommodated itself to his hand. It didn't struggle or try to escape but simply pressed itself against his wrist and the trailing sleeve of his sweater as if it understood, as if it were grateful. In the next moment he was cradling it against his chest, the pulse of its heart already slowing. He went to the couch and sank into it, uncertain what to do next. The rat gazed up at him, shivered the length of its body, and promptly fell asleep.

The situation was novel, to say the least. Gerard had never touched a rat in his life, let alone allowed one to curl up and sleep in the weave of his sweater. He watched its miniature chest rise and fall, studied the intricacy of its naked feet that were like hands, saw the spray of etiolated whiskers and felt the suppleness of the tail as it lay between his fingers like the suede fringe of the jacket he'd worn as a boy. The fire faltered but he didn't rise to feed it. When finally he got up to open a can of soup, the rat came with him, awake now and discovering its natural perch on his shoulder. He felt its fur like a caress on the side of his neck and then the touch of its whiskers and fevered nose. It stood on its hind legs and stretched from his lap to the edge of the table as he spooned up his soup by candlelight, and he couldn't resist the experiment of extracting a cube of potato from the rich golden broth and feeding it into the eager mincing mouth. And then another. And another. When he went to bed, the rat came with him, and if he woke in the dark of the night—and he did, twice, three times—he felt its presence beside him, its spirit, its heart, its heat, and it was no reptile, no cold thankless thing with a flicking tongue and two dead eyes, but a creature radiant with life.

The house was very cold when he woke to the seeping light of morning. He sat up in bed and looked round him. The face of the clock radio was blank, so the electricity must still have been down. He wondered about that, but when he pushed himself up and set his bare feet on the floor, it was the rat he was thinking of—and there it was, nestled in a fold of the blankets. It opened its eyes, stretched and then climbed into the palm he offered it, working its way up inside the sleeve of his pajamas until it was balanced on his shoulder. In the kitchen, he turned on all four gas burners and the oven too and shut off the room to trap the heat. It wasn't until the kettle began to boil that he thought about the fireplace—and the snake stretched out in its terrarium—but by then it was too late.

He returned to the pet store the following day, reasoning that he might as well convert the snake's lair into a rat's nest. Or no, that didn't sound right—that was what his mother used to call his boyhood room; he'd call it a rat apartment. A rat hostel. A rat—Bozemen grinned when he saw him. "Not another rat," he said, something quizzical in his eyes. "He can't want another one already, can he? But then with Burms you've got to watch for obesity—they'll eat anytime, whether they're hungry or not."

Even under the best of conditions, Gerard was not the sort to confide in people he barely knew. "Yes," was all he said, in answer to both questions. And then he added, "I may as well take a couple of them while I'm here." He looked away. "To save me the trip."

Bozeman wiped his hands on the khaki apron he wore over his jeans and came out from behind the cash register. "Sure," he said, "good idea. How many you want? They're six ninety-nine each."

Gerard shrugged. He thought of the rat at home, the snugness of it, the way it sprang across the carpet in a series of little leaps or shot along the baseboard as if blown by a hurricane wind, how it would take a nut in its hands and sit up to gnaw at it, how it loved to play with anything he gave it, a paper clip, an eraser, the ridged aluminum top of a Perrier bottle. In a moment of inspiration he decided to call it Robbie, after his brother in Tulsa. Robbie. Robbie the Rat. And Robbie needed company, needed playmates, just like any other creature. Before he could think, he said: "Ten?"

"Ten? Whoa, man, that is going to be one fat snake."

"Is that too many?"

Bozeman slicked back his ponytail and gave him a good long look. "Hell, no—I mean, I'll sell you all I've got if that's what you want, and everything else too. You want gerbils? Parakeets? Albino toads? I'm in business, you know—pets for sale. This is a pet shop, *comprende*? But I tell you, if that Burm doesn't eat them PDQ, you're going to see how fast these things breed. . . . I mean, the females can go into heat or whatever you want to call it at five weeks old. Five *weeks*." He shifted his weight and moved past Gerard, gesturing for him to follow. They stopped in front of a display of packaged food and brightly colored sacks of litter. "You're going to want Rat Chow," he said, handing him a ten-pound sack, "and a bag or two of these wood shavings." Another look. "You got a place to keep them?"

By the time he left the store, Gerard had two wire cages (with cedar plank flooring so the rats wouldn't contract bumblefoot, whatever that was), twenty pounds of rat food, three bags of litter and two supersized doggie bags with five rats in each. Then he was home and shutting the door to keep out the cold even as Robbie, emerging from beneath the pillows of the couch, humped across the floor to greet him and all the lights flashed on simultaneously.

It was mid-April by the time my wife and I returned from Switzerland. Tim and Tim II, who'd been cared for in our absence by our housekeeper, Florencia, were there at the door to greet us, acting out their joy on the doorstep and then carrying it into the living room with such an excess of animation it was all but impossible to get our bags in the door before giving them their treats, a thorough back-scratching and a cooed rehearsal of the little endearments they were used to. It was good to be home, back to a real community after all that time spent living in a sterile apartment in Basel, and what with making the rounds of the neighbors and settling back in both at home and at work, it wasn't till some weeks later that I thought of Gerard. No one had seen him, save for Mary Martinson, who'd run into him in the parking lot at the mall, and he'd refused all invitations to dinner, casual get-togethers, ice-skating on the lake, even the annual Rites of Spring fund-raiser at the clubhouse. Mary said he'd seemed distracted and that she'd tried to engage him in conversation, thinking he was still locked in that first stage of grieving and just needed a little nudge to get him on track again, but he'd been abrupt with her. And she didn't like to mention it, but he was unkempt—and he smelled worse than ever. It was startling, she said. Even outdoors, standing over the open trunk of his car, which was entirely filled, she couldn't help noticing, with something called Rat Chow, even with a wind blowing and a lingering chill in the air, he gave off a powerful reek of sadness and body odor. Someone needed to look in on him, that was her opinion.

I waited till the weekend, and then, as I'd done back in December, I took the dogs down the wide amicable streets, through the greening woods and over the rise to Gerard's cottage. The day was glorious, the sun climbing toward its zenith, moths and butterflies spangling the flower gardens, the breeze sweetened with a scent of the south. My neighbors slowed their cars to wave as they passed and a few people stopped to chat, their engines rumbling idly. Carolyn Porterhouse thrust a bouquet of tulips at me and a mysterious wedge-shaped package wrapped in butcher's paper, which proved to be an Emmentaler—"Welcome home," she said, her grin anchored by a layer of magenta lipstick—and Ed Saperstein stopped right in the middle of the road to tell me about a trip to the Bahamas he and his wife had taken on a chartered yacht. It was past one by the time I got to Gerard's.

I noticed right off that not much had changed. The windows were streaked with dirt, and the yard, sprouting weeds along the margins of the unmowed lawn, looked as neglected as ever. The dogs bolted off after something in the deep grass and I shifted the bouquet under one arm, figuring I'd hand it to Gerard, to cheer him up a bit, and rang the bell. There was no answer. I tried a second time, then made my way along the side of the house, thinking to peer in the windows—for all anyone knew, he could be ill, or even, God forbid, dead.

The windows were nearly opaque with a scrim of some sort of pale fluff or dander. I rapped at the glass and thought I saw movement within, a kaleidoscopic shifting of shadowy forms, but couldn't be sure. It was then that I noticed the odor, saturate and bottom-heavy with ammonia, like the smell of a poorly run kennel. I mounted the back steps through a heavy accounting of discarded microwave dinner trays and a tidal drift of feed bags and knocked uselessly at the door. The wind stirred. I looked down at the refuse at my feet and saw the legend *Rat Chow* replicated over and over in neon-orange letters, and that should have been all the information I needed. Yet how was I to guess? How was anyone?

Later, after I'd presented the bouquet and the cheese to my wife, I tried Gerard's phone, and to my surprise he answered on the fourth or fifth ring. "Hello, Gerard," I said, trying to work as much heartiness into my voice as I could, "it's me, Roger, back from the embrace of the Swiss. I stopped by today to say hello, but—"

He cut me off then, his voice husky and low, almost a whisper. "Yes, I know," he said. "Robbie told me."

If I wondered who Robbie was—a roommate? a female?—I didn't linger over it. "Well," I said, "how're things? Looking up?" He didn't answer. I listened to the sound of his breathing for a moment, then added, "Would you like to get together? Maybe come over for dinner?"

There was another long pause. Finally he said, "I can't do that."

I wasn't going to let him off so lightly. We were friends. I had a responsibility. We lived in a community where people cared about one another and where the loss of a single individual was a loss to us all. I tried to inject a little jocularity into my voice: "Well, why not? Too far to travel? I'll grill you a nice steak and open a bottle of Côtes du Rhône."

"Too busy," he said. And then he said something I couldn't quite get hold of at the time. "It's nature," he said. "The force of nature."

"What are you talking about?"

"I'm overwhelmed," he said, so softly I could barely hear him, and then his breathing trailed off and the phone went dead.

They found him a week later. The next-door neighbors, Paul and Peggy Bartlett, noticed the smell, which seemed to intensify as the days went on, and when there was no answer at the door they called the fire department. I'm told that when the firemen broke down the front door, a sea of rodents flooded out into the yard, fleeing in every direction. Inside, the floors were gummy with waste, and everything, from the furniture to the plasterboard walls and the oak beams of the living room ceiling, had been gnawed and whittled till the place was all but unrecognizable. In addition to the free-roaming animals, there were hundreds more rats stacked in cages, most of them starving and many cannibalized or displaying truncated limbs. A spokeswoman for the local ASPCA estimated that there were upwards of thirteen hundred rats in the house, most of which had to be euthanized at the shelter because they were in no condition to be sent out for adoption.

As for Gerard, he'd apparently succumbed to pneumonia, though there were rumors of hantavirus, which really put a chill into the community, especially with so many of the rodents still at large. We all felt bad for him, of course, I more than anyone else. If only I'd been home through the winter, I kept thinking, if only I'd persisted when I'd stood outside his window and recognized the odor of decay, perhaps I could have saved him. But then I kept coming back to the idea that there must have been some deep character flaw in him none of us had recognized—he'd chosen a snake for a pet, for God's sake, and that low animal had somehow morphed into this horde of creatures that could only be described as pests, as vermin, as enemies of mankind that should be exterminated, not nurtured. And that was another thing neither my wife nor I could understand—how could he allow even a single one of them to come near him, to fall under the caress of his hand, to sleep with him, eat with him, breathe the same air?

For the first two nights I could barely sleep, playing over that horrific scene in my mind—how could he have sunk so low? How could anyone?

The ceremony was brief, the casket closed (and there wasn't one of us who wanted to speculate on the reason, though it didn't take an especially active imagination to picture Gerard's final moments). I was very tender with my wife afterward. We went out to lunch with some of the others and when we got home I pressed her to me and held her for a long while. And though I was exhausted, I took the dogs out on the lawn to throw them their ball and watch the way the sun struck their rollicking fur as they streaked after the rumor of it, only to bring it back, again and again, and lay it in my palm, still warm from the embrace of their jaws.

(2007)

Anacapa

The boat left at eight a.m., and that wouldn't have presented a problem, or not especially, if Damian hadn't been in town. But then Damian was the whole reason for being here on this dock in the first place, the two of them hunkered over Styrofoam cups of coffee and shuffling in place with an assemblage of thirty or so males and two females (one of whom would turn out to be the deckhand), waiting in a kind of suppressed frenzy to board and lay claim to the prime spots along the rail. Hunter didn't like boats. Didn't especially like fish or fishing. But Damian did, and Damian—his roommate at college fourteen years ago and a deep well of inspiration and irritation ever since—always got his way. Which was in part why eight a.m. was such an impossible hour on this martyred morning with the sun dissolved in mist and the gulls keening and his head pounding and his stomach shrunk down to nothing. The other part of it, the complicating factor, was alcohol. Gin, to be specific.

They'd drunk gin the night before because gin was what they'd drunk in college, gin and tonic, the drink of liberation, the drink of spring break and summer vacation and the delirium of Friday and Saturday nights in the student clubs with the student bands pounding away and the girls burning like scented candles. Never mind that Hunter stuck almost exclusively to wine these days and had even become something of a snob about it ("Right over the hill in the Santa Ynez Valley? Best vineyards in the world," he'd tell anyone who would listen), last night it was gin. It had started in the airport lounge when he'd arrived an hour early for Damian's flight and heard himself say "Gin and tonic" to the bartender as if a ventriloquist were speaking for him. He'd had three by the time Damian arrived, and then for the rest of the night, wherever they went, the gin, which had managed to smell almost exactly like the scent of the jet fuel leaching in through the open window, continued to appear in neat little glasses with rectangular cubes of ice and wedges of lime till he and Damian collapsed at the apartment five short hours ago.

He stared blearily down at the blistered boards of the dock and the tired sea churning beneath them. For a long moment he watched a drift of refuse jerking to and fro in the wash beneath the pilings and then he leaned forward to drop a ball of spit into the place where, he supposed, waxing philosophical, all spit had originated. Spit to spit. The great sea. Thalassa, roll on. The water was gray here, transparent to a depth of three or four feet, imbued with a smell of fish gone bad. He spat again, watching transfixed as the glistening fluid, product of his own body, spiraled through the air to vanish in the foam. And what was spit anyway? A secretion of the salivary glands, serving to moisten food—and women's lips. His first wife—Andrea—didn't like to kiss while they were having sex. She always turned her head away, as if lips had nothing to do with it. Cee Cee, who'd left him three weeks ago, had been different. In his wallet, imprisoned behind a layer of scratched plastic, was a picture of her, in profile, her chin elevated as if she were being stroked, her visible eye drooping with passion, the red blaze of a carnation tucked behind her ear like a heat gauge. He resisted the impulse to look at it.

Damian's voice—"Yeah, man, that's what I'm talking about, *fortification*!"—rang out behind him and Hunter turned to see him tapping his Styrofoam cup to those of a couple in matching windbreakers, toasting them, as if there were anything to celebrate at this hour and in this place. Damian had a flask with him. Hunter had already been the recipient of a judicious shot of brandy—not gin, thank God—and he presumed Damian was sharing the wealth. The woman—she was small-boned, dark, with her hair wrapped like a muffler round her throat—looked shy and sweet as she sipped her infused coffee and blinked her eyes against the burn of it. In the next moment, Damian had escorted the couple over to the rail and was making introductions. "Hey, Hunt, you ready for another?" he said, and Hunter held out his cup, hoping to deaden the pain, and then they were all four tapping the rims of the spongy white cups one against the other as if they were crystal flutes of Perrier-Jouët.

"This is Ilta's maiden voyage, can you believe it?" Damian crowed, his voice too loud, so that people had begun to stare at him.

"This is cor-rect," she said in a small voice animated by the occasion, and, he supposed, the brandy. "I do it for Mock." And here she looked to the man in the matching windbreaker, whose name seemed to be either Mack or Mark, Hunter couldn't be sure.

"I'm a regular," the man said, grinning as he tipped back his cup and then held it up for Damian to refresh, "but my wife's never been out." He looked harmless enough, one of those ubiquitous, fleshy-faced, pants-straining, good-time boys in his forties who probably sat behind a computer five days a week and dreamed in gigabytes, but Hunter would have killed him in a minute for the wife, whom he clearly didn't deserve. She was a jewel, that was what she was, and that accent—what was it? Swedish? "She eats the fish, though," Mack or Mark went on. He gave her a good-natured leer. "Don't you, dumpling?"

"Who doesn't?" Damian put in, just to say something. He was the type who needed to be at the center of things, the impresario, the star of all proceedings, and that could be charming—Hunter loved him, he did—but it could be wearing too. "I mean, fresh fish, fresh from the sea like you never get it in the store?" He paused to tip the flask over the man's cup. "I mean, come on, Ilta, what took you so long?"

"I do not like the, what do you say? The rocking." She made an undulating motion with her hands. "Of this boat."

They all looked to the boat. It was big enough, a typical party boat, seventy, eighty feet long, painted a crisp white and so immovable it might have been nailed to the dock. In that moment Hunter realized he hadn't taken his Dramamine—the label advised taking two tablets half an hour to an hour before setting out—and felt in his jeans pocket for the package. His throat was dry. His head ached. He was wondering if the little white pills would have any effect if he took them now, or if they worked at all no matter when you took them, remembering the last time he'd been talked into this particular sort of adventure and the unrelenting misery he'd experienced for the entire six and a half hours of the trip ("There's nothing more enjoyable—and tender, tender too—than seeing somebody you really admire puking over the rail," Damian had kept saying). The memory ran a hot wire through him and before he could think he had the package out and was shaking four pills into the palm of his hand and offering them to Ilta. "Want a couple of these?" he asked. "Dramamine? You know, for motion sickness?" He pantomimed the act of gagging.

"We gave her the patch," the husband said.

Ilta waved a finger back and forth, as if scolding Hunter. "I do it for Mock," she repeated. "For the anniversary. We are married today three years ago."

Hunter shrugged, cupped his palm to his mouth and threw back all four pills, figuring the double dose had to do something for him.

"In Helsinki," the husband put in, his face lit with the blandest smile of possession and satisfaction. He put an arm around his wife and drew her to him. They kissed. The gulls squalled overhead. Hunter looked away. And then suddenly everyone snapped to attention as the other woman—the deckhand in waiting—pulled back the bar to the gangplank. It was then, just as they'd begun to fumble around for their gear, that the man with the spider tattoo thrust himself into the conversation. Hunter had noticed him earlier—when they were in the office paying for their tickets and renting rods and tackle and whatnot. He was a crazy, you could see that from across the room, everything about him wired tight, his hair shaved down to a black bristle, his eyes like tracers, the tattoo of a red-and-black spider—or maybe it was a scorpion—climbing up the side of his neck. "Hey," he said now, pushing past Ilta, "can I get in on this party?" And he held out his cup.

Damian never flinched. That was his way. Mr. Cool. "Sure, man," he said, "just give me your cup."

In the next moment they were shuffling forward to the reek of diesel as the captain fired up his engines and the boat shivered beneath them. Everything smelled of long use, fishermen here yesterday and fishermen coming tomorrow. The decks were wet, the seats damp with dew. Fish scales, opalescent, dried to a crust, crunched underfoot. They found a place in the cabin, room for four at one of the tables lined up there cafeteria style, and the spider man, aced out, made his way to the galley. Hunter had a moment to think about Cee Cee, how she would have hated this—she was a downtown girl, absolutely, at home in the mall, the restaurant and the movie theater and nowhere else—and then there was a lurch, the boat slipped free of the dock and beyond the salt-streaked windows the shore broadened and dipped, and very slowly fell away into the mist.

It was an hour and a half out to the fishing grounds. Hunter settled in gingerly, his stomach in freefall, the coffee a mistake, the brandy compounding that mistake and the Dramamine a dissolve of pure nothing, not even worthy of a placebo effect. It wasn't as if it was rough—or as rough as it might have been. This was June, when the Santa Barbara Channel was entombed in a vault of fog that sometimes didn't burn off till two or three in the afternoon—June Gloom, was what they called it in the newspaper—and as far as he knew the seas were relatively calm. Still, the boat kept humping over the waves like a toboggan slamming through the moguls at the bottom of a run and the incessant dip and rise wasn't doing him any good. He glanced round him. No one else seemed much affected, the husband and wife playing cards, Damian ordering up breakfast in the galley at the front of the cabin, the others snoozing, reading the paper, scooping up their eggs over easy as if they were in a diner somewhere on upper State Street, miles from the ocean. After a while, he cradled his arms on the tabletop, put his head down and tumbled into a dark shaft of sleep.

When he woke, it was to the decelerating rhythm of the engines and a pulse of activity that rang through the cabin like a fire alarm. Everybody was rising en masse and filing through the doors to the deck. They'd arrived. He felt a hand on his shoulder and lifted his head to see Damian looming over him. "You have a nice sleep?"

"I dreamed I was in hell, the ninth circle, where there's nothing moving but the devil." The boat rolled on a long gentle swell. The engines died. "And maybe the sub-devils. With their pitchforks."

The flask appeared. Damian pressed it to his lips a moment, then held it out in offering. "You want a hit?"

Hunter waved him away. He still hadn't risen from his seat.

"Come on, man, this is it. The fish are waiting. Let's go."

There was a shout. People were backed up against the windows, clumsy with the welter of rods that waved round them like antennae. Somebody had a fish already, a silver thrashing on the boards. Despite himself, he felt a vestigial thrill steal over him. He got to his feet.

Damian was halfway to the door when he turned round. "I put our stuff out there in back on the port side—Mark said that was the best spot. Come on, come on." He waved a hand impatiently and Hunter found his balance all at once—it was as if he'd done a backflip and landed miraculously on his feet. Just then the sun broke through and everything jumped with light. Damian went flat as a silhouette. The sea slapped the hull. Someone else cried out. "And wait'll you get a load of Julie," he said under his breath.

"Julie? Who's Julie?"

The look Damian gave him was instructive, teacher to pupil. After all, as Damian had it he'd come all the way down here for the weekend—for this trip, for last night and tonight too—to cheer up his old buddy, to get him out of the house and back among the living, waxing eloquent on the subject of Hunter's failings into the small hours of the day that was just now beginning. "The deckhand, man. Where you been?"

"Sleeping."

"Yeah, well maybe it's time to wake up."

And then they were out in the light and the world opened up all the way to the big dun humps of the islands before them—he'd never seen them so close—and back round again to the boat and its serried decks and the smell of open water and Julie, the deckhand, freshly made-up and divested of the shapeless yellow slicker she'd worn back at the dock, Julie, in a neon-orange bikini and sandals with thin silver straps that climbed up her bare ankles, waiting to help each and every sportsman to his bait.

So they fished. The captain, a dark presence behind the smoked glass of the bridge that loomed over them, let his will be known through the loudspeakers on deck. *Drop your lines,* he commanded, and they dropped their lines. *Haul in,* he said, and they hauled in while he revved the engines and motored to another spot and yet another. There were long stretches of boredom after the initial excitement had passed and Hunter had an abundance of time to reflect on how much he hated fishing. At long intervals, someone would connect, his rod bent double and a mackerel or a big gape-mouthed thing variously described as either a rockfish or a sheephead would flap in over the rail, but Hunter's rod never bent or even twitched. Nor did Damian's. Before the first hour was up, Damian had left his rod propped on the rail and drifted into the cabin, emerging ten minutes later with two burgers wrapped in waxed paper and two beers in plastic cups. Hunter was hunched over his knees on one of the gray metal lockers that held the life jackets and ran along both sides of the boat, his stomach in neutral, trying all over again to get used to the idea of lateral instability. He accepted the burger and the beer.

"This sucks," Damian said, settling in beside him with a sigh. Their rods rode up and down with the waves like flagpoles stripped of their flags.

"It was your idea."

Damian gazed out across the water to where the smaller island, the one separated from the bigger by a channel still snarled in fog, seemed to swell and recede. "Yeah, but it's a ritual, it's manly. It's what buddies do together, right? And look at it, look where we are—I mean is this beautiful or what."

"You just said it sucks."

"I mean this spot. Why doesn't he move us already?" He jerked his head around to shoot a withering glare at the opaque glass of the bridge. "I mean, I haven't caught shit—what about you? Any bites?"

Hunter was unwrapping the burger as if it were crystal, thinking he'd maybe nibble at it—he didn't want to press his luck. He set it down and took the smallest sip of beer. In answer to Damian's question, he just shrugged. Then, enunciating with care, he said, "Fish are extinct."

"Bullshit. This guy on the other side got a nice-sized calico, like eight or nine pounds, and they're the best eating, you know that . . ." He took a massive bite out of the hamburger, leaning forward to catch the juices in the waxed-paper wrapping. "Plus," he added through the effort of chewing, "you better get on the stick if you want to win the pool."

Hunter had been so set on simply enduring that he'd forgotten all about the pool or even the possibility of connecting, of feeling some other force, something dark and alien, pulling back at you from a place you couldn't imagine. "What are you talking about?"

"The pool, remember? Everybody on the boat put in ten bucks when they gave you the bag with your number on it? You must really be out of it—you put in a twenty for both of us, remember, and I said I'd get the first round?"

"I'm not going to win anything." He let out a breath and it was as if the air had been sucked out of his lungs.

Mostly, the night before, they'd talked about sex. How when you didn't have it you were obsessed with it, how you came to need it more than food, more than money. "It's the testosterone clogging your brain," Damian had said, and Hunter, three weeks bereft, had nodded in agreement. "And I'll tell you another thing," Damian had added after a lengthy digression on the subject of his latest girlfriend's proclivities, "once you have it, I'm talking like five minutes later, it's like, 'Hey, let's go shoot some hoops.' " Now, because he couldn't seem to resist it, because they were in college all over again, at least for the weekend, he said, "Just keep your rod stiff, 'cause you never know."

And then Mark was there, in a pair of disc sunglasses and a baseball cap that clung like a beanie to his oversized head. He had his own burger in one hand and a beer in the other. The boat slipped into a trough and rose up again on a long debilitating swell. "Any luck?" he asked.

"Nada," Damian said, his voice tuned to the pitch of complaint. "The captain ought to move us. I mean with what we're paying you'd think he'd work his fish-finding mojo just a little bit harder, wouldn't you?"

Mark shrugged. "Give him time. I know the man. He can be a bit of a hard-ass, but if they're out there he'll find them. He always does. Or almost always." He looked thoughtful, his lower face arranged around his chewing. "I mean, sometimes you get skunked. It's nature, you know, the great outdoors. Nobody can control that."

"How about Ilta?" Hunter heard himself say. "She get any?"

Mark drew a face. "She's not feeling so well, I guess. She's in the head. Been in the head for the past fifteen minutes."

"Green in the gills," Damian said with a joyful grin, and Hunter felt his stomach clench around the tiniest morsel of burger and bun.

"Something like that," Mark said, gazing off into the distance.

"She just needs to get her sea legs, is all."

"I shouldn't have brought her. She only did it for me—to please me, you know? The only time she's been on a boat before this was the ferry between Copenhagen and Göteborg and she said she vomited the whole time—but that was years ago and I figured, we both figured, this would be different. Plus, we got her the patch."

Hunter thought about that a moment, even as Damian started in weighing the relative merits of patch and pill as if he'd just stepped out of pharmacy school. He was feeling bitter. Bitter over the day, the place, the fish, the lack of fish, over Cee Cee and Ilta and Julie and all the rest of the unattainable women of the world. He was picturing Mark's wife in the cramped stinking head, cradling the stainless steel toilet, alone and needful while her husband gnawed his burger and guzzled beer, and he was about to say something cutting like "I guess that just proves the sea's no place for a woman," when the captain's voice droned through the speakers. *Haul in,* the captain commanded, and Hunter went to his pole and began to crank the reel, the weight of the sinker floating free, and the hook, when it was revealed, picked clean of the wriggling anchovy that Julie, in her bikini, had threaded there for him.

Mark didn't move. "I'm already in," he said, by way of explanation. "But you watch, he's going to take us southeast now, nearer the tip of the island." He paused, chewing. "That's Anacapa, you know. It's the only one of the Channel Islands with an Indian name—the rest are all Spanish."

Hunter didn't resent him showing off his knowledge, or not exactly—after all, Mark was the authority here, the regular, the veteran of scute and scale and the cold wet guts and staring eyes of the poor brainless things hauled up out of the depths for the sake of machismo, buddyhood, the fraternity of hook, line and sinker—but he didn't want to be here and his stomach was fluttering and for all he knew he'd be next in the head, like a woman, like a girl, and so he said, "Don't tell me—it means Soupcan in the Indian language, right? Or no: Microwave, Microwave Oven."

"Come on, Hunt, you know they didn't have any of that shit." Damian had set down his burger to reel in, the plastic cup clenched between his teeth so that his words were blunted. He was warning him off, but Hunter didn't care.

"It means illusion," Mark said, as the boat swung round and everybody, as one, fought for balance. "Like a mirage, you know? Because of the fog that clings to it—you can never be sure it's really there."

"Sounds like my marriage," Hunter said, and then, as casually as if he were bending over the coffee table in his own living room to pick up a magazine or the TV remote, he leaned over the rail, the sudden breeze catching his hair and fanning it across his forehead, and let it all heave out of him, the burger and bun, the beer, the coffee and brandy and Dramamine, and right there at the end of it, summoned up from the deepest recess, the metallic dregs of the gin.

The next spot, which as Mark had predicted, was closer to the island, didn't look much different from the last—waves, birds, the distant oil rigs like old men wading with their pants rolled up—but almost immediately after the captain dropped anchor, people began to hook up and a pulse of excitement beat through the crowd. One after another, the rods dipped and bent and the fish started coming over the rail. In the confusion, Hunter dropped his burger to the deck, even as Damian's rod bowed and his own began to jerk as if it were alive. "You got one!" Damian shouted, stepping back to play his own fish. "Go ahead, grab it, set the hook!"

Hunter snatched up the rod and felt something there. He pulled and it pulled back, and so what if he'd inadvertently slipped on the catsup-soaked bun with its extruded tongue of meat and very nearly pitched overboard—this was what he'd come for. A fish. A fish on the line! But it was tugging hard, moving toward the front of the boat, and he moved with it, awkwardly fumbling his way around the others crowding the rail, only to realize, finally, that this was no fish at all—he was snagged on somebody else's line. In that moment, three people up from him, the spider man was coming to the same realization.

"Jesus Christ, can't you watch your own fucking line?" the man snarled as they separately reeled in and the tangle of their conjoined rigs rose shakily from the water. "I mean you're down the other fucking end of the boat, aren't you?"

Yeah, he was. But this moron was down on his *fucking* end too. It wasn't as if it was Hunter's fault. It was nobody's fault. It was the fault of fishing and lines and the puke-green heaving ocean that should have stayed on the front of a postcard where it belonged. Still, when he'd finally made his way down the deck and was staring the guy in the face, he ducked his head and said only, "I'll get my knife."

That decision—to shuffle back alongside the glassed-in cabin and across the open area at the stern of the boat, to dig into the tackle box Damian had brought along and come up with the bare blade of the gleaming Swiss-made knife there and measure it in his hand while everyone on the boat was hooking up and the deck had turned to fish and a wave bigger than any of the others that had yet hit rocked the boat like a potato in a pot—was regrettable. Because the captain, hooded above, outraged, pressed to the very limit, let his voice of wrath tear through the speakers: "You with the knife—you, yeah, you! You trying to stab somebody's eye out?"

Hunter lurched like a drunken man. He squinted against the sun and up into the dark windows that wrapped round the wheelhouse till it seemed as if the boat were wearing a gigantic pair of sunglasses. He saw the sky reflected there. Clouds. The pale disc of the sun. "No, I'm just—" he began, but the captain's voice cut him off. "Put that goddamned thing away before I come down there and throw it in the goddamned ocean!"

Everyone was looking at him while they pumped their bent rods or hustled across the deck with one writhing fish or another suspended by the gills, and he wanted to protest, wanted to be the bad guy, wanted to throw it all right back at the dark god in his wheelhouse who could have been Darth Vader for all he knew, but he held himself back. Shamefaced, he staggered to the tackle box and slammed the knife into it, the very knife Damian had insisted on bringing along because men in the outdoors always had knives because knives were essential, for cutting, hewing, stabbing, pinning things down, and when he turned round, one hand snatching at the rail for balance—and missing—Julie was there. The wind took her hair—dark at the roots, bleached by the sun on the ends—and threw it across her face. She gave him a wary look. "What's the problem?" she asked.

"I didn't do anything," he said. "I just wanted to cut a tangle, that's all, and he—this guy up there, your precious captain, whoever he is, unloads on me . . ." He could hear the self-pity in his voice and knew it was all wrong.

"No open knives allowed on deck," she said, looking stern. Or as stern as a half-naked woman with minute fish scales glittering on her hands and feet could manage to look on the deck of a party boat in the middle of a party.

He could have blown it, could have been a jerk, but he felt the tension go out of him. He gave her a smile that was meant to be winning and apologetic at the same time. "I'm sorry, I guess I didn't know any better. I'm not a regular, but you already knew that, didn't you—just from looking at me, right? Tell you the truth, I feel a whole lot better experiencing the mighty sea from a barstool in that place back at the wharf—Spinnakers, you know Spinnakers?—with a cocktail in my hand and the fish served up on a plate, and maybe a little butter-lemon sauce? To dip? And lick off your fingers?"

When he mentioned Spinnakers, she'd nodded, and now she was smiling too. "It's all right," she said. "Here, let me help you." She took him by the sleeve then and led him across the deck to where the spider man, his face at war with itself, stood waiting.

What happened next remained a bit fuzzy, but as it turned out Hunter wasn't destined to be the bad actor, not on this trip. The spider man stepped forward to claim that role, and his transformation from bit player to full-blown menace needed no rehearsal. There was Julie, quick and efficient, her legs flexed and breasts swaying with the motion of the boat as she pulled in the tangle and cut the lines free with a pair of nail clippers she'd magically produced, and in the next moment she was handing each of them their rigs. She looked to Hunter first—and he was deep inside himself, fixated on the question of the nail clippers and where she could possibly have kept them given those two thin strips of cloth and the way they seemed to grow out of her flesh—and asked if he needed help rigging up again. Before he could say yes, because he did need her help in unraveling the mystery of the sinker so that it would swing away from the leader instead of snarling up the minute he dropped it overboard, and because he liked the proximity to her, liked looking at her and hearing her voice in the desert of this floating locker room, the spider man spoke up. His voice was ragged, jumping up the scale. "What about me?" he demanded. "This dickhead's the one that snagged me and I'm the one losing out on fishing time. You going to give me a refund? Huh? He can wait. He doesn't know what the fuck he's doing anyway."

The boat lurched and Hunter grabbed the rail to steady himself. "Go ahead," he said, "do him first, I don't care. Really. I don't."

The spider man looked away, muttering curses, as she bent to retie his rig. "What about bait," he said. "This clown"—he jerked a thumb at Hunter—"fucked up my bait. I need bait. Fresh bait."

She could have told him to fetch it himself—she was there to help and smile and show off her physique in the hope and expectation of tips, sure, but she was nobody's slave and any five-year-old could bait a hook—and yet she just gave him a look, padded over to the bait well and came back with a live anchovy cradled in one hand. But he was off now and there was no bringing him back, his harsh cracked voice running through its variations—she was wasting his time, and the whole thing, the whole fucking boat, was a conspiracy and he wanted a refund and he was damned fucking well going to get it too and they could all kiss his ass if they thought he was going to put up with this kind of cheat and fraud because that's what it was, screwing over the customer, eight bucks for a goddamned burger that tasted like warmed-over shit—and when finally she'd threaded the anchovy on his hook he said, loud enough for everybody to hear, "Hey, thanks for nothing. But I guess you're peddling your little ass for tips, right, so here you go"—and before she could react he stabbed a rolled-up bill into the gap between her breasts.

It wasn't a happy moment. Because Julie wasn't frail and wilting, wasn't like Ilta, whose sweet suffering face stared out of the vacancy of the head every time one of the sportsmen pulled back the door in an attempt to go in and relieve himself. She was lean and muscular, knots in her calves and upper arms, her shoulders pulled tight. In a single motion she dug out the bill and threw it in his face without even looking at it, and then she slapped him, and this was no ordinary slap, but an openhanded blow that sent him back against the rail.

For a split second it looked as if he was going to go for her and Hunter braced himself because there was no way he was going to let this asshole attack a woman in front of him, even if he had to take a beating for it, and he would, he would take a beating for Julie. Gladly. But the spider man, a froth of spittle caught in the corners of his mouth, just glared at her. "All right!" he shouted. "All right, fuck it," and he swung round, whirled the rented pole over his head like a lariat and flung it out into the chop, where gravity took it down just as if it had never existed.

Later, after the captain had come down personally from his perch to restrain the spider man and the command went up to haul in and the engines revved and the boat began hammering the waves on the way back to the dock, Hunter took a seat in the cabin to get out of the wind and for the first time since the night before he felt a kind of equilibrium settle over him. Mark and Damian were at the counter, leaning back on their elbows and sipping beer out of their plastic cups. Ilta was stretched out on a bench in the far corner, her face to the wall, a blanket pulled up over her shoulders. The others milled round in a happy mob, eating sandwiches, ordering up cocktails, reliving their exploits and speculating on who was going to win the pool, because apparently it wasn't over yet. In announcing the problem that had arisen with one of the passengers, the captain had promised to make up the lost time with a little inshore fishing—an hour or so, for halibut—once they'd deposited the unhappy sportsman back at the dock. An hour more. Hunter would have preferred an hour less, but he found himself drifting up to the counter to order a gin and tonic—as a calmative, strictly as a calmative—and then taking it outside, in the breeze, to where Julie stood over a pitted slab of wood at the rear of the boat, filleting the day's catch.

Behind her, a whole squadron of gulls, interspersed with half a dozen pelicans, cried havoc over the scraps. She looked tired. Gooseflesh stippled her shoulders and upper arms. Her makeup was fading. She dipped mechanically to the burlap sacks to extract the fish, slamming them down one after another before gutting them with an expert flick of her knife, half of them alive still and feebly working their tails. Next she ran the blade against the grain to remove the scales, a whole hurricane of translucent discs suddenly animated and dancing on the breeze as if by some feat of prestidigitation, and then she teased out the fillets and shook them into plastic bags, dumping the refuse overboard with a clean sweep of the knife. A few sportsmen stood around watching her. The engines whined at full throttle, the wake unraveling from the stern as if from an infinite spool, the birds vanishing in the froth. Hunter steadied himself against the rail and lifted the plastic cup to his lips, his fingers stinking of baitfish, wishing he had a dripping sack of plunder to hand her, but he didn't. Or not yet anyway. "You look like you've done that a time or two before," he said.

She looked up with a smile. "Yeah," she said. "One or two." Up close, he saw that her torso glittered with the thin wafers of the scales, scales everywhere, caught in the ends of her hair, fastened between her breasts, on her calves and the place where her thighs came together.

"Could I get you a drink?" he asked, and when she didn't answer, he added, "I'm having a gin and tonic. You like gin?"

The knife moved as if it had a life of its own. The fish gave in, lost their heads, ribs and tails, while the fillets, white and yielding, disappeared into ice chests, all ready for freezer or pan. And here was Damian's bag, #12, laid out before her like an offering. He could hear Damian crowing even now because Damian had hooked a lingcod that was bigger by a pound and a half than his nearest competitor's catch and he hadn't been shy about letting everybody know it—"I'm going to win that pool, you wait and see," he'd said before sidling up to the bar with Mark, "and I'm going to tip Julie a hundred and ask her to have a drink with us later, for your sake, your sake only, buddy, believe me." The thought of it made him feel queasy all over again. "Sure," Julie said. "I like gin, who doesn't? But I can't drink while I'm on duty—it's against regulations. And plus, the captain—"

"Yeah," he said, "the captain."

The boat slammed down hard and jerked back up so that he had to brace himself, but the knife never paused. After a moment he said, "Well, what about afterwards then, after we're back in, I mean? Would you like to have a drink then? Or dinner? After you get cleaned up and all?"

"That might be nice," she allowed. "But we've still got a whole lot of fishing to do. So let's not get premature here—"

He leaned back and let the gin wet his lips. He could see the way things would unfold—he was going to fish like the greatest fisherman on earth, like Lucky Jim himself, and he was going to catch a fish twice the size of Damian's. A hundred dollars? He'd tip her the whole thing, all three hundred, and she'd hold on to his arm while the spider man stalked off to haunt some other ship and Anacapa faded away in the mist and Damian went back home to sleep on the couch. That was the scenario, that was what was going to happen, he was sure of it. Of course, on the other hand, she must have had a dozen propositions a day, a girl as pretty as that, doing what she did for a living, and besides what would he do with all that fish? Was there room for it in the freezer even? Or would it just sit on a shelf in the refrigerator, turning color, till he dropped it in the trash?

"Right?" she said. "Agreed?"

He took another sip of his drink, felt the alcohol quicken in him even as his stomach sank and sank again. The gulls screeched. The knife flashed. And the shore, dense with its pavement and the clustered roof tiles and the sun caught in the solid weave of the palms, came up on him so quickly it startled him. "Yeah," he said, "yeah, sure. Agreed." He held to the rail as the captain gunned the engines and the boat leaned into an arc of exploding light, then tipped the cup back till he could feel the ice cold against his front teeth. "And just you wait," he said, grinning now. "I'm going to nail the granddaddy of all the halibut from here to Oxnard and back."

Of course, given the vicissitudes of the day, that wasn't how it turned out. If there was a granddaddy out there cruising the murk of the bottom, he kept his whereabouts to himself. Still, Hunter took a real and expanding satisfaction in watching the spider man, his wallet lightened by the price of the rod, reel and rigging he'd tossed, slink off the boat with his head down, while the rest of them—the true sportsmen, the obedient and fully sanctioned—got their extra hour of bobbing off the coast on a sea reduced to the gentlest of swells while the sun warmed their backs and almost everybody took their shirts off to enjoy it. A few people hooked up, Damian among them, and then the captain gave the order to haul in and Damian was declared winner of the pool for his lingcod and he got his picture taken with his arm around Julie in her bikini. As it happened, Hunter and Damian were the last ones off the boat, Julie standing there at the rail in her official capacity to help people up onto the gangplank and receive her tips. "It was awesome," Damian told her, his plastic bag of fish fillets in one hand, five twenties fanned out in the other, "really awesome. Best trip we've ever had—right, Hunt?"

Hunter had dipped his head in acknowledgment, distracted by Julie and the promise he'd come so close to extracting from her out there on the rolling sea. He was about to remind her of it—he was waiting, actually, till Damian went up the ladder so he could have a moment alone with her—when Damian, with a sidelong glance at him, said, "Hey, you know, we'd really take it as an honor, Hunter and me, if you'd come out to dinner with us. To celebrate, I mean. What about champagne? Champagne sound cool?"

Julie looked first to Hunter, then Damian, and let a slow grin spread across her face. "Real nice," she said. "Spinnakers? In, say, one hour?"

Which was what had brought them to this moment, in the afterglow of the trip, the three of them seated at a table up against the faded pine panels of the back wall, looking out to the bar crowded with tourists, fishermen and locals alike, and beyond that to the harbor and the masts of the ships struck pink with the setting sun. Julie was in a sea-green cocktail dress, her legs long and bare, a silver Neptune's trident clasped round her neck on a thin silver chain. Damian was on one side of her, Hunter on the other. They'd clinked champagne glasses, made their way through a platter of fried calamari with aioli sauce. Music played faintly. From beyond the open windows, there was the sound of the gulls settling in for the night.

Gradually, as he began to feel the effects of the champagne, it occurred to Hunter that Damian was monopolizing the conversation. Or worse: that Damian had got so carried away he seemed to have forgotten the purpose of this little outing. He kept jumping from one subject to another and when he did try to draw Julie out he was so wound up he couldn't help talking right through her. "So what's it like to be a deckhand?" he asked at one point. "Pretty cool job, no? Out on the water all day, fresh air, all that? It's like a dream job, am I right?" Before she could say ten words he'd already cut her off—he loved the outdoors too, couldn't she tell? He was the one who'd wanted to come out on the boat—"I practically had to drag Hunt, here"—and it wasn't just luck that had hooked him up with that lingcod, but experience and desire and a kind of worship of nature too deep to put into words.

Hunter tried to keep up his end of the conversation, injecting sardonic asides, mimicking the tourists at the bar, even singing the first verse of a sea chantey he made up on the spot, but Julie didn't seem especially receptive. Two guys, one girl. What kind of odds were those?

Damian had shifted closer to her. The second bottle of champagne went down like soda water. Hunter nudged Damian under the table with the toe of his shoe—twice, hard—but Damian was too far gone to notice. Halfway through the main course—was he really feeding her shrimp off the tines of his fork?—Hunter pushed back his chair. "Men's room," he muttered. "I'll be right back." Julie gave him a vague smile.

To get to the men's, he had to go out on the deck and down a flight of stairs. All the tables on the deck were occupied, though the fog was rolling in and there was a chill on the air. People were leaning over their elbows, talking too loud, laughing, lifting drinks to their lips. Jewelry glinted at women's throats, fingers, ears. A girl in her teens sat at the far table, the one that gave onto the stairs, looking into the face of the boy she was with, oblivious to the fact that she was sitting at the worst table in the house. Hunter thumped down the stairs and felt a sudden flare of anger. Son of a bitch, he was thinking. He wasn't going to sleep on the couch. No way. Not tonight. Not ever.

He slammed into the men's room and locked the door behind him. The stalls were empty, the sinks dirty, the overhead light dim in its cage. He smelled bleach and air freshener and the inescapable odor they were meant to mask. It had come in on the soles of deck shoes, sandals and boots, ammoniac and potent, the lingering reek of all those failing bits of protoplasm flung up out of the waves to be beached here, on the smudged ceramic tile of the men's room beneath Spinnakers. The smell caught him unawares and he felt unsteady suddenly, the floor beneath him beginning to rise and recede. But that wasn't all—the room seemed to be fogging up all of a sudden, a seep of mist coming in under the door and tumbling through the vent as if a cloud had touched down just outside. The far wall faded. The mirror clouded over. He rubbed a palm across the smeared glass, then a paper towel, until finally he put both hands firmly down on the edge of the sink and stared into the mirror, hoping to find something solid there.

(2008)

Three Quarters of the Way to Hell

Snow he could take, but this wasn't snow, it was sleet. There was an inch of it at least in the gutters and clamped atop the cars, and the sidewalks had been worked into a kind of pocked gray paste that was hell on his shoes—and not just the shine, but the leather itself. He was thinking of last winter—or was it the winter before that?—and a pair of black-and-whites he'd worn onstage, really sharp, and how they'd got ruined in slop just like this. He'd been with a girl who'd waited through three sets for him that night, and her face was lost to him, and her name too, but she had a contour on her—that much he remembered—and by the time they left she was pretty well lit and she pranced into the street outside the club and lifted her face to the sky. *Why don't we walk?* she sang out in a pure high voice as if she wanted everybody in New York to hear her. *It's so glorious, isn't it? Can't you feel it?* And he was lit himself and instead of taking her by the wrist and flagging down a cab he found himself lurching up the street with her, one arm thrown over her shoulder to pull her to him and feel the delicious discontinuous bump of her hip against his. Within half a block his cigarette had gone out and his face was as wet as if he'd been sprayed with a squirt gun; by the time they turned the corner his shoes were gone, and there was nothing either he or the solemn *paisano* at the shoe repair could do to work the white semicircular scars out of the uppers.

He dodged a puddle, sidestepped two big-armed old ladies staring at a Christmas display as if they'd just got off the bus from Oshkosh, and pinched the last drag out of the butt of his cigarette, which hissed as he flicked it into the gutter. For a minute, staring down the length of Fifth Avenue as it faded into the beating gloom like something out of an Eskimo's nightmare, he thought of hailing a cab. But there were no cabs, not in weather like this, and the reason he was walking the thirty-odd blocks to the studio in the first place, he reminded himself bitterly, was because he didn't have money to waste on anything so frivolous as carfare. He lifted his feet gingerly and turned into the blow, cursing.

It was cold in the apartment—the landlady was a miser and a witch and she wouldn't have turned on the heat for two free tickets to Florida—and Darlene felt her body quake and revolt against the chill as she stood before the mirror plucking her eyebrows after a lukewarm shower. She couldn't muster much enthusiasm for the session. It was grim outside, the windows like old gray sheets tacked to the walls, and she just couldn't feature bundling up and going out into the storm. But then it was grimmer inside—peeling wallpaper, two bulbs out in the vanity, a lingering sweetish odor of that stuff the landlady used on the roaches—and she never missed a date, not to mention the fact that she needed the money. She was in her slip—she couldn't find her robe, though she suspected it was balled up somewhere in the depths of the laundry basket, and there was another trial she had to get through, the machine in the laundry room inoperative for two weeks now. Her upper arms were prickled with gooseflesh. There was a red blotch just to the left of her nose, tracing the indentation of the bone there. The eye above it, staring back at her like the swollen blown-up eye of a goldfish at the pet store, was bloodshot. Bloodshot. And what was she going to do about that?

On top of it all, she still wasn't feeling right. The guy she'd been seeing, the guy she'd been saving up to go to Florida with for a week at Christmas—Eddie, second trumpet with Mitch Miller—had given her a dose and her backside was still sore from where the doctor had put the needle in. The way her head ached—and her joints, her right shoulder especially, which burned now as she positioned the tweezers above the arch of her eyebrow—she began to wonder if there'd actually been penicillin in that needle. Maybe it was just water. Maybe the doctor was pinching on his overhead. Or maybe the strain of gonorrhea she'd picked up—that Eddie had picked up in Detroit or Cleveland or Buffalo—wouldn't respond to it. That's what the doctor had told her anyway—there was a new strain going around. His hands were warm, the dab of alcohol catching her like a quick cool breeze. *Just a little sting,* he said, as if she were nine years old. *There. Now that's better, isn't it?*

No, she'd wanted to say, it's not better, it's never better and never will be because the world stinks and the clap stinks and so do needles and prissy nurses and sour-faced condescending M.D.s and all the rest of it too, but she just opened up her smile and said *Yeah.*

She was tired of every dress in the closet. Or no, not just tired—sick to death of them. All of them. The hangers clacked like miniature freight cars as she rattled through them twice, shivering in her slip and nylons, her feet all but frozen to the linoleum. *Christ,* she said to herself, *Jesus Christ, what the hell difference does it make?* and she reached angrily for a red crepe de chine with a plunging neckline she hadn't worn in a year and pulled it over her head and smoothed it across her hips, figuring it would provide about as much protection from the cold as a swimsuit. She'd just have to keep the cloth coat buttoned up to her throat, and though it was ugly as sin, she'd wear the red-and-green checked scarf her mother had knitted her . . . what she really needed—what she deserved, and what Eddie, or somebody, should give her and give her soon—was a fur.

A gust threw pellets of ice against the windowpane. For a moment she held the picture of herself in a fur—and not some chintzy mink stole, but a full-length silver fox—and then it dissolved. A fur. Yeah, sure. She wasn't exactly holding her breath.

The hallway smelled like shit—literally—and as he stomped the slush off his shoes and bent to wipe the uppers with the paper towels he'd nicked from the men's room at Benjie's, where he'd stopped to fortify himself with two rye whiskeys and a short beer, he wondered what exactly went on on the ground floor when they weren't recording. Or maybe when they were. Neff would press just about anything anybody wanted to put out, whether it was boogie-woogie, race records or that rock and roll crap, and who knew how many junkies and pill heads came in and out of the place so stewed they couldn't bother to find the bathroom? He took off his hat, set it on the extinct radiator and ran both hands through his hair. There was a slice of broken glass in a picture frame on the wall and that at least gave him back his reflection, though it was shadowy and indistinct, as if he'd already given up the ghost. For a moment there, patting his hair back into place while he stared down the dim tunnels of his eyes, he had a fleeting intimation of his own mortality—he was thirty-eight and not getting any younger, his father ten years dead and his mother fading fast; before long it would be just him and his sister and one old wraith-like spinster aunt, Aunt Marta, left on this earth, and then he'd be an old man in baggy pants staring at the gum spots on the sidewalk—but suddenly the door opened behind him and he turned round on a girl in a cloth coat and he was immortal all over again.

"Oh, hi, Johnny," she said, and then she gave the door a look and leaned back into it to slam it shut. "God, it's brutal out there."

At first he didn't recognize her. That sort of thing happened to him more and more lately, it seemed, and he told himself he had to cut back on the booze—and reefer, reefer was the worst, sponging your brain clean so you couldn't recognize your own face in the mirror. He'd come into some joint—a bar, a club, his manager's office—and there'd be somebody there he hadn't expected, somebody transposed from some other scene altogether, and he'd have to fumble around the greeting and give himself a minute or two to reel his brain back in. "Darlene," he said now, "Darlene Delmar. Wow. I haven't seen you in what, years? Or months anyway, right?"

She was wearing sunglasses though it was as dark as night outside and there was some sort of welt or blemish under the left lens, right at the cheekbone. She gave him a thin smile. "Six months ago, Cincinnati. On what was that station? W-something."

"Oh, yeah," he said, faking it, "yeah. Good times, huh? But how you been keeping?"

A rueful smile. A shrug. He could smell her perfume, a faint fleeting whiff of flowers blooming in a green field under a sun that brought the sweat out on the back of your neck, spring, summer, *Florida,* but the odor of the streets drove it down. "As well as can be expected, I guess. If I could get more work—like in a warmer climate, you know what I mean?" She shook out her hair, stamped her feet to knock the slush off her heels, and he couldn't help looking at her ankles, her legs, the way the coat parted to reveal the flesh there.

"It's been tough all over," he said, just to say something.

"My manager—I've got a new manager, did I tell you that? Or how could I, since I haven't seen you in six months . . . ?" She trailed off, gave a little laugh, then dug into her purse for her cigarettes. "Anyway, he says things'll look up after the New Year, definitely. He was talking about maybe sending me out to L.A. Or Vegas maybe."

He was trying to remember what he'd heard about her—somebody had knocked her up and she'd had a back-room abortion and there'd been complications. Or no, that wasn't her, that was the girl who'd made a big splash two years back with that novelty record, the blonde, what was her name? Then it came to him, a picture he'd been holding awhile, a night at a party somewhere and him walking in to get his coat and she was doing two guys at once, Darlene, Darlene Delmar. "Yeah," he said, "yeah, that'd be swell, L.A.'s the place, I mean palm trees, the ocean . . ."

She didn't answer. She'd cupped her hands to light the cigarette—which he should have lit for her, but it was nothing to him. He stood rooted to the spot, his overcoat dripping, and his eyes drifted to the murky window set in the door—there was movement there, out on the street, a tube of yellow extending suddenly to the curb. Two guys with violin cases were sliding out of a cab, sleet fastening on their shoulders and hats like confetti. He looked back to her and saw that she was staring at him over the cigarette. "Well, here come the strings," he said, unfolding an arm to usher her up the hall. "I guess we may as well get to it."

He hadn't bothered to light her cigarette for her—hadn't even moved a muscle for that matter, as if he were from someplace like Outer Mongolia where they'd never heard of women or cigarettes or just plain common courtesy. Or manners either. His mother must have been something, a fat fishwife with a mustache, and probably shoeless and illiterate on top of it. Johnny Bandon, born in Flatbush as Giancarlo Abandonado. One more wop singer: Sinatra, Como, Bennett, Bandon. She couldn't believe she'd actually thought he had talent when she was growing up, all those hours listening alone to the sweet tenor corroboration of his voice and studying his picture in the magazines until her mother came home from the diner and told her to go practice her scales. She'd known she was working with him today, that much her manager had told her, but when she'd come through the door, chilled right to the marrow, she'd barely recognized him. Rumor had it he'd been popping pills, and she knew the kind of toll that took on you—knew firsthand—but she hadn't been prepared for the way the flesh had fallen away from his face or the faraway glare of his eyes. She'd always remembered him as handsome—in a greasy sort of way—but now here he was with his cueball eyes and the hair ruffled like a duck's tail feathers on the back of his head, gesturing at her as if he thought he was the A&R man or something. Or some potentate, some potentate from Siam.

Up the hall and into the studio, a pile of coats, hats and scarves in the secretary's office, no place to sit or even turn around and the two fiddle players right on their heels, and she was thinking one more job and let's get it over with. She'd wanted to be pleasant, wanted to make the most of the opportunity—enjoy herself, and what was wrong with that?—but the little encounter in the hallway had soured her instantly, as if the pain in her backside and the weather and her bloodshot eye wasn't enough. She unwound the scarf and shrugged out of her coat, looking for a place to lay it where it wouldn't get sat on.

Harvey Neff—this was his studio and he was producing—emerged from the control booth to greet them. He was a gentleman, a real gentleman, because he came up to her first and took her hand and kissed her cheek and told her how terrific it was to be working with her again before he even looked at Johnny. Then he and Johnny embraced and exchanged a few backslaps and the usual words of greeting—*Hey, man, long time no see* and *How's it been keeping?* and *Cool, man, cool*—while she patted down her hair and smoothed her skirt and debated removing the dark glasses.

"Listen, kids," Harvey was saying, turning to her now, "I hope you're up for this, because as I say we are going to do this and do it right, one session, and I don't care how long it takes, nobody leaves till we're all satisfied, right? Because this is a Christmas record and we've got to get it out there, I mean, immediately or there's no sense in making it at all, you know what I mean?"

She said she did, but Johnny just stared—was he going to be all right for this?—until Fred Silver, the A&R man for Bluebird, came hurtling into the room with his hands held out before him in greeting and seconded everything Harvey had said, though he hadn't heard a word of it. "Johnny," he said, ignoring her, "just think if we can get this thing out there and get some airplay, because then it slips into the repertoire and from Thanksgiving to New Year's every year down the road it's there making gravy for everybody, right? I mean look at 'White Christmas.' 'Santa, Baby.' Or what was that other thing, that Burl Ives thing?"

The room was stifling. She studied the side of Fred Silver's head—bald to the ears, the skin splotched and sweating—and was glad for the dress she was wearing. But Johnny—maybe he was just a little lit, maybe that was it—came to life then, at least long enough to shrug his shoulders and give them all a deadpan look, as if to say I'm so far above this you'd better get down on your knees right now and start chanting hosannas. What he did say, after a beat, was: "Yeah, that I can dig, but really, Fred, I mean really—'Little Suzy Snowflake'?"

They walked through it twice and he thought he was going to die from boredom, the session men capable enough—he knew most of them—and the girl singer hitting the notes in a sweet, commodious way, but he was for a single take and then out for a couple drinks and a steak and some *life,* for Christ's sake. He tried to remind himself that everybody did novelty records, Christmas stuff especially, and that he should be happy for the work—hell, Nat King Cole did it, Sinatra, Martin, all of them—but about midway through the arrangement he had to set down the sheet music and go find the can just to keep from exploding. *Little Suzy Snowflake.* It was stupid. Idiotic. Demeaning. And if he'd ever had a reputation as a singer—and he had, he did—then this was the kiss of death.

There were four walls in the can, a ceiling and a floor. He locked the door behind him, slapped some water on his face and tried to look at himself long enough in the mirror to smooth his hair down—and what he wouldn't have given to have been blessed with hair that would just stay in place for ten minutes instead of this kinky, nappy mess he was forever trying to paste to the side of his head. Christ, he hated himself. Hated the look in his eyes and the sunken cheeks and the white-hot fire of ambition that drove him, that had driven him, to this, to make this drivel and call it art. He was shit, that was what he was. He was washed up. He was through.

Without thinking twice he pulled the slim tube of a reefer from the pack of Old Golds in his jacket pocket and lit up, right there in the can, and he wouldn't have been the first to do it, God knew. He took a deep drag and let the smoke massage his lungs, and he felt the pall lift. Another drag, a glance up at the ceiling and a single roach there, making its feelers twitch. He blew smoke at it—"Get your kicks, Mr. Bug," he said aloud, "because there's precious few of them in this life"—and then, without realizing just when he'd slipped into it, he found he was humming a Cab Calloway tune, biggest joke in the world, "Reefer Man."

She must have looked like the maternal type—maybe it was the dress, or more specifically, the way it showed off her breasts—because Harvey prevailed upon her to go down the hall to the restroom and mother the star of the proceedings a little bit because the ticker was ticking and everybody, frankly, was starting to get a little hot under the collar, if she knew what he meant. "Like pissed off? Like royally?" Darlene took a moment, lowered her head and peeped over the sunglasses to let her eyes rove over the room. "Poor man," she said in her sweetest little-girl-lost voice, "he seemed a bit confused—maybe he can't find his zipper." Everybody—she knew them all, except the strings—burst out in unison, and they should have recorded *that.* George Withers, the trombonist, laughed so hard he dropped his mouthpiece on the floor with a thud that sounded like a gunshot, and that got them all laughing even harder.

There was a dim clutter of refuse in the hallway—broken music stands, half a smashed guitar, a big waist-high ashtray lifted from the Waldorf with the hotel's name etched in the chrome and a thousand extinguished butts spilling over onto the floor—and a lingering smell of stopped-up toilets. She nearly tripped over something, she didn't stop to see what, and then she was outside the restroom and a new smell came to her: he was smoking reefer in there, the moron. She'd dragged herself all the way out here in the cold to do a job, hoping for the best—hoping for a hit—and here he was, the great Johnny Bandon, the tea head, getting himself loaded in the can. Suddenly she was angry. Before she knew what she was doing she was pounding on the door like a whole van full of narcs. "Johnny!" she shouted. "Johnny, people are waiting." She tried the doorknob. "Open up, will you?"

Nothing. But she knew that smell. There was the sound of water running, then the toilet flushed. "Shit," she hissed. "Damn you, open up. I don't know about you, but I need this, you hear me? Huh?" She felt something rise in her, exactly like that geyser she'd seen in *Life* magazine, red-hot, white-hot. She rattled the knob.

There was the metallic click of the bolt sliding back and then he pulled open the door and told her in an even voice to keep her shirt on, only he was smiling at her, giving her the reckless grin of abandon that ten years ago had charmed half the women in the country. She was conscious of the fact that in her heels they were the same height and the crazy idea that he'd be the perfect dance partner flitted through her head as he stood there at the door and the marijuana fumes boiled round him. What he said next totally disarmed her, his voice pitched to the familiar key of seduction: "What's with the glasses? Somebody slug you, or what?"

The world leapt out at her when she slipped the sunglasses from her eyes, three shades brighter, though the hallway was still dim as a tomb. "It's my eye," she said, touching a finger to her cheekbone at the right orbit. "I woke up with it all bloodshot."

From down the hall came the muted sound of the band working their way through the arrangement without them, a sweeping glide of strings, the corny cluck-cluck-knock of a glockenspiel and the tinkling of a triangle, and then the horns, bright and peppy, Christmas manufactured like a canned ham. "You're nuts," he said. "Your eye's no more bloodshot than mine is—"

She couldn't help smiling. "Oh, yeah? Have you looked in the mirror?"

They were both laughing suddenly, and then he took her by the arm and pulled her into the restroom with him. "You want some of this?" he said.

There was something about the moment—the complicit look she gave him, the way she showed her teeth when she laughed, the sense he had of getting away with something, as if they were two kids ducking out of school to have a smoke under the fire escape—that just lit him up, just like that, like a firecracker. Neff could wait. They could all wait. He passed her the reefer and watched her eyes go wide with greed as she inhaled and held it in, green eyes, glassy and green as the bottom of a Chianti bottle. After a moment the smoke began to escape her nostrils in a sporadic way, as if there was something burning inside of her, and he thought first of the incinerator in the basement of the tenement he'd grown up in, and the smell of it, of cardboard and wet newspaper and everything scraped off a plate, cat litter, dead pets, fingernail parings, and then, as if that sponge had wiped his brain clean, of church. Of votive candles. Of incense. Jesus, he was high as a kite.

"What?" she said, expelling the smoke through her mouth. "What's that grin for?"

He let out a laugh—or no, a giggle. "I just had this image," he said. "Very strange. Like you were on fire inside—"

Her eyes were on him, green and unblinking. She was smiling. "Me? Little old me? On fire?"

"Listen," he said, serious suddenly, and he was so far out there he couldn't follow his own chain of thought, "did you go to church when you were a kid? I want to know. You're Catholic, right?"

Her eyes went away from him then, up to where one very stewed roach clung to the ceiling, and they came back again. "Yeah," she said, ducking her head. "If you can believe it, I was in the choir."

"You were? Wow. Me too. I mean, that was how I—"

She put a hand on his arm as if to emphasize the connection. "I know exactly what you mean—it's probably how ninety percent of the singers out there got started. At least the ones I met anyway."

"Church."

"Church, yeah." She was grinning at him, and when she grinned her dimples showed and her face opened up for him till he had to back up a step for fear of falling right into it.

He wanted to banter with her, say something clever, charming, keep it going, but instead he said, "You ever go anymore?"

She shook her head. "Not me. Uh-uh. It's been years." Her lips were pursed now, the dimples gone. "You?"

"Nah," he said. "All that was a long time ago. When I was a kid, you know?"

An achingly slow moment revealed itself in silence. She passed him the reefer, he took a drag, passed it back. "I guess we're both about halfway to hell by now," she said.

"Oh, I don't know," he said, and everything seemed to let go of him to make way for that rush of exhilaration he'd been feeling ever since she'd stepped into the can with him, "I'd say it's more like three quarters," and they were laughing all over again, in two-part harmony.

It was Harvey himself who finally came to fetch them and when Johnny opened the door on him and the smoke flowed out into the hallway she felt shamed—this wasn't what she'd come for, this wasn't professional or even sensible. Of course, Harvey had seen it all in his day, but still he gave her a sour look and it made her feel like some runaway or delinquent caught in the act. For a moment she flashed on the one time she'd been arrested—in a hotel room in Kansas City, after a night when she'd felt the music right down in her cells, when she'd felt unbeatable—but she stopped right there amidst the clutter and shook out her hair to compose herself. Harvey was white-faced. He was furious and why wouldn't he be? But Johnny chose to ignore it, still riding the exhilaration they'd felt in the bathroom—and it wasn't the reefer, that wasn't it at all, or not all of it—and he said, "Hey, Harvey, come on, man, don't sweat it. We're ready to slay 'em, aren't we, babe?"

"Sure," she said, "sure," and then they were back in the studio, dirty looks all around, Harvey settling into the control booth with Fred Silver, and the opening strains of "Little Suzy Snowflake," replete with glockenspiel and tinkling triangle, enveloping the room.

"No, no, no, no," Johnny shouted, waving his arms through the intro, "cut, cut, cut!"

Neff's face hung suspended behind the window of the control booth. "What's the matter now?" his voice boomed, gigantic, disproportionate, sliced three ways with exasperation.

Johnny was conscious of his body, of his shoulders slipping against the pads of his jacket and the slick material of his pants grabbing at his crotch as he turned and gestured to the booth with both palms held out in offering. "It's just that Darlene and me were working something out back there—warming up, you know? I just think we need to cut the B-side first. What do you think?"

Nobody said a word. He looked at Darlene. Her eyes were blank.

There was a rumble from the control booth, Harvey with his hand over the mike conferring with Fred Silver, the session men studying the cuffs of their trousers, something, somewhere, making a dull slippery hissing sound—they were running tape, and the apprehension of it brought him back to himself.

"I think"—the voice of God from the booth, *Domine, dirige nos*—"we should just get on with it like we planned or we're going to be here all night. Know what I'm saying, Johnny?" And then Silver, a thinner voice, the Holy Ghost manifesting Himself in everything: "Keep it up, Johnny, and you're going to make me pick up the telephone." Neff's hand went back to the mike, a sound like rubbing your sleeve over a trumpet mute, and there was more conferring, the two heads hanging there behind the glass like transparencies.

He felt scared suddenly, scared and alone and vulnerable. "Okay," he said to the room, "okay, I hear you." And he heard himself shift into another mode altogether, counting off the beat, and there were the strings pouring like syrup out of the corners and the whisper of the brushes and the high hat and he was singing in the unshakable pure tenor that was Johnny Bandon's trademark, and forget Harvey, forget the asinine lyrics, he was singing here, singing: only that.

Something happened as soon as Johnny opened his mouth, and it had happened to her before, happened plenty, but it was the last thing she'd expected from a session like this. She came in on the second verse—*Little Suzy Snowflake/Came tumbling down from the sky*—and felt it, the movement inside of her, the first tick into unconsciousness, what her mother used to call opening up the soul. *You're a soul singer,* her mother used to say, *you know that, little sister? A real soul singer.* She couldn't help herself. She took Johnny's lead and she flew, and so what if it was corny, so what if the glockenspiel was a cliché out of some fluffy nostalgic place and time nobody could remember and the arrangement was pure chintz? She flew and so did he.

And then the B-side, warmer, sweeter, with some swing to it—"Let it snow, let it snow, let it snow"—and they traded off, tit for tat, call and response, *But baby it's cold outside.* When Harvey's voice came at them—"That's it, kids, you nailed that one down"—she couldn't quite believe it was over, and from the look of Johnny, his tie tugged loose, the hair hanging in his eyes, he couldn't believe it either.

The musicians were packing up, the streets and the night awaiting them, the sleet that would turn to snow by morning and the sky that fell loose over everything because there was nothing left to prop it up. "Johnny," she murmured, and they were still standing there at the mike, both of them frozen in the moment, "that was, I mean that was—"

"Yeah," he said, ducking his head, "we were really on, weren't we," and from the way he turned to her she was sure he was going to say *Let's go have a drink* or *Your place or mine?* but he didn't. Instead he just closed his eyes and began to sing, pure, sweet and high. Nobody moved. The ghostly heads in the recording booth pivoted toward them, the horn players looked up from their instrument cases and their felt rags and fragile mouthpieces. Even the strings—longhairs from the Brooklyn Academy of Music—hesitated. And then, on the third bar, she caught up to him, their two voices blended into one: *It is the night/Of our dear Savior's birth.*

The moment held. They sang the song through, then sang it again. And then, without pause, as if they were reading from the same sheet, they swept into "Ave Maria," "O Come All Ye Faithful," "What Child Is This," the sweet beat of the melody as much a part of her as the pulsing of the blood in her veins. She didn't know what time it was, didn't know when Harvey and the A&R man deserted the booth, didn't know anything but the power of two voices entwined. She knew this only—that she was in a confined space, walls and floor and ceiling, but that didn't make any sense to her, because it felt as if it opened up forever.

(2003)

Wild Child

1

During the first hard rain of autumn, when the leaves lay like currency at the feet of the trees and the branches shone black against a diminished sky, a party of hunters from the village of Lacaune, in the Languedoc region of France, returning cold and damp and without anything tangible to show for their efforts, spotted a human figure in the gloom ahead. The figure appeared to be that of a child, a boy, and he was entirely naked, indifferent to the cold and the rain. He was preoccupied with something—cracking acorns between two rocks, as it turned out—and didn't at first see them coming. But then one of the party—Messier, the village smith, whose hands and forearms had been rendered the color of a red Indian's with the hard use of his trade—stepped in a hole and lost his balance, lurching into the boy's field of vision. It was that sudden movement that spooked him. One moment he was there, crouched over his store of raw acorns, and the next he was gone, vanishing into the undergrowth with the hypersensitivity of a stoat or weasel. None of them could be sure—the encounter had been so brief, a matter of seconds—but they unanimously claimed that the figure had fled on all fours.

A week later, the boy was spotted again, this time at the verge of a farmer's fields, digging potatoes from the ground and bolting them as they were, without benefit of cooking or even rinsing. The farmer's instinct was to chase him off, but he restrained himself—he'd heard the reports of a wild child, a child of the forest, *un enfant sauvage,* and he crept closer to better observe the phenomenon before him. He saw that the child was very young indeed, eight or nine years old, if that, and that he used only his bare hands and broken nails to dig in the sodden earth, like a dog. To all outward appearances, the child seemed normal, having the fluid use of his limbs and hands, but his emaciation was alarming and his movements were swift and autonomous—at some point, after the farmer had approached to within twenty yards of him, the child reared his head and made eye contact. It was difficult to see the child's face because of the unbarbered thatch of his hair and the way it masked his features. Nothing moved, not the flock on the hill, nor the clouds in the sky. The countryside seemed preternaturally silent, the birds in the hedgerows holding their breath, the wind stilled, the very insects mute underfoot. That look—the unblinking eyes, black as coffee poured straight from the pot, the tightening of the mouth around discolored canines—was the look of a thing out of Spiritus Mundi, deranged, alien, hateful. It was the farmer who had to turn away.

That was how it began, the legend brewing, stewing, simmering in every pot throughout the district through the fall of 1797, in the fifth year of the new French Republic, and into the year that succeeded it. The Terror was over, the King was dead, life—especially in the provinces—returning to normal. People needed a mystery to sustain them, a belief in the arcane and the miraculous, and any number of them—mushroom gatherers and truffle diggers, squirrel hunters, peasants bent under the weight of faggots or baskets of turnips and onions, kept watch in the woods, but it wasn't until the following spring that the boy was sighted again, this time by a party of three woodcutters, led by Messier, the smith, and this time they gave chase. They chased the boy without thinking, without reason, chased him because he ran from them, and they might have been chasing anything, a cat, a hind, a boar. Eventually, they ran him to tree, where he hissed and flailed the branches, flinging things down on them. Each time one of them attempted to mount into the branches and snatch for the boy's callused foot, he was pummeled and bitten, until finally they decided to smoke him out. A fire was built beneath the tree, the boy all the while watching these three bipeds, these shagged and violent and strangely habited and gibbering animals, out of the deep retreat of his eyes. Picture him there, crouched in the highest branches, his skin so nicked and abraded it was like a hide haphazardly tanned, the scar at his throat a bleached white tear visible even from the ground, his feet dangling, arms limp, as the smoke rose about him.

Picture him, because he wasn't able to picture himself. He knew nothing but the immediate, felt only what his senses transmitted to him. When he was a child of five, small and undernourished, the stubborn thirteenth child of a stubborn peasant family, his mind lax and pre-lingual, he was taken out into the forest of La Bassine by a woman he hardly knew or acknowledged, his father's second wife, and she didn't have the strength to do what she had to do, and so when she took him by the hair and twisted his head to expose the taut flesh of his throat she shut her eyes fast and the kitchen knife missed its stroke. Still, it was enough. His blood drew steam from the leaves and he lay there in a shrunken, skeletal nest, night coming down and the woman already receding into the trees.

He had no memory of any of it, no memory of wandering and foraging until his blouse and crude pantaloons were torn, were mesh, were string, no memory at all. For him, there was only the moment, and in the moment he could catch things to feed his hunger, things that had no names and no qualities except their desire to escape him, frogs, salamanders, a mouse, a squirrel, nestling birds, the sweet and bitter sacs of the eggs themselves. He found berries, mushrooms, ate things that sickened him and at the same time sharpened his senses of gustation and olfaction so that he could distinguish what was edible from what was not. Was he lonely? Scared? Superstitious? No one can say. And he couldn't have said himself, because he had no language, no ideas, no way of knowing he was alive or in what place he was alive or why. He was feral—a living, breathing atavism—and his life was no different from the life of any other creature of the forest.

The smoke irritated his eyes, interrupted his breathing. Below him, the fire built and climbed and everything was obscured. When he fell, they caught him.

2

Fire he knew, remnants of the blazes the farmers made of last year's stalks and the stubble of the fields, and he'd learned through trial that a potato in the ashes turns to meal, savory and fragrant, but the smoke of the woodcutters' blaze overcame him so that the air was poisoned all around him and he fell into another state. Messier took him up and bound his limbs and the three men brought him back to the village of Lacaune. It was late in the afternoon, the night already gathering round the trunks of the trees and consolidating the leaves of the bushes as if they'd been tarred. All three were eager to be home, to warm themselves at the hearth—it was cold for April and the sky spitting rain—but here was this marvel, this freak of nature, and the astonishment of what they'd done sustained them. Before they'd passed the first outlying houses, the boy flung comatose over Messier's shoulder, the whole village knew they were coming. Père Fasquelle, the oldest man in Lacaune, whose memory stretched back to the bloodline of the dead king's father's father, was out in the street, his mouth hanging open, and every child danced away from courtyards and doorways to come running in a mob even as their parents put down hoes and ladles and stirring spoons to join them.

They took the boy to the tavern—where else, but the church, and there was no sense in that, or not yet anyway—and he seemed to come to life then, just as Messier was handing him through the door to DeFarge, the tavern keeper. The smith had a proprietary hold on the boy's legs, supporting him at the small of the back, and DeFarge took possession of the shoulders and head in his soft white taverner's hands. Behind them, Messier's two companions and the surging crush of the village, children crying out, men and women alike jostling for position and everyone focused on the open door so that a stranger coming on the scene would have thought the mayor had declared a holiday and the drinks on the house. There was a moment suspended in time, the crowd pressing, the child caught between the outdoors and the interior of that fabricated structure, the feral and the civilized in balance. That was when the child's black eyes flashed open and in a single savage movement he jerked his head forward and upward, clamping his teeth on the excess flesh beneath DeFarge's chin.

Sudden panic. DeFarge let out a scream and Messier tightened his grip even as the taverner let go in pain and terror and the child crashed to the floor, rending flesh, and those who saw it said it was just as if a swamp turtle, dredged out of the muck, had whipped round its viridian head and struck out blindly. The blood was there, instant, paralyzing, and within seconds the taverner's beard flowered with it. Those already in the room jerked away from him while the crush at the door fell back precipitately and the child, Messier gone down with him, bucked and writhed in the doorway. There were shouts and cries and two or three of the women let out with fierce draining sobs that seemed to tear the heart out of the crowd—this was a wild thing among them, some beast or demon, and there it was at their feet, a twisting shape in the shadow of the doorway, blood on its snout. Startled, even Messier gave up his hold and jerked to his feet, his eyes staring as if he were the one who'd been attacked.

"Stab it!" someone hissed. "Kill it!"

But then they saw that it was only a child, measuring just over four and a half feet tall and weighing no more than seventy bone-lashed pounds, and two of the men covered his face with a rag so he couldn't bite and pressed their weight into him until he stopped writhing and the claws of his hands, which had worked out of the knots, were secure again. "There's nothing to fear," Messier proclaimed. "It's a human child, that's all it is." DeFarge was led away, cursing, to be treated, and no one—not yet—had thought of rabies, and they crowded in close then, poking at the bound-up child, the *enfant sauvage* stripped from the fastness of the forest. They saw that his skin was roughened and dark as an Arab's, that the calluses of his feet were thick and horned and his teeth so yellowed they were like a goat's. The hair was grease itself and protected them from the unflinching glare of his eyes where it fell across his face and the rough corners of the cloth jammed deep in his mouth. No one thought to cover his genitals, the genitals of a child, two acorns and a twig.

The night wore on and nobody wanted to leave the room, the excess prowling round the open door, queuing up for a second and third look, the drink flowing, the darkness steeping in its post-winter chill, DeFarge's wife throwing wood at the fire and every man, woman and child thinking they'd seen the miraculous, a sight more terrifying and wonderful than the birth of the two-headed calf at Mansard's the year past or the adder that had borne a hundred adders just like it. They poked the child, prodded him with the toes of their sabots and boots—some of the more curious or courageous leaned in close to catch the scent of him, and every one of them pronounced it the smell of the wild, of the beast in its lair. At some point, the priest came to bless him, and though the wild Indians of America had been brought to the fold of God and the aborigines of Africa and Asia too, the priest thought better of it. "What's the matter, Father?" someone asked. "Is he not human?"

But the priest—a very young man with an angelic face and hardly a trace of beard—just shook his head and walked out the door.

Later, when people grew tired of the spectacle and eyelids began to collapse and chins give way to gravity, Messier—the most vocal and possessive of the group—insisted that the prodigy be locked in the back room of the tavern overnight so that news of his capture could be spread throughout the province in the morning. They'd removed the gag to enable the child to eat and drink, and a number of people, women among them, had attempted to coax him to taste one thing or another—a heel of bread, a scrap of stewed hare, wine, broth—but he'd twisted and spat and would take nothing. Someone speculated that he'd been raised by wolves, like Romulus and Remus, and would consume only the milk of a she-wolf, and he was given a very small quantity of the nearest simulacrum—the deposit of one of the village bitches that had just given birth—and yet that too was rejected. As were offal, eggs, butter, *boudin* and cheese. After a while, and after half the citizens in the place had stood patiently over the bound and writhing form with one thing or another dangling from tentative fingertips, they gave up and went home to their beds, excited and gratified, but weary, very weary, and bloated with drink.

Then it was quiet. Then it was dark. Traumatized, numb, the child lay there in a state between waking and sleeping. He was trembling, not from the cold because he was hardened to the weather, even to winter and the bitterest of days, but because of fear. He couldn't feel his limbs, the cords so tightly wound they were like ligatures, cutting off circulation, and he was terrified of the strangeness of the place where he was confined, a place that was enclosed on six planes and gave no sign of the stars overhead and no scent of pine or juniper or water in its flight. Animals, bigger and more powerful than he, had taken him for their pleasure, for their prey, and he had no expectation but fear because he had no word for death and no way to conceptualize it. He caught things, quick frightened things, and he killed them and ate them, but that was in a different place and a different time. Perhaps he made the connection, perhaps not. But at some point, when the moon rose and the thinnest sliver of light cut between the jointure of two stones in the near wall, he began to stir.

He had no awareness of time. Flexing, rocking, pushing off with his flexible toes and scrabbling with his nails, he shifted in space and shifted again and again till the cords began to give up their grip. When they were loose, he tore them off as if they were strips of vegetation, the vines and tendrils and entangling branches that snatched at his wrists and ankles as he perambulated through the forest, and a moment later he was stalking the room. There were two doors, but he didn't know what a door was and the rigidity of his terror had kept him from discovering its function when he was brought into this place and laid on the compacted floor in a scattering of straw. Nonetheless, he felt them, felt the wood as a texture to itself and a contrast to the stone, and thrust his weight into them. Nothing happened. The doors—the one leading back into the tavern, the other to the yard—were latched, and even if they weren't he wouldn't have been able to uncover the secret of their hinges or their method either. But above him was the roof, thatch over a frame of stripped poles laid close as fingers and toes. A single leap took him there, where he clung upside down like an oversized insect, and then it was a small thing to separate two poles and begin to dig upward toward the scent of the night.

3

For two years and more he eluded capture, hovering like a *cauchemar* at the margins of people's thoughts, and when the mistral raked the roofs and shrieked down the chimneys, they said he was stirring up the spirits of the forest. If a hen went missing, they blamed the *enfant,* though he'd never been seen to consume flesh or even to know what it was; if it rained too much or too little or if rust afflicted the grain or aphids the vines, people crossed themselves and cursed his name. He wasn't a child. He was a spirit, a demon outcast like the rebel angels, mute and staring and mad. Peasants reported seeing him capering in moonlit meadows, swimming like a rat in the rivers, basking in the sun in summer and darting through the scabs of snow that lay on the winter hills, oblivious to the cold. They called him the Naked One. *L'Animal.* Or, simply, the Savage.

For his part, he scraped and dug and followed his nose. On the primal level, he had only to feed himself, and if he raided the fields like any other creature of the forest, he took the same risks as they, to be trapped or shot or startled to immobility by the sudden flapping of a scarecrow's rags. Still, his diet was barely adequate, as might be imagined, consisting almost entirely of vegetable matter, and in winter he suffered just as the birds did. But he survived. And he grew. Haunting the barnyards, the middens and granaries, he became bolder, quicker, stronger, and farmers took to setting the dogs on him, but he was cannier than any dog and too smart to go to tree. Did he somehow come to understand that people were his tribe in the way that a bear instinctually consorts with other bears rather than foxes or wolves or goats? Did he know he was human? He must have. He had no words to form the proposition, no way of thinking beyond the present moment, but as he grew he became less a creature of the forest and more of the pasture, the garden, the dim margin where the trees and the *maquis* give way to cultivation.

Then came the winter of 1799, which was especially bitter. By this time, wary of the forest of La Bassine and wandering in search of the next trove of mushrooms or wild grapes or berries and the grubs he extracted from the pulp of decaying trees, he'd worked his way up over the mountains, across the plain between Lacaune and Roquecézière, and then down again along the bed of the Lavergne until he arrived in the environs of the village of Saint-Sernin. It was early January, just after the New Year, and the cold held a grip on everything. When night fell, he made himself a nest of pine branches, but slept fitfully because of his shivering and the hunger that clawed at his insides. At first light he was up and pawing through the scattered clods of a dormant field, looking for anything to feed into his mouth, tubers, onions, the chaff and scraps of crops long since harvested, when a ghostly drifting movement caught his eye: smoke, rising above the trees at the far end of the field. He was crouched on all fours, digging. The ground was wet. A crow mocked him from the trees. Without thinking, without knowing what he was doing or why, he rose and trotted toward the smoke and the cottage that gave rise to it.

Inside was the village dyer, François Vidal, who'd just gotten out of bed and started up the fire to warm the place and make himself a bit of porridge for breakfast. He was childless, a widower, and he lived alone. From the rafters of his one-room cottage hung the drying herbs, flowers and marsh weeds he used in his receipts—he was the only man in the region who could produce a *bon teint* of royal purple in lamb's wool, employing his own mixture and mordant, and he was of necessity extremely secretive. Did his competitors want his receipts? Yes, they did. Did they spy on him? He couldn't have said for certain, but he wouldn't have put it past them. At any rate, he went out to the yard, to the crude shed in which he kept his cow, so that he could feed and milk her, thinking to skim off the cream to complement his porridge. That was when he saw something—the dark streak of an animal—moving upright against the dun earth and the stripped backdrop of the trees.

He had no prejudices. He hadn't heard the rumors from Lacaune or even from the next village over. And when his eyes adjusted and registered the image in his brain, he saw that this was no animal, but a human child, a boy, filthy, naked to the elements and in need. He held out his hand.

What ensued was a test of wills. When the boy didn't respond, Vidal extended both his hands, palms up, to show he was unarmed, and he spoke to him in soft, coaxing tones, but the boy didn't seem to understand or even to hear. As a child, Vidal had a half-sister who was deaf, and the family had evolved its own home signs to communicate with her, though the rest of the village shunned her as a freak; it was these signs that began to come back to him as he stood there in the cold, contemplating the naked child. If the boy was a deaf-mute, as it appeared, then perhaps he would respond to the signs. The dyer's hands, stained with the residue of his trade, spoke in quick elegant patterns, but to no avail. The boy stood rooted, his eyes flitting past the dyer's face to the house, the shed, the smoke that flattened and billowed against the sky. Finally, fearful of driving him off, Vidal backed slowly to the house, made a welcoming gesture at the door, and then stepped inside, leaving the door open wide in invitation.

Eventually, with the dyer bent over the hearth and the cow—Rousa—unmilked and lowing with a sound that was like the distant intermittent report of a meteorological event in the hills, the boy came to the open door and Vidal was able to get a good look at him. Whose child was this, he wondered, to be allowed to run wild like an animal, the filth of the woods ingrained in the very pores of his skin, his hair matted with twigs and burrs and leaf mold and his knees callused like the soles of his feet? Who was he? Had he been abandoned? And then he saw the scar at the child's throat and knew the answer. When he gestured toward the fire, toward the blackened pot and the wheat porridge congealing within it, he was thinking of his dead sister.

Cautiously, one tentative step at a time, the boy was drawn to the fire. And just as cautiously, because he was afraid that any sudden movement would chase him through the door and back out into the fields, Vidal laid sticks on the hearth till the fire leapt up and he had to remove the pot, which he set on the fender to cool. The door stood open. The cow lowed. Using his hands to speak, the dyer offered the boy a bowl of porridge, fragrant with the steam rising from it, and he meant to fetch milk and pull the door shut, once he had his trust. But the boy showed no interest whatever in the food. He was in constant motion, rocking back and forth on his feet, his eyes fixed on the fire. It came to Vidal that he didn't know what porridge was, didn't know a bowl or a spoon or their function either. And so he made gestures, pantomiming the act of eating in the way of a parent with an infant, bringing the spoon to his lips and tasting the porridge, making a show of masticating and swallowing and even going so far as to rub his abdomen in a circular fashion and smiling in satisfaction.

The boy was unmoved. He simply stood there, rocking, fascinated by the fire, and the two of them might have stayed in position all day long if it weren't for an inspiration that suddenly came to the old man. Perhaps there were simpler, ruder foods, he reasoned, foods of the forest and fields, that the child would take without prejudice, nuts and the like. He looked round him—he had no nuts. Nuts were out of season. But in a basket against the far wall there was a small quantity of potatoes he'd brought up from the root cellar to fry in lard with his evening meal. Very slowly, communicating with his body and his hands so as not to alarm the child, he got to his feet, and slowly—so slowly he might have been a child himself playing a game of statues—crossed the room to the basket. He lifted the straw lid, and still pantomiming, held up the basket to display its contents.

That was all it took. In an instant the child was there, inches away, the wild odor rising from him like musk, his hands scrabbling in the basket till he was clutching every last potato in his arms—a dozen or more—and then he was at the fire, throwing them into the flames in a single motion. His face was animated, his eyes leaping. Short, blunted, inarticulate cries escaped his lips. Within seconds, in the space of time it took Vidal to move to the door and pull it closed, the boy had reached into the coals to extract one of the uncooked potatoes, burning his fingers in the process. Immediately, as if he had no concept of what cookery involved, he began gnawing at it. When it was gone, he reached for another and then another and the same sequence of events played out, only now the potatoes were blackened on the outside and hard within and his fingers visibly scarred.

Appalled, Vidal tried to instruct him, showing him the use of the fire irons, but the boy ignored him—or worse, stared right through him as if he didn't exist. The dyer offered him cheese, bread, wine, but the child showed no interest, and it was only when he thought to pour him a cup of water from the pitcher on the table that the child responded. He tried at first to lap the water from the cup, but then he understood and held it to his lips until it was drained and he wanted more, which Vidal, as fascinated as if a fox had got up on two legs and come to join him at table, kept pouring until he was sated. After which, naked and filthy, the child pulled his limbs to his chest and fell into a deep sleep on the stones of the hearth.

For a long while, the dyer merely sat there, contemplating this apparition that had blundered into his life. He got up from time to time to feed the fire or light his pipe, but he didn't attempt to do any work, not that day. All he could think of was his half-sister, Marie-Thérèse, an undersized child with a powerfully expressive face—she could say more with her face alone than most people with their tongues. She was the product of his father's first marriage to a woman who had died of puerperal fever after bearing only this one damaged child, and his mother never accepted her. She was always last to be fed and first to receive the slap to the face or the back of the head when things went wrong, and she took to wandering off by herself, away from the other siblings, until one night she didn't come back. He was eight or nine at the time, and so she must have been twelve or so. They found her body at the bottom of a ravine. People said she must have lost her way in the dark and fallen, but even then, even as a child, he knew better.

Just then Rousa bellowed and he started. What was he thinking, leaving her to burst like that? He got up quickly, slipped into his coat and went out to her. When he returned, the child was pinned against the far wall, huddled and afraid, staring at him as if they'd never encountered one another before. Things were out of place, the table overturned, candlesticks on the floor, all his painstakingly gathered and hoarded plants torn down from the rafters and scattered like drift. He tried to calm the boy, speaking with his hands, but it did no good—every movement he made was matched by a corresponding movement, the child keeping his back to the wall and maintaining the distance between them, rocking on his feet, ready to leap for the door if only he knew what the door was. And his jaws, his jaws seemed to be working. What was it? What was he eating, another potato? It was then that the dyer saw the naked tail of the thing dangling like a string of saliva from the corner of the boy's mouth, and the boy's yellowed teeth, chewing round the dun wad of fur.

If he'd felt sympathy, if he'd felt kinship and pity, now all the dyer felt was disgust. He was an old man, fifty-four years on this earth, and Marie-Thérèse had been dead nearly half a century. This was none of his affair. None of it. Cautiously, warily, all his senses on alert as if he'd found himself locked in a cage with a ravening beast, he backed toward the door, slipped outside and pulled it shut behind him.

Late that afternoon, as a cold rain pelted the streets of Saint-Sernin and fell hard over the countryside, the wild child was given up to science, and through science, to celebrity. After having rolled one of his big cast-iron dye pots across the yard and up against the door to secure it, Vidal had gone directly to Jean-Jacques Constans-Saint-Estève, the government commissioner for Saint-Sernin, to make a report and give over responsibility for the creature immured in his cottage. The Commissioner, a man who traveled widely about the district, had heard the rumors from Lacaune and elsewhere, and he was eager to see this phenomenon with his own eyes. Here was a chance, he reasoned—if this creature wasn't just some bugbear or an African ape escaped from a private menagerie—to put Rousseau's notion of the Noble Savage to the test. What innate ideas did he have? Did he know of God and Creation? What was his language—the ur-language that gave rise to all the languages of the world, the language all men brought with them from Heaven? Or was it the gabble of the birds and the beasts? He could barely restrain himself. The light was fading from the sky and he'd had no dinner, but dinner was nothing compared to what this opportunity meant. He took Vidal by the arm. "Lead me to him," he said.

By the time the Commissioner had concluded his audience with Vidal and hurried with him out into the rain to see this prodigy for himself, he was surprised to see people in the street, heading in the same direction as he. "Is it true, Citizen Commissioner?" people asked. "They've captured the wild child?"

"I hear," someone else said, and there was a mob of them now, men, women and children, plodding through the rain to Vidal's cottage, "that he has six fingers on each hand—"

"And toes," another chimed in. "And he has claws like a cat to climb straight up a wall."

"He leaps fifty meters in a bound."

"Blood, he lives on blood that he sucks from the sheep at midnight."

"Nonsense, nonsense"—one of the village women, Catherine Thibodeaux, appeared at his shoulder, hooded against the storm—"it's only an abandoned child. Where's the curé? Call out the curé."

When they approached the yard, the Commissioner swung round furiously to hush them—"Stay back," he hissed, "you'll frighten him"—but the crowd had worked itself into a frenzy of fear and wonderment and they pressed forward like a flock heading to pasture. Everyone crowded round the door, pressing their faces to the windows, and if it weren't for the impediment of the dye kettle they would have rushed into the room without thinking. Now they hesitated, their voices dropping to a whisper, while Vidal and the Commissioner shifted the kettle aside and stepped into the room, pulling the door fast behind them. The child was there, crouched before the fire, no different from how Vidal had left him, though he didn't seem to be masticating anything at the moment. Thankfully. What was strange, however, was that he didn't look up, though certainly he must have been aware of the alien presence in the room and even of the credulous faces pressed to the windows.

The Commissioner was dumbstruck. This child—this thing—was scarred, hunched, filthy, and it gave off a stench of the barnyard, as wild and forlorn as the first upright creature created by God in His own image, the man Adam who was given dominion over the animals and named them in turn. But this *was* an animal, a kind of ape, the sort of degraded thing Linnaeus must have had in mind when he placed men and apes in the same order of being. And if there was any doubt, there was the fresh coil of its dung, gleaming on the rough planks of the floor.

The fire snapped and hissed. There was a murmur from the crowd pressed up against the windows. "Good God," he exclaimed under his breath, and then, turning to the dyer, he put to him the only question he could manage, "Is it dangerous?"

Vidal, his house a shambles so that he was embarrassed in front of the Commissioner, merely shrugged. "He's just a child, Citizen Commissioner, a poor abandoned child, flesh and blood, just like anyone else. But he's unschooled. He doesn't know porridge, doesn't know a bowl, a cup, a spoon, doesn't know what to do with them—"

Constans-Saint-Estève was in his early forties and dressed in the fashion of Paris as it was before the Revolution. He had a fleshy face and the pouting lips of an epicene. His back still pressed to the door, his eyes locked on the child, he whispered, "Does he speak?"

"Only cries and whimpers. He may be—I think he's a deaf-mute."

Overcoming his initial shock, the Commissioner crossed the room and stood over the boy a moment, murmuring blandishments. His scientific curiosity had been re-aroused—this was a rare opportunity. A wonder, really. "Hello," he said finally, bending at the knees and bringing his bland face into the child's line of vision, "I am Jean-Jacques Constans-Saint-Estève, Commissioner for Saint-Sernin. And who might you be? What is your name?"

The child stared through him, as if he were insubstantial.

"Do you have a name?"

Nothing.

"Do you understand me? Do you understand French? Or perhaps some other language?" Judging from the coloration of the child's skin, he might have been Basque, Spanish, Italian. The Commissioner tried out a greeting on him in the languages of these regions, and then, frustrated, clapped his hands together as loudly as he could, right in front of the child's nose. There was no reaction whatever. The Commissioner looked to Vidal and the pale buds of the faces hung as if on a branch at the near window and pronounced, *"Sourd-muet."*

It was then that the villagers could stand it no longer and began to push into the room, one at a time, until the place was crowded to the walls, people trampling the dried leaves and roots scattered across the floor, examining everything—trying, Vidal thought, to discover his secret methods and receipts, which made him uneasy in the extreme, made him suspicious and angry—and it was then that the child came to life and made a bolt for the open door. A cry went up and people leapt back as if a mad dog were among them; in a trice the child was out in the yard, in the rain, galloping on all fours for the curtain of trees at the edge of the field. And he would have made it, would have escaped again back into nature, but for two of the strongest men in the village, men in their twenties, great runners, who brought him to ground and wrestled him back to the open door of the dyer's cottage. The child writhed in their grip, making a repetitive sound that rattled in his windpipe—*uh-uh-uh-uh*—and snaking his head round to bite.

It was fully dark now, the light of the fire and a single candle falling through the open door to illuminate the scene. The Commissioner stood there in the doorway, looking down at the child for a long moment, and then he began to stroke the child's face, pushing the hair back from his brow and out of his eyes so that everyone could see that he was a human child and no dog or ape or demon, and the stroking had the effect it would have on any sentient thing: the child's breathing slowed and his eyes went distant. "All right," the Commissioner said, "let him go," and the men loosened their grip on his limbs and stepped back. For a moment the child just slumped there on the doorstep, glistening with wet and mud, his limbs thin as a cow's shins, and then he took hold of the hand the Commissioner held out to him and rose quietly to his feet.

It was as if some switch had been turned off in the *enfant's* inner apparatus—he came docilely, holding on to the Commissioner's hand like a novice on the way to church, while the village followed in solemn processional. Along the way, the rain still lashing down and the streets a soup of mud, people tried to get close enough to touch the child, and they shouted out that he fed only on nuts and roots in the woods—and what would he eat now, a *blanquette de veau*? *Boeuf bourguignon? Langouste?* The Commissioner didn't bother to answer, but he was determined to make his own experiment. First he would clothe the boy's nakedness and then he would offer him an array of foods to see what he would take and in the process he would try to learn something of this prodigy that would benefit society and the understanding of mankind.

Once home, he shut the door on the villagers and instructed his servant to find a garment for the child, and then, while he ordered up his own dinner, he installed the child in the room he used as his study and offices. A fire was laid and the boy went directly to it. In the room were several chairs, a desk, shelves of legal volumes and volumes of natural history and philosophy, the Commissioner's papers, a freestanding globe and a birdcage of wrought iron. Inside the cage was a gray parrot his late father had brought back from a voyage to Gambia thirty years earlier; her name was Philomène and she could ask, in penetrating tones, for grapes, cherries and nuts, comment on the weather and the state of inebriation of dinner guests and whistle the opening figure of Mozart's Piano Sonata in A minor. Excited by the prospect of examining the boy at his leisure, the Commissioner stepped out of the room only long enough to mollify his wife and give orders to have various foodstuffs brought to him; when he returned, the boy's face was pressed against the bars of the cage and Philomène was vainly serenading him with the Mozart.

He took the boy gently by the hand and led him to the desk, where a servant had laid out a selection of foods, both raw and cooked. There was meat, rye and wheat bread, apples, pears, grapes, walnuts, chestnuts, acorns, potatoes, parsnips and a solitary orange. Of all this, the child seemed only to recognize the acorns and potatoes, the latter of which he immediately threw into the fire, while cracking the acorns between his teeth and sucking the pulp from them. The potatoes he devoured almost instantly, though they were as hot as the coals themselves; bread meant nothing to him. Again, and for many patient hours, the Commissioner tried speaking to the child, first aloud and then in dumbshow, but nothing would rouse him; he seemed no more aware than a dog or cat. And no noise, not even the beating of a drum, affected him. Finally, after making sure the windows were secure and the doors latched, the Commissioner left the child in the room, snuffed the candles and went off to bed. Where his wife scolded him—what was he thinking bringing that savage thing into their house? What if he arose in the night and murdered them all?—and his two sons, Guillaume and Gérard, four and six respectively, informed him that they were too frightened to sleep in their own beds and would have to share his.

In the morning, he approached his study on silent feet, though he kept telling himself there was no need because the child was almost certainly deaf. He lifted the latch and peered into the room, not knowing what to expect. The first thing he saw was the child's garment, a shift of gray cloth that had been forced over his head the previous night; it lay on the carpet in the center of the room beside a shining loop of excrement. The next thing was the child himself, standing in the far corner, staring at the wall and rocking back and forth on his feet and moaning as if he'd been wounded in some vital place. Then the Commissioner noticed several of his volumes of Buffon's *Histoire naturelle, générale et particulière* lying facedown on the floor, their leaves scattered to the wind. And then, finally, he noticed Philomène, or what was left of her.

That afternoon the wild child was sent to the orphanage at Saint-Affrique.

4

He was brought to Saint-Affrique in a fiacre, the jolting and swaying of which caused him a great deal of discomfort. Four times during the journey he became sick on the floor of the carriage and the servant Constans-Saint-Estève had sent along to accompany him did little to relieve his distress, other than daubing at the mess with a rag. The child was dressed in his gray shift, which was knotted tightly at the waist to prevent his removing it, he was barefooted and he'd been provided with a small sack of potatoes and turnips for his sustenance. The horses seemed to terrify him. He rocked on the seat and moaned the whole way. On arriving at the orphanage, he made a bolt for the woods, down on all fours and squealing like a rodent, but his guardian was too quick for him.

Inside the walls, it was apparent that he was no ordinary child. The director of the orphanage—Citizen R. Nougairoles—observed that he had no notion of sitting at table or of relieving himself in the pot or even the latrine, that he tore at his garment as if the very touch of the cloth seared his skin and that he refused to sleep in the bed provided for him, instead curling up in a pile of refuse in the corner. When threatened, he used his teeth. The other children, curious at first, soon learned to give him his distance. Still, in the short time he was there, a mere two weeks, he did become acculturated to the degree that he seemed to appreciate the comforts of a fire on a bitter day and he extended his dietary range to include pease soup improved with hunks of dark bread. On the other hand, he displayed no interest whatever in the other orphans (or in anyone, for that matter, unless they were in immediate possession of the simple foods he liked to eat). People might as well have been trees for all he responded to them—except when they got too close, of course—and he had no conception either of work or recreation. When he wasn't eating or sleeping, he crouched over his knees, rocking and vocalizing in a curious inarticulate way, but every moment he looked for his chance to escape and twice had to be chased down and forcibly restrained. Finally, and this was the one thing Nougairoles found most disturbing, he showed no familiarity with the forms and objects of holy devotion. The Director concluded that he was no impostor, but the real thing—Linnaeus' *Homo ferus* in the flesh—and that the orphanage could hardly be expected to contain him.

In the meanwhile, both he and Constans-Saint-Estève wrote up their observations of the child and posted them to the *Journal des débats,* and from there the other Parisian periodicals took hold of the story. Soon the entire nation was mad for news of this prodigy from Aveyron, the wild child, the animal in human form. Speculation galloped through the streets and echoed down the alleys. Was he Rousseau's Noble Savage or just another aborigine? Or perhaps—thrilling conjecture—the *loup-garou,* or werewolf, of legend? Or was he more closely related to the orangutan, the great orange ape of the Far East, an example of which, it had been proposed, should be mated to a prostitute in order to discover its issue? Two prominent and competing naturalists—Abbé Roche-Ambroise Sicard, of the Institute for Deaf-Mutes in Paris, and Abbé Pierre-Joseph Bonnaterre, professor of natural history at the Central School for Aveyron, located in Rodez—applied to take possession of the child in order to observe and record his behavior before it was further tainted by contact with society. Bonnaterre, being closer at hand, won out, at least in the short term, and he personally took charge of the boy at Saint-Affrique and transferred him to the school at Rodez. For the child, bewildered and aching only to get free of it all, it meant another fiacre, another assault of horses, another unfamiliar face. He was sick on the floor. He clutched the sack of turnips and potatoes to his side and would not let it out of his sight.

For the next several months, at least until the Minister of the Interior acted decisively in Sicard's favor, Bonnaterre had the boy to himself. He assigned a servant to see to the boy's corporal needs and then set about staging various experiments to gauge the child's reactions and store of knowledge. Since it had been assumed that the child was deaf, all contact with him thus far had been in dumbshow, but Bonnaterre laid out a number of instruments, from the triangle to the drum to the bass viol, and led the child to them, playing on each one in succession as best he could. Beyond the windows it was a clear, bright winter's day. Bonnaterre's servant—his gardener, to whom the boy had seemed at least minimally to relate, perhaps because of the smell of the earth about him—was stationed by the door to prevent the child's escape and to discipline him if he should act out (and he did defeat all notions of modesty, pulling his smock up to the cincture at the waist in order to warm himself at the fire, for instance, and playing with his penis as if it were a toy soldier).

At any rate, Bonnaterre—a stern and imposing man with a face as flagrant as a ham against the pure white curls of his periwig—persisted for some time, beating at the drum, drawing the bow across the strings of the bass viol, clapping, shouting and singing till the gardener began to suspect he'd lost his mind. The child never reacted, never winced or smiled or turned his head at one plangent sound or another. But then the gardener, in his idleness, reached for a walnut from the bowl of them set on a sideboard at the rear of the room, out of sight of the boy, and applied the nut cracker to it with a sound barely discernible in the general racket fomented by his master, and—it was like a miracle—the boy's head jerked round. In an instant, he was at the gardener's side, snatching at the nuts; in the next, he was atop the sideboard, pounding the shells against the gleaming mahogany surface with the nearest thing that came to hand, a silver candlestick, as it turned out.

Despite the damage to the furniture, Bonnaterre was encouraged. The child was not deaf, not deaf at all, but rather his senses had been so attuned to the sounds of nature that any noise of human agency, no matter how strident or articulate, failed to impress him: there were no human voices in the wild, nor bass viols either. Creeping about the woods in an eternal search for food, he listened only for the fall of the apple or chestnut or the cry of the squirrel, or even, perhaps, on some miraculous level, for the minute vibrations sent out by the escargot as it rides along its avenue of slime. But if food was the child's exclusive focus throughout his feral life, then how would he react now that food was abundant and his for the asking? Would he begin to develop an interior life—a propositional life—rather than being exclusively fixated on exterior objects?

Bonnaterre pondered these questions, even as he observed the boy day by day and watched as he acquired rudimentary signs to make his desires understood, pointing to the water jug, for instance, when he was thirsty or taking his caretaker by the hand and leading him to the kitchen when he was hungry, there to point at one object or another. If he wasn't immediately gratified he went to the floor, moving rapidly on hands and feet and dragging his posterior across the finished boards, at the same time setting up a withering deep-throated sort of howl that peaked and fell and rose again from nothing.

When he was given what he wanted—potatoes, walnuts, broad beans, which he shelled with amazing swiftness and dexterity—he ate until it seemed he would have to burst, ate more than any five of the other children could consume at a sitting, and then gathered up the leftovers in his gown and stole away to the courtyard, where he buried them for future reference, no different from a dog with a bone. And when he was fed with others he displayed no sense of courtesy or fairness, but took all the food to himself, whether by a bold snatch or the furtive gesture, with no thought for his fellows. During the third week of observation he began to accept meat when it was offered, raw at first, and then cooked, and eventually he came to relish potatoes browned in oil in the pan—when the mood struck him he would go to the kitchen, take up the knife and the pan and point to the cabinet in which the potatoes and cooking oil were kept. It was a rude life, focused on one thing only—on food—and Bonnaterre was able to recognize in him the origins of uncivilized humanity, untouched by culture, by awareness, by human feeling. "How could he possibly be expected to have known the existence of God?" Bonnaterre wrote. "Let him be shown the heavens, the green fields, the vast expanse of the earth, the works of Nature, he does not see anything in all that if there is nothing there to eat."

For the boy's part, he began, very gradually, to adjust. His food came to him not from a hole in the earth or a chance encounter with carrion or the wild thing that was slower than he, but from these animals that had captured him, strange animals with heavy faces and snouts, with their odd white pelage and the hairless smooth second skin of their legs. He was with the one in charge of him at some point, the one all the others deferred to, and on an impulse he snatched at the man's pelt, the whiteness there, the gleam of it, and was startled to see it detached from the man's head and dangling from his own fingers. The man—the big flushed face, the veins like earthworms crawling up his neck—leapt from his seat with a cry and made to snatch the thing back, but the child was too quick for him, darting round the room and hooting over this thing, this hide that smelled of musk and the friable white substance that gave it its color. Gabbling, the man came after him, and, terrified now, the child ran, ran to a kind of stone that was transparent and gave a view of the outdoors and the courtyard. This was glass, though he had no way of knowing it, and it was an essential component of the walls that imprisoned him. The man shouted. He ran. And the stone shattered, biting into his forearm with its teeth.

They put a bandage of cloth on his wound, but he used his own teeth to tear it off. Blood was a thing he knew, and pain, and he knew to avoid brambles, the hives of the wasps, the scaled stone of the ridges that shifted underfoot and cut at his ankles with mindless ferocity, but this was different, a new phenomenon: glass. A wound of glass. It puzzled him and he took up a shard of it when no one was looking and ran it over his finger till the pain came again and the blood showed there and he squeezed and squeezed at the slit of his skin to see the brightness of it, vivid with hurt. That night, just before supper, he tugged at the other man's hand, the one who smelled of manure and mold, till the man took him out into the courtyard; the instant the door was opened he made a run for the wall and scaled it in two desperate bounds and then he was down on the far side and running, running.

They caught him again, at the foot of the woods, and he fought them with his teeth and his claws but they were bigger, stronger, and they carried him back as they always had and always would because there was no freedom, not anymore. Now he was a creature of the walls and the rooms and a slave to the food they gave him. And that night they gave him nothing, neither food nor water, and locked him in the place where he was used to sleeping at night, though he did not want to sleep, he wanted to eat. He chewed at the crack of the door till his lips bled and his gums tightened round the pain. He was wild no more.

When they took him to Paris, when the Minister of the Interior finally intervened on behalf of Sicard and gave instructions that the child should be brought north to the City of Light, he traveled through the alien countryside with Bonnaterre and the gardener who had acted as his caretaker all the while he was in Rodez. At first, he wouldn't enter the fiacre—as soon as he was led out of the gates and saw it standing there flanked by the three massive and stinking draft horses with their stupendous legs and staring eyes, he tried to bolt—but Bonnaterre had foreseen the event and placed a cornucopia of potatoes, turnips and small, hard loaves on the seat, and his weakness led him to scramble up the step and retreat inside. As a precaution against any further mischance, Bonnaterre had the gardener affix a lead to the cord round the child's waist, a simple braid of rope, the other end of which was held loosely in the abbé's hand as the public coach made its appointed stops and took on the odd passenger along the way. Was this a leash, such as might be used on a dog? It was an interesting question, one with pointed philosophical and humanitarian implications—certainly Bonnaterre didn't want to call it a leash, nor did the gardener—and as the boy rocked on the seat and made sick on the floor, the abbé kept hold of it with the lightest touch. The coach heaved on its springs, the gardener made himself small, Bonnaterre looked straight ahead. And when a blanched, imposing lady and her maid boarded the fiacre in a market town along the way, he went out of his way to assure them that the child was no threat at all and that the lead was solely for his own protection.

Nonetheless, when they stopped that evening at an inn along the way, the child (he was taller now and he'd put on weight, hardly a child any longer) did manage to create a scene. As the coachman held the door for the lady, the child gave a sly, sudden jerk at the lead, tearing it from the abbé's hand; in the next moment, using the lady's skirts as a baffle, he bounded down from the coach and lit out up the road in his curious, loping, lopsided gait, the leash trailing behind him. The lady, thinking she was being attacked, let out with a shriek that startled the horses into motion even while Bonnaterre and his servant clambered down to give chase and the hostler fought the reins. As can be imagined, the abbé was in no condition to be running footraces along the rutted dirt byways of a country lane, and he hadn't gone twenty feet before he was bent double and gasping for air.

This time, however, and to everyone's relief, the child apparently wasn't attempting an escape, but instead stopped of his own accord no more than a hundred yards off, where a ditch of stagnant water ran along the road. Before they could prevent him, he threw himself down on his stomach and began to drink. The surface of the water was discolored with duckweed, strands of algae, roadside offal. Mosquitoes settled on the child's exposed limbs. His garment was soiled in the muck. Both Bonnaterre and the gardener stood over him, remonstrating, but he paid them no mind: he was thirsty; he was drinking. When done drinking, he rose and defecated on the spot (another curiosity: he defecated while standing and squatted to micturate), dirtying the skirts of his gown without a second thought. And then, as if this weren't enough, he made a snatch for something in the reeds and had it in his mouth before they could intervene—a frog, as it turned out, mashed to pulp by the time the gardener was able to pry it from his jaws.

After that, he came docilely enough to the inn, where he settled himself in the far corner of the room provided for him, gurgling and clicking over his sack of roots and tubers, to all appearances content and wanting the society of no one. But before long the villagers got wind of his arrival and crowded the inn for the rest of the night, straining to get a look at him—people clamoring at the doorway and scuffling in the halls, dogs yammering, the whole neighborhood in an uproar. He shrank into his corner, his face to the wall, and still the furor persisted till long after dark. And, of course, the closer he and his guardians got to the capital, where the influence of the newspapers was strongest, the bigger and more insistent the crowds grew. Despite himself, and despite the Minister of the Interior's strict injunction to bring the child to Paris without harm or impediment, Bonnaterre couldn't help gratifying the people along the way with at least a glimpse of the prodigy. And no, he didn't feel at all like a circus crier or a gypsy sword-swallower or anything of the kind—he was a scientist presenting the object of his study, and if the pride of possession gave him an internal glow of special privilege and authority, well, so be it.

It might have been the contact with all those people or the breathing of the night air or the miasma that hung over the roadside ditches where he liked to drink, but the child fell ill with smallpox along the way and had to be confined in the back room of an inn for a period of ten days while he broke out in spots and alternately shivered and burned with the fever. Blankets were brought, the local physician was consulted, there was talk of purging and bloodletting, and Bonnaterre was in a state—it was his head that was on the line here. Perhaps literally. The Minister of the Interior, Lucien Bonaparte, brother of Napoléon, was an exacting man, and to present him with the mere corpse of a wild child would be like bringing him the hide of some rare creature from the African jungle, its anatomical features lost, its vibrant colors already faded. The abbé got down on his knees before the writhing, bundled, sweating form of the child, and prayed.

Drifting in and out of sleep, the child watched the walls fade away and the roof dissolve to present the stars and the moon and then he was capering through a meadow while the Midi shook the trees till they bent like individual blades of grass and he was laughing aloud and running, running. He saw back in time, saw the places where he'd gorged on berries, saw the vineyard and the grapes and the cellar where a farmer had stored his crop of potatoes, new-dug from the earth. Then there were the boys, the village boys, urchins, quick-legged animals, discovering him there in the forest and giving chase, pelting him with sticks and rocks and the hard sharp stabs of their cries, and then the men and the fire and the smoke. And this room, where the walls re-erected themselves and the roof came back to obliterate the sky. He felt hunger. Thirst. He sat up and threw off the bedclothes.

Three days later, he was in Paris, though he didn't know it. All he knew was what he saw and heard and smelled. He saw confusion, heard chaos, and what he smelled was ranker than anything he'd come across in all his years of wandering the fields and forests of Aveyron, concentrated, pungent, the reek of civilization.

5

The Institute for Deaf-Mutes sprawled over several acres just across the boulevard Saint-Michel from the Luxembourg Gardens. It was formerly a Catholic seminary, which the revolutionary government had given over to Abbé Sicard for the training and advancement of the deaf and dumb. Employing a method of instruction in the language of signs he had adopted from his predecessor, De l'Epée, Sicard had become famous for the amazing transformations he'd wrought in several of his pupils, turning the all-but-hopeless into productive citizens who not only could articulate their needs and wants with perfect clarity but expound on philosophical issues as well. One of them, a well-made young man by the name of Massieu, was the cynosure of a number of Sicard's public demonstrations of his pupils' speaking and writing ability, in which the pupils answered questions written on cards by the audience, and he came to address a number of learned societies with confidence and dignity and in an accent not much worse than an educated foreigner's. Even more astonishing, this young man, who'd come to the Institute as dumb as a stone, was eventually able to dine in company and entertain people with his own original *bon mots,* memorably defining gratitude as *la mémoire du coeur* and distinguishing between desire and hope by pronouncing that "Desire is a tree in leaf, hope is a tree in bloom, enjoyment is a tree with fruit." And so, when the wild child was delivered up to Sicard by Bonnaterre, all of Paris awaited the result, the miracle that was sure to follow as the boy acquired the ability of language and the gift of civilization; it was hoped that one day he too would stand before an entranced audience and give shape to the thoughts and emotions he'd felt while living as an animal.

Unfortunately, things proved different.

After the initial flurry of excitement, after the crowds had dissipated and half the haut monde of Paris had trooped up the stairs of the Institute to observe him rocking in the corner of his room on the fifth floor, after he was brought to the chambers of the Minister of the Interior for a private interview (where he sat on his haunches in a corner and stared vacantly into the distance before relieving himself on the carpet), after the newspapers had recorded his every move and common citizens had gathered on street corners to debate his humanity, he was given over to neglect. Sicard, a man preoccupied with his more tractable pupils, the text of the book he was writing on the education of deaf-mutes and his duties as one of the founders of the Society of Observers of Man, examined the boy over the course of several days and pronounced him an incurable idiot—he wasn't about to risk his reputation on a creature that recognized no signs whatever and hadn't the sense or even the hygiene of a house cat. Thus, the child was abandoned again, but this time within the walls of the institution, where there was no one to look after him and where the other children made it their duty to chase, taunt and torment him.

He slunk about the corridors and grounds, moving from shadow to shadow as if afraid of the light, and whenever he heard the clamor of the deaf-mute students in the stairwell he ran in the opposite direction, ascending rapidly when they were below him, descending when they were above. Out of doors, he kept his back to the rough stone of the buildings, watchful and frightened, and when the others were released from their classes, he darted for the nearest tree. If he thought to escape during this period, he was frustrated not only by the fact that the keeper locked him in at night, but by the walls that delimited the grounds of the Institute—he could have scaled them in his efficient squirrel-like way, but what lay beyond the walls was the city, and he was a creature and prisoner of it now.

His only relief was in the privacy of his room, and even that was denied him more often than not because members of the scientific community continued to haunt the corridors of the Institute, one philosopher or naturalist after the other poking his head in the door or following him as he trotted the halls in his freakish sidelong gait or climbed up into the branches of the nearest tree to get away from the crush of people, people all around him where before there had been none. He took his food privately, in his room, hoarding it, and if he were to get wet—in a rainstorm or in the ornamental pond, where the other children delighted in cornering him—he had the disconcerting habit of drying himself with ashes from the hearth so that he looked like a ghoul haunting the halls. He tore the straw from his bed, refused to bathe, defecated beside the chamberpot as if in defiance. Twice, lashing out at mild Monsieur Guérin, the old man employed to maintain the grounds, he inflicted bite wounds. Sicard and all his staff gave him up for hopeless. There was even talk of sending him to the Bicêtre, where he would be locked away with the retarded and the insane, and it might have happened if it weren't for the fact that it would have reflected so poorly on Sicard, who had, after all, insisted on bringing the child to Paris. By the fall of 1800, things stood at an impasse.

It was then that a newly fledged doctor from the Val-de-Grâce Hospital came to work as medical officer at the Institute. His name was Jean-Marc Gaspard Itard, he was twenty-five years old and he'd been schooled in Marseilles prior to his internship in Paris; he was given an apartment in the main building and a modest—very modest—salary amounting to sixty-six francs per annum. The first time he encountered the wild child was after he'd bandaged a bite wound on the forearm of one of the female students and learned that the boy who'd inflicted it was even then crouched in the denuded crown of the big elm that dominated the grounds, refusing to come down. Itard had, of course, heard rumor of the child—everyone in Paris had, and Sicard had mentioned him in passing as a failed experiment—but now, angry and disturbed, he marched out of the building and into the naked wind to confront him.

The grounds were deserted; the light was fading from the sky. A cold spell had settled over the city, slops freezing in the streets, citizens wrapping up in greatcoats and scarves even as their breath steamed around them. In his haste, Itard had forgotten his own coat—he was in his jacket only—and almost immediately a chill ran through him. He hurried across the brittle grass to where the elm stood silhouetted against the faint red streaks of the sky. At first he couldn't see anything in the maze of slick black branches rattling composedly in the wind, but then a pigeon shot from the tree in a helter-skelter of wings and there was the boy, a white glow clinging like a fungus to the upper reaches of the trunk. He moved closer, his eyes fixed on the tree, until he stumbled over something, a shadow at his feet. When he bent to examine it, he saw that it was a simple shift of gray cloth, the boy's garment, flung down like an afterthought.

So he was naked, the Savage was naked, up in the tree, and he'd bitten a girl. Itard almost turned his back on him—Let him freeze, he was thinking, the animal. If that's what he wants, let him freeze. But then his eyes went to the tree again and he saw with a sudden clarity, saw the boy's neutral wedge of a face, the dark vacancy of his eyes, his pale splayed limbs, and he rode up out of his own body for a moment and inhabited the boy's. What must it have been like to be abandoned, to have your throat cut, to be captured and imprisoned and without defense except to sink your teeth into the slowest and weakest of your tormentors? To throw off your clothes, indifferent to the cold? To cower and hide and hunger? Very slowly, very deliberately, Itard lifted himself up and began to climb.

The first thing Itard did was arrange for the groundskeeper's wife, Madame Guérin, to take charge of the boy's needs, to provide a woman's touch, to mother him. Henceforth, the boy would take his meals in her apartments, along with Monsieur Guérin, whose attitude, Itard was sure, would soften toward the boy over time. Madame Guérin was then in her forties. She was a squat, uncomplaining woman, formerly of the peasantry but now, like all members of the Republic, a citizen; she was broad of bosom and hip and wore her abundant, graying hair tied up in a knot on the crown of her head. Her own children—three daughters—lived with her sister in a cottage in Chaillot and she saw them when she could.

Itard himself—unmarried, utterly devoted to his deaf-mute charges and yet ambitious and eager to prove himself—saw something in the boy the others failed to notice. High in the branches of the elm, the city spread out beneath him and the flights of birds intersecting over the rooftops, he held out his hand against the wind, murmuring blandishments, coaxing, until the boy took it. He didn't attempt to pull the child to him or to apply any force or pressure—it was far too dangerous; any sudden movement could precipitate a fall—but he just held the hand offered to him, communicating his warmth to the boy in the most elemental way. After a while, the boy's eyes settled on him, and he saw a whole world there, shuttered and excluded perhaps, but there nonetheless. He saw intelligence and need. And more: a kind of bargain in the making, a trust that sprang up automatically because they both knew that there was no one, not even the most agile of the deaf-mutes, who would have followed the Savage into that tree. When he finally let go of the boy's hand, gesturing to the ground below, the boy seemed to understand him and followed him down the trunk of the tree, each movement, each hand- and foothold synchronized to his. At the base of the tree Itard held out his hand again and the boy clasped it and allowed himself to be led back into the big stone building and up the steps to his room and the fire Itard laid there. The two of them knelt on the rough planks of the floor for a long while, warming their hands as the wind lashed at the window and night came down like an axe.

Sicard gave his permission for Itard to work with the child. What else could he do? If the neophyte failed to civilize the Savage, failed to teach him to speak and behave himself in society—and Sicard was certain he would fail—it was nothing to him. In fact, it was something of a relief, as he himself was no longer responsible, and yet if the Savage did somehow manage miraculously to acquire speech, it would reflect well on the whole enterprise; Sicard could even fleetingly envision the child, dressed in a proper suit of clothes, standing beside Massieu in an auditorium and wittily reflecting on his former life, speaking of raw tubers as *la nourriture des animaux et des Belges* or some such thing. But no, that would never happen. And it was best to lay the blame on someone else's shoulders. Still, he did manage to extract an annual stipend of five hundred francs from the government for the child's care and education and the unique experiment Itard was prepared to carry out to put to the test the thesis propounded by Locke and Condillac: Was man born a tabula rasa, unformed and without ideas, ready to be written upon by society, educable and perfectible? Or was society a corrupting influence, as Rousseau supposed, rather than the foundation of all things right and good?

For the next five years Itard would devote himself seven days a week to finding out.

The boy took to the regime warily. On the one hand, he basked in the protection Madame Guérin and Itard gave him against the mob of deaf-mutes clamoring for his destruction and he relished the unending supply of food in the Guérins' cabinet, and yet, on the other, he resisted with all his heart the doctor's attempts to control him. He'd put on weight, grown softer, paler (once he'd come in from the woods and the burning effect of the sun, his skin was seen to be as fair as any other child's), and he wanted only to crouch in a corner of his room and rock back and forth or sit by the edge of the pond and watch the light play over the water. And now, suddenly, here was this man with his insistent eyes and prodding nose haunting his every waking moment, pursuing him to his room to attack him there and even sitting down at table with him to interfere as he hoarded his food, the sausages he'd come to love and the potatoes fried in oil and the beans, the broad beans stewed into a pottage, the bread hot from the oven.

Every day, without relief, he was made to perform. And this was especially hard because for the first few weeks Itard had let him do as he pleased, taking him for long ambles in the park, allowing him to eat what and when he wanted and to hunker in his corner or curl up to sleep at any time of day or night, and that was a kind of heaven to the child because he was the leader, his whims were Itard's whims, and with Itard at his side he could defy the deaf-mutes, especially one lean, quick whipcord of a boy who was forever creeping up on him to administer wet blows with his open hands or to wrestle him to the floor and press his weight into him till he couldn't breathe. Itard was there for him now, there to watch over him, but also, very slowly and subtly, to mold him to his will. On the morning of the first snowfall, when the whole institution was clothed in slumber and every sound damped by the steady, silent accumulation, the child woke with a frantic pounding joy and darted naked down the flights of stairs to the yard where he held his face to the sky and cried out at the descending swirl of pristine crystals and burrowed into the drifts, insensible to the cold, and no one attempted to stop him. The stone buildings loomed like cliffs calling down the storm out of the sky. Shapes formed and fragmented in the air, visions playing there in the courtyard for him and him alone. And then he looked up, sensing something, a presence, and there the man was, Itard, wrapped in his greatcoat and scarf, the dark curls of his hair whitening, his lashes, his eyebrows, the sharp projection of his nose.

The next day, the regime commenced and ever so gradually heaven receded.

Itard began by taking hold of the boy immediately after breakfast and giving him a long hot bath, a bath that lasted three hours and more, Madame Guérin heating pot after pot of water, the boy frolicking, splashing, diving, spouting, at play like any other child bathed in sustaining warmth and free to express himself, but there was a purpose here, a civilizing purpose, and the fact that the child was made clean and free of offensive odors was merely the ancillary benefit. No, what Itard was doing—and these baths continued every day for the next month—was sensitizing the Savage, making him aware of his body, his self, in a way the life of the animal could never have done. After the bath each day, another hour would be spent in massage, as Itard and Madame Guérin took turns rubbing his limbs, the small of his back, soothing him, giving him pleasure, allowing him to appreciate an interaction he'd never before experienced: he was being touched by one of his fellow creatures, and there was no fear in it, no violence. Sure enough, within the month, he would fall into a tantrum if the water wasn't hot enough or the hands of his masseur sufficiently firm, and he began dressing himself without prompting, because now he felt the cold like any other domesticated creature and there was no going back. So too with his food. The Savage who had subsisted on raw roots and tubers, who had plucked potatoes from the fire and devoured insects and torn rodents with his teeth, turned up his nose at a plate of food that contained something he didn't care for or that was contaminated by a single shining example of Madame Guérin's silvered, flowing hair.

There were other things too that showed him coming awake in his senses. He learned to use a spoon to remove potatoes from a boiling pot, rather than simply thrusting in his oblivious fingers. He came to recognize himself in a hand mirror and to manipulate it so that it caught the light and tossed it from one corner of the room to the other. His fingers sought out the softness of Madame Guérin's skirts and the delicious ripple of the corduroy of Itard's suits. When he caught his first cold and sneezed, perhaps for the first time in his life, he was terrified and ran to his bed to bury himself beneath the counterpane, afraid that his own body was assaulting him. But then he sneezed again and again and before long, with Itard standing over him and murmuring reassurance, he came to anticipate the sneeze and ride its currents, exaggerating the sound of it, laughing, capering around the room as if propelled by an internal wind.

The next step—and here the boy began to chafe under his teacher's demands—was the commencement of the second stage of the regime, designed to focus his vision and sharpen his hearing in the way that his taste and tactile sensitivity had been stimulated. To this point he had engaged in a kind of selective hearing, registering only the sounds connected with eating, the rattle of spoon in bowl, the hiss of the flames under the pot, the cracking of a nut, but human speech—aside from inflection, as when either Itard or the Guérins lost patience with his tantrums or attempted to warn him away from things that might injure him—failed to register. Speech was a kind of background music, no different from the incomprehensible twitter of the birds of the forest or the lowing of the cow or bark of the dog. Itard set out to train him first by imitation, reasoning that this was how infants acquired language, miming what was said to them by their parents. He broke the language down into simple vowel and consonant sounds, and repeated them over and over, in the hope that the boy would echo him, and always he held up objects—a glass of milk, a shoe, a spoon, a bowl, a potato—and named them. The boy's eyes dodged away from his. He made no connection whatever between these rude noises and their referents and after months of study he could produce no sounds other than a kind of dull moaning and the laughter that awakened in him at the oddest and most frustrating moments. Still, he did react to the blunted speech of his deaf-mute tormenters—running from the noise of them, as he would have run from any startling sound in nature, a clap of thunder or the crash of a cataract—and one evening, when Itard had just about given up hope, he finally managed his first articulate expression.

It was in February, the sky stretched low and gray over the city, dinner stewing in a thousand pots, the eternal thumping and slamming and bellowing of the other students quietened both by the weather and the usual pre-prandial lull. Itard was seated in the kitchen of the Guérins' apartment as Madame Guérin prepared the meal, quietly smoking and observing the boy, who was always at his most alert when food was the focus. It happened that while the boy was at the stove, overseeing the boiling of his potatoes, the Guérins, husband

and wife, began an animated discussion of the recent death of one of their acquaintances in an accident involving a carriage. Madame Guérin claimed it was the fault of the coachman—that he was negligent, perhaps even drunk—while her husband defended him. Each time she made a claim, he said, "Oh, but that's different," and put in a counterclaim. It was that simple exclamation, that vowel sound, that "o" that caused the boy to turn his head, as if he could distinguish it from the rest. Later, when he was preparing for bed (and, incidentally, showing a marked preference for freshly laundered sheets and a featherbed to the nest of sticks and refuse and the cold planks he'd formerly insisted upon), Itard came to him to say good night and drill him on his vowels, thinking that the agency of sleep might somehow help impress the sounds on the empty tablet of the boy's mind.

"Oh," Itard said, pointing to the window. "Oh," he said, pointing to the bed, to his own throat, to the round and supple sound hanging in the air.

To his amazement, from deep in the boy's throat, the same sound came back at him. The boy was in his nightgown, tugging at the blankets. There was no show of ablutions or pretense of prayers to a non-conceptualized God; when the child felt sleepy, he retired to his room and plunged into the bed. But now, as he lay there, he repeated the sound, as if struck by the novelty of it, and Itard, excited, bent over him, repeating "oh, oh, oh," until the child fell asleep.

It only seemed natural then, that in the morning, when the boy came to him, Itard called him by his new name, the one he'd suggested for himself, an august and venerable name borne proudly by any number of Frenchmen before and since, a name in which the accent fell heavily on the open second syllable: Victor. His name was Victor, and though he couldn't pronounce the first part of it and perhaps didn't even hear it and never would, he learned to respond to the second. He was Victor. Victor. After thirteen years on this earth, he was finally somebody.

6

It was around the time of his naming that Victor—or rather, Itard, on Victor's behalf—received an invitation to attend the salon of Madame Récamier. This was a great opportunity, not only for Victor, whose cause could be promoted among the most powerful and influential people in France, but for Itard too, who, despite himself, had unrealistic social expectations, and like any other man, yearned for recognition. Madame Récamier was then twenty-four years old, a celebrated beauty and wit, wife of a wealthy banker three times her age and doyenne of a château in Clïchy-la-Garenne, just outside the city; anyone who was anyone came there to pay her homage and to be seen. Accordingly, Itard bought himself a new jacket and had Madame Guérin make Victor a suit of clothes replete with a high-collared shirt, waistcoat and cravat, so that he looked like a gentleman in miniature. For a full week before the date of the salon, Itard devised various games and stratagems to teach Victor how to bow in the presence of a lady, with mixed results.

On the evening of the party they hired a carriage, Victor by now having lost his fear of horses to the extent that he stuck his head out the window and shrieked with glee the whole way, startling pedestrians, gendarmes and dogs alike, and proceeded through a cold rain to Clïchy-la-Garenne. At first things seemed to go well, the *bon ton* of Paris making way for the doctor and his charge, the former savage who was now dressed and comporting himself like any other boy of thirteen, though Victor failed to bow to anyone, let alone his hostess, and persisted in trotting from one corner of the grand hall to the other, smearing his face with whatever foods he was able to find to his liking, the beaded eggs of fish presented on wafers of bread, fungus that had been stuffed, breaded and fried in hot oil, the remains of songbirds skewered nose-to-anus.

Madame Récamier gave him the seat of honor beside herself and even fussed over Itard a bit, trying to draw him out for the benefit of her guests, hoping he might, like a circus trainer, persuade Victor to show off some trick or another. But Victor didn't show off any tricks. Victor didn't know any tricks. Victor was mute, unable—or unwilling—even to pronounce his own name, and he wasn't in the least susceptible to Madame Récamier's legendary beauty and celebrated eyes. After a while she turned to the guest seated on her other side and began to regale the table at large with an involved story concerning the painter who had recently done her portrait in oils, how he'd made her sit frozen in a single position and wouldn't even allow one of the servants to read aloud to her for fear of breaking her concentration. The tedium she'd endured. The suffering. What a beast this painter was. And at a gesture from her everyone looked up and there it was, like a miracle, the very portrait of the inestimable Madame Récamier—couchant, her feet tantalizingly bare and her face wearing a dignified yet seductive look—displayed on the wall behind them. Itard was transported. And he was about to say something, searching for the right words, something charming and memorable that would rise above the self-satisfied gabble of his fellow diners, when a crash, as of priceless statuary upended, silenced the table.

The sound had come from the garden, and it was followed, sharply, by a second crash. Itard looked to Madame Récamier, who looked to the vacant seat beside her even as one of the notables at the far end of the table cried out, "Look, the Savage—he's escaping!" In the next moment, the whole party was thrown into turmoil, the men springing up to burst through the doors in pursuit, the ladies gathering at the windows and fanning themselves vigorously to keep from fainting with the excitement of it all, the servants fluttering helplessly round the vacated places at the table and the hostess herself trying to look as if this were all part of the evening's entertainment. Itard, mortified, threw back his chair in confusion, the napkin clutched like a lifeline in his right hand. He was immobilized. He didn't know what to do.

By the time Itard came to his senses, Victor was zigzagging back and forth across the lawn, pursued by a dozen men in wigs, frilled shirtfronts and buckled pumps. Worse, the boy was divesting himself of his garments, flinging the jacket from his shoulders, tearing the shirt down the middle, running right out of his shoes and stockings. A moment later, despite the hot baths, the massages and the training of his senses, he was as naked to the elements as he'd been on the day he stepped out of the woods and into the life of the world—naked, and scrambling up the trunk of one of Madame Récamier's plane trees like an arboreal ape. Itard moved through the doors as if in a trance, the shouts of prominent citizens—including the august General Jean Moreau, Jean-Baptiste Bernadotte, future king of Sweden and Norway, and old Monsieur Récamier himself—ringing in his ears. With the whole party looking on, he stood at the base of the tree, pleading with Victor to come down, until finally he had to remove his own jacket and begin climbing.

The humiliation of that evening stayed with Itard for a long while, and though he wouldn't have admitted it, it played a role in his attitude toward his pupil in the ensuing weeks and months of his training. Itard cracked down. No longer would he allow Victor to get away with the tantrums that too often put an end to his lessons, no longer would he tolerate any deviance from civilized behavior, which most emphatically meant that Victor would henceforth and strictly keep his clothes on at all times. And there would be no more tree climbing—and no more forays into society. Society could wait.

At this stage in Victor's education, in addition to constantly drilling him on his vowels, Itard began to employ the method Sicard had used in training his deaf-mutes to read, write and speak. He began by having Victor attempt to match everyday objects—a shoe, a hammer, a spoon—with simple line drawings of them, the idea being that once Victor had mastered the representation, then the symbols that depicted them in language, the words, could be substituted for the drawings. On the table in Victor's room, Itard laid out a number of these objects, including the key to Madame Guérin's food closet, an article of which the boy was especially enamored, and then fastened the drawings to the opposite wall. When he pointed to the drawing of the key, for instance, or the hammer, he demonstrated to Victor that this was the object he wanted. Unfortunately, Victor was unable to make the connection, though Itard persisted, perfecting his drawings and drilling the boy over and over while simultaneously pronouncing the appropriate word: "*La clé,* Victor, bring me *la clé.*" Occasionally, Victor did bring the correct object, but just as often, despite a thousand trials, he brought the hammer when the key was wanted or the shoe when it was the spoon his teacher had requested.

Itard then hit on the idea of having his pupil manually match the objects to the drawings, a less complex task surely. He began by arranging each of the articles on a hook beneath the corresponding drawing. He and Victor sat on the bed in Victor's room and studied the arrangement—key, hammer, spoon, shoe—until Victor had had time to associate each object with the drawing above it, then he rose, gathered up the objects and handed them to Victor to put up again. For a long while, Victor merely looked at him, his eyes soft and composed, then he got to his feet and put the objects back in their proper order. He was able to do this repeatedly, without hesitation, but when Itard changed the sequence of the drawings, Victor continued to place the objects in their original order—he was relying on his spatial memory alone. Itard corrected him, over and over, and just as often, no matter how Itard arranged the drawings or the objects, Victor placed the things where they had originally been, always relying on memory. "All right," Itard said to himself, "I will complicate the task." Soon there were a dozen articles, then fifteen, eighteen, twenty, so many that Victor could no longer remember the order in which they had been arrayed. Finally, after weeks of drills, of firmness, of pleading, of insistence, Itard was gratified—or no, he was delighted, ecstatic—to see his pupil making careful comparison of drawing and object and ultimately mastering the task at hand.

Next, it was the words. Itard went back to the original four objects, set them on their hooks, printed the signifiers for each in clear block letters—LA CLÉ, LE MARTEAU, LA CUILLER, LE SOULIER—and removed the drawings. Nothing. It was just as before—Victor made no connection whatever between what must have seemed to him random markings and the tangible things on the hooks. He was able only to arrange the items from memory, and no amount of study, no number of repetitions, could enlighten him. Weeks passed. Victor began to balk at the drills. Itard persisted. Nothing happened. Puzzled, he went to Sicard.

"The boy is congenitally infirm," the abbé said, sitting behind his great mahogany desk and stroking one of the cats that roamed the Institute's grounds.

"He is, I am sorry to say, an idiot—and not an idiot because he was abandoned but a true idiot, a cretin, and it was his idiocy that was the cause of his abandonment."

"He's no idiot, I can testify to that. He's making progress. I see it in his eyes."

"Yes, and imagine the parents, ignorant peasants, a succession of squalling and filthy children clinging to their knees and little or nothing in the pot and they have this child—this Victor, as you call him—who cannot speak or respond normally. Of course they abandon him. It's a sad fact of life, and I've seen it time and again with my deaf-mutes."

"With all due respect, Abbé, he is no idiot. And I'll prove it. Just give me time."

Sicard leaned down to release the cat, a spoiled fat thing which was the brother or uncle or perhaps even the father (no one could remember) of the nearly identical one Madame Guérin kept in her apartments. When he sat back up again, he leveled his eyes on Itard and observed, in a quiet voice, "Just as you did at Madame Récamier's, I suppose?"

"Well, I—" This was a low blow, and Itard wasn't prepared for it. "That was unfortunate, I admit, but—"

"Unfortunate?" The abbé tented his hands before him. "The boy is an embarrassment—to you, to me, to the Institute and all we've accomplished here. Worse: he's an insult." He lowered his voice to a whisper: "Give it up, Itard. Give it up while you can—it will destroy you, can't you see that?"

But Itard wouldn't give up. Instead, he abandoned Sicard's method and went all the way back to the beginning. As he saw it, Victor's problem was one of perception—and it went deeper, far deeper, than in any of the Institute's deaf-mutes, whose visual acuity had been honed as an adaptation to their disability so that the thing and its representation in symbols was readily apparent to them. They had little difficulty in discerning the fine gradations in contour that separate one letter from another, a printed *b* from an *h*, an *l* from a *t*, and once they recognized the system they were able to appreciate it in all its variations. Victor, on the other hand, simply did not see the letters of the words because he couldn't distinguish simple shapes. And so, Itard came up with the idea of training Victor to recognize basic figures—cardboard triangles, circles, squares, parallelograms—and to match them to the spaces from which they'd been cut. At first, Victor took the new regime as a kind of game, and he was easily able to fit the pieces back in the holes, but then Itard, excited by the boy's progress, made the drills increasingly complicated, varying the shapes, colors and sequences of the pieces until finally, predictably, Victor revolted.

Imagine him. Imagine the wild child in his suit of clothes with his new name and his newly acquired love of comfort, with the mother-figure Madame Guérin had come to represent there to comfort and caress him and the demanding father, Itard, filling his every waking moment with impossible, frustrating tasks as in some tale out of the Brothers Grimm, and it's no surprise that he broke down, that his initial spirit, his free spirit, his wild spirit, reasserted itself. He wanted only to roam in some uncontained place, to sleep in the sun, to put his head in Madame Guérin's lap and sit at the table and eat till he burst, and yet every time he looked up, there was Itard, the taskmaster, with his fierce eyes and disapproving nose. And more, and worse: there were changes coming over his body, the hormonal rush of puberty, coarse hair sprouting under his arms and between his legs, his testes descending, his appendage stiffening of its own accord, morning and night. He grew confused. Anxious. Angry.

The blowup came on a fine spring afternoon, all of Paris redolent with the perfume of lilac and lily, the southern breeze as soft and warm as a hand laid against a cheek, the pond on the Institute's grounds giving rise spontaneously to ducklings, whole fleets of them, even as the deaf-mutes capered over the lawns, squealing and whinnying in their high, strained, unnatural voices. Itard had devised an especially complex configuration of shapes and cutouts, posters nailed up on the walls and three-dimensional figures spread across the table, and he could see that Victor was growing frustrated. He was feeling frustrated himself—this morning, like a hundred others before it, offering up hope in such niggardly increments that it seemed as if the glaciers of the Alps and Pyrenees would meet before Victor could learn to perform a task any four-year-old would have mastered in a minute.

The shapes wouldn't cohere. Victor backed away, flung himself sullenly on the bed. Itard took him by the arm and forced him to stand and confront the problem, just as he'd done over and over again all morning long, the grip of his iron fingers on the yielding flesh of the boy's upper arm as familiar to both of them as breathing in and breathing out. But this time, Victor had had enough. With a violence that startled them both, he snatched his arm away and for one suspended moment made as if to attack his teacher, his teeth bared, fists raised in anger, until he turned on the hated objects—the spheres, pyramids and flat geometric figures—and tore them to pieces. He raged round the room, ducking away from his teacher with the animal dexterity that had yet to abandon him despite the weight he was putting on, heaving the scraps out the open window, then rushing to the fireplace to fling ashes round the room and ripping at the sheets of the bed with his teeth until they were shredded, and all the while Itard trying to wrestle him down. Finally, ululating in a new oppressive voice that might have been the call of some carrion bird, Victor threw himself on the floor and fell into convulsions.

The convulsions were authentic—the eyes sunk back in the boy's head, his teeth gnashing, tongue bloodied—but they were self-generated for all that, and Itard, who'd witnessed this scene innumerable times in the past, lost control himself. In a flash, he was on the boy, jerking him up off the floor and dragging him to the open window—shock treatment, that was what he needed, a force that was greater than he, implacable, irresistible, a single act of violence that would tame him forever. And here it was, ready to hand. Clutching him by the ankles, Itard thrust the boy through the frame of the open window and dangled him there, five long stories from the ground. Victor went rigid as a board, the convulsions dissolved in the terror of the moment. What must he have thought? That after all the kindness and blandishments, all the food, warmth and shelter, his captors—and this man, this man in particular who had always forced these strange, useless labors on him—had finally shown their true colors. That his teacher was in league with Madame Guérin, that they'd softened him in order to destroy him as surely as the deaf-mutes would have done if they'd had their way, and before them the merciless boys of the villages at the edge of the forest. He'd been betrayed. The ground would rush to meet him.

For those few minutes, Itard didn't care what the boy was feeling. All the pain and humiliation of the scene at Madame Récamier's came rushing back to him, all the endless wasted hours, the unceasing contest of wills, Sicard's skepticism, the sharpened blade of the world's ready judgment and failure waiting in the wings. Victor whimpered. He wet his trousers. A pigeon, disturbed on its roost, let out a soft flutter of concern. And then, after all the blood had rushed to Victor's face, after the sky seemed to explode across the horizon and close back up on itself in a black ball and the deaf-mutes began to gather below, pointing and shouting, Itard tightened his grip and hauled the boy back into the room.

He didn't lay him on the bed. Didn't set him in the chair or back on the floor. He held him up until Victor's muscles flexed and he was able to stand on his own. Then, very firmly and without hesitation, he made the boy gather up what scraps of cardboard remained, and recommenced the lesson.

After that excoriating afternoon, Victor seemed to come round. He still balked at his lessons, but not as often—or as violently—as before, and Itard had only to motion to the window to subjugate him completely. There were no more tantrums, no convulsions. Dutifully, his shoulders slumped and head bowed, Victor did as he was told and applied himself to his lessons, gradually acquiring a modicum of skill at matching the geometric shapes to their receptacles. At this point, Itard decided to move forward, attempting to teach him the alphabet through the agency of both his tactile sense and his burgeoning ability to make visual distinctions; to this end, he created a sort of board game in which there were twenty-four compartments, each marked with a letter of the alphabet, and twenty-four corresponding metal cutouts. The idea was for Victor to remove the cutouts from the compartments and then replace them properly, which he seemed able to do right from the beginning with relative ease. It was only by observing him closely, however, that Itard saw that Victor hadn't learned the letters at all, but was instead painstakingly setting aside the cutouts and simply reversing the order in which he'd removed them. And so Itard complicated the game, as he'd done with the representational drawings, until Victor could no longer memorize the order of the letters but had to concentrate on matching the shapes. Which he finally did. Victoriously.

This led, shortly thereafter, to Victor's pronouncing his first word aloud. It came about that one late afternoon, Madame Guérin had poured out a bowl of milk for Sultan, her pampered cat, and then a glass for Victor while the metal letters of the alphabet happened to be laid out on the table in her kitchen, and Itard, always looking for an opportunity of instruction, took up the glass before Victor could reach for it and manipulated four of the cutouts to spell the word for milk: l-a-i-t. Pronouncing it simultaneously—"Lait, lait"—he scrambled the letters and pushed them back across the table to Victor, who immediately arranged them to spell: t-i-a-l. "Good, Victor, very good," he murmured, realizing his mistake—Victor had seen the word upside down—and quickly rearranging the letters. Again the exercise, and this time Victor spelled the word properly. "Lait, lait," Itard repeated, and Madame Guérin, at the stove now, took it up too, a chant, a chorus, a panegyric to that simple and nourishing liquid, all the while pointing from the letters on the table to the milk in the glass and back again to his lips and tongue. Finally, with effort, because he'd come to relish milk as much as the cat did, Victor fumbled out the word. Very faintly, with his odd intonation, but clearly and distinctly, he echoed them: "Lait."

Itard was overjoyed. Here it was, at long last, the key to unlock the boy's mind and tongue. After praising him, after losing all control of himself and pulling Victor to him for a rib-rattling hug and pouring him a second and third glass of milk till his lips shone with a white halo, Itard ran off to the abbé's office to report this *coup de foudre,* and Sicard, for all his dubiety, withheld judgment. He could have remarked that even cretins can pronounce a few simple words, that infants of eighteen months can mouth "mama" and "papa," but instead he simply said, "Congratulations, *mon frère.* Keep up the good work."

The doctor went to bed happy that night and the next night and the night after that, and he remained happy through his mornings and afternoons until he took his dinner with Victor and the Guérins on the third evening after his pupil's triumph and Victor exclaimed "Lait!" when Madame Guérin poured him a glass of water, cried "Lait!" when she sliced him a piece of lamb, and "Lait, lait, lait!" when she set his potatoes, hot in their jackets, on the plate before him.

Was the doctor disappointed? Was he crushed, annihilated in the deepest fortress of his spirit? Was he rehearsing the abbé's words—"Give it up; it will destroy you"—over and over again? Yes, of course he was—how could he not be?—and he showed it in his face, in his gestures, in his attitude toward his ward and pupil, angry at the sight of him, of his thin wrists and too-big head and the flab beginning to accrue at his waist and in his cheeks and breast and under his chin even as Victor matched the metal cutouts to their compartments, singing out "Lait!" every time he succeeded.

Itard could never be sure if it was his own antagonism and harshness in those days following his disappointment that prompted the first major crisis in Victor's sojourn at the Institute, but when he came up the five flights of stairs in the morning to find the boy's bed empty, he blamed himself. Victor was not at the Guérins', not in Sicard's offices or mooning over the pond, and a search of the deaf-mutes' dormitories and of the grounds, extending even to the farthest walls, proved futile. Once again, as if he'd been a figment of the collective imagination, the wild child had vanished.

7

Outside in the dark, beyond the gates of the Institute, Victor was adrift. There was too much noise. There were too many people. Nothing seemed familiar, nothing seemed real. The sky was jagged, unrecognizable, the city a flower carved of stone, blooming under a moonless spring night, its petals radiating out in a thousand alleys and turnings and dead ends. Something had driven him out of his bed, down the flights of stairs and then across the grounds and up through the gates and into the streets, but he couldn't remember what it was. Some slight, some injury, the continuing and immitigable frustration of trying to please this man with his fierce grip and seething eyes—yes, and something else too, something he couldn't take hold of because it was inside of him, beating with the pulse of his blood.

Earlier, just after dinner, one of the deaf-mutes (not like him, a she, a new inmate arrived that morning with hair that hung down her back and a screen of heavy folded cloth concealing her legs and the other thing that was there, the potent physical mystery he could divine in the way he could sense the presence of an animal in a silent glen or sniff out the sodden secret pocket of earth that gave up the gift of a mole or truffle) had come to him in the hallway outside his room and held out her hand. She was offering him something, a sweet thing, small and sweet from the oven, and he didn't like such things and slapped it from her hand. There it was, on the floor, between them. She drew in her breath. Her face changed. And suddenly her eyes sprang at him, her arms jerking and her elbows knifing as her fingers bent and flexed and contorted themselves in some mad show, and he backed away from her. But when she reached down to retrieve the sweet, he came at her from behind and put his hands there, in the place where her limbs joined beneath the cloth, and he didn't know what he was doing or why he did it.

And yet there were repercussions. The she jumped as if she'd been stung, whirling round at the same time to rake her nails across his face, and he didn't understand and struck back at her and suddenly she was making the noise of an animal, a rising complaint that echoed down the hallway till the man appeared, his jacket askew and his face rigid with the expression Victor knew to be dangerous, and so he shrank away even as the man took hold of him roughly and made his voice harsh and ugly till it too rang out from the stone. This booming, this racket, and what was it? The teeth clenched, the parceled sounds flung out, each syllable a blow, and why, why? There was the physical pain of that enraged grip, and any creature would have felt it, any dog grabbed by the collar, but that was as nothing to the deeper pain—this was the man who demanded everything of him and who hugged him and petted him and gave him good things to eat when he complied, and to see him transformed was a shock. Victor remembered the window—and the closet into which he'd been thrust whenever he balked in those first months of his training—and he let himself go limp even as the man dragged him through the door, across the floor of his room and into the closet. And so, when it was time for bed, when the man's footsteps approached and the key turned in the lock and the closet door was pulled open, Victor would not make it up with him, would not hold his arms out for a hug as he'd done so many times before, and when the night came he hid by the gates till he heard the stamp and shudder of the horses and the chime of the wheels and the gates swung open to release him.

At first, in the freedom of the night, he'd felt supercharged with excitement, and he stole away from the walls with a sense of urgency, something in the smell of the air, polluted as it was, bringing him back to his old life when everything was untainted and equally divided between the kingdoms of pleasure and pain. He kept to the shadows instinctively, the noise of the carriages like thunder, people everywhere, emerging from the mist like specters, shouting, crying, their clogs beating at the stones, and dogs—how he hated them—making their racket in the alleys and snarling behind the fences. This new energy, this new feeling, drove him on. He walked till his shoes nagged at his feet and then he walked out of them and left them standing there in an alley behind him, two neat leather shoes, one set in front of the other in mid-step as if he'd been carried off by some great winged thing. A light rain began to fall. He turned one way to avoid a group of men bawling in their rumbling, low, terrible voices, and then he was running and he turned another way and was lost. The rain quickened. He huddled beneath a bush and began to shiver. All the urgency had gone out of him.

When he woke, the night had gone silent but for the hiss of the rain in the trees along the street and the trill of it in the gutters. He didn't know where he was, didn't know who he was, and if someone had stooped down under the bush and called him Victor—if Madame Guérin in her apron had appeared at that moment with her soft face and pleading hands and called him to her—he wouldn't have recognized his name. He was cold, friendless, hungry. Just as he'd been before, in the woods of La Bassine and the high cold plain of Roquecézière, but it was different now because now he felt a hunger that wasn't for food alone. He shifted position, tried to draw his wet clothes around him as best he could. One side of his face was smeared with filth where he'd lain in the mud. The soles of both feet were nicked and bleeding. He shivered till his ribs ached.

At first light, a man in uniform saw him curled beneath the bush and prodded him with the glistening toe of a boot. He'd been somewhere else, dislocated in his dreams, and he sprang up in a panic. The man—the gendarme—spoke something, the quick, harsh words like a drumbeat, and when he made a snatch for Victor's arm, he was just half a beat too slow. Suddenly Victor was running, the paving stones tearing at his feet, and the gendarme ran too, till the rain and the mist intervened and Victor found himself sitting beneath a tree overlooking the rush and chop of the moving river. Somewhere else, not half a mile distant, Itard and the Guérins roamed the streets, stopping pedestrians to inquire of him—Had anyone seen him, a boy of fifteen, his sharp nose, clipped hair the color of earth, in blue shirt and jacket, the wild boy, the Savage escaped from the Institute for Deaf-Mutes? People just stared. Itard turned away from them, calling "Victor, Victor!" with a ringing insistence, even as Madame Guérin's voice grew increasingly plaintive and hollow.

The city awoke and arose. Fires were lit. Raw dough fell into hot oil, eggs cracked, pike lost their heads, civilization progressed. Victor sat there in the rain, running his hands over his body, over the stiffening thing between his legs and the heavy roll of flesh round his midsection, the miracle of it, and then he pushed himself up and followed his nose across the street to where an open doorway gave onto a courtyard blossoming with the scent of meat in a pan. The rain slackened here, caught and held fast by the eaves. There was pavement underfoot. He could see a woman moving behind a window that was cracked an inch or two to let in the air, and he went to the window and stood watching her as she tended the meat and the pan and the odor of it rose up to communicate with him. It took a moment before she saw him there, his face smeared with mud, his hair wet and hanging, his black eyes fixed on her hands that spoke to the pan on the stove and the licking of the fire and the rhythm of the long two-pronged fork. She said something then, her face flaring in anger, her voice growling out, and in the next moment she vanished, only to reappear at a door he hadn't seen. There were more words flung out into the rain, and then there was the dog, all teeth and clattering nails, and Victor was running again.

But four legs outrun two, and just as he made the street the animal's jaws closed on him, on his right leg, in the place where the buttock tapers into the long muscle beneath it. The animal held on, raging in its own language, and he knew he had to stay upright, knew he had to fight it from the vantage of his height and not give in and fall beneath its teeth. They jerked there, back and forth, the animal releasing its grip only to attack again and again, the blood bright on the black ball of its snout, and he beat at the anvil of its head with both fists until something fell away inside him and his own teeth came into play, clamping down on the thing's ear. Then the snarls turned to pleas, to a high, piping, bewildered protest that was no domesticated sound at all, and he held tight to the furious jerking anvil till the ear was his and the dog was gone. He tasted hair, tasted tissue, blood. People stared. A man came running. Someone called out to God as his witness, a common-enough phrase, but Victor knew nothing of God or of witness either. For the first time in a long buried while, he chewed without a thought for anything else but that, and he was chewing still as he turned on his heel and trotted up the street in his torn pants, his own blood hot on the back of his thigh.

He thought nothing. He didn't think of Madame Guérin or the food locker or of Itard or the she who'd offered him the sweet thing in the bleak familiar hallway outside the door of his room, and he didn't think of the room or the fire or his bed. Walking, he felt the pain in his feet and this new fire burning in the flesh of his thigh, and he limped and shuffled and stayed as close to the walls as he could. Everything that had come before this moment had been erased. He kept walking round the same block, over and over, his head down, shoulders slumped, in search of nothing.

Itard had fallen into a deep, exhausted sleep when one of the deaf-mutes who'd been sent out to scour the neighborhood came to him with a pair of scuffed leather shoes in hand. The boy—he was Victor's age, lean, clear-eyed, his hair cut too close to the scalp by the Institute's incompetent barber—was fluent in the manual language of the deaf-mutes and was able to tell Itard where he'd found the shoes and to lead him there and even demonstrate in which direction they'd been pointed. Itard felt stricken. He felt sick. The shoes—he turned them over in his hand—were worn unevenly along the inside seam where Victor's lurching, pigeon-toed gait punished the leather. There was no doubt. These shoes, these artifacts, were as familiar to him as his own boots.

It was raining, the cobblestones glistening as if they'd been polished. Pigeons huddled on the windowsills and under the eaves. Itard bent to touch the spot the boy indicated and then looked off down the dripping alley to where the walls seemed to draw together in the distance. He was afraid suddenly. The experiment was over. Victor was gone for good.

Even as he got to his feet and hurried down the alley, the deaf-mute at his side, he pictured Victor passing swiftly through the city, guided by his nose and ears, throwing off his suit of clothes like a yoke, working his way up along the bank of the Seine till the fields opened around him and the trees went dense in the ravines. He didn't stop to think what the boy would eat or that he was dependent now and grown heavy with surfeit and luxury, but thought only of Victor's eyes and teeth and how he would stoop to snatch up a frog or snail and crush it between his jaws—yes, and how well had all the eternal hours of exercises, of matching shapes and letters and forming vowels deep in the larynx prepared him for that? It was nothing. Life was nothing. He—Itard—for all his grand conception of himself and his power and his immutable will, was a failure.

A moment later they emerged from the alley and were back out on a wet, twisting street crowded with people and the baggage they hauled and carried and pressed to their bodies as if each loaf or sausage or block of paraffin was as vital as life itself, no chance of finding him here, no chance, and he thought of Victor's room, empty, and in the same moment that he was struck by the pang of his loss he felt a clean swift stroke of liberation slice through him. The experiment was over. Done. Finished. No more eternal hours, no more exercises, no more failure and frustration and battling the inevitable—he could begin to live the rest of his life again. But no. No. Victor's face rose up before him, the trembling chin and retreating eyes, the narrowed shoulders and the look of pride he wore when he matched one shape to another, and he felt ashamed of himself. He could barely lift his feet as he made his way back to the Institute through the bleak, unsettled streets.

It was Madame Guérin who wouldn't give up. She searched the streets, the paths of the Luxembourg Gardens where she took Victor for his walks, the cafés and wineshops and the alleys out back of the grocer's and the baker's. She quizzed everyone she met and displayed a crude charcoal sketch she'd made of him one night as he sat rocking by the fire, tending his potatoes, and she alerted her daughters and sent old Monsieur Guérin out to limp along the river and look for the inadmissible in the slow, lethal slip of the current. Finally, on the third day after he'd gone missing, one of the women who sold produce to the Institute's kitchens came to her and said she'd seen him—or a boy like him—across the river, begging in the marketplace at Les Halles.

She set out immediately, the woman at her side, her feet chopping so swiftly she was out of breath by the time she reached the bridge, but she went on, her blood clamoring and the color come into her face. The day was warm and close, puddles in the streets, the river a flat, stony gray. She was sweating, her blouse and undergarments soaked through by the time they reached the marketplace, and then, of course, the boy was nowhere to be found. "There," the woman shouted suddenly, "over there by the flower stall, there he is!" Madame Guérin felt her heart leap up. There, sitting on the pavement beneath a wagon and gnawing at something clenched in his two fists, was a boy with a dark thatch of hair and shoulders narrowed like a mannequin's, and she hurried to him, his name on her lips. She was right there, right at his side, bent over him, when she saw her mistake—this was a wasted scrap of a boy, starved and fleshless and staring up hostilely out of eyes that were not Victor's. Her legs felt unaccountably heavy all of a sudden and she had to sit on a stool and take a glass of water before she could think to offer the woman her thanks and start back for the Institute.

She was walking slowly, deliberately, her eyes on the pavement so as to avoid stepping into a puddle and ruining her shoes, and in her mind she was trying to get hold of her loss and fight down her sense of desolation—he would turn up, she knew he would, and if he didn't, she had her daughters and her husband and her cat, and who was he anyway but a poor, hopeless, wild boy who couldn't pronounce two words to save his life—when she glanced up to avoid a skittish man with a cane and locked eyes with Victor. He was on the far side of the street, carriages rattling by, the humped shoulders and floating heads of pedestrians intervening, all of Paris moving in concerted motion as if to frustrate her, as if to take him away again, and when she stepped into the road to go to him she didn't bother to look right or left and she ignored the curses of the ham-fisted man in his wagon and the stutter of his horses' hooves, because nothing mattered now, nothing but Victor.

For one uncertain moment, he didn't react. He just stood there, pressed against the wall of the building that loomed behind him, his face small and frightened and his eyes losing their focus. She saw how he'd suffered, saw the mud layered in his hair, the torn clothes, the blood at the seat of his pants. "Victor!" she called, sharply, angrily. What was he thinking? What was he doing? "Victor!"

It was as if those two syllables had become palpable and hard, fastened to a stone that hurtled out of the sky and struck him down. He fell to his knees and sobbed aloud. He tried to speak, tried to say her name, but there was nothing there. *"Uh-uh-uh-uh,"* he said, his voice ragged with emotion, *"uh-uh-uh-uh,"* and he crawled the last few penitential steps to her and took hold of her skirts and wouldn't let go.

While that scene in the streets was unfolding, Itard was back in his rooms, working with a mute boy who was functionally deaf but had retained some measure of hearing. This boy—his name was Gaspard and he was Victor's age, fair-haired, well-made, with a quick smile and tractable disposition—had progressed rapidly since coming to the Institute from a remote village in Brittany the preceding year. He could communicate readily by means of signs and he quickly mastered the exercises designed to allow him to associate an object and its graphic representation and then the object and the written word assigned it. For the past month, Itard had been drilling him in the shaping of the sounds of these words with the palate, lips, tongue and teeth, and the boy was beginning to string together discrete bits of sound in a comprehensible way, something Victor had been unable to do, though two years had gone by since he'd first come to the Institute—and Victor had the advantage of normal hearing. It was a conundrum, since Itard refused to believe that Victor was mentally deficient—he'd spent too much time with him, looked too deeply into his eyes, to believe that. At any rate, he was putting Gaspard through his drills and thinking of Victor, of Victor lost and wandering somewhere out there in the city, at the mercy of common criminals and sexual inverts, when Monsieur Guérin knocked at the door with the news that he'd been found.

Itard jumped up from the desk, knocking over the lamp in his excitement, and if it weren't for Gaspard's quick thinking and active feet, the whole room might have gone up in flames. "Where?" Itard demanded. "Where is he?"

"With Madame."

A moment later, with the reek of lamp oil in his nostrils and permeating his clothes, Itard was downstairs in the Guérins' apartment, where he found Victor lying rigid in the bath while Madame Guérin tended to him with soap and washcloth. Victor wouldn't look at him. Wouldn't so much as lift his eyes. "The poor child," Madame Guérin said, swiveling her neck to gaze up at him. "He's been bitten by some animal and lying in filth." Steam rose from the bath. Two vast pots of water were heating on the stove.

"Victor, you've been bad, very bad," Itard said, letting his intonation express everything he felt except relief, because he had to be stern, had to be like his own father, who would never let a child have his way in anything. Especially this. Running off as if he didn't belong here, as if he hadn't been treated with equanimity and even affection—and if he didn't belong here, then where did he belong? "Victor!" He raised his voice. "Victor, look at me."

No response. The boy's face was a wedge driven into the surface of the water, his hair a screen, his eyes focused on nothing.

"Victor! Victor!" Itard had moved closer until he was leaning over the tub, both hands gripping the sides. He was angry suddenly, angry out of all proportion to the way he'd felt just a moment earlier when Monsieur Guérin had brought him the news. What had changed? What was wrong? He wanted to be acknowledged, that was all. Was that too much to ask? "Victor!"

He couldn't be sure, because of the bathwater and the influence of the steam, but the boy's eyelids seemed to be wet. Was he crying? Was he movable too?

Madame Guérin's voice came at him out of the silence. "Please, Monsieur le Docteur—can't you see that he's upset?"

In the morning, first thing, though it might have been perverse, though it might have been his overzealousness that had precipitated the crisis in the first place, Itard went back to work on Victor, redoubling his efforts. Some elementary principal had been re-established over that bath, a confirmation of the order of being, he the father and Victor the son, and he was determined to take advantage of it while he could. He'd seen the influence of his own and Sicard's methods on Gaspard and some of the other deaf-mutes, and so he went back to drilling Victor on the simple objects and the words, written out on cardboard, that represented them. At first, Victor was as incapable of making the connection as he'd been at an earlier stage, but as the months progressed a kind of intellectual conversion gradually occurred so that Victor was finally able to command some thirty words—not orally, but in written form. Itard would hold up a card that read BOUTEILLE or LIVRE and Victor, making a game of it, would scramble out the door, mount the stairs to his room and unfailingly fetch the correct object. It was a breakthrough. And after endless repetitions, with several bottles and several books, papers, pens and shoes, he even began to generalize, understanding that the written word did not exclusively refer to the very specific thing in his room but to a whole class of similar objects. Now, Itard reasoned, he was ready for the final stage, the leap from the written word to the spoken that would engage all his faculties and make him fully human for the first time in his life.

For the next year—an entire year, with its fleeing clouds and intermittent rains, its snows and blossomings and stirrings in the trees—Itard trained him in the way he'd trained Gaspard, staring at him face to face and working the cranio-facial muscles through their variety of expressive gestures, inserting his fingers into the boy's mouth to manipulate his tongue and in turn having the boy touch his own and feel the movement of it as speech was formed. They drilled vowels, reached for consonants, for the simplest phones. It was slow going. "Fetch *le livre,* Victor," Itard would say, and Victor would simply stare. Itard would then get up and cross the room to hold the book in his hand, simultaneously pointing to Victor. "Tell me, Victor. Tell me you want the book. The book, Victor. The book."

In the meanwhile, whenever a breeze would stir the curtains or the clouds would close over the grounds or lightning knife through the sky, Victor would go to the window, no matter what they were doing or to what crucial stage the lesson had attained, deaf to all remonstrance. He had put on weight. He was taller now, by two inches and a half. Stronger. More and more he had the bearing of a man—unnaturally short, yes, and with the unformed features of a boy, but an incipient man for all that. There was the evidence of the hair under his arms and radiating out from his pubes and even the faint translucent trace of a mustache above his upper lip. During this period he was more easily distracted and he seemed to go blank at times, staring, humming, rocking, just as he'd done when he first came out of the woods. Increasingly, he seemed agitated too, and as his body continued to change, he became more of a problem about the grounds.

In addition to the incident with the deaf-mute girl, there was further cause for worry. While Itard couldn't imagine Victor's doing serious physical harm to anyone, male or female, the boy continually overstepped the bounds of propriety so that Sicard began to regard him as an immoral influence on the other children, and with good reason. There was no more sense of shame in him than in an arctic hare or an African ape that lived in its skin, and when the mood took him he would pull out his phallus and masturbate no matter the situation or the company (though thankfully, to this point, the abbé was unaware of it). He would rub up against people inappropriately, male and female alike. Increasingly, on awakening, he would dispense with his trousers and sometimes his undergarments too. No amount of discipline or punishment could make him feel shame or even modesty.

Once, when Madame Guérin's three daughters were present and they were all of them—the Guérins, Itard and Victor—having a picnic on the grounds of the Observatory in the Gardens, Victor made a fumbling amorous approach to Julie, his favorite of the three. He was used to seeing Julie, who often came to visit her mother—"Lee, Lee!" he would cry when she came into the room—and she seemed genuinely sympathetic toward him, not simply for her mother's sake, but because she was good-hearted and compassionate. On this day, however, no sooner had they spread the blanket and opened the hamper, than Victor made a snatch at the lion's share of the sandwiches and ran off with them to hide in a cluster of trees. This was his usual behavior—he had little sense, after all his training and humanizing, of anyone outside of himself, of pity or fellow-feeling or generosity—but this time there was a twist. A few moments later he came sidling back to the group, his face smeared with fish paste and mayonnaise, and began stroking the hair first of one sister, then another, his fingers visibly trembling as he touched them; then, with each in turn, he laid his head in her lap a moment until finally he got up and seized her by the back of the neck, his grip firm and yet gentle too. When they ignored him, he seemed hurt and pushed himself awkwardly away. The last was Julie, and she was more tolerant than her sisters. The same scenario played out, but then, showing a leap Itard felt he was incapable of, the boy took Julie firmly by the hand, pulled her to her feet and then led her across the grass to the clump of trees where he'd secreted the sandwiches.

The sisters shared a glance and made a remark as suggestive as they could in the presence of their parents, and Madame Guérin gave out with a little laugh of embarrassment, while her husband, stoic, elderly, his considerable nose reddened by the sun, gave all his attention to the sandwich before him. "Our Savage has grown civilized under the spell of feminine charm, eh?" Itard observed. "And who could blame him?" All eyes, but for Monsieur Guérin's, focused on the clump of trees and the pronounced sunstruck movement there. Intrigued, and with a lifted eyebrow for the party to show that he was amused and not at all concerned on a deeper level, though he was, of course, knowing Victor's rudimentary conception of propriety, Itard went to investigate.

Victor, his face bloodless and sober, was gently squeezing Julie's knees as if they were balls of malleable wax he was trying to shape into something else altogether, and at the same time he kept gesturing to his cache of sandwiches. The sandwiches, four or five of them—all showing conspicuous marks of his teeth—lay in a bed of fresh-picked leaves. Julie tried her best to look bemused, though she was plainly uncomfortable, and after she let Victor stroke her hair and mold her knees for some minutes, she smiled brightly and said, "That's enough, Victor. I want to go back to *Maman* now."

Victor's face took on a defeated look as Julie rose in a fragrant swirl of skirts and began to retrace her steps back to the party. "Lee!" he cried piteously, patting the depression in the grass where she'd been sitting, "Lee! Lee!" And then, in a kind of desperation, he held up the remains of a half-eaten sandwich as the ultimate expression of his love.

Itard was moved by this, of course—he was only human. But he couldn't conceive of how to instruct his pupil in morals or decorum when he was unable to implant words in his head—Victor couldn't formulate his own desires, let alone express them, and each day's exercises seemed to take him further from the goal. Six months went by, then another year. Victor began to chafe under the regimen in a way that recalled the early days, and no matter how many times they worked their facial muscles and their tongues and drilled over the same words, Victor simply could not pronounce them. Itard himself, a man with the patience of the gods, came to dread their sessions, until finally, reluctantly, he had to face the truth—Victor was regressing. Gaspard came and went, working now as a shoemaker's apprentice, able to read, write and speak with some degree of fluency, and others appeared in his place and learned and developed and moved on too. Sicard was growing impatient, as was the Minister of the Interior, who had authorized the funds for Victor's care and expected some sort of tangible return on the public investment. But there was some block here, some impediment Victor just couldn't seem to overcome, and despite himself Itard was forced to admit that it was the irremediable result of those years of estrangement, those years of inhumanity and wandering without any human voice to speak to him. He began to give up hope.

Then there came a day, a bright day of spring with a scent of renewal on the warm breeze blowing up out of the south, when Sicard appeared in the doorway to the doctor's rooms. Itard had been expecting a student and had left the door ajar, and he looked up in surprise—never, in all his time at the Institute, had the abbé come to visit him in his rooms, and yet here he was, wrapped in his soutane, his features pinched round the tight disapprobation of his mouth. This was trouble, and no doubt about it.

"The Savage," Sicard spat, and he was so worked up he could barely get the words out.

Itard got up from his desk in alarm and took up the water pitcher and the glass beside it. "Abbé," he said, already pouring, "can I get you a glass of water? Would you—?"

Sicard was in the room now, swiping one open palm across the other, his robe in a riot of motion. "That animal. That—God help me, but he's incurable. That idiot. That self-polluter, that, that—"

Itard gave him a stricken look. "What's he done?"

"What's he done? He's exposed himself in the flesh before the assembled female inmates and Sister Jean-Baptiste as well. And, and manipulated himself like one of the idiots in the Bicêtre—which is where he belongs. Either there or prison." He glared at Itard. His breathing—the ratcheting of the air through his nostrils—was thunderous. His eyes looked as if they were about to dissolve.

"But we can't just abandon him."

"I will not allow him to corrupt this institution, to pollute the innocent minds of these children—our wards, doctor, our wards. And worse—what if he acts on his impulses? What then?"

From outside the open window came the cries of the children at their games, the sound of a ball thumped and bodies colliding. Laughter. Shouts. Children at play, that was all it was. Only the sound of children at play, and yet it depressed him. Victor didn't play. Victor had never played. And now he was a child no longer.

Itard had tried everything, removing meat from the boy's diet, as well as any other foods that might contribute to unnatural excitation, giving him long baths again in the hope of calming him, and when he was most worked up, bleeding him till the tension flagged. Only the bleeding seemed to work, and then only for a few hours at a time. He saw Victor's face suddenly, rising before him in his consciousness, saw the pale descending slash of it in the corner of his room as he sat rocking over his feet and jerking at himself, saw the sheen of the eyes that pulled the whole world back into that primeval pit from which the first civilized man had crawled an eon ago. "He's not like that," he said lamely.

"He's incurable. Ineducable. He must be sent away."

There was a solution that had occurred to Itard, but it was something he couldn't discuss with anyone, certainly not the abbé or Madame Guérin. If Victor were able to express himself carnally, to experience the release every healthy male needs if he's not to become mad, then maybe there was hope yet, because this regression of his, this inability to focus and absorb his lessons—to speak like a human being—was perhaps somehow tied to his natural needs. Itard thought of hiring a prostitute. For months he'd wrestled with the notion, but finally he saw that he couldn't do it—it was one thing to rescue a child from savagery, hold him up to examination as a specimen, train his senses and his mind, and it was quite another to play God. No man had that right.

"We can't do that," he insisted. "He's a ward of the state. He's our responsibility. We took him from the woods and civilized him and we can't just throw up our hands and send him back—"

"Civilized him?" Sicard had spread his feet apart as if he expected to crouch down and grapple over the issue. He'd refused a seat, refused the water. He wanted one thing and one thing only. "You have no more to say about it."

"What about the Minister of the Interior? My report to him?"

"Your report will say that you've failed." His expression softened. "But not for lack of trying. I appreciate the energy you've put into this, we all do—but I told you this years ago and I'll tell you now: give it up. He's an idiot. He's filthy. An animal. He deserves only to be locked up." He snatched up the glass of water as if to examine its clarity, then set it down again. "And more: he should be castrated."

"Castrated?"

"Like a dog. Or a bull."

"And should we put a ring through his nose too?"

The abbé was silent a long while. The breeze picked up and rustled the curtains. A shaft of sunlight, golden as butter, struck the floor at his feet. Finally—and he had to raise his voice to be heard over the cries of the children—he cleared his throat and said, "I don't see why not. Truly, I don't."

8

The report, the final report Itard prepared for the Minister of the Interior, was a trial, a kind of crucifixion of the soul that made him want to cry out every time the quill touched the page. It was an admission that he'd wasted five years of his life—and of Victor's—in assaying the impossible, and that for all his brashness and confidence, all his repeated assurances to the contrary, he had failed. Ultimately, he had come to understand that the delimiting factors of Victor's abandonment were insurmountable—that he was, as Sicard insisted, ineducable. In the interest of science and in small measure to justify his own efforts, Itard listed these factors for the official record: "(1) Because he cannot hear the speech of others and learn to speak himself, Victor's education is and will remain incomplete; (2) His 'intellectual' progress will never match that of children normally brought up in society; (3) His emotional development is blocked by profound egotism and by the impossibility of channeling his awakening sexual feeling toward any satisfactory goals."

As he wrote, the pen seemed to drag across the page as if it were made of lead, every moment of hope he'd experienced in his association with Victor—the boy's rapid progress in those first few months, his first word, his naming, the leap he'd made in distinguishing written words—rising up before him and then vaporizing in despair. It took him several days and pot after pot of coffee before he began to understand that even in his failure there had been at least a muted success. Victor shouldn't be compared to other children, he argued, but only to himself—he was no more sentient than a plant when he'd first come out of the woods, differing only from the vegetative state in that he could move and vocalize. He was then the Savage of Aveyron, an animal-man, and now he was Victor, a young man who despite his limitations had learned to make himself useful to society, or at least the society of his guardians, Monsieur and Madame Guérin, for whom he was not only able but eager to perform household tasks such as cutting wood for the fire and setting the table for meals, and in the course of his education he had developed some degree of moral sensibility.

Some degree. He had no sense of shame, but then neither did Adam and Eve before the serpent came into the Garden, and how could he be blamed for that? Perhaps the most wrenching lessons Itard had felt compelled to give him were the ones designed to make him stretch beyond himself, to understand that other people had needs and emotions too, to feel pity and its corollary, compassion. Early on, when Victor was used to stealing and hoarding food in his room, Itard had tried to teach him a version of the Golden Rule in the most direct way he could think of—each time Victor filched some choice morsel from Itard's plate or old Monsieur Guérin's, Itard would wait his opportunity and swipe something back from Victor, even going so far as to slip into his room in his absence and remove his hoard of potatoes, apples and half-gnawed crusts of bread. Victor had reacted violently at first. The minute he turned his attention to his plate and saw that his *pommes frites* or broad beans were missing—that they were now on his teacher's plate—he threw a tantrum, rolling on the floor and crying out in rage and pain. Madame Guérin made a face. Itard held firm. Over time, Victor eventually reformed—he no longer took food from others' plates or misappropriated articles he coveted, a glittering shoe buckle or the translucent ball of glass Itard used as a paperweight—but the doctor could never be sure if it was because he'd developed a rudimentary sense of justice or, simply, that he feared reprisal in the way of the common criminal.

That was what led the doctor, sometime during the third year of the boy's education, to the most difficult lesson of all. It was on a day when they'd drilled with shapes for hours and Victor had been particularly tractable and looking forward to the usual blandishments and rewards Itard customarily gave him at the end of a trying session. The sun was sinking in the sky. Beyond the windows, the clamor of the deaf-mutes in the courtyard rose toward the release of dinnertime. The scent of stewing meat hung on the air. For several minutes now Victor had been looking up expectantly, awaiting the conclusion of the exercises and anticipating his reward. But instead of reward, Itard gave him punishment. He raised his voice, told Victor that he'd been bad, very bad, that he was clumsy and stupid and impossible to work with. For a long while he continued in this vein, then rose abruptly, seized the boy's arm and led him to the closet where he'd been confined, as punishment, when he'd been particularly recalcitrant during the early days of his education.

Victor gave him a look of bewilderment. He couldn't fathom what he'd done wrong or why his teacher's face was so contorted and red and his voice so threatening. At first, mewling plaintively, he let himself be led to the door of the closet, but then, as Itard was about to force him into it, Victor turned on him in outrage, his face flushed and his eyes flashing, and for a long moment they struggled for dominance. Victor was bigger now, stronger, but still he was no match for a grown man, and Itard was able to shove him, pleading and crying, into the closet. The door wouldn't shut. Victor wouldn't allow it. He braced his feet against the inside panel and pushed with all his strength and when he felt himself losing the battle he lurched forward suddenly to sink his teeth into Itard's hand before the door slammed shut and the key turned in the lock. It was an emotional moment for the doctor. His hand throbbed—he would have to treat the wound—and the boy would hate him for weeks, but he rejoiced all the same: Victor had developed a sense of justice. The punishment was undeserved and he'd reacted as any normal human being would have. Perhaps it was a small victory—would the Savage of Aveyron, dragged down from his tree, have grasped the concept?—but it was proof of Victor's humanity and Itard included mention of it in his report. Such a child—such a young man—he argued in conclusion, was deserving of the attention of scientists and of the continued support and solicitude of the government.

The report ran to fifty pages. The Minister of the Interior had it published at government expense, Sicard included with it a letter praising Itard's efforts, and Itard received some measure of the recognition and celebrity he'd craved. But the experiment was over, officially, and Victor's days at the Institute were numbered. Sicard militated for the boy's removal, writing the Minister of the Interior to the effect that for all Itard's heroic efforts the boy remained in a state of incurable idiocy, and that further he was a growing menace to the other students. It took some time—months and then years of depletion and vacancy—but eventually the government agreed to continue in perpetuity Madame Guérin's annual stipend of one hundred fifty francs to care for Victor and to award her an additional five hundred francs to relocate, with her husband and the boy, to a small house around the corner from the Institute on the impasse des Feuillantines.

If Victor was at all affected by the move from the only home he'd known, from the room he'd occupied all this time and the grounds he'd roamed till he had every twig and leaf, furrow and rock memorized, he didn't show it outwardly. He was a great help in moving the Guérins' furnishings, and the new environment seemed to excite him so that he got down on all fours and sniffed at the baseboards of the walls and examined each of the rooms minutely, fascinated to see the familiar objects—his bed and counterpane, the pots and pans, the twin chairs the Guérins liked to pull up to the fire—arrayed in this new place. There wasn't much of a yard, but it was free of deaf-mutes, and it was a place where he could study the sky or apply the axe and saw to the lengths of wood Madame Guérin required for the stove, where he could lie in the sun alongside Sultan, who had grown yet fatter and more ponderous as he aged. And each day, just as she'd done for years, Madame Guérin took him for a walk in the park.

And Itard? He made an effort to visit, at least at first, and on hearing his voice, the boy would come running to him for a hug, and the reward—a bag of nuts or an orange—the doctor never failed to produce. Victor was in his twenties now, shorter than average—short as a child—but his face had broadened and he'd developed a rudimentary beard that furred his cheeks and descended as far as the scar on his throat. When he went out for his walks he still trotted along in his unique way, but around the house and the yard he began to shamble from place to place like an old man. Itard regarded the Guérins as old friends—almost as comrades in arms, as they'd all gone through a kind of war together—and Madame always insisted on cooking for him when he visited, but there was an awkwardness between him and his former pupil now, all the physical intimacy of their years together reduced to that initial hug. What was the point? What could they possibly say to each other? Victor spoke with his eyes, with certain rude gestures of his hands, but that was a vocabulary in which Itard was no longer interested. He was a busy man, in constant demand, his fame burgeoning, and with time his visits became less and less frequent until one day they stopped altogether.

At the same time, the Guérins, now effectively retired from the Institute, were aging in a way that made it seem as if the weeks were months and the months years piled atop them. Monsieur Guérin, ten years his wife's senior, fell ill. Victor hovered in the doorway of the sickroom, looking out of his neutral eyes, uncomprehending—or at least that was the way it seemed to Madame Guérin. The more her husband needed her, the more Victor seemed to regress. He demanded her attention. He tugged at her dress. Insisted that she come into the next room to fix him his *pommes frites* at any hour of the day, to pour him milk or massage his legs or simply to look and marvel at something he'd discovered, a spider making its web in the corner where the chimney met the ceiling, a bird perched on the windowsill that was gone by the time she turned her head. And then Monsieur Guérin was gone too and Victor stood bewildered over the coffin and shrank away from the strange faces gathered above it.

The day after the funeral, Madame Guérin didn't get out of bed until late in the afternoon and Victor spent the day staring out the window, beyond the projection of the building across the street, and into the view of the open lot beyond. He poured himself glass after glass of water, the original liquid, the liquid that took him back to his time of freedom and deprivation, and stared out to where the grass stood tall and the branches of the trees caught the wind. When the light shifted toward evening he moved to the cupboard and set the table as he'd been trained to do: three bowls, three mugs, three spoons and the twice-folded cloth napkins. Ducking his head, he went into Madame Guérin's room and stood over the bed gazing at the heaviness of her face, her skin gone the color of ash, the lines of grief that dropped her chin and tugged at the corners of her eyes. He was hungry. He hadn't been fed all day. The fire was dead and the house was cold. He motioned to his mouth with his right hand and when Madame Guérin began to stir he took her arm and led her to the kitchen, pointing at the stove.

As soon as she came through the doorway, he knew that something was wrong. She pulled back, and he could feel her arm trembling against his, and there was the table, set for three. "No," she said, her voice strained and caught low in the back of her throat, "no," and it was a word he understood. Her shoulders shifted and she began to cry then, a soft wet insuck of grief and despair, and for a moment he didn't know what to do. But then, as tentatively and cautiously as he'd stalked the things he trapped in the grass a whole lifetime ago, he moved to the table and took up the bowl, the cup, the spoon and the napkin and silently put them back where they belonged.

In the years to come, Victor rarely left the house or the small square of the yard, hemmed in as it was by the walls of the surrounding buildings. Madame Guérin became too frail eventually to take him for his walks in the park and so he stood at the window instead for hours at a time or lay in the yard watching the clouds unfurl overhead. He took no pleasure in eating and yet he ate as if he were starved still, still roaming La Bassine with his stomach shrunken in disuse. The food thickened him around the middle and in the haunches. His face took on weight till he was nearly unrecognizable. No one knew. No one cared. He'd once been the sensation of Paris, but now he was forgotten, and even his name—Victor—was forgotten too. Madame Guérin no longer called him by name, no longer spoke at all except to her daughters, who rarely visited, wrapped up as they were in their own lives and passions. And the citizens of Paris, if they remembered him in passing, as they would remember the news of another generation or a tale told round the fire late at night, referred to him only as the Savage.

One morning Sultan vanished as if he'd never existed and before long there was another cat asleep in the chair or in Madame's lap as she sat and knitted or stared wearily into the pages of her Bible. Victor barely noticed. The cat was a thing of muscle and hidden organs. It stalked grasshoppers against the wall in the sun and ate from a dish in the kitchen, and with a long, languid thrust of its tongue it would probe itself all over, even to the slit beneath its tail, but mostly it lay inert, sleeping its life away. It was nothing to him. The walls, the ceiling, the glimpse of the distant trees and the sky overhead and all the power of life erupting from the earth at his feet: this was nothing. Not anymore.

He was forty years old when he died.

(2005)

PART IV

A Death in Kitchawank

My Pain Is Worse Than Your Pain

I like my wife fine and we had a pretty smooth run of it over the years but there was a sort of—oh, what do I want to say here?—*expectedness* to the days that sometimes bore down on me till I felt like a piece of furniture that hasn't been moved in a lifetime. An end table maybe, made of maple, with some fine beveling that serves no other purpose than to collect dust. Which is why—and I'm not making excuses, just stating the facts—I pulled on my black jeans and turtleneck that night, dug my ski mask out of the closet and climbed up the backside of Lily Baron's cabin to the patch of roof where the deck projects on the second floor and peeped in the window with no other intention but to see what she was doing at eleven forty-five at night, and maybe, if that was what she wanted, to surprise her. Give her a little jolt. In the best possible sense, that is, by way of amiability and with the promise of mutual enjoyment.

You see, Lily has had it rough this past year. She's only forty-three, but Frank, her husband who's no longer with us, was in his sixties, and when he retired, she quit her job as a legal secretary and came up here to Big Timber to live out the rest of her days in tranquility amidst the giant sequoias. They built their dream house on the double lot Frank had bought back in the eighties and became full-timers (or dream *cabin,* I should say, since the twenty-eight of us who live here year-round as well as the fifty or so part-timers like to think of ourselves as roughing it, and while a couple of us do have actual log cabins built from kits out of actual peeled logs, most of us settle for houses with alpine touches, like cedar paneling, stone fireplaces and mounted animal heads over our hand-hewn mantelpieces. To a man, woman, child and dog, we call them cabins).

Frank volunteered for neighborhood watch and he helped out in winter with snow removal, and Lily, with her heartbreaking face and a figure unruined by childbearing because she'd borne no children, not to Frank or her previous husband, who, I understand, worked for the Forest Service over at Mineral King before he drank himself senseless and pitched headlong over the rail of the fire lookout, began organizing potlucks and bridge nights down at the lodge, that sort of thing. And she began drinking more than was probably good for her. As did Frank. This—and we've all joked about it—is just one of the hazards of living in a fishbowl community at seventy-two hundred feet and a good twisting brake-eating hour from the nearest town in a place of natural beauty so all-encompassing God might have thought to set it aside for His wife. If He even bothered to get married.

Anyway, Frank liked nature, liked the hills, and despite his age he was always out there hiking no matter the weather. You'd look up from the fire or the TV or your first double vodka and tonic on a snow-bleared winter morning and there he'd be, with his daypack and alpenstock, heading off into the woods without a thought as to trails, compasses or the weather, and if he had a cell phone it really wouldn't have mattered since the reception here is what they invented the *Call Failed* indicator for. He went out one spring afternoon with his fly rod and a daypack containing a pint of Jim Beam and two cream cheese and olive sandwiches Lily had sealed in plastic wrap and he never came back. As they later reconstructed it, he was fishing Hellbore Creek for goldens when he must have taken a tumble because his leg was broken in two places, though with his eyes gouged out by the ravens and the way the bear had frolicked with the corpse no one could be sure. He'd been missing four days by the time Search and Rescue found him, the sandwiches gone along with the soft stuff of his eyes and the bourbon drawn down to less than a finger in its intact glass shell. Lily said she was sure he'd suffered and we all tried to reassure her, citing the solace of the bourbon, the soothing rhapsody of the stream and the sun that made way for the stars as if to give him a glimpse of eternity when the nights came on, but privately we knew she was right.

Of course he'd suffered. Alone with his pain. Hopeless. Fighting off the ravens till he could no longer lift his arms. He'd tried to crawl his way out of the canyon, according to Bill Secord, who was one of the first on the scene, but the pain in his leg was too bad apparently and he didn't make it more than maybe two hundred yards despite all the scratching in the undergrowth and the way his fingernails were abraded down to the nub.

As if that wasn't enough to lay on any woman, especially one as sweet and undeserving of it as Lily, there was the further complication of her accident. And this wasn't much more than maybe three or four months after the funeral, when she was just starting to climb out of her own personal canyon and was entertaining a man whose name I don't want to mention here because the sound of that name—hell, the look of him with his fat gloating face hanging out the open window of his pickup—makes me burn up with jealousy like a dry stick of pine laid on the coals. That's funny too, I mean, that this particular image should pop into my head, because Lily's accident involved just exactly that: burning. She had one of these old-fashioned popcorn makers, with the hot oil bubbling in the guts of it, and the way I see it she was a bit flustered when this particular individual showed up at the door with a bottle in one hand and a fistful of wilting wildflowers in the other, no way ready even to start thinking along those terms with Frank still intact in the ground, or mostly so, and maybe she was rushing a little, overcompensating in her role as hostess, and when she settled into the couch with her second drink her foot got tangled in the cord and the whole business, scalding oil, Orville Redenbacher's crackling yellow kernels and the gleaming aluminum cylinder of the popcorn maker itself, came down on her.

The oil melted the skin across half her back down to the pantyline and wrapped a big annealed scar around her left shoulder and upper arm and burned what looks like two teardrops into the flesh under her left eye, which the plastic surgeon says he can remove and smooth over just like new once she saves up for the next round of operations, because, of course, Frank, who never even bothered to carry a compass with him out into the woods, didn't have adequate health coverage from his insurer. Or life insurance, for that matter. I remember we all chipped in to defray the funeral expenses, but inevitably we fell well short of the actual cost. Which Lily had to absorb with no help from anybody, not Frank's sister in Missoula or his one-armed son Lily'd had to put up with through the first ten years of her marriage.

So I was on her roof. With cause. And Jessica, my wife, who likes to turn in early—she's yawning and gaping and stretching her arms out like she's drowning come seven-thirty or eight—was at home, oblivious, snoring lightly in the frigid cavern of the bedroom we shared with its view in summer of the blistered duff at the ankles of the trees and in winter the piled-up drifts that look like waves rolling across a stormy white sea. If I'd expected Lily to be, oh, I don't know, putting her hair up before the bathroom mirror so that her breasts rose and fell with the action of her arms in a baby-blue see-through negligee or something of the like, I was disappointed. At first I could see nothing but the upper hallway leading to her bedroom and the head of the mounted mule deer that graced the top of the stairway (the rock-hard nose of which I'd kissed for luck any number of times when Jessica and I were over for drinks and dinner and drinks when Frank was alive). There was a light on there, glowing faintly in the cheap smoked-glass sconce they'd got for twelve ninety-five at the Home Depot in Porterville, but there was no sign of movement. Or of her. They had a dog—she had a dog, I should say, a Chihuahua mix—but it was so old and withered and blind and deaf and pathetic it couldn't have raised the alarm if an entire armored division rolled through the living room. So I waited. And watched.

Did I mention, by the way, that this was in winter?

The night was clear all the way up to where the stars slid across their tracks, which meant that it was cold, maybe ten or twelve above, and I was having a little trouble seeing through the eye-slits of my mask, plus my breath was condensing around the opening for my mouth and freezing there so that my lips had begun to sting even before I'd got to Lily's (on foot, because I didn't want to just pull up there out front in my truck, because that would have spoiled the surprise—that, and you never knew who was watching up here where everybody's business is everybody's business). At least the roof was clear. Frank had gone metal, with a steep pitch that overhung the upper deck, and the sun had taken the three feet of snow the last storm had dropped and deposited it down below. All to the good. I broke the crust of ice around my mouth and was just about to ease myself down on the deck to get a look in the window there, the bedroom window, when the slick thin all-but-invisible sheet of ice that had replaced the snow took my boots out from under me and I lost my balance.

We don't have gutters here, for obvious reasons—the weight of the snow shearing over the side would rip them off in a heartbeat—so there was nothing between me and a two-story drop but corrugated sheet metal and the odd rivet. I was a little drunk. I admit it. We'd been over to the Ringsteads' for drinks and cards earlier and after we got home I guess I kept on pouring even as I was thinking about how lonely Lily must have been because half the mountain was there but she never showed. Anyway, I did not plummet over the side and go down two stories to where the big granite boulders protruded like bad teeth from the drifts, or not yet anyway, but instead just managed to catch myself on one of the steel chimney supports Frank had been obliged to install after a Jeffrey pine came down and obliterated the chimney last winter. I was spared. But the noise I'd made in trying to save myself got the blind and deaf Chihuahua barking and that barking apparently roused Lily.

I was spread-eagled on the slick roof and just trying to inch my way across to the deck when the door there flew open and Lily appeared, dressed in the baby-blue nightie of my dreams which I guess I must have seen hanging on the hook in the bathroom when I went in to relieve myself on one of those happy drinks-dinner-drinks nights, only with a big off-white cable-knit sweater obscuring the parts of her anatomy I'd most come to see. She let out a low exclamation in her sweet girlish voice that was like the trickle of a pure mountain spring, the dog at her feet yapping and the weight of all those stars beginning to crash down on me, and then she said, "Don't you move, you son of a bitch, because I've got a gun." And she did have a gun. We all have guns up here, twenty guns per person, as if it were a rule of the community. Of course I didn't have one, or not then anyway. My twenty guns were back home in my own cabin.

But here was my problem. I'd come to reconnoiter, albeit with the hope and maybe even expectation of a whole lot more, but I'd lost the element of surprise and wondered now whether I ought to say something to identify myself as me and not some crazed rapist paroled out of Lompoc Prison and dressed all in black with a black ski mask concealing his face and bad intentions in his heart.

And it wasn't getting shot that motivated me, believe me, because I would have welcomed it at that point—it was what my mother, my poor dead overworked and long-suffering mother, used to call mortification. If I revealed myself now, now that she'd got the drop on me, as they say, how could I hope to convince her that my purpose was essentially romantic—and beyond that consolatory even?

As it turned out, that decision was taken from my hands by the action of what some people would call fate but that I'm here to tell you was just bad luck, pure and simple. I lost my grip. The roof was like a skating rink if you could take a skating rink and cant it at a forty-five degree angle. Suddenly the night deserted me and I was gone. And it was my bad luck—my very bad, catastrophic luck—that I did not land among the drifts but on a big unforgiving incisor of rock that broke my leg just as thoroughly and nastily as Frank's had been broken out there among the boulders of Hellbore Creek.

While I was lying there, concealed behind my mask like a second-string superhero and unable to move because the pain was like a comet trapped inside my body, I began thinking—and I don't know why—of the stepson, of Frank Jr. He'd lost his arm in an incident at the San Diego Zoo when he was fourteen, which you may have read about because it made all the papers at the time. There was still a controversy surrounding the whole business, as to whether he really was high on angel dust and provoking the polar bear where it was only trying to cool off in its fetid little pond of greenish water or whether he honestly slipped and fell, but the result was he lost his right arm right to the shoulder and maybe a little beyond. You look at him now—he's thirty-two years old, handsome as a TV anchorman, with Frank's blond hair and squared-off features—and from the left side he could be doing Marine Corps recruiting posters, but on the right there's just nothing there, and when he walks it really throws him off balance so he's got a kind of funny hitch in his step. Lily, who's just eleven years older than he is, more the age of a big sister than a mother, had to put up with him under her roof when she and Frank lived down in the flats all those years because with his disability Frank Jr. couldn't support himself, and believe me, he's about as pleasant to be around as a cage full of rats, angry at the world and always pissing and moaning about the indescribable pain he feels in his missing limb. Which he invariably goes on to describe in detail. Ad nauseam.

But let me get back to it, because this connects in to what I'm trying to say here, about pain, about my pain and Lily's pain and everybody else's too, the upshot being that about three minutes later I'm exposed for who I am. To Lily, who's standing over me with a flashlight and her snubnose .38 Special that Frank gave her for her birthday year before last, because here's the kid—Frank Jr., who's supposed to be living down the hill in Porterville in some sort of halfway house—appearing out of nowhere to swoop down with the one hand he's got left to him and tear the mask off my face.

I don't think I ever talked and wheedled and apologized and extenuated as much as I did that night, stretched out on my back in the snow and freezing my ass off while Lily looked at me as if I were something she'd stepped on in the parking lot at Costco and Frank Jr. ran in to phone for the sheriff, the fire department and every last living soul on the mountain, including old Brick Sternreit, who'd won the title of Mountain Man three times running during the Memorial Day chili cookoff despite the fact that he was closing in on ninety, Bart Bliss, who ran the lodge and sported the longest beard on the mountain, three widows, two widowers and my own sharp-honed steel-eyed rapier of a wife, Jessica. There was an interval there, Frank Jr. in the house and phones ringing everywhere, when it was just me and Lily and the dead cold of the night. Lily had lowered the .38, thumbed the safety and dropped the thing in the pocket of the big cardigan sweater, which I now saw was decorated with a pair of prancing reindeer done up in red stitching, but the flashlight was still leveled on my face. "Lily," I gasped, fighting for breath against the pain, "could you lower that light? Please? Because my leg's broke"—I almost said, *Just like Frank's,* but suppressed it—"and I can't move and the light's right in my eyes."

The beam never wavered. "What in hell were you thinking?" This was framed in an accusatory tone, and her voice was anything but melodious and sweet.

"I love you," I said. "I've loved you since the day Frank brought you up here and we all got drunk on pitchers of margaritas down at the lodge . . . remember?"

Her voice was flat. "You don't love me."

"I do."

"You have a funny way of showing it. What did you think, you'd see me naked or something?"

There was the sound, in the distance, of snow tires crunching the crust of ice on the blacktop road that twisted below us past the Turners' place, and already the headlights were dancing in the tops of the stripped aspens out front of Lily's. "You must think I'm like a Peeping Tom or something, but really, I just, I mean—"

"No," she said, cutting me off, "I don't think you're a Peeping Tom—I think you're a slime. I mean, really, how could you? With Frank barely cold in the ground and what about Jessica, what about her, what about your *wife*?"

The pain—the comet that was shooting from my lower leg to my brain and back again, fighting to explode into the night—seized me up a minute and I had no reasonable answer to give her. I wanted to say, *She won't mind,* or *She doesn't have to know,* or *I don't love her, I love you,* but I couldn't.

"And the mask? What's with the mask? I mean, that's just sick."

And so I wheedled and protested but it did no good because those tires and those headlights belonged to Bill Secord, first responder, and before I could blink twice the whole community was gathered there to contemplate me in my sprawled and broken disgrace (wildly, it came to me that I could say I was just checking the chimney braces as a favor to Frank, in memory of Frank, that is, and to help out a poor widow who didn't know the first thing about winter maintenance). Voices drifted over me. Two dogs slunk up to sniff my boots. I noticed a bottle of vodka passing from hand to hand, but no one thought to offer me any, not even to wet my lips. People debated whether or not I should be moved and Bill was all official about back injuries and the like and the sheriff appeared out of the shadows to take his report while the ambulance was jerking its lights in and out of the trees and Jessica, my bedmate, my companion, my old rug and sweet married bride, lurched up and leaned over me with her face so disarranged with hurt and confusion and rage I barely recognized her as she let loose with a cold wad of spit that wound up freezing right there on my cheek as the paramedics lifted me onto the stretcher and the doors of the ambulance slammed shut on the night and the mountain, which until that very moment had been my home and my hideout and my refuge from the bad old world.

You want pain? Jessica filed for divorce before they even got the pin in my leg, and when I had to rely on the jerk whose name I won't mention to drive me home from the hospital and help me up the steps to my own house and then make a second trip out to the car for the wheelchair, she was gone. As was about eighty-seven percent of the furniture and the plasma TV that had been my only solace the last couple of years, that and the squirrels, that is, and she'd cleaned out most of the microwave dinners and canned goods so that I had nothing to eat on top of nothing to watch. Oh, that was a cold house. And I tell you, for the rest of that winter, I never showed my face for the humiliation of what had gone down, and if I drank bourbon, I drank it alone.

If we're anything, though, we're a community that forgets if not forgives—hell, half of them up here have done things twice as bad as looking in on a woman out of concern and love in the dead of a winter's night—and by spring I was feeling almost back to normal. So much so that I even took the wheelchair down to the lodge one night, up and down those looping murderous hills for a good mile till my palms were bleeding, and sat there over a medium-rare steak, a pitcher of Firestone and a shot glass that never stayed dry for long because everybody who came through the door stood me a round and slapped me on the back and said how good it was to see me out and about. And that was fine. Time heals all wounds and such. Except that my nerves were like guitar strings twisted too tight and my heart was undergoing cardiac arrest at the thought that Lily might walk through that door at any minute. Which she didn't. I tried calling her when I got back home—Bill Secord gave me a ride, thank God, or I'd probably still be down there—but she had caller I.D. and wouldn't pick up.

It must have been a few weeks later that I ran into that kid out on Tamarack Lane. Tamarack intersects my street, Aspen, and then swerves past our little man-made lake and continues on to the lodge and the main road beyond, so that if I want to go anywhere at all ninety percent of the time it's going to be down Tamarack. We only have a couple of roads up here anyway, snaking wide frost-buckled blacktop thoroughfares to nowhere, hemmed in by the towering sequoias, ponderosa pines and the like that give the place its name, with maybe a cabin tucked back in the woods every couple of hundred yards, and these roads loop around back on themselves so the plan of the development is like a big hamster maze, one way in and one way out. Beyond that, there's the state route winding its way down to Porterville to the north in case anybody would want to go down there and buy a plasma TV to replace the one lost to them, and to Kernville on the other side, where there's nothing much but a couple run-down bars and trinket shops for the tourists. In winter, the Kernville road is closed due to the fact that nobody lives out there and the snow, which averages twenty-four feet per annum and goes to as much as forty and more in an El Niño year, isn't worth the expense of plowing. Which puts us, for a good four or five months of the year, at the end of the road, for all that indicates or implies about the quality of people we sometimes unfortunately wind up with.

This kid was one of them, though I didn't know it at the time. I was getting around pretty good by then with my cane, my leg still shrunken and white as a grub where the cast had constricted it, and I'd just turned onto Tamarack, thinking to hobble down to the lodge for a little exercise and maybe check the mail and see who was around, have a drink or two, get social, when there he was, striding along in this jaunty hey-look-at-me kind of way. Now, it was pretty rare to see strangers walking around the development—somebody goes by my house and nine out of ten I can tell you their first, middle and last name and all the regrets they've had since they got out of elementary school—but there are hikers and day-trippers and whatnot coming by occasionally, so it wasn't unheard of. Anyway, the kid looks to be twenty or so and he's tall and greyhound skinny, with a little soul patch just like mine, and so of course I'm neighborly and call out my standard greeting ("What up?"), which he returns with a big doggy smile that shows off the gap where three of his teeth are missing in front, one upstairs, two down. Next thing we're standing there chatting, and if I was vaguely aware of one of the house alarms going off up the street (we're always getting cabins broken into up here because you leave a place vacant long enough and somebody's going to notice), I barely gave it a thought.

He was pretty winning, this kid, a real talker. Within sixty seconds he was asking me about the quality of the construction up on the mountain—he was a big aficionado of cabin architecture as well as being a master carpenter, or so he said, and why not believe him?—and three minutes later I found myself humping back up Aspen with him to show off what I'd done vis-à-vis layout, exposed beams, roof pitch and all the rest when I took early retirement and built the place for Jessica six years ago. We got talking. I made a pot of coffee. He leaned back in the one armchair my wife had left behind and observed that the place was pretty spare. I agreed that it was. And I said to myself, *What the hell, what have I got to lose?* So I told him my story. When I was done—and I have to admit I went to some length to wring the very bitterest dregs out of it—I offered to freshen up his coffee with a shot of Jim Beam and he took me up on it and then, because we were just being neighborly as all hell and maybe I hadn't had as many people to talk to as I might have liked these past months, I encouraged him to sit right there and open up. What was his story? How'd he wind up on the mountain? Was he somebody's kid? Grandkid?

Let me tell you, if you thought Lily had troubles, this kid went her one better. Or worse, I guess. He just looked at me a long moment over the rim of his cup, as if deciding whether to trust me or not, and he never flinched when the sheriff's four-by went up and down the road two if not three times, siren screaming, and then he said, "You ever hear about that kid the parolee snatched in the back of Safeway when he was nine years old and then kept him traveling around the country till the kid didn't know where he was or even who he was? Not to mention the dirty things he made that scared little kid do just to earn a candy bar—or, shit, a half-rotten scrap of meat? The handcuffs—you hear about the handcuffs?"

Well, that was a story. How he had to eat dog food out of the can with the only present the man ever gave him, which was a bent spoon. How the man made him split wood for the stove and clean the house like a slave all day and wouldn't let him get within a mile of a newspaper and never let him out of the house and didn't even have a TV. I still don't know how much of it was the truth, but I watched the tears come up in his eyes and you know he had trouble whatever it was. We sat talking for the better part of an hour and then the sheriff, siren stifled now but his lights still flashing, pulled into the driveway, and who was with him but Bill Secord, stepping out carefully so as not to trample the irises Jessica planted along the drive last year, and right behind him, in her red cowgirl boots and skintight jeans, was Lily.

The kid gave me a look. "I need to tell you something—" he started, and I cut him off.

"You been breaking into cabins?"

"Not really."

"What do you mean *not really*? Either you did or you didn't." There was the thump of the sheriff's footfall on the weathered cedar planks of the front deck and then the accompanying thump of Bill's boot and a lighter tread altogether, which was Lily's, I knew. Can I tell you that I was torn in two directions in that instant, that I felt something for the kid despite myself and that the thought of seeing Lily's pale white oval of a face and maybe catching a whiff of that hundred-and-twenty-five-dollar-an-ounce perfume she dabs so prettily under the twin points of her jawbone had me all but paralyzed?

The kid's voice came at me like a tape on high speed. "Listen, I didn't steal anything, I mean, look at me—where would I hide it? I was hungry, that was all. Because it wasn't normal, what happened to me, you know? And I—I'm sorry, I just get these food cravings." He was on his feet now and he was pleading. "I only escaped three years ago."

I didn't say anything. Lily was right outside the door.

"Listen, I'm begging you," the kid said, drifting like a shadow across the room. "I just want to—could I just go in the bedroom a minute and close the door?"

So he did and I opened the front door to the sheriff (his name's Randy Juniper, he's thirty-six years old and he has a permanent hair up his ass, which is to say I don't like him and never have liked him and never will), Bill Secord and Lily. Lily looked like she was drowning. Water up to her neck and the river in flood. She and Bill stepped in the room and Bill closed the door behind him and stared down at his shoes. Randy, I noticed, had his three-foot-long flashlight in one hand, though it was broad daylight, and he squinted at me in my own living room as if it was an interrogation cell in Guantánamo or someplace, and then, in his official sheriffese, he said, "You see anybody suspicious out there this morning?"

"They broke into my cabin," Lily whispered, not looking at me.

"Who?" I said, playing for time.

Now she did glance up, her eyes, which are the exact color of Coca-Cola poured into a clear spotless glass, hardening with the contemplation of how much had been laid on her and laid on her again. "This kid," she said, her voice gone soft, "like a teenager or maybe twenties, real gawky and skinny and stupid-looking—I pulled into the drive because I was down the lodge for breakfast and I saw him coming round the back of the cabin and when he saw me he just took off into the woods."

Next question, and I didn't like the way Sheriff Randy was looking at me, not at all: "Did they get anything?"

They hadn't. But the screen over the kitchen sink had been slit open and that was enough for her. And the sheriff.

"You," the sheriff said finally, "wouldn't know anything about it, would you?"

My answer was a long time coming—seconds, I guess, five, maybe ten even. I didn't like the implication here because what they were hinting at was that I was a criminal, a thief, maybe a colluder with thieves, and all because I fell off Lily's roof with the best of intentions, with love in my heart, and so I just looked Randy right in the face and shook my head no.

Time passes slowly up here, the hours squeezing out like toothpaste at the flattened end of the tube. I noticed that the days got a little longer and then they started to get a little shorter. The sun hung up in the trees. I fed the birds and the squirrels, stared at the faded place on the wall where the TV had been and thought about various projects I might embark on to fill the lonely hours, building a chicken coop maybe (though chickens wouldn't last half an hour up here what with the coyotes and the bear and his cousins), buying a horse or a dirt bike so I could get out in the woods more, overhauling the engine on my snow machine. None of these came to fruition. And if I'd taken some satisfaction in how much my neighbors drank, half of them with corrupted livers and at least two I know of working on a single kidney each, now I was drinking so heavily I found myself waking up all day long and in places I didn't even know I could get to, like on top of the refrigerator or underneath the pickup.

Lily was the problem, of course. And Jessica, who'd moved in with her mother in Sacramento and refused to return my calls. I did give Jessica some thought, remembering the good times like when I held her head down for a full hundred and ten seconds during an apple-bobbing contest at the county fair or how we'd make up a big pot of chili beans and sit out on the deck and listen to the sounds of nature, but it was Lily who occupied my thoughts. My leg was getting stronger and more and more I found myself drifting past her cabin on my daily walks or driving by after dark just to see if her lights were on.

One day, late afternoon, September touching the leaves of the aspens so they went from green to gold overnight and the breath of winter impatient on the air, I just couldn't take it any longer and decided to dig out my bird-watching binoculars and maybe just stroll through the woods a bit—and if I wound up on the ridge across from Lily's with an unobstructed view of the lower deck and the Weber grill giving off smoke in the corner there, so much the worse. No one was in sight, but the smoke told me Lily was barbecuing. The thought of that—not just the way she did tri-tip with her special sauce that managed to be both sweet and sour in equal proportions and how she leaned over you to refresh your drink so you could smell the bourbon on her breath and her perfume at the same time, but also the sad fact that I'd once shuffled across the boards of that very deck as an honored guest—got me feeling nostalgic. I sat there on a hard lump of rock, the binoculars trained on the windows, nostalgia clogging my veins like sludge, till the sun shifted and shadows tipped back from the trees and Lily finally appeared, a platter of meat in one hand and a spatula and tongs in the other. She was wearing a pair of red shorts that emphasized the creases front and rear and a low-cut white blouse. Her feet were bare. I wanted to kiss those feet, wanted to come down off my perch and worry over the splinters that were certainly a danger on that deck that hadn't been treated since Frank died, wanted to warn her, make a joke, see her smile.

We all have binoculars up here, by the way, which are necessary to the enjoyment of nature, or so we tell ourselves, and we like to compete as to whose are the most powerful, just as we compete over our four-by-fours, snow machines and the like. Jessica got my good ones, the Bushnell Elites that allow you to count the whiskers on a marmot's snout half a mile away, but the ones she left me—bargain basement Nikon 7x20s—were more than adequate to the purpose. I could see not only that Lily'd had her toenails done, in a shade of red that came as close to the hue of those clinging shorts as was humanly possible, but that both of her big toes sported a little white rose painted right in the middle. She was wearing her hoop earrings, the silver glinting in the long tube of sunlight as she bent to lift the top off the Weber and employ the tongs, and though I was maybe a football field away, it was close enough to hear the first startled sizzle of the meat hitting the grill. Or maybe I was imagining that. But I could see that she was all made-up, beautiful as a porcelain doll, with her eyebrows penciled in and her lashes thick as fur.

So I'm only human. And what I was thinking was that even if she wasn't ready for my company, even if she wouldn't glance up when I mounted the steps to the deck with a sad forgiving smile and invite me to sit down and break bread with her—or, in this case, slice tri-tip—she would at least have to acknowledge me and maybe even hear me out on the subject of the ski mask and the roof and all the rest. Because I loved her purely and I wanted her to know that. As if it had been decided all along, I pushed myself up from the rock just like that and kept to the cover of the trees while she fussed around the little picnic table on the deck, and as I got closer I could hear the strains of some eighties band leaching out through the screen door in front. At the foot of the driveway, I bent to secrete the binoculars under a bush so as not to give her the wrong impression, and then came silently up on her, looking to the surprise factor, though I wasn't yet sure if I was going to chime out "Guess who?" or just "Hi" and add that I was in the neighborhood (a joke: we were all in the neighborhood twenty-four/ seven) and just thought I'd say hello.

As it turned out, I didn't have the opportunity, because at that moment Frank Jr. came backing his way out through the screen door, a big wooden bowl of salad clutched to his chest under the pressure of his arm and the rim of a sloshing cocktail glass clenched between his teeth. When he saw me—I was at the landing of the six steps that led up to the lower deck—he just about spit the glass into the bowl. As it was, he fumbled the bowl awkwardly for half a second before it hit the deck, spewing romaine and cherry tomatoes across the bleached boards, and I was worried he was going to bite through the glass, but he caught himself. Lily saw me then. Her look was blank at first, as if she didn't recognize me, or more likely couldn't place me in context, so far had she gone in wiping me off her personal slate.

Frank Jr. broke the silence. "Jesus, you got brass."

I couldn't be sure but Lily looked as if she was smiling at me—or maybe, considering what happened next, she was grimacing. Honestly, I don't know.

Frank Jr. moved across the deck to put himself between me and her, as if I was some sort of threat, which I wasn't and never have been, and I couldn't help comparing him with the skinny kid who'd come up here to violate people's space and steal what little they had for his own use. Frank Jr. was older, better-looking, but they were both kids to me and they shared the same general look, a kind of twitching around the mouth that only showed the kind of contempt they had for older people, and in that moment I half-wished I'd turned the kid in. I never did find out what happened to him. They found a stolen Mustang convertible abandoned on one of the logging roads not a mile and a half from the development, but whether he was responsible or not no one could say. For my part, I just pushed open the bedroom door after the sheriff left and found the room empty, as if the kid was nothing more than my own invention.

Frank Jr. was real enough though. And he let out a low curse and said, "Neither me or Lily want to see you on this property, not now or ever." And he turned to her and squeezed her to him and I saw something there that made my heart jump. "Right, Lily?"

I don't know how it happened, but I found myself all the way up the six steps and standing there on the deck as if I belonged, and I started to explain, but that was one of the hardest things I ever had to do in my life because all the factors had been churning around in me through all those washed-out months, so I just said what I'd said to her that night. "Lily," I said, "I'm sorry if I offended you or whatever"—I paused, and her eyes weren't so much hateful as just stunned—"but you know why I did it."

She said nothing.

Frank Jr. took a step forward. "No," he said, low and nasty, "she doesn't."

"Because I love her," I said, and maybe I took a step toward him too so that we were three feet apart and the next thing I knew I heard the sound of one fist clapping. Against my cheekbone. Frank Jr.—and he has a lot of power in that arm because when you think of it that arm has to do the work of two—lashed out and hit me and I tell you it was bad luck, pure and simple, that sent me into the rail that maybe wasn't up to code with regard to height requirements and then pitched me right over it into the duff ten feet down. On my leg. My bad leg. Which broke all over again with a snap you could have heard in Sacramento.

But that wasn't the worst. The worst was that Lily, instead of coming to my aid as even an anonymous stranger would have, instead took hold of Frank Jr. with both her strong shapely bare suntanned arms and pulled her to him for a long soul kiss that left not a single doubt in my mind. And I tell you, he was the stepson. The *stepson,* for Christ's sake. I mean, morally speaking, isn't that what they call incest?

I won't go into detail about Bill Secord and the sheriff and the whole playing out of the same charade of the winter past, but I will say that when you talk about pain, it comes in varieties and dominions nobody can even begin to imagine. And when you talk about fate, which I reject as a useful proposition, you talk about some kind of wheel you can never get off of. Fate doesn't leave you any margin for hope or redemption or even change. With fate, the fix is in, but I'm going to tell you that luck is different, bad luck anyway. Bad luck can change. I sit here in my rented wheelchair and look out into the trees present and see the ghosts of the trees past and tell myself it has to, because nobody—not Lily with her scarred back and two permanent tears or Frank Jr. with his missing arm or the snatched kid who had to degrade himself every minute of every day without hope even of the faintest flicker of love—could stand to be as lonely and miserable as this.

(2009)

The Silence

Dragonfly

What a dragonfly was doing out here in the desert, he couldn't say. It was a creature of water, a sluggish slime-coated nymph that had metamorphosed into an electric needle of light, designed to hover and dart over pond and ditch in order to feed on the insects that rose from the surface in soft moist clouds. But here it was, as red as blood if blood could shine like metal, hovering in front of his face as if it had come to impart some message. And what would that message be? *I am the karmic representative of the insect world, here to tell you that all is well among us. Hooray! Jabba-jabba-jabba!* For a long while, long after the creature had hurtled away in shearing splinters of radiance, he sat there, legs folded under him in the blaze of one-hundred-and-eighteen-degree heat, thinking alternately: *This is working* and *I am losing my mind.*

And this was only the first day.

Yurt

What he wanted, more than he wanted the air to sink into the alveoli of his lungs or the blood to rush through the chambers of his heart, was to tell his wife about it, about this miracle of the dragonfly in the desert. But of course he couldn't, because the nature of this retreat, under the guidance of Geshe Stephen O'Dowd and Lama Katie Capolupo, was silence, silence rejuvenant, unbroken, utter. Three years, three months and three days of it, the very term undertaken by the Dalai Lamas themselves in their quest for enlightenment. He had signed on, drawn down his bank account, paid his first wife a lump sum to cover her maintenance and child support for the twins, married the love of his soul on a sere scorched afternoon three weeks ago and put the finishing touches to his yurt. In the Arizona desert. Amidst cholla and saguaro and sun-blistered projections of rock so bleak they might have confounded the Buddha himself. The heat was an anvil and he was the white-hot point of steel beaten under the hammer.

Though he felt light-headed from the morning and afternoon group meditation sessions and the trancing suck of the desert sun, he pushed himself up and tottered back to the yurt on legs that might as well have been deboned for all the stability they offered him, this perfect gift of the dragonfly inside him and no way to get it out. He found her—Karuna, his wife, the former Sally Barlow Townes of Chappaqua, New York—seated in the lotus position on the hemp mat just inside the door. She was a slim, very nearly emaciated girl of twenty-nine, with a strong sweep of jaw, a pouting smallish mouth and a rope of braided blond hair that drew in the light and held it. Despite the heat, she was wearing her pink prayer shawl over a blue pashmina meditation skirt. Her sweat was like body paint, every square millimeter of exposed flesh shining with it.

At first she didn't lift her eyes, so deeply immersed in the inner self she didn't seem to be aware of him standing there before her. He felt the smallest stab of jealousy over her ability to penetrate so deeply, to go so far—and on the first day, no less—but then he dismissed it as selfish and hurtful, as bad karma, as *papa*. They might have been enjoined from speaking, he was thinking, but there were ways around that. Very slowly he began to move his limbs as if he were dancing to an unheard melody, then he clicked his fingers, counting off the beat, and at last she raised her eyes.

Chickpeas

Dinner for their first evening of the retreat, after the meager portions of rice and lentils doled out for the communal morning and afternoon meals, had been decided on in a time when they could express themselves aloud—yesterday, that is. It was to consist of tahini, lemon juice and chickpeas blended into hummus, basmati rice and naan bread. He was at the stove watching the chickpeas roiling in a pan of water over the gas jet, which was hooked up to the propane tank half-buried in a pit behind the yurt. It must have been seven or so in the evening—he couldn't be sure because Geshe Stephen had encouraged them all to remove their watches and ceremonially grind them between two stones. The heat had begun to lift and he imagined the temperature dipping into the nineties, though numbers had no value here and whether it was diabolically hot or, in winter, as he'd been forewarned, unforgivingly cold, really didn't matter. What mattered were the chickpeas, golden in the pot. What mattered was the dragonfly.

He'd done his best to communicate the experience to Karuna, falling back on his admittedly rusty skills at charades. He led her to the entrance of the yurt and pointed to the place where he'd been sitting in the poor stippled shade of a palo verde tree and then used the distance between his forefinger and thumb to give her an idea of the creature and its relative size, jerking that space back and forth vigorously to replicate its movements and finally flinging his hand out to demonstrate the path it had taken. She'd gazed at him blankly. *Three syllables,* he indicated digitally, making his face go fierce for the representation of dragon—he breathed fire, or tried to—and then softening it for the notion of fly, and he'd been helped here by the appearance, against the front window, of an actual fly, a fat bluebottle that had no doubt sprung from the desiccating carcass of some fallen toad or lizard. She'd blinked rapidly. She'd smiled. And, as far as he could see, didn't have the faintest idea of what he was attempting to convey, though she was trying her hardest to focus on the bliss in his face.

But now she was bending to the oven, where the flattened balls of dough were taking on the appearance of bread, her meditation skirt hitched up in back so that he was able to admire the shape of her ankles, a shape as miraculous as that of the dragonfly—or no, a thousand times more so. Because her ankles rose gracefully to her calves and her calves to her thighs and from there . . . he caught himself. This was not right-mindfulness, and he had to suppress it. There would be no touching, no kissing, no sex during the length of the retreat. And that length of time looped out suddenly before him like a rope descending into an infinite well: three years, three months, three days. Or no: two. One down, or nearly down. A quick calculation: 1,189 to go.

He reached for the handle of the pot and had actually taken hold of it, so entranced was he by the poured gold of the chickpeas, before he understood that the handle was hot. But not simply hot: superheated, all but molten. He managed to drop the pot back on the burner without upsetting it, the harsh clatter of metal on metal startling his wife, who shot him a glance out of enlarging eyes, and though he wanted to cry out, to curse and shout and dance through his pain, he just bit his finger at the knuckle and let the tears roll down both flanges of his nose.

Tarantula

The first night came in a blizzard of stars. The temperature dropped till it was almost bearable, not that it mattered, and he stared hard at the concentric rings of the yurt's conical ceiling till they began to blur. Was he bored? No, not at all. He didn't need the noise of the world, the cell phones and TVs and laptops and all the rest, transient things, distractions, things of the flesh—he needed inner focus, serenity, the Bodhisattva path. And he was on it, his two feet planted firmly, as he dropped his eyes to study the movements of Karuna while she prepared for bed. She was grace incarnate, swimming out of her clothes as if emerging from a cool clean mountain stream, naked before him as she bent for the stiff cotton nightshirt that lay folded beneath her pillow on the raised wooden pallet beside his own. He studied the flex of her buttocks, the cleft there, the way her breasts swung free as she dipped to the bed, and it was so right, so pure and wholly beautiful that he felt like singing—or chanting. Chanting in his own head, *Om mani padme hum.*

And then suddenly she was recoiling from the bed as if it had burst into flame, pinning the nightshirt to her chest and—it was her turn now—jamming a fist into her mouth to keep from screaming. He jumped to his feet and saw the tarantula then, a miracle of creation as stunning in its effect as the dragonfly, if more expected, because this was its environment, its home in the world of appearances. Big as a spread hand, it paused a moment on the pillow, as if to revel in its glory, and then, on the unhurried extension of its legs that were like walking fingers, it slowly ascended the adobe wall. Karuna turned to him, her eyes fractured with fear. She mouthed, *Kill it,* and he had to admire her in her extremity, because there was no speech, not even the faintest aspiration, just the drawn-back lips and the grimace of the unvoiced verb.

He shook his head no. She knew as well as he that all creatures were sacred and that the very worst *papa* attached to taking a life.

She flew to the drainboard where the washed and dried pot lay overturned, snatched it up and shoved it in his hand, making motions to indicate that he should capture the thing and take it out into the night. Far out. Over the next ridge, if possible.

And so he lifted the pot to the wall, but the tarantula, with its multiple eyes and the heat of its being, anticipated him, shooting down the adobe surface as if on a hurricane wind to disappear, finally, in the mysterious dark space beneath his wife's bed.

Geshe

In the morning, at an hour he supposed might be something like 3:30 or 4:00, the first meditation session of the day began. Not that he'd slept much in any case, Karuna insisting, through gestures and the overtly physical act of pinching his upper arm between two fingers as fiercely tuned as any tarantula's pedipalps, on switching beds, at least for the night. He didn't mind. He welcomed all creatures, though lying there in the dark and listening to the rise and fall of his bride's soft rasping snores he couldn't help wondering just what exactly the tarantula's message had been: *I am the karmic representative of the arachnid world, here to tell you that all is well among us, which is why I've come to bite your wife. Hooray! Jabba-jabba-jabba!*

Geshe Stephen, who'd awakened them both with a knuckle-rap at the door that exploded through the yurt like a shotgun blast, was long-nosed and tall, with a slight stoop, watery blue eyes and two permanent spots of moisture housed in his outsized nostrils. He was sixty-two years old and had ascended to the rank of Geshe—the rough equivalent of a doctor of divinity—through a lifetime of study and an unwavering devotion to the Noble Eightfold Path of the Gautama Buddha. He had twice before sought enlightenment in a regimen of silence and he was as serene and untouched by worldly worry as a breeze stirring the very highest leaves of the tallest tree on the tallest mountain. Before the retreat began, when the thirteen aspirants were building their domiciles and words were their currency, he'd delivered up any number of parables, the most telling of which—at least for this particular aspirant—was the story of the hermit and the monk.

They were gathered in the adobe temple, seated on the floor in a precise circle. Their robes lay about them like ripples on water. Sunlight graced the circular walls. "There was once a monk in the time of the Buddha who devoted his life to meditation on a single mantra," the Geshe intoned, his wonderfully long and mobile upper lip rising and falling, his voice so inwardly directed it was like a sigh. "In his travels, he heard of an ancient holy man, a hermit, living on an island in a vast lake. He asked a boatman to row him out to the island so that he could commune with the hermit, though he felt in his heart that he had reached a level at which no one could instruct him further, so deeply was he immersed in his mantra and its million-million iterations. On meeting the hermit he was astonished to find that this man too had devoted himself to the very same mantra and for a number of years equal to his own, and yet when the hermit chanted it aloud the monk immediately saw that the hermit was deluded and that all his devotion had been in vain—he was mispronouncing the vowels. As a gesture of compassion, of *karuna*"—and here the Geshe paused to look round the circle, settling on Karuna with her shining braid and her beautiful bare feet—"he gently corrected the hermit's pronunciation. After which they chanted together for some time before the monk took his leave. He was halfway across the lake when the oarsman dropped both oars and stared wildly behind him, for there was the hermit, saying, 'I beg your pardon, but would you be so kind as to repeat the mantra once more for me so that I can be sure I have it right?' How had the hermit got there? He had walked. On the water." Again the pause, again the Geshe's eyes roaming round the circle to settle not on Karuna, but on him. "I ask you, Ashoka: what is the sound of truth?"

Ashoka

His name, his former name, the name on his birth certificate and his New York State driver's license, was Jeremy Clutter. He was forty-three years old, with a B.A. in fine arts (he'd been a potter) and an M.A. in Far Eastern studies, a house in Yorktown which now belonged to his first wife, Margery, and a middle-aged paunch of which he was—or had been—self-conscious. He'd met Sally at a week-long Buddhist seminar in Stone Mountain, Georgia, and she'd pointed out to him that the Buddha himself had sported a paunch, at the same time touching him intimately there. In his former life he'd made a decent income from a dot-com start-up, thepotterswheel.com, that not only survived the '01 crash but had become robust in its wake. Money built his yurt. Money paid off Margery. Money embellished the Geshe's grace. And the Geshe gave him his true name, Ashoka, which when translated from the Sanskrit, meant "Without Sadness."

Ironwood

The second morning's meditation session, like all the ensuing ones, was held out of doors on a slightly pitched knob of blasted dirt surrounded by cactus and scrub. There was a chill to the air that belied the season, but to an aspirant they ignored it. He chanted his mantra inside his head till it rang like a bell and resolved to bring a jacket with him tomorrow. Geshe Stephen kept them there till the sun came hurtling over the mountains like a spear of fire and then he rose and dismissed them. Bowing in his holy, long-nosed way, the Geshe took Ashoka gently by the arm and held him there until the others had left. With a steady finger, the finger of conviction, the Geshe pointed to a dun heap of dirt and rock in the intermediate distance and then pantomimed the act of bending to the ground and gathering something to him. Ashoka didn't have a clue as to what the man was trying to impart. Geshe Stephen repeated the performance, putting a little more grit and a little less holiness into it. Still, he didn't understand. Did he want him, as an exercise, a lesson, to measure the mountain between the space of his two arms extended so as to reduce it to its essence? To dirt, that is?

Finally, exasperated, the Geshe pulled a notepad and pencil from his pocket [illegible] rawled his redemptive message: *Go up to the mountain and gather iron-* [illegible] *he winter fires in the temple. Then report—report,* that was the word he [illegible] *temple kitchen to peel potato and daikon for the communal stew.*

Flypaper

The days stuck to him like flypaper. The moment was all there was. He went inward. Still, very gradually, the days became unglued, loosening and flapping in the wind that swept the desert in a turmoil of cast-off spines and seed pods. Nights came earlier, mornings later. One morning, after group meditation, the Geshe pressed a note into his hand. The note asked—or no, instructed—him to meet the water truck that came bimonthly from the nearest town, Indio Muerto, which lay some thirty-five miles across the motionless plain.

The truck, painted an illusory forest green, appeared as a moving speck in the distance, working haltingly over the ruts and craters of what was once and occasionally a dirt road. He sat cross-legged in the infertile soil and watched it coming for what might have been hours or even days, all sense of time and the transient rush of things foreign to him now. There would come a moment when the truck would be there before him, he knew that, and so he spun a prayer wheel and chanted inwardly until it was in fact there, planted before him and obscuring the horizon as if it had sprung up out of the ground.

He saw that there was a new driver to replace the expressionless old man who'd come in the past, a lean monkey-faced boy of nineteen or twenty with tattooed arms and a cap reversed on his head, and that the kid had brought his similarly tattooed and capped squeeze along for the desolate ride across the waste. No problem there. Ashoka didn't begrudge him. In fact, as he watched them climb down from the cab of the truck he couldn't help remembering a time when he and Margery had driven across country together in a car that had no radio and how Margery had said afterward that he'd never shut up for one instant the whole way, singing and laughing and spinning out one story after another, because for him, at least in those days, conversation wasn't about truth or even communication—it was there for its entertainment value, pure and simple.

"So, uh," the kid began, startling him out of his reverie—or no, shocking him with the impact of those two syllables spoken aloud and reverberating like thunderclaps—"where you want me to pump it?"

He pressed his hands to his ears. His face reddened. In that moment, rising, he caught a glimpse of himself in the big blazing slab of the truck's side-view mirror and it was as if he'd been punched in the chest. What he saw reflected there was the exact likeness of one of the *pretas,* the restive spirits doomed to parch and starve because of their attachments to past lives, his hair white as death and flung out to every point of the compass, his limbs like sticks, face seared like a hot dog left too long on the grill.

"Whoa," the kid said, even as the girl, her features drawn up in a knot of fear and disgust, moved into the protection of his arm, "you all right there?"

What could he say? How could he begin to explain?

He produced a gesture to wave him off. Another for reassurance. And then, turning so gradually he could have been a tree growing toward the light, he lifted a hand and pointed, shakily, to the water tank, where it floated on wooden struts behind the two whitewashed yurts that housed Geshe and Lama respectively and rose like twin ice-cream cones from the dead blasted earth.

Air-horn

Everyone in the community, all thirteen of them plus Geshe Stephen and Lama Katie and including their nearest neighbors, the former Forest and Fawn Greenstreet (now Dairo and Bodhi respectively), had an air-horn. For emergencies. If there was an accident, an illness, a fire, the air-horns were to be used to summon help. He spent a long while each day in contemplation of the one he and Karuna had been given, for what reason he couldn't say. Perhaps because it represented a link to the renounced world, a way out. Or because it had a pleasing shape. Or because it was the only object of color, real color, in the yurt.

Karuna was at the cutting board, dicing cucumbers. She'd lost weight. But she was firm and lean and beautiful, not that it mattered, and he was enjoying the sight of her there, her elbows flashing beneath her robes that pulled back to reveal the pink thermal longjohns beneath. Outside it was dark. There was a fire in the woodstove. Karuna's elbows flashed. Earlier, she'd been trying to tell him something of her day, of what she'd experienced on her walk out into the desert, but he couldn't really catch much of it, despite the fact that she was leagues ahead of him when it came to charades. Something about a hillside and a moment and something she'd seen there, tracks, he thought, and a discarded water bottle. He'd smiled and nodded, feigning comprehension, because he liked the way her eyes flared and jumped and sank back again, liked the purse of her mouth and the ghost of her breasts bound up and held tight in the thermal weave that fit her like a new skin.

These thoughts were unhealthy, he knew that. And as he watched her now, he couldn't help feeling even more unhealthy—aroused, even—and so he shifted his gaze to the air-horn, where it stood on an adobe shelf like a work of art. And it *was* a work of art. The milk-white canister topped with a red rooster's comb of plastic which was to be depressed in an emergency, the matching red lettering (SPORTS/MARINE, and below it, BIG HORN) and the way the sound waves were depicted there as a flaring triangle of hard red slashes.

Big horn, he said to himself. *Sports/Marine. Big horn. Sports/Marine.* And for that moment, for that night, it became his mantra.

Bup-Bup-Bah

That was a problem, a growing problem, as the days wore on. The mantra, that is, because as the Buddha taught, life means suffering and the origin of suffering is attachment and the cessation of suffering is only attainable by taking the Bodhisattva path, and yet his mantra became mangled in its eternal repetition until other mantras, meaningless phrases and snatches of tunes, blotted it out altogether. *Big horn* lasted a week or more. And then one chill afternoon, sitting buttock to buttock with Fawn Greenstreet—Bodhi—on one side of him and Karuna on the other, staring through the long-nosed ascetic face of Geshe Stephen and digging inward, shovelful by shovelful, *bup-bup-bah* came to him. It was a musical phrase, from a tune of the great and towering giant of inwardness, John Coltrane, a tune called "Bakai." The horns chanted it rhythmically, *bup-bup-bah, bup-bup-bah,* with a rising inflection on the first *bah* and a descending on the second. He tried to fight it off with *Om mani padme hum,* tried with all his concentration and practice, but it wouldn't budge. It was there, *bup-bup-bah, bup-bup-bah,* like a record stuck in the groove, repeating over and over, repeating endlessly. And worse: his proximity to Bodhi on one side and his own wife on the other, given the day and the cold of the ground and the warm inviting odor arising from them both—*bup-bup-bah*—was giving him an erection.

Twins

Another note, this one handed to him by Lama Katie after the morning cleanup in the temple and the incantatory scraping of the baked-on oatmeal from the depths of the communal cook pot. Lama Katie, squat, big-breasted, her hair the color of midnight in a coal mine and her eyes even darker, gave him a smile of encouragement that radiated down the two deeply etched lines defining her chin and into the billowing plumpness beneath. She knew the contents of the note: she'd written it herself. According to the date marked on the calendar secreted in a chest in the back corner of her yurt, the twins—his twins, Kyle and Kaden—were due to appear this evening for the first of their biannual visits. He should wait for them half a mile out, Lama Katie suggested, so that the noise and presence of the rental vehicle their mother was driving wouldn't impede his fellow aspirants on their journey down the Bodhisattva path.

It was mid-afternoon, the winter sun bleached white and hanging motionless overhead, when he turned away from Karuna, who was shucking a bushel of corn delivered to them via muleback by one of the Geshe's more worldly followers, plucked up a prayer wheel and went on down the dirt track to wait for them. The desert ran before him. Birds visited. Lizards. He sat on a rock and stared off in the distance, chanting beneath his breath, his mantra beating as steadily in the confines of his skull as the heart beating in his chest, the Coltrane riff retired to another life in another universe and the Buddha, the very Buddha, speaking through him.

The car was unremarkable, but strange for all that, its steel shell, the glint of the sun on its windshield, the twin plumes of dust trailing away behind it till it was there and motionless and he could see his ex-wife's face, a shadow clenched in distaste, as the two boys, nine years old now—or were they ten?—spun out of the doors in a flurry of leaping limbs. He caught them in his arms and rocked them round him in a mad whirl, their voices like the cries of birds descending to a feast. He showed them the prayer wheel, let them spin it. Sat with them and listened to their ten thousand questions (When was he coming back? Where was Karuna? Could they see his yurt? Did he have a pet lizard? Could they have a pet lizard?) He found that his mimetic skills had blossomed and he answered them with his hands, his eyes, the cast of his mouth and the movement of his shoulders. Finally, when the novelty had begun to wear off and they started to look round them for a means of escape—he could only imagine what their mother must have been telling them about their father's mental state on the long flight and longer drive out here—he produced a pad and pencil and wrote them a note.

What he was doing, he reiterated, was seeking the truth, *prajna,* wisdom. Liberation from the cycle of rebirth in which all beings are trapped. If one soul achieves liberation, that soul can guide others toward achieving it too. They crouched beside him, staring at the pad in his lap, their faces numb, eyes fixed on the words as if the words had no meaning. *I'm doing it for you,* he wrote, underlining fiercely, *for you, for both of you.*

"Mom too?" Kaden asked.

He nodded.

They gave each other a look, smiles flowering, and in the next instant they sprang up in a sudden delirium of joy and ran to her where she sat in the car, carrying the note like a gift of infinite worth, the paper fluttering in the breeze their moving limbs stirred in the air. She took it, her face a simulacrum of itself behind the reflective windshield, then ordered them into the car. There was the abrupt thunderclap of the engine turning over, the screech of the front end as the car wheeled round, pale miniature hands fluttering their goodbyes out the open window, and then, finally, silence.

Rattlesnake

The rattlesnake was itself a shadow, pooled there on the trodden dirt floor of the yurt as if shadows ruled and light was abject. He didn't see it until it was too late. Karuna, her hair released from the tight braid and exerting a life and movement of its own, was washing her face over a pan of water he'd heated for her on the woodstove and he'd been watching her idly, remembering their first night together after they'd realized to their delight—karma, it was karma—that they lived no more than half an hour's drive from each other through the dense hilly woodlands of Westchester County. They were in Georgia then, the last night of the conference, and they'd lingered over beers, exchanging information, and she was so stunned by the coincidence that she'd slid away from the table in a slow sinuous dance, then taken him by the hand and led him back to her room.

When the snake bit her just above the ankle, where the swell of her calf rose from the grip of the heavy white sweatsock she wore as protection against the evening chill, it was just doing what it was designed to do. There was warmth in the yurt. It had come to the warmth. And she, inadvertently, had stepped on it. She didn't cry out, not even then, not even when the snake snapped back into the shadows as if it were attached to a spring, but just looked down in bewilderment at her bare calf and the two neat spots of blood that had appeared there in commemoration of the puncture wounds. He didn't think of what the snake's message had been, not yet, not before Karuna stretched herself out on the bed and he twisted the tourniquet round her calf and her eyes fluttered and the fire hissed in the stove and the leg began to swell and darken and he took the air-horn to the door of the yurt and annihilated the silence in a single screaming stroke.

The snake's message—and he knew it even as Dairo and Bodhi flew up out of the darkness with faces like white darting bats, Geshe Stephen and the others not far behind—was this: *I am the karmic representative of the reptile world and all is not well among us. There is nothing inside and no cessation of pain. Hooray! Jabba-jabba-jabba!*

Without Sadness

A tangle of hands moved like thought, juggling mute phrases and tracing the edges of panic. Everyone was gesturing at once, the yurt shrunk round them, the snake vanished, the fire dying in the stove. Karuna's eyes had stopped blinking. She seemed to be in a deep trance, gone as deep as any soul can go, focused on the rising swirls of the ceiling and the circular hole that gave onto the night and the stars and the dead black face of the universe above.

His hands trembled as he gripped the pencil and scribbled a note for Geshe Stephen, who was standing stooped over the bed, looking lost. *We need to get the doctor.*

The Geshe shrugged. There was no doctor. There was no telephone. The nearest town was Indio Muerto. They all knew that—they'd all signed on with that knowledge and its implications implanted like splinters in their brains.

What about the car?

Another shrug. The community's only automobile was a boxy white Prius belonging to Geshe Stephen, which was housed beneath a formfitting cloth out back of his yurt where its shape wouldn't tempt anyone from the path or interfere with the business at hand. Its wheels were up on blocks and the Geshe, in a first-day ceremony, had drained the fuel tank and removed the distributor cap as a symbolic gesture while the gathered aspirants looked rapturously on.

We need to get her to the hospital! he screamed across the page in angry block letters.

The Geshe nodded. He was in agreement. He dipped his shoulders, produced a tight grin that tapered to a grimace at both corners of his mouth. His expression said: *But how?*

Into that silence that was fraught with the shuffling of feet, bare and slippered both, the faint hiss of the stove and the sub-aural racket of neurons firing in brains that were no longer in touch with souls, no longer calm and meditative, neurons nudged from the path and straining to find their way back, there came a deep harsh ratcheting cry from the figure on the bed, from Karuna. They turned to her as one. Her face was twisted. Her leg was swollen to twice its size. The skin was black around the wound. They all looked shocked, Bodhi especially, shocked and offended, wondering why she hadn't stifled that human noise with a fist, with a knuckle stuffed between her teeth. The silence had been broken, and it was Karuna who had broken it, consciously or not.

What he wanted to say—to roar so that they could have heard him all the way to Indio Muerto and back—was *Christ, what is wrong with you people? Can't you see she's dying?* But he didn't. Habit, conditioning, the reflex of the inner path kept him silent, though he was writhing inside. This was attachment and that sigh was the sound of truth.

Your Boat

Later, after they'd all filed uselessly out, he built up the fire and sat beside her while her breathing slowed and accelerated and finally caught in her throat for the last time. It might have taken an hour or mere minutes, he couldn't say. Into his head had come a new mantra, a jingle from a commercial on TV when he was growing up as a child of baseball fields and macadam basketball courts with their bent and rusted hoops and the intense otherworldly green of a New York summer, a green so multivalent and assertive it was like a promise of life to come. The jingle was for a toothpaste and it made its own promises, and yes, you did wonder where the yellow went when you brushed your teeth with Pepsodent. The new mantra sang in his head and danced a tarantella, double speed, triple, and then it became a dirge. Just before dawn he found himself running back even further, reaching down to take hold of the earliest mantra he could recall as it marched implacably across the field of his consciousness, beating out its own tempo with two pounding knees on the underside of a metal desk in the back corner of a just-arisen classroom, *Row, row, row your—Om mani padme hum—Gently down the stream. Row, row, row—Om.*

At dawn he got up from the bed and without looking behind him pushed open the door and walked out into the desert.

Dragonfly

In the desert, he walked without purpose or destination. He walked past the hill where his wife had found the discarded water bottle, past the place where the green truck had appeared on the horizon, beyond the mountain where he'd gathered ironwood and down into the hot bleached plain it gave onto. He needed a mantra, but he had none. Into his head it came, the mantra the Geshe had given him, but he couldn't sustain it, his mind swept clear of everything now. The sun was the eye of God, awake and staring. After a while his feet seemed to desert him and he sat heavily in the lee of a jagged boulder.

What he awakened to were voices, human voices, speaking aloud. He blinked open his eyes and looked up into three terrified faces, man, woman and child, their wide straw hats framing their skulls like halos. They were speaking to him in a language he didn't understand. They said, *"Necesita usted socorro?"* They said, *"Tiene agua?"* And then one of them, the woman, went down on her knees and held a plastic jug of water to his lips and he drank, but sparingly, and only because he knew they wouldn't go away, wouldn't stop *talking,* unless he did. He didn't need water. He was beyond water, on a whole different path altogether. He reassured them with gestures, thanked them, blessed them, and then they were gone.

The sun moved till the projection of rock gave up its shade. His eyes closed but the lids burned till he opened them again and when he opened them the dragonfly was there. He studied it for a long while, the delicate interplay of its wings, the thin twisting calligraphy of its legs and the perfect jointed tube of its thorax. And what was its message? It had no message, he saw that now. It was merely a splinter of light, hovering for just a moment—just this moment—over the desert floor.

(2009)

A Death in Kitchawank

Saturday, just after two, the sun a hot compress on her shoulders and scalp, the shrieks and catcalls of the children as they splash in the shallows a kind of symphony of the usual. Behind her, the sharp *thwock* of the dense black rubber ball as it rockets from the paddle and slaps the wall, regular as a heartbeat till one of the men miscalculates and it freezes in cardiac arrest on the tail of a stifled curse. One beat, two, and here it comes again: *thwock*. She's thinking she should have brought her straw hat to the beach with her because she wouldn't want a thin red line of sunburn etched into the parting of her hair, but she'll worry about that later—or maybe not at all. She hasn't worn her hat in a week or more now—she hates hats, hats are a thing of her mother's day—and her tan is deep, even at her hairline. She's wearing a pair of oversized sunglasses new from the drugstore yesterday and last year's black one-piece, which is maybe a little tight around the hips and waist, but so what? She's not on display here. This is her beach, her community, her lake. These are her friends and neighbors gathered in their beach chairs and sprawled across their fluffed-up towels and beach blankets with their paperbacks and newspapers and Hebrew National wieners. This is the peace at the center of life. This, this Saturday in July when her mind runs free all the way up to the arch of the sun and back and her only worry is to shift the straps on her shoulders and gloss her lips to keep them from drying out.

In the house, which she could see if she craned her neck to look back over her shoulder past the concession stand and the paddleball courts and the big open grassy field where teenage couples are strolling hand in hand and boys playing pickup baseball, is the refrigerator, new three years ago and as cluttered as if it had been there a century. In its cool dark depths are the steaks in a covered dish of honey-ginger marinade, the potato salad and coleslaw she put up after breakfast and the Rose's lime juice and vodka for the gimlets. All is well. And so what if the warm shifting sand beneath her feet has to be trucked in every other year at the expense of the Kitchawank Colony Association, its hundreds of billions of individual grains disappearing into the high grass, washing into the lake, adhering to toes and arches and tanned sinewy ankles only to wind up on bathroom tiles and beneath the kitchen sink? It's as essential as air, as the water itself: how could you have a beach without it?

When she next opens her eyes it's to the quick cold shock of Susan, her youngest, snuggling in beside her, everything wet suddenly as if a whole basket of fish has been upended in her lap. She feels the cold bunched knees poking at her, the shuddering ribcage and chattering teeth, hears her own voice jump up: "Get off, honey, you're all wet!" And Susan, freckled, stick-limbed, ten years old, snuggling tighter. "I'm cold, Mommy." She reaches behind her for the beach bag and the towel she's brought for herself, never bothering to ask where her daughter's own towel is because she knows it'll turn up at the edge of the ball field or draped over the welded frame of the monkey bars, as soaked through as a dishrag. And then she's wrapping her and holding her close till the shivering stops and her daughter springs loose to chase half a dozen other kids to the concession stand. For Coke, winter in a bottle, and the wiener snug in its bun. With chopped onion and sweet pickle relish and plenty of mustard. She lifts her sunglasses for a moment to watch after her and here are the Sollovays, the Greens, the Goldsteins, settling in around her in a wash of greeting and banter and sheer high spirits. Marsha Goldstein, her legs silken and her lips fluttering around her smile, offers a cigarette, but she prefers her own and they both light up and let the tobacco lift them, until in unison, as if they've rehearsed it, they throw back their heads and exhale in long twin plumes of blue. "What time did you want us tonight?" Marsha asks. "Fiveish?"

"Yes," she says, "yes, that'll be perfect," and she glances over her shoulder, past the courts and the chain-link fence and the screen of trees to where her house sits tranquilly on its own little rise—the only house, of all the two hundred and more in the community, that looks directly onto the lake, a fact of which she tries not to be too sinfully proud. There's the Buick, last year's model, at rest in the drive like a picture out of a magazine, and the swing set they put up for Susan and her friends, though you could throw a stone and hit the big metal-framed one in the playground at the lake. The Japanese maple she planted when her daughter was born stands out in relief against the near wall of the house, throwing a delicate patterned shade over the flagstone path up to the kitchen door, its leaves the color of the claret Sid likes to sip after dinner. She lets her eyes linger there a moment before lifting them to the house itself. And it's funny, because with the way the light comes off the lake and the big picture window stands in shadow, she can see into her own kitchen and the table there, already set for dinner, the clock on the yellow wall, time ticking by, and it's almost as if she's in two places at once.

[Forgive me for stepping in here but I do want to get this right—the fact is, I may have been there that day, the threads of the past so snarled now that thirty-five years on I've lost the ability to separate them with any clarity. But if I was there, I would have been on the paddleball court, playing in a fiercely competitive and very physical foursome with Miriam's husband Sid and her two sons—Alan, who was twenty-six, and Lester, my best friend, who was then twenty-two, like me. And I would have entered the next scene too, the dinner scene, preceded by cocktails and the long unwinding of a muggy Saturday afternoon, fresh from the lake and the shower, the corded muscles of my legs gone limp in the afterglow of exercise and the long slow seep of alcohol.]

She's got both fans going, the one at the kitchen window and the big lazy ceiling fan revolving in a slow slippage of optical illusion over the table, and yet still she's dripping. Marsha's with her, their drinks perspiring on the counter while they stand elbow to elbow at the cutting board, slicing long squared-off strips of carrot and wafer-thin slivers of Vidalia onion for the salad, dicing cucumbers and halving cherry tomatoes still warm from the garden, Marsha, who'd been maid of honor at her wedding to Sid just as she'd been Marsha's maid of honor when she married David in a time when there were only the four of them. Now the boys are in their twenties, Susan's ten and Marsha's daughter Seldy is sixteen, or no, seventeen.

"I don't know," she's saying, in reference to the two young couples, summer people, who've become fixtures at the beach, "if you've got it, flaunt it, though seeing the one girl in her two-piece suit makes me feel like I put on a hundred pounds—yesterday. And another hundred this morning."

"No, no, I agree, but the shorter one, what's her name—?"

"Barbara, isn't it? Or is that the other one?"

"The other one's Rachel, and she's really very sweet, though you wouldn't know it from the look on her face, which to me, I don't know, is so *forbidding*—but what I was saying is to walk around in a two-piece when you're eight months' pregnant is just—"

"Too much."

"Right," she says, and then they're both laughing. "Way too much."

From the living room comes the sound of the men, their voices rich and pleased, as they call down the questions of the day, revile Nixon, trade quips with the boys. Les has begun to wear his hair long and dress in bell-bottoms and spangled shirts, in confraternity with his friend T., who looks so satisfied he could be flying across the room on his own magic carpet ride. And she's had her moments of worry—or not worry, really, just concern—over whether the boys have been experimenting with tea or grass or whatever they call it these days, but she's never said anything. And won't. She doesn't want to harp. Let them do what they're going to do because no one, not even a mother, can legislate for them. Once they're grown, that is, and her boys, with the shoulders and arms they inherited from Sid, are definitely grown.

They're just sitting down to dinner—to the artichokes, one per plate, the grill out on the deck sending up smoke under the steaks—when Seldy, in a yellow sundress that shows off the figure she's been growing into over the past year, drifts into the room, late as usual. Her mother says, "It's about time," and her father makes a quip about how she must've gotten lost on the long grueling four-minute drive from the house, but Sid and the three boys are dumbstruck for one thunderous instant. This is the face of beauty, and though they're all family here, though Seldy's like a daughter to Sid and a sister to the boys, Miriam's boys anyway, none of that matters. Sid's the first to break the spell, his voice rising to emphasize the joke: "Well, Jesus Christ, we thought we were going to wilt away and starve waiting for you." And then the boys are falling all over themselves to wave and grin and ante up the wit ("Yeah, and think how starved the first caveman must've been to discover you *could* eat one of these things"), and Seldy, flushing, slides into the empty seat between Alan and Les, letting the steam from the artichoke rise gently about her face and the long trailing ends of her hair slip from her shoulders to sway gracefully over her plate.

It is then, just as Sid rises to check on the steaks (nobody here wants anything but rare and rarer and he'd be offended if they did), that the first eruption of thunder rolls across the lake to shake the house and rattle the ice cubes in the drinks Miriam has just freshened all the way around. The sky goes instantly dark and it's just as if a shade has been drawn over the day. She's wondering if she should go out to the kitchen and rummage through the drawer for the candles left over from Hanukkah when the storm chases a cool breeze through the screens and Marsha waves her napkin in front of her face, letting out a sigh of relief. "Thank God," she says. "Oh, yes, bring it on."

The first raindrops, big and slow and widely dispersed, begin to thump at the shingles and there's Sid, with his muscled arms and bald head, out on the deck, hustling the lid off the grill and flipping the steaks, the worn boards spotted all around him. Another blast of thunder. "Better hurry, Sid!" David calls and then it's really coming down, the original deluge, and this is funny, deeply, infectiously funny, Sid flipping steaks and wet through in an instant, because there's no harm, no harm at all, and if there's a drop or two on the platter of meat, which he's covering even now, what does it matter? They'll have candles, they'll eat, and the evening, with its rising fertile smell of grass and the earth at the edge of the woods, will settle in around them, as cool and sweet as if the whole neighborhood were air-conditioned.

[I see I've written myself into the scene after all, a refugee from my own fractured family, at peace in the moment. Fair enough. But peace neither lasts nor suffices, and the fact was that Lester and I pursued the available pharmacopoeia far more assiduously than Miriam could ever have imagined. We were stoned at that very moment, I'm sure of it, and not merely on anything so innocuous as marijuana—stoned, and feeling blessed. Feeling, in the midst of all that radiant love and the deepest well of tranquillity, that we were getting away with something.]

Time jumps and jumps again, the maples struck with color, the lake giving up a thin sheet of wrinkled ice along the shore, then there's the paucity of winter with its skeletal trees and the dead fringe of reeds stuck like an old man's beard in the gray jaws of the ice. Twice the car gets away from her on the slick streets, the passenger's side door taking the brunt of it so she has to go through all sorts of gyrations to lean over the back seat and swing open the door there for Susan when she picks her up from ballet or violin lessons. It seems like it's always raining. Or sleeting. And if there's a sun up there in the sky, somebody ought to get out a camera and show her the evidence. She lives for summer, that's what she tells Marsha on the phone and anybody else who'll listen, because she's got thin blood, and dark at four-thirty in the afternoon is no way to live. Yes. Sure. But it seems like the summer's gone before it even begins and then it's winter again and the winter after that, months spinning out until the pointer stops on a day in March, gray as death, Susan working against the chill in the unheated basement with the girls from the Explorers' Club at school, building a canoe from a kit shipped in all the way from Minnesota while Miriam tiptoes around upstairs, arranging warm-from-the-oven oatmeal cookies on a platter and pouring hot cocoa from the thermos into six porcelain teacups, each with its own marshmallow afloat in the center like a white spongy island.

When she opens the basement door there's an overpowering smell of epoxy and the distilled vinegar Sid got for cleanup, and she worries about that, about the fumes, but the girls seem oblivious. They cluster around her in a greedy jostling pack, hands snatching at the cookies and the too-hot cups, all except for Janet Donorio, a poised delicate girl with fade-away eyes who lifts the last cup from the tray as if she's dining with the Queen of England at Buckingham Palace, and why can't Susan be more like that? But Susan has no sense of herself—she already has three cookies clenched in her hand, privilege of the house, as she stabs her tongue at the marshmallow in her cup, a mustache of chocolate sketching itself in above her upper lip.

"Shouldn't you girls have some ventilation in here?" she says, just to hear herself, but they're fine, they assure her, and it's going great, it really is.

The canoe, lying overturned on a pair of sawhorses, has been a long winter's project, Sid doing the lion's share of the work on weekends, though the girls have been fairly diligent about the hand-sanding, the cutting and fitting of the fiberglass cloth and the slow smoothing of the epoxy over it. It's just that they're at an age when gathering for any purpose outside of school is a lark and they can't help frittering away their time gossiping, spinning records, dancing to the latest beat or craze or whatever it is, their thin arms flailing, hair in motion, legs going like pogo sticks. They make fast work of the cookies and chocolate. And now, sated, they watch her warily, wondering why she's lingering when it's clear her motherly duties have been dispensed with, and so she collects the cups, sets them on the tray and starts back up the stairs.

Thanks to Sid, who's a father like no other despite the fact that he has to drag himself home every night after a stifling commute and the kind of hard physical labor on one jobsite after another that would prostrate a man half his age, the canoe is ready for its maiden voyage by the time the ice shrinks back from the shore and the sun makes its first evanescent return. Miriam sits stiffly on the bench by the playground, Marsha beside her—freezing, actually, because with the way the wind's blowing down the length of the lake from the north a windbreaker just isn't enough—while the girls divide themselves democratically into two groups of three, roll up their jeans in the icy shallows and see the first group off in a mad frantic windmilling of forearms and paddles. "Be careful now!" she calls, and she's pleased to see that her daughter has been gracious or at least patient enough to wait her turn in the second group. As Susan leans forward to push the canoe off, her ankles chapped with the cold, her face long and grave and bursting with expectation, it's too much for Miriam and she has to look away to where the paddles flash in the pale depleted sunlight and the canoe cuts back and forth across the black surface like the blade of her pinking shears.

Marsha, who's come to lend moral support, lights a second cigarette off the end of her first and flicks the still-smoldering butt into the dun grass at their feet, exhaling with a long complicated sigh. "Too cute by half," she says.

Miriam's on her feet—she can't help herself—listening to her own voice skitter over the water and ricochet back again: "Don't get too far out! Girls! Girls?"

"I heard from Seldy last night," Marsha's saying as Miriam eases back down on the bench. Seldy's at Stony Brook. A junior. On scholarship and majoring in math, she's that smart.

"And how is she?"

A pause. The canoe, far out now—halfway to the other shore and its dense dead accumulation of shoulder-high weed—makes a wobbly, long-stemmed turn and starts back, the girls paddling in unison, finally getting it. "Terrible. Awful. Worse than"—Marsha's voice, wadded with grief and anger, chokes in her throat—"I don't know, *anything.*"

"What? What is it? She isn't—"

"She's dropping out."

Miriam is so surprised she can't help repeating the phrase, twisting it with the inflection of disbelief—"She's dropping out?" Caught up in the moment, with the girls on the lake, Susan and the others waiting their turn and the wind tugging a wedge of geese overhead, she doesn't stop to consider that both her own sons dropped out in their time too.

"It's that boy."

"What boy?"

"You know, the one from high school that went to the community college for all of half a semester—Richie?"

For a moment Miriam's confused, the name caught on her lips like an invocation—*Richie, Richie?*—and then suddenly she can picture him, tall and rangy in a swimsuit so tight you could see every crease and fold, the washboard stomach, hair that fell across his face like a raven's wing, Richie, Richie Spano, the wiseguy, the joker, with his braying laugh and the look on his face when you caught him out that said, *I am so far above this.*

"You're kidding."

"I wish."

And here's the canoe, scraping at the sand that will have to be replaced again this spring or they'll all be hip-deep in mud, and Susan's there now, trading places with the girl in back, the power position, raising her paddle high as if it were the honed glistening spear of a warrior out for conquest.

A puff of smoke. A long mournful inhalation and Marsha won't look her in the eye. "They're going to get a place in the Village, she says. Live free. Do their thing." The canoe, Miriam sees, is stuck there under the weight of the girls, stuck in the mud, and she has to restrain herself from interfering until finally Susan digs her paddle into the bottom to push them off and the canoe rides free in a shimmer of light. "Or some such crap," Marsha says.

[I was already gone by then, trying to redeem myself in grad school, and Les was in San Francisco, managing the first Cajun-style restaurant to appear there, but I knew Richie Spano from the time Les and I rented a house in the Colony three years earlier. There was a lot of traffic in that

> house—friends, musicians, druggies, friends of friends, friends of druggies—and Richie drifted in from time to time. He was quick on his feet, cocky, borderline obnoxious, with a mean streak that was something sick. One night, apropos of nothing, he plucked the darts out of the board on the kitchen wall and nailed my girlfriend's cat with one of them—which stuck there in the stripe of fur along its spine, quivering like a bandillera, until the cat vanished and bled all over the carpet in the back room and cost thirty-five dollars at the vet's to repair, money I paid out of my own pocket because Richie Spano wasn't about to pay anybody anything.]

Miriam is there at the window one soft mist-hung morning in the spring of a year when the canoe has been all but forgotten, chained to a rail on a grassy strand off to the far side of the beach in a mismatched tumble of upended boats, the girls on to other pursuits now, most of them boy-related. Susan is seventeen, too nervous by half over her college applications, her AP courses, the way Mr. Honer presses her to practice though she's only third violin and Mr. Davies rides roughshod over the Thespian Club, but her room is decorated with posters of shirtless, long-haired boys posing with guitars in their hands. And there was junior prom last year when Miriam had to pull strings behind the scenes till the boy her daughter liked finally asked her, though thank god nothing more came of it beyond the gown, the flowers and home by one.

She's sipping a cup of tea while her cigarette levitates smoke at her elbow, caught in a recollection of her own seventeen-year-old self when she first came up from Stelton for the summer to stay with her cousins in a bungalow not three city blocks from where she's sitting now. No one would have described her as shy back then, and when she went to the beach with her cousin Molly that first afternoon and saw a group of boys sweating over a little black ball on the paddleball court, she went right up to them, not five feet away, and watched as they leapt and grimaced and slammed at the ball with all the raw frustrated adolescent power boiling up out of them until they began to falter, to hit out, to lose the rhythm of the game—and it was no secret why. It was because she was there, with her pretty dark features that everyone said were just like Rita Hayworth's, with her nails freshly done and a white towel slung insouciantly over one shoulder, dressed in the swimsuit she'd spent the better part of an hour admiring in the full-length mirror at Genung's before she said yes and counted out the money at the cash register. There were four boys playing and half a dozen others sprawled on the grass at the edge of the court, but the one who caught her eye—the tall one, with his slicked-back dirty blond hair, his shrinking T-shirt and the black high-top basketball shoes he wore without socks—was Sid.

She shifts in her seat, lifts the cigarette to her lips to consolidate the recollection, but the cigarette is dead. And the tea—the tea's gone cold. She's about to push herself up and light the gas under the kettle when a movement on the ball field catches her eye. There's someone out there—two people, a boy and a girl—and that strikes her as odd because it's a school day and though it's officially spring the leaves of the trees are wound tight in the grip of their buds and it's cold still, especially with the way the mist is pushing in off the lake. Hardly beach weather.

She's already put up dinner—a pot roast simmering in the crock pot Les gave her for her birthday last year—and she's been through the newspaper twice and blackened the crossword puzzle till she can't make a thing of it. Is she bored? Lonely? In need of stimulation? She supposes so. She's been spending an awful lot of time sitting at the window lately, talking on the telephone or just dreaming, and she's been putting on weight too. But what *are* they doing out there?

In the next moment she's in the front hall, shrugging into her faded blue parka with the mismatched mittens stuffed deep in the pockets amidst various wads of Kleenex and expired notes to herself, and then she's out in the air, the day brisk and smelling faintly of something left too long in the refrigerator, heading down the path to where her property ends and the single-lane gravel road loops through the high chain-link gates and peters out in the beach area. She veers left, onto the grass of the outfield, and feels it wet on the worn suede moccasins she slipped on at the door. When she gets closer—when she's halfway to the two figures bent over what looks to be a big gray-green stone protruding from the grass—she recognizes Seldy. Seldy, in bell-bottom jeans and a serape and some sort of leather cowboy hat pulled down so far it masks her eyes. And who's that with her? Richie. Richie, looking as if he's dressed for Halloween with his long hair, his tie-dyed shirt and the ragged cloth overcoat he might have dug out of the pile at the Salvation Army.

She's not thinking, really—and the way she's dressed and with her hair uncombed and no makeup on she's not especially in the mood to see anybody at the moment—but she's here now and that thing on the ground, she realizes, is no rock. It's moving. And the boy—*Richie*—is stabbing at it with a fallen branch. In the very instant she opens her mouth to say "Hi," startling them both, she sees what it is: a turtle. One of the big ridge-backed things that come up out of the lake to lay their eggs on the apron of sand at the edge of the ball field.

Seldy tries for a smile and only partly succeeds. Richie ignores her. "Hi," Seldy murmurs.

"Are you up visiting?" she hears herself say, even as Richie forces the stick into the animal's mouth and the jaws clamp down with an audible crack.

"See that?" he says. "One of these things can take your hand off if you're not careful."

Very softly, as if she's afraid to raise her voice, Seldy says, "Yes," but that's puzzling, because Marsha didn't breathe a word and it takes a moment for her to realize they must be staying with Richie's parents on the other side of the lake—or not even on the lake, really, but in a development off Amazon Road. And then a scenario from a year ago presents itself, a dinner party she was giving for a new couple, the Abramsons—he's a doctor in the city—and how Seldy, up for the weekend, had sat rigidly between her parents and barely said a word all night. Except to be negative. At one point, early on, before the Abramsons and the others arrived, Miriam had been rearranging the flowers in the big cut-glass vase she'd inherited from her mother, soliciting Marsha's opinion, just chattering, that was all, when Seldy, her face sour and her lips drawn down, snapped at her out of nowhere. "Jesus, Miriam, it's only the Colony, only the *sticks*," she said, and her voice was like a saw cutting the house in two. "You'd think you were Mrs. Dalloway or something."

It's cold—raw—and she tightens the parka around her. She's about to say something inane like "That's nice," when Richie jerks the branch from the turtle's mouth and brings it down hard on the slick gleaming carapace, not once but twice. He's lifting it again, lifting it high, when she steps forward and takes hold of the end of it so quickly she surprises herself. "What are you doing?" she demands, her voice gone harsh in her throat.

To his credit, he doesn't resist, and the stick is hers now, to drop in the grass at her feet while the turtle, hissing, thrashes its head back and forth as if it can't pinpoint the source of the threat. "Thing doesn't deserve to live," he says, and his eyes are unfocused, fully dilated, as if he's dreaming on his feet. "They're just trash anyway. They kill fish, ducks even. They—"

"No," she says, cutting him off, "no. They belong here. They have a right to live just like everything else." She wants to go on, wound up all of a sudden, angry out of all proportion, but he's already turned his back on her, stalking across the grass in his high-heeled boots—purple, purple boots—and she's left there with Seldy. Who has nothing to say. Her best friend's daughter, a girl she's known since she was in the cradle, and she has nothing to say. Miriam wants to invite her up to the house for tea, a bagel, a good long chat about dropping out, about fashion and respect for nature and life in the Village—*freaks, they call themselves freaks*—but she finds, in that moment, that she has nothing to say either.

[I remember stopping by one year on spring break and finding Miriam in a lawn chair out on the fringe of the ball field, wrapped in an old sleeping bag, keeping watch over a pair of nesting turtles while a pickup game went on behind her. I must have spent an hour crouched there beside her, catching up on things as the turtles patiently extruded their eggs as if time had gone back a millennium and there were no lawnmowers or automobiles or boys with sticks and rocks and baseball bats poised to annihilate them. And where was Sid? Working. Always working. He'd had his reverses on the stock market and elsewhere, a tough year, but he was still a member of the tin knockers' union and always had work. As far as I could tell, he didn't even know turtles existed.]

And it's another day, a year further on, Susan at Rutgers and loving it, or at least liking it, or so she says on the odd nights when she bothers to call, and Miriam has just got off the phone with her cousin Molly, who lives in Connecticut now and whose youngest—Mark, just twenty-four—has had some sort of nervous breakdown. Or worse. He's been in treatment since he was a teenager and nobody wants to call it schizophrenia because you don't come back from that. They say it runs in families, and when Miriam comes to think of it, Molly's father was no mental paragon, scared of his own face in the mirror, hearing voices, talking nonsense half the time. She just thanks her lucky stars her own children turned out normal, though sometimes she wonders about Les, out there on the West Coast, unmarried at thirty and running with a fast crowd, restaurant people, bar people, people who use drugs and don't go to bed till the sun rises.

She pushes herself up from the table, aching in her joints—and there's a sharp pain in the calf of her left leg, a kind of thrilling or buzzing that goes away almost as soon as she puts a name to it. She actually pads to the stove and lights the burner under the kettle before she realizes it's not tea she wants. Or a cigarette either. The house is a mess—she's never been much of a housekeeper, except on special occasions, holidays, dinner parties, when she can get herself motivated—but she's in no mood to start sifting through the papers and magazines and books, the pots and pans and dead and dried-up flowers that seem to accumulate like drift, that will one day bury the house like the sands of Arabia and no one here to care one way or the other. From the window she can see the wall of the paddleball courts, which are empty at this hour on a weekday, and beyond them Rose Shapiro—eighty and stooped—pacing the beach as if she were making her way across the steppes of Russia like poor Dr. Zhivago, and the sight only depresses her the more. You marry, have children, cook, clean, get sick, get old, pace the beach till you can't even remember who you are anymore. That's life. That's what it is.

It is then that she thinks of the canoe. Susan had it out last summer once or twice, but aside from that it's just sat there inert for as long as she can remember. She's suddenly seized with the idea of it, its smooth white skin pressed to the belly of the water, clouds scudding by overhead, the release of it, gliding, just gliding. She makes herself a sandwich at the kitchen counter, pours juice into the thermos, selects a paperback from the shelf in the den and goes out into the day and the sunlight, which flares with sudden brilliance, feeling as if she's going off on an adventure. The lake gives back the sun in a fine glaze of light. There's a ripple of wind across the water, an infinity of scalloped black wavelets riding out as far as she can see. Birds spangle the grass.

She has some trouble with the combination lock—it's just rusty, that's all—and then, once she's got the chain free and tries to flip the boat over, she finds it's unaccountably heavy. There's no one to see her, really, aside from Mrs. Shapiro, who barely glances up from her own shoelaces, but still she feels embarrassed to think that she can't even flip over a canoe, a thing she must have done a hundred times when she was a girl. Is she really that old and weak? She sucks in her breath and gives it another try, like one of those puffed-up Russian weight lifters in the Olympics on TV, and there it is, like a miracle, right side up and thumping reverberantly to the ground. The sound echoes out over the water and comes back again, thrilling with the chatter of birds and the soughing of the breeze in the branches overhead. It's April. She's fifty-eight years old. And her feet, her bare feet, are in the water now, the canoe hovering before her and threatening to tip first one way and then the other until all at once she's firmly planted in the seat and the paddle is working in her sure tight grip and the shore retreats behind her.

It's a joy. A lark. And almost immediately she finds her rhythm, the motion—dip and rise and dip again—coming back to her as if it were ingrained in her muscle memory, and maybe it is, though it's been more years than she can count. She feels the sun on her face and when she shifts position it wraps itself across her shoulders like an electric blanket, warming and gentle. By the time she thinks to look back to where her house sits reduced on the horizon, she's nearly to the far side of the lake. What she's thinking is that she should do this more often—get out, enjoy life, breathe the air—and she makes a promise to herself that starting tomorrow, she will. It's not even noon yet when she lays the paddle athwart the gunwales and unwraps her sandwich, pastrami on rye, just letting the boat drift, and isn't this the best pastrami on rye she's ever had? The canoe rocks. She lies back, for just a moment, and closes her eyes.

When she wakes, she can't imagine where she is, despite the evidence all around her. It takes her a minute, so inured is she to her own home, to her kitchen and den and the walls and doors and ceilings that contain her, to come fully to herself. The sun is gone, the clouds bleeding across the sky. And the wind is stronger now, damper, sweeping out of the south with a scent of rain. She's not wearing her watch—she left it home for fear of getting it wet—and that further disorients her, as if to know the time would put everything back in its place. Nothing for it but to paddle, but which way? She can't see the shore from here, not through the low-bellied clouds—as best she can figure the canoe must have been carried all the way down the lake while she dozed. All right. She'll just orient herself, that's all. She swivels round, scanning both shores till she finds a fixed point, the pale white tower of the seminary all the way up on Stony Street emerging suddenly from the clouds and the canopy of the distant trees, which means she has to go in . . . that direction, there, behind her now. She feels the relief wash over her—at least she knows where she is—until she reaches for the paddle, or the place where the paddle was, and finds it gone.

> [This became a family legend, trotted out at dinner parties over the years, the story of how Miriam used her hands to paddle the boat to the nearest point, which unfortunately lay on the far side of the lake, and how she'd walked a good mile and a half barefoot and with her windbreaker and the blouse beneath it soaked through before she got to Kitchawank Village and the pay phone in front of the liquor store there and realized she didn't have a cent to her name, let alone a dime. How she'd turned around and walked another three blocks on the cold hard unforgiving pavement till she got to Lowenstein's Deli and Sy Lowenstein let her use the store phone to call Sid, who was installing heating ducts in a four-plex in Mount Kisco where thank God they had a phone already hooked up on the ground floor, to please come get her before she froze to death. And how Sid had let out one of his arpeggiated *Jesus Christs!* and went twenty miles over the limit all the way back and then had to take her out to Fiorvanti's because there was no dinner on the table that night.]

She's never much liked the autumn, even when Susan was in Brownies and she took the girls out into the woods to collect leaves and hickory nuts and they made campfires and cooked wieners over the open coals, because autumn prefigures winter and winter lasts forever. But it's an autumn day in an advancing year, the trees brilliant around the lake, each leaf painted a distinctive shade and the whole blended as in a Monet, when the phone rings and she picks up to hear from Molly, all the way out in Connecticut, that Marsha's daughter Seldy is getting married. To Richie Spano. Who, at thirty-four, is assistant manager of some sort of appliance store in Yorktown Heights and apparently making a decent living, though no one would have thought it from the way he was raised.

What goes through her mind first is a quick envious accounting—neither Alan nor Les is married yet, nor do they look to be soon, and Susan's been so busy studying for the Bar she hasn't had a date in months, or not that Miriam knows of anyway—and then, as she forms the words *She hasn't told me anything about it,* the hurt sets in. This is Marsha, her best friend all these years, maid of honor at her own wedding, and she can't call her with the news? Yes, well maybe they have been like strangers lately, because things are different now, everybody getting older and more stay-at-home, the Colony breaking down as people die off or move away to Florida and the new people don't want to pay their dues and drop out—plus in most cases they're not even Jewish—but that doesn't mean you can't pick up a telephone.

As soon as she hangs up—before it occurs to her that maybe Marsha's ashamed to have such a son-in-law, not to mention a daughter throwing her life away—she's dialing. What she wants to say is *Hello, how are you?* so that she can ease into the situation as gracefully as possible, but her lips betray her. "Marsha?" she says. "How come you didn't tell me the good news?"

"Hello, Miriam, is that really you?" Marsha returns, her rasping voice as familiar as Miriam's own. "It's been too long, hasn't it, what with one thing and another? But news? What news are you talking about?"

"Seldy. Getting married. Are you planning a spring wedding then—June? Like you and David? And Sid and me?"

There's a pause. The sound of a match striking and Marsha drawing smoke into her lungs. "No," she breathes finally, "no, that's not the way it is anymore."

And then there's the exegesis, a story stewed in its details and leaning heavily toward Richie and Richie's feelings. Richie—he grew up Catholic, did she know that?—hates religion, just *hates* it, and so does Seldy, or that's what she claims. They don't want a fuss. Don't want anybody there—and it was like pulling teeth just to get them to say that she and David could stand as witnesses when they go before the justice of the peace. And they want to do it as soon as possible.

There's a pause. Silence on both ends of the line. "Well, could we at least host the reception?" Miriam puts in, feeling nothing but shame and disappointment for Marsha—and for herself, herself too.

Very softly: "No, I don't think so. I think the Spanos—Rich Senior and Carlotta, the parents?—I think they have something planned."

She wants to shout back at her *You think?* but she goes numb all over, the phone pressed to her ear like a weight, like one of the dumbbells Alan had left in the far corner of the basement from when he was in junior high. She gazes out across the lake and hears herself peep and chirp back at Marsha as the conversation runs to the sorrows and sicknesses of people they know, to the sad state of the Colony, how hardly anybody goes to the Association meetings anymore and how they could barely raise a crew to take the raft out of the water this fall, and then finally stalls. "Call soon," she hears herself say.

"Yes, I will."

"Promise?"

"Promise."

There are half a dozen people she wants to call, she's so wrought up, but for a long while, as the sun softens and the colors fade from the trees on the far side of the lake, she just sits there, feeling as if someone has died. What will Sid think? Sid's always had a soft spot for Seldy, as if she were his own daughter, and he's never liked Richie Spano, never liked what he stood for or where he came from or how he'd managed to get his hooks into her. And then she's remembering the time, years ago now, down at the lake, when she snapped awake from a sun-soaked dream to a clamor of voices raised in anger. Sid's voice she recognized right away, a low buzz of outrage that meant he was right on the verge, but the other voice—a high querulous whine that seemed to choke on itself—she didn't know.

It was Richie Spano's. She turned to look over her shoulder and there he was, incandescent in the light, flailing his arms and screaming in Sid's face. He didn't want to wait for a court and he'd been waiting too long already, shouting it out as if he'd been gored, shouting that the whole idea of holding the court when you never lose was just bullshit, that was all. She pushed herself up from the beach chair in the moment that the two of them came at each other—and Sid, though he was slow to anger, could have torn him apart and would have but for the intervention of David, who forced himself between them before the shoves could turn to blows. But that wasn't enough for Richie. He danced out of reach, spewing his obscenities till Sid broke loose and came for him, but there was no way Sid could catch him in the open and that just made it worse. The next week, at the very next meeting of the Association, she raised her hand and made a motion to ban people from the beach who weren't even members of the Colony—and she named Richie Spano specifically, because whose guest was he anyway?

[My memories of Sid are of a man secure in himself, a big man—huge for his generation, six-three and two-twenty and none of it gone to fat—who gave the impression of power held in reserve, even when he was flipping steaks in a rainstorm or revolving a gimlet so that the pale green viscid liquid swirled like smoke in a crystal ball. He was quick-witted and light on his feet, as verbally wicked as we ourselves were, and if you were admitted to his inner circle—and I was, I was—he would defend you against all comers. He'd fought the Germans, done a stint as a beat cop in Harlem and then come home to the house on the lake to raise his family. I remember walking into a bar with him once, an unfamiliar place, down and dirty—and he must have been in his mid-sixties then—and feeling untouchable, as secure as if I were sitting in my own living room.]

The tragic days of our lives, the days of accounting, begin like any other, with routine, with the bagel in the toaster and the coffee on the stove. So this is a morning. Sunlight streams through the big picture window though it's cold, down to zero overnight, and the lake is sealed beneath a hard uneven tegument of ice so thick you could drive a truck across it. Miriam is feeling good, the pain in her hip subsiding under the ministrations of the prescription the doctor gave her while Sid, home from work because things are slow, is sitting across the table from her, his head bowed to the paper, jaws working at the bagel she's smeared with cream cheese and decorated with a transparent wafer of lox and a sprinkle of capers. They're silent, she absorbed in her thoughts, he in the paper. The only sounds are the little ones, the tap of a spoon on the rim of a cup, the sigh of the knife as it divides another bagel. The smell of fresh-brewed coffee is as rich and intoxicating as if they were sitting on a carpet in some bazaar in the Orient.

"You want juice?" she says. "Fresh-squeezed, I can make fresh-squeezed, with the oranges Molly sent us from Florida?"

He glances up from the paper, his eyes a roving watery blue above the little wire reading glasses clamped to the bridge of his nose. His fringe of hair, so thin now it's barely there, sticks up awkwardly in back. He's dressed in blue jeans, moccasins, a thin gray sweatshirt she's washed so many times it's almost white. "Yeah," he breathes, "I guess. But don't go to any trouble."

She's already pushing herself up, about to say, *They're going to go bad soon anyway,* when she glances reflexively out the window, just as she does a hundred times a day. There's a scattering of snow over the beach, the lake, the long low building that houses the concession stand, snow like dust. Everything is still, not even a bird moving among the stripped black branches of the trees. Susan says that she needs a hobby, needs to get out more, and maybe she does spend too much time at the window, more interested in what's outside of her than what's here inside the house—if this is what old women do, biddies, yentas, then she guesses she's one of them. Yet when Les flew in from San Francisco for her sixty-fifth two weeks back she felt the resistance rising in her—was she really that old? And the cake—the cake was like the flank of some animal set ablaze in a conflagration, only it wasn't running away. It was right there on the table in front of her.

But here's the juicer, here the crate of oranges. She dips forward to dig into the crate, her gaze running across the table, past Sid and out to the familiar scene as if it were a picture in a frame. But it's not a picture and something's wrong, something's out of place. She spots it then, a moving shadow in the deeper gloom cast by the overhanging roof of the concession stand, a man there, furtive, jerking back the door and ducking inside. "Sid," she says, her blood quickening, "there's somebody out there. I just—I think somebody just broke into the concession stand."

"Who? What are you talking about?" He's set down the paper now and he's leaning forward to peer out the window, his lips pursed in concentration. "I don't see anything."

"He just went inside. I'm telling you. There's somebody in there."

This is an old story. There've always been problems with the place, the lake an irresistible draw for teenagers looking for trouble, and over the years the outbuildings have periodically been broken into, though there's not much to steal, not in the off-season. They don't seem to care. They just want to smash things, carve epithets into the counters, spray-paint their dirty slogans in the corners where children can't miss them come summer. It's been that way since the first truckload of sand was laid down, though it's worse now, always and progressively worse, because the community isn't what it was. And never will be.

Sid doesn't want to be bothered, she can see that. He thinks she's crazy, calling him at work every time a strange car pulls into the lot, sitting out there over her turtles and chasing dogs away from the Canada geese, ringing up the Yorktown cops so many times they don't even bother to send a patrol car anymore. He's already turned back to the paper—"It's nothing, Miriam, nothing, don't worry yourself"—when she drops the oranges right back in the crate and snatches up the binoculars. At first she can't make out a thing, but then she focuses on the door, and sure enough, it's standing open and there's movement there, a man's face showing like an image in a slide projector, presented and withdrawn all in the space of an instant. "Sid. Sid!"

The look he gives her is not a loving look. He sighs in that way he has when he's feeling put-upon, a sigh that could contain a novel's worth of martyrdom and resentment. But then she's handing him the binoculars and he's standing there erect at the window, focusing in. After a moment, he emits a low curse.

"Son of a bitch," he mutters, and he strides across the room to the door even as she calls out, "Take a coat!" and tries to fumble into her parka and slip on her boots all at the same time.

By the time she reaches the gates—and the big brass padlock there is hanging open, no question about it—he's already at the paddleball courts, moving swiftly, his shadow jogging on ahead of him. It's cold and she's forgotten her glasses. She digs into her pockets, but can only come up with one mitten. The pain in her hip is back, as sharp as a scalpel. She's forcing herself on, breathing hard, breathing as if she's about to have a heart attack, when she hears the shouts ring out, and she makes the open door just in time to see Richie Spano, in a black peacoat and with the dark slash of a mustache slicing his face in two, standing over Sid, who's stretched out supine on the gray concrete floor. What she doesn't know, not yet, because she hardly ever talks to Marsha anymore, is that Vic Janove, who's run the concession stand for the past twenty years and who's become as close to the Goldsteins as she and Sid used to be when they were young together, has asked Richie, as a favor, to look after the place while he's in Florida.

Sid is down on the concrete. He's sixty-eight years old and he's just been in a fistfight. And Richie, the breath issuing from his mouth like one of those dialogue balloons in the funny papers, squares his shoulders, swings round and walks right past her and out the door, and all he says, his voice so fierce and choked he can barely get it out, is, "You bitch. You stupid interfering bitch."

> [This too is family legend, though it's etched in pain. Sid, who had suffered what the neurologists quaintly call an insult to the brain when his head struck the concrete, was too stubborn to go to the doctor. He'd been knocked down before. It was nothing. He took a fistful of aspirin to quell his headache, asked Miriam to make him a cup of tea and maybe some soup, borscht or chicken noodle, it didn't matter, because he wasn't really hungry anyway. Three days later, when finally he relented, and she, unsteady on her feet herself, tried to help him down to the car, he collapsed in the driveway. He was dead before she could get the car door open.]

It's a Saturday in July, another Saturday, the voices of children careening about her and the steady *thwock* of the dense black rubber ball punctuating her thoughts. These are new children, of course, the children and grandchildren of her friends and of the new people too. She barely glances at the men on the paddleball court—they're interchangeable, their bare legs furred in dark swirls, T-shirts glued to their torsos, sweatbands at their wrists. Their voices rise and fall, immemorial. Someone laughs. A radio buzzes, seeking the signal. *Thwock. Thwock.* She knows it will all be lost, everything we make, everything we love, everything we are.

Her eyes close, the sun pressing at her lids like a palpable weight. She can feel everything, every molecule of the hot aluminum slats of the chair and the fading grains of sand, she can taste the air and smell the cold depths of the lake, where no one ever drowns and every child comes home safely. There's a splashing in the shallows, a dog raising its voice in ecstasy, the sharp tocsin of the lifeguard's whistle. And then peace, carving out a space where the big green turtles rise lazily from the depths and the geese float free and a little girl, somebody's daughter, comes wet and shivering to her mother's sun-struck embrace.

(2009)

What Separates Us from the Animals

When the new doctor first moved in—it was a year ago now, in January—my husband Wyatt and I had him over to dinner. We were being neighborly, of course, that goes without saying, but we were also curious to see what he was like when his guard was down. After he'd had two Cutty Sarks and water, that is, and maybe half a bottle of chablis, and he was sitting by the fire with his legs stretched out before him and the remains of a platter of my cranberry tarts balanced on the swell of his belly. That was when you found out what a man was really like, in the afterglow of dinner, when he was digesting, and believe me the doctor had been no slouch at the table, putting away two steaming helpings of lobster bisque, a grilled haddock fillet with rosemary potatoes and my own tartar sauce, three buttered slices of homemade sourdough and a wilted spinach salad with bacon bits and roasted pine nuts. Of course, we weren't the only ones to invite him over—probably half the families on the island had the same idea—but we were the first. I'd been chair of the committee that brought him here, so I had an advantage. Plus, that was me standing out there in the cold to greet him when he drove off the ferry in an old Volvo wagon the color of jack cheese.

He'd begged off that first night—too much to do, he'd said, what with unpacking and all, and that was understandable, though I really did fail to appreciate why he wouldn't accept my offer of help, especially in the absence of a wife or children or any sort of family, if you discount the two slope-shouldered Siamese cats staring out the front window of the car—but he agreed to come the following night. "Just name the time," he said with a little click of his fingers, "and I'll be there."

"We tend to eat early this time of year," I said, trying not to make my voice sound too apologetic. We were standing on the porch of the house he was seeing for the first time and I'd just pushed open the door for him and handed him the key. There was a breeze out of the northeast, bitter as the salt smell it carried. The cats mewed in unison from the confines of the car, which sat in the driveway, sagging under its load. I was thinking of the city, how they ate at all hours there, and trying to balance Wyatt's needs—he was a bear if he didn't get fed—with what my mother, when she was alive, used to call etiquette.

"How early?" He lifted a pair of eyebrows thick as spruce cuttings.

"Oh, I don't know—would four-thirty be all right?" He frowned then and I added quickly, "For cocktails, that is. Dinner can always wait."

Whether he was put out or not, I'll say this for him: he was prompt. There he was rapping at the door the next evening just as the light was fading from the sky and Venus brightening out over the water. He'd come at four-thirty on the dot and that showed consideration on his part, but both Wyatt and I were surprised to say the least when we got a look at what he was wearing. I don't know what we expected, not a tux and tails certainly, but he was a doctor after all, an educated man, and from the city too, and you'd think he'd have some notion of what it meant to accept an invitation. I don't know how to put this politely so I'll just say I was dumbfounded to see him standing there on the front porch dressed in the very same paint-spattered blue jeans, shapeless gray sweatshirt and pinched little baseball cap he'd been wearing the previous day (which I'd excused at the time because he was in the process of moving and nobody wears their Sunday finest for lugging boxes and hauling furniture, not that he had much—medical equipment, mainly—but then the Trumbull House *was* furnished. That was the whole point, wasn't it?).

Of course, I'm nothing if not adaptable, and I did manage to recover myself quickly enough to give him as gracious a smile as I could muster under the circumstances and usher him in out of the cold. I didn't have time to worry over the peculiar odor he was bringing in with him or where I could possibly seat him without having to think about the furniture, because there he was, stamping around in the anteroom and clapping his arms to his shoulders as if he'd walked twenty miles in an arctic blast instead of just kitty-corner across the street, and the moment had come for me to act the role of hostess—and Wyatt too. Or, in his case, host.

Wyatt was looking chicken-necked in the white shirt and tie I'd made him put on, and his eyes dodged away from the doctor's even as he took the man's meaty big-knuckled hand in his own. "Pleased to meet you," the doctor whispered so you could barely hear him and ran a hand through his beard. Did I mention he had a beard? A doctor with a beard? That set me back, I'll tell you, but at least I'd seen him the previous day and this was Wyatt's first exposure to him. (Not that there's anything wrong with beards—half the lobstermen wear them. So does Wyatt, for that matter.)

As planned, we got sociable over the scotch whiskey, the doctor sitting in the wooden rocker by the fire and Wyatt and I settling into the couch with its linen slipcovers and ecru pillows that are nothing but dirt magnets and why I didn't go for a darker shade—or gray even, a nice charcoal gray—I'll never know. Of course, I didn't want to dominate the conversation but I'm afraid there were long stretches when I was pretty much resigned to listening to my own voice as I filled him in as best I could on our institutions, our likes and dislikes, and some of our more colorful types like Heddy Hastings, who at eighty-seven years old ignored everybody's advice and named a whole litter of Pekinese puppies after her deceased siblings and then went around talking to them as if they were living, breathing people. The doctor didn't seem surprised, or not particularly—I guess he'd seen just about everything in the city. He was more a listener than a talker, in any case, and Wyatt wasn't much of a conversationalist unless he was sitting down at the fishermen's shack with the Tucker brothers and some of the other old boys he'd grown up with, and that was a problem right from the start. But I'd given Wyatt a couple of prompts, and as he got up to refresh our drinks, he cut me off in the middle of a description of the sins and venalities of the summer people and blurted, "So you're divorced then, is that it?"

The doctor—he'd said right off *Call me Austin,* but the way my mother raised me I just couldn't bring myself to address him as anything other than Doctor—held out his glass and gave us two words on the subject: "Never married."

"Really?" I said, trying to cover my surprise. I looked at him closely, looked at him in a whole new light. I thought of the two cats in the car—Siamese, no less—and made a leap. Was he gay, was that it? Because if he was he hadn't mentioned a thing about it when he applied for the position, and though we didn't have a whole lot of choice (there was one other applicant, a black woman from Burkina Faso who was still working toward her certification), I don't know if we would have wanted a gay doctor. I tried to read Wyatt's face, to see how he was taking it, but he turned his back to me as he measured out the scotch whiskey.

"Wyatt and I've been married twenty-eight years now," I said into the silence that had descended over the room, "and to answer your unasked question, no, we were never blessed with children." Something came over me then, a kind of sadness that catches me unawares at the oddest times. My face felt like putty all of a sudden, as if it had just been molded from big wet globs of the stuff, and I thought for a minute I was going to start to cry. "It was me," I told him, fighting to master my voice. "My tubes. They—but you'll learn all that soon enough." I drew in a deep breath to compose myself before turning the focus back on him. "What about you? Never found a . . . a *person*—you hit it off with?"

He laughed and waved his hand as if he were swatting flies. "No, I don't swing that way, if that's what you're thinking." He dropped his eyes, a big overgrown man in dirty clothes who was probably just shy, that was all, and if I thought of Mary Ellen Burkhardt's daughter Tanya, who'd recently come back to us after her divorce on the mainland, so much the worse. "I like women as much as the next man," he said, but he never raised his eyes to look at me, just studied the pattern of the carpet as if it were the most fascinating thing in the world. And then—I did think this was a bit excessive—he laughed again, and I couldn't help feeling it was at our expense. I mean, we may be provincial—how could we help but be, living out here a good twelve and a half miles from the coast with just five hundred year-round residents and one bar, one café, one church and a single supermarket that's anything but super?—but we were still part of the modern world. Eileen McClatchey's son, Gerald, was queer, as he insisted on calling himself, and we did have the summer people, after all.

But then we were at the table, eating, and he never paused for grace or removed his cap, though I told myself not to be judgmental. He praised my cooking in the usual way—I'm known from one end of this island to the other for my lobster bisque, not to mention my pork roast with onion and peanut sauce—and then, as I've said, we wound up by the fire. I was trying to pinpoint the odor he gave off, something between perspiration, naphtha and a heap of old sweat socks left out in the rain, and I was just about to offer to do a load of wash for him as a way of getting him to open up, but he wasn't the sort of man to open up, even when he was digesting. In fact, right then, with the crumbs on his lips and the platter of cranberry tarts still balanced on his stomach, he began, ever so softly, to snore.

It was a while before I saw him again, other than to wave at him when he passed by in his Volvo going God knows where, and in that time just about everybody we knew invited him to dinner (the better class, that is, the ones who gave two hoots whether a township functioned smoothly or even at all). I know the Caldwells had him over, Betsy Fike, John and Junie Jordan, all sorts of people. And if he wasn't dining out, he could be found down at the Kettle at seven o'clock on the stroke, forking up a plate of fish and chips or deep-fried scallops, which are delicious, I admit it, but maybe not so beneficial for your heart health, as any doctor ought to know. At any rate, I doubted if he cooked for himself at all, not even to the extent of heating up a can of soup over the range or popping a frozen dinner in the microwave.

Then there was the question of his office hours. Our agreement—the township was paying him $75,000 a year, plus the use of the Trumbull House, gratis—stipulated that he hold office hours, morning and afternoon, five days a week, and be available for house calls as needed. But Betsy Fike, whose wrist never really healed properly after her boating accident, went in to see him at ten o'clock on a Tuesday morning—in pain, real pain—and the door was locked and he never answered her knock. Even worse, when you could get in—and I had this from Fredericka Granger—he just sat there behind his desk, which even back then, right in the beginning, was a mess, heaped high with forms and papers and grease-stained sandwich wrappers, empty potato chip bags and the like, and you practically had to move heaven and earth to convince him to take you into the back room for an examination. And that was a mess too.

I guess he'd been here six weeks or so by the time I decided to go in and see for myself. There was nothing wrong with me—Wyatt says I'm as healthy as a horse—but I invented something (female troubles, and though I'd turned forty-six and long since given in to the inevitable, I still wanted to see what he had to say about it, if that makes any sense). At any rate, I went in after lunch on one of those crusted-over March days when you think winter will never end, and took a seat in the deserted waiting room. The doctor didn't have a nurse, so you just rang a bell and waited. I rang, took a seat and began leafing through the finger-worn magazines Dr. Braun had left behind when he lost his license in a prescription pill sting on the mainland and had to leave us.

Dr. Murdbritter (yes, that's right, it does sound Jewish and we batted that around like a shuttlecock before we made him the offer) wasn't prompt at all, not this time. I sat there a good ten or fifteen minutes, listening for sounds from within, until I got up and rang again, twice, before resuming my seat. When he finally appeared, in a faintly grayish-looking white shirt with an open collar, no jacket, he looked as if he'd been asleep. His hair—have I mentioned his hair?—was as kinky as a poodle's and it tended to jut up on one side and lie flat on the other, and so it was now, as if he'd just raised his head from the pillow. He looked old, or older than his documentation claimed (which was my age exactly—we were even born in the same month, six days apart) and I had to wonder about that. Had he fudged a bit there? And if so, what of his qualifications, not to mention previous experience?

"Hello, Doctor," I said, trying not to chirp, which I unfortunately find myself doing in such circumstances—running into people, that is, at the market or the gas station or the library or wherever. *You're chirping,* Wyatt'll say, and I'm forever trying to rein myself in.

The doctor's face was unreadable. He was squinting at me. He gave a little tug at his beard. "Mrs. McKenzie," he said, his voice as flat as if he were reading from a phone book.

"Call me Margaret," I said, appending a little laugh. "After all, we have broken bread together—"

He didn't appear to have heard this—or if he did he chose to ignore it. This wouldn't be a sociable visit, I could see that. "What seems to be the problem?" he asked, stepping back to hold the door open so that I could see through to his heaped-up desk, and beyond it, the examining room, which looked little better.

"Oh, nothing, really," I said, settling into the chair stationed in front of the desk while he eased himself into the swivel chair behind it with an audible sigh, "and I don't want to trouble you—" Was that really a boot, a mud-encrusted *boot,* peeping out from beneath the examining table in the back room? And where were the oil paintings of dories and seabirds and the sun setting over Penobscot Bay Alva Trumbull had left behind when she bequeathed the place to the township?

"Yes?" He was waiting, his fingers knitted, his eyes roving over me.

"I'm having pains."

"What sort of pains?"

I glanced away, then turned back to him, indicating, as best I could, the region of my lap. "Women's pains. A kind of, I don't know, just pain."

"Bloating?"

I shook my head.

"Blood? Any discharge at all?"

I shook my head again, even more emphatically. There had been something, a faint discoloration I sometimes found in the crotch of my panties when I did the wash, but it was ordinary, the sort of thing women my age can be prone to once menopause comes, and I'd thought nothing of it till he put a name to it: *discharge.* I felt strange all of a sudden, as if I'd gone too far, too deep, and my little fib had come back to bite me.

He asked the usual questions then, looked at the charts Dr. Braun had left, probing gently about my previous history, and when we got to a point where we could go no further, he rose and said, "If you'll step inside," indicating the examining room.

"But I, I don't really—" I began, pushing myself up from the chair in confusion, all the while silently cursing Fredericka Granger. Here he was leading me into the examining room without a hint of hesitation, but as far as I was concerned there was nothing to be examined, or no point to it, at any rate, because I was here to check up on him, not vice versa.

"It's all right," he said, and for a moment I saw beyond the beard and the dingy shirt and the tumult of the place, and saw him for what he was—a good doctor, a friend, a man who'd come to fulfill our collective need. I bowed my head and complied.

Still, as soon as I was inside, in his inner sanctum, I have to tell you I was shocked all over again. Everything I'd heard was true. The paper on the examining table looked as if it hadn't been changed since Dr. Braun's time. The linoleum was in serious need of wax, let alone a good mopping, the wastebaskets were overflowing—I saw fluffs of cotton stained with blood, syringes, throwaway thermometers, yet more fast-food wrappers and paper cups—and there must have been half an inch of dust scattered over everything. Worse, there was that muddy boot peeping out at me from beneath the table, and his jacket, his white coat, thrown across the back of a chair like an afterthought.

"Sit here, please," he said, indicating the table, and he went through the usual routine, taking my temperature, peering into my eyes, listening to my heart and lungs. "Now, if you'll just lie back," he said finally, puffing for breath as if he'd just climbed a steep hill. I lifted my legs to the table and lay back, wondering about that, and then it came to me: he was out of condition, that was what it was, as disordered on the inside as he was on the outside, overweight, sloppy, with an appetite for deep-fried food and no wife or mother to anchor him. I felt sorry for him suddenly, felt as if I wanted to reach out and console him, help him, but then he was there leaning over me, his fingers pressing at my abdomen, roving from one spot to another, liver, kidneys and lower. Was this painful? This?

I was unconsciously holding my breath, his odor—it was B.O., plain and simple, and I saw myself gift-wrapping one of the spare bottles of Old Spice Wyatt's sister sends every Christmas and leaving it on his porch in an anonymous gesture—settling over me like a miasma. Listerine. Maybe I'd leave some Listerine too.

"You understand you'll have to go to the mainland, to a gynecologist, for a complete exam," he offered at the conclusion of our little visit. "I can't really do an exam without a nurse present—for my own protection, you understand—and since we don't seem to have funding for a nurse . . ."

"Yes," I said, feeling nothing but relief.

He was writing a prescription for some sort of pain medication—or a placebo, more likely—and saying, "Just take one of these every four hours for pain, and if it gets worse, or if there's any bleeding or unusual discharge, you let me know right away."

I smiled as best I could, and then, ignoring everything—the mess of the room, his beard, the fact that his lower teeth were as yellow as a dog's—I made a leap, envisioning a little dinner party, my shrimp scampi or maybe linguine, Tanya Burkhardt and her mother Mary Ellen sitting across the table from the doctor and Wyatt mixing the drinks. "I was wondering," I said, as he handed me the prescription, which I was determined to tear up the minute I was out the door, "if maybe you wouldn't want to come over to dinner again sometime soon? Thursday, maybe? How does Thursday sound?"

Tanya and Mary Ellen arrived first, and I saw right away that Tanya hadn't managed to gain back any of the weight she'd lost from the strain of the divorce and trying to manage the twins all by herself (though I couldn't understand why, since she'd been back nearly three months now and living at home, where she didn't have to lift a finger and Mary Ellen heaped up enough food three times a day to choke a lumberjack). And her hair. Tanya had always had the most beautiful hair, her best feature really, since it hid her ears and contoured her face, but here she was shorn like a nun. Which only emphasized those unfortunate ears she'd inherited from her father, Michael, now deceased but living on in his daughter's flesh. Or cartilage, I suppose, in this case.

Anyway, we were all settled in around the fire, presenting the cozy sort of scene I hoped would awaken some long-forgotten notion of hearth and family in Dr. Murdbritter, when he called to say he'd be late—something about a last-minute patient suffering from an asthma attack, which could only have been Tom Harper, who went around wheezing like a sump pump and should have given up smoking the day he was born—and that put me off my mood. When the doctor did finally arrive, we were just finishing our second cocktail—Wyatt had made up a batch of his famous cranberry margaritas—and I'm afraid Tanya was looking a bit flushed.

I don't know if I was overcompensating by getting everybody to the table as expeditiously as possible (yes, the doctor had his drink, white wine, and precisely three of my Swedish meatballs and two slices of cheese folded onto half a cracker amidst a smattering of small talk orchestrated by Mary Ellen and me), but I did really feel that we had to get something on our stomachs. I seated the doctor between Tanya and her mother, across from Wyatt and myself, and served the bread hot from the oven with pats of fresh creamery butter and little individual dipping plates of my own garlic-infused olive oil, which I figured would keep them busy long enough for me to excuse myself and dress the salad. I was in the kitchen, trying to listen to the conversation wafting in from the dining room while I tossed the salad and grated Romano, when Tanya sashayed through the open door and helped herself to a glass of the Italian red I'd set aside for the pasta course, filling it right to the very rim. "It's a nice wine," I said absently, but she just put her lips to the glass, shrugged, and drank half of it in a gulp before topping off the glass and drifting back into the dining room to take her seat at the table. Was this a recipe for trouble? I couldn't say, not at the time, but my thinking was charitable and if I was foolish enough to try to play matchmaker, well, maybe I got what I deserved.

It seemed that Tanya took a dislike to the doctor right off, asking him all sorts of pointed (rude, that is) questions about his past and why he'd ever want to maroon himself in a craphole (her exact phrase) like this. I tried to intercede, to have a *general* conversation, but the doctor, chuffing slightly and making short work of the bread, butter and olive oil, didn't seem fazed, or not particularly. "Oh, I don't know," he breathed, snatching a look at her before dropping his eyes to his plate, "I guess I'd just had enough of the rat race in the city. Know what I mean?"

"No, I don't," Tanya returned, with real vehemence. "People look at me like I'm some sort of wounded bird or something just because I've crawled back here to my mother, but I can't wait to get away again. Just give me the opportunity—give me a ticket anywhere and five hundred bucks and I'm gone."

"Tanya," Mary Ellen said, coming down sharply on the first syllable.

"But you can't mean that, Tanya," I said. Wyatt stared at the paneled wall behind her. The doctor studied her as if seeing her for the first time.

"Damn straight I do." Tanya lifted her glass and drained it, and this wasn't just a run-of-the-mill red but an imported Chianti that cost twenty-two dollars a bottle on the mainland and was meant to be sipped and sniffed and appreciated. She glared round the room, then pushed herself up from the table. "And if you"—she pointed a finger at me—"and my mother think you can shove me off on some man I've never laid eyes on in my life just because you've got nothing better to do than play matchmaker, then you don't need his kind of doctor, you need a head doctor."

We tried, both Mary Ellen and I, but Tanya wouldn't sit back down and eat. She wandered away from the table and into the living room, where she sank into the easy chair by the fire, and I was so involved in that moment with getting dinner on the table—the green beans were within ten seconds of being overcooked to the point of losing their texture—that I didn't notice her slip out the door. What could I do? I put on a brave face and served the pasta and the green beans and we all seemed to find common ground in the vacancy Tanya left behind. The doctor perked up, Wyatt regaled us with a story about the young kayaker killed by a shark that apparently mistook the silhouette of his boat for a basking seal (a story so fresh I'd only heard it twice before), and Mary Ellen used her people skills to bring the doctor out—at least as far as he was willing to come.

We learned what had become of the oil paintings, which were now stored in the closet on the ground floor ("Too nautical for a landlubber like me," he said with a chuckle) and discovered that his family name was of Franco-German origin. He had a brandy after dinner, his eyes at half mast and his big hands folded over his abdomen, and he never mentioned Tanya or the scene she'd created. And when his eyes fell shut and his breathing began to slow, Mary Ellen gently shook him awake and he looked at us all as if trying to recollect who we were and where he was, before rising massively and murmuring that he'd a lovely evening and hoped he could repay us someday with an invitation of his own.

Spring came in a long succession of downpours that flooded the streets and got the peepers peeping and the birds winging in from the south, a spell of nice weather took us by surprise in mid-May, and then it was June and the summer people began their annual migration. I saw Tanya around town with her two boys (three-year-olds, and a real handful), but we didn't stop to chat because no matter what she'd been through with her ex or how sympathetic and forgiving a person I might be, her behavior in my dining room had been inexcusable, just inexcusable. As for the doctor, I did slip out one evening and leave a few anonymous gifts on his front porch—the shaving lotion and mouthwash, along with a plastic bucket of cleaning supplies and a mustache trimmer I found at the drugstore—but I was busy with a thousand things and hadn't got round to inviting him over again and, of course, we were still waiting for him to live up to his parting promise and have us over one night in return. Not that I blamed him for putting us off. He had enough on his hands with the influx of summer people and the rash of contusions and snapped bones they suffered pitching headlong over the handlebars of their mopeds or careening down the rocks at Pilcher's Head without having to worry about entertaining (though certainly it wouldn't have killed him to host a cocktail party in that magnificent front room of the Trumbull House—if it still was magnificent, that is). In fact, all I knew of the doctor during the ensuing months came to me on the wings of rumor and complaint. Everybody had something to say on the subject, it seemed, and at the next town meeting, sure enough, Betsy Fike, who could hone the knife blade of a grudge for months if not years, stood up and declared that something had to be done about the state of the doctor's office, not to mention the house, which was common property of the township and needed to be kept up out of consideration for the next generation and beyond.

Mervis Leroy, who was chair of the meeting, asked if she'd actually been in the house since the doctor's occupation thereof and could testify to any lack of upkeep or deterioration, and Betsy (she's five foot one, whip-smart, with two grown daughters and a husband about as expressive as a wall) admitted that she hadn't. "But I've been to his office twice, after that first time when he wouldn't even answer the door, and I can tell you the place is a pigsty. Worse. Even a pig wouldn't put up with it."

Voices piped up all around her and Mervis pounded his gavel and recognized one speaker after another, everybody supplying anecdotal evidence but pretty much saying the same thing: that Dr. Murdbritter seemed all right as a doctor, neither conspicuously bad nor conspicuously good, but that the way he maintained his office and his person was a disgrace. Someone, I forget who, pointed out that his Volvo had been sitting at the curb with a flat tire for two months now and that when he did make house calls he did it on foot, which was no way to operate if a crisis ever arose. Especially if you were overweight. And then there was the garbage situation and the way the dogs would get into his cans and scatter trash (and worse: medical waste) all over his back lawn and how he never bothered to do a thing about it. Junie Jordan said that while she was in the waiting room Wednesday last she'd peeked in the door at the main room of the house and saw that it hadn't been touched since the day he moved in, except that the chairs were all covered in cat hair and there were dust bunnies sprouting up everywhere and cobwebs in the corners like in a horror movie, big ropes of them. People looked angry.

Then came the question: what to do about it? Send him a letter of official condemnation? Tell him to clean up or ship out? Start all over again searching for a replacement, one who was a model of personal hygiene? Do nothing and hope for the best? Finally—and this was my inspiration, because I had so much invested in making this work and could always see my way to a compromise, unlike some of my neighbors, who will go unmentioned here—it was moved that the township should allocate two hundred dollars a month out of the general fund for the purpose of hiring a maid to go into the Trumbull House once a week and straighten up. Betsy Fike seconded the motion. The chorus of ayes was resounding.

We found a young immigrant woman from Lincolnville and she took the ferry out and marched up the street with her own mop and broom slung like weapons of war over one shoulder. I watched her mount the steps, try the door handle—the door was left unlocked during office hours—and vanish inside. Five minutes later, she was back on the porch, the doctor hovering in the doorway like some dark presence while the young woman—a girl really—seemed to be giving him what for. I only wished I could have heard what they were saying, and I did go to the front door and ease it open, but at that moment a pack of tourists went buzzing by on their mopeds and all sense was lost to the racketing of their engines.

I waited ten minutes, watching the erstwhile maid head off down the street, the mop and broom dragging behind her in the dirt in the very picture of defeat, before I rang the doctor's number. He answered on the second ring. "Dr. Murdbritter," he announced in his official voice.

"I just wanted to know why you turned that girl away," I started in without preliminary, and I guess that was a mistake. "We allocated the funds. For you. To help you with, well, to give you a hand keeping the place up—"

"Who is this?"

"It's me, Margaret. Margaret McKenzie."

"I suppose you were watching all along."

"Well, I just happened to be in the front yard and I couldn't help but . . . She's a good girl, with the best references. And she came all the way out here on the ferry just to—"

"I'm sorry," he said, cutting me off, and I was startled by the tone of his voice, "but I just can't have any interference in my personal life. You people brought me here to establish a practice and that's what I'm doing. If you find funding for a nurse, you let me know—otherwise, stay clear, do you hear me?"

Of course, I had no choice but to report this turn of events, not to mention the doctor's rudeness, to just about everyone I could think of, my phone tied up for the rest of the day and well into the evening so that Wyatt had to wait on his supper, which wound up being leftovers spruced up with a garden salad. We hashed it over at the next meeting, but no one had a good solution beyond giving the doctor his notice and that would have left us in a vulnerable position until we could find a replacement. I took it on myself to try to contact the woman from Burkina Faso in the hope that she'd completed her requirements and received her license in the interim, but a recording told me her telephone was no longer in service and my follow-up letter came back stamped *Addressee Unknown.*

We were at a stalemate. The tourists and summer people thronged the doctor's porch with their blood-stained T-shirts and improvised bandages even as we islanders took our place in line and shuffled into his ever-filthier offices to announce our ailments because we had no choice in the matter. *Would you let him put a needle in you?* Betsy Fike demanded over the phone one day. *Even in an emergency? Or blood—would you want him drawing blood?* I felt very tired that day, crushed really, and I could barely rise to his defense and point out that his syringes were disposable and the blood things too. *I know,* I said finally, my voice ragged and weary, *I know.*

Autumn came early, blowing off shore with a cold wind just after Labor Day. The summer people departed, leaves flamed and died, the geese flapped overhead and showed up in roasting pans and crockpots. The first snow fell at the end of October and I felt so low and depressed it might as well have been the frozen white lid of my coffin, and when Thanksgiving rolled round I just didn't feel up to it. Normally, Wyatt and I opened the house to a dozen or more guests and really made it festive—I baked for a week, served cod chowder, broiled oysters and turkey with all the trimmings, and it was one of the highlights of the year, and not just for Wyatt and me, but for our neighbors too. Yet this year was different, and it wasn't just because I would have had to invite the doctor—that was a given. Truthfully, I didn't even realize what it was till Wyatt brought it up.

"You know, you're running yourself into the ground, worrying over every little detail all the time," Wyatt said one night when he came in the door from work. "Have you had a look at yourself in the mirror? You're as white as"—I watched him mentally juggling clichés before he gave up—"I don't know, just white. Pale, you know."

What I hadn't told him, what I hadn't told anybody, was that I'd begun spotting again. And this wasn't just a faint discoloration, but blood, actual blood, crusted and dried till it was brown as dirt. I'd spent a long afternoon at our little one-room library (open Tuesday and Thursday, ten to four), masking the computer screen while I searched the Internet for information and that only scared and depressed me the more. I read about endometrial polyps, cancer of the uterus and fallopian tubes, anemia, hysterectomy, sonar and radiation treatments, the sickness that lingers and kills. I didn't want to go to the mainland, didn't want to pick doctors out of the phone book, didn't want them probing and cutting and laying me up in some hospital in the city while strangers haunted the corridors and shot by obliviously in their shiny little Japanese cars. I went to the drugstore and stocked up on iron pills, multipurpose vitamins, a calcium supplement, and I hid my underthings at the bottom of the hamper as if that would solve anything.

One afternoon—it was just after Christmas, which I'd tried to make as cheerful for Wyatt as I could, though I didn't feel up to caroling, not this time around—I was sitting at the front window, sipping tea and looking out into the fog that had begun to drift in. It was a typical winter fog, dense and shifting, so that the far side of the street just seemed to evaporate one minute only to reappear the next. At some point a stray shaft of sunlight cut through it all and lit up the front of the Trumbull House like a movie set and I could see something hanging on the door there, a sheet of white cardboard, it looked like. I plucked my binoculars from the table and focused in. It was a note of some sort, big and boxy, outsized like everything about Dr. Murdbritter, even his mess, but I couldn't make out what it said. I knew in my heart that I needed to see him, confide in him, have him examine me even if I had to drag Wyatt into the room along with me, but I was afraid—not only of the tests he'd insist on and what they might show, but of letting him touch me there, and of the dirt, the dirt above all else.

I put on my coat, looked both ways on the porch to be sure no one was watching, and crossed the street to the doctor's house. His car—he'd had Joe Gilvey replace the tire for him after Mervis drafted an official letter of complaint—was gone, and that was strange. After those first few weeks when he'd traced each of our six blacktop roads to where they petered out in a salt marsh or bay, he'd given up exploring, and then he'd had the flat and the car had just sat there like a natural feature of the environment for I don't know how long. When I got to his porch, the mystery cleared itself up: the note said that he was taking the ferry to the mainland on personal business and would be back the following afternoon, directing all emergencies that might arise in his absence to the sheriff's office. I don't know what I felt at that moment. One part of me had been ready to ring the bell, slink into his office and confess what was happening to me and how scared I was, while the other part held back.

I can't explain what I did next, not in any rational way, but I somehow had the duplicate key in my hand, the one that had hung on its little hook above the calendar on the bulletin board in my kitchen, and why I'd thought to put it in my pocket I'll never know. In the next moment, I was inside, the house cold and dank and smelling of things I wouldn't want to name, let alone the cat box, which must have been changed sporadically, if at all. I found the coffeepot in the kitchen set atop a stove so stained and blackened you couldn't tell what color it was—he had been cooking after all, I thought, but it was a small consolation. I brewed the strongest coffee I could stand and began looking through the closets for the cleaning supplies, the mop and broom and vacuum cleaner Dr. Braun had left behind in his haste to vacate the place.

Can I tell you that all the lethargy that had come over me in the past months vanished the moment I went to work? I keep the tidiest house on the island, take my word for it, though some of the other wives and homemakers might make the same claim for themselves. Cleanliness, the desire for order where there is none, the struggle to fight down the decay all around us, is what separates us from the animals, at least in my opinion. I'm alert to everything, every tarnish and scuff and speck of mold, and I can't sit still till it's gone. It's just me, it's just the way I am. My father told me that when the Nazis were retreating across France ahead of the Allies, they'd vacate a farmhouse one morning and the Allies would occupy it that evening, and the most common booby trap the Nazis left behind was this: they'd leave a picture just slightly askew on the wall and when a soldier went to straighten it, goodbye. *They'd have got you, Missy, the very first day,* my father used to say, and he'd say it with pride.

Anyway, I went at that mess as if I were possessed, working past dinnertime so that Wyatt and I had to go out to the Kettle to eat and I ordered the fried scallops and polished them off with a vengeance, not caring a hoot if they hardened my arteries or not. I couldn't sleep that night thinking of the shambles of the doctor's bedroom and his filthy sheets—how could anybody sleep like that?—and of all that remained to be done not only in the house itself but in the office, especially the office. The ferry would be back at two, I knew that, but I wouldn't rest till I had that desk cleared, the floors gleaming, the examining room and all the stainless-steel cabinets and instruments shining as if they gave off a light of their own. This place was a shrine, didn't he realize that? A place of shriving and forgiveness and healing as sacred as any church. By God, I thought, *by God.*

I got lost in the rhythm of the work and when two o'clock rolled round I was still at it, which is why I really couldn't say when he came in. I was down on my knees scrubbing the floor under the examining table till I thought I was going to take the finish right off it, my hand moving automatically from brush to pail and back again, and for a moment I didn't realize he was there in the room with me. Somewhere in the distance I could hear the washer going and the dryer tossing his clothes with a rattle and clack. He might have cleared his throat, I don't know, but I looked up then and saw him whole, from his clunky shoes and ill-fitting pants right on up to the look of shock and astonishment on his big whiskered face. He didn't say a word. I got slowly to my feet, wiping my hands on the apron I'd run through the washer before dawn, the dial set to hot and a quarter cup of bleach poured in on top of it. "Doctor," I said, and then I used his given name for the first time in my life, "Austin. I'm sorry, but I just had to—talk to you. About me. About my problem, that is."

He might have said something then, a faint murmur of reassurance escaping his lips, but his face was so comical, so caught between what he'd been yesterday and what he was now, I wouldn't have noticed it anyway. Was he angry? A little, I suppose. Or maybe he was just relieved, because finally the ice had been broken, finally we were getting down to the bottom of things. For the longest moment we simply stood there, ten feet apart, and let me tell you, everything in that room and the room beyond it shone as if we were seeing it for the first time, both of us, and when the sun broke free and poured through those spotless windows to pool on the shining floor, the glare was almost too much for us.

(2010)

Good Home

He always took Joey with him to answer the ads because Joey was likable, the kind of kid anybody could relate to, with his open face and wide eager eyes and the white-blond hair of whoever his father might have been. Or mother. Or both. Royce knew something about breeding and to get hair like that there must have been blonds on both sides, but then there were a lot of blonds in Russia, weren't there? He'd never been there, but from what his sister Shana had told him about the orphanage they must have been as common as brunettes were here, or Asians and Mexicans anyway, with their shining black hair that always looked freshly greased, and what would you call *them,* blackettes? His own hair was a sort of dirty blond, nowhere near as extreme as Joey's, but in the same ballpark, so that people often mistook Joey for his son, which was just fine with him. Better than fine: perfect.

The first place they went to, in Canoga Park, was giving away rabbits, and there was a kid there of Joey's age—ten or so—who managed to look both guilty and relieved at the same time. A FOR SALE sign stood out front, the place probably on the verge of foreclosure (his realtor's brain made a quick calculation: double lot, maybe 3,500 square feet, two-car garage, air, the usual faux-granite countertops and built-ins, probably sold for close to five before the bust, now worth maybe three and a half, three and a quarter), and here was the kid's father sauntering out the kitchen door with his beer gut swaying in the grip of his wife-beater, Lakers cap reversed on his head, goatee, mirror shades, a real primo loser. "Hey," the man said. He was wearing huaraches, his toes as blackened as a corpse's.

Royce nodded. "What's happening?"

So there were rabbits. The kid's hobby. First there'd been two, now there were thirty. They kept them in one of those pre-fab sheds you get at Home Depot and when the kid pulled back the door the stink hit you in the face like a sucker punch. Joey was saying, "Oh, wow, wow, look at them all!" but all Royce was thinking was *Get me out of here,* because this was the kind of rank, urine-soaked stench you found in some of the street fighters' kennels, if they even bothered with kennels. "Can we take two?" Joey said, and everybody—the father, the kid and Joey—looked to him.

He gave an elaborate shrug, and how many times had they been through this charade before? "Sure," he said, "why not?" A glance for the father. "They're free, right? To a good home?"

The father—he wasn't much older than Royce, maybe thirty-four, thirty-five—just nodded, but on the way out Royce bent to the kid and pressed a five into his palm, feeling magnanimous. The next stop yielded a black Lab, skinny, with a bad eye, but still it would have to have its jaws duct-taped to keep it from slashing one of the dogs, and that was fine except that they had to sit there for half an hour with a cadaverous old couple who made them drink lukewarm iced tea and nibble stale anise cookies while they went on about Slipper and how she was a good dog, except that she peed on the rug—you had to watch out for that—and how sad they were to have to part with her, but she was just too much for them to handle anymore. They struck out at the next two places, both houses shuttered and locked, but all in all it wasn't a bad haul, considering these were just bait animals anyway and there was no need to get greedy.

Back at home, the minute they pulled up under the oaks in front, Joey was out the door and dashing for the house and his stash of Hansen's soda and barbecue chips, never giving a thought to the rabbits or the black Lab confined in their cages in the back of the Suburban. That was all right. There was no hurry. It wasn't that hot—eighty-five maybe—and the shade was dense under the trees. Plus, he felt like a beer himself. Just driving around the Valley in all that traffic was work, what with the fumes radiating up off the road and Joey chattering away about anything and everything that entered his head till you couldn't concentrate on the music easing out of the radio or the way the girls waved their butts as they sauntered down the boulevard in their shorts and blue jeans and invisible little skirts.

He left the windows down and kicked his way across the dirt expanse of the lot, the hand-tooled boots he wore on weekends picking up a fine film of dust, thinking he'd crack a beer, see what Steve was up to—and the dogs, the dogs, of course—and then maybe grill up some burgers for an early dinner before he went out. He'd have to lift the Lab down himself, but Joey could handle the rabbits, and no, they weren't going to bait the dogs tonight no matter how much Joey pleaded, because tonight was Saturday and he and Steve were going out, remember? But what Joey could do, before he settled down with his video games, was maybe give the bait animals a dish of water, or would that be asking too much?

The house was in Calabasas, pushed up against a hillside where the oaks gave way to chaparral as soon as you climbed up out of the yard on the path cut through the scrub there, the last place on a dirt road that threw up dust all summer and turned into a mudfest when the rains came in December. It was quiet, private, nights pulled down like a shade, and it had belonged to Steve's parents before they were killed in a head-on collision with a drunk three years back. Now it was Steve's. And his. Steve paid the property taxes and they split the mortgage each month, which for Royce was a whole lot cheaper than what he'd be paying elsewhere—plus, there was the barn, formerly for horses, now for the dogs. They had parties every couple of weeks, various women circulating in and out of their lives, but neither of them had ever been married, and as far as Royce was concerned, he liked it that way. Tonight, though, they were going out—cruising, as Steve liked to call it, as if they were in some seventies disco movie—and Joey would be on his own. Fine. No problem. Joey knew the score: stay out of the barn, don't let anybody in, bed at ten, call him on the cell if there were any problems.

Steve drove. He'd never had a DUI, but Royce had, and Royce needed his license up and running in order to ferry people around to his various listings, as if that would make a difference since nobody in his office had sold anything in recent memory. Or at least he hadn't anyway. They took the 101 into town, wound their way down Laurel Canyon and valeted the car in a lot off Sunset. It was just getting dark. A continuous line of cars, fading to invisibility behind their headlights, pulsed up and down the boulevard. This was the moment he liked best, slamming the car door and stepping out into the muted light, the street humming with the vibe of the clubs, the air so compacted and sweet with exhaust it was like breathing through your skin, the night young, anything possible.

Their first stop was a Middle Eastern restaurant that hardly served any food, or not that he could see anyway. People came here to sit at the tables out front and smoke Starbuzz or herbal shisha through the hookahs the management provided for a fee. Every once in a while you'd see a couple inside the restaurant picking over a lamb kebab or pita platter, but the real action was outside, where just about everybody surreptitiously spiked the tobacco with something a little stronger. The waitress was slim and young, dark half-moons of makeup worked into the flesh under her eyes and a tiny red stone glittering in one nostril, and maybe she recognized them from the week before, maybe she didn't. They ordered two iced teas and a hookah setup and let the smoke, cool and sweet, massage their lungs, their feet propped up on the wrought-iron rail that separated them from the sidewalk, eyes roaming the street. After a moment, just to hear his own voice over the shush of tires and the rattling tribal music that made you feel as if you were running on a treadmill, Royce said, "So what nationality you think these people are—the owners, I mean? Iranian? Armenian?"

Steve—he was a rock, absolutely, six-two, one-eighty, with a razor-to-the-bone military haircut though he'd never been in the military—glanced up lazily, exhaling. "What, the waitress, you mean?"

"I guess."

"Why, you want a date with her?"

"No, I just—"

"I can get you a date with her. You want a date with her?"

He shrugged. "Just curious, that's all. No biggie. I just figured, you're the expert, right?" This was a reference to the fact that Steve had dated an Iranian girl all last winter—or Persian, as she liked to classify herself, and who could blame her? She was fleshy in all the right places, with big bounteous eyes and a wide-lipped smile that really lit her face up, but she'd wanted things, too many things, things Steve couldn't give her.

"Yeah, that's me, a real expert, all right. I don't know why you didn't just hit me in the face with a two-by-four the minute Nasreen walked through the door"—he held it a beat, grinning his tight grin—"*Bro.*" He was about to bring the hose to his lips, but stopped himself, his eyes fixed on a point over Royce's shoulder. "Shit," he breathed, "isn't that your brother-in-law?"

Feeling caught out all of a sudden, feeling exposed, Royce swung round in his seat to shoot a glance up the boulevard. Joe—Big Joe, as Shana insisted on calling him after she came back from Russia with Joey, who was just a baby in diapers then—was nobody he wanted to see. He'd left Shana with a fractured elbow and a car with a bad transmission and payments overdue and she'd been working double shifts on weekends ever since to catch up. Which was why Royce took Joey Friday through Sunday—Joey needed a man's influence, that's what Shana claimed, and besides, she couldn't afford a babysitter. "Ex-brother-in-law," he said.

But there he was, Big Joe, easing his way in and out of the clusters of people making for the clubs and restaurants, his arm flung over the shoulder of some woman and a big self-satisfied grin on his face, just as if he was a regular human being. Even worse, the woman—girl—was so pretty the sight of her made Royce's heart clench with envy. If he was about to ask himself how a jerk like Joe had managed to wind up with a girl like that, he never got the chance because Steve was on his feet now, up out of his seat and leaning over the rail, calling out, "Joe, hey, Joe, what's happening?" in a voice deep-fried in sarcasm.

Joe was no more than twenty feet away and Royce could see him exchange a glance with the girl, as if he was going to pat down his pockets and pretend he'd left his credit card on the bar at the last place, but he kept on coming because he had no choice at this point. He wasn't that big—just big in relation to Joey and

Shana—but he carried himself with a swagger and he had one of those faces that managed to look hard even when he was smiling at you. Which he definitely wasn't doing now. He just froze his features, tightened his grip on the girl, and made as if to ignore them. But Steve wouldn't have it. Steve was over the railing in a bound, waving his arms like a game-show host. "Hey, man, good to see you," he was crowing in his put-on voice. "What a coincidence, huh? And look, look who's here"—and now the voice of wonder—"your brother-in-law!"

That moment? Nobody really liked it. Not the couple with the pita platter or the waitress or the other smokers, who only wanted to suck a little peace through a tube and dissolve the hassles of the day, and certainly not Joe. Or the girl he was with. She was involved now, giving him a look: *brother-in-law?*

"Ex," Joe said, looking from her to Royce and shooting him a look of hate. He was stalled there, against his will, the girl about to say something like *Aren't you going to introduce me?* and people beginning to turn their heads. Steve—he was amped up, clowning—kept saying, "Hey, come on, man, come on in and have a toke with us, like a peace pipe, you know?"

Joe ignored him. He just kept staring at Royce. Very slowly, in disgust, he began to shake his head, as if Royce were the one who'd walked out on his wife and kid and refused to pay child support or even leave a forwarding address, then he tightened his grip on the girl's arm, sidestepped Steve, and made a show of strutting off down the street as if nothing had happened. And nothing had happened. What was he going to do, have Steve fight his battles for him? It wasn't worth it. Though if he was Steve's size, or even close, he would have gone over that rail himself, and he would have had a thing or two to say, and maybe more—maybe he would have gone for him right there on the sidewalk so people made way and the pretty girl let out a soft strangled cry.

By the time they settled in at the first bar up the street, he'd put it out of his head. Or mostly. He and Steve talked sports and spun out a couple of jokes and routines and he found himself drifting, but then Joe's face loomed up in his consciousness and he was telling himself he should have followed him to see what he was driving, get a license plate number so Shana could clue the police or child services or whoever. Something. Anything. But he hadn't, and the moment was gone. "Forget it," Steve told him. "Don't let that fucker spoil the night for you."

They went to the next place and the next place after that, the music pounding and the lights flashing, and for a while there he felt loose enough to go up to women at random and introduce himself and when they asked him what he did for a living, he said, "I'm a dog man." That got them interested, no doubt about it, but it was the rare woman who didn't turn away or excuse herself to go to the ladies' when he began to explain just what that meant. Still, he was out on the town and the alcohol began to sing in his blood and he didn't feel tired or discouraged in the least. It was around eleven when Steve suggested they try this hotel he'd heard about, where they had a big outdoor pool area and a bar scene and you could sit out under the stars and watch girls jump in and out of the pool in their bikinis. "Sure," he heard himself say, "why not?" And if he thought of Joey, he thought of him in bed, asleep, the video remote still clenched in his hand and the screen gone blank.

He was feeling no pain as he followed Steve up the steps of the hotel and into the darkened lobby. Two doormen—studiously hip, mid-thirties, with phone plugs in their ears and cords trailing away beneath their collars—swung back the doors on a big spreading space with low ceilings, concrete pillars and a cluster of aluminum and leather couches arranged in a grid against the wall on the right. People—various scenesters, mostly dressed in black—lounged on the couches, trying their best to look as if they belonged. Beyond them, the pool area opened up to the yellow night sky and the infinite lights of the city below. A minute later he and Steve were crowding in at the pool bar—glasses that weren't glass but plastic, a rattle of ice cubes, scotch and soda—while the music infected them and the pool sucked and fell in an explosion of dancing blue light. Girls, as promised. And swimming like otters. "Pretty cool, huh?" Steve was saying.

He nodded, just taking in the scene, thinking nothing at this point, his mind sailing free the way it did when somebody else's dogs were fighting and he had no betting interest in the outcome. Suddenly he felt a wave of exhaustion sweep over him—or was it boredom? After a moment he excused himself to find his way to the men's, and that was when the whole world shifted on him.

Right in the lobby, set right there in the wall above the long curving sweep of the check-in desk, was a lit-up glass cubicle, maybe eight feet long, four high, with a mattress and pillow and a pale pink duvet turned back on itself—how could he have missed it on the way in? It was like the window of a furniture store, or no, a stage set, because there was a girl inside, propped up against the back wall as if she were in her own bedroom. She was wearing pajamas—nothing overt like a teddy or anything like that—just pajamas, button-up top and draw-string bottoms rolled up at the ankles. She had a cell phone stuck to one ear and a book open in her lap. Her hair was dark and long, brushed out as if for bed—a brunette, definitely a brunette—and her feet were bare and pressed to the glass so you could see the pale flesh of her soles. That was what got him, that was what had him standing there in the middle of the lobby as if he'd been nailed to the floor: the soles of her feet, so clean and white and intimate in that darkened arena with its scenesters and hustlers and everybody else doing their best to ignore her.

"Can I help you?" The man behind the desk—big-frame glasses, skinny tie—was addressing him.

"I was"—but this was genius, wasn't it, the hotel advertising what you could do there, in private, in a room, if you had a girl like that?—"just looking for the men's . . ."

"Down the hall to your right."

He should have moved on, but he didn't, he couldn't. The guy behind the desk was studying him still—he could feel his eyes on him—probably a heartbeat away from informing him that he couldn't stand there blocking traffic all night and another heartbeat away from calling security. "Does she have a name?" Royce murmured, his voice caught low in his throat.

"Chelsea."

"Does she—?"

The man shook his head. "No."

When Steve finally came looking for him, he was squeezed in at the end of one of the couches in the dark, just watching her. At first, she'd seemed static, almost like a mannequin, but that wasn't the case at all—she blinked her eyes, flipped the hair out of her face, turned the pages of her book with a flick of enameled nails, each gesture magnified out of all proportion. And then, thrillingly, she shifted position, stretching like a cat, one muscle at a time, before flexing her arms and abdomen and pushing herself up into the lotus position, her feet tucked under her, the book in her lap and the cell cupped to one ear. He wondered if she was really talking to anybody—a boyfriend, a husband—or if it was just part of the act. Did she eat in there? Take bathroom breaks? Brush her teeth? Floss?

"Hey, man, I've been looking all over for you," Steve said, emerging from the shadows with the dregs of a drink in one hand and all trace of his grin gone. "What are you doing? You know what time it is?"

He didn't. He just shook his head in a slow absent way as if he were waking from a deep sleep, and then they were down the steps and out on the street, the cars crawling past in a continuous illuminated loop and a sliver moon caught like a hook in the jaws of the yellow sky. The cell in his left front pocket began to vibrate. It was Joey. "What's up, big guy?" he said without breaking stride. "Shouldn't you be asleep? Like long asleep?"

The voice was soft, remote. "It's the Lab."

"What about her?"

"She's crying. I can hear her all the way from my bedroom."

"Yeah, okay, thanks for telling me—really—but don't you worry about it. You just get to sleep, hear me?"

Even softer: "Okay."

He wanted to add that they'd work the dogs in the morning, that they'd devote the whole morning to them because there was a match next weekend and if Joey was good he was going to bring him along, first time ever, because he was old enough now to see what it was all about and why they had to put so much time into training Zoltan and Zeus the way they did, baiting them and watching their diet and their weight and all the rest of it, but Joey had broken the connection.

Most of them were creeps, pure and simple—either that or old men who stood there gaping at her when they checked in with their shrink-wrapped wives—and she never had anything to do with any of them, no matter if they sent her ten-page letters and roses and fancy candy assortments, the latter of which she just gave to the maids in any case because sweets went straight to her hips and thighs. In fact, it was against the rules to make eye contact—Leonard, the manager, would jump down your throat if you even glanced up at somebody because that was like violating the fourth wall of the stage. *This is theater,* he kept telling her, *and you're an actress. Just keep that in mind.* Right. The only thing was, she didn't want to be an actress, unlike ninety-nine percent of the other girls clawing their way through the shops and bars and clubs seven days a week—she was two years out of college, waitressing mornings in a coffee shop and doing four nights a week here, representing some sort of adolescent wet dream while saving her money and studying for her LSATs.

Was it demeaning? Was it stupid? Yes, of course it was, but her mother had danced topless in a cage during hippie times—and that was in a bar where people could hoot and throw things and shout out every sleazy proposition known to humankind. She wasn't an actress. Anybody could be an actress. She was going to go into immigration law, help give voice to people who didn't have a say for themselves, do something with her life—and if using her looks to get her there, to get paid to study, was part of the deal, then that was fine with her.

So she was in her cubicle, embracing the concept of the fourth wall and trying to make sense of the logical reasoning questions TestMasters threw at her, good to go sometimes for an hour or more without even looking up, but she wasn't blind. The scene drifted past her as if she were underwater, in a submarine, watching all the strange sea creatures interact, snatch at each other, pair up, stumble, glide, fade into the depths, and her expression never changed. She recognized people from time to time, of course she did, but she never let on. Matt Damon had been in one night, with a girl and another guy, and once, just after she clocked in, she thought she'd seen George Clooney—or the back of his head anyway—and then there were people she'd gone to college with, an older couple who were friends of her parents, even a guy she'd dated in high school. Basically, and it wasn't that hard, she just ignored them all.

On this particular night though, a Saturday, when the throngs were out and the words began to blur on the page and nobody, not even her mother, would answer the phone, she stole a glance at the lobby and the guy who'd just stood there watching her for the last five minutes till Eduardo, the desk man, said something to him. In that instant, when he was distracted by whatever Eduardo was saying, she got a good look at him and realized, with a jolt, that she knew him from somewhere. Her eyes were back on the page but his image stayed with her: a lean short tensed-up guy with his hands in his pockets, blond hair piled up high on the crown of his head and a smooth detached expression, beautiful and dangerous at the same time, and where did she know him from?

It took her a while. She lost him when he drifted across the room in the direction of the lounge and she tried to refocus on her book but she couldn't. It was driving her crazy: where had she met him? Was it at school? Or here? Had she served him at the coffee shop, was that it? Time passed. She was bored. And then she snatched a look again and there he was, with another guy, moving tentatively across the lobby as if it were ankle-deep in mud—drunk, both of them, or at least under the influence—and it came to her: he was the guy who'd adopted the kittens, the one with the little kid, the nephew. It must have been six weeks ago now. Missy had had her second—and last—litter, because it was irresponsible to bring more cats into the world when they were putting them down by the thousands in the shelters every day and she'd decided to have her spayed once the kittens were weaned, all nine of them, and he'd showed up in answer to her ad. And what was his name? Roy or something. Or no: Royce. She remembered because of the boy, how unusual it was to see that kind of relationship, uncle and nephew, and how close they seemed, and because Royce had been so obviously attracted to her—couldn't keep his eyes off her, actually.

She'd just washed her hair and was combing out the snarls when the bell rang and there they were on the concrete landing of her apartment, smiling up at her. "Hi," he said, "are you the one with the kittens?"

She looked from him to the boy and back again. She'd given one of the kittens away to a guy who worked in the hotel kitchen and another to one of her girlfriends, but there were seven left and nobody else had called. "Yeah," she said, pushing the door open wide. "Come on in."

The boy had made a real fuss over the kittens, telling her how cute they all were and how he couldn't make up his mind. She was just about to ask him if she couldn't get him something to drink, a glass of lemonade, a Coke, when he'd looked up at his uncle and said, "Could we take two?"

They were in a hurry—he apologized for that—and it was just a chance encounter, but it had stayed with her. (As had three of the kittens, which she hadn't been able to find homes for.) Royce told her he was in real estate and they'd lingered a moment at the door while the boy cradled his kittens and she told him she was looking to buy a duplex, with her parents' help, so the rent on the one apartment could cover her mortgage—like living for free—but she hadn't pushed it and he hadn't either.

Now, as she watched him square up his shoulders at the door, she wondered if he'd recognized her. For an instant her heart stood still—he was going, gone—and then, on an impulse, she broke her pose, set down the book and flicked off the light. In the next moment she was out of the cubicle, a page torn from her book in one hand and her pen in the other, rushing across the cold stone floor of the lobby in her bare feet. She scribbled out a note on the back of the page—*How are the kittens? Call me. Chelsea*—and handed it to Jason, the doorman.

"That guy," she said, pointing down the street. "The one on his cell? Could you run and give this to him for me?" In her rush, she almost forgot to include her number, but at the last second she remembered, and by the time Jason put his fingers to his lips and whistled down the length of the block, she was hurrying back across the lobby to the sanctuary of her cubicle.

It took three cups of coffee to clear his head in the morning, but he was up early all the same and took time to make an omelet for Joey—"No onions, no tomatoes," Joey told him, "just cheese"—before they went out to see to the dogs. The Lab was in her cage outside the door to the barn, still whining, and he didn't even glance at her. He'd have Joey feed her some of the cheap kibble later, but first he had to work Zoltan and Zeus on the treadmills and make sure Zazzie, who'd thrown six pups out of Zeus' sire, the original Zeus, got the feed and attention she needed while she was still nursing. Zeus the first had been a grand champion, ROM, Register of Merit, with five wins, and the money he'd brought in in bets alone had been enough to establish Z-Dogz Kennels—and a dozen or more of his pups were out there on the circuit, winning big in their own right. Royce had never had a better pit dog, and it just about killed him when Zeus couldn't scratch after going at it with Marvin Harlock's Champion Kato for two and a quarter hours and had to be put down because of his injuries. Still, he'd been bred to some sixteen bitches and the stud fees alone had made up a pretty substantial part of Royce's income—especially with the realty market dead in the water the last two years—and Zeus the second, not to mention his brother Zoltan, had won their first matches, and that boded well for stud fees down the road.

The dogs set up their usual racket when he and Joey came in—happy to see them, always happy—and Joey ran ahead to let them out of their cages. Aside from the new litter and Zoltan, Zeus and Zazzie, he and Steve had only three other dogs at the time, two bitches out of Zeus the first, for breeding purposes with the next champion that caught their eye, and a male—Zeno—that had lost the better part of his muzzle in his first match and would probably have to be let go, though he'd really showed heart. For now, though, they were one big happy family, and they all surged round Royce's legs, even the puppies, their tongues going and their high excited yips rising up into the rafters where the pigeons settled and fluttered and settled again. "Feed them all except Zeus and Zoltan," he shouted to Joey over the noise, "because we're going to work them on the mills first, okay?"

And Joey, dressed in yesterday's blue jeans with smears of something on both knees and a T-shirt that could have been cleaner, swung round from where he was bending to the latch on Zeno's cage, his eyes shining. "And then can we bait them?"

"Yeah," he said. "Then we'll bait them."

The first time he'd let Joey watch while they set the dogs on the bait animals, he'd been careful to explain the whole thing to him so he wouldn't take it the wrong way. Most trainers—and he was one of them—felt that a fighting dog had to be blooded regularly to keep him keyed up between matches and if some of the excess and unwanted animals of the world happened to be lost in the process, well that was life. They were just going to be sent to the pound anyway, where some stoner working for minimum wage would stick a needle in them or shove them in a box and gas them, and this way was a lot more natural, wasn't it? He no longer remembered whether it was rabbits or cats or a stray that first time, but Joey's face had drained and he'd had to take him outside and tell him he couldn't afford to be squeamish, couldn't be a baby, if he wanted to be a dog man, and Joey—he was all of nine at the time—had just nodded his head, his mouth drawn tight, but there were no tears, and that was a good sign.

He didn't want to wear the dogs out so close to their next match, so he clocked half an hour on the treadmill, then put Zeus in the pit he'd erected in the back corner of the barn and had Joey bait him with one of the rabbits, after which it was Zoltan's turn. Finally, he took the Lab out of her cage, taped her jaws shut and let both dogs have a go at her, nothing too severe, just enough for them to draw some blood and get the feel of another body and will, and whether it fought back or stood its ground or rolled over to show its belly didn't matter. Baiting was just part of the regimen, that was all. After five minutes, he had to wade in and break Zeus' hold on the animal. "That's enough for today, Joey—we want to save the Lab for maybe two days before the match, okay?"

Joey was leaning against the plywood sides of the pit, his expression unreadable. There was something in his hair—a twig or a bit of straw the dogs had kicked up. He didn't say anything in response.

The Lab was trembling—she had the shakes, the way dogs did when they'd had enough and wouldn't come out of their corner—and one of her ears was pretty well gone, but she'd do for one more go around on Thursday, and then they'd have to answer another ad or two. He bent to the dog, which tried to look up at him out of its good eye but was trembling so hard it couldn't quite manage to raise its head, clipped a leash to its collar, and led it out of the pit. "Put her back in her cage," he told Joey, handing him the leash. "And you can feed and water her now. I'll take care of Zeusy and Zoltan. And if you're good, maybe later we'll do a little Chicken McNuggets for lunch, how's that sound? With that barbecue sauce you like?"

He turned away and started for the house. He hadn't forgotten the note in his pocket—he was just waiting till a reasonable hour (ten, he was thinking) before he called her, figuring she'd been up even later than he and Steve. *Call me,* she'd written, and the words had lit him up right there on the street as if he'd been plugged into a socket—it was all he could do to keep himself from lurching back into the hotel to press his face to the glass and mouth his assent. But that would have been uncool, terminally uncool, and he'd just floated on down the street, Steve ribbing him, all the way to the car. The mystery was the reference to the cats and he'd been trying to put that together all morning—obviously he and Joey must have answered an ad from her at some point, but he couldn't remember when or where, though maybe she did look familiar to him, maybe that was part of it.

He crossed the yard and went in the kitchen door, but Steve was sitting at the table in the breakfast nook, rubbing the bristle of his scalp with one hand and spooning up cornflakes with the other, so Royce stepped out back to make the call on his cell. And then, the way these things do, it all came back to him as he punched in the number: the kittens, a potted bird of paradise on the landing, the condo—or no, duplex—she was looking to buy.

She answered on the first ring. Her voice was cautious, tentative—even if she had caller I.D. and his name came up it wouldn't have meant anything to her because she didn't know him yet, did she?

"Hi," he said, "it's me, Royce, from last night? You said to call?"

She liked his voice on the phone—it was soft and musical, sure of itself but not cocky, not at all. And she liked the fact that he'd been wearing a nice-fitting sport coat the night before and not just a T-shirt or athletic jersey like all the rest of them. They made small talk, Missy brushing up against her leg, a hummingbird at the feeder outside the window like a finger of light. "So," he said after a moment, "are you still interested in looking at property? No obligation, I mean, and even if you're not ready to buy yet, it would be a pleasure, a privilege and a pleasure, to just show you what's out there . . ." He paused. "And maybe buy you lunch. You up for lunch?"

He worked out of an office on a side street off Ventura, not ten minutes from her apartment. When she pulled up in the parking lot, he was there waiting for her at the door of a long dark bottom-heavy Suburban with tires almost as tall as her Mini. "I know, I know," he said, "it's a real gas hog and about as environmentally stupid as you can get, but you'd be surprised at the size of some of the family groups I have to show around . . . plus, I'm a dog man."

They were already wheeling out of the lot, a book of listings spread open on the console between them. She saw that he'd circled a number of them in her price range and the neighborhood she was hoping for. "A dog man?"

"A breeder, I mean. And I keep this vehicle spotless, as you can see, right? But I do need the space in back for the dogs sometimes."

"For shows?"

A wave of the hand. They were out in traffic now and she was seeing him in profile, the sun flaring in his hair. "Oh, no, nothing like that. I'm just a breeder, that's all."

"What kind of dogs?"

"The best breed there is," he said, "the only breed, pit bull terriers," and if she thought to ask him about that, which she should have, she didn't get the chance because he was already talking up the first property he'd circled for her and before she knew it they were there and all she could see was possibility.

Over lunch—he took her to an upscale place with a flagstone courtyard where you could sit outside beneath a huge twisting sycamore that must have been a hundred years old and listen to the trickling of the fountain in the corner—they discussed the properties he'd showed her. He was polite and solicitous and he knew everything there was to know about real estate. They shared a bottle of wine, took their time over their food. She kept feeling a mounting excitement—she couldn't wait to call her mother, though the whole thing was premature, of course, until she knew where she was going to law school, though if it was Pepperdine, the last place, the one in Woodland Hills, would have been perfect. And with the sun sifting through the leaves of the trees and the fountain murmuring and Royce sketching in the details of financing and what he'd bid and how much the attached apartment was bringing in—and more, how he knew a guy who could do maintenance, cheap, and a great painter too, and didn't she think the living room would look a thousand percent better in maybe a deeper shade of yellow, gold, really, to contrast with the oak beams?—she knew she would get in, she knew it in that moment as certainly as she'd ever known anything in her life.

And when he asked if she wanted to stop by and see his place, she never hesitated. "It's nothing like what you're looking for," he said, as they walked side by side out to the car, "but I just thought you'd like to see it out of curiosity, because it's a real sweet deal. Detached house, an acre of property, right up in the hills. My roommate and I, we're co-owners, and we'd be crazy to sell, especially in this market, but if we ever do, both of us could retire, it's that sweet."

The thing was—and he was the one to ask—did she want to stop back at the office for her car and follow him? Was she all right to drive? Or did she just want to come with him?

The little decisions, the little moments that can open up forever: she trusted him, liked him, and if she'd had any hesitation three hours ago he'd more than won her over. Still, when he put the question to her, she saw herself in her own car—and she wouldn't have another glass of wine, though she was sure he was going to offer it when they got there—because in her own car she could say goodbye when she had to and make certain she got to work on time. Which on a Sunday was eight p.m. And it was what, three-thirty now?

"I'll follow you," she said.

The streets were unfamiliar, narrow twisting blacktop lanes that dug deeper and deeper into the hills, and she'd begun to wonder if she'd ever be able to find her way back again when he flicked on his signal light and led her onto a dirt road that fell away beneath an irregular canopy of oaks. She rolled up her window, though it was hot in the car, and followed at a distance, easing her way over the washboard striations that made the doors rattle in their frames. There was dust everywhere, a whole universe of it fanning out from the shoulders of the road and lifting into the scrub oak and mesquite till all the lower leaves were dulled. Mailboxes sprang up every hundred yards or so, but the houses were set back so you couldn't see them. A family of quail, all skittering feet and bobbing heads, shot out in front of her and she had to brake to avoid them. Scenery, a whole lot of scenery. Just as she was getting impatient, wondering what she'd got herself in for, they were there, rolling in under the shade of the trees in front of a low rambling ranch-style house from the forties or fifties, painted a deep chocolate brown with white trim, a barn set just behind and to the right of it and painted in the same color combination.

The dust cleared. He was standing there beside the truck, grinning, and here came the boy—Joey—bouncing across the yard as if he were on springs. She stepped out of her car, smelled sage and something else too, something sweet and indefinable, wildflowers she supposed. From the barn came the sound of dogs, barking.

Royce had an arm looped over Joey's shoulder as they ambled toward her. "Great spot, huh? You want end of the road, this is it. And you should see the stars—nothing like the city where you get all that light pollution. And noise. It's quiet as a tomb out here at night." Then he ducked his head and introduced Joey—or reintroduced him.

The boy was taller than she'd remembered, his hair so blond it was almost white and cut in a neat fringe across his eyebrows. He gave her a quick smile, his eyes flashing blue in the mottled sun beneath the trees. "Hi," she said, "bending to take his hand, "I'm Chelsea. How are you doing?"

He just stared. "Good." And then, to Royce, "Mr. Harlock's been ringing the phone all day looking for you. Where have you *been*?"

Royce was watching her, still grinning. "Don't you worry," he said, glancing down at the boy, "I'll call him first chance I get. And now"—coming back to her—"maybe Chelsea'd like to sit out on the porch and have a nice cold soda—or maybe, if we can twist her arm, just one more glass of that Santa Maria Chard we had over lunch?"

She smiled back at him. "You really have it? The same one?"

"What you think, I'm just some amateur or something? Of course, we have it. A whole case straight from the vineyard—and at least one, maybe two bottles in the refrigerator even as we speak . . ."

It was then, just as she felt her resolve weakening—what would one more hurt?—that the screen door in front sliced open and the other guy, the taller one from last night, stuck his head out. "It's Marvin on the phone," he called, "about next week. Says it can't wait."

"My roommate, Steve," Royce said, nodding to him. "Steve," he said, "Chelsea." He separated himself from her then, spun around on one heel and gestured toward the porch. "Here, come on, why don't you have a seat out here and enjoy the scenery a minute while I take this call—it'll just be a minute, I promise—and then I'll bring you your wine. Which, I can see from your face, you already decided to take me up on, right?"

"Okay, you convinced me," she said, feeling pleased with herself, feeling serene, everything so tranquil, the dogs fallen silent now, not a man-made sound to be heard anywhere, no leaf blowers, no backfiring cars or motorcycles or nattering TVs, and it really was blissful. For one fraction of a moment, as she went up the steps to the porch and saw the outdoor furniture arrayed there, the glass-topped table and the armchairs canted toward a view of the trees and the hillside beyond, she pictured herself moving in with Royce, going to bed with him and waking up here in the midst of all this natural beauty, and forget the duplex—she'd be even closer to school from here, wouldn't she? She settled into the chair and put her feet up.

And then the door slammed and Joey, having bounced in and back out again, was standing there staring at her, a can of soda in his hand. "You want some?" he asked, holding it out to her. "It's good. Kiwi-strawberry, my favorite."

"No, thanks. It's a tempting offer, but I think I'll wait for your uncle." She bent to scratch a spot on the inside of her calf, a raised red welt there, thinking a mosquito must have bitten her, and when she looked up again her eyes fell on the cage standing just outside the barn door in a flood of sunlight. There was a dark figure hunched there, a dog, and as if it sensed she was looking, it began to whine.

"Is that one of your dogs?" she asked.

Joey gave her an odd look, almost as if she'd insulted him. "That? No, that's just one of the bait animals. We've got real dogs. Pit bulls."

She didn't know what to say to that, the distinction he was making—a dog was a dog as far as she was concerned, and this one was obviously in distress. "Maybe it needs water," she said.

"I already watered her. And fed her too."

"You really like animals, don't you?" she said, and when he nodded in response, she added, "And how are the kittens doing? Did you litter-train them? And what are their names—you name them yourself?"

She was leaning forward in the chair, their faces on a level. He didn't answer. He shuffled his feet, his eyes dodging away from hers, and she could see the lie forming there—*bait animals*—even before he shrugged and murmured, "They're fine."

Royce was just coming through the door with two glasses of white wine held high in one hand and a platter of cheese and crackers in the other. His smile died when he saw the look she was giving him.

"Tell me one thing," she said, shoving herself up out of the chair, all the cords of her throat strung so tight she could barely breathe, "just one thing—what's a *bait* animal?"

The darkness came down hard that night. It was as if one minute it was broad day, bugs hanging like specks in the air, the side of the barn bronzed with the sun, and then the next it was black dark. He was out on the porch, smoking, and he never smoked unless he was drunk, and he was drunk now, because what was he going to do with an open bottle of wine—toss it? He hadn't made Joey any supper and he felt bad about that—and bad about laying into him the way he did—but Shana would be here soon to pick him up and she could deal with it. Steve was out somewhere. Everything was still, but for the hiss and crackle of Joey's video game leaching down from the open bedroom window. He was about to push himself up and go in and put something on his stomach, when the Lab bitch began to whine from across the yard.

The sound was an irritant, that was what it was, and he let out a soft curse. In the next moment, and he didn't even think twice about it, he had the leash in his hand. Maybe it didn't make sense, maybe it was too late, but Zeus could always use the exercise. And when he was done, so could Zoltan.

(2010)

In the Zone

People told her she'd get cancer in her bones, that the mice were growing into monsters the size of dogs, that if she planted a tomato or a cucumber in her own garden she wouldn't be able to eat it because of the poison in the ground. And the mushrooms she loved so? The ones that sprouted in the shady places after a rain, the big brown-capped porcini that were like meat in your mouth? They were the worst. They concentrated the poison and put it in your body where it gathered and glowed and killed you dead. Was that really what she wanted? Was she touched in the head?

Well, no, she wasn't. And when the opportunity came to move back to the deserted ruins of her village after living for nearly three years in an inhuman space in a crumbling apartment block for evacuees in Kiev, she took it. Leonid Kovalenko, sixty-seven years old and with a pair of ears as big as a donkey's, who'd been a friend of her late husband, Oleski, and whose wife wouldn't budge from the apartments because she was afraid, knew of a man with a car who knew of a border guard who, for a bribe, would let you in. Back in. Where you belonged. Where the forest was cool and moist and striped with shade and the smoke unfurled from your chimney like a flag all twenty-four hours of the day so that when you went out to the well on a moonlit night you could see it there, a presence, hovering above the roof on the suspired breath of your ancestors.

"How much do you want?" she asked Leonid as they browsed among the inferior cabbages and pulpy potatoes at the market, rutabagas like wet cardboard, overpriced honey in a jar without the comb. "Because I have little."

He shrugged, weighing a cabbage in one hand while rich people, the educated rich and the corrupt rich alike, went by on the street in their automobiles that roared and belched and gave back the sun in glistening sheets of light. "For you?" he mused, gazing at her appraisingly from beneath the overgrown hedges of his eyebrows. He was a hairy man, hair creeping out from beneath his collar and sleeves, curling out of his nostrils and the pits of his great flapping ears, nothing at all like Oleski, who was smooth as a baby till the day he died, but for his private hair and his beard that came in so sketchily it was barely there at all. "For you," he repeated, as if the deal had already been struck, "a little is more than enough."

*

The man with the car was young, in his thirties, she guessed, and he wore a leather jacket like a hoodlum. He smoked the whole time, lighting one cigarette off the other. In place of conversation he had the radio that thrummed and buzzed with a low-level static and snatches of what someone in Prague or Moscow might have called music but to her was just noise. She sat in back with her two bags of possessions while Leonid, his great wide shoulders sagging against the torn vinyl of the seat, sat up front with the driver. It was night. The road was rutted. From the ditches came the sounds of the spring peepers, awakening from the frost to glory in life and love and the spewing of their eggs that were like pale miniature grapes all bound up in transparent tissue. When they came to the checkpoint and the fence that enclosed the Zone of Alienation for thirty kilometers around, the young man got out and conferred with the guard while Leonid lit his first cigarette of the night and shifted in the seat to study her face in the dim light cast by the guard's kiosk. "A small bribe," he said. "Nothing to worry over."

She wasn't worried, or not particularly. Word had it that the Ministry of Emergencies was looking the other way and allowing a small number of people—old people, over fifty only—to return to their villages because they knew no other way of life and because they were expendable. The sooner they died, either from natural or unnatural causes, the sooner their pensions would be released to the state. There were rumors of criminals roaming the Zone, of looters dismantling machinery and mining the deserted apartment blocks of Pripyat, the city closest to the reactor, for television sets and stereos and the like, then smuggling them, radiant with poison, out into the larger world. She didn't care. She peered past Leonid to where the driver was having a laugh with the guard and sharing something out of a bottle. Beyond them was night absolute, the black night of the primordial forest where there were no apartments or automobiles or shops. "I don't like him," she whispered. "I don't like him and I don't trust him."

In the half-light of the car, Leonid's hand, blocky and work-hardened, snaked its way between the front seats to rest ever so lightly on her knee, and that was a revelation to her, that was when she began to understand things in the way the peepers in their ditches understood. Leonid's own bags lay at his feet, two dark humps that were his life compacted. "Everything," he murmured, his voice gone thick in his throat, "is going to be all right."

And then the hoodlum was back in the car and the gate swung aside as if by magic and they were on a road that was no longer a road, jostling and scraping, shrieking through the brush of the dried and dead plants from the years past, dodging fallen trees no one had bothered to cut because there was no one to bother. They hadn't gone more than a mile when the hoodlum tugged violently at the wheel and the car spun round in an exaggerated loop and came to a stop, the motor still ratcheting beneath them. "This is as far as I go," he said.

"But it's still seven miles to the village," Leonid protested. And then, a wheedling tone came into his voice, "Maryska Shyshylayeva is an old woman—don't make her walk all that way. Not in the dark and the cold of night."

Before she knew she was going to speak, the words were out: "I'm sixty-two years old and while I may be stout—I don't deny it—I can out-walk you, Leonid Kovalenko, with your creaky knees and big fumbling feet." She could picture the cabin she and Oleski had built of peeled logs cut from the forest and the thatch they'd laid across the roof that bloomed with wildflowers in the spring—and the stove, her pride, that had never gone cold a day in her life, until the order came to evacuate, that is. "And you too," she said, turning to the black-jacketed driver and honing her voice, "whatever your name is."

*

She hadn't thought to bring a flashlight but Leonid had and that was a good thing because the night was moonless and the road she'd reconstructed in her dreams a hundred nights running all but invisible beneath her feet. It wasn't cold for April, or not particularly, but her breath hung before her like a veil and she was glad of the sweater and cloth coat she was wearing. Out here, the peepers were louder, shrieking as if their lives were going out of them. There were other noises too—the irregular hooting of owls from their hidden perches, a furtive dash and rustle in the brush, and then, startlingly, a sudden rising open-throated cry she'd hadn't heard even the faintest trace of since she was a girl. "Do you hear that?" she said, her feet driving on, the straps of the bags digging into her shoulders.

"Wolves," he said, between breaths. She'd been walking long distances lately to build up her stamina and she didn't feel winded or tired in the least, but after the first mile or so she had to adjust her pace so that he could keep up. He breathed hollowly through his smoker's lungs and in that moment she found herself worrying for him: what if he couldn't make it? What would she do then?

"So the rumors are true," she said. "About the animals returning."

His feet shuffled through the mat of dead grasses that had colonized the cracks of the road. "I'm told there are moose now," he said, pausing to catch his breath. "Roe deer like flocks of sheep, boar, rabbits, squirrels. Like in the time of Adam. Or our grandparents anyway."

She held that picture a moment, even as something scurried across the road ahead of them. She saw her cabin restored to what it was, the deer clustered round, the fields standing high and green, rabbits jumping out of their skins and right into the pot even as she set it on the stove to boil, but then the image dissolved. "What of the poison? They say you can't eat a tomato from your own garden, let alone a rabbit that's grazed here all along—"

"Ridiculous. Rumors, nonsense. They just want to have an excuse to keep us out. What do you think, the meat's going to glow? Nobody can tell, nobody, and if you don't think poachers are feasting on venison and rabbit and goose even now, then you're crazy. We'll eat it, you can bet we will. Just think of it, all that game, all the fish in the lakes and rivers no one's touched in three years now."

She wanted to agree with him, wanted to say that she didn't care about radiation or anything else because we all have to die and the sooner the better, that all she cared about was the peace of the forest and her home where she'd buried her husband fourteen years ago, but she was afraid despite herself. She pictured rats with five legs, birds without wings, her own self sprouting a long furred tail beneath her skirts while the meat shone in the pan as if it were lit from within. The night deepened. Leonid huffed for air. She hurried on.

*

When the order came to evacuate, after the explosion that jolted people from their beds and combusted the sky in the dead hours of the night, after the preternaturally darkened days—nearly a week of them—in which rumors flew and everybody who wasn't in the fields or milking or out in the orchards hovered over their radios, the government sent in troops to force compliance. The core of the reactor was heating up again—there could be a second explosion. It wasn't safe. Everyone must board the buses that rolled through the villages, no exceptions made. Two bags only, that was what the radio said and it was reiterated by the loudspeakers blaring from the jeeps and army trucks that stopped outside each house. What of our things? people wanted to know. What of the livestock, our pets? The government reassured them, one and all, that they would be able to return in three days' time, and that the livestock would be evacuated too. The dogs—and the government didn't reveal this—were to be shot on sight, nearly ten thousand of them across Polissia, for fear of rabies. And the livestock, including her own milk cow, Rusalka, were ultimately to be slaughtered en masse and mixed with the flesh of uncontaminated animals for feeding to luckier dogs and cats living in places were there were no evacuations and life went on as usual.

She believed the voice of the radio. Believed the reports of the invisible poison. Believed what she was told. There was no alternative. She had electricity in the cabin, a loop of wire strung from a pole that connected to another pole and on and on ad infinitum, but no telephone, and so she went in that suspended week when no one knew anything to the cottage of the Melnychenkos to pay for the use of theirs. What had they heard? They'd heard that to the north of them the city of Pripyat stood deserted, all forty-nine thousand inhabitants shunted onto buses and whisked away; beyond that, they knew no more than she. She stood by the stove in the Melnychenkos' front room, the log walls of which were decorated with ikons and pages torn from color magazines, just like her own, and placed a call to her son, Nikolai, the professor of language studies in Kharkov. He would know what to do. He would know the truth. Unfortunately, however, the receiver only gave back a buzz in her ear and when the bus came she carried her two bags up the steps and found a seat among her neighbors.

And so now, in the black hours of night in a haunted place that was the only place she'd ever wanted to be, she trudged up the overgrown road with Leonid Kovalenko, waiting for the light of dawn so that she could see what had become of her life. Had the looters been here? Or the animals? What of her sheets and comforter—her bed? Would there be a place to sleep even? Four walls? A roof? Her father used to say that if you ever wanted to get rid of a barn or a shed or even a house all you had to do was poke a hole in the roof and nature would bring it down for you. Her left shoe began to rub against the place where her toes fought the grip of the worn leather. Her ankles felt swollen and her shoulders burned under the weight of her bags.

Leonid had long since fallen silent, the shaft of his flashlight growing dimmer as they walked on, moving ever more slowly, to his pace. She wanted to leave him behind, maddened by his wheezing and shuffling—he was an old man, that was what he was—and it was all she could do to keep from snatching the flashlight away from him and rushing off into the night. She heard the wolves again, a sound like interference on the radio, starting low and tailing off in a high broken whine. There was a smell of bog and muck and fallow land. She was focusing on putting one foot in front of the other, all the while mentally sorting through her cupboards, the tinned goods there, the rice, flour and sugar she stored in jars on the highest shelf to frustrate the rodents, her spices, her crockery, her cookware, when the sky to the east began to grow pale and she saw the world as it once had been. Five minutes later, hurrying on, no thought for Leonid or his flashlight now, she was there, in her own yard with the spring flowers gone to riot and the apple tree she'd planted herself already in bloom and the dark horizontal lines of the cabin materializing from the grip of the shadows as if she'd never been away at all.

*

That first day was among the happiest of her life. She felt like a songbird caged all these years and suddenly set free, felt giddy, a girl all over again. And the house, the house was a miracle, everything as she'd left it, the smells awakening a thousand recollections, of Oleski, of the good times, the summer nights when the light seemed as if it would never fade, the snowbound winters when the two of them sat playing chess and checkers in front of the stove while the cat purred in her lap and the samovar steamed and the silence was so absolute you could wrap yourself in it. Her bed was still made, though the comforter was damp with mold and the pillowcase slick to the touch, but they could be washed, everything could be washed and no harm done. Of course, there was damage, she could see that at a glance. A pane of glass in the back window lay shattered on the carpet and a birch tree thick around as her waist had fallen against the roof. What had been her garden was now a forest of weeds and saplings, there were mice in the stove and birds nesting atop the cupboard, but the looters hadn't come—they'd stuck to the cities, to Chernobyl and Pripyat—and if you could ignore the dust that lay over everything and the dirt of the spiders and mice and birds, there was nothing a broom and a mop and a good strong back couldn't put to rights.

She was at the stove, arranging sticks of three-year-old kindling in the depths of the firebox, thinking the mice could look out for themselves, thinking she'd warm the place, dry it out, then tape newspaper over the broken pane, boil water to wash the sheets and scrub the tabletop and sink—and here, right at hand, was her sturdiest pot hanging on its hook where she'd left it, ready to receive the soup she would prepare from the pork, cabbage and potatoes she'd brought along and maybe something off the shelves of her larder too because unless the cans had burst they were good, weren't they?—when she heard a noise behind her and turned to see Leonid there, his face drained of everything but exhaustion. He came forward heavily and sank into her armchair. "I just need to rest a moment," he said, his breath leaving him in a thin wheeze that made her think of a child releasing a balloon.

"Rest," she said, her smile blooming so that her cheeks felt flushed with it, "I'll make us tea." And then, because she couldn't contain herself, she swept across the room to plant a kiss on his cheek. "Nobody's been here," she crowed, "nobody at all!"

It was at that precise moment that the hinges of the cupboard below the sink gave a short sharp groan and the slick head and labile shoulders of a weasel emerged, one paw arrested. The animal shot them an indignant look, its body a dun writhe of snakelike muscle flowing from the cabinet to the floor, before it vanished through a hole in the wall no wider around than a wind-drift apple. Leonid caught her eye, grinning himself now, and said, "Nobody?" before they both dissolved in laughter.

*

She fetched water from the well while he fell into a heavy sleep in the armchair, then filled all her pots and stoked the stove till the water came to a furious boil and the room began ever so gradually to take on warmth. Next, she washed her cutting board and knives and all the dishes she could lay hands on, just to remove any hint of grime from them—and the poison, the poison too—then stripped the sheets from the bed and washed them, along with the comforter, in her big tub. In the yard—it was so overgrown with weeds it was as if no one had lived here in a century—she discovered that her clothesline had been snapped in two by a fallen branch, the ends of the frayed rope lying sodden on the ground, but she was able to knot them and hang out the sheets and her comforter in the hope they'd dry by nightfall. When she came back through the door, she found Leonid awake and alert.

"Where's that cup of tea I was promised?" he asked, his voice rising in merriment as if he'd just delivered the punchline of a joke. He was feeling exactly the same way she was, feeling liberated, relieved, as joyful and rejuvenated as if he'd just won the lottery.

She poured them each a cup, but she wouldn't sit down, taking hers to the cutting board, where she began to cube the pork and dice the vegetables and feed them into the pot. There were so many things to do, infinite things, and the funny part of it was that she didn't feel tired at all, though she'd been up all night and walked those seven miles in the dark.

From the armchair, Leonid lifted his voice in supposition: "That's the meat you brought along, isn't it? And the vegetables?"

"What do you think—I shot a boar while you were snoring there in the chair? And sprouted a whole garden outside the window like in some fairy tale?" She turned to face him, hands on her hips, and here was where the doubt crept in, here was where she was glad to have him there with her if only to get a second opinion on the parameters of this tentative new world they were inhabiting. "But the rice in this jar? I'm going to use it, because we are going to have to eke out every bite till we can grow a garden and snare rabbits and catch fish from the river. The poison can't invade glass, can it? Or tins?"

He was on his feet now, setting down the empty tea cup and taking up the broom, which he began to whisk across the floor in a running storm of dust and leaves. Had she really said "we"? As if it were already decided that he wouldn't go home to his own cottage but stay on here with her?

"No," he said, over his shoulder, "I don't think so, not after three years. But anything you've canned, tomatoes, snap beans, we have to be careful if the seal's broken, because then we'll get the real poison, ptomaine or what have you—"

"Yes," she said, cutting him off, "and die fast, right here tonight, instead of waiting for the radiation to do the job."

She'd meant to be funny, or irreverent at any rate, but he didn't laugh. He just went on sweeping till he threw open the door and swept all the litter out into the yard. Then he set the broom carefully aside and said, "I'd better get the saw from my place and cut that birch tree away from the eaves. *We,*" he said, emphasizing the pronoun, "wouldn't want a leaky roof, now would we?"

*

That first night they slept together in her marriage bed, but not as lovers—more in the way of brother and sister, in the way of practicality, because where else would he sleep except between his own slimy sheets in his cottage three quarters of a mile away? In the morning they each had a bowl of soup fortified with rice and then he went out the door and vanished up the road while she busied herself with all manner of things, not the least of which was scrubbing the mold from the walls with the remains of an old jug of bleach. It was past noon, the sun high, birdsong like a symphony, deer nosing through the yard and the evicted weasel sunning itself atop the woodpile, when he returned, pushing a wheelbarrow filled with foodstuffs from his own larder, another set of bedsheets, a fur comforter, his rifle and fishing pole and a coil of rope for snares. And more: there was a dog trotting along behind him. It was no dog she'd ever seen before, not among the pets of her neighbors, or not that she could remember anyway. She regarded it dubiously, its ribs showing like stripes and the scrap of its tail wagging feebly over the scent of the soup drifting out the open door. It was of medium size, not big enough to be a proper watchdog, its coat the color of suet shading to a dark patch over one eye. "We can't keep it," she said flatly. "It'll be a struggle just to feed ourselves."

"Too late," he said, grinning wide. "I've already named him."

"As if that means anything."

"Sobaka," he called, appending a low whistle, and the dog came to him even as he set the wheelbarrow down in the high weeds.

"'Dog'? You've named him 'dog'? What kind of a name is that?"

He was on the doorstep now, proffering the fur, which smelled of ancient history. His ears shone. He was grinning through the gap in his beard, which seemed to have grown even thicker and grayer overnight. Then he took her in his arms, hard arms, lean and muscular, not an old man's arms at all, and squeezed her to him. "What kind of name? The perfect name. Maybe, just maybe, if you behave yourself, Maryska Shyshylayeva, I'll call you 'woman.' What do you think of that?"

And when night came and the lantern burned low, they slept together again, only this time there was no euphemism interposed between them.

*

Time went on. The days broadened. Her garden, planted from the seed packets she'd brought with her from Kiev, grew straight and true, as if it had arisen from virgin soil. Leonid put up wire fencing borrowed from a derelict field to discourage the rabbits and used his rifle on the hogs that stole in to dig up her potatoes, so that the smell of smoking meat hung thick over the yard and attracted a whole menagerie of fox, lynx, raccoon dog, bear and wolf. When the wolves came, and they came as much for the deer crowding the meadows as for the scent of Leonid's meat, Sobaka kept close to the house, and in time he began to thicken around the ribs and haunches and his bark rang out in defiance of the interlopers. He was a superior mouser, better even than the big striped cat—Grusha, that was her name—she'd had to leave behind. Three years was an eon in a cat's life. As soft and old as she'd become, the cat would have been an easy target for a fox or hawk or one of the big white-tailed eagles that had reappeared to soar over the Zone on motionless wings—or the poison, the poison would have gotten her by now, sure it would. Still, if this dog had survived, she couldn't help thinking, maybe Grusha had too. Maybe one day she'd be there meowing at the door as if the calendar had stood still. And wouldn't that be a miracle, among so many others?

The thing was—and she couldn't put this out of her mind—the fact of the poison increasingly seemed less a liability than a benefit. The government that had collectivized all the big farms to the north and east of them and suppressed any notion of individual effort and freedom was gone, withdrawn to the safety of its eternal offices in all the sanitized regions of the country. And the people who for centuries had tamed and beaten and leached the land were gone too, while in their absence the animals had come back to thrive in all their abundance. Neither she nor Leonid had been sick a day—he was leaner now, his shoulders thrust back, his face tanned, and the work of the place had hardened her too so that she'd lost the excess flesh she'd put on in the apartments—and the dire warnings, the predictions of cancers and mutations and all the rest seemed nothing more than wives' tales now. What more would she want? A cow, so they could have dairy. And Grusha returned to her. But she was content, and when she served Leonid a plate of dumplings or *holubtsi,* she saw nothing but love in his face. About his wife, he never spoke a word.

And then one morning as they were lingering over breakfast—porridge, a fresh loaf she'd baked the night before, strawberry preserves she'd put up all those years ago and a pot of the good rich China tea Leonid had discovered in an abandoned house on one of his jaunts through the woods—a strange terrible mechanical sound suddenly erupted out of nowhere and drove down the chatter of the birds and the symphony of the bees. At first she thought the reactor had blown again, thought they were doomed, but then the noise began to settle into a pattern she recognized from long ago: somebody was driving a vehicle down the forgotten street out front of the house.

In the next moment they were both on their feet. They moved as if entranced to the door that stood open to admit the breeze and saw a car there, a jeep with battered fenders and no top and a single man behind the wheel, turning that wheel now and pulling right on up to the door. They couldn't have been more astonished if the premier himself had showed up—or a man from space. Her heart sank. They were going to be evicted, that was it, she was sure of it. But then she got a good look at the man behind the wheel and understood in a flash: it was Nikolai, his face flushed, his blond hair in a tangle, his eyes obscured behind a pair of dark glasses.

"Mama," he said, stepping down from the jeep and coming to her embrace, holding her tight to him in a mad whirling hug. Then there was the awkward introduction to Leonid, whom he knew, of course, from his days here as a boy before he went off to the state school and never returned, and then he was handing her packages, gifts of food from the city and a book by William Faulkner, the American agrarian writer he was forever translating, though she'd told him years ago that the Bible and Chekhov were enough for her.

Oh, but he was fat! Ushering him to the table and fussing over the loaf and his tea, she couldn't help noticing the girth of him that wouldn't allow him to button his shirt around the midsection and the way his cheeks sagged with the weight of easy living. He was thirty-six years old. He was her son, the professor. And in all those days, weeks and months of the three years she was entombed in those apartments, he had visited her exactly once.

At first, they talked of the little things—the weather, the strikes and movements and tragedies of the outside world, the health of his fragile and childless wife—but then, within minutes of his stepping through the door, he started in on the subject he'd come expressly to address, or not simply to address, but to harangue her with: the poison. Did she know the danger she was exposing herself to? Did she understand? Could she imagine? His hands were like balls of butter, his eyes sunk to glittering blue slits in the reddened globe of his face. He pushed the bread aside. He wouldn't touch the tea.

After a moment he snatched up the jar of honey—wild honey, honey they'd collected themselves, with the comb intact—and waved it in her face. "Do you have any idea how radioactive this is? You couldn't poison yourself more thoroughly if you stirred arsenic into your tea. Bees collect pollen, don't you know that? Every grain of it shot through with radionuclides—they concentrate it, Mama, don't you understand?"

There was something attached to his belt, a little machine with a white plastic cover, and he took it up now, depressed the button on top and held it to the jar. Immediately, it began to release a quick breathless high-pitched chirp, as if a field of crickets were trapped inside. "Do you hear that?" he demanded, and he got up from the table to run the little machine across the walls, the plates, the food in the cupboard, and all the while it chirped and chirped again. "That," he said, "is the sound of cancer, Mama, of disease. You're getting it from the environment, from everything you touch, but more than that from the food, the meat, the vegetables in your garden. It's suicide to be here, Mama, suicide, slow and sure."

It was then that Leonid pushed himself up from the table with a sigh and ambled out the door, his bulky frame shimmering in the wash of golden summer light. She was left with her son, the professor, and his little white machine. He ran it over the antlers of the deer Leonid had hung on the wall above the sofa and it screeched out its insectoid warning—"Strontium-90, concentrated in the bones, Mama, in your bones too"—and then over the ashes in the bucket by the stove. "The worst," he said, "the very worst, because the radionuclides are bound up in the wood and when you burn it they're released all over again into the atmosphere. To breathe. For you to breathe. And Leonid. And your dog."

She looked at him bitterly. What was he trying to do—terrify her? Ruin her life? Give her bad dreams so she couldn't sleep at night?

"Mama," he said, and he had his hand on her arm now, "I've come to take you back."

And now she spoke for the first time since he'd brandished his little chirping machine: "I won't go."

"You will."

Suddenly Leonid was back in the room, the dog at his side. He seemed to have something in his hand, an axe handle, as it turned out. Sobaka, who'd slunk away when the jeep approached, stood his ground now and showed his teeth. Leonid said: "You heard your mother."

*

She couldn't sleep that night, imagining the poison in her bones, illuminating her from the inside out like in the X-rays they took of her lungs when she was in the apartments. The rot was working in her and she'd been fooling herself all along. Any day now she'd fall sick—or Leonid would, sinking into himself till the flesh dropped away and she would have to haul him out by his attenuated ankles and bury him beside Oleski. She saw that, saw him dead, even as he lay next to her, oblivious, stretched out like a fallen tree, snoring mightily. She listened to him in the dark and heard the creatures of the night rustling outside the window, and finally, near dawn, fell asleep to the ancient sound of the wolves on their hunt.

Next morning she was up as usual, working in the garden, and when she was done, she cooked, washed and cleaned, no different from any other day, but the heaviness stayed with her. Leonid was tentative around her, as if sensing her thoughts. He brought her a pair of rabbits he'd caught in his snares and then went about doing what he did best: repairing things. She tried to drive down her uneasiness, but it wasn't till late in the day, the rabbits roasting on a bed of onions, carrots and potatoes and the breeze as sweet as a hand on your cheek, that she began to relax. She took a chair out into the yard and sat there in the sun with Leonid, sipping a glass of the *zubrovka* he'd very patiently distilled from bison grass, drop by drop, and thought about one of the stories he'd told her from his time when he'd slipped across the border into Turkey and gone to sea as a merchantman.

He'd had a shipmate from a place called Tobago, an island in a tropical sea, and this man—his skin as weathered and black as an old bicycle horn—had a disease called ciguatera. It came from eating certain reef fishes from his native waters, fishes that accumulated poison in them, and it attacked his nervous system so that he was always twitching and jerking about. All his teeth but one had fallen out and his eyes were affected too, so that he wore the thickest lenses just to see. One day, when they were all on shore leave in a tropical port, Leonid and another shipmate were strolling by a café and saw this man there, a beer in hand, a plate of barracuda set before him. "What are you doing, my friend?" Leonid said. "Don't you realize that barra is the very fish that gives you the disease?" And the man just smiled at him, his mouth full now, and said, "Yes, this I know, but it's de sweetest fish in de sea."

That was it, exactly. And she glanced at Leonid, at his big ears and drooping stolid features, and raised her glass to him. His own glass rose to click the rim of hers and he gave her his broad toothy grin. "To your health," she said.

*

The first frost arrived late that year and when it came to swab the trees with color and shrivel the leaves of her tomato plants, it was immediately succeeded by a brief return to summer, one of those autumn idylls that comes round every once in a lucky year. She was out in her garden under the full force of the sun, harvesting her squash and cucumbers and beans while the pots boiled away on the stove and Leonid gave up all his time to her and the canning that consumed their every waking moment, when she heard the sound of hooves on the road out front. She glanced up, expecting one of the moose or big strutting red deer that thronged the woods and gave her pleasure every time she saw one, but she was surprised. There was a man on the road, a young man in his twenties with the same look as the hoodlum who'd driven the car for them last spring, and for a moment she caught her breath, expecting trouble. But then she saw he was dressed in simple clothes—no boots and leather jacket—and that his face was shaded by the broad-brimmed felt hat of a farmer. Even more surprising—startling, amazing—he was leading two milk cows on a tether, both of them laden with his possessions wrapped up in burlap.

He started when he saw her there, rising from her knees and wiping her hands on her skirts, but then he called out a greeting and in the next moment he was in the yard, coming up the path to her. She didn't know what to do. They'd seen no one since Nikolai, all sense of grace and propriety lost to her, and even as she called out a hello in response, her voice seemed out of practice.

He was no more than twenty feet from her, the cows lurching this way and that on their tether and finally dipping their heads to the grass, when she saw that he wasn't alone. Coming round the bend in the road was a young woman hunched under the weight of a backpack, her blond hair wrapped high on her head and shining in the sun, and behind her were two children, lean and long-legged and striding right along, though they couldn't have been more than seven or eight. "Hello," the man called out again, and now Sobaka was there, barking and showing his teeth, and the figure of Leonid shadowed the doorway, his rifle in hand. "I didn't know anyone was living out here now," the man said, and if the dog intimidated him—or the sight of Leonid in the doorway—he didn't let it show. In fact, he seemed so relaxed he might have been standing in his own yard, with his own dog, and she and Leonid the outsiders.

One of the children let out a cry and then both of them were running across the yard in a bright flash of bare knees and working arms as Sobaka danced round their heels and the young woman strode into the yard behind them to shrug out from under her backpack and set it down in the high grass. "Do you know if the Ilyenok place is still standing?" the woman asked, coming forward till she stood shoulder to shoulder with her husband.

"Ilyenok?" Maryska echoed stupidly, but she could feel something opening up inside her—the notion of what was going on here, what this promised, settling into her brain like a little bird winged down from the trees.

"Aren't you Maryska Shyshylayeva?" the man said, but he was hardly a man—he was an overgrown boy, that was what he was. "I'm Sava, Sava Ilyenok—don't you recognize me?"

In the next moment, Leonid was out of the house, the rifle forgotten, embracing this boy, son of deceased parents, son of the earth, son of the village, come home again. "Yes," Leonid boomed, rocking back from the boy to take in the sight of the pretty young wife and the two children, who were frolicking with the dog now, "we know you, of course we know you, and welcome, welcome!"

And Maryska, coming back to herself, held out her hands in delight. "You must be exhausted," she said. "Come, come in. I've got soup on the stove, hot tea, bread and jam for the children." She paused to gaze longingly on the cows. "But no cheese, I'm afraid."

Husband and wife exchanged a glance, then turned their faces to her. He was the one who spoke. "Oh, I don't know," he said, shrugging his shoulders, "I think we can fix that."

*

When the snow came, the first snow, it was light and wet, limning the bare branches of the poplars and bowing the evergreens. The stove ticked and hissed throughout the day. Everything was still. In the oven was the pheasant Leonid had shot that morning, which she planned to serve with potato dumplings and sour cream. She was reading, for the tenth time, the tenth time at least, the Chekhov story about the peasants and their miserable lives and how one misery propagates another, when she set the book aside and went out into the yard to smell the air and watch the heavy snowflakes whirl down out of the sky.

The trees stood sentinel, black lines etched against the accumulation of snow. A pair of squirrels were busy at the base of the apple tree, darkening the whiteness with their miniature digging. She wasn't worried about herself any longer or about Leonid either, but she did worry for the children, for Ilya and Nadia Ilyenok, and what the days might bring them. What of *their* bones? What of the strontium-90 in the grass the cows chewed all day long? What would Nikolai say about it? He would say that they were crazy, suicidal, that to live in nature under the open sky and walk the earth that gave up everything, even its poisons, was somehow unnatural—as if the apartments, with their crush and stink of humanity, were some sort of heaven.

She was about to turn and go back into the house, to her roasting bird and

Leonid and the *zubrovka* they would sip over the chessboard before dinner, when a movement beside the woodshed caught her eye. There was something there, small, compact, lithe, and at first she thought it was the weasel come back to them, but then she saw her mistake: it was a cat. Gray, striped, with a long fluff of hair and a tail tipped in white.

"Grusha," she called softly, "can it really be you?" The cat—Grusha had been darker, hadn't she?—gave her a long steady gaze before melting away behind the shed. She didn't want to spook it, and so she moved forward very slowly, step by step, but by the time she got there, it was gone, nothing left but fading tracks in a wet snow.

(2010)

Los Gigantes

At first they kept us in cages like zoo animals, but that was too depressing. After a while we began to lose interest in what we'd been brought there to do. We didn't think about it, or not much anyway. We were just depressed, that was all, and when they brought the women to us it was inevitable that we went about the business in a halfhearted way. In any case, it was soon over and then it was time for a meal, another meal. They fed us well, I'll say that for them. No expense was spared. And the food was good, the best I'd ever tasted, prepared for us by a man who was rumored to have been first assistant to the pastry chef at the presidential palace before he was replaced by a Frenchman who didn't speak a word of Spanish.

Originally we were ten, but one of our number was suspect and soon rooted out. It happened that a woman refused to go with him and when Corporal Carrera, who held the keys, wanted to know why, she said, *Just look at him.* And he did. We all did. (This was during the first week when we really hadn't had a chance to get to know one another yet and no one had given the man much thought. Why would we? We were being fed. We had women. Life was good.) Anyway, once this woman had spoken up we all began to scrutinize him and saw what she meant: he was damaged goods. He was tall enough, three or four inches taller than me, in fact, and thick in the limbs, but his face was like an anvil and his eyes couldn't seem to focus. And when he talked it was in disconnected monosyllables that seemed to dredge themselves up out of some deep fissure in his digestive tract. The man in the cage beside mine whispered, "Pituitary freak," and in that instant I saw what I'd missed. Yes: damaged goods. No sense in wasting the stipend, the ex-assistant pastry chef's culinary concoctions and all those prescribed women on him. I felt a sense of outrage that was as much about my own humiliation as anything else: whoever had chosen him had chosen me too, and what did that say about me?

Even worse, for the first time in my life I had to contend with the fact that I wasn't the biggest man around. At six feet ten inches and four hundred and twenty-odd pounds I wasn't far off, but there were two men heavier, in addition to the pituitary case (freak or not, he'd still looked down at me). All my life I'd been the one looking down on the world, the biggest boy and then the biggest man not only in my own bustling port city but in the entire province. I was strong too. At the Fiesta de Primavera I once lifted two sheep above my head, one in each hand, and for a prank when I was in my teens I hauled the Mayor's shining black Duesenberg coupe up the steps of the Ministry of Justice and left it there at the feet of the gilded statue of the President. By the time I turned twenty I was earning a good wage cranking the capstan that lifted the wooden drawbridge in the center of town so that the high-masted fishing vessels could pass beneath it—and if that seems unremarkable, just consider that formerly three mules had been required to do the job, mules that were now free to pull plows through the fields of maize that ring the city, while the muleskinner himself was able to retire on a small pension and move into the house his mother had left him at the place where the river runs brown into the moss-green sea. People would come out to watch me work—families with picnic baskets, nubile women, strongmen, grandmothers, sailors. My legend grew. Of course, to be a legend, to attain that status, is to court attention. That was how they found me. And truly? I wish they never had.

Within the month the first rumors of discontent began to circulate among us. If in the beginning it had seemed as if we'd arrived in paradise, our days given over to leisure and nothing expected of us but the essentials, the routine began to wear on us. We were free to roam the compound by day and we had books and a communal radio and we played games of cards and dice, the usual sort of thing, but we were locked in at night, and the cages—though they were roomy enough and each equipped with a toilet, desk, couch and reading lamp in addition to a gargantuan steel-frame bed—were an oppression of the spirit. The man I was to become closest to—Fruto Lacayo, a former circus fat man who stood seven inches shorter but outweighed me by some forty pounds—was the first to voice his complaints.

We were in the courtyard one afternoon, smoking, chatting, getting our bearings in this place that was not, despite appearances, a former zoo, but in fact a camp where the regime had kept dissidents in a time before dissidence had been so radically discouraged as to eliminate it altogether. Fruto had been pacing along the path that traced the outer walls under the beneficent gaze of the guard in the tower (who wasn't a guard at all, we were told, but rather a *facilitator*) when he came directly across the courtyard to where I was sitting in the shade with the latest issue of *Hombre,* examining the photographs of the slim-ankled women who stared out from its pages with looks of air-brushed longing. "Jesus Christ," he muttered, gasping for breath, "I feel like my joint's about to fall off."

I gave him a wary smile. He was a fat man. I was a giant. And if you don't see the distinction, then you have no access to my soul and no appreciation either. I shrugged. "Better than working, isn't it?"

There was a sheen of sweat on his jowls. It was winter then, thank the Lord and the Blessed Virgin, but still the humidity was high and the afternoon temperatures were in the eighties and even nineties so that we were always uncomfortable, especially where our parts chafed. "I'm not so sure," he said. "It's these cages. We're not animals."

"No," I said, "we're not."

"Do you know what the President did before he joined the army—professionally, I mean?"

I didn't. He'd been president before I was born and I expected he'd be president still when I moved on to the next world.

Fruto winked, as if he were letting me in on a great secret. "You don't? You really don't?"

I shook my head.

"Well, let me tell you, let me awaken you: he was a cattle breeder."

The initial breakout wasn't a serious attempt—it was perfunctory, at best—but at least it made a statement, at least it was a beginning. Early one night, after we'd lain with the evening's women and were gathered around the radio in the courtyard half-listening to the tail end of one of the President's speeches (rumba music, that was what we wanted, and "Rumba Ciudad" was due to come on at eight), Fruto heaved himself up from his chair, and addressing us all, growled, "I don't know about you, but I've had it. I'm going home. Tonight. Soon as it's dark."

There was a flutter of astonished voices: *You can't be serious! Have you gone mad? Leave here?* Melchior Arce, a former stevedore who was nearly as wide across the shoulders as me though his head was disproportionately small and his left hand had been mangled in an accident so that it looked like a crushed tarantula dangling from his shirtsleeve, gave a whistle of surprise. "The only way they'll get me out of here," he said, "is in a coffin." He paused to bite off the end of his cigar and spit it in the dirt. "What's wrong with you, fat man—you a *maricón*?"

"You want to know the truth?" Fruto went on, ignoring the insult. "I don't like big women. Never have. I like them petite, the way women should be—if I want to see fat I can just look in the mirror."

If I'd been feeling the stirrings of my own discontent, now I went rigid with longing: all I could see was the face of Rosa, my Rosita, the girl I'd left behind when I'd signed the agreement and come all the way across the country to be cooped up here in this stifling compound with its jungle reek and chicken-wire cages that showed us for what we really were. Rosita was petite by any measure, a hundred pounds, if that, and an inch short of five feet. I too had always been attracted to the sleek and unencumbered, to the girls who looked more like children than women, and why was that? Because opposites attract, of course they do—otherwise we'd all be pygmies or giants instead of something proportional, something in between. I'd asked her to wait for me. *I'll be gone six months,* I told her, *a year at most. And we'll save the stipend—every penny of it—so we can be married when I come back.* She asked what the government wanted of me—pressed me, over and over—but I couldn't tell her. *Secret work,* I'd said. And she'd looked up at me out of her saucer eyes, beseeching, wanting more, the truth. *Top secret,* I said. *For the military.*

But now, as soon as Fruto spoke the words, I knew I was going with him. We gathered a few things—sliced meat, bread, chocolate bars left over from dinner—and waited till lights out at ten, when the nocturnal clamor of the jungle rose to a crescendo and our fellow *gigantes,* exhausted from their venereal labors, turned over in their massive beds and began to snore. Then we made our way across the courtyard to the main gate, which was secured by a padlocked chain doubled over on itself. The guard was asleep. Nothing moved but for a solitary rat silhouetted against the faint glow of the village that lay three miles to the west of us. I took hold of the chain in the grip of my two hands and snapped it without even trying (it was nothing, a child's toy, a poor weak thing designed to forestall ordinary men), and then I rolled back the gate on its lubricated rail and in the next moment we were outside in the darkness.

The problem was Fruto. We hadn't gone five hundred yards down the dirt lane that would take us to the village where there were taxis, buses, even a rail line that would give us access to the whole of the country, to freedom, to the slim and beautiful, to Rosita, when he sat ponderously on a wet stump overgrown with black twisted vines and, wheezing heavily, croaked, "I can't go on."

"Can't go on? What are you talking about? We just left the place!" I crushed mosquitoes against the back of my neck. Something flapped across the darkened road.

"Give me a minute. Let me catch my breath." I could barely make out the shape of him there in the dense clot of shadows. I heard him slapping at his own host of mosquitoes. "You don't have one of those sandwiches handy, do you?" he asked.

"Look," I said, "if we expect to get out of this, to go home—you do want to go home, don't you?—we'll need to get to the village and purchase a bus ticket or hire a taxi and be gone before they bring in the morning's women."

"Go on without me," he said. The air seemed to tear through his lungs. "I'll follow you after I've had a bit of rest. And a sandwich. Let's split up the provisions now. Just in case."

"In case of what?"

"In case we don't meet up again."

So I left him there. It was no less than he deserved. The worst that would happen was that they would take him back to his cage, to food and leisure and the manipulation of the flesh. For my part I made it as far as the village, where I found myself distracted by the lights of a cantina. I had to duck to get through the door. Everyone stared. I should say in my own defense that I'm not one of these men who drink themselves senseless, but they didn't allow us liquor in the compound—for fear it would affect our performance, I suppose—and the taste of it after more than a month without made me want another taste and another after that. I slept somewhere, I don't remember where. And in the morning, when they came for me, I went along with them as docilely as one of the sheep I'd lifted above my head as if they were no more than woolly clouds trailing across a serene blue sky.

The following afternoon, after we'd eaten our lunch and ministered to the women who joined us each day at siesta time, Fruto and I were summoned to the military barracks on the far side of the village. A truck painted in camouflage colors took us through town (ordinary men, ordinary women, bicyclists, street vendors, dogs that were so ordinary even the bitches that whelped them wouldn't have given them a second glance) and into another compound, this one made of whitewashed brick, with a three-story building at the center of it. Corporal Carrera led us up the stairs and into a big office on the second floor that was presided over by a monumental oil portrait of the President and a dozen limp flags representing each of the country's provinces. There was a bank of windows, spilling light. Beneath them stood a mahogany desk, very grand in size, though to us it was like the sort of thing children make use of in elementary school, and seated at the desk, in full military uniform replete with epaulettes and layered decorations, was a man we recognized as Colonel Lázaro Apunto, Director of Educational and Agricultural Resources for the Western Region. There were no seats for us, or no seats large enough, and so we were made to stand.

A long moment elapsed, Corporal Carrera stationed at the door, the Colonel gazing up at us with a look caught halfway between irascibility and awe. Finally, he spoke. "So, I'm given to understand that you two have been abrogating your patriotic duties, is that correct?"

I said, "Yes, that is correct."

"You have complaints—legitimate complaints?"

This started Fruto going in the way that a molded steel crank, in the hands of the President's chauffeur, might fire up a balky engine. "We are not animals," he said, "and we want our privacy. We can't be expected to be, be *intimate,* in a chicken-wire cage where anyone can see for himself how we go about our business, and the heat is intolerable. And the insects. And—"

"And the food?" the Colonel asked, cutting him off. "Is that not of the highest order, rich in protein, flavorful? And your stipends, the money we send on each week to your families—your loved ones, whose home addresses we scrupulously maintain—aren't they sufficient? And what of work? It's not as if we're asking you to work."

"The food is excellent," I said, stifling the impulse to append *Your Excellency* to the assessment.

"Good," the Colonel sighed, leaning back in his chair, "very good." He was a little man, with mustaches. But then they were all little men, everyone in the military, everyone on the street, even the President himself. "For a moment there I'd thought you were going to renege on your contract with the government, but here I see the whole matter is nothing really, just a question of adjustments. You want stucco walls built over the chicken wire? Fine. It will not be a problem. In fact"—he scrawled something on a pad—"we'll see to it immediately."

"Tile floors," Fruto put in. "For the sake of the coolness on our feet. A fan. Two fans. And a radio in each—*room*—and, and a day off. Once a week. Sundays. Sundays off." He bowed his head, mopped sweat. His grin was like a grimace. "The day of rest, eh? Our Lord's day."

The Colonel tented his fingers, smiled benignly at us. He waved a hand. "All this can be arranged. Your needs are our needs. If you haven't already divined the importance of the project in which you're participating, let me enlighten you. The President—the country—has many enemies, I don't have to tell you that. They are building up their armed forces, constantly building and accelerating, and who can guess what their purposes are—but we must counter them. Do you know your Greeks?"

"Greeks?" I echoed, mystified.

"Homer. Aeschylus. Euripides. They had their heroes, their champions, their Achilleses and Ajaxes, and that is what the President envisions for our country's forces—and not simply individual heroes but an entire regiment of them, do you see?"

"Like Samson?" Fruto put in.

The Colonel shot him a look. "Not the Hebrews, the *Greeks.* They knew how to win a war."

"The President must be a very patient man," I offered. "It'll take generations."

A shrug. " 'Prescient' is the word. That is why he is the father of our country. And don't concern yourself: we will breed the issue of your labors—the females, that is—once they reach puberty. And when that issue reaches puberty, we will breed them as well." He fumbled for something on his desk, sifting through the papers there until he held up a single sheet, transparent in the light glazing the windows. "Do you see this? This is a sample requisition form to be sent out to the boot makers of the future, calling for boots in exactly your size, señor, eighteen, triple E. Just think of it." He settled back in his chair. "Helmets the size of birdbaths, jerseys like tents. No, my friends, the President is a man of foresight, a futurist you might say, and his vision is all-encompassing. Are you not proud of your country? Do you not want, with all your heart, to protect and nourish her?"

Fruto stood there dazed. I nodded in assent, but it was only for show. Was I seething inside? Not just then, perhaps—we'd already had a pretty fair idea of what was wanted from us and we had, after all, signed on the dotted line, as venal as any other men—but I could see the months to come, years even, stretching out before me like a sentence in the penitentiary.

Corporal Carrera pulled open the door behind us, our signal to vacate the room: our business here was concluded. But just as we reached the door, my legs working autonomously and Fruto heaving for breath and wiping at his massive face with the great sopping field of his handkerchief, the Colonel called out to us. "Now go and do your duty, for the love of your country and of the President. Go to your female volunteers—whose stipends are but half of yours, incidentally, and so it should be—and, in your throes, think of him."

The Colonel was as good as his word. Improvements came rapidly, laborers from the village appearing the very next day to reinforce the frames of the cages with four-by-four posts, enclose them in walls of lath and stucco and lay tile in a handsome herringbone pattern you could stare at for hours. There were tin roofs. Each of us got a radio. At night, electric fans stirred the breezes and mosquito netting held the insects at bay. I'd volunteered to help with the work—let's face it, I was bored to the point of vacuity with all that sitting around—but the Colonel wouldn't hear of it. "No," he said, on one of his inspections of the compound. "You must conserve your energy"—and here the hint of a smile appeared beneath the dark cantilever of his mustaches—"for your President and your country."

In the interim, we were bused to the women's compound, which, as it turned out, lay some three miles to the north of the men's facility, on the banks of a nameless oozing watercourse that bred mosquitoes and stinging flies in the pestilent millions so that we were all of us, men and women alike, scratching furiously the entire time we were there. What distinguished their compound from ours, aside from the increase of insects? Not much. They too lived in cages, but they were crammed in, four or five of them to a cage, and their camp stretched as far as the eye could see. If we were nine, the women numbered in the hundreds, and this of course reflected a simple calculus any cattle breeder could have worked out on a single sheet of paper.

The women I was put in with the first night were among the biggest in the camp, selected especially for me. And by big I don't necessarily mean the heaviest—such women were reserved for Fruto and his ilk—but the tallest and broadest, with the longest limbs and thickest bones. These women could have felled forests, collapsed mines, held back the sea just by linking arms. Where the President had found them, I couldn't imagine—not till one of them called me by name.

I'd just set down my overnight bag and taken possession of the bed, as uninterested in these women as I'd been in the phalanxes that had trooped in and out of my cage at the men's compound, when one of them broke ranks and came across the dirt floor to me, my name on her lips. She was Magdalena Duarte, she'd been raised in the city I called home and—in a shy voice—told me she'd often come to the drawbridge to watch me at work when she was just a girl. "Before my growth spurt," she said, covering her mouth with one hand as she laughed at her own joke.

Later, after we'd coupled by rote while the insects whined and the other women, utterly indifferent, unfurled straw mats and lay down to sleep, she asked me how I was adjusting to my new role in life. Did I like it?

"Anything for the President," I said.

Her voice was soft, with a scratch in it. "All work and no play, eh?"

"Something like that. But what of you—do you like serving your country?"

I could just make out her features in the light of the guard tower where it fell across the wire mesh of the cage. She glowed a moment, her face like a moon rising over a dim horizon. "They move us to a nicer place once we're pregnant," she said. "And the stipend is all my parents have to live on in these times. You see, I come from a large family"—she caught herself, giggled softly—"of many children, that is, thirteen of us, and so when the recruiter came to us, I did my duty. To the President, yes, and to my family as well."

I was quiet a moment, thinking about that—duty—when she dropped her voice even lower and whispered: "You know, there's another compound. Two other compounds."

"No," I said, "I had no idea." Beside us, in the dark, the giantesses heaved and blew and let their stertorous snores crash through their dreams.

"For little people."

"Little? What do you mean little?" Forgive me if in that moment I thought of Rosa, my Rosa, my Rosita, and her perfect diminutive feet that were the size of a child's, of her mouth, her lips, the way she would tease me good-naturedly every time I had to bend double and squeeze sideways through a doorway or avoid the chairs in her parents' parlor for fear of splintering them.

"Not dwarves, not midgets—the President wants normal stock only—but people who, by the grace or whim of God, are very fine and very small." She left the thought hanging there, the darkness seizing me, the mosquitoes raging till the furious cacophony of their wings drove down every sound in that place.

"But why? Why would he want—*little* people?"

I couldn't see anything but her face in the mosaic shadow of the wire, but I could feel her shrug animate the mattress. "They say he wants to create a race no more than two feet high and normal in every other way, intelligent, active, people like cats who can come and go in the night without detection."

"Spies?"

Another shift of the mattress. She was nodding now. "Our fatherland has many enemies," she said, whispering still, as if fearful of being overheard. "We must be ready for them."

I couldn't sleep that night, not a wink, not after what Magdalena had told me. I kept picturing Rosa in a camp like this one, stepping into a cage where a wiry little man like a human Chihuahua lay waiting for her, though I knew it was absurd. Rosa was an innocent. She would never volunteer, never allow herself to be conscripted no matter what pressures were brought to bear. Or would she? Would she feel moved in her heart (in her loins!) to serve her country like all these patriotic women laid out snoring in the darkness around me? The thought seared me, burned in my brain like the perpetual flame illuminating the grave of our President's lamented mother. It was dawn by the time I finally dozed off, my dreams poisoned and my heart constricted as if a noose had been drawn tight around it.

After that, I bided my time, and when they moved us back to our new apartments in the men's compound—the very night—I broke out again. This time I went straight for the bus terminal and soon experienced the giddy release of the wheels revolving beneath me as a dark curtain of vegetation lurched past the windows and the striped margins of the road home came clear in the first light of dawn. What I didn't yet appreciate was that after our first abortive attempt at escape the Colonel had issued an alert to all carriers to be on the lookout for any big man seeking passage out of the province. They were waiting for me at the end of the line.

Did I go quietly? No, I didn't. When I saw them there in their Black Maria with its chopping blue light, I came down off the bus like a hurricane and laid that vehicle over on its roof till the men it contained came crawling out the windows and I snatched them up two at a time and flung them behind me like so many paper dolls. Sadly, they'd anticipated me here too, and their chloroform canisters brought me down as swiftly and surely as if I were that king ape in the cinema show we'd all marveled at in simpler times, when the images played across the screen like waking dreams and Rosa breathed quietly at my side.

I awoke in a damp subterranean place that smelled of the raw dirt of the floor and the whitewash slathered over the rough stone of the walls. Here was a huge vault of a room, lit dimly by a pair of gray bulbs in wall sconces, a silent place where no one would hear my cries of outrage or pleas for freedom. I was laid out on my back on one of the big industrial-strength beds, and my hands and ankles were bound up in chains—and not merely run-of-the-mill chains, but the heavy steel links they use to moor boats in the harbor of my ancestral home by the sea. It took me no more than sixty seconds to intuit where I was—that is, in the basement of the three-story brick building where the Colonel had his offices overlooking the poor huts and open sewers of the village beyond. If I listened carefully I could hear the sound of footsteps on the floor above and of a chair rolling back and forth on its casters. I tugged at my chains, of course, but they held me fast, secured not to the posts of the bed but to the great ceiba pillars that rose out of the shadows at the four corners of the room to disappear in the ceiling above.

Almost as soon as I opened my eyes a door swung to at the far end of the room and a woman entered bearing a tray of food. She was of average height and weight, this woman—no Amazon—and as I soon discovered, it was her task to spoon-feed me as I lay there under the burden of my chains. "Release me," I whispered, but she shook her head. "Just one hand—so I can eat. I feel like an infant lying here. Please. I beg you." She shook her head again and pressed a spoonful of the rich seafood stew we know as *zarzuela* to my lips. If I'd had any notion of refusing it, of going on a hunger strike in protest of the way I was being treated—*mistreated*—the scent and taste of that *zarzuela* drove it away. You can't begin to imagine what it takes to fuel the cells of this body that entraps me. I ate. Ate hungrily and gladly.

And then the women started coming to me, three a day, morning, afternoon and evening, the big women, the giantesses, lowering themselves over me as I lay chained and helpless beneath them. Did I want to perform the act? No. But I was devoured by lust, perpetually aroused, no matter that I was rebelling inside or that I found the women gross and the task odious. They must have been putting something in my food—one of the coarse brown powders easily attainable at any Chinese herbalist's shop, the ground horn of the rhinoceros or the friable bones of the tiger infused in alcohol. The women came. I stared at the ceiling. My rage grew.

It must have been the third or fourth day when the Colonel appeared. He was seated in a wicker chair drawn up to my bed as I awakened one afternoon from a bludgeoning dream and he began lecturing me without preliminary. "You may be interested to know," he said, "that you've obtained excellent results, superior, the best of your cadre."

"Release me," I said, my voice tense and caught deep in my throat.

He was studying a notepad. He took a minute to smooth the top sheet with his fingers. "Some seventy-six percent of the women you've"—he broke off, searching for the right phrase—"*been with* have become impregnated. Congratulations."

"If you release me, I promise, I swear on my mother's soul, that I will do my duty without complaint, without—"

He held up a hand. "Speaking of your mother, she's doing very well for herself, better than she's ever done in all her life, thanks to the stipend you're providing. She appreciates your service, as does the President." Here he leaned in close to me and I saw that a small glittering object was dangling by a ribbon from his right hand—a medal, such as the military doles out to its heroes. In the next moment I felt the pressure of his fingers as he pinned it to the breast of my shirt. "You'll be released in good time," he said, "so that you can go back to the compound where you'll be more comfortable, but we all feel that for the present, given your, what shall we say, recalcitrance, not to mention dereliction of duty, you'll be better off here. Really, it's for your own good. And the President's too, that goes without saying."

Later, in my boredom and the solitude that ground me down till my consciousness floated free—*Rosa, Rosa, where are you?*—I shifted my neck and forced my head as far back against the pillow as it would go so that I was able to squint down the vast slope of my chest and get a look at the medal the President had devised as a token of his gratitude. Dangling from the ribbon was a figure cast in metal—either gold or brass, I never did discover which. It took me a moment—squinting, as I say—to see what it represented: a bull, rampant, with a thin golden puff of steam spewing from his nostrils.

That was it. That was the end. I didn't care what became of me after that, but I knew then that I hadn't been born on this earth to serve anybody, let alone the President, that I didn't love him, didn't even know him, and that the rage building in me, beat by beat, was a force no man could contain, not even a giant. I waited till the mute who served me had left with the remains of the evening meal and the last giantess had done with me and waddled her way out the door, and then I went deep inside myself, working like a Hindu fakir through every cell of my body, from my smallest toes to the truncheons of my legs and my torso that was like a bucket of iron and on up to my shoulders, my biceps and forearms and down into the reservoirs of my fingers, one digit at a time.

Then I began worrying the chain that bound my right arm, thrusting and jerking back again, over and over, through a thousand repetitions, till finally it gave way and the arm was free. After that, it was easy. I came up off the bed, chains rattling loose around me, telling tales, and if the guard who must have been watching through a hidden peephole came hurtling into the room, I barely noticed. I could have gone through the door and taken the guard with me, but I didn't. No, I just leaned into the nearest pillar and shoved till the whole edifice began to quake and quake again.

That was six months ago. I wasn't blinded, no one cut my hair, and when the building came down around me—inferior construction; the termites would have got to it if I hadn't—I found a pocket of air trapped beneath a beam and was spared. I dug my own way out and if the authorities presumed I was buried beneath the rubble, along with the Colonel and his functionaries and the great glistening oil portrait of the President, I wasn't about to disabuse them. This time I avoided public transport, making my way home in the depths of a freight car designed to carry livestock from one place to another.

Rosa and I escaped to the high fractured plains caught fast in the mountains that separate our country from that of our enemies to the south, where we are living now as man and wife in a village populated by Indians whose teeth are eroded by the leaves they chew to give them energy in the high altitudes where they must scrape a poor living from the earth. I earn my own keep here through main strength, as I always have, hauling loads up and down the stony trails that vanish around each bend and drop off thousands of feet to the distant featureless land below. Am I a beast of burden? Yes. But I'm nobody's beast but my own. And Rosa's. Rosa is pregnant now, incidentally, and if we're lucky she'll bear our first son come spring, and if we're even luckier he'll be neither giant nor dwarf, but something in between. As for me, I try to keep my head down and avoid attracting notice, but inevitably they'll find me, I know that. How could anybody, let alone a man like me, expect to blend in in a land where the people are so very, very small?

(2011)

The Way You Look Tonight

He was in the teachers' lounge, seven-fifteen a.m., sipping the latte he'd picked up on his way to work and checking his e-mail before classes started, when he clicked on a message from his brother Rob and a porno filled the screen. His first reaction was annoyance, shading rapidly through puzzlement to fear—in the instant he recognized what it was (a blur of color, harsh light, movement) he hit escape and shot a look round the room to see if anyone had noticed. No one had. The lounge was sparsely populated at this hour, and those who were there were sunk deep inside themselves, staring into their own laptops and looking as if they'd been drained of blood overnight. It was Monday. The windows were dark with the drizzle that had started in just before dawn. The only sound was the faint clicking of keys.

All of a sudden he was angry. What had Rob been thinking? He could be fired. Would be. In a heartbeat. The campus was drug-free, alcohol-free, tobacco-free, and each teacher, each year, was required to take a two-hour online sexual harassment course, just to square up the parameters. Downloading porn? At your workplace? That was so far beyond the pale the course didn't even mention it. His fingers trembled over the keys, his heart thumped. He clicked on the next message—some asinine joke his college roommate had sent out to everybody he'd ever known, all thirty or so of them with their e-mail addresses bunched at the top of the screen—and deleted it before getting to the punchline. Then there was a reminder from the dentist about his appointment at three-thirty, after school let out, and a whole long string of the usual sort of crap—orphans in Haiti, Viagra, An Opportunity Too Unique To Miss Out On—which he hammered with the delete key, one after another, with a mounting irascibility that made Eugenie McCaffrey, the math teacher, look up vaguely and then shift her eyes back to her own screen. Rob had left no message, just the video. And the subject heading: *I Thought You'd Want To Know.*

By lunch he'd forgotten all about it, but when he checked his phone messages there was a text from Rob, which read only: *??????* Sandwich in hand, the noontime buzz of the lounge reverberating round him—food, caffeine, two periods to go—he called Rob's number, but there was no answer and the message box was full. Of course. He summoned his brother's face, the hipster haircut, the goofball grin, eyes surfing the crest of some private joke—when was he going to grow up?—then dialed Laurie at work because it came to him suddenly that they were supposed to go out to dinner tonight with one of her co-workers and her husband, whom he'd never met, and he was wondering how that might or might not interfere with the football game on TV, but she didn't answer either.

Then the day was over and he was in his car, heading to the dentist's. The drizzle had given way to a drifting haze that admitted the odd column of sunlight so that the last he saw of the school, for today at least, was a brightly lit shot of glowing white stucco and orange-tile roof rapidly dwindling in the rearview mirror. Traffic was light and he was fifteen minutes early for the dentist, whose office was on the second floor of a vaguely Tudorish building that anchored an open-air mall—bank below, Italian restaurant with outdoor seating bottom floor left, then a realtor and a sandwich shop and on and on all the way round the U-shaped perimeter. A patch of lawn divided the parking lot. There were the usual shrubs and a pair of long-necked palms rising out of the grass to let you know you weren't in Kansas, appearances to the contrary.

He debated whether to drift over to the sandwich shop for a bite of something, but thought better of it, remembering the time the dentist had chastised him in a high singsong voice because he hadn't brushed after lunch, the point of which had escaped him, since he'd been coming in to get his teeth cleaned in any case. The thought made him shift the rearview and pull back his lips in a grimace to study his gums and then work a fingernail between his front teeth, after which he took a swig of bottled water and swished it around in his mouth before rolling down the window and spitting it out. That was just the way he was, he supposed—the kind of person who did what was expected of him, who wanted to smooth things out and take the path of least resistance. Unlike Rob.

It was then that he thought of the video. He looked round him, his blood quickening, but no one was paying any attention to him. The cars on either side were empty and the only movement was at the door of the bank, where every few minutes someone would come in or out and the guard stationed there (slab-faced, heavy in the haunches, older—forty, forty-five, it was hard to say) would casually nod his head in recognition. Shielding the laptop with the back of the seat and the baffle of his own torso, he brought up the video—porn, he was watching porn right there in the dentist's parking lot where anybody could see, and he wasn't thinking about students or students' parents or the rent-a-cop at the bank or the real thing either, because all at once the world had been reduced to the dimensions of the screen on the seat beside him.

He saw an anonymous room, a bed, the incandescence of too-white flesh and the sudden thrust of bodies cohering as the scene came into focus. In the center of the bed was the woman, on all fours, the man standing behind her and working at her, his eyes closed and his face drawn tight with concentration. The woman had her head down so that her own face was hidden by the spill of her hair, red-gold hair parted in the middle and swaying rhythmically as she rocked back into him. He saw her shoulders flex and release, her fingers spread and wrists stiffen against the white field of the sheets, and then she lifted her head and he saw her face and the shock of it made something surge up and beat inside of him with a fierce sudden clangor that was like the pounding of a mallet on a steel rail. He watched as she stared into the camera, her eyes receding beneath the weight of the moment—Laurie's eyes, his wife's—and then he slapped the screen shut. *I Thought You'd Want To Know.*

For a long moment he sat there frozen, unable to move, unable to think, the laptop like a defused bomb on the seat beside him. He wanted to look again, wanted to be sure, wanted to feel the surge of shock and fear and hate pulse through him all over again, but not now, not here. He had to get home, that was all he could think. But what of the dentist? Here he was in the parking lot, staring up at the bank of windows where Dr. Sedgwick would be bent over his current patient, finishing up with the pads and the amalgam and all the rest in anticipation of his three-thirty appointment. But he couldn't face the dentist now, couldn't face anybody. He was punching in the dentist's number, the excuse already forming on his lips (food poisoning, he was right out there in the lot, but he was so sick all of a sudden he didn't think he could, or should . . . and maybe he'd better make another appointment?), when he became aware that there was someone standing there beside the car window. A girl. In her twenties. All made up and in a pair of tight blue pants of some shiny material that caught the light and held it as she bent to the door of the car next to his while another girl clicked the remote on the far side and the locks chirped in response. She didn't look at him, not even a glance, but she was bending over to slip something off the seat, on full display, every swell and cleft and crease—inches from him, right in his face—and all at once he was so infuriated that when the dentist's secretary answered in her bland professional tone he all but shouted into the phone, "I can't make it. I'm sick."

There was a pause. Then the secretary: "Who is this? Who's speaking, please?"

He pictured her, a squat woman with enormous breasts who doubled as hygienist and sometimes took over the simpler procedures when Dr. Sedgwick was busy with an emergency. "Todd," he said. "Todd Jameson?"

Another pause. "But you're the three-thirty—"

"Yeah, I know, but something's come up. I'm sick. All of a sudden, and I—" The car beside him started up, the long gleaming tube of the chassis sliding back and away from him, and there was the lawn, there were the palm trees, but all he could see was Laurie, the way her fingers stiffened on the sheets and her eyes went on gazing into the camera but didn't register a thing.

"Our policy is for a twenty-four hour cancellation or else we have no choice but to charge you."

"I'm sick. I told you."

"I'm sorry."

The moment burst on him like one of those rogue waves at the beach and he came within a hair of shouting an obscenity into the receiver but he caught himself. "I'm sorry too," he said.

At home, he found he was shaking so hard he could barely get the key in the door, and though he didn't want to, though it wasn't even four yet, he went straight to the kitchen and poured himself a shot of the tequila they kept on hand for margaritas when people came over. He didn't bother with salt or lime but just threw it back neat and if this was the cliché—your wife has sex with another man and you go straight for the sauce—then so be it. The tequila tasted like soap. No matter. He poured another, downed it, and still he was trembling. Then he sat down at the kitchen table, opened the laptop, clicked on Rob's e-mail and watched the video all the way through.

This time the blow was even harsher, a quick hot jolt that seared his eyes and shot through him from his fingertips to his groin. The whole thing lasted less than sixty seconds, in medias res, and what had preceded it—disrobing, a kiss, foreplay—remained hidden. The act itself was straightforward as far as it went, no acrobatics, no oral sex, just him behind her and the rhythmic swaying that was as earnest and inevitable as when any two mammals went at it. Dogs. Apes. Husbands and wives. At the moment of release, she looked back at the guy doing it to her and as if at a signal rolled over and here were his knees in the frame now and his torso looming as he covered her with his own body and they kissed, their two heads bobbing briefly in the foreground before the screen went dark. The second time through, details began to emerge. The setting, for one thing. Clearly, it was a dorm room—there was the generic desk to the left of the bed, a stack of books, the swivel chair with the ghosts of their uninhabited clothes thrown over it, Levi's, a belt buckle, the silken sheen of her panties. And Laurie. This was Laurie before she'd cut her hair, before her implants, before he'd even met her. Laurie in college. Fucking.

The tequila burned in his stomach. There was no sound but for the hum of the refrigerator as it started up and clicked off again. Very gradually, the light began to swell round him as the sun searched through the haze to fill the kitchen and infuse the walls with color—a cheery daffodil yellow, the shade she'd picked out when they bought the condo two years ago on her twenty-ninth birthday. "This is the best birthday present I ever had," she'd said, her voice soft and steady, and she'd leaned in to kiss him in the lifeless office where the escrow woman sat behind her block-like desk and took their signatures on one form after another as if she'd been made of steel and they'd run out of movable parts.

They'd celebrated that night with a bottle of champagne and dinner out and sex in their old apartment on their old bed that had come from Goodwill in a time when neither of them had a steady job. He looked round the room now—the most familiar room in the world, the place where they had breakfast together and dinner most nights, sharing the cooking and the TV news and a bottle of wine—and it seemed alien to him, as if he'd been snatched out of his life and set down here in this over-bright echoing space with its view of blacktop and wires and the inescapable palm with its ascending pineapple ridges and ragged wind-blown fronds.

The next thing he knew it was five o'clock and he heard her key turn in the lock and the faint sigh of the door as she pushed it shut behind her and then the drumbeat of her heels on the glazed Saltillo tile in the front hall. "Todd?" she called. "Todd, you home?" He felt his jaws clench. He didn't answer. Her footsteps came down the hall, beating, beating. "Todd?"

He liked her in heels. *Had* liked her in heels, that is. She was a surgical nurse, working for a pair of plastic surgeons who'd partnered to open the San Roque Aesthetics Institute five years back, and she changed to flats while assisting at surgery but otherwise wore heels to show off her legs beneath the short skirts and calibrated tops she wore when consulting with prospective patients. "Advertising," she called it. The breast implants—about which he'd been very vocal and very pleased—had come at a discount.

He was still at the table when she walked into the kitchen, the bottle on the counter, the shot glass beside him, the laptop just barely cracked. "What's this?" she said, lifting the bottle from the counter and giving it a shake. "You're drinking?" She came across the room to him, laid a hand on his shoulder and ran it up the back of his neck, then bent forward to lift the empty glass to her nose and take a theatrical sniff.

"Yeah," he said, but he didn't lift his eyes.

"That's not like you. Tough day?"

"Yeah," he said.

"Well, if you're partying"—and here her voice fluted above him, light and facetious, as if the world were still on its track and nothing had changed—"then I hope you won't mind if I pour myself a glass of wine. Do we have any wine left?" Her hand dropped away and he felt a chill on the back of his neck where her palm had been. He heard her heels tapping like typewriter keys, then the wheeze of the vacuum seal on the refrigerator door, the cabinet working on its hinges, the sharp clink as the base of the wine glass came into contact with the granite counter, and finally the raucous celebratory splash of the wine. Still he didn't look up. Her attitude—this sunniness, this self-possession, this blindness and blandness and business-as-usual crap—savaged him. Didn't she know what was coming? Couldn't she feel it the way animals do just before an earthquake strikes?

"That guy you used to date in college," he said, his voice choked in his throat, "what was his name?"

He looked up now and she was poised there at the counter, leaning back into it, the glass of wine—sauvignon blanc, filled to the top—glowing with reflected light. She let out a little laugh. "What brought that up?"

"What color hair did he have? Was it short, long, what?"

"Jared," she said, her eyes gone distant a moment. "Jared Reed. From New *Joisey.*" She lifted the glass to her lips, took a sip, the gold chain she wore at her throat picking up the light now too. She was wearing a blue silk blouse open to the third button down. She put a hand there, to her collarbone. Sipped again. "I don't know," she said. "Brown. Black maybe? He wore it short, like Justin Timberlake. But why? Don't tell me you're jealous"—the facetious note again when all he could think of was leaping up from the table and slapping every shred of facetiousness out of her—"after all these years? Is that it? I mean, what do you care?"

"Rob sent me a video today."

"Rob?"

"My brother. Remember my brother? *Rob?*" His voice got away from him. He hadn't meant to shout, hadn't meant to be accusatory or confrontational—he just wanted answers, that was all.

She said nothing. Her face was cold, her eyes colder still.

"Maybe"—and here he flipped open the laptop—"maybe you ought to have a look at it and then you tell me what it is." He was up out of the chair now, the tequila pitching him forward, and he didn't care about the look on her face or the way she cradled the wine and held out her hands to him and he didn't touch her—wouldn't touch her, wouldn't touch her ever again. The kitchen door was a slab of nothing, but it slammed behind him and the whole house shook under the weight of it.

Later, as faces wheeled round him and the flat-screen TV behind the bar blinked and shifted over the game that was utterly meaningless to him now, he had the leisure to let his mind go free. School didn't exist—lesson plans, papers to grade, none of it. Laurie didn't exist either. And Jared Reed was just a ghost. And whether he had brown hair or black or muscles on top of muscles or a dick two feet long, it didn't matter because he was just a ghost on a screen. Nothing. He was nothing. Less than nothing.

But here was the bartender (thirties, with a haircut like Rob's and dressed in a cowboy shirt with embroidery round the pockets like icing on a cake) looming over him with the Jameson bottle held aloft. "Yeah," he said, and he would have clarified by adding, *Hit me again,* but that would have been too much like being in a movie, a bad movie, bad and sad and pathetic. He wasn't a drinker, not really, and he hadn't wanted the tequila except that it was there because they didn't keep anything in the house beyond that and a couple bottles of wine they got when it was on sale, but when they went out, he always ordered Jameson. Jameson was all he ever drank, aside from maybe a beer chaser, which he wasn't having tonight, definitely wasn't having. Rob drank it too. And their father, when he was alive. It was a family tradition, and how many times had they sat at dinner when they were kids and their father would say, *Just wait till old man Jameson kicks off, then we'll be rich,* and they would chime, *Who's Jameson?,* and he'd say, *Who's Jameson? The Whiskey King, of course.* And their mother: *Don't hold your breath.*

And then the drink was there and he was sipping it, thinking of the last thing Rob had sent him as an attachment, and when was it? A week ago? Two? It was an article he'd downloaded from some obscure Web site and he'd forwarded it under the heading *Look What Our Glorious Ancestor Was Up To.* The ancestor in question—if he was an ancestor, of course, and there was the joke—was James Jameson, heir to the whiskey fortune. In 1888 Jameson was thirty-one years old, same age as Todd was now, and he was a wastrel and an adventurer, and because he was limp with boredom and had done all the damage he could in the clubs and parlors of Ireland, England and the Continent, he signed on for an African expedition under Henry Morton Stanley, of Livingston fame. They were in the Congo, in the heart of the heart of darkness, stuck on some river Todd had forgotten the name of though he'd read through the article over and over with a kind of sick fascination—stuck there and going nowhere. One morning when Stanley was away from camp, Jameson got the idea that he might like to visit one of the cannibal tribes to see how they went about their business and make a record of it in his sketchbook. From the beginning of the expedition, he'd made detailed drawings of tribesmen, game animals, the erratic vegetation and crude villages scattered along the banks of the rivers, and now he was going to draw cannibals. At work. For six handkerchiefs—not a dozen or two dozen, just six—he bought a ten-year-old slave girl and gave her as a gift to the cannibals, then sat there on a stump or maybe a camp chair, one leg crossed over the other, and focused his concentration. He drew the figure of the girl as she was stripped and bound to a tree, drew her as the knife went in under the breastbone and sliced downward. She never struggled or pleaded or cried out but just stood there bearing it all till her legs gave way and he drew that too, his hand flashing and the pencil growing duller while the mosquitoes hummed and the smoke of the cookfire rose greasily through the overhanging leaves.

Was there a theme here? Was he missing something? Laurie had run out the door shouting, *You don't own me!* as he'd backed the car out of the drive, the window up and the motor racing. And Rob had sent him the video. And the article too. Just then, a groan went up from a booth in the corner behind him and he glanced vaguely at the TV before digging out his phone and hitting Rob's number. The referee on the screen waved his arms, music pounded, the bottles behind the bar glittered in all their facets. He got a recording. The message box was full.

The strangest thing, the worst thing, had been those first few minutes when he had to struggle with himself to keep from bulling his way back into the kitchen to see the look on her face, to see her shame, to see tears. He'd slammed the door so hard the cheap windows vibrated in their cheap frames and one of Laurie's pictures—the silhouette of a couple on a moonlit beach he'd always hated—crashed to the floor, glass shattering on the tiles. He didn't stoop to clean it up. Didn't move, not even to shift his feet. He just stood there rigid on the other side of the door, picturing her bent over the screen, her face stricken, the wine gone sour in her throat. But then the thought came to him that maybe she liked it, maybe it turned her on, maybe she was proud of it, and that froze him inside.

When she did come through the door—and she'd had enough time to watch the thing three or four times over—she didn't look contrite or aroused or whatever else he'd expected, only angry. "Jared is such an asshole," she hissed, glaring at him. "And so's your brother, so's Rob. What was he thinking?"

"What was *he* thinking? What were you thinking? You're the one on the sex tape."

"So? So what? Did you think I was a virgin when we got married?"

"You tell me—how many men *did* you have? Fifty? A hundred?"

"How many women did you have?"

"I'm not the one putting out sex tapes."

She stood her ground, tall on her heels, her face flushed and her arms folded defensively across her chest. "You want to know something—you're an asshole too."

If ever he was going to hit her, here was the moment. He took a step toward her. She never even flinched.

"Listen, Todd, I swear I didn't know that creep was making a video—he must have had a hidden camera going or something, I don't know. I was in college. He was my boyfriend."

"What about the lights?"

She shrugged. An abortive smile flickered across her lips. "He always liked to do it with the lights on. He said it was sexier that way. He was an artist, I told you that, really visual—"

Everybody had past lovers, of course they did, but they were conveniently reduced to shadows, memories, a photo or two, not this, not this hurtful flashing resurrection in the flesh, the past come home in living color. *An artist.* All he knew was that he hated her in that moment.

"How was I to know? Really, I'm sorry, I am. To put that online—where's it posted, even?—I mean, it's really disgusting and stupid. He's a shit, a real shit."

"You're the shit," he said. "*You're* disgusting."

"I can't believe you. I mean, really—what does it have to do with you?"

"You're my wife."

"It's my body."

"Yeah? Well you can have it. I'm out of here."

And that was when she chased him down the drive and put on a show for the neighbors, her voice honed to a shriek like something out of the bell of an instrument, a clarinet, an oboe, abuse of the reed, the pads: *You don't own me!*

It was getting late. The game was over, long over, and he was sitting there in a kind of delirium, waiting for his phone to ring, waiting for Rob—or maybe her, maybe she'd call and pour her soul out to him and they could go back to the way they were before—when he noticed the couple sitting at the end of the bar. They were kissing, long and slow, clinging fast to each other as if they were out in a windstorm, as if all the contravening forces of the universe were trying to tear them apart, two untouched drinks standing sentinel on the bar before them and the bartender in his cowboy shirt steering round them as he poured and wiped and polished. The girl's arms were bare, her jacket—blue suede, with a fake-fur collar—draped over the chair behind her. He couldn't see her face, only the back of her head, her shoulders, her arms, beautiful arms, stunning actually, every muscle and tendon gently flexed to hold her lover to her, and he looked till he had to look away.

He became aware of the music then, some syrupy love song seeping out of the speakers, and what was it? Rod Stewart. Rod Stewart at his worst, hyper-inflated love delivered in a whisper, as manufactured as a pair of shoes or a box of doughnuts, and here was this couple sucking the breath out of each other, and what was he doing here, what was he thinking? He was drunk, that was what it was. And he hadn't had anything to eat, had he? Eating was important. Vital. He had to eat, had to put something on his stomach to absorb the alcohol—how else could he get behind the wheel? Drunk driving on top of everything else. He pictured it: the cuffs, the cell, his corner in the teachers' lounge deserted and Ed Jacobsen, the principal, wondering where he was—not a phone call? Couldn't he even have called?

The thought propelled him up off the stool, down the length of the bar past the stupefied sports fans and the clinging couple and the bartender with the haircut like Rob's, *You have a good night now,* and out onto the street. He stood there a moment outside the door, patting down his pockets, wallet, keys, cell phone, taking stock. The air was dense and moist, fog working its way up the streets as if the streets were rivers and the fog a thing you could float on. He could smell the ocean, the rankness of it. He thought he'd go to the next place, get a burger and coffee, black coffee—wasn't that how it was done? Wasn't that taking the cliché full circle? That was how it had been in college after he'd gone out cruising the bars with his dormmates, lonely, aching, repressed, gaping at the girls as they took command of the dance floor and never knowing what to do about it. A burger. Black coffee.

He started down the street, everything vague before him, trying to think of where to go, of who would be open at this hour. Things glittered in the half-light, the pavement wet, trash strewn at the curbs. A single car eased down the street, headlights muted, taillights bleeding out into the night. Neon thickened and blurred. He made a left on the main street, heading toward a place he thought might be open still, a place he and Laurie sometimes went to after a late movie, focused now, or as focused as he could be considering the whiskey and the hammer beating inside him, reverberating still, when a woman's voice cut through the night. She was cursing, her delivery harsh, guttural, as if the words were being torn from her, and then there was the wet clap of flesh on flesh and a man's voice, cursing back at her—figures there, contending in the shadows.

He wanted to call out, wanted to defy them, bark at them, split them apart, get angry, get furious—there they were, just ahead of him, the woman lurching into the man, the man's arms in dark rapid motion, their curses propulsive, shoes shuffling on the concrete in a metastasized dance—but he didn't. There was a suspended moment when they felt him there and they switched it off, in league against him, and then he was past them, his footsteps echoing and the curses starting up behind him in a low seething growl of antipathy.

How he made it home he couldn't say, but he remembered standing at the door of the car fumbling with his keys on a street so dark it might as well have been underground and feeling the cell buzz in his pocket. Or thinking he felt it. He kept it on vibrate because of teaching, because of class—the embarrassment factor—but half the time he never felt it there against his skin and wound up missing his calls. Which was why he had to check messages all the time . . . but it was buzzing and he had it in his hand and flipped it open, the only light on the street and a dim light at that. Rob. Rob calling.

"Hello?"

"Hey, Todd, hey, bro—you okay? I mean, I been calling for like three hours now and I'm worried about you, because I mean, it's tough, I know, but it's not like the end of the world or anything—"

"Rob," he said, his voice ground down so that he barely recognized it himself. "Rob, can you hear me?"

"Yeah, yeah, I can hear you."

"Good. Because screw you. That's my message: screw you." And then he'd turned the phone off and thrust it deep in his pocket.

When he came in the door the house was silent. There was a lamp on in the hallway and the nightlight in the kitchen was on too, but Laurie, in her meticulous way, had turned off all the rest and gone to bed. Or so it seemed. He moved slowly, heavily, his breath coming hard and his feet working as if independent of him, far away, down there in the shadows where the baseboard ran the length of the hall and conjoined with the frame of the bedroom door. If she had a light on in there—if she was up, waiting for him, waiting for what came next—he would have seen it in the crack at the bottom of the door, the tile uneven there, treacherous even, shoddy workmanship like everything else in the place. Very slowly, he turned the handle and eased the door open, wincing at the metallic protest of the hinges that needed a shot of WD-40, definitely needed WD-40, and then he was in the room and looking down at the shadow of her where she lay in bed, on her side, her back to him. It took him a moment to see her there, his eyes adjusting to the dark and the stripes of pale trembling light the streetlamp outside the window forced through the shades, but very gradually she began to take on shape and presence. Laurie. His wife.

He saw the way she'd tucked her shoulder beneath her, saw the rise there, the declivity of her waist and the sharp definition of her upthrust hip. He'd always loved her hips. And her legs. The indentation of her knees. The way she walked as if carrying a very special prize for someone she hadn't quite discovered yet. He was remembering the first time he'd ever seen her, a hot summer day with the sun arching overhead and her walking toward him with a guy from school he liked to hang out with on weekends, and he didn't know a thing about her, didn't know her name or where she came from or that they liked the same books and bands and movies or that her whole being would open up to his and his to hers as if they had the same key and the key fit just exactly right. What he saw was the sun behind her and the shape of her revealed in silhouette, all form and grace and the light like poured gold. What he saw was the sway of her hips against the fierce brightness of the sun and the shadow of her legs caught in the grip of a long diaphanous dress, her legs, sweet and firm and purposeful, coming toward him.

He remembered that. Held that vision. And then, as quietly as he could, he pulled back the covers and got into bed beside her.

(2011)

The Night of the Satellite

What we were arguing about that night—and it was late, very late, 3:10 a.m. by my watch—was something that had happened nearly twelve hours earlier. A small thing, really, but by this time it had grown out of all proportion and poisoned everything we said, as if we didn't have enough problems as it was. Mallory was relentless. And I was feeling defensive and maybe more than a little paranoid. We were both drunk. Or if not drunk, at least loosened up by what we'd consumed at Chris Wright's place in the wake of the incident and then at dinner after and the bar after that. I could smell the nighttime stink of the river. I looked up and watched the sky expand overhead and then shrink down to fit me like a safety helmet. A truck went blatting by on the interstate and then it was silent but for the mosquitoes singing their blood song while the rest of the insect world screeched either in protest or accord, I couldn't tell which, thrumming and thrumming till the night felt as if it was going to burst open and leave us shattered in the grass.

"You asshole," she snarled.

"You're the asshole," I said.

"I hate you."

"Ditto," I said. "Ditto and square it."

The day had begun peaceably enough, a Saturday, the two of us curled up and sleeping late, the shades drawn and the air conditioner doing its job. If it weren't for the dog we might have slept right on into the afternoon because we'd been up late the night before at a club called Gabe's, where we'd danced, with the assistance of well rum and two little white pills Mallory's friend Mona had given her, till our clothes were sweated through and the muscles of our calves—my calves anyway—felt as if they'd been surgically removed, hammered flat and sewed back in place. But the dog (Nome, a husky, one blue eye, one brown) kept laying the wedge of his head on my side of the bed and emitting a series of truncated violin noises because his bladder was bursting and it was high time for his morning run.

My eyes flashed open, and despite the dog's needs and the first stirrings of a headache, I got up with a feeling that the world was a hospitable place. After using the toilet and splashing some water on my face, I found my shorts on the floor where I'd left them, unfurled the dog's leash and took him out the door. The sun was high. The dog sniffed and evacuated. I led him down to the corner store, picked up a copy of the newspaper and two coffees to go, retraced my steps along the quiet sun-dappled street, mounted the stairs to the apartment and settled back into bed. Mallory was sitting up waiting for me, still in her nightgown but with her glasses on—boxy little black-framed things that might have been an example of the generic reading glasses you find in the drugstore but for the fact that they were ground to the optometrist's specifications and she wore them as a kind of combative fashion statement. She stretched and smiled when I came through the door and murmured something that might have been "good morning," though, as I say, the morning was all but gone. I handed her a coffee and the *Life* section of the newspaper. Time slowed. For the next hour there were no sounds but for the rustle of newsprint and the gentle soughing suck of hot liquid through a small plastic aperture. We might have dozed. It didn't matter. It was summer. And we were on break.

The plan was to drive out to the farmhouse our friends Chris and Anneliese Wright were renting from the farmer himself and laze away the hours sipping wine and maybe playing croquet or taking a hike along the creek that cut a crimped line through the cornfields which rose in an otherwise unbroken mass as far as you could see. After that, we'd play it by ear. It was too much trouble to bother with making dinner—and too hot, up in the nineties and so humid the air was like a flak jacket—and if Chris and Anneliese didn't have anything else in mind, I was thinking of persuading them to join us at the vegetarian place in town for the falafel plate, with shredded carrots, hummus, tabouleh and the like, and then maybe hit a movie or head back over to Gabe's till the night melted away. Fine. Perfect. Exactly what you wanted from a midsummer's day in the Midwest the week after the summer session had ended and you'd put away your books for the three-week respite before the fall semester started up.

We didn't have jobs, not in any real sense—jobs were a myth, a rumor—and we held on in grad school, semester after semester, for lack of anything better to do. We got financial aid, of course, and accrued debt on our student loans. Our car, a hand-me-down from Mallory's mother, needed tires and probably everything else into the bargain. We wrote papers, graded papers, got A's and B's in the courses we took and doled out A's and B's in the courses we taught. Sometimes we felt as if we were actually getting somewhere, but the truth was, like most people, we were just marking time.

At any rate, we made some sandwiches, put the dog in the car and drove through the leafy streets of town until the trees gave way and the countryside opened up around us, two bottles of marked-down shoppers' special Australian zinfandel in a bag on the floor in back. The radio was playing (bluegrass, a taste we'd acquired since moving out here in the heart of the country) and we had the windows rolled down to enjoy the breeze we were generating as the car humped through the cornfields and over a series of gently rolling hills that made us feel as if we were floating. Nome was in the back seat, hanging his head out the window and striping the fender with airborne slaver. All was well. But then we turned onto the unmarked blacktop road that led out to Chris and Anneliese's and saw the car there, a silver Toyota, engine running, stopped in our lane and facing in the wrong direction.

As we got closer we saw a woman—girl—coming toward us down the center of the road, her face flushed and her eyes wet with what might have been the effects of overwrought emotion or maybe hay fever, which was endemic here, and we saw a man—boy—then too, perched on the hood of the car, shouting abuse at her retreating back. The term "lovers' quarrel" came into my head at the very moment the girl lifted her face and Mallory yelled, "Stop!"

"It's a lovers' quarrel," I said, ever so slightly depressing the accelerator.

"Stop!" Mallory repeated, more insistently this time. The guy was watching us, something like an angry smirk on his face. The girl—she was no more than a hundred feet away now—raised her hand as if to flag us down and I eased up on the gas, thinking that maybe they were in trouble after all, something wrong with the car, the engine overheating, the fuel gauge on empty. It was hot. Grasshoppers flung themselves at the windshield like yellow hail. All you could smell was tar.

The car slowed to a halt and the girl bent to my window, letting her face hover there a moment against the green tide of corn. "You need help?" I asked, and those *were* tears in her eyes, absolutely, tears that swelled against her lids and dried in translucent streaks radiating out from her cheekbones.

"He's such a jerk," she said, sucking in her breath. "He's, he's"—another breath—"I hate him."

Mallory leaned over me so the girl could see her face. "Is he your—?"

"He's a jerk," the girl repeated. She was younger than us, late teens, early twenties. She wore her blond hair in braids and she was dressed in a black tank top, cut-off jeans and pink Crocs. She threw a look at the guy, who was still perched on the hood of the car, then wiped her nose with the back of her hand and began to cry again.

"That's right," he shouted. "Cry. Go ahead. And then you can run back to your mommy and daddy like the little retard you are!" He was blond too, more of a rusty blond, and he had the makings of a reddish beard creeping up into his sideburns. He was wearing a Banksy T-shirt, the one with the rat in sunglasses on it, and it clung to him as if it had been painted on. You could see that he spent time at the gym. A lot of time.

"Get in the car," Mallory said. "You can come with us—it'll be all right."

I turned to Mallory, blocking her view of the girl. "It's between them," I said, and at the same time, I don't know why, I hit the child lock so the door wouldn't open. "It's none of our business."

"None of our business?" she shot back at me. "She could be abused, or I don't know, *abducted,* you ever think of that?" She strained to look around me to where the girl was still standing there on the blacktop as if she'd been fixed in place. "Did he hit you, is that it?"

Another sob, sucked back as quickly as it was released. "No. He's just a jerk, that's all."

"Yeah," he crowed, sliding down off the hood now, "you tell them all about it, because you're little Miss Perfect, aren't you? You want to see something? You, I'm talking to you, you in the car." He raised one arm to show the long red striations there, evidence of what had passed between them. "You want her? You can have her."

"Get in," Mallory said.

Nome began to whine. The house was no more than half a mile up the road and probably he could smell Chris and Anneliese's dog, a malamute named Boxer, and maybe the sheep the farmer kept behind the fence that enclosed the barn. The girl shook her head.

"Go ahead, bitch," the guy called. He leaned back into the hood of the car and folded his arms across his chest as if he'd been at this awhile and was prepared to go on indefinitely.

"You don't have to put up with that," Mallory said, and her voice was honed and hard, the voice she used on me when she was in a mood, when I was talking too much or hadn't got around to washing the dishes when it was my turn. "Come on, get in."

"No," the girl said, stepping back from the car now so that we got a full view of her. Her arms shone with sweat. There were beads of moisture dotting her upper lip. She was pretty, very pretty.

I eased off the brake pedal and the car inched forward even as Mallory said, "Stop, Paul, what are you doing?" and I said, "She doesn't want to," and then, lamely, "It's a lovers' quarrel, can't you see that?" Then we were moving up the channel the road cut through the greenest fields in the world, past the pissed-off guy with the scratched forearms and a hard harsh gloating look in his eyes, down into a dip and up the next undulating hill, Mallory furious, thumping at the locked door as if it were a set of drums and straining her neck to look back as the whole scene receded in the rearview mirror.

By the time we got to Chris and Anneliese's, Mallory was in full crisis mode. The minute we pulled into the driveway I flicked off the child lock, but she just gave me a withering look, slammed out of the car and stalked up the steps of the front porch, shouting, "Anneliese, Chris, where are you?" I was out of the car by then, Nome shooting over the front seat to rocket past me even as Boxer came tearing around the corner of the house, a yellow Lab pup I'd never seen before at his heels. The dogs barked rhapsodically, then the screen door swung open and there were Chris and Anneliese, spritzers clutched in their hands. Chris was barefoot and shirtless, Anneliese dressed almost identically to the girl on the road, except that her top was blue, to match her eyes, and she was wearing open-toed flats to show off her feet. Before grad school she'd been a hosiery model for Lord & Taylor in Chicago and she never missed an opportunity to let you know it. As for the rest of her, she was attractive enough, I suppose, with streamlined limbs, kinky copper-colored hair and the whitest teeth I'd ever seen or imagined. My own teeth tended toward the yellowish, but then neither of my parents was a dentist and both of hers were.

Mallory didn't say hello or how are you or thanks for inviting us, but just wheeled around in exasperation and pointed down the road. "I need a bicycle," she said. "Can I borrow somebody's bicycle?"

Anneliese showed her teeth in an uncertain smile. "What are you talking about? You just got here."

The explanation was brief and vivid and unsparing with regard to my lack of concern or feeling. All three of them looked at me a minute, then Anneliese said, "What if he's dangerous?"

"He's not dangerous," I said reflexively.

"I'm going with you," Anneliese said, and in the next moment she was pushing a matching pair of ten-speed bicycles out the door, hers and Chris'.

Chris waved his glass. "You think maybe Paul and I should go instead? I mean, just in case?"

Mallory was already straddling the bike. "Forget it," she said, with a level of bitterness that went far beyond what was called for, if it was called for at all. I'd done what anyone would have done. Believe me, you just do not get between a couple when they're in the middle of a fight. Especially strangers. And especially not on a sweltering afternoon on a deserted country road. You want to get involved? Call the cops. That was my feeling anyway, but then the whole thing had happened so quickly I really hadn't had time to work out the ramifications. I'd acted instinctively, that was all. The problem was, so had she.

Mallory shot me a look. "You'd probably just wind up patting him on the back." She gave it a beat, lasered in on Chris. "Both of you."

That was when things got confused, because before I could respond—before I could think—the women were cranking down the drive with the sun lighting them up as if we were all in the second act of a stage play, and the dogs, spurred on by the Lab pup, chose that moment to bolt under the lowest slat of the bleached wooden fence and go after the sheep. The sheep were right there, right in the yard, milling around and letting off a sweaty ovine stink, and the two older dogs—mine and Chris'—knew they were off limits, strictly and absolutely, and that heavy consequences would come down on them if they should ever lapse and let their instincts take over. But that was exactly what happened. The pup, which, as it turned out, was a birthday present from Chris to Anneliese, didn't yet comprehend the rules—these were sheep and he was a dog—and so he went for them and the sheep reacted and that reaction, predator and prey, drove the older dogs into a frenzy.

In that instant we forgot the women, forgot the couple on the road, forgot spritzers and croquet and the notion of chilling on a scalding afternoon, because the dogs were harrying the sheep and the sheep had nowhere to go and it was up to us—grad students, not farmers, not shepherds—to get in there and separate them. "Oh, shit," Chris said and then we both hurdled the fence and were right in the thick of it. I went after Nome, shouting his name in a fury, but he'd gone atavistic, tearing wool and hide from one bleating animal after another. I had him twice, flinging myself at him like a linebacker, but he wriggled away and I was down in the dirt, in the dust, a cyclone of dust, the sheep poking at my bare arms and outthrust hands with their stony black hooves. There was shit aplenty. There was blood. And by the time we'd wrestled the dogs down and got them out of there, half a dozen of the sheep had visible gashes on their faces and legs, a situation that was sure to disconcert the farmer—Chris' landlord—if he were to find out about it, and we ourselves were in serious need of decontamination. I was bleeding. Chris was bleeding. The sheep were bleeding. And the dogs, the dogs we scolded and pinched and whacked, were in the process of being dragged across the front yard to a place where we could chain them up so they could lie panting through the afternoon and contemplate their sins. That was the moment, that was what we were caught up in, and if the women were on their bicycles someplace wearing a scrim of insects or stepping into somebody else's quarrel, we didn't know it.

A car went by then, a silver Toyota, but I only caught a glimpse of it and couldn't have said if there were two people in it or just one.

We never did get around to playing croquet—Mallory was too worked up, and besides, just moving had us dripping with sweat—but we sat on the porch and drank zinfandel and soda with shaved ice while the dogs whined and dug in the dirt and finally settled down in a twitching fly-happy oblivion. Mallory was mum on the subject of the couple in the Toyota except to say that by the time she and Anneliese got there, the girl was already in the car, which pulled a U-turn and shot past them up the road, and I thought—foolishly, as it turned out—that that was the end of it. When six o'clock rolled around we wound up going to a pizza place because I was outvoted, three to one, and after that we sat through a movie Anneliese had heard good things about but which turned out to be a dud. It was a French film about three non-specifically unhappy couples who had serial affairs with one another and a troupe of third and fourth parties against a rainy Parisian backdrop that looked as if it had been shot through a translucent beach ball. At the end there was a close-up of each of the principals striding separately and glumly through the rain to separate destinations. The three actresses, heavily made-up, suffered from smeared mascara. The music swelled.

Then it was Gabe's and the pounding air-conditioned exhilaration of an actual real-life band and limitless cocktails. Chris and Anneliese were great dancers, the kind everybody, participants and wallflowers alike, watches with envy, and they didn't waste any time, not even bothering to find a table before they were out there in the middle of the floor, their arms flashing white and Anneliese's coppery flag of hair draining all the color out of the room. We danced well too, Mallory and I, attuned to each other's moves by way of long acquaintance, and while we weren't maybe as showy as Chris and Anneliese, we could hold our own. I tried to take Mallory's hand, but she withheld it and settled into one of the tables with a shrug of irritation. I stood there a moment in mute appeal, but she wouldn't look me in the eye, and it was then that I began to realize it was going to be a long night. What did I want? I wanted to dance, wanted joy and release—summer break!—but I went to the bar instead and ordered a spritzer for Mallory and a rum and Coke for myself.

The bar was crowded, more crowded than usual, it seemed, even though most of the undergrads had gone home or off to Europe or Costa Rica or wherever they went when somebody else was paying for it. There were two bartenders, both female and both showing off their assets, and it must have taken me five minutes just to get to the bar and another five to catch the attention of the nearest one. I shouted my order over the furious assault of the band. The drinks came. I paid, took one in each hand and began to work my way back through the crowd. It was then that someone jostled me from behind—hard—and half the spritzer went down the front of my shirt and half the rum and Coke down the back of a girl in front of me. The girl swung round on me with an angry look and I swung round on whoever had jostled—pushed—me and found myself staring into the face of the guy from the blacktop road, the guy with the distraught girlfriend and the silver Toyota. It took a beat before I recognized him, a beat measured by the whining nasal complaint of the girl with the Coke-stained blouse—"Jesus, aren't you even going to apologize?"—and then, without a word, he flashed both palms as if he were performing a magic trick and gave me a deliberate shove that tumbled me back into the girl and took the drinks to the floor in a silent shatter of glass and skittering ice cubes. The girl invoked Jesus again, louder this time, while the guy turned and slipped off into the crowd.

A circle opened around me. The bartender gave me a disgusted look. "Sorry," I said to the girl, "but you saw that, didn't you? He shoved me." And then, though it no longer mattered and he was already passing by the bouncer and swinging open the door to the deepening night beyond, I added, my own voice pinched in complaint, "I don't even know him."

When I got back to the table, sans drinks, Mallory gave me a long squint through her glasses and said—or rather, screamed over the noise of the band—"What took you so long?" And then: "Where're the drinks?"

That was the defining moment. My shirt was wet. I'd been humiliated, adrenaline was rocketing through my veins and my heart was doing paradiddles, and what I was thinking was, *Who's to blame here? Who stuck her nose in where it wasn't wanted?* So we got into it. Right there. And I didn't care who was watching. And when the band took a break and Chris and Anneliese joined us and we finally got a round of drinks, the conversation was strained to say the least. As soon as the band started up again I asked Anneliese to dance and then, out of sympathy or etiquette or simple boredom, Chris asked Mallory and for a long while we were all out on the dance floor, Chris eventually going back to Anneliese, but Mallory dancing with a succession of random guys just to stick it to me, which she succeeded in doing, with flying colors and interest compounded by the minute.

And that was how we found ourselves out in that dark field on the night of the satellite, letting things spill out of us, angry things, hurtful things, things that made me want to leave her to the mosquitoes and go off and rent a room on the other side of town and never talk to her again. She'd just told me she hated me for maybe the hundredth time—we were drunk, both of us, as I've said, the encounter on the road the tipping point and no going back—and I was going to retort, going to say something incisive like, "Yeah, me too," when I felt something hit my shoulder. It was a blow, a palpable hit, and my first thought was that the Toyota guy had followed us in order to exact some sort of twisted vengeance for an incident that never happened, that was less than nothing—the girl *hadn't* got in our car, had she?—but then I felt whatever it was skew off me and drop into the wet high grass with an audible thump. "What was that?" Mallory said.

I wasn't making the connection with the streak of light that had shot overhead as we'd climbed out of the car—or not yet, anyway. "I don't know."

"Here," she said, pulling out her phone to shine the light on the ground.

The object was right there, right at our feet, cradled in a gray-green bowl of broken stalks. It was metallic, definitely metallic, some sort of steel or titanium mesh six inches long and maybe three wide, like a sock, the size of a sock. And it wasn't hot, as you'd expect, not at all. In fact—and this was when it came to me—the heating had taken place twenty-three miles up and by the time it had got here, to earth, to me, it was as lukewarm as a carton of milk left out on the counter.

It was a sign, but of what I wasn't sure. I went online the next day and found an article confirming that the streak in the sky had been produced by the reentry of a decommissioned twenty-year-old NASA climate satellite scientists had been tracking as it fell out of orbit. The satellite had been the size of a school bus and weighed six and a half tons and that fact alone had caused considerable anxiety as it became increasingly clear that its trajectory would take it over populated areas in Canada and the U.S. A picture of it, in grainy black and white, showed the least aerodynamic structure you could imagine, all sharp edges and functional planes, the whole overshadowed by a solar panel the size of the screen at a drive-in movie. The article went on to claim that all debris of any consequence had most likely been incinerated in the upper atmosphere and that the chances of any fragment of it hitting a given person anywhere within its range had been calculated at 1 in 3,200. All right. But it had hit *me,* and either they needed to recalculate or Mallory and I should get in the car and go straight to Vegas. I brought my laptop into the kitchen, where she was sitting at the table in the alcove, working a serrated knife through the sections of her grapefruit.

"What did I tell you?" I said.

She took a moment to scan the article, then glanced up at me. "It says it was incinerated in the upper atmosphere."

"*Most likely,* it says. And it's wrong, obviously. You were there. You saw it." I pointed through the doorway to the living room, where the piece of mesh—

stiff, twisted, blackened from the heat of reentry—occupied a place on the bookcase where formerly a vase had stood between Salinger and Salter in the American Lit section. "Tell me that's not real."

The night before, out in the field, she'd warned me not to touch it—"It's dirty, it's nothing, just some piece of junk"—but I knew better, I knew right away. I took it up gingerly between thumb and forefinger, expecting heat, expecting the razor bite of steel on unprotected flesh and thinking of *The War of the Worlds* in its most recent cinematic iteration, but after we'd had a moment to examine it under the pale gaze of the cell phone and see how utterly innocuous it was, I handed it to her as reverently as if it were a religious relic. She held it in one hand, running her thumb over the braid of the mesh, then passed it back to me. "It feels warm," she said. "You don't really think it came from that meteor or whatever it was?" She turned her face to the sky.

"Satellite," I told her. "Last I heard they said it was going to come down in Canada someplace."

"But they were wrong, is that what you're saying?"

I couldn't see her features, but I could hear the dismissiveness in her voice. We'd been fighting all day, fighting to the point of exhaustion, and it infuriated me to think she wouldn't even give me this. "They've been wrong before," I said, and then I cradled the thing under one arm and started back across the field without bothering to see if she was coming or not.

Now she said, "Don't be crazy. It's just some piece of a car or a tractor or something, or a lawnmower—it fell off a lawnmower, I'll bet anything."

"A lawnmower in the sky? It hit me. Right here, on the shoulder." I jerked at the neck of my T-shirt and pulled it down over my left shoulder in evidence.

"I don't see anything."

"There's a red mark there, I'm telling you—I saw it in the mirror this morning."

She just stared at me.

A week slid by. The heat never broke, not even after a series of thunderstorms rumbled in under a sky the color of bruised flesh—all the rain managed to do was drive up the humidity. We were supposed to be enjoying ourselves, we were supposed to be on vacation, but we didn't do much of anything. We sat around and sweated and tried to avoid contact as much as possible. Dinner was salad or takeout and we ate at the kitchen table, where the fan was, books propped in our hands. It was hard on the dog, what with the complication of his fur that was made for another climate altogether, and I took him for increasingly longer walks, just to get out of the house. Twice I brought him to the park where the satellite had sloughed its skin, and if I combed the grass there looking for evidence—metal, more metal, a screw, a bolt—I never said a word about it to anybody, least of all Mallory. What did I find? A whole world of human refuse—bottle caps, cigarette lighters, a frayed length of shoelace, plastic in its infinite varieties—and the bugs that lived in and among it, oblivious. I came back from the second of these excursions and found Mallory on the couch where I'd left her, her bare feet and legs shining with sweat, magazine in one hand, Diet Coke in the other. She never even glanced up at me, but I could see right away there was something different about her, about the way she was holding herself, as if she knew something I didn't.

"I took the dog to the park," I said, looping his leash over the hook in the entryway. "Hotter down there than here, I think."

She didn't say anything.

"You want to go down to Gabe's for a drink? How does a G and T sound?"

"I don't know," she said, looking up at me for the first time. "I guess so. I don't care."

It was then that my gaze happened to fall on the bookcase, on the gap there, where the old paperback of *Nine Stories* had fallen flat. "Where's the thing?" I said.

"What thing?"

"The mesh. My *mesh*."

She shrugged. "I tossed it."

"Tossed it? Where? What do you mean?"

In the next moment I was in the kitchen, flipping open the lid to the trashcan, only to find it empty. "You mean outside?" I shouted. "In the Dumpster?"

When I came thundering back into the room she still hadn't moved. "Jesus, what were you thinking? That was mine. I wanted that. I wanted to keep it."

Her lips barely moved. "It was dirty."

I must have spent half an hour out there poking through the side-by-side Dumpsters that served our building and the one across the alley from it. I was embarrassed, I'll tell you, people strolling by and looking at me like I was one of the homeless, a can man, a bottle redeemer, and I was angry too, and getting angrier. She had no right, that was what I kept telling myself—she'd done it just to spite me, I knew it, and the worst thing, the saddest thing, was that now I'd never know if that piece of mesh was the real deal or not. I could have sent it to NASA, to the JPL, to somebody who could say yea or nay. But not now. Not anymore.

When I came back up the stairs, sweating and with the reek of rotting vegetables and gnawed bones and all the rest hanging round me like a miasma, I went right for her. I took hold of her arm, slapped the magazine away and jerked her to her feet. She looked scared and that just set me off all the more. I might have pushed her. She might have pushed back. Next thing I was out the door, out on the street, fuming, the sun still glaring overhead, everything before me looking as ordinary as dishwater. There was a bar down the street—air-conditioning, music, noise, people, a change of mood that was as easy to achieve as switching channels on the TV—and I was actually on my way there, my shoulders tense as wire, when I stopped myself. I patted down my pockets: wallet, keys, cell phone, a dribble of dimes and quarters. I didn't have a comb or a toothbrush or a change of underwear, I didn't have books or my iPod or the dog, but none of that seemed to matter, not anymore. A couple in shorts and running shoes flashed by me, breathing noisily. A motor scooter backfired across the street.

We kept the car in the lot out back of the apartment. I went the long way around the building, keeping close to the wall in case Mallory was at the front window looking to see where I'd gone off to. The tank showed less than a quarter full and my wallet held three fives and three singles—along with the change, that gave me a grand total of nineteen dollars and ninety-five cents. No matter. I'd stop at the ATM on the way out of town and if things got desperate I did have a credit card, which we reserved for emergencies only, because we really struggled just to make the minimum payment every month. Was this an emergency? Mallory wouldn't think so. The geniuses from NASA might not think so either—or the farmer whose sheep bore crusted-over scabs on their legs and throats and sad white faces. But as I wheeled the car out of the lot I couldn't help thinking it was the biggest emergency of my life.

I didn't know where I was going, I had no idea beyond the vague notion of putting some miles behind me, heading north maybe till the corn gave way to forest, to pines as fragrant as the air that went cold at night and seeped in through the open window so you had to pull a blanket over you when you went to sleep. The car—the rusted-out Volvo wagon Mallory's mother used to drive to work back in Connecticut—shuddered and let out a grinding mechanical whine as I pulled up in front of the bank. I got out, mounted the three steps to the concrete walkway where the ATM was and waited the requisite six feet, six inches away from the middle-aged woman in the inflated khaki shorts who was just then feeding in her card. The heat was staggering. My shirt was wet as a dishrag, my hair hanging limp. I wasn't thinking, just doing.

It was then that I glanced up and noticed the silver Toyota parked in the lot of the ice-cream parlor next door. A woman and two kids emerged from the building, licking cones, and went off down the street, and then the door swung open again and there was the blond girl, her own cone—the pale green of pistachio—held high and her face twisted in a grimace as she said something over her shoulder to the man behind her. He was wearing the same T-shirt he'd worn that day on the road and he didn't have an ice cream of his own, but as he came through the door he twisted his face too and jerked hold of the girl's arm. She let out a cry, and then the ice cream, double scoop, which had already begun to melt in green streaks across the back of her hand, slipped from the cone to plop wetly at her feet, just like anything else subject to the law of gravity.

"You creep," she said. "Look what you did." And he said something back. And then she said something. And then I was no longer watching them because as far as I was concerned they could go careering around the world on any orbit they wanted, just so long as it never intersected mine again. Space debris collides in two wide bands of low earth orbit, at 620 and 930 miles up, fragmenting and fragmenting again, things as big as satellites and rocket boosters and as small as the glove the astronaut Ed White lost on the first U.S. spacewalk. Eventually, it's all going to come down, and whether it'll burn up or crush a house or tap somebody on the shoulder in a dark field on a dark night is anybody's guess.

The woman at the ATM seemed to be having trouble with her card—no bills had yet appeared and she kept punching at the keys and reinserting the card as if sheer repetition would wear the machine down. I had time. I was very calm. I pulled out my cell and called Mallory. She answered on the first ring. "Yeah?" she snapped, angry still. "What do you want?"

I didn't say anything, not a word. I just pressed my thumb to the off switch and broke the connection. But what I'd wanted to say was that I'd taken the car and that I'd be back, I was pretty sure I'd be back, and that she should feed the dog and pay the rent, which was due the first of the month, and if she went out at night—if she went out at all—she should remember to look up, look up high, way up there where the stars burn and the space junk roams, because you never can tell what's going to come down next.

(2012)

Slate Mountain

The sun was a little gift from the gods, pale as a nectarine and hanging just above the treetops on a morning the weatherman on the local NPR affiliate had assured him would begin with a cold misting drizzle and progress to rain. Well, the weatherman—or actually, she was a woman, a weatherwoman, with a soft whispery voice that made you think of a whole range of activities that had nothing whatever to do with the weather—had been wrong before. More times than he could count. Satellites, ocean sensors, hygrometers, anemometers, barometers—they were all right in their way, relaying messages to people stuck in cities who might want to know when to break out their galoshes and umbrellas, but more often than not he could just step out the back door, take a sniff of the air and tell you with ninety-five percent accuracy what the day was going to bring. Of course he could. And he did it now, riding a rush of endorphins as he shifted the coffee cup from his right hand to his left to swing open the back door, stroll out onto the deck with its unimpaired views of the humped yellow fields and freestanding oaks and the blue-black mountains hanging above them, and take in the air. It was damp, no doubt about that, but the sky was clear, or mostly clear, and even if it did spit a little rain—even if it snowed up there at the higher elevations—there was no way in the world he was going to cancel the hike.

It was a Saturday at the end of October, the leaves bronzing on the lower slopes, deer season safely in the can and the mosquitoes gone to mosquito hell till spring at least, and seventeen people had signed up, including Mal Warner, who'd been a member of the group executive committee of the Los Padres Chapter for as long as Brice could remember. "So we'll have two executives along for this little stroll," Syl had pointed out at dinner last night. It hadn't really occurred to him to think of it in those terms—he and Mal went back forty-five years, to the time of Brower and the fight over the Grand Canyon, though they'd grown apart in recent years—but he'd looked up from his vegetarian lasagna and salad of nopal and field greens to give her a little nod of recognition. "Yes," he'd said, acknowledging the point—he was on the executive committee of the Kern-Kaweah Chapter, after all, not to mention leader of a dozen or more group hikes a year—"I guess so."

He'd set down his fork and gazed across the room, beyond Syl and the calendar on the wall and out the window to where the evening sun burnished the top rail of the fence till it shone as if it had been waxed, wondering all over again why

Mal had decided to drive all this way to join them—and not for dinner or a drink or a night of reminiscence out on the deck but for a routine day hike up a mountain that held no challenges for either of them. Plus, Mal had chosen to e-mail rather than telephone, as if he couldn't bother to waste his breath, though the message itself was amiable enough: *See you're leading one of your 60-plus hikes up Slate Mt. next week and thought I'd come join you. You've got to admit I qualify. And some. Looking forward. Yours, Mal. P.S. Say hi to Syl.*

Now, as the breeze shifted and a high vanguard of cirrostratus crept into place around the sun like dirty wash, he sipped his coffee and thought of the pleasures of the trail. It had been over a month since he'd been up in the mountains because of what he liked to call the special use tax of the hunting season, Fish and Game making their pile out of it and everybody else left to duck for cover. You'd have to be suicidal to leave the paved roads when the hunters were on the loose, whether you were dressed in Day-Glo orange and carrying an air-raid siren strapped to your back or not—Christ, if it was up to him he'd impose a ban on all hunting, even of rodents, and make it permanent. Over a month. He was looking forward to stretching his legs.

Just as he was about to go in and urge Syl to get a move on—it took nearly an hour to drive the switchbacks up to the seven-thousand-foot elevation of the trailhead where the group would assemble, and he, as leader, had to be there first to reassure them as they emerged from their vehicles in a confusion of coolers, daypacks and binoculars and the like, no dogs allowed, thank you, and alcoholic beverages discouraged—a glint of light caught his eye and he looked up to see a boxy silver car swing off the main road and start up the drive toward him. It took him a moment—the flash of wire-frame spectacles, the outsized head, the gleam of a perfect set of old man's choppers working over a wad of gum—to realize that this was Mal behind the wheel, and it took him a further moment to recollect and replay the unhappy occasion of their last meeting, which had nearly brought them to blows over the very pettiest of things, so petty it embarrassed him to recall it: a dinner check.

How long ago was it? Five or six years anyway. They'd been entertaining a party of Angels—donors in excess of the $100,000 range—after a horseback trip into the Golden Trout Wilderness, regaling them with a feast at the local lodge, no expense spared and everybody aglow with the camaraderie of the trail, when the check came. It was pretty hefty, but that was only to be expected, the overheated faces up and down the table glutted with filet mignon and lobster tail and the cocktails and wine and desserts and after-dinner drinks that preceded and rounded out the meal, but he and Mal had agreed beforehand to split the cost between their chapters. The waitress had brought the check to him, and while he was fumbling with his reading glasses and frowning over the figures that seemed to swell and recede in the candlelight, Mal had pushed himself up to come jauntily round the table, lean in and whisper in his good ear, "You're going to have to cover this—I must have left my wallet in my other pants." Which was exactly what he'd said, word for word, the last time. And the time before that. The upshot was a discussion out in the parking lot that managed to exhume some buried resentments, not the least of which involved Syl, who'd been Mal's lean leggy golden-braided hiking companion before Brice had ever met her, on a hike, with Mal, some forty years ago. He'd said some harsh things. So had Mal.

And now here he was, easing out of the car and slinging a daypack over his shoulder in one fluid motion, looking not a minute older than he had in the parking lot that day, though he must have been, what? Sixty-eight? Or no: sixty-nine. Sixty-nine and loping up the walk without the slightest hesitation, no hitch in *his* stride, no tics or palsies or spastic readjustment of the lower back muscles after the long drive, just forward momentum. When he reached the bottom step, Brice came down to him and they shared a solemn handshake. "Brice," Mal said.

"Mal."

"Hope you don't mind my stopping off here instead of meeting you up top. Thought it'd be nice to drive up with you. Plus"—and here he grinned, as if in acknowledgment of what had come between them—"it sure saves fuel."

Before he could respond, Syl came tearing out the door. "Mal!" she cried, scooting across the porch in her hiking boots, no-nonsense jeans and down vest to fall into his arms for a sisterly embrace that might have lasted just a beat too long. "It's so good to see you."

"Yeah," Mal said, his jaws working and his eyes shining, "you too."

Hiking wasn't a competitive activity, or that was the party line anyway, but of course it was. It was about endurance, about knowledge, wisdom, woodcraft, and it was as testosterone-fueled as any other sport, which was why he liked leading the sixty-and-up groups—it eliminated the young studs with their calf-length shorts and condescending attitudes, the kind who were always pressing to pass you on the trail. He could really get worked up about that if he let himself, because the first rule of the group hike, to which they'd all sworn allegiance beforehand, was never to pass the leader (or, for their opposite number, the bloated ex-athletes and desk jockeys and their top-heavy wives, never to lag behind the rear leader). Now, as they stood assembled at the trailhead, he went over the printed rules for the twelve hikers who'd showed up: four couples in their early to late sixties, a single man wearing lace-up knee boots who looked to be seventy-five or so and three stocky women in matching pastel hoodies he took to be widows or divorcées. "And remember," he said, "always keep in sight of the person ahead of you in case there're forks in the trail and you're not sure which way to go. Any questions?"

"What about bears?" one of the stocky women asked.

He shrugged, gave her a slow smile. "Oh, I don't know—what did you bring for lunch?"

"Tuna. On rye."

"Uh-huh, well that just happens to be their favorite. They're probably all lifting their muzzles in the air right now, taking a sniff." He waited for laughter, but there was none. "But seriously, it shouldn't be a problem. I rarely see bears up here, especially this time of year after the hunters have got through with them. But if a bear should come for you, you know the drill: stand up tall, wave your arms and shout. And if that doesn't do it, abandon your pack. And lunch. Better to go hungry than have a four-hundred-pound black bear pinning you down and licking your face, don't you think?"

That got a chuckle out of them, at least a couple of them anyway. He gave the group a quick once-over, looking for weakness or instability, thinking of the woman who'd had some sort of nervous breakdown on the Freeman Creek trail last spring, repeating a single word—"dirigible"—over and over in an array of voices till she was screaming it at the treetops. Or the bone-thin guy dressed in motorcycle regalia who'd gone into convulsions and had to have a stick thrust between his teeth while the ravens buzzed overhead and an untimely snow sifted down to whiten his face and sculpt miniature pyramids on both ends of the stick before help could arrive. That had been a nightmare. And if it hadn't been for one of the group, a dental hygienist who knew her way around emergencies, the guy probably would have died there on the trail. But that was an anomaly, the chance you take, whether you're out on a mountaintop in the Sierras or pushing a cart at Walmart.

There wouldn't be any problems today, he could see that at a glance. A cluster of mild-looking faces hung round him like pale fruit, old faces—*older* faces—that had seen their senses of humor erode along with everything else. They looked obedient, respectful, eager. And all of them, the seventy-five-year-old and the stocky women included, looked fit enough for what had been advertised as a moderate-to-strenuous hike of six hours' duration and a two-thousand-foot elevation gain, lunch at the summit, back before dark. No problem. No problem at all.

He collected the liability waivers, checked his watch to give the two no-shows the requisite fifteen minutes to pull into the lot, then announced, "We're all set then. Just follow me and I'll try to point out anything interesting we might encounter along the way." And he'd actually started out, the group falling into line behind him, before he swung round and added, pointing to Mal, "The rear leader today is Mal Warner, in the plaid shirt there?"

Until he pronounced it aloud, he hadn't realized he was going to select Mal, but after being stuck in the car with him for the better part of an hour, listening to him jaw on about everything from his stock-market losses to the line of hiking gear he was trying to get off the ground with the help of a major investor and his devotion to Pilates, weight training and the modified butterfly stroke he'd devised to take pressure off his hips, Brice couldn't help thinking it might be best all the way round if he put some distance between himself and Mal. Mal would have been the logical choice in any case, since Brice didn't know the first thing about any of the others and Syl could get herself lost walking to the grocery store. They'd have plenty of time to catch up on things later on—at least that's what he told himself. He even foresaw a conciliatory dinner, at which he would insist on picking up the check.

"Please be sure to stay ahead of him," he went on, in official mode. "And if you have trouble, whether it's a stone in your shoe or a blister or you need to catch your breath, just give a holler. We want everybody to have a super experience today, okay?" Heads nodded. People shuffled in place. "So let's just go and enjoy the heck out of it, are you with me?"

The first sour note was struck before they'd gone half a mile. Someone—hunters, was his best guess—had scattered trash all over the trail, fire-blackened cans, plastic bags, a slurry of corn cobs, ground meat and chili beans in a sauce like congealed blood, the de rigueur half-crumpled beer cans and empty liquor bottles. Today it was bourbon and vodka, generic brands, the mainstay of the middle-aged sportsman. If they were younger, it would have been Jägermeister, and what the appeal of that sugary medicinal crap was, he could never figure. Of course, in his day it was sloe gin, which you gulped down without pausing for breath, telling yourself you loved it, till it came up in the back of your throat. No matter—he made a point of carrying a biodegradable trash bag with him anywhere he went, even along the back roads down below, and now he bent patiently to the trash and began stuffing it into the mouth of the bag.

"People have no respect," somebody said.

"You can say that again," the woman who'd been worried about the bears put in, and in the next moment she was kneeling beside him, scooping up trash with hands like risen dough and nails done in two colors, magenta and pink. "They're like animals." And then, lowering her voice to address him so he had to turn his face to hers and see that she was wearing mascara and blusher—on a hike—she said, "I'm Beverly, by the way. Beverly Slezak? I thought you might have known my husband Hal, from down in Visalia? He was a great one for hiking—before the cancer got to him. Lung," she added, her shoulder brushing against his as she leaned forward to dump a handful of cans into the bag.

"No," he said, scuttling forward with the bag as some of the others brought him offerings, "I don't think I know him. Or knew him, that is."

Mal's voice, from somewhere behind him: "People *are* animals. Apes. The third chimpanzee, along with the bonobo and the common chimp."

"Right," Syl put in. "And that's why we're out here in the woods, cleaning up trash. It's what apes do."

Somebody laughed. And then the old guy (*old:* he was ten years older than Brice, if that) opined in a flat voice that it was probably Mexicans because the whole world's just a dump to them and one of the other men—tall, with swept-back features and a long white braid trailing down his back—objected. "Hey, I resent that. I'm Mexican and you don't see me throwing shit all over the place—"

"All right," Brice heard himself say, and he was straightening up now and twisting a knot in the neck of the bag, "it's nothing to get worked up over, sad as it is—it's just the kind of thing we want to educate people about. But what we'll do? We'll leave the bag here beside the trail and collect it when we come back down, because no litterer's going to spoil my day, are you with me?"

After that, they went on up along a series of meadows and he pointed out the frost-withered remains of the various plants that flowered here in July—corn lilies, sneezeweed, columbine, rein orchids, geraniums—and promised he'd lead a summer hike if anybody was interested in seeing the meadows in bloom. "Right," said Beverly, who seemed to have taken up post position just behind him, "and get eaten alive by the mosquitoes. And gnats. And those biting things, what are they? They look like houseflies but they sure make you dance."

He turned his head to look at her without breaking stride—and where was Syl? There, back toward the rear, in animated discussion with Mal. She was matching him stride for stride, her hands juggling ideas, the brim of her baseball cap pulled down so he couldn't make out the upper half of her face, only her outthrust chin and the gleam of her moving lips. "Deerflies," he said.

"Not the yellow ones, the black ones."

A breeze stirred the tops of the pines. He could taste the moisture on the air. The sun was gone. "I don't know," he said. "Some sort of horsefly maybe. But you don't have to worry today, do you?"

"No," she said, taking the grade with short powerful thrusts of her legs, and he saw that she wasn't so much overweight as muscular, her calves swelling against the woolen knee socks and her thighs caught in the grip of a pair of tight blue nylon shorts. "No, I guess not."

"That's the beauty of a fall hike," he said, swinging round to fling out his arms as if he'd created it all, the meadows, the views, the soaring pines and big granite boulders ranged like giants' skulls along the trail. Soon it would all be covered in snow and you'd need skis to get up here.

The old man—he was second behind Beverly—took the opportunity to ask an involved question about the geology of the mountain, throwing around terms like "pre-cretaceous" and "metamorphic," and the best Brice could do was to say he honestly didn't know but that up top, up at nine thousand feet, there were all sorts of rare plants, like purple mountain parsley, which hadn't even been discovered—or identified, that is—till 1976.

"Dead now, I suppose," the old man said.

Brice acknowledged the point, taking a quick glance behind him to be sure everybody was still there, the group in single file now as the trail steepened and the switchbacks dug into the slope in the thinning air. "Just like the bugs."

Two miles up was a saddle with a scatter of downed trees, where he liked to call a rest stop so people could catch up, refer to their water bottles and power bars and take in the view of the granite spires known as the Needles where they rose up like outstretched fingers from the grip of the mountain opposite. The group settled in, some of them spreading groundcloths, others easing down in the pine needles to sort through their packs. Everyone seemed companionable enough at this point, all the hang-ups and anxieties of their daily lives washed clean on the flow of blood pumping through their hearts and lungs and down into the loose working muscles of their legs. As advertised. And what had John Muir said? *I never saw a discontented tree.* Exactly.

He was unwrapping the avocado and bean-sprout sandwich he'd prepared in the kitchen before first light when Syl, the bill of her cap set at a rakish angle, eased down beside him and began sorting through her own pack. She was on a diet—a perpetual diet, though to his eyes her figure had scarcely changed over the years, her legs firm, her stomach flat and her small, perfectly proportioned breasts still right where they should be, whether she was wearing a bra or not, and never mind the striations above her upper lip or the way her throat sagged to give away her age—and so she'd passed on his offer to make her a sandwich, relying on her cache of low-cal fiber bars instead. She unwrapped one now and gave him a grin.

He grinned back. He was feeling good, better than good—he could have climbed up over Slate and kept on going down the far side and into the foothills, along the river course and all the way home. Car? What car? Who needed a car? "What were you two talking about back there?" he asked. "From what I could see it looked like you barely had time to catch your breath."

"What? Mal and me? He's a talker, that's for sure. He's still upset about his last wife—Gloria, the one we never met? They lasted two years, I gather, if that. Plus, he keeps repeating himself, starts on one story and then suddenly he's off on another one and then another till he doesn't even know what the subject is and you have to guide him back to it."

"If you've got the patience." He took a bite of the sandwich, gazed across the massed treetops below them to where the Kern River cut its canyon and then to the mountains beyond, mountains that rolled into other ranges altogether, on and on till they dropped off into the deserts to the east.

"I don't know what it is between you two—I mean, after all these years. He's Mal, what can I say? He's got his charms. Still."

The notion irritated him. "I thought he was a real bore."

"That's just because he was nervous."

"Nervous? About what?"

"You. The situation. Seeing us both after all this time. You know what he said? He said I was as beautiful as the day we first met."

He didn't have anything to say to this. He studied her a moment, her legs sprawled in front of her, her lips pursed, her gaze eclipsed by some private memory. She took a bite of the fiber bar, a smear of chocolate caught in the corner of her mouth, then unscrewed the cap of her water bottle and took a long swallow.

"But what about you?" she said finally. "You seemed pretty friendly with your groupie there, what was her name—the one with the nails and face job and the hair dyed the color of a brick wall? What is she, a cosmetologist or something?"

He just smiled. "Beats me."

"But she's hot for something, isn't she?"

"Yeah," he agreed, smiling wider. "Aren't they all?"

It had begun to rain, a light pattering in the dust that had people rising to their feet and briskly stuffing things back into their packs. Mal had already shrugged into his poncho and was making his way toward them, so he pushed himself up and clapped his hands to get everyone's attention. "All right, everybody," he said, raising his voice to be heard over the scrape and shuffle of activity, "gather round a minute. I don't think the rain's going to amount to much—"

"Scattered showers," the old man put in, cutting him off. "That's what the TV said."

"Right, well, we can head down now or go on up to the summit—what do you think, show of hands?"

The majority, Mal and Syl included, raised their hands, while the remainder just stood there watching him. "Good," he said finally. "I'd hate for a little weather to spoil the fun, so let's go on as planned and see what it's like up top—anybody has a problem, don't be shy. Just let me know and we'll head back down anytime you say. But really, I agree with"—gesturing to the old man—"what was your name?"

"Louis."

"With Louis here. The forecast, I mean. A little rain never hurt anybody, right?"

They were up at eight thousand feet, moving along easily, the rain sucked back up into the clouds, the trail barely slick and the black sheared-off face of Slate Mountain looming over the treetops as if it had just dropped down out of the sky, when the cries of what must have been a whole flock of ravens broke the silence. The trees held fast. There was the scrape of hiking boots. Then a pair of the birds appeared from below, beating upslope, their wings creaking to gain purchase on the air, and everybody stopped to watch them go. "What's that all about, you think?" Beverly asked, and there she was, right behind him, her hair clamped beneath a floppy pink hat now as a concession to the damp. "Something dead up there?"

"Probably a deer," he said, "or the offal anyway. The stuff the hunters leave behind."

"For a raven party."

"Yeah, I guess so," he said, moving on, talking over his shoulder while keeping one eye on the snaking line behind him. He was thinking of the way a carcass disappears up here, beetles coming up out of the ground, flies laying their eggs, vultures and ravens at it, rot, bacteria, coyotes, even the mice sneaking out under cover of darkness to gnaw calcium from the bones. He wanted to say, *Everything dies to give life to something else,* but he didn't want to come off sounding pompous—or morbid, especially with a group like this, when they were all out here to deny the proposition or at least forget about it for the time it took them to get to the summit of a mountain and back down again—and so he left it at that.

He turned his head and kept moving on up the trail, Beverly doing her best to keep pace, to show him she was fit, a fit widow, if that was what she was, as if he were in the market and this was some kind of test. Which, he supposed, it was. Why should there be limits? If you felt good, what did age matter? It was only a number. He didn't feel any different than he had at fifty—or forty, even. His blood pressure was in the acceptable range, he and Syl had sex once a week and he slept through the night and woke each morning with the sense that there was something new out there in the world, something reserved for him and him alone if only he had the strength to go out and find it. His feet dug at the trail. He wasn't even breathing hard.

When they got close, he could see that the ravens were squabbling over something just off the trail. They hung in the trees like ornaments, fought along the ground in a black flap of wings, their voices harsh and constricted. He sliced away from the trail then, dodging through waist-high brush until he was there and the ravens lifted off silently and he saw what it was they'd been disputing: a bear. The carcass of a bear, its paws removed and its gut slit open, but otherwise intact. Before he had time to think (Rule #2: Never leave the trail), Beverly was there at his elbow and he could hear the others following behind, their voices muted, legs scissoring through the brush. He hadn't wanted this: these people were old, they could misstep, break a leg, break everything.

"What is it," Beverly said, breathless, "—a bear? Is that a bear?"

There was an anger churning in him—poachers, and they'd got the gallbladder and the paws to sell on the black market and left the rest to rot. What was wrong with the world? Christ, you couldn't even take a hike anymore, not without this, this obscenity, this *shit.* Suddenly he was shouting. "Get back, all of you! Back on the trail!" But it was too late. Half of them were already gathered round, gaping at the swollen dead thing before them, its eyes gone, tongue discolored, the stumps of the legs rigid as poles, and the rest picking their way toward him. Beverly had her cell phone out, taking pictures. And here came Syl and Mal and then the old man, high-stepping his way through the bushes as if they were about to come to life and take him down.

"We ought to report this," Beverly said. "What number do we call? You know what number?"

He would have told her it was useless, useless because there was nothing anybody could do about it, nothing that would put the animal together again and breathe the life back into it or eliminate the superstition and ignorance that drove the market for animal parts, for degradation, for destruction, but instead he just said, "There's no signal up here."

It was then that the trees began to stir, a breeze there, a sound like distant freight. When the rain came, it came in earnest, a heavy pounding that slicked everything even as they struggled back to the trail and fumbled with their rain gear, and then it was sleet, and then it was snow.

This time there was no debate, no show of hands, no further pretense: if they wanted to make the summit it would have to be another day because he was in charge here—he was the captain of this ship—and they were turning back. "We're calling it a day," he said, and he wanted to tail it with a joke, a quip about the weather or maybe the weatherwoman on the radio and how she'd been right after all, but all the lightness had gone out of him. It was always rougher on the way down than the way up—people never seemed to realize that—and with the wet snow the footing would be worse than usual. He'd have to keep an eye on the old guy—Louis—and on Beverly, who'd already slipped twice, the rear of her shorts sporting a long dark vertical smear that ran down the back of her right leg as if she'd just stepped out of the mineral bath at the spa. They hadn't gone a hundred yards before he almost lost it himself, looking back over his shoulder to keep everyone in sight when he should have been watching his own two feet, but he managed to catch himself at the last minute. That would have been something, the group leader taking a muddy pratfall, and whether he'd have wound up hurting himself or not, he could imagine the sort of multi-faceted joke Mal would have made of it—and you didn't see *him* slipping. Not Mal. He had the agility of a surfer, all out-flung arms and flapping lips.

No one had much to say, not even Beverly, who was right behind him (and Louis behind her, as if they'd drawn lots). Every once in a while, negotiating the sharp corner of a switchback, he'd hear a snatch of Mal's voice in mid-discourse, but the rest were quiet, focusing on their own thoughts and maybe their disappointment too, because if you didn't reach the summit, no matter how illuminating the scenery or soothing the exercise, the hike was a failure. For his part, he was disappointed too—the bear had cast a pall over everything and then the weather had come down on top of that, and if he had to think about it, there was Mal too, Mal as pure irritant, and why he'd ever agreed to get back together with him he'd never know. Some misguided notion of being cool or democratic or nostalgic or whatever it was. His neck ached from looking back over his shoulder and his left knee was sore where he'd strained it to keep from falling. He was thinking he'd beg off on dinner plans, thinking maybe Mal could get a ride back with somebody else—*Next time,* he'd tell him, we'll do it *next time*—and then they were down at the seventy-five-hundred-foot level and the snow tapered off to sleet and then a light rain and by the time they reached the parking area it had stopped altogether.

He stood there patiently at the trailhead, making a checkmark by each name on his reservation list as people filed by him. Most just nodded or gave him a muted thanks, eager to get to their cars and back to their recliners and sofas and wide-screen TVs, but the old man stopped to jaw awhile—*Hell, I could have made it to the top, no problem, but I respect your decision, what with the women, but maybe next time we'll do an all-male hike and really put some miles under our boots, huh, what do you say?*—and Beverly stopped too, standing there beside him as if she were ready to hand out certificates of achievement.

Five minutes passed. Ten. He kept looking up the long flat final stretch of the trail, expecting to see Syl and Mal come striding round the corner at any minute, but they never showed. The old man climbed into his car. The lot cleared. Beverly snapped open her compact and touched up her lipstick, making a kissing noise that seemed unnaturally loud in the silence that had descended after the last of the cars rattled up the rutted road to the highway. "Where could they be?" she murmured, as if thinking for him. "They were right behind us, weren't they?"

He looked back across the dirt lot to where his car stood beside a bulky black SUV that must have been Beverly's, straining his eyes to see into the darkened interior, as if somehow Syl and Mal had slipped by him and were waiting there for him, talking quietly, making jokes, wondering why he was lingering here with this boxy widow while the sky darkened and everybody just grew colder and hungrier.

At fifteen minutes he cupped his hands and began to shout. "Syl!" he called, "Syl!," until he was bleating it. At twenty, he started back up the trail, Beverly tagging along like a dog, though he tried to dissuade her. "You don't have to feel responsible," he told her. "It's nothing. I'm sure it's nothing."

"I want to help. I can't just leave you out here by yourself."

He had nothing to say to this. He could feel the incline in the long muscles of his legs. His breath steamed before him. "I can't imagine what happened," he said, moving quickly now, but not panicking, not yet. "They're both experienced in the woods and they're both—Syl especially—in good shape."

"Maybe she turned an ankle. Maybe—" Beverly let the thought trail off. She was eager, keeping pace, her arms swinging at her sides.

He didn't want to think about heart attack or stroke or even broken bones. He called out till his voice went hoarse and the shadows deepened and the trail was gone and they had to turn back. It was full dark by the time they got back to his car. He sat there, the heater going, Beverly shivering beside him, and tapped the horn at intervals, signaling into the night. An hour crept by. The battery light kept going on and he had to keep starting the car up to run the heater and then shutting it off again. What they talked about, he and Beverly—this stranger who was sitting beside him in the dark while his thoughts raced and collided—he had no recollection of afterward. But at seven, when there was still no sign of Syl, he backed the car around and drove the three miles to the lodge, where there would be a telephone available to him, a ground line that could get him through to anybody, to the county sheriff, the paramedics, Search and Rescue, and what was he going to say? Just this: *I've got two people missing.*

He was in a brightly lit place, voices swelling round him, an undercurrent of jaunty guitar and country baritone washing through the speakers at either end of the room. The man from the local SAR team—mid-forties, squat, carrying a big breadbasket of flesh round his waist like a badge of authority—had told him they'd be on the case as soon as they could, volunteers and sheriff's department people driving up the mountain even as they spoke, but that they really couldn't expect to do much till first light in the morning. The temperature was likely to go down into the teens overnight—that was what he'd heard on the radio anyway—but the snow was expected to hold off, so there was that. Were they dressed for the elements, these two? Did they have a space blanket? A tent? The means to make a fire?

Brice had just shaken his head. He had everything he needed for an emergency in his pack, but who knew what Syl was carrying? Or Mal. Mal should have known better, should have been prepared, but then he'd always been a free spirit—give him a minute and he'd tell you all about it—and whether he'd thought beyond a couple sandwiches and a bottle of water for a routine day hike, who could say? And then he was picturing them up there on the mountain in the fastness of the night, lost and cold and hungry, huddling together for warmth, maybe injured—maybe that was it, maybe Mal had broken a leg or knocked himself unconscious doing the butterfly face-first into a tree—and then he was staring down at the plate set on the bar before him, a sandwich there, untouched, and the drink beside that, bourbon and water, no ice. "I don't blame you," Beverly was saying, "because if I was in your place the last thing I'd be thinking about is food, but you've got to keep yourself up."

She was perched on the stool beside him, the remains of a steak and salad scattered about the plate at her elbow, a drink in one hand. She'd gone to the ladies' and cleaned herself up, the smear of mud gone now, her makeup freshened, her legs crossed at the knee. He saw Syl again, up there in the dark. Huddling. With Mal. And then he saw himself in bed with this woman, with Beverly, who'd confessed to him in a breathless voice that she'd signed up for the hike under false pretenses: "I'm really only fifty-three, and that's the truth. But then you didn't exactly I.D. me, did you?"

He kept telling himself that everything was going to turn out all right, that Mal and Syl must have missed the turnoff and taken the trail that led in the other direction altogether, eight miles down to Coy Flat, and that once it got dark they would have seen it was too late to retrace their steps—and he'd told the Search and Rescue man the same thing. *They must have missed the fork, that's all,* but the man had just said, *How old did you say they were?*

What if she died? What if Syl died up there?

He tried to put the thought out of his head, tried to focus: here was the emergency he'd always thought he was prepared for, but when it came to it, he wasn't prepared for anything. How could he be? How could anybody? The whole world was just chance and misstep, that was all. A bear wandered too far afield and wound up gutted and dead, you took the wrong turn and died of exposure on the flank of a mountain under a thin black sky that was no covering at all. The truth was, he hadn't taken Syl away from Mal. Mal hadn't wanted her. He'd gone to South America, to the Andes and Tierra del Fuego, to climb mountains and tramp the wide world, but he couldn't wait for Syl to finish college and so he left her behind. And Brice had been there for her. Every Friday, no matter the weather or how beaten down he was from the shit job he'd taken out of college just to pay the bills, he drove the two hundred miles up the cleft of the San Joaquin Valley to take her to dinner or a movie or to cruise the student bars and then sit in the lounge of the dorm sucking at her tongue and feeling for her breasts till the lights flickered for curfew. Then they were together. Then they were married. And then, childless by design because children were an extravagance in a world already stressed to the limits, they devoted themselves to right living and ecology, to education and preservation. They grew old together. *Older.*

Beverly leaned into him, the toe of her hiking boot grazing his leg. He saw that she'd removed the knee socks so that her legs were bare, solid legs, smooth, descending to the sculpted hollows of her ankles. "So what do you want to do?" she asked, and they might have been on a date in some anonymous place, not a care in the world that wasn't immediate and erotic. "You can't sit up in your car all night long, you're not going to do that, are you?"

He was. That was the least he could do. There was a sleeping bag in the trunk. He'd wrap himself in that.

"Because, well, you're going to have to drive me back to get my car, and I'm perfectly willing to sit there with you for as long as you want and we can honk the horn every once in a while, to signal, but you should know I took a room here for the night, very reasonable actually, and you're welcome—I mean, no strings attached—if you want to get some sleep, that is . . ."

In some way it was Syl's own fault, trusting Mal like that, keeping up the chatter—the flirtation—till neither of them was paying the slightest bit of attention to the trail or where it went or what had happened to the rest of the group, which must have been around the next turn, sure it was, and why worry? It wouldn't have fazed Mal. Or Syl. He would have liked a bed—and whatever else Beverly was offering—but he could already foresee exactly what was going to happen.

He was going to drive her to her car where it sat beneath the trees in the impenetrable dark and he was going to say no to her, but gently, and there'd be a kiss and maybe a bit more—he wasn't dead yet—but then she'd get in her car and the brake lights would flash and she'd be gone, back to the lodge and the lights and the music. And he'd sit there wrapped up in the sleeping bag, stiff and miserable, till dawn broke and the Search and Rescue team hurried up the path he was too drained to negotiate and within the hour they'd be back, bearing Mal on a stretcher because Mal was too far gone with cold and disorientation to stand upright on his own. A few minutes—five, ten?—would elapse, each one thunderous, dropping down on him like a series of explosions. He'd be out of the car, moving toward the trailhead, and there she'd be, dehydrated maybe, suffering from exposure, but tall still, and erect, her head held high and her step firm, Syl, the old lady he was married to.

(2011)

Sic Transit

There was a foul odor coming from the house—the odor, as it turned out, of rotting flesh—but nobody did anything about it, at least not at first. I was away at the time, my business taking me to the East Coast for a series of fruitless meetings with a consortium of inadequate and unserious people whose names I forgot the minute I settled into the first-class cabin for the trip back home, and so I had the story from my wife's walking partner, Mary Ellen Stovall, who makes her living in real estate. We'd always wondered about that house, which was something of an eyesore in the neighborhood—or would have been an eyesore, that is, if it was visible from the street. We went by the place nearly every day, my wife Chrissie and I, running errands or strolling down to the beach club or one of the shops and restaurants on the main road. The houses around it—tasteful, well-kept and very, very pricey—were what you'd expect from a California coastal community, in styles ranging from craftsman to Spanish mission to contemporary, most of them older homes that had been extensively remodeled, in some cases taken right down to the frame or even the original slab. But what this one looked like was anybody's guess because the trees and shrubbery had long since gone wild so that all you saw was a curtain of green enclosing a gravel drive, in the center of which stood—or rather, listed—an ancient, rust-spattered Buick the size of our two Priuses combined.

As it happened, the man who lived there—*had* lived there—was a recluse in his early sixties whom no one, not even the next-door neighbors, could recall ever having seen. The properties on either side of him featured eight-foot walls topped with bougainvillea that twisted toward the sun in great puffed-up balls of leaf and thorn and flame-red flower, and as I say, his property had reverted to nature so that his flat acre on a bluff with ocean views might as well have been sectioned out of the Amazonian jungle for all anybody could see into—or out of—it. Isolation, that was what he had. Isolation so absolute it took that odor and a span of eight full days after he'd expired for the police and firemen, who'd arrived simultaneously in response to the neighbors' complaints, to force open the door and find him sunk into his bed, his mouth thrown open and the mattress so stained with his fluids it had to be burned once the coroner and the forensics people had got done with him.

Why am I telling you all this? Because of what came next, of what I discovered both on my own and with Mary Ellen Stovall's help, and because I'm in a period of my life—I just turned fifty—when I've begun to think less about the daily struggle and more of what awaits us all in the end. Here was an anonymous death, unattended, unmourned, and the thought of it, of this man, whoever he was, drawing his last breath in a run-down house on a very valuable piece of property not two blocks from where Chrissie and I had bought in at top dollar during the very crest of the boom, spoke to me in some deep way I couldn't define. Had he suffered? Had he lain there for days, weeks, a month, too ill or derelict in his soul to call for help? Had he slowly starved? Mary Ellen—who was to get the listing once the surviving relative, a brother, equally bereft, in some godforsaken place like Nebraska or Oklahoma, had given her the go-ahead—claimed that the body had been practically engulfed in a litter of soda cans, half-filled containers of microwave noodles, and (this really got to me) blackened avocado skins from the tree out back.

According to the ten-line story that appeared in the local paper the day after I got back, the dead man had been identified as Carey Fortunoff, and he'd once been a member of an obscure rock band called Metalavox, after which he disappeared from public view, though he continued to write the occasional song for other bands and singers, a few of whom were named in the article, but they must have been equally obscure since neither Chrissie nor I had ever heard of them. Out of curiosity I googled the band and came up with a single paragraph that was virtually a duplicate of what the paper had run. There was a photo, in black and white, of the five band members in a typical pose of the era, which looked to be late seventies, early eighties, judging from their haircuts and regalia. They were in a cemetery, variously slouching against one tombstone or another, wearing mirror sunglasses and wasp-waisted jackets, their hair judiciously mussed. As to which one was Carey Fortunoff—the dead man—I couldn't say, though for the two or three minutes I invested in staring at the photo I imagined he was the one standing—slouching—just slightly to the left of the four others and staring out away from the camera as if he had better things on his mind than posing for a cheesy promotional shot. And that was it. I clicked on something else, which led me to another thing altogether and before I knew it half an hour had vanished from my life. Then I went down to see what Chrissie wanted to do about dinner.

The next day was Sunday and I was up early, still running on East Coast time. I awakened in the dark and for a long while just lay there on my side watching the numbers mutate on the face of the ancient digital clock Chrissie's mother had left behind when she'd died the previous year. I hadn't wanted that clock—I always tried to sleep through the night and didn't like knowing what time it was if I woke to use the bathroom, which was increasingly common now that I'd reached the age when the prostate seems programmed to enlarge—but, of course, out of sensitivity to Chrissie and her loss, I'd given in. "It reminds me of her," Chrissie had claimed the day she'd cleared space on the bureau and knelt to plug the thing in. "I know it's crazy," she added, turning to give me a plaintive look, "but it's like she's right here watching over me." Again, out of sensitivity, I didn't point out to my wife that she couldn't see the thing anyway since she wore a sleep mask to bed (along with a medieval-looking dental appliance designed to prevent her from snoring, which, occasionally, it did). At any rate, I watched the numbers reorganize themselves until the window took on a grayish glow that reminded me of the test pattern on the TV we'd had when I was a boy, then I pushed myself up, pulled on a pair of shorts, a T-shirt and sandals, and slipped out the door, thinking to walk down to the village for croissants and coffee.

It was utterly still, the new-made light just touching the tops of the trees in a glad, dependable way. There was no sound but for the distant hiss of the freeway, a kind of white noise we all get so used to we barely know it's there. A crow started up somewhere and then the other birds chimed in, variously clucking and whistling, but hidden from view. I wasn't thinking about Carey Fortunoff or anything else for that matter beyond maybe the way the smell of fresh coffee and croissants hot from the oven hit you when you stepped in the door of the bakery, but then I found myself passing by his house—or jungle, that is—and I couldn't help stopping right there in the street to wonder all over again about the kind of person who could let his property deteriorate like that.

The car was still there, still listing, still enclosed in a shadowy pocket of vegetation. The bushes were woven as tight as thatch, the trees—eucalyptus, black acacia, oak and Catalina cherry—struggling above them. Looking closer, I could see the bright globes of oranges and—what was it, Meyer lemon?—choked in the gloom, and there, to the side of the car, a splash of pink begonias run wild. I glanced over my shoulder. Did I feel guilty? Ghoulish, even? Yes. But a moment later I was trespassing on a dead man's property.

It was nothing to duck down the tunnel of the drive to where a crude path twisted through the undergrowth in the direction of what must have been the house itself. The shadows congealed. I felt a chill. People always describe the odor of dead things as being vaguely sweetish, but the smell here was more of the earth, the smell of compost or what's left at the bottom of the trash can on a summer morning. I'd gone maybe a hundred feet before I spotted a window up ahead, the light puddled there, dense and gray, and then the front of the house emerged from the tangle like a stage prop, single story, flat roof, stucco in a shade of brown so dark it was almost black. Coffee grounds, that was what I thought of, a house the color of coffee grounds, and what was wrong with beige or white or even lime green for that matter? But now the path widened, branches broken off, bushes trampled, and it came to me that this was where the police had gone in to bundle up the corpse in some sort of plastic sheet or body bag, something impervious to leakage.

I could have stopped there. I suppose I should have. But I was curious—and I'd come this far, Chrissie asleep still, the croissants on the warming tray in the display case at the bakery and the coffee brewing, and, as I say, I felt some deeper compulsion, no man an island and all that—and without even thinking I went right up the front steps and tried the door. It was locked, as I'd expected it to be, though in this neighborhood we have an exceptionally low incidence of crime and people have grown pretty casual about security. Half the time—and I'm at fault here, I know it, because you've got to be prepared for the unexpected—Chrissie and I forget to set the house alarm when we turn in at night. Still, there I was on the front porch of Carey Fortunoff's house and the door was locked—and whether he'd locked it himself before climbing into bed for the final time or the firemen had secured it after breaking in was something I didn't want to think about. Next thing I knew, I was fighting my way through jasmine and oleander gone mad, clinging to the skin of the house and trying the windows successively till I reached the back and found the door there, a windowless slab of pine painted the same color as the house, only two shades lighter. I tried the knob. It turned in my hand till it clicked and the door eased open.

Inside, the smell was more intense, as you might expect, but it wasn't overpowering—there was a chemical component to it, an astringency, and I realized that the firemen must have used some sort of dispersal agent to contain the odor. Everything was dim, the windows overgrown, the shades pulled, the shadows intact. Very gradually—and it was absolutely still in that room, which turned out to be the kitchen—my eyes began to adjust and I was surprised to see that things were orderly enough, no cascading bags of garbage, no blackened pans piled up in a grease-smeared sink, no avocado skins strewn across the floor. Orderly—and ordinary too. He had the same sort of things in his kitchen we did, dishwasher, Viking range, coffee maker, refrigerator.

For a long while I just stood there, ignoring the voice in my head that advised me to get out, screamed at me to get out while I could, because if anybody should catch me here the humiliation factor would be off the scale, *Neighbor Caught Looting Dead Rocker's House,* but then, almost as if I were working from a script, I crossed the room and pulled open the refrigerator door. The light blinked on and I saw the usual stuff arrayed there—catsup, mayonnaise, Dijon mustard, horseradish, chunky peanut butter, pickles, a six-pack of Hires root beer. Half a dozen eggs resided in the sculpted plastic container built into the door. There was butter in the butter compartment and in the rack on the door a carton of one percent milk, expired. Did I actually unscrew the lid of the pickle jar, pluck one out with thumb and forefinger and savor the cold crunch of it between my teeth? I'm not sure. Maybe. Maybe I did.

Again, there was something operating in me here that I'm not proud of—that I wasn't even in control of—and I'm telling you about it simply to get it down, get it straight, but really, what was the harm? I was curious, all right? Is curiosity a crime? And sympathetic too, don't forget that. A thought flashed through my head—if those East Coast people could see me now they'd be the ones vetoing the arrangement and not me—but the thought crumpled like foil and in the next moment I was moving down the hall to the living room, or great room, as the realtors like to call it. Great or not, it was an expansive space with a raised ceiling that must have taken up a third of the square footage of the place and had once featured a view out to sea, where water and sky met in a shimmering translucent band that shrank and enlarged and changed color through all the phases of the day, the same view Chrissie and I enjoy, albeit more distantly, from our upstairs bedroom window. The shades hadn't been drawn here, but there was nothing to see beyond the cascading leaves and the bare branchless knuckles of the shrubs pressed up against the glass.

There was a grand piano in one corner (Steinway, white) and across from it an electric version hooked up via a nest of wires to a pair of speakers that stood on either side of it. I had an impulse to lift the lid on the Steinway and try a key or two—and who in this world has ever entered a room with a piano and failed to go to it and tinkle out something, be it "Chopsticks" or the opening bars of Tchaikovsky's "Marche Slave"?—but I fought it down. The neighbors might have been behind an eight-foot wall but how could they fail to remark on the sound of a dead man playing the piano at six-thirty of a Sunday morning? No. No piano playing. Chrissie would be waking soon, the paper was still in the driveway and the croissants waiting. I had to go. Had to leave right this minute . . . but what was this on the walls, these rectangular forms giving back the soupy light? Photos. Framed photos.

A glance showed me I'd been wrong in identifying Carey Fortunoff as the brooder in the group photograph. Here was his face replicated in half a dozen discrete scenarios, with and without his bandmates; with a pair of rockers even I recognized, famous men; with a sweet-faced woman sporting teased blond hair and holding an infant daughter, her hair teased too—and I realized, by process of elimination, that he was the one in the original photo partially obscured by a tombstone and staring straight into the camera. Not as dynamic maybe as the one I'd mistaken him for or as good-looking either, but solid in his own way.

I imagined him as the composer, the arranger, the mad genius behind the band, because didn't every band, if it was to succeed at any level, require a mad genius?

I didn't know. But suddenly I felt something, a presence, an aura, and I came back to myself. I needed to stop prying. I needed to leave. I needed croissants, coffee, my wife. And no, I had no interest in entering that bedroom down the hall or wherever it was. I turned to go, was actually on my way across the room and out the door, when my eye fell on the bookshelf, and if there's an impulse every bit as compelling as to lift the lid on a piano and finger a few keys, it's to inspect a bookcase, whether a friend's or a stranger's, just to get a sense of the titles some other person, someone other than you or your wife, would select and read. Without trying to sound overly dramatic, this was the moment where the fates intervened, because what drew my attention was a uniform set of leather-bound books, hand-numbered and dated. Journals. The journals of a third-tier musician who'd died alone in what sort of extremis I could only imagine—Carey Fortunoff's journals. The one I picked at random was dated 1982, and I didn't flip back the cover and leaf through it, because another impulse was at work in me, even stronger than the ones I'd already given way to.

I never hesitated. Ignoring the warning voices rattling round my head, I tucked the volume under my arm and slipped out the way I'd come.

I tried to be inconspicuous on the street, just another man—citizen, neighbor, innocent—heading down to the bakery in the early morning with a favorite book, but in any case there was no one around to doubt or question me. The walls stood tall and mute. A soft breeze swayed in the treetops. On the main road, the one that arcs gracefully through the lower village, a pair of cars, pinked by the early sun, rolled silently to a halt at the four-way stop sign, then rolled on. I bought the newspaper from one of the machines ranged like staring eyes outside the bakery, folded the book inside it, and went on up the steps and into the shop, where the smells were sweet and comforting.

Coffeed and croissanted, I took a table in back and made a show of studying the headlines before sliding the book out from between the Real Estate and Style sections. I won't say my heart was hammering—it wasn't—but I did feel the quickening pulse of an illicit thrill. I looked up. There were three other people in the place, aside from the girl behind the counter: two women and a man, each sitting separately, and each absorbed in laptop or phone. I didn't recognize them—and if I didn't recognize them, then they wouldn't have recognized me. I opened the journal and spread it flat on the table.

The first page simply stated the date in bold black numerals three inches high. Beneath it was the leering cartoon figure of what I at first took to be a devil—horns, goatee, cloven hooves—and I was put off. Here was the same old pubescent trope: devils and grinning skulls, phallic snakes, witch women and graves, a kind of wet dream of death you saw in one form or another on every band poster of the era. But then I saw my mistake—the figure was actually meant to be that of a satyr, as indicated by the definition of satyriasis written out in block letters at the bottom of the page: *Excessive or abnormal sexual craving in the male.* Which was at least more interesting. I turned the page.

What followed, beginning with the first entry for January 1, the day after the band had performed for a New Year's Eve party at a place called the Whisky, alternated between descriptions of random sexual encounters (groupies), drug use (cocaine, Percodan) and recording sessions for the group's first album, which apparently was being released that May by Warner Brothers, one of the big companies of the time. It was the usual sort of thing, the rock and roll cliché interlarded with detailed descriptions of various sex acts and demeaning depictions of the females involved, forays into new pharmaceutical experiences, visits to the doctor for burns, contusions and sexually transmitted diseases, set lists, the names of cities, restaurants, venues. I have to admit I began to skip ahead. What was I looking for? Introspection. Connection. Some sort of insight into a life, this life, a life lived coevally with my own. And pain, of course—the sort of pain and hurt and trauma that defines and delimits any life on this earth.

I wasn't disappointed. In May, once the band went on tour, the entries began to shrink away to virtually nothing, a single line, the name of a city (*Cincinnati, encore "Hammerhead" & "Corti-Zone," vomit on shoes, whose?*), and then in June the pages went blank altogether. What happened—and this was revealed in the first long entry for July, the longest entry in the journal thus far—was that Carey Fortunoff, mad genius of Metalavox or no, had quit the band in mid-tour, kicking out the windshield of the van they were traveling in after a dispute with the drummer over credit for a song he (the drummer) claimed he'd co-written.

Carey was uncompromising. He had a temper. And no matter how his bandmates pleaded with him, or the drummer (Topper Hogg, another name to look up) prostrated himself, Carey walked away from the whole thing. Just crossed the road, stuck out his thumb and spent two deprived and miserable weeks flagging rides west, sleeping rough, haunting Dumpsters outside fast-food restaurants and listening to every sort of country western and pop atrocity his thumbed rides inflicted on him, till he finally made it back to L.A. And his wife. His wife, Pamela, mentioned now for the first time, as if she'd been supplied by a casting company, as if she'd carried no more weight in his life than one of the Cindys and Susies and Chantals he picked up after every gig, as he called it. (*Lost 22 pounds by the time I got back to Pamela, my head splitting open like a big ripe cantaloupe.*

Why didn't you call me? she said. And what'd I do? I just shrugged, because how you could you even begin to put it into words?)

Imagine my surprise. But then, of course, I didn't have access to the earlier volumes, which for all I knew might have portrayed an awkward first meeting, a tender courtship and a marriage as deep and committed and sweetly strong as the one Chrissie and I have been able to make together. So give him credit. If anyone's at fault here, it's me, for having entered his story at random, for hovering over it like some sort of vulture, for being a thief, an expropriator—and yet as I look back on it now, everything I did, even if it was questionable, even if it was ultimately futile, was for a reason. For the better, that is. But I'll let you be the judge of that.

The next surprise was his daughter. Two lines after he mentioned the wife, in trotted the daughter. A three-year-old. Terri. And whether she was a prodigy or autistic, tall or short or fat or thin, dark or blond (and here something clicked: the pouf-haired toddler in the photo?), I couldn't have said, not yet, not without reading on. I looked up. My coffee cup was empty and the plate before me held nothing but crumbs, so I closed the book, slipped it back into the newspaper and went home to my wife.

That night I took Chrissie out to La Maison, the new restaurant in the village that was so popular you couldn't get in the door unless you had connections, but, of course, I always had connections. I walked her the long way around, avoiding Carey Fortunoff's street, making up some excuse about wanting to stop off at the ATM for cash, when, in fact, I had more than enough with me, not to mention half a dozen credit cards, all fully paid up. The maitre d', who was fooling nobody with his simulated French accent, practically went down on his knees when we came through the door, and we were soon sitting at our favorite table on the patio, where we liked to watch the evening light mellow over the village and cling to the mountains beyond till everything was in shadow but for the highest peak. Our daughter, Patricia, was away for the summer on a fellowship in Florence, studying art restoration, and though we both missed her, it was nice to be free to come and go as we pleased, almost as if we were dating again. When the waiter poured out our first glass of wine, I took Chrissie's hand and raised my glass to her.

We were on our second glass, Chrissie as ebullient as ever, her voice rising and falling like birdsong as she gossiped about this neighbor or that and filled me in on the details of Mary Ellen Stovall's marital tribulations, when she suddenly glanced up and said, "Oh, you remember that house? The one on Runyon?"

"What house?" I said, though I knew perfectly well what she was talking about.

"The one where the guy died? The musician?"

This was my chance to come clean, to tell her about the leather-bound volume I'd secreted in the garage behind a shelf of old *National Geographics*, but I held back, and I still don't know why. I shifted my eyes. Broke off a crust of bread and chased a dollop of tapenade across my plate.

"Mary Ellen says there's no way they can ever get the smell out of the house—it's like that boat in the harbor, remember, where the seal climbed up and then fell through the skylight into the galley and couldn't get out?" She gestured with her glass. "And rotted there, for what, weeks, wasn't it? Or months. Maybe it was months."

"So what are they going to do?"

She shrugged, her bracelets faintly chiming as she worked her fork delicately in the flaking white flesh of the halibut Provençal, which was her favorite thing on the menu. Mine too, actually, as neither of us eats much meat anymore. "I don't know—but it's got to be a teardown, don't you think?"

There had been problems with Carey Fortunoff's marriage almost from the start. Pamela was one of the hangers-on, one of the original groupies, when the band had first formed and was still rehearsing in somebody's mother's garage. She was nineteen years old, shining like a rocket blazing across the sky (Carey's words, not mine), and she had musical ambitions of her own. She played guitar. Wrote her own songs. She'd been performing in a local coffeehouse since she was fourteen (this was in Torrance, from what I could gather, the town where Carey had been raised by a single mother with a drinking problem), and for a while she'd sat in with the band during rehearsals and they'd even covered one or two of her songs. But then she got pregnant. And Topper Hogg joined the band and felt they should go in a different direction. So she stayed home. And Carey, a self-confessed sex addict, went on the road.

All this came out in the July entries, this and more—how she'd refused to have an abortion, how she swore she'd stick to him till the seas boiled and the flesh melted from her bones no matter what he threw at her, whether he gave her a dose of the clap (twice) or chlamydia (once) or whether he loved her or not. It came out because he was back with her now, living in a two-room apartment in Redondo Beach and trying both to shake off the uneasiness—fright—of having burned his bridges with Metalavox and forge on with new music for a solo album. He was feeling introspective. Or confused. Or both. At any rate, this was where the journal became something more than a compilation of trivia and deepened into something more—a life, that is. I was hooked. That night, after Chrissie had gone to bed, I went out to the garage and read it through to the end.

For the first few weeks, they went to the beach nearly every day—to "kick back," as he put it. There was the sun, the sand, there were the surfboards he and Pamela paddled out on the ocean while whoever they could grab hold of watched the little girl so she didn't drown herself, the days lazy and long and memorialized by the potent aroma of suntan oil and the hiss of cold beer in the can. But Carey wasn't much of a surfer and the waves were all taken in any case (prioritized, that is, by a clique of locals who resented outsiders and one another too), and by August he and his family were headed north, for the Russian River, where they were going to stay for the remainder of the summer with another couple—friends from high school, from what I could gather. Jim and Francie. Jim was a writer, Francie taught school. And they'd rented a "funky" cabin in the redwoods just three blocks from the river and a place called Ginger's Rancho, where local bands played six nights a week and on Mondays there were poetry readings.

It was an ongoing party, shared meals, a surfeit of beer and wine and drugs, swimming in the river, dancing in the club at night, yet what Pamela didn't know—or Jim either—was that Carey was having sex with Francie every chance he could get. They'd make excuses, going out to the market while Jim was writing and Pamela babysitting, taking long walks, swimming, canoeing, berry picking, their eyes complicit and yet no one the wiser. Then came a sultry afternoon in mid-August when they all went down to Ginger's in their shorts and swimsuits to sit in the bar there, at a table in the corner where the window was thrust open and they could gaze out on the river as it made its swift dense progress to the sea. Francie was wearing her two-piece—a leopard-skin pattern, gold and black like the sun spotting the floor of the jungle—and Carey, in a pair of cut-off jeans, leaned into the table to admire the pattern of moles in the cleft between her breasts. (Orion's Belt, he liked to call it—privately, of course—and he was writing a song named after one of the three stars of the constellation, Alnilam, though how he expected to find a rhyme for it I couldn't imagine.) Pamela was in a one-piece and a baggy T-shirt and was trying her best to keep the little girl—Terri—entertained. Jim was Jim, with hair that hung in his eyes, a chain-drinker and chain-smoker who seemed content to let the world roll on by.

An hour passed. They took turns buying rounds for the table. There was music on the jukebox and time slowed in the way it does when simply drawing breath is all that matters. Even Terri seemed content, sprawled on the floor and playing with her Barbies. Then, at a signal, Carey got up to go to the men's room and a moment later Francie went to the ladies', making sure the coast was clear before pulling him in with her and locking the door. It was risky, it was mad, but that made it all the more intensely erotic, a hurried bottomless grinding up against the sink while the jukebox thumped through the wall and the shouts of children at play in the shallows ricocheted eerily round them in that echoing space. Francie came back to the table first, after having hastily dabbed at herself with a wad of paper towels, and if her smooth tanned abdomen showed a trace of Carey's fluids shining there, no one noticed. A moment later Carey sauntered across the room, four fresh gin and tonics cradled against his chest. "What took you so long?" Pamela wanted to know. He set down the drinks, one at a time, shrugged. "There was a line like you wouldn't believe."

And where was Terri? She was at the next table over, being entertained by an old woman in a bleached straw hat who must have been a retired elementary school teacher or a grandmother or something of the like because she took right to Terri as if she'd been waiting for her all her life. The two of them were playing word games, playing patty-cake, the woman had her on her lap. Pamela said it was cute. The drinks went down. The conversation jumped and sparked, longtime friends spinning out jokes and routines and gossiping about every soul they knew in common who didn't happen to be sitting at the table in that moment. And then, at some point, Pamela glanced up and saw that the old woman in the straw hat was gone. Along with Terri. The little girl. Her daughter.

It took a minute for Carey to grasp the situation—and when he did, when he got up dazedly from his chair, the first stirrings of alarm beating in him, he went methodically through the place, jerking out chairs to look under the tables, going down on his hands and knees, startling people, Pamela right behind him and Jim and Francie right behind her. Then it was the restrooms, the kitchen, then out the door to where the river, cold and muscular, framed the shore. He saw a maze of bare limbs, people spread out on mats and blankets, huddled beneath beach umbrellas in bruised puddles of shade, radios going, kids shouting, dogs shaking themselves dry. But he didn't see Terri. And now it began to build in him, the shock and fear and hate—hate of the old woman, of all these people, these oblivious *people,* and of Pamela too, for doing this to him, for giving him this daughter he loved in that moment more than anything in the world. He began shouting his daughter's name, his voice high and tight, as if he were onstage howling into the microphone at the climax of one his concerts, and here were Pamela and Jim and Francie, their faces shrinking away from his like stones dropped down a well. "Terri!" he called. "Terri!"

But wasn't that the old woman? Wasn't that her, laid out on her back like a corpse, her flabby legs spread in a V and the straw hat pulled down over her face?

He was on her in the next instant, snatching the hat away. "Where is she?" he demanded. "My daughter. What did you do with her?"

The old lady blinked under the harshness of the sun. It was hot. Mid-afternoon. She was glazed in sweat. "Who?"

"My daughter. Terri. The little girl you had in your lap. *Terri!*"

Something like recognition slid across the woman's face, the faintest spark, and he realized she was drunk, no grandmother, no schoolteacher, just a drunken fat old slut he could have choked to death right there on the beach and nobody would have blamed him. And what did he get out of her? Blinking, holding up a hand to shield her eyes, her voice cracked and the fat of her arms shining like grease, she came up on one elbow and gave him a grimace. "I thought she was with you."

He was making promises to himself as he ran up and down the beach, wading now, calling out his daughter's name over and over—he'd been wrong, he'd sinned, he'd been selfish, stupid, stupid, stupid, and if they found her, if she was all right, saved, fine, whole, he would change his ways, he swore it. If only—

That was when Pamela let out a cry from the far end of the beach where the trail wound through a scrub of bushes and low trees and he ran toward the sound of it, people jerking their heads around, Jim just behind him and Francie too, the sand burning under his feet and the sun knifing at him. In the next moment, Pamela was stepping out of the shadows as if out of an old photograph, and he saw the smaller figure there beside her, Terri, in her pink playsuit and with her face clownishly smeared with the juice of the huckleberries she'd been picking all by herself.

What happened next? I didn't know. Curiously, there were no entries after that, the year drawn down in a succession of blank white pages. It happened that I had to go back east again on business in any case (not with the first group—I had no patience with them—but for another investment opportunity, which ultimately turned a nice little profit for Chrissie and me), and when I got back I treated her to a week at a resort in Cabo we like to use as a getaway. Time passed. I forgot about the journal, forgot about Carey Fortunoff and his unplumbed life. And then one day Mary Ellen stopped by to pick up Chrissie for their afternoon walk just as I was coming in the door, and it all came back to me.

"So what's new?" I asked. "Anything interesting out there?"

"Well, *duh,*" she said. "Haven't you been reading the paper? Things are going through the roof—my last two listings sold the day they came on the market. For above asking." She was wearing a yellow sun visor and a white cotton tennis dress. Her eyes jumped out at me as if they held more than they could contain. She wasn't aggressive, or not exactly, but she never seemed far off message.

"What about that place on Runyon?" I asked. "That ever sell?"

"Why? You interested?" She was giving me a coy look, dropping one hand to tug at the hem of her skirt as if to draw my attention there. She had great legs, her best asset, tanned and honed by countless hours of tennis and power-walking. I realized I'd never seen her in a pair of pants, but then why would I? Her standard outfit was a skirt and heels and a blouse cut just low enough to keep the husbands interested while the wives paced off the living room to determine where the hutch was going to go.

She held the look just a beat too long. "Because Chrissie never said a word. But that's a prime piece of property, two blocks closer to the beach than your place, and with better views—or potential views. I'll tell you, that's where I'd build my dream house if I had the wherewithal. Or the peace of mind." This was a reference to the fact that her life was unsettled now that she'd separated from her husband and moved into a condo with views of nothing.

I shrugged. "Just curious."

"I'll show it to you if you want." A door eased shut upstairs and here was Chrissie coming down the staircase in her walking shorts, her own legs long and bare and shining like tapered candles in the light from the open doorway. Mary Ellen shot me a look. "Tomorrow? Say, four?"

I went in the front door this time, Mary Ellen Stovall leading the way. The first room we entered, just off the hallway, was a den, wood-paneled, with floor-to-ceiling bookcases filled not with books but CDs, thousands of them, and on the bottom two shelves, running along all four walls, records—old-fashioned vinyl records in their original jackets. Mary Ellen flicked on an overhead light and the spines leapt out at me, dazzling slashes of color in every shade conceivable. There were speakers, an amp, turntable and CD player, and a single ergonomic chair covered in black velvet. This was his sanctum, I realized, the place where he came to *listen*.

"He had quite a collection," Mary Ellen said, clicking across the parquet floor in her heels to pull out a CD at random. " 'Throbbing Gristle,' " she read, turning it over in her hand so that the cover flashed like a beacon. "Ever hear of them?"

"No," I said.

"Not your kind of music, is it?"

"Not so much, no."

"But listen, if you see anything you want, go ahead and take it, because aside from the piano, which I've got somebody coming in to pick up—and the appliances for the recycler—the rest is going to the dump. I mean, the brother doesn't want it and since there's no other heirs . . ." She gestured with the CD to complete the thought, then slid it back in its place on the shelf.

"I thought he had a daughter?"

"Not that I know of. But don't you want to see the rest of the place? Just out of curiosity?" She paused, took a moment to cross one ankle in front of the other and tap her heel so that the sound, faint as it was, seemed to etch its way into the silence. "Of course, the house has got to go—that goes without saying. But it's a steal, a real steal at the price. And you can't beat the location."

"Yes, definitely," I said. "But give me a minute—you go on ahead."

What I was thinking was that the 1982 volume of Carey Fortunoff's journals didn't have to go back at all and that if I wanted to I could just waltz out the door with any one I liked. Or better yet, now that I had a legitimate purpose in being here, I could come in at my leisure and read through them all. But then why would I want to? He was nothing to me. In fact—and here I bent to leaf through the records—I'd never even heard his music, not a note. The records, incidentally, were alphabetized, and I went through the M's pretty thoroughly (Metallica, Montrose, Motörhead and the like), thinking to put the Metalavox album on the turntable, just for my own interest, but I couldn't find it. What I did find, up above on a separate shelf, was a complete set of CDs labeled by year in magic marker, each one featuring multiple discs with the names of the compositions neatly written out, Carey Fortunoff's music ordered in the way he'd ordered the events of his life in the journals. I even found one that was called *Alnilam.*

Mary Ellen tapped down the hall, stuck her head in the door. "Come on, I want to show you the grand room, because that's where the views are going to be once we get rid of all the undergrowth—or overgrowth or whatever you want to call it—and isn't that just the worst shame about this place, that he let it go like that?" She sighed, ran a hand through her hair. "But to each his own, huh?"

I followed her up the hallway, her hips swaying over the high heels, until she paused at a closed doorway. "You might want to hold your nose," she whispered, as if Carey Fortunoff were still in there, still doing whatever he'd been doing before the breath went out of him. "The master bedroom," she mouthed. "I've never even opened the door. Really, I think I'm afraid to."

And then we were in the grand room, the light muted and leafy. Mary Ellen went to the window as if she could see out across the channel to the islands, the million-dollar view (or in this case, more likely three- or four-million-dollar view) she would earn her commission on. I stood in the doorway, gazing at the bookcase, where the gap for the 1982 volume stood out like a missing tooth. I tried to be casual, moving toward it as if I'd never seen it before, as if I were a potential buyer contemplating a move to a better location, as if I weren't some sort of hyena sniffing out the death of a neighbor I never knew, but then time seemed to compress and two things happened that continue to trouble me to this day.

The first was my discovery, in the gap on the shelf where it must have slipped out of the volume I'd removed, of a newspaper clipping, yellowed with age and dated August 16, 1982. The headline read, "Toddler Drowns in Russian River," and below it: "The body of Teresa Fortunoff, age 3, was found by sheriff's deputies late yesterday afternoon. The current had apparently swept the girl nearly a mile downriver from where she was first reported missing. The cause of death was given as drowning. She is survived by her parents, Carey Fortunoff, former member of the rock group Metalavox, and Pamela Perry Fortunoff, both of Los Angeles."

Before I could absorb the shock of it—Carey had lied to me, to himself, to posterity—the purposive clack of Mary Ellen's heels made me turn my head and I had a second shock (or surprise, I suppose, would be a better word). She'd stripped off her blouse and dropped her skirt right there on the floor. I saw that she was wearing an elaborate set of undergarments, in black lace, with matching garters, an arrangement that had taken some forethought. "I'm so lonely since Todd left," she whispered, wrapping her arms around me. I felt the heat of her, smelled her perfume that rose and wafted and overwhelmed every other odor there was or ever had been. "Hold me," she said, whispering still. And then, because I hadn't reciprocated—or not yet—she added, "I won't breathe a word."

Carey Fortunoff's last year wasn't at all like what I'd imagined. He was in good health (but for a knee injury he'd sustained in a motorcycle accident twenty years back that left him with a slight limp), he was composing the score for a film being shot in Bulgaria and a record label was interested in bringing out an album that would collect the best of his songs, both the ones he'd written for himself and for other artists, including "Alnilam," which had apparently been a top twenty hit for a band called Mucilage. He was sixty-two. Pamela was long gone. Francie too. But he had a new girlfriend he'd met online and he wrote passionately about her, in love—genuine love that went beyond the quick fix of sex, or at least that's how I read it—for the first time in years. (*Just to be with her is all the heaven I need, put on a record, an old movie, just sit there holding hands. All gravy.*) If he had a problem it was with people, with society, with all the hurry and the wash of images, strange faces, the jabber of day-to-day life. Increasingly, he'd withdrawn into himself and his music, sleeping through the day and emerging only at night and only then to take care of the necessities, groceries and the like. Pickles. One percent milk. Root beer. He wore a hooded sweatshirt and dark glasses to hide his face. He let the trees and shrubs go mad.

I really can't say if it was the death of his daughter that broke him, but he marked the anniversary of the day in subsequent volumes and wrote what from its description seemed to be a symphony called "The Terri Variations," though, as far as I know, no one ever heard it. Thirty years passed before he admitted the truth of what had happened that day on the Russian River—in the 2012 volume, which he had no idea of knowing would be his last. Or maybe he did. Maybe he had some intuition of what was coming, of the common cold his new girlfriend would give him on one of her conjugal visits, the cold he ignored till it turned to pneumonia and cost him his life in a dark neglected house.

There was no lifeguard on that beach. It wasn't much of a beach even, just an irregular strip of sand spat up by the river during the winter rains, its configuration changing year to year so that one summer it would be a hundred yards across and the next fifty. Daytime temperatures reached into the nineties and sometimes higher, but the river remained cold, flowing swiftly, dark with its freight of sediment. Carey found the old woman and the old woman was drunk. She didn't know what he was talking about. Little girl? She hadn't seen any little girl. She cursed him and he cursed her back. Then he and Jim—the cuckold—chased up and down the shore, calling out till they had no breath left in them, while the women, Pamela and Francie, searched the parking lot and the street out front where the speed limit was posted at thirty-five but people tended to do fifty or more. Twenty minutes after Pamela first looked up and saw that their daughter was missing, they called the police.

What were they hoping? That Terri had been found wandering and been picked up by a good Samaritan, a real schoolteacher, an actual grandmother, someone with a stake in things, someone who cared, someone who would deliver her to the authorities—who was driving her to the police station even then. They didn't want to think about abduction, didn't want to think about the river. But they had to. And so Carey was up to his waist in the water, beating along the shore, ducking under obstructions, feeling with bare feet in the mud that blossomed in dark plumes to the surface and just as quickly dissolved in the current. He was wet through. Chilled. Exhausted. Even when the police and firemen arrived and they sent boats out onto the river with nets to drag and hooks to poke under obstructions, he kept at it, kept going through all the plummeting hours and all the horror and futility of it. And when they found her, still in her pink playsuit and with her limbs so white and bloodless they might have been bleached right on down to the bone, he pressed her to him though she was as cold as the river in its deepest and darkest hole.

Mary Ellen Stovall was right about the house. We didn't bid on it, of course, Chrissie and I, because that was only the thought of the moment and we're content where we are. In fact, I never even told Chrissie about the afternoon I'd gone over there and what had happened between her walking partner and me, which I'm not proud of, believe me, and when Mary Ellen stops by these days I always find that I seem to be busy elsewhere. I look at Chrissie and the way the light shines in her hair or how her smile opens up when I come in the door and I know that I love her and only her.

The bulldozers—there were two of them—came in and leveled everything on that lot, the car hauled off to the wrecking yard, the trees splintered, the walls of the house collapsing as if they'd been made of paperboard and all that was Carey Fortunoff's life—his journals, his music, the things on the shelves and the room where they'd found him—lifted into an array of clanking trucks and carted off to the landfill so that only the bare scraped dirt remained. And the views, of course.

Why I kept that volume of his journal, the one I pulled off the shelf on a hushed Sunday morning nearly a year ago now, and why it's still out there in the garage behind a barricade of *National Geographics* no one will ever look at again, I can't really say. Call it a memento, call it testimony. After all, you might ask, who was he, Carey Fortunoff, and why should anyone care? The answer is simple: he was you, he was me, he was any of us, and his life was important, all-important, the only life anybody ever lived, and when his eyes closed for the final time, the last half-eaten carton of noodles slipping from his hand, we all disappeared, all of us, and every creature alive too, and the earth and the light of the sun and all the grace of our collective being. That was Carey Fortunoff. That was who he was.

(2012)

Burning Bright

Tara

She was born in captivity at an English zoo in 1978, one of a litter of three Bengal tiger cubs. Once she was weaned, she was tranquilized, lifted into a cage and flown across Europe, the Middle East and the Indian Ocean to Delhi, where she was put in the back of a pickup truck and driven north to the Dudhwa National Park in Uttar Pradesh, not far from the Nepalese border. There she came under the care of Billy Arjan Singh, hunter turned conservationist, who'd had success in rewilding leopards and now wanted to try his hand with tigers—and not out of any sort of vanity, as with the maharajahs and nouveaux riches who bred tigers for their own sport, but as a practical measure to reinvigorate the gene pool and save the species from extinction. The sad truth was that there were more tigers in captivity than in the wild.

He gave Tara the run of his house and yard, which was hemmed in by the serried vegetation of the park surrounding it, and he took her for excursions into the jungle in order to acclimate her. The first time the superintendent saw her ambling along at Billy's side, he called out, "Why, she's just like a dog." And Billy, grinning, ran a hand through the soft fur at her throat. "Yes," he called back, "but she's just a big kitty, aren't you, darling?" and then he bent to her and let her lick the side of his face with the hot wet rasp of her tongue. At first he fed her slabs of meat hacked from donated carcasses, then progressed to living game—rats, geese, francolin, civets—working up the food chain till she was stalking and running down the swamp deer and sambar that would constitute her natural prey. When she came into maturity—into heat—she left him to mate with one of the males he'd heard coughing and roaring in the night, but she allowed him to follow her to her den beneath the trunk of a downed sal tree and examine her first litter, four cubs, all apparently healthy.

What the tiger felt can only be imagined, but certainly to be removed from an enclosure in a cold alien place and released into the wild where her ancestors had roamed free through all the millennia before roads and zoos and even humans existed, must have been gratifying in some deep atavistic way. Billy's feelings are easier to divine. He felt proud, felt vindicated, and for all the naysayers who claimed that captive-bred animals could never be reintegrated into the wild, here was Tara—and her cubs—to prove them wrong. Unfortunately, two problems arose that Billy hadn't foreseen. The first was that the zoo in England had kept inaccurate stud records—shoddy, that is—so that genetic testing of her siblings would eventually show that Tara was not in fact a pure-bred Bengal but rather a hybrid whose father was of a different subspecies altogether—a Siberian. Billy's critics rose up in condemnation: he'd polluted the gene pool, whether intentionally or inadvertently, and there was no going back because the animals were at large and the damage was done.

Still, this was nothing compared with the second problem. Within six months of Tara's release, a resident of one of the local villages—a young woman, mother of four—was killed and partially eaten by a tiger that emerged in daylight and stalked down the center of the main street as if it had no fear of people whatever.

Siobhan

Her mother was going to keep a tight leash on her—that's what she'd said, what she'd been saying all week, as the house swelled with relatives, and the Fongs, Dylan's family, kept coming and going and the presents mounted and the flowers filled every vase in the living room and the family room and spilled out onto the patio too. Siobhan was in the sixth grade and she didn't need any sort of leash, tight or loose, because she was dutiful and good and did what she was told, or mostly anyway. It was her mother. Her mother was in a state, yelling into her cell phone at the caterers, the florist, even the Unitarian minister she'd picked out to perform the ceremony, and if anybody needed a leash it was her.

Siobhan tried not to let it bother her. What she focused on, dwelled on, called up as if in some secret fantasy of glamour and excitement no one could begin to enter but her, was the fact that in less than an hour she would be leading the bridesmaids down the aisle at her sister's wedding, dressed in a mint-green taffeta gown she'd picked out herself. Plus, it was New Year's Eve, there would be fireworks at the pier and her mother had promised her she could stay up till midnight. Even better—and this had been the subject of a stream of breathless texts to her friends in Mrs. Lindelof's class for the past month—was where the wedding was being held. It wasn't going to be in a church or some cheesy reception hall or somebody's backyard, but in the outdoor pavilion at the San Francisco Zoo, where you'd be able to hear the animals cooing and trumpeting and roaring just as if you were in the jungle. It was the coolest thing she'd ever heard of.

The limo came, a white one, longer than two cars put together, and she and her mother and father and Aunt Katie had it all to themselves. There was a bar in it, with Coke and 7UP and liquor and little packages of pretzel sticks, M&M's and macadamia nuts. "Don't," her mother warned, snatching at her hand as she reached for the M&M's. "The last thing I need is to have you with chocolate smears all over your dress."

The last thing. Everything was the last thing, everything she did. But her mother was distracted, holding three conversations at once, with Aunt Katie and her father on either side of her and with Megan on the cell because Megan was in the other limo with her bridesmaids, and before they'd gone two blocks Siobhan had managed to stuff three crinkling packages of M&M's into her purse. Very carefully, watching for her moment, she snuck a handful of the candy-coated pellets into her mouth, the dark rich savor of the chocolate melting away on her tongue because she didn't dare chew. Her mother's eyes, framed in eyeliner like an actress's, were huge, twice the size of normal, and they flared from one thing to another, out the window, to the back of the driver's head, to Aunt Katie, her father, but not to her, not then, not while the chocolate lay secretly on her tongue and the excitement built in her like a beating drum.

"You damn well better," her mother said into the phone and then ended the call. "I don't know, Tom," her mother said, her voice jerking at the words as if each one was attached to a string that went all the way down her throat. "I don't know. I really don't."

Aunt Katie—young, blond, pretty, with a face just like Siobhan's mother's, only without all the lines—said, "It's all right. Everything's fine. Relax, Janie, just relax."

Her father let out a curse. "Christ," he said. "What is it now?"

"I just can't get used to it."

"What? Oh, shit, don't tell me—"

"Dylan's father, with those teeth. And the mother—she's the nicest person, it's not that, but she's so pushy and now we have to sit around and eat, I don't know, sea cucumber and squid at our own daughter's reception—"

"Just say it—they're Chinese, right? Well, I've got news for you—they've been Chinese since the kids started dating. Can't you give it a rest? Or are you just going to go ahead and spoil it for everybody?"

"I know, I know: you're right. But she's so dark. And short. Even in heels. I mean, really, have you *looked* at her?"

"What are you talking about? Who?"

But her mother, her eyes bugging like those cue-ball eyes the boys always brought to class on the last day of school, just jerked her head to stare out the window, both her feet in their ivory patent-leather heels tapping so furiously it sounded as if the limo was falling apart.

Vijay

A week earlier, on Christmas Day, he'd awakened feeling rinsed out and headachy, just maybe half a beat away from getting up and being sick in the toilet. He'd made the rounds of the parties the night before with his older brother Vikram, who was twenty-one and already had his associate's degree in pharmacology, and his best friend, Manny, who was his classmate at Lincoln High. There'd been pot and plenty of booze, tequila and vodka mostly. And beer, of course—beer was like water to him now. He could drink with the best of them—had been drinking since his sophomore year—and he didn't get silly or weepy like some of the retards in his class and he didn't let it affect his grades either. He'd applied to Berkeley, Davis and San Diego State as his first-choice schools and six backup schools too, and he intended to get into at least one of the top three and win a scholarship while he was at it. But right now everything was a little hazy and the smell of his mother's cooking seeping in under the door didn't make things any better.

Curry. The eternal curry. But then why should she cook anything special today, which meant nothing to them, after all. If Jesus had gone and gotten born on some day approximating this one two thousand years ago and then went on to get nailed to a cross, sacrificed like a lamb or some Hazuri goat, what did it matter? His parents were Sikhs, both of them born in Punjab, and he and Vikram were American, pure and simple, and all the hocus-pocus of priests and incense and kneeling and chanting that Manny's family bought into as if it were the biggest thing in the world was beyond irrelevant. He knew firsthand. Because he'd gone to the big drafty church on Ashton Avenue for Manny's confirmation when he was fourteen, and while the whole thing was interesting in a kind of anthropological way—Manny in a suit, Manny mumbling back at the priest, Spanish and Latin and English all leaching into one another, people dipping their fingers in a trough of water that was no different from what came out of the tap except that it had been blessed by the priest—it was the party afterward that had lit him up. There was a piñata. Tamales. And Manny's father—because this was an initiation and they were grown up now—allowed them each a glass of thin red wine that tasted like the wax of the white candles blazing over the shrine in the living room.

The sheets felt stiff. And there was a smell, a vague nameless funk that seemed to rise around him every time he shifted position. Were they stained? Had he come home and masturbated last night? He couldn't remember. He lay there a moment longer, then pushed himself up and went into the bathroom across the hall and drank down two glasses of water. Vikram's door was closed. What time was it? It felt late, past breakfast anyway. He padded back into his bedroom and pulled his cell from the front pocket of his jeans and checked the time: 12:30. Then he thought of his mother downstairs cooking and his father, on this universal day off, sitting there in front of the TV, watching soccer on the Spanish-language channel, though he didn't understand a word of the language—*What do I care, Vijay? I see the ball, I see the referee, I see the ball go into the net*—and then, on an impulse, he hit Manny's number.

"Hey," he said, when Manny answered.

"Hey."

"How you feeling?"

"I don't know. Hungover. How about you?"

He shrugged, no big deal, though Manny wasn't there to see it. "Maybe a little. But I just got to get out of here today, what with my dad watching soccer and moms doing whatever, cooking, the crossword puzzles, I don't know. I was thinking—you cool with it, you done with the family stuff?"

"I don't know, sure. What do you got in mind?"

"There's nobody going to be at the zoo today, it'll be like *deserted,* so I thought, once I tear Vik away from his sexy dreams, maybe we just go over there and hang out, you know?"

No response. But he could hear Manny breathing on the other side.

"We can like grab a burger on the way. And Vik still has that Stoli from last night—so even if the stores are closed . . . And weed—weed, of course. What do you say?"

Tatiana

She was a Siberian, four and a half years old, with the wide head, heavy frame and pale fur that distinguished her subspecies of *Panthera tigris.* Like Tara, she'd been born in captivity—at the Denver Zoo—and then transferred to San Francisco for breeding purposes two years earlier. That first day, when she came out of sedation, she found herself in the cage she'd been forced into just before dawn in the thin dry air of the Rocky Mountains, the only air she'd ever known, but there was something different about the cage now and it took her a moment to apprehend it: the front panel stood open. The smell must have come to her then, dank and lingering, the reek of the sea that was less than a quarter mile away, and then all the other smells she would have recognized from that morning and the morning before and all the mornings of her life, animal smells, the scent of urine and feces and the riveting anal discharge big cats use to mark their territory.

She didn't emerge right away, not that first day. She seemed to prefer the cage, with its impermeable top and the fading odors of her home, safe there from whatever loomed over her, above the high concrete walls of the outdoor enclosure in which the cage had been placed. Sounds came to her: the harsh broken cries of parrots and macaws, the noise of traffic out on the street and the engines of planes that were like insects droning across the sky, the trumpeting of an elephant, a snarl, a roar, and over it all the screeching of monkeys, monkeys and apes.

Vijay

He hadn't confessed it to anyone, not even his brother, because he wasn't a dork and didn't want to be taken for one, like all the other Indians and Chinese he'd been lumped together with in school since kindergarten, but his secret love, his true love, wasn't for the engineering degree his parents kept pushing him toward, but for animals. He wanted to be a zoologist—or better yet, a field biologist, studying animals in a state of nature, just like on the TV shows. Both Vik and Manny would say things like, *Why the zoo all the time, man, what's the deal? You in love with a gorilla, or what?* And he would shrug and say, *I don't know, you got a better suggestion?* And they didn't. Because the zoo was five blocks from the house and he and Vik had been going there since they were kids, just to get out from under the critical eye of their mother, who would have objected if they were going to just hang out on the street like hooligans (*Hooligans and I don't know,* gangbangers, *isn't that what they call them?)* but found the idea of the zoo vaguely educational. It was a place where they weren't going to get in trouble anyway—or that was the way she saw it.

By the time they got to the burger place on Sloat across from the zoo, it was already three in the afternoon and it just seemed natural to doctor their Cokes with a hit or two from the bottle, especially since it was a holiday and it was a hair-of-the-dog kind of thing, though Manny said it was disgusting to waste good vodka like that so he ordered an orange drink to go with his. It was a gray day, heavy with mist rolling in off the ocean. The burger place was deserted, the streets were empty. Christmas. They stared out the window on nothing, chewing.

"What time you got to be home?" he asked Manny. "It's like a special dinner today, right? With like your aunts and uncles and all that?"

Manny ducked his head, took a pull of his orange and vodka. He was in his board shorts and a black hoodie and he was wearing a brand-new Warriors cap, a Christmas present from his sister. "I don't know," he said. "Six, six-thirty. And yeah, I got to be there."

Vik hadn't said much to this point, his eyes raw and red, his cheeks puffed out as if the burger was repeating on him. "Hey, if we're going to go," he said now, "we ought to go because we can't smoke here and I think I've had about enough of sitting and staring out the window on nothing—anybody comes by and sees us here they're going to think we're losers, right? Primo losers."

So they got up and shuffled out the door, Vijay secretly pleased it was his brother who'd got them motivated instead of him because he wouldn't want to seem too eager, but the fact was the zoo would be closing at dusk and they didn't really have all that much time. Out on the sidewalk, Vik lit a joint and they passed it hand to hand as they crossed the street to the zoo's entrance. "So Christmas," Vik was saying to Manny. "Do you have a tree and all that?"

Manny had his head down as if he had to watch his feet to be sure where they were going. He seemed rocked already. "Yeah," he murmured.

"That cool?"

"Yeah. We put lights on it, ornaments, colored balls."

"Spangles? Those silver things, I mean?"

"Tinsel, yeah."

They were almost at the ticket kiosk now, Vijay digging into his wallet for the family pass their mother renewed each year. All he had to do was flash it at whoever was behind the window, usually a bony red-haired girl with no tits and an onyx stud like a mole under her lip, and she just waved them in—Manny, with his dark skin and black buzz cut, passing for just another brother in the Singh family.

Vik said, "That's a German thing, you know."

"What, tinsel?"

"The tree. 'O Tannenbaum.' Didn't you guys have to sing that in elementary school?" Then he was laughing, one of those warm-up laughs that promised more but really wasn't out of control yet. "I mean, it's not Mexican or even American, but *German*. Can you picture it, all those Nazis handing out these scrawny little trees to cheer up the Jews at what, Auschwitz?"

They were there now, at the window, and Vijay was flashing the family membership card, and though the girl wasn't there—*Christmas*—but some fat old man instead, it wasn't a problem. He barely glanced up from his iPhone, the old man—fat, fat as a Butterball turkey stuffed with sausage and chestnuts and cranberries and whatever—fixing them for half a second with his beady brown dog's eyes, and then he waved them in.

Siobhan

Of course, the wedding didn't start right away (and the groom couldn't see the bride because that was bad luck), so she had to go into this little back room that looked like somebody's office with her sister and her friends, everybody putting on makeup and texting like mad and passing around a silver flask with Sambuca in it. Nobody offered her any, which she wouldn't have taken anyway, even out of curiosity, because liquor was for adults and she wasn't an adult and was in no particular hurry to be one. She did have a Red Bull though, and it made her feel as if she were in the final lap of a race at school and beating everybody by a mile.

Then her mother came for them and they were outside in the damp air, the fog misting around them and the smell of the animals sharp in her nostrils. There was a hooting in the distance, one of the monkeys, the ones with voices like fire alarms. It just kept going, this monkey, and when you thought it was going to stop, when it slowed down and the hoots were softer and spaced further apart, it was only gathering breath for the next blast. That was the thing about having the wedding at the zoo—it was weird, but in a good way, because you never knew what was going to happen. Unlike in a church. Here was this thing out of a jungle someplace that didn't care in the slightest about weddings and caterers and the volume of the string quartet her mother had hired to play the wedding march as they came down the walk and under the roof of the open-air pavilion.

She was watching her feet, afraid to trip or stumble or do something wrong, all the adults standing now and looking back over their shoulders to get a glimpse of the bride, while the string quartet strained to drown out the monkey. All the men were in tuxedos. Some of the women wore hats. There were flowers everywhere. And then, just as she got to where the minister was waiting along with Dylan and the best man, she saw Dylan's little brother Jason, who was thirteen and a secret smoker of clove cigarettes, Jason, dressed in a suit and tie and giving her his starving zombie look to make her laugh. But she didn't laugh, though the Red Bull was pulsing through her. She just swept up the aisle the way she'd practiced it at the rehearsal, smiling at everybody as if she were the one getting married—and maybe someday she would be.

Afterward, when people were standing in line for food and drinks and the DJ was setting up his equipment, Jason came up to her with a plate of pot stickers and offered her one. "Did you hear that monkey?" he said. "I thought he was going to bust a gut."

She hadn't noticed till that moment that the sound was gone, long gone, replaced now by the prandial buzz of the adults poised over their plates and wine glasses. "It was *so* funny," she said, using her fingers to pluck a pot sticker from the edge of the plate.

"If any monkey knows any reason why these two should not be joined together, let him speak now or forever hold his peace."

She laughed at the very moment she bit into the pot sticker, which caused a dribble of grease to run down the front of her dress. She glanced up guiltily to see if her mother was watching, but her mother was on the far side of the pavilion with Aunt Katie, waving a glass of yellowish wine as if it were a baton.

"Hey," Jason said, his smile narrowing till it was gone, "you want to see something?"

"What?"

He shot his eyes at the adults bent over their canapés and drinks, then came back to her. He lifted his chin to point behind her, down the steps of the pavilion where the walk wound its way into the depths of the zoo. "Out there, I mean?"

She didn't know what to say. The zoo was closed, yellow crime-scene tape—*Do Not Cross*—stretched across the path, and her mother had strictly forbidden her even to think for a single second about leaving the pavilion. And her mother meant it. The whole last week she'd been in a fury, constantly on the phone with her lawyer and the zoo people and the mayor's office and anybody else she could harangue because they were threatening to cancel the permit for the wedding. Because of what had happened on Christmas. The accident. The attack. It was on the news, on Facebook, Twitter, everywhere—the police were investigating and the zoo was closed until further notice. But her mother had prevailed. Her mother had connections. Her mother always got what she wanted—and they'd reserved the pavilion a whole year in advance, because Megan and Dylan had met here at the zoo as interns on summer vacation from college and it was the only place in the world they would even consider exchanging vows. They'd hired the caterers, the DJ, sent out invitations. There was only one answer her mother would accept. Megan and Dylan got their pavilion, but the rest of the zoo was off-limits. To everybody. Period.

She just looked at him. He knew the situation as well as she did.

"I found something," he said. "On the walk there? It's like two hundred feet away."

"What?" she said.

"Blood."

Tara

Typically, there had been one or two tiger attacks in the reserve each year, usually during the monsoon season when people went into the park to collect grasses for their animals. Over the years, going all the way back to the last century, long before the park existed—and long before that too, as long as people and wild animals had been thrust together in the same dwindling patchwork of bush and farmer's fields—the region had had its share of man-eaters, but these had been hunted down and eliminated. Now, after the second and third victims were found lying in a tangle of disarticulated limbs along a path that lay just a mile from the site of the first attack, Billy Arjan Singh began to have second thoughts. Publicly he continued to maintain that the attacks could have come from any of the park's tigers, especially those that had been injured or were too old and feeble to hunt their customary prey—and Tara, demonstrably, was as young and vigorous as any animal out there—but privately he began to admit the possibility that his experiment had gone terribly wrong.

There came a respite. Several months went by without report of any new victims, though one man—a woodcutter—went missing and was never heard from again. Billy dismissed the rumor. People went missing all the time—they ran off, changed their names, hitchhiked to Delhi, flew to America, died of a pain up under the ribcage and lay face-down in some secret place till the jackals, carrion birds and worms had done with them. All was quiet. He began the process of obtaining permits to bring another animal into the country, this one from the zoo at Frankfurt.

Then it all went to hell. A woman—a grandmother barely five feet tall—was snatched while hanging laundry out to dry and half the village witnessed it—and before the week was out, a bicyclist was taken. In rapid succession, all along the perimeter of the park, six more people were killed, always in daylight and always by a tiger that seemed to come out of nowhere. Outrage mounted. The newspapers were savage. Finally, Billy gave in to the pressure and mounted a hunt to put an end to the killings—and, he hoped, prove that it was some other animal and not Tara that was responsible.

In all, before the tiger—*a* tiger—was shot, twenty-four people lost their lives. Billy was there for the kill, along with two of the park's rangers, though when the tiger came to the bait—a goat bleating out its discomfort where it had wound itself around the stake to which it was tethered—his hand fluttered on the trigger. They followed the blood spoor to a copse and stood at a safe distance as the tiger's anguished breathing subsided, then Billy moved in alone to deliver the coup de grace. The animal proved to be young—and female—but it had no distinguishing marks and to the last Billy insisted it wasn't Tara. Whether it was or not, no one will ever know, because he chose to bury the carcass there deep in the jungle, where the mad growth of vegetation would obliterate the evidence in a week's time. In any case, the attacks ceased and life in the villages went back to normal.

Vijay

He always had specific things he wanted to see—the African savanna, where zebra, kudu, ostrich and giraffe wandered back and forth as if there were no walls or fences and you could watch them grazing, watch them pissing and shitting and sometimes frisking around, and the koalas, he loved the koalas, and the bears and the chimps, the little things that were different about them each time he visited—but Vik and Manny didn't care about any of that. For them the zoo was just a place where they could watch girls, get stoned and kick back without anybody coming down on them. He didn't mind. He felt that way himself sometimes—today, for instance. Today especially. It was Christmas. They were out of school. He'd worked hard all term and now it was time to let loose.

They barely glanced at the savanna but went on into the primate center as if they'd agreed on it beforehand. There was hardly anybody around. The chimps looked raggedy, the gorillas were asleep. Vik wrinkled up his nose. "Man, it *stinks* in here. Don't these things ever take a bath?"

"Or use underarm deodorant," Manny put in. "They could at least use deodorant, couldn't they? I mean, for our sake?" And then he was lifting his voice till he was shouting: "Hey, all you monkeys—yeah, I'm talking to you! You got no consideration, you know that?"

And this was funny, flat-out hilarious, because they were all feeling the effects of the weed and weed made everything hilarious. He laughed till he began to feel oxygen deprivation, Vik's face red and Manny's too.

"Remember the time," he was saying, trying to catch his breath, "like maybe two years ago or something, when we were here and those dudes were painting the cage?"

"Oh, yeah, yeah," Manny gasped, and they were all laughing again at the thought of it, the day they'd come into the ape house and there were two workers inside one of the empty cages, painting the back wall, and they'd all crowded up to the bars making jokes about the new species of ape on exhibit and how clever it was—*Look, it's Bigfoot, and look, look, it can dip a paintbrush, coooooool*—until one of the workers turned around and told them to go fuck themselves.

Was it really all that funny? Yes. Yes it was. Because it was a routine now and they could call it up anytime they wanted, the three of them united and the rest of the world excluded.

So they laughed, drifting from one exhibit to another, not really paying attention, and if there were any girls to look at they were few and far between. Because it was a holiday. Because it was Christmas. At some point they were out front of the snack bar—the Leaping Lemur Café, another joke—and Manny said he wanted a fresh orange drink to make the vodka go down and maybe some nachos. "Anybody want nachos?"

Vijay got himself a Coke because his throat was dry and watched the kid behind the counter pour a glob of neon-orange cheese over Manny's nachos while the only other people there—a mother with a baby in a stroller and an older couple gobbling hot dogs—looked on as if the whole world had come to a stop. The kid behind the counter had the name of some pathetic metal band tattooed across his knuckles—*Slayer*—but since there were six letters and only five knuckles, the *er* had been squeezed in on the last knuckle, which was the smallest one, and what did that say about planning and foresight? Not to mention basic IQ? After that, they drifted over to the big cats, hoping to see them up and about, if only for the sake of breaking the tedium, but the lions—a male and two females—were lying there unconscious. "Shit, look at them," Vik said. "They might as well be rugs."

"Zoned out," Manny said. And then he got up on the metal rail where you're not supposed to be and started waving his arms and shouting—"Hey, lions, hey! Hey, I'm *talkin'* to you!"

Vik joined in and this was funny too, the two of them goofing, the lions stretched out as if they were dead, the sky closing in and everything as dim and gray and depressing as only a winter's afternoon in San Francisco could be. They began to roar then, roar like lions, and he joined in just for the sheer crazy throat-rattling rush of it, but still the lions never moved, not even to twitch their tails. They all three roared till they were almost out of breath and then they broke down and laughed till they were.

Finally Vik straightened up and said, "I don't know—this is boring. I'm ready to bag it, how about you?"

Manny shrugged.

And then, surprising himself because it really didn't matter one way or the other and they were going to have to go home eventually, everybody knew that, he said, "What about the tiger?"

Siobhan

Her mother wasn't watching, her mother was busy air-kissing everybody and waving her wine glass, and once the music got going people started dancing, which provided a natural screen. She ducked away under the cover of swaying gowns and tuxedoed shoulders and met Jason in the bushes just off the path, where nobody could see them. "Come on," he whispered, taking her by the hand, "it's this way."

She could feel her heart going. Her mother would kill her if she found out. Absolutely kill her. Plus this was Jason, a boy two years older, and he was holding her hand. He led her through a fringe of low palms and then back onto the walk where it looped away out of sight of the pavilion. It was dusk now and the bushes seemed denser, dangerous suddenly, as if anything could have gotten loose and hidden itself there in the shadows, waiting to spring out at them. The birds were chattering, the ones in the trees and the ones in the cages somewhere up ahead. Suddenly Jason let go of her hand and darted up the path, his dress shoes slapping at the pavement. She hurried on, nearly frantic with excitement, the smells coming to her now, the sounds of furtive movement, the low coughs and snorts and muffled roars. But there he was, just ahead, down on his knees and gesturing to her, the soles of his shoes palely glowing and his suit jacket bunched at the shoulders. "Over here," he said, trying to keep his voice down. "Hurry!"

When she came up to him she saw that he was bent over a dark uneven stain on the concrete, a spot no bigger around than one of the desktops in school. "See it?" he whispered.

She looked down, leaned closer, then straightened up, hands on hips. "That's just a wet spot."

"Yeah?" he said. "And why do you think it's wet? And it's not just water, believe me"—and here he pressed his palm to the stain and then spread open his hand for her. "See that? See it? That's blood."

She saw nothing. Just his five fingers, the ones he'd wrapped around hers a minute ago, and his palm, which might have been slightly darker—or damper. "That's not blood," she said.

"Is so." He gave her a strained look, his features melting into shadow. The sound of the music from the pavilion suddenly came clear, drowning out the birds and whatever else was out there. He held her eyes and wiped his hands on his pants. "Diluted blood anyway."

Vijay

If the lions were comatose at this point, the tiger gave them what they wanted. The minute they appeared there at the edge of its enclosure—an open pit with a dry moat at the bottom of the wall and some fake rocks and a raked-over tree stump in the background—it looked up at them and started pacing. Or more than pacing—it was slinking, flowing like water from one place to another, its feet almost a blur and the muscles flexing hard in its shoulders. They all just stood there for a moment, watching it. He could feel the weed blurring things and the vodka trying to counteract it, burning through him. He felt rocked, dizzy almost, as if everything were floating a couple of inches off the ground. Vik said, "Now that's what they're supposed to do—give us some action. I mean, we're paying customers, right? Or at least moms is."

And then, without warning, Vik jumped atop the restraining bar and began roaring down at the tiger. The effect was immediate: the tiger froze, staring up at him in confusion. Vik roared, flapped his arms. The tiger seemed to cringe, then its hackles rose and all of a sudden it was flowing faster, around and around, down into the moat below them and then back up and around again. Next thing Manny climbed up and they were both roaring and Manny started sailing nachos out into the void, one after the other, the tiger shrinking away from them as if they were on fire. "Ka-boom!" Manny shouted. "Ka-boom!"

They laughed. They were excited. And though Vijay knew it was wrong, knew they could get in trouble, knew the animals shouldn't be disturbed, let alone harassed, and that every sign warned against it, he found himself scrabbling around for something to throw—a pine cone, here was a pine cone in the dirt and he was snatching it up and rushing back to take aim. Why? He couldn't have said, then or afterward. It was something primal, that was all. They had this thing on the run, this big jungle cat that was as scared as the fluffed-up little Pomeranian in the apartment next door, and when the first pine cone went skittering across the concrete floor of the enclosure he took off running for another one, for a stick, for anything.

That was when he heard the sound Manny made—it wasn't a scream but something hoarser, deeper, worse—and he turned round to see the tiger's head burst up right there at the lip of the enclosure and the tiger's claws digging in, the big paws and clenched forearms clinging impossibly to the molded concrete for the smallest fraction of an instant before the striped flanks came surging into the picture and it was there like some CGI demon, grabbing hold of Manny and taking him down on the pavement in a quick thrash of limbs and a noise that was like a generator cranking up again and again. Vik's face. Manny down. The noise. And then the cat was on Vik and Vik was screaming and before he could think the thing was on him, tearing at the back of his neck and dropping him to the pavement as if he'd been sledge-hammered. He was trying to ball up and protect his head, the smell of blood and rot and the froth of saliva hot in his face, thinking nothing, thinking death, his shoulders and forearms raked and bitten and his feet a thousand miles away, when the tiger suddenly let go of him.

Tatiana

In the wild, a Siberian of Tatiana's age might have a range as extensive as sixty square miles, but she'd never been in the wild, had never known anyplace but this and the zoo in Denver, and her territory was measured in square feet, not miles. Industry standards vary on the minimum size of big cat exhibits, but restraining walls are mandated at sixteen and a half feet, a height no tiger, no matter the provocation or duress, could ever hope to surmount. Unfortunately, in the aftermath of the incident at the San Francisco Zoo, the wall was found to be substandard, measuring just twelve and a half feet from the floor of the moat to its highest point.

Siobhan

She managed to make it back without her mother catching her—and what her mother didn't know would never hurt her, would it? That's what Jason said anyway, and, giggling, she agreed with him as he led her to the bar through the dense swaying forest of adults, who were dancing now, their arms in motion and heads bobbing to the beat. The DJ was playing Beyoncé, Fergie, Adele, Megan's favorites. Megan was dancing with Dylan and the bridesmaids all had their boyfriends out on the dance floor now too. The bass was so strong it was like an earthquake and she could feel it thrumming through the soles of her shoes. People made way for them at the bar as if they were celebrities—and they were, or she was anyway, *flower girl*, sister of the bride—and she asked for a Diet Coke, no ice, and Jason got a club soda and cranberry with two cherries and a shot of grenadine, then they lined up at the food table for dim sum and ribs and still her mother never came looking for her.

Jason piled up his plate and then set it back down again on the table. "Oh, shit," he said, "I better go wash my hands. Watch my plate?"

"*Jason,* it wasn't blood."

He gave her a look of disbelief. He was tall for his age and his head seemed to bob up over his neck like E.T.'s, and she wondered about that, if she could give him a secret moniker—just two initials—when she texted Tiffany and Margaret to tell them she was hanging out with a boy at the wedding. She liked the way his hair was clipped in two perfect arches around his ears. She liked the way he was grinning at her now. "I wouldn't want to catch AIDS," he said, holding out his palms as if to deny it.

And then he was gone and she started eating by herself at a table in the far corner of the pavilion, but when he came back, conspicuously wiping his hands on the legs of his suit pants, he picked up his plate and came right to her. They didn't say anything for a long while, eating in silence and staring out at the adults as if they were going to have to take a quiz on the party. She heard her mother's high whinnying laugh and the next minute her father was leading her mother out onto the dance floor and she watched them settle into some weird gyrating sort of dance they must have learned in college back in the seventies. "You know what?" she said. "I don't think I've ever seen my parents dance before."

"My parents would never dance," Jason said. She followed his eyes to where they sat stiffly in two chairs pushed up against the rail, Jason's grandmother just to the right of them and just as stiff. "Even if somebody picked up an AK and said 'Dance or die!' "

"What about you?" she asked and she felt her cheeks color. "I mean, do you dance?"

"Me?" He held the moment, straight-faced, before he broke into a grin. "I'm the number one best dancer in the world," he said, letting his eyes flick over the dance floor before turning back to her. "Now that Michael Jackson's dead."

Vijay

What he did, and it was nothing anybody in any movie he'd ever seen would have done, was run. As soon as the tiger let go of him—to slam back into Manny so hard it was like a rocket flashing across the pavement—he scrambled to his feet and ran as fast as he could through the gloom of the day that was closing down around him, looking frantically for a way out, a tree to climb, anything, before he realized he was making for the snack bar, where there were people, where they could call 911, call the cops, call an ambulance. He didn't think of Vik till Vik came pounding up behind him, blood all over, his clothes in strips and his eyes rolled back in his head. They didn't say anything, not a word, just ran. It was maybe three hundred yards to the snack bar, three football fields, but it seemed to take forever to get there, as if they were running in place in some waking nightmare—and that was what this was, exactly what it was.

But when they got there, frantic, the doors were locked and they could see the guy inside, the metal head, the moron, and he wasn't moving toward them—*he was backing away!* Vik was beating on the glass, they both were, shouting for help, shouting to open up because there was an animal loose, a tiger loose, open up, open up!

The kid didn't open up. He just backed into a corner and tried to stare them down, but he had his cell in his hand and he was punching in a number (as it later turned out he *was* dialing 911, not because he believed them but because he thought they were on drugs and trying to rob the place). They kept beating on the glass and they would have broken right through it if they could, beating with the palms of their hands and shouting out for help, until they watched the kid's face go slack and turned to see the tiger coming right at them, its feet churning and its head down—following the blood trail, following the spoor. Vijay felt it like a hot wind as it blew past him to careen into Vik, its paws raking and batting, and though he flattened himself against the glass, shouting "Vik! Vik!" there was nothing he could do but wait to die as the flashing teeth and furious claws worked his brother over.

Tatiana

This world. This world of apes, this screeching world. She was out in it, terrified, enraged, doing the only thing she knew to do, one down and dead and another beneath her, all the power of all the generations invested in her and burning bright. She roared. She showed her fangs. And she would have gone for the other one, the one frozen there by the shimmering wall, if it weren't for the distraction of this solid rolling thing with its flashing lights and screaming siren and the hot quick shock of surprise that ended her life.

Siobhan

She danced till she was soaked through—and he was right, Jason, he was the best dancer in the world. The music seeped through her skin and into her blood. Her father danced with her, then she danced with her sister and everybody was taking pictures with their cell phones. And then there was a slow song and Jason put an arm around her waist and she watched what everybody else was doing, all the adults, and rested her head on his shoulder, on his chest, right where she could feel the flutter of his heart. She couldn't hear any of the animals anymore, couldn't have heard them even if they'd been roaring, because the music was everything. The night settled in. Jason rocked with her. And if she knew where she was at all, it was because of the smell, the furtive lingering odor of all those animals locked in their cages.

(2012)

The Marlbane Manchester Musser Award

If you'd happened to spot Riley on the train that afternoon, your eyes drifting up momentarily from your BlackBerry, iPod or other hand-held device, you probably wouldn't have made much of him. He was in his fifties then, taller than average, thinner than average, with a tendency to hunch inside the black leather coat he affected (knee-length, of a style thirty years out of date, replete with once-shining buckles, zippers and studs in the shape of miniature starbursts) and hair that would have been gray or even white but for the providence of the Clairol Corporation. He'd applied a mixture called "Châtain Moyen" in the shower just that morning, expecting, as the label promised, medium brown, but getting instead something between the color of a new penny and a jar of marinara sauce. In any case, he was oblivious. He had his head down, studying the stained typescript of his generic acceptance speech, abbreviating in the left-hand margin the title of the award he was now on his way to receive, though he already had it by heart: The Marlbane Manchester Musser Award in Regional Depiction from the Greater Stuyvesant Area Chamber of Commerce and Associated Libraries. He just didn't want any slip-ups, that was all. Especially if alcohol was involved. And alcohol was always involved.

He'd left Buffalo at seven-forty a.m. and expected to be in Albany by two—at least that was what the Amtrak timetable proposed, and whether or not Amtrak would deliver was beyond his control. In Albany, he was to be met by Donna Trumpeter, of the Greater Stuyvesant Women's Service Club, who would drive him in her own personal blue-black SUV the remaining forty-eight point five miles to the town itself. There would be a dinner, served either in the town hall or a school cafeteria gussied up with crepe paper and a banner, he would give his speech and read a passage from his latest novel, *Maggie of the Farm,* accept a plaque and a check for $250 and drink as much scotch as was humanly possible before he was presented at the local Holiday Inn for a lukewarm shower, a stab at sleep and, in the morning, acidic coffee and rubberized waffles, after which Donna Trumpeter or one of her compatriots would return him to the train station so he could reverse the journey he was now undertaking.

"Why do you even bother?" his third wife, Caroline, had thrown at him as he was shrugging into his coat that morning for the drive to the station. "It's not as if you don't have a trunk full of awards already—awards you never even glance at, as far as I can see."

He had his hand on the doorknob, the slab of the door thrown back on the awakening light of a bitter morning desecrated with sleet, an inch of it already on the ground and more coming. "For the publicity."

"Publicity? What kind of publicity you think the Greater Stuyvesant area is going to give you? Nobody in New York's ever heard of it. I'll bet they've never even heard of it in Albany. Or Troy either. Or what, *Utica*."

"It all adds up."

"To what?"

He sighed. Let his shoulders slump into the cavernous hollows of the coat. "For the money then."

"The money? Two hundred fifty bucks? Are you kidding? That'd barely cover dinner at Eladio."

"Yes," he said, the draft raw on the left side of his face.

"Yes, *what*?"

"Yes, I'm kidding."

She might have had something more to say about it, but really, what did it bother her what he did—she had a car and a credit card, and a night alone never killed anybody—but she just bunched her chin and squinted her eyes as if to get a better read on him. The sleet whispered over the pavement. The air tasted of metal. "My god," she said. "What did you do to your hair?"

He was in the club car, scarring his palate with superheated coffee out of a cardboard container and masticating an ancient sandwich advertised as chicken salad on wheat but which managed to taste of absolutely nothing, when a powerfully built middle-aged man came swaying down the aisle, pushing a boy before him. Riley glanced up, though he wasn't naturally curious, despite his profession. What he knew of people he knew from his early wild years—and from the newspaper and movies, or *films* as he liked to call them—and that had been enough to get him through fourteen novels and counting. He believed in giving people their space and if he didn't really have much use for the rest of humanity, that was all right—he led a pretty hermetic existence these days, what with his books, the cats (six of them) and Caroline, Caroline, of course. He liked to say, only half-joking, that he resented strangers because they always seemed to be in his way but that he was willing to tolerate them—and here he'd shrug and grin—because, who knew, they might just buy his books.

At any rate, there was something about these two that caught his attention, and it might have had to do with the fact that they were the only other people in the car but for the attendant, a recessive little man of indeterminate age and origin who looked as if he'd rolled over more miles than all the truckers in western

New York State combined. Still, they made an odd pair. The man was white, fleshy in the face, with eyes that seized on Riley and then flung him away just as quickly, and the boy—he looked to be eight or nine—was dark-skinned, Hispanic maybe. Or maybe Indian—from India. All this went through Riley's head in an instant and then he dismissed it and returned to his sandwich and the newspaper he'd spread out on the plastic tabletop, even as the big man and the boy settled into the booth directly behind him.

After a while he felt the booth heave as the man got up and went to the counter to order a coffee for himself and hot chocolate and a sticky bun for the boy. It took no more than a minute or two for the attendant to irradiate the drinks in the microwave and hand over the cellophane packet with the bun smeared inside, but the whole while the big man kept his gaze fixed on Riley, a gaze so steady and unrelenting Riley began to wonder if he somehow knew him. A single jolt of paranoia sizzled through him—could this be the deranged yahoo who'd called up early one morning to say how disgusted he was by *Maggie of the Farm* because Maggie was such a slut, and go on to wonder, in a pullulating spill of profanity, why that had to be, why every woman in every book and movie and TV show had to be such a *fucking slut*?—when he realized that the man wasn't looking at him at all. He was looking beyond him to where the boy sat, as if the boy was a piece of luggage he was afraid somebody was going to dash by and snatch.

Then the man was swaying down the aisle again, this time more gingerly—and dangerously—because he had his hands full, a cardboard cup in each hand and the sticky bun dangling from two fingers in its shrink-wrapped package. Again the booth heaved. There was the faintest rasp as the cardboard containers made contact with the table. The rails clacked. Scenery rushed past the windows. The man said something (Spanish, was he talking in Spanish?) and it was followed by the noise of crinkling cellophane as the treat was unwrapped—whether by the boy or the man, Riley couldn't say.

All of a sudden he was irritated with himself—what did he care? Since these two had come into the car he'd been stuck on the same paragraph, reading it over and over as if the words had no meaning. Exasperated, he glanced out the window as a lone clapboard house flashed by, then a series of brown rippled fields, then another house and another expanse of field, equally brown and equally rippled. He'd just brought his eyes back to the paper when the man's voice started up behind him.

"Hello, Lon?" A pause. "I am on the train, yes. Just passing Syracuse. Were you able to place that bet for me? Two hundred, the over/under on the Bills, yes?" The voice was needling, breathy, the vowels elongated and the diction too precise, as if it were being translated, and here it was stuck in Riley's head. In disgust, he folded up the paper and slid out of the booth, leaving the empty cup and sandwich wrapper for the attendant to deal with. He didn't glance behind him, though he wanted to give the guy a look—cell phones, God, he hated cell phones. Instead he just brushed imaginary crumbs from the front of his coat and started up the aisle.

"But I just wanted to tell you," the man's voice flew up and batted round the molded aluminum ceiling like an asthmatic bird, "don't wait for me at the Albany station—change of plan. I'm going to be taking a different route." He pronounced it "rowt," but then what would you expect? "Yes, that's right: I have something I need to dispose of. A package, yes. That's right, a package."

Anent Riley: he was a committed technophobe, forever pushed to the brink by the machines that controlled his life, from the ATM to the ticket dispenser at the parking garage and the clock radio that kept him awake half the night with its eternally blinking light. Card keys baffled and frustrated him—he could never seem to get the elevator to work or open the door to his own room in a hotel, and once he did manage to get inside, the TV remote, with its gang-piling options, invariably defeated him. He distrusted computers, preferring to write by hand, the way he'd always done. And the keyless car Caroline had talked him into buying put him in a rage every time he got behind the wheel—it seemed to change its agenda randomly, confronting him with all sorts of warning beeps and whistles, not to mention a sinuous female voice with an Oxbridge accent that popped up out of nowhere and never seemed to have anything good to say, when all he wanted was to turn a key, shift into gear and go. To drive. To get somewhere—his *destination*—without having to take a mechanical aptitude test. Was that too much to ask? Wasn't that what cars were for?

Worst of all was the cell phone. He refused to carry one—*If you want to know the truth, there's nobody I want to talk to*—and it irritated him to see the things stuck to the sides of people's heads as if generating a nonstop stream of vapid chatter was essential to life, like breathing or eating or shitting. What he valued was simplicity, pen to paper, the phone on its stand in the front hallway where it belonged, starry nights overhead, wood split and stacked beside the fireplace in the hundred-year-old farmhouse he and Caroline had bought six years ago (though admittedly the farm itself was long gone, replaced by tract houses, another irritant). Simplicity. Unmediated experience. Maggie, on her farm, tossing feed to the chickens or tugging at a cow's udders in the absence of electronic babble. Still, for all that, as he settled back into his seat after his annoying encounter in the club car, he couldn't help patting his pocket to feel the burden of the alien weight there—Caroline's iPhone, which she'd insisted he take in the event anything went wrong on the other end of the line. What if Donna Trumpeter failed to show? What if the train derailed? What if terrorists bombed the Albany station? *Then I'll just go ahead and die,* he'd said. *Gladly. Because I won't have to carry, this, this*—but she'd thrust it on him and that was the end of the argument.

He'd set the newspaper aside and had just opened the new novel by one of his former classmates at Iowa—Tim McNeil, whose skyrocketing fame made his stomach clench with envy—when the pneumatic doors at the end of the car hissed back and the big man entered, pushing the boy before him with one oversized hand and clutching a valise in the other. Riley noticed the man's clothes for the first time now—an ill-fitting sport coat in a checkered pattern, pressed pants, shoes so black and glistening he must have shined them three times a day—and what was he? Some sort of foreigner, that was evident, even to someone as indifferent as Riley. The term "Pole" jumped into his head, which was immediately succeeded by "Croat," though he couldn't say why, since he'd never been to Poland or Croatia and had never known anyone from either country. *Russian,* he thought next, and settled on that. But Jesus, the guy wasn't going to sit across from him, was he? If he was, he'd just get up and—

But no—the man chose a seat facing him, two rows up. There were other people on the car, a trio of nuns bent over their cell phones, a young mother with two comatose babies, a few salesman types, what looked to be a college girl with a book spread open in her lap though she too was busy with her phone, texting wisdom out into the world, and nobody so much as glanced up. The man made a show of heaving the valise up onto the overhead rack, then deposited the ticket strips in the metal slot on the seatback, pushed the boy into the inner seat and sat heavily in the other, his eyes raking over Riley so that he felt that tympanic thump of discomfort all over again. Enough, he told himself, dropping his eyes—he wasn't going to let it bother him. Nothing was going to bother him. He was on his way to pick up an award and he was going to have a good time because that was what this was all about, a break in the routine, a little *celebration* for work well done, an a-ward, a re-ward, something Caroline could never even begin to understand because she was about as artistic as a tree stump. And it all added up, it did, no matter what she thought. He was in the game still and any one of his books could go big the way McNeil's had. Who knew? Maybe there'd be a movie, maybe Spielberg would get involved, maybe word of mouth was operating even now . . .

He bent to the book—a sequel to the *New York Times* bestselling *Blood Ties,* which immediately made him wonder if he shouldn't attempt a sequel to *Maggie*—and followed the march of the paragraphs up and down the page for as long as he could, which was no more than five minutes, before he fell off to sleep, his chin pinioned to his breastbone.

Riley wasn't one to dream—sleep came at him like a hurtling truck—and when he felt the hand on his shoulder, the gentle but persistent pressure there, he was slow to come back to the world. He found himself blinking up into the face of the erstwhile Russian, the big man with the careful accent, who was saying this to him: "Sir. Sir, are you awake?"

He blinked again, the phrase *I am now* coming into his head, but he merely murmured, "Huh?"

The man's face hung over him, pores cratered like the surface of the moon, tangled black eyebrows, eyes reduced to slits—*Cossack's eyes*—and then the man was saying, "Because I must use the facilities and I am wondering if you would watch over the boy for me." And there was the boy, his head no higher than the seatback, standing right there. Riley saw he was younger than he'd first thought, no more than five or six. "I will thank you," the man went on, making as if to usher the boy into the seat beside Riley but hesitating, waiting for assent, for permission. Caught by surprise, Riley heard himself say, "Sure. I guess." And then, before he could think, the boy was sitting limply beside him and the big man leaning in confidentially. "I am grateful. There are bad people everywhere, unfortunately, and one doesn't like to take chances." He said something to the boy in a different voice, the tone caustic and admonitory—Spanish, it was definitely Spanish, but then why would a Russian be speaking Spanish, if he was a Russian, that is?—then gave Riley's shoulder a brief squeeze. "Very bad people."

Riley craned his neck to watch the man's heavy shoulders recede down the length of the car behind him before the door to the restroom swung open to block his view and the man disappeared inside. He turned to the boy, more baffled and irritated than anything else, and simulated a smile. He'd never done well with children—to him they were alien beings, noisy, hyper, always scrabbling and shouting and making incomprehensible demands, and he thanked God he'd never had any of his own, though his second wife, Crystal, formerly one of the students in the itinerant workshops he'd given over the years, had twice been pregnant and had actually thought of giving birth before he'd managed to make her see the light. But here was this boy, lost in a nylon ski jacket two sizes too big for him, his eyes fixed on the floor and a cheap tarnished cross suspended from a chain round his neck. Riley turned back to his book, but he couldn't focus. A minute passed. Then another. Scenery flashed by. And then, over the rattling of the wheels and the shrieking metallic whine of the brakes—were they already coming into the Schenectady station, the stop before his?—he heard the boy's voice, whispering, a voice no louder or more forceful than the breath expelled from his lungs, and turned to him.

The boy's eyes jumped to his. "Socorro," he whispered, then glanced over his shoulder before dropping his gaze again. Very softly—the screeching brakes, the shudder of the car, the rafters of the station fixed in the window—the boy repeated himself: "Socorro."

It took him a moment—French had been his language, both in high school and college, though he recalled little of it now and had no access to Spanish whatever, if this *was* Spanish the boy was speaking—before he said, "Is that your name? Socorro?"

The boy seemed to shrink away from him, down, down into the depths of his jacket and the scuffed vinyl of the seat that loomed over him as if it would swallow him up. He didn't say yes, didn't say no, didn't even nod—all he did was repeat the word or phrase or whatever it was in a voice so small it was barely audible. There was a whistle, a shout, the train lurched and the wheels began to revolve again. Riley wasn't slow on the uptake, or not particularly—it was just that he wasn't used to people, to *complication*—but an unraveling skein of thoughts began to suggest themselves to him now. He glanced up at the rack above the seat the big man had vacated and saw that the valise was no longer there and then he thrust his face to the window, jerking his eyes back to the platform and the receding crowd there—men, women, strollers, backpacks, luggage, the nuns, a seeing-eye dog and a woman in dark glasses, all that color and movement, too much, way too much, so that he couldn't be sure what he was seeing even as the checkered sport coat flickered suddenly into view and vanished just as quickly.

What went through his head in those first few ruptured moments as he turned away from the window? That his eyes had deceived him, that the big man was in the restroom still and would be back any second now to claim the boy, who must have been his nephew or an adopted son or even his own natural child by a Hispanic woman, a Latina, an immigrant maybe with a green card or even citizenship. Wasn't that how the Russians did it? Marry a citizen and get a free pass? He glanced up and down the car but no one had got on and the conductor was nowhere to be seen. The boy was hunched inside his jacket, absolutely motionless, his eyes on the floor. Riley saw now that he wasn't wearing a shirt under the ski jacket, as if he'd dressed—or been dressed—hurriedly. And his shoes—he was wearing only one shoe, a scuffed and dirt-smeared sneaker. His socks were wet, filthy. He looked—and here the awful truth slammed at Riley like a ballistic missile—*abused.*

He came up out of the seat so suddenly he cracked his skull on the luggage rack and for just an instant saw lights dancing before his eyes. "Stay here, I'll be right back," he breathed, and then he was out in the aisle and heading for the restroom, the skirts of his coat flapping behind him like great enveloping wings. He seized hold of the handle, flung open the door. There was no one inside.

A quick glance into the car beyond—nothing, nobody—and then he was easing himself down beside the boy and the boy was shrinking, getting smaller by the moment. The boy's limbs were sticks, his eyes two puddles gouged out of a muddy road. Riley bent his face toward him, fighting to control his voice. "Where's your father?" he said. "Where'd he go? *Votre père?* Papa? Where's your papa? Or uncle? Is he your uncle?"

The boy said nothing. Just stared down at the floor as if Riley were speaking a foreign language. Which, in fact, he was.

"Where are you going? What town? Where do you live—do you know where you live?"

More nothing. Advanced nothing. Nothing feeding off of nothing.

What he had to do, *right this minute,* was find the conductor, the engineer, anybody—the nuns, where were the nuns when you needed them?—to take this, this *situation* off his hands. He'd actually started to get to his feet again before he realized how sketchy this all was—he couldn't very well leave the kid there. What if the big man came back? What if somebody else—? What if they thought *he* was somehow responsible? He shot his eyes round the car. Something came up in his throat. It was then that he thought of the phone, Caroline's phone, this miracle of instant communication secreted in his pocket *for just such a moment as this.*

He eased to one side to slip it from his pocket, a hard mute monolithic thing, cold in his hand, its screen decorated with the imprint of his wife's fingertips. He'd call Amtrak, that was what he was thinking—the emergency number. There had to be an emergency number, didn't there? Or 911. He'd call 911 and have the police meet him at the Albany station. All right. But how to turn it on? He'd seen Caroline do it a hundred times, her fingers flicking lightly over the screen as a steady stream of colorful icons rolled dutifully into position. He pressed the screen, expecting the thing to jump to life, but nothing happened. Again he pressed it. The kid was watching him now out of the reddened pools of his eyes—had he been crying, was that it? "It's okay," he heard himself say. "Everything's fine. Just give me—give me a minute here."

The car rocked. Bleak dead trees flailed at the windows. The sky was made of stone. Finally—and he felt a surge of satisfaction so powerful he nearly sang out in triumph—he found the on/off switch hidden in the frame and indistinguishable from it, as if the manufacturer, clearly a sadist, had put all the company's resources into making its function as obscure as possible. No matter. The screen flashed at him, a parade of icons there, and they shimmied at the merest touch of his finger. But where were the numbers? How did you make a call? Why were—?

And now the train was slowing and the loudspeakers suddenly crackled with a mechanical voice announcing *Station stop Albany/Rensselaer* even as he shoved the phone back in his pocket and sprang up to jerk his bag down from the overhead rack, the decision already forming in his brain because it was the only decision he could have made—anyone in his position would have done the same thing and you didn't have to be Albert Schweitzer to weigh the moral balance of it. He took the kid by the hand, pulled him up out of the seat and down the aisle to the door, which at that moment clattered open on the platform in a burst of noise and confusion, people swarming everywhere, and where was a cop? He needed a cop.

A dirty white pigeon fluttered into the air. Somebody said, "Laura Jean, you look terrific, I hardly recognize you," and a pair of policemen surfaced amidst the crowd, moving toward him now, and here was a too-thin vaguely blondish woman rushing for him with her hands outstretched and the light of redemption in her cracked blue eyes, and she was going to say, "Mr. Riley?" and he was going to say, "Ms. Trumpeter?" but that never happened, because the policemen wrestled him to the pavement even as he felt the cold metallic bite of the handcuffs gnaw into his flesh.

Sometime later—he didn't know how much later because they'd taken his watch—he found himself in a desperate place, a place even the wildest of his wild years couldn't have begun to prepare him for. There were strange smells, unsettling noises, the rhythmic tapping of heels on linoleum. Cold steel. Corridors within corridors. Here he was in the midst of it, his hands shaking as if he'd had a hundred cups of coffee, and he couldn't stop pacing back and forth across the stained concrete floor of the solitary cell they'd put him in, the guard or deputy or whatever he was giving him a rude shove and announcing in an overheated voice that it was for his own protection. "The people we got in here, they don't like creeps like you. And you want to know something? Neither do I." And then he added, as a kind of oral postscript, "Scumbag."

Donna Trumpeter, aflutter with righteousness, had tried to explain that they'd made a mistake, that he—Riley, the man in handcuffs with the heart rate surging like Krakatoa—was a famous writer, a celebrity, *an award winner,* but the cops wouldn't listen. They produced a blanket for the boy, as if he were cold, as if that were the extent of his problem, and another cop—a female with a face like a blazing gun—wrapped the boy up and led him away. Riley talked himself hoarse. He protested in a high buzzing whine while they led him in cuffs through the cavernous station, and everybody, even the crackheads and bums, stared at him; fulminated while they strong-armed him into the back seat of the cruiser and drove him down the bleak cold street; alternately raged, threatened and pleaded as they read him his rights, took his fingerprints and photo—his mug shot!—and booked him. Was he allowed a phone call? Yes. On a real phone greased with the slime of ten thousand penitential hands, a phone attached to a wall with an actual cord that disappeared inside it before connecting with a vast seething network of wires that ran all the way to Buffalo and beyond. It took four rings for Caroline to answer, each one an eternity, and what was the name of that attorney they'd used when the neighbor's pinhead of a kid set fire to the fence?

"Hello?" Her voice was guarded, caller I.D. alerting her to the suspect number. Absurdly he wanted to throw his voice and pretend to be a telemarketer, make her laugh, goad her, but things were too desperate for that.

"It's me," he said. "I'm in trouble." He felt as if he were in a submarine deep under the sea and all the air had gone out of it. The walls were squeezing in. He couldn't breathe. "I'm in jail. I've been arrested."

"Listen, I'm just sitting down to a salad and a glass of wine and I really don't have time for whatever this is—humor, is that it? You think you're funny? Because I don't."

He dredged something out of his voice, something real, that stopped her. "Caroline," he said, and now he was sobbing—or almost, right on the verge of it—"I'm in jail. Really. It's crazy, I know, but I need you to . . . I need your help. That lawyer, remember that lawyer, what was his name?"

"Lawyer? What are you talking about?"

He repeated himself for the third time, angry now, the humiliation burning in him, and what if the papers got hold of this? "I'm in jail."

Her voice tightened. "For what?"

"I don't know, it's all a mistake."

Tighter yet: "For what?"

There was a deputy right there, pointing emphatically at his watch. The corridor smelled of cleaning solution, vomit, bad shoes, bad feet, bad breath.

It took everything in him to get the words out. "They're calling it"—and here he emitted a strained whinnying laugh—"child abuse."

"Jesus," she snapped. "Why don't you get a life? I told you I'm trying to have a bite of dinner here—*in peace* for once? Go try your routine on one of your groupies, one of the literary ladies of where is it? Greater Stuyvesant. I'm sure they'll all love it." And then, because Riley must have committed some sin he wasn't aware of in another life and another time, something truly heinous and compoundedly unforgivable, the phone went dead.

Four hours later—half-past eight by the watch they'd returned to him, along with his wallet, his belt and the flat inanimate slab of Caroline's iPhone—he was sitting across from Donna Trumpeter in a booth at the bar/restaurant of the Stuyvesant Marriott, trying to nurse his pulse rate back to normal with judicious doses of Johnnie Walker Black. He'd ordered a steak, blood-raw, but it wasn't there yet. Donna Trumpeter flipped the hair away from her face. She leaned into the table on both her elbows and cupped her chin in her hands. She'd just finished telling him, for the tenth time, how very sorry she was about all of this and that of course the ladies of the service club and her book group and the mayor and all the citizens of the Greater Stuyvesant area who'd driven who knew how many miles to hear him speak all understood that the circumstances were unavoidable. They'd held the ceremony anyway, apparently, the mayor's wife reading aloud from *Maggie of the Farm* in the booming tones she'd employed as a high school thespian a quarter century earlier, and everyone—at least at last report—had been satisfied with the evening, the high point of which was the turkey schnitzel, garlic mashed potatoes, brown gravy and peas provided by the high school cafeteria staff doing overtime duty. "But," and here she drew in a vast quavering breath, "of course, they all wanted you." Her eyes, giving back the nacreous sheen of the overhead lights, fluttered shut and then snapped open again. "There's no substitute for genius."

This last comment, coupled with the tranquilizing effect of the scotch, made him feel marginally better. "I guess that'll teach me," he said, sounding as doleful and put-upon as he knew how.

"Oh, no," she said, "no. You did the right thing. The *only* thing."

"If I had to do it again—" he began and then trailed off. He'd been trying to catch the waitress' eye for a refill, and here she was—a huge woman, titanic, as slow on her feet as mold creeping across a petri dish—backing her way out of the double doors to the kitchen, his steak balanced on one arm, Donna Trumpeter's Cobb salad on the other. The cops had realized their mistake after an interpreter was brought in to question the boy in Spanish and then they'd hurried to release him, their apologies rattling round the station like a dry cough. They didn't care. He meant nothing to them. They'd branded him a pervert and a pervert he remained, just another perp, another scumbag, innocent or not. He could go ahead and sue. They were just doing their job and no jury was going to give him a nickel. If anything, he was at fault—for interfering, for letting the real abductor get away when all along they'd been waiting to take him at the station.

The waitress, breathing heavily—puffing, actually, as if she were trying to keep an imaginary feather afloat—set the plates down on the table and as the smell of the steak rose to him he realized how hungry he was. "Another scotch," he said, and because he was calming down now, the earth solid beneath his feet the way it always had been and always would be, he added, "please," and then, "if it's not too much trouble." He cut meat, lifted it to his lips, sipped scotch. Donna Trumpeter kept up a soft soothing patter which revolved around what an honor it was to be in his presence—she couldn't believe it; it was like a dream—and how deeply each of his books had moved her, *Maggie of the Farm* most of all. "Really," she said, "the way you portray day-to-day life—and the insight you have into women, my God!—it's almost Tolstoyan. Or no: better. Because it's real. In the here and now."

He gently reminded her that the book was set in the nineteen thirties.

"Of course. What I mean is it's not *nineteenth century*, it's not *Russia*."

"No," he agreed, "it's not." It was about then that he noticed she wasn't wearing a wedding ring. And that her eyes, for all the coiled springboard of theories and embroidery, vegetarian cookery, cats and poetry he saw lurking there, were really quite beautiful. Stunning, actually. And her mouth. She had a sensual mouth, full-lipped, just like the one he'd imagined for Maggie. And though she was thin, too thin for his taste, she had a pair of breasts on her. There they were, clamped in the grip of the tight pink angora sweater she was wearing, and what was he thinking? That skinny women, skinny literary women with full lips and syntactical adulation shining in their eyes, could be lavishly receptive in another arena altogether. And further: that he'd had a scare, a bad scare, and could do with a little soothing.

He was about to lay his hand on hers when she suddenly pulled back to pantomime a smack to her forehead. "Oh, my God, I almost forgot," she said, and then he was studying the crown of her skull, the parting there, as she bent to her purse, which she'd tucked away beneath the table when they'd sat down. In the next moment she was straightening up, slightly flushed from the effort, and smiling so forcefully her teeth shone. "Here," she said, and she was handing what he at first took to be a breadboard across the table—the plaque, the plaque, of course—and along with it an envelope embossed with the logo of the Greater Stuyvesant Chamber of Commerce. "God, if I'd forgotten . . ."

He must have looked surprised—he'd been through an emotional wringer, but not, he reminded himself, anything even close to the sort of horror that poor abused kid must have endured, and he didn't give a damn what anybody thought, whether it was random chance that had put him there or not, he *was* a hero, he *was,* and he'd suffered for it—because she said, "I know it's not much. Especially, well, considering."

"It's plenty," he said, and was he tearing up? "And I want to thank you, all of you, but you especially, you, Donna, from the bottom of my . . ." He lifted his head, cast a watery eye on the shadow of the waitress drifting by on the periphery. "But what I'd really like, what I *need,* that is, I mean after all we've been through together—oh, hell, let me just come out and say it. Do you want to come up to the room with me?"

He watched her smile retract, lips tightening like wire. "I'm seeing somebody," she said.

He was desperate. He'd been in jail. He'd never even got to deliver his speech. "He doesn't have to know."

"I'm sorry," she said firmly and then she got up from the table. "I'll take care of the check," she added in a softer voice, and touched his hand in parting. The smile flickered back. "Sleep tight."

He staggered up the stairs to his second-floor room like an octogenarian, as drained as he'd ever been in his life. For a long while he fumbled with the card key, trying it forwards, backwards, upside down, till finally the light went mercifully green and he was inside. The room was like any other. Stucco walls, beige lampshades, plastic night tables with some sort of fake wood-grain pattern worked in beneath the surface. Industrial carpeting. Sheets and blankets stretched tight as drumskin over the bed by immigrant women who'd seen too much in their own place and time and now had to rake through the daily leavings of the class of people who had the wherewithal to couple here and gulp booze and do drugs and clip their nails over the sink. He didn't want to think about the women's children and the hopes they might have had for them, about the boy and the big man and a room just like this one in Chicago or Detroit or wherever the bad people, the very bad people, did what they were going to do.

He went to the window and looked out into a vast parking lot, a great dark sinkhole illuminated by the sad yellow light of the arc lamps rising hazily out of it. It took him a moment, his reflection caught there in the window, his jacket like a dead thing wrapped around him, to realize it was snowing. Or no, this was sleet, definitely sleet, the storm that had hit Buffalo finally caught up with him.

In the morning, he took the train back, and if he lifted his head from the newspaper when anyone came down the aisle, it was a reflex only. The rails thumped beneath him with a pulverizing regularity that seemed to work so deeply inside him it was as if he were being eviscerated with each thrust of the wheels. His breath fogged the window. He tried Tim McNeil's novel again and again it put him to sleep. Back at home, Caroline seemed to find the whole business hilarious and he just couldn't summon the strength to give her the hard truth of it. Still, she did warm to him when they went out to Eladio and blew the two-hundred-fifty-dollar honorarium on abalone flown in from California, Kobe beef and a bottle of Veuve Clicquot Demi-Sec chilled to perfection. Two days later he learned from the newspaper that the boy's name was Efraín Silva and that he'd wandered away from his mother at the Home Depot in Amherst and was now reunited with her, though there seemed to be some question regarding her legal status, which had only come to light because of her going to the police. As for the abductor, the big man in the pressed pants and checked jacket, he was still at large, and whether he was Russian or Croatian or Fijian for that matter, no one knew. No one knew his name either. All they knew was what he'd done to the boy and where he'd done it and they knew too that he'd do it again to some other boy in some other place.

If Riley felt a vague unease in the coming days, he chalked it up to the cold he seemed to have caught somewhere along the line. And when the next invitation came—from Kipper College of the Dunes in Kipper, Oregon, informing him that he was one of three finalists for the Evergreen Award in Creative Literature for his novel *Magpie of the Farm*—he didn't show it to Caroline or anyone else. He just went in through the house to the fireplace, stacked up the kindling there, and used the creamy soft vellum to guide the flame of the match into the very heart of the fire.

(2012)

Birnam Wood

It rained all that September, a grim cold bleached-out rain that found the holes in the roof and painted the corners with a black creeping mold that felt greasy to the touch. Heat would have dried it up, or at least curtailed it, but there was no heat—or insulation either—because this was a summer rental, the price fixed for the season, Memorial Day to Labor Day, and the season was over. Long over. Back in May, when Nora was at school out west and I'd sent her a steady stream of wheedling letters begging her to come back to me, I'd described the place as a cottage. But it wasn't a cottage. It was a shack, a converted chicken coop from a time long gone, and the landlord collected his rent in summer, then drained the pipes and shut it down over the winter so that everything in it froze to the point where the mold died back and the mice, disillusioned, moved on to warmer precincts.

In the summer, we'd been outside most of the time, reading and lazing in the hammock till it got dark, after which we'd either listened to records or gone out to a club or to somebody's house. We had a lot of friends—my friends, that is, people I'd grown up with—and we could just show up anytime, day or night, and get a party going. On weekends, I'd unfold the geological survey maps of Fahnestock or Harriman Park and we'd pick out a lake in the middle of nowhere and hike in to see what it looked like in the shimmering world of color and movement. Almost always we'd have it to ourselves, and we'd swim, sunbathe, pass a joint and a bota bag of sweet red wine and make love under the sun while the trees swayed in the breeze and the only sound was the sound of the birds. Nora didn't have a tan line all summer. Neither did I.

But then it was September and it was raining and I had to go back to work. I was substitute-teaching at the time, a grinding chaotic thankless job, but I didn't really have a choice—we needed money to stay alive, same as anybody else. Nora could have worked—she had her degree now and she could have substituted, could have done anything—but the idea didn't appeal to her and so on the three or four days a week I was summoned to one school or another, she was at home, listening to the rain drool from the eaves and trickle into the pots we'd set out under the worst of the leaks. I sprang for a cheap TV to keep her company, and then an electric heater the size of a six-pack of beer that nonetheless managed to make the meter spin like a 45. But then, we weren't paying utilities—the landlord was. I'd given him a lump sum at the end of May—for the season—and now we were getting our own back. One morning when I was at work, he used his key to let himself in and found Nora in bed, the blankets pulled up to her neck and the TV rattling away, and he'd backed out the door, embarrassed, without saying a word. The next day we got the eviction notice. The day after that, he cut off the electricity.

I was cooking by candlelight over the gas stove a few nights later (Chef Boyardee cheese ravioli, out of the can, with a side of iceberg lettuce cut in wedges), when Nora edged up beside me. We'd been drinking burgundy out of the gallon jug we kept under the sink as a way of distracting ourselves from the obvious. The house crepitated around us. It wasn't raining, at least not right then, but there was a whole lot of *dripping* going on, dripping that had emerged as the defining soundtrack of our lives in the absence of music, and I couldn't remember a time, not a single minute going all the way back to the day we first met, when there wasn't a record on or at least the radio.

Her hair shone greasily in the candlelight. She'd twisted it into pigtails for convenience because the water heater, which ran not on gas but electricity, was defunct now, definitely defunct, and there was no way to take a shower unless we went over to a friend's house—and that involved the hassle of actually getting in the car and going someplace when it was so much easier just to pile up the blankets on the bed, get stoned and watch the shadows creep over the beams that did such an admirable job of holding up the slanted portion of the roof. Nora gazed into the pot on the stove. "I can't live like this," she said.

"No," I said, and I was in full agreement here, "neither can I."

The first place we looked at was also a seasonal rental, but the seasons were reversed. It was another crumbling outbuilding in the same summer colony, but it had been tricked up with heat and insulation because the landlady—eighty, ninety maybe, with eyes like crushed glass and hair raked back so tightly you could make out the purple-splotched ruin of her scalp beneath—saw the advantage of renting through the winter and spring to whoever was left behind when the summer people went back to the city. I didn't begrudge her that. I didn't begrudge her anything. I didn't even know her. Nora had circled an ad in the *Pennysaver,* dialed the number, and now here she was, the old lady, waiting for us on the porch, out of the rain, and the minute we pulled into the driveway she began waving impatiently for us to jump out of the car, hurry up the steps and get the business over with.

There were two problems with the house, the first apparent to all three of us, the second only to Nora and me. That problem, hovering over us before we even walked in the door, was that we were looking for a deal because we didn't have the kind of money to put down for a deposit or first and last months' rent, just enough for now, for the current month—enough, we hoped, to get us out of the converted chicken coop and into someplace with heat and electricity till we could think what to do next. The old lady—Mrs. Fried—didn't look as if she would let things slide. Just the opposite. She gazed up at us out of her fractured eyes with the expectation of one thing only: money.

But then there was the first problem, which obviated the need to dwell on the second. The place was too small, smaller even than the shack we were living in, and we saw that the minute we stepped through the door. There were two rooms, bedroom and living room/kitchen, and to the right of the door, in a little recess, a bathroom the size of the sweatbox in *The Bridge on the River Kwai*. We never got that far. We just stood there, the three of us, and gazed into the bedroom, which was off the narrow hall. The bedroom was too cramped for anything but the single bed squeezed into it. A second single, made up with an army blanket and sheets gone gray with use, was pushed up against the wall in the hallway so that you had no more than a foot's leeway to get around it and into the front room. The old lady read our faces, read our minds—or thought she did—and gestured first at the bed in the hallway and then the one in the bedroom. "Ven you vant," she said, shrugging, her delicate wheeze of a voice clinging to the hard consonants of her youth, "you come."

If Nora found it funny, laughing so hard she couldn't seem to catch her breath as we ducked back into the car, I didn't. I was the one put in the awkward position here, I was the provider, and what was she? It was the sort of question you didn't ask, because it stirred resentment, and resentment was what had brought us down the first time around. I put the car in gear and drove down the dark tree-choked tunnel of the street, turned right, then right again, and swung into the muddy drive where the shack stood awaiting us. Inside, it smelled like a tomb. I could see my breath, even after I'd flicked on all four burners of the stove. Not sixty seconds went by before Nora said something that set me off and I came right back at her—"We wouldn't be in this fucking mess if you'd get up off your ass and find a job"—and when we went to bed, early, to save on candles, it was for the warmth and nothing else.

There was no call next morning, and I had mixed feelings about that. I dreaded those calls, but they meant money—and money was the beginning and end of everything there was, at least right then. When the phone did finally ring it was half-past twelve and it went off like a flash bomb in the dream I was having, a dream that made me so much happier than the life I jolted awake to I wanted it to go on forever. My eyes opened on the slanted ceiling and my first thought was that even the chickens must have hated staring up at it, the sameness of it, day after day, until you lost your head and your feathers and somebody dropped you into a frying pan. Nora was propped up beside me, reading. Rain rapped insistently at the roof. "Well," she said. "Aren't you going to answer it?"

The cold pricked me everywhere, like acupuncture, and I clutched my jeans to my groin, fumbled with a sweatshirt and hobbled across the room to snatch up the phone. It was my best friend, Artie, whom I'd known since elementary school. He didn't bother with a greeting. "You find a place yet?"

"Uh-uh, no."

"Well, I might've found something for you—"

I glanced at Nora. She'd put down her book and she was watching me now, her eyes squinted to slits in the fierceness of her concentration. *Who is it?* she mouthed, but I ignored her.

"I'm listening," I said.

"I didn't know if you'd be interested, because it's not a real rental—it's more like housesitting—and it's only temporary, like from next week through the end of April. It's a friend of my father's. An old guy and his wife. They go to Florida every winter and they want somebody in the house—or the apartment, there's an apartment in the basement, above ground, with windows and all—just so they don't get anybody breaking in. I was there once when I was a kid. It's nice. On a private lake. A place called Birnam Wood. You ever hear of it?"

"No," I said.

"Would you be interested at all?"

"You got a phone number?"

I told Nora not to get too excited because chances were it wouldn't work out. Either we wouldn't want the place—there had to be something wrong with it, right?—or they, the old couple, wouldn't want us, once they got a look at us. Still, I phoned right away and the old man answered on the first ring. I introduced myself, talking fast, too fast maybe, because it wasn't till I dropped the name of Artie's father that the voice on the other end came to life. "Yes, we are expecting your call," the old man said, and he had some sort of accent too, hesitating over the *w* in "we," as if afraid it would congeal on him, and in a sudden jolt of paranoia I wondered if he and Mrs. Fried were somehow in league—or worse, if he *was* Mrs. Fried, throwing her voice to catch me unawares. But no, the place was miles away, buried in the woods in the hind end of Croton, well beyond the old lady's reach. He gave the address, then directions, but they were so elaborate I stopped listening midway through, thinking instead of what Artie had said: the place was on a lake. A private lake. I'd find it, no problem. How many private lakes could there be? I told the old man we'd like to come have a look—at his earliest convenience, that is.

"When"—the hesitation again—"would you like to come?"

"I don't know—how about now? Now okay?"

There was a long pause, during which Nora flapped both hands at me as if to say *Don't sound too eager,* and then the old man, in his slow deliberate way, said, "Yes, that will suit us."

We were late getting there, very late, actually, one snaking blacktop road looking much like the next, the rain hammering down and Nora digging into me along the lines of *You're a real idiot, you know that?* and *Why in God's name didn't you write down the directions?* For a while it looked like a lost cause, trees crowding the road, nobody and nothing around except for the odd mailbox and the watery flash of a picture window glimpsed through the vegetation, but finally, after backing in and out of driveways and retracing our path half a dozen times, we came to a long low stone wall with a gated entrance flanked by two stone pillars. The gate—wrought-iron coated in black enamel so slick it glowed—stood open. A brass plaque affixed to the pillar on the right read BIRNAM WOOD. I didn't want to bicker but I couldn't help pointing out that we'd passed by the place at least three times already and Nora should have kept her eyes open because I was the one driving and she was the one doing all the bitching, but she just ignored me because the gravel of the private lane was crunching under our tires now and there were lawns and tennis courts opening up around us. Then the first house rose up out of the trees on our left, a huge towering thing of stone and glass with a glistening black slate roof and too many gables to count, even as the lake began to emerge from the mist on the other side of the road.

"Wow, you think that's it?" Nora's voice was pitched so low she might have been talking to herself. "Artie did say it was a mansion, right?" I could feel her eyes on me. "Well, didn't he?"

I didn't answer. A moment ago I'd been worked up, hating her, hating the broken-down car with its bald tires and rusted-out panels that was the only thing we could afford, hating the trees and the rain, hating nature and rich people and the private lakes you couldn't find unless you were rich yourself, unless you had a helicopter, a whole fleet of them, and now suddenly a different mix of emotions was surging through me—surprise, yes, awe even, but a kind of desperation too. Even as the next house came into view on the right—ivy-covered brick with three wings, half a dozen chimneys and a whole fairway of lawn sweeping down to the lake and the two red rowboats pulled up on a perfect little crescent of beach—I knew I had to live here or die and that I'd do anything it took, right down to licking the old man's shoes, to make that happen.

"What's the number?" I said. "You see a number on that house?"

She didn't. She'd lost her glasses—she was always losing her glasses—and in our rush to get out the door she hadn't bothered with her contacts either. No matter. The road took us over a stone bridge and swept us directly into the driveway of the house we were looking for—number 14. We got out of the car, the rain slackening now, and just stared up at the place, a big rearing brown-timbered Tudor that sat right on the lake itself. Around the corner I could make out a gazebo and a little dock with a rowboat tethered to it, this one painted green. And swans. Swans on the lake.

Everything seemed to brighten suddenly, as if the sun were about to break through. "All right," I said, "here goes," and I took Nora by the hand and led her up the flagstone steps to the front door.

I introduced Nora as my wife, though that was a lie. Old people, that's what they wanted to hear. If you were married, you were mature, reliable, exactly like them, because in their day men and women didn't just live together—they made a commitment, they had children and went on cruises and built big houses on lakes and filled them with all the precious trinkets and manufactured artifacts they collected along the way. Mr. and Mrs. Kuenzli—Anton and Eva—were just like that. They met us at the door, two dwarfish old people who were almost identical, except that she was wearing a dress and had dyed her hair and he wasn't and hadn't. They gave us tea in a big room overlooking the lake and then escorted us around the house to show off their various collections—Mexican pottery, jade figurines, seascapes painted by a one-armed man they'd encountered in Manila. Every object had a story connected to it. They took turns filling in the details, no hurry at all. I knew what they were doing: checking us out, trying to get a read on us. I shrugged it off. If they were alarmed at the sight of us (this was in a time when people our age wore beads and serapes and cowboy boots and grew their hair long for the express purpose of sticking it to the bourgeoisie), they didn't show it. Still, it was a good hour before we went downstairs to the basement, which was where we were going to live, after all. That is, if things worked out.

They did. I made sure they did. The minute we walked down the stairs I was hooked—and I could see that Nora was too. Here was a huge room—low-ceilinged, but the size of a basketball court—with a kitchen off to the left and next to it a bedroom with curtains, framed pictures on the walls and twin beds separated by matching night tables fitted out with ashtrays and reading lamps, just like the room every TV couple slept in, chastely and separately, so as not to confront the American family with the disturbing notion that people actually engaged in sexual relations. Nora gave me a furtive glance. "Ven you vant, you come," she said under her breath, and we both broke up.

Then it was back out into the main room and the real kicker, the deal-sealer, the sine qua non—a regulation-size slate-topped pool table. A pool table! All this—leather armchairs, Persian carpets, gleaming linoleum, heat, twin beds, the lake, the rowboat, swans—and a pool table too? It was too much. Whatever the old man was asking for rent, because this wasn't strictly housesitting and we were willing to make a token monthly payment, I was ready to double. Triple. Anything he wanted. I squeezed Nora's hand. She beamed up at me as the old couple looked on, smiling, moved now by the sight of us there in the depths of that house that had no doubt harbored children at one time, grandchildren even.

I felt a vast calm settle over me. "We'll take it," I said.

At the end of the first week, after checking on us six or seven times a day (or spying on us, as Nora insisted, Mrs. Kuenzli fretting over how we were getting along—*Fine, thanks*—and even one night creaking down the stairs with a pot of homemade chicken-spaetzle soup), the old couple climbed into a limousine and went off to the airport, leaving us in possession. The main house was sealed off, of course, but I didn't care about that. What I cared about was getting out of the shack. What I cared about was Nora. Making her happy. Making myself happy—and everybody else too. Within days of the Kuenzlis' departure, my friends began showing up unannounced for the purpose of shooting 8-ball and cranking up the volume on the Bang & Olufsen sound system the Kuenzlis had at some point so fortuitously installed, then maybe getting wrecked and taking the rowboat out on the glittering surface of the lake while the trees flamed and the swans bobbed in our wake. Even the weather cooperated. If September had been a loss, one of the coldest and rainiest on record, October tiptoed in on a streak of pure sunshine and temperatures that climbed into the seventies.

I was shooting pool one Saturday afternoon with Artie and another friend, Richard, all three of us wired on Black Beauties and chain-drinking cheap beer, when Nora came in the door looking flushed. She had news. While we'd been frittering our time away—that was how she put it, "frittering," but she was smiling now, hardly able to contain herself—she'd gone out on her own to interview for a job.

I loved her in that moment, loved the way the color came into her face because she was addressing all three of us now, not just me, and that made her self-conscious no matter the news, which was good, very good, I could see that in an instant. "Well," I said, "you get it?"

The smile stalled, came back again. She nodded. "It's not much," she said, already retreating. She looked from me to Artie and Richard. "Minimum wage—but it's six nights a week."

I'd set down my pool cue and was coming across the room to her, that big room with its buffed floors and the carpets thick enough for anything, when I noticed she was all dressed up, and not in business clothes but in the fringed boots and gauzy top she wore when we were going bar-hopping. "What is it," I said, "that hostessing thing?"

She nodded.

"At Brennan's?"

Her smile was gone now. Her eyes—she was wearing her false lashes and pale blue eyeshadow—sank into mine. I was the one who'd told her about the job, which Richard had heard about from the bartender there. *All you have to do is smile,* I'd told her. *All you have to do is say 'Party of four?' and let them follow you to the table. You can do that, can't you?* I hadn't meant to be demeaning. Or maybe I had. She was strong-willed but I wanted to break her down, make her dependent, make her mine, but at the same time I wanted her to hold up her end, because we were a couple and that was what couples did. They worked. Both of them.

I took her by the hand, tried to peck a kiss to her cheek, but she pulled away.

"It means I'll be gone nights."

I shrugged. I could feel Artie and Richard watching me. There was a record on the stereo—I remember this clearly—something drum-based, with a churning polyrhythmic beat that seemed to fester under my words. "At least it's something," I said.

Artie lined up a shot. The balls clacked. Nothing dropped. "Hey, it's great news," he said, straightening up. "Congrats."

Nora gave him a look. "It's only temporary," she said.

We settled into a routine. The phone rang in the dark and I got up, answered it and found out what school I was going to because somebody who just couldn't stand another day of it had called in sick—either that or hung himself—and I was back home by three-thirty or four, at which point she'd be drinking coffee and making herself scrambled eggs and toast. Then I'd drive her to work and either sit there at the bar for a couple (depending on how I was feeling about our financial situation), or go back home and shoot pool by myself, pitting Player A against Player B and trying not to play favorites, until she got off at ten and I went to pick her up. Sometimes we'd linger at the bar, but most nights—weeknights anyway—we'd go back home because I needed the sleep. We climbed into our separate beds, snug enough, warm and dry and feeling pampered—or if not pampered, at least secure—and when I switched off my reading lamp and turned to the wall the last image fading in my brain was of the steady bright nimbus of Nora's light and her face shining there above her book.

The weather held all that month, even as the leaves persisted and the lake rippled under the color of them. Whenever we could, we went out in the rowboat, and though we never acknowledged it I suppose we were both thinking the same thing—that we'd better take advantage of it while we could because each day of sun might be the last. I'd row and Nora would lie back against the seat in the stern, her eyes closed and her bare legs stretched out before her. What did I feel? Relaxed. As relaxed as I've ever felt in my life, before or since. There was something more to it too. I felt powerful, in command, the muscles of my arms flexing and releasing while Nora dozed at my feet and the rest of the world went still as held breath.

It was a feeling that couldn't last. And it didn't. Less than a week into November there was frost on the windshield when I got up for school and the sun seemed to have vanished, replaced by a low cloud cover and winds out of the north. Finally, reluctantly, I pulled the rowboat ashore and turned it over for the winter. Two days later there was a rim of ice around the lake and the temperature went down into the teens overnight. But, as I say, the house was warm and well-insulated, with a furnace that could have heated six houses, and when we went to bed at night we couldn't resist joking about the shack, what we'd be suffering if we were still there. "My feet," Nora would say, "they'd freeze to the floor like when you touch the tip of your tongue to the ice-cube tray." "Yeah," I'd say, "yeah, but you wouldn't even notice because by then we'd be dried up and frozen like those mummies they found in the Andes." And she'd laugh, we'd both laugh, and listen to the whisper of the furnace as it clicked on and drove the warm air through the bedroom and into the big room beyond where the pool table stood draped in darkness.

And then came the night when I dropped her off at Brennan's and had my first drink and then another and didn't feel like going home. It was as if some gauge inside me had been turned up high, all the way, top of the dial. I felt like that a lot back then, and maybe it was just an overload of testosterone, maybe that was all it was, but on this night I sat at the bar and kept on drinking. I knew the regulars, an older crowd that came in for dinner and gradually gave way to people like Nora and me, the music shifting from a soft whisper of jazz to the rock and roll we wanted to hear as the late diners gathered up their coats and gloves and doggie bags and headed out into the night. I'd been talking a lot of nothing to a guy in a sport coat who must have been in his thirties, a martini drinker, and when he got up and left a guy my own age slid onto the stool beside me. He asked me what was happening at the same time I asked him, then he ordered a drink—tequila and tonic, very West Coast, or *hip,* that is—and we started talking. His name was Steve, he had rust-red hair kinked out to his shoulders and he wore a thin headband of braided leather.

What did we talk about? The usual, bands, drugs, what concerts we'd been to, but then we started in on books and I was pleased and surprised because most of the people I ran into in that time and place didn't extend themselves much beyond the Sunday comics. We were debating some fine point of *Slaughterhouse Five,* testing each other's bona fides—he could quote passages from memory, a talent I've never had—when Nora leaned in between us to brush a kiss to my lips, then straightened up and shook out her hair with a quick neat flip of her head. "My heels are killing me," she said. "And this top—Jesus, I'm freezing." She stole a look around, gave Steve a vacant smile, picked up my drink and downed it in a single gulp. Then she was gone, back to her post at the station by the door.

Steve gave a low whistle. "Wow," he said. "That your old lady?"

I just shrugged, nonchalant, elevated in that instant above everybody in the place. I wouldn't have admitted it, but something stirred in me whenever I looked up and saw the way the men watched her as she tapped across the floor in her heels, trailing husbands and wives and sometimes even kids behind her, but it wasn't something good or admirable.

"Man, I'd love to—" he began, and then caught himself. "You are one lucky dude."

Another shrug. My feelings were complicated. I'd been drinking. And what I said next was inexcusable, I know that, and I didn't mean it, not in any literal sense, not in the real world of twin beds and Persian carpets and all the rest, but what I was trying to convey here was that I wasn't tied down—*old lady*—wasn't a husband, not yet anyway, and that all my potentialities were intact. "I don't know," I said, "she can be a real pain in the ass." I took a sip of my drink, let out a long withering sigh. "Sometimes I think she's more trouble than she's worth, know what I mean?"

That was all I said, or some variant of it, and then there was another drink and the conversation went deeper and I guess somehow Steve must have got the impression that we weren't really all that committed, that living together was an experiment gone sour, that we were both—she and I—on the brink of something else. There was an exchange of phone numbers and addresses (*Birnam Wood? Cool. I used to swim in the lake there when I was a kid*) and then he was gone and the crowd at the bar began to thin. The minute he left I forgot him.

Next thing I knew, Nora was there, dressed in her long coat and her knit hat and gloves, perched high on the platform of her heels.

"You've been drinking," she said.

"Yeah," I admitted.

She gave me a tired smile. "Have fun?"

"Yeah." I smiled back.

"Did you know it's snowing out?"

"Really?"

"Really." And then a beat. "You want me to drive?"

It was a long way home, twenty, twenty-five minutes under the best of conditions, but with the snow and the worn tires and the fact that Nora didn't see too well at night, it must have taken us twice as long as that. We were the only ones on the road. The snow swept at the headlights and erased everything out in front of us. I tried not to be critical but every time we went around a curve the car sailed out of control and I suppose I got vocal about it because at one point she pulled over, her lips drawn tight and her eyes furious in the sick yellow glare of the dashboard. "You want to drive?" she said. "Go ahead, be my guest."

When we got home (finally, miraculously), the phone was ringing. I could hear it from outside the door, making its demands. It took me a minute, pinning a glove under one arm and struggling to work the key in the lock as the snow sifted down and Nora stamped impatiently. "Hurry up, I have to pee," she said between clenched teeth. Then we were in, the phone ringing still—it must have been the sixth or seventh ring—and I flicked on the lights while Nora made a dash for the bathroom and I crossed the room to answer it.

"Hello?" I gasped, out of breath and thinking it must be Artie, because who else would be calling at that hour?

"Hey, what's happening," said the voice on the other end of the line. "This Keith?"

"Yeah," I said. "Who's this?"

"Steve."

"Steve?"

"From the bar, you know. Like earlier? Brennan's?" I heard Nora flush the toilet. The cover was off the pool table because I'd left in the middle of the climactic match between Player A and Player B, all the angles still in play. I listened to the water rattle in the pipes. And then Steve's voice, low, confidential, "Hey, I was just wondering. Is Nora there?"

The bathroom door clicked open. There was a buzzing in my skull. Everything was wrong. "No," I said, shaking my head for emphasis though there was no one there to see it, "she's not in."

"When'll she be back?"

I said nothing. I watched her swing open the bathroom door, saw her face there, the pristine towels on the rack and the copper-and-gold wallpaper Mrs. Kuenzli must have gone to some special store to pick out because she wanted the best, only the best. The voice on the other end of the line was saying something else, insinuating, whispering in my ear like a disease, and so I bent down to where the phone was plugged into the wall and pulled it out of the socket.

"Who was that?" Nora asked.

"Nobody," I said. "Wrong number."

She gave me a doubtful look. "You were on the line long enough."

I wanted to do something right for a change, wanted to take hold of her and press her to me, confess, tell her I loved her, but I didn't. I just said, "You feel like a game of pool? I'll spot you two balls—"

"You play," she said. "I'm beat. I think I'll get ready for bed and read for a while." She paused at the bedroom door to give me a sweet tired smile. "You've got to admit, Player B's a lot better than I am anyway."

No argument there. I turned on the light over the table, cued up a record and took up the game where I'd left off. I was deep into my third game, on a real roll on behalf of Player A, the balls dropping as if I didn't even have to use the stick, as if I were willing them in, when suddenly there was a knock at the door. Two thumps. A pause. And then two thumps more.

I was just laying down the stick, any number of scenarios going through my head—it was a stranded motorist, the guy who drove the snowplow come to complain about the tail end of the car sticking out into the street, Artie braving the elements for a nightcap—when Nora came out of the bedroom, looking puzzled. She was in her pajamas, the kind kids wear, with a drawstring round the waist and a fold-down collar. Pink. With a flight of bluebirds running up and down her limbs and flapping across her chest. Her feet were bare. "Who's that?" she asked. "Artie?"

I didn't know what was coming, couldn't have guessed. I was in my own house, shooting pool and listening to music while the snow fell outside and the furnace hummed and my girlfriend stood there in her pajamas. "Must be," I said, even as the knock came again and a voice, muffled by the door, called out, "Keith? Nora? Knock-knock. Anybody home?"

I opened the door on Steve, his hair matted now and wet with snow. He was holding a bottle of tequila by the neck and raised it in offering as he stamped in through the door. "Hey," he said, handing me the bottle, "cool place." He shrugged out of his jacket, dropping it right there on the floor. "Anybody down for a little action? Nora, how about you? A shot? Want to do a shot?"

She looked at him, bewildered—or maybe it was just that she wasn't wearing her glasses and had to squint to take him in. I just stood there, the bottle like a brick in my hand—or no, a cement block, a weight, avoirdupois, dragging me down.

Steve never hesitated. He crossed the room to her, digging in his pocket for something, grinning and glassy-eyed. "Here," he said, producing an envelope. "After I saw you tonight? You're so beautiful. I don't even know if you know how beautiful—and sexy. You're really sexy." He handed her the envelope, but she wasn't looking at the envelope, she was looking at me. "I wrote you a poem," he said. "Go ahead. Read it."

"Steve," I was saying, "look, Steve, I think—" but I couldn't go on because of the way Nora was staring at me, her lips parted and her eyes come violently to life.

"Read it," he repeated. "I wrote it for you, just for you—"

"Look," I said, "it's late," and I moved toward him and actually took hold of his arm in an attempt to steer him away and out the door, back into the snow and out of our lives. "Nora's tired," I said.

He never turned, never even acknowledged me. "Let *her* say it. You're not tired, are you?"

For the first time, she shifted her eyes to him. "No," she said finally. "No, I'm not tired at all."

Before I knew what I was doing, I'd set the bottle down on the desk and I was pulling on my coat, furious suddenly, and then I was out the door and into the night, the snow swirling overhead and Steve's voice—"So you want a hit of tequila?"—trailing off behind me with a soft hopeful rising inflection.

Outside, the snow made a noise, a kind of hiss, as if the night had come alive. I walked twice round the house, cursing myself—and I wouldn't go back in, I wouldn't, not till whatever was going to happen happened and he was gone—and then I found myself huddling under the gazebo. I turned my collar up, pulled on my gloves. There was a wind now and a taste of cold northern forests on the air. I walked out on the dock and stood there for I don't know how long, the lake locked up like a vault below me. That was when I noticed the light in the house directly across from ours, the one with all the chimneys and the two red rowboats that were turned over now, twin humps like moguls in the snow. It was the only light visible anywhere, a single lamp burning in a window on the ground floor of the wing nearest the lake. What came over me, I can't say—what the impulse was, I mean—but I lowered myself down off the edge of the dock and started across the lake. The wind was in my face. There were no stars. And the footing was bad, drifting powder over ice as clear as if it had come out of a machine. I went down twice, hard, but picked myself up and kept on.

When I got close, when I came up the crescent of beach past the rowboats and on up the slope of the whitening lawn, I saw that the curtains were open, which explained the resiliency of the light. The people there—and I didn't know them, not at all, not even by sight—must have left them open purposely, I realized, because of the snow, the romance of it, first snow of the season. It came to me that I was trespassing. Peeping. That anybody could have seen my tracks. But as soon as the thought entered my head I dismissed it, because I didn't care about any of that—I'd gone out of myself, fixated on that light. Still, I kept to the shadows. I might even have crouched down in the bushes there, I don't know.

What I saw was an ordinary room, a bedroom, lit like a stage. I saw a bed, an armoire, pictures on the wall. A shadow flickered across the room, then another, but for the longest time I didn't see anything. And then the man came into view, padding back and forth, undressing, getting ready for bed. How old was he? I couldn't tell, not really. Older than me, but not old. He settled into the bed—a double bed, queen-sized maybe—flicked on the lamp there and picked up a magazine and began reading. At some point, he set it down and seemed to be saying something to the other person in the room—the wife, I guessed—but of course it was just a murmur to me. And then, as if she'd heard her cue and stepped out of the wings, there she was, in a nightgown, fussing around her side of the bed before finally settling in and turning on her own light.

I felt guilty. I felt sick. And I didn't see anything revealing—or sexual, that is—no snuggling or stroking or even a kiss. They were night owls, those people. That light burned a long time. I know. Because I stayed there till it went out.

(2012)

Acknowledgments

Grateful acknowledgment is made to the following magazines, in which these stories first appeared:

After the Plague: Esquire, "Peep Hall"; *GQ,* "Death of the Cool"; *Granta,* "Rust"; *The New Yorker,* "She Wasn't Soft," "Killing Babies," "Captured by the Indians," "Achates McNeil," "The Love of My Life," "Friendly Skies," "My Widow" and "The Underground Gardens"; *The Paris Review,* "Going Down"; *Playboy,* "Termination Dust," "The Black and White Sisters" and "After the Plague."

"Killing Babies" also appeared in *The Best American Short Stories 1997,* edited by E. Annie Proulx (Houghton Mifflin); "The Underground Gardens" in *Prize Stories 1999: The O. Henry Awards,* edited by Larry Dark (Anchor Books); and "The Love of My Life" in *Prize Stories 2001: The O. Henry Awards,* edited by Larry Dark (Anchor Books).

Tooth and Claw: GQ, "The Kind Assassin"; *Harper's,* "Rastrow's Island" and "Here Comes"; *The New Yorker,* "When I Woke Up This Morning, Everything I Had Was Gone," "Swept Away," "Dogology," "Chicxulub" and "Tooth and Claw"; *Playboy,* "Jubilation," "Up Against the Wall" and "The Swift Passage of the Animals"; *StoryQuarterly,* "All the Wrecks I've Crawled Out Of"; *Zoetrope,* "Almost Shooting an Elephant."

"Swept Away" also appeared in *The O. Henry Prize Stories, 2003,* edited by Laura Furman (Anchor Books); and "Tooth and Claw" in *The Best American Short Stories 2004,* edited by Lorrie Moore (Houghton Mifflin).

The author would also like to cite the following works as sources of certain factual details in "Dogology": *The Wolf Children: Fact or Fantasy,* by Charles Maclean; *Wolf-Children and Feral Man,* by the Reverend J. A. L. Singh and Robert M. Zingg; and *The Hidden Lives of Dogs,* by Elizabeth Marshall Thomas.

Wild Child: Best Life, "Bulletproof"; *Harper's,* "Question 62" and "Admiral"; *The Kenyon Review,* "Hands On"; *McSweeney's,* "Wild Child"; *The New Yorker,* "La Conchita," "Sin Dolor," "The Lie," "Thirteen Hundred Rats" and "Ash Monday"; *The Paris Review,* "Balto"; *Playboy,* "The Unlucky Mother of Aquiles Maldonado" and "Three Quarters of the Way to Hell"; *A Public Space,* "Anacapa."

"Balto" also appeared in *The Best American Short Stories 2007,* edited by Stephen King (Houghton Mifflin); and "Admiral" in *The Best American Short Stories 2008,* edited by Salman Rushdie (Houghton Mifflin).

The author would also like to acknowledge Harlan Lane's *The Wild Boy of Aveyron* and Roger Shattuck's *The Forbidden Experiment* as sources of certain factual details in "Wild Child."

A Death in Kitchawank: The Atlantic, "The Silence"; *Harper's,* "My Pain Is Worse Than Your Pain," "What Separates Us from the Animals" and "Sic Transit"; *The Kenyon Review,* "In the Zone" and "Slate Mountain"; *McSweeney's,* "Burning Bright"; *The New Yorker,* "A Death in Kitchawank," "Los Gigantes," "Birnam Wood" and "The Night of the Satellite"; *Playboy,* "Good Home," "The Way You Look Tonight" and "The Marlbane Manchester Musser Award."